JOHN STEINBECK

JOHN STEINBECK

TRAVELS WITH CHARLEY AND LATER NOVELS 1947–1962

The Wayward Bus

Burning Bright

Sweet Thursday

The Winter of Our Discontent

Travels with Charley in Search of America

THE LIBRARY OF AMERICA

The paper used in this publication meets the
minimum requirements of the American National Standard for
Information Sciences—Permanence of Paper for Printed
Library Materials, ANSI Z39.48—1984.

Distributed to the trade in the United States
by Penguin Putnam Inc.
and in Canada by Penguin Books Canada Ltd.

Library of Congress Catalog Number: 2006048757
For cataloging information, see end of Notes.
ISBN 978-1-59853-004-9

First Printing
The Library of America—170

Manufactured in the United States of America

Robert DeMott
and Brian Railsback
wrote the notes for this volume

Contents

THE WAYWARD BUS

I pray you all gyve audyence,
And here this mater with reverence,
By fygure a morall playe;
The somonynge of Everyman called it is,
That of our lyves and endynge shewes
How transytory we be all daye.

—EVERYMAN

For
GWYN

Chapter 1

FORTY-TWO miles below San Ysidro, on a great north-south highway in California, there is a crossroad which for eighty-odd years has been called Rebel Corners. From here a county road goes at right angles toward the west until, after forty-nine miles, it connects with another north-south highway that leads from San Francisco to Los Angeles and, of course, Hollywood. Anyone who wishes to go from the inland valley to the coast in this part of the state must take the road that begins at Rebel Corners and winds through hills and a little desert and through farmland and mountains until, at last, it comes to the coastal highway right in the middle of the town of San Juan de la Cruz.

Rebel Corners got its name in 1862. It is said that a family named Blanken kept a smithy at the crossroads. The Blankens and their sons-in-law were poor, ignorant, proud, and violent Kentuckians. Having no furniture and no property, they brought what they had with them from the East—their prejudices and their politics. Having no slaves, they were ready, nevertheless, to sell their lives for the free principle of slavery. When the war began, the Blankens discussed traveling back across the measureless West to fight for the Confederacy. But it was a long way and they had crossed once, and it was too far. Thus it was that in a California which was preponderantly for the North, the Blankens seceded a hundred and sixty acres and a blacksmith shop from the Union and joined Blanken Corners to the Confederacy. It is also said that they dug trenches and cut rifle slits in the blacksmith shop to defend this rebellious island from the hated Yankees. And the Yankees, who were mostly Mexicans and Germans and Irish and Chinese, far from attacking the Blankens, were rather proud of them. The Blankens had never lived so well, for the enemy brought chickens and eggs and pork sausage in slaughter time, because everyone thought that, regardless of the cause, such courage should be recognized. Their place took the name of Rebel Corners and has kept it to this day.

After the war the Blankens became lazy and quarrelsome

and full of hatreds and complaints, as every defeated nation does, so that, pride in them having evaporated with the war, people stopped bringing their horses to be shoed and their plows for retipping. Finally, what the Union Armies could not do by force of arms the First National Bank of San Ysidro did by foreclosure.

Now, after eighty-odd years, no one remembers much about the Blankens except that they were very proud and very unpleasant. In the following years the land changed hands many times before it was incorporated into the empire of a newspaper king. The blacksmith shop burned down and was rebuilt and burned again, and what was left was converted into a garage with gas pumps and then into a store-restaurant-garage and service station. When Juan Chicoy and his wife bought it and got the franchise to run a public conveyance between Rebel Corners and San Juan de la Cruz, it became all these and a bus station too. The rebel Blankens have, through pride and a low threshold of insult which is the test of ignorance and laziness, disappeared from the face of the earth, and no one remembers what they looked like. But Rebel Corners is well known and the Chicoys are well liked.

There was a little lunchroom in back of the gas pumps, a lunchroom with a counter and round, fixed stools, and three tables for those who wanted to eat in some style. These were not used often for it was customary to tip Mrs. Chicoy when she served you at a table and not to if she served you at the counter. On the first shelf behind the counter were sweet rolls, snails, doughnuts; on the second, canned soups, oranges, and bananas; on the third, individual boxes of cornflakes, riceflakes, grapenuts, and other tortured cereals. There was a grill at one end behind the counter and a sink beside it, beer and soda spouts beside that, ice cream units beside those, and on the counter itself, between the units of paper napkin containers, juke-box coin slots, salt, pepper, and ketchup, the cakes were displayed under large plastic covers. The walls, where there was room, were well decorated with calendars and posters showing bright, improbable girls with pumped-up breasts and no hips—blondes, brunettes and redheads, but always with this bust development, so that a visitor of another species might judge from the preoccupation of artist and audience that the seat of procreation lay in the mammaries.

Alice Chicoy, Mrs. Juan Chicoy, that is, who worked among the shining girls, was wide-hipped and sag-chested and she walked well back on her heels. She was not in the least jealous of the calendar girls and the Coca-Cola girls. She had never seen anyone like them and she didn't think anyone else ever had. She fried her eggs and hamburgers, heated her canned soup, drew beer, scooped ice cream, and toward evening her feet hurt and that made her cross and snappish. And as the day went on the flat curl went out of her hair so that it hung damp and stringy beside her face, and at first she would brush it aside with her hand and finally she would blow it out of her eyes.

Next to the lunchroom was a garage converted from the last blacksmith shop, its ceiling and beams still black from the soot of the old forge, and here Juan Chicoy presided when he was not driving the bus between Rebel Corners and San Juan de la Cruz. He was a fine, steady man, Juan Chicoy, part Mexican and part Irish, perhaps fifty years old, with clear black eyes, a good head of hair, and a dark and handsome face. Mrs. Chicoy was insanely in love with him and a little afraid of him too, because he was a man, and there aren't very many of them, as Alice Chicoy had found out. There aren't very many of them in the world, as everyone finds out sooner or later.

In the garage Juan Chicoy fixed flat tires, got the air locks out of gas lines, cleaned the diamond-hard dust from choked carburetors, put new diaphragms in tubercular gasoline pumps, and did all the little things that the motor-minded public knows nothing whatever about. These things he did except during the hours from ten-thirty until four. That was the time he drove the bus, carrying passengers who had been deposited at Rebel Corners by the big Greyhound busses to San Juan de la Cruz and bringing passengers back from San Juan de la Cruz to Rebel Corners, where they were picked up either by the Greyhound bus going north at four-fifty-six or by the Greyhound going south at five-seventeen.

While Mr. Chicoy was gone on his route his duties at the garage were carried out by a succession of overgrown boys or immature young men who were more or less apprentices. None of them lasted very long. Unwary customers with dirty carburetors could not know in advance the destruction these apprentices could heap on a carburetor, and while Juan Chicoy himself was a magnificent mechanic, his apprentices usually were cocky adolescents who spent their time between jobs putting slugs in the juke box in the lunchroom and quarreling mildly with Alice Chicoy. To these young men opportunity beckoned constantly, drawing them ever southward toward Los Angeles and, of course, Hollywood, where, eventually, all the adolescents in the world will be congregated.

Behind the garage were two little outhouses with trellises, one of which said "Men" and the other "Ladies." And to each one a little path led, one around the right-hand side of the garage and one around the left-hand side of the garage.

What defined the Corners and made it visible for miles among the cultivated fields were the great white oaks that grew around the garage and restaurant. Tall and graceful, with black trunks and limbs, bright green in summer, black and brooding in winter, these oaks were landmarks in the long, flat valley. No one knows whether the Blankens planted them or whether they merely settled near to them. The latter seems more logical; first, because the Blankens are not known to have planted anything they could not eat, and second, because the trees seemed more than eighty-five years old. They might be two hundred years old; on the other hand, they might have their roots in some underground spring which would make them grow large quickly in this semidesert country.

These great trees shaded the station in summer so that travelers often pulled up under them and ate their lunches and cooled their overheated motors. The station itself was pleasant too, brightly painted green and red, a deep row of geraniums all around the restaurant, red geraniums and deep green leaves thick as a hedge. The white gravel in front and around the gas pumps was raked and sprinkled daily. In the restaurant and in the garage there was system and order. For instance, on the shelves in the restaurant the canned soup, the boxed cereals, even the grapefruits, were arranged in little pyramids, four on the bottom level, then three, then two, and one balanced on top. And the same was true of the cans of oil in the garage, and the fan belts hung neatly in their sizes on nails. It was a very well kept place. The windows of the restaurant were screened against flies, and the screen door banged shut after every entrance or exit. For Alice Chicoy hated flies. In a world that was not easy for Alice to bear or to understand, flies were the final and malicious burden laid upon her. She hated them with a cruel hatred, and the death of a fly by swatter, or slowly smothered in the goo of fly paper, gave her a flushed pleasure.

Just as Juan usually had a succession of young apprentices to help him in the garage, so Alice hired a succession of girls to help her in the lunchroom. These girls, gawky and romantic and homely—the pretty ones usually left with a customer within a few days—seemed to accomplish little in the way of work. They spread dirt about with damp cloths, they dreamed over movie magazines, they sighed into the juke box—and the most recent one had reddening eyes and a head cold and wrote long and passionate letters to Clark Gable. Alice Chicoy suspected every one of them of letting flies in. Norma, this most recent girl, had felt the weight of Alice Chicoy's tongue many times about flies.

The routine of the Corners in the morning was invariable. With the first daylight or, in the winter, even before, the lights came on in the lunchroom, and Alice steamed up the coffee urn (a great godlike silver effigy which may, in some future archaeological period, be displayed as an object of worship of the race of Amudkins, who preceded the Atomites, who, for some unknown reason, disappeared from the face of the earth). The restaurant was warm and cheerful when the first truck drivers pulled wearily in for their breakfast. Then came the salesmen, hurrying to the cities of the south in the dark so as to have a full day of business. Salesmen always spotted trucks and stopped, because it is generally believed that truck drivers are great connoisseurs of roadside coffee and food. By sun-up the first tourists in their own cars began to pull in for breakfast and road information.

The tourists from the north did not interest Norma much, but those from the south or those who came over the cut-off from San Juan de la Cruz and who might have been to Hollywood fascinated her. In four months Norma personally met fifteen people who had been to Hollywood, five who had been on a picture lot, and two who had seen Clark Gable face to face. Inspired by these last two, who came in very close together, she wrote a twelve-page letter which began, "Dear Mr. Gable," and ended, "Lovingly, A Friend." She often shuddered to think that Mr. Gable might find out that she had written it.

Norma was a faithful girl. Let others, featherbrains, run after the upstarts—the Sinatras, the Van Johnsons, the Sonny Tufts. Even during the war, when there had been no Gable pictures, Norma had remained faithful, keeping her dream warm with a colored picture of Mr. Gable in a flying suit with two belts of 50-caliber ammunition on his shoulders.

She often sneered at Sonny Tufts. She liked older men with interesting faces. Sometimes, wiping the damp cloth back and forth on the counter, her dream-widened eyes centered on the screen door, her pale eyes flexed and then closed for a moment. Then you could know that in that secret garden in her head, Gable had just entered the restaurant, had gasped when he saw her, and had stood there, his lips slightly parted and in his eyes the recognition that this was his woman. And around him the flies came in and out with impunity.

It never went beyond that. Norma was too shy. And, besides, she didn't know how such things were done. The actual love-making in her life had been a series of wrestling matches, the aim of which was to keep her clothes on in the back seat of a car. So far she had won by simple concentration. She felt that Mr. Gable not only would not do things like that, but wouldn't like them if he heard about them.

Norma wore the wash dresses featured by the National Dollar Stores, though, of course, she had a sateen dress for parties. But if you looked closely you could always find some little bit of beauty even on the wash dresses. Her Mexican silver pin, a representation of the Aztec calendar stone, was left to her in her aunt's will after Norma had nursed her for seven months and really wanted the sealskin stole and the ring of baroque pearls and turquoise. But these went to another branch of the family. Norma had also a string of small amber beads from her mother. She never wore the Mexican pin and the beads at the same time. In addition to these, Norma possessed two pieces of jewelry which were pure crazy and which she knew were pure crazy. Deep in her suitcase she had a gold-filled wedding ring and a gigantic Brazilian-type diamond ring, the two of which had cost five dollars. She wore them only when she went to bed. In the morning she took them off and hid them in her suitcase. No one in the world knew that she owned them. In bed she went to sleep twisting them on the third finger of her left hand.

The sleeping arrangements at the Corners were simple. Directly behind the lunchroom there was a lean-to. A door at the end of the lunch counter opened into the Chicoys' bed-sitting room, which had a double bed with an afghan spread, a console radio, two overstuffed chairs and a davenport—which group is called a suite—and a metal reading lamp with a marbled green glass shade. Norma's room opened off this room, for it was Alice's theory that young girls should be watched a little and not let to run wild. Norma had to come through the Chicoys' room to go to the bathroom—that, or slip out the window, which she ordinarily did. The apprentice-mechanic's room was next to the Chicoys' on the other side, but he had an outside entrance and used the vine-covered cubicle marked "Men" behind the garage.

It was a nice compact grouping of buildings, functional and pleasant. The Rebel Corners of the Blankens' time had been a miserable, dirty, and suspicious place, but the Chicoys flourished here. There was money in the bank and a degree of security and happiness.

This island covered by the huge trees could be seen for miles. No one ever had to look for road signs to find Rebel Corners and the road to San Juan de la Cruz. In the great valley the grain fields flattened away toward the east, to the foothills and to the high mountains, and toward the west they ended nearer in the rounded hills where the live oaks sat in black splotches. In the summer the yellow heat shimmered and burned and glared on the baking hills, and the shade of the great trees over the Corners was a thing to look forward to and to remember. In the winter when the heavy rains fell, the restaurant was a warm place of coffee and chili beans and pie.

In the deep spring when the grass was green on fields and foothills, when the lupines and poppies made a splendid blue and gold earth, when the great trees awakened in yellow-green young leaves, then there was no more lovely place in the world. It was no beauty you could ignore by being used to it. It caught you in the throat in the morning and made a pain of pleasure in the pit of your stomach when the sun went down over it. The sweet smell of the lupines and of the grass set you breathing nervously, set you panting almost sexually. And it was in this season of flowering and growth, though it was still before daylight, that Juan Chicoy came out to the bus carrying an electric lantern. Pimples Carson, his apprentice-mechanic stumbled sleepily behind him.

The lunchroom windows were still dark. Against the eastern hills not even a grayness had begun to form. It was so much night that the owls were still shrieking over the fields. Juan Chicoy came near to the bus which stood in front of the garage. It looked, in the light of the lantern, like a large, silver-windowed balloon. Pimples Carson, still not really awake, stood with his hands in his pockets, shivering, not because it was cold but because he was very sleepy.

A little wind blew in over the fields and brought the smell of lupine and the smell of a quickening earth, frantic with production.

Chapter 2

THE electric lantern, with a flat downward reflector, lighted sharply only legs and feet and tires and tree trunks near to the ground. It bobbed and swung, and the little incandescent bulb was blindingly blue-white. Juan Chicoy carried his lantern to the garage, took a bunch of keys from his overalls pocket, found the one that unlocked the padlock, and opened the wide doors. He switched on the overhead light and turned off his lantern.

Juan picked a striped mechanic's cap from his workbench. He wore Headlight overalls with big brass buttons on bib and side latches, and over this he wore a black horsehide jacket with black knitted wristlets and neck. His shoes were round-toed and hard, with soles so thick that they seemed swollen. An old scar on his cheek beside his large nose showed as a shadow in the overhead light. He ran fingers through his thick, black hair to get it all in the mechanic's cap. His hands were short and wide and strong, with square fingers and nails flattened by work and grooved and twisted from having been hammered and hurt. The third finger of his left hand had lost the first joint, and the flesh was slightly mushroomed where the finger had been amputated. This little overhanging ball was shiny and of a different texture from the rest of the finger, as though the joint were trying to become a fingertip, and on this finger he wore a wide gold wedding ring, as though this finger was no good for work any more and might as well be used for ornament.

A pencil and a ruler and a tire pressure gauge protruded from a slot in his overalls bib. Juan was clean-shaven, but not since yesterday, and along the corners of his chin and on his neck the coming whiskers were grizzled and white like those of an old Airedale. This was the more apparent because the rest of his beard was so intensely black. His black eyes were squinting and humorous, the way a man's eyes squint when he is smoking and cannot take the cigarette from his mouth. And Juan's mouth was full and good, a relaxed mouth, the underlip slightly protruding—not in petulance but in humor and self-confidence—the upper lip well formed except left of center where a deep scar was almost white against the pink tissue. The lip must have been cut clear through at one time, and now this thin taut band of white was a strain on the fullness of the lip and made it bunch in tiny tucks on either side. His ears were not very large, but they stood out sharply from his head like seashells, or in the position a man would hold them with his hands if he wanted to hear more clearly. Juan seemed to be listening intently all the time, while his squinting eyes seemed to laugh at what he heard, and half of his mouth disapproved. His movements were sure even when he was not doing anything that required sureness. He walked as though he were going to some exact spot. His hands moved with speed and precision and never fiddled with matches or with nails. His teeth were long and the edges were framed with gold, which gave his smile a little fierceness.

At his workbench he picked tools from nails on the wall and laid them in a long, flat box—wrenches and pliers and several screwdrivers and a machine hammer and a punch. Beside him Pimples Carson, still heavy with sleep, rested his elbow on the oily wood of the bench. Pimples wore the tattered sweater of a motorcycle club and the crown of a felt hat cut in saw teeth around the edge. He was a lank and slender-waisted boy of seventeen, with narrow shoulders and a long foxy nose and eyes that were pale in the morning and became greenish-brown later in the day. A golden fuzz was on his cheeks, and his cheeks were rivuleted and rotted and eroded with acne. Among the old scars new pustules formed, purple and red, some rising and some waning. The skin was shiny with the medicines that were sold for this condition and which do no good whatever.

Pimples' blue jeans were tight, and so long that they were turned up ten inches on the bottoms. They were held to his narrow middle by a broad, beautifully tooled leather belt with a fat and engraved silver buckle in which four turquoises were set. Pimples kept his hands at his sides as much as he could, but in spite of himself his fingers would move to his pitted cheeks until he became conscious of what he was doing and put his hands down again. He wrote to every company that advertised an acne cure, and he had been to many doctors, who knew that they could not cure it but who also knew that it would probably go away in a few years. They nevertheless gave Pimples prescriptions for salves and lotions, and one had put him on a diet of green vegetables.

His eyes were long and narrow and slanted like the eyes of a sleepy wolf, and now in the early morning they were almost sealed shut with mucus. Pimples was a prodigious sleeper. Left to his own devices, he could sleep nearly all the time. His whole system and his soul were a particularly violent battleground of adolescence. His concupiscence was constant, and when it was not directly and openly sexual it would take to channels of melancholy, of deep and tearful sentiment, or of a strong and musky religiosity. His mind and his emotions were like his face, constantly erupting, constantly raw and irritated. He had times of violent purity when he howled at his own depravity, and these were usually followed by a melancholy laziness that all but prostrated him, and he went from the depression into sleep. It was opiatic and left him drugged and dull for a long time.

He wore pierced white and brown saddle oxfords on bare feet this morning, and his ankles, where they showed below the turned-up jeans, were streaked with dirt. In his periods of depression Pimples was so prostrated that he did not bathe nor even eat very much. The felt hat crown notched so evenly was not really for beauty but served to keep his long light brown hair out of his eyes and to keep the grease out of it when he worked under a car. Now he stood stupidly watching Juan Chicoy put the tools in his box while his mind rolled in great flannel clouds of sleepiness, almost nauseating in their power.

Juan said, "Get the work light on the long cord connected. Come on, Pimples. Come on now, wake up!"

Pimples seemed to shake himself like a dog. "Can't seem to come out of it," he explained.

"Well, get the light out there and take my back board out. We've got to get going."

Pimples picked up the hand light, basketed for protection of the globe, and began unwinding the heavy rubber-guarded cable from around its handle. He plugged the cord into an outlet near the door and the hand light leaped into brilliance. Juan lifted his toolbox and stepped out of the door and looked at the darkened sky. A change had come in the air. A little wind was stirring the young leaves of the oaks and whisking among the geraniums and it was an uncertain, wet wind. Juan smelled it as he would smell a flower.

"By God, if it rains," he said, "that would be one too many."

To the east the tops of the mountains were just becoming visible in outline with the dawn. Pimples came out carrying the lighted hand lamp and unkinking the cable behind him on the ground. The light made the great trees stand out, and it was reflected on the yellow-green of the new little oak leaves. Pimples took his light to the bus and went back to the garage for the long board with casters on the bottom on which a man could lie and wheel himself about when he worked under a car. He flung the board down beside the bus.

"Well, it's like to rain," he said. "Take nearly every year in California it rains this season."

Juan said, "I'm not complaining about the season, but with this ring gear out and the passengers waiting, and the ground is pulpy with rain—"

"Makes good feed," said Pimples.

Juan stopped and looked around at him. His eyes crinkled with amusement. "Sure," he said, "it sure does."

Pimples looked shyly away.

The bus was lighted by the hand lamp now and it looked strange and helpless, for where the rear wheels should have been were two heavy sawhorses, and instead of resting on axles the rear of the bus rested on a four-by-four which extended from one horse to the other.

It was an old bus, a four-cylinder, low-compression engine with a special patented extra gear shift which gave it five speeds ahead instead of three, two below the average ratio, and two speeds in reverse. The ballooning sides of the bus, heavy and shining with aluminum paint, showed nevertheless the bumps and bends, the wracks and scratches, of a long and violent career. A home paint job on an old automobile somehow makes it look even more ancient and disreputable than it would if left in honorable decay.

Inside, the bus was rebuilt too. The seats which had once been woven of cane were now upholstered in red oilcloth, and while the job was neatly done, it was not professionally done. There was the slightly sour smell of oilcloth in the air and the frankly penetrating odor of oil and gasoline. It was an old, old bus, and it had seen many trips and many difficulties. Its oaken floorboards were scooped and polished by the feet of passengers. Its sides were bent and straightened. Its windows could not be opened, for the whole body was slightly wracked out of shape. In the summer Juan removed the windows and in the winter put them back again.

The driver's seat was worn through to the springs, but in the worn place was a flowered chintz pillow which served the double purpose of protecting the driver and holding down the uncovered springs. Hanging from the top of the windshield were the penates: a baby's shoe—that's for protection, for the stumbling feet of a baby require the constant caution and aid of God; and a tiny boxing glove—and that's for power, the power of the fist on the driving forearm, the drive of the piston pushing its connecting rod, the power of person as responsible and proud individual. There hung also on the windshield a little plastic kewpie doll with a cerise and green ostrich-feather headdress and a provocative sarong. And this was for the pleasures of the flesh and of the eye, of the nose, of the ear. When the bus was in motion these hanging items spun and jerked and swayed in front of the driver's eye.

Where the windshield angled in the middle and the center of support went up, sitting on top of the dashboard was a small metal Virgin of Guadalupe painted in brilliant colors. Her rays were gold and her robe was blue and she stood on the new moon, which was supported by cherubs. This was Juan Chicoy's connection with eternity. It had little to do with religion as connected with the church and dogma, and much to do with religion as memory and feeling. This dark Virgin was his mother and the dim house where she, speaking Spanish with a little brogue, had nursed him. For his mother had made the Virgin of Guadalupe her own personal goddess. Out had gone St. Patrick and St. Bridget and the ten thousand pale virgins of the North, and into her had entered this dark one who had blood in her veins and a close connection with people.

His mother admired her Virgin, whose day is celebrated with exploding skyrockets, and, of course, Juan Chicoy's Mexican father didn't think of it one way or another. Skyrockets were by nature the way to celebrate Saints' Days. Who could think otherwise? The rising, hissing tube was obviously the spirit rising to Heaven, and the big, flashing bang at the top was the dramatic entrance to the throne room of Heaven. Juan Chicoy, while not a believer in an orthodox sense, now he was fifty, would nevertheless have been uneasy driving the bus without the Guadalupana to watch over him. His religion was practical.

Below the Virgin was a kind of converted glove box, and in it were a Smith & Wesson 45-caliber revolver, a roll of bandage, a bottle of iodine, a vial of lavender smelling salts, and an unopened pint of whisky. With this equipment Juan felt fairly confident that he could meet most situations.

The front bumpers of the bus had once borne the inscription, still barely readable, "*el Gran Poder de Jesus*," "the great power of Jesus." But that had been painted on by a former owner. Now the simple word "Sweetheart" was boldly lettered on front and rear bumpers. And the bus was known as "Sweetheart" to all who knew her. Now she was immobilized, her rear wheels off, her end sticking up in the air and resting on a four-by-four set between two sawhorses.

Juan Chicoy had the new ring and pinion gears and he was rolling them carefully together. "Hold the light close," he said to Pimples, and he turned the pinion in the ring all the way around. "I remember once I put a new ring on an old pinion and she went out right away."

"Busted tooth sure makes a noise," said Pimples. "It sounds like it's coming through the floor at you. What do you suppose knocked that tooth out?"

Juan held the ring gear up sideways and in front of the light turned the pinion slowly, inspecting the fit of tooth against tooth as he went. "I don't know," he said. "There's lots nobody knows about metal and about engines too. Take Ford. He'll make a hundred cars and two or three of them will be no damn good. It's not just one thing that's bad, the whole car's bad. The springs and the motor and the water pump and the fan and the carburetor. It just breaks down little by little and there don't nobody know what makes them. And you'll take another car right off the line, you'd say it was just exactly the same as the others, but it's not. It's got something the others haven't got. It's got more power. It's almost like a guy with a lot of guts. It won't bust down no matter what you do."

"I had one of them," said Pimples. "Model A. I sold her. Bet she's still running. Had her three years and never spent a dime on her."

Juan laid his ring gear and pinion on the step of the bus and picked up the old ring from the ground. With his finger he traced the raw place where the tooth had broken out. "Metal's funny stuff," he said. "Sometimes it seems to get tired. You know, down in Mexico where I came from they used to have two or three butcher knives. They'd use one and stick the others in the ground. 'It rests the blade,' they said. I don't know if it's true, but I know those knives would take a shaving edge. I guess nobody knows about metal, even the people that make it. Let's get this pinion on the shaft. Here, hold the light back here."

Juan put his little platform behind the bus and he lay on it on his back and scooted himself under with his feet. "Hold the light a little more to the left. No, higher. There. Now shove me my toolbox, will you?"

Juan's hands worked busily and a little oil dropped down on his cheek. He rubbed it off with the back of his hand. "This is a mean job," he said.

Pimples peered underneath the bus at him. "Maybe I could hook the light over that nut," he said.

"Oh, you'd just have to move it in a minute," said Juan.

Pimples said, "I sure hope you get her going today. I'd like to sleep in my own bed tonight. You don't get no rest in a chair."

Juan chuckled. "Did you ever see madder people in your life when we had to come back after that tooth broke out? You'd think I did it on purpose. They were so mad they gave Alice hell about the pie. I guess they thought she made it. When people are traveling they don't like anything to interrupt them."

"Well, they got our beds," Pimples observed. "I don't see what they got to squawk about. You and me and Alice and Norma were the ones slept in chairs. And them Pritchards was the worst. I don't mean Mildred, the girl, but her old man and old lady. They figure they've been getting gypped someway. He tells me a hundred times how he's a president or something and he's going to make somebody suffer for this. Outrage, he says it was. And him and his wife had your bed. Where'd Mildred sleep?" Pimples' eyes glowed a little.

"On the davenport, I guess," said Juan. "Or maybe with her father and mother. That fellow from the trick company got Norma's room."

"I kinda liked that guy," Pimples said. "He didn't say nothing much. He said he'd just as soon set up. He didn't say what line he was in. But them Pritchards made up for it, all except Mildred. You know where they're going, Mr. Chicoy? They're going on a trip down to Mexico. Mildred's been studying Spanish in college. She's going to interpret for them."

Juan drove a key pin into the shaft and pounded it gently into place. He pulled himself from under the bus. "Let's get that rear-end assembly now."

Light was creeping up the sky and over the mountains. The colorless dawn of grays and blacks moved in so that white and blue things were silver and red and dark green things were black. The new leaves on the big oaks were black and white, and the mountain rims were sharp. Lumpish, heavy clouds that rolled in the sky like dumplings were beginning to take on a faint rose-pink color on their eastern edges.

Suddenly the lights in the lunchroom sprang on and the geranium border around the building leaped into being. Juan glanced toward the lights. "Alice is up," he said. "Won't be long till the coffee's ready. Come on, let's move the rear end in now."

The two men worked together well. Each understood what was to be done. Each did his piece. Pimples lay on his back too, tightening the housing nuts, and in the teamwork a good feeling came to him.

Juan strained a tight forearm against a nut and his wrench slipped and he took skin and flesh off his knuckle. The blood ran thick and black out of his greasy hand. He put the knuckle in his mouth and sucked it and made a line of grease around his mouth.

"Hurt it bad?" Pimples asked.

"No, it's good luck, I guess. You can't finish a job without blood. That's what my old man used to say." He sucked the blood again and already the flow was lessening.

The warmth and pinkness of the dawn sneaked in about them so that the electric light seemed to lose some of its brilliance.

"I wonder how many will come in on the Greyhound," Pimples asked idly. And then a strong thought came to him out of the good feeling for Mr. Chicoy. It was a thought so sharp that it almost hurt him. "Mr. Chicoy," he began uncertainly, and his tone was fawning, craven, begging.

Juan stopped turning the nut and waited for the request for a day off, for a raise, for something. There was going to be a request. That was inherent in the tone, and to Juan it was trouble. Trouble always started this way.

Pimples was silent. He couldn't get the words.

"What do you want?" Juan asked guardedly.

"Mr. Chicoy, could we fix it—I mean—could you fix it so you don't call me Pimples any more?"

Juan took his wrench from the nut and turned his head sideways. The two were lying on their backs, their faces toward each other. Juan saw the craters of old scars and the coming eruptions and one prime, tight, yellow-headed pustule about to burst on the cheek. As he looked, Juan's eyes softened. He knew. It came on him suddenly, and he wondered why he had not known before.

"What's your name?" he asked roughly.

"Ed," said Pimples. "Ed Carson, distant relative of Kit Carson. Before I got these in grammar school, why, they used to call me Kit." His voice was studied and calm, but his chest rose and fell heavily and the air whistled in his nostrils.

Juan looked away from him and back at the bulbous lump of the rear-end housing. "O.K.," he said, "let's get the jacks underneath." He rolled out from under the bus. "Get the oil in there now."

Pimples went quickly into the garage and brought out the pressure gun, trailing the air hose behind him. He turned the pet cock and the compressed air hissed into the gun behind the oil. The gun clicked as he filled the housing with the oil until a little ran thickly out. He screwed in the plug.

Juan said, "Kit, wipe your hands and see if Alice has got any coffee ready, will you?"

Pimples went toward the lunchroom. Near the door where one of the great oaks stood there was a patch of near darkness. He stood there for a moment, holding his breath. He was shaking all over in a kind of a chill.

Chapter 3

WHEN the rim of the sun cleared the mountains to the east, Juan Chicoy stood up from the ground and brushed the dirt from the legs and seat of his overalls. The sun flashed on the windows of the lunchroom and lay warm on the green grass that edged the garage. It blazed on the poppies in the flat fields and on the great islands of blue lupines.

Juan Chicoy went to the entrance door of the bus. He reached in, turned the ignition key, and pushed down the starter with the heel of his hand. For a while the starter whined rustily, and then the engine caught and roared for a moment until Juan throttled it down. He pushed down the clutch with his hand, put the gear in compound low, and let up the clutch. The rear wheels turned slowly in the air and Juan went around to the rear to listen to the action of the gears, to try to hear any uneven matching of the assembly.

Pimples was washing his hands in a flat pan of gasoline in the garage. The sun warmed a brown leaf left by the past year and blown into a corner of the garage doorframe. After a while a little night-laden fly crawled heavily out from under the leaf and stood in the clear sun. Its wings were muddily iridescent and it was sluggish with night cold. The fly rubbed its wings with its legs and then it rubbed its legs together and then it rubbed its face with its forelegs while the sun, slanting under the great puffed clouds, warmed its juices. Suddenly the fly took off, circled twice, fluttered under the oaks and crashed against the screen door of the lunch room, fell on its back and buzzed against the ground, upside down for a second. Then it righted itself and flew up and took its position on the frame beside the lunchroom door.

Alice Chicoy, haggard from the night of sitting up, came to the door and looked out toward the bus. The screen door opened only a few inches, but the fly flung himself through the opening. Alice saw him come through and whacked at him with the dish towel she carried in her hand. The fly buzzed crazily for a moment and then settled under the edge of the counter. Alice watched the rear wheels of the bus idly turning in the air and then she went in back of the counter and turned off the steam valve of the coffee urn.

The brown fluid in the glass pipe on the side of the urn looked thin and pale. She ran her towel over the counter and in doing so noticed that the big white coconut cake in its transparent plastic cover was ragged on one edge with a "V" cut out of it. She took a knife from the silver tray, lifted the cover, trimmed the cake's edge, and put the crumbs in her mouth. And just before the cover went back into place the fly lunged under the edge and flung himself on the coconut filling. He clung under a slight overhang so that he was not visible from above, and he dug and struggled hungrily into the sweet filling. He had a high, huge mountain of cake and he was very happy.

Pimples came in, smelling of gasoline and grease, and he took his place on one of the round stools. "Well, we got that done," he said.

"You and who else?" Alice asked satirically.

"Well, of course, Mr. Chicoy done the expert work. I'd like to have a cup of coffee and a piece of cake."

"You been in that cake already, before I got up." She brushed her hair out of her eyes with one hand. "You can't cover up," she said.

"Well, charge it to me," said Pimples. "I'm paying for my feed, ain't I?"

"What do you want to eat all that sweet stuff for?" Alice said. "You're at the candy tray all day long. You don't get hardly any pay. All goes for sweet stuff. I bet that's what makes all them pimples. Why don't you lay off for a while?"

Pimples looked shyly down at his hands. The nails were rimmed with black where the gasoline had not reached. "It's rich in food energy," he said. "Fellow's going to work, he needs food energy. Take about three o'clock in the afternoon when you get a let-down. Why, you need something rich in food energy."

"It's rich in lead in the pants," Alice observed. "You need food energy about as much as I need a—" and she left it in the air. Alice was a very profane woman but she never said the words, she only led up to them. She drew a cup of coffee from the spout—a thick, flat-bottom cup with no saucer—spurted in some milk and slipped the cup across the counter.

Pimples, looking hazily at the Coca-Cola girl who swung provocatively over the juke box, put in four spoonfuls of sugar and stirred the coffee around and around with the spoon straight up.

"I like to have a piece of cake," he repeated patiently.

"Well, it's your funeral. You're going to have a can on you like a balloon."

Pimples looked at Alice's well-formed behind and then quickly away. Alice took the knife from behind the counter and cut a wedge of coconut cake. The cliff of cake toppled on the fly and pressed him down. Alice shoveled the cake onto a saucer and slid it along the counter. Pimples went at it with his coffee spoon.

"Those folks didn't get up yet?" he asked.

"No, but I heard them stirring around. One of them must have used up all the hot water. I haven't got a bit in the lunch-room."

"That must be Mildred," said Pimples.

"Huh?"

"The girl. Maybe she took a bath."

Alice looked at him levelly. "You get to your food energy and keep your mind where it belongs," she said sharply.

"I never said nothing. Hey, there's a fly in this cake!"

Alice stiffened. "You had a fly in your soup yesterday. I think you carry flies in your pocket."

"No, look here. He's still kicking."

Alice came near. "Kill him," she cried. "Squash him! You want him to get loose?" She picked up a fork from behind the counter and mashed the fly and cake crumbs together and scraped the whole thing into the garbage can.

"How about my cake?" Pimples asked.

"You'll get another piece of cake. I don't know why you always get flies. Nobody else does."

"Just lucky, I guess," Pimples said softly.

"Huh?"

"I said I was—"

"I heard what you said." She was unrested and nervous. "You watch your mouth or you'll go out of here so fast you'll think you're on fire. I don't care if you are a mechanic. To me you're just a punk. A pimple-faced punk." Pimples had withered. His chin had settled lower and lower against his chest as her anger rose. And he didn't know that she was making him the depositary of a number of things.

"I didn't say nothing," he said. "Can't a guy even make a joke?"

Alice had reached a point where she had either to go on into a crazy, hysterical rage that tore the living daylights out of herself and everyone else around her, or she had to begin to taper off quickly, for she could feel the uncontrollable pressure rising in her chest and throat. In a second she appraised the situation. Things were tight. The bus had to get out. Juan had not rested either. The people who were using the beds would hear her rage and come out and Juan might hit her. He had once. Not hard, but accurately, and timed so perfectly that she imagined he had nearly killed her. And then the black fear that was always on the edge of her mind—Juan might leave her. He had left other women. How many she didn't know because he'd never spoken of it, but a man of his attractiveness must have left other women. All of this happened in a split second. Alice decided on no rage. She forced the pressure down in her chest. Woodenly she raised the plastic cake cover and cut an oversized wedge and put it on a saucer and she carried this down the counter and set it in front of Pimples.

"Everybody's nervous," she said.

Pimples looked up from his fingernails. He saw how the little lines of age were sneaking down her neck, and he noticed the thickness of her upper eyelids. He saw that her hands had lost the tightness of skin of young girls. He was very sorry for her. Unblessed with beauty as he was, he thought that youth was the only thing in the world worth having and that one who had lost youth was already dead. He had won a great victory this morning, and now when he saw the weakness and indecision in Alice he pressed for a second victory.

"Mr. Chicoy says he ain't going to call me Pimples no more," he said.

"Why not?"

"Well, I asked him not. My name's Edward. They used to call me Kit in school on account my last name's Carson."

"Is Juan calling you Kit?"

"Uh-huh."

Alice didn't really understand what it was about, and behind her in the bedroom there was movement, footsteps between the rugs and a little low talking. Now that she was aware of the strangers, Pimples became closer to her because he was not quite a stranger. "I'll see how it goes," she said.

The sun had been shining in through the front windows and the door, making five bright splashes on the wall, illuminating the grapenuts packages and the pyramids of oranges behind the counter. And now the bright squares dimmed and went out. There was a roll of thunder, and without warning the rain began. It whisked down on the roof.

Pimples went to the door and looked out. The rain sheeted down, obscuring the country, splashing high on the cement road. There was a steely look to the wet light. Pimples saw Juan Chicoy inside the bus for shelter. The back wheels were still turning around slowly. As he watched, Juan leaped to the ground and made a run for the lunchroom. Pimples held the door open for him and he bolted through, but even in the little run his overalls were dark with water and his shoes squidged sloppily on the floor.

"God Almighty," he said, "that's a real cloudburst."

The gray wall of water obscured the hills and there was a dark, metallic light with it. The heads of the lupines bent down, heavy with water. The petals of the poppies were beaten off and lay on the ground like gold coins. The already wet ground could absorb no more water, and little rivulets started immediately for the low places. The cloudburst roared on the roof of the lunchroom at Rebel Corners.

Juan Chicoy had taken one of the tables by the lunchroom window and he drank well-creamed coffee and chewed a doughnut and looked out at the downpour. Norma came in and began to wash the few dishes on the stainless steel sink behind the counter.

"Bring me another cup of coffee, will you?" Juan asked.

She came listlessly around the end of the counter. The cup was too full. A little stream of coffee dripped off the bottom of it. Juan pulled out a paper napkin and folded it as a blotter for the wet cup.

"Didn't get much rest, did you?" he asked.

Norma was drawn, and her dress was wrinkled. You could see now that she would be an old-looking woman long before she was old. Her skin was muddy and her thin hands were splotched. Many, many things gave Norma the hives.

"Didn't get any sleep at all," she said. "I tried the floor but I couldn't sleep."

"Well, we'll see it doesn't happen again," said Juan. "I should have got a car to take them into San Ysidro."

"Giving them our beds!" Alice said derisively. "Now, where did you get that idea? Where else do you suppose they could have got the owners' beds? They don't have to work today. They could just as well of sat up."

"Slipped up on me, I guess," said Juan.

"You don't care if your wife sleeps in a chair," Alice said. "You'd give away her bed any time." Again Alice could feel rage rising in her and it frightened her. She didn't want it to rise. She knew it would spoil things, and she was afraid of it, but there it was, rising and boiling in her.

A sheet of rain whisked over the roof like a heavy broom and left silence as it moved on, and almost immediately another flat of rain took its place. The drip and gurgle of water from the roof eaves and from the drains was loud again. Juan had been looking reflectively at the floor, a small smile tightening his mouth against the white band of the scar on his lip. And this was another thing Alice was frightened of. He had set her out to observe her. She knew that. All relations and all situations to Alice were person-to-person things in which she and the other were huge and all others were removed from the world. There was no shading. When she talked to Juan, there were only the two of them. When she picked at Norma, the whole world disappeared, leaving only Norma and her in a gray universe of cloud.

But Juan, now, he could shut everything out and look at each thing in relation to the other. Things of various sizes and importance. He could see and judge and consider and enjoy. Juan could enjoy people. Alice could only love, like, dislike, and hate. She saw and felt no shading whatever.

Now she tucked her loosening hair back. Once a month she used a rinse on her hair which was guaranteed to give it the mysterious and glamorous glints that capture and keep men in slavery. Juan's eyes were distant and amused. This was a matter of horror to Alice. She knew he was seeing her, not as an angry woman who darkened the world, but as one of thousands of angry women to be studied, inspected, and, yes, even enjoyed. This was the cold, lonely horror to her. Juan blotted out the universe to her and she sensed that she blotted out nothing to him. He could see not only around her but through her to something else. The remembered terror of the one time he had hit her lay not in the blow—she had been hit before, and far from hating it had taken excitement and exuberance from it—but Juan had hit her as he would a bug. He hadn't cared about it much. He hadn't even been very angry, just irritated. And he had hit a noisy thing to shut it up. Alice had only been trying to attract his attention in one of the few ways she knew. She was trying to do the same thing now, and she knew from the changed focus in his eye that he had slipped away from her.

"I try to make a nice little home for us; nice, and with a carpet and a velveteen suite, and you got to give it away to strangers." Her voice was losing its certainty. "And you let your own wife sit up in a chair all night."

Juan looked up slowly. "Norma," he said, "bring me another cup of coffee, will you? Plenty of cream."

Alice braced herself for the rage she knew was coming, and then Juan looked slowly toward her. His dark eyes were amused and warm, the focus changed again, and he was looking at her and she knew that he saw her.

"It didn't hurt you any," he said. "Make you appreciate the bed tonight."

Her breath caught. A hot wave flooded over her. Rage was transmuted to hot desire. She smiled at him vacantly and licked her lips. "You bastard," she said very softly. And she took a huge, shuddering sigh of air. "Want some eggs?" she asked.

"Yeah. Two in the water, about four minutes."

"I know how you like them," she said. "Bacon on the side?"

"No. A. piece of toast and a couple of doughnuts."

Alice went behind the counter. "I wish they'd come out of there," she said. "I'd like to use my own bathroom."

"They're stirring around," said Juan. "They'll be out in a little."

And they were stirring. There were footsteps in the bedroom. A door inside opened and a woman's voice said sharply, "Well, I think you could knock!" And a man replied, "I'm sorry, ma'am. The only other way was to go out the window."

Another man's voice with a brittle singsong of authority said, "Always a good idea to knock, my friend. Hurt your foot?"

"Yes."

The door at the end of the counter opened and a small man came out into the lunchroom. He was dressed in a double-breasted suit; his shirt was of that light brown color worn by traveling men and known as a thousand-miler because it does not show dirt. His suit was a neutral pepper-and-salt for the same reason, and he wore a knitted dark green tie. His face was sharp, like a puppy's face, and his eyes were bright and questioning, like a puppy's eyes. A small, carefully trimmed mustache rode his upper lip like a caterpillar, and when he talked it seemed to hump its back. His teeth were white and even except for the two front uppers, and these were glittering gold. He had a brushed look about him, as though he had cleaned the lint from his suit with his hairbrush; and his shirt had the strained appearance that comes from washing the collar in the hand basin and patting it flat on the dresser top to dry. There was a kind of shy confidence in his manner and a wincing quality in his face, as though he protected himself from insult with studied techniques.

"Morning, folks," he said. "I just wondered where you all slept. And I'll bet you sat up all night."

"Well, we did," Alice said sourly.

"It's all right," said Juan. "We'll get to bed early tonight."

"Get the bus fixed? Think we'll make it in this rain?"

"Oh, sure," said Juan.

The man limped around the end of the counter and sat painfully down at one of the little tables. Norma brought a glass of water and a handful of silver wrapped in a paper napkin.

"Eggs?"

"Fried, with their eyes open, crisp bacon, and buttered toast. Buttered—get it? Hardest thing in the world is to get buttered toast. Now you butter that toast, plenty of butter, and let it melt in so there's no yellow lumps showing and you'll get yourself a nice tip." He lifted his foot shod in a perforated and decorated brown oxford and looked at it and grunted with pain.

"Sprain your ankle?" Juan asked.

The door at the end of the counter opened and a medium-sized man came out. He looked like Truman and like the vice-presidents of companies and like certified public accountants. His glasses were squared off at the corners. His suit was gray and correct, and there was a little gray in his face too. He was a businessman, dressed like one, looked like one. In his lapel buttonhole there was a lodge pin so tiny that from four feet away you couldn't see what it was at all. His vest was unbuttoned one notch at the bottom. Indeed, this bottom button was not intended to be buttoned. A fine gold watch and key chain crossed this vest and ducked in and out of a buttonhole on the way.

He said, "Mrs. Pritchard will have scrambled eggs, moist if they're fresh, toast and marmalade. And Miss Pritchard only wants orange juice and coffee. I'll have grapenuts and cream, eggs turned over and well done—don't let the yolk be running —dry toast and Boston coffee—that's half milk. You can bring it all in on a tray."

Alice looked up with fury. "You better come out here," she said. "We haven't got tray service."

Mr. Pritchard looked at her coldly. "We got held up here," he said. "I've already lost one day of my vacation. It isn't my fault that the bus broke down. Now the least you can do is to bring that breakfast in. My wife isn't feeling so good. I'm not used to sitting on a stool and Mrs. Pritchard isn't either."

Alice lowered her head like an angry milk-cow. "Look, I want to go to the toilet and wash my face and you're holding up my bathroom."

Mr. Pritchard touched his glasses nervously. "Oh, I see." He turned his head toward Juan and the light reflected from his glasses so that there were two mirrors with no eyes behind them. His hand whipped his watch chain out of his vest pocket. He opened a little gold nail file and ran the point quickly under each nail. He looked about and a little shudder of uncertainty came over him. Mr. Pritchard was a business-man, president of a medium-sized corporation. He was never alone. His business was conducted by groups of men who worked alike, thought alike, and even looked alike. His lunches were with men like himself who joined together in clubs so that no foreign element or idea could enter. His religious life was again his lodge and his church, both of which were screened and protected. One night a week he played poker with men so exactly like himself that the game was fairly even, and from this fact his group was convinced that they were very fine poker players. Wherever he went he was not one man but a unit in a corporation, a unit in a club, in a lodge, in a church, in a political party. His thoughts and ideas were never subjected to criticism since he willingly associated only with people like himself. He read a newspaper written by and for his group. The books that came into his house were chosen by a committee which deleted material that might irritate him. He hated foreign countries and foreigners because it was difficult to find his counterpart in them. He did not want to stand out from his group. He would like to have risen to the top of it and be admired by it; but it would not occur to him to leave it. At occasional stags where naked girls danced on the tables and sat in great glasses of wine, Mr. Pritchard howled with laughter and drank the wine, but five hundred Mr. Pritchards were there with him.

And now, at the end of Alice's ugly statement about a toilet, he looked about the lunchroom and found that he was alone. There were no other Mr. Pritchards here. For a moment his glance rested on the little man in the business suit, but there was something queer about him. True, there was some kind of a pin in his buttonhole, a little blue enamel bar with white stars on it, but it was no club Mr. Pritchard recognized. He found himself hating these people and hating even his vacation. He wanted to go back to the bedroom and close the door, but here was this stout woman who wanted to go to the toilet. Mr. Pritchard cleaned his nails very rapidly with the gold nail file on his watch chain.

At bottom, and originally, Mr. Pritchard was not like this.

He had once voted for Eugene Debs, but that had been a long time ago. It was just that the people in his group watched one another. Any variation from a code of conduct was first noted, then discussed. A man who varied was not a sound man, and if he persisted no one would do business with him. Protective coloring was truly protective. But there was no double life in Mr. Pritchard. He had given up his freedom and then had forgotten what it was like. He thought of it now as youthful folly. He put his vote for Eugene Debs alongside his visit to a parlor house when he was twenty. Both were things to be expected of growing boys. He even occasionally mentioned at a club luncheon his vote for Debs, to prove that he had been a spirited young man and that such things were, like a kid's acne, a part of the process of adolescence. But although he excused and even enjoyed his prank in voting for Debs, he was definitely worried about the activities of his daughter Mildred.

She was playing around with dangerous companions in her college, professors and certain people considered Red. Before the war she had picketed a scrap-iron ship bound for Japan, and she had gathered money for medical supplies for what Mr. Pritchard called the Reds in the Spanish war. He did not discuss these things with Mildred. She didn't want to talk it out with him. And he had a strong feeling that if everyone was quiet and controlled she would get over it. A husband and a baby would resolve Mildred's political uneasiness. She would then, he said, find her true values.

Mr. Pritchard's visit to the parlor house he did not remember very well. He had been twenty and drunk, and afterward he had had a withering sense of desecration and sorrow. He did remember the subsequent two weeks when he had waited in terror for symptoms to develop. He had even planned to kill himself if they did; to kill himself and make it look like an accident.

Now he was nervous. He was on a vacation he didn't really want to take. He was going to Mexico which, in spite of the posters, he considered a country not only dirty but dangerously radical. They had expropriated the oil; in other words, stolen private property. And how was that different from Russia? Russia, to Mr. Pritchard, took the place of the medieval devil as the source of all cunning and evil and terror. He was nervous this morning because he hadn't slept either. He liked his own bed. It took him a week to get used to a bed, and here he was in for three weeks of a different bed practically every night, and God knew how some of them would be populated. He was tired and his skin felt grainy. The water was hard here so that when he shaved he knew he would have a ring of ingrown hairs around his neck within three days.

He took a handkerchief from his breast pocket, removed his glasses and polished them. "I'll tell my wife and daughter," he said. "We didn't know we were discommoding you so."

Norma liked that word and she said it over under her breath. "Discommode—I wouldn't want to discommode you, Mr. Gable, but I think you should know . . ."

Mr. Pritchard had gone back into the bedroom. His voice was audible, explaining the situation, and women's voices were questioning.

The man with the mustache got up from his chair and limped painfully to the counter, groaning under his breath. He brought the sugar bowl back with him and sank, with grimaces, back into his chair.

"I would have got that for you," Norma said with concern.

He smiled at her. "I wouldn't want to trouble you," he explained bravely.

"It wouldn't discommode me none," said Norma.

Juan put down his coffee cup.

Pimples said, "I'd like to have a piece of that coconut cake."

Alice absently cut him a piece and slid the saucer down the counter and made a note on a pad.

"I guess there ain't never one on the house," said Pimples.

"I figure there's plenty on the house the house don't know about," Alice replied.

"Looks like a bad sprain you've got there," Juan observed to the little man.

"Crushed," he said, "toes crushed. Here, I'll show you."

Mr. Pritchard came out of the bedroom and took a seat at the remaining table.

The little man unlaced his oxford and took it off. He slipped his sock off and laid it carefully in the oxford. His foot was bandaged from the instep to the ends of the toes, and the bandage was spotted and soaked with bright red blood.

"You don't need to show us," Alice said quickly. Blood made her faint.

"I ought to change the bandage anyway," said the little man, and he unwound the gauze and exposed the foot. The big toe and the two next to it were horribly crushed, the nails blackened and the ends of the toes tattered and bloody and raw.

Juan had arisen. Pimples came close. Even Norma could not stay away.

"My God, that's an awful smash," Juan said. "Let me get some water and wash it. You ought to have some kind of salve. You'll get an infection. You might lose that foot."

Pimples whistled shrilly between his teeth to indicate interest and a kind of enthusiasm for the quality of the hurt. The little man was looking into Juan's face, his eyes shining with pleasure and anticipation.

"You think it's bad?" he demanded.

"You're damn right, it's bad," said Juan.

"You think I should get a doctor?"

"Well, I would if it was me."

The little man chuckled with delight. "That's all I wanted to hear," he said. He ran his thumbnail down his instep, and the top of his foot lifted off—the skin, the blood, the mashed toes—and underneath there was his foot whole and unhurt and his toes untouched. He put back his head and laughed with glee.

"Good, isn't it? Plastic. New product."

Mr. Pritchard had come close, a look of disgust on his face.

"It's the 'Little Wonder Artificial Sore Foot,'" the man said. He pulled a flat box from his side pocket and handed it to Juan. "You've been so nice to me, I want you to have one. Compliments of Ernest Horton representing the Little Wonder Company." His voice raced with his enthusiasm. "It comes in three sizes—one, two, or three crushed toes. This one I'm giving you is the three-toe number, just like the one you just saw. It's got bandage and a bottle of artificial blood to keep the bandage looking terrible. Instructions inside. You've got to soften it in warm water the first time you put it on. Then it fits like skin and nobody can tell. You can have a barrel of fun with it."

Mr. Pritchard leaned forward. Way in the back of his mind he could see himself taking off his sock at a board meeting. He could do it right after he got back from Mexico, tell some story about bandits first.

"What do you get for them?" he asked.

"Dollar and a half, but I hardly ever sell for retail," Ernest Horton said. "The trade snaps them up as fast as I can get them. I sold forty gross to the trade in two weeks."

"No?" said Mr. Pritchard. His eyes were wide with appreciation.

"Show you my order book if you don't believe it. It's the fastest selling novelty I've ever handled. Little Wonder is cleaning up with it."

"What is the mark-up?" Mr. Pritchard demanded.

"Well, I wouldn't like to say unless you're in the trade. Business ethics, you know."

Mr. Pritchard nodded. "Well, I'd like to try one at the retail price," he said.

"Get you one right after I eat. You got that buttered toast?" he asked Norma.

"Coming up," said Norma, and she went guiltily behind the counter and switched on the toaster.

"You see, it's the psychology that sells it," Ernest said exultantly. "We've stocked artificial cut fingers for years and they moved slow, but this—it's the psychology of taking off your shoe and sock. Nobody ever thinks you'd go to the trouble of doing that. The fellow that figured that out got himself a very nice fee."

"I guess you're making a little something out of it yourself," said Mr. Pritchard with admiration. He was feeling much better now.

"I do all right," said Ernest. "I got one or two other little things that might interest you in my sample case. Not for sale except to the trade, but I'll demonstrate them. It might give you a laugh."

"I'd like to take half a dozen of the sore feet," said Mr. Pritchard.

"All the three toes?"

Mr. Pritchard considered. He wanted them for gifts, but he didn't want competition. Charlie Johnson could sell the tricks better than Mr. Pritchard could. Charlie was a natural comic.

"Suppose you let me have one three-toe and three two-toe

and two one-toe," he said. "That'd be about right for me, I guess."

The quality of the rain was changing. It came with great, gusty, drenching downpours and with short, drippy intervals between. Juan sat with his coffee by the window. Half a brown doughnut lay in the saucer.

"I think she's going to let up a little," said Juan. "I'd like to turn over that rear end some more before we start."

"I'd like to have a piece of that coconut cake," said Pimples.

"No you don't," Alice said. "I've got to keep a little cake for customers."

"Well, I'm a customer, ain't I?"

"I don't know if we'll get deliveries from San Ysidro today," said Alice. "I got to keep a little cake on hand."

At the very end of the counter there was a candy tray arranged like steps, with wrapped and packaged candy bars in it. Pimples got up from his stool and stood in front of the display. He considered the bright little packages a long time before he made his selections. Finally he picked out three bars and put them in his pocket. "One Baby Ruth, one Love Nest, and one Coconut Sweetheart," he said.

"Coconut Sweethearts are a dime. They got nuts," said Alice.

"I know," said Pimples.

Alice picked up her pad from behind the counter. "You're one jump ahead of your pay now," she said.

Chapter 4

THE moment the Pritchards came out of the bedroom Norma said quickly, "I got to brush my hair and clean up a little bit." And she bolted for the door. Alice was right behind her.

"After me in the bathroom," Alice said coldly. Norma went across the bedroom of Mr. and Mrs. Chicoy and into her own bedroom. She closed the door behind her and, as there was no key, she snapped the little catch beside the lock to secure her privacy. Her narrow iron Army cot was unmade, and Ernest Horton's big sample case stood against the wall.

It was a very narrow room. A dresser with a bowl and pitcher stood against one wall, a silken pillow top, fringed and shiny, was tacked up over the dresser. It was pink and had a picture of crossed cannons in front of a bunch of red roses. And printed on the pillow top was a poem called "A Soldier's Prayer to His Mother."

> Midst shot and shell I think of you, Mother dear
> I hope your prayers will keep me clear
> And when the war is o'er and won,
> I will come back to you, my Number One.

Norma looked quickly at the window, murky with rainy light, and then she reached inside the neck of her dress and turned back the material. On a safety pin, fastened to the turned edge, was a small key. Norma unpinned it. She pulled her suitcase from under the dresser, unlocked and opened it. A shiny picture of Clark Gable in a silver frame lay on top, and it was signed "With Best Regards—Clark Gable." She had bought the picture and frame and signature in a gift shop in San Ysidro.

She ran her hand quickly to the bottom of the suitcase. Her fingers came on a little square ring box. She pulled it out and jerked it open, saw that the rings were there, and shoved the box back to the bottom of the suitcase. She closed and locked the case, pushed it under the dresser, and pinned the key back inside her dress. She opened the dresser drawer, lifted out a brush and comb, and went to the window. On the wall beside the red-and-green-flowered cretonne drapes there was a framed mirror. Norma stood in front of it and looked at herself.

A lead-colored light came through the window and fell on her face. She widened her eyes with intensity and then she smiled, showing all her teeth, smiled vivaciously. She stood on her toes a little and waved to an immense crowd and smiled again. She ran the comb through her thin hair and tugged as the teeth caught in the marceled ends. She got a pencil from the dresser and worked the dull point through her pale eyebrows, accentuating the curve in the middle so that her face took on a surprised look. Then she began to brush her hair, ten strokes on one side and ten on the other. And while she brushed, she raised and flexed the muscles of one leg and then the other to develop the calves. It was a routine recommended by a picture star who had never willingly taken any exercise of any kind but who had beautiful legs.

Norma glanced quickly at the window as the light grew still dimmer. She would have hated to be observed in the grotesque dance. Norma was even more submerged than an iceberg. Only the tiniest part of Norma showed above the surface. For the greatest and best and most beautiful part of Norma lay behind her eyes, sealed and protected.

The doorknob of her bedroom turned and then there was pressure against the door. Norma stiffened and stood rigid. Only one hand moved, and it frantically rubbed at her eyebrows and succeeded in making gray smudges on her forehead. And now there came a knocking at the bedroom door. A light, courteous knocking. She put her brush on the dresser, smoothed down her dress, and went to the door. She pushed the catch and opened the door a crack. The face of Ernest Horton was looking in at her. His tight, hairy mustache arched over his mouth.

"I thought I'd take my sample case out of your way," he said.

Norma still held the door open only a crack.

"You folks have been so nice and all," he went on. "I don't want to be any more nuisance than I have to."

Norma slowly relaxed, but she was still breathing a little hard. She opened the door and stepped back. Ernest, with a smile of embarrassment, came into the room. He went to the bed.

"I should have made this bed," he said, and he drew the sheet and blanket up and began to pat the wrinkles out.

"No, I'll do that," said Norma.

"You didn't even wait for your tip I promised you," said Ernest. "But I've got it for you." He made the bed neatly, as though he had done it many times before.

"I could have done that just as well," said Norma.

"Well, it's done now," he said. He went to his big sample case. "Mind if I open this? I want to get some stuff out."

"Go ahead," said Norma. Her eyes filled with interest.

He laid the big sample case on her bed and snapped the catch and threw back the lid. There were wonderful things in the case. There were cardboard tubes and handkerchiefs that changed color. There were exploding cigars and stink-bombs. There were voice-throwers and horns and paper hats for parties and pennants and funny buttons. There were silken pillows like the one on the wall. Ernest was extracting six of the artificial sore feet in their flat packages, and Norma had moved close to look into the wonderful sample case. Her eyes had been caught by a series of photographs of picture stars. They were not like any she had ever seen. The pictures were pressed and molded into thick sheets of sheer plastic at least a quarter of an inch through. And there was another curious thing about them. The pictures did not look flat. By some trick of bending, or possibly of refracted light, the faces were rounded and had depth. They seemed to be three-dimensional, and the frames were eight by ten inches in size.

On top was a lifelike, smiling picture of James Stewart, and projecting from under that was a second picture of which she could only see the hair and a part of the forehead, but she knew that hair and that forehead. Her lips parted and a shine came into her eyes. Slowly her hand moved into the case and lifted James Stewart aside. And there he was, Clark Gable, looking round and full. It was a serious, intense pose, the chin out, the eyes level and intent. It was such a picture as she had never seen. She sighed deeply and tried to control her breath so that it could not be heard. She lifted the picture out and stared into the eyes, and her own were wide and hypnotized.

Ernest watched her and saw her interest. "Isn't that a knockout?" he said. "It's a new idea. Notice how it looks round, almost like a statue?"

Norma nodded, speechless.

"I make a prophecy," Ernest said. "I go down the line and lay my word on it. That little number is going to wipe every other kind of pictures right off the map. It's acid-proof, moisture-proof, lasts forever, won't ever turn brown. It's molded and baked right inside the frame. It'll last forever."

Norma's eyes never left the picture. Ernest reached for the picture and her fingers tightened on it like claws.

"How much?" Her voice came out a throaty, rasping growl.

"It's just a sample," said Ernest. "It's something to show to the trade. It's not for sale. You order them."

"How much?" Her fingers were white with pressure. Ernest looked at her closely. He saw her face intent and set, jaw muscles rigid and nostrils flaring a little with controlled breathing.

Ernest said, "They bring two bucks retail, but I said I was going to give you a nice tip. Would you rather have that than a nice tip?"

Norma's voice was hoarse. "Yes."

"Well, then, you can have it."

The whiteness went slowly out of her fingers. There was a light of glory in her eyes. She licked her lips. "Thanks," she said. "Oh, thanks, mister!" She turned the face of the picture toward her and pressed it against her. The plastic was not cold, like glass, but warm and soft-feeling.

"I guess I can get along with only one sample," Ernest said. "See, I'm swinging south. I won't go back to the head office for six weeks. I figured to spend two weeks in L.A. That's a great place for novelties."

Norma carried the picture to her dresser and opened the drawer and shoved the picture down under a pile of clothes and closed the drawer. "I suppose you'll get to Hollywood," she said.

"Oh, sure. That's even better than L.A. for novelties. Then, it's kind of like my vacation too. I've got a lot of friends there. I have my vacation and get around and see things and I see the trade too. Kills two birds. I don't lose any time. I got an Army friend works in a studio there. I always run around some with him. Last time we had a party it started out in the Melrose Grotto. That's over on Melrose, right next to RKO. And that really was a party! I wouldn't really like to tell you what we did do, but I never had so much fun in my life. And then my friend, of course, had to go back to work at the studio.

Norma had become as intent as a setter pup watching a bug. "Your friend works in a studio?" she asked casually. "Which one?"

"Metro-Goldwyn-Mayer," said Ernest. He was repacking his sample case and not looking up at her. He did not hear the rasp of breath in her throat or the unnatural tone that came into her voice.

"You go into the studio lots?"

"Yeah. Willie gets me a pass. I go and watch them shoot sometimes. Willie's a carpenter. Worked there before the war and now he's back there. I soldiered with him. Awful nice fellow. And what a guy at parties! He knows more dames, he's got more phone numbers than you ever saw. A big thick black book full of phone numbers. Even he can't remember who half the dames are he's got the phone numbers of."

Ernest was warming to his subject. He sat down on the little straight chair beside the wall. He chuckled. "Willie was stationed in Santa Ana first of the war, before I even knew him. Well, the officers got to know about his black book and they'd take Willie into Hollywood and he'd get dames for them and then Willie got a pass when he wanted it. He was making out good when they shipped his outfit out."

Norma's eyes took on a quick look of annoyance during this recital. Her fingers picked at her apron. Her voice became high and then low. "I wonder if it would discommode you to do a favor for me?"

"Sure," said Ernest. "What do you want?"

"Well, if I was to give you a letter and you was—er—were on the MGM lot and you happened to see Mr. Gable, why I wonder if you'd give it to him?"

"Who's Mr. Gable?"

"Mr. Clark Gable," said Norma sternly.

"Oh, him. You know him?"

"Yes," said Norma frostily, "I'm—I'm his cousin."

"Oh, I see. Well, sure I will. But maybe I don't go. Why don't you put it in the mail?"

Norma's eyes narrowed. "He don't get his mail," she said mysteriously. "There's a girl, a secretary like, that just takes it and burns it up."

"No!" said Ernest. "What for?"

Norma stopped to consider this. "They just don't want him to see it."

"Not even from his own relatives?"

"Not even from his cousin," said Norma.

"Did he tell you that?"

"Yes." Her eyes were wide and blank. "Yes. Course I'll go there pretty soon," she said. "I've had offers and once I was just about to go and my cousin—Mr. Gable, that is—he said, 'No, you've got to get experience,' he said. 'You're young. You're not in any hurry.' So I'm getting experience. You learn a lot about people in a lunchroom. I study them all the time."

Ernest looked at her a little skeptically. He knew the fantastic stories about waitresses who became dramatic stars overnight, but Norma didn't have the bubs for it, he thought, nor the legs. Norma's legs were like sticks. But, then, he knew about two or three picture stars who were so plain without make-up that no one would recognize them off the screen. He'd read about them. And Norma, even if she didn't look it—well, they could pad her out, and if her cousin was Clark Gable, why, that was an "in" you couldn't beat. That was the breaks.

"Well, I hadn't thought much about asking Willie to get me a pass this time," he said. "I've been out there quite a few times but—well, if you want me to I'll go right in, find him, and give him your letter. What do you suppose they throw away his mail for?"

"They just want to work him to death and then throw him away like an old shoe," said Norma passionately. Wave after wave of emotion swept over her. She was in an ecstasy, and at the same time panic was crowding up on her. Norma was not a liar. She had never done anything like this before. She was going out on a long teetering plank and she knew it. One question, one bit of knowledge on Ernest's part, would throw her off and hurtle her into a chasm, and yet she couldn't stop.

"He's a great man," she said, "a great gentleman. He don't like the parts they make him do because he isn't like that. Even Rhett Butler—he didn't like to play that because he's not a rat and he don't like to play rat parts."

Ernest had lowered his eyes and was studying Norma through his eyelashes. And Ernest was beginning to understand. The key to it was creeping into his brain. Norma was as pretty now as she was ever likely to be. There was dignity in her face, courage, and a truly great flow of love. There were only two things for Ernest to do—to laugh at her or play along. If there'd been any other person in the room—another man, for instance—he probably would have laughed to protect himself from the other person's scorn, and he would have been ashamed and more boisterous because he could see that it was a powerful, pure, and overwhelming thing shining in this girl. This was the thing that kept the neophytes lying through the nights on the stone floors in front of the altars. This was an outpouring of an attar of love, of a naked intensity that Ernest had never seen before in anyone.

"I'll take the letter," he said. "I'll tell him it's from his cousin."

A look of fright came on Norma's face. "No," she said, "I'd rather surprise him. Just tell him it's from a friend. Don't tell him a single other thing."

"When do you think you'll be going down there to take a job?" Ernest asked.

"Well, Mr. Gable says I ought to wait another year. He says I'm young and need experience studying people. I get pretty tired of it sometimes, though. Sometimes I wish I was there in my own house with them—those—big, thick curtains and a long couch, like, and I'd see all my friends—Bette Davis and Ingrid Bergman and Joan Fontaine, because I don't mess around with that other kind that's always getting divorced and things like that. We just sit around and talk about serious things, and we study all the time because that's how you get ahead and be a great actress. And there's lots that treat their fans mean; won't sign autographs and things like that, but not us! Not our kind, I mean. We even have girls right off the streets sometimes in for a cup of tea and talk and just like they were us because we know we owe everything we got to the loyalty of our fans." She was quaking inside with fear and she couldn't stop. She was getting far out on the plank and she couldn't stop and it was about to throw her.

Ernest said, "I didn't understand at first. You've already been in pictures. Are you a star already?"

"Yes," said Norma. "But you wouldn't know me by the name I'm using here. I have another name I use in Hollywood."

"What is it?"

"I couldn't tell," said Norma. "You're the only person anywhere around here that knows anything about me. Now, you won't tell, will you?"

Ernest was shaken. "No," he said, "I won't tell if you don't want me to."

"Keep my secret inviolate," said Norma.

"Sure," said Ernest. "Just give me the letter and I'll see he gets it."

"You'll see who gets what?" said Alice from the doorway. "What are you two doing alone in a bedroom?" Her eyes roved suspiciously about for evidence, skimmed over the sample case on the bed, stopped on the pillow, inspected the spread, and then moved to Norma. Alice's eyes traveled up her feet and legs, lingered a moment on her skirt, hesitated on her waist, and then settled on her flaming face.

Norma was almost sick with embarrassment. Her cheeks were splotched with blood. Alice put her hands on her hips.

Ernest said placatingly, "I was just getting my sample case out of the way and she asked me to take a note to a cousin of hers in L.A."

"She's got no cousin in L.A."

"Yes, she has too," Ernest said angrily, "and I know her cousin."

And now the rage that had been trying to get out of Alice all morning burst from her. "You listen to me," she shouted. "I won't have you drummers diddling my hired girls."

"Nobody's touched her," Ernest said. "Nobody laid a hand on her."

"No? Well, then, what'cha doing in her bedroom? Take a

look at her face." The hysteria boiled over in Alice. A heavy, throaty, screaming voice came from her throat. Her hair fell about her face and her eyes rolled and watered and her lips became cruel and tight, as a fighter's do when he is slugging a half-conscious opponent. "I won't have it. You think I want her knocked up? You think I want bastards all over the place? We give you our beds and our rooms!"

"I tell you nothing happened!" Ernest shouted at her. He was overwhelmed with hopelessness in the face of this craziness. His denials sounded in his ears almost like admissions. He didn't understand why she was doing it, and the injustice made him sick to his stomach and rage was rising in him too.

Norma's mouth was open and she was catching the microbe of hysteria. Whinnying cries came from her with every panting breath. Her hands fought in front of her as though they were trying to destroy each other.

Alice advanced on Norma and her right fist was doubled, not like a woman's fist, but with the fingers folded tightly and the knuckles up and outstuck, the thumb laid close against the first joints. Her words were thick and moist. "Get out of here! Get out of the whole place! Get out in the rain!" Alice descended on Norma and Norma backed away and a terrified scream came from her mouth.

There were quick steps in the doorway and Juan said sharply, "Alice!"

She stopped. Her mouth sagged open and her eyes grew afraid. Juan came slowly into the room. His thumbs were hooked in his overalls pockets. He moved toward her as lightly as a creeping cat. The gold ring on his amputated finger glimmered in the leaden light from the window. Alice's rage poured over into terror. She cringed away from him, passed the end of the bed and into the blind alley until she came up against the wall, and there she was stopped.

"Don't hit me," she whispered. "Oh, please don't hit me."

Juan came close to her and his right hand moved slowly to her arm just above the elbow. He was looking at her, not through her or around her. He swung her gently about and led her across the room and through the door and he closed the door on Norma and Ernest.

They stared at the closed door and hardly breathed. Juan led

Alice to the double bed and turned her gently and she sagged down like a cripple and fell back, staring wildly up at him. He picked a pillow from the top of the bed and put it under her head. His left hand, the one with the stump finger and the wedding ring, stroked her cheek gently. "You'll be all right now," he said.

She crossed her arms over her face and her sobs were strangled and harsh and dry.

Chapter 5

BERNICE PRITCHARD and her daughter Mildred and Mr. Pritchard sat at the small table to the right of the entrance door of the lunchroom. The little group had drawn closer together. The two older people because they felt that in some way they were under attack, and Mildred in a kind of protective sense toward them. She often wondered how her parents had survived in a naughty and ferocious world. She considered them naïve and unprotected little children, and to a certain extent she was right about her mother. But Mildred overlooked the indestructibility of the child and the stability, its pure perseverance to get its own way. And there was a kind of indestructibility about Bernice. She was rather pretty. Her nose was straight and she had for so long worn pince-nez that the surfaces between her eyes were shaped by the pressure. The high, gristly part of her nose was not only very thin from the glasses, but two red spots showed where the springs regularly pressed. Her eyes were violet colored and myopic, which gave her a sweet, inward look.

She was feminine and dainty and she dressed always with a hint of a passed period. She wore jabots occasionally and antique pins. Her shirtwaists had always some lace and some handwork, and the collars and cuffs were invariably immaculate. She used lavender toilet water so that her skin and her clothing and her purse smelled always of lavender, and of another, almost imperceptible, acid odor which was her own. She had pretty ankles and feet, on which she wore very expensive shoes, usually of kid and laced, with a little bow over the instep. Her mouth was rather wilted and childlike, soft, and without a great deal of character. She talked very little but had in her own group gained a reputation for goodness and for sagacity; the first by saying only nice things about people, even people she did not know, and the second by never expressing a general idea of any kind beyond perfumes or food. She met the ideas of other people with a quiet smile, almost as though she forgave them for having ideas. The truth was that she didn't listen.

There had been times when Mildred wept with rage at her mother's knowing, forgiving smile after one of Mildred's political or economic deliveries. It took the daughter a long time to discover that her mother never listened to any conversation that had not to do with people or places or material things. On the other hand, Bernice never forgot a detail about goods or colors or prices. She could remember exactly how much she had paid for black suede gloves seven years ago. She was fond of gloves and rings—any kind of rings. She had a rather large collection, but she wore with anything else, always, her small diamond engagement ring and her gold wedding band. These she removed only to bathe. She left them on when she washed her combs and brushes in ammonia water in the hand basin. The ammonia cleaned the rings and made the little diamonds shine brightly.

Her married life was fairly pleasant and she was fond of her husband. She thought she knew his weaknesses and his devices and his desires. She herself was handicapped by what is known as a nun's hood, which prevented her experiencing any sexual elation from her marriage; and she suffered from an acid condition which kept her from conceiving children without first artificially neutralizing her body acids. Both of these conditions she considered normal, and any variation of them abnormal and in bad taste. Women of lusty appetites she spoke of as "that kind of woman," and she was a little sorry for them as she was for dope fiends and alcoholics.

Her husband's beginning libido she had accepted and then gradually by faint but constant reluctance had first molded and then controlled and gradually strangled, so that his impulses for her became fewer and fewer and until he himself believed that he was reaching an age when such things did not matter.

In her way she was a very powerful woman. She ran an efficient, clean, and comfortable house and served meals which were nourishing without being tasty. She did not believe in the use of spices, for she had been told long ago that they had an aphrodisiac effect on men. The three—Mr. Pritchard, Mildred, and herself—did not take on any weight, probably because of the dullness of the food. It did not stimulate any great appetite.

Bernice's friends knew her as one of the sweetest, most unselfish people you will ever meet, and they often referred to her as a saint. And she herself said often that she felt humbly lucky, for she had the finest, most loyal friends in the whole world. She loved flowers and planted and pinched and fertilized and cut them. She kept great bowls of flowers in her house always, so that her friends said it was like being in a florist's shop, and she arranged them herself so beautifully.

She did not take medicines and often suffered in silence from constipation until the accumulated pressure relieved her. She had never really been ill nor badly hurt, and consequently she had no measuring rod of pain. A stitch in her side, a backache, a gas pain under her heart, convinced her secretly that she was about to die. She had been sure she would die when she had borne Mildred, and she had arranged her affairs so that everything would be easy for Mr. Pritchard. She had even written a letter to be opened after her death, advising him to marry again so that the child could have some kind of mother. She later destroyed this letter.

Her body and her mind were sluggish and lazy, and deep down she fought a tired envy of the people who, so she thought, experienced good things while she went through life a gray cloud in a gray room. Having few actual perceptions, she lived by rules. Education is good. Self-control is necessary. Everything in its time and place. Travel is broadening. And it was this last axiom which had forced her finally on the vacation to Mexico.

How she reached her conclusions not even she knew. It was a long, slow process built up of hints, suggestions, accidents, thousands of them, until finally, in their numbers, they forced the issue. The truth was that she didn't want to go to Mexico. She just wanted to come back to her friends having been to Mexico. Her husband didn't want to go at all. He was doing it for his family and because he hoped it would do him good in a cultural way. And Mildred wanted to go, but not with her parents. She wanted to meet new and strange people and through such contacts to become new and strange herself. Mildred felt that she had great covered wells of emotion in her, and she probably had. Nearly everyone has.

Bernice Pritchard, while denying superstition, was nevertheless profoundly affected by signs. The bus breaking down so early in the trip frightened her, for it seemed to portend a series of accidents which would gradually ruin the trip. She was sensitive to Mr. Pritchard's unrest. Last night, lying sleepless in the Chicoys' double bed, listening to the sighing breaths of her husband, she had said, "This will turn into an adventure when it's over. I can almost hear you telling it. It will be funny."

"I suppose so," Mr. Pritchard answered.

There was a certain fondness between these two, almost a brother-and-sister relationship. Mr. Pritchard considered his wife's shortcomings as a woman the attributes of a lady. He never had to worry about her faithfulness. Unconsciously he knew that she was without reaction, and this was right in his mind. His nerves, his bad dreams, and the acrid pain that sometimes got into his upper abdomen he put down to too much coffee and not enough exercise.

He liked his wife's pretty hair, always waved and clean; he liked her spotless clothes; and he loved the compliments she got for her good housekeeping and her flowers. She was a wife to be proud of. She had raised a fine daughter, a fine, healthy girl.

Mildred was a fine girl; a tall girl, two inches taller than her father and five inches taller than her mother. Mildred had inherited her mother's violet eyes and the weakness that went with them. She wore glasses when she wanted to see anything clearly. She was well formed, with sturdy legs and strong, slender ankles. Her thighs and buttocks were hard and straight and smooth from much exercise. She played tennis well and was center on her college basketball team. Her breasts were large and firm and wide at the base. She had not inherited her mother's physiological accident, and she had experienced two consummated love affairs which gave her great satisfaction and a steady longing for a relationship that would be constant.

Mildred's chin was set and firm like her father's, but her mouth was full and soft and a little frightened. She wore heavy black-framed glasses, and these did give her a student look. It was always a surprise to new acquaintances to see Mildred at a dance without glasses. She danced well, if a little precisely, but she was a practicing athlete and perhaps she practiced dancing too carefully and without enough relaxation. She did have a slight tendency to lead, but that could be overcome by a partner with strong convictions.

Mildred's convictions were strong too, but they were variable. She had undertaken causes and usually good ones. She did not understand her father at all because he constantly confused her. Telling him something reasonable, logical, intelligent, she often found in him a dumb obtuseness, a complete lack of thinking ability that horrified her. And then he would say or do something so intelligent that she would leap to the other side. When she had him catalogued rather smugly as a caricature of a businessman, grasping, slavish, and cruel, he ruined her peace of conception by an act or a thought of kindliness and perception.

Of his emotional life she knew nothing whatever, just as he knew nothing of hers. Indeed, she thought that a man in middle age had no emotional life. Mildred, who was twenty-one, felt that the saps and juices were all dried up at fifty, and rightfully so, since neither men nor women were attractive at that age. A man or a woman in love at fifty would have been an obscene spectacle to her.

But if there was a chasm between Mildred and her father, there was a great gulf between Mildred and her mother. The woman who had no powerful desires to be satisfied could not ever come close to the girl who had. An early attempt on Mildred's part to share her strong ecstasies with her mother and to receive confirmation had met with a blankness, a failure to comprehend, which hurled Mildred back inside herself. For a long time she didn't try to confide in anyone, feeling that she was unique and that all other women were like her mother. At last, however, a big and muscular young woman who taught ice hockey and softball and archery at the university gained Mildred's confidence, her whole confidence, and then tried to go to bed with her. This shock was washed away only when a male engineering student with wiry hair and a soft voice did go to bed with her.

Now Mildred kept her own counsel, thought her own thoughts, and waited for the time when death, marriage, or accident would free her from her parents. But she loved her parents, and she would have been frightened at herself had it ever come to the surface of her mind that she wished them dead.

There had never been any close association among these three although they went through the forms. They were dear and darling and sweet, but Juan and Alice Chicoy regularly established a relationship which Mr. or Mrs. Pritchard could not have conceived. And Mildred's close and satisfying friendships were with people of whose existence her parents were completely ignorant. They had to be. It had to be. Her father considered the young women who danced naked at stags depraved, but it would never have occurred to him that he who watched and applauded and paid the girls was in any way associated with depravity.

Once or twice, on his wife's insistence, he had tried to warn Mildred against men just to teach her to protect herself. He hinted and believed that he had considerable knowledge of the world, and his complete knowledge, besides hearsay, was his one visit to the parlor house, the stags, and the dry, unresponding acquiescence of his wife.

This morning Mildred wore a sweater and pleated skirt and low, moccasin-like shoes. The three sat at the little table in the lunchroom. Mrs. Pritchard's three-quarter-length black fox coat hung on a hook beside Mr. Pritchard. It was his habit to shepherd this coat, to help his wife on with it and to take it from her, and to see that it was properly hung up and not just thrown down. He fluffed up the fur with his hand when it showed evidence of being crushed. He loved this coat, loved the fact that it was expensive, and he loved to see his wife in it and to hear other women speculate upon it. Black fox was comparatively rare, and it was also a valuable piece of property. Mr. Pritchard felt that it should be properly treated. He was always the first to suggest that it go into summer storage. He had suggested that it might be just as well not to take it to Mexico at all, first, because that was a tropical country, and second, because of bandits who might possibly steal it. Mrs. Pritchard held that it should be taken along, because, in the first place, they would be visiting Los Angeles and Hollywood where everyone wore fur coats, and second, because it was quite cold in Mexico City at night, so she had heard. Mr. Pritchard capitulated easily; to him, as well as to his wife, the coat was the badge of their position. It placed them as successful, conservative, and sound people. You get better treatment everywhere you go if you have a fur coat and nice luggage.

Now the coat hung beside Mr. Pritchard, and he ran his fingers deftly up through the hairs to clear the long guard hairs from the undercoat. Sitting at the table, they had heard through the bedroom door Alice's hoarse, screaming attack on Norma, and the animal vulgarity of it had shocked them deeply, had driven them as nearly close together as they could be. Mildred had lighted a cigarette, avoiding her mother's eye. She had done this only in the six months since she had turned twenty-one. After the initial blow-up the subject had never verbally come up again, but her mother disapproved with her face every time Mildred smoked in front of her.

The rain had stopped and only the drips from the white oaks fell on the roof. The land was soggy, water-beaten, sodden. The grain, fat and heavy with the damp, rich springtime, had lain heavily down under the last downpour, so that it stretched away in tired waves. The water trickled and ran and gurgled and rushed to find low places in the fields. The ditches beside the state highway were full, and in some places the water even invaded the raised road. Everywhere there was a whisper of water and a rush of water. The golden poppies were all stripped of their petals now, and the lupines lay down like the grain, too fat, too heavy, to hold up their heads.

The sky was beginning to clear. The clouds were tattering, and there were splashes of lovely clear sky with silks of cloud skittering across them. Up high a fierce wind blew, spreading and mixing and matting the clouds, but on the ground the air was perfectly still, and there was a smell of worms and wet grass and exposed roots.

From the area of the lunchroom and garage at Rebel Corners the water ran in shallow ditches to the large ditch beside the highway. The bus stood shining and clean in its aluminum paint, and the water still dripping from its sides and its windshield flecked with droplets. Inside the lunchroom it was a little overwarm.

Pimples was behind the counter, trying to help out, and this would never have occurred to him before today. Always, in other jobs, he had hated the work and automatically hated his employer. But the experience of the morning was still strong in him. He could still hear Juan's voice saying in his ears, "Kit, wipe your hands and see if Alice got the coffee ready yet." It was the sweetest-sounding sentence he had ever heard. He wanted to do something for Juan. He had squeezed orange juice for the Pritchards and carried coffee to them, and now he was trying to watch the toaster and scramble eggs at the same time.

Mr. Pritchard said, "Let's all have scrambled eggs. That'll make it easier. You can leave mine in the pan and get them good and dry."

"O.K.," said Pimples. His pan was too hot and the eggs were ticking and clicking and sending up an odor of wet chicken feathers that comes from too fast frying.

Mildred had crossed her legs and her skirt was caught under her knee, so that the side away from Pimples must be exposed. He wanted to get down that way and look. His darting, narrow eyes took innumerable quick glances at what he could see. He didn't want her to catch him looking at her legs. He planned it in his mind. If she didn't move he would serve the eggs and he would take a napkin over his arm. Then, after he set down their plates, he would pass their table and go on about ten feet and drop the napkin as though by accident. He would lean down and look back under his arm, and then he would be able to see Mildred's leg.

He had the napkin ready and he was mixing the eggs to get them done before she moved. He stirred the eggs. They were stuck by now so he scooped shallowly to leave the burned crust in the pan. The odor of burning eggs filled the lunch room. Mildred looked up and saw the flash in Pimples' eye. She looked down, noticed how her skirt was caught, and pulled it clear. Pimples saw her without looking directly at her. He knew that he had been caught and his cheeks stung with blood.

A dark smoke rose from the egg pan and a blue smoke rose from the toaster. Juan came in quietly from the bedroom and sniffed.

"God Almighty," he said, "what are you doing, Kit?"

"Trying to help out," said Pimples uneasily.

Juan smiled. "Well, thanks, but I guess you'd better not help out with eggs." He came to the gas stove, took the hot pan of burned eggs, put the whole thing into the sink, and turned the water on. It hissed and bubbled for a moment and then subsided, complaining, in the water.

Juan said, "Kit, you go out and try to start the engine. Don't choke her if she won't start. That'll only flood her. If she doesn't start right away, take off the distributor head and dry the points. They may have got wet. When you get her started, put her in low for a few minutes and then shift her to high and let the wheels turn over. But be careful she doesn't shake herself off those sawhorses. Just let her idle."

Pimples wiped his hands. "Should I open the grease cock first and see if she's still full?"

"Yeah. You know your stuff. Yeah, take a look. That gudgeon grease was pretty thick this morning."

"It might of shook down," said Pimples. He had forgotten the last look at Mildred's leg. He glowed under Juan's praise.

"Kit, I don't figure anybody would steal her, but keep an eye on her." Pimples laughed in sycophantic amusement at the boss's joke and went out the door. Juan looked over the counter. "My wife's not feeling very well," he said. "What can I get for you folks? More coffee?"

"Yes," said Mr. Pritchard. "The boy was trying to scramble some eggs and he burned them up. My wife likes hers moist—"

"If they're fresh," Mrs. Pritchard interposed.

"If they're fresh," said Mr. Pritchard. "And I like mine dry."

"They're fresh, all right," said Juan. "Right fresh out of the ice."

"I don't think I could eat a cold-storage egg," said Mrs. Pritchard.

"Well, that's what they are, I wouldn't lie to you."

"I guess I'll just have a doughnut," said Mrs. Pritchard.

"Make mine the same," said Mr. Pritchard.

Juan looked frankly and with admiration at Mildred's legs. She looked up at him. Slowly his eyes rose from her legs, and his dark eyes were filled with so much pleasure, were so openly admiring, that Mildred blushed a little. She warmed up in the pit of her stomach. She felt an electric jar.

"Oh—!" She looked away from him. "More coffee, I guess. Well, maybe I'll take a doughnut too."

"Only two doughnuts left," said Juan. "I'll bring two doughnuts and a snail and you can fight over them."

The engine of the bus exploded into action outside and in a moment was throttled down to a purr.

"She sounds good," said Juan.

Ernest Horton came quietly, almost secretly, out of the bedroom door and closed it softly behind him. He walked over to Mr. Pritchard and laid the six thin packages on the table. "There you are," he said, "six of them."

Mr. Pritchard pulled out his billfold. "Got change for twenty?" he asked.

"No, I haven't."

"You got change for twenty?" Mr. Pritchard asked Juan.

Juan pushed the "No Sale" button on the cash register and raised the wheel weight on the bill compartment. "I can give you two tens."

"That will do," said Ernest Horton. "I've got a dollar bill or so. You owe me nine dollars." He took one of the tens and gave Mr. Pritchard a dollar.

"What are they?" Mrs. Pritchard asked. She picked one up but her husband snatched it out of her hand. "No you don't," he said mysteriously.

"But what are they?"

"That's for me to know," said Mr. Pritchard playfully. "You'll find out quick enough."

"Oh, a surprise?"

"That's right. Little girls better keep their noses out of what doesn't concern them." Mr. Pritchard always called his wife "little girl" when he was playful, and automatically she fell into his mood.

"When do iddle girls see pretty present?"

"You'll find out," he said, and he stuffed the flat packages in his side pocket. He wanted to come in limping when he got the chance. He had a variation on the trick. He would pretend that his foot was so sore that he couldn't take off his shoe and sock himself. He would get his wife to take off the sock for him. What a kick that would be to watch her face! She'd nearly die when she saw that sore foot on him.

"What is it, Elliott?" she asked a little peevishly.

"You'll find out, just keep your pretty hair on, little girl."

"Say," he went on to Ernest, "I just thought up a new wrinkle. Tell you about it later."

Ernest said, "Yup, that's what makes the world tick. You get a new wrinkle and you're fixed. You don't want to go radical.

Just a wrinkle, like they call it in Hollywood, a switcheroo. That's with a story. You take a picture that's made dough and you work a switcheroo—not too much, just enough, and you've got something then."

"That makes sense," said Mr. Pritchard. "Yes, sir, that makes good sense."

"It's funny about new wrinkles," said Ernest. He sat down on a stool and crossed his legs. "Funny how you get a wrong idea. Now, I've got a kind of an invention and I figured I could sit back and count my money, but I was wrong. You see, there's lot of fellows like me traveling around living out of a suitcase. Well, maybe there's a convention or you've got a date that's pretty fancy. You'd like to have a tuxedo. Well, it takes a lot of room to pack a tuxedo and maybe you only use it twice on a whole trip. Well, that's when I got this idea. Suppose, I said, you've got a nice dark business suit—dark blue or almost black or oxford—and suppose you got little silk slipcovers like little lapels and silk stripes that just snap on the pants. In the afternoon you've got a nice dark suit and you slip on the silk covers to the lapels and snap on the strips and you've got a tuxedo. I even figured out a little bag to carry them in."

"Say!" cried Mr. Pritchard, "that's a wonderful idea! Say, why I've got to take up room in my suitcase right now for a tuxedo. I'd like to get in on a thing like that. If you get up a patent and put on a campaign, a big national advertising campaign, why, you might maybe get a big movie star to endorse it—"

Ernest held up his hand. "That's just the way I figured," he said. "And I was wrong and you're wrong. I drew it all out on paper and just how it would go on and how the trousers leg would have little tiny silk loops for the hooks for the stripes to go on, and then I had a friend who travels for a big clothes manufacturer"—Ernest chuckled—"he put me right mighty quick. 'You'd get every tailor and every big manufacturer right on your neck,' he said. 'They sell tuxedos anywhere from fifty to a hundred and fifty bucks and you come along with ideas to take that business away with a ten-dollar gadget. Why, they'd run you right out of the country,' he said."

Mr. Pritchard nodded gravely. "Yes, I can see the point. They have to protect themselves and their stockholders."

"He didn't make it sound too hopeful," said Ernest. "I figured I'd just sit and count the profits. I figured that a fellow, say, traveling by air—he's got the weight limitations. He's got the right to save room in his suitcase. It'd be like two suits for the weight of one. And then I figured maybe the jewelry companies might take it up. Set of studs and cuff links and my lapels and stripes all in a nice package. I haven't got around to that yet. Haven't asked anybody. Might still be something in it."

"You and I ought to get together for a good talk," said Mr. Pritchard. "Have you got it patented?"

"Well, no. I didn't want to go to the expense until I could see if anybody was interested."

"Oh," said Mr. Pritchard. "I guess maybe you're right. Patent attorneys and all, they cost quite a bit of money. Maybe you're right." Then he changed the subject. "What time can we get started?" he asked Juan.

"Well, the Greyhound gets in around ten. They bring regular freight and some passengers. We should get started at ten-thirty. That's the schedule. Can I get you folks anything else? Some more coffee?"

"Some more coffee," said Mr. Pritchard.

Juan brought it to him and looked out the window at the bus with its wheels turning over in the air. Mr. Pritchard looked at his watch.

"We've still got an hour," he said.

A tall, stooped old man came around the side of the building. The man who had slept in Pimples' bed. He opened the door to the lunchroom, came in, and sat down on a stool. He had his head bent permanently forward on the arthritic stalk of his neck so that the tip of his nose pointed straight at the ground. He was well over sixty, and his eyebrows overhung his eyes like those of a Skye terrier. His long, deeply channeled upper lip was raised over his teeth like the little trunk of a tapir. The point over his middle teeth seemed to be almost prehensile. His eyes were yellowish gold, so that he looked fierce.

"I don't like it," he said without preliminaries. "I didn't like it yesterday when you broke down, and I like it even less today."

"I've got the rear end fixed," said Juan. "Turning over right now."

"I think I'll cancel and go on back to San Ysidro on the Greyhound," said the man.

"Well, you can do that."

"I've got a feeling," said the man. "I just don't like it. Something's trying to give me a warning. I've had 'em before a couple of times. I didn't pay any mind to them once and I got into trouble."

"The bus is all right," said Juan, his voice rising a little in exasperation.

"I'm not talking about the bus," said the man. "I live in this county, native of it. The ground's full of water. San Ysidro River will be up. You know how the San Ysidro rises. Right under Pico Blanco it comes down that Lone Pine Canyon and makes a big loop. Ground gets full of water and every drop runs right off into the San Ysidro. She'll be raging right now."

Mrs. Pritchard began to look alarmed. "Do you think there's danger?" she asked.

"Now, dear," said Mr. Pritchard.

"I've got a feeling," said the man. "The old road used to go around that loop of the river and never cross it. Come thirty years ago Mr. Trask got himself made roadmaster of this county. The old road wasn't good enough for him. He put in two bridges and saved what? Twelve miles, that's what he saved. It cost the county twenty-seven thousand dollars. Mr. Trask was a crook."

He turned his stiff neck and surveyed the Pritchards. "A crook. Just about to indict him for another job when he died, three years ago. Died a rich man. Got two boys in the University of California right now living on the taxpayers' money." He stopped and his upper lip waggled from side to side over his long yellow teeth. "If those bridges get any real strain on them they'll go out. The concrete isn't stout enough. I'll just cancel and go back to San Ysidro."

"The river was all right day before yesterday," said Juan. "Hardly any water in it."

"You don't know the San Ysidro River. She can get up in a couple of hours. I've seen her half a mile wide and covered with dead cows and chickenhouses. No, once I get this kind of feeling I won't go. I'm not superstitious, either."

"You think the bus might go through the bridge?"

"I don't say what I think. I know Trask was a crook. Left an estate of thirty-six thousand five-hundred dollars. His boys are up at college spending it right now."

Juan came out from behind the counter and went to the wall phone. "Hello," he said. "Give me Breed's Service Station out on the San Juan road. I don't know the number." He waited a while and then he said, "Hello. Say, this is Chicoy down at the Corners. How's the river? Oh, yeah? Well, is the bridge all right? Yeah. Well, O.K., I'll see you pretty soon." Juan hung up. "The river is up pretty high," he explained. "They say the bridge is all right."

"That river can rise a foot an hour when Pine Canyon dumps a cloudburst into it. Time you get there the bridge might be gone."

Juan turned a little impatiently to him. "What do you want me to do? Not go?"

"You do just as you like. I only want to cancel and get back to San Ysidro. I'm not going to fool around with this kind of nonsense. Once I had a feeling like this and I didn't pay attention and I broke both legs. No, sir, I got that feeling when you broke down yesterday."

"Well, consider yourself canceled," said Juan.

"That's what I want, mister! You're not an old-timer here. You don't know what I know about Trask. Salary of fifteen hundred a year and he leaves thirty-six thousand five-hundred, and a clear title to a hundred and sixty acres of land. Tell me!"

Juan said, "Well, I'll see you get on the Greyhound."

"Well, I'm not telling you anything about Trask, I'm just telling you what happened. You figure it out for yourself. Thirty-six thousand five-hundred dollars."

Ernest Horton asked, "Suppose the bridge is out?"

"Then we won't go across it," said Juan.

"Then what'll we do? Turn around and come back?"

"Sure," said Juan. "We'll either do that or jump it."

The stooped man smiled about the room in triumph. "You see?" he said. "You'll come back here and there'll be no bus here for San Ysidro. You'll sit around here for how long?

Months? Wait for them to build a new bridge? You know who the new roadmaster is? A college boy. Just out of college. All books and no practice. Oh, he can draw a bridge, but can he build one? We'll see."

Suddenly Juan laughed. "Fine," he said. "The old bridge isn't washed out yet and already you're having trouble with the new one that isn't built."

The man turned his aching neck sideways. "Are you getting lippy?" he demanded.

For a moment a dark red light seemed to glow in Juan's black eyes. "Yes," he said. "I'll get you on the Greyhound, don't you worry. I wouldn't want you on this run."

"Well, you can't kick me off, you're a common carrier."

"O.K.," said Juan wearily. "Sometimes I wonder why I keep the bus. Maybe I won't much longer. Just a headache. You've got a feeling! Nuts!"

Bernice had been following this conversation very closely. "I don't believe in these things," she said, "but they say it's the dry season down in Mexico. It's like autumn. Summer's when it rains."

"Mother," said Mildred, "Mr. Chicoy knows Mexico. He was born there."

"Oh, were you? Well, it's the dry season, isn't it?"

"Some places," said Juan. "I guess it is where you'll be going. Other places there isn't any dry season."

Mr. Pritchard cleared his throat. "We're going to Mexico City and to Puebla and then to Cuernavaca and Tasco, and we may take the trip to Acapulco and we'll go to the volcano if it's all right."

"You'll be all right," said Juan.

"You know those places?" Mr. Pritchard demanded.

"Sure."

"How are the hotels?" Mr. Pritchard asked. "You know how the travel agencies are—everything is wonderful. How are they really?"

"Wonderful," Juan said, smiling now. "They're great. Breakfast in bed every morning."

"I didn't mean to cause trouble this morning," said Mr. Pritchard.

"Sure, it's all right" He leaned his arms on the counter and spoke confidentially. "I get fed up a little sometimes. I drive that damn bus back and forth and back and forth. Sometime I'd like to take and just head for the hills. I read about a ferry-boat captain in New York who just headed out to sea one day and they never heard from him again. Maybe he sunk and maybe he's tied up on an island some place. I understand that man."

A great red truck with a trailer slowed down on the highway outside. The driver looked in. Juan moved his hand rapidly from side to side. The truck went into second gear, gathered speed, and went away.

"I thought he was coming in," said Mr. Pritchard.

"He likes raspberry pie," said Juan. "He always stops when we got some. I just told him we haven't got any."

Mildred was looking at Juan, fascinated. There was something in this dark man with his strange warm eyes that moved her. She felt drawn to him. She wanted to attract his attention, his special attention, to herself. She had thrown back her shoulders so that her breasts were lifted.

"Why did you leave Mexico?" she asked, and she took off her glasses so that when he answered he would see her without them. She leaned on the table, and put her forefinger to the corner of her left eye, and pulled the skin and eyelid backward. This changed the focus of her eye. She could see his face more clearly that way. It also gave her eyes a long and languorous shape, and her eyes were beautiful.

"I don't know why I left," Juan said to her. His warm eyes seemed to surround her and to caress her. Mildred felt a little weak and sirupy in the pit of her stomach. "I'll have to stop this," she thought. "This is crazy." A quick and sexual picture had formed in her mind.

Juan said, "People down there, unless they're rich, have to work too hard and for too little money. I guess that's the main reason I left."

"You speak very good English," Bernice Pritchard said as though it were a compliment.

"Why not? My mother was Irish. I got both languages at once."

"Well, are you a Mexican citizen?" Mr. Pritchard asked.

"I guess so," said Juan. "I never did anything about it."

"It's a good idea to take out your first papers," said Mr. Pritchard.

"What for?"

"It's a good idea."

"It doesn't make any difference to the government," said Juan. "They can tax me and draft me."

"It's still a pretty good idea," said Mr. Pritchard.

Juan's eyes were playing with Mildred, touching her breasts and sliding down over her hips. He saw her sigh and arch her back a little, and deep in Juan an imp of hatred stirred. Not strongly because there wasn't much of it in him, but the Indian blood was there, and in the dark past lay the hatred for the *ojos claros*, the light eyes, the blonds. It was a hatred and a fear of a complexion. The light-eyed people who had for centuries taken the best land, the best horses, the best women. Juan felt the stirring like a little heat lightning, and he felt a glow of pleasure knowing that he could take this girl and twist her and outrage her if he wanted to. He could disturb her and seduce her mentally, and physically too, and then throw her away. The cruelty stirred and he let it mount in him. His voice grew softer and more rich. He spoke directly into Mildred's violet eyes.

"My country," he said, "even if I don't live there, it is in my heart." He laughed inside at this, but Mildred did not laugh. She leaned forward a little and pulled back the corners of both eyes so that she could see his face more clearly.

"I remember things," said Juan. "In the square of my town there were public letter-writers who did all the business for the people who couldn't read or write. They were good men. They had to be. The country people would know if they weren't. They know many things, those people of the hills. And I remember one morning when I was a little boy I was sitting on a bench. There was a fiesta in this town in honor of a saint. The church was full of flowers and there were candy stands and a ferris-wheel and a little merry-go-round. And all night the people shot off sky-rockets to the saint. In the park an Indian came to the letter-writer and said, 'I want you to write a letter to my patron. I will tell you what to say and you will put it in good and beautiful form so he will not find me discourteous.' 'Is it a long letter?' the man asked. 'I don't know,' said the

Indian. 'That will be one peso,' said the man. And the little Indian paid him, and he said, 'I want you to say to my patron that I cannot go back to my town and my fields for I have seen great beauty and I must stay behind. Tell him I am sorry and I do not wish to give him pain, nor my friends, either, but I could not go back. I am different and my friends would not know me. I would be unhappy in the field and restless. And because I would be different my friends would reject me and hate me. I have seen the stars. Tell him that. And tell him to give my chair to my friend brother and my pig with the two little ones to the old woman who sat with me in fever. My pots to my brother-in-law, and tell the patron to go with God, with loveliness. Tell him that.' "

Juan paused and saw that Mildred's lips were open a little, and he saw that she was taking his story as an allegory for herself.

"What had happened to him?" she asked

"Why, he had seen the merry-go-round," said Juan. "He couldn't leave it. He slept beside it, and pretty soon his money was gone and he was starving, and then the owner let him turn the crank that ran the merry-go-round and fed him. He couldn't ever leave. He loved the merry-go-round. Maybe he's still there." Juan had become foreign in the telling. A trifle of accent had come into his speech.

Mildred sighed deeply. Mr. Pritchard said, "Let me get this straight. He gave away his land and all his property and he never went home because he saw a merry-go-round?"

"He didn't even own his land," said Juan. "Little Indians never own their land. But he gave away everything else he had."

Mildred glared at her father. This was one of the times when she found him stupid to the point of nausea. Why couldn't he see the beauty in this story? Her eyes went back to Juan to tell him silently that she understood, and she thought she saw something in his face that had not been there before. She thought there was a cruel, leering triumph in his face, but it was probably her eyes, she thought. Her damnable eyes that couldn't see very well. But what she saw was a shock to her. She looked quickly at her mother and then at her father to see whether they had noticed anything, but they were regarding Juan vacantly.

Her father was saying in his slow and, to Mildred, maddening way, "I can understand how he would think it was fine if he had never seen a merry-go-round before, but you get used to anything. A man would get used to a palace in a few days and then he'd want something else."

"It's just a story," Mildred said with so much fierceness that her father turned surprised eyes on her.

Mildred could almost feel Juan's fingers on her thighs. Her body tingled with desire, aroused and unsatisfied. She itched with a pure sexual longing, and her anger arose against her father as though she had been interrupted in the midst of connection. She put on her glasses, looked quickly at Juan and then away, for his eyes were veiled although he looked at all of them. He was enjoying a kind of triumph. He was laughing at her and also at the thing her father and mother did not know was happening. And suddenly her desire hardened into a knot in her stomach and her stomach ached and she felt a revulsion. She thought she would be sick.

Ernest Horton said, "I always intended to get down Mexico way. Thought I might ask the head office about it some time. Might make some pretty valuable contacts down there. Like these fiestas they have. They sell novelties, don't they?"

"Sure," said Juan. "They sell little rosaries and holy pictures and candles and things like that, candy and ice cream."

"Well, if a guy went down and got a line on that stuff, why, we could probably turn it out a lot cheaper than they can. We could stamp out those rosaries—well, nice ones—out of pot metal. And skyrockets. My company supplies some of the biggest celebrations, all kinds of fireworks. It's an idea. I think I'll write a letter."

Juan looked at the increasing pile of dirty dishes in the sink. He stared over his shoulder at the door to the bedroom and then he opened the door and looked in. The bed was empty. Alice had got up, but the bathroom door was shut. Juan came back and began to scrub the dirty dishes in the sink.

The sky was clearing fast now, and the clean yellow sun was shining on the washed land. The young leaves of the oaks were almost yellow in the new light. The green fields looked incredibly young.

Juan smiled shortly. He cut two slices of bread.

"I think I'll walk around a little bit," said Mr. Pritchard. "Want to come, dear?" he asked his wife. She looked quickly at the bedroom door.

"Pretty soon," she said, and he understood her.

"Well, I'll just go outside," he said.

Chapter 6

AFTER Juan left her Alice lay a long time on her back with her arms crossed over her face. Her sobbing stopped gradually, like a child's. She could hear the murmuring talk out in the lunchroom. The inside of her arm was warm and wet over her eyes. She was flooded with a kind of comfort, and the release from tension was as though a tight mesh had been loosened from her body. As she lay in relaxed comfort, her mind jumped back to what had happened. She didn't remember the woman who had screamed at Norma. The morning was beginning to be hazy to her. She had not yet found her own rationalization for her action. Now that she thought of it, she knew she had not really suspected Norma of misconduct, and if she had she really wouldn't have cared very much. She did not love Norma. She didn't care a thing for Norma. Poor little washed-out cat.

When Norma had come to work, Alice, of course, put her senses on the girl and on Juan like a stethoscope, and when she had found no reaction on Juan's part, no quickening, no little creeping and trailing with the eye, Alice had lost interest in Norma except as an organism for carrying coffee and washing dishes. Alice was not very aware of things or people if they did not in some way either augment or take away from her immediate life. And now, as she lay relaxed and warm and quiet, her mind began to work and terror came with her thoughts.

She went back over the scene. Her terror grew out of Juan's gentleness. He should have hit her. His failure to do so worried her. Maybe he didn't care about her any more. Casual kindness in a man she had found to be the preliminary to a brush-off. She tried to remember what the Pritchard women looked like, and she tried to remember whether Juan had looked with warmth on either of them. She knew Juan. His eyes heated up like a stove when his interest was aroused. Then, with a little shock, she remembered that he had given up their bed to the Pritchards. She could smell the lavender on the bedclothes right now. A hatred and a distaste for that odor came to her.

She listened to the murmur of voices through the door. Juan was feeding them. He wouldn't have done it if he hadn't been interested. Juan would say the hell with it and go on out to work on the bus. A restless fear arose in Alice. She had mistreated Norma. That was easy. With Norma's kind you showed weakness, and Norma would melt and run down over herself. Take a girl like that, why, she had so little love that even a stink of it on a wind would knock her ass over teacup. Alice was contemptuous of this starvation for love. She could not tie her own up with Norma's. Alice was big in herself and everyone else was very little, everyone, that is, except Juan. But, then, he was an extension of herself. She thought it might be just as well to put Norma on her feet before anything else. She needed Norma to run the lunchroom, because Alice intended to get drunk just as soon as Juan went away in the bus. She would tell him when he came back that she had a toothache that was killing her.

She didn't do it very often, but she looked forward to it now. And if she was going to do it, she'd better begin covering her tracks. Juan didn't like drunk women. She uncrossed her arms from over her face. Her eyes were sunken from the pressure and it took a moment to get them to track. She saw how the sun was flooding sweetly over the green plain behind the bedroom, and how it flowed over the rising hills far to the west. A sweet day.

She struggled her body upright and went to the bathroom. There she dampened one end of a bath towel in cold water and patted it against her face to take out the creases where her arms had pressed down against her plump cheeks. She rubbed the end of the towel around her face and over her nose and along the edge of her hairline. A brassière strap was broken. She slipped open her dress and found that the little safety pin that held it was still there, so she pinned the strap to the brassière again. It was a little tight but she'd sew it after Juan had gone. She wouldn't, of course. When enough of the strap was broken she'd buy a new brassière.

Alice brushed her hair and put on lipstick. Her eyes were still red. She put some eyedrops in the corners with a medicine dropper and rubbed the lids against her eyeballs with her fingers. For a moment she inspected herself in the medicine-chest mirror and then went out. She slipped off her wrinkled dress and put on a clean print.

Quickly she crossed the bedroom to Norma's door and knocked softly. There was no answer. She knocked again. From inside the room came a rustling of paper. Norma came to the door and opened it. Her eyes were glazed, and she seemed to have been just awakened. In her hand she held the stub pencil she had used for the eyebrows earlier.

When she saw Alice a look of alarm came upon her face. "I didn't do nothing wrong with that fellow," she said quickly.

Alice stepped into the room. She knew how to handle the Normas when she had her wits. "I know you didn't, honey," Alice said. She cast down her eyes as though she were ashamed. She knew how to handle girls.

"Well, you shouldn't of said it. Suppose somebody heard it and believed it? I'm not that kind. I'm just trying to make my living and no trouble." Her eyes suddenly swam in tears of self-pity.

Alice said, "I shouldn't of done it but I just felt so bad. It's my time of the month. You know yourself how miserable you feel. Sometimes you go kind of crazy."

Norma inspected her with interest. This was the first time she'd ever found softness in Alice. This was the first time that Alice had ever needed to enlist Norma. She didn't like women and girls. There was a streak of cruelty in Alice toward other women, and when she saw Norma's eyes brim with tears of sympathy she felt triumphant.

"You know how it is," Alice said. "You just get a little crazy."

"I know," said Norma. Soft tentacles of warmth stretched out from her. She ached for love, for association, for some human being in the world to be friendly with. "I know," she said again, and she felt older and stronger than Alice and a little protective too, which was what Alice wanted.

Alice had seen the pencil in her hand. "Maybe you had better come out now and help. Mr. Chicoy's doing it all alone."

"I will in just a moment," said Norma.

Alice closed the door and listened. There was a pause, a slipping sound, and then the sharp sound of the bureau drawer closing. Alice pushed back her hair with her hand and walked softly toward the door into the lunchroom. She felt fine. She had gathered a great deal of information about Norma. She knew how Norma felt about things. She knew where Norma had put the letter.

Alice had tried to get into Norma's suitcase before but it was always locked, and while she could have taken it apart with her fingers—it was only cardboard—the marks would have showed tampering. She would wait. Sooner or later, if she was careful, Norma would neglect to lock her suitcase. Alice was clever, but she didn't know that Norma was clever too. Norma had worked for Alices before. When Alice went through Norma's dresser drawers and looked at her things and read the letters from her sister, she didn't notice the paper match carelessly lying on the drawer's edge. Norma always put it there, and when it was displaced she knew someone had been going through her things. She knew it couldn't be Juan or Pimples, so it must be Alice.

Norma was not likely to leave her suitcase unlocked. For all her dreams Norma was not stupid. In a toothpaste box in her locked suitcase there was twenty-seven dollars. When she had fifty dollars Norma would go to Hollywood and get a job in a restaurant and wait her chance. The fifty dollars would rent her a room for two months. Food she would get where she worked. Her high, long-legged dreams were one thing, but she could take care of herself too. Norma was no fool. True, she didn't understand Alice's hatred of all women. She didn't know that this apology was a trick. But she would probably find it out in time to save herself. And while Norma believed that only the best and most noble thoughts and impulses resided in Clark Gable, she had a knowledge of and a lack of respect for the impulses of the people she met and came in contact with in everyday life.

When Pimples came scratching softly at her window at night she knew how to take care of that. She locked her window. He wouldn't dare make too much noise trying to get in for fear Juan in the next room would hear him. Norma was nobody's fool.

Now Alice stood in front of the door between the bedroom and the lunchroom. She ran her finger down either side of her nose and then she opened the door and went behind the counter as though nothing at all had happened.

Chapter 7

THE big and beautiful Greyhound bus was pulled in under the loading shed at San Ysidro. Helpers put gasoline into the tank and checked the oil and the tires automatically. The whole system worked smoothly. A colored man cleaned between the seats, brushing the cushions and picking up gum wrappers and matches and cigarette butts from the floor. He ran his fingers behind the last seat, which stretched across the rear. Sometimes he found coins or pocketknives behind this seat. Loose money he kept, but most other articles he turned in to the office. People made an awful stink about things they left, but not about small change. Sometimes the swamper managed as much as a couple of dollars behind that seat. Today he had dug out two dimes, a fifty-cent piece, and a hip-pocket wallet with a draft card, driver's license, and a Lions Club membership card.

He glanced inside the bill section. Two fifty-dollar bills and a certified check for five-hundred dollars. He put the wallet in his shirt pocket and brushed the seat with his whisk broom. He breathed a little hard. The money was easy. He could take it out and leave the wallet behind the seat for some other swamper to find down the line. The check would be left too. There was too much danger in checks. But those two sweet fifties—those sweet, sweet fifties! His throat was tight and would be until he got those sweet fifties out and the wallet behind the seat.

But he couldn't get to them because the punk kid was washing the outside of the windows where they were splashed with dirty mist from the highway. The swamper had to wait. If they caught him they'd put him away.

There was a little rip in the cuff of his blue serge trousers. He figured he would slip those two sweet fifties in there, inside the cuff, before he got off the bus. Then he'd get sick before he went off the job. He'd be sick, all right. Like enough he wouldn't be back for a week. If he got sick on the job and still stayed out the day till quitting time, they wouldn't figure anything if he didn't show up for a few days and it would save his job. He heard a step on the bus and stiffened a little. Louie, the driver, looked in.

"Hi, George," he said. "Say, did you find a wallet? Guy says he lost it."

George mumbled.

"Well, I'll come back and look," said Louie.

George swung around, still on his knees. "I found it," he said. "I was going to turn it in as soon as I finished."

"Yeah?" said Louie. He took the wallet from George's hand and opened it. The punk kid looked in through the window. Louie smiled sorrowfully at George and flicked his eyes toward the punk.

"Too bad, George," Louie said. "I guess they've got 'em stacked against us. Two fifties the guy said and two fifties it is." He pulled out the bills and the check so the punk looking through the window could see them. "Better luck next time, George," Louie said.

"Suppose the guy pays a reward," said George.

"You'll get half," said Louie. "If it's under a buck, you'll get it all."

Louie moved out of the bus and into the waiting room. He handed the wallet in at the desk.

"George found it. He was just bringing it in," said Louie. "That's a good nigger."

Louie knew the wallet's owner was right beside him so he said to the cashier, "If it was me that lost this, I'd give George a nice little present. Nothing don't turn a guy bad like no appreciation. I remember a guy found a grand and he turned it in and he didn't even get a thank-you. The next thing you know he robbed a bank and killed a coupla guards." Louie lied easily and without strain.

"How many going south?" Louie asked.

"You're full up," said the clerk. "You got one for Rebel Corners, and don't forget the pies like you did last week. I never had so much trouble with fifty pies in my life. Here's your wallet, sir. Will you inspect it to see if it's all right?"

The owner paid a five-dollar reward. Louie figured to give George a buck sometime. He knew George wouldn't believe him, but what the hell. It was a stinker's game and a muddy track. Everybody had to take his chance. Louie was big, a little on the stout side, but a dresser. His party friends called him "meat-face." He had a fast line and was smart and liked to be known as a horse player. He called race horses dogs and spoke of all situations as parlays. He would have liked to be Bob Hope or, better, Bing Crosby.

Louie saw George looking in from the loading platform doors. An impulse of generosity seized him. He walked over and gave George a dollar bill. "Cheap son of a bitch!" he said. "Here, you take the buck. Over five-hundred dollars he gets back and he puts out a buck!"

George looked into Louie's face, just one quick, brown flash of the eyes. He knew it was a lie and he knew there wasn't anything he could do about it. If Louie was mad at him he could make it tough. And George had wanted that drunk. He had almost felt the liquor take hold of him. If only that punk kid had kept his big nose out of it.

"Thanks," said George.

The kid went by with his bucket and sponge. George said, "You call those windows clean?" And Louie made it up to George. He said to the kid, "You want to get any place, you better get on the ball. Those windows stink. Do them again."

"I ain't taking orders from you. I'll wait till I get some kind of complaints from the super."

Louie and George exchanged glances. It was just a punk. In less than a week he'd be out on his ass if Louie thought of it.

The big Greyhounds came in and out of the covered loading shed heavy and high as houses. The drivers slipped them smoothly and beautifully into place. The station smelled of oil and diesel exhaust fumes and candy bars and a powerful floor cleaner that got in the nose.

Louie went back toward the front. His eyes had caught a girl coming in from the street. She was carrying a suitcase. All in one flash Louie caught her. A dish! A dish like that he wanted to ride in a seat just behind his own raised driver's chair. He could watch her in the rear-view mirror and find out about her. Maybe she lived somewhere on his route. Louie had plenty of adventures that started like this.

The light from the street was behind the girl so he couldn't see her face, but he knew she was a looker. And he didn't know how he knew it. There might have been fifty girls come in with a light behind them. But how did he know this one was a looker? He could see a nice figure and pretty legs. But in some subtle way this girl smelled of sex.

He saw that she had carried her suitcase over to the ticket window so he did not go directly toward her. He went into the washroom. And there he stood at the wash basin and dipped his hands in water and ran them through his hair. From his side pocket he took a little comb and combed his hair back smoothly and patted it behind where the suggestion of a duck tail stood out. And he combed his mustache, not that it needed combing for it was very short. He settled his gray corduroy jacket, tightened the belt, and pulled his stomach in a little bit.

He put the comb back in his pocket and inspected himself again in the mirror. He ran his hand over the sides of his hair. He felt behind to see that no strands were out and that the duck tail was lying down. He straightened his regulation black ready-made bow tie and he took a few grains of sen-sen out of his inner shirt pocket and threw them in his mouth. And then he seemed to shake himself down in his coat.

Just as his right hand went to the brass knob of the washroom door, Louie's left hand flipped fingers up and down his fly to be sure he was buttoned up. He put on his face a little crooked smile, half worldliness and half naïveté, an expression that had been successful with him. Louie had read someplace that if you looked directly into a girl's eyes and smiled it had an effect. You must look at her as though she were not only the most beautiful thing in the world, but you must keep looking into her eyes until she looked away. There was another trick too. If it bothered you to look into people's eyes, you should look at a point on the bridge of the nose right between the eyes. To the person looked at it appeared that you were looking into the eyes, only you weren't. Louie had found this a very successful approach.

Nearly all his waking hours Louie thought about girls. He liked to outrage them. He liked to have them fall in love with him and then walk away. He called them pigs. "I'll get a pig," he would say, "and you get a pig, and we'll go out on the town."

He stepped through the door of the washroom with a kind of lordliness, and then had to back up because two men came down between the benches carrying a long crate with slats to let air in. The side of the crate said in large white letters MOTHER MAHONEY'S HOME-BAKED PIES. The two men went in front of Louie and through to the loading platform.

The girl was sitting on a bench now, her suitcase beside her on the floor. As he moved across the room Louie took a quick look at her legs and then caught her eyes and held them as he walked. He smiled his crooked smile and moved toward her. She looked back at him, unsmiling, and then moved her eyes away.

Louie was disappointed. She hadn't been embarrassed as she should have been. She had simply lost interest in him. And she was a looker too—fine well-filled legs with rounded thighs and no stomach whatever and large breasts which she made the most of. She was a blonde and her hair was coarse and a little broken at the ends from a too-hot iron, but well-brushed hair that had good lights in it and a long, curling bob that Louie liked. Her eyes were made up with blue eyeshadow and some cold cream on the eyelids and plenty of mascara on the lashes. No rouge, but a splash of lipstick that was put on to make her mouth look square, like some of the picture stars. She wore a suit, a tight skirt and a jacket with a round collar. Her shoes were tan saddle-leather with white stitching. Not only a looker but a dresser. And the stuff looked good.

Louie studied her face as he walked. He had a feeling that he had seen her someplace before. But then, she might look like someone he knew, or he might have seen her in a movie. That had happened. Her eyes were wide set, almost abnormally wide-set, and they were blue with little brown specks in them and with strongly marked dark lines from the pupil to the outer edge of the iris. Her eyebrows were plucked and penciled in a high arch so that she looked a little surprised. Louie noticed that her gloved hands were not restless. She was not impatient nor nervous, and this bothered him. He was afraid of self-possession, and he did feel that he had seen her somewhere. Her knees were well-covered with flesh, not bony, and she kept her skirt down without pulling at it.

As he strolled by Louie punished her for looking away from his eyes by staring at her legs. This usually had the effect of making a girl pull down her skirt, even if it was not too high, but it hadn't any effect on this girl. Her failure to react to his art made him uneasy. Probably a hustler, he said to himself. Probably a two-dollar hustler. And then he laughed at himself. Not two dollars with that stuff she's wearing.

Louie went on to the ticket window and smiled his sardonic smile at Edgar, the ticket clerk. Edgar admired Louie. He wished he could be like him.

"Where's the pig going?" Louie asked.

"Pig?"

"Yeah. The broad. The blonde."

"Oh, yes." Edgar exchanged a secret man-look with Louie. "South," he said.

"In my wagon?"

"Yeah."

Louie tapped the counter with his fingers. He had let the little fingernail on his left hand grow very long. It was curved, like half a tube, and sanded to a shallow point. Louie didn't know why he did this, but he was gratified to notice that some of the other bus drivers were letting their little fingernails grow too. Louie was setting a style and he felt good about it. There was that cab driver who had tied a raccoon's tail on his radiator cap and right overnight everybody had to have a piece of fur flapping in the breeze. Furriers made artificial fox tails, and high-school kids wouldn't be seen in a car without a tail whipping around. And that cab driver could sit back and have the satisfaction of knowing he had started the whole thing. Louie had been letting his little fingernail grow for five months and already he'd seen five or six other people doing it. It might sweep the country, and Louie would have started the whole thing.

He tapped the counter with the long, curved nail, but gently, because when a nail gets that long it breaks easily. Edgar looked at the nail. He kept his left hand below the counter. He was growing one too, but it wasn't very long yet, and he didn't want Louie to see it until it was much longer. Edgar's nails were brittle, and he had to put colorless nail polish on his to keep it from breaking right off. Even in bed it broke once. Edgar glanced toward the girl.

"Figure to make some time with the—pig?"

"No harm trying," said Louie. "Probably a hustler."

"Well, what's wrong with a good hustler?" Edgar's eyes flicked up. The girl had recrossed her legs.

"Louie," he said apologetically, "before I forget, you'd better see to the loading of that crate of pies yourself. We had a complaint last week. Someplace along the line somebody dropped the crate and a raspberry pie got all mixed up with a lemon pie and there was raisins all over hell. We had to pay the claim."

"It never happened on my run," said Louie truculently. "It goes to San Juan, don't it? That jerk line from Rebel Corners done it."

"Well, we paid the claim," said Edgar. "Just kind of check it, will you?"

"There wasn't no pies dropped on my run," Louie said dangerously.

"I know. I know you didn't. But the front office told me to tell you to check it."

"Why don't they come to me?" Louie demanded. "They got complaints, why don't they call me up instead of sending messages?" He tended his anger as he would a fire. But he was angry at the blonde. The god-damned hustler. He looked up at the big clock on the wall. A hand two feet long jerked seconds around the dial, and in the reflection of the glass Louie could see the girl sitting with crossed legs. Although he couldn't be sure because of the curve of the glass, he thought she was looking at the back of his head. His anger melted away.

"I'll check the pies," he said. "Tell them there won't be any raspberries in the lemon pie. I guess I'll make a little time with the pig." He saw the admiration in Edgar's eyes as he turned slowly and faced the waiting room.

He was right. She had been looking at the back of his head, and when he was turned she was looking in his face. There was no interest, no nothing, in her glance. But she had beautiful eyes, he thought. God-damn, she was a looker! Louie had read in a magazine that wide-set eyes meant sexiness, and there was no doubt that this girl put out a strong, strong feeling of sex. She was the kind of girl everybody watched walk by. Why, she walked in a place and everybody turned and looked at her. You could see their heads turn, like watching a horse race. It was something about her, and it wasn't make-up and it wasn't the way she walked, although that was part of it too. Whatever it was, it projected all around her. Louie had felt it when she came in from the street and the light was behind her so he couldn't really see her then. And now she was looking in Louie's face, not smiling, not putting out anything, just looking, and he still felt it. A tightness came into his throat and a little flush rose out of his collar. He knew that in a moment his glance would slide away. Edgar was waiting, and Edgar had faith in Louie.

There were a few lies in Louie's reputation but actually he did have a way, he did make time with pigs. Only now he wasn't easy. This pig was getting him down. He wanted to slap her face with his open hand. His breath was rising painfully in his chest. The moment was going to be over unless he did something. He could see the dark raylike lines in her irises and the fullness of her jowls. He put on his embracing look. His eyes widened a little and he smiled as though he had suddenly recognized her. At the same time he moved toward her.

Carefully he made his smile a little respectful. Her eyes held onto his, and a little of the coldness went out of them. He stepped near to her. "Man says you're going south on my bus, ma'am," he said. He almost laughed at that "ma'am," but it usually worked. It worked with this girl. She smiled a little.

"I'll take care of your bag," Louie went on. "We leave in about three minutes."

"Thanks," said the girl. Her voice was throaty and sexy, Louie thought.

"Let me take your suitcase. I'll put it on now and then you'll have a seat."

"It's heavy," said the girl.

"I ain't exactly a midget," said Louie. He picked up her suitcase and walked quickly out to the loading platform. He climbed into the bus and put the suitcase down in front of the seat that was right behind his seat. He could watch the girl in his mirror and he could talk to her some when they got rolling. He came out of the bus and saw the punk and another swamper putting the crate of pies on top of the bus.

"Careful of that stuff," Louie said loudly. "You bastards dropped one last week and I got the beef."

"I never dropped nothing," said the punk.

"The hell you didn't," said Louie. "You watch your step." He went through the swinging doors to the waiting room.

"What's eating him?" the other swamper asked.

"Oh, I sort of jammed him up," said the punk. "The nigger found a wallet and I seen it, so they figured they got to turn it in. It was a big roll of jack too. They're both sore at me 'cause I seen it. Louie and that nigger was gonna split them up a coupla half centuries and I guess I jammed it for 'em. Course they had to turn it in when they seen I saw 'em."

"I could use some of that," said the swamper.

"Who couldn't," said the punk.

"I can take me a century and I can go out and I can get very nice stuff for that there." They went on for a time with ritual talk.

In the waiting room there was a little burst of activity. The crowd for the southbound bus was beginning to collect. Edgar was busy behind his counter, but not too busy to keep his eye on the girl. "A pig," he said under his breath. It was a new word to him. From now on he would use it. He glanced at the little fingernail on his left hand. It would be long before he would have as good a one as Louie's. But why kid himself? He couldn't make time like Louie anyway. He always ended up by going down the line.

There was a last-minute flurry of customers at the candy counter, at the peanut vending machines, at the gum dispensers. A Chinaman bought copies of *Time* and *Newsweek* and rolled them carefully together and put them in his black broadcloth overcoat pocket. An old lady restlessly turned over magazines on the newsstand without any intention of buying one. Two Hindus with gleaming white turbans and shining black curly beards stood side by side at the ticket window. They glanced fiercely about as they tried to make themselves understood.

Louie stood by the entrance to the loading platform and glanced continually at the girl. He noticed that every man in the room was doing the same thing. All of them were watching her secretly, and they didn't want to get caught at it. He turned and looked through the swinging glass doors and saw that the punk and the swamper had got the crate of pies safely on top of the bus and the tarpaulin pulled down over it. The light in the waiting room dimmed to dusk. A cloud must have covered the sun. And then the light rose again as though controlled by a rheostat. The big bell over the glass doors clamored. Louie looked at his watch and went through the door to his big bus. And the passengers in the waiting room got up and shuffled toward the door.

Edgar was still trying to make out where the Hindus wanted to go. "The god-damned rag heads," he said to himself. "Why'nt they learn English before they start running around?"

Louie climbed into the high seat enclosed by a stainless steel bar and glanced at the tickets as the passengers got on. The Chinaman in the dark coat went directly to the back seat, took off his coat, and laid the *Time* and *Newsweek* in his lap. The old lady clambered breathlessly up the step and sat down in the seat directly behind Louie.

He said, "I'm sorry, ma'am, that seat's taken."

"What do you mean, taken?" she said belligerently. "There aren't any reserved seats."

"That seat's taken, ma'am," Louie repeated. "Don't you see the suitcase beside it?" He hated old women. They frightened him. There was a smell about them that gave him the willies. They were fierce and they had no pride. They never gave a damn about making a scene. They got what they wanted. Louie's grandmother had been a tyrant. She had got whatever she wanted by being fierce. From the corners of his eyes he saw the girl on the lower step of the bus, waiting behind the Hindus to get in. He was pushed into a spot. Suddenly he was angry.

"Ma'am," he said, "I'm the boss on my bus. There's plenty of good seats. Now will you move back?"

The old woman set her chin and scowled at him. She switched her behind a little, settling into the seat. "You've got that girl in this seat, that's what you've got," she said. "I've got a mind to report you to the management."

Louie blew up. "All right, ma'am. You just get out and report me. The company's got lots of passengers, but it hasn't got many good drivers." He saw that the girl was listening, and he felt pretty good about it.

The old woman saw that he was angry. "I'm going to report you," she said.

"Well, report me then. You can get off the bus," Louie said loudly, "but you're not going to sit in that seat. The passenger in that seat got a doctor's order."

It was an out, and the old woman took it. "Why didn't you say so?" she said. "I'm not unreasonable. But I'm still going to report you for discourtesy."

"All right, ma'am," Louie said wearily. "That I'm used to."

The old woman moved back one seat.

"Going to hang out her big ear and catch me off base," Louie thought. "Well, let her. We got more passengers than drivers." The girl was beside him now, holding out her ticket. Involuntarily Louie said, "You only going as far as the Corners?"

"I know, I've got to change," said the girl. She smiled at his tone of disappointment.

"That's your seat right there," he said. He watched the mirror while she sat down and crossed her legs and pulled down her skirt and put her purse beside her. She straightened her shoulders and fixed the collar of her suit.

She knew Louie was watching every move. It had always been that way with her. She knew she was different from other girls, but she didn't quite know how. In some ways it was nice always to get the best seat, to have your lunches bought for you, to have a hand on your arm crossing the street. Men couldn't keep their hands off her. But there was always the trouble. She had to argue or cajole or insult or fight her way out. All men wanted the same thing from her, and that was just the way it was. She took it for granted and it was true.

When she'd been young she'd suffered from it. There had been a sense of guilt and of nastiness. But now she was older she just accepted it and developed her techniques. Sometimes she gave in and sometimes she got money or clothes. She knew most of the approaches. She could probably have foretold everything Louie would do or say in the next half hour. By anticipating, she could sometimes stave off unpleasantness. Older men wanted to help her, put her in school or on the stage. Some young men wanted to marry her or protect her. And a few, a very few, openly and honestly simply wanted to go to bed with her and told her so.

These were the easiest because she could say yes or no and get it over with. What she hated most about her gift, or her failing, was the fighting that went on. Men fought each other viciously when she was about. They fought like terriers, and she sometimes wished that women could like her, but they didn't. And she was intelligent. She knew why, but there wasn't anything she could do about it. What she really wanted was a nice house in a nice town, two children, and a stairway to stand on. She would be nicely dressed and people would be coming to dinner. She'd have a husband, of course, but she couldn't see him in her picture because the advertising in the women's magazines from which her dream came never included a man. Just a lovely woman in nice clothes coming down the stairs and guests in the dining room and candles and a dark wood dining table and clean children to kiss good night. That's what she really wanted. And she knew as well as anything that that was not what she would ever get.

There was a great deal of sadness in her. She wondered about other women. Were they different in bed than she was? She knew from watching that men didn't react to most women the way they did to her. Her sexual impulses were not terribly strong nor very constant, but she didn't know about other women. They never discussed this kind of thing with her. They didn't like her. Once the young doctor to whom she had gone to try to have the pain of her periods relaxed had made a pass at her, and when she had talked him out of that he had told her, "You just put it out in the air. I don't know how, but you do it. Some women are like that," he said. "Thank God there aren't many of them or a man would go nuts."

She tried wearing severe clothes, but that didn't help much. She couldn't keep an ordinary job. She learned to type, but offices went to pieces when she was hired. And now she had a racket. It paid well and it didn't get her in much trouble. She took off her clothes at stags. A regular agency handled her. She didn't understand stags or what satisfaction the men got out of them, but there they were, and she made fifty dollars for taking off her clothes and that was better than having them torn off in an office. She'd even read up on nymphomania, enough, anyway, to know that she didn't have it. She almost wished she had. Sometimes she thought she'd just go into a house and make a pile of dough and retire to the country—that, or marry an elderly man she could control. It would be the easiest way.

Young men who were attractive to her had a way of turning nasty. They always suspected her of cheating them. They either sulked or tried to beat her up or they got furious and threw her out.

She'd tried being kept and that was the way it ended. But an old man with some money—that might be the way. And she would be good to him. She'd really make it worth his money and his time. She had only two girl friends, and both of them were house girls. They seemed to be the only kind who weren't jealous of her and who didn't resent her. But one was out of the country now. She didn't know where. She followed troops somewhere. And the other was living with an advertising man and didn't want her around.

That was Loraine. They had had an apartment together. Loraine didn't care much about men; still, she didn't go for women. But then Loraine got caught short with this advertising man and asked her to move out. Loraine explained everything when she told her not to come around.

Loraine was working in a house and this advertising man fell for her. Well, Loraine had got gonorrhea, and before she even had a symptom she gave it to this advertising man. He was a nervous type and he blew his top and lost his job and came bellyaching to Loraine. She felt responsible in a way so she took him in and fed him while they both got cured. That was before the new treatment, and it had been pretty rough.

And then this advertising man went on a sleeping-pill pitch. She'd find him passed out and he was pretty vague, and his temper was bad unless he had his pills, and he took more and more of them. Twice Loraine had to have him pumped out.

Loraine was a really good girl and things were hard because she couldn't work in the house until she was cleared up. She didn't want to infect anybody she knew, and still she had to have money for doctor's bills and rent and food. She had to work the streets in Glendale to make it, and she wasn't feeling good herself. And then, with everything else, the advertising man turned jealous and didn't want her to work at all in spite of the fact that he didn't have a job. It would be nice if the whole thing had blown over by now and she and Loraine could have the apartment together. They had been a good pair together. They had had fun, good, quiet fun.

There had been a whole series of conventions in Chicago and she had saved some money from the stags. She was taking busses back to Los Angeles to save money. She wanted to live quietly a while. She hadn't heard from Loraine for a long time. The last letter said this advertising man was reading her mail so not to write.

The last passengers were coming through the doors and getting into the bus.

Louie had his legs crossed. He was a little timid with this girl. "I see you're going to L.A.," he said. "Do you live there?"

"Part of the time."

"I like to try and figure people out," he said. "A guy like me sees so many people."

The motor of the bus breathed softly. The old woman was glaring at Louie. He could see her in the mirror. She would probably write a letter to the company.

"Well," Louie said to himself, "the hell with the company." He could always get a job. The company didn't pay much attention to old ladies' letters anyway. He glanced back down the bus. It looked like the two Hindus were holding hands. The Chinaman had both *Time* and *Newsweek* open on his lap and he was comparing stories. His head swung from one magazine to the other, and a puzzled wrinkle marked his nose between his brows. The dispatcher waved at Louie.

Louie swung the lever that closed the door. He eased his gear into compound-reverse and crept out of the concrete slip, then swung delicately and wide so that his front fender cleared the north wall by a part of an inch. He swung wide again in compound-low and cleared the other side of the alley by a fraction of an inch. At the entrance to the street from the alley he stopped and saw that the street was clear for him. He turned the bus and it took him over to the other side of the street. Louie was a good driver with a perfect record. The bus moved down the main street of San Ysidro and came to the outskirts and to the open highway.

The sky and the sun were washed and clean. The colors were sharp. The ditches ran full of water; and in some places, where the ditches were clogged, the water extended out onto the highway. The bus hit this water with a great swish, and Louie could feel the tug at the wheel. The grass was matted down from the force of the rain, but now the warmth of the sun was putting strength into the rich grass and it was beginning to rise up again on the high places.

Louie glanced in the rear-view mirror at the girl again. She was looking at the back of his head. But something made her look up at the mirror and right into Louie's eyes, and the eyes with their dark lines and the straight, pretty nose and the mouth painted on square photographed permanently in Louie's brain. When she looked into his eyes she smiled as though she felt good.

Louie knew that his throat was closing, and a rising pressure was in his chest. He thought he must be nuts. He knew he was shy, but mostly he convinced himself that he was not, and he was going through all the symptoms of a sixteen-year-old. His eyes flicked from road to mirror, back and forth. He could see that his cheeks were red. "What the hell is this?" he said to himself. "Am I going to go ga-ga over a chippie?" He looked at her more closely to find some thought to save himself, and then he saw deep forceps marks along her jaws. That made him feel more comfortable. She wouldn't be so god-damned confident if she knew he saw the forceps marks. Forty-two miles. The figures came into his head. She'd get off in forty-two miles. Louie would have to make time. He couldn't waste a minute if he wanted to throw a line over this little hustler. And when he tried to speak his voice was hoarse.

She leaned close behind him. "I couldn't hear you," she said.

Louie coughed. "I said the country looks nice after the rain."

"Yes, it does."

He tried to get back to his usual opening. He noticed in the mirror that she was still leaning forward to listen.

"Like I said," he began, "I try to figure people out. I'd say you was in the movies or on the stage."

"No," said the girl. "You'd be wrong."

"Aren't you in show business?"

"No."

"Well, do you work?"

She laughed, and her face was very charming when she laughed. But Louie noticed that one of her upper front teeth was crooked. It leaned over and interfered with its neighbor. Her laughter stopped and her upper lip covered the tooth. "Conscious of it," Louie thought.

She was ahead of him. She knew what he was going to say. It had happened so many times before. He was going to try to find out where she lived. He wanted her telephone number. It was simple. She didn't live anywhere. She had a trunk stored with Loraine with some books in it—*Captain Hornblower*, and a *Life of Beethoven*, and some paper books of the short stories of Saroyan, and some old evening dresses to be made over. She knew Louie was having trouble. She knew that blush that rose out of a man's collar and the thickness of labored speech. She saw Louie glance apprehensively in the mirror at the rear of the bus.

The Hindus were smiling a little at each other. The Chinaman was staring up in the air, trying to work up in his mind some discrepancy in the stories he had been reading. A Greek in the rear seat was cutting an Italian cigar in two with a pocketknife. He put one piece in his mouth and thoughtfully placed the other half in his breast pocket. The old woman was working herself up into a rage at Louie. She directed an iron look at the back of his head, and her chin quivered with fury and her lips were white with the tension of their compression.

The girl leaned forward again. "I'll save you time," she said. "I'm a dental nurse. You know, I do all those things in a dentist's office." She often used this. She didn't know why. Perhaps because it stopped speculation and there were never any more questions after she said it. People didn't want to talk much about dentistry.

Louie digested this. The bus came to a railroad crossing. Automatically Louie set his air brakes and stopped. The brakes hissed as he released them and went through the gears to cruising speed again. He sensed that things were closing in on him. The old bitch was going to start trouble any minute now. He didn't have forty-two miles at all. Once the old bitch put in her oar the thing would be over. He wanted to make time while he could, but it was too soon according to Louie's methods. He shouldn't make a play for a good half hour, but the old bitch was going to force his hand.

"Sometimes I get into L.A.," he said. "Is there someplace I

could call you and maybe we could—have dinner and go to a show?"

She was friendly about it. There wasn't anything mean or bitchy about her. She said, "I don't know. You see, I haven't any place to live now. I've been away. I want to get an apartment as soon as I can."

"But you work someplace," said Louie. "Maybe I could call you there."

The old woman was squirming and twitching in her seat. She was mad because Louie had kicked her out of the front seat.

"Well, no," said the girl. "You see, I haven't got a job. Of course, I'll get one right away because you can always get a job in my profession."

"This isn't a brush-off?" Louie asked.

"No."

"Well, maybe you could drop me a line when you get settled."

"Maybe."

"Because I'd like to know someone to take out in L.A."

And now here it came, the voice as shrill as a whetstone. "There's a state law about talking to passengers. You watch the road." The old woman addressed the whole bus. "This driver's putting our lives in danger. I'm going to ask to get off if he can't keep his attention on his driving."

Louie closed up. This was serious. She really could make trouble. He looked in the mirror and found the girl's eyes. With his lips he said, "The god-damned dried up old bitch!"

The girl smiled and put her fingers to her lips. In a way she was relieved and in another she was sorry. She knew that sooner or later she would have trouble with Louie. But she also knew that in many ways he was a nice guy and one she could handle up to a certain point. She knew from his blush that she could probably stop him by hurting his feelings.

But it was over and Louie knew it. The girl wasn't going to get herself in a mess. He had to make time while the bus was rolling. He knew that. Once you got to a station the passengers wanted out as quick as possible. Now he'd lost out. At Rebel Corners he would stop only long enough to let her off and unload that god-damned crate of pies. He hunched over the wheel. The girl had folded her hands in her lap and her eyes would not raise to meet his in the mirror. There were lots of girls prettier than this one. Those forceps scars were damned ugly. They'd give a guy the shivers. Of course, she wore her hair long and forward to cover them. A girl like that couldn't wear her hair up. Louie liked hair up and, Jesus! suppose you woke up in bed and saw those scars. There were plenty of pigs in the world and Louie could get along. But in his chest and his stomach there was a weight of sorrow. He fought at it and picked at it but it wouldn't move. He wanted this girl more than he had ever wanted anyone, and in a different way. He felt a dry and grainy sense of loss. He didn't even know her name, and now he wouldn't get to know her. He could see Edgar's eager eyes questioning him when he came back to San Ysidro. Louie wondered if he would lie to Edgar.

The great tires sang on the road, a high, twanging song, and the motor throbbed with a heavy beat. There were big, wet, floppy clouds in the sky, dark as soot in the middle and white and shining on the edges. One of them was creeping up on the sun now. Already, ahead on the highway, Louie could see the shadow of it rushing toward the bus, and far ahead on the highway he could see the towering green mound of the oaks that grew about the lunchroom at Rebel Corners. He was filled with disappointment.

Juan Chicoy came to the side of the bus as it pulled in.

"What you got for me?" he asked as the door opened.

"One passenger and a flock of pies," said Louie. He got up from his seat, reached around, and lifted the girl's suitcase. He climbed down to the ground and held up his hands, and the girl put her hands on his arms and stepped down. They walked toward the lunchroom.

"Good-by," she said.

"Good-by," said Louie. He watched her go through the door, her little behind bobbing up and down.

Juan and Pimples had the crate of pies off the top of the bus. Louie climbed back into the bus.

"So long," said Juan.

The old woman had moved up into the front seat. Louie levered the door shut. He went into gear and moved away. When he was in cruising speed and the tires were ringing on the highway, he looked in the mirror. The old woman wore a look of mean triumph.

"You killed it," Louie said to himself. "Oh, you murdered it."

The woman looked up and caught his eyes in the mirror. Deliberately Louie made silent words with his lips. "You god-damned old bitch!" He saw her lips grow tight and white. She knew what he meant.

The highway sang along ahead of the bus.

Chapter 8

JUAN and Pimples carried the crate of Mother Mahoney's Home-Baked Pies near to the door of the lunchroom and set it down on the ground. Both of them watched the blonde go through the door. Pimples whistled a low gurgling note. The palms of his hands turned suddenly sweaty. Juan's eyes had lowered until only a little glint of light shone between his lashes. He licked his lips quickly and nervously.

"I know what you mean," said Juan. "Want to take time out and go over and lift your leg on a tree?"

"God Almighty," said Pimples. "Whew!"

"Yeah," said Juan. He bent over, turned the latch on the crate, and raised the hinged side. "I'll take a small bet, Kit."

"What's that?" Pimples asked.

"I bet," said Juan, "I bet two to one you already got in your mind the idea that you didn't have a day off for two weeks and you'd like to take today and ride over to San Juan with me. Maybe it would even help if the bus breaks down again."

Pimples started to blush around his eruptions. He raised his eyes uneasily and looked at Juan, and there was so much humor without poison in Juan's eyes that Pimples felt better. "God damn!" he thought, "there is a man. Why'd I ever work for anybody else?"

"Well," Pimples said aloud, and he felt he was talking to a man. Juan understood how a guy looked at things. When a cookie went by, Juan knew how a guy felt. "Well," he said again.

"Well," Juan mimicked him, "and who's gonna take care of the gas pumps and fix the flats?"

"Who done it before?" Pimples asked.

"Nobody," said Juan. "We used to just put a sign on the garage—Closed For Repairs. Alice can pump gas." He slapped Pimples on the shoulder.

"What a guy," Pimples thought. "What a guy!"

The pies were held by little traylike slots which gripped the edges of the pans and left each pie separate from all the others. There were four stacks of twelve pies—forty-eight pies.

"Let's see," said Juan, "we get six raspberry, four lemon cream, four raisin, and two caramel custard cream." He pulled out the pies as he spoke and laid them on top of the crate. "Take them in, Pim—Kit, I mean."

Pimples took a pie in each hand and went into the lunchroom. The blonde was sitting on a stool drinking a cup of coffee. He couldn't see her face but he felt the electricity or whatever it was she had. He put the pies on the counter.

As he turned to go out again he felt the silence in the room. Mr. Pritchard and the crabby old guy and the young fellow, Horton, were entranced. Their eyes rose and washed the blonde and fell away. Miss Pritchard and her mother looked pointedly at the piles of bran in back of the counter. Alice was not there, but Norma was in front of the blonde, wiping the counter with her rag.

"Like to have a snail?" Norma asked.

Pimples paused. He had to hear the tone of the blonde's voice.

"Yes, I guess so," she said. A quick spasm kinked Pimples' stomach at the throaty tone. He hurried outside and gathered up more pies.

"Get moving," Juan said. "You can look at her all the way over to San Juan, unless you'd rather drive."

Pimples rushed the pies in. Sixteen pies out. That left thirty-two. Juan closed the side of the crate and turned the catch. When Pimples came out the last time he helped Juan put the pie crate in the big black trunk of "Sweetheart," the bus. She was ready now. Ready to go. Juan stood back and looked at her. She was no Greyhound but she wasn't bad. Around the windows a little rust showed through the aluminum paint. He would have to touch that up. And the hub caps could take a new coat too.

"Let's get going," he said to Pimples. "Lock the garage doors. Right between the benches under the radiator hose connections you'll find the sign to put on the door. Jump now if you want to get your clothes changed."

Pimples leaped for the garage door. Juan straightened up and stretched his arms from his sides and moved toward the lunchroom.

Mr. Pritchard's right leg was crossed over his left and his

suspended toe made little convulsive jumps. He had glanced into the blonde's face when she came in and now there was a pleasant excitement in him. But he was puzzled. Somewhere, he thought, he had seen this girl. Maybe she'd worked in one of his plants, maybe a secretary, maybe in some friend's office. But he'd seen her. He felt sure he had. He truly believed that he never forgot a face, when the truth was that he rarely remembered one. He didn't look closely at any face unless he planned to do business with its owner. He wondered about the sense of sin he got out of the recognition. Where could he have seen this girl?

His wife was looking secretly at his swinging foot. Ernest Horton was frankly gazing at the blonde's legs. Norma liked the girl. In one respect Norma was like Loraine. She didn't love anyone—well, except one—so she had nothing to be taken away, nothing to lose. And this girl was nice. She was pleasant-spoken and polite. Actually the girl felt good toward Norma too, sensing that this girl could like her.

Just before the Greyhound came in Alice had said to Norma, "Watch the counter, will you? I'll be right back." And then the bus and the blonde and getting the coffee had taken up Norma's thoughts. But now a certain knowledge struck her, made her turn cold and nauseous inside. She knew what was happening as though she could see it. She knew, and knowing, many calculations came into her head around her sick anger. The little roll of money in small bills. That could be used until she could get a job. And why couldn't she go now? She was going to sometime. She opened the cabinets beneath the shelves in back of the lunch counter and shoved the pies in, all except one of each kind. One raspberry, one raisin, one lemon cream, and one caramel custard cream she lined up on the counter, and the smell of them made her sicker. She still didn't quite know what to do.

Juan came through the front door and stood looking at the back of the blonde's head.

Norma said, "Will you watch the counter a minute, Mr. Chicoy?"

"Where's Alice?" Juan asked.

"I don't know," said Norma. She could see Alice in her mind. Alice's eyes weren't so good. She would take the letter to the window and hold it up to the light. She wasn't really interested. It was a casual, vague kind of curiosity. She would lean sideways to the light and her hair would fall in her eyes so she would blow it, and her fingers would scrabble through the pages. Norma shivered. She saw herself hurtling into the room. She saw herself snatch the letter, and her fingers flexed. She felt Alice's skin against her fingernails and her nails striking and clawing for Alice's eyes, those horrible, wet, juicy eyes. Alice would fall on her back and Norma would come down on that great, soft stomach with her knees, and she'd scratch and tear at Alice's face and the blood would run in the scratches.

Juan, looking at Norma, said, "What's the matter? Are you sick?"

"Yes," said Norma.

"Go ahead before you get sick here."

Norma edged down the counter and opened the bedroom door softly. The door to her own room was open just a crack. She closed the door into the lunchroom and moved silently toward her own door. She was cold now and shivering. Cold as ice. Noiselessly she pushed her door open. And there it was—Alice, by the window, holding the letter to Clark Gable up to her eyes and blowing her hair sideways.

Alice blew her hair and looked up and saw Norma standing in the doorway. Her mouth was open, her face avid. She couldn't change her expression. Norma took a step into the room. Her chin was set so hard that the lines receded from her mouth. Alice stupidly held the letter out to her. Norma took it, folded it carefully, and tucked it in her bodice. And then Norma went to her bureau. She drew her suitcase from underneath. She unpinned the key from the inside of her dress and unlocked the suitcase. Heavily she began to pack. She emptied the bureau drawers into the suitcase and pressed the mound of clothes down with her fist. From the closet she dragged out her three dresses and her coat with the rabbit collar and she laid the coat on the bed and rolled the dresses up around the hangers and poked them in the suitcase too.

Alice couldn't move. She watched Norma, her head swinging as the girl passed back and forth. In Norma's brain there was a silent scream of triumph. She was on top. After a life of being pushed around, she was on top and she was silent. She felt good about that. Not one word did she say and not one word would she say. She threw two pairs of shoes into the suitcase and put the lid firmly down and locked it.

"You going right now?" Alice asked.

Norma didn't answer. She wouldn't break her triumph. Nothing could force her.

"I didn't mean to do anything wrong," Alice said.

Norma didn't look up.

"You'd better not tell or I'll fix you," Alice suggested uneasily. Still Norma did not speak. She went to the bed and got her black coat with the rabbit collar. Then she picked up her suitcase and walked out of the room. Her breath was whistling in her nose. She went in back of the lunch counter and pushed the "No Sale" button on the cash register. Norma took out ten dollars, a five and four ones and a half and two quarters. She shoved the money in the side pocket of her black coat. Her weak mouth was set in a hard line.

Juan said, "What's going on here?"

"I'm going to San Juan with you," said Norma.

"You've got to help Alice," said Juan. "She can't stay here alone."

"I've quit," said Norma. She saw that the blonde watched her as she came around the edge of the counter. Norma went out the screen door. She carried her suitcase to the bus and she climbed in and took a seat toward the rear. She stood her suitcase up on its end beside her. She sat very straight.

Juan watched her go out of the door. He shrugged his shoulders. "What do you suppose that was?" he asked of no one in particular.

Ernest Horton was scowling. He hated Alice Chicoy. He said, "What time you think we'll get started?"

"Ten-thirty," said Juan. "It's ten-ten now." He glanced at the Pritchards. "Look, I've got to change my clothes. If you folks want coffee or anything, just come back here and get it."

He went into the bedroom. He slipped the shoulder straps of his overalls and let the pants fall down around his shoes. He had on shorts with narrow blue stripes. He peeled his blue chambray shirt over his head and kicked off his moccasins and stepped out of the overalls, leaving shoes and socks and overalls in a pile on the floor. His body was hard and brown, colored not by the sun but by brown ancestry. He moved over to the bathroom and knocked on the door. Alice flushed the toilet and opened the door. She had been washing her face again and a wet strand of hair was plastered to her cheek. Her mouth was lax and her eyes were swollen and red.

"What's going on?" Juan asked. "You're having one hell of a time for yourself, aren't you?"

"I've got a toothache," Alice said. "I can't help it. I've got a jumping pain right here."

"What's the matter with Norma?" Juan asked.

"Let her go," Alice said. "I knew I'd catch up with her sometimes."

"Well, what did she do?"

"She's just a little light-fingered," said Alice.

"What did she take?"

"Just thought I'd see. Remember that bottle of Bellodgia you gave me for Christmas? Well, it was gone and I found it in her suitcase. She came in when I found it and she got huffy and I told her she could go."

Juan's eyes veiled. He knew it was a lie, but he didn't much care what the truth was. Women fights didn't interest him at all. He got in the tub and pulled the shower curtain about him.

"You've been a mess all morning," he said. "What's the matter with you?"

"Well, it's my time," said Alice, "and then this toothache."

Juan knew the first was not true. But he only suspected the second could be false. "Take yourself a slug of liquor when we go. That'll be good for both ends," he said.

Alice was pleased. She wanted him to suggest it.

"You've got to take care of everything," Juan went on. "Pimples is going along with me today."

Excitement surged in Alice. She would be alone, all by herself. But she couldn't let Juan know that was what she wanted. "What's Pimples going for?" she asked.

"He wants to get some things over in San Juan. Say, why don't we close up the place? You can go to the dentist in San Juan."

"No," Alice said. "It's not a good idea. I'll go in to San Ysidro tomorrow or the next day. It's not a good idea to close the lunchroom."

"O.K. It's your tooth," said Juan, and he turned on the water. He poked his head out of the curtain. "Go on out there and take care of the passengers."

Ernest Horton had moved in on the blonde when Alice came into the lunchroom.

"Now, let's have a couple of cups of coffee," he said. And to the blonde, "You rather have a coke?"

"No. Coffee. Cokes make me fat."

Ernest had been making time. He had asked her name and the blonde had said it was Camille Oaks. It wasn't, of course. It was a quick grouping of a Camel advertisement on the wall—another blonde on a poster with balloon-like breasts—and a tree she could see through the window. But Camille Oaks she was from now on, for this trip at least.

"I heard that name recently some place," Ernest said. He passed the sugar dispenser politely to her.

Mr. Pritchard's foot was swinging in little jerks and Mrs. Pritchard was watching. She knew Mr. Pritchard was getting irritable at something, but she didn't know why. She had no experience with this kind of thing. Her women friends were not of a kind to put Mr. Pritchard's foot swinging. And she knew nothing about his life outside of her own social movements.

He uncrossed his legs, stood up, and went to the counter. "You're thinking of the Oakes murder trial," he said to Ernest. "I'm sure this young lady wasn't murdered or vice versa," he chuckled. "A little more coffee," he said gallantly to Alice.

His daughter pulled her right eye sideways to look at him. There was a quality in his voice she had never heard before. And there was a little grandeur in his tone. He was broadening his "a" and putting an unnatural formality into his speech. It shocked his daughter. She peered at the girl and suddenly she knew what it was. Mr. Pritchard was reacting to Camille Oaks. He was making a play—a kind of fatherly play. His daughter didn't like it.

Mr. Pritchard said, "I have an impression I have met you. Could that be?"

In her head Mildred paraphrased it, "Ain't I seen you somewheres?"

Camille looked at Mr. Pritchard's face and her eyes flicked to the club button on his lapel. She knew where he had seen her. When she took off her clothes and sat in the bowl of wine she very carefully didn't look at the men's faces. There was something in their wet, bulging eyes and limp, half-smiling mouths that frightened her. She had a feeling that if she looked directly at one he might leap on her. To her, her audiences were blobs of pink faces and hundreds of white collars and neat four-in-hand ties. The Two Fifty—Three Thousand Clubs usually wore tuxedos.

She said, "I don't remember."

"Ever been in the Middle West?" Mr. Pritchard insisted.

"I've been working in Chicago," said Camille.

"Where?" Mr. Pritchard asked. "The impression is very strong."

"I'm a dental nurse," said Camille.

Mr. Pritchard's eyes brightened behind his glasses. "Say, I'll bet that's it. Dr. Horace Liebholtz, he's my dentist in Chicago."

"No," said Camille, "no, I never worked for him. Dr. T. S. Chesterfield, that was my last job." She got that from a poster too and it wasn't clever. She hoped he wouldn't notice right over his shoulder the sign, "Chesterfields—They Satisfy."

Mr. Pritchard said gaily, to his daughter's disgust, "Well, I'll remember sooner or later. I never forget a face."

Mrs. Pritchard had caught her daughter's eyes and she saw the distaste in Mildred's expression. She glanced at her husband again. He was acting queerly. "Elliott," she said, "will you bring me a little coffee?"

Mr. Pritchard seemed to shake himself into reality. "Oh, yes—sure," he said, and his voice returned to normal. But he was irritated again.

The screen door opened and banged shut. Pimples Carson entered, but a Pimples transformed. His face was heavily powdered in an attempt to cover up the eruptions, and this succeeded in turning their redness to a rich purple. His hair was slicked back and stuck with pomade. He wore a shirt with a very tight collar, a green tie with a small knot, and the shirt collar was pinned under the knot with a gold collar pin. Pimples seemed to be strangling a little, so tight was his collar. Shirt and tie rose and fell slightly when he swallowed. His suit was a chocolate brown, a hairy material, and on the sides of the trousers were the almost indistinguishable print of bedsprings. He wore white shoes with brown saddles and woolen socks of red and green plaid.

Alice looked up at him in astonishment. "Well, will you look what just come in!" she said.

Pimples hated her. He sat on a stool in the place Mr. Pritchard had only just vacated to take coffee to his wife. "I'd like to have a piece of that new raspberry pie," he said. He glanced nervously at Camille and his voice strangled a little. "Miss, you ought to have a piece of that pie."

Camille looked at him and her eyes grew warm. She knew when a man was having trouble. "No thanks," she said kindly. "I had breakfast in San Ysidro."

"It's on me," said Pimples frantically.

"No, really, thanks. I couldn't."

"Well, he could," said Alice. "He could eat pies standing on his head in a washtub of flat beer on Palm Sunday." She whirled a pie and got out a knife.

"Double, please," said Pimples.

"I don't think you got any pay coming," said Alice cruelly. "You've eaten yourself right through your salary this week."

Pimples winced. God, how he hated Alice! Alice was watching the blonde. She'd caught it. Every man in the room was alert, his senses feeling toward this girl. Alice was nervous about it. She would know when Juan came in. A moment ago she had wanted the bus to be on its way so she could have a good big drunk. But now, now she was getting nervous.

Ernest Horton said, "If I can get to my sample case I'll show you some cute gadgets I'm selling. New stuff. Very cute."

Camille said, "How long you been out of the Army?"

"Five months," said Ernest.

She dropped her eyes to his lapel with the blue bar and white stars. "That's a nice one," she said. "That's the real big one, isn't it?"

"That's what they tell me," said Ernest. "It don't buy any groceries, though." They laughed together.

"Did the big boss pin it on you?"

"Yeah," said Ernest.

Mr. Pritchard leaned forward. It bothered him that he didn't know what was happening.

Pimples said, "You ought to try some of this raspberry pie."

"I couldn't," said Camille.

Alice said, "You find a fly in that and I'll let you have the rest of the pie right in the kisser."

Camille knew the symptoms. This woman was getting ready to hate her. She glanced uneasily at the other two women in the room. Mrs. Pritchard wouldn't bother her. But the girl, there, who was trying to go without her glasses. Camille just hoped she didn't cross with her. That could be a tough babe. She cried in her mind, "Oh, Jesus, Loraine, get rid of that jerk and let's live in the apartment again." She had a dreadful sense of loneliness and weariness. She wondered how it would be to be married to Mr. Pritchard. He was something like the man she had in mind. It was probably not very hard being married to him. His wife didn't look as though he gave her much trouble.

Bernice Pritchard was in the dark. She didn't hate Camille. Vaguely she knew that some change had come over the room, but she didn't know what it was. "I guess we'd better get our things together," she said brightly to Mildred. And this in spite of the fact that their things were together.

Now Juan came out of the bedroom. He was dressed in clean corduroy trousers, a clean blue shirt, and a leather windbreaker. His thick hair was combed straight back and his face was shiny from shaving.

"All ready, folks?" he said.

Alice watched him as he walked around the end of the lunch counter. He didn't look at Camille at all. Alice felt a stir of alarm. Juan looked at all girls. If he didn't there was something wrong. Alice didn't like it.

Mr. Van Brunt, the old gentleman with the stiff neck, came in from outside and held the screen door open a little. "Looks like more rain," he said.

Juan addressed him shortly. "You'll get on the next Greyhound north," he said.

"I changed my mind," said Van Brunt. "I'm going along

with you. I want to see that bridge. But it's going to rain more, I tell you that."

"I thought you didn't want to go."

"I can change my mind, can't I? Why don't you call up again about that bridge?"

"They said it was all right."

"That was some time ago," said Van Brunt. "You're a stranger here. You don't know how fast the San Ysidro can rise. I've seen it come up a foot an hour when the hills dump into her. You better call up."

Juan was exasperated. "Look," he said, "I drive the bus. I've been doing it for some time. Would you mind? You just ride and take a chance on me, or don't, but let me drive it."

Van Brunt turned his face up sideways and stared at Juan coldly. "I don't know whether I'll go with you or not. I might even write a note to the railroad commission. You're a common carrier, you know. Don't forget that."

"Let's go, folks," said Juan.

Alice kept secret eyes on him, and he didn't look at Camille, didn't offer to carry her suitcase. That was bad. Alice didn't like it. It wasn't like Juan.

Camille picked up her suitcase and scuttled out of the door. She didn't want to sit with any of the men. She was tired. Quickly her mind had gone over the possibilities. Mildred Pritchard was unattached and already Mildred didn't like her. But the girl who had quit was out there in the bus. Camille hurried out the door and climbed in. As quickly as they could, Ernest Horton and Mr. Pritchard followed, but Camille was in the bus. Norma sat quite still. Her eyes were hostile and her nose red and shiny. Norma was very much frightened at what she had done.

Camille said, "Would you mind if I sit with you, honey?"

Norma turned her head stiffly and regarded the blonde. "There's plenty of seats," she said.

"Would you mind? I'll tell you why later."

"Suit your own convenience," said Norma grandly. She could tell that this girl was expensively dressed. It didn't make sense. People didn't want to sit with Norma. But there was a reason. Maybe a mysterious reason. Norma knew her movies.

Things like this could turn into nine reels of pure delight. She moved over near the window and made room.

"How far are you going?" Norma asked.

"To L.A."

"Why, I'm going there too! Do you live there?"

"Off and on," said Camille. She noticed that the men who had come piling out of the lunchroom had seen her sit down with Norma. Their drive slowed down. There was going to be no competition. They clustered around the rear end of the bus to have the bags put in the luggage compartment.

Juan lingered at the lunchroom door with Alice looking through the screen at him. "Take it easy," he said. "Had a god-damn mess all morning. Try to get it cleared up before I get home."

A sharpness came on Alice's face. She was about to answer.

Juan went on, "Or one of these days I won't get home."

Her breath caught. "I just don't feel good," she whined.

"Well, start feeling good, then, and don't run it into the ground. Nobody likes sick people very long. Nobody. Get that straight." His eyes were not looking at her but around her and through her, and panic came over Alice. Juan turned away and walked toward the bus.

Alice leaned her elbows on the cross piece of the screen door. Big soft tears filled her eyes. "I'm fat," she said quietly, "and I'm old. Oh, Jesus, I'm old!" The tears ran into her nose. She snorted them back. She said, "You can get young girls, but what can I get? Nothing. An old slob." She sniffled quietly behind the screen.

Mr. Pritchard would have liked to have sat behind the blonde to watch her, but Mrs. Pritchard took a seat near the front and he had to sit down beside her. Mildred sat alone on the other side and behind them. Pimples climbed on and he got the seat Mr. Pritchard wanted, and Ernest Horton sat with him.

Juan noticed with dismay that Van Brunt took the seat directly behind the driver's seat. Juan was nervous. He hadn't had much sleep and some kind of hell had been popping since early morning. He got the bags neatly stacked in the rear trunk, pulled the canvas cover down, and closed the door of the trunk. He waved his hand at Alice leaning inside the screen door. He knew from her posture that she was crying and he intended that she should. She'd got out of hand. He wondered why he stayed with her. Just pure laziness, he guessed. He didn't want to go through the emotional turmoil of leaving her. In spite of himself he'd worry about her and it was too much trouble. He'd need another woman right away and that took a lot of talking and arguing and persuading. It was different just to lay a girl but he would need a woman around, and that was the difference. You got used to one and it was less trouble. Besides Alice was the only woman he had ever found outside of Mexico who could cook beans. A funny thing. Every little Indian in Mexico could cook beans properly and no one up here except Alice—just enough juice, just the right flavor of the bean without another flavor mixed up with it. Here they put tomatoes and chili and garlic and such things in the beans, and a bean should be cooked for itself, with itself, alone. Juan chuckled. "Because she can cook beans," he said to himself.

But there was another reason too. She loved him. She really did. And he knew it. And you can't leave a thing like that. It's a structure and it has an architecture, and you can't leave it without tearing off a piece of yourself. So if you want to remain whole you stay no matter how much you may dislike staying. Juan was not a man who fooled himself very much.

He was almost to the bus when he turned back and walked quickly to the screen door. "Take care of yourself," he said. His eyes were warm. "Get a slug of liquor for that tooth." He turned away and walked back to the bus. She'd be drunker than a skunk when he got back, but maybe that would blow out her tubes and she'd feel better. He would sleep in Norma's bed if Alice passed out. He couldn't stand the smell of her when she was drunk. She had an acid, bitter smell.

Juan glanced up at the sky. The air was still but up high a wind was blowing, bringing legions of new clouds over the mountains, and these clouds were flat and they were joining together and moving in on one another as they hurried across the sky. The big oaks still dripped water from the morning rain and the geranium leaves held shining drops in the centers. There was a hush on the land and a great activity.

Much as he hated to give Van Brunt any credit, Juan was

afraid it was going to rain some more, and soon. He climbed up the steps of the bus. Van Brunt caught him before he even sat down.

"Know where that wind's coming from? Southwest. Know where those clouds are coming from? Southwest. You know where our rain comes from?" he demanded triumphantly. "Southwest."

"O.K., and we're all gonna die sometime," said Juan. "Some of us pretty horribly. You might get run over by a tractor. Ever seen a man run over by a tractor?"

"How do you figure that?" Van Brunt demanded.

"Let it rain," said Juan.

"I don't own a tractor," said Van Brunt. "I got four pair of the best horses in this state. How do you figure that tractor?"

Juan stepped on the starter. It had a high, thin, scratchy sound, but almost immediately his motor started and it sounded good. It sounded smooth and nice. Juan turned in his seat.

"Kit," he called, "keep listening to that rear end."

"O.K.," said Pimples. He felt good about Juan's confidence.

Juan waved his hand to Alice and closed the bus door with his lever. He couldn't see what she was doing through the screen. She would let him get out of sight before she brought out a bottle. He hoped she wouldn't get into any trouble.

Juan drove around the front of the lunchroom and turned right into the black-top road that led to San Juan de la Cruz. It wasn't a very wide road but it was fairly smooth and the crown had a high arch so that it shed the water nicely. The valley and the hills were splashed with gouts of sunlight, and they were fenced with the moving shadows of clouds rushing across the sky. The sun spots and the shadows were somber gray, threatening and sad.

"Sweetheart" bumped along at forty. She was a good bus and the rear end sounded good too.

"I never liked tractors," said Mr. Van Brunt.

"I don't either," Juan agreed. He felt fine all of a sudden.

Van Brunt couldn't let it alone. Juan had succeeded beyond his hopes. Van Brunt turned his head sideways on his stiff neck. "Say, you're not one of these fortunetellers or anything like that?"

"No," said Juan.

"Because I don't believe any stuff like that," said Van Brunt.

"Neither do I," said Juan.

"I wouldn't have a tractor on the place."

Juan was about to say "I had a brother who was kicked to death by a horse," but he thought, "Aw, nuts, the guy's a pushover. I wonder what he's scared of."

Chapter 9

THE highway to San Juan de la Cruz was a black-top road. In the twenties hundreds of miles of concrete highway had been laid down in California, and people had sat back and said, "There, that's permanent. That will last as long as the Roman roads and longer, because no grass can grow up through the concrete to break it." But it wasn't so. The rubber-shod trucks, the pounding automobiles, beat the concrete, and after a while the life went out of it and it began to crumble. Then a side broke off and a hole crushed through and a crack developed and a little ice in the winter spread the crack, so the resisting concrete could not stand the beating of rubber and broke down.

Then the county maintenance crews poured tar in the cracks to keep the water out, and that didn't work, and finally they capped the roads with an asphalt and gravel mixture. That did survive, because it offered no stern face to the pounding tires. It gave a little and came back a little. It softened in the summer and hardened in the winter. And gradually all the roads were capped with shining black that looked silver in the distance.

The San Juan road ran straight for a long way through level fields, and the fields were not fenced because cattle didn't wander any more. The land was too valuable for grazing. The fields were open to the highway. They terminated in ditches beside the road. And in the ditches the wild mustard grew rankly and the wild turnip with its little purple flowers. The ditches were lined with blue lupines. The poppies were tightly rolled, for the open flowers had been beaten off by the rain.

The road ran straight toward the little foothills of the first range—rounded, woman-like hills, soft and sexual as flesh. And the green clinging grass had the bloom of young skin. The hills were rich and lovely with water, and along the smooth and beautiful road "Sweetheart" rolled. Her washed and shining sides reflected in the water of the ditches. The little tokens swung against the windshield—the tiny boxing gloves, the baby's shoe. The Virgin of Guadalupe on her crescent moon on top of the instrument board looked benignly back at the passengers.

There was no rough or ill sound from the rear end, just the curious whine of the transmission. Juan settled back in his seat prepared to enjoy the trip. He had a big mirror in front of him so that he could watch the passengers, and he had a long mirror out the window in which he could see the road behind. The road was deserted. Only a few cars passed, and none came from the direction of San Juan. At first this puzzled him unconsciously, and then he began to worry actively. Perhaps the bridge was out. Well, if it was he would have to come back. He'd take the whole crowd of passengers into San Ysidro and turn them loose there. If the bridge was out, there would be no bus line until it was in again. He noticed in his mirror that Ernest Horton had got his sample case open and was showing Pimples some kind of gadget that whirled and flashed and disappeared. And he noticed that Norma and the blonde had their heads together and were talking. He increased his speed a little.

He didn't think he was going to do anything about the blonde. There wasn't any possible way to get at her. And Juan was old enough not to suffer from something that was out of possibility. Given the opportunity there wasn't any question about what he would do. He had felt a wrench in the pit of his stomach when he first saw the blonde.

Norma had been stiff with Camille so far. She was so frozen up it took her some time to thaw. But Camille needed Norma as a kind of a shield, and they had their destination in common.

"I've never been in L.A. or Hollywood," Norma confided softly so that Ernest could not hear. "I won't know where to go or anything."

"What are you going to do?" Camille asked.

"Get a job, I guess. Waitress or something. I'd like to get in pictures."

Camille's mouth tightened in a smile. "You get a job waitressing first," she said. "Pictures are a very tough racket."

"Are you an actress?" Norma asked. "You look like you might be an actress."

"No," said Camille. "I work for dentists. I'm a dental nurse."

"Well, do you live in a hotel, or a room, or a house?"

"I don't have any place to live," said Camille. "I used to have an apartment with a girl friend before I went to Chicago to work."

Norma's eyes grew eager. "I've got a little money put away," she said. "Maybe we could get an apartment together. Say, if I got a job in a restaurant it wouldn't cost hardly anything for food. I could bring stuff home." A hunger was growing in Norma's eyes. "Why, maybe sharing the rent it wouldn't be much. I could make good tips, maybe."

Camille felt a warmth for the girl. She looked at the red nose and the dull complexion, the small pale eyes. "We'll see how it goes," she said.

Norma leaned close. "I know your hair's natural," she said. "But maybe you could show me how to kind of touch mine up. My hair's mousy. Just mousy."

Camille laughed. "You'd be surprised if you knew what color my hair is," she said. "Hold still a minute." She studied Norma's face, trying to visualize what cold cream and powder and mascara could do for her, and she thought of the hair shining and waved, and the eyes made a little larger with eye-shadow, and the mouth reshaped with lipstick. Camille hadn't any illusions about beauty. Loraine was a washed-out little rat without make-up but Loraine did all right. It would be fun and company to make this girl over and to give her some confidence. It might even be better than Loraine.

"Let's think about it," she said. "This is pretty country. I'd like to live in the country some time." A picture had projected itself on her mind, the pattern of what would happen. She would fix Norma up. She could be kind of pretty if she was careful. And then Norma would meet a boy and naturally she'd bring him home to show him off and the boy would make passes at Camille and Norma would hate her. That's the way it would happen. That's the way it had happened. But what the hell! it would be fun before it happened. And maybe she could anticipate it and never be in when Norma brought a boy home.

She felt warm and friendly. "Let's think about it," she said.

On the highway ahead Juan saw a crushed jackrabbit. Lots of people liked to run over things like that, but Juan didn't. He moved his steering wheel so that the flattened carcass passed between the wheels and there was no crunching under the tires. He had the bus at forty-five. The big highway busses sometimes went sixty miles an hour, but Juan had plenty of time. The road was straight for another two miles before it began wandering into the soft foothills. Juan took one hand off the wheel and stretched.

Mildred Pritchard felt the telegraph poles whipping by as little blows on her eyes. She had her glasses on again. She watched Juan's face in the mirror. She could see little more than a profile from her angle. She noticed that he raised his head to look back at the blonde every minute or so, and she felt a bitter anger. She was confused about what had happened that morning. No one knew, of course, unless Juan Chicoy had guessed. She was still a little swollen and itchy from the thing. A sentence kept repeating itself in her mind. She's not a blonde and she's not a nurse and her name is not Camille Oaks. The sentence went on, over and over. And then she chuckled at herself inwardly. "I'm trying to destroy her," she thought. "I'm doing a stupid thing. Why not admit I'm jealous? I'm jealous. All right. Does admitting it make me any less jealous? No, it does not. But she forced my father to make a fool of himself. All right. Do I care whether my father is a fool? No, I do not—if I'm not with him. I don't want people to think I'm his daughter, that's all. No, that's not true either. I don't want to go to Mexico with him. I can hear everything he'll say." She was uncomfortable and the movement of the bus was not helping. "Basketball," she thought, "that's the stuff." She flexed the muscles of her thighs and thought about the engineering student with the crew-cut hair. She pictured her affair with him.

Mr. Pritchard was bored and tired. He could be very irritating when he was bored. He twitched. "This looks like rich country," he said to his wife. "California raises most of the vegetables for the United States, you know."

Mrs. Pritchard could hear herself talking after she got home. "Then we drove through miles and miles of green fields with poppies and lupines, just like a garden. There was a blond girl got on at a funny little place and the men made fools of themselves, even Elliott. I joshed him about it for a week afterward." She'd write it in a letter. "And I'm pretty sure the poor little painted thing was just as nice and sweet as could be. She said she was a nurse, but I think she was probably an actress—little parts, you know. There are so many of them in Hollywood. Thirty-eight thousand listed. They've got a big casting agency. Thirty-eight thousand." Her head nodded a little. Bernice was sleepy and hungry. "I wonder what adventures we'll have now," she thought.

When his wife slipped into her daydream Mr. Pritchard knew it. He had been married to her long enough to know when she wasn't listening to him, and ordinarily he went right on talking. He often clarified his thinking about business or politics by telling his thoughts to Bernice when she wasn't listening. He had a trained memory for figures and for bits of information. He knew approximately how many tons of sugar beets were produced in the Salinas valley. He had read it and retained it in spite of the fact that he had no use whatever for the information. He felt that such information was good to know and he had never questioned its value or why it might be good to know. But now he had no inclination toward knowledge. A powerful influence was battering at him from the rear of the bus. He wanted to turn around and look at the blonde. He wanted to sit where he could watch her. Horton and Pimples were behind him. He couldn't just sit opposite and look at her.

Mrs. Pritchard asked, "How old do you think she is?" And the question shocked him because he had been wondering the same thing.

"How old who is?" he asked.

"The young woman. The blond young woman."

"Oh, her. How should I know?" His answer was so rough that his wife looked a little bewildered and hurt. He saw it and tried to cover his mistake. "Little girls know more about little girls," he said. "You could tell better than I could."

"Why? I don't know. Well, with that make-up and the hair tint it's hard to tell. I just wondered. Somewhere between twenty-five and thirty, I guess."

"I wouldn't know about that," said Mr. Pritchard. He looked out the window at the approaching foothills. His palms were a little damp and the magnet drew at him from the rear of the bus. He wanted to look around. "I don't know about that," said Mr. Pritchard. "But I'm interested in that young Horton. He's young, and he's got lots of get-up, and he's got ideas. He really caught my fancy. You know, I might find a place for a man like that in the organization." This was business.

Bernice too could draw a magic circle around herself, with motherhood, or say, menstruation, a subject like that, and no man could or would try to get in. Business was her husband's magic circle. She had no right to go near him when it was business. She had no knowledge nor interest in business. It was his privacy and she respected it.

"He seems a nice young man," she said. "His grammar and his background—"

"My God, Bernice!" he cried irritably. "Business isn't background and grammar. It's what you can produce. Business is the most democratic thing in the world. It's what you can do that counts."

He was trying to remember what the blonde's lips looked like. He believed that full-lipped women were voluptuous. "I'd like to have a little talk with Horton before he gets away," Mr. Pritchard said.

Bernice knew that he was restless.

"Why don't you talk to him now?" she suggested.

"Oh, I don't know. He's sitting with that boy."

"Well, I'm sure that boy will move if you ask him nicely." She was convinced that anyone would do anything if nicely asked. And in her case she was right. She claimed and got the most outrageous favors from strangers simply by asking nicely. She would ask a bellboy to carry her bags four blocks to the station because it was too close, really, to get a cab, and then thank him nicely and give him a dime.

Now she knew she was helping her husband to do something he wanted to do. What it was she didn't quite know. She wanted to get back to writing the imaginary letter about their trip. "Elliott is so interested in everything. He had long talks with everyone. I guess that's why he's so successful. He takes such an interest. And he's so thoughtful. There was a boy with big pimples and Elliott didn't want to disturb him, but I told him just to ask nicely. People do love nice manners."

Mr. Pritchard was cleaning his nails again with the gold appliance he wore on his watch chain.

Pimples' eyes were on the back of Camille's head. But first when he had sat down he made sure that he couldn't see her legs under the seat, not even her ankles. Now and then she turned to look out of the window, and he could see her profile, the long, darkened eyelashes which curled upward, the straight, powdered nose, nostrils a little coated with tobacco smoke and the dust of traveling. Her upper lip curved upward to a sharp line before it pillowed out in its heavy red petal, and Pimples could see the downy hair on her upper lip. For some reason this aroused him agonizingly. When her head was turned straight ahead he could see one of her ears where the hair parted a little and exposed it. He could see the heavy lobe and the crease behind her ear where it fitted so close to her head. The edge of her ear was fluted. As he stared at the ear she almost seemed to be conscious of his look, for she raised her chin and shook her head from side to side so that the part in her hair fell together and concealed the ear. She got a comb from her purse because the backward shake had uncovered the deep forceps scars along her jaw. Now Pimples saw the ugly scars for the first time. He had to lean sideways to see them, and a stab of pain entered his chest. He felt a deep and unreasoning sorrow, but the sorrow was sexual too. He imagined himself holding her head in his arms and stroking the poor scars with his finger. He swallowed several times.

Camille was saying softly to Norma, "Then there's this Wee Kirk i' the Heather. I guess that's the prettiest cemetery in the world. You know, you have to get a ticket to get in. I like just to walk around in there. It's so beautiful and the organ plays nearly all the time and you find people buried there that you've seen in pictures. I always said I'd like to be buried there."

"I don't like to talk about things like that," said Norma. "It's bad luck."

Pimples had been vaguely discussing the Army with Ernest Horton. "They say you can learn a trade and travel all over. I don't know. I'm taking a course in radar engineering. It starts next week by mail. I guess radar is going to be pretty hot stuff. But you can get a real good course in radar in the Army."

Ernest said, "I don't know how it would be in peacetime. You can have it when there's a war."

"Did you get to do some real fighting?"

"I didn't ask for it but I got it."

"Where were you?" Pimples asked.

"All over hell," said Ernest.

"Maybe I could get a good line and get in selling, like you," Pimples suggested.

"Oh, that's just plain starvation till you get your contacts," Ernest said. "It took me five years to build up my contacts and then I got drafted. I'm just getting back on my feet now. You can't just step into it and you've got to work at it. It doesn't look like work but it is. If I was to start over again I'd learn a trade so I could have a home. Pretty nice to have a wife and a couple of kids." Ernest always said this. When he was drunk he believed it. He didn't want a home. He loved moving around and seeing different people. He would run away from a home immediately. Once he had been married, and the second day he had walked out, leaving a thoroughly frightened and angry wife, and he never saw her again, nor wrote to her. But he saw her picture once. She was picked up for marrying five men and drawing Army allotments from each one. What a dame. A real hustler. Ernest almost admired her. There was hustling that paid dividends.

"Why don't you go back to school?" he asked Pimples.

"I don't want no fancy stuff," said Pimples. "Them college boys are just a bunch of nances. I want a man's life."

Camille had leaned close to Norma and was whispering in her ear. The two girls were shaking with laughter. The bus surged around the bend and entered the hill country. The road cut between high banks, and the soil of the cuts was dark and dripping with water. Little goldy-backed ferns clung to the gravel and dripped with rain. Juan put his right hand on the wheel and let his elbows hang free. There would be fifteen minutes of twisting hill road now with no straight stretches at all. He glanced in his rear-view mirror at the blonde. Her eyes were puckered with laughter and she'd covered her mouth with spread fingers the way little girls do.

Mr. Pritchard, going back, was not careful, and when the bus took a curve he was flung sideways. He clutched at the seat-back, missed it, and fell sprawling on Camille's lap. His right hand reaching to break his fall whipped her short skirt up and his arm went between her knees. Her skirt was slightly torn. She helped him disengage himself and she pulled down her skirt. Mr. Pritchard was blushing violently.

"I'm very sorry," he said.

"Oh, it's all right."

"But I've torn your skirt."

"I can mend it."

"But I must pay to have it mended."

"I'll just patch it up myself. It isn't bad." She looked at his face and knew that he was prolonging the affair as much as he could. "He'll want to know what address to send the money to," she thought.

Mrs. Pritchard called, "Elliott, are you trying to sit in that lady's lap?"

Even Juan laughed then. Everyone laughed. And suddenly the bus was not full of strangers. Some chemical association was formed. Norma laughed hysterically. All the tension of the morning came out in her laughter.

Mr. Pritchard said, "I must say, you take it very well. I didn't come back here to sit in your lap. I wanted to have a few words with this gentleman. Son," he said to Pimples, "would you mind moving for just a little while. I have some business I'd like to talk over with Mr.—I don't think I heard your name."

"Horton," said Ernest, "Ernest Horton."

Mr. Pritchard had a whole series of tactics for getting on with people. He never forgot the name of a man richer or more powerful than he, and he never knew the name of a man less powerful. He had found that to make a man mention his own name would put that man at a slight disadvantage. For a man to speak his own name made him a little naked and unprotected.

Camille was looking at her torn skirt and talking softly to Norma. "I always wanted to live on a hill," she said. "I love hills. I love to walk in hills."

"It's all right after you're rich and famous," Norma said firmly. "I know people in pictures that every chance they get, why, they go hunting and fishing and wear old clothes and smoke a pipe."

Camille was bringing Norma out. She had never in her whole life felt so excited and free. She could say anything she wanted. She giggled a little.

"It's nicer to wear old dirty clothes if you've got a closet full of nice fresh clean ones," she said. "Old clothes are the only kind I've got and I'm god-damned sick of it." She glanced at Camille to see how she'd react to such candor.

Camille nodded. "You aren't kidding, sister." Something very strong and sympathetic was growing up between these two. Mr. Pritchard tried to hear the conversation but he couldn't.

The ditches beside the highway ran full with water descending toward the valley. The heavy clouds were massing for a new attack.

"It's coming on to rain," Van Brunt said happily.

Juan grunted. "I had a brother-in-law kicked to death by a horse," he observed.

"Couldn't have used any sense," said Van Brunt. "Horse kicks a man, it's usually the man's fault."

"Killed him anyway," said Juan, and he settled into silence.

The bus was nearing the top of the grade and the turns were becoming tighter all the time.

"I was very much interested in our little talk this morning, Mr. Horton. It's a pleasure to talk with a man with some get-up and go. I'm always on the look-out for men like that for my organization."

"Thanks," said Ernest.

"We're having trouble right now with these returning veterans," said Mr. Pritchard. "Good men, you understand. And I think everything should be done for them—everything. But they've been out of the run. They're rusty. In business you've got to keep up every minute. A man that has kept up is twice as valuable as a man that has been out of the mill, so to speak." He looked at Ernest for approval. Instead he saw a kind of hard, satiric look come into Ernest's eyes.

"I see your point," Ernest said. "I was four years in the Army."

"Oh!" said Mr. Pritchard. "Oh, yes—you're not wearing your discharge button, I see."

"I've *got* a job," Ernest said.

Mr. Pritchard fumbled with his thoughts. He had made a bad mistake. He wondered what the thing was in Ernest's lapel button. It looked familiar. He should know. "Well, they're a fine bunch of boys," he said, "and I only hope we can put in an administration that will take care of them."

"Like after the last war?" Ernest asked. It was a double brush, and Mr. Pritchard began to wonder if he'd been right about Horton. There was a kind of a brutality about Horton. He had a kind of swagger and a headlong quality so many ex-soldiers had. The doctors said they would get over it just as soon as they lived a good normal life for a while. They were out of line. Something would have to be done.

"I'm the first one to come to the defense of our veterans," Mr. Pritchard said. He wished to God he could get off the subject. Ernest was looking at him with a slightly crooked smile that he was beginning to recognize in applicants for jobs. "I just thought I'd like to interview a man with your get-up and go," Mr. Pritchard said uneasily. "When I get back from my vacation I'd be very glad to have you call on me. We can always make room for a man who's got it."

"Well, sir," said Ernest, "I get very sick of running around the country all the time. I often thought I'd like to have a home and a wife and a couple of kids. That's the real way to live. Come home at night and lock the whole world outside, and a boy and a girl, maybe. This sleeping in hotels isn't living."

Mr. Pritchard nodded. "You're four-square right," he said, and he was very much relieved. "I'm just the right man to say that to. Twenty-one years married and I wouldn't have it any other way."

"You've been lucky," said Ernest. "Your wife's a fine-looking woman."

"And she's a fine woman," said Mr. Pritchard. "The most thoughtful person in the world. I often wonder what I'd do without her."

"I was married once," said Ernest. "My wife died." His face was sad.

"I'm sorry," said Mr. Pritchard. "And this may sound silly. Time does heal wounds. And maybe some day—well, I wouldn't give up hope."

"Oh, I don't."

"I didn't mean to pry into your affairs," said Mr. Pritchard, "but I've been thinking about your idea for those lapel slipcovers for a dark suit to convert into a tuxedo. If you're not tied up with anyone I thought we might—well, talk about doing a little business."

"Well," said Ernest, "it's like I told you. Clothes manufacturers won't want something that will rule out some of their business. I just don't see the angle right now."

Mr. Pritchard said, "I forget whether you said you had applied for a patent."

"Well, no. I told you. I just registered the idea."

"How do you mean, registered?"

"Well, I wrote out a description and made some drawings and put it in an envelope and mailed it to myself, registered mail. That proves when I did it because that envelope is sealed."

"I see," said Mr. Pritchard, and he wondered whether such a method would have any standing in court. He didn't know. But it was always better to take the inventor in on a percentage. Only the really big fellows could afford to lift an invention whole. The big fellows could afford a long fight. They figured it was cheaper than cutting in an inventor and the figures proved they were right. But Mr. Pritchard's firm wasn't big enough and, besides, he always thought that generosity paid off.

"I've got an idea or two that might work out," he said. "Course, it'll take some organization. Now, suppose you and I could make a deal. This is just a supposition, you understand. I'd handle the organization and we would take a percentage of profit after expenses."

"But they don't want it," Ernest said. "I've asked around."

Mr. Pritchard laid a hand on Ernest's knee. He had a hollow feeling that he ought to shut up, but he remembered the satiric look in Ernest's eyes and he wanted Ernest to admire him and to like him. He couldn't shut up.

"Suppose we formed a company and we protected the idea?" he said. "Patent it, I mean. Now we organize to manufacture this product, a national advertising campaign—"

"Just a moment," Ernest broke in.

But Mr. Pritchard was carried away. "Now suppose these layouts just happened to fall into the hands of, say, oh, Hart, Schaffner and Marx or some big manufacturer like that, or maybe the association. They'd get ahold of it by accident, of course. Well, maybe they'd like to buy us out."

Ernest began to look interested. "Buy the patent?"

"Buy not only the patent but the whole company."

"But if they bought the patent then they could kill it," Ernest said.

Mr. Pritchard's eyes were slitted and his pupils shone through his glasses and a little smile lay on the corners of his mouth. For the first time since she had got off the bus from San Ysidro he had forgotten Camille. "Look ahead a little further," he said. "When we sell and dissolve the company we only pay a capital gain tax on the profits."

"That's smart," said Ernest excitedly. "Yes, sir, that's very smart. That's blackmail and a very high-class blackmail. Yes, sir, nobody could touch us."

The smile vanished from Mr. Pritchard's mouth. "What do you mean, blackmail? We would intend to go ahead and manufacture. We could even order machinery."

"That's what I mean," said Ernest. "It's very high class. It's all wrapped up. You're a smart man."

Mr. Pritchard said, "I hope you don't think it's dishonest. I've been in business thirty-five years and I've climbed to the head of my company. I can be proud of my record."

"I'm not criticizing you," Ernest said. "I think you've got a very sound idea there. I'm for it, only—"

"Only what?" said Mr. Pritchard.

"I'm kind of low on dough," said Ernest, "and I'm gonna need a quick buck. Oh, well, I can borrow it, I guess."

"What do you need money for? Maybe I could advance—"

"No," said Ernest, "I'll get it myself."

"Is it some new wrinkle you figured out?" Mr. Pritchard asked.

"Yes," said Ernest. "I gotta get this idea into the patent office by carrier pigeon."

"You don't think for one minute—"

"Of course not," said Ernest. "Certainly not. But I'm gonna be happier when that envelope gets to Washington alone."

Mr. Pritchard leaned back in his seat and smiled. The highway whirled and twisted ahead, and between two great abutments was the pass into the next valley.

"You'll be all right, son. I think we can do business. I don't want you to think I'd take advantage though. My record speaks for itself."

"Oh, I don't," said Ernest. "I don't." He looked secretly at

Mr. Pritchard. "It's just that I've got a couple of very luscious dames in L.A. and I don't want to get in that apartment and forget everything." He saw the reaction he wanted.

"I'm going to be two days in Hollywood," Mr. Pritchard said. "Maybe we could talk a little business."

"Like in these dames' apartment?"

"Well, a man needs some kind of relaxation. I'm going to be at the Beverly Wilshire. You could call me there."

"I sure will," said Ernest. "What color dame you like best?"

"Don't misunderstand me," said Mr. Pritchard. "I like to sit and have a scotch and soda but I've got a position, you know. I don't want you to misunderstand."

"Oh, I don't," said Ernest. "I could maybe pick up the blonde ahead here, if you want."

"Don't be silly," said Mr. Pritchard.

Pimples had moved forward in the bus. On the underside of his jaw he felt an itching burn and he knew an eruption was forming. He sat down in the seat across from Mildred Pritchard. He didn't want to touch the new place but he was powerless over his hands. His right hand moved upward and his forefinger rubbed the lump under the chin. It was a very sore lump. This one was going to be a devil. He knew already what it would look like. He wanted to squeeze it, to scratch it, to rip it out. His nerves were on edge. He forced his hand into his coat pocket and clenched his fist there.

Mildred was staring vacantly out of the window.

"I wish I could go to Mexico," Pimples said.

Mildred looked around at him in surprise. Her glasses caught the light from his window and glared blindly at him.

Pimples swallowed. "I never been there," he said weakly.

"Neither have I," said Mildred.

"Yeah, but you're going."

She nodded. She didn't want to look at him because she couldn't keep her eyes from his eczema and that embarrassed him. "Maybe you can go soon," she said uneasily.

"Oh, I'll go," said Pimples. "I'll go everywhere. I'm a great traveler. I'd rather travel than anything. You get experience that way."

She nodded again and took off her glasses in protection against him. Now she couldn't see him so clearly.

"I thought maybe I'd be a missionary like Spencer Tracy and go to China and cure them of all those diseases. You ever been to China?"

"No," said Mildred. She was fascinated by his thinking.

Pimples took most of his ideas from moving pictures and the rest from the radio. "It's very poor people there in China," he said, "some of them so poor they just starve to death right outside your window if some missionary don't come along and help them. And if you help them, why, they love you, and let any Jap come around and make trouble and they stick a knife right in him." He nodded solemnly. "I think they're just as good as you and me," he said. "Spencer Tracy just came along and he cured them up and they loved him—and you know what he done? He found his own soul. And there was this girl and he didn't know whether he ought to marry her because she had a past. Of course, it came out it wasn't her fault and it wasn't even true, but this old dame told lies about her." Pimples' eyes glowed with pity and enthusiasm. "But Spencer Tracy didn't believe those lies and he lived in an old palace that had secret passages and tunnels and—well, then the Japs come."

"I saw the picture," Mildred said.

The bus went into second gear for the last climb. Now it was in the gap at the top and then it emerged and turned sharp left, and below was the valley gloomy with gray clouds, and the great loop of the San Ysidro River gleamed like dark steel under the glowering light. Juan eased the bus into high gear and began the descent.

Chapter 10

THE San Ysidro River runs through the San Juan valley, turning and twisting until it discharges sluggishly into Black Rock Bay under the protection of Bat Point. The valley itself is long and not very wide, and the San Ysidro River, having not very far to run, makes the most of what distance it has by moving from one side of the level stretch to the other. Here it cuts under a cliff, against a mountain, and then it spreads thinly out on sandbanks. During a good part of the year there is no surface water at all, and the sandy bed grows full of willows which stretch their roots down toward underground water.

Rabbits and raccoons and small foxes and coyotes make their homes in the willows of the river bottom when the water is down. At the head of the valley to the north and east the river rises, not as one head, but in many little branches, so that the source on a map looks like a tree with small, leafless branches. The dry and stony hills with shoulders and gullies and canyons do not supply water to the river during all the year, but when the rains fall in the late winter and spring the rocky shoulders absorb a little of the water and cast the rest in black torrents to the little streams that tumble out of the creases, and the streamlets combine and join larger creeks and the creeks come together at the northern end of the valley.

So it is that in the late spring, when the hills have digested as much rain as they can, a heavy storm may swell the San Ysidro River to a raging flood in a very few hours. Then the foamy yellow water cuts at the banks and great hunks of farmland cave into the river. Then the bodies of cows and sheep go tumbling and rolling in the yellow flood. It is an unstable and precocious river; dead during part of the year and deadly during another part.

In the middle of the valley, which is on a direct line between Rebel Corners and San Juan de la Cruz, the river makes a great loop, ranging from side to side of the level valley, casting its coil against the mountain on the eastern edge and moving away to cross the fields and farmlands. In the old times the road followed the loop of the river and crawled up the side of the hill to avoid crossing. But with the coming of engineers and steel and concrete, two bridges had been thrown over the river, and these cut out twelve miles of the San Ysidro's playfulness.

They were wooden bridges, backed and suspended by steel rods, and each one was supported in the middle and at the ends by concrete piers. The wood was painted dark red and the iron was dark with rust. On the river side of each bridge backwaters of piles and braided, mattressed willow deflected the water toward the spans and kept the gnawing current from undermining the bridgeheads.

These bridges were not very old, but they had been built at a time when the tax rate was not only low, but much of it uncollectable because of what was called "hard times." The county engineer had found it necessary to build within a budget that allowed only the simplest construction. His timber should have been heavier and his struts more numerous, but he had to build a bridge within a certain cost and he did. And every year the farmers of the middle valley watched the river with cynical apprehension. They knew that some time there would be a quick and overwhelming flood that would take the bridges out. Every year they petitioned the county to replace the wooden bridges, but there weren't enough votes in the rural section to make the petitions mandatory. The large towns, which had not only the votes but the taxable assets, got the improvements. People were not moving to the medium-rich farmlands. A good service-station corner in San Juan had a higher assessed valuation than a hundred acres of grainland in the valley. The farmers knew that it was only a question of time before the bridges were destroyed and then, they said, the county would god-damned well come to its senses.

A hundred yards from the first bridge toward Rebel Corners there was a little general store on the highway. It stocked the groceries, the tires, the hardware a man bought on Saturday afternoon or when he didn't have time to drive either to San Juan de la Cruz or to San Ysidro over the range. This was Breed's General Store. And of late years it had, as did all country stores, added gas pumps and a stock of automobile accessories.

Mr. and Mrs. Breed were unofficial custodians of the bridge, and at flood time their phone rang constantly and they supplied information about the river's rise. They were used to this. Their one great fear was that some day the bridge would go out and the new one might be a quarter of a mile down the river, and then they would have to move their store or build a new one near the new bridge.

At least half of their trade nowadays was in soft drinks, sandwiches, gasoline, and candy bought by travelers on the highway. Even the bus between Rebel Corners and San Juan invariably stopped there. It brought express packages, and the passengers drank soft drinks. Juan Chicoy and the Breeds were old and good friends.

And now the river was up, and not only up, but, as Mr. Breed said to his wife, "there's a backwash cutting in under the piles above the bridge, and if it cuts a channel in back, there goes your ball game." He had made half a dozen trips to the bridgehead since daylight. This was a bad one and Mr. Breed knew it. Thin-lipped and unshaven, he had stood on the bridge at eight o'clock this morning and watched the tumbling yellow water laced with yellow foam and dotted with uprooted scrub oak and cottonwood. And he had seen a few planks of planed lumber come twisting down, and then a piece of roof with shingles still on, and then the drowned, bobbing body of McElroy's black Angus bull, square and short-legged. As it went under the bridge it rolled over on its back, and Breed could see the wild upturned eyes and the flapping tongue. It made Breed sick to his stomach.

Everyone knew McElroy's barn was too close to the bank and that bull cost eighteen hundred dollars. McElroy didn't have that kind of money to throw away. He didn't see any of the rest of the herd come down, but the bull would be enough. Mac had put a lot of faith in that bull.

Breed walked farther out on the bridge. The water was only three feet below the timbers now and Breed could feel the plunging water plaguing the caissons to protest under his feet. He rubbed his unshaven chin with his fingers and walked back to the store. He didn't tell his wife about McElroy's black Angus. It would only make her sad.

When Juan Chicoy called up about the bridge Breed told him the truth. The bridge was still in, but God knew for how long. The water was still rising. The bare, stony hills were still emptying their freshets into the river, and it was clouding up again.

At nine o'clock the lower timbers cleared the flood only by eighteen inches. Once the pressure came on those struts and braces and a few uprooted trees banged into the bridge, it was only a question of time. Breed stood inside his screen door and drummed his fingers on the wire.

"Let me fix you some breakfast," his wife said. "You'd think you owned the bridge."

"I guess I do in a way," said Breed. "If it went out they'd say it was my fault. I've called the supervisor's office and I've called the county engineer. They're both closed. If that channel gets back of the pier, there goes your ball game."

"You'd better eat some breakfast. I'll make you some wheat cakes."

"All right," Breed said. "Don't make them too thick."

"I never make them thick," said Mrs. Breed. "Want an egg on top?"

"Sure," said Breed. "I don't know whether Juan is going to make it or not. He's not due for more than an hour yet and, Jesus! how the water is coming up!"

"No reason to swear," said Mrs. Breed.

Her husband looked around at her. "I'd say this was one of the times when there's every reason to swear. I'm going to take a drink."

"Before breakfast?"

"Before anything."

She didn't know about the black bull, of course. He went to the wall phone and rang McElroy's, a three-two ring, and he kept it up until Pinedale, two miles this side of McElroy's, answered.

"I've been trying to get him too," Pinedale said. "His line's dead. I'm going to ride up and see if he's all right."

"I wish you would," said Breed. "His new bull went under the bridge this morning."

Mrs. Breed raised frightened eyes. "Walter!" she cried.

"Well, it's true. I didn't want you to fret."

"Walter! Oh, my God!" said Mrs. Breed.

Chapter 11

Alice Chicoy stood inside the screen door and watched the bus pull away. She let the tears dry on her cheeks. When the bus passed beyond her view from the door she went to the side window from which she could see the county road. The bus ran into a patch of sunlight and gleamed for a moment, and then she couldn't see it any more. Alice drew a great breath and released it in a luxurious sigh. It was her day! She was alone. She felt happy and secret, and she felt sinful too. Slowly she smoothed her dress down over her hips and caressed her thighs. She looked at her nails. No, later for that.

She looked slowly around the lunchroom. She could still smell cigarette smoke. There were things to be done, yet it was her day and she went about them slowly. First she got from the cupboard a cardboard sign that said "Closed" in large letters. She went outside and hung the sign on a nail on the edge of the screen door. Then she went inside and closed and latched the screen door. And she pulled the inner door and turned the key in it. Next she went from window to window and let down the Venetian blinds and pulled the slats downward so no one could see in.

The lunchroom was dusky and very quiet. Alice worked deliberately. She washed and put away the dirty coffee cups and she washed the lunch counter and the tabletops. The pies she put out of sight under the counter. Then she brought a broom from the bedroom and swept the floor and put the dust and the mud and the cigarette butts in the garbage can. The counter gleamed a little in the dusky light and the tabletops looked white and clean.

Alice came around the counter and sat on one of the stools. It was her day! She felt silly and giddy. "Well, why not?" she said aloud. "I don't have much fun. Bring me," she said, "bring me a double whisky and hurry it up."

She put her hands on the counter and looked at them carefully. "Poor work-ruined hands," she whispered, "dear hands." Then in a shout, "Where the hell is that whisky?" And she answered herself, "Yes, ma'am, it's coming right up, ma'am."

"Well, that's better," said Alice. "I just want you to know who you're talking to. Don't put on any lip because you can't get away with it. I've got my eye on you."

"Yes, ma'am," she answered herself. And she got up and went in back of the counter.

At the far end and low to the floor there was a small cabinet. Alice bent over, opened the door, and reached blindly in and brought out a fifth of Old Grandad bourbon. She picked a water glass from the rack and carried the bottle and the glass to the counter in front of the stool where she had been sitting.

"Here you are, ma'am."

"Take it over to that table. Do you think I look like someone that stands up at bars?"

"No, ma'am."

"And bring another glass. And a bottle of cold beer."

"Yes, ma'am."

She carried all these things to the table beside the door and laid them out. "You can go now," she said, and answered, "Yes, ma'am."

"But don't go far, I might want something."

As she poured out the beer she giggled to herself. If anybody heard me they'd think I was crazy. Well, maybe I am. She poured out a fine shot in the other glass. "Alice," she said, "ready, set, go!" She waved the glass and drank slowly. She did not toss it. She let the hot, straight whisky ease and burn and flow over her tongue and in back of her tongue, and she swallowed slowly and felt the bite on her palate, and the warmth of the whisky went into her chest and into her stomach. Even after she had emptied the glass she still held it to her lips. She put down the glass and she said, "Ah!" and breathed outward harshly.

She could taste the sweet whisky again on her returning breath. Now she reached for the tumbler of beer. She crossed her legs and drank very slowly until the glass was empty.

"God!" she said.

It seemed to Alice she had never realized how utterly comfortable and charming the lunchroom was, the light glimmering down between the slanting blinds. She heard a truck go by on the highway and it disturbed her. Suppose something happened to interfere with her day? Well, they'd have to break the door down. She wouldn't let anyone in. She poured two fingers of whisky in one glass and four fingers of beer in the other glass.

"There's more than one way to skin a drink," she said, and she tossed the whisky in and tossed the beer right in after it. Now, there's an idea. It doesn't taste the same. The way you drink changes the taste. Why had no one else ever found that out, only Alice. Somebody should write that down—"The way you drink makes the taste." There was a little tension in her right eyelid, and a curious but pleasant pain ran down the veins of her arms.

"Nobody has time to find out things," she said solemnly. "No time." She poured half a glass of beer and filled the glass with whisky. "I wonder if anybody ever tried this before?"

The metal paper-napkin holder was in front of her and she could see her face in it. "Hello, kid," she said. She waved the glass, and it was as distorted in the shining metal as her face. "Here's a go, kid. Your health, kid." And she drank the beer and the whisky the way a thirsty man drinks milk. "Ah," she said, "that's not so god-damned bad. No sir. I think I've got something there. That's good."

She adjusted the paper-napkin holder so that she could see herself better. But a bend in the metal surface made her nose look broken at the top and fat and bulbous at the bottom. She got up and went around the counter and into the bedroom, and she brought a round hand mirror back to the table and propped it against the sugar dispenser. She settled herself and crossed her legs. "Now there! I'd like to invite you for a drink." She poured whisky in each glass. "No beer," she said. "All out of beer. Well, we'll fix that."

She went to the icebox and brought another bottle of beer. "Now, you see," she said to the mirror, "we first put a little whisky—not too much—not too little—and we add just the right amount of beer. And there you are." She pushed one glass toward the mirror and drained the other one. "Some people are afraid to take a drink," she said. "They can't handle it."

"Oh, you don't want it? Well, that's your privilege. I'm not going to make you take it. I'm not going to let it go to waste, either." And she drank off the other glass. Her cheeks were tingling now as though a frost were stinging the surface. She brought the mirror close and inspected herself. Her eyes were damp and shiny. She whipped back a strand of loose hair.

"No reason to let yourself run down just because you're having a good time." And without warning a vision flipped into place in her head and she turned the mirror face down. The vision struck so hard and so quickly that it was like a blow. Perhaps it was the darkened room. Alice cried, "I don't want to think about that. I hate to think about that."

But the thought and vision were in. A darkened room and a white bed and her mother paralyzed, rigid, unmoving, the eyes staring straight up, and then the white hand rising from the counterpane in a gesture of despair, a gesture for help. Alice could creep in, no matter how stealthily, and that hand would rise in frightful helplessness, and Alice would hold it for a moment and then put it gently down and go out. Every time she came into that room she would beg the hand not to rise, to lie still, to be dead, like the rest of the body.

"I don't want to think about that," she cried. "How did that get in?" Her hand shook and the bottle rattled against the glass. She poured an enormous drink and drained it, and it caught in her throat so that she coughed, and she just saved herself from being sick. "That'll fix you," she said. "I want to think about something else."

She imagined herself in bed with Juan, but her mind slipped on past that. "I could have had any man I wanted," she boasted. "Enough made passes at me, God knows, and I didn't give in much." Her lips writhed away from her teeth a little salaciously. "Maybe I should of while I could. I'm getting along— That's a god-damned lie," she shouted, "I'm as good as I ever was. I'm better! Who the hell wants a skinny bitch that don't know what to do? No real man wants stuff like that. I could go right out now and pick them off like flies."

The bottle was a little less than half full now. She spilled some in pouring and giggled at herself. "I do believe I'm getting a little drunk," she said.

There came a great knocking at the screen door and Alice froze and sat silent. The knocking came again. A man's voice called, "Nobody here. I thought I heard talking."

"Well, try it again. They might be in back," a woman's voice answered.

Alice picked up the hand mirror gently and looked at herself. She nodded her head and closed one eye in a large wink. The knocking came again.

"I tell you there's nobody here."

"Well, try the door."

Alice heard the rattling of the screen door.

"It's locked up," the man said, and the woman replied, "It's locked on the inside. They must be in there."

The man laughed and his feet scraped on gravel. "Well, if they're in there they want to be alone. Don't you ever want to be alone, baby? With me, I mean."

"Oh, shut up," said the woman. "I want a sandwich."

"For that you'll have to wait."

Alice wondered why she hadn't heard the car or the footsteps on the gravel before the knock. "I'll bet I'm plastered," she thought. She could hear the car drive away all right.

"Can't take 'no' for an answer," Alice said aloud. "Just because a person wants to take a day to rest and get pulled together, why, they've got to have a god-damned sandwich."

She held up the bottle and squinted judiciously through the glass. "Not a lot left." She became frightened. Suppose she should run out before she was ready? And then she nodded and smiled to herself. There were two bottles of port wine right in the back of that cabinet. They gave her a sense of security and she poured herself a big drink and sipped at it. Juan didn't like to be around women when they were drinking. He said their faces got crooked and he hated that. Well, Alice would just show him. She drank half the whisky in her glass and stood up heavily.

"Now, you just stay here and wait for me," she said politely to the glass. Turning the edge of the counter she swayed a little, and the corner bit into her side just above the hip. "That's going to be black and blue," she said. She crossed the bedroom and went into the bathroom.

She dampened the washcloth and rubbed soap into it till she had a thick paste and then she scrubbed her face. She scrubbed hard beside her nose and in the little crease that crossed her chin. She put the cloth over her little finger and twisted it into her nostrils and she washed her ears. Then, with her eyes squinted shut, she rinsed the soap off and looked at herself in the mirror over the basin. Her face seemed very red and her eyes were a little bloodshot. For a long time she worked on her face. Cream, and then that rubbed off on a towel. She inspected the towel for dirt and found it. She worked at her eyebrows with a brown eyebrow pencil. The lipstick gave her some trouble. She got a blob of carmine red too low on her under lip and had to wipe it all off on the towel and start again. She made her lips very full and then put them together and rolled one against the other, and she looked at her teeth and rubbed some lipstick off with her towel. She should have washed her teeth before she put on the lipstick. Now powder. That would take the redness out of her face. Then she brushed her hair. She had never liked her hair. Holding it this way and that for effect, she began to lose interest.

In the bedroom she dug out a close-fitting black felt hat with a kind of a visor. She pushed her hair up inside the hat and angled the brim rakishly.

"Now," she said, "now we'll see how a woman's face gets crooked. I wish Juan would come home right now. He'd change his tune."

In the bedroom she got the bottle of Bellodgia from her dresser drawer and put perfume on her bosom and on the lobes of her ears and at her hair line. And she patted a little on her upper lip. "I like to smell it too," she said.

She walked back to the lunchroom, carefully avoiding the corner that had struck her before. It was even darker than it had been, for the clouds were getting thick and very little light was coming through. Alice sat down at her table and adjusted her hand mirror. "Pretty," she said, "you're kind of pretty. What are you doing this evening? Would you like to go dancing?"

She poured off the drink in her glass. Suppose that driver for the Red Arrow Line should come by and knock on the door. She'd let him in. He was a great kidder. She'd give him a drink or two and then she'd show him a thing or two.

"Red," she'd say, "you set yourself up as a great kidder but I'm going to show you something. There's some kidding on the level." She let her mind dwell on his narrow waist and heavy muscled forearms. He wore a broad belt around his blue jeans, and the jeans—well, the guy was O.K. Something about thinking of those jeans. There was a copper rivet at the bottom where the fly started. And something about that rivet brought sorrow to Alice. Bud had had one. A copper rivet just there. She tried to evade this vision too, and failing, gathered it—gathered it to her mind. He had begged her over and over again. And finally they walked four miles out to the picnic grounds. Bud carried the lunch—hard-boiled eggs and ham sandwiches and an apple pie. Alice bought the pie but she told Bud she made it. And he didn't even wait for the lunch.

He hurt her. And after, she said, "Where are you going?"

"I've got work to do," Bud said.

"You said you love me."

"Did I?"

"You aren't going to leave me, Bud?"

"Listen, sister, you got laid, that's all. I didn't sign no long-term contract."

"But it's the first time, Bud."

"There's got to be a first time for everybody," he said.

Alice was crying over herself now. "It's no damn good!" she shouted at herself in the mirror. "None of it's any damn good." She blubbered while she drank off another whisky and poured the last of the bottle into her glass.

All the others were no damn good, either, and what had she now? A stinking job with bed privileges and no pay. That's what. And married to a stinking greaser, that's what. Married to him! Too far out in the country to go to the movies. Got to sit in a stinking lunchroom.

She put her head down on her arms and cried brokenheartedly. And a second Alice could hear her crying. A second Alice stood at her shoulder and watched her. Got to walk on eggs all the time to keep him happy. She raised her head and looked in the mirror. The lipstick was smeared all over her upper lip. Her eyes were red and her nose was running. She reached for the napkin container, pulled out two paper napkins, and blew her nose. She balled up the paper and threw it on the floor.

What did she want to keep this joint clean for? Who cared? Who gave a damn about her? Nobody! But she could take care of herself. Nobody was going to kick Alice around and get away with it. She emptied the last of the whisky.

Getting out the port wine was a job. She staggered and fell

against the sink. There was hot pressure against the inside of her nose and her breath whistled in her nostrils. She stood the bottle of port wine on the counter and got a corkscrew. The bottle fell over when she tried to get the corkscrew into it, and the second time the cork broke into small pieces. She pushed the rest of it into the bottle with her thumb and lunged back to the table.

"Soda pop," she said. She filled her glass full of the dark red wine. "Wish there was some more whisky." Her mouth was dry. She drank half the tumbler of wine thirstily. "Why, that's good," she giggled. Maybe she'd always have whisky first to give flavor to the wine.

She drew the mirror close to her. "You're an old bag," she said bitterly. "You're a dirty drunken old bag. No wonder nobody wants you. I wouldn't have you myself."

The image in the mirror was not double but it had double outlines, and at the outside of her range of vision Alice could feel the room begin to rock and sway. She drank the rest of the glass and choked and sputtered and the red wine ran out of the corners of her mouth. She missed the glass and poured wine over the tabletop before she got her glass filled. Her heart was pounding. She could hear it, and she could feel it beat in her arms and shoulders and in the veins on her breasts. She drank solemnly.

I'm gonna pass out, and a damn good thing. I wish I would never come to. I wish that would be the end of it—the end of it—the end of it— Show these bastards I don't have to live if I don't want to. I'll show 'em.

And then she saw the fly. He wasn't an ordinary house-fly but a newborn bluebottle, and his body shone with an iridescent blue sheen. He had come to the table and was standing on the edge of the pool of wine. He dipped his proboscis and went back to cleaning himself.

Alice sat perfectly still. Her flesh crawled with hatred. All her unhappiness, all her resentments, centered in the fly. With an effort of will she forced the two images of the fly to be one image. "You son of a bitch," she said softly. "You think I'm drunk. I'll show you."

Her eyes were wary and smart. Slowly, slowly, she slipped sideways from the table and crouched low to the floor, supporting herself with her hand. She kept her eyes on the fly. He had not moved. She crept over to the counter and went behind it. A dish towel was lying on the stainless steel sink. She took it in her right hand and folded it carefully. It was too light. She dampened it under the tap and squeezed out the excess water. "I'll show the son of a bitch," she said, and she moved catlike along the counter. The fly was still there, still shining.

Alice raised her hand and let the towel fall back on her shoulder. Step by careful step she moved close, her hand raised and flexed. She struck. Bottle and glasses and sugar dispenser and napkin holder all crashed to the floor. The fly zoomed and circled. Alice stood still, following him with her eyes. He landed on the lunch counter. She lunged, striking at him, and when he rose again she flailed the air with the towel.

"That's not the way," she said to herself. "Creep up on him. Creep up on him." The floor tilted under her feet. She put out her hand and supported herself on the stool. Where was he now? She could hear the buzz. The angry, sickening whine of his wings. He's got to land sometime, somewhere. She felt sickness rising in her throat.

The fly made a series of loops and eights and circles and then settled down to low, swooping flights from one end of the room to the other. Alice waited. There was darkness crowding in on the edges of her vision. The fly landed with a little plop on the box of cornflakes on the top of the great pyramid of dry cereals on the shelf behind the counter. He landed on the "C" of "corn" and moved restlessly over to the "O." He stood very still. Alice snuffled.

The room was rocking and whirling but with will power the fly and the area around him were unblurred. Her left hand reached back to the counter and her fingers crept across it. She moved silently, slowly, around the end of the counter. She raised her right hand very, very carefully. The fly sprang forward a step and paused again. He was ready to take off. Alice sensed it. She sensed his rise before he rose. She swung with all the weight of her body. The wet towel smashed against the pyramid of cardboard boxes and followed through. Boxes and a row of glasses and a bowl of oranges crashed to the floor behind the counter and Alice fell on top.

The room rushed in on her with red and blue lights. Under her cheek a broken box spilled out its cornflakes. She raised her head once and then put it down again and a rolling darkness dropped over her.

The lunchroom was dusky and very quiet. The fly moved to the edge of the drying pool of wine on the white tabletop. For a moment he sensed in all directions for danger, and then deliberately he dipped his flat proboscis into the sweet, sticky wine.

Chapter 12

THE clouds piled in gray threat on threat and a blue darkness settled on the land. In the San Juan valley the darker greens seemed black and the lighter green of grass, a chilling wet blue. "Sweetheart" came rolling heavily along the highway and the aluminum paint on her gleamed with the evil of a gun. Away to the south a bank of dark cloud fringed off into rain and the curtain of it descended slowly.

The bus pulled in close to the gas pumps in front of Breed's store and stopped. The little boxing gloves, the baby shoe, swung back and forth in little pendulum jerks. Juan sat in the seat after the bus had stopped. He raced the motor for a moment, listening to it, and then he sighed and turned the key and the engine stopped.

"How long are you going to wait here?" Van Brunt asked.

"I'm going to take a look at the bridge," said Juan.

"It's still there," Van Brunt said.

"So are we," said Juan. He pulled the lever to open the door.

Breed came out of his screen door and walked toward the bus. He shook hands with Juan. "Aren't you a little late?"

"I don't think so," said Juan, "unless my watch is off."

Pimples climbed down and stood beside them. He wanted to be ahead so he could see the blonde get off the bus.

"Got any coke?" he asked.

"No," said Breed. "Few bottles of Pepsi-Cola. Haven't had any coke for a month. It's the same stuff. You can't tell them apart."

"How's the bridge?" Juan asked.

Mr. Breed shook his head. "I think here goes your ball game. Take a look for yourself. I don't like it."

"There's no break yet?" Juan asked.

"She could go like that," said Breed, and he sideswiped the palms of his hands together. "She's got a strain on her that makes her cry like a baby. Let's take a look."

Mr. Pritchard and Ernest climbed down from the bus and

then Mildred and Camille, with Norma behind her. Camille was expert. Pimples didn't see anything.

"They got some Pepsi-Cola," Pimples said. "You like to have one?"

Camille turned to Norma. She was beginning to see how Norma could be valuable. "Like a drink?" she asked.

"Well, I wouldn't mind," said Norma.

Pimples tried not to show his disappointment. Breed and Juan strolled down the highway toward the river. "Going to look at the bridge," Juan called over his shoulder.

Mrs. Pritchard called from the step, "Dear, do you think you could get me a cold drink? Just water if there isn't anything else. And ask where the 'you-know-what' is."

"It's around back," said Norma.

Breed fell into step beside Juan as they strode toward the bridge. "I've been expecting her to go out every year," he said. "I wish we'd get a bridge so when a big rain came I could sleep at night. I just lay in bed and hear the rain on the roof, but I'm listening for the bridge to go out. And I don't even know what kinda sound she'll make when she goes."

Juan grinned at him. "I know how that is. I remember in Torreón when I was a little kid. We used to listen at night for the popping that meant fighting. We kinda liked the fighting, but it always meant my old man would go away for a while. And at last he went away and he didn't come back. I guess we always knew that would happen."

"What became of him?" Breed asked.

"I don't know. Somebody got him, I guess. He couldn't stay home when there was any fighting. He had to get in it. I don't think he much cared what they were fighting about. When he came home he was full of stories every time." Juan chuckled. "He used to tell one about Pancho Villa. He said a poor woman came to Villa and said, 'You have shot my husband and now I and the little ones will starve.' Well, Villa had plenty of money then. He had the presses and he was printing his own. He turned to his treasurer and said, 'Roll out five kilos of twenty-peso bills for this poor woman.' He wasn't even counting it, he had so much. So they did and they tied the bills together with wire and that woman went out. Well, then a sergeant said to Villa, 'There was a mistake, my general. We did not shoot that woman's husband. He got drunk and we put him in jail.' Then Pancho said, 'Go immediately and shoot him. We cannot disappoint that poor woman.' "

Breed said, "It don't make any sense."

Juan laughed. "I know, that's what I like about it. God, that river is eating around the back of the breakwater."

"I know. I tried to phone and tell them," said Breed. "I can't get anybody on the phone."

They walked together out on the wooden bridge. And the moment Juan stepped on the flooring he could feel the thrumming vibration of the water. The bridge shivered and trembled. And there was a deep hum in the timbers that was louder than the rush of the water. Juan looked over the side of the bridge. The supporting timbers were under water and the river foamed and bubbled under it. And the whole bridge trembled and panted, and there were little strained cries from the timbers where the iron turn-bolts went through. As they watched, a great old live oak tree came rolling heavily down the stream. When it struck the bridge and turned, the whole structure cried out and seemed to brace itself. The tree caught in the submerged underpinning and there came a shrill, ripping sound from under the bridge. The two men moved quickly back off the bridgehead.

"How fast is she coming up?" Juan asked.

"Ten inches in the last hour. Of course, she might start to go down now. Might have reached flood."

Juan looked at the side of the supporting streamers. His eye found a brown bolthead on the edge of the water and he kept his eyes on it. "I guess I could make it all right," he said. "I could make a run for it. Or I could get the passengers to walk across and I could drive over and pick them up on the other side. How's the other bridge?"

"I don't know," said Breed. "I tried to phone and find out but I can't get anybody. And suppose you cross this one and the other one's out, and you come back and this one's out? You'd be trapped in the bend. You'd have some mighty sore passengers."

"I'm going to have some mighty sore passengers anyway," said Juan. "I've got one—no, two—that are going to raise hell no matter what happens. I know the signs. You know a man named Van Brunt?"

"Oh, that old fart! Yes, I know him. He owes me thirty-seven dollars. I sold him some alfalfa seed and he claimed it was no good. Wouldn't pay for it. He's got bills all over the county. Nothing he buys is any good. I wouldn't sell him a candy bar on credit. He'd claim it wasn't sweet. So you got him along?"

"I got him," said Juan. "And I got a man from Chicago. Big business bug. He's going to be pretty sore if things don't come out the way he wants them to."

"Well," said Breed, "you got to make up your own mind."

Juan looked at the threatening sky. "I guess it's going to rain, all right. And with the hills full up it'll all dump right into the river. I could get over all right, but about what chance have I got to get back?"

"About ten per cent," said Breed. "How's your wife?"

"Not too good," said Juan. "She's got a toothache."

"It pays to keep your teeth up," said Breed. "Should go to the dentist every six months."

Juan laughed. "I know. Are you acquainted with anybody that does?"

"No," said Breed. He liked Juan. He didn't even consider him a foreigner.

"I don't either," said Juan. "Well, there's one other way to stay out of trouble with the passengers."

"What's that?"

"Let them decide. This is a democracy, isn't it?"

"They'll just get to fighting."

"Well, what's wrong with that if they fight each other?" said Juan.

"You've got something there," Breed said. "But I'll tell you one thing. Whatever side everybody else is on, Van Brunt is gonna be on the other side. There's a fellow wouldn't vote for the second coming of Christ if it was a popular measure."

"He's all right," said Juan. "You just gotta know how to handle him. I had a horse once that was so ornery that if you reined left he'd turn right. I fooled him. I did everything opposite and he thought he was getting his own way. You could get Van Brunt to do almost anything by disagreeing with him."

"I'm going to forbid him to pay that thirty-seven dollars," said Breed.

"It might work at that," Juan said. "Well, the river isn't at flood. That bolthead is covered. I'm going to see what the passengers want to do."

Back in the store Pimples felt a little cheated. He had been maneuvered into buying both Norma and Camille a Pepsi-Cola. Try as he would, he couldn't separate Camille from Norma. And it wasn't Norma's fault. Camille was using her.

Norma was flushed with pleasure. She had never been so happy in her life. This beautiful creature was nice to her. They were friends. And she didn't say they'd live together. She said she'd see how things worked out. For some reason this gave Norma a great deal of confidence. People had not been nice to Norma. They had said "yes" to things and then wormed out of them. But this girl, who looked like everything Norma wanted to be, said "she'd see." In her mind Norma could see the apartment they would get. It would have a velvet davenport and a coffee table in front of it. And the drapes would be wine-colored velvet. They'd have a radio and phonograph combination, of course, and plenty of records. She didn't like to think past that. It was almost like spoiling her luck to think past that. There was a kind of an electric blue for the davenport.

She raised her glass of Pepsi-Cola and let the sweet, biting drink run down her throat, and in the middle of the swallow despair settled down on her like a heavy gas. "It won't ever happen," her mind cried. "It'll get away! It'll be just like always and I'll be alone again." She squeezed her eyes shut and wiped the back of her hand across them. When she opened her eyes again she was all right. "I'll save it," she thought. "Little by little I'll make the apartment, and then if it doesn't happen I'll still have it." A hardness came over her and an acceptance. "If any of it comes through it'll just be gravy. But I can't expect it, I can't let myself expect it. That will take it away from me."

Pimples said, "I've got plenty of plans. I'm studying radar. That's going to be a very important job. Fellow that knows radar is going to be fixed pretty nice. I think a person's got to look ahead, don't you? You take some people, they don't look ahead into the future and they end up right where they started." A little smile was fixed on Camille's lips.

"You've got something there," she said. She wished she could get away from this kid. He was a nice kid, but she just wished she could get away from him. She could practically smell him. "Thank you very much for the drink," she said. "I think I'll just go and freshen up a little. You want to come, Norma?"

A look of devotion came on Norma's face. "Oh, yes," she said, "I guess I ought to freshen up too." Everything Camille said was right, was dainty and fine. "Oh, Jesus Christ, let it happen!" Norma cried in her mind.

Mrs. Pritchard was sipping a lemonade. It had taken a little time to get it because they didn't serve lemonade. But when Mrs. Pritchard had pointed out the lemons in the grocery section and had even offered to squeeze them herself—well, there was nothing Mrs. Breed could do, and she'd made it.

"I just can't drink old bottled things," Mrs. Pritchard explained. "I like just the pure fruit juice." Mrs. Breed resentfully went down under this wave of sweetness. Mrs. Pritchard sipped her lemonade and looked through a rack of postcards on the novelty counter. There were pictures of the courthouse in San Juan de la Cruz and of the hotel in San Ysidro which was built over a hot spring of epsom salts. A fine old hotel much frequented by rheumatic people who bathed in the strong waters. The hotel was called a Spa on the postcards. There were other items on the novelty counter. Painted plaster dogs and glass pistols full of colored candy and bright kewpie dolls and fancy redwood boxes of glacée California fruits. And there were lamps whose shades turned when the lights were on so that the forest fires and ships under full sail moved and shone in a very lifelike manner.

Ernest Horton stood at the counter too and looked at the display with a certain amount of contempt. He said to Mr. Pritchard, "Sometimes I think I ought to open a novelty store with all new stuff. Some of this old stuff's been on the market for years and nobody buys it. Now my company has nothing but up-and-coming stock, all new."

Mr. Pritchard nodded. "Gives a man confidence to work for a firm he knows is on its toes," he said. "That's why I think you might like to work for us. You could be sure we're on our toes every hour of the day."

Ernest said, "Excuse me, I'm going to get my case. I've got an item that really isn't before the public yet but it's gone like hot cakes to the trade already, just to the trade. I'd like to place a few here, maybe."

He went out quickly and lugged his sample case in. He opened it and brought out a cardboard box. "Plain wrapping, you see. That's for the surprise." He opened the box and took out a perfect little high tank toilet twelve inches high. There was the box and a little chain with a brass knob on the bottom, and the toilet bowl was white. And it even had a little seat cover colored to look like wood.

Mrs. Breed had moved down in back of the counter. "My husband does all the buying," she said. "You'll have to see him."

"I know," said Ernest. "I just want you to look at this item. It sells itself."

"What's it for?" Mr. Pritchard asked.

"You just watch," said Ernest. He pulled the little chain and immediately the toilet bowl flushed with a brown fluid. Ernest lifted the toilet seat right out of the bowl and it was a small glass. "That's one ounce," he said triumphantly. "If you want a double shot, say for a highball, you pull the chain twice."

"Whisky!" cried Mr. Pritchard.

"Or brandy, or rum," said Ernest. "Anything you want. See, here in the tank is the place you fill it, and the tank is guaranteed plastic. It knocks 'em cold. I've got orders for eighteen hundred of this little item already. It's a knockout. It gets a laugh every time."

"By George, that's clever," Mr. Pritchard said. "Who thinks these things up?"

"Well," Ernest explained, "we've got an idea department. Everybody puts ideas in. This item was suggested by our salesman in the Great Lakes area. He'll make himself a nice bonus. Our company gives two per cent of the profits to any employee who sends in a workable idea."

"It's clever," Mr. Pritchard repeated. In his mind he could see Charlie Johnson when he first saw it. Charlie would want to rush right out and get one for himself. "What do you get for them?" Mr. Pritchard asked.

"Well, this one retails for five dollars. But if you don't mind my making the suggestion, we have a model that sells for twenty-seven fifty."

Mr. Pritchard pursed his lips.

"But look what you get," Ernest went on. "This one is plastic. The better item is—well, the box is oak and is made of old whisky barrels so that it'll take the liquor fine. The chain is real silver and it has a Brazilian diamond for a knob. The bowl is porcelain, real toilet quality porcelain, and the seat is hand-carved mahogany. And on the box there's a little silver plate for, if, like you wanted to present it to a lodge or a club, your name goes on that."

"It sounds like a good value," Mr. Pritchard said. His mind was made up. He knew how he would get the better of Charlie Johnson now. He would give one of the toilets to Charlie. But on the plate he would put "Presented to Charlie Johnson, the all-American soandso, by Elliott Pritchard," and then let Charlie show off all he wanted to. Everybody would know who had the idea first.

"You haven't got one with you, have you?" he asked.

"No, you have to order."

Mrs. Pritchard spoke up. She had moved close, quietly. "Elliott, you're not going to get one of those. Elliott, they're vulgar."

"I wouldn't have it around if there were ladies, of course," said Mr. Pritchard. "No, little girl. Know what I'm going to do? I'm gonna send one of them to Charlie Johnson. That'll get back at him for sending me that stuffed skunk. Yes, sir, I'll fix him."

Mrs. Pritchard explained. "Charlie Johnson was Mr. Pritchard's roommate in college. They have the wildest jokes. They're like little boys when they get together."

"Now," said Mr. Pritchard seriously, "if I ordered one, could you have it sent to an address I'll give you? And could you have it engraved? I'll write what I want you to put on the plate."

"What are you going to say?" Bernice asked.

"Little girls keep their noses out of big man's business," said Mr. Pritchard.

"I'll bet it'll be awful," said Bernice.

Mildred was in the dumps. She felt heavy and tired and she wasn't interested in anything. She was sitting in a twisted wire candy-store chair all by herself at the end of the counter. Cynically she had watched Pimples trying to get the blonde alone. The trip had let her down. She was disgusted with herself and what had happened. What kind of a girl was she if a bus driver could set her off? She shivered a little with distaste. Where was he now? Why didn't he come back? She smothered her impulse to get up and go look for him. Van Brunt's voice sounded beside her so that she jumped.

"Young lady," he said, "your skirt shows. I thought you'd like to know."

"Oh, yes. Thank you very much."

"You might have gone all day thinking you were all fixed up if somebody didn't tell you," he said.

"Oh, yes, thank you." She stood up and, leaning backward, pushed her skirt against her legs so that she could see. There was an inch of slip showing behind.

"I think it's better to be told things like that," Van Brunt said.

"Oh, it is. I guess I broke a shoulder strap."

"I don't care to hear about your underwear," he said coldly. "My only remark is—and I repeat it—your skirt shows. I don't want you to think I had any other motive."

"I don't," said Mildred helplessly.

Van Brunt went on, "Too many young girls get self-conscious of their legs. They think everybody is looking at them."

Suddenly Mildred was laughing wildly like a sick woman.

"What's so funny?" Van Brunt demanded angrily.

"Nothing," said Mildred. "I just thought of a joke." She had remembered that Van Brunt had never missed any show of legs all morning.

"Well, if it's that funny, tell it," he said.

"Oh, no. It's a personal joke. I'll go out and fix my strap." She looked at him and then, deliberately, she said, "You see, there are two straps on each shoulder. One is for the slip and the other supports the brassière and the brassière holds the breasts up firmly." She saw Van Brunt's color come up out of his collar. "There isn't anything below that until the panties, if I wore panties, which I don't."

Van Brunt turned and walked away quickly and Mildred felt

better. Now the old fool wouldn't have a comfortable moment. She could watch him and maybe later trick him and catch him in the act. She got up, laughing to herself, and went out around the back of the store to the lean-to marked "Ladies."

A lattice covered the door and the morning glory was beginning to climb up. Mildred stood in front of the closed door. She could hear Norma talking to the blonde inside. She listened. Maybe this would make the trip worth while, just listening to people talk. Mildred liked to eavesdrop on people. Sometimes her liking to bothered her. She could listen to inanities with interest. But of all the listening, the best was in women's rest rooms. The freedom of women in any room where there was a toilet, a mirror, and a washbowl had interested her for a long time. She had once written a paper in college, which had been considered daring, in which she had maintained that women lost their inhibitions when their skirts were up.

It must be either that, she thought, or the certainty that man, the enemy, could never invade this territory. It was the one place in the world where women could be certain there would be no men. And so they relaxed and became outwardly the people they were inwardly. She had thought a great deal about it. Women were more friendly or more vicious to one another in public toilets, but on personal terms. Perhaps that was because there were no men. Because, where there were no men, there was no competition, and their poses dropped from them.

Mildred wondered whether it was the same in men's toilets. She just didn't think it was likely, because men had many competitions besides women, while most of women's insecurities had to do with men. Her paper on the subject had been returned marked "Not carefully thought out." She planned to do it over again.

Out in the store she had not been friendly toward Camille. She just didn't like her. But she knew her dislike would not carry into the rest room. She thought, "Isn't it strange that women will compete for men they don't even want?"

Norma and Camille were talking on and on. Mildred put her hand on the door and pushed it open. In the small room were a toilet stall and a washbowl with a square mirror over it.

A dispenser of paper seatcovers was on one wall, and paper towels beside the basin. A slot machine for sanitary pads was on the wall beside the frosted glass window. The concrete floor was painted dark red and the walls were thick with layers of white paint. There was a sharp smell of perfumed disinfectant in the air.

Camille was seated on the toilet and Norma stood in front of the mirror. They both looked at Mildred as she came in.

"Want to get in here?" Camille asked.

"No," said Mildred. "I've got a drooping strap on my slip."

Camille looked down at the skirt. "You have all right. No, not that way," she said to Norma. "You see the way your hair line goes? Well, make the eyebrows go up a little on the outside, just a little. Wait, honey. Wait a minute and I'll show you."

She stood up and moved to Norma. "Turn around so I can see you. There, now. And there, now look at yourself. See how it kind of brings down your hairline a little bit? Your forehead's high so you try to bring it down. Now look, close your eyes." She took the eyebrow pencil from Norma and rubbed it gently on the lower lids just below the lashes, making the line a little darker as it passed the outside corners.

"You've got the mascara on too thick, honey," she said. "See how the lashes stick together? Use more water and take a little more time. Wait a minute." She brought out of her purse a little plastic case of eyeshadow. "Now you go careful with this stuff." She dipped her finger into the blue paste, rubbed a little on each of Norma's upper eyelids, making it heavier toward the outside corners. "Now, let me see." She inspected her work. "Look, honey, you keep your eyes too wide, like a rabbit. Let your upper lids down a little bit. No, and don't squint. Just let your upper lids droop down a little bit. There, like that. Now look at yourself. See the difference?"

"My God, I look different," Norma said. Her voice was awed.

"Sure you do. Now, you've got the lipstick on all wrong. Look, honey, your lower lip is too thin. So is mine. Bring the lipstick down a little bit here, and a little here."

Norma stood still like a good child and let her work.

"See? Heavier in the corners," Camille said. "Now your lower lip looks fuller."

Mildred said, "You're good. I could use some advice too."

"Oh, well," said Camille. "It's pretty simple."

"That's theatrical make-up," Mildred said. "I mean it's a kind of theatrical type make-up."

"Well, you know, dealing with the public—dentists use their nurses almost like receptionists."

"Oh, damn it!" Mildred exclaimed. "This strap isn't loose, it's broken." She peeled her dress off her shoulder and she had a little silken string in her hand.

"You'll have to pin it," Camille said.

"But I haven't got a pin and my needle and thread's in one of the suitcases!"

Camille opened her purse again, and in the lining were half a dozen tiny safety pins. "Here," said Camille, "I always go heeled." She unfastened one of the pins. "You want me to fix it for you?"

"If you don't mind. My damned eyes. I can't see anything."

Camille pulled the loose slip up, folded the end of the strap, and pinned it firmly to the edge of the slip. "That's hardly all right, but at least it doesn't show. It's still a pin job. You always been shortsighted, honey?"

"No," said Mildred. "I was all right until—well, right when I was about fourteen. One doctor said it had to do with puberty. He said some girls get their eyesight back when they have their first baby."

"That's tough," said Camille.

"It's a damn nuisance," Mildred said. "I don't care how much they make new shapes of glasses. They still aren't very good looking."

"Ever heard of that kind that fit right down against the eyes?"

"I've thought about it and I haven't done anything about it. I guess I'm scared to have anything touch my eyes."

Norma was still regarding herself with wonder in the mirror. Her eyes had suddenly become larger and her lips fuller and softer and the wet rat look had gone from her face.

"Isn't she wonderful?" Norma said to no one. "Isn't she just wonderful?"

Camille said, "She's gonna be a pretty kid when she learns a few tricks and gets some confidence. We'll touch up that hair, honey, as soon as we get in."

"You mean you've thought it over?" Norma cried. "You mean we'll get the apartment?" She whirled on Mildred. "We're going to have an apartment," she said breathlessly. "We're going to have a davenport and Sunday morning we'll wash and set our hair—"

"We'll see," Camille broke in. "We'll just have to see how things work out. Here's the two of us without jobs and already she's got a duplex rented. Hold your horses, honey."

"It's a funny trip," Mildred said. "We're on our way to Mexico. Everything's gone wrong from the start. My father wanted to see the country. He thinks we might settle in California some time. So he wanted to take the bus to Los Angeles. He thought he could see the country better."

"Well, he can," said Camille.

"He can see too much of it maybe," Mildred said. "But did you ever see such a collection of people as we've got?"

"They're all about the same," said Camille.

"I like Mr. Chicoy," said Mildred. "He's part Mexican, you know. But that boy! I've got a feeling he'd climb all over you if you weren't careful."

"Oh, he's all right," Camille said. "He's just a little goaty. Most kids are like that. He'll probably get over it."

"Or maybe he won't," said Mildred. "Did you take a good look at that old fellow, Van Brunt? He didn't get over it. It just ingrew. That's a pretty filthy man in his mind."

Camille smiled. "He's pretty old," she said.

Mildred went into the little cubicle and sat down. "There's something I wanted to ask you," she said. "My father thinks he's seen you somewhere. He's got a pretty good memory. Did you ever see him?"

For a second Mildred saw the hostility in Camille's eyes, saw the tightened mouth, and she knew she'd touched something sore. And instantly Camille's face was placid again.

"I think I must look like somebody else," she said. "This time he's made a mistake unless he saw me in the street somewhere."

"On the level?" Mildred asked. "I'm not trying to catch you now. I just wondered."

The friendliness, the companionship, the relaxation, slipped from the room. It was as though a man had entered. Camille's eyes stabbed at Mildred. "He made a mistake," she said coldly. "You can take that any way you want."

The door opened and Mrs. Pritchard came in. "Oh, there you are," she said to Mildred. "I thought you'd wandered off."

"Oh, I broke a strap on my slip," said Mildred.

"Well, hurry up. Mr. Chicoy's back and there's quite an argument going on— Thank you, dear," she said to Norma, who had moved away from the basin to make room for her. "I'll just moisten my handkerchief and take a little of the dust off— Why don't you have a lemonade?" she said to Mildred. "That nice woman doesn't mind making them at all. I told her she'd be quite famous if she just served pure fruit juices."

Suddenly Camille said, "I wish we could get something to eat. I'm getting hungry. I'd like something good."

"So would I," said Mrs. Pritchard.

"I'd like a cold cracked crab with mayonnaise and a bottle of beer," Camille said.

"Well, I've never had crab that way," said Mrs. Pritchard, "but I wish you could have tasted the way my mother fried butterfish. She used to take an old-fashioned cast-iron skillet— and the fish, it had to be very fresh and very carefully trimmed. She'd make a batter with brown toasted crumbs—bread crumbs, not cracker crumbs—and she'd put a whole tablespoon —no, two tablespoonfuls—of Worcestershire sauce in a beaten egg. I think that was the secret."

"Mother," said Mildred, "don't start on the butterfish recipe."

"You'd better have a lemonade," said Mrs. Pritchard. "It'd clean up your skin. A good long trip makes a person blotchy."

"I wish we'd get moving," Mildred said. "We can get lunch in the next town. What's its name?"

"San Juan de la Cruz," said Norma.

"San Juan de la Cruz," Mrs. Pritchard repeated softly. "I think the Spanish names are so pretty."

Norma took a long, astonished look at herself in the mirror before they went out. She drooped her eyes. It was going to take practice to remember to do that all the time, but it changed her whole appearance and she liked it.

Chapter 13

JUAN sat on a stool drinking a Pepsi-Cola and rubbing the shiny end of his amputated finger over the corduroy ridges of his trousers. When the women came around from the back and entered the store he looked up at them and the rubbing of his finger became a tapping.

"Is everybody here?" he asked. "No, there's one missing. Where's Mr. Van Brunt?"

"I'm over here." He spoke from behind the counter on the grocery side, where, concealed by a stacked wall of canned coffee, he was inspecting the shelves idly.

Mr. Pritchard said, "I want to know when we can get started. I have connections to make."

"I know," Juan said gently, "and that's what I want to talk about. The bridge is not safe. I can probably get across it. But there's another bridge and it may be out, or it may go out. We can't get any news about it. If we get into the bend of the river with both bridges out, we'd be caught, and nobody could make any connections. Now, I'm willing to take a vote and do anything the majority of the passengers want to do. I'll make a run for it and take a chance, or I'll take you back and you can make other plans. It's up to you. But when you make up your minds I want you to stick to the verdict."

He raised the bottle and drank the Pepsi-Cola.

"I haven't the time," Mr. Pritchard said loudly. "Look, my friend. I've had no vacation since the war started. I've been making the implements of war that gave us the victory, and this is my first vacation. I just haven't the time to go gallivanting all over the country. I need a rest. I only have a few weeks and this is eating them up."

Juan said, "I'm sorry. I'm not doing it on purpose, you know, and if you got caught in the bend of the river you might lose a lot more time and I might lose the bus getting it across. The bridge is strained to the breaking point. It may come down any minute. The only other choice is to go back."

Van Brunt came from behind the stack of coffee. He had a

two-and-a-half pound can of sliced peaches in his hand. He crossed the store to Mrs. Breed. "How much?" he asked.

"Forty-seven cents."

"My God! For a can of peaches?"

"The profit hasn't changed," she said. "We've just got to pay more for them."

Van Brunt threw a half-dollar violently down on the counter. "Open 'em up," he said. "Forty-seven cents for a mean little can of peaches!"

Mrs. Breed put the can in a wall opener, turned the crank, and stopped just as the edge raised. She passed the can over the counter to Van Brunt. He drank off part of the juice first, then reached in and picked out a yellow slice with his fingers. He held it over the open can to drip.

"Now I heard what you said," he observed. "You think you can waste our time. I've got to get in to the courthouse and I've got to get in this afternoon. And it's up to you to get me through. You're a common carrier, subject to the rules of the railroad commission."

"That's what I'm trying to do," said Juan. "And one of the rules of the commission is don't kill the passengers."

"It comes of not knowing the country," Van Brunt went on. "There ought to be a strict law that you've got to know the country before you can drive a bus." He waved a slice of peach and flipped it into his mouth and picked up another slice between his thumb and forefinger. He was enjoying himself.

"You said there was only two things to do. Well, there's three. You don't know about the old road that was there before they put in those damn-fool bridges. It goes right around the outside of the bend. The stagecoaches used to use it."

Juan looked questioningly at Mr. Breed. "I heard about it, but what condition is it in?"

"Stages used it for over a hundred years," said Van Brunt.

Mr Breed said, "I know it's all right for a couple of miles, but I don't know it beyond that. It goes up the side of the mountain to the east, there. It might be washed out. I haven't been over it since way before the rains."

"You've got your choice," Van Brunt said. He waved his piece of peach, flung it into his mouth, and talked around it. "I told you it was going to rain. I told you the river would be up, and now, when you're stuck, I tell you how to get out of it. Do I have to drive your god-damned bus too?"

Juan bawled, "Keep your pants on and watch your language. There's ladies here."

Van Brunt tilted the can and drank the rest of the juice, straining the peaches out with his teeth. The thick juice ran down his chin and he wiped it off with his sleeve. "God, what a trip!" he said. "Right from the beginning."

Juan turned and faced the other passengers. "Well, there it is. My franchise says I'm supposed to go on the highway. I don't know the old road. I don't know if I could get through or not. It's up to you to decide what you want to do. If we get hung up I don't want to be to blame."

Mr. Pritchard said, "I like to see things get done. Now, I've got to get to Los Angeles, man. I've got airplane tickets for Mexico City. Do you know what they cost? And the planes are booked solid. We've got to get through. Let's get some action on this. You think the bridge is dangerous?"

"I know it's dangerous," said Juan.

"Well," said Mr. Pritchard, "you say you don't know whether you can get through on the old road?"

"That's right," said Juan.

"So you've got two gambles and one sure thing. And the sure thing don't get you through either. Hmmmm," said Mr. Pritchard.

"What do you think, dear?" Mrs. Pritchard said. "We've got to do something. I haven't had a good bath for three days. Dear, we've got to do something."

Mildred said, "Let's try the old road. It might be interesting." She glanced at Juan to see how he would take this attitude, but already his eyes had moved from her to Camille.

Something about the recent association made Camille say, "I vote for the old road. I'm so tired and dirty now, nothing would make much difference to me."

Juan looked down and his eyes sharpened when he saw Norma's face. She didn't look like the same girl. And Norma knew he had noticed. "I say the old road," she said breathlessly.

Ernest Horton found a chair, the one Mrs. Breed ordinarily

used when her legs swelled up in the afternoons. He had been watching the counting of noses.

"I don't much care," he said. "Of course, I'd like to get to L.A., but it don't make much difference. I'll stick with the others, whatever they say."

Van Brunt put the can down loudly on the counter. "It's going to rain," he said. "That back road can get awful slippery. You might not make it up over the hill, to the eastward. It's steep and slick. If you mired down there I don't know how you'd ever get out."

"But you're the one that suggested it," Mildred said.

"I'm just getting all the objections down," Van Brunt said "Just getting them in order."

"How would you vote?" Juan asked.

"Oh, I won't vote. That's the silliest thing I ever heard of. Seems to me the driver ought to make the decisions, like a captain of a ship."

Pimples went to the candy counter. He laid down a dime and picked up two Baby Ruths. He put one in his side pocket to give to Camille when he could get her alone, and the other he unwrapped slowly. A wild, exciting thought had just popped into his mind. Suppose they went over the bridge and right in the middle the span broke and the bus fell into the river? Pimples would be thrown clear, but the blonde would be trapped in the bus. And Pimples dived and dived and he was nearly dead, but at last he broke a window and pulled Camille out and he swam ashore and laid her, unconscious, on the green grass and he rubbed her legs to get the circulation started. But better, he turned her over and he put his hands under her breasts and gave her artificial respiration.

But suppose they took the old road and the bus mired down? Then they'd be there all night, with maybe a fire going, and they'd be together and sit together in front of the fire with a light on their faces and maybe a blanket thrown over the two of them.

Pimples said, "I think we'd better try the old road." Juan looked at him and grinned.

"You've got real Kit Carson blood in you, haven't you, Kit?" And Pimples knew it was a joke, but it wasn't a mean joke.

"Well, I guess that's everybody but one, and he won't vote. What's the matter? Do you want to be able to sue?"

Van Brunt swung around to the others. "You're all being crazy," he said. "Know what he's doing? He's pulling out from under. If anything should happen he won't get the blame because he could say he only did what you told him to. No, he's not going to trap me that way."

Mr. Pritchard cleaned his glasses on his white linen handkerchief. "It's an idea," he said. "I hadn't thought of it quite that way. We're really giving up our rights."

Juan's eyes glowed with rage. His mouth grew thin and tight. "Get in the bus," he said. "I'm taking you back to San Ysidro and dumping you. I'm trying to get you through and you act as though I were trying to murder you. Come on, get in the bus. I'm sick of it. Since last night I've had my life turned upside down for your comfort and I'm tired of it. So come on. We're going back."

Mr. Pritchard walked over to him. "No, I didn't mean that," he said. "I appreciate what you've done. We all do. I was just trying to think clearly on all sides of the subject. That's what I do in business. Don't do anything until you've thought it through."

"I'm sick of it," Juan said again. "You had my bed last night. I just want to get rid of you."

Van Brunt said, "Don't forget, it was your bus that broke down. It wasn't our fault."

Juan said evenly, "Mostly, I think, I want to get rid of you."

"Watch yourself," Van Brunt said. "Don't forget, you're a common carrier with a franchise. After this example it wouldn't be hard to get the franchise removed."

Juan changed suddenly. He laughed. "Boy, that would be a relief. I'd be free of people like you, and I can think where I would put that franchise, rolled up and tied with barbed wire."

Camille laughed aloud and Ernest Horton giggled happily. "I've got to remember that," he said, "yes, sir. Look, Mr. Chicoy, these two men have been talking. The rest of us want to go. We'll take our chance. Why don't you just draw a line and anybody over the line wants to go, the rest stay here. That's fair enough."

Mildred said, "Mr. Chicoy, I want to go."

"O.K.," said Juan. "That big crack there in the floor. Everybody that don't want me to take the back road get over on the other side with the vegetables."

Nobody moved. Juan looked carefully into each face.

"It isn't legal," Van Brunt said. "It won't hold in any court."

"What won't hold?"

"What you're doing."

"It isn't in any court."

"It may be," said Van Brunt.

"You can't come even if you want to," said Juan.

"You just try to keep me off. I've got a ticket and I've got a right to go on the bus. You just try to keep me off and I'll have you up so fast it'll make your head spin."

Juan hunched his shoulders. "And you would too," he said. "O.K., let's get started." He turned to Mr. Breed. "Could you lend me a few tools? I'll bring them right back."

"What kind of tools?"

"Oh, a pick and shovel."

"Oh, sure. You mean in case you get stuck?"

"Yeah, and have you got a block and tackle?"

"Not a very good one. The blocks are all right, but there's just some old half-inch line on them. I don't know how much strain it would take. That's a pretty heavy bus."

"Well, it would be better than nothing," Juan said. "Haven't got any new line I could buy here, have you?"

"I haven't had a new piece of Manila line since the war started," said Breed. "But you're welcome to what I have got. Come along. Pick up what you want."

Juan said, "Come along, Kit, and give me a hand, will you?" The three went out of the store and around to the back.

Ernest said to Camille, "I wouldn't have missed this. I wouldn't for anything."

"I just wish I wasn't so tired," she said. "I've been riding busses for five days. I want to get out of my clothes and get some real sleep for a couple of days."

"Why didn't you take the train? Chicago, you said?"

"Yes, Chicago."

"Well, you coulda got on the Super Chief and slept all the way to L.A. That's a nice train."

"Saving pennies," said Camille. "I've got a little piece of

change and I want to lay around for a few weeks before I got to work. And I'd rather do it in a double bed than a berth."

"Did I catch you right?" he asked.

"You did not," said Camille.

"O.K., you're the boss."

"Look, let's not play," Camille said. "I'm too damn tired to play guessing games with you."

"O.K., sister, O.K. I'll play any way you want."

"Well, then, let's just sit this one out. Do you mind?"

"You know? I like you," Ernest said. "I'd like to take you out when you get rested up."

"Well, we'll see how it goes," Camille said. She liked him. She could talk to him. He knew a few answers and that was a relief.

Norma had been watching them, listening. She was full of admiration for Camille. She wanted to learn just how it was done. Suddenly she realized that her eyes were wide open as a rabbit's and she drooped the upper lids.

Mrs. Pritchard said, "I hope I'm not going to get a headache. Elliott, see if they have any aspirins, will you?"

Mrs. Breed tore a cellophane bag off a big cardboard display. "You want one of them? That's a nickel."

"We better have half a dozen," Mr. Pritchard said.

"That'll be twenty-six cents with tax."

"You needn't have got so many, Elliott," Mrs. Pritchard said. "I have a bottle of five hundred in my bag."

"It's best to be prepared," he answered. He knew her headaches and they were dreadful. They twisted her face and reduced her to a panting, sweating, grinning, quivering blob of pain. They filled a room and a house. They got into everyone around her. Mr. Pritchard could feel one of her headaches through walls. He could feel it all over his body, and the doctor said there was nothing to do about it. They injected calcium and they gave her sedatives. The headaches usually came when she was nervous and when things, through no fault of her own, were not going well.

Her husband would have liked to protect her. They seemed to be selfish, these headaches, and yet they were not. The pain was real. No one could simulate such agonizing pain. Mr. Pritchard dreaded them more than anything in the world. A good one could make the whole house vibrate with horror. And they were a little like conscience. Try as he would, Mr. Pritchard could never lose the feeling that they were in some way his fault. Not that Mrs. Pritchard ever said anything or indicated that this might be so. In fact she was very brave. She tried to muffle her screams with a pillow.

Mr. Pritchard didn't bother her much in bed—very seldom, in fact. But in a curious way he tied up his occasional lust and his loss of self-control with her headaches. It was planted deep in his mind that this was so, and he didn't know how it had got planted. But he did have a conscience about it. His bestiality, his lust, his lack of self-control, were the cause. And he didn't have any means of saving himself. Sometimes he found himself hating his wife very deeply because he was unhappy. He stayed in his office overtime when she had a headache, and sometimes he just sat at his desk for hours, staring at the brown paneling, his body throbbing with his wife's pain.

In the middle of one of her worst spells she would try to save him. "Go to a movie," she would moan. "Go over to Charlie Johnson's. Take some whisky. Get drunk. Don't stay here. Go to a movie." But it was impossible. He couldn't.

He put the six little transparent bags into his coat pocket. "Would you like to take a couple now, just in case?" he asked.

"No," she said. "I think I'm going to be all right." She smiled her brave, sweet smile.

Mildred, when she heard the first mention of aspirin, went to the grocery side and studied the OPA price-ceiling chart on the wall. Her mouth pinched tight and her throat was convulsed. "Oh, Jesus Christ," she said softly under her breath. "Oh, Christ, is she going to start that already?" Mildred didn't quite believe the headaches. She'd never had a bad headache herself, only mild periodic ones and a few hangover headaches at school. She called her mother's psychosomatic and psychotic, and she dreaded them even more than her father did. As a little girl she had run from them and gone to earth in the cellar or in the space behind the cabinet in the sewing room. And usually she was pulled out and taken in to her mother because when mother had a headache she needed love and she needed to be petted. Mildred thought of the headaches as a curse. She hated them. And she hated her mother when she had them.

For a time Mildred had thought them pure sham, and even now, when through reading she knew the pain was real, Mildred still considered the headaches a weapon her mother used with complete cunning, with complete brutality. The headaches were pain to her mother, truly, but they governed and punished the family too. They brought the family to heel. Certain things her mother didn't like were never done because they brought on a headache. And when she was at home, Mildred knew that her fear about getting into the house not later than one in the morning was caused by the almost certainty that her mother would get a headache if she didn't.

Between headaches you forgot how devastating they were. Mildred thought that a psychiatrist was what her mother needed. And Bernice would have done anything. She wanted to do anything. It was Mr. Pritchard who put his foot down. He didn't believe in psychiatrists, he said. But actually he did believe in them, so much that he was afraid of them. For Mr. Pritchard had gradually come to depend on the headaches. They were in a way a justification to him. They were a punishment on him and they gave him sins to be atoned for. Mr. Pritchard needed sins. There were none in his business life, for the cruelties there were defined and pigeonholed as necessity and responsibility to the stockholders. And Mr. Pritchard needed personal sins and personal atonement. He denounced the idea of a psychiatrist angrily.

Mildred forced herself to turn around and go back to her mother. "Are you all right, dear?"

"Yes," Bernice said brightly.

"No headache?"

Bernice was apologetic. "I just had a twinge and it frightened me," she said. "I could never forgive myself if I had one of those horrible things and ruined papa's trip."

Mildred felt a little shiver of fear at this woman who was her mother—at her power and her ruthlessness. It must be unconscious. It had to be. Mildred had seen and heard the engineering of this trip to Mexico. Her father hadn't wanted to go. He would have liked to take a vacation by just staying home from the office, which would mean that he would go to the office every day; but by going at odd hours and returning, not by the clock but by his feeling, he would have had a sense of vacation and rest.

But the trip to Mexico had been planted. When and how? Mildred didn't know and her father didn't know. But gradually he became convinced not only that it was his idea, but that he was forcing his family with him. And this gave him a fine sense of being boss in his own home. He had walked through closing door after closing door in the maze. It was rather like a trap nest. A hen finds a hole, looks in, sees there is a bit of grain, steps through the door—the door closes. Well, here is a nest. It's dark and quiet. Why not lay an egg? It'd be a good joke on whoever left that door open.

Her father had almost forgotten that he didn't want to go to Mexico. Both Mr. and Mrs. Pritchard were doing it for Mildred. That was really the safe thing. She was studying Spanish in college, a language she was incapable of understanding, just as her instructors were. Mexico would be just the place to practice up. Her mother said there was no way of learning a language like having to use it.

Mildred, looking at her mother's sweet, relaxed face, simply could not believe that this woman could engineer a thing and then destroy it. Why? And she would do it. She had planted the idea. Sure as hell she was going to have a headache. But she would wait until she was out of touch with doctors, until her headache would cause the greatest possible impression. It was hard to believe. Mildred didn't think her mother really knew what she was doing. But there was a doughy lump in Mildred's chest and it weighed down on her stomach. The headache was coming. She knew it.

She envied Camille. Camille was a tramp, Mildred thought. And things were so much easier for a tramp. There was no conscience, no sense of loss, nothing but a wonderful, relaxed, stretching-cat selfishness. She could go to bed with anyone she wanted to and never see him again and have no feeling of loss or insecurity about it. That was the way Mildred thought it was with Camille. She wished she could be that way, and she knew she couldn't. Couldn't because of her mother. And the unbidden thought entered her mind—if her mother were only dead Mildred's life would be so much simpler. She could have a secret little place to live somewhere. Almost fiercely, she brushed the thought away. "What a foul thing to think," she said to herself ceremoniously. But it was a dream she often had.

She looked out the front window. Pimples had helped to put the block and tackle into the bus, and the Manila line had grease on it and the grease had got on Pimples' chocolate brown trousers. He was trying to rub out the spot with a handkerchief. "Poor kid," Mildred thought, "that's probably his only suit." She was going to tell him not to touch it when she saw him go to the gasoline pump and put a little of the gas on his handkerchief and go to work expertly on the spot.

And there was Juan calling, "Come on, you folks."

Chapter 14

THE back road around the San Ysidro River bend was a very old road, no one knew how old. It was true that the stage coaches had used it, and men on horseback. In the dry seasons the cattle had been driven over it to the river, where they could lie in the willows during the heat of the day and drink from holes dug in the river bed. The old road was simply a slice of country, uncultivated to start, marked only by wheel ruts and pounded by horses' hoofs. In the summer a heavy cloud of dust arose from its surface when a wagon went by, and in winter, pastelike mud spurted from under horses' feet. Gradually the road became scooped out so that it was lower than the fields through which it traveled, and this made it a long lake of standing water in the winter, sometimes very deep.

Then it was that men with plows made ditches on either side, with the embankments toward the road. And then cultivation came in and the cattle became so valuable that the owners of the property along the road put up fences to keep their cattle in and other people's cattle out.

The fences were split redwood posts set in the ground with one-by-six planks nailed halfway up connecting them. And along the top of the posts was old-fashioned barbed wire, a strip of twisted metal with sharpened spikes. The fences weathered in the sun and rain, the redwood planks and the posts turned light gray and gray-green, and lichens grew on the wood and moss formed on the shady sides of the posts.

Walking men burning with messages came by and painted their messages on the planks. "Repent, for the Kingdom of Heaven is at hand"—"Sinner, come to God"—"It is late"—"Wherefore shall it profit a man . . ."—"Come to Jesus." And other men put other signs on the fence with stencils. "Jay's Drugs"—"Cyrus Noble—The Doctors' Whisky"—"San Ysidro Bicycle Shop." These signs were all weathered and dimmed now.

As the fields were used less for grazing and more for wheat and oats and barley, the farmers began to remove from their fields the weeds, the field turnip, the yellow mustard, the poppies and thistles and milkweeds, and these refugees found a haven in the ditches beside the road. The mustard stood seven feet high in the late spring, and red-winged blackbirds built their nests under the yellow flowers. And in the damp ditches the water cress grew.

The ditches beside the road under the high growth of weeds became the home of weasels and bright-colored water snakes, and the drinking places for birds in the evening. The meadow larks sat all morning on the old fences in the spring and whistled their yodeling song. And the wild doves sat on the barbed wire in the evening in the fall, shoulder to shoulder for miles, and their call rang down the miles in a sustained note. At evening the night hawks coursed along the ditches, looking for meat, and in the dark the barn owls searched for rabbits. And when a cow was sick the great ugly turkey buzzards sat on the old fence waiting for death.

The road was well-nigh abandoned. Only a few families who had farms that could not be reached in any other way ever used it any more. Once there had been many little holdings here, with a man living close to his acres and his farm behind him and his vegetable patch under the parlor window. But now the land stretched away, untenanted, and the little houses and the old barns stood windowless and gray and unpainted.

As noon came on the clouds hurried in from the southwest and bunched together. It is the rule that the longer the clouds prepare, the longer the rain will continue. But it was not ready yet. There were still some patches of blue sky and now and then a blinding flash of sun struck the ground. Once a tall cloud cut sun streaks into long, straight ribbons.

Juan had to drive back a little along the highway to reach the entrance to the old road. Before he turned into it he stopped the bus and got down and walked ahead. He felt the greaselike mud under his feet. And Juan knew a sense of joy. He had been trying to push his carload of cattle bodily about their business in which he had no interest. There was almost a feeling of malice in him now. They had elected this road, and it might be all right. He had a happy vacation-feeling. They wanted it, now let them take it. He would see what they would do if the bus stalled. He dug his toe into the mixed mud and gravel before he turned back. He wondered what Alice was doing. He knew damn well what Alice was doing. And if he wrecked the bus—well, he might just walk away from it, just walk away and never come back. It was a very happy vacation-feeling he had. His face was glowing with pleasure when he climbed into the bus.

"I don't know whether we'll make it or not," he said happily. And the passengers were a little nervous at his exuberance.

The passengers were seated in a bunch, as far forward as they could get. Every one of them felt that Juan was their only contact with the normal, and if they had known what was in his mind they would have been very much frightened. There was a high glee in Juan. He closed the door of the bus and he put his foot twice on the throttle to race his engine before he set the bus in low gear and turned it into the muddy country road.

The clouds were almost prepared for the stroke now. He knew that. In the west he could see one cloud fraying down. There it was starting, and it would move over the valley in another spring downpour. The light had turned metallic again with a washed, telescopic quality that meant only violent rain.

Van Brunt said brightly, "The rain's coming."

"Looks like," said Juan, and he turned his bus into the road. He had good tread on his tires, but as he left the blacktop he could feel the rubber slip a little on the greasy mud and the rear end swing in a small arc. But there was a bottom to it, and the bus lumbered over the road. Juan put it in second gear. He would keep it there probably for the whole distance.

Mr. Pritchard called above the beat of the motor, "How long is this detour?"

"I don't know," said Juan. "I've never been over it. They say thirteen or fifteen miles—something like that." He hunched over the wheel and his eyes lifted from the road and glanced at the Virgin of Guadalupe in her little shrine on top of his instrument board.

Juan was not a deeply religious man. He believed in the Virgin's power as little children believe in the power of their uncles. She was a doll and a goddess and a good-luck piece and a relative. His mother—that Irish woman—had married into the Virgin's family and had accepted her as she had accepted her husband's mother and grandmother. The Guadalupana became her family and her goddess.

Juan had grown up with this Lady of the wide skirts standing on the new moon. She had been everywhere when he was little—over his bed to supervise his dreams, in the kitchen to watch over the cooking, in the hall to check him in and out of the house, and on the *zaguán* door to hear him playing in the street. She was in her own fine chapel in the church, in the classroom in school, and, as if that wasn't ubiquitous enough, he wore her on a little gold medal on a golden chain about his neck. He could get away from the eyes of his mother or his father or his brothers, but the dark Virgin was always with him. While his other relatives could be fooled or misled and tricked and lied to, the Guadalupana knew everything anyway. He confessed things to her, but that was only a form because she knew them anyway. It was more a recounting of your motives in doing a certain thing than a breaking of the news that you had done it. And that was silly too, because she knew the motives. Then, too, there was an expression on her face, a half smile, as though she were about to break out into laughter. She not only understood, she was also a little amused. The awful crimes of childhood didn't seem to merit hell, if her expression meant anything.

Thus Juan as a child had loved her very deeply and had trusted her, and his father had told him that she was the one set aside especially to watch over Mexicans. When he saw German or Gringo children in the streets he knew that his Virgin didn't give a damn about them because they were not Mexicans.

When you add to this the fact that Juan did not believe in her with his mind and did with every sense, you have his attitude toward Our Lady of Guadalupe.

The bus slithered along the muddy road, moving very slowly and leaving deep ruts behind. Juan flicked his eyes to the Virgin and he said in his mind, "You know that I have not been happy and also that out of a sense of duty that is not natural to me I have stayed in the traps that have been set for me. And now I am about to put a decision in your hands. I cannot take the responsibility for running away from my wife and my little business. When I was younger I could have done it, but I am soft now and weak in my decisions. And I am putting this in your hands. I am on this road not of my own volition. I have been forced here by the wills of these people who do not care anything for me or for my safety or happiness, but only for their own plans. I think they have not even seen me. I'm an engine to get them where they are going. I offered to take them back. You heard me. So I am leaving it to you, and I will know your will. If the bus mires down so that ordinary work will let me get it out and proceed, I will get it out. If ordinary precaution will keep the bus safe and on the road, I will take that precaution. But if you, in your wisdom, wish to give me a sign by dropping the bus into the mud up to the axles, or sliding it off the road into a ditch where I couldn't do anything about it, I will know you approve of what I want to do. Then I will walk away. Then these people can take care of themselves. I will walk away and disappear. I will never go back to Alice. I will take off my old life like a suit of underwear. It is up to you."

He nodded and smiled at the Virgin, and she had the little smile on her face too. She knew what was going to happen but, of course, there was no way of finding that out. He couldn't run away without sanction. He had to have the approval of the Virgin. It was directly up to her. If she felt strongly about his going back to Alice, she would smooth the road and get the bus through, and he would know that he was set for life with what he had.

He breathed high in his lungs with excitement and his eyes shone. Mildred could see his face in the rear-view mirror. She wondered what terrible joy there was in his mind to make his face light up. This was a man, she thought, a man of complete manness. This was the kind of a man that a pure woman would want to have because he wouldn't even want to be part woman. He would be content with his own sex. He wouldn't ever try to understand women and that would be a relief. He would just take what he wanted from them. Her disgust for herself passed, and she felt pretty good again.

Her mother was writing another letter in her mind. "There we were on that muddy road, miles from any place. And even the driver didn't know the road. Well, just anything could happen. Anything. There wasn't a house in sight and the rain was starting."

The rain was starting. Not like the gusts and spurts of the

morning, but a heavy, driving, drumming, businesslike rain that delivered so many gallons an hour in a given area. And there was no wind. This was downpour, pure, straight rainfall. The bus hissed and splashed over the level road, and Juan, when he turned the front wheels a little, could feel the rear end slide.

"You got any chains?" Van Brunt called.

"No," said Juan happily. "Haven't been able to get chains since before the war."

"I don't think you're going to make it," said Van Brunt. "You're all right on the level but you've got to start going uphill pretty soon." He motioned to the east and the mountains toward which they were crawling. "The river cuts right up against a bluff," he shouted to the other passengers. "The road goes up over that bluff. I don't think we're going to make it."

To Pimples it had been a morning of conflicts and stresses. There weren't many relaxed moments in his life anyway, but this day had been particularly tearing. His body burned with excitements. Pimples was loaded with the concupiscent juices of adolescence. His waking and his sleeping hours were preoccupied with the one goal. But so variable was the reaction to the single stimulus that he found himself one moment as lustful as a puppy on a curtain, the next floundering in thick and idealistic sentiment, and the next howling with self-condemnation. He felt then that he was alone, that he, alone, was the great sinner of the world. He looked with fawning adoration at the self-control of Juan and other men he knew.

Since she had come into his sight all of his body and his brain yearned toward Camille, and his yearning went from lustful pictures of himself and her to visions of himself married to her and settled down with her. One moment he felt almost forward enough to just out and out ask her, and the next, her glance in his direction forced a quivering embarrassment on him.

Again he had tried to get a seat where he could watch her without being noticed, and again he had failed. He could see the back of her head, but he could see Norma's profile. So it was that only at this late time did Pimples notice the change in Norma and, noticing, he drew a deep breath. She was not the same. He knew that it was only make-up, for he could see the eyebrow pencil and the lipstick from where he sat, but that wasn't what sent his blood coursing hotly in his stomach. She was changed. There was a conscious girlness about her that had not been there before, and Pimples' wild juices whispered to him. If, as he really knew deep in his heart, he couldn't have Camille, he might maybe get Norma. He wasn't as frightened of her as he was of the goddess Camille. Unconsciously he began to make plans for trapping Norma, overwhelming her. A new pustule was forming right in front of his left ear. Automatically he scratched it, and the angry red of his tainted flesh spread outward on his cheek. He looked secretly at the fingernail that had done the business and put it in his pocket and cleaned it. He had made his cheek bleed. He took out his handkerchief and held it to his face.

Mr. Pritchard was worried about getting through and making his connection. There was a gnawing in him that would not let him rest or relax. He had tried to laugh it off to himself. He had used all the ordinary methods for throwing out unpleasant thoughts, and they didn't work.

Ernest Horton had said Mr. Pritchard's plan was blackmail, and Ernest had almost indicated that he thought Elliott Pritchard would steal his slipcover for a dark suit if he wasn't watched. This had at first outraged Mr. Pritchard—a man of his reputation and standing. And then he had thought, "Yes, I have standing and reputation in my own community, but here I have nothing. I am alone. This man thinks I am a crook. I can't send him to Charlie Johnson so he can get an idea of how wrong he is." This bothered Mr. Pritchard very much. Ernest had gone even further. He had indicated that he thought Mr. Pritchard was the kind of man who would go to an apartment with blondes. He had never done that in his life. He had to prove to Ernest Horton that his judgment had been wrong. But how could he do it?

Mr. Pritchard's arm was over the back of the seat, and Ernest was sitting alone in the seat behind him. The engine of the bus, traveling in second gear, was loud, and the old body vibrated noisily. There was only one way—to offer Ernest Horton something, something open and honest, so that he would see that Mr. Pritchard was not a crook.

A vague thought came back to him. He turned in his seat. "I

was interested in what you said about what your company does with ideas that come in."

Ernest looked at him with amusement. The guy wanted something. He suspected the old boy wanted to get in on a party or two. Ernest's boss was that way. He wanted conferences at night and always ended up in a whorehouse and was always surprised at how he got there.

"We've got a very nice relationship," Ernest said.

"This idea is nothing much that I had," Mr. Pritchard said. "It's just something that came to me. You can have it if you want it and if it'll do you any good."

Ernest waited without comment.

"You take cuff links," Mr. Pritchard said. "Now, I always wear French cuffs and cuff links, and once you get the links in—well, you've got to take them out before you can take off the shirt. And if you want to push up your sleeves to wash your hands you've got to take out the cuff links. It's easy to put in cuff links before you put on the shirt, but you can't get your hands through. When you've got the shirt on it's hard to get the cuff links in. See what I mean?"

"There's that kind that clicks together," Ernest said.

"Yes, but they aren't popular. You're always mislaying or losing part."

The bus stopped. Juan put the car in low gear and moved quickly on. There was a jar as he hit a hole and a second jar as the rear wheels went through it, and the bus moved slowly on. The rain drummed heavily on the roof. The windshield wiper squeaked on the glass.

Mr. Pritchard leaned back farther in his seat and pulled up his sleeve so that his plain gold cuff links showed. "Now, suppose," he said, "instead of links or a bar, there was a spring. When you put the cuff on over your hand the spring would give and you could push the cuff up your arm to wash, and then the spring would go right back into place." He watched Ernest's face closely.

Ernest's eyes were half closed in thought. "But how would it look? It would have to be a steel spring or it wouldn't last."

Mr. Pritchard said eagerly, "I thought that through. On the cheaper ones you could gold-plate the spring or silver-plate it. But on the expensive ones, like pure gold or platinum—the quality ones—why, instead of a bar it's a tube, and when the cuff is at your wrist, why, the little spring has disappeared right into the tube."

Ernest nodded slowly. "Yes," he said. "Yes, sir. Sounds pretty good."

"You can have it," said Mr. Pritchard. "It's yours to make anything you want out of it."

Ernest said, "My company goes in for a different kind of novelties, but maybe—maybe I could talk them into it. The best-selling things in the world—for men, that is—are razors or razor gadgets, pens and pencils, and personal jewelry. The fellow that don't write five lines a year will buy a tricky fountain pen for fifteen dollars any day. And jewelry? Yes, sir, it might work out. What would you want out of it if they thought it was a good idea?"

"Nothing," Mr. Pritchard said. "Absolutely nothing. It's yours. I like to help an up-and-coming young fellow." He was beginning to feel good again. But suppose the thing worked out, this idea he'd cooked up. Suppose it made a million dollars. Suppose—but he had said it and his word was good. His word was his bond. If Ernest wanted to show appreciation, that was up to him. "I don't want a single thing," he repeated.

"Well, that's mighty nice of you." Ernest took a notebook from his pocket, made an entry, and tore out the page. "Of course, in a thing like that I'd have to get an assignment," he said. "If you've got a moment while you're in Hollywood, maybe you could give me a call and we'll talk some business. We might be able to do business." His left eye drooped a little as he said it, and then his eyes turned and rested a moment on Mrs. Pritchard. He passed the slip to Mr. Pritchard and said, "Aloha Arms, Hempstead 3255, apartment 12B."

Mr. Pritchard colored a little, took out his wallet and put the paper in it, and he pushed the paper down in the back of the slot. He didn't really need to keep it. He could throw it away the first chance he got, for his memory was good. It would be years before he would forget that phone number. The system had clicked in his head, his old system. Three and two are five and repeat. And Hempstead. Hemp is rope. Yellow hemp, and you can't use anything instead of hemp. He used hundreds of memory tricks like that. Yellow hemp, blond hemp. His fingers itched to throw the paper away. Sometimes Bernice looked in his wallet for some change. He told her to. But he felt danger in his stomach—the miserable feeling of having been called a thief.

He said to his wife, "You feel all right, little girl?"

"Yes," she said. "I think I fought it off. I just said to myself, 'I won't let it come. I won't let it interfere with my darling's vacation.'"

"I'm glad," said Mr. Pritchard.

"And, dear," she went on, "how do you men get such ideas?"

"Oh, they just come to you," he said. "That new shirt with the small buttonholes is the cause of this one. I got caught in it a few days ago and nearly had to call for help."

She smiled. "I think you're very nice," she said. And he reached over and put his hand on her knee and squeezed her leg. She slapped his hand playfully and in a moment he took it away.

Norma had her head turned so that her mouth was close to Camille's ear. She spoke as softly as she could because she knew that Pimples was trying to listen. She was conscious of his gaze, and in a way she was gratified. She had never been so confident in her life as she was now.

"I haven't really got any family, like you'd call a family," she said. She was tumbling herself out in front of Camille. She was explaining and pouring out her life. She wanted Camille to know all about her, the way she was before this morning and the way she was now, and that would make Camille her family and would tie this beautiful and sure creature to her.

"When you're alone you do such funny things," she said. "I used to lie to people. I'd pretend things to myself. I would—well, do things like the things I was pretending were true. You know what I'd do? I'd picture like a certain movie star was—well, was my husband."

It had jumped out. She hadn't intended to go so far. She blushed. She shouldn't have told that. It was kind of like letting Mr. Gable down. But she inspected this and found it wasn't so. She didn't feel quite the same about Mr. Gable as she had. Her feeling had moved on to Camille. It was a shock to realize it. She wondered if she were being inconstant.

"It's when you don't have any family and no friends," she

explained. "I guess you just make them up if you haven't got them. But now, well, if we could get an apartment I wouldn't have to make up anything."

Camille turned her face away so she couldn't see the nakedness in Norma's eyes, the complete defenselessness. "Oh, brother!" Camille thought. "What have I let myself in for now? I've got a baby. I've gone and got caught in something. How did this happen? I'm going to have to make her over and live her life and in a little while it'll probably bore the hell out of me and I'll be in too deep to get out of it. If Loraine's shucked off that advertising man and we can go back together, what am I going to do with this? How did it start? How the hell did I get into it?"

She turned to Norma. "Listen, honey," she said crisply. "I didn't say we could do it. I said we'd have to see how it worked out. There's a lot you don't know about me. For one thing, I'm engaged to be married, and my boy friend, he thinks it might be pretty soon. So you see, if he wants to now, why I couldn't go along with you."

Camille saw the despair come into Norma's eyes, like a cold horror, and the sagging of her cheeks and mouth and how the muscles of her shoulders and arms collapsed. Camille said to herself, "I can get a room in the next town and hide out till she gets lost. I can run out on her. I can—oh, Jesus, how did I let myself in for this? I'm too tired. I need a hot bath."

Aloud she said, "Don't take it so hard, honey. Maybe he isn't ready. Maybe—oh, look, honey, maybe it will work out. Maybe it will. Really. We'll just see how it goes."

Norma compressed her lips tightly and squinted her eyes. Her head jiggled with the vibration of the bus. Camille didn't want to look at her. After a time Norma got herself under control. She said quietly, "Maybe you're ashamed of me, and I wouldn't blame you. I can only be a waitress, but if you'd show me I could maybe get to be a dental nurse like you. I'd study nights and I'd work as a waitress in the daytime. But I'd do it, and then you wouldn't have to be ashamed of me. It wouldn't be so hard with you to help me."

Camille felt a rolling wave of nausea in her stomach. "Oh, God Almighty! Now I'm really trapped. What do I say? Tell her another lie? Would it be better to tell this girl exactly what

I do for a living? Or would that make it worse? That might shock her so she wouldn't want me for a friend. Maybe that'd be the best thing. No, it would be best just to lose her in a crowd, I guess."

Norma was saying, "I'd like to have what you'd call a profession that had some dignity to it, like you."

Camille said in despair, "Look, honey, I'm awful tired. I'm too tired to think. I've been traveling for days. I'm too worn out to think about anything. Let's just let it lay for a while. We'll just see how it goes then."

"I'm sorry," Norma said. "I got excited and I forgot. I won't talk about it any more. We'll just see how it goes, huh?"

"Yes, we'll see how it goes," said Camille.

The bus jerked to a stop. They were coming near to the foothills now and the green billows of land were dimly visible through the rain. Juan half stood up to look down at the roadbed. There was a hole in the road, a hole full of water, no telling how deep. It might drop the bus clear out of sight. He glanced quickly at the Virgin. "Shall I take a chance?" he said under his breath. His front wheels were on the edge of the pool. He grinned, put the bus in reverse, and backed up twenty feet.

Van Brunt said, "You going to try a run for it? You'll get stuck."

Juan's lips moved silently. "My dear little friend, if you only knew," he whispered. "If all of the rest of you only knew." He put the bus in first gear and ran at the hole. The water splashed away with a rushing hiss. The rear wheels went into the hole. The bus slipped and floundered. The rear wheels spun and the motor roared and the spinning wheels edged the bumbling body slowly across and slithered it out on the other side. Juan slipped the gears to second and crawled on.

"Must have been a little gravel mixed in with that," he said over his shoulder to Van Brunt.

"Well, you wait till you start up the hill," Van Brunt said ominously.

"You know, for a man that wants to get through you put more things in the way," Juan said.

The road began to climb and the water did not stand anymore. The ditches along the side were running full. The driving wheels of the bus slipped and churned in the ruts. Juan suddenly knew what he was going to do if the bus piled up. He hadn't known. He had thought he might go to Los Angeles and get a job driving a truck, but he wouldn't do that. He had fifty dollars in his pocket. He always carried that much for repair emergencies, and that would be enough too. He would walk away, but not far. He'd get under cover and wait until the rain stopped. He might even sleep some place. For food he would grab one of those pies. Then, when he was rested, he would walk over to the highway, bum a ride, just wait at a service station until someone picked him up. He would thumb his way to San Diego and then he'd go across the border to Tijuana. It would be nice there, and he might just lie on the beach for two or three days. The border wouldn't bother him. On this side he'd say he was American. On the other side he'd be Mexican. Then, when he was ready, he'd go out of town, maybe catch a ride or maybe just walk over the hills and by the little streams, perhaps as far as Santo Tomás, and there he'd wait for the mail carrier. He would buy a lot of wine in Santo Tomás, and he'd pay the mail carrier, and then down the peninsula he would go, through San Quintin, past Ballenas Bay. It might take two weeks through the rocks and the prickly desert and then across to La Paz. He would see that he had some money left. At La Paz he would catch a boat across the gulf to Guaymas or Mazatlán, maybe even to Acapulco, and in any of those places he would find tourists. More at Acapulco than at Guaymas or Mazatlán. And where there were tourists floundering around with the Spanish language in a strange country Juan would be all right. Gradually he'd work his way up to Mexico City and there were really tourists. He could conduct tours, and there were plenty of ways of getting money. He wouldn't need much.

He chuckled to himself. Why in God's name had he stuck to this as long as he had? He was free. He could do whatever he wanted to. Let them look for him. He might even see a note about it in the L.A. papers. They'd think he was dead and they'd look for his body. Alice would raise hell for a while. It would give her a great sense of importance. Plenty of people could cook beans in Mexico. He might lay up with one of those

American women in Mexico City who lived down there to beat the taxes. With a few good suits of clothes Juan knew he was presentable enough. Why in hell hadn't he gone back before?

He could smell Mexico in his nose. He couldn't think why he hadn't done it before. And the passengers? Let them take care of themselves. They weren't very far out. They'd got so used to throwing their troubles on other people they had forgotten how to take care of themselves. It would be good for them. Juan could take care of himself and he was going to start doing it too. He'd been living a silly kind of life, worrying about getting pies from one town to the next. Well, that was over.

He glanced up with secret eyes at the Guadalupana. "Oh, I'll keep my word," he said under his breath. "I'll get them through if you want me to. But even then I'm not so sure I won't walk away."

His mind plunged with pictures of the sun-beaten hills of Lower California and the biting heat of Sonora, the chill morning air on the plateau of Mexico with the smell of pine knots in the huts and the popcorn smell of toasting tortillas. And a homesickness fell on him like a sweet excitement. The taste of fresh oranges and the bite of chili. What was he doing in this country anyway? He didn't belong here.

The curtain of the years rolled back, and superimposed on the muddy country road he saw and heard and smelled Mexico, the chattering voices of the market, the squawking parrot in the garden, the quarreling pigs in the street, the flowers and fish and the little modest dark girls in blue *rebozos*. How strange that he had forgotten for so long. He yearned toward the south. He wondered what crazy trap could have kept him here. Suddenly he was impatient to be away. Why couldn't he just slam on the brakes and open the door and walk away through the rain? He could see their stupid faces looking after him and hear their outraged comments.

He glanced again at the Virgin. "I'll keep my word," he whispered. "I'll get through if I can." He felt the wheels slip in the mud and he grinned at the Virgin of Guadalupe.

The river cut in close to the hills now, bringing its border of willows with it. And the road dodged sideways, away from it. The rain was thinning out, and from the road they could see the light yellow water whirling in the broad basin of the river and dragging lines of dirty foam in twisting streaks. Ahead the road climbed up the hill, and at the top there was a yellow cut, a kind of cliff, and the road ran in front of it. At the very top of the yellow cliff, in great faint letters, was the single word REPENT. It must have been a long and dangerous job for some wild creature to put it there with black paint, and it was nearly gone now.

In the cliff of sandstone there were erosion caves cut by the wind and dug out by animals. The caves looked like dark eyes peering out of the yellow cliff.

The fences were fairly strong here, and in the upland grass red cows stood dark and wet and some of them had already borne their spring calves. The red cows turned their heads slowly and watched the bus as it ground by, and one old fool of a cow became panic-stricken and ran away, kicking and bucking as though that would remove the bus.

The roadbed had changed. The gravel gave the bus better footing. The body bumped and jarred over the rain-rutted gravel, but the wheels did not slip. Juan looked suspiciously at the Virgin. Was she tricking him? Would she get him through and force him to make his own decision? That would be a dirty trick. With no sign from Heaven Juan didn't know what he would do. The road took a long loop around an old farm and then climbed toward the cliff in earnest.

Juan had the bus in low gear again and a wisp of steam came out of the overflow pipe and curled up in front of the radiator. The high point of the road was right in front of the cliff with its dark caves. Almost angrily Juan speeded his motor. The wheels threw gravel. There was a place where the ditch was plugged and water and topsoil flowed across the road. Juan raced at the dark streak. The front wheels crossed it and the back wheels spun in the greasy mud. The rear end swung around and the wheels spun and the hind end of the bus settled heavily into the ditch.

Juan's face had a fierce grin. He raced his motor and the wheels dug deeper and deeper. He reversed his direction and spun his wheels, and the spinning tires dug holes for themselves and settled into the holes, and the differential rested on the ground. Juan idled his motor. In the rear-view mirror he could see Pimples looking at him in amazement.

Juan had forgotten that Pimples would know. Pimples' mouth was open. Juan knew better than that. When you come to a soft place you don't spin the wheels. Juan could see the questions in Pimples' eyes. Why had he done it? He wasn't that stupid. He caught Pimples' eye in the mirror and all he could think to do was to wink secretly. But he saw relief come over Pimples' face. If it was a plan it was O.K. If there was something in back of it Pimples would go along. And then a horrible thought crossed Pimples' mind. Suppose it was Camille. If Juan wanted her Pimples wouldn't have a chance. He couldn't compete with Juan.

The angle of the bus was sharp. The rear wheels were buried and the front end stood high up on the road. "Sweetheart" looked like a crippled bug. Now Van Brunt's face cut out Pimples' reflection in the mirror. Van Brunt was red and angry and his bony finger cut the air under Juan's nose.

"So you did it," he cried. "So you tied us up. I knew you'd do it. By God, I knew you would! How am I going to get into the courthouse now? How are you going to get us out of this?"

Juan knocked the finger aside with the back of his hand. "Take your finger out of my face," he said. "I'm sick of you. Now get back to your seat."

Van Brunt's angry eyes wavered. He suddenly realized that this man was out of control. He wasn't afraid of the railroad commission or anybody. Van Brunt backed up a little and sat down on the angled seat.

Juan turned off the ignition and his motor died. The rain pattered on the roof of the bus. He tapped his palms on the steering wheel for a moment and then he turned in his seat and faced his passengers. "Well," he said. "That does it."

They stared back at him, shocked at the situation. Mr. Pritchard said softly, "Can't you get us out?"

"I haven't looked yet," said Juan.

"But it seems to me like we're in pretty deep. What are you going to do?"

"I don't know," said Juan. He wanted to see Ernest Horton's face, to see if he knew the thing had been deliberate, but Ernest was hidden behind Norma. Camille showed no effect at all. She had waited too long to be impatient.

"Sit tight," Juan said. He pulled himself upright against the angled bus and pushed the door lever. The lock clicked but the door was sprung. It did not open. Juan stood up and put his foot against the door and pushed it open. They could hear the hiss of rain on the road and on the grass. Juan stepped out into the rain and walked around to the back of the bus. The slanting rain felt cold on his head.

He had done a good job. It would probably take a wrecking car or maybe even a tractor to get it out. He leaned down and looked underneath to verify something he already knew. The axles and the differential were resting on the ground. Through the windows the passengers were looking out, their faces distorted by the wet glass. Juan straightened up and climbed back into the bus.

"Well, folks, I guess you'll just have to wait. I'm sorry, but don't forget you all wanted to come this way."

"I didn't," Van Brunt said.

Juan whirled on him. "God damn it, keep out of this! Don't get me mad because I'm right on the point of getting mad."

Van Brunt saw that he meant it. He looked down at his hands, pinched up the loose skin on his knuckles, and rubbed his left hand with his right.

Juan sat sideways in the driver's seat. His eyes flicked over the Virgin. "All right, all right," he thought to her, "so I cheated a little bit. Not much, but a little. I guess you're justified now in making it pretty uncomfortable for me." Aloud he said, "I'll just have to walk on ahead and phone for a wrecking car. I'll tell them to send out a taxi for you folks. That shouldn't take very long."

Van Brunt spoke with restraint. "There isn't a place in four miles. The old Hawkins place is about a mile, but it's standing empty since the Bank of America took it over. You'll have to go to the county road and that's a good four miles."

"Well, if I have to go, I have to go," said Juan. "I can only get just so wet."

Pimples had a rush of friendliness. "I'll go," he said. "You stay here and let me go."

"No," said Juan, "this is your day off." He laughed. "You just enjoy it, Kit." He reached over to the instrument board, unlocked the glove box, and opened the little door. "There's some emergency whisky here," he said.

He paused. Should he take the pistol—a good Smith & Wesson 45-caliber revolver with a 6-inch barrel? It would be a shame to leave it. But it would be a nuisance to have it too. If he got into any kind of trouble the gun would go against him. He decided to leave it. If he was going to leave his wife, he could surely leave his gun too. He said lightly, "If you get jumped by tigers, there's a gun in here."

"I'm hungry," Camille said.

Juan smiled at her. "You take these keys and open up the back. There's a lot of pies there." He grinned at Pimples. "Don't eat 'em all, son. Now, you can stay in the bus or you can get out the tarpaulin from the back and put it on the ground up in those caves if you want. You might even build a fire in there if you can find any dry wood. I'll get a car sent out to you soon as I can."

"I'd like to go instead of you," Pimples said.

"No, you stick around and look after things," said Juan, and he saw a flash of pleasure on Pimples' face. Juan buttoned his jacket tightly over his chest. "Just sit tight," he said, and he stepped down out of the bus.

Pimples clambered down after him. He followed Juan a few steps until Juan turned and waited for him. "Mr. Chicoy," he said softly, "what is it you got on your mind?"

"On my mind?"

"Yeah. You see—well, you spun them wheels."

Juan put his hand on Pimples' shoulder. "Look, Kit, I'll tell you sometime. You just hold on for me, will you?"

"Well, sure, Mr. Chicoy, only—I'd just like to know."

"I'll tell you all about it when we get a minute alone," Juan said. "You just keep these folks from killing each other for a little while, will you?"

"Well, sure," Pimples said uneasily. "How long you think it'll be before you get back?"

"I don't know," Juan said impatiently. "How can I tell? You do like I say."

"Sure. Oh, sure," said Pimples.

"And eat all the pie you want," said Juan.

"But we'll have to pay for it, Mr. Chicoy!"

"Sure," said Juan, and he strode away along the road in the

rain. He knew that Pimples was looking after him and he knew that Pimples sensed something. Pimples knew he was running out. Juan didn't feel good about it now. Not the way he thought he would. It didn't seem as good or as pleasant or as free. He stopped and looked back. Pimples was just getting into the bus.

The road went past the cliff with its eroded stone caves. Juan turned off the road and went into the shelter for a moment. The caves and their overhang were larger than they looked from outside and they were fairly dry too. In front of the entrance to the largest cave there were three fire-blackened stones and a battered tin can. Juan stepped back to the road and walked on.

The rain was thinning out. To his right, down the hill, he could see the great bend of the river and how it turned and headed back across the valley through the sodden green fields. The country was too wet. There was an odor of decay in the air, the fat green stems fermenting. The road ahead was rain-beaten and rotted by water, but not by wheels. Nothing had been over it for a long time.

Juan bowed his head into the rain and walked faster. It wasn't so good. He tried to remember the sunny sharpness of Mexico and the little girls in blue *rebozos* and the smell of cooking beans, and instead Alice came into his head. Alice, looking out of the screen door. And he thought of the bedroom with its flowered curtains. She liked things nice. She liked pretty things. The bedspread, now, a giant afghan she had knitted herself in little squares, and no two the same color. She said she could get over a hundred dollars for it. And she had knitted every bit of it herself.

And he thought of the big trees, and how nice it was to lie in a tub full of hot water in the bathroom, the first real bathroom he had ever had outside of hotels. And there was always a bar of sweet-smelling soap. "It's just a god-damned habit," he said to himself. "It's a damned trap. You get used to a thing and so you think you like it. I'll get over it the way I'd get over a cold. Sure, it'll be painful. I'll worry about Alice. I'll be sorry. I'll accuse myself, and it might be I won't sleep good. But I'll get over it. After a while I won't think about it. It's just a damned trap." And Pimples' face, trusting and warm, came up before him. "I'll tell you later. I'll tell you all about it, Kit Carson." Not many people had trusted Juan that way.

He tried to think of the lake at Chapala, and over its pale smooth water he saw "Sweetheart," the bus, sagged down in the mud.

Ahead and down the hill to the left, in an indentation of the foothills, he saw a house and a barn and a windmill with the blades broken and hanging. That would be the old Hawkins place. Just the set-up he'd been thinking about. He would go in there, maybe in the house, but more likely in the barn. An old barn is usually cleaner than an old house. There was bound to be a little hay or straw in the barn. Juan would crawl in there and sleep. He wouldn't think about anything. He would sleep until maybe this time tomorrow, and then he'd walk on to the county road and pick up a ride. What difference did it make to him about the passengers? "They can't starve. It won't hurt them at all. It'll be good for them. It isn't any business of mine."

He hurried his steps down the hill toward the old Hawkins place. They'd look for him. Alice would think he was murdered and she'd call in a sheriff. Nobody ever thought he'd run off like this. That's what made it such a good joke. Nobody thought he could do it. Well, he'd show them. Get to San Diego, cross the border, pick up the mail truck to La Paz. Alice would have the cops out.

He stopped and looked back at the road. His footprints were clear enough, but the rain would probably wash them out, and he could cover his tracks if he wanted to. He turned in off the road toward the Hawkins place.

The old house had gone to pieces very quickly once it was abandoned. A few wandering boys broke out the windows and stole the lead pipe and the plumbing, and the doors soon banged themselves silly and fell off their hinges. The old dark wallpaper, pulled down under wind-driven rain, revealed under-sheets made from old newspapers with old cartoons—"Foxy Grandpa" and "Little Nemo" and "Happy Hooligan" and "Buster Brown." Tramps had been there and had left their litter and burned the door casings in the old black fireplace. The smell of desertion and damp and sourness was in the house. Juan looked in the doorway, walked through and smelled the odor of the vacant house, and went out the back door toward the barn.

The corral fence was down and the big door off, but inside the barn smelled fresh. The stalls were polished where the horses had rubbed against the wood. The corners were cobwebbed. Between the manure windows were still the candle-boxes with the worn brushes and rusty currycombs. And an old collar and hames and a set of tugs hung on a rack beside the door. The leather of the collar was split and the padding stuck out.

The barn had no loft. The whole central part had been used to store hay. Juan walked around the end of the last stall. It was dusky inside and the light of the sky lanced through broken shakes in the roof. The floor was covered with short straw, dark with age, and with a slightly musty smell. Standing still in the entrance, Juan could hear the squeaking of mice and he could smell the colonies of mice too. From a rafter two cream-colored barn owls looked down at him and then closed their yellow eyes again.

The rain had diminished so that there was only a faint puttering on the roof. Juan went to a corner and with his foot kicked aside a layer of the dusty top straw. He sat down and then lay back and thrust his hands behind his head. The barn was alive with secret little sounds, but Juan was very tired. His nerves itched and he felt mean. He thought perhaps if he slept he would feel better.

Back in the bus he had felt, in anticipation, a bursting, orgasmic delight of freedom. But it was not so. He felt miserable. His shoulders ached, and now that he was relaxed and stretched out he wasn't sleepy. He wondered, "Won't I ever be happy? Isn't there anything to do?" He tried to remember old times when it seemed to him that he was happy, when he had felt pure joy, and little pictures came into his mind. There was a very early morning with chill air and the sun was coming up behind the mountains and in a muddy road little gray birds were hopping. There wasn't any reason for joy, but it had been there.

And another. It was evening and a shining horse was rubbing his lovely neck on a fence and the quail were calling and there was a sound of dropping water somewhere. His breath came short with excitement just remembering it.

And another. He rode in an old cart with a girl cousin. She was older than he—he couldn't remember what she looked like. The horse shied at a piece of paper and she fell against him, and to right herself she put out her hand and touched his leg, and delight bloomed in his stomach and his brain ached with delight.

And another. Standing at midnight in a great, dim cathedral with a sharp, barbaric smell of copal smarting his nose. He held a skinny little candle with a white silk bow tied about it halfway up. And like a dream, the sweet murmur of the mass came from far away at the high altar and the drowsy loveliness drew down over him.

Juan's muscles relaxed and he slept in the straw of the deserted barn. And the timid mice sensed his sleep and came out from under the straw and played busily and the rain whispered quietly on the barn roof.

Chapter 15

THE passengers watched Juan walk away and disappear over the brow of the hill. They didn't speak, not even when Pimples climbed back into the bus and took his place in the driver's seat. The seats were tilted and each passenger tried to get comfortable.

At last Mr. Pritchard asked, generally, "How long do you suppose it'll take him to get a car out here?"

Van Brunt rubbed his left hand nervously. "Can't possibly expect it under three hours. He's got a four-mile walk. Even if he can get a car to come out, it'll take them an hour to get started and an hour to get here. That is, if they'll come out at all. I'm not sure anybody will come over this road. We should have walked in with him and caught a ride at the county road."

"We couldn't," said Mr. Pritchard. "We've got all our baggage."

Mrs. Pritchard said, "I didn't want to say anything when you got this crazy idea, Elliott. After all, it is your vacation."

She had been wanting to explain to the other passengers how people of the obvious position of the Pritchards should come to find themselves on a bus—should put themselves in the way of this kind of thing. They must have been wondering, she thought. Now she turned and addressed them. "We came out on a train, a nice train—the City of San Francisco, a very comfortable extra-fare train. And then my funny husband had this crazy idea of coming down on a bus. He thought he would see the country better that way."

"Well, we're seeing it, little girl," he said bitterly.

She went on, "My husband said he had been out of touch. He wanted to see what the people, the real people, were talking about." A delicate malice was creeping into her voice. "I thought it was silly but it's his vacation. He's the one who's worked so hard for the war effort. The wives didn't have much to do, just trying to make out with rationing and all, and no food in the stores. Why, once for two months we didn't taste beef. Nothing but chicken."

Mr. Pritchard looked at his wife in some surprise. It was not a common thing for this edge to come into her voice and it had a strange effect on him. Suddenly he found himself getting angry, getting wildly, unreasonably angry. It was her tone that did it. "I wish we'd never come," he said. "I didn't want to come anyway. I'd have had a real rest playing a little golf and sleeping in my own bed. I never wanted to come."

The other passengers watched with curiosity and interest. They were bored. This might be good. The anger of these two was beginning to fill the bus.

Mildred said, "Mother, Dad, cut it out."

"You stay out of this," Mr. Pritchard said. "I didn't want to come. I didn't want to at all. I hate foreign countries, particularly dirty ones."

Mrs. Pritchard's mouth pinched white and her eyes were cold. "This is a fine time to tell me about it," she said. "Who made all the plans for it and bought all the tickets? Who got us on this bus, stalled in the middle of nowhere? Who did all that? Did I?"

"Mother!" Mildred cried. She had never heard this tone in her mother's voice before.

"And it seems a strange thing"—Mrs. Pritchard's voice broke a little—"I try so hard. This trip, when you get it all paid for, is going to cost three or four thousand dollars. If you didn't want to come I could have built the little orchid house I've wanted so long, just a little, tiny orchid house. You said it wouldn't be a good example, getting it during war, but the war is over now and we take a trip you didn't want to take. Well, you spoiled it for me now too. I won't enjoy it. You spoil everything. Everything!" She covered her eyes with her hand.

Mildred stood up. "Mother, stop it. Mother, stop this right now!"

Mrs. Pritchard moaned a little.

"If you don't stop it I'm going to walk away," Mildred said.

"Go away," said Mrs. Pritchard. "Oh, go away. You don't understand anything."

Mildred's face set. She picked up her gabardine topcoat and put it on. "I'm going to walk to the county road," she said.

"That's four miles," Van Brunt said. "You'll spoil your shoes."

"I'm a good walker," said Mildred. She had to get out, her hatred for her mother was rising in her and making her sick.

Mrs. Pritchard's handkerchief was out and the scent of lavender filled the bus.

"Pull yourself together," Mildred said harshly. "I know what you're going to do. You're going to get a headache and punish us. I know you. One of your fake headaches," she said viciously. "I'm not going to sit around and see you get away with it."

Pimples watched, fascinated. He was breathing through his mouth.

Mrs. Pritchard looked up at her daughter with horror. "Dear! You don't believe that!"

"I'm beginning to," said Mildred. "Those headaches come too opportunely."

Mr. Pritchard said, "Mildred, stop it."

"I'm going on."

"Mildred, I forbid it!"

His daughter whirled on him. "Forbid and be damned!" She buttoned her coat over her chest.

Mr. Pritchard put out his hand. "Mildred, please, dear."

"I've had enough," she said. "I need the exercise." She stepped out of the bus and walked rapidly away.

"Elliott," Mrs. Pritchard cried. "Elliott, stop her. Don't let her go."

He patted her arm. "Now, little girl, she'll be all right. We're just irritable. All of us."

"Oh, Elliott," she groaned, "if only I could lie down. If only I could get some rest. She thinks my headaches aren't true. Elliott, I'll kill myself if she believes that. Oh, if I only could stretch out."

Pimples said, "Ma'am, we got some tarpaulins in the back end. We use 'em to cover the baggage when we carry it on top. If your husband would take one of them up in that cave, why, you could lay down there."

"Why, that's a wonderful idea," said Mr. Pritchard.

"Lie on the old damp ground?" she demanded. "No."

"No, on a canvas. I could fix you a sweet little bed for a sweet little girl."

"Well, I don't know," she said.

"Look, dear," he insisted. "Look, I'm going to roll up my topcoat. Now you just put your head down there, like that. Now, in a little while I'll come and get you and take you to your own little bed."

She whimpered.

"And rest your head on the pillow and close your eyes."

Pimples said, "Mr. Chicoy told me to bring out the pies if anybody got hungry. There's four flavors and they're pretty good too. I could eat a piece right now."

"Let's get that tarpaulin first," Mr. Pritchard said. "My wife is exhausted. She's about at the end of her strength. You help me fix her a bed, will you?"

"O.K.," said Pimples. He felt that he was doing all right in Juan's absence. He felt fine and jaunty. His posture showed his mood for his shoulders were back and his pale wolf eyes were bright and confident. There was only one worry in Pimples. He wished he had had sense enough to throw an old pair of shoes into the bus. His two-toned oxfords were likely to take a beating from the mud, and that would mean a long job with a toothbrush to clean them up again. And he couldn't appear to protect his shoes for that would indicate to Camille that he was not a devil-may-care fellow. She wouldn't be impressed by a man who was careful of his shoes even if they were new white and brown oxfords.

Ernest said, "I'm going to have a look at those caves," and he got up and climbed to the door of the bus. Van Brunt grumbled and followed.

Mrs. Pritchard nestled her cheek in Mr. Pritchard's coat and closed her eyes. She was filled with dismay. How could she have fought with him in public—with her own husband? It had never happened before. When it was necessary to quarrel she always managed that they should be alone. Not even Mildred was permitted to hear a quarrel. She felt it was vulgar to fight when people could hear, and, besides, it broke a pattern she had been years building, the story that because of her sweetness her marriage was ideal. Everyone she knew believed that. She believed it herself. Through her own efforts she had built a beautiful marriage and now she had slipped. She had quarreled. She had let it get out about the little orchid house.

For a number of years she had wanted such a house. Ever

since, in fact, she had seen an article in *Harper's Bazaar* about a Mrs. William O. MacKenzie who had one. The pictures had been lovely. People would say of Mrs. Pritchard that she had the darlingest little orchid house. It was precious and valuable. It was better than jewelry or furs. People she didn't even know would hear about her little orchid house. Secretly she had learned a great deal about such projects. She had studied plans. She knew costs of heating systems and humidifiers. She knew where the original stock was bought and how much it cost. She had studied books on propagation. And all of this very secretly because she knew that if and when the time came that she could have it Mr. Pritchard would want to find out these things and tell her. It was the only way. She didn't even resent it. That was simply a way of life, the way she had made her marriage successful. She would be impressed with his knowledge and she would ask his advice about everything.

But she was worried because she had let the thing slip in anger. Such a mistake might set her back six months or more. She had planned to have him suggest it, and by careful reluctance cause him to overcome her opposition. But now the subject had been mentioned in anger and he would have a block against it. Unless she was very careful in the future he might never come around. It had been stupid of her and vulgar of her.

She could hear Norma and Camille talking softly behind her. Her eyes were closed and she looked so little and so ill that they couldn't imagine she was listening.

Norma was saying, "One of the things I'd like to have you show me is how you handle—well, fellas."

Camille laughed shortly. "What do you mean?" she asked.

"Well, you take Pimples. I can see how he's been—trying, and he can't get to first base with you, and at the same time you don't even seem like you're doing it. And you take that other fella. That salesman. Well, he's pretty clever and you handled him just like nothing. I wish I knew how you did it."

Camille was pleased. Much as she might be worried by this incipient millstone, it was pleasant to have admiration. Now was the time to tell Norma she wasn't a dental nurse, to tell her about the giant wine glass and the stags, and yet she couldn't. She didn't really want to shock Norma. She wanted to be admired.

"Thing I like is you never are mean or nasty about it and still they never lay a finger on you," Norma continued.

"I never noticed," Camille said. "I guess it's kind of like an instinct." She chuckled. "I've got a girl friend that can really handle men. She just don't give a hoot and she's kind of mean with men anyway. Well, Loraine—that's her name—was—well, she was kind of engaged to this fellow and he had a good job and so he wasn't any trouble. Loraine wanted a fur coat. Of course, she had a short wolf jacket and she had a couple of white fox furs because Loraine is a very popular girl. She's pretty and little and when she's with girls she'll keep you laughing all the time. So Loraine wanted a mink coat, not a short one, but a real full-length one, and they cost three, four thousand dollars."

Norma whistled between her teeth. "Jesus God!" she said.

"Well, one afternoon Loraine said, 'I guess I'll get my fur coat now.' And I said, 'You're kidding.'

" 'You think I'm kidding? Eddie's going to give it to me.'

" 'When did he tell you?' I asked her.

"Loraine just laughed. 'He didn't tell me. He don't even know it yet.'

" 'Well,' I said. 'Look, you're nuts.'

" 'You wanna bet?' Loraine will take a bet on anything.

"I don't bet on things so I said, 'How are you going to go about it?'

" 'If I tell you, will you keep it to yourself?' she said. 'It's easy. I know Eddie. I'm gonna needle him tonight and keep needling him till he gets mad. And I'm gonna keep right on until he throws a punch at me. I may even have to step into one because when Eddie's a little drunk he misses pretty bad. Well, then I'm gonna let Eddie stew in his own juice. I know Eddie. He'll get to feeling mean and sorry. You want to take that bet?' she said. 'I'll even lay down a time. I'll bet you I have that coat by tomorrow night.'

"Well, I don't bet anything, so I said, 'Two bits you don't.' "

Norma's mouth was open with excitement, and a gleam of reflected light came from between Mrs. Pritchard's closed lashes.

"Did she get it?" Norma demanded.

"Well, I went over to her place Sunday morning. Loraine

had a mouse all right, a real blue shiner, and she had a patch over it and her nose was cut up too."

"Well, did she get the coat?"

"She got the coat all right," Camille said. There was a frown on her face, a puzzled look. "She got the coat and it was a beauty. Well, then she took off all her clothes. There were just two of us there. She turned that coat inside out and she put it right on next her skin with the hair next her skin. And then she rolled and rolled on the floor and she laughed and giggled like she was crazy."

Norma's held breath exhaled slowly. "God," she said, "why did she do that?"

"I don't know," said Camille. "It was like she—well, it was like she was a little crazy, kinda nuts."

Mrs. Pritchard's face was glowing. She breathed very rapidly. Her skin tingled, and there was an aching, itching feeling in her legs and stomach she had never felt before, and there was an excitement in her that she had had only once in her life and that was on horseback a long time ago.

Norma said judiciously, "I don't think it was nice. If she really loved Eddie and he was going to marry her, I don't think it was a nice thing to do."

"I don't either," said Camille. "It kind of bothered me about Loraine and I told her so, but she said, 'Well, some girls just take the longer way around. I wanted it quick. It'll be the same thing in the end, anyway. Somebody was gonna work Eddie over.' "

"And did she marry him?"

"Well, no. She didn't."

"I'll bet maybe she never loved him at all," Norma said heatedly. "I'll bet she just gold-dug Eddie."

"Maybe," said Camille, "but she's been my girl friend for a long time, and if I ever needed anything she was right there. One time when I had pneumonia she sat up with me for three days and nights, and I was broke and she paid the doctor."

"I guess you just can't tell," Norma said.

"No, I guess not," said Camille. "Anyway, you asked me about how to handle men."

Mrs. Pritchard was beating herself with words. Her reaction had frightened her. She said to herself, even whispering the words, "What a horrible, vulgar story. What animals those young girls are. So this is what Elliott means by 'getting down to the people.' Oh, that's horrible. We just forget how people are, how nasty they can be. Dear Ellen," she wrote frantically, and the excitement was still tingling on the insides of her legs. "Dear Ellen, the trip was terrible between San Ysidro and San Juan de la Cruz. The bus went into a ditch and we just sat and waited for hours. My Elliott was very sweet and made me a bed in a funny cave. You said I would have adventures. Remember? You said I always would have adventures. Well, I did. There were two vulgar, illiterate girls on the bus, one of them a waitress and the other was rather pretty. She was a you-know-what. I was resting and I guess they thought I was asleep and they went right on talking. I couldn't put in a letter what they said. I'm still blushing. Gentle people just don't know how these little things live. It's incredible. I always think it's ignorance. If we only had better schools and if—well, if you want the truth—if we who should be examples were just better examples, I'm sure the whole picture might change, gradually, but certainly."

Ellen would read the letter over and over to people. "I just had a letter from Bernice. She's having the most exciting adventures. You know, she always does. Why, I want you to hear what she says. I've never known anyone who could see the good sides of people the way Bernice can."

Norma was saying, "If I liked a fella I wouldn't think of doing a thing like that to him. If he wanted to give me a present he'd have to think of it himself."

"Well, that's the way I feel about it too," said Camille. "But I haven't got a fur coat, not even a chubby. And Loraine's got three."

"Well, I don't think it's fair," said Norma. "I don't think I'd like Loraine."

"God Almighty!" Camille cried in her mind. "You don't know if you'd like Loraine. I wonder if you've got any idea what Loraine would think of you?" No, she thought, that isn't true. Loraine would probably take this girl and fix her up and help her. Whatever you could say about Loraine, nobody could say she wasn't a good scout.

Chapter 16

MILDRED put her head down to keep the rain from misting her glasses. The gravelly road felt good under her feet and the exercise made her draw her breath deeply. It seemed to her that the day was getting darker. It couldn't be very late, and still an evening light was creeping in, making light things, such as pieces of quartz and limestone, seem lighter, and dark things, such as the fence posts, seem black.

Mildred walked quickly, her feet stabbing at the ground and her heels striking into the gravel. She was trying to push the quarrel out of her mind. She did not remember having seen her mother and father fight before. But this had been a practiced thing with a routine-like quality that indicated it was a far from uncommon process. Her mother must maneuver the quarrels into the bedroom where no one could hear them. She had built up and maintained a story of the perfect marriage. This time the tension had got to a breaking point and there was no bedroom to retire to. There had been mean little drops of yellow venom in the quarrel that disturbed Mildred. It was a poison that seeped subtly in, not an open, honest rage but rather a secret, creeping anger that struck with a thin, keen blade and then concealed the weapon quickly.

And there was this endless trip to Mexico ahead. Suppose Mildred didn't come back? Suppose she walked on and caught a ride and disappeared—rented a room someplace, perhaps on the coast by the sea, and spent the time on the rocks or on the beach? The idea was very pleasant to her. She could cook for herself and get to know other people on the beach. The idea was ridiculous. She hadn't any money. Her father was very generous—but not with cash. She could charge her clothes and sign checks in restaurants, but her actual money was always very short. Her father was generous but very curious. He wanted to know what she bought and where she ate, and he could find these things out on the monthly bills.

Of course, she could go to work. She would pretty soon anyway, but not right yet. No, she had to weather it out. She had to stumble through this horrible Mexican trip, which could be so wonderful if she were alone, and then go back to college. It wouldn't be long until she would go to work, and her father would approve of that. He would say to Charlie Johnson, "I'd give her anything she wants, but no, sir, she's got too much get-up-and-go. She's making her own living." And he would say it with pride, as though some virtue of his own was involved, and he would never know that she was working for the sake of privacy, so she could have her own apartment and some spending money, for things he didn't know about.

At home, for instance, she was free to go to the liquor cabinet any time she wanted, but she knew that her father had in his memory the exact level of liquid in every bottle, that if she took three drinks he would know it immediately. He was a very curious man.

She took off her glasses and wiped them on the lining of her coat and put them on again. In the road she could see Juan's tracks, long strides. There were places where his foot had slipped on a rock, and there were muddy stretches where the whole prints of his feet were visible, with the line broken by the drives of his toes. Mildred tried to walk in his tracks, but his step was too long for her, and she felt the pull on her thighs after she had kept it up for a while.

He was a strange, compelling man, she thought. She was glad she had got out of that crazy experience of the morning. No sense in it, she knew. Irritation and functioning glands interplaying—she knew all that. And she also knew herself to be a girl of strong sexual potential. There would come a time in the not far future when she would either have to get married or make some kind of permanent arrangement. Her times of restlessness and need were growing more frequent. She thought of Juan's dark face and shining eyes and she was not affected. But there was warmth in him and honesty. She liked him.

As she cleared the hill she saw the deserted farm below and was fascinated. She could feel the despondency of the place. She knew she couldn't pass the house without looking through it. Her steps quickened. All her interest was aroused.

"Bank foreclosed," Van Brunt had said, "and the family had to move, and the bank wouldn't be interested in an old house. It was the land they were taking."

Her strides were almost as long as Juan's now. She came swinging down to the foot of the hill to the muddy entrance of the farm and suddenly she stopped. Juan's tracks turned in. She walked along the road a little to find whether they emerged and continued, but she could find no other footsteps ahead.

"He must still be in there," she said to herself. "But why? He was going out to the county road. There couldn't be a telephone here." She grew cautious as she realized she didn't know what was going on, and she didn't know much about this man. She walked slowly into the entrance and moved out on the grass so that her feet would not make a rasping sound on the gravel.

There was something dangerous about the deserted house. She recalled old newspaper stories of murders in places like this. Her throat tightened with fear. "Well," she consoled herself, "I can turn right around and go out. Nobody's stopping me. Nobody's pushing me in, but I know I must. I know I won't leave. Maybe those murdered girls could have got away too. Maybe they were asking for it."

She saw a vision of herself lying on the floor of one of the rooms, strangled or stabbed, and there was something in the vision that made her laugh—her glasses were still on. And what did she know about Juan? He had a wife and a business. Then there was a headline she remembered. "Father of three in sadist murder. Parson murders choir singer." Why are so many choir singers and organists murdered, she wondered. There seems to be a high occupational hazard about choir singing. Choristers are always being found choked behind the organ. She laughed. She knew she was going into this house. Should she just clump on in or should she steal in and catch Juan Chicoy at whatever he was doing? Maybe he was just going to the toilet.

She put a careful foot on the step and paused when the floorboard creaked under her weight. She went through the house opening cupboards. There was an overturned pepper can in the kitchen and a coat hanger in the closet of the bedroom. She turned her head sideways to look at the old comic pages under the peeled wallpaper. She read a strip of "Happy Hooligan." The mule, Maud, drew back her legs and kicked and Cy sailed through the air, and on the seat of Cy's pants were the imprints of the mule's hoofs.

She straightened her head. Why hadn't she thought of the barn before? Mildred crept back to the front porch and looked closely at the boards. She could see the wet track of Juan's shoes. She followed the track to the living room and lost it. Then she went to the open back door and looked out. What a fool she had been, creeping about! There were the footprints going out, headed, in fact, for the barn.

She went down the broken steps and followed the trail across the lot and passed the old windmill. She entered the barn and stood listening. There was no sound. She thought of calling out and gave it up. Slowly she moved down the line of stalls and around the end stall. It had taken a little while for her eyes to adjust to the light. She stood in the entrance to the central part. All the little mice flicked out of sight. Then she saw Juan lying on his back, his hands cupped behind his head. His eyes were closed and he was breathing evenly.

"I can go away," Mildred said. "Nobody's keeping me. It will be my fault. I just want to remember that. He's minding his own business. Oh, what's this nonsense?"

She took off her glasses and put them in her pocket. The outline of the man was fuzzy to her now, to her unfocused eyes, but she could still see him. She walked slowly, carefully, across the straw-covered floor and when she was beside him she crossed her ankles and let herself down and sat on her crossed feet. The scar on his lip was white and he breathed shallowly and evenly. "He was just tired," she said to herself. "He lay down to rest a moment and he fell asleep. I shouldn't wake him up."

She thought of the people back in the bus—suppose neither she nor Juan ever came back. What would they do? Her mother would collapse. Her father would wire the governor—two or three governors. He would call the FBI. There would be hell to pay. Yet what could they do? She was twenty-one. When they caught up with her she could say, "I'm twenty-one and doing what I want to do. Whose business is it?" And suppose she went to Mexico with Juan? That would be quite a different story, quite a different thing.

And now little irrelevancies invaded her mind. If he's an Indian or has Indian blood, how is it someone can creep up on him? She held her eye corners back to bring his face into focus. It was a scarred, leathery face, but it was a good face, she thought. The lips were full and humorous, but they were kind. He would be gentle while he was with a woman. He might not stay with her for very long, but he would be nice to her. But he had that wife, that horrid wife, and he stayed with her. God knows how long. She must have been pretty when he married her, but she was ugly now. What had happened there? How did that horrid woman hold him? Maybe he was just like everyone else, like her father. Maybe he was just held in line by fears and by habit. Mildred didn't see how it could happen to anyone, but she knew it did. When people got old they grew frightened of smaller and smaller things. Her father was frightened of a strange bed or a foreign language or a political party he didn't belong to. Her father truly believed that the Democratic party was a subversive organization whose design would destroy the United States and put it in the hands of bearded communists. He was afraid of his friends and his friends were afraid of him. A rat race, she thought.

She moved her eyes down over Juan's body, a tough, stringy body that would get tougher and stringier as he got older. His trousers were a little wet from the rain and they hugged close to his legs. There was a neatness about him—a neatness of a mechanic who has just washed up. She looked at his flat stomach and at his broad chest. She saw no change in his breathing, no muscular change, but his eyes were open and he was looking at her. And his eyes were not sleep-heavy, but bright.

Mildred started. Perhaps he hadn't been asleep at all. He might have watched her come into the barn. She found herself explaining, "I needed exercise. You know, I've been sitting a long time. I thought I'd walk to the county road and pick up the car there. And then I saw this old place. I like old places."

Her feet were going to sleep. She leaned sideways and, supporting herself with one hand, moved her legs and feet to one side and covered her knee carefully with her skirt. Her feet buzzed and burned with returning blood.

Juan did not answer. His eyes were on her face. Slowly he rolled on his side and supported his head with a hand under his ear. A dark gleam came into his eyes, and his mouth curled up a little at the corners. His face was hard, she thought. No way of getting past the eyes into the head. It was either all on the surface or else it was too completely protected ever to get at.

"What are you doing here?" she asked.

His lips parted a little. "What are you doing here?"

"I told you, I needed exercise. I told you."

"Yes, you told me."

"But what are you doing here?"

He didn't seem really awake. "Me? Oh, I sat down to rest. I went to sleep. No sleep last night."

"Yes, I remember," she said. She had to go on talking. She was wound up. "I wondered about you. You don't belong here. I mean, driving a bus. You belong someplace else."

"Like where?" he asked playfully. His eyes dropped to where the lapels of her coat crossed.

"Well," she said uneasily, "I had a funny kind of a thought while I was walking. I thought maybe you wouldn't come back. You might just keep going and maybe go back to Mexico. I could see how I might do that if I were you."

His eyes squinted and he peered into her face. "Are you nuts? What made you think that?"

"Well, it was just something that came to me. Your life, driving the bus, I mean, must be pretty dull after—well, after Mexico."

"You haven't been in Mexico?"

"No."

"Then you don't know how dull it is there."

"No."

He raised his head and straightened his arm and put his head down on his arm. "What do you think would happen to those people back there?"

"Oh, they'd get back somehow," she said. "It isn't far. They wouldn't starve."

"And what do you think would happen to my wife?"

"Well—" She was confused. "I hadn't thought of that."

"Yes, you did," said Juan. "You don't like her. I'll tell you something. Nobody likes her except me. One of the reasons I like her is because nobody likes her." He grinned. "What a liar," he said to himself.

"It was just a crazy thought I had," she said. "I even thought

I might run away too. I thought I would disappear and live by myself and—well, never see anyone again that I knew." She rose up on her knees and sat down again on the other side.

Juan looked at her knee. He put out his hand and pulled her skirt down over it. She flinched when his hand came toward her and then relaxed uneasily.

"I don't want you to think I followed you in here," she said.

"You don't want me to think it, but you did," said Juan.

"Well, what if I did?"

His hand came out again and rested on her covered knee and fire raced through her.

"It's not you," she said. Her throat was dry. "I don't want you to think it's you. It's me. I know what I want. I don't even like you. You smell like a goat." Her voice staggered along. "You don't know the kind of life I lead. I'm all alone. I can't tell anyone anything."

His eyes were hot and shiny and they seemed to bathe her in heat.

"Maybe I'm not like anyone else," she went on. "How do I know? But it's not you. I don't even like you."

"You give yourself a hell of an argument, don't you?" said Juan.

"Look, what are you going to do about the bus?" she demanded. "Are you going to the road?"

The weight of his hand on her knee increased and then he took his hand away. "I'm going back and pull the bus out, pull those people through," he said.

"Then why did you come here?"

"Something went haywire," he said. "Something I figured out went haywire."

"When are you going back?"

"Pretty soon."

She looked at his hand, relaxed on the straw in front of her, its skin dark and shiny and a little wrinkled. "Aren't you going to make a pass at me?"

Juan smiled and it was a good, open smile. "Yes, I guess so. After you get through arguing with yourself. You're on both sides now. Maybe pretty soon you'll decide whether you're for or against and I'll have something to work on."

"Don't you—don't you want me?"

"Sure," said Juan. "Sure."

"Is it that you know I'll fall into your lap anyway, so you won't have to take any trouble?"

"Don't get me into your argument," said Juan. "I'm older than you are. I like this thing very much. I like it so much that I can wait. I can even go without for a while."

"I could dislike you very much," she said. "You don't give me any pride. You don't give me any violence to fall back on later."

"I thought you'd have more pride to be left to make up your own mind."

"Well, I don't."

"I guess not," he said. "The women in my country are like that too. They have to be begged or forced. Then they feel good about it."

"Well, are you always this way?"

"No," said Juan, "only with you. You came here for something. You said yourself it didn't have anything to do with me."

She looked at her fingers. "It's funny," she said. "I'm what you'd call an intellectual girl. I read things. I'm not a virgin. I know thousands of case histories, but I can't make the advances." She smiled quickly and warmly. "Can't you force me a little?"

His arms stretched out and she fell into place beside him in the straw.

"You won't hurry me?"

"We've got all day," he said.

"Will you despise me or laugh at me?"

"What do you care?"

"Well, I do, whether I want to or not."

"You talk too much," he said. "You just talk too much."

"I know it and it goes on all the time. Will you take me away? Maybe to Mexico?"

"No," said Juan. "Let's see if you can shut up for a little while."

Chapter 17

PIMPLES took the keys from the ignition lock on the instrument board and went to the rear of the bus. He unlocked the padlock which defended the luggage and threw up the lid. The smell of pies came sweetly to his nose. Mr. Pritchard looked in over his shoulder. The luggage was stacked tightly in the compartment.

"I guess I'll have to take it all out to get those tarps," said Pimples, and he began to pull at the wedged suitcases.

"Wait," said Mr. Pritchard. "Let me lift and you pull and we can leave them all in." He stood on the bumper and strained upward at the bottom suitcase while Pimples yanked at the heavy fold of canvas. Pimples worked it from side to side and gradually it came free from under the luggage.

"Maybe we'd better get a couple of pies while we got it open," Pimples said. "There's raspberry and lemon cream and raisin and caramel custard cream. A piece of caramel custard cream would go pretty good now."

"Later," said Mr. Pritchard. "Let's get my wife settled first." He took one side of the heavy cloth and Pimples the other and they proceeded toward the cliff with its caves.

It was a fairly common formation. The side of the little hill had dropped away in some old time, leaving a smooth surface of soft limestone. Gradually wind and rain cut under from below, while the top of the cliff was held in place by topsoil and grass roots. And over the ages several caves were formed under the overhanging cliff. Here a coyote littered her pups, and here, in the old days when there were such things, a grizzly bear came to sleep. And in the higher caves the owls sat during the day.

Three deep, dark caves developed at the bottom of the cliff and a few small ones higher up. All the cave entrances were now protected from the rain by the high overhang of the cliff itself. The caves were not entirely the inventions of nature, for bands of Indians hunting antelopes had rested here and lived here, and had even fought forgotten battles here. Later it became a stopping place for white men riding through the country, and the men had enlarged the caves and built their fires under the overhang.

The smoke stains on the sandstone were old and some fairly new, and the floors of the caves were comparatively dry, for this little hill, one side of which had dropped away, did not receive the drainage from other, higher hills. A few initials had been scratched on the sandstone cliff, but the surface was so soft that they soon became illegible. Only the large, weathering word "Repent" was still clear. The wandering preacher had let himself down with a rope to put up that great word in black paint, and he had gone away rejoicing at how he was spreading God's word in a sinful world.

Mr. Pritchard, carrying his end of the tarpaulin, looked up at the word "Repent." "Somebody went to a lot of trouble," he said, "a lot of trouble." And he wondered who had financed such a venture. Some missionary, he thought.

He and Pimples dropped the tarpaulin under the cliff's overhang while they went to inspect the caves. The shallow holes were nearly alike, about five feet high and eight or nine feet wide and ten or twelve feet deep. Mr. Pritchard chose the cave the farthest toward the right because it seemed to be drier and because it was a little darker inside. He thought the darkness would be good for his wife's coming headache. Pimples helped him spread the tarpaulin.

"I wish we could get some pine boughs or some straw to put underneath the canvas," Mr. Pritchard said.

"Grass is too wet," said Pimples, "and there ain't a pine tree in fifty miles."

Mr. Pritchard rubbed the canvas with the butt of his hand to see whether the cloth was dirty. "She can lie on my overcoat," he said, "and she can put her fur coat over her."

Ernest and Van Brunt came in to look at the cave.

"We could stay here for weeks if we had anything to eat," Ernest said.

"Well, we may be quite a time at that," said Van Brunt. "If that bus driver isn't back by tomorrow morning I'm going to walk in. I've had about all the nonsense I can take."

Pimples said, "I can break out a couple of pies if you folks want."

"That might be a good idea," said Ernest.

"What kind you like?" Pimples asked.

"Oh, any kind."

"The caramel custard cream is nice. It's got graham crackers instead of crust."

"That'll be fine," said Ernest.

Mr. Pritchard went back to the bus for his wife. He was feeling ashamed about his anger of a little time ago. He had the hard knot in his stomach he got when things were not going well, a fistlike knot. Charlie Johnson said he must have an ulcer, and Charlie was pretty funny about it. He said no one under twenty-five thousand dollars a year got an ulcer. It was a symptom of a bank account, Charlie said. And unconsciously Mr. Pritchard was a little proud of the pain in his stomach.

When he climbed into the bus, Mrs. Pritchard's eyes were closed.

"We've got your little bed all fixed," Mr. Pritchard said.

Her eyes, opened and she stared wildly about.

"Oh!"

"Were you asleep?" he said. "I shouldn't have wakened you. I'm sorry."

"No, dear. It's all right. I was just dozing."

He helped her to her feet. "You can lie on my overcoat and put your little fur coat over you."

She smiled weakly at his tone.

He helped her down the steps. "I'm sorry I was rude, little girl," he said.

"It's all right. You're just tired. I know you didn't mean it."

"Well, I'm going to buy you a great big dinner in Hollywood to make up for it, maybe at Romanoff's, with champagne. Would you like that?"

"You can't be trusted with money," she said playfully. "It's all forgotten now. You were just tired."—"Dear Ellen, we had the nicest dinner at Romanoff's and you'll never guess who was at the next table."—"Why, it's hardly raining at all," she said.

"No, and I want my little girl to get some sleep so she'll be well and strong."

"Are you sure it's not damp and there aren't any snakes?"

"No, we looked around."

"And no spiders?"

"Well, there weren't any spider webs."

"But how about big, hairy tarantulas? They don't have webs."

"We can look around some more," he said. "The walls are smooth. There's no place for them to hide." He conducted her to the little cave. "See how nice? And you can lie with your head up this way so you can look out if you want to."

He spread his coat and she sat down on it.

"Now, lie down and I'll cover you up."

She was very docile.

"How's my girl's head?"

"Well, it's not as bad as I was afraid it would be."

"That's good," he said. "You get a little nap. Are you comfy?"

She made a little moan of comfort.

"If you want anything just call out. I'll be near."

Pimples came to the cave entrance. His mouth was full and he carried a pie tin in his hand. "You like to have a piece of pie, ma'am?"

Mrs. Pritchard raised her head and then she shivered and put her head down. "No, thank you," she said. "It was nice of you to think of me, but I couldn't eat pie."—"Elliott just treated me like a queen, Ellen. How many people can say that after they've been married twenty-three years? I just feel lucky all the time."

Mr. Pritchard looked down at her. Her eyes were closed and there was a small smile on her lips. He felt the sudden lonely sorrow that came so often. He remembered, really remembered, the first time it had happened. He had been five when his little sister was born, and suddenly there were doors closed against him and he couldn't go into the nursery and he couldn't touch the baby and the feeling came on him that he was always a little dirty and noisy and unworthy and his mother was always busy. And then the cold loneliness had fallen on him, the cold loneliness that still came to him sometimes, that came to him now. The little smile meant that Bernice had retired from the world into her own room, and he couldn't follow her.

He took his gold nail pick from his pocket and opened it and cleaned his nails as he walked away. He saw Ernest Horton sitting against the cliff on the other side of the overhang. The high cave was over his head. Ernest was sitting on some newspapers and as Mr. Pritchard approached he slipped a double sheet of paper from under him and held it out.

"Most useful things in the world," he said. "You can do anything with them except read them."

Mr. Pritchard chuckled, took the paper, and sat down on it beside Ernest. "If you read it in the paper it isn't true," he said, quoting Charlie Johnson. "Well, here we are. Two days ago I was in a suite in the Hotel Oakland and now we're in a cave. It just shows, you can't make plans."

He stared at the bus. Through the window he could see that Pimples was in there with the two girls and they were eating pie. He felt a strong urge to join them. He could eat a piece of pie.

Ernest said, "Everything goes to show something. I have to laugh sometimes. You know, we're supposed to be a mechanical people. Everybody drives a car and has an icebox and a radio. I suppose people really think they are mechanical minded, but let a little dirt get in the carburetor and—well, a car has to stand there until a mechanic comes and takes out the screen. Let a light go off, and an electrician has to come and put in a new fuse. Let an elevator stop, and there's a panic."

"Well, I don't know," said Mr. Pritchard. "Americans are pretty mechanical people all in all. Our ancestors did pretty well for themselves."

"Sure, they did. So could we if we had to. Can you set the timer on your car?"

"Well, I—"

"Go further," said Ernest. "Suppose you had to stay out here two weeks. Could you keep from starving to death? Or would you get pneumonia and die?"

"Well," said Mr. Pritchard, "you see, people specialize now."

"Could you kill a cow?" Ernest insisted. "Could you cut it up and cook it?"

Mr. Pritchard found that he was getting impatient with this young man. "There's a kind of cynicism running around the country," he said sharply. "It seems to me young people have lost their faith in America. Our ancestors had faith."

"They had to eat," Ernest said. "They didn't have time for

faith. People don't work much any more. They've got time for faith."

"But they haven't any faith," Mr. Pritchard cried. "What's got into them?"

"I wonder," Ernest said. "I've even tried to figure it out. My old man had two faiths. One was that honesty got rewarded some way or other. He thought that if a man was honest he somehow got along, and he thought if a man worked hard and saved he could pile up a little money and feel safe. Teapot Dome and a lot of stuff like that fixed him on the first, and nineteen-thirty fixed him on the other. He found out that the most admired people weren't honest at all. And he died wondering, a kind of an awful wondering, because the two things he believed in didn't work out—honesty and thrift. It kind of struck me that nobody has put anything in place of those two."

Mr. Pritchard shook this out of his head. "You can't be thrifty because of taxes," he said. "There was a time when a man could build up an estate, but now he can't. Taxes take it all. You're just working for the government. I tell you, it knocks initiative on the head. No one has any ambition any more."

"It don't make a lot of difference who you work for if you believe in it," said Ernest. "The government or anybody else."

Mr. Pritchard interrupted him. "The returning soldiers," he said, "they're the ones I'm worrying about. They don't want to settle down and go to work. They think the government owes them a living for life and we can't afford it."

Ernest's forehead was beaded with perspiration now, and there was a white line around his mouth and a sick look in his eyes. "I was in it," he said softly. "No, no, don't worry. I'm not going to tell you about it. I wouldn't do that. I don't want to."

Mr. Pritchard said, "Of course, I've got the greatest respect for our soldiers, and I think they should have a voice."

Ernest's fingers crept to his lapel buttonhole. "Sure," he said, "sure, I know." He spoke as though he addressed a child. "I read in the papers about our best men. They must be our best men 'cause they got the biggest jobs. I read what they say and do, and I've got a lot of friends that you might call bums, and there's awful little difference between them. I've heard some of the bums get off stuff that sounded even better than the stuff that the Secretary of State gets off— Oh, what the hell!" He laughed. "I've got an invention, and it's a rubber drum that you beat with a sponge. It's for the drunks that want to play traps in the orchestra. I'm going to take a little walk."

"You're nervous," said Mr. Pritchard.

"Yeah, I'm nervous," Ernest said. "Everybody's nervous. And I'll tell you something. If we've got to fight somebody again, you know what's the most awful thing? I'll go too. That's the most awful thing." And he got up and walked away, back in the direction from which the bus had come.

His head was down and his hands were in his pockets and his feet beat against the gravel of the road and he was holding his mouth very tight and he couldn't stop. "I'm nervous," he said, "I'm just nervous. That's all it is."

Mr. Pritchard stared after him and then he lowered his eyes to his hands and got out his nail file again and cleaned his nails. Mr. Pritchard was shaken and he didn't know why. With all Mr. Pritchard's pessimism about government interference with business, there was always in the back of his mind a great hopefulness. Somewhere there was a man like Coolidge or like Hoover, who would come along and take the government out of the hands of these fools in the administration, and then everything would be all right. The strikes would stop and everybody would make money and be happy. It was just around the corner. Mr. Pritchard believed it. He had no idea that the world had changed. It has just made a few mistakes and the right man would come along—say, Bob Taft—and everything would get on an even keel again and these damned experiments would stop.

But this young man bothered him because this was a bright young man, and he had a feeling of hopelessness. Although he hadn't said it, Mr. Pritchard knew that Ernest Horton wouldn't even vote for Bob Taft if he were nominated. And Mr. Pritchard, like most of his associates, believed in miracles, but he was deeply shaken. Horton hadn't attacked Mr. Pritchard directly but—now, about the carburetor. Mr. Pritchard let his mind create the shape of a carburetor. Could he take it apart? Vaguely he knew that there was a little float in a carburetor, and in his mind he could see the brass screen and the gaskets.

But he had more important things to think about, he told himself. Horton had said "if the lights went out"—and Mr. Pritchard tried to think where the fuse boxes were in his house, and he didn't know. Horton had been attacking him. Horton didn't like him. Suppose they were stranded as the young man had said.

Mr. Pritchard closed his eyes and he was standing in the aisle of the bus. "Don't worry," he said to the other passengers, "I'm going to take care of everything. I haven't built a big business organization without some ability, you know. Let's reason this out," he said. "We need food first. There's some cows in that field back there." And Horton had said he didn't know how to kill a cow. Well, he'd show him. Probably Horton didn't know there was a pistol in the compartment on the instrument board. But Mr. Pritchard knew.

Mr. Pritchard took out the pistol. He got out of the bus and walked away toward the field and climbed a fence. He held the big black pistol in his hand. Mr. Pritchard had been to a great many movies. His mind unconsciously made a dissolve. He didn't see himself kill the cow or cut it up, but he saw himself come to the overhang again with a great slab of red meat. "There's food for you," he said. "Now for a fire." And again he dissolved, and the fire was leaping and a big piece of meat hung on a stick over the blaze.

And Camille said, "But what about that animal? It belongs to someone."

Mr. Pritchard answered, "Expediency knows no law. The law of survival comes first. Nobody could expect me to let you people starve."

And suddenly he dissolved again and he shook his head and opened his eyes. "Stay off that," he whispered to himself. "Keep away from that." Where had he seen her? If he could just talk to her a little while he ought to be able to place it. He knew he wasn't wrong because her face had given him a clutching sensation in his chest. He must not only have seen her, but something must have happened. He looked toward the bus. Pimples and the two girls were still inside.

He got to his feet and brushed the seat of his trousers as though the paper had not protected him from dust. The rain was only misting a little now, and in the west there were patches of blue sky. Everything was going to be all right. He walked over to the bus and climbed the steps. Van Brunt was stretched out on the seat at the rear which went across the width of the bus. Van Brunt seemed to be asleep. Pimples and the girls were talking softly so that they wouldn't disturb him.

"What I want in a wife is to be true," Pimples said.

"How about you?" Camille asked. "You figure to be true too?"

"Sure," said Pimples, "if she's the right kind of wife I will."

"Well, suppose she isn't?"

"Well, then I'll show her a thing or two. I'll show her two can play that game, like Cary Grant done in that movie."

An empty pie tin and another with only a quarter of a pie left were on the seat across from the group. The two girls sat together and Pimples, sitting sideways on the seat ahead of them, dropped his arm over the back.

They all looked up as Mr. Pritchard came in. "You mind if I sit in?" he said.

"Sure, come on in," said Pimples. "You like to have a piece of pie? Here's a piece right here." And he handed the pie to Mr. Pritchard and moved the empty tins so he could sit down.

"Have you got a girl now?" Camille continued.

"Well, kind of a one. But she's—er—well, she's kind of silly."

"Is she true to you?"

"Sure," said Pimples.

"How do you know?"

"Well, I never could—I mean—yeah, I'm sure."

"I guess you'll be getting married pretty soon," Mr. Pritchard said playfully, "and going in business for yourself."

"No, not for a while," said Pimples, "I'm studying by mail. There's a big future in radar. Make up to seventy-five dollars a week inside of a year."

"You don't say?"

"There's fellas that took that course that wrote in and said that's what they're making," said Pimples. "One of them is a district manager already, after one year."

"District manager of what?" Mr. Pritchard asked.

"Just district manager. That's what he said in his letter, and it's printed right in the ad."

Mr. Pritchard was beginning to feel good again. Here was ambition. Not everybody was cynical.

Camille said, "When do you think you'll get married?"

"Oh, not right yet," said Pimples. "I think a fella ought to see the world a little before he settles down. He ought to get around some. I might get on a ship. If you know radar, why, you know radio too. I thought I might get on a ship and be a radio operator for a while."

"But when are you going to finish your course?" Mr. Pritchard asked.

"Well, the lessons are going to start pretty soon now. I've got the coupon all made out and I'm saving up for the down payment. I took a test and they say I got plenty of talent. I had three or four letters from them."

Camille's eyes were very weary. Mr. Pritchard looked at her face. He knew his eyes were shielded by his glasses. He thought she had a fine face when you looked at it closely. Her lips were so full and friendly now, and only her eyes were tired. All the way from Chicago on a bus, he thought. She didn't look strong enough. He could see the fullness of her breasts under her suit and the suit was wrinkled. She had turned the French cuffs of her shirt inside out so that the edges would be clean. Mr. Pritchard noticed this. It meant neatness to him. He studied little details.

He felt this girl almost like a perfume. He felt an excitement and a hunger. It's just that you don't often see a girl like this, so attractive and so nice, he told himself. And then he heard himself talking and he hadn't even known he was going to talk.

"Miss Oaks," he said, "I've been thinking, and it occurred to me that you might like to listen to a little business idea I had. I'm president of quite a large corporation and I thought—well, I'm sure these young people would excuse us for a little while if you'd care to hear my ideas. Would you step over to the cliff there? I have some newspapers to sit on." He was astonished at his own words.

"Oh, Jesus!" Camille said to herself. "Here it comes."

Mr. Pritchard got down first and gallantly helped Camille off the bus. He held her elbow as she stepped across the ditch and he guided her gently to the spread newspapers where he and Ernest had sat. He pointed downward.

"Oh, I don't know," Camille said. "I've been sitting a long time."

"Well, maybe the change in position will rest you," said Mr. Pritchard. "You know, when I'm working long hours at my desk I change the height of my chair about every hour, and I find it keeps me fresh." He helped her to sit down on the newspapers. She covered her knees with her skirt and sat hugging her knees against her breast.

Mr. Pritchard sat down beside her. He took off his glasses. "I've been thinking," he said. "You know, a man in my position has to look ahead and plan. Now, technically, I'm on a vacation." He smiled. "Vacation—I wonder what a real vacation would be like."

Camille smiled. The ground felt very hard. She wondered how long this was going to take.

"Now the main raw product of a successful company is human beings," Mr. Pritchard said. "I'm always looking for human beings. You can get steel and rubber any time, but brains, talent, beauty, ambition—that's the difficult product."

"Look, mister," Camille said, "I'm awful tired."

"I know, my dear, and I'll come to the point. I want to employ you. That's as simply as I can say it."

"As what?"

"As a receptionist. It's quite a specialized job, and from there you could become—well, you might even become my personal secretary."

Camille was played out. She looked toward the cave entrance where Mrs. Pritchard was. She couldn't see anything. "What'll your wife have to say about that?"

"Well, what's she got to do with it? She doesn't run my business."

"Mister, like I said, I'm tired. We don't have to go through all that. I'd like to be married. I'd be a good wife, and with a settlement so I wouldn't have to worry for a while, why, I could even be good to a man."

"I don't see what you're getting at," Mr. Pritchard said.

"Yes, you do," said Camille. "You won't like me because I don't play it your way. You'd like to take months to get around to it and surprise me with it, but I'm nearly broke. You say your wife doesn't run your business, but I say she does. You and your business and everything about you. I'm trying to be nice but I'm tired. She probably picks your secretaries and you don't even know it. That's a tough woman."

"I don't know what you're talking about."

"Yes, you do," Camille said. "Who bought your tie?"

"Well—"

"She would know about me in a minute. She would. Now let me talk a little bit. You couldn't ask a girl outright. You'd have to go round about. But there's only two ways, mister. You either fall in love or you make a business proposition. If you'd said, 'Here's the way it is. So much for an apartment and so much for clothes,' why, I could have thought it out and I could have come to a conclusion, and it might have worked. But I'm not going to be nibbled to death by ducks. Did you want to surprise me after two, three months of me sitting at a desk? I'm getting too old to play."

Mr. Pritchard's chin was stuck out. "My wife does not run my business," he said. "I don't know where you got that idea."

"Oh, skip it," said Camille. "But I'd just as soon come up against a nest of rattlesnakes as your wife if she didn't like me."

"I'm a little surprised at your attitude," Mr. Pritchard said. "I hadn't thought of any of these things. I was just trying to offer you a job. You can take it or leave it."

"Oh, brother!" said Camille. "If you can kid yourself into believing that, God help any girl you get. She'll never know where she stands."

Mr. Pritchard smiled at her. "You're just tired," he said. "Maybe when you get rested you'll think it over."

The enthusiasm was gone out of his voice and Camille was relieved. She thought maybe she had made a mistake because he'd be very easy to handle, a real sucker. Loraine could have taken his shirt in one day.

Mr. Pritchard saw her face differently now. He saw hardness in it and defiance, and now that he was this close he saw the make-up and how it was put on, and he felt naked before this girl. It bothered him to have her talk this way. He had thought if everything worked out—well, he would—well—but the trouble was that she knew. Only he wouldn't have called it—well, there was such a thing as being a lady about such things.

He was confused, and in his confusion he was getting angry again. Twice in one day to be angry was unusual with him. His neck was getting red with anger. He had to cover up. He had to for his own sake. He said crisply, "I simply offered you a job. You don't want it—all right. There's no reason to be vulgar about it. There's such a thing as being a lady."

An edge came into her voice. "Look, Mac," she said, "I can play rough too. This lady business does it. I'm going to tell you something. You thought you recognized me. Now, do you belong to any clubs like The Octagon International or The Birds of the World or The Two Fifty—Three Thousand Club?"

"I'm an Octagon," Mr. Pritchard said stiffly.

"You remember the girl that sits in the wine glass? I've seen what you boys look like. I don't know what you get out of it and I don't want to know. But I know it isn't pretty, mister. And maybe you'd know a lady if you saw one. I don't know." Her voice came in little breaks and there was almost a hysteria of weariness in her. She jumped to her feet. "I'm going to take a stroll now, Mac. Don't give me any trouble because I know you, and I know your wife."

She walked away quickly. Mr. Pritchard watched her go. His eyes were wide and there was a heavy weight in his chest, a kind of played-out, physical horror. He watched her pretty body swaying as she went, and he saw her pretty legs, and his mind took her clothes off, and she was standing beside the huge glass and the wine was running down in red streams over her stomach and thighs and buttocks.

Mr. Pritchard's mouth was open and his neck was very red. He looked away from her and studied his hands. He took out his gold nail file and put it back in his pocket again. A dizziness came over him. He stood up uncertainly and walked down under the cliff to the little cave where Mrs. Pritchard lay.

She opened her eyes and smiled as he entered. Mr. Pritchard lay down beside her quickly. He pulled up her coat and crawled under it.

"Dear, you're tired," she said. "Elliott! what are you doing? Elliott!"

"Shut up," he said. "You hear me? Shut up! You're my wife, aren't you? Hasn't a man got any rights with his wife?"

"Elliott, you're mad! Someone'll—someone'll see you." She fought him in panic. "I don't know you," she said. "Elliott, you're tearing my dress."

"I bought it, didn't I? I'm tired of being treated like a sick cat."

Bernice cried softly in fear and in horror.

When he left her she cried with her face nestled close to her fur coat. Gradually her crying stopped and she sat up and looked out the cave entrance. Her eyes were ferocious. She raised her hand and set her nails against her cheek. She drew them down experimentally once and then she bit her lower lip and slashed downward with her fingernails. She could feel the blood oozing from the scratches. She put out her hand and dirtied it on the cave floor and rubbed the dirt into her bleeding cheek. The blood flowed down through the dirt and down her neck to the collar of her waist.

Chapter 18

MILDRED and Juan came out of the barn and she said, "Look, the rain has stopped. Look at the sun on the mountains. It's going to be beautiful."

Juan grinned.

"You know, I feel wonderful," she said. "I feel wonderful."

"Sure," said Juan.

"Do you feel wonderful enough to hold my mirror? I couldn't see in there." She took a little square mirror from her purse. "Here. No, a little higher." She combed her hair quickly and patted some powder on her cheeks and put on lipstick. She peered very closely in the mirror because she could see only at short range. "Do you think I'm flippant for a violated girl?"

"You're all right," he said. "I like you."

"But just that? No more?"

"Do you want me to lie?"

She laughed. "I guess I do a little. No, I don't. And you won't take me to Mexico?"

"No."

"This is the end then? There isn't any more?"

"How do I know?" Juan asked.

She put the mirror and the lipstick back in her purse and smoothed the lipstick on, one lip over the other. "Brush the straw off my coat, will you?"

She turned as he brushed her coat with his hand. "Because," she went on, "my father and mother don't know about these things. I'm sure I was conceived immaculately. My mother planted me, a number one bulb, before the snow came and covered me with soil and sand and manure." She was giddy. "Can't go to Mexico. What do we do now?"

"Go back and dig out the bus and drive to San Juan." He walked toward the entrance gate of the old farm.

"Can I take your hand just for a little?"

He looked at the hand with the amputated finger and started to move to the other side to give her his whole hand.

"No," she said, "I like that one." She took his hand and rubbed her finger over the smooth skin of the amputation.

"Don't do that," he said. "It makes me nervous."

She clutched his hand tightly. "I won't have to put on my glasses," she said.

The ranges to the east of them were glowing and gold with the setting sun. Juan and Mildred turned to the right and started up the hill toward the bus.

"Will you tell me something as—well, as a payment for my whoring?"

Juan laughed. "What do you want?"

"Why did you come down here? Did you think I'd follow you?"

"You want the truth or do you want to play games?" he asked.

"Well, I'd like both. But no—er—I guess I want the truth first."

"Well, I was running away," said Juan. "I was going to beat my way back to Mexico and disappear and let the passengers take care of themselves."

"Oh, and why don't you?"

"I don't know," he said. "It went sour. The Virgin of Guadalupe let me down. I thought I fooled her. She doesn't like fooling. She cut the heart out of it."

"You don't believe that," she said seriously. "I don't believe it either. What was the real reason?"

"For what?"

"For you coming down to that old place?"

Juan walked along and his face broke into a wide smile and the scar on his lip made the smile off-center. He looked down at her and his black eyes were warm. "I came down here because I hoped you would go for a walk, and then I thought I might—I might even get you."

She wrapped her arm around his arm and pulled her cheek hard against the sleeve of his jacket. "I wish it could go on a little more," she said, "but I know it can't. Good-by, Juan."

"Good-by," he said. And they walked slowly back toward the bus.

Chapter 19

VAN BRUNT lay outstretched on the back seat of the bus. His eyes were closed but he was not sleeping. His head rested on his right arm and the weight of his head cut off the full flow of blood to his right hand.

When Camille and Mr. Pritchard left the bus Pimples and Norma were silent for a while.

Van Brunt listened to age creeping in his veins. He could almost feel the rustle of blood in his papery arteries, and he could hear his heart beat with a creaking whistle in it. His right hand was going to sleep, but it was his left hand that worried him. There wasn't much feeling in his left hand. The skin was insensitive, as though it were a thick rubber. He rubbed and massaged his hand when he was alone to bring the circulation back, and he really knew what was the matter although he hardly admitted it even to himself.

A few months ago he had fainted, just for a moment, and the doctor had read his blood pressure and told him to take it easy and he'd be all right. And two weeks ago another thing had happened. There had been an electric flash in his head behind his eyes, a feeling like a blinding blue-white glare for a second, and now he couldn't read any more. It wasn't that he couldn't see. He saw clearly enough, but the words on a page swam and ran together and squirmed like snakes, and he couldn't make out what they said.

He knew very well he had had two little strokes, but it was a secret he kept from his wife and she kept from him and the doctor kept from both. And he waited, waited for another one, the one that would flash in his mind, would flash through his body, and if it didn't kill him, it would numb out all feeling. Knowing it had made him angry, angry at everyone. Physical hatred of everyone around him crowded in his throat.

He tried on all possible glasses. He used magnifying glasses on the newspapers because he himself, with half of his mind, was trying to keep his condition secret from himself. His angers had a habit now of bursting from him without warning, but the real horror to him was that he cried, uncontrollably sometimes, and couldn't stop. Recently he had awakened early in the morning saying to himself, "Why should I wait for it?"

His father had died of the same thing, but before he died he had lain like a gray, helpless worm in a bed for eleven months, and all the money he had saved for his old age was spent on doctor bills. Van Brunt knew that if the same thing happened to him the eight thousand dollars he had in the bank would be gone, and his old wife would have nothing after she buried him.

As soon as the drugstores opened that day, he went in to see his friend Milton Boston of the Boston Drug Store.

"I've got to poison some squirrels, Milton," he said. "Give me a little cyanide, will you?"

"That's damn dangerous stuff," Milton said. "I kinda hate to sell it. Let me give you some strychnine. It'll do the job just as well."

"No," Van Brunt said, "I've got a government bulletin with a new formula and it calls for cyanide."

Milton said, "Well, all right. You'll have to sign the poison book, of course. But look out for that stuff, Van. Look out for it. Don't leave it around."

They'd been friends for many years. They'd gone in the Blue Lodge together and had been through the Chairs, and in succeeding years they had been Worshipful Master of the San Ysidro Lodge, and then Milton went into the Royal Arch and the Scottish Rite and Van Brunt never went beyond the third degree. But they had remained friends.

"How much of the stuff do you want?"

"About an ounce, I guess."

"That's an awful lot, Van."

"I'll bring back what I don't use."

Milton was worried. "Don't touch it at all with your hands, will you?"

"I know how to handle it," Van Brunt said.

Then he went into his office in the basement of his house, and with a sharp pocketknife he pricked the back of his hand. When there was a little blood coming out, he opened the glass tube of crystals. And then he stopped. He couldn't do it. He just couldn't tip the crystals into the cut.

After an hour he took the tube to the bank and put it in his safety-deposit box along with his will and his insurance policies. He thought of buying a little ampule to wear around his neck. Then, if the big one came, he could maybe get it to his mouth the way those people in Europe did. But he couldn't take it now. Maybe it wouldn't happen.

There was a weight of disappointment on him, and there was anger in him too. All the people around him who weren't going to die angered him. And there was another thing that bothered him. The stroke had knocked the cap off one set of his inhibitions. He had suddenly reachieved powerful desires. He was pantingly drawn toward young women, even little girls. He couldn't keep his eyes and his thought from them, and in the midst of his sick desires he would burst into tears. He was afraid, as a child is afraid of a strange house.

He was too old to accommodate the personality change of his stroke and the new nature it gave him. He had never been a reader, but now that he could not read he was famished for reading. And his temper grew sharper and more violent all the time until people he had known for years began to avoid him.

He listened to time passing in his veins and he wanted death to come and he was afraid of it. Through half-shut eyes he saw the golden light of the sunset come into the bus. His lips moved a little and he said, "Evening, evening, evening." The word was very beautiful, and he could hear the whistling in his heart. A fullness of feeling came on him, swelled in his chest, swelled in his throat, pulsed in his head. He thought he was going to cry again. He tried to clench his right hand, but it was asleep and it wouldn't clench.

And then he became rigid with tension. His body seemed distended, like a blown-up rubber glove. The evening light blazed in. In back of his eyes a terrible flickering flash came. He felt himself tumbling and tumbling toward grayness and toward darkness and into black, black. . . .

The sun touched the western hills and flattened itself, and its light was yellow and clear. The saturated valley glittered under the level light. The clean, washed air was crisp. In the fields the flattened grain and the thick, torpid stems of the wild oats tightened themselves, and the sheathed petals of the golden poppies loosened a little. The yellow river boiled and swirled and cut viciously at the banks. In the back seat of the bus Van Brunt snored hoarsely against his palate. His forehead was wet. His mouth was open and so were his eyes.

Chapter 20

PIMPLES moved into the seat beside Norma and she gathered her skirts daintily against her and slid a little toward the window.

"What do you suppose that old guy wants with that girl?" he asked suspiciously.

"I don't know," said Norma. "But I tell you one thing. She can handle him. She's a wonderful girl."

Pimples said, "Oh, I don't know. There's other wonderful girls."

Norma flared up. "Like who?" she said, derisively.

"Like you," said Pimples.

"Oh!" She hadn't expected this. She put her head down and stared at her laced fingers, trying to regain her balance.

"What did you have to go and quit for?" Pimples said.

"Well, Mrs. Chicoy wasn't nice to me."

"I know. She isn't nice to anybody. But I wish you didn't quit. We could have got together, maybe."

Norma didn't answer. Pimples said, "If you say the word I'll get out one of the raisin pies. They're pretty nice."

"No. No, thanks. I couldn't eat anything."

"You sick?"

"No."

"Well, if you'd only come back to work at the Corners we could maybe go into San Ysidro Saturday nights and dance and stuff like that."

"You didn't think of that before," she said.

"I didn't think you liked me."

She became a little arch now. This was a delightful game. "What makes you think I like you now?" she said.

"Well, you're different now. You kinda changed. I like the way you done your hair."

"Oh, that," she said. "Well, there wasn't any reason to kinda fix myself up back at the lunchroom. Who'd see me?"

"I would," Pimples said gallantly. "Come on back. They'll give you your job again. I guarantee that."

She shook her head. "No, when I quit, I quit. I don't go crawling back. Besides, there's a future. We've got plans."

"What kind of plans?"

Norma wondered whether she ought to tell. In some ways it was bad luck, but she found she couldn't help herself. "We're going to get a little apartment with a nice davenport and a radio. And we're going to have a stove and an icebox and I'm going to study to be a dental nurse." Her eyes were shining.

"Who's 'we'?"

"Me and Miss Camille Oaks, that's who. When I'm a dental nurse I can dress good and we'll go to shows and maybe give little dinners."

"Nuts," he said. "You won't never do that."

"What makes you say that?"

"You just won't. Now, why don't you come back to the Corners? I'm studying radar and we'll go out together sometimes and you can't tell—we might get together. You take a girl—she's gonna want to get married. I'm a young guy. It's—er—it's good for a young guy to have a wife. It gives him kind of—ambition."

Norma looked into his face, a level, questioning look, to see whether he was making fun of her. And there was something so direct in her look that Pimples misinterpreted it and glanced away in embarrassment.

"I know," he said bitterly. "You think you couldn't go with a guy that's got these things. I done everything. I spent over a hundred dollars going to doctors and for stuff at the drugstore. But it don't do no good. There was one doctor says they won't last. He says they'll go away in a couple more years. But I don't know if that's the truth. Go ahead," he said fiercely. "Get your damn apartment. Maybe I got ways of having fun you never heard of. I don't have to take no guff from nobody." His voice was completely miserable and he stared down into his lap.

Norma looked at him in amazement. She had never known this kind of abject pain in anyone but herself. No one ever needed Norma for sympathy or reassurance. A bubble of warmth burst in her and a kind of gratefulness.

She said, "Don't you think like that. You don't have to, because if a girl cared for you she wouldn't think like that. The doctor knew what he was talking about. I knew three other young fellows, and them things went away after a while."

Pimples kept his head down. There was still misery in him but an imp was stirring too. He felt the advantage coming to his side and he began to use it, and it was a new thing to him, a new discovery. Always he had blustered with girls and bragged, and this was so easy. A sly imp began to operate.

"Well, it just gets so you can't stand it," he said. "Sometimes I think I'll just kill myself." He forced a half sob.

"Now don't you say like that," said Norma. This was a new function for her too, but one she fitted into probably better than any other.

"Nobody likes me," Pimples said. "Nobody won't have nothing to do with me."

"Don't you say like that," Norma repeated. "It's not true. I always liked you."

"No, you never."

"I did too." She laid her hand on his arm in reassurance.

Blindly he reached up and held her hand against his arm. And then his hand clasped hers and he squeezed her fingers and automatically she squeezed back. He turned in his seat and flung his arms about her and pushed his face into hers.

"Don't!" she cried. "Stop that!"

He gripped her more tightly.

"Stop it," she said. "Stop it. That old man back there."

Pimples whispered, "Listen to the old bastard snore. He's pounding his ear. Come on, come on."

She wedged her elbows against his chest to hold him away. His hands began plucking at her skirt. "Stop," she whispered. "You just stop." She knew now that she had been tricked. "Stop it! Let me get out of here!"

"Come on," he said frantically. "Please come on." Pimples' eyes were glazed and he was fighting with her skirt.

"Stop it, please stop. Suppose—suppose Camille came in? Suppose she saw what you're—"

Pimples' eyes cleared for a moment. He looked at her evilly. "Suppose she did. What do you care what that god-damned tramp sees?"

Norma's mouth fell open and her muscles relaxed. She looked at him in unbelief. She looked at him as though she hadn't heard what he said. Then her rage was cold and murderous. Her work-hardened muscles set rigidly. She tore her hand free and hit him in the mouth. She leaped to her feet and swung at him with both her fists, and he was so startled that he covered his face with his hands to protect himself.

She was spitting at him like a cat. "You skunk!" she said. "Oh, you dirty little skunk." And she kicked and shoved and pushed him out into the aisle, and she ran up the aisle and out of the bus. His feet were tangled in the stanchions of the seats and he tried to roll over.

A sickness and a weakness came over Norma. Her lips were quivering and her eyes were streaming. "Oh, the dirty skunk," she cried. "The filthy, dirty skunk."

She crossed the ditch and flung herself down in the grass and put her head down on her arms. Pimples got to his feet and peeked out the window. He didn't know what in the world to do.

Camille, walking slowly back along the road, saw Norma lying face down in the grass. She stepped across the ditch and leaned over her. "What's the matter? Did you fall down? What's the matter with you?"

Norma raised her tearful face. "I'm all right," she said.

"Get up," said Camille shortly. "Get up out of that wet grass." She reached down and jerked Norma to her feet and led her under the cliff and sat her down on the folded newspapers. "Now, what in the hell is the matter with you?"

Norma wiped her wet face with her sleeve and destroyed the last of her lipstick. "I don't want to talk about it."

"Well, that's your business," said Camille.

"That Pimples. He grabbed me."

"Well, can't you take care of yourself? Do you have to pull a nosedive?"

"That wasn't why."

"Well, what was why?" Camille wasn't really interested. She had her own troubles.

Norma rubbed her red eyes with her fingers. "I hit him," she said. "I hit him because he said you was a tramp."

Camille looked quickly away. She stared across the valley where the last of the sun was disappearing behind the mountains and she rubbed her cheek with her hand. Her eyes were dull. And then she forced them to take on life and she forced them to smile and she gave the smile to Norma.

"Look, kid," she said. "You'll just have to believe this until you find it out for yourself—everybody's a tramp some time or other. Everybody. And the worst tramps of all are the ones that call it something else."

"But you aren't."

"Let it lay," said Camille. "Just let it lay. Come on, let's try to do something with your face. New lipstick isn't as good as a bath but it's better than nothing."

Camille opened her purse and dug into it and got out a comb.

Chapter 21

JUAN quickened his footsteps so that Mildred had trouble keeping up with him.

"Do we have to run?" she asked.

"It'll be a lot easier digging the bus out while it's still light than floundering around in the dark."

She trotted along beside him. "Do you think you can get it out?"

"Yes."

"Well, why didn't you do that in the first place instead of walking away?"

He slowed his footsteps for a moment. "I told you," he said. "I told you twice."

"Oh, yes. You really meant that, then."

"I really mean everything," said Juan.

They came to the bus after the sun had slipped below the range. But the high clouds were lighted with rose and they threw a rose transparency over the land and the hills.

Pimples skulked out from behind the bus when Juan approached. There was a hostile cringing about him. "When are they coming out?" he asked.

"I can't get anyone," Juan said shortly. "We'll have to do it ourselves. We're going to need help. Where the hell is everybody?"

"Scattered around," said Pimples.

"Well, get out the tarpaulin."

"That lady's got it laying down up there."

"Well, get her up. I want rocks if you can find any and I want planks or some posts. We may have to tear down some fence. But leave the barbed wire up so the stock won't get out. And, Pimples—"

Pimples' mouth dropped open and his shoulders sagged. "You said—"

"Get all the men. I'm going to need help. I'll get the big jack out from under the back seat."

Juan climbed into the bus. It was a little dark in the bus

now. He saw Van Brunt lying on the seat. "You'll have to move so I can get the jack," he said.

Suddenly Juan leaned close. The eyes of the old man were open and rolled up, and a harsh, labored snoring came from his mouth, and there was spittle around the corners of his mouth. Juan turned him over on his back and his tongue fell into his throat and his in-breathing was plugged. Juan reached into the open mouth with his fingers and pushed the tongue down and forward. He shouted, "Pimples! Pimples!" and with his free hand he knocked on the window with his gold wedding ring.

Pimples climbed into the bus.

"This man's sick, goddammit. Call some help. Blow the horn."

It was Mr. Pritchard who took over Van Brunt. He hated it and yet he had to do it. Juan cut a little piece of stick and showed him how to hold down the tongue and wedge the stick against the roof of the mouth so that the old man could breathe. Mr. Pritchard was revolted by the look of the man, and the sour odor that came from the laboring chest sickened him. But he had to do it. He didn't want to think about anything. His mind wanted to stop. A series of chilling agonies ran through him. His wife came into the bus and saw him and took the first seat inside the door, as far from him as possible. And even in the dusky light he could see the scratches and the blood on her collar. She didn't speak to him.

He said in his mind, "I must have been crazy. I don't know how I could have done it. Dear, can't you just think I was sick, out of my head?" He said it in his head. He would give her the little orchid house, and not such a little one. He'd build her the finest orchid house money could buy. But he couldn't even mention it for a long time. And the Mexican trip—they would have to go through with it. It would be horrible, but they would have to go through with it. How long would it be before the look would go out of her eyes, the reproach, the hurt, the accusation? She wouldn't speak for several days, he knew, or when she did it would be with perfect politeness; short replies and a sweet voice, and her eyes would not meet his. "Oh, God," he thought, "how do I get into these things? Why can't it be me here, dying, instead of this old man? He's never going to have to go through anything again."

He felt the men working under him on the bus. He heard the shovel bite and the suck of mud and he heard the stone thrown under the wheels. His wife sat stiffly and her lips were set in a tolerant smile. He didn't know yet how she was going to handle the situation, but it would come to her.

She was sad and she said to herself, "I must think no evil. Just because Elliott went down under a brutishness is no reason for me to lose beauty and toleration." There was a flicker of triumph in her. "I have conquered anger," she whispered, "and I have conquered disgust. I can forgive him, I know I can. But for his own sake it must not be too soon—for his own good. I'll have to wait." Her face was full of dignity and hurt.

Outside, Pimples was performing miracles of muscle and fortitude. His two-toned oxfords were destroyed with mud. Almost purposely he destroyed them. There was a layer of mud on his chocolate trousers. He violated his fine clothes. He drove his shovel into the earth and dug down behind the wheels and underneath the sides and he threw the mud out. He got down on his knees in the mud to use his hands. His wolf eyes glittered with effort and the sweat stood out on his forehead. Out of the corner of his eye he watched Juan. Juan had forgotten, and just at a time when Pimples needed him most. Pimples drove his shovel into the ground with gusty bursts of strength.

Ernest Horton took a pickax and crossed the ditch. He picked away the turf and roots and topsoil until he found what he wanted. The broken stone from the ancient crash of the hill. He lifted the stones out and piled them on the grass beside his hole.

Camille came over to him. "I'll help you carry some of these down."

"You'll get all dirty," said Ernest.

"You think I can get any dirtier than I am?" she asked.

He rested the pick head on the ground. "You wouldn't like to give me your phone number? I'd take you out."

"That was the truth," said Camille. "I don't live any place yet. I haven't got a number."

"Have it your own way," said Ernest.

"No, this is straight. Where are you going to stay?"

"Hollywood Plaza," said Ernest.

"Well, if you're in the lobby about seven o'clock day after tomorrow, I might come by."

"Fair enough," said Ernest. "I'll take you to Musso-Franck's for dinner."

"I didn't say I would," she said. "I said I might. I don't know how I'm going to feel. If I don't show up, don't drop your watch. I'm too pooped to figure anything out."

"Fair enough," said Ernest. "I'll stick around till seven-thirty."

"You're a good guy," said Camille.

"I'm just another sucker," said Ernest. "Don't take those big ones. I'll bring those. You take the little ones."

She picked a rock up in each hand and walked toward the bus.

Juan went to the old fence and tore the posts out of the earth. He tore down eight of them, but alternate posts, so that the barbed wire would not fall down. He carried the posts down and went back for more.

The rose afterglow was turning pale pink and a duskiness settled on the valley. Juan set his jack against a post and under the flange of the wheel rim, and he lifted one side of the bus. As the wheel rose, Pimples filled the hole under the tires with rocks.

Juan took another bite and lifted again, and gradually one side of the bus rose out of the mud. Juan moved his jack to the other side and raised the other wheel.

Camille and Norma were carrying rocks to fill the holes, while Ernest dug them out.

Mildred asked, "What can I do?"

"Steady this post while I get a new pinch," said Juan. He was working furiously against the coming dark. His forehead was glistening with sweat. Pimples, on his knees in the mud, packed rocks under the wheels, and the other side of the bus rose out of the mud.

"Let's get it extra high," said Juan, "so we won't have to do it all over again. I'd like to have these posts in under the wheels."

It was almost dark when they were ready. Juan said, "I want

everybody to give a push when I start. If we can just make three feet we'll be all right."

"How's the road ahead?" Pimples asked.

"It looked all right to me. God! You raised hell with your clothes."

Pimples' face was sick with disappointment. "It don't amount to nothing," he said. "What good is clothes?" His tone was so despondent that Juan stared at him in the half darkness.

A tight smile raised Juan's lips. "You'll have to take charge back here, Kit, while I drive. Make them throw their weight on it when I go ahead. You know how. You take charge back here, Kit."

Pimples threw down his shovel. "Come on, everybody," he shouted. "Come on, snap into it! I'll take the right side. Girls too. Everybody got to shove." He marshaled his people at the back of the bus. For a second he looked hungrily at Mrs. Pritchard sitting inside. "She'd just be in the way, I guess," he said.

Juan climbed into the bus. "Get out and give a shove," he said to Mr. Pritchard.

The engine started easily enough. Juan let it turn over for a moment. He eased it into compound-low and then he knocked twice on the side of the bus and heard Pimples knock back twice on the rear wall. He speeded his engine a little and let his clutch in. The wheels caught, slipped, groaned, and caught, and "Sweetheart" waddled drunkenly over the bed of rocks and climbed out onto the road. Juan pulled ahead out of the mud on the road and then he set his hand brake. He stood up and looked out the doorway.

"Just pile the tools in here on the floor," he said. "Come on, let's get moving."

He turned on his lights and the beam lighted the gravel road as far as the top of the little hill.

Chapter 22

JUAN took the bus very slowly over the hill and down the water-scarred gravel road past the deserted house. As he turned, his headlights picked out the eyeless house and the broken windmill and the barn.

The night was very black, but a new breeze had come up, bearing the semenous smell of grass and the spice of lupine. The headlights tunneled the night over the road and an owl flew flashing in and out of the light. Far ahead a rabbit crossing the road looked into the lights so that its eyes glowed red, and then it hopped clear into the ditch.

Juan kept the bus in second gear and missed the water-scored ruts with his wheels. The inside of the bus was dark except for the dash lights. Juan let his eyes dart to the Virgin. "I ask only one thing," he said in his mind. "I gave up the other, but it would be nice if you could make it so she was sober when I get back."

Mrs. Pritchard was not rigid any more. Her head swayed with the movement of the bus and she was dreaming. She was dressed in—what—what would she have on? Something light. It would have to be white. And she was taking Ellen through her little orchid house. "You wonder why I keep a few purple orchids?" she asked Ellen. "Well, everybody has relatives who like purple ones. Even you have, Ellen, you know that. But look over here. These are just coming—the lovely browns and greens. Elliott ordered those from Brazil. They came from a thousand miles up the Amazon."

On the floor of the bus the pickax clinked against the shovel.

Pimples leaned close to Juan's ear. "I could take her over, Mr. Chicoy. You're tired out. I'll drive if you want."

"No, thanks, Kit, you've had enough."

"But I ain't tired."

"It's all right," said Juan.

Mildred could see Juan's profile against the lighted road. "I wonder how long I can make the day last. Like a peppermint stick. I'll have to hold onto today until I can get another one as good."

Over the banging and the bouncing of the bus Mr. Pritchard listened for the breathing of Van Brunt. He could just barely see the face against the seat. He found that he hated this man because he was dying. He inspected his hatred in amazement. He felt that he could strangle this man easily and get it over with. "What kind of a thing am I?" he cried. "What makes these horrible things in me? Am I going crazy? Maybe I've been working too hard. Maybe this is a nervous breakdown."

He leaned close to make sure that the breathing of the sick man was not cut off. There would be a bad bruise in the roof of his mouth where the stick was wedged. He heard a little stir and saw that Ernest Horton had come back and taken the next seat.

"You want me to take over?"

"No," said Mr. Pritchard. "I guess everything's all right. What do you suppose it is?"

"It's a stroke," said Ernest. "I didn't mean to blast you today. I was just nervous."

"Just one of those days," said Mr. Pritchard. "When things are pretty bad my wife says, 'It'll be funny some time.' "

"Well, that's a good way to look at it if you can do it," said Ernest. "I'll be at the Hollywood Plaza if you want to give me a call. Or try that apartment some night—that number I gave you."

"I'm going to be all tied up, I'm afraid," said Mr. Pritchard. "I wish you'd look in at the plant some time, though. We might do business yet."

"We might at that," said Ernest.

Norma sat next to the window now and Camille was by her side. Norma leaned her elbow on the window sill and looked out at the fluttering dark. There was a little rim of lighter sky around the edge of a great dark cloud over the western mountains, and then as the cloud lifted the evening star shone out of it, clear and washed and steady.

"Star light, star bright, first star I see tonight, wish I may, wish I might, get the wish I wish tonight."

Camille turned her head sleepily. "What did you say?"

Norma was silent for a moment. Then she asked softly, "We'll see how it goes?"

"Yeah, we'll see how it goes," said Camille.

Far ahead and a little to the left a cluster of lights came into view—little lights winking with distance, lost and lonely in the night, remote and cold and winking, strung on chains.

Juan looked at them and called, "That's San Juan up ahead."

BURNING BRIGHT

A Play in Story Form

Tyger! Tyger! burning bright
In the forests of the night,
What immortal hand or eye
Could frame thy fearful symmetry?

—WILLIAM BLAKE

To,
for,
and because of
Elaine

Contents

Foreword

Burning Bright is the third attempt I have made to work in this new form—the play-novelette. I don't know that anyone else has ever tried it before. Two of my previous books—*Of Mice and Men* and *The Moon Is Down*—essayed it. In a sense it is a mistake to call it a new form. Rather it is a combination of many old forms. It is a play that is easy to read or a short novel that can be played simply by lifting out the dialogue.

My reasons for wanting to write in this form are several and diverse. I find it difficult to read plays, and in this I do not find myself alone. The printed play is read almost exclusively by people closely associated with the theater, by students of the theater, and by the comparatively small group of readers who are passionately fond of the theater. The first reason for this form, then, is to provide a play that will be more widely read because it is presented as ordinary fiction, which is a more familiar medium.

The second reason for the creation of the play-novelette is that it augments the play for the actor, the director, and the producer, as well as the reader. The usual description of a character in a play—"Businessman, aged forty"—gives them very little to go on. It can be argued that with this terse description the burden of character portrayal must lie in the dialogue and in seeing the actor onstage. It can further be argued that terse description gives the director and the set designer greater leeway in exercising their own imagination in production.

Against these arguments it can be said, first, that it can do no harm for theatergoers or theater people to have the fullest sense of the intention of the writer; and, second, that director, actor, and set designer cannot be limited, and may even be helped, by a full knowledge of the details pertinent to the action. And for the many people who have not seen the play, and will never see it, this becomes an aid to which they are entitled.

It is generally accepted that writers of regular fiction do not care, or are not able, to submit themselves to the discipline of the theater. They do not wish to keep the action within the boundaries of the proscenium arch; they do not wish to limit themselves to curtains and to scenes projected by dialogue alone. The usual play, then, would seem to be highly confining—and so it is. There must be no entrance into the thoughts of a character unless those thoughts are clearly exposed in the dialogue. People cannot wander around geographically unless the writer has provided some physical technique for making such wanderings convincing onstage. The action must be close-built, and something must have happened to the characters when the curtain has been lowered on the final line. These working principles are applicable both to the regular play form and to the play-novelette. There is one further limitation. The piece must be short.

On the rewarding side of the picture lie the concentration and discipline of the theater and the impossibility of setting down any vaguenesses either intellectual or physical. You must be clear and concise. There can be no waste, no long discussion, no departure from a main theme, and little exposition. As in any good play, the action must be immediate, dynamic, and dramatic resolution must occur entirely through the characters themselves.

The difficulties of the technique are very great. The writer whose whole training has lain in the play is content to leave physical matters to his director or set designer and has not learned to use description as a fiction writer does. On the other hand, the fiction writer has been trained to let his description pick up his dialogue, and he tends to depart from the tight structure of the theater. If a writer is not accustomed to *seeing* his story before his eyes, his use of this form is not likely to be successful.

Despite its difficulty, the play-novelette is highly rewarding. It gives a play a wide chance of being read and a piece of fiction a chance of being played without the usual revision. I think it is a legitimate form and one that can stand a great deal of exploration.

JOHN STEINBECK

ACT ONE

The Circus

THE canvas walls of the dressing tent were discolored with brown water spots, with green grass stains and grey streaks of mildew, and the prickles of sun glittering came through. On the ground the close-cut barley stubble stood in bunches with the black 'dobe earth between. Near to one cloth wall there was a large and travel-beaten trunk with dull brass straps and corners, its lid upraised and a mirror the whole size of the top disclosed.

Joe Saul sat on a folding canvas chair before the trunk. He was naked to the waist but he had on tights and slippers. He dabbed the yellow powder on his face and painted his eyes with black—not carefully.

A lithe and stringy man of middle age, Joe Saul. His jaws muscled against strain and cables down the sides of his neck. His arms were white and blue-veined, with the long cords of clinging and hanging rather than the lumps of lifting. His hands were white, the fingers spatulate, and palms and fingers calloused from the rope and bar.

Joe Saul's face was rough and a little pock-marked; his eyes looked large and dark and glittering within their penciled edges. He finished his make-up and took a little bottle of dark hair dye from the trunk, poured some on a brush and worked the stain into his thick, graying hair, particularly at the temples. Then neatly he packed his powder and bottles back in the trunk and slipped on the shirt of his tights and cinched his canvas belt. Only a small bulge showed over the belt. He leaned back in his chair and flexed his hands, so that the thin muscles of his forearms squirmed.

From outside the dressing room came sounds of the developing show—call of barker and skirl of calliope and thin waltz of merry-go-round backed by the chutter of gathering people. And nearer sounded grunts of lions and whoosh of elephants, grunt and squeal of pigs and discontented snort of horses against the brass wail of a circus trombone.

And Joe Saul flexed his hands and looked down at them. From outside the flap came three short whistles in place of knocking.

"Come in," said Joe Saul, and Friend Ed stepped through the flap. Friend Ed was broader, taller, heavier, than Joe Saul, slower in motion and speech. He was dressed and made up too, a big pants clown ruffed at neck, wrists, and ankles, white suit with big red polka dots, and feet as long and curved as barrel staves: a white face, red rubber nose, sad black mouth and black lines over the eyelids. High on his forehead were painted the inverted V's of astonishment. He had created on his face a look of surprised perplexity. Only his thick dark hair and hands were his own. He carried the bald head with fringe of bright red hair and the big false hands.

Joe Saul closed the trunk lid to make a place for him to sit, and Friend Ed dropped his hair piece and his false hands on the trunk and seated himself on its edge and swung his big floppy clown foot gently back and forth.

"Where's Mordeen?" he asked.

"She went to sit with Mrs. Malloy's baby," said Joe Saul. "Mrs. Malloy's gone off to the post office to send a money order to her son Tom," he said monotonously. "Her son Tom, '*my-son-Tom.*' He's in college, you know." Joe Saul sat up tight-straight. "I'm sure, Friend Ed, I don't tell you for the first time that Mrs. Malloy has got a son Tom that's in college and only nineteen. Did you hear about that, Friend Ed? Did you hear about it twenty thousand times?"

Friend Ed opened his black mouth so that the red inner lips and little white teeth showed. "Don't curse him, Joe Saul," he said. "Or her."

"Who's cursing?" Joe Saul leaned back and flexed his hands on his knees. "She's a nice woman," he said. "And I guess if you've got a son Tom in college you've got a little fringe of God Almighty on your head, but I wouldn't curse her. I'm glad for her. She's a nice woman."

"Now look, Joe Saul, you're nervy."

"No."

Friend Ed glanced down at the flexing hands. "That's a new thing, you're doing there. That's a nervy thing." His foot stopped its swinging.

Joe Saul looked at his hands. "I didn't know I was doing it," he said. "But you are right, Friend Ed. I've got a rustle in me. It's a little itching rustle under my skin."

"I see it coming on you, Joe Saul. It's not a thing of surprise to me except it's late. It's very late—I wonder why so late. Three years it is since Cathy died. You were strong in your wife-loss. You were not nervy then. And it's eight months since Cousin Will missed the net. You were not nervy then. Victor's a good partner, isn't he? You said he was. And it's not the first time a Saul missed the net in all the generations. What's the matter with you, Joe Saul? You're putting an itch in the air around you like a cloud of gnats in a hot evening."

Joe Saul flexed his hands, looked at them, and then he grappled them together to keep them still. "Victor's all right," he said. "Maybe better than Cousin Will. It's what you get used to. I could feel the tuning of Cousin Will. I knew his breathing and his pulse. Cousin Will was my blood and my being; we were the products of a thousand years, the end products. I have to think about Victor, think about what he'll do. I could feel Cousin Will in my nerve ends. Maybe I'll get used to Victor, but he's a stranger. His blood is not my blood. He has no ancestry in it."

Outside the tent a band struck up, playing an overture fast and hot.

"Is Mordeen made up, Joe Saul?"

"Sure. She wouldn't have gone else." His hands flexed again in spite of him, and Friend Ed noticed it.

"Is it your nerve? I've seen that happen. Do you fear for your hands? I knew a man once going blind and he ran about looking at color, looking and staring so he'd remember. He was afraid he might forget what color was like when he was blind. Do your hands trouble you?"

"I don't think so. Why should they? They've never slipped or lost their grip."

Friend Ed leaned over and touched Joe Saul on the shoulder. "Do I have the friend-right to ask a question, Joe Saul?"

"Always."

"Is there any trouble with Mordeen?"

"No—oh, no!"

"You're sure?"

"I'm—sure."

"It's a fine girl, Joe Saul, a fine wife. See you remember it. She's young—but very good. See you never doubt that. No man ever had better. Don't compare her with your Cathy—she's different but just as good, and lovely and true."

"I know."

"What I came to say is this. I'm having a little birthday party for the twins. They wanted only kids, but they asked for you and for Mordeen. Will you come and bring some little twist of a present?"

"Do they really ask for me?"

"They did—and will you keep your god-damned hands still?"

Joe Saul leaped up, and his slippers rustled in the stubble. He paced, holding his hands against their restlessness in front of him. He bit his underlip.

Friend Ed spoke quietly. "I'll take some of the itch from you, if you'll let me. I held you weeping when your Cathy died. I lifted Cousin Will off the ring rim, and I stood left hand to you with Mordeen. I think I know your sickness but you will have to say it first, Joe Saul."

The pacing stopped. "She's taking a long time to get a money order," he said. "I think you do know. I think your twins know. I wonder—whether Mordeen knows."

"Will you say it, then, for your mind's rest and your hands' peace? Maybe there's some kind of answer."

Joe Saul sighed. "I wonder is it age coming on me? I think of old times. They say old men think back. I think of my grandfather talking—that was after his hands were gone weak, and his timing gone and the certainty of his eye. When it didn't matter any more, he'd drink wine in the afternoon. He'd lesson us on the training mat, and when we were resting sometimes Grandfather would talk. He did a lot of reading, that old man, and more thinking. Maybe he made up things, but we believed him. You never knew him, Friend Ed."

"No, I never knew him. Talk it out, Joe Saul! Let's find the bitter seed that's like the inside of a peach pit."

Joe Saul sat in his chair and leaned back, thinking. "We were real proud kids," he said, "with one hip up and our chests stuck out. We believed everything he said because he was Old Joe Saul. I'm named for him. He used to say that we were nature spirits once—you know, in trees and streams. We lived in the wind and in the black storms. 'That's what your great-granddads were,' he'd say. Remember how white his hair was? No—you never saw him. Then he said we were the first doctors, but witch doctors. We troubled the waters and drove the thunder back over the edge, and we jumped like the streams over rocks, and we sailed—arms out—like the wind.

"Well, then he said we were doctors against hurt, and we had to make the form of hurt and sickness to drive it out, so that we were crooked for fits and spastic for poison, and we bent like rubber for a broken leg. He had it all down, and we'd squat and listen on the training mat." And Joe Saul squatted beside his chair to show how it was.

"It's a strange telling for children," Friend Ed interposed. "Would you sometime tell it to the twins?"

"Of course I will. The twins have the blood. They'd understand. Old Joe Saul said then in Greece we wore high shoes and wooden masks and we were gods. He said in Rome we tumbled in the red sand of the arena after the blood had run, and we juggled burning sticks in front of the set-up crosses and their burdens.

"Then in the dark centuries, he said, we laughed and played in the miracles, and we were the only gay in that laughter-starving time. From then on, he said, everybody knows."

"I'll want the twins to hear," said Friend Ed.

"I told you he'd drink a little in the afternoon when he didn't go up any more and it didn't matter. Kings, he'd say, princes, counts, Astors, Vanderbilts, or Tudors, Plantagenets, Pendragons for that matter—who knows their great-granddads with any certainty? Old Joe Saul would stand there, tall and one finger out like a dry stick. He had a full head of hair and every tooth his own. He'd stand there, a white cloud, and we were proud kids squatting on the mat, all knee and elbow burned from the workout.

" 'Two ancient families there are,' he'd say, 'known and sure and recognized—and only two. Clowns and acrobats. The rest are newcomers.' "

Friend Ed breathed deep with satisfaction. "You can tell the twins at their birthday party, after the cake."

Joe Saul's face twisted with remembering now. He stood

and his hands went to their gripping. "And he'd say to us, 'Have kids—have lots of kids! Be not ever without a baby on the fingers, a child on the mat, and a boy on the bar.' He'd scowl down on us sitting there."

Joe Saul was silent, and Friend Ed was silent. The sound of lightly tripping, snorting ring horses came through the tent. Friend Ed looked strongly at Joe Saul. "There's your bitter seed," he said. "There it is. Cathy had no child—but Mordeen?"

"It's been three years," Joe Saul said. "Three years."

"Do you begin to think it's you?"

"I don't know what it is—I don't know what it is. But a man can't die this way."

"Nor a woman either."

Joe Saul cried, "A man can't scrap his blood line, can't snip the thread of his immortality. There's more than just my memory. More than my training and the remembered stories of glory and the forgotten shame of failure. There's a trust imposed to hand my line over to another, to place it tenderly like a thrush's egg in my child's hand. You've given your blood line to the twins, Friend Ed. And now—three years with Mordeen."

"Maybe it's you should go to doctors. There might be a remedy you haven't thought of."

"What do they know?" Joe Saul cried. "There's some dark kind of curse on me, and I feel it."

"On you alone, Joe Saul?" Friend Ed smiled. "Do you feel singled out, pinned up alone in a museum? It's time we sing this trouble out into the air and light. Else it will grow with poisoned fingers like a cancer in your mind. Rip off the cover. Let it out! Maybe you're not alone in your secret cave."

"I know!" Joe Saul said quietly. "I guess I'm getting that way—digging like a mole into my own darkness. Of course, Friend Ed, I know it is a thing that can happen to anyone in any place and time—a farmer or a sailor, or a lineless, faceless Everyone! I know this—and maybe all of these have the secret locked up in loneliness."

"That would do it. And now that I know, I'll try to help. I'll try to think—and help."

Suddenly Joe Saul said nervously, "I wonder what's keeping Mordeen. That's a long time to get a money order. Her baby—Mrs. Malloy's too old to have a baby. She's too old—she's forty-five."

"But she had it," said Friend Ed. And automatically to an unseen, unheard cue he put his hair piece on and smoothed the bald skin over his thick hair and patted the edges down on his forehead just above the incredulous eyebrows. "Now that I know, Joe Saul, I'll try to help. I'm on—" He put on his false hands, shuffled his big feet in a mincing dance step, and flopped out of the tent.

Joe Saul lifted the lid of the trunk and pulled his little chair close and peered at himself in the mirror. He leaned close and inspected his face. Suddenly Friend Ed looked in again. "I didn't mean that—I didn't mean it that way."

"Mean what?"

"I heard it in my ears, the way it sounded when I said, 'But she had it.' I didn't mean it that way, Joe Saul."

"I didn't hear it—that way," Joe Saul said uneasily. "You're on, Friend Ed." And sure enough, the shrill band played the march of elephants and white horses, giraffes and hippopotamuses and pinwheeling clowns. Friend Ed whirled, and the canvas dropped behind him. He called a greeting outside. "Run, Mordeen, he's waiting for you."

Now the flap lifted and Mordeen came in. Her tights were white and silver and over her shoulders she wore a long silver and blue cape which fell in heavy folds to her ankles. Mordeen was fair and very beautiful, her golden hair in short tight curls, her eyes blued, her make-up carefully applied. She was smiling, her face alight with a pleasant memory.

Joe Saul swung around to her, his face dark and serious. "Have you seen Victor, Mordeen?"

"No, I haven't. That baby, Joe Saul, he crows, really crows, and rocks back and forth. He grabbed at a shaft of sunshine with his hand. You should have seen his face when his hand went through it, amazed and disappointed all at once." She laughed and then, seeing him and his posture, "What's the matter, Joe Saul? Aren't you well?"

"I'm all right." He stood up.

"Angry then? You must be angry. Your eyes are so black, but when you are angry they seem to have a red glow. Are you angry with me, Joe Saul?"

He moved very quickly to her and put his arms around her, and there was hunger and eagerness in his body and in his face.

"Not angry," he said. "No, not angry—and still angry." He stroked her cheek. "Angry at Time when you were away. Angry at Time. Irritated with the minutes when you aren't with me."

"I like that," she said. "It's good to be missed. I came back as soon as I could. It's good to be away a little. Then I know how well and strongly I love you."

He strained her tight to him. "I get frightened," he said. "My mind plays games. It whispers that you don't exist. It sneers that you have gone away. It whines to me that there is no Mordeen. It's a cruel, mischievous game."

She was smiling and her voice was sleepy, languourous. "It's a child's game to make good things better," she said. "I remember holding a piece of white cake with black frosting and pretending it was not mine. That was to make it nicer when I tasted it. Now, Joe Saul, that's better. The red is gone out of your eyes. You have the blackest eyes—like new split coal—that black! But you were angry, or very troubled."

"If I was, I am not now," he said. "Everything bad evaporates when I touch you. I love you, Mordeen—starvingly."

"Then you are not satisfied?"

"No—never—I never am. What a dull thing that would be—like the slight, painful sluggishness of an overfull stomach, like too much food or too much sleep. No, you keep me fed and hungry, and that is the best."

She pushed him a little bit away from her so she could look clearly into his face. "Will you tell me what is worrying you, Joe Saul?"

"It's nothing," he said.

"Is it Victor?"

"A little."

"Is it—" she paused—"anything else?"

"No—no."

"Am I a good woman to you?"

He held her tight. "Oh, my God! My God, Mordeen! You're a burning flower in my heart. See—I am harsh breathing like a boy. I'm full of you."

The flap opened again and Victor entered. Joe Saul released Mordeen, slowly and proudly, and turned to face him.

Victor was large and powerful, dark and young. His mouth was full and arrogant, his eyes sullen. He wore flannel slacks and a white T-shirt, and a gold medallion on a golden chain hung at his throat. His skin bloomed with youth. He held his right arm across his stomach, and the wrist was tightly bandaged with surgical tape. He stood defiantly in the entrance. Mordeen slipped quietly around until she stood behind Joe Saul.

As for Joe Saul, he stared at Victor, first with perplexity and then with growing anger.

"Why aren't you ready?" he asked, and then he saw the tape. "What's that?"

Victor put threat and self-sufficiency on his face to cover fear. "I sprained my wrist," he said. "I just came from the doctor."

For a long moment Joe Saul regarded him and then he asked very quietly, "How?"

Victor expected anger. He was not prepared for quietness—he was not braced for quietness. He had been set and poised to repel a rage, he carried rage to defend himself. In the ominous quiet he was off balance and he could not change his pattern of defense.

"No need to get mad," he said loudly. "I couldn't help it. I tell you it was an accident. Might happen to anybody—might happen any time."

Joe Saul turned slowly back and forth like a gun turret, and he was silent. But Victor blustered on. "I was playing, just playing around with some of the fellows—touch football. That's all, just playing, and one guy just put out his foot—didn't mean it. Say, what's the matter with you?" He shifted back uneasily, for Joe Saul had stood up and moved slowly near to him. And Joe Saul's voice recited without rise or fall, monotonously.

"You went to high school in a little town," he said, "Ohio, was it?" He did not wait for an answer. "Athlete, half mile, pole vault, tumbling team. And funny—like a clown. And everyone said that you should be on the stage, wasting your time there in the little town. Ran away with a circus—the old dream, every little boy's escape."

He stopped and licked his lips.

And Victor said, "The doctor says three days. It's only a strained tendon. What are you yelling about?"

Joe Saul went on quietly as though he had not heard. "It isn't that you didn't know but that you can't ever know. If you were a musician, you'd bat a tennis ball with your violin. If you were a surgeon, you'd sharpen pencils with a scalpel."

Victor said, "Don't shout at me!"

Joe Saul said quietly, "It sounds like that to you, does it? You're stronger, quicker, younger, even more sure than Cousin Will, but now I know what it is. Whatever you do is an accident of youth and muscle. You have not the infinite respect for your tools and your profession—Profession! You have made it a trade."

Joe Saul's tone had sharpened in contempt. "And you have not even learned your trade. You did not hang clinging to your father's forefingers. You have no blood in it." He paused uneasily and looked away.

Mordeen moved closer to him, shivering a little at his quietness. And her movement caught Victor's attention and gave him his weapon. Almost with relief he put her up as a shield against the lashing.

"What's the matter—feeling old?" His eyes went to meet Mordeen.

Joe Saul asked blankly, "What?"

Victor pressed forward, like a yammering boy after a hurt cat. "What's the matter—jealous? What's the matter—afraid you can't keep up with a young girl? Is she too much for you?"

Joe Saul was staring at the ground. He sighed and he said softly, "I'll go and report that we can't go on for three days." Slowly he moved very near and struck Victor hard in the face with his open palm. Then he turned and walked lightly on his toes out of the dressing tent.

Mordeen went quickly to the open trunk, dropped her cape over the little chair, sat down and rubbed cold cream on her face. But Victor stood in shock, unable to get over the nausea of the insult. His eyes were glazed with hatred and the inability to put it to violent use. He moved dumbly, nearer to Mordeen.

"I couldn't hit an old man, a man old enough to be my father," he said.

Mordeen rubbed the cold cream into her skin and wiped it off on a little towel. She did not look around.

"You notice I didn't raise a hand against him?" Victor said.

"He knew he was safe. He knew I wouldn't hit him back—an old man like that."

"He can't hear you," Mordeen said. She wiped the eye shadow from around her eyes.

"I wouldn't care if he could. You heard me say the same thing right in his face."

"And I saw what he did to you," said Mordeen.

"I could break him with my hands," said Victor, and with his hands he showed how he could do it. "I could throw him like an old sack. Why, I could crush him—but I didn't. That wouldn't be fair."

Mordeen turned toward him. The yellow and blue and red streaked towel was in her hand. "You're really afraid of him," she said softly.

Victor surged toward her, his chest up and the muscles rippling on his shoulders. "How do you mean afraid? I tell you I could tear him apart."

Mordeen looked at him for a long minute. "Why didn't you then?" she asked.

"Because—" He fought the question because he did not know. Then he formed his answer. His voice grew silky. "Because—I'll tell you why. I have respect for you." He considered his solution. "Because I don't want trouble or fighting when there's a girl I—I am in love with."

Mordeen looked up at him in wonder. "In love with?" Her mouth stayed open after she had said it.

Victor moved closer. He put out his hand to touch her shoulder, but when she looked at his hand he took it away. "I didn't tell you," he said. "I tried to keep it in. I want to be fair. I'm not the kind of guy that creeps on his partner. But he hit me—in the face."

Mordeen said quietly, "You hit him below the belt. That's how fair you are."

Victor began, "I didn't lay a hand—oh, yes," he said, chuckling, "I see what you mean. That got him, didn't it? Next time he whips out that tongue of his, I'll get him again. I know how—now." His lips curled with hatred. He was poisoned with insult. "I don't need to hit him. I can just stand back and punch him with a word. He's old, and you can't get cured of that."

Mordeen smiled up at him. "Besides, you respect and love me," she said sardonically.

Victor shook his head, like a bruised fighter with a steady left hand in his face. And suddenly he fell back on the surest defense there is—none. It was a wrestling tactic to go limp against strain. "I'm a fool," Victor said. "Joe Saul is right. I don't know my ass from a teacup. Of course he's right. But maybe I'll learn. Maybe I'll grow up someday." His face was young and eager. "I admire Joe Saul more than anybody in the world. That's why it hurt so much when he hit me the way you'd hit a dog. That's why I hit back—because I was hurt. That's why I did it.

"Let's start fresh, Mordeen. I'll apologize to Joe Saul. He'll understand why I did it when I tell him how hurt I was. I don't know my ass from a teacup. Coming from high school, being with famous people, trying to be like them when I don't know enough. Why, it's a privilege to be taught by Joe Saul. I know it. I'm sorry I lost myself, Mordeen."

She watched him, believing and not believing, and then deciding to believe because she couldn't see what there was to lose. "I can see how that is," she said. "Oh, I've had things like that happen to me, things that made me dumb and sick. You see, Victor, we're a kind of a little world inside a world. We have a whole life and pattern most people just don't know about. Lots of people resent us or envy us. And so we're proud and maybe a little bit afraid of people. Maybe we protect ourselves too much."

"I see what you mean," he said, although he didn't at all.

"When you argue with a child," she said warmly, "you give a good argument and the child says yah, yah! You understand him and he doesn't listen, so the child wins."

"I see what you mean," he aid softly. A little purr crept into his voice. She looked up for a moment in apprehension. "I see what you mean," he repeated, and the purr was gone.

He hurried on. "I never think of you growing up—here."

"But I did." Her voice was very soft. "My whole life. I was born in a sleeping car, raised in the ring. I rode in a hoodah before I could walk."

Victor's unfortunate choice it was always to mis-see, to mishear, to misjudge. He read softness into her because of the softness of her voice, when she was only remembering. His was the self-centered chaos of childhood. All looks and thoughts, loves and hatreds, were directed at him. Softness was softness toward him, weakness was weakness in the face of his strength. He preheard answers and listened not. He was full colored and brilliant—all outside of him was pale.

"You knew Joe Saul's first wife?" he asked.

"Oh, yes."

"Did Joe Saul love her?"

"Oh, yes! Oh, very yes."

He paused and his lashes fell over his fine eyes. He dropped on one knee so that his eye level was a little below hers. He studied her face, or seemed to—brows, eyes, nose, upper lip well bowed, lower lip full and passionate, tight with exquisite nerves. He spoke softly but with the purr of insinuation in his voice.

"Why did you marry him?"

She raised her head, astonished. "Why?"

"Yes, why? A fifty-year-old man, or nearly, a man near-finished when you've only started. Why did you marry him?"

Mordeen smiled then with kindness at him, smiled almost with affection, as one does when a little boy first asks, "What is God?"

"I married him because—because I loved him."

"That was three years ago. Do you love him now?"

Her lips stood apart as though she listened to faintly heard music outside a summer window. "More," she said. "Much more."

He brought his malformed wisdom, his pool-hall, locker-room, jokebook wisdom to the front. "Joe Saul must be like a father in your mind," he said meanly.

"Oh, no."

He laughed. "I know more about women than you give me credit for," he said. "Isn't it true—you don't have to answer, you don't have to say anything—isn't it true that you sometimes wish for, maybe even crave, the hard arms of a young man and the smooth skin of a young man"—his voice rose—"the force, and body lust, and crushing passion of a young man?"

"No," she said softly. "That is not true. That is not true."

"I don't believe you," he said. "I know more than that."

Her kindness toward him lasted on as though there were enough warm blanket over her life so that she could spare a corner for his shoulders.

"I guess you really don't believe me," she said. "Maybe that will be your sorrow. Maybe sometime in a cold perplexity you'll wonder what you missed, and maybe you'll only be dimly aware of missing something."

"I'm not a baby," he cried. "I've been around. I've known women."

"Happy women?"

"When I got through with them they were happy."

"For how long?"

He boasted, "They weren't happy until they could have me again. They always wanted me again."

"Of course. And they'll be wondering what they missed. I'm not telling any secret—Joe Saul knows that I had some other life. I know the tricks, techniques of duration, of position, games, perverse games to drive the nerves into a kind of hysterical laughter."

Victor's mouth was wet now, and he breathed through his mouth and his tongue went over his lips. "I told you I didn't believe you."

She said, "Joe Saul knows one trick, one ingredient. You haven't heard about it. Maybe you never will. Without that trick you'll one day go screaming silently in loss. Without it there are no good methods or techniques. You know I've wondered how it is that one act can be ugly and mean and enervating, like a punishing drug, and also most beautiful and filled with energy, like milk."

Victor stood up and he spoke with uneasy truculence. "What is this trick that makes a young girl fall in love with Old Joe Saul? Do you think he can do anything I can't do?"

"Yes."

"What is this ingredient?"

"Affection," she said softly. "You have never learned it. Very many people never do."

Victor was uneasy, and he felt failure—that he had been caught in a failure. He said loudly, "You mean I'm not as good a man as Old Joe Saul? Let me try, and I swear to God you'll never go back to him. Ah! we're all alike, men, women. What are you telling me? A jump in the hay is a jump in the hay. What's this breathless thing?"

"All alike," she said. "Surely—all alike. And everyone who hammers out a tune makes great music, and when one rough line rhymes with another that's great poetry, and every daub on canvas is a great painting."

"What are you getting at?" he asked uneasily.

Mordeen said, "I used to wonder why this love seemed sweeter than I had ever known, better than many people ever know. And then one day the reason came to me. There are very few great Anythings in the world. In work and art and emotion—the great is very rare. And I have one of the great and beautiful. Now say your yah, yah, Victor, like a child unanswerably answering Wisdom. You will have to do that, I think."

Victor said, "If it's so goddamn good, why does he have the jerks? Why does he go stepping around like a cat on hot rocks? Why's his temper short and the gray coming into his sick face? Tell me that if it's so goddamn good."

Mordeen had become rigid, her mouth tight and her eyes veiled.

"You do have a gift," she said. "Instinctively you know where to put the knife and how to twist it. I know what you mean, but you don't know. You groped blindly and found a thing as precious as a porcelain doorknob in the dark." She stood up and stepped close to him. Her face was cold and her voice icy. "I want to tell you this," she said. "Maybe I'm telling myself. I will do anything—anything—anything to bring content to him. See you remember that, Victor."

His guard was up now and he wasn't listening; he was only angry because here was a world he could not enter and so he had to disbelieve in its existence. He fell back on the world he knew. He said, "You're setting yourself high. What makes you so special?"

"Joe Saul," she said quickly.

"You're a woman like any other woman—same equipment, no more, no less. Everything else is the same too. You need what every girl in the world needs—a little bit of forcing so you can claim it wasn't your fault. Maybe you need the back of the hand, maybe you need—" He grabbed her in his arms, holding her elbows against her sides. "Maybe you need—me." He leaned over to kiss her and she sagged and relaxed so that, holding her, he could not reach her mouth with his mouth. Her head fell limply away from him and her body hung dead in his arms.

Victor was puzzled now. He had instinctively pinned her arms against resistance. Her eyes were closed, and she was still. Outside the tent flap there were three short whistles instead of knocking. But neither Victor nor Mordeen heard. The whistles were repeated, and then Friend Ed stepped through the flap. His make-up was off but he still wore his polka-dot clown suit. He stood looking at Victor's back. Then slowly he moved toward them.

Victor was worried. "Mordeen," he said, "Mordeen, are you all right?" He released his arms, and as he did, she stepped quickly back away from him. Her face was snarling with hatred and contempt. Then she saw Friend Ed and she stared at him.

Victor looked around and his hand went up protectively. Friend Ed stepped closer. "Go away," he said softly. "Go away now! I'll never tell. I think Joe Saul would kill you."

Victor said, "I didn't—"

"Go away. It wouldn't be good for Joe Saul to kill you—not good for Joe Saul. Even if they didn't catch him he'd carry a sourness all his life. You're not worth that much to him or to me. Tell him you have to leave the show—your mother died, anything. But go!"

"I—you don't know—"

Friend Ed dropped his shoulders and moved closer. "Maybe I'll have to take the sourness myself. Please, please go away!"

Victor said, "Nobody can make me go away." He looked at his taped wrist. "You watch yourself."

"All right, but go away now, go away."

Victor hesitated. "Don't think I'm afraid," he said, but he walked to the flap and disappeared.

Mordeen and Friend Ed watched him go and then they turned sluggishly and looked at each other, and they seemed to look through cloudy water so that they had to stare to see at all. A wall of slowness separated them.

Mordeen said in a dreaming voice, "You saw all that, Friend Ed?"

"Yes, I saw."

"What do you believe?"

"I believe what I saw."

"Do you think Joe Saul would?"

"He would want to—he would have to, and if he couldn't I would try to make him."

Mordeen sighed deeply. She said, "Victor knowing nothing and feeling very little has an instinct for finding frail places and areas of pain. I'm sure he doesn't know anything, and still he feels and probes like a blind leech and he gets blood."

Friend Ed looked at her for a long moment. "Joe Saul reported the act couldn't go on and then he went to a bar. He's getting drunk, Mordeen."

She sat down wearily, started to speak. "I must—" and she was silent.

"Do you want to talk to me?" Friend Ed asked.

"Yes—yes, I do. There's a cloud coming down. I want to talk. He's getting drunk. Is that part of the cloud?"

"Do you know what the cloud is?"

"Yes. Do you?"

"Yes."

Friend Ed asked quickly, "Will you tell me this: can you have a baby?"

Mordeen looked away from him. "Yes, I can."

"How do you know?"

"The only way I could know. I know."

"When did it happen?"

"Five years ago."

"Does Joe Saul know?"

"No, he doesn't. It was before. It was all dead and done, before Joe Saul."

Friend Ed said, "I don't understand it. He hasn't never been sick that I know of. He's a twisting mass of strength and force."

She said softly, "He was sick once. He told me. It was the only time and when he was a boy. Growing pains, they called it. His bones and his joints ached and the fever burned him. For a year he was whipped with pain."

Friend Ed's eyebrows rose. "And you took his account and discovered—"

"Yes, rheumatic fever."

"And could that be the cause?"

"Yes," she said. "It could. It need not but it could." She said passionately, "Can't we tell him? Could we bring this in the open? We need a baby. We can get one, adopt it, and it will be ours. Maybe if this thing were certain and understood the cloud would go away. Maybe—"

"I don't think you can tell him that," Friend Ed said. "I don't think that would be good. Do you know what happens to a man when he knows he is sterile?"

"I know he is miserable now and hungry, starving for a child. I know it has always been, but now it's frantic."

"Is he a good lover?"

"Oh, wonderful! Gentle and fierce and—wonderful."

Friend Ed said quietly, "When the bodies of man and woman meet in love there is a promise—sometimes so deep buried in their cells that thinking does not comprehend—there is a sharp promise that a child may be the result of this earthquake and this lightning. This each body promises the other. But if one or the other knows—knows beyond doubt that the promise can't be kept—the wholeness is not there; the thing is an act, a pretense, a lie, and deeply deep, a uselessness, a thing of no meaning."

"I know," she said.

"How it is with a woman I'm not sure," he continued. "But with a man—perhaps he may feel free because he is in no danger; and perhaps the woman may feel wildly free in lust without consequence, but in her tissues there is contempt for a sterile man. And in a man there is a searching for the contempt he knows is there. Then, no matter how she pretends and protests and covers the sadness of the sterile love, he knows and feels it. And since we do not willingly do futile things, the man's body gradually refuses to perform a useless act, and the woman—oh, very slowly—has no need for him and her senses turn away from the dark double disappointment."

Mordeen looked down at her hands and she said, "I don't think that is so with me. I think I would do anything—anything my mind or heart or body can conceive—to give contentment to Joe Saul."

Friend Ed replied, "That is because he does not know. Once he knows—knows beyond every hiding, boding doubt that his seed is dead—he will not permit you even to try. The fog of his self-contempt will settle over him, and you will not be able ever to find him again in his gray misery."

"Then what should I do?" she asked.

"I don't know," he said. "It would be different if his mind and energy could rove creatively in the stars of mathematics or build out of eight notes a pattern of music new and living—then he might survive. But these things he does not have, and most men do not. Swinging on his high bar, timing his swing to catch your turning body—this is as old and instinctive to him as chewing when meat is in his mouth."

"What shall I do?"

"Don't make him know."

"But suppose it is not true. Suppose by some accident he became alive; suppose the fault is mine, an organ disarranged, an acid improperly applied by my own body, a poisoned thought lying concealed but toxic."

"You don't believe that," Friend Ed said. "I know you. You've had all the tests. You know."

She put her forehead in her hands. "Do you know how I love this man, Friend Ed?"

"I think I do. I hope I do."

"Do you know I would protect him from hurt if I were ripped and burned in the process?"

"That would be only a double burning."

"Do you know I am capable of any lie or cheat or violence—any good or bad that a human can conceive—for his content and joy?"

"I think you are. And I wonder what tiny mote of chance there is of its succeeding."

She looked at him closely. "You know what I am considering, don't you?"

"I think so."

"If I were very careful, took every precaution, don't you think there is a possibility?"

"I can't advise you. I don't know."

"But without it what chance is there?"

"I don't know. I will not advise you. I might be wrong."

"But of only two choices and both wrong, and one long waiting and it wrong too—must I not choose the least wrong of three?"

Friend Ed beat his hands together. "I don't know. I tell you I will not advise you. I will not offer my responsibility, I will not endorse your note of happiness. Anything, anything else. I wish I didn't know, I wish I did not even a thread suspect what you are thinking and planning."

Mordeen sat very straight. "I know you are his friend," she said. "I suppose I put too much burden on friendship. It isn't a rope that can take that much strain. I should have made the pattern by myself, Friend Ed. But I was lonely and unsure. I thought I needed some strength outside myself to help me. I'm sorry."

"Then you will—"

"Hush," she said softly. "I will close everything away in a dark self. If I am wrong about anything it will be *my* wrongness, and you need not think it or touch it."

He bowed his head.

Mordeen said, "He would not like me to see him drunk, particularly if his drinking is not happy. Find him, Friend Ed, stay with him. And when he is tired beyond wakefulness, take him to the sleeping car and cover him well. See his clothes are off. You'll find his night things in the black case under the lower berth—and wind his watch—and see his chest is covered when he sleeps."

"You?" he asked.

"Oh, yes—tell him I had a little headache and I will walk for a while. Tell him I will come to him very soon."

"I'm afraid," he said.

"I was. I was more afraid than I have ever been in a small, terrified life. But now I am not. Maybe I needed your weakness to build my own strength. Go out and find Joe Saul and comfort him. Hurry! He might be in need. Hurry, Friend Ed. Change your clothes quickly and find him. Put him to sleep before the night show. Do this for us." She took him by the arm and led him to the flap and held it back for him. And Friend Ed went uncertainly away.

Then quickly she came back and leaned over the mirror in the trunk lid and brushed her short hair. She was putting on her lipstick when the flap opened and Victor stepped quietly in. Victor wore slacks and a bright shirt, a sport coat and a painted tie. His shoes were white and brown. Across his tie hung a gold chain from which a small gold football dangled. She saw him in the mirror of her trunk. She turned halfway toward him and spoke in flat, quick voice. "Why did you come back?"

He said sullenly, "Did you think I could be frightened away? No, I want to square things off. I followed Joe Saul into town and then came back. I waited for that one to go. I want to square some things away with you."

She made a great effort. "I'm sorry and ashamed, Victor. I was going to try to find you—to say I'm sorry."

He scowled at her. "What changed you then? Have a fight with your old man? He's getting drunk, you know—or did you know?—pig drunk. I stood beside him in the bar, and he looked at me with juicy red eyes and he didn't even know me—that happy man, that good old lover with his trick."

"I'm sorry, Victor, really sorry."

"What changed you then?" he asked. "Did you suddenly find out that maybe I was right, that maybe this soggy stuff you thought was love might be a wizened imitation?"

"No, not quite that," she said.

"Or did you dig down through your pile of sticky words and find out that they were only words, when you needed hard and young action?"

"No, not quite that," she said.

"I came in to tell you once and finally what I think of the crap you were shoveling around. I want you to know that I won't have any of it. You were pretty tough, pretty sure. You know, you sit on the very peak top of the dunghill and look down on all the other chickens. You're perfect and me, I—I'm filth. Well, I tell you, I'm only honest. I'm not caught up in your stinking cloud." He paused and then continued, "And I don't believe you are either."

She said, "I was going to try to find you and tell you I was sorry."

"Why should you be sorry? What do you want of me?"

"After you left, I knew you were hurt," she said. "I told you how tight and clannish we are in this business. I'm afraid we have a way of rejecting everyone who was not born in it and descended from parents and grandparents who were born in it."

"You sure made me feel welcome!" he said sneeringly, and his eyes were very hostile.

"That's what I thought about," she said. "You are in our profession. If you stay you will have children born to it. We—I should not have cut you off the way I did. An act like ours is a kind of family, Victor. We—I should have made you feel more part of us."

"It's too late now. Your old man hit me in the face and you played dead, and the goddamned clown—did you hear what he said to me? Does he think I'll run away?"

"He didn't understand," she said. "Maybe we're so close-clotted that none of us understood. I'd like to make you feel welcome."

"How are you going to go about that" he asked.

"I don't know," she said. "If we have hurt you so deeply, I don't know. I thought of a possible way, but I don't know."

He eyed her foxily and a secret triumph began to creep over him. He said vulgarly, "Well, I know one way you could make a start."

Her eyes were wide on him. "I would like to be friends with you, Victor. I mean that. And maybe the others—maybe I can help to make you welcome."

He came close to her. "I guess I don't care so much about the others."

"Yes, you do. I think you do. Victor, I thought of something. When I was a little girl I had a time of sharp loneliness. I guess everyone has. I felt unwanted and cold, rejected. I took all the pennies I had and bought presents and wrapped them and gave them to myself. I thought that if the other children saw how I got presents they would know I was very popular and they would want to be my friends. But it didn't work. And then, Victor, an older girl got into trouble. She stole a ring. She was afraid and she was wary of the friends she had. She came to me for help, and I helped her, and—listen, Victor—I felt warm and wanted. I felt good when I could give something so frantically needed, and I was not lonely any more."

He said, "You're funny. You always tell stories. What's this one about? What do you want me to get from it? Your stories are loaded, Mordeen." But his voice had lost its sullenness. And he smiled a little in spite of himself. "Tell me," he said. "What's your story about?"

"Well," she began hesitantly, "it is about making you feel welcome. And I thought that if you would help me, when I need help, it might be good rich thing for both of us."

His truculence was going out of him and in spite of himself a jauntiness crept in. "Now who would think you needed help?" he said. "I thought I was the one needed help. That's what you said."

"Victor, you saw yourself that there is a trouble on us. Maybe if I could explain it so that you could understand it, you might be willing to help me." Her eyes appealed to him, and Victor went past understanding, went into triumph. He put his hand out to touch her shoulder—withdrew it when her shoulder moved imperceptibly away. Suddenly he laughed and his hand settled with authority on her shoulder.

"Why, I'd do anything for you, baby," he said. And then, "I'm sorry I was rough with you before. I know better than that. I guess I was afraid of you. I've got over that now." He stared at her. "Maybe you've changed. But they say women and horses know when a man isn't sure of himself. They can tell no matter how much he bluffs."

Mordeen's eyes veiled with pain, and she withdrew a little into herself. "I thought you might understand," she said softly.

"I do," he cried. "Christ, what a fool a man can be! I hear the signals, I see the lights, and I'm just dumb. I know a dame can't make the first move. How stupid can I be? Here you've thought it over, and I'm dragging my toe like a country boy."

He laughed again. "Let's get the hell out of here. Your old man's drunk. We'll go to a show. We'll go to town and have dinner. Say, how would it be if I rent a car and we go for a ride?"

Her face had tightened now. She turned away from him

toward the trunk. She picked up a lipstick and drew on full lips. Her throat was tight, but she had made her decision. Her haggard face smoothed out and imperceptibly her posture became soft and provocative.

"How about it?" he demanded.

When she turned to him again she was different.

"How about what, Victor?" she said huskily.

"How about dinner and we go for a ride?"

She looked up at him, studying his face. "That will be very nice," she said. Her intonation had changed. "I don't get out very much." She continued to stare at him.

"What do you see?" he asked gaily.

"See? Oh, I was noticing how black your eyes are."

"Don't you like them?"

"Oh, yes. I was thinking how some families have a black-eyed child and a blue-eyed child. It's strange."

"Not in my family," he crowed. "There hasn't been a light eye on either side that anyone knows."

"That's strange," she said. "Families have such strange qualities. I knew a family that had fits and, do you know, in every second generation there was insanity."

"You know funny people. I guess we're lucky. Old age is the only thing that can kill us. My grandparents, all four, are still alive, and my great-grandfather on my father's side knocked off at a hundred and four. No, we're tough. But what are we doing here? Let's get the hell out of here."

"Yes," she said, "that will be nice." She stood up and pulled her long cape over her shoulders. "I'll go back to the sleeping car and dress," she said. "I'll have to look nice. We'd better not be seen. Where can I meet you?"

He studied her. "No," he said slowly, "I guess you won't stand me up. Baby, there's a Chinese joint—nice booths. It's on Twelfth Street, but around the corner from the bank. It's like in an alley. I'll be in the first booth with the curtains drawn." He smiled down on her, his teeth flashing. "I'll take care of you, honey. I won't get you in any trouble. You just trust me."

She stood up and moved toward the flap. "Don't come out with me. I'll meet you in an hour." She stopped, and the spirit almost left her.

Victor stood beside her and he felt the change. He slipped his arm cozily about her waist. "I bet I know what you're thinking," he said. "Don't worry about it. We didn't invent this—it happens every day. It's nobody's fault. Don't you feel bad. Why, it can happen to anybody! We aren't so special. It can happen to anybody."

"Don't come out with me," she said.

She went out and left him. And almost instantly she was back. "He's coming. I saw him coming. Quick, get out! Quick!"

He went to the other side of the tent, lifted the canvas from the ground, and slipped underneath.

Mordeen breathed deeply. She parted the flap and looked out. She seemed about to go and then withdrew. But the next moment she was gone—gone in a flash.

The light was golden and soft now. The afternoon slid down the tent. From outside, the circus band struck up the recessional march, and below the music there was the thud of elephants' feet and the whinnying of horses. A lion roared in hunger, and suddenly a whole family of pigs went squealing.

Then the tent flap opened and Joe Saul looked in. His eyes rolled vacantly and his mouth was wet and loose. His shoulders hung askew and his tie was crooked in his unbuttoned shirt collar.

"Mordeen," he said thickly. "Mordeen, I'm drunk. I'm sorry but I'm drunk." He peered at the trunk standing open. He staggered to the little chair and sat down. His hands fluttered lovingly over the trunk. He picked up her lipstick, smelled it, and he smiled. Clumsily he put the trunk in order and patted the tray that held the powder and grease paint and cold cream. He caught sight of himself in the mirror and stared at his loose, drunken face. Then suddenly he slammed the trunk lid shut. The tinkle of broken mirror sounded through its sides. He put his head down on his arm, cradled his face against his forearm. His right fist struck the trunk top hard, then more softly. "Mordeen," he said, "I hurt Friend Ed. Sent him away." His fist fell and the fingers slowly opened.

Friend Ed looked in at the flap. He saw Joe Saul, watched him a moment, and then entered silently. Friend Ed squatted down on the ground and crossed his ankles. He crossed his arms lightly and took up his vigil over Joe Saul.

ACT TWO

The Farm

THE June morning sun peered over the ridgepole of the barn and fell across the farmhouse porch and tumbled bright and yellow through the windows into the kitchen. The light reflected from the polished metal of the stove and glittered on the pie tins set up in the warmer to dry. It was a kitchen to live in: a square table covered with oil cloth, for eating and figuring and sewing and reading; straight chairs with little pads in their seats for comfort; a big calendar from an implement house, but a calendar for keeping notes, with room around the dates to fill in plans projected for seeding and cultivating and harvesting. It was a self-sufficient kitchen. There was even a cot under the window where a tiring wife might rest while the bread was baking. On a shelf beside the sink stood a little radio playing the sprightly music of the morning, a record of a circus band playing a wild recessional.

This was a warm and old and comfortable kitchen, beaten into ease by generations. From outside came the farmyard noises of chickens cackling, of pigs grunting, of horses snorting and whinnying in their stalls. And a late rooster crowed as though he could not give up his morning song even though the sun was risen. A teakettle hummed steam on the stove, a coffee pot grunted and bumped beside it. The farm clock ticked, its pendulum flashing by the little glass window.

Joe Saul, the farmer, sat by the table, his head down on his elbow. His right hand held a pen, and in front of him was an open ink bottle. Friend Ed, who owned a neighboring farm, sat hunched down in a chair beside him. Both men were dressed in blue jeans and blue shirts open at the throat. Their coffee cups stood on the table in front of them.

Friend Ed got up and took his coffee cup to the stove and filled it. "Want a refill?" he asked.

Joe Saul raised his head and shoved his coffee cup over to the edge of the table. "Thanks," he said.

Friend Ed filled his cup. "You ought to get a bookkeeper to

do it for you. That's what I do. There's getting to be so much paper work a man hasn't time to bring in a crop."

Joe Saul sipped his coffee, then added sugar and cream. "When I can't keep books on my own farm I ought to give up farming," he said. "I've always been good at arithmetic, but there's just too much of it. But it's not only that. I've got to do everything myself—or at least be there."

"Isn't Victor working out?" Friend Ed asked.

"Oh, he's a good enough worker—tries anyway. But he's got no blood for it, Friend Ed. Before Cousin Will was killed I could send him out to cultivate and know and be sure it would be done right. But Victor's a town boy. Sometimes he does things right, but you can't be sure. I have to be with him all the time. You know how it is, Friend Ed, with you and me, and how it was with Cousin Will and our fathers and grand- and great- and great-great-grandfathers—we do things, and we don't know how or why but it's right. You can't be told about the land or read about it. It's got to be in the blood. I'm not criticizing Victor: he tries hard and mostly he's all right, but I just can't be sure. I've always got to go and look."

"I know," Friend Ed observed. "A funny thing happened like that with the twins. Al said at breakfast yesterday, 'I've got a feeling about something I should do.' And Eddie said, 'I know. Your green beans want poles.' Just like that, as if the green beans were calling to him."

"That's what I mean," Joe Saul said. "They've got the blood. You'd never have to look at a patch of corn if the twins did the hoeing. Oh, my God almighty!"

"Now stop this," Friend Ed said. "Now stop this! You're tearing yourself like a rupture."

Joe Saul said, "I get a nightmare sometimes. I see this land—this sweet flat black land—and in my nightmare it goes back to fallow, and then the sumac comes back in clumps, and then the forest trees, and this house molders away until there's only a chimney and cellar hole. The farm goes back the way it was when Old Joe Saul pulled up and took salt and pepper and tobacco, gunpowder and seed corn, from his saddlebags. That's all he had, Friend Ed, those and an ax. He cut five trees and planted his seed corn with a pointed stick. He used to tell about it when we were little kids tending our first calves." He gestured toward the door with his hand. "And look at it now—flat and black and sweet, shining like steel when the spring plow cuts in. And in ten years it could be nearly the way it was, with no one to keep it up. I get nightmares, too, of strangers—maybe from the towns, who don't know how to drain and damp."

"Stop it, Joe Saul. You worry at yourself like a puppy with a pig's ear. Get back to your paper work and stop mauling yourself. How's Mordeen?"

"Well, I don't know. She's a little sickly the last two weeks. There's one thing worries me, Friend Ed. She's had an ache or two before and you'd never know it. She's farm stock—get up and do her work and never a complaint or a shirk in her. And now—well, her stomach *is* upset, sure, and she's a little dizzy sometimes, but she's different. She went to the doctor yesterday. She says he told her it was nothing serious but she'd have to take it easy. It's funny. She's almost lah de dah! This morning she said, 'Would you mind if I didn't get up for a while, I don't feel quite well.' Now you know that's not like her. And then she stretched her arms and got a funny little smile. Didn't look sick at all, but her stomach *is* upset."

"She'll be all right," Friend Ed said quietly. "Women go through queer times." And he changed the subject. "One thing I've been meaning to ask you. Does Victor seem to hold a grudge for that bawling out you gave him?"

"Why, no. I don't think so. He's pretty quiet, doesn't talk much. Seems to go about his business and do his work. I think it did him good maybe."

"I was a little worried," said Friend Ed. "I thought maybe you shouldn't have hit him."

"I'm sorry about that," Joe Saul said. "I lost my temper. I told him I was sorry. I think he's forgot it."

"It wasn't like you to hit him or any man, Joe Saul."

"He said a thing. He said a thing that made me red mad. Do you hear Mordeen stirring around? I thought I heard her."

"I guess she's up," said Friend Ed. "I should be going. With all the work I've got to do on my place, I sit around in your kitchen after sun-up. Is your clock right?"

"Set it with the radio—it's always right."

A record started softly on the radio, a wailing torch song.

Joe Saul looked over at it. "I don't know how we managed before we had it. We hardly ever turn it off. It's like another person in the house. And Mordeen listens while she does the work." He sighed. "Let's have a fresh cup of coffee. Here, give me your cup. I'll wash it out."

He carried the cups to the sink and rinsed them.

The door opened and Mordeen came in. Her face was blooming and there was a small, satisfied smile on her mouth. She wore a quilted flowered dressing gown which reached almost to the floor.

Both men looked at her, and Joe Saul said, "Feeling better, Mordeen?"

"Oh, yes. Yes, much better."

Friend Ed said, "You look fine to me."

She moved to the couch under the window and sat down on it. "How beautiful a day," she said in wonder, as though it were the first day in the world.

"It's growing weather," Joe Saul said. "Shall I get you a little breakfast? There's oatmeal and crisp bacon in the warmer."

"You cook for me?" She laughed a low, happy laugh. "I should have got your breakfast. But it's nice to hear you offer, Joe Saul, it's very nice. No, I don't want breakfast."

"Coffee then? I'm just going to empty the pot and make a fresh one. Would you like some nice fresh coffee?"

"No," she said. "But I'm not really sick. I think I'm just indulging myself."

"It will be the first time," Joe Saul said. "It's a new thing with you."

She drew a deep breath, started to speak. "I—"

"Yes?" Joe Saul asked.

"I don't know what I started to say. My mind went flying off."

Joe Saul carried the filled cups of coffee to the table. "If you aren't going to have some, I won't make another pot, but maybe, if you don't feel well, I'd better. Victor will be in for his midmorning coffee soon."

Mordeen moved slowly in on what she had to say. She smiled to herself, and then her face was serious, and then she smiled again. She looked down at her hands, palm upward on her lap, one holding one, and the fingers relaxed and like a nest. "The doctor told me to take it very easy for a while," she said.

Joe Saul put down his cup and looked at her, twisting his chair around. "But he said you were all right. What does he think is the matter?"

And now she said it straight and clearly. "Joe Saul, I'm going to have a baby—*we're going to have a baby.*"

He did not hear at first because he had not been listening for it, but the words repeated themselves silently in his ears. His face set, looking at her, and the words repeated themselves again deep in his brain. For a moment Joe Saul fought his trembling chin. And then he put his head down on his arms and wept.

Friend Ed was looking at Mordeen, looking closely.

She looked back and her face was grave. She nodded. And then she smiled again.

An earthquake of emotion shook Joe Saul. Friend Ed looked away from him. But Mordeen smiled inwardly, watching her hands loving each other in her lap. Her face was withdrawn in mystery. The secrets of her body were in her eyes—the zygote new thing in the world, a new world but formed of remembered materials: the blastoderm, the wildly splitting cells, and folds and nodes, the semblance of a thing, projections to be arms and legs and vague rays of ganglia, gill slits on the forming head, projections to be fingers and two capacities from which to see one day, and then, a little man, whole formed, no bigger than the stub of a pencil and bathed in warm liquor, drawing food from the mother bank and growing. This frantic beingness lay under her loving hands embraced in a slow ecstasy in her lap.

And then Joe Saul stood up and walked heavily on his heels to the window and he looked out on his farm. He grasped his arms behind his back and pulled his shoulders up.

"Now," he said, "now it's all right." He raised his voice as though he called to the land. "Now it's all right." He laughed and turned his fierce delighted face back to the room. He released his arms and patted his hips gently as he spoke. "I've heard that in some parts of Europe they go out to the barns and tell the cattle. Why, every form is good and every ceremony." And he said, "Now that the black is lifted I can speak of blackness. So many of us nested in this land that we were it and it was part of us, so that the spring grass grew out of our pores and the green daggers of the corn came sprouting from our stomachs. You know, Friend Ed, how the unseasonable drought is like a dryness in the chest and how unplanned heat is a fever in us." He went on softly, "The generations of us—a totem, man on man, back to the first man—and the plans for future men and future great-grand men—all lying orderly in the blueprint chromosomes."

Friend Ed smiled. "I think you might like to give a party. I'll bring the twins. I'll get ice cream and whisky and I'll kill a turkey. This is a moment of great joy, Joe Saul. And where did I hear that?"

Joe Saul said, "Now that the black is up I can speak of black, but I can't remember it very well. I can't remember how it felt now the triumph is in me." He went to Friend Ed. "I see myself and myself's torment whirling away out of range of sight and feeling—torment in blood and heart that the line, a preciousness carried and shielded through the stormy millennia, is snapped, the product discontinued, the stamen mildewed."

"It's all over, Joe Saul. Would you like to invite some friends? Does Mordeen want it known so soon?"

They looked at her, and Friend Ed said more loudly to catch her attention, "Mordeen, do you want it known?"

She smiled. "Oh, yes. Why should I not? What is the matter, Joe Saul? Aren't you glad?"

"Glad? Oh, yes. But remembering—remembering the pain—it's like looking last in a coffin—there it is. The face is dead and you can forget it. But if you do not look, the face is never dead and you cannot in your back mind say good-by. And so I am looking back at the sadness so deep dug in. The top mind denies sterility. I remember how it was. Being convinced, I denied the desolation or made a joke of it—a bitter joke. I can remember only vaguely now the slow suspicious hatred that can grow and flower between man and woman while they say, 'Not now. We can't afford a child. We don't want a child if we can't take perfect care of it.' Or they say, 'We have great things to do in the world—great work that would be inhibited by a child. Our time is too precious for the squalling and noise and mess and—the expense.'"

"Would a party tire you, Mordeen?" Friend Ed asked. "Don't you think we should have a laughing party?"

"I do," she said. "I want a great scrabbling party full of noise, violent and crazy. That's what I want, Joe Saul. Come from your blackness now, Joe Saul."

"It's going fast," he said. "It's like a wound that, healing, leaves no memory, but only a scar of insensitive skin. Only the fecund can mention sterility at all. The sterile feel in their guts the desolate secret knife. Only the sterile really know through default the great two laws, that one must live and one must pass that life along—carry the fire and pass it down. The blood must flow, and the genes are ordered to communicate." He paused and shook his head violently.

Victor came up on the porch and entered the kitchen. He wore overalls and an open blue shirt. His arms were brown. "I thought I'd come in for a cup of coffee," he said. He caught some feeling from the room and was silent.

Joe Saul moved to Mordeen and looked at her as though she were new and unknown in his eyes. And she raised her head and her eyes brushed over Victor for a moment and then rose to face Joe Saul.

He said "Mordeen" softly, experimentally, as though he had never pronounced this name before. There was a wonder in his eyes. He sighed the great shuddering sigh that follows active love. He said, "Mordeen, we have a child," not telling her but tasting the words.

Victor's head snapped up. "What did you say?"

Then Joe Saul whirled on him. "You heard. We have a child," he shouted. "There's going to be a baby in this house. There's going to be a child playing in that dust. There's going to be a growing thing discovering the sky and kicking the chickens aside and finding eggs!" Joe Saul's body wove from side to side. He laughed hysterically in a surge of great joy. "There'll be great questions asked and answered. Do you understand that? We will rediscover the whole world. Can you hear that? This land will have its own plant growing out of it—born to it, knowing it."

His voice grew soft, almost whispered, and his eyes saw. "Our child will lie chest-flat, cheek-flat, against the ground.

His toes will kick the dirt and his ear will listen and the earth will speak to him."

Victor smiled, a tight, concealing smile, and his eyes met Joe Saul's and then passed on to Mordeen, and his smile deepened. "Congratulations, Joe Saul," he said. "This calls for celebration. But you say 'he.' How do you know it will be a boy?"

Joe Saul shouted, "How do I know? What do I care? I am not dead. My blood is not cut off. My immortality is preserved. I am not dead! Boy? Girl? There will be more—and boys or girls." He went close and pounded his fist gently on Victor's chest, forcing him back a little. "We have got a child," he said. "It's right there growing. It came from me—do you hear? It came from me. And it will be a piece of me, and more, of all I came from—the blood stream, the pattern of me, of us, like a shining filament of spider silk hanging down from the incredible ages."

Joe Saul sat down, exhausted. But in a moment he threw back his head and laughed.

Then Joe Saul rose up, prancing like a heavy horse, dancing unguilefully, and laughing too. He waltzed, his arms held out as though he balanced a partner; heavy footed he was, and his knees were bent. And the little radio played the waltz for him. And he was silly, as a joy-stuffed child is silly. Mordeen watched him, smiling, and Victor's eyes followed him, and Victor went disgustedly to fill the coffee pot. Friend Ed laughed at his antic clumsiness.

"I never have seen you this way, Joe Saul," he cried.

"I never had reason," said Joe Saul, and he stopped in his dancing.

"Well, reason or none, I have chores to do. They don't understand reasons—good or bad."

Joe Saul drew himself up in towering mock majesty.

"I here declare a holiday, a holy day," he orated. "I here declare that chores do not exist. Let your twins do them, or let them not be done. Argue with me, and I will flick my hand—like this—and your farm will disappear." He laughed at his own funniness. "Give me more argument, and I will flick twice—like this—and you will disappear." He whirled, "Victor, in the cabinet—get the whisky—get glasses. You want a party—it begins now. This empress"—he bowed toward Mordeen and, looking at her, his throat closed and the play went nearly out of him—"this queen, this mother wants a party. She has it. Hurry, Victor, before the party gets away," and Joe Saul ran to help to bring the glasses. He poured large portions.

Mordeen said, "None for me. I'd like it but I can't. I'll have to leave such things for a while."

In the middle of his gaiety Joe Saul became stone. He walked to the cot where she sat. He kneeled in front of her and put his hands on her knees. "Take care," he said. "Walk tenderly. Oh, take gentle care. Rest, and let your thoughts be high and beautiful." And he added hoarsely, "I order you to lift no burden, to encourage no weariness. You are to call me—me—when any work heavy or hard or long or even tiresome is to be done. Do you hear me? I order this."

She put her hand on his head affectionately and moved her fingers in his hair. "I will obey you," she said. "And it's a pleasant thing. I will take care. But I'm not as delicate as you would think. There's a frightening endurance in expectant women. I will obey. Now have your drink." She put her hands under his elbows and raised him to his feet. "Drink! Begin your party."

His mood changed then. He stepped to the table and raised his glass. "To the Child!" he shouted, and he drained his glass, and Friend Ed and Victor drank after him.

Quickly he filled the glasses. And Friend Ed raised his glass high. "To the Mother," he cried. They drank again. "That's good," Joe Saul said. "That's the one I should have said first. That's good, Friend Ed." He choked. "Ah! it's strong. I need a little water." He went to the sink and drew water and poured it down so quickly that the water ran from the corners of his mouth and dampened his blue shirt.

Victor was close to the table, passing the glasses. Victor's eyes burned with the quick impact of the whisky. A boldness was growing on him. He waited until Joe Saul came back to the table and then he raised his glass and looked at Mordeen.

"To the Father," he said.

Suddenly Joe Saul's eyes were wet. He drank his drink and slowly put down his glass. He went to Victor and put his arm around the broad young shoulders. "Thank you," he said. "Oh, thank you, Victor."

And Victor in triumph looked again at Mordeen. And he saw hatred in her face as he had never experienced—hatred so cold and dangerous that he could not counter it. His eyes wavered and fell and he turned away, and his eyes met Friend Ed's eyes, and there he saw an executioner looking at him with lethal, detached sternness, as though judging where to put the rope. He coughed and said loudly, "A few more toasts like that and I'd be drunk. I guess I'd better get to work." He went out of the kitchen and his footsteps hammered on the porch boards.

Joe Saul idly poured more whisky into the glasses. "I'm as skittish as a horse," he said, and he chuckled. "Strange, one moment I want to shout and I find myself weeping. I'm touchy as a range horse in the blowing papers of a picnic ground."

Mordeen stood up carefully. "If we're to have a party, I'd better rest," she said. "The excitement has tired me, tired me out."

"You should eat," Joe Saul said.

"No, not now. Later I'll drink some milk and eat a little toast."

"Lie down then. And if a party is too much, we'll have no party."

"Oh, I want a party—all the friends, the twins, the neighbors. But who's to cook and make the punch?"

"You go," Joe Saul said. "I'll get everything in town. I'll have it sent all ready. It would be a sad thing if I couldn't do this to celebrate our child."

She walked by him and her hand drew lovingly across his back.

Joe Saul watched her go and then he sat down and regarded his poured drink. "I'm tired," he said. "I'm suddenly very tired, as though the blood had poured out of me."

"It's akin to shock," Friend Ed said. "I guess it is a kind of shock. And now if you run true to form, you'll have morning nausea worse than hers, and when there is a little pain in her, your guts will twist in agony. And in labor—oh, God help you, Joe Saul, in labor!"

Joe Saul said, "I want to bring a present to her—some preciousness, some new beautiful thing to delight her, so that her eyes will dance, and she will say, 'Who could ever have thought that I would have a beauty thing like this.'"

"I think she has it."

Joe Saul stirred. "Yes, I know that. But something like a ceremony, something like a golden sacrament, some pearl like a prayer or a red flaring ruby of thanks. Some hard, tangible humility of mine that she can hold in the palm of her hand or wear dangling from a ribbon at her throat. That's a compulsion on me, Friend Ed. Come with me." He was excited again. "I must get this thing. My joy requires a symbol. Come with me to town. We'll get the partiness—all cooked and carved and poured. She's worked so hard before every party that only a little unweariness was left to enjoy it. I'll be the hands to do her work tonight. And then we'll look—I don't know what the beauty is—but I'll know it when I see it."

Now he had made up his mind he was excited again. "Hurry, Friend Ed. Drink your whisky and come with me. I don't feel trustful of myself to be alone." He walked to the door, and back to the door and back, like a terrier begging to be let out.

Friend Ed stood up slowly. He said satirically, "Be careful, Joe Saul. Remember the child. See you don't overdo. You must conserve your strength." And then he said seriously, "You don't want to be alone, but do you want Mordeen to be alone?"

"Ah!" Joe Saul said. "It's hard to remember. She has always been so complete and competent. Thank you for remembering. I'll call Victor, tell him to stay close. I'll take the old dinner bell to her. Then if she needs anything she can clang the bell and he will come."

Friend Ed said quietly, "I don't think Victor—" and then he knew that he could never say what he had thought.

"Victor's all right. Didn't you hear him? He's forgot I hit him in the face. Victor's a good boy." He opened the door and shouted "Victor!" and a far answer came. Joe Saul cupped his hands. "Victor, come here, I want to talk to you. Come on, Friend Ed." The two men went out and the door closed behind them. Alone on its shelf the little radio played on, the kettle bustled with steam. The ticking of the clock was very loud.

Now there were steps on the porch. Victor opened the door quietly and stood in the doorway, looking out, while an automobile engine roared and the sound whined up the gears and slowly rose to silence in the distance. Then Victor gently closed the door and walked lightly to the table. He poured himself a drink and drained the glass and quickly poured another. The neck of the bottle clashed against the tumbler. And through the open door to the bedroom Mordeen's voice called, "Is it you, Joe Saul?"

Victor sat quietly and sipped his drink, and his glance rose and remained on the door. He sat down in one of the straight chairs and leaned back, and the old chair creaked. Mordeen called anxiously, "Who's there?" And in a moment she stood in the doorway. She saw Victor and stopped and her hands went out and braced against the door frame. "Oh!" she said. "It's you. Why didn't you answer?"

Victor rocked his chair a little on its hind legs and he sipped the straight whisky in his glass. "Joe Saul asked me to take care of you while he's in town. He told me to, ordered me to."

"What do you want, Victor?" she asked in alarm. "You shouldn't be drinking now."

He finished the drink and idly poured another. His eyes felt over her body. "Come in," he said. "Come in and sit and talk to me."

For a moment she hesitated, and then her face became a mask, closed and wary and waiting. She crossed behind the table and sat down on the cot under the window. Outside a cow bawled mournfully for her calf.

Mordeen said woodenly, and softly, "What do you want, Victor?"

He swung his chair around, facing her. He rested his elbow on the table and he crossed his legs. "Just wanted to pass the time of day with you," he said. "I never seem to get to talk to you. Isn't that funny? I'd think you'd want to talk to me."

She stared at him, her eyes expressionless.

Victor tasted his drink and made himself more comfortable. His body slouched in his chair. The small gold medal shone at his throat. "And now I hear this interesting news, but not from you. I hear it from Old Joe Saul. It just seemed to me that you yourself would want to tell me all about it."

She said finally in a monotone, "When you finish your game, maybe you'll tell me what you want."

Victor smiled. "You don't want to pretend that you don't know what I'm talking about, do you?"

"I know what you're talking about," she said, "but I don't know what you are trying to say."

He uncrossed his legs and leaned toward her. "Do you think I have no interest in my child?" he asked.

She said without emphasis, "It's not your child, Victor. It's Joe Saul's child."

Now he laughed loudly. "Mordeen," he said, "do you think that if you say that often enough it will be true?"

"It is true," she said.

Now he leaped up angrily. "That's a lie," he cried. "You know it is and I know it is. You know Joe Saul can't have a child. You know that. I don't like being used. I don't like being shut out of something that's mine. Don't try tricks because I don't like them. This is my baby. I've got a lot of girls in trouble so I know *I'm* all right—but this is the first one that will be born. Don't you think I have some feeling for my own blood? Do you think I want to be used like a stud animal for the comfort of Joe Saul? Is that fair? He gets everything, and I get put back in the corral."

"You got what you said you wanted," she said coldly. "You got what you can understand."

"Don't do that again," he said angrily. "What I can understand and what I can't understand! I think I proved to you I could understand anything you can. Even if you wouldn't come near me again afterwards."

She said, "Victor, don't bother me."

"Don't bother you. First I don't understand and now don't bother you. I understand enough to be sure it's my child, and I'll bother you when you have my baby. Understand that!" He leaned toward her in rage, beating out his intention on the table with his closed fist.

His anger raised anger in her. She stood up and her voice fought against the control she put on it. "I told you, Victor, and asked and even begged you to believe that I would do anything in the world for Joe Saul's content because of my love for him."

"Yah!" he said snarlingly.

"I tell you again. I warn you to believe it."

"What's he going to say when he knows it's my baby, when

he knows you were out in the barn with me when he was drunk?"

She cried fiercely, "It's Joe Saul's baby, conceived in love for him. I saw his face hovering over me. I felt his arms—not yours. You don't exist in this, Victor. The little seed may have been yours, I have forgotten. But no love was given or offered or taken. No! It's Joe Saul's baby. Joe Saul's and mine."

She glared at him like a mother cat, and her claws were out. And then she backed to the cot, her teeth bared and her nostrils flaring. She breathed in little bursts. "And no one, nothing will take that away. I had to do an alien thing, had to hide my hurt in a mountain cave of love to do it. You nor any consideration will take this child away from Joe Saul. Believe it, Victor. If I could do that thing before—think what I could do now."

Victor's body and his face were beaten by her force. He stood, walked toward the door. And suddenly he flung himself on the floor in front of her and embraced her ankles and laid his face down on her feet.

"Oh, God! I'm lonely." His despair was heavy as a gray stone. "What have I done, Mordeen? What crime have I committed? In the night I've thought of the things you said. Mordeen, I've laughed at them and I've run out to women to prove those words weren't true—and they are." He raised his face and looked at her. "I wish I had never seen Joe Saul. I wish I had never seen your eyes on him hot and happy and shining. If I had not known, I could go to the town girls, fumble at their dresses, quiet their giggling and rut with them. But now I hear your voice over their little shrill squeals of pleased protest. I feel your strong sure warmth behind their chilly pimpled breasts." He said miserably, "I love you. And it's not like anything I have ever known. It is as different as—as—you said it once—as milk."

Her face had grown compassionate as she looked down at him. "Poor Victor, you will find it. If you are open to it, capable of returning it, this will come to you."

"I've argued this way, argued to myself, Mordeen. But I have found this kind of love, and it cries in my mind that it can't happen twice." He rose up to his knees. "It shouts to me that if I do not save this—this one I know beyond all doubt—I will lose my chance. Mordeen," he cried, "I'm frantic. I do not think I can live. I don't say this the way such things are said—I do not think I can live. I have a crazy animal clawing in my guts." And indeed he was doubled up with pain.

"Now you know," she said softly. "Now you know why I did what I did. I didn't think you were capable of knowing." In pity she put her hand on his forehead and smoothed his hair back. Outside, a thunderhead throttled the sun and the light in the kitchen grew dusky. The radio turned low intoned prices of wheat, barley, corn, oats, hay, hogs, steers, calves, sheep, in a murmured litany.

Mordeen said, "I guess a shower is coming. Can't you go away, Victor? If you feel so, wouldn't it be better if you were not here, because this pattern will not change? Nothing can change it. You've thought of killing Joe Saul, haven't you, Victor?"

"Yes," he said almost under his breath.

"That would not change it. I would still be Joe Saul's wife, and this one here would be his child. And you, Victor, would be colder than a lonely cold; you would die in the cold of hatred. Think carefully of going away. The year will turn, and it will be better and then better and then—gone in some best new thing."

The kitchen was quite dark now and a very far thunder rumble shook the air. Victor put his cheek down on her knees, and time and the year rolled over and over as the earth rolls, swaying like a tiring top. The year changed and the world swung through the great ellipse. The year and the season swung on about the house. In Mordeen the baby grew. And the year rolled on.

"I've thought of that too," Victor said. "I can say with my mind that I will go—but I would refuse it. That I know. For I think of the summer ending now and the stubble on the ground and the hay brushing the ridge pole in the barn and windfall apples on the orchard earth. And you—a swelling below your breasts and my child kicking against the soft wall, and turning, and I not able to put my hand there and feel its moving life."

"Hush, Victor. It is not your child. A year will draw—is drawing—out your sorrow like a basting thread."

"A year," he said in the darkened room. And thunder crashed distantly and a blue flickering flash shook the room. "I know the passing year. The fall is chilling down and the hoar frost does crisp and yellow the strong grasses near the stream under the tattering cottonwoods. The blackbirds flocked nervously a week and now they are gone. The wind and the arrowing wild ducks are driving to the south over the burning sumac. And you—you walk heavily on your heels, your shoulders back to balance the growing weight of my child, and your face is glorious and your eyes smile all day long and your mouth perhaps turns upward, smiling in your sleep."

"Hush, Victor," she said wearily. "It's not your child. And don't you think it is a little cold in here? The rain will turn to sleet, I think."

The year slipped past, and the endless business of the aging earth continued.

The wind whined a little ghost howl around the corners of the house.

"A man can forget nearly anything in a year, Victor."

"I know this year," he said miserably. "I know the white drifts curving down to the silver ice in the shallows above the pond. I know the black lashing branches of the pear trees and the dogs snuffling and moaning in the storm porch. I can feel the ice-air burning in my nose and blue aching fingernails and the acid cider. They're bringing in a Christmas tree from the forest today. And you, Mordeen, quiet and tired with waiting —you move silently, with eyes and ears and touch turned inward to hear and see and feel my child."

She stirred in the steely light, moved heavily. "It's not your child. It's Joe Saul's child," she said with heavy monotony. "Turn on the light, Victor, and build up the fire. The cold is creeping in. The winter's really here. My year of bearing is nearly done. And very soon Friend Ed and Joe Saul will be coming with the Christmas tree. Shovel a wider path down to the road so they can get the tree in. They said it would touch the ceiling. And, Victor, I wish you could find the strength to go away. I've seen your suffering in this livelong year. But the birth will be soon now, Victor. Please try to go away. I have not changed my mind in the year. It's Joe Saul's child. I will protect him in this child. I threaten you, Victor."

He cried, "Mordeen, I love you. I cannot go away."

He stood up and turned on the light, opened the stove and poked the dying fire to flame. The light was nearly gone. The windows were edged with white and big feathered flakes were drifting down.

The steel winter lay on the land and crept to the doors and windows and peered whitely in. And the snow put silence on the earth. Mordeen pushed herself heavily up from the couch. Her shoulders were back and the child was low and large in her body. She shuffled across the room, filled the teakettle, and put it on the stove. One of her hands stayed on her abdomen, as though to help support the weight which bore her down. Then she stood listening. "I think they're coming in. Go help them, Victor; help them get it through the door. And please remember what I said."

Victor looked out, and then he opened the porch door. A tumble of snow came in. Friend Ed and Joe Saul were sliding the fine fir tree butt forward up the path. They edged it up the stairs to the open door and Victor grabbed it and pulled the snowy branches through the door. Joe Saul and Friend Ed stood on the storm porch, stamping and beating their shoulders. They stood laughing there, taking off their coats and kicking the arctics from their feet, and then they came into the pleasant kitchen. Their cheeks were pink with cold and their eyes watered. They rubbed their hands together in the warmth.

"We'll have to cut it off," Friend Ed observed. "I told you it was too big."

Mordeen had brought a broom to sweep up the scattered snow before it melted. She moved slowly with a careful rolling step.

Joe Saul cried, "I'd rather have it too big and cut it off than too small and have to stretch it. Here, give me that broom, Mordeen. You shouldn't be doing that. Here, you sit down and let us do all this."

She smiled, saying, "It's been hard learning not to do my own work. You may regret you've made a sluggard of your wife."

"You'll learn to do it again." Joe Saul laughed. "But not now. The work you are doing is much more important. I was telling Friend Ed how startled I was when the baby moved—lying in bed, and I guess I was half asleep, and then I felt this little secret movement, and it wakened me." He looked upward, smiling in his remembering. "At first it was as though someone had touched me to catch my attention, but very gently. And then I felt a creeping like a soft cat—stealthy. And then there was a little push, and then—you can believe this or not—there was a shaking like silent laughter and then a scrabbling movement. I felt it climb up my spine and then come tumbling down again. And then the small shake of laughing. Well, it startled me. I thought at first one of the dogs had crawled in bed with us. And I sat up and turned on the light. Mordeen didn't even wake up. And do you know what it was?" He pointed. "It was that one playing in the darkness of his mother." He laughed with pleasure, and Mordeen smiled. Victor moved restlessly.

Friend Ed said, "I know how that is. And if you want to feel a real rumpus, you have twins sometime. I think they play volley ball. The doctor didn't say it's twins, did he, Mordeen?"

"No," she said, "it's only one. And it's turned and perfect. I saw it," she said in wonder. "I saw it on the X-ray plate. At first I didn't know what it was. Know what it looked like? Well, it looked like the nave of a cathedral with a vaulted roof and one great column—that was ribs and spine. At first I couldn't make out the child until Dr. Zorn showed me, and then, there he was, upside down and balled up like a kitten."

Joe Saul said excitedly, "What did he look like, what could you see?"

"Why, everything," she said. "His head and little arms and his legs and feet curled up. He's been a great jumper but now he's quiet. That worried me. I thought something might be wrong. But Dr. Zorn says he's just fine. He will be quiet now, the doctor says. He will sleep until he has to make the big fight."

Victor said nervously, "If you aren't going to set up the tree right now, I'd like to go out to my room. I don't feel clean."

"Go ahead," Joe Saul agreed. "We'll put up the tree after dinner." And Victor said, "I don't feel clean," and he almost ran from the room. Mordeen watched him go.

"I don't know how we'll get around that monster tree," Mordeen said. "It will nearly fill the room."

"And ought to," Joe Saul crowed. "Say, I'd like to see that picture. I wonder if I could get it."

"The doctor wants to study it," Mordeen said. "But if you go to his office I'm sure he'll show it to you."

"Maybe afterwards he'll let me have it to keep," said Joe Saul. He sat down by the table and stretched his arms in luxury. "Next Christmas, Friend Ed, next tree we bring in—why, he'll be sitting under it. And he'll have his own presents. I wonder what I'll get him his first Christmas. I'll have to think about that. But I've got a whole year to think."

"Something round or soft or shiny the first year," Friend Ed advised. "That's about all that interests them the first year. Say, you'd better not call him 'him' all the time. It might be a girl."

"I don't care," Joe Saul said. "I'd like a girl. I'll like what I get." He turned to Mordeen. "You go in the bedroom and lie down and rest," he ordered. "I'm going to get dinner now. I'll call you when it's ready. Friend Ed is going to eat with us. He'll help me."

She stood up slowly and obediently. "I'm really spoiled," she said, smiling. "And I like it very well. You have a lazy wife, and it is your fault."

He stood and went to her and took her face between his hands and looked in her eyes, holding her chin tilted up at him. And he chuckled with delight. "Look, only look, Friend Ed. Isn't she beautiful?" And suddenly his lips trembled and he looked away. And Mordeen moved heavily through the door.

Joe Saul stirred the fire and put a big pan on the heat. "It's going to be a fry supper," he said. "Whether you like it or not, that's what you'll get, Friend Ed." He moved quickly about at his preparation. "Fried liver and stewed tomatoes and milk and tapioca for dessert. Would you like a drink of whisky, Friend Ed?"

"I wouldn't mind."

Joe Saul brought bottle and glasses to the table and poured two big drinks. "It will take a minute for the pan to heat," he said. "Everything's ready. I did it all this morning. When I fry the liver we can eat." He drank half of his whisky and set the glass down on the table. "It's strange, Friend Ed," he said. "Of course you know the baby's there—of course it's there—but it's a mystery. I suppose you don't quite believe it until it is really born. But she has *seen* it, really see the head and arms and legs. That's different! That's a very different thing. That makes it real. It's not just an idea any more or a wish or a prayer. It's a real thing. Oh, I'll have to see that picture! I'll have to see it. I'll go tomorrow."

"I see what you mean, Joe Saul. That's true."

The door burst open and Victor stood before them. His eyes were wild. He was wrapped in an overcoat and he carried a suitcase in his hand.

"I can't stand it. I'm getting out. I'm going—going now—right now!"

Joe Saul looked at him in amazement. "Going? What's wrong with you, Victor?"

"Well, I—I can't stand it, that's all."

"Can't you tell me what's the matter?" Joe Saul asked.

A torturing struggle was taking place in Victor's mind. His eyes were filled with fierce suffering, with hatred and longing and love.

Joe Saul asked, "Is it because I hit you in the face, Victor?"

For a moment Victor was still weighing, fighting with himself, and at last he chose his course. He looked at Joe Saul almost with compassion. "That's it," he said. "I can't stay in a place where I was hit in the face."

"But I apologized," said Joe Saul. "I said I was sorry. Did it hurt so much, Victor?"

"Yes, it did."

"I'm sorry. In a time of such joy, it seems a shame. Isn't there anything I can do?"

Victor fought himself, and his emotion overcame him. "No," he cried. "No. I'm going." He turned and ran as though he could not trust himself. He ran out of the door and left it standing open.

Joe Saul sighed. He went to the door and looked out and then he closed it gently and came back to the table. "I thought he had forgotten," he said. "I'm sorry he feels this way. He didn't even tell me where to send his pay."

Friend Ed spoke uneasily. "Let him go. He's young, and

that's a brooding time, Joe Saul. That's a time when you inspect your hurts like little rocks. Let him go. There are many Victors. There will always be a Victor."

"I suppose you are right. I wish I had not hit him. I'm ashamed of that."

"Maybe he is ashamed too."

"Of what?"

"Of—running away."

"I'm sad because I was weak. I would not like to give weakness to my child."

He drank the rest of his whisky. "Remember, I said next year he'll have a present of his own. But he's a real thing now, with the picture. He's there and I can see him. He's closer than in another room. There's just a little soft wall between. Maybe he can hear and feel. I'm giving him a present soon."

"You're crazy, Joe Saul. You're just dog crazy."

"Maybe I am, but that's how I hope I stay. I had a strange thought. He's there, he's here. Why shouldn't he have a present this year? Why should he not?"

Friend Ed grinned. "Might be a little difficult to give to him. You're crazy, Joe Saul."

"Well, I could give him a present. I thought what I could give him. If I had the weakness to hit Victor, maybe I have others. I thought of it when I wanted to go in to Dr. Zorn to see the picture and now I think of it more. I want to give my son clean blood."

"You have," Friend Ed said uneasily. "What are you talking about."

"I want to give him the proof. That's what I mean—attested. I can get Zorn to go over me, head, heart, stomach, everything. Maybe I can say to this child—that's what your father gave you first of all—strength and health and cleanliness. That would not be a bad present, Friend Ed."

"I think you're really crazy," he said anxiously. "This is a silly thing. I don't like it. I don't want you to do it."

"*You* don't. Why don't you? I can give him the papers all signed by Dr. Zorn—maybe rolled like a parchment with a big seal and tied with a red ribbon like a diploma. I could hang it on the tree for him. His first present and the best."

"Don't do it. Zorn might think you're crazy, the way I do. He might put that in your paper."

But Joe Saul poured whisky in both glasses. He leaned across the table toward Friend Ed. "Don't tell Mordeen. I'll do it as a secret and as a kind of joke, but not a joke too. I haven't ever had a thorough check-up. It will please her, Friend Ed; don't tell her."

Friend Ed stood up. "I don't want you to do this. I don't like this. It's—it's crazy."

Joe Saul said quietly, "I think it is the sanest thing I have ever done. I don't know why I haven't done it before."

He raised his glass and cried, "I'm giving him a present. I must be sure it is perfect. I'm giving him the greatest present in the world. I'm giving my son *life*."

ACT THREE, SCENE I

The Sea

THE tiny cabin of the little freighter was old and comfortable and well used. On one side stood a little mess table with a retaining ridge; good swivel chairs were bolted to the floor, and water bottles and glasses were placed in racks on a small sideboard. The walls were paneled in dark wood well oiled and rubbed for many years, and the brass brightwork shone. Against one wall, under hanging sea coats, was a broad chest upholstered as a bench. Two deep leather chairs stood in front of a small coal grate in a tile mantel, and on the mantel itself there was a model of a schooner complete and beautiful in its detail; beside it was a small artificial Christmas tree decorated with tinsel and silver and red glass balls. On the little hearth was a small rack of fire tools—a short heavy poker, a shovel, and tongs. On the wall under the portholes hung the trophies of many voyages to many places, assegai and knobkerries from Africa, war clubs and shark-toothed spears from the Polynesian south, daggers and stilettos, a witch mask or two, and a shrunken head, black and baleful, hanging by its hair.

The door stood open to the rail of the flying bridge and beyond—the night city of docks and behind them tall lighted buildings, and neon signs glowing in the sky. A second closed door led to the sleeping cabins. A small coal fire glowed in the iron grate.

From outside came the sounds of the harbor, toot of tugs and mutter of engines, and steam hiss and rumble of deck winches and creak of lines in running gear. Behind the harbor sounds the city talked with streetcars and truck engines, with auto horns and juke-box music.

Mr. Victor in a blue mate's uniform and cap came into the cabin. He looked around nervously, then went to the little grate and stirred the coals, rattled the poker on the iron. A tug whistled a passing signal in the stream. And in the city a fire siren whined up the scale and down again. Mr. Victor stood looking at the little Christmas tree on the mantel. From the other side of the closed door Mordeen's voice came, muffled, calling, "Joe Saul!" Mr. Victor's head swung around. "Joe Saul!" the voice called with a note of alarm in it.

Mr. Victor went to the door and opened it. "He's not here," he said. "Come out, I want to talk to you." He went back to the grate and rubbed his hands close to the coals, and he said again toward the open door, "Come here, Mordeen. I want to talk to you."

In a moment she stood in the doorway, her hair disheveled from the pillow and her eyes wild and uncertain with sleep. She said, "I had a dream." And then as her mind came out of sleep, "Where did Joe Saul go?"

"He went ashore," said Mr. Victor. "He told me to stand by in case you needed anything."

"The time is close, Victor," she said. "I've had the first ragged pains. Maybe false pains, but my time is close. I want Joe Saul here with me. I want him here." She walked back and forth in the heavy, rolling pace that restlessly precedes birth.

"Sit down," said Mr. Victor.

"No," she said. "I'm not comfortable sitting down." And then she laughed shortly. "A woman told me she always could tell when a child was due because she cleaned the bottom drawers of her bureau. Well, I just remembered the dust in the bottom of my cabinet, and I wanted to bend down, way down, to clean it out. I guess that's my sign. I want Joe Saul here. If he does not come back soon, I want you to look for him, Victor. It will be soon—oh, very soon."

A seething excitement filled Victor. He moved one of the big chairs a little. "No," he said at last, quietly but with a force controlled in his throat. "I can't! I tried, Mordeen. I tried to force myself. And I know that if it goes on a little more I will not—I will not know what I am doing." He held out his arms and he cried, "See, a chill is going on in me. My hands won't be quiet. Mordeen, I can't let you go."

"Let me go, Victor? What are you saying?" Her face was alarmed.

"I've given it every thought," he cried. "I can't do it. You are my woman and that is my child. I must have you."

"Are you crazy?" She stood in front of him. "I am not your woman!"

"Maybe crazy," he said. "And maybe I will get crazier. You must come away with me now. You are my woman and I cannot have my child born here."

"Mr. Victor," she said in command. "Go to your quarters. Go instantly. If Joe Saul heard you, he would have you off the ship or he would kill you. Go to your quarters!"

"No," he said, wondering. "It's too late. I must have you and my child." The hysterical intensity grew in his voice. "I must have that. It would be good if you wanted me as much as I want you, but I must have you whether you wish it or not. This is my whole life. I won't throw it away no matter what comes of it. Look!" he cried. "I tried to run away and leave you and my child to Old Joe Saul. And I couldn't do it. I came back. And I tried to be wise—to stand by like a cuckolded goat and see my woman and my child in Joe Saul's arms. *And I cannot do it.*"

"Victor," she said, "I've told you over and over why I need this child: I love Joe Saul. This is crazy."

"Crazy or not, that's the way it is," he said dully. "I will not lose the one life I have ever had—even if the world burns up."

She said kindly, "Poor Victor. You do not understand many things, and this you don't seem to understand at all."

"Maybe I don't have to understand," he said. "You are going away with me—now, tonight. I have a place for you. I have a doctor. You will come with me now. You must come with me now"—his voice rose—"if I have to tear you free."

She was frightened at him now, sensing his growing hysteria. "I will not go, Victor. Don't you know that? Nothing can make me go. Don't you know that?"

His head was down and he shook it slowly from side to side. "There's only one other thing," he said. "We can wait here—just as we are. When Joe Saul comes I will tell him. I will tell him everything. I don't think you can look into his eyes and say, 'This is not true.' Then he will throw you out, and I will take you. In his rage he may hurt you—and the child. Is this worth doing, Mordeen? Or suppose he didn't—suppose he let it pass and you had to live with his covered hatred for you and his hatred for my child. I will surely tell him, Mordeen. Even if I don't want to, I will surely do it."

Her body bent over with pain. She leaned forward and her eyes distended and she bit her lips until the pain receded.

"It's starting. Give me time," she begged. "Please, Victor, give me time to think. I can't think now. Can't you see?"

"No," he said. "I've been over it too often in my mind. I don't dare give you time. No. I can't afford to give you time. It would cheat me," he shouted. "I tell you I don't dare. You must come away."

"I won't go," she said. "He will understand, and it will be all right."

"You don't believe that, Mordeen. If that were so, why didn't he adopt a child? Why his constant talk about blood and family? No, you don't believe that."

She came to him, pleading then. "Please, Victor, don't destroy three people for the sake of one. He has never hurt you. Why will you kill him, and through him me? What will you have then? Please, Victor. At least give me a little time."

"No," he said. "Time? Time is my enemy."

Suddenly she was calm and very tired. "Victor, many things have happened. With the child forming and growing in my womb, there is also a change in my mind. I am not the same as before. The hard self-corners are smoothed."

He asked uneasily, "Is this some trick?"

"No," she said quietly. "I don't think it is a trick unless it is a trick on me too. At first when I asked your help I was closed off in a little house of pain. There were no others in my world except Joe Saul and me. But in the long heavy months my world has grown. It is not closed off."

Victor said restlessly, "What are you trying to do?"

"I'm trying to tell you that you could be welcome now."

"How about Joe Saul?" he demanded.

"That has not changed. I love Joe Saul. I will not have him hurt. I am his wife."

"What kind of a fool do you think I am? Are you saying you would love both of us?" he demanded.

"Not in the way you mean, Victor. But I would try to open the family like a garment and take you in."

"Do you think you could be wife to two men?"

"No, Victor. I can be wife only to Joe Saul."

"Then I say no," he cried. "No!"

She looked at him closely then to make sure he would not change. "Please, Victor."

"No."

"Victor," she cried, "you don't know what your choice means! You don't know me. Please, Victor. You don't know. Why should you throw your life away? Don't do it, Victor! I beg you not to do it."

He said dully, "I've thought about it long, Mordeen. Lying in my bunk, hearing you laughing and planning with Joe Saul —how do you think that feels? Mordeen, if my choice were made with the certainty that I would die tomorrow, I would still make it. You must come away."

"You're sure, Victor? Can't there be some change? Can't you give me—at least a little time? Please, Victor—time."

"No," he said. "I can't go back now. I'm in a long narrow tunnel and I can't turn."

For a long moment she looked at him, and her eyes were full of tears. Neither of them saw Friend Ed standing in the doorway, looking in at them. His dark blue captain's uniform concealed his figure in the half-darkness.

Mordeen shook her head slowly. "I don't have a choice?" she said.

"No, you don't have a choice. Get a coat. That's all you are to take. Everything will be new—everything."

She sighed deeply. "Don't you know I will kill you, Victor?"

"Hurry," he said. "Only a coat. I don't want anything more from this old life."

She looked at him quietly, and her eyes set with resolve. She moved to the rack of coats and lifted down a long gray cloak.

"Victor," she said, "will you get the suitcase under my bunk?"

"What suitcase?" he demanded suspiciously. "I don't want anything from this life."

She turned toward him. "It's for the hospital," she said. "I've had it packed for weeks."

He hesitated.

"Get it, Victor," she said.

He went to the door, and as he passed through she hurried to the relics on the wall and drew a short thick knife from its sheath and concealed it in the folds of her cloak. And as she did, she saw Friend Ed standing just inside the door, shaking his head slowly at her. She stood perfectly still, her mouth open a little.

Victor came from the sleeping cabin carrying the suitcase. He saw Friend Ed. He dropped the suitcase on the floor and moved quickly toward him.

"What the hell do you want?" he demanded.

But Friend Ed looked past him at Mordeen. "Once I wouldn't help you," he said. "I wouldn't take the responsibility. Now I will."

"Get out of here!" Victor said.

"Hush," said Friend Ed.

Mordeen said, "I did it all myself. I don't need your help."

"But you have it now," Friend Ed said. "Whether you want it or not, you have it."

"Stay clear!" she shouted at him. "Stay clear of this! What I have started I will finish."

"I have my sailing orders," he said. "I sail at midnight. I came to say good-by." He looked at Victor. "Will you come on deck with me?" he asked. "I have a message for you."

"Say it here," Victor said harshly.

"No, it's a secret. Come!" He gently urged Victor through the door, and the two disappeared into the night.

Mordeen stood rigid, her eyes wide with fright. She waited for what she expected—then came the crunching blow, the expelled moaning cry, and in a moment the little splash. She shivered.

She was still staring straight ahead when Friend Ed came in again. He walked over to her and gently took the knife from her and replaced it in its sheath. He came back to her and took her arm and helped her to a chair and seated her.

He said, "Where's Joe Saul? I came to say good-by."

She roused herself from shock. "He was not bad, Friend Ed. He was not evil."

"I know," he said.

"I can't think," she said. "It's coming—the pains are coming."

Joe Saul stood in the open door, his legs apart, his shoulders down; his chin was hard with rage and his eyes flared with fury.

Mordeen moved toward him. Then she saw his hard eyes that looked through and past her, and she moved timidly to the chest under the hanging coats, as though to hide.

Friend Ed cried, "I've been looking for you. I've got my orders. I'm sailing at midnight. What's the matter with you, Joe Saul? Have you been drinking?"

"Drinking? No!" he cried in rage. "I'm a sick man. That's what. I'm—sick!"

Friend Ed spoke in despair. "You went to Dr. Zorn!"

"Yes, I went. I went. I went all by myself. No one asked me to go. Goddamit, no one asked me to go!"

Friend Ed said hopelessly, "You went to Dr. Zorn. You know!"

Mordeen embraced herself in silent agony.

Joe Saul's eyes became wary. He did not meet Friend Ed's eyes. He did not look at Mordeen. "It's my heart. Doc Zorn says I have a bad heart. Me—a bad heart. I was sick once when I was a boy. That caused it."

Friend Ed spoke to Joe Saul as though he were a child. "Well, is it dangerous?"

Joe Saul cried, "Dangerous! He says I'll have to take it easy. Take it easy—me!"

Friend Ed sat in a swivel chair at the end of the table and laughed and laughed. "What's wrong with that? Might be a good thing to take it easy. I'd like to myself. Give you more time with the baby."

Joe Saul said venomously, "I guess so. Mr. Victor has read all the books—now he can do some work."

Mordeen covered her face with her hands.

Friend Ed said, "Forget Victor. Victor is not here."

But Joe Saul went on, unhearing. "Someday he'll be master of a big liner, ladies and the captain's dinner, and he'll go up to the bridge once every watch just to see that everything's all right—but the sea's not in him. It will be a big hotel floating back and forth—maybe so big that they don't even turn it around—like a ferry boat."

"Stop it," Friend Ed said. "Don't blame Victor."

And Joe Saul said harshly, "At the bleak opening of the world we edged along the points in burned-out logs, feeling the coasts. We were sailors. Then with rush sails on cross-tied sticks we moved over the waters, and we raised a little light on the world so that it was not edged in darkness. We shipped long sweeps to beat against the winds and currents. We ranged up the coasts, up and down, from Sidon to Cornwall, from Carthage to Good Hope. And then—oh, timidly we put out into the blackness, crept blindly out and found it was not black at all but another bright world. We knew by roll and creak, by smell and the patterned flight of birds, by brown mud in the sea or floating weeds or a tormented school of herring how it was with the world and with the weather."

Friend Ed said quickly, "Be sure you aren't lying, Joe Saul."

But Joe Saul went on bitterly, "Mr. Victor's all right, and if he's not sure he has a book. But he does not see without looking nor hear without listening. When we came in the harbor he nearly ran down a scow because his hand did not swing over. He had to think and we nearly cut the scow in two. But I was there. Maybe now I will not be there. Maybe another time I'll be in my bunk, a sick man, and on the bridge—Mr. Victor. And I'm the one who wanted to give a present—a present of perfection—a Christmas present."

Friend Ed stood up and walked to the grate and warmed his hands for a moment while he thought. He moved the glowing coals with the short poker. And suddenly he made his decision. He touched Mordeen on the shoulder and strode back to stand over Joe Saul. "You're lying to me, Joe Saul. I don't remember any time before when you had to lie to me. And I would let you lie and gradually come out with your nasty truth, but there's no time. I'm sailing at midnight. So drop your lie."

Joe Saul asked, "What lie?"

"You know what lie. Your heart. That's not it, Joe Saul, and you know it. After all this time you've dug up your hard icy fact and finally you've got to face it. And if I'm to help you as my right and duty say, then I've got to help you with the truth. Name it, Joe Saul, name it, goddam you!"

Joe Saul shivered and his body shrank and he sat down heavily in one of the swivel chairs. His mouth worked helplessly. He said, "I forced it. Zorn didn't want me to see. I forced him. I made him let me see. I was crazy with power and joyfulness. I told him I would go to another man if he did not let me see. I made him let me look in the microscope."

Mordeen stood up and gripped the mantel with her hands. Friend Ed glanced at her and then moved a little to cover the sight of her from Joe Saul. Friend Ed said, "For a fool a happy lie is good enough. But I had hoped you were a little wiser. If you were wiser, the truth could be a glory for you."

Joe Saul went on, "I made him let me look. I saw the slide—big as a porthole it looked, and blinding with light. I turned the knob, and there they were. I saw them—shrunken and crooked and dead, corpses of sperm—dead. And, oh, my God!" Joe Saul covered his eyes with his hands.

Friend Ed got up and stood over his friend in pity. He tried to think. "I haven't much time," he said. "What can I do for you, Joe Saul?"

Joe Saul spoke behind his hands. "What can anyone do? It is finished. My line, my blood, all the procession of the ages is dead. And I am only waiting a little while and then I die."

Friend Ed sighed. He looked to Mordeen for help and then he chose his hard course.

"What are you going to do, Joe Saul?" he said harshly. "Take down your hands. Stop trying to hide in the dark behind your fingers. The world still goes on outside. What are you going to do? What are you going to think? I haven't got much time."

Joe Saul raised his head. "I haven't had much time to think," he said.

"You've had all your life to think. You haven't dared."

Now rage came flooding up in Joe Saul's body and in his mind. "I'll have to kill him," he said hoarsely. "There is no place in the whole world for him to live, knowing and sneering, maybe never telling but always knowing. I cannot have his mind living in the same world with me."

Friend Ed said, "Forget Victor, forget Victor. How about Mordeen?"

Joe Saul bared his teeth and looked at the wall in front of him. "I can't get my mind open to her treachery. I feel that if I let myself look at her or think even for a second about her that I'll go down in a horrible pit with my hands on her throat. Stop torturing me, Friend Ed! Stop torturing me!" And Joe Saul covered his eyes again and his body shook. "There's no place for me to live in the whole world," he said.

Mordeen crept to the chair and hid in it.

Friend Ed's voice cut into Joe Saul like a wet rawhide thong. "Stand up, you cowardly, dirty thing! Stand up, or by Christ I'll hit you sitting down! Stand up!"

Joe Saul looked up in wonder at this rage. He came slowly to his feet. "What's this, Friend Ed?"

"Friend nothing. So much I can take and no more. What is this crawling, whining ego of yours that's so important? How can you dare out of your silly self to crush a lovely thing? Have I wasted my life being friend to a whimpering nastiness?"

"Friend Ed, what are you saying? Don't you understand?"

"I do understand. I understand that you are offered a loveliness and you vomit on it, that you have the gift of love given you such as few men have ever known and you throw on it the acid of your pride, your ugly twisted sense of importance."

"Friend Ed, Friend Ed, don't you understand? It's not my child, it can't be."

"It *is* your child. More than you can conceive in your sick soul. Soul? I wonder what your soul looks like. I think I know —it looks like those dead shrunken sperm." Friend Ed's voice spat at him so that Joe Saul raised his hands as though to protect himself from blows.

"She is giving you a child—yours—to be your own. Her love for you is so great that she could do a thing that was strange and foul to her and yet not be dirtied by it. She ringed herself with love and beauty to give you love and beauty. How wrong she must have been to love a fool—and a filthy fool."

"But why couldn't she tell me? Why did I have to discover—"

"Because you couldn't receive it. Because in your smallness you had not the graciousness to receive this gift. You cannot live because you have not ever looked at life. You crush loveliness on the rocks of your stinking pride. I wonder if you ever could understand." Friend Ed stood towering over Joe Saul and suddenly, without warning, struck him in the face with his open hand, struck him with complete contempt.

Joe Saul's eyes were wide. His hand rose slowly and touched his reddening cheek. And he looked at his fingers. His body sank slowly into the chair, but his eyes, wide with wonder and confusion and pain, did not leave Friend Ed's face.

And Friend Ed's mouth trembled and his eyes were sad. He

kneeled down beside the chair and put his arm around Joe Saul's shoulders. "I've given you everything a friend can give, Joe Saul—even contempt, and that's the hardest thing of all. Killing is easy compared to that." And he said, "You didn't hear what I had to say. I'm sailing at midnight. I've done everything I can—everything. Now you will be all alone on your particular dark ocean. Maybe your soul will require the destruction of everything beautiful around it for its small integrity. But I always thought it might be a little braver soul than that, Joe Saul. It is so easy a thing to give—only great men have the courage and courtesy and, yes, the generosity to receive."

Joe Saul looked blankly away from Friend Ed and closed his eyes.

Friend Ed went on, "Now you are alone. I don't know what you will do or think. But I can't believe, I can't think, that all my life I have been a friend to meanness."

Joe Saul's eyes wandered away and then came back. "Don't leave me, Friend Ed! For God's sake, don't leave me alone! I'm afraid. I don't know what to do." His voice was pleading. "Don't leave me alone."

Friend Ed spoke softly. "I told you—I have my sailing orders. I have to go."

"I'm afraid. I don't know what to do."

"I don't know what you'll do, Joe Saul. But I would hope that some greatness might be left in you. They say that crippled men have compensations which make them stronger than the strong. I could wish that you would know and understand that you are the husband and the father of love. The gift you have received is beyond the furthest hope of most men. It's not that you should try to excuse or explain. You should—you must—search in your dark crippled self for the goodness and the generosity to receive."

Joe Saul looked at him in wonder. "Are you sure that this is true, Friend Ed?"

"I am sure—oh, I am sure. But you—if you ever require sureness you have a long twilight way to go."

Joe Saul said, "It's a new, an unknown road. I don't know that I can find it alone."

"You'll never find it any other way. Come say good-by to

me, Joe Saul. Say a good wish to me standing off to sea, and to yourself—standing off. Come, Joe Saul. Take the first steps. Come, Joe Saul." His hand put a little pressure behind Joe Saul's shoulders and almost forced him to his feet. Friend Ed took Joe Saul's cap from the table and put it on his head and straightened it. And he buttoned the two top gold buttons of Joe Saul's uniform.

Joe Saul said brokenly, "Friend Ed—"

"Hush. You'll have to work it out. You'll have to work it out—alone."

He pushed Joe Saul out and stood with him against the rail. And then Friend Ed came back and stood in the doorway looking into Mordeen's eyes. And he bowed with respect and love. Then he went quickly away. Joe Saul stood gazing after him.

Mordeen got up and moved toward the door, and then a great convulsion shook her and beat her down, and another struck her to her knees. She struggled and writhed on the floor and at last she screamed hoarsely in labor.

Joe Saul rushed in. "Mordeen," he cried. He saw her twisting on the floor. He ran to her and gathered her against his breast. He raised his head and shouted, "Mr. Victor! Mr. Victor, hurry, goddam you! Victor, come help me!"

ACT THREE, SCENE II

The Child

THE small square room was white, impersonal, undecorated, a cell, a little sterile box with a wide door on one side. And in its center stood a high hospital bed and bedside table with a glass of water and a glass straw. And the room was muffled and silent, secret and cut off from every world.

Mordeen lay in the bed, her hair spread over the pillow, and a bundle, silent and covered, was beside her. Her face was masked with gauze and she lay very still, but her breathing was hoarse and her chest rose fiercely, struggling to bring a rush of pure air to her lungs. Then slowly her head turned from side to side and she muttered and moaned, fighting her way up from drugged unconsciousness.

The wide swing door opened and he stood in the entrance. He wore cap and long white tunic. The face, except for the eyes, was covered with a surgical mask. He came softly around the bed and looked down at her under the soft night light. And then he looked down at the muffled bundle that lay beside her. And his gloved hand gently pulled the covering aside.

"Mordeen!" he said softly.

As though she heard him, she took a great gasp of air into her lungs and her head twisted from side to side. "Dead," she whispered. "Dead—the whole world—dead—Victor dead."

He said, "No, Mordeen, not dead—here and alive, always."

She threshed her head violently and she whimpered, "Friend Ed, I wanted—I wanted him to have his child. I wanted—but it's dead. Everything is dead."

Joe Saul said, "Listen to me, Mordeen. He is here—and resting. He's had great effort and now he's sleeping—a little wrinkled and very tired—and the soft hair—" He looked down. "And his mouth—the sweet mouth—like your mouth, Mordeen."

Her eyes snapped open and she struggled up. "Joe Saul, where are you? Joe Saul? Why did you go? Where did you go?"

He pressed her back against the pillow and took a cloth from the table and dried her wet forehead.

"I'm here, Mordeen. I didn't go away, or, if I did, I came back. I'm here."

And she muttered, "Who is dead? Is Joe Saul dead?"

"I'm here," he said. "I went away into an insanity but now I'm back."

"Maybe he'll never know," she said secretly. "Maybe he'll never guess. Maybe Joe Saul will be content." Her chest constricted and she held her breath.

He wiped her forehead until her throat relaxed. "Rest," he said. "I do know and I know more. I know that what seemed the whole tight pattern is not important. Mordeen, I thought, I felt, I knew that my particular seed had importance over other seed. I thought that was what I had to give. It is not so. I know it now."

She said, "You are Joe Saul? Faceless—only a voice and a white facelessness."

"I thought my blood must survive—my line—but it's not so. My knowledge, yes—the long knowledge remembered, repeated, the pride, yes, the pride and warmth, Mordeen, warmth and companionship and love so that the loneliness we wear like icy clothes is not always there. These I can give."

"Where is your face?" she asked. "What's happened to your face, Joe Saul?"

"It's not important. Just a face. The eyes, the nose, the shape of chin—I thought they were worth preserving because they were mine. It is not so.

"It is the race, the species that must go staggering on. Mordeen, our ugly little species, weak and ugly, torn with insanities, violent and quarrelsome, sensing evil—the only species that knows evil and practices it—the only one that senses cleanness and is dirty, that knows about cruelty and is unbearably cruel."

She tried to sit up, tried to raise herself. "Joe Saul, the baby was born dead."

"The baby is alive," he said. "This is the only important thing. Be still, Mordeen. Lie quietly and rest. I've walked into some kind of hell and out. The spark continues—a new human—only being of its kind anywhere—that has struggled without strength when every force of tooth and claw, of storm and cold, of lightning and germ was against it—struggled and survived, survived even the self-murdering instinct."

"Where is he?" she asked.

"Look down. Here he lies sleeping, to teach me. Our dear race, born without courage but very brave, born with a flickering intelligence and yet with beauty in its hands. What animal has made beauty, created it, save only we? With all our horrors and our faults, somewhere in us there is a shining. That is the most important of all facts. *There is a shining.*"

Her eyes were clearing now and her brain climbed up out of the gray ether cloud. "You are Joe Saul," she said. "You are my husband—and you know?"

"I know," he said. "I had to walk into the black to know—to know that every man is father to all children and every child must have all men as father. This is not a little piece of private property, registered and fenced and separated. Mordeen! This is *the Child.*"

Mordeen said, "It is very dark. Turn up the light. Let me have light. I cannot see your face."

"Light," he said. "You want light? I will give you light." He tore the mask from his face, and his face was shining and his eyes were shining. "Mordeen," he said, "I love the child." His voice swelled and he spoke loudly. "Mordeen, I love our child." And he raised his head and cried in triumph, "Mordeen, *I love my son.*"

SWEET THURSDAY

For Elizabeth with love

Prologue

One night Mack lay back on his bed in the Palace Flophouse and he said, "I ain't never been satisfied with that book Cannery Row. *I would of went about it different."*

And after a while he rolled over and raised his head on his hand and he said, "I guess I'm just a critic. But if I ever come across the guy that wrote that book I could tell him a few things."

"Like what?" said Whitey No. 1.

"Well," said Mack, "like this here. Suppose there's chapter one, chapter two, chapter three. That's all right, as far as it goes, but I'd like to have a couple of words at the top so it tells me what the chapter's going to be about. Sometimes maybe I want to go back, and chapter five don't mean nothing to me. If there was just a couple of words I'd know that was the chapter I wanted to go back to."

"Go on," said Whitey No. 1.

"Well, I like a lot of talk in a book, and I don't like to have nobody tell me what the guy that's talking looks like. I want to figure out what he looks like from the way he talks. And another thing—I kind of like to figure out what the guy's thinking by what he says. I like some description too," he went on. "I like to know what color a thing is, how it smells and maybe how it looks, and maybe how a guy feels about it—but not too much of that."

"You sure are a critic," said Whitey No. 2. "Mack, I never give you credit before. Is that all?"

"No," said Mack. "Sometimes I want a book to break loose with a bunch of hooptedoodle. The guy's writing it, give him a chance to do a little hooptedoodle. Spin up some pretty words maybe, or sing a little song with language. That's nice. But I wish it was set aside so I don't have to read it. I don't want hooptedoodle to get mixed up in the story. So if the guy that's writing it wants hooptedoodle, he ought to put it right at first. Then I can skip it if I want to, or maybe go back to it after I know how the story come out."

Eddie said, "Mack, if the guy that wrote Cannery Row *comes in, you going to tell him all that?"*

Whitey No. 2 said, "Hell, Mack can tell anybody anything. Why, Mack could tell a ghost how to haunt a house."

"You're damn right I could," said Mack, "and there wouldn't be no table-rapping or chains. There hasn't been no improvement in house-haunting in years. You're damn right I could, Whitey!" And he lay back and stared up at the canopy over his bed.

"I can see it now," said Mack.

"Ghosts?" Eddie asked.

"Hell, no," said Mack, "chapters. . . ."

1. What Happened in Between

WHEN the war came to Monterey and to Cannery Row everybody fought it more or less, in one way or another. When hostilities ceased everyone had his wounds.

The canneries themselves fought the war by getting the limit taken off fish and catching them all. It was done for patriotic reasons, but that didn't bring the fish back. As with the oysters in *Alice*, "They'd eaten every one." It was the same noble impulse that stripped the forests of the West and right now is pumping water out of California's earth faster than it can rain back in. When the desert comes, people will be sad; just as Cannery Row was sad when all the pilchards were caught and canned and eaten. The pearl-gray canneries of corrugated iron were silent and a pacing watchman was their only life. The street that once roared with trucks was quiet and empty.

Yes, the war got into everybody. Doc was drafted. He put a friend known as Old Jingleballicks in charge of Western Biological Laboratories and served out his time as a tech sergeant in a V.D. section.

Doc was philosophical about it. He whiled away his free hours with an unlimited supply of government alcohol, made many friends, and resisted promotion. When the war was over, Doc was kept on by a grateful government to straighten out certain inventory problems, a job he was fitted for since he had contributed largely to the muck-up. Doc was honorably discharged two years after our victory.

He went back to Western Biological and forced open the water-logged door. Old Jingleballicks hadn't been there for years. Dust and mildew covered everything. There were dirty pots and pans in the sink. Instruments were rusted. The live-animal cages were empty.

Doc sat down in his old chair and a weight descended on him. He cursed Old Jingleballicks, savoring his quiet poisonous words, and then automatically he got up and walked across the silent street to Lee Chong's grocery for beer. A well-dressed man of Mexican appearance stood behind the counter, and only then did Doc remember that Lee Chong was gone.

"Beer," said Doc. "Two quarts."

"Coming up," said the Patrón.

"Is Mack around?"

"Sure. I guess so."

"Tell him I want to see him."

"Tell him who wants to see him?"

"Tell him Doc is back."

"Okay, Doc," said the Patrón. "This kind of beer all right?"

"Any kind of beer's all right," said Doc.

Doc and Mack sat late together in the laboratory. The beer lost its edge and a quart of Old Tennis Shoes took its place while Mack filled in the lost years.

Change was everywhere. People were gone, or changed, and that was almost like being gone. Names were mentioned sadly, even the names of the living. Gay was dead, killed by a piece of anti-aircraft fallback in London. He couldn't keep his nose out of the sky during a bombing. His wife easily remarried on his insurance, but at the Palace Flophouse they kept Gay's bed just as it was, before he went—a little shrine to Gay. No one was permitted to sit on Gay's bed.

And Mack told Doc how Whitey No. 1 took a job in a war plant in Oakland and broke his leg the second day and spent three months in luxury. In his white hospital bed he learned to play rhythm harmonica, an accomplishment he enjoyed all the rest of his life.

Then there was the new Whitey, Whitey No. 2, and Mack was proud of him, for Whitey No. 2 had joined First Marines and gone out as a replacement. Someone, not Whitey No. 2, said he had won a Bronze Star, but if he had he'd lost it, so there was no proof. But he never forgave the Marine Corps for taking his prize away from him—a quart jar of ears pickled in brandy. He'd wanted to put that jar on the shelf over his bed, a memento of his service to his country.

Eddie had stayed on his job with Wide Ida at the Café La Ida. The medical examiner, when he looked at his check sheet and saw what was wrong with Eddie, came to the conclusion that Eddie had been technically dead for twelve years. But Eddie got around just the same, and what with the draft taking everybody away he very nearly became a permanent bartender for Wide Ida. Out of sentiment he emptied the wining jug into a series of little kegs, and when each keg was full he bunged it and buried it. Right now the Palace is the best-endowed flophouse in Monterey County.

Down about the middle of the first quart of Old Tennis Shoes, Mack told how Dora Flood had died in her sleep, leaving the Bear Flag bereft. Her girls were broken-hearted. They put on a lady-drunk that lasted three days, stuck a "Not Open for Business" sign on the door, but through the walls you could hear them doing honor to Dora in three-part harmony—"Rock of Ages," "Asleep in the Deep," and "St. James Infirmary." Those girls really mourned—they mourned like coyotes.

The Bear Flag was taken over by Dora's next of kin, an older sister who came down from San Francisco, where for some years she had been running a Midnight Mission on Howard Street, running it at a profit. She had been a silent partner all along and had dictated its unique practices and policies. For instance, Dora had wanted to name her place the Lone Star, because once in her youth she had spent a wonderful weekend in Fort Worth. But her sister insisted that it be called the Bear Flag, in honor of California. She said if you were hustling a state you should do honor to that state. She didn't find her new profession very different from her old, and she thought of both as a public service. She read horoscopes and continued, after hours at least, to transform the Bear Flag into a kind of finishing school for girls. She was named Flora, but one time in the Mission a gentleman bum finished his soup and said, "Flora, you seem more a fauna-type to me."

"Say, I like that," she said. "Mind if I keep it?" And she did. She was Fauna ever afterward.

Now all this was sad enough, but there was a greater sadness that Mack kept putting off. He didn't want to get to it. And so he told Doc about Henri the painter.

Mack kind of blamed himself for Henri. Henri had built a boat, a perfect little boat with a nice stateroom. But he'd built it up in the woods, because he was afraid of the ocean. His boat sat on concrete blocks and Henri was happy there. One time, when there wasn't much else to do, Mack and the boys played a trick on him. They were bored. They went down to the sea rocks and chiseled off a sack of barnacles and took them up and glued them on the bottom of Henri's boat with quick-drying cement. Henri was pretty upset, particularly since he couldn't tell anybody about it. Doc could have reassured him, but Doc was in the Army. Henri scraped the bottom and painted it, but no sooner was the paint dry than the boys did it again, and stuck a little seaweed on too. They were terribly ashamed when they saw what happened. Henri sold his boat and left town within twenty-four hours. He could not shake the persistent and horrifying notion that the boat was going to sea while he was asleep.

And Mack told how Hazel had been in the Army too, although you couldn't get anybody to believe it. Hazel was in the Army long enough to qualify for the G.I. bill, and he enrolled at the University of California for training in astrophysics by making a check mark on an application. Three months later, when some of the confusion had died down, the college authorities discovered him. The Department of Psychology wanted to keep him, but it was against the law.

Hazel often wondered what it was that he had gone to study. He intended to ask Doc, but by the time Doc got back it had slipped his mind.

Doc poured out the last of the first bottle of Old Tennis Shoes, and he said, "You've talked about everything else. What happened to you, Mack?"

Mack said, "I just kind of stayed around and kept things in order."

Well, Mack had kept things in order, and he had discussed war with everybody he'd met. He called his war the Big War. That was the first one. After the war the atom-bomb tests interested him, in a Fourth-of-July kind of way. The huge reward the government offered for the discovery of new uranium deposits set off a chain reaction in Mack, and he bought a secondhand Geiger counter.

At the Monterey bus station the Geiger counter started buzzing and Mack went along with it—first to San Francisco, then to Marysville, Sacramento, Portland. Mack was so scientifically interested that he didn't notice the girl on the same bus. That is, he didn't notice her much. Well, one thing led to another, which was not unique in Mack's experience. The girl was taking the long way to Jacksonville, Florida. Mack would have left her in Tacoma if his Geiger counter hadn't throbbed him eastward. He got clear to Salina, Kansas, with the girl. On a hot muggy day the girl lunged at a fly on the bus and broke her watch, and only then did Mack discover that he had been following a radium dial. Romance alone was not enough for Mack at his age. He arrived back in Monterey on a flatcar, under a tarpaulin that covered a medium-sized tank destined for Fort Ord. Mack was very glad to get home. He had won a few dollars from a guard on the flatcar. He scrubbed out the Palace Flophouse and planted a row of morning glories along the front, and he and Eddie got it ready for the returning heroes. They had quite a time when the heroes straggled back.

Over Doc and Mack a golden melancholy settled like autumn leaves, melancholy concocted equally of Old Tennis Shoes and old times, of friends lost and friends changed. And both of them knew they were avoiding one subject, telling minor stories to avoid a major one. But at last they were dry, and their subject confronted them.

Doc opened with considerable bravery. "What do you think of the new owner over at the grocery?"

"Oh, he's all right," said Mack. "Kind of interesting. The only trouble is he can't never take Lee Chong's place. There was never a friend like Lee Chong," Mack said brokenly.

"Yes, he was wise and good," said Doc.

"And tricky," said Mack.

"And smart," said Doc.

"He took care of a lot of people," said Mack.

"And he took a few," said Doc.

They volleyed Lee Chong back and forth, and their memories built virtues that would have surprised him, and cleverness and beauty too. While one told a fine tale of that mercantile Chinaman the other waited impatiently to top the story. Out of their memories there emerged a being scarcely human, a dragon of goodness and an angel of guile. In such a way are the gods created.

But the bottle was empty now, and its emptiness irritated Mack, and his irritation oozed toward Lee Chong's memory.

"The son-of-a-bitch was sneaky," said Mack. "He should of

told us he was going to sell out and go away. It wasn't friendly, doing all that alone without his friends to help."

"Maybe that's what he was afraid of," said Doc. "Lee wrote to me about it. I couldn't advise him—I was too far away—so he was safe."

"You can't never find out what a Chink's got on his mind," said Mack. "Doc, who would of thought he was what you might say—plotting?"

Oh, it had been a shocking thing. Lee Chong had operated his emporium for so long that no one could possibly have foreseen that he would sell out. He was so mixed up in the feeding and clothing of Cannery Row that he was considered permanent. Who could have suspected the secret turnings of his paradoxical Oriental mind, which seems to have paralleled the paradoxical Occidental mind?

It is customary to think of a sea captain sitting in his cabin, planning a future grocery store not subject to wind or bottom-fouling. Lee Chong dreamed while he worked his abacus and passed out pints of Old Tennis Shoes and delicately sliced bacon with his big knife. He dreamed all right—he dreamed of the sea. He did not share his plans or ask advice. He would have got lots of advice.

One day Lee Chong sold out and bought a schooner. He wanted to go trading in the South Seas. He dreamed of palms and Polynesians. In the hold of his schooner he loaded the entire stock of his store—all the canned goods, the rubber boots, the caps and needles and small tools, the fireworks and calendars, even the glass-fronted showcases where he kept gold-plated collarbuttons and cigarette lighters. He took it all with him. And the last anyone saw of him, he was waving his blue naval cap from the flying bridge of his dream ship as he passed the whistle buoy at Point Pinos into the sunset. And if he didn't go down on the way over, that's where he is now—probably lying in a hammock under an awning on the rear deck, while beautiful Polynesian girls in very scanty clothes pick over his stock of canned tomatoes and striped mechanics' caps.

"Why do you suppose he done it?" Mack asked.

"Who knows?" said Doc. "Who knows what lies deep in any man's mind? Who knows what any man wants?"

"He won't he happy there," said Mack. "He'll be lonely out among them foreigners. You know, Doc, I figured it out. It was them goddam movies done it. You remember, he used to close up every Thursday night. That's because there was a change of bill at the movie house. He never missed a movie. That's what done it, the movies. I and you, Doc, we know what liars the movies are. He won't be happy out there. He'll just be miserable to come back."

Doc gazed at his run-down laboratory. "I wish I were out there with him," he said.

"Who don't?" said Mack. "Why, them South Sea Island girls will kill him. He ain't as young as he used to be."

"I know," said Doc. "You and I should be out there, Mack, to help protect him from himself. I'm wondering, Mack, should I step across the street and get another pint or should I go to bed?"

"Why don't you flip a coin?"

"You flip the coin," said Doc. "I don't really want to go to bed. If you flip it I'll know how it's going to come out."

Mack flipped, and he was right. Mack said, "I'd just as lief step over for you, Doc. You just set here comfortable—I'll be right back." And he was.

2. *The Troubled Life of Joseph and Mary*

MACK came back with a pint of Old Tennis Shoes and he poured some in Doc's glass and some in his own.

Doc said, "What kind of a fellow is the new owner over there—Mexican, isn't he?"

"Nice fellow," said Mack. "Classy dresser. Name of Joseph and Mary Rivas. Smart as a whip, but kind of unfortunate, Doc—unfortunate and funny. You know how it is, when a pimp falls in love it don't make any difference how much he suffers—it's funny. And Joseph and Mary's kind of like that."

"Tell me about him," said Doc.

"I been studying him," said Mack. "He told me some stuff and I put two and two together. He's smart. You know, Doc, there's a kind of smartness that cuts its own throat. Haven't you knew people that was so busy being smart they never had time to do nothing else? Well, Joseph and Mary is kind of like that."

"Tell me," said Doc.

"I guess you couldn't find no two people oppositer than what you and him is," Mack began. "You're nice, Doc, nice and egg-heady, but a guy would have to be nuts to think you was smart. Everybody takes care of you because you're wide open. Anybody is like to throw a sneak-punch at Joseph and Mary just because he's in there dancing and feinting all the time. And he's nice too, in a way."

"Where'd he come from?" Doc asked.

"Well, I'll tell you," said Mack.

Mack was right. Doc and Joseph and Mary were about as opposite as you can get, but delicately opposite. Their differences balanced like figures of a mobile in a light breeze. Doc was a man whose whole direction and impulse was legal and legitimate. Left to his own devices, he would have obeyed every law, down to pausing at boulevard stop signs. The fact that Doc was constantly jockeyed into illicit practices was the fault of his friends, not of himself—the fault of Wide Ida, whom the liquor laws cramped like a tight girdle, and of the Bear Flag, whose business, while accepted and recognized, was certainly mentioned disparagingly in every conceivable statute book.

Mack and the boys had lived so long in the shadow of the vagrancy laws that they considered them a shield and an umbrella. Their association with larceny, fraud, loitering, illegal congregation, and conspiracy on all levels was not only accepted, but to a certain extent had become a matter of pride to the inhabitants of Cannery Row. But they were lamblike children of probity and virtue compared to Joseph and Mary. Everything he did naturally turned out to be against the law. This had been true from his earliest childhood. In Los Angeles, where he had been born, he led a gang of pachucos while he was still a child. The charge that he lagged with loaded pennies, if not provable, at least seems reasonable. He rejected the theory of private ownership of removable property almost from birth. At the age of eight he was a pool hustler of such success that Navy officers had been known to put him off limits. When the gang wars started in the Mexican district of Los Angeles, Joseph and Mary rose above pachucos. He set up an ambulatory store, well stocked with switch knives, snap guns, brass knuckles, and, for the very poor, socks loaded with sand, cheap and very effective. At twelve he matriculated at reform school, and two years later emerged with honors. He had learned nearly every criminal technique in existence. This fourteen-year-old handsome boy with sad and innocent eyes could operate the tumblers of a safe with either fingers or stethoscope. He could make second stories as though he had suction cups on his feet. But no sooner had he mastered these arts than he abandoned them, reasoning that the odds were too great. He was always a smart boy. Joseph and Mary was looking for a profession wherein the victim was the partner of the predator. The badger game, the swinging panel, and the Spanish treasure were nearer to his ideal. But even they fell short. He had never made a police blotter and he wanted to keep it that way. Somewhere he felt there was a profession illegal enough to satisfy him morally and yet safe enough not to outrage his instinctive knowledge of the law of averages. You might have said he was well launched on his career when, suddenly, puberty smote him, and for a number of years his activities took a different direction.

In the fields of larceny and fraud Joseph and Mary vegetated for a number of years. He was a man when the fog cleared from before his eyes and he could see again. Then just when he was set to go, the Army got him and kept him as long as it could in good conscience. It is said that his final dishonorable discharge is a masterpiece of understatement.

J and M never could get set. He started again on his career and took a wrong turning, for he fell under the influence of a young and understanding priest, who drew him into the warm bosom of Mother Church, into which Joseph and Mary had been born anyway. Now Joseph and Mary Rivas approved of confession and forgiveness, and he felt, as perhaps François Villon had, that under the protection of the cloth he might find some outlet for his talent. Father Murphy taught him the theory of honest labor, and when Joseph and Mary had got over the shock of the principle he decided to give it a try. He was still malleable, and he succeeded, where Villon had failed, in keeping his hands off church property. With the help of Father Murphy, who had influence in the city government, Joseph and Mary found himself the possessor of a city job, a position of dignity, with a monthly check to be cashed without fear of fingerprinting.

The Plaza in Los Angeles is a pretty square, ornamented with small gardens, palms in great pots, and many, many flowers. It is a landmark, a tourist center, a city pride, for it preserves a Mexican-ness unknown in Mexico. Joseph and Mary, then, was in charge of watering and cultivating the plants in the Plaza—a job that was not only easy and pleasant but kept him in direct touch with those tourists who might be interested in small packets of art studies. Although Joseph and Mary realized he could never get rich in this job, he took a certain pleasure in being partly legal. It gave him the satisfaction most people find in sin.

At about this time the Los Angeles Police Department had a puzzle on its hands. Marijuana was being distributed in fairly large quantities and at a greatly reduced price. The narcotics squad conducted raid after raid without finding the source. Every vacant lot was searched from San Pedro to Eagle Rock. And then the countryside was laid out on graphing paper and the search for the pointed leaves of the marijuana went on in ever-widening circles: north past Santa Barbara; east to the Colorado River; south as far as the border. The border was sealed, and it is well known that muggles does not grow in the Pacific Ocean. Six months of intensive search, with the cooperation of all local officials and the state police, got absolutely nowhere. The supply continued unabated, and the narcotics squad was convinced that the pushers did not know the source.

Heaven knows how long the situation might have continued if it had not been for Mildred Bugle, thirteen, head of her class in Beginning Botany, Los Angeles High School. One Saturday afternoon she crossed the Plaza, picked some interesting leaves growing around a potted palm, and positively identified them as Cannabis Americana.

Joseph and Mary Rivas might have been in trouble but for the fact that the Los Angeles Police Department was in worse trouble. They could not bring him to book. How would it look if the newspapers got hold of the story that the Plaza was the source of supply? that the product had been planted and nurtured by a city employee, freshened with city water, and fed with city manure?

Joseph and Mary was given a floater so strongly worded that it singed his eyelashes. The police even bought him a bus ticket as far as San Luis Obispo.

Doc chuckled. "You know, Mack," he said, "you're almost building a case for honesty."

"I always put in a good word for it," said Mack.

"How did he get in the wetback business?" Doc asked.

"Well, he was casing the field for a career," said Mack, "and wetbacks looked like a gold-brick cinch. Joseph and Mary figured the angles and the percentage. You look at it and you see it couldn't flop." He put up his fingers to count facts, then took a quick drink to tide him over the period when his hands would be tied up.

Mack touched the little finger of his left hand with his right forefinger. "Number one," he said. "J and M talks Mexican because his old man and his old lady was Mexican before they come to L.A." He touched his third finger. "Number two, the wetbacks come in by theirself. Nobody makes them come. There's a steady supply. Number three, they can't talk English and they don't know a cop from a bucket. They *need* somebody like Joseph and Mary to take care of them and get them jobs and take their pay. If one of them gets mean, all J and M got to do is call the federal men, and they deport him without no trouble to J and M. That's what he was always looking for—a racket with the percentage stacked for the house. He figures he's got three or four crews working in fruit and vegetables and he can kind of lay back and rest, the way he always wanted. That's why he bought out Lee Chong. He figured to make the grocery a kind of labor center, where he could rest up his men and sell them stuff at the same time. And what he's doing ain't very much against the law."

Doc said, "I can tell, from your tone, it didn't work. What happened?"

"Music," said Mack.

Now it is true that Joseph and Mary did know all the angles, averages, and percentages. His systems couldn't lose, but they did. The odds are against making your point with the dice, and that law holds until magic intervenes and someone makes a run.

There were literally millions of wetbacks in the country—quiet, hard-working, ignorant men, content to bend their backs over the demanding earth. It was a setup; it couldn't lose. How did it happen, then, that in Joseph and Mary's crew there should be one tenor and one guitar player? Under his horrified eyes an orchestra took shape—two guitars, a guitarón, rhythm and maraca men, a tenor, and two baritones. He would have had the whole lot deported if his nephew, Cacahuete, had not joined them with his hot trumpet.

Joseph and Mary's wetbacks abandoned the carrot and cauliflower fields for the dance floors of the little towns in California. They called themselves the Espaldas Mojadas. They played "Ven á Mi, Mi Chica Dolorosa" and "Mujer de San Luis" and "El Nubito Blanco que Llora."

The Espaldas Mojadas dressed in tight *charro* costumes, wore huge Mexican hats, and played for dances in the Spreckel Fireman's Hall, the Soledad I.O.O.F., the Elks of King City, the Greenfield Garage, the San Ardo Municipal Auditorium. Joseph and Mary stopped fighting them and started booking them. Business was so good he screened new wetbacks for talent. It was Joseph and Mary's first entrance into show business, and its native dishonesty reassured him that his course was well chosen.

"So, you see," said Mack, "it was music done it. You can't trust nothing no more. You take Fauna now—the Bear Flag ain't like any hookshop on land or sea. She makes them girls take table-manner lessons and posture lessons, and she reads the stars. You never seen nothing like it. Everything's changed, Doc, everything."

Doc looked around his moldy laboratory, and he shivered. "Maybe I'm changed too," he said.

"Hell, Doc, you can't change. Why, what could we depend on! Doc, if you change a lot of people are going to cash in their chips. Why, we was all just waiting around for you to get back so we could go on being normal."

"I don't feel the same, Mack. I'm restless."

"Now you get yourself a girl," said Mack. "You play some of the churchy music to her on your phonograph. And then I'll come in and hustle you for a couple of bucks. Make a try, Doc. You owe it to your friends."

"I'll try," said Doc, "but I have no confidence in it. I'm afraid I've changed."

3. *Hooptedoodle (1)*

LOOKING back, you can usually find the moment of the birth of a new era, whereas, when it happened, it was one day hooked on to the tail of another.

There were prodigies and portents that winter and spring, but you never notice such things until afterward. On Mount Toro the snow came down as far as Pine Canyon on one side and Jamesburg on the other. A six-legged calf was born in Carmel Valley. A cloud drifting in formed the letters O-N in the sky over Monterey. Mushrooms grew out of the concrete floor of the basement of the Methodist Church. Old Mr. Roletti, at the age of ninety-three, developed senile satyriasis and had to be forcibly restrained from chasing high-school girls. The spring was cold, and the rains came late. Velella in their purple billions sailed into Monterey Bay and were cast up on the beaches, where they died. Killer whales attacked the sea lions near Seal Rocks and murdered a great number of them. Dr. Wick took a kidney stone out of Mrs. Gaston as big as your hand and shaped like a dog's head, a beagle. The Lions' Club announced a fifty-dollar prize for the best essay on "Football—Builder of Character." And last, but far from least, the Sherman rose developed a carnation bud. Perhaps all this meant nothing; you never notice such things until afterward.

Monterey had changed, and so had Cannery Row and its denizens. As Mack said, "The tum-tum changes, giving place to new. And God tum-tums himself in many ways."

Doc was changing in spite of himself, in spite of the prayers of his friends, in spite of his own knowledge. And why not? Men do change, and change comes like a little wind that ruffles the curtains at dawn, and it comes like the stealthy perfume of wildflowers hidden in the grass. Change may be announced by a small ache, so that you think you're catching cold. Or you may feel a faint disgust for something you loved yesterday. It may even take the form of a hunger that peanuts will not satisfy. Isn't overeating said to be one of the strongest symptoms of discontent? And isn't discontent the lever of change?

Before the war Doc had lived a benign and pleasant life, which aroused envy in some gnat-bitten men. Doc made a living, as good a living as he needed or wanted, by collecting and preserving various marine animals and selling them to schools, colleges, and museums. He was able to turn affable and uncritical eyes on a world full of excitement. He combined the beauty of the sea with man's loveliest achievement—music. Through his superb phonograph he could hear the angelic voice of the Sistine Choir and could wander half lost in the exquisite masses of William Byrd. He believed there were two human achievements that towered above all others: the *Faust* of Goethe and the *Art of the Fugue* of J. S. Bach. Doc was never bored. He was beloved and preyed on by his friends, and this contented him. For he remembered the words of Diamond Jim Brady who, when told that his friends were making suckers of him, remarked, "It's fun to be a sucker—if you can afford it." Doc could afford it. He had not the vanity which makes men try to be smart.

Doc's natural admiration and desire for women had always been satisfied by women themselves. He had few responsibilities except to be a kindly, generous, and amused man. And these he did not find difficult. All in all, he had always been a fulfilled and contented man. A specimen so rare aroused yearning in other men, for how few men like their work, their lives—how very few men like themselves. Doc liked himself, not in an adulatory sense, but just as he would have liked anyone else. Being at ease with himself put him at ease with the world.

In the Army there had been times when he longed for his music, for his little animals, and for the peace and interest of his laboratory. Coming home, forcing open the water-swollen door, was a pleasure and a pain to him. He sighed as he looked at his bookshelves. It took him ten minutes to decide which record to play first. And then the past was gone and he was faced with the future. Old Jingleballicks had kept the little business going in a manner even more inefficient than Doc had, and then had left it to founder. The stocks of preserved animals were depleted. The business contacts had lapsed. The bank that held his mortgage was no longer checked by patriotism. There was some question whether Doc could ever build back his marginal business. In the old days he would have forgotten such considerations in multiple pleasures and interests. Now discontent nibbled at him—not painfully, but constantly.

Where does discontent start? You are warm enough, but you shiver. You are fed, yet hunger gnaws you. You have been loved, but your yearning wanders in new fields. And to prod all these there's time, the bastard Time. The end of life is now not so terribly far away—you can see it the way you see the finish line when you come into the stretch—and your mind says, "Have I worked enough? Have I eaten enough? Have I loved enough?" All of these, of course, are the foundation of man's greatest curse, and perhaps his greatest glory. "What has my life meant so far, and what can it mean in the time left to me?" And now we're coming to the wicked, poisoned dart: "What have I contributed in the Great Ledger? What am I worth?" And this isn't vanity or ambition. Men seem to be born with a debt they can never pay no matter how hard they try. It piles up ahead of them. Man owes something to man. If he ignores the debt it poisons him, and if he tries to make payments the debt only increases, and the quality of his gift is the measure of the man.

Doc's greatest talent had been his sense of paying as he went. The finish line had meant nothing to him except that he had wanted to crowd more living into the stretch. Each day ended with its night; each thought with its conclusion; and every morning a new freedom arose over the eastern mountains and lighted the world. There had never been any reason to suppose it would be otherwise. People made pilgrimages to the laboratory to bask in Doc's designed and lovely purposelessness. For what can a man accomplish that has not been done a million times before? What can he say that he will not find in Lao-Tse or the *Bhagavad-gita* or the Prophet Isaiah? It is better to sit in appreciative contemplation of a world in which beauty is eternally supported on a foundation of ugliness: cut out the support, and beauty will sink from sight. It was a good thing Doc had, and many people wished they had it too.

But now the worm of discontent was gnawing at him. Maybe it was the beginning of Doc's middle age that caused it—glands slackening their flow, skin losing its bloom, taste buds weakening, eyes not so penetrating, and hearing dulled a little. Or it might have been the new emptiness of Cannery Row—the silent machines, the rusting metal. Deep in himself Doc felt a failure. But he was a reasonably realistic man. He had his eyes examined, his teeth X-rayed. Dr. Horace Dormody went over him and discovered no secret focus of infection to cause the restlessness. And so Doc threw himself into his work, hoping, the way a man will, to smother the unease with weariness. He collected, preserved, injected, until his stock shelves were crowded again. New generations of cotton rats crawled on the wire netting of the cages, and four new rattlesnakes abandoned themselves to a life of captivity and ease.

But the discontent was still there. The pains that came to Doc were like a stir of uneasiness or the flick of a skipped heartbeat. Whisky lost its sharp delight and the first long pull of beer from a frosty glass was not the joy it had been. He stopped listening in the middle of an extended story. He was not genuinely glad to see a friend. And sometimes, starting to turn over a big rock in the Great Tide Pool—a rock under which he knew there would be a community of frantic animals—he would drop the rock back in place and stand, hands on hips, looking off to sea, where the round clouds piled up white with pink and black edges. And he would be thinking, What am I thinking? What do I want? Where do I want to go? There would be wonder in him, and a little impatience, as though he stood outside and looked in on himself through a glass shell. And he would be conscious of a tone within himself, or several tones, as though he heard music distantly.

Or it might be this way. In the late night Doc might be working at his old and battered microscope, delicately arranging plankton on a slide, moving them with a thread of glass. And there would be three voices singing in him, all singing together. The top voice of his thinking mind would sing, "What lovely little particles, neither plant nor animal but somehow both—the reservoir of all the life in the world, the base supply of food for everyone. If all of these should die, every other living thing might well die as a consequence." The lower voice of his feeling mind would be singing, "What are you looking for, little man? Is it yourself you're trying to identify? Are you looking at little things to avoid big things?" And the third voice, which came from his marrow, would sing, "Lonesome! Lonesome! What good is it? Who benefits? Thought is the evasion of feeling. You're only walling up the leaking loneliness."

Sometimes he would leave his work and walk out to the lighthouse to watch the white flail of light strike at the horizons. Once there, of course, his mind would go back to the plankton, and he would think, It's a protein food of course. If I could find a way to release this food directly to humans, why, nobody in the world would have to go hungry again. And the bottom voice would sing, "Lonesome, lonesome! You're trying to buy your way in."

Doc thought he was alone in his discontent, but he was not. Everyone on the Row observed him and worried about him. Mack and the boys worried about him. And Mack said to Fauna, "Doc acts like a guy that needs a dame."

"He can have the courtesy of the house any time," said Fauna.

"I don't mean that," said Mack. "He needs a dame around. He needs a dame to fight with. Why, that can keep a guy so goddam busy defending himself he ain't got no time to blame himself."

Fauna regarded marriage with a benevolent eye. Not only was it a desirable social condition, but it sent her some of her best customers.

"Well, let's marry him off," said Fauna.

"Oh no," said Mack. "I wouldn't go that far. My God! Not Doc!"

Doc tried to solve his problem in the ancient way. He took a long, leisurely trip to La Jolla, four hundred miles south. He traveled in the old manner, with lots of beer and a young lady companion whose interest in invertebrate zoology Doc thought might be flexible—and it was.

The whole trip was a success: weather calm and warm, tides low. Under the weed-wreathed boulders of the intertidal zone Doc found, by great good fortune, twenty-eight baby octopi with tentacles four or five inches long. It was a little bonanza for him if he could keep them alive. He handled them tenderly, put them in a wooden collecting bucket, and floated seaweed over them for protection. An excitement was growing in him.

His companion began to be a little disappointed. Doc's enthusiasm for the octopi indicated that he was not as flexible as she. And no girl likes to lose center stage, particularly to an octopus. The four-hundred-mile trip back to Monterey was made in a series of short dashes, for Doc stopped every few miles to dampen the sack that covered the collecting bucket.

"Octopi can't stand heat," he said.

He recited no poetry to her. The subject of her eyes, her feelings, her skin, her thought, did not come up. Instead Doc told her about octopi—a subject that would have fascinated her two days before.

Doc said, "They're wonderful animals, delicate and complicated and shy."

"Ugly brutes," said the girl.

"No, not ugly," said Doc. "But I see why you say it. People have always been repelled and at the same time fascinated by octopi. Their eyes look baleful and cruel. And all kinds of myths have grown up around octopi too. You know the story of the kraken, of course."

"Of course," she said shortly.

"Octopi are timid creatures really," Doc said excitedly. "Most complicated. I'll show you when I get them in the aquarium. Of course there can't be any likeness, but they do have some traits that seem to be almost human. Mostly they hide and avoid trouble, but I've seen one deliberately murder another. They appear to feel terror too, and rage. They change color when they're disturbed and angry, almost like the rage blush of a man."

"Very interesting," said the girl, and she tucked her skirt in around her knees.

Doc went on, "Sometimes they get so mad they collapse and die of something that parallels apoplexy. They're highly emotional animals. I'm thinking of writing a paper about them."

"You might find out what causes human apoplexy," said the girl, and because he wasn't listening for it, Doc didn't hear the satire in her tone.

There's no need for giving the girl a name. She never came back to Western Biological. Her interest in science blinked out like a candle, but a flame was lighted in Doc.

The flame of conception seems to flare and go out, leaving man shaken, and at once happy and afraid. There's plenty of precedent of course. Everyone knows about Newton's apple. Charles Darwin said his *Origin of Species* flashed complete in one second, and he spent the rest of his life backing it up; and the theory of relativity occurred to Einstein in the time it takes to clap your hands. This is the greatest mystery of the human mind—the inductive leap. Everything falls into place, irrelevancies relate, dissonance becomes harmony, and nonsense wears a crown of meaning. But the clarifying leap springs from the rich soil of confusion, and the leaper is not unfamiliar with pain.

The girl said good-by and went away, and Doc did not know she was gone. For that matter he did not know she had been with him.

With infinite care Doc scrubbed out a big aquarium, carpeted it with sea sand, and laid in stones populated with sponges and hydroids and anemones. He planted seaweeds and caught little crabs and eels and tide-pool Johnnys. He carried buckets of sea water from the beach and set up a pump to circulate the water from tank to aquarium and back. He considered every factor within his knowledge—relations of plant and animal life, food, filtering, oxygenation. He built an octopus world within walls of glass, trying to anticipate every octopus need and to eliminate every octopus enemy or danger. He considered light and heat.

Eight of his octopi were dead, but the twenty living ones scuttled to the bottom of their new home and hid themselves, throbbing and blushing with emotion. Doc drew a stool close and peered into the little world he had made, and his mind was filled with cool green thoughts and stately figures. For the moment he was at peace. The pale expressionless eyes of the octopi seemed to be looking into his eyes.

In the days that followed, Doc's disposition was so unpredictable that Mack exhausted every other possibility before he moved in on Western Biological for the two dollars he thought he needed.

Mack's campaign was probably the most elaborate of his career. It began quietly, and only after a thorough preparation did it begin to take shape. Then spinnerets of emotion laced in and the heavy notes of tragic necessity began to be faintly heard. Drama grew, as it should, out of its inherent earth. Mack's voice was controlled and soft—no trembling yet—just a reasonable, clear, but potentially passionate growth. Mack knew he was doing well. He could hear himself, and he knew that if he were on the receiving end he would find it impossible not to weaken. Why, then, did not Doc turn his eyes from the dimly lit aquarium? He had certainly said "hello" when Mack came in. A little shakily Mack cut in the *vox angelica*, the *vox dolorosa*, and finally a *bendiga stupenda* so moving that Mack himself was in tears.

Doc did not turn his head.

Mack stood stunned. It is a frightening thing to lay out everything you have, to finish, and have no response. He didn't know what to do next. He said loudly, "Doc!"

"Hello," said Doc.

"Don't you feel good?"

"Sure, Mack. How much do you want?"

"Two dollars."

Doc reached in his hip pocket for his wallet without lifting his eyes. Mack's great performance had been wasted. He might just as well have simply come in and asked for the money. He knew he could never reach such a height again. A sudden anger came over him, and he considered refusing the money, but his natural good sense saved him. He stood there rolling the dollar bills between his fingers. "What's got into you, Doc?" he asked.

Doc turned slowly toward him. "There's going to be one great difficulty," he said. "How am I going to light them? It's always a problem, but in this case it might be insuperable."

"Light what, Doc?"

"We start with two obvious problems," Doc continued. "First, they can't stand heat, and second, they are to a certain extent photophobic. I don't know how I'm going to get enough cold light on them. Would it be possible, do you suppose, to condition them, to light them constantly, so that the photophobia subsides?"

"Oh sure," said Mack uneasily.

"Don't be too sure," said Doc. "The very process of conditioning might, if it did not kill them, change their normal reactions. It's always difficult to evaluate responses that approximate emotions. If I place them in an abnormal situation, can I trust the response to be normal?"

"No," said Mack.

"You cannot dissect for emotion," Doc went on. "If a human body were found by another species and dissected, there would be no possible way of knowing about its emotions or its thoughts. Now, it occurs to me that the rage, or rather the symptom that seems like rage, must be fairly abnormal in itself. I have seen it happen in aquariums. Does it occur on the sea bottom? Is the observed phenomenon not perhaps limited to the aquarium? No, I can't permit myself to believe that, or my whole thesis falls."

"Doc!" Mack cried. "Look, Doc, it's me—Mack!"

"Hello, Mack," said Doc. "How much did you say?"

"You've already give it to me," said Mack, and he felt like a fool the moment he'd said it.

"I need better equipment," said Doc. "Goddam it, I can't see without better equipment."

"Doc, how's about you and me stepping over and getting a half-pint of Old Tennis Shoes?"

"Fine," said Doc.

"I'll buy," said Mack. "I've got a couple of loose bucks."

Doc said sharply, "I'll have to get some money. Where can I get some money, Mack?"

"I told you, I'll buy, Doc."

"I'll need a wide-angle binocularscope and light. I'll have to find out about light—maybe a pinpoint spot from across the room. No, they'd move out of that. Maybe there are new kinds of lights. I'll have to look into it."

"Come on, Doc."

Doc bought a pint of Old Tennis Shoes and later sent Mack out with money to buy another pint. The two of them sat in the laboratory side by side, staring into the aquarium, resting their elbows on the shelf, and they got to the point where they were mixing a little water with the whisky.

"I got an uncle with an eye like them," said Mack. "Rich old bastard too. I wonder why, when you get rich, you get a cold eye."

"Self-protection," said Doc solemnly. "Conditioned by relatives, I guess."

"Like I was saying, Doc. Everybody in the Row is worried about you. You don't have no fun. You wander around like you was lost."

"I guess it's reorientation," said Doc.

"Well, some people think you need a dame to kind of nudge you out of it. I know a guy that every time he gets feeling low he goes back to his wife. Makes him appreciate what he had. He goes away again and feels just fine."

"Shock therapy," said Doc. "I'm all right, Mack. Don't let anybody give me a wife though—don't let them give me a wife! I guess a man needs a direction. That's what I've been needing. You can only go in circles so long."

"I kind of like it that way," said Mack.

"I'm going to call my paper 'Symptoms in Some Cephalopods Approximating Apoplexy.' "

"Great God Almighty!" said Mack.

4. *There Would Be No Game*

As he got to know him, Joseph and Mary regarded Doc with something akin to love—for love feeds on the unknown and unknowable. Doc's honesty was exotic to Joseph and Mary. He found it strange. It attracted him in spite of the fact that he could not understand it. He felt that there was something he had missed, though he could not figure what it was.

One day, sitting in Western Biological, Joseph and Mary saw a chess board and, finding that it was a game and being good at games, he asked Doc to teach him. J and M easily absorbed the characters and qualities of castles and bishops and knights and royalty and pawns. During the first game Doc was called to the telephone, and when he returned he said, "You've moved a pawn of mine and your queen and knight."

"How'd you know?" the Patrón asked.

"I know the game," said Doc. "Look, Joseph and Mary, chess is possibly the only game in the world in which it is impossible to cheat."

Joseph and Mary inspected this statement with amazement. "Why not?" he demanded.

"If it were possible to cheat there would be no game," said Doc.

J and M carried this away with him. It bothered him at night. He looked at it from all angles. And he went back to ask more about it. He was charmed with the idea, but he couldn't understand it.

Doc explained patiently, "Both players know exactly the same things. The game is played in the mind."

"I don't get it."

"Well, look! You can't cheat in mathematics or poetry or music because they're based on truth. Untruth or cheating is just foreign, it has no place. You can't cheat in arithmetic."

Joseph and Mary shook his head. "I don't get it," he said.

It was a shocking conception, and he was drawn to it because, in a way, its outrageousness seemed to him like a new, strange way of cheating. In the back of his mind an idea stirred. Suppose you took honesty and made a racket of it—it might be the toughest of all to break. It was so new to him that his mind recoiled from it, but still it wouldn't let him alone. His eyes narrowed. "Maybe he's worked out a system," he said to himself.

5. Enter Suzy

It is popular to picture a small town constable as dumb and clumsy. In the books he plays the stock bumpkin part. And people retain this attitude even when they know it's not true. We have so many beliefs we know are not true.

A constable, if he has served for a few years, knows more about his town than anyone else and on all levels. He is aware of the delicate political balance between mayor and councilmen, Fire Department and insurance companies. He knows why Mrs. Geltham is giving a big party and who is likely to be there. Usually he knows, when Mabel Andrews reports a burglar, whether it is a rat in the dining room, a burglar, or just wishful thinking. A constable knows that Mr. Geltham is sleeping with the schoolteacher and how often. He knows when high-school boys have switched from gin to marijuana. He is aware of every ripple on the town's surface. If there is a crime the constable usually knows who didn't do it and often who did. With a good constable on duty a hundred things don't happen that might. Sometimes there's a short discussion in an alley; sometimes a telephone call; sometimes only his shadow under a street light. When he gets a cat down out of a tree he knows all about the owner of the cat. And many weeping, parent-prodded little boys and girls put small things, stolen from the Five-and-Dime, in the constable's hands, and he, if he is a good constable, gives them a sense of mercy-in-justice without injuring the dignity of the law.

A stranger getting off the Del Monte Express in Monterey wouldn't be aware that his arrival was noted, but if something happened that night he would know it all right.

Monterey's Joe Blaikey was a good constable. He wouldn't ever be chief—didn't much want to be. Everybody in town liked Joe and trusted him. He was the only man in town who could stop a husband-and-wife fight. He came by his techniques in both social life and in violence from being the youngest of fifteen nice but violent children. Just getting along at home had been his teacher. Joe knew everyone in Monterey and he could size up a stranger almost instantly.

When a girl named Suzy got off the Greyhound bus, she looked up and down the street, fixed her lipstick, then lifted her beat-up suitcase and headed for the Golden Poppy Restaurant. Suzy was a pretty girl with a flat nose and a wide mouth. She had a good figure, was twenty-one, five-feet-five, hair probably brown (dyed blond), brown cloth coat, rabbit-skin collar, cotton print dress, brown calf shoes (heel taps a little run over), scuff on the right toe. She limped slightly on her right foot. Before she picked up her suitcase she opened her brown purse of simulated leather. In it were mirror, comb with two teeth missing, Lucky Strikes, matchbook that said "Hotel Rosaline, San Francisco," half pack of Peppermint Life Savers, eighty-five cents in silver, no folding money, lipstick but no powder, tin box of aspirin, no keys.

If there had been a murder that night Joe Blaikey could have written all that down, but now he wasn't even aware that he knew it. Joe acted pretty much by instinct. He got into the Golden Poppy just as the waitress was putting a cup of coffee on the counter in front of Suzy.

Joe slipped onto the stool next to her. "Hi, Ella," he said to the waitress. "Cup of coffee."

"Coming up," said Ella. "How's your wife, Joe?"

"Oh, pretty good. Wish she'd get her strength back, though."

"Takes it out of you," said Ella. "Man can't understand that. Give her a tonic and let her rest. I'll have fresh coffee in a minute if you want to wait."

"Yeah," said Joe.

Ella went to the head of the counter, put coffee in the Silex, and filled the bowl.

Joe said quietly to Suzy, "What's on your mind, sister?"

"Not a thing," said Suzy. She didn't look at him but she could see him in the shine of a malted machine behind the counter.

"Vacation?"

"Sure."

"How long?"

"Don't know."

"Looking for a job?"

"Maybe."

Ella started toward them, saw what was happening, and got busy at the other end of the counter.

Joe asked, "Know anybody here?"

"I got an aunt here."

"What's her name?"

"That your business?"

"Yep."

"All right, I got no aunt."

Joe smiled at her, and Suzy felt better. She liked a guy who was worried about his wife.

He said to her, "On the bum?"

"Not yet," said Suzy. "You gonna give me trouble, mister?"

"Not if I can help it," said Joe. "You got a Social Security card?"

"Lost it," said Suzy.

Joe said, "It's a tough town. All organized. Don't work the street. The authorities won't have it. If you need a buck to blow town, come to me. My name's Joe Blaikey."

"Thanks, Joe. But I ain't hustling, honest."

"Not yet, you ain't," said Joe. "It's a hell of a town to get a job in since the canneries closed. Take it easy." He stood up and stretched. "I'll get the coffee later, Ella," he said and went out.

Ella's work seemed to be all done. She mopped the counter with a damp cloth. "Swell fella," she said. "More coffee? Fresh is ready."

"Seemed like," said Suzy. "Yeah."

Ella brought a fresh cup. "Where you staying?"

"Don't know yet."

"My sister rents rooms—pretty nice. Four dollars a week. I can give her a ring, see if she's got one vacant."

"I think I'll look around town a little," said Suzy. "Say, mind if I leave my suitcase here? It's kind of heavy."

"Sure. I'll put it back of the counter here."

"Well, s'pose you're off shift when I come back?"

Ella looked levelly at Suzy. "Sister," she said, "I ain't never off shift."

Suzy looked in the store windows on Alvarado Street and then she went to the wharf and watched the fishing boats at their moorings. A school of tiny fish always lay in the shade of the pier and two little boys fished with hand lines and never caught anything. About four o'clock she strolled along deserted Cannery Row, bought a package of Lucky Strikes at the grocery, glanced casually at Western Biological, and knocked on the door of the Bear Flag.

Fauna received her in the combination bedroom and office.

"I'll tell you the truth," said Fauna, "business ain't been good. It may pick up some in June. I wish I could put you on. Ain't you got a hard-luck story that would kind of sway me?"

"Nope," said Suzy.

"You broke?"

"Yep."

"But you don't make nothing of it." Fauna leaned back in her swivel chair and squinted her eyes. "I used to work a Mission," she said. "I know hard-luck stories from both ends. I guess if you laid all the hard luck I've heard end to end, why, the Bible would look short. And some of them stories was true. Now, I could make a guess about you."

Suzy sat silent—posture, hands, face, noncommittal.

"Lousy home," said Fauna. "Fighting all the time. Probably you wasn't more than fifteen or sixteen when you married the guy, or maybe he wouldn't. Done it just to get away from the fighting."

Suzy made no reply.

Fauna looked away so that she wouldn't see the hands slowly grip each other. "Got in a family way right off," said Fauna. "That made the guy restless, and he powdered. What did you say?"

"I didn't say nothing," said Suzy.

"Where's the baby?"

"I lost it."

"Do you hate the guy?"

"I got nothing to say," said Suzy.

"Okay with me. I ain't really very interested. There's some dames born for this business. Some are too lazy to work and some hate men. Don't hardly none of them enjoy what they're doing. That would be like a bartender that loves to drink. You don't look like a natural-born hustler to me. You ain't lazy. Why don't you get a job?"

"I worked waitress and I worked Five-and-Dime. Only

difference is, you get took to a movie instead of three bucks," said Suzy.

"You trying to make a stake?"

"Maybe."

"Got a boy?"

"Nope."

"Hate boys?"

"Nope."

Fauna sighed. "You got me, sister. I can feel myself being got. You're a tough kid. Doing your own time, like an old con. I like that. It works better with me than a hard-luck story. Tell me, you hot?"

"Huh?"

"Under raps, I mean. Anybody got anything on you?"

"Nope."

"Ever done time?"

"Once. Thirty days. Vagrancy."

"Nothing else on the blotter?"

"Nope."

"Can you give off a smile? You'd freeze the customers." Suzy grinned at Fauna.

"Good God Almighty!" said Fauna. "You look like somebody's sister! I'm afraid you'll cost me. Why do I have to be a pushover? Ever worked a house?"

"Nope."

"Well, it ain't as bad as the street. Doc Wilkins will be in tomorrow."

Suzy asked, "Can I get my suitcase?"

"I guess so." Fauna opened a wallet on her desk. "J. C. Penney's is open till six. Get yourself a dress—fancy but cheap. Get a new toothbrush. And when you come back, for God's sake go to work on your hair. You could be a good-looking kid if you worked it up."

"I been riding a bus," said Suzy.

"That'll do it," said Fauna. "We eat at half-past six. How long since you ate?"

"Yesterday."

"Beef stew tonight, creamed carrots, cherry Jello for dessert."

On her way to the door Suzy paused and her hand patted

the doorframe. "Cop worked me over today," she said. "Name's Joe Blaikey."

"He's a nice fella. Why, he'd lend you dough," said Fauna.

"That's what he said," Suzy replied. "I love beef stew."

At the Golden Poppy, Ella handed the suitcase over the counter. "You look like a kid with a job," said Ella.

"Looks like. Say, where's J. C. Penney?"

"Turn right and go a block and a half. Yellow front. Be seeing you."

"Sure," said Suzy.

On the sidewalk Joe Blaikey fell into step beside her and took her suitcase from her hand. "That's a good woman," he said. "You just keep your nose clean and you'll be all right."

"How'd you know?" Suzy asked.

"She called me," said Joe. "See you around."

"Okay," said Suzy.

She took her suitcase from him and turned into J. C. Penney's.

"Can I help you?"

"Dress. Not too dear."

"Over here."

"I like that tomatoey one."

"That's a new shade, 'Love Apples.'"

"Tomato color."

"It's rayon. It'll give you good service."

"It better. Size twelve."

"Shoes to match?"

Suzy took a very deep breath. "Yes, by God!" she said.

6. *The Creative Cross*

For days the flame burned in Doc, his phoenix thought. True, he didn't have a proper microscope, but he had eyes and he had, thank God, an analytic mind that could slough off sensations, emotions, pains. As he stared at the octopi his thesis took form. With a glass needle he stimulated one to fear and rage until it attacked and killed its brother. He removed one passive octopus to a separate jar where he subjected it to mild solutions of menthol, of Epsom salts, sickening it a little and then bringing it back to health again. Then he aroused rage, and when the body colors pulsed and changed he introduced a small amount of cocaine sulphate and saw the emotion disappear into sleep, if you can say an octopus sleeps. Then he aroused it with saline and touched it here and there with the frustrating needle, noted the flush, the growing intensity of color, the uncertain whipping and groping of the arms, until suddenly it collapsed and died. Doc removed the body and dissected the tissue, trying to find burst vesicles.

"It works!" he said aloud. "I haven't proper equipment to see how it happens, but this animal dies with the appearance of apoplexy. There must be leakage even if I can't see it. I can start my paper with observation."

Doc bought a package of yellow pads and two dozen pencils. He laid them out on his desk, the pencils sharpened to needle points and lined up like yellow soldiers. At the top of a page he printed: OBSERVATIONS AND SPECULATIONS. His pencil point broke. He took up another and drew lace around the O and the B, made a block letter of the S and put fish hooks on each end. His ankle itched. He rolled down his sock and scratched, and that made his ear itch. "Someone's talking about me," he said and looked at the yellow pad. He wondered whether he had fed the cotton rats. It is easy to forget when you're thinking.

Watching the rats scrabble for the food he gave them, Doc remembered that he had not eaten. When he finished a page or two he would fry some eggs. But wouldn't it be better to eat first so that his flow of thought would not be interrupted later? For some days he had looked forward to this time of peace, of unbroken thought. These were the answer to his restlessness: peace and the life of the mind. It would be better to eat first. He fried two eggs and ate them, staring at the yellow pad under the hanging light. The light was too bright. It reflected painfully on the paper. Doc finished his eggs, got out a sheet of tracing paper, and taped it to the bottom of the shade below the globe. It took time to make it neat. He sat in front of the yellow pad again and drew lace around all the letters of the title, tore off the page, and threw it away. Five pencil points were broken now. He sharpened them and lined them up with their brothers.

A car drove up in front of the Bear Flag. Doc went to the window and looked out. No one he knew, but he saw Mack go into the grocery. He remembered he wanted to ask Mack something.

It's always hard to start to concentrate. The mind darts like a chicken, trying to escape thinking even though thinking is the most rewarding function of man. Doc could take care of this. When you know what you're doing you can handle it. He set his jaw and was starting to turn back to his desk when he saw out of the corners of his eyes the flash of a skirt. He looked out the window again. A girl had come out of the Bear Flag and was walking along Cannery Row toward Monterey. Doc couldn't see her face, but she had a fine walk, thigh and knee and ankle swinging free and proud, no jerk and totter the way so many women walked as they fell from step to step. No, this girl walked with her shoulders back and her chin up and her arms swinging in rhythm. It's a gay walk, Doc thought. You can tell so much by a walk—discouragement or sickness, determination. There are squinched-up mean walks and blustering walks, shy creeping walks, but this was a gay walk, as though the walker were going happily to a meeting with someone she loved. There was pride in the walk too, but not vanity. Doc hoped she would not turn the corner, but she did. There was a flick of skirt and she was gone. But Doc could see in his mind her swinging limbs, the melody of her lithe, swift movement. Probably ugly as a mud fence, he thought, and then he laughed at himself. "That's full circle," he said. "Mind, I congratulate you. You jumped me to sex, translated it to aesthetics, and ended with sour grapes. How dishonest can I be? And all because I don't want to go to work. I'll work my head off to avoid work. Come, mind. This time you don't get away with it—back to the desk."

He picked up a pencil and wrote, "The observed specimens were twenty small octopi taken in the intertidal zone near the town of La Jolla. Specimens were placed in a large aquarium under conditions as nearly approximating their natural habitat as possible. Sea water was continuously filtered and replaced every twenty-four hours. Animals from a typical ecological community were introduced, together with sand, rock, and algae taken from the collecting point. Small crustaceans were supplied. In spite of precautions, five individuals died within one week. The remaining fifteen seemed to become acclimatized and readily captured and consumed the small grapsoid crabs placed in the aquarium. The lights—" His pencil point broke. He took another, and it broke with a jerk, making a little tear in the paper. He read what he had written; dull, desiccated, he thought. Why should I presume that an animal so far removed from the human—perhaps I'm fooling myself. The middle voice sang subtly, "Looking for yourself in the water—searching, little man, among the hydroids for your soul—looking for contentment in vanity. Are you better than Mack that you should use the secret priestly words of science to cover the fact that you have nothing to say?"

And the bottom voice mourned, "Lonesome! Lonesome! Let me up into the light and warmth. Lonesome!"

Doc jumped up and went to the aquarium and stared into the lighted water. From under a rock an octopus looked out and one of its arms flicked rhythmically, as though it led an orchestra, and the beat was gay and free and fluid—like the swinging thigh and knee and ankle.

Doc put his face in the palm of his hand and pressed blackness on his eyes until specks of green and red light swarmed on his vision. And then he got up and went across the street for beer.

7. Tinder Is as Tinder Does

JOSEPH and Mary Rivas liked Fauna, even admired her. But he did feel that it was a little indecent for a woman to own the Bear Flag, a paying institution with a steady income. Operate it, yes, but not own it. The proprieties told Joseph and Mary there should be a man in the background to drain off the profits. It was his observation that when women had access to money they got nervous. To his mind, a healthy woman was a broke woman. A dame with money was a kind of a half-assed man. She stopped working at being a woman, and, as everybody knows, the finest thing about a woman is that she is a woman.

Joseph and Mary had given some thought to relieving Fauna of the responsibility of the profits: if he owned the Bear Flag and Fauna ran it, there would be a natural and practical balance. Fauna had so far figured her way out from under his philanthropy, but Joseph and Mary did not give up, particularly when it was no trouble not to.

A good stock manipulator reads the financial page and looks for the stock he has, but he also notices other quotations too, just in case. Joseph and Mary kept that kind of eye on the Bear Flag. He felt that someday Fauna might look away from the dealer for a moment. Now that his own affairs ran smoothly, he was able to cast a benevolently rapacious eye about him. He knew about Suzy before she had even got her clothes washed, and he felt that Fauna was slipping.

"You got a quail there," he told Fauna. "That's Mary trouble if I ever seen it."

"I guess so," said Fauna.

"Why'd you take her on?"

"I let myself make a mistake once in a while," said Fauna. "She ain't a good hustler, but when I get through with her she might make somebody a damn fine wife."

"She's making a patsy of you," said the Patrón.

"People got to be a patsy now and then," said Fauna. "You never feel real good if you never been a sucker. Once I went missionary down in South America."

"Why?" asked the Patrón.

"Can't remember right off."

"What did you do?"

"Taught them to love one another."

"What did they do?"

"Taught me to shrink heads."

"Savages!" said the Patrón.

"No they wasn't. Them headhunters was pretty nice people —honest too. When they sell you a head they give good value. But there's always a wise guy. Like this Athatoolagooloo—a natural-born head-hustler. He'd worked out a way to push monkey heads. Gave them a close shave, didn't have to shrink them much. There's people will buy anything."

"I know," said the Patrón.

"Well, the Bishop come through," said Fauna, "and he give me holy hell for buying up them monkey heads."

"You mean to say *you* bought them?" said the Patrón.

"Sure I bought them. I got a box of them in the wood-shed. Everybody said I was a fool, but it paid off."

"How'd it pay off?"

"Well, look," said Fauna. "My bunch was honest and they shrunk honest heads. S'pose a shipment goes out and this joker Athatoolagooloo slips in a couple of his monkey heads—pretty soon nobody don't trust nobody. Why, people would get to looking asspants at a real nice head. I bought them up to keep them off the market. I had my reputation to think of."

"Yeah, but this joker—" the Patrón began.

"I know what you're going to say—and he done it too. He had me. He charged me more for them monkey heads than I paid for the real article. He knew he had me."

"That's what I thought. Anybody would," said the Patrón.

"Oh, it all worked out," said Fauna. "If you ever buy a Chungla head you'll know you got the best."

"Yeah, but how about the joker?" said the Patrón.

Fauna opened up her desk drawer and took out a beautiful little item, black as polished ebony and no bigger than a lemon. "He made up real nice, didn't he?" said Fauna.

The Patrón looked nervously away. "I got to get back," he said. "I left my nephew in the store."

"Don't he play trumpet?"

"Drives me crazy," said Joseph and Mary. "Got a new trumpet. Can't get away from it. Made him go practice down on the beach. Figured the waves and the sea lions would kind of drown him out. The other night he give a passing signal to a Navy tug, and they're still looking for what passed them. But last night was the worst. He was practicing down on the beach and he aimed his damn trumpet into that sewer pipe. Got resonance, he said. I don't know if it's true, but I heard that every toilet in the whole neighborhood give off with 'Stormy Weather.' Old lady Somers was taking an enema. I don't believe what they said happened. I got to get back. That kid can break glass with a high note."

"Come over and visit again," said Fauna.

"You mind what I said about Suzy."

"I will," said Fauna.

It's a funny thing, but you never like to trade at your own place. The store across the street has always got fresher cigarettes than you have. The girls at the Bear Flag never got cigarettes from the slot machine at the Bear Flag. When they wanted Luckies or a 7 Up they went to the Patrón's. For that matter, nearly everyone in Cannery Row went nearly every place in Cannery Row nearly every day.

Joseph and Mary had hardly got back to the grocery before Suzy came in. You wouldn't recommend Joseph and Mary as a celebrator of God's loveliest creation, but if you wanted a quick assay on a babe you couldn't ask for better than Joseph and Mary's. If he was not involved in an emotional way he was good. Between the time Suzy got change and the time she pushed the Lucky Strike button on his cigarette machine, each had gone over the other and registered the result.

Suzy's note: "Greaseball, smart and mean. Look out if he gives you something. A percentage boy. Smiles with his mouth. Eyes like a snake. May trip himself someday by being too smart."

Patrón's note: "Lousy risk for a house. A character. Won't play the rules. Might reverse the field. Too friendly. If she likes a guy she might toss in her roll."

The Patrón would have kicked her out of the Bear Flag. He knew that the only person you can trust is an absolutely selfish person. He always runs true to form. You know everything he'll do. But you take somebody with an underlying kindness, and he might fool you. The only satisfactory sucker is the one who is entirely selfish. You never have any trouble with that kind. Fauna was laying herself wide open.

Joseph and Mary tabulated Suzy the way he might have bought a used car. Pretty good figure, good ankles and legs, too light in the butt and too heavy in the chest. That's a bad sign: a good hustler is flat-chested. Face kind of pretty if she felt like it. Face reflected how she felt. Good-looking if she felt good. A good hustler has a mask, looks the same to everybody, pretty, but you don't remember what she looked like the next morning. Suzy you wouldn't forget. A real bad risk. Suzy liked people or she didn't like them. That in itself was bad.

Cacahuete, the Patrón's nephew, was dusting shelves, and he flashed a gold smile at Suzy.

Suzy lighted up. She didn't smile—she grinned. Her lips were full and her mouth wide, and when she grinned her eyes crinkled and something warm and scary came out of her. That's a bad risk. On top of this was toughness, but not dependable dull toughness. Suzy might take a poke at Jack Dempsey. She wasn't smart. All in all, Joseph and Mary would've dumped Suzy in a minute. She'd be the kind of dumb dame who'd fall for some guy without finding out his bank balance. She was the kind, he thought, who'd give one guy a helluva lot of trouble but who'd be lousy playing the field. She had something of the same quality Doc had. The Patrón decided to warn Fauna again. This kid could be pure murder in a hookshop. Such was the Patrón's reasoned opinion, and the Patrón was a professional. If you'd take a doctor's advice about a disease, you'd surely take the Patrón's about a hustler. Both could be wrong, of course.

The appraisals and judgments were almost instantaneous, so that by the time Suzy had opened her cigarettes, put one in her mouth, and lighted it, the judgment was complete.

"How are you?" Joseph and Mary asked.

"Okay," said Suzy. "Fauna wants some yellow pads and a couple of pencils—soft pencils."

The Patrón laid them out. "She does a lot of writing," he said. "She's used six pads in about a month."

"She's doing astrology."

"You believe that stuff?"

"No, but it don't do no harm."

"I knew a guy made a good living with it," said the Patrón.

"Oh, she don't charge nothing," said Suzy.

"I know," said the Patrón. "I can't figure why not. Fauna ain't dumb."

"She sure ain't," said Suzy.

Doc came in with two empty beer bottles. "Get a couple of cold ones back on the ice, will you?" he asked.

Suzy glanced at him, took him in, and looked away. His beard shocked her a little. She didn't stare at him the way you don't stare at a cripple.

The Patrón said, "Why don't you put in an icebox? Then you can take a case at a time."

"It's easier to let you keep the ice," said Doc.

"You know Suzy here? She's new at the Bear Flag."

"How do you do," said Doc.

"How do you do," said Suzy. She would have said "Hi" to anyone else.

When Doc had gone the Patrón said, "That's a funny guy."

"It takes all kinds," said Suzy.

"He knows stuff I ain't even heard of." The Patrón was defending Doc the way everyone did.

"Kind of hoity-toity?" asked Suzy.

"Hell no! That's the way he always talks. He don't know no other way."

"Well, I guess it takes all kinds," said Suzy.

"He gets bugs and stuff out of the ocean and sells them."

"Who to?"

"Why, there's people'll buy anything," said the Patrón.

"I guess so. Why don't other people do it?"

"Too much work, and you got to know what to get."

"Say, why does he wear that beard? I used to know a wrestler wore one."

"I don't know why," said the Patrón. "Why'd the wrestler?"

"Thought it made him look tough."

"Well, maybe Doc the same—but no, he don't want to be tough." The Patrón went on, "In the Army they made a guy with a beard shave it off. Said a guy with a beard wanted to be different, and the best way to not get along in the barracks is to be different."

"Maybe that's it," said Suzy. "I don't mind a different guy if he ain't too different."

"Dames can take it," said the Patrón. "They don't like it but they can take it. What the hell am I doing all this talking for? I got work to do!"

Suzy asked, "You Mexican?"

"American. My old man was Mexican."

"Can you talk that spick talk?"

"Sure."

"Polly-voo?"

"That ain't the same kind," said the Patrón.

"Be seeing you," said Suzy, and she went out and let the screen door slam.

She ain't a bad kid, the Patrón thought, but I'd sure kick her the hell out of the Bear Flag.

Doc looked out the window of Western Biological. He watched Suzy walk past the vacant lot and up to the front porch of the Bear Flag. Just as she was about to climb the steps she turned and looked around. She thought someone was looking at her. She didn't see Doc.

8. The Great Roque War

PACIFIC GROVE and Monterey sit side by side on a hill bordering the bay. The two towns touch shoulders but they are not alike. Whereas Monterey was founded a long time ago by foreigners, Indians and Spaniards and such, and the town grew up higgledy-piggledy without plan or purpose, Pacific Grove sprang full blown from the iron heart of a psycho-ideo-legal religion. It was formed as a retreat in the 1880s and came fully equipped with laws, ideals, and customs. On the town's statute books a deed is void if liquor is ever brought on the property. As a result, the sale of iron-and-wine tonic is fantastic. Pacific Grove has a law that requires you to pull your shades down after sundown, and forbids you to pull them down before. Scorching on bicycles is forbidden, as is sea bathing and boating on Sundays. There is one crime which is not defined but which is definitely against the law. Hijinks are or is forbidden. It must be admitted that most of these laws are not enforced to the hilt. The fence that once surrounded the Pacific Grove retreat is no longer in existence.

Once, during its history, Pacific Grove was in trouble, deep trouble. You see, when the town was founded many old people moved to the retreat, people you'd think didn't have anything to retreat from. These old people became grumpy after a while and got to interfering in everything and causing trouble, until a philanthropist named Deems presented the town with two roque courts.

Roque is a complicated kind of croquet, with narrow wickets and short-handled mallets. You play off the sidelines, like billiards. Very complicated, it is. They say it develops character.

In a local sport there must be competition and a prize. In Pacific Grove a cup was given every year for the winning team on the roque courts. You wouldn't think a thing like that would work up much heat, particularly since most of the contestants were over seventy. But it did.

One of the teams was called the Blues and the other the Greens. The old men wore little skullcaps and striped blazers in their team colors.

Well, it wasn't more than two years before all hell broke loose. The Blues would practice in the court right alongside the Greens but they wouldn't speak to them. And then it got into the families of the teams. You were a Blue family or a Green family. Finally the feeling spread outside the family. You were a partisan of the Blues or a partisan of the Greens. It got so that the Greens tried to discourage intermarriage with the Blues, and vice versa. Pretty soon it reached into politics, so that a Green wouldn't think of voting for a Blue. It split the church right down the middle. The Blues and the Greens wouldn't sit on the same side. They made plans to build separate churches.

Of course everything got really hot at tournament time. Things were very touchy. Those old men brought a passion to the game you wouldn't believe. Why, two octogenarians would walk away into the woods and you'd find them locked in mortal combat. They even developed secret languages so that each wouldn't know what the other was talking about.

Well, things got so hot and feeling ran so high that the county had to take notice of it. A Blue got his house burned down and then a Green was found clubbed to death with a roque mallet in the woods. A roque mallet is short-handled and heavy and can be a very deadly weapon. The old men got to carrying mallets tied to their wrists by thongs, like battle-axes. They didn't go any place without them. There wasn't any crime each didn't charge the other with, including things they'd outgrown and couldn't have done if they'd wanted to. The Blues wouldn't trade in Green stores. The whole town was a mess.

The original benefactor, Mr. Deems, was a nice old fellow. He used to smoke a little opium, when it was legal, and this kept him healthy and rested so that he didn't get high blood pressure or tuberculosis. He was a benevolent man, but he was also a philosopher. When he saw what he had created by giving the roque courts to the Pacific Grove retreat he was saddened and later horrified. He said he knew how God felt.

The tournament came July 30, and feeling was so bad that people were carrying pistols. Blue kids and Green kids had gang wars. Mr. Deems, after a period of years, finally figured that as long as he felt like God he might as well act like God. There was too much violence in town.

On the night of July 29 Mr. Deems sent out a bulldozer. In the morning, where the roque courts had been, there was only a deep, ragged hole in the ground. If he'd had time he would have continued God's solution. He'd have filled the hole with water.

They ran Mr. Deems out of Pacific Grove. They would have tarred and feathered him if they could have caught him, but he was safe in Monterey, cooking his yen shi over a peanut-oil lamp.

Every July 30, to this day, the whole town of Pacific Grove gets together and burns Mr. Deems in effigy. They make a celebration of it, dress up a life-size figure, and hang it from a pine tree. Later they burn it. People march underneath with torches, and the poor helpless figure of Mr. Deems goes up in smoke every year.

There are people who will say that this whole account is a lie, but a thing isn't necessarily a lie even if it didn't necessarily happen.

9. Whom the Gods Love They Drive Nuts

To a casual observer Cannery Row might have seemed a series of self-contained and selfish units, each functioning alone with no reference to the others. There was little visible connection between La Ida's, the Bear Flag, the grocery (still known as Lee Chong's Heavenly Flower Grocery), the Palace Flophouse, and Western Biological Laboratories. The fact is that each was bound by gossamer threads of steel to all the others—hurt one, and you aroused vengeance in all. Let sadness come to one, and all wept.

Doc was more than first citizen of Cannery Row. He was healer of the wounded soul and the cut finger. Strongly entrenched in legality though he was, he found himself constantly edged into infringements by the needs of his friends, and anyone could hustle him for a buck without half trying. When trouble came to Doc it was everybody's trouble.

What was Doc's trouble? Even he didn't know. He was deeply, grievingly unhappy. For hours on end he sat at his desk with a yellow pad before him and his needle-sharp pencils lined up. Sometimes his wastebasket was full of crushed, scribbled pages, and at others not even a doodle went down. Then he would move to the aquarium and stare into it. And his voices howled and cried and moaned. "Write!" said his top voice, and "Search!" sang his middle voice, and his lowest voice sighed, "Lonesome! Lonesome!" He did not go down without a struggle. He resurrected old love affairs, he swam deep in music, he read the *Sorrows of Werther*; but the voices would not leave him. The beckoning yellow pages became his enemies. One by one the octopi died in the aquarium. He had worn thin the excuse of his lack of a proper microscope. When the last octopus died he leaped on this as his excuse. When his friends visited him he would explain, "You see, I can't go on without specimens, and I can't get any more until the spring tides. As soon as I have specimens and a new microscope I can whip the paper right off."

His friends sensed his pain and caught it and carried it away with them. They knew the time was coming when they would have to do something.

In the Palace Flophouse a little meeting occurred—occurred, because no one called it, no one planned it, and yet everyone knew what it was about.

Wide Ida brooded hugely. The Bear Flag was represented by Agnes, Mabel, and Becky. All the boys were accounted for. The meeting began casually and obliquely, as all meetings should.

Hazel said, "Wide Ida throwed out a drunk last night and sprained her shoulder."

"I ain't as young as I used to be," Wide Ida said gloomily.

"The drunk dared her," said Hazel. "He didn't even touch the sidewalk going out. If they was an Olympic event for A and C, Wide Ida would win it easy."

"Sprained my shoulder up," said Wide Ida.

They kept skirting their problem.

Mack said, "How's Fauna been?"

"Pretty good. She got problems," said Agnes.

Becky was delicately picking off nail polish. "That Fauna," she said, "she's a wonder. She's giving us table-setting lessons. I bet if they was thirty-five forks, she'd know what every one of them was for."

"Ain't they to eat with?" Hazel asked.

"Jesus, what a ignorant!" said Becky. "I bet you don't know a dessert fork from a hole in the ground."

Hazel said belligerently, "You know what a Jackson fork is for?"

"No, what?"

"Just leave it lay and see who's a ignorant," said Hazel.

Wide Ida asked, "Any change with Doc?"

"No," said Mack. "I went over to see him last night. I wisht there was something we could do."

They fell to musing. If the times were hard on Doc, they were equally hard on his friends who loved him. Once he had been infallible. There was nothing he could not do because there was nothing he wanted to do very much. And in spite of themselves a little contempt for him was growing in his friends—a kind and loving contempt that might never have happened if he had not once been so great. People who had once spoken his name with awe now felt better than he because he was no better than they.

"I ain't got an idea's how to proceed," said Mack.

Hazel said, "How's about if we ask Fauna to do his horoscope? She's doing me right now."

"You ain't got no future," said Mack.

"I have too," said Hazel. "I bet Fauna could tell us what to do about Doc."

Mack looked interested. "It's better than nothing," he said. "Hoc sunt. Eddie, you dig up one of them kegs you buried during the war. Hazel, you ask Fauna to come over for a drink. Tell her to bring her star stuff."

"Maybe she's got me finished," said Hazel.

It was a matter of some sorrow to Fauna that she didn't entirely believe in astrology, but she had found that nearly everyone wants to believe that the stars take notice of us. Her science gave her a means for telling people what they ought to do, and Fauna had definite ideas about what everybody ought to do.

In spite of her secret skepticism, every once in a while she turned up a reading that astonished her. Hazel's horoscope had her breathless and baffled. She seriously considered burning it and never telling him.

Hazel led her to the Palace Flophouse and Mack poured her a drink from the keg. She tossed it off, still deep in thought.

"You got my stars wrote down?" Hazel demanded anxiously.

Fauna regarded him sorrowfully. "I don't want to tell you," she said.

"Why not? Is it bad?"

"Awful," said Fauna.

"Come on, tell me. I can take it."

Fauna sighed. "I've checked it over and over," she said. "You sure you give me your true birthday?"

"Sure."

"Then I don't see how it can be wrong." She turned wearily and faced the others. "The stars say Hazel's going to be President of the United States."

There was a shocked silence.

"I don't believe it," said Mack.

"I don't want to be President," Hazel said, and he didn't.

"There is no choice," said Fauna. "The stars have spoke. You will go to Washington."

"I don't want to!" Hazel cried. "I don't know nobody there."

"I wonder where we could all go," said Whitey No. 2. "I seen some islands in the Pacific that was pretty nice. But hell, Hazel would have them too. The U.S. got a mandate."

"I won't take it," said Hazel.

Mack said, "We could kill him."

"His stars don't say it," Fauna said. "He's going to live to seventy-eight and die from a spoiled oyster."

"I don't like oysters," said Hazel.

"Maybe you'll learn in Washington."

Mack said, "Maybe you made a mistake."

"That's what I hoped," said Fauna. "I went over and over it. No, sir! Hazel is going to be President."

"Well, we've weathered some pretty bad ones," Eddie offered forlornly.

"Ain't they no way I can tell them I won't do it? Hell, I'll hide out!" said Hazel desperately.

Fauna shook her head dismally. "I'll check again," she said, "but I don't think you got a prayer. You got nine toes, Hazel?"

"I don't know."

"Well, count."

Hazel took off his shoes and moved his lips. "Nine," he said bitterly.

"That's what the horoscope said. We can only pray it's for the best."

"Lord!" said Whitey No. 2. "That's what I call a nine-to-one prayer. Fauna, now you've went and made a president out of a sow's ear, how about getting Doc's paper wrote?"

"Who's a sow's ear?" Hazel demanded.

"William Henry Harrison."

"Oh!" said Hazel. "Oh yeah!"

Agnes piped up in her hoarse soprano, "Doc just ain't himself. I took him a pint and he didn't hardly pass the time a day. Just set there looking at that yellow paper. Know what was on that paper?"

"Eggs," said Whitey No. 1.

"No. I don't like to tell. It ain't nice."

"Hot damn!" said Mack. "Maybe he's getting well. Go on—what?"

"Well," said Agnes in a shocked voice, "he'd drew a picture of a lady without no clothes on, and right beside that was one of them damn devilfish, only it was smoking a pipe. Don't hardly seem like the old Doc."

Wide Ida shook herself out of a mountainous lethargy. "He used to be the easygoinest guy in the world. Now he's got a wild hair. Anybody else but Doc, I'd figure it was a dame. But hell! Doc can take dames or let them alone."

Mack said, "He could even take dames *and* let them alone."

Fauna put her hands on her hips. "You fellas sure there ain't a girl hiding out where he can't get to her?"

"No," said Hazel. "I wisht he'd snap out of it. Go over and talk to him, and he don't say nothing and he don't listen."

"Let's run a few dames past him and see if he picks up," said Whitey No. 2.

Mack said, "I don't believe in it but I wish Fauna would do a job on Doc. Might give us an idea."

Fauna said, "I never seen nobody that wanted me to do a horoscope that believed in it. I ain't sure I believe in it myself. Sure I'll do Doc. When's his birthday?"

With surprise they realized that no one could remember.

"Seems like it was in autumn," said Eddie.

"Got to have it," Fauna said. "Mack, you think you could find out?"

"I guess so. Say, Fauna, if you ain't got too much integrity, could you maybe rig it a little?"

"How do you mean?"

"Well, kind of tell him to lay off his goddam paper and get back to horsing around."

"What's wrong with his paper if only he gets it wrote?" Hazel demanded.

Mack, scratched his stomach. "I guess we got to face it," he said. "Doc wants to write that crazy paper. Driving himself nuts with it. Know what I think? Doc ain't never going to write that paper."

Hazel stood up. "What d'you mean?"

"Well, you know them kind of people they call accident prone? No matter what they do they get hurt. It's like they *want* accidents. Well, I think Doc don't really want to write that paper."

Whitey No. 1 said, "He sure goes about it the hard way."

"Ever hear of a substitute?" said Mack.

"You mean like on the bench at football?" Eddie asked.

"Hell no!" said Mack. "I mean like a guy is using something to cover up something else—and maybe he don't even know it himself."

Hazel demanded, "You running Doc down?"

"Take it easy," said Mack. "I think Doc's scared to write that paper because he knows it's crazy. Quod erat demonstrandum."

"Huh?" asked Fauna.

"Q.E.D.," said Mack.

"Oh!" said Fauna. "Sure."

10. There's a Hole in Reality Through Which We Can Look if We Wish

Doc had made changes. His desk was drawn in front of the window. He sat writing rapidly on his yellow pad. "Color change," he wrote, "seems to be not only a concentration of fluids to the surface but also a warping of tissue, which, perhaps, refracts the light, giving an impression of color."

A door slammed. Doc looked out at the street. Fauna was teetering down the chicken walk that led from the Palace Flophouse.

Doc looked back at his pad. There were footsteps on the pavement. He looked up. Wide Ida was going toward her bar. Joseph and Mary came out of the Heavenly Flower and crossed the street, climbed the stairs of Western Biological, and knocked.

"Come in," Doc cried, and there was relief in his voice.

"Thought I'd shovel the dirt a little. That band of mine is practicing upstairs. Drives me crazy."

"Well, I'm pretty busy," said Doc.

J and M gazed about the room. "Why do you keep snakes?"

"To sell."

"Who'd buy snakes?" said J and M. "Say, what you looking at?" He craned his neck. "That's the new dame. She's going to give Fauna trouble. Little Mary trouble."

"Who?" Doc asked.

"You wasn't listening, I guess."

"I must get to work," said Doc.

"You know, I still don't get it."

"What?"

"There must be some way to kind of bend the odds in chess."

"There isn't. I've got to go."

"What's the rush?"

"Tide!" said Doc.

Doc walked on the beach beyond the lighthouse. The waves splashed white beside him and sometimes basted his ankles. The sandpipers ran ahead of him as though on little wheels. The golden afternoon moved on toward China, and on the horizon's edge a lumber schooner balanced.

On Doc's left the white sand dunes rounded up, and behind them the dark pine trees seemed to hold a piece of night throughout the day.

Doc thought, Under stimulation there is increased pulsing like a man under physical or emotional strain, something like the release of adrenalin—but no way to prove it. No more specimens until the spring tides.

His middle voice argued, "Maybe you don't believe any of it. Why can't you laugh at yourself? You could once. You're trapped in a cage of self-importance."

"Lonesome!" the low voice cried in his guts. "No one to receive from you or give to you. No one warm enough and dear enough."

Doc wanted desperately to go back to his old life—the hopeless wish of a man wanting to be a little boy, forgetting the pain of little boys. Doc dropped to his knees and dug a hole in the damp sand with a scooped hand. He watched the sea water seep in and crumble the sides of the hole. A sand crab scuttled away from his digging fingers.

From behind him a voice said, "What are you digging for?"

"Nothing," said Doc without looking around.

"There are no clams here."

"I know it," said Doc. And his top voice sang, "I just want to be alone. I don't want to talk or explain or argue or even to listen. Now he'll tell me a theory he's got on oceanography. I won't look around."

The voice behind him said, "There's so much metal in the sea. Why, there's enough magnesium in a cubic mile of sea water to pave the whole country."

I always get them, Doc thought. If there's a bug-houser within miles he's drawn to me.

"I'm a seer," said the voice.

Doc rocked angrily back on his heels. "Okay," he said. "It's just my business but you tell me about it." He didn't remember ever having been discourteous to a stranger before.

This one was a big, bearded stranger with the lively, innocent eyes of a healthy baby. He wore ragged overalls and a blue shirt washed nearly white, and he was barefooted. The straw hat on his head had two large holes cut in the brim, proof that it had once been the property of a horse.

Doc found his interest rising.

"It is my custom to invite a stranger to dinner," said the seer. "Not original, of course. Harun al-Rashid did the same. Please follow me."

Doc stood up from his squatting position. The tendons in back of his knees creaked with pain. The seer towered above him, and on closer inspection it was true that his blue eyes had the merry light of a wise baby. But his face was granitic—chiseled out of the material of prophets and patriarchs. Doc found himself wondering if some of the saints had not looked like this. From the ragged sleeves of the blue shirt wrists like big grapevines protruded, and hands sheathed in brown calluses crisscrossed with barnacle cuts. The seer carried a pair of ancient basketball shoes in his left hand, and, seeing Doc look at them, he said, "I only wear them in the sea. My feet aren't proof against urchins and barnacles."

In spite of himself Doc felt surrounded by the man. "Harun," said Doc, "was visited by djinni and the spirits of earth, fire, and water. Do the djinni visit you?" Doc thought, Oh Lord!

Am I going to play along with this nonsense? Why can't I cross my fingers and spit and walk away? I can still walk away.

The seer looked downward at an angle into Doc's face. "I live alone," he said simply. "I live in the open. I hear the waves at night and see the black patterns of the pine boughs against the sky. With sound and silence and color and solitude, of course I see visions. Anyone would."

"But you don't believe in them?" Doc asked hopefully.

"I don't find it a matter for belief or disbelief," the seer said. "You've seen the sun flatten and take strange shapes just before it sinks in the ocean. Do you have to tell yourself every time that it's an illusion caused by atmospheric dust and light distorted by the sea, or do you simply enjoy the beauty of it? Don't you see visions?"

"No," said Doc.

"From music, don't forms of wishes and forms of memory take shape?"

"That's different," said Doc.

"I don't see any difference," said the seer. "Come along—dinner's ready."

In the dunes there are deep little creases where the wind-crouching pines have made a stand against the moving sand, and in one of these, only a hundred yards back from the beach, the seer had his home. The little valley was protected from the wind. The pine boughs covered it, and the sand was deeply carpeted with sweet pine needles. Once down in the little cup you could hear the wind sweeping the pine tips overhead, and a perpetual dusk hung under the warped trees. The pines survived only by following the suggestions of the stronger forces—crouching low and growing their limbs in the direction of the wind, nourishing the little trailing plants which slow up the pace of the walking dunes. Under the trees a fire was burning, and on a hearth of flat stones blackened tin cans steamed.

"This is my home," the seer said. "You are welcome here. I have a wonderful dinner." He brought a tin box from the fork of a tree, took out a loaf of French bread, and sliced off two thick slices. Then he brought sea urchins from a dripping sack, cracked them on a rock, and spread the gonads on the bread. "The males are sweet and the females sour," he said. "I like to mix the two."

"I've tasted them," said Doc. "The Italians eat them. It's about as strong a protein as you can get. Some people think it's aphrodisiac."

There was an iron simplicity in the seer. He was like a monolith of logic standing against waves of angry nonsense.

"Next we'll have steamed limpets," said the seer. "I have a pin here to eat them with. Do you like sea lettuce? It's an acquired taste. And then I have a stew—a kind of universal bouillabaisse—I won't tell you what's in it. You'll see."

"Do you take all of your food from the sea?"

The seer smiled at him. "No, not all. I wish I could. It would be simpler. I take all the protein I need, and more, but my human stomach still craves starch. I want a little bread and some potatoes. I love acid with the protein. See—I have a bottle of vinegar and some lemons. And last, I indulge myself with herbs: rosemary and thyme and sage and marjoram."

"How about sugars?" Doc asked. "You won't find sugars in a tide pool."

The seer dropped his eyes and watched a black ant try to climb an avalanche of sand, losing ground all the way. When he spoke his voice was shy and ashamed. "I steal candy bars," he said. "I can't seem to help it."

"The flesh is weak," said Doc.

"Oh, I don't mind that," the seer cried. "Appetites are good things. The more appetites a man has, the richer he is, but I was taught not to steal. I don't believe in stealing. It hurts my feelings when I do, and I don't enjoy the candy bars as much as I would if I didn't steal them, but I love Baby Ruths and Mounds."

They picked the limpets from their shells with pins and dipped them in lemon juice. The stew contained mussels and clams and crabs and little fish, seasoned with garlic and rosemary.

"Some people don't like it," said the seer.

After they had finished Doc lay back in the pine needles, and a fine peacefulness settled on him. The air, the softness of the needles, the odors of kelp and pine and yerba buena, the music of surf against wind-plucking pine needles, the fullness of belly, made a little room of contentment around him.

He said, "I'm surprised they don't lock you up—a reasonable

man. It's one of the symptoms of our time to find danger in men like you who don't worry and rush about. Particularly dangerous are men who don't think the world's coming to an end."

"It's coming to an end, all right," the seer said. "That started the moment it was born."

"I don't know why they don't put you in jail. It's a crime to be happy without equipment."

"Oh, they do," said the seer, "and they put me under observation every once in a while."

"I forgot," said Doc. "You are crazy, aren't you?"

"I guess so," said the seer, "but not dangerous. And they've never caught me stealing candy bars. I'm very clever at that, and I steal only one at a time."

"Don't ever gather disciples," said Doc. "They'd have you on a cross in no time."

"There's not much danger of that. I don't teach anybody anything."

"I'm not so sure," said Doc. "The doctrine of our time is that man can't get along without a whole hell of a lot of stuff. You may not be preaching it, but you're living treason."

"I'm lazy," said the seer. "Did you ever drink yerba buena tea?"

"No."

"It's strong and aromatic and a mild physic. Can you drink it out of a beer bottle?"

"I don't know why not."

"Look out! The bottle's hot! Here, wrap a twig around it."

After a while the seer asked, "What's aching you, or don't you want to talk about it?"

"I'd just as soon talk about it if I knew what it was," said Doc. "As a matter of fact, it's gone away for the moment."

"Ah, one of those," said the seer. "Do you have wife or children?"

"No."

"Do you want wife or children?"

"I don't think so."

The seer said, "I saw a mermaid last night. You remember, there was a half moon and a thin drifting mist. There was color in the night, not like the black and gray and white of an ordinary night. Down at the end of the beach a shelf of rock reaches out, and the tide was low so that there was a smooth bed of kelp. She swam to the edge and then churned her tail, like a salmon leaping a rapid. And then she lay on the kelp bed and made dancing figures with her white arms and hands. She didn't go away until the rising tide covered the kelp bed."

"Was she a dream? Did you imagine her?"

"I don't know. But if I did I'm proud that I could imagine anything so beautiful. What is it you want?"

"I've tried to think," said Doc. "I want to take everything I've seen and thought and learned and reduce them and relate them and refine them until I have something of meaning, something of use. And I can't seem to do it."

"Maybe you aren't ready. And maybe you need help."

"What kind of help?"

"There are some things a man can't do alone. I wouldn't think of trying anything so big without—" He stopped. The heavy waves beat the hard beach, and the yellow light of the setting sun illuminated a cloud to the eastward, a clot of gold.

"Without what?" Doc asked.

"Without love," said the seer. "I have to go to the sunset now. I've come to the point where I don't think it can go down without me. That makes me seem needed." He stood up and brushed the pine needles from his threadbare overalls.

"I'll come to see you again," said Doc.

"I might be gone," the seer replied. "I've got a restlessness in me. I'll probably be gone."

Doc watched him trudge over the brim of the dune and saw the wind flip up the brim of his straw hat and the yellow sun light up his face and glisten in his beard.

11. Hazel's Brooding

After Mack left the Palace Flophouse (and, incidentally, did not find Doc at home), Hazel sat brooding. Things came through slowly to Hazel. He had heard Mack advance his theory about how Doc would never get his paper written, but the impact of the statement did not strike home until he was alone. It is true that all over Cannery Row the feeling was growing that Doc was not infallible, but the news had not seeped through to Hazel. He knew that Doc was in trouble, but the friendly feeling of contempt had not penetrated. If Hazel had wanted to know the day and hour of the world's demise, he would have gone to Doc and Doc's answer would have been final. Alone he brooded, not about Doc's weakness, but about the treachery of Doc's friends who could question him, who would *dare* to question him.

Hazel beat his hand on the arm of his rocking chair for a while and then he got up and went to Wide Ida's. Eddie was behind the bar, so Hazel had two shots of whisky and paid for a Coke.

He walked between two canneries to the beach. A seagull with a broken wing engaged his kindly interest. He chased it, trying to help it, until it swam to sea and drowned.

Hazel had experienced an earthquake and he searched for the shaker. He walked along the rocks to Pacific Grove Beach, and even the brown young men standing on their hands for the girls did not hold interest. He went up the hill and toured the basement of Holman's Department Store. The floor manager accompanied him, an honor and a precaution few people received. But Hazel didn't even see the shining display of small tools.

You cannot cut the ground from under a man and expect him to act normally. On his way back to Cannery Row, Hazel passed a funeral home where an impressive group was gathering. Ordinarily Hazel would join any kind of celebration with enthusiasm. But now he watched the mounds of gladiolas being carried out and no sense of participation stirred in him. The festive dead would have to be buried without Hazel.

In New Monterey, Hazel walked, not around, but right through a dog fight. All the preceding manifestations would have troubled his friends, but if they had known what Hazel was thinking they would have been horrified.

Thinking is always painful, but in Hazel it was heroic. A picture of the process would make you seasick. A gray, whirling furor of images, memories, words, patterns. It was like a traffic jam at a big intersection with Hazel in the middle trying to get something to move somewhere.

He strolled back to Cannery Row but he did not go to the Palace Flophouse. By instinct, he crept under the branches of the black cypress tree in the vacant lot where he had lived for so many years in pre-Palace days. Hazel's thoughts were not complicated. It was just remarkable that he had them at all.

Hazel loved Doc. Doc was in trouble. Somebody was responsible. Who? That it might be a situation rather than a person was beyond his grasp. The person who was hurting Doc must be made to stop it even if he had to be killed. Hazel had nothing against murder. That he hadn't killed anybody was only because he hadn't needed to or wanted to. He tried to recall everything he had heard concerning Doc's frustration, and it was all nebulous, all vague, except for one thing: Mack had said Doc couldn't write his paper. That was the only clear statement that had been made. Mack was the one. If Mack knew about it, he must be responsible for it. This was a matter of sorrow to Hazel, because he liked Mack very much. He hoped he wouldn't have to kill him.

It was getting dark under the cypress tree, too dark to read. Hazel always judged light by whether or not you could read by it, in spite of the fact that he never read anything. The front-porch light of the Bear Flag came on. Western Biological was still dark. Up the hill in the Palace Flophouse the kerosene lantern made a dim glow through the windows. Again and again, Hazel tried to turn to sweet thoughtlessness, but it was no use. Mack was responsible. Mack had to do something about it.

Hazel got up and brushed the cypress dirt from his clothes. He walked up past the rusty pipes and the empty boiler, crossed the railroad track, and went up the chicken walk. Behind him, muffled by the canneries, he could hear Cacahuete playing "Stormy Weather" on his trumpet and the sea lions on China Point barking.

In the Palace, Mack and the boys were playing ticktacktoe with a piece of chalk on the floor. The wining jug was set conveniently near.

"Hi, Hazel," said Mack. "Draw up."

"Mack," Hazel said sadly, "I want you should step outside with me and put up your dukes."

Mack rocked back on his heels. "What!"

"I'm going to beat the holy hell out of you," said Hazel.

"Why?" Mack asked.

This was just the question Hazel was afraid of. He tried to find a quick, tough answer. "You just step out and you'll find out," he said.

"Hazel—" Mack stood up. "Hazel baby, what's eating you? Tell me. See if I can't make it right."

Hazel felt the whole situation leaving his hands. "You can't treat Doc that way," he said fiercely. "Not Doc!"

"What way am I treating him? I ain't done nothing to Doc, except maybe hustle him a little. But we all done that—even you tried."

"You said he can't write his paper, that's what you done."

"Oh, for God's sakes!" said Mack.

"You're yellow then."

"Okay, I'm yellow. Sometime when I ain't feeling yellow I'll paddywhack you. Sit down. Have jolt from the jug."

They babied Hazel and pampered him until his eyes were damp with appreciation. But when Hazel's mind dug in it would not let loose. "You got to help him," he repeated. "He ain't happy, he just mopes. You got to help him."

Mack said, "It ain't entirely our fault. Trouble is, Doc lets concealment like a worm in the bud feed on his damask cheek."

"He sure as hell does," said Whitey No. 2.

"I ain't going to stand for no excuses," said Hazel.

Mack studied the problem from every angle. "Hazel's right," he said at last. "We've been selfish. We never in our lives had such a good friend as Doc, and we're letting him down. Makes me feel ashamed. It's Hazel showed the way. If I was in trouble I wouldn't want Hazel to do no figuring but I sure would like to have him for a friend."

Hazel ducked his head in embarrassment. In his life so few compliments had come his way that he didn't know how to cope with them.

Mack went on, "I make a solemn move we all stand up and drink a toast to Hazel—a noble, noble soul!"

"Aw, hell, fellas," said Hazel, and he wiped his eyes on his sleeve.

They stood in a circle around him, Mack and Eddie, Whitey No. 1 and Whitey No. 2, and each one tipped the jug over his elbow and drank to Hazel. Good feeling was running so high they did it again, and were about to do it a third time when Hazel said, "Ain't there something we can drink to so I can get a drink?"

"To Lefty Grove!" said Eddie.

That broke the ice. An era of good feeling set in. They dug up another keg of the private stock Eddie had saved during the war. He started the bung and smelled it delicately.

"I remember this one," he said. "They was some guys up from South America and they brought in a bottle of absinthe."

"Perfumes the whole house," said Mack.

It was like old times, they reminded one another. If Gay were only here—let's drink a toast to good old Gay, our departed friend.

The absinthe had soothed the mixture in the keg and added something sweet and old-fashioned. A courtliness crept into the speech of the dwellers of the Palace Flophouse, an old-world courtesy. Everyone vied to be last, not first, at the refilled jug.

"Next dough we get we'll go up to Woolworth's and get some glasses," said Mack.

"Hell," said Whitey No. 2, "they'll just get broke. But I see what you mean."

Somehow they felt they were living in a moment when history pauses and takes stock and changes course. They knew they would look back on this night as a beginning. At such times men feel the nudge toward oratory.

Mack steadied himself against the stove and begged their attention by rapping on the stovepipe. "Gentlemen," he said, "let us here highly resolve to get Doc's ass out of the sling of despond."

Eddie said, "Remember we done something like that once and damn near ruined him."

Mack's golden mood held. "We were younger then," he said. "This time we're going to think her out and she's going to be foolproof."

Hazel was so far won back into comradeship that he had relaxed into happy incoherence. "To Lefty Grove!" he said.

Mack opened the oven door and sat on it. "I've give it a lot of thought," he said. "Lately I done hardly nothing else."

"You never do hardly nothing else," said Whitey No. 2.

Mack ignored him. "I got a theory—"

"Aw, shut up!" said Eddie.

"Who you talking to?" said Whitey No. 2.

"I don't know," said Eddie innocently, "but if the shoe fits—"

"I got a theory, if you ain't too pie-eyed to listen," said Mack. When he had them quiet he went on, "When you hear my theory you might get kind of violent. I want you to sleep on it before you talk. I think Doc needs a wife."

"*What!*"

"Well, hell, he don't have to marry her," said Mack. "You know what I mean . . . ." If the absinthe had not given them tolerance he might have had a series of fights right then. "Kindly do not interrupt," he said. "I will now review the dame situation in the U.S. You take a look at divorces and the reasons for them and you can only think one thing: the only guy that shouldn't have nothing to do with picking out a wife is the guy that's going to marry her. That's a fact. It's a fact that if he's left alone a guy practically always marries the wrong kind of dame."

"Play it safe and don't marry nobody," said Whitey No. 2.

"There's some guys can't operate that way," said Mack.

"Are you suggesting we turn Doc, our true friend, in?"

"I asked you not to shoot off your face until you slept on it," said Mack with dignity.

Hazel tugged at his sleeve. "Ain't you joking, Mack?"

"No," said Mack, "I ain't joking."

"If anything bad come to Doc, you know what I'd do to you?" Hazel asked.

"Yes," said Mack. "I think I do—and I think I'd have it coming."

Hazel's bed was a four-poster on which the bedposts were two-by-fours topped by a quilt. He had built it from memory of a moving picture. When the Palace Flophouse was quiet at last, Hazel lay in his bed and looked up at the log-cabin pattern of his canopy. His mind was whirling. He wished there were some simpler way to help Doc than by the major operation Mack had suggested. Once he got up and looked out the door and saw that the green shaded light was on in the laboratory.

"The poor bastard," he whispered.

He didn't sleep well and his dreams were shaped like mushrooms.

12. Flower in a Crannied Wall

JOE ELEGANT was a pale young man with bangs. He smoked foreign cigarettes in a long ebony holder and he cooked for the Bear Flag. The girls said he made the best popovers in the world, and he could give a massage that would shake the kinks out of a Saturday night when the fleet was in. He sneered most of the time, and except at mealtime kept to himself in his little lean-to behind the Bear Flag, from which the rattle of his typewriter could be heard late at night.

One morning soon after she had come Suzy was having her coffee while Joe Elegant cleared the table of crumbs from earlier breakfasts.

"You make good coffee," Suzy said.

"Thank you."

"You don't look like a guy would work here."

"It's temporary, I assure you."

"I got a wonderful recipe for gumbo. Want me to give it to you?"

"Fauna designs the meals."

"You ain't very friendly."

"Why should I be?"

He was passing behind her. Suzy reached up, hooked her fingers in his shirt collar, twisted and yanked his face down level with her own. "Listen you," she began, and she scowled into his popping eyes. "Oh, the hell with it," said Suzy and released him.

Joe Elegant stepped back and massaged his throat and smoothed his shirt.

"Sorry," said Suzy.

"It's quite all right."

"What makes you so mean?"

"You said it. I don't belong here."

"Where do you belong?"

"I don't think you'd understand."

"You too good for the place?"

"Let's say I'm different."

"No kidding!" said Suzy.

"I'm writing a novel."

"You are? What about? I love novels."

"You wouldn't like this one."

"Why not?"

"You wouldn't understand it."

"Then what good is it?"

"It isn't intended for the mass."

"I'm the mass, huh? I guess you got something there. I bet you could write a pretty nice hunk of stuff."

Joe Elegant swallowed and his face twitched convulsively. "Sometime I'll read you some of it."

"Say, that would be nice. But you said I couldn't understand it."

"I'll explain it as I go along."

"I'd like that. There's one whole hell of a lot I don't understand."

"Do you like brownies?" he asked.

"I love them."

"I'll make you some. Maybe you'll come to my apartment some afternoon. I could give you a cup of tea."

"Say, you're a nice fella! Got any more coffee?"

"I'll make a fresh pot."

13. Parallels Must Be Related

Doc spent a restless night. His head was full of yellow pads and seers and octopi. Ordinarily he would have worked or read since he couldn't sleep, but now if he turned on a light he would see the yellow pad and the marshaled pencils.

As the dawn crept over the bay he decided to go for a very long walk, perhaps to follow the shoreline all the way around to Carmel. He arose, and since it was still dusky in the laboratory he turned on the lights to make his coffee.

Wide Ida, from the entrance of La Ida, saw his lights come on. She put an unlabeled pint bottle of brown liquor in a paper bag and crossed the street to Western Biological.

"Doc," she said, "would you work this stuff over?"

"What is it?"

"They say it's whisky. I just want to know if it'll kill anybody. I got a pretty good buy. They make it up in Pine Canyon."

"That's against the law," said Doc.

"Killing people is against the law too," said Wide Ida.

Doc was torn between bootlegging and murder. He thought sadly that he was always involved in something like this—not good or bad but bad and less bad. He made a fairly quick analysis. "It's not poison," he said, "but it won't build good healthy stomachs. There's some fusel oil in it. But I guess it's no worse than Old Tennis Shoes."

"Thanks, Doc. What do I owe you?"

"Oh, maybe a quart—but not this stuff."

"I'll send over some Old Taylor."

"You don't have to go off the deep end," said Doc.

"Doc, I hear you got trouble."

"Me? What kind of trouble?"

"I just heard," said Wide Ida.

Doc said angrily, "I've got no trouble. What's all the talk! God Almighty, everybody treats me as though I had a disease. What kind of trouble?"

"If there's anything I can do," she said and went out quickly, leaving the pint behind.

Doc took a sip of it, made a face, and took a swig. His heart was pounding angrily. He could not admit that the pity of his friends only confirmed his frustration. He knew that pity and contempt are brothers. He set his chin. "I *will* get the spring tides at La Jolla," he said to himself. "I *will* get a new microscope." And the very lowest voice whispered, "Somewhere there's warmth."

He sat down at his desk and wrote viciously: "Parallels must be related." He took another drink from the pint and opened yesterday's mail. There was an order for six sets of slides—starfish, embryonic series, for the Oakland Polytechnic High School. He was almost glad to do the old and practiced work. He got his collecting buckets together, threw rubber boots in his old car, and drove out to the Great Tide Pool.

14. *Lousy Wednesday*

SOME days are born ugly. From the very first light they are no damn good whatever the weather, and everybody knows it. No one knows what causes this, but on such a day people resist getting out of bed and set their heels against the day. When they are finally forced out by hunger or job they find that the day is just as lousy as they knew it would be.

On such a day it is impossible to make a good cup of coffee, shoestrings break, cups leap from the shelf by themselves and shatter on the floor, children ordinarily honest tell lies, and children ordinarily good unscrew the tap handles of the gas range and lose the screws and have to be spanked. This is the day the cat chooses to have kittens and housebroken dogs wet on the parlor rug.

Oh, it's awful on such a day! The postman brings overdue bills. If it's a sunny day it is too damn sunny, and if it is dark who can stand it?

Mack knew it was going to be that kind of a day. He couldn't find his pants. He fell over a box that had crept out in his path. He cursed each brother in the Palace Flophouse, and on his way across the vacant lot he went out of his way to kick a dandelion flower. He was sitting gloomily on a pipe when Eddie came by, and so naturally he walked with Eddie to Wide Ida's to try to do something about it. He hung around waiting for Wide Ida to go so that Eddie could slip him a drink. But Wide Ida was bending over the bar, cursing a letter.

"Taxes," she said. "Every time you get going there's more taxes. You're lucky, Mack. You don't own nothing and you don't make nothing. Until they start taxing skin, you're safe."

"What's the beef?" Mack asked.

"City and county taxes," said Wide Ida.

"On what?"

"On this place. It ain't much, but I was fixed to put a down payment on a new Pontiac."

It was a statement that ordinarily would have aroused a detached compassion in Mack, together with mild self-congratulation that he was not burdened with taxable assets. But now a nagging worry fell on him, and he went back to the Palace Flophouse to worry in greater comfort. He went over the history of the Palace in his mind.

It had belonged to Lee Chong. Long before the war Mack and the boys had rented it from him for five dollars a month, and, naturally enough, they had never paid any rent. Lee Chong would have been shocked if they had. Then Lee Chong sold out to Joseph and Mary. Did the Palace go with the rest? Mack didn't know, but if it did, the Patrón didn't know it. He was no Lee Chong. He would have demanded the rent. But if the Patrón did own the place, he would get a tax bill. If he got a tax bill, he was sure to be on the necks of Mack and the boys. The Patrón was not a man to pay out money without getting more money back, that was certain.

It seemed very unjust. Their home, their security, even their social standing, were cast in the balance. Mack lay on his bed and considered what could be done. Suppose the Patrón demanded back rent—clear back for years. You couldn't trust a man like that. What a lousy day it was! Mack didn't know what to do, so he called a meeting of the boys, even sent Hazel to bring Eddie back from Wide Ida's bar.

It was a grim and shaken assembly. Mack explained all the angles until even Hazel seemed to understand the danger. The boys studied their fingers, looked at the ceiling, blew on their knuckles. Eddie got up and walked around his chair to change his thinking luck.

At last Whitey No. 2 said, "We could steal his mail so he won't get no tax bill."

"It ain't practical," said Mack. "Even if it wasn't a crime."

Hazel offered, "We could kill him."

"You ain't heard that's against the law too?" Mack asked.

"I mean, make it like an accident," said Hazel. "He could fall off Point Lobos."

"Then somebody else inherits the joint and we don't even know who."

The injustice in the theory of private ownership of real estate was descending on them.

"Maybe we could get Doc to talk to him. He likes Doc." This was Whitey No. 1's offering.

"That would only draw it to his attention," said Mack. "Hell, he might even raise the rent."

"He might even try to collect it," said Eddie.

Hazel was going into a slow but luminous burn. He gazed about the whitewashed walls of the Palace Flophouse, at the Coca-Cola calendar girls, at the great and ancient woodstove, at the grandfather clock, at the framed portrait of Romie Jacks. There were honest, unabashed tears in Hazel's eyes. "The son-of-a-bitch," he said. "After all our work he takes away our home—the only place where I ever been happy. How can a guy be so goddam mean?"

"He ain't done it yet," said Mack. "He don't even know about it maybe."

"I wish Doc owned the place," said Eddie. "We wouldn't have no trouble with Doc."

Mack looked at him quickly. "What put that in your head?" he demanded.

"Hell, Doc don't open his mail for weeks on end. Doc would forget to collect the rent and he'd forget to open a tax bill."

Excitement shone in Mack's eyes. "Eddie," he said, "maybe you put your finger in it."

"In what?"

"I got to think it over," said Mack, "but just maybe our darling Eddie here is a genius."

Eddie blushed with pleasure. "What'd I do, Mack?"

"I can't tell you now."

"Hell, Mack, I want to know what I done."

"It was smart," said Mack. "It was a stroke of just pure wonderful. Now let's give the Patrón a going-over. How much guts you think he's got?"

"Plenty," said Hazel. "And he's plenty wise."

Mack spoke slowly, thinking aloud. "Let's see. Joseph and Mary, you might say, is a con man in a general kind of way—"

"He's a nice dresser," said Hazel.

"A con man can't make enemies unless, of course, he wants to get out of town. He got to keep everybody happy and friendly."

"Come on, Mack," Whitey No. 1 demanded. "Tell us!"

"Fellas," said Mack, "if I blowed it now and it wasn't no good, why, you'd kind of lose face in me. I want to think this one out and see if I can't kind of surround him. But if we do her, you'll all have to help."

"Do what?"

"Let me alone now, boys," said Mack, and he went back to his bed and put his head on his crossed hands and studied the rafters of the Palace Flophouse.

Hazel came quietly to his bedside. "You won't let nobody take our home away, will you, Mack?"

"I promise!" said Mack fervently. "Where's Eddie?"

"Went back to Wide Ida's."

"Will you do something for me, Hazel?"

"Sure, Mack."

"Take that lard can over there and see can Eddie fill it full of beer without too much fuss. It'll help me to think better."

"You'll get your beer," said Hazel. "You just keep thinking, Mack. Say, Mack, how do you think Eddie always got a stroke of genius even when he don't know it and I don't never have none?"

"Come again?" said Mack.

"How come—oh, the hell with it!" said Hazel.

15. The Playing Fields of Harrow

FAUNA had made a success of three improbable enterprises. More than likely she could have held her own in steel or chemicals, maybe even in General Electric, for Fauna had the proper ingredients for modern business. She was benevolent and at the same time solvent, public-spirited and privately an individualist, open-handed but with a delicate sense of double-entry bookkeeping, sentimental but not soft. She could easily have been chairman of the board of a large corporation. And Fauna took a deep personal interest in her girls.

Shortly after she took over the Bear Flag, Fauna set aside and decorated the Ready Room. It was a large and pleasant apartment with three windows overlooking the vacant lot. Fauna put in deep chairs and couches covered with bright, flower-littered glazed chintz. The drapes matched the furniture, and the pictures were designed to soothe without arousing interest—engravings of cows in ponds, deer in streams, dogs in lakes. Wet animals seem to serve some human need.

For recreation Fauna provided a table-tennis set, a card table, and a parchesi board. The Ready Room was a place to relax, to read, to gossip, to study, and some of these things were actually done by the girls of the Bear Flag.

One wall was dominated by a large framed board on which were pasted enormous gold stars, and this was Fauna's personal pride. The Ready Room was gay and feminine. It had an exotic, oriental odor from the incense which burned in the blackened lap of a crouching plaster Buddha.

At about a quarter to three Agnes and Mabel and Becky were relaxing in the Ready Room. It was the time of languor. The vacant lot was washed in clear pale sunshine, which made even the rusty pipes and the old boiler look beautiful. The tall mallow weeds were as sweetly green as a garden. A sleek, gray, lazy Persian cat hunted gophers in the grass and didn't care whether she caught one or not.

Mabel stood at the window. She said, "I heard some people used to live in that old boiler."

Agnes was painting her toenails and waving her feet to dry

the enamel. "That's before your time," she said. "Mr. and Mrs. Malloy, they had it fixed up nice—awning out front, oriental rug. Once you got inside, through the firedoor, it was real nice. She was a homemaker."

"Why'd they leave?" Becky asked.

"They got to arguing. She kept wanting curtains. He wouldn't let her because there wasn't no windows. When they argued it kind of echoed in there and got on their nerves. He said there wasn't room inside to take a swing at her. He's in the county jail now—trusty. Mrs. Malloy's slinging hash in a grease joint over at Salinas, waiting for him to get out. They was real nice people. He's a high Elk."

Mabel moved away from the window. "You heard the Rattlesnake Club is coming from Salinas tonight? Took the whole house over."

"Yeah," said Becky. "They're having a memorial meeting for dead members. Fauna give them a rate."

Agnes lifted her left leg and blew on her toenails. "Like this color?" she asked.

"It's nice," said Becky. "Looks a little like you was rotting. Say, where in hell is Suzy? She'll find out when Fauna says three o'clock she means three o'clock. Gee, Fauna's a funny name."

Mabel said, "Her name used to be Flora. What is a fauna anyway? I never knew nobody named that."

"Oh, it's like a baby deer," said Becky. "I don't think Suzy'll be here long. She's kind of nuts—got a nuts look in her eye. Goes out walking."

Mabel said, "Well, it's two minutes to three. Suzy better get here."

On the stroke of three a door opened and Fauna came in from her bedroom. A silver headband was tied around her orange hair, and it made her look like a certain social leader recently deceased. Fauna had the elegance found only in the drawing rooms of the old rich and in *haute monde* brothels. She was heavy but she moved with light, deft steps. She carried a large basket.

"Where's Suzy?" she asked.

"I don't know," said Mabel.

"Well, look in her room."

Mabel went out.

Fauna moved to the parchesi board. "Somebody's been shooting craps with the parchesi dice," she said.

"How'd you know?" Becky asked.

"There's two bucks in the corner pocket. I don't want gambling in the Ready Room. If a young lady wants to run a few passes with a customer, that's different, but I don't want to find no more pencil marks on the lump sugar either. Gambling's a vice. I knew many a good hooker with a future that's throwed it away on games of chance."

"Hell, Fauna, you play poker," said Becky.

"Poker ain't a game of chance," said Fauna. "And you watch your language, Becky. Vulgarity gives a hookshop a bad name." She took a linen tablecloth from her basket and spread it over the parchesi board. Then she laid out a napkin, a plate, wineglasses, and a heap of flat silver.

Mabel and Suzy came in.

Fauna said, "I don't like my young ladies to be late." She took a teacher's pointer from her basket. "Now, what young lady wants to be first?"

Agnes said, "I'll do her."

"You done it yesterday," said Mabel. "Goddam it, it's my turn!"

Fauna said sternly, "Young ladies, suppose some nice dumb young fellow was to hear you. Now, Mabel—" She indicated the items on the tablecloth with a pointer, and Mabel began, like a child reciting poetry, "Oyster fork . . . salad fork . . . fish fork . . . roast fork . . . savory fork . . . dessert fork . . . plate . . . dessert knife . . . savory knife . . . roast knife . . . fish knife—"

"Good!" said Fauna. "Now here." And Mabel went on, "Water . . . white wine . . . claret . . . burgundy . . . port . . . brandy."

"Perfect," said Fauna. "Which side does the salad go on?"

"Left side, so you can get your sleeve in the gravy."

Fauna was deeply gratified. "By God, that's good! I wouldn't be surprised if Mabel wasn't one of them stars before too long." She indicated the gold stars on the wall.

"What are they?" Suzy asked.

Fauna said proudly, "Every one of them stars represents a

young lady from the Bear Flag that married, and married well. That first star's got four kids and her husband's manager of an A and P. Third from the end is president of the Salinas Forward and Upward Club and held the tree on Arbor Day. Next star is high up in the Watch and Ward, sings alto in the Episcopal church in San Jose. My young ladies go places. Now, Suzy—"

"Huh?"

"What's that?"

"That funny kind of fork?"

"What's it for?"

"I don't know."

"Cooperate, Suzy. What do you eat with it?"

Suzy mused, "You couldn't get much mashed potatoes on it. Pickles maybe?"

"It's a clam fork," said Fauna. "Now say it. *Clam fork.*"

Suzy said vehemently, "I wouldn't eat a clam if you was to give me a scoop shovel."

"What a mug!" said Agnes.

Suzy turned on her. "I ain't no mug!"

Mabel cried, "Double negative! Double negative!"

"What you talking about?" said Suzy.

Mabel said, "When you say you ain't no mug, that means you're a mug."

Suzy started for her. "Who's a mug?"

Fauna bellowed, "If certain young ladies don't come to order they're going to get a paste in the puss! Now—posture. Where's the books?"

Agnes said, "I think Joe Elegant's reading them."

"Damn it," said Fauna, "I picked them books special so's nobody'd take them. What's he reading them for? *Breeder's Journal*, *California Civil Code*, and a novel by Sterling North—what the hell is there to read? Well, we'll just have to use the basket, I guess. Agnes, put the basket on your head."

Fauna inspected her. "Now look here, young ladies," she said. "Just because you got your ankles together and your hips flang forward—that don't necessarily mean posture. Agnes, tuck in your butt! Posture's a state of mind. Real posture is when a young lady's flat on her ass and still looks like she got books on her head."

There came a knock on the door and Joe Elegant handed Fauna a note. She read it and sighed with pleasure. "That Mack," she said. "What a gent! I guess he'd drain the embalming fluid off his dead grandma, but he'd do it nice."

"Is his grandma dead?" Agnes asked.

"Who knows?" said Fauna. "Listen to this, young ladies. 'Mack and the boys request the pleasure of your company at their joint tomorrow aft. to drink a slug of good stuff and talk about something important. Bring the girls. R.S.V.P.'" Fauna paused. "He could of yelled outside the window, but not Mack—he requests the pleasure of our company." She sighed. "What a gent! If he wasn't such a bum I'd aim one of you young ladies at him."

Agnes asked, "What's the matter with Mack's grandma?"

"I don't even know he's got a grandma," said Fauna. "Now when we go over there tomorrow, you young ladies keep your traps shut and just listen." She mused, "Something important—well, it might be like Mack needs twenty bucks, so just keep your heads shut and let me do the thinking."

Suddenly Fauna beat her forehead with the heel of her hand. "I nearly forgot! Joe Elegant baked a great big goddam cake. Suzy, you take four cold cans of beer and that cake and go over and give them to Doc to cheer him up."

"Okay," said Suzy. "But it'll probably molt in his stomach."

"His stomach ain't none of your business," said Fauna.

And when Suzy had gone Fauna said, "I wisht I could stick up a star for that kid. She don't hardly pull her own weight here."

16. The Little Flowers of Saint Mack

Doc laid ten big starfish out on a shelf, and he set up a line of eight glass dishes half filled with sea water. Although he was inclined to carelessness in his living arrangements his laboratory technique was immaculate. The making of the embryo series gave him pleasure. He had done it hundreds of times before, and he felt a safety in the known thing—no speculation here. He did certain things and certain other things followed. There is comfort in routine.

His old life came back to him—a plateau of contentment with small peaks of excitement but none of the jagged pain of original thinking, none of the loneliness of invention. His phonograph played softly, played the safe and certain fugues of Bach, clear as equations. As he worked, a benign feeling came over him. He liked himself again as he once had; liked himself as a person, the way he might like anyone else. The self-hatred which poisons so many people and which had been irritating him was gone for the time. The top voice of his mind sang peacefulness and order, and the raucous middle voice was gentle; it mumbled and snarled but it could not be heard. The lowest voice of all was silent, dreaming of a warm safe sea.

The rattlesnakes in their wire cage suddenly lifted their heads, felt the air with their forked tongues, and then all four set up a dry buzzing rattle. Doc looked up from his work as Mack came in.

Mack glanced at the cage. "Them new snakes ain't got used to me yet," he said.

"Takes a little time," said Doc. "You haven't been here much."

"Didn't feel no welcome here," said Mack.

"I'm sorry, Mack. I guess I've been off my feed. I'll try to do better."

"You going to let up on them devilfish?"

"I don't know."

"They was making you sick."

Doc laughed. "It wasn't the octopi. I guess it was trying to think. I'd got out of the habit."

"I never got the habit," said Mack.

"That's not true," said Doc. "I never knew anyone who devoted more loving thought to minisculae."

"I never even heard of them," said Mack. "Say, Doc, what do you think of the Patrón—your honest, spit-in-the-lake opinion?"

"I don't think I understand him. We're kind of different."

"You ain't kidding," said Mack. "He ain't honest."

Doc said, "I'd call that expert testimony."

"What do you mean?"

"I mean you bring some experience to bear."

"Oh, I know what you mean," said Mack earnestly, "but you search your heart, Doc, and see if I ain't dishonest in a kind of honest way. I don't really fool nobody—not even myself. And there's another thing—I know when I'm doing it. Joseph and Mary can't tell the difference."

"I think that might be true," said Doc.

"What I'm wondering is—well, I don't think the Patrón wants any trouble around here, do you?"

"Nobody wants any trouble."

"He's got a stake here," Mack went on. "If the whole Row took a skunner to him, why, he just couldn't take that chance, don't you think?"

"If I knew what you were talking about, it might help," said Doc.

"I'm just trying to figure something," said Mack.

"Well, if you mean that the Patrón is in kind of a sensitive position—"

"That's what I do mean," said Mack. "He can't afford to have no enemies."

"Nobody wants enemies," said Doc.

"I know. But he could get his ass in a sling. He got a business and he's got property."

"I see what you mean," said Doc. "You're going to pressure him and you want to know what he'll do. What are you going to try to take away from him, Mack?"

"I'm just thinking," said Mack.

"I never knew you to think idly. When you think, somebody gets hurt."

"I never hurt nobody, Doc."

"Well, not bad. I will say your bite is not deadly."

Mack was uneasy. He had not intended the conversation to turn to him. He changed the subject.

"Say, Doc, did you hear? The whole country club took a loyalty oath on the eighteenth green. Whitey No. 2 was caddying. Them members all took off their hats and swore they would not destroy the U. S. government."

"I'm glad," said Doc. "I was worried. Did the caddies take the oath too?"

"Some of them did, but not Whitey. He's kind of an idealist, you might say. He says if he gets an idea to burn down the Capitol he don't want no perjury rap to stand in his way. They won't let him caddy no more."

"Does he want to burn down the Capitol?" Doc asked.

"Well, no. He says he don't want to now, but he don't know what he'll want to do next month. He give us quite a talk about it. Says he was a Marine, went through a lot of fighting for the country, figures he's got a kind of personal interest. He don't want nobody to tell him what to do."

Doc laughed. "So he can't carry golf clubs any more because of his ideals?"

"They say he's a security risk," said Mack. "Whitey claims he ain't got a good enough memory to be a security risk. Besides, they don't talk about nothing out there on the golf course except money and dames."

Doc said, "Heroes always get punished at first."

"Speaking of dames, Doc—"

"Let's," said Doc.

"Whatever happened to that swell-looking babe in the fur coat used to come over?"

"She's not been very well."

"That's too bad," said Mack. "What's she got?"

"Oh, something obscure. Can't seem to track it down."

"I guess with that kind of dough—"

"What do you mean?"

"I seen it happen so many times," said Mack. "You take a dame and she's married to a guy that's making twenty-five bucks a week. You can't kill her with a meat ax. She's got kids and does the washing—may get a little tired but that's the worse that can happen to her. But let the guy get raised to seventy-five bucks a week and she begins to get colds and take vitamins."

"That's a new theory of medicine," said Doc.

"It ain't new. Hell, just use your eyes. Guy gets up to a hundred a week and this same dame reads *Time* magazine and she's got the newest disease before she even finished the page. I've knew dames that can give doctors cards, spades, and big cassino about medicine. They got stuff called allergy now. Used to call it hay fever—made you sneeze. Guy that figured out allergy should of got a patent. A allergy is, you get sick when there's something you don't want to do. I've knew dames that was allergic to dishwater. Married guy starts making dough—he's got a patient on his hands."

"You sound cynical," said Doc.

"No, I ain't. You just look around and show me one well dame with her old man in the chips."

Doc chuckled. "You think that's what happened to my friend?"

"Oh, hell no," said Mack. "That's big stuff. When you get dough like that it's different. She got to have something that don't nobody know what it is. She can't have nothing common that you can take salts for. She goes around puzzling doctors. They stand around her and they shake their heads and they scratch and they never seen nothing like her case before."

"I haven't heard you go on like this for a long time," said Doc.

"You ain't been in the mood to listen. You think them doctors is honest?"

"I haven't any reason to doubt it. Why?"

"I bet I could fix rich dames up," said Mack. "At least for a while."

"How would you go about it?"

"Well, sir, first I'd hire me a deaf-and-dumb assistant. His job is just to set and listen and look worried. Then I'd get me a bottle of Epsom salts and I'd put in a pretty little screwcap thing and I'd call it Moondust. I'd charge about thirty dollars a teaspoonful, and you got to come to my office to get it. Then I'd invent me a machine you strap the dame in. It's all chrome and it lights colored lights every minute or so. It costs the dame twelve dollars a half-hour and it puts her through the motions she'd do over a scrub board. I'd cure them! And I'd make a fortune too. Of course they'd get sick right away again, so I'd have something else, like mixed sleeping pills and wake-up pills that keeps you right where you was when you started."

Doc said, "Thank God you haven't got a license to practice!"

"Why?"

"As a matter of fact, I don't know why," said Doc. "How about preventive medicine?"

"You mean how to keep them from getting sick?"

"Yes."

"That's easy," said Mack. "Stay broke!"

Doc sat silent for a while. He glanced at the starfish and saw the reproductive fluid beginning to ooze from between their rays. "Say, Mack," he asked, "did you come over to try to get something out of me?"

"I don't think so," said Mack. "If I did I've forgot what it was. I'm sure glad you got over it, Doc."

"Got over what?"

"Oh, them goddam sooplapods."

"Look, Mack!" Sudden anger welled up in Doc. "Don't get any funny ideas. I am going to write that paper. I am going to La Jolla for the spring tides."

"All right, Doc, all right. Have it your own way."

But back in the Palace Flophouse Mack reported to the boys, "Seemed like he was better, but he ain't over the hump yet. We got to help him not to write that goddam paper."

17. Suzy Binds the Cheese

SUZY was light on her feet. She was up the stairs and knocking on the door of Western Biological before the snakes rattled. Doc called, "Come in," without looking up from his microscope.

Suzy stood in the doorway. She held a gigantic flop cake on one hand and carried a paper bag of canned beer in the other. "How do you do," she said formally.

Doc looked up. "Oh, hello. For God's sake, what's that?"

"A cake. Joe Elegant made it."

"Why?" Doc asked.

"I think Fauna told him to."

"Well, I hope you like cake," said Doc.

Suzy laughed. "I don't think this is a eating cake. This is a looking cake. Fauna sent you some beer."

"That's more like it," said Doc. "What's Fauna want?"

"Nothing."

"That's funny."

"Where shall I put the cake?" said Suzy.

Now Doc looked at Suzy and Suzy looked at Doc and they both had the same thought and they burst into laughter. Tears streamed from Suzy's eyes. "Oh, Lord!" said Suzy. "Oh, Lord!" She laughed with her mouth wide and her eyes pinched shut. Doc slapped his leg and threw back his head and roared. And the laughter was so pleasant they tried to keep it going after its momentum was spent.

"Oh, Lord," said Suzy, "I got to wipe my eyes." She put the cake down on top of the rattlesnake cage, and hysterical rattling filled the room. Suzy jumped back. "What's that?"

"Rattlesnakes."

"What you got them for?"

"I take their venom and sell it."

"I'd hate to live with a bunch of dirty snakes."

"They're not dirty. They even change their skins. That's more than people do."

"I hate them," said Suzy, and she shuddered.

"You wouldn't, once you knew them."

"Well I ain't likely to get to know them," said Suzy. "They're dirty."

Doc leaned back in his chair and crossed his legs. He said, "You know, this interests me. Snakes are cleaner than most animals. Wonder why you call them dirty?"

Suzy looked at him levelly. "You want to know why?"

"Sure I do."

"Because you run Fauna down."

"Wait a minute," said Doc. "What's that got—I did not!"

"You said Fauna's trying to get something out of you. She just done it to be nice."

Doc nodded his head slowly. "I see. So you got even by calling snakes dirty."

"You got it, mister. Nobody don't run Fauna down when I'm around."

"It was just a joke," said Doc.

"Didn't sound like no joke to me."

"Why, Fauna's one of my best friends," said Doc. "Let's have a can of beer and make peace."

"Okay," said Suzy. "You make the first move."

Doc said, "Tell Joe Elegant it's an incredible cake."

"Got marshmallow frosting," said Suzy.

"And tell Fauna the beer saved my life."

Suzy's face relaxed. "Okay," she said. "I guess that's okay. Where's the opener?"

"Right in the sink back there."

Suzy brought the two punched cans to Doc's work table. "Say, what you doing?"

"Making slides. When I started I put starfish sperm and ova in each of these glasses. Then every half-hour I kill one glass of the developing embryos, and when I have the whole series, I mount them on slides like this, and one slide shows the whole development."

Suzy bent over the dishes. "I don't see nothing."

"They're too small. I can show you in the glass."

Suzy backed up. "What do you do it for?"

"So students can see how starfish get to be."

"Why do they want to know?"

"Well, I guess because that's the way people get to be."

"Then why don't they study people?"

Doc laughed. "It's a little difficult to kill unborn babies every half-hour. Here, take a look." He pushed a glass dish under the microscope.

Suzy peered in the eyepieces. "God Almighty!" she said. "Did I look like that once?"

"Something like."

"Sometimes I feel like that now. Say, Doc, you got a funny business—bugs and all like that."

"There are funnier businesses," he said sharply.

She stiffened. "Meaning my business? You don't like my business, huh?"

"It doesn't matter whether I like it or not. There it is. But it does seem to me a kind of sad substitute for love—a kind of lonesome substitute."

Suzy put her hands on her hips. "And what've you got, mister? Bugs, snakes? Look at this dump! It stinks. Floor ain't been clean in years. You ain't got a decent suit of clothes. You probably can't remember your last hot meal. You sit here breeding bugs—for Chrissake! What do you think that's a substitute for?"

In the old days Doc would have been amused, but now his guard was down and he caught her anger like a disease. "I do what I want," he said. "I live the way I want. I'm free—do you get that? I'm free and I do what I want."

"You ain't got nothing," Suzy said. "Bugs and snakes and a dirty house. I bet some dame threw you over. That's what you're substituting for. Got a wife? No! Got a girl? No!"

Doc found himself shouting, "I don't want a wife. I have all the women I want!"

"Woman and women is two different things," said Suzy. "Guy knows all about women he don't know nothing about a woman."

Doc said, "This guy is happy that way."

"Now you're happy!" said Suzy. "You're a pushover! If no dame's got you it's because no dame wants you. Who the hell would want to live with bugs and snakes in a joint like this?"

"Who'd want to go to bed with anybody that's got three bucks?" said Doc cruelly.

Suzy said icily, "A smart guy. A real smart guy. He's got what he wants. Seems to me I heard you're writing a great big goddam highfalutin paper."

"Who told you that?"

"Everybody knows about it. Everybody's laughing at you behind your back—and you know why? Because everybody knows you're kidding yourself. You ain't never going to write that paper because you can't write that paper. You're just sitting here like a kid playing wish games."

She saw her words go home as surely as though she had watched arrows drive into his chest, and misery and shame overwhelmed her. "I wish I didn't say that," she spoke softly. "I wish to God I never said that."

"It might be true," said Doc quietly. "Maybe you put your finger on the truth. Is everybody laughing at me? Is everybody laughing—?"

"My name's Suzy," she said.

"Are they laughing, Suzy?"

"They got no right to," she said. "I was just fighting back—honest to God I was. I didn't mean any of that stuff I said."

"I love true things," said Doc. "Even when they hurt. Isn't it better to know the truth about oneself?" And he asked it of himself. "Yes, I think it is. I think it is. You're quite right, I've got nothing. That's why I built up the whole story about my paper until I believed it myself—a little man pretending to be a big man, a fool trying to be wise."

"Fauna will kill me," Suzy moaned. "She'll wring my neck. Say, Doc, you got no right to take mad talk from a two-bit hustler—you got no right."

"What's it matter where the truth comes from," he said, "if it's the truth?"

Suzy said, "Doc, I never felt so lousy in my life. Get mad at me, won't you?"

"Why should I get mad? Maybe you've stopped a bunch of nonsense. Perhaps you've nipped a fool in the bud."

"Get mad at me," she begged. "Here! Take a punch at me."

Doc chuckled. "I wish it could be that easy."

Suzy said sadly, "Then I ain't got any choice," and she shrilled at him, "Why you goddam bum! You lousy stinking fool! Who the hell d'you think you are?"

There was a flutter of footsteps and the door burst open.

It was Becky. "Suzy! You're late. The Rattlesnakes are here. Come on! Get into your tomato dress."

"It's called 'Love Apples,'" said Suzy quietly. "So long, Doc," and she followed Becky out.

Doc watched them go. He said aloud, "That's probably the only completely honest human I have ever met." His eyes wandered to the table and suddenly he bellowed, "*Goddam it!* She made me miss the time. The dirty bitch! I got to do it all over." And he dumped the contents of the glass dishes into his slop bucket.

18. A Pause in the Day's Occupation

NOT the least important and valuable custom Fauna brought to the Bear Flag was the little time of rest and contemplation in the Ready Room after work and before sleep. Grievances were brought out and inspected, quarrels were settled, and all the little matters of interest and despair were turned over and examined for their actual value. Then praise or blame were assigned and plans for improvement were laid out with lore and tact learned in other fields. Fauna warped and nudged and bunted her young ladies toward good nature and kindliness, which are the parents of restful sleep. It was not unusual for light refreshments to be served, and on occasion the young ladies' voices joined in song—"Home Sweet Home," "Old Black Joe," "Down by the Old Mill Stream," "Harvest Moon." Dog watch in the Ready Room was a medicine to weary nerves and frayed bodies.

The Bear Flag was shorthanded the night of the memorial meeting for dead members sponsored by the Rattlesnake Club of Salinas. Helen and Wisteria were doing sixty days for a lady fight that is still discussed with admiration in Cannery Row.

When the last Rattlesnake had gone and the big front door was closed, the girls wandered wearily into the Ready Room, sat down, and kicked off their shoes. Becky said, "One of them Rattlesnakes tonight called us an institution and a landmark."

Agnes said acidly, "We get a few more like Suzy and it'll be a institution all right. I got an uncle in a institution. He goes right on fighting the battle of San Juan Hill. Where is Suzy?"

"I'm right here," said Suzy, entering. "I was getting that cracked record out of the juke-box. Am I pooped! Let's put it in the sack."

"Before Fauna gives us good night? You crazy?" Mabel said. "She'd bust a gut."

Becky sighed. "What a night! This is one time the group rate paid off. Them Rattlesnakes ain't turned a trick since midnight but they sure was active."

"They was going fine until they run out of liquor," said Mabel. "That new stuff Wide Ida sent in must be made of jumping beans."

Suzy said, "I figured if that short one told me once more how his little boy cut a worm in two with a shovel—"

"Oh, you got it too, huh? Know what the little bastard said? Only four years old too. He said, 'I cut a wum.' Now if he said he cut a camel I could listen to it three or four times."

"That bald one!" said Mabel. "Did *his* wife have an

operation! They turned her inside out. Sounded like they was pelting her. He got crying so hard I never did find out what she had."

"A malignant artichoke," said Becky. "I made him say it slow."

Agnes asked, "Say, who is this guy Sigmund Ki they was singing about?"

"Never heard of him," said Becky. "I once knew a dame said she was the original Frankie though."

"I've personally knew three original Frankies," said Mabel. "Suzy, you got to stop arguing with the customers."

Suzy said, "If that's the live members of the Rattlesnake Club, the dead ones is what I call dead. I can scream twice at a rubber lizard and then the hell with it."

Fauna came out of the bedroom office and stood in the doorway, rubbing lotion into her hands. She had changed to a peach-colored dressing gown. She said seriously, "Young ladies, you can make fun of the Rattlesnakes if you want to, but if you ever get in the administration end you will welcome good solid citizens like them. Why, there was some very important people here from Salinas! I give them a good rate, but you notice there's no busted furniture. Them free-spending sailors last Saturday night cost me eighty-five dollars in repairs. That nice boy give Becky a five-dollar tip—but he busted two windows and run off with the deer-antler halltree."

Suzy said, "God, I'm sleepy."

Fauna said sharply, "Suzy, I got one rule: never let the sun rise on a cross word or an unbalanced book." She scratched her nose with a pencil. "I just wish there was more Rattlesnakes," she said.

"I wish there was more dead members," Suzy said.

"That's a cross word, Suzy!" said Fauna. "The birds are chirping happily, so why can't we? Now let's relax. Who wants a beer?"

Becky said, "If I say I want it I'll have to get it for everybody. My dogs are tired! You know what I was dancing? A quadrille!"

Fauna said dryly, "I seen you. I'll have to give you some lessons, I guess. You done a kootch quadrille. It ain't your feet should be tired. After all the posture lessons I give you, you still dance like a harlot."

"What's a harlot?" Becky asked.

"A whore," said Mabel.

"Oh, harlot, huh?" said Becky.

Agnes said, "Fauna, I want you should tell Suzy when she goes on errands she should come back. She stayed over Doc's about an hour while the Rattlesnakes was really active."

Suzy asked, "Say, Fauna, what's wrong with Doc?"

"Wrong? Ain't nothing wrong with him," said Fauna. "He's one of the nicest fellas ever lived on Cannery Row. You'd think he'd turn bitter the way everybody hustles him. Wide Ida gets him to analyze her booze, Mack and the boys throw the hook into him for every dime that sticks out, a kid cuts his finger on the Row and he goes to Doc to get it wrapped up. Why, when Becky got in a fight with that Woodman of the World and got bit in the shoulder, she might of lost her arm if it wasn't for Doc. Show her the scar, Becky."

Suzy asked, "Don't Doc never come here?"

"No, he don't. But don't let nothing ever give you the idea he's strange. There's girls goes in there with fur coats and stuff and he plays that churchy kind of music. Doc's all right. He gets what he wants. Dora said every girl made a play for him. I put a stop to that."

"Why'd you do that?" Suzy asked.

"I'm saving him—that's why. You look at them gold stars over there—every star, one of my girls has married well."

Suzy said, "Who marries hustlers?"

"Now that's a bad attitude to take," Fauna said coldly. "That's the kind of attitude I try to discourage. You look at that third star from the end over there. I admit she's kind of snooty, but why shouldn't she be? She's a reader in a big church in San Luis Obispo. I tell you, my girls marry, and marry well!"

Suzy said, "What's that got to do with Doc?"

"I got him staked out for Miss Right," said Fauna. "Someday I'll draw a bead on him."

"Hell," said Suzy, "he said he don't want to marry nobody."

"Watch your language, Suzy," said Fauna. And then with interest she asked, "How'd you get along with him?"

"We got in a hassle," said Suzy. "He made me mad and I made him mad. All them goddam bugs—and a paper about nervous breakdowns in devilfish! Someday a guy in a white coat's going to tap him on the shoulder."

Fauna said, "Don't believe it! Why, some of them bugs he gets as much as ten bucks for."

"Not *apiece*?" said Suzy.

Fauna went on, "Why, he takes an old beat-up cat he paid a quarter for and he shoots red and blue and yellow paint in it and he gets fifteen bucks for it."

"Why, for Chrissake?" Suzy asked.

"Suzy, if you don't watch your language I'll wash out your mouth. Now you just get up and bring the beer for that. You're an ignorant girl but I'll be goddamned if I'll let you get common."

Suzy went out, and Fauna said, "I wonder if she might be for Doc—she's got an awful big mouth. She'd talk her way out of an apple dumpling."

Suzy came back with a tray of beer bottles.

Becky said, "Fauna, why don't you read Suzy's horoscope?"

"You mean stars and like that?" said Suzy. "What for?"

Becky said, "To see if you're going to marry Doc."

Suzy said angrily, "I like a joke as good as anybody but don't get rough with me."

Becky said, "Who's rough?"

"I don't believe that crap about stars," said Suzy. "And you lay off talking about Doc. He's been to college—he's read so many books he can't count 'em—and not comic books neither. You lay off talking about him and me."

Fauna said, "That will be enough, miss. You see that chart? Just look at them gold stars. And look particular at that gold star that's got a gold star on it. That young lady is married to a professor at Stanford. He's got about a million books, and she used to take all day Sunday figuring out Jiggs and Maggie. You know what she does? If somebody points to all them books and says, 'Does the little lady read all of them?' she just smiles kind of quiet and mysterious. When they ask her a question, you know what she does? You can learn, Suzy, if you just pay attention. She repeats the last three words anybody says, and first thing you know, they think she said it. Why, her own husband thinks she can read and write! You get smart, Suzy. Doc don't want no dame that knows as much as him. What would he have to talk about? Let him tell you for once. Don't tell him."

Becky said, "She won't. She loves to shoot off her face."

"She damn well better learn to shut up or she won't be no gold star," said Fauna. "That's a good idea about the horoscope. When's your birthday, Suzy?"

"February twenty-third."

"What time was you born?"

"God knows, but I think it was leap year."

Agnes said, "I bet she was born at night. I can always tell."

Fauna went into her room and brought back a chart and pinned it to the wall. And she brought out her schoolroom pointer again. "Now this here's you, Pisces—that's fish."

Suzy said, "You mean I'm fish?"

"You're fish," said Fauna.

"I don't believe a goddam word of it. I don't even like fish," Suzy said. "Why, hell, I break out if I look at a fish!"

"Don't look at them then," said Fauna. "But if you ain't lied about your birthday you're fish. Now let's see—fish is to Jupiter, carry two in the Saturn, and three left over in the House of Venus—"

"I don't believe none of it," Suzy said.

Fauna looked up from her figuring. "Tell her some of that stuff I done, Mabel."

Mabel said, "I seen her do wonderful stuff. I had a pup one time. Fauna, she done a horoscope on him. It says on that pup's third birthday, ten o'clock, he's going to explode."

Suzy asked, "Did he?"

"Well, no. Something went haywire with the chart, I guess. Ten o'clock on that dog's third birthday he caught fire. I was taking a lemon rinse."

"You could use one now," Fauna said.

"What caught him on fire?" Suzy asked.

"He just caught. Spontaneous something or other. He was a pretty good dog but he wasn't very bright. Never could housebreak him. He used to wet on Joe Elegant."

Suzy said, "I bet Joe Elegant set him on fire."

"That's a lie!" said Mabel. "Joe Elegant was in the hospital."

Suddenly Fauna clapped her hands to her brow. "God Almighty!"

"What is it?" said Becky. "What's the matter?"

Fauna said impressively, "Suzy, you know what you're going to marry? You're going to marry a Cancer!"

"Thought you caught it," said Suzy. "I didn't know you had to marry it."

"Don't get funny," said Fauna. "Cancer, that's a crab—and that's also July. Now you just think—who works with crabs and stuff like that?"

Becky said, "Joe Anguro's fish market."

Fauna exploded, "Doc! And if his birthday's in July he's a gone goose. Agnes, when's Doc's birthday?"

"I don't know. Mack's gonna ask him."

"Well, we'll have to find out. Can't let him know why we want to know."

Agnes said, "Mack will find out. Mack's used to hustling Doc."

"Well, I want to know right away. Now you young ladies get some sleep, you hear me? You know what's coming in today?" Fauna stuck the pencil in her hair. "A great big fat juicy destroyer! And you know what day it is?"

The girls spoke in a chorus. "Lord-God-Almighty," they said, "payday!"

It took Fauna about five minutes to put up her hair and then she was ready to make her final rounds to see that the garbage was out and all the lights turned off. In the dark Ready Room she saw a glowing cigarette.

"Who's there?" she called.

"Me," said Suzy.

"Why ain't you in bed?"

"I was thinking."

"Now I know you'll never make a hustler. What you thinking about, your horoscope?"

"Yeah."

"You like Doc, huh?"

"I put the knife in him. He made me mad."

"Whyn't you let me handle it?" said Fauna. "I think I could maybe get him for you."

"He don't want a wife, and if he did, he don't want nobody like me."

"People don't know what they want," said Fauna. "They got to be pushed. Why would guys in their right mind want to get married? But they do."

"Maybe they fall in love," said Suzy.

"Yeah—and that's the worst that can happen. Know something, Suzy? When a man falls in love it's ninety to one he falls for the dame that's worst for him. That's why I take matters in my own hands."

"How do you mean?" Suzy asked.

"Well, when a guy picks out a dame for himself he's in love with something in himself that hasn't got nothing to do with the dame. She looks like his mother, or she's dark and he's scared of blondes, or maybe he's getting even with somebody, or maybe he ain't quite sure he's a man and has to prove it. Fella that studied stuff like that told me one time—a man don't fall for a dame. He falls for new roses, and he brings his own new roses. The best marriages are the ones pulled off by someone that's smart but not sucked in. I think you'd be good for Doc."

"Why?"

"Because you ain't like him. You want I should try?"

"No," said Suzy. "I wouldn't sandbag no guy. Especially Doc."

"Everybody sandbags everybody," said Fauna.

Suzy said softly, "You know, you was right, Fauna. I was sixteen when it happened. But you know, he talked to me like I was a girl. I can't even remember how it sounds—talked to like a girl."

Fauna put her hand on Suzy's shoulder. "Maybe you'll find out again," she said. "If I pull this off I'll put a red ring around your gold star. You ready to go to sleep now?"

"I guess so," said Suzy. "Let's don't sandbag Doc."

Suzy waited until Fauna had rustled to her bed and then she crept out the front door. The light was still burning in Western Biological. She went across the street, past the street light, and up the stairs, and she tapped with her fingertips. Doc didn't answer. She opened the door and saw him sitting at his table, his eyes red, the glass dishes in front of him. He looked very tired and the skin above his beard was gray.

"You're working late," she said.

"Yes. You made me ruin the first set. I had to do it over. It takes time."

"I'm sorry. Doc, you got to write that paper. I don't know nothing about it, but you got to write it."

"I think you were right the first time," he said. "Maybe I can't."

"Sure you can," said Suzy. "You can do anything you want to."

"Maybe that's it. Maybe I don't want to."

"I want you to."

"What have you got to do with it?"

Suzy blushed and looked at her fingers for an answer. "Everybody wants you to," she said. "You'll let everybody down if you don't do it."

He laughed. "That's not a good reason, Suzy."

She tried another tack. "Everybody hates a coward—"

"If I'm a coward, whose business is it?"

"You got to write it, Doc."

"I won't!"

"I'd help you if I could."

"What in the world could you do?"

Her face flamed. "Maybe give you a kick in the ass. Maybe that's what you need."

"Why can't you leave me alone?" he said. And then, "God-dam it! You've done it again—you made me pass over the time!"

"You done it yourself," said Suzy, "you lousy stiff! You blame everybody else. You done it yourself."

"Get on back to the whorehouse!" he shouted. "Go on! Get out!"

In the doorway she stopped and looked back. "God, how I hate a fool!" she said, and she slammed the door behind her.

In a moment there was a tap on the glass.

"Go on home!" Doc shouted.

Mack opened the door. "It ain't Suzy, it's me."

"You were listening."

"No, I wasn't. Say, Doc, would you say a piece of property on Cannery Row was a good investment?"

"No," said Doc.

"She's quite a dame," said Mack.

"I thought you said you weren't listening."

"Listen, Doc, nobody in this block was listening—but everybody heard. You know, they say there's three good reasons for marrying a hustler."

"What are you talking about?" said Doc.

Mack counted on his fingers. "Number one, she ain't likely to wander—she's done all her experimenting. Number two, you ain't likely to surprise her or disappoint her. And number three, if a hustler goes for you she ain't got but one reason."

Doc watched him, hypnotized. "What reason?"

"She likes you. Good night, Doc."

"Sit down—have a drink."

"I can't. I got to get some sleep. I got work to do tomorrow. 'Night, Doc."

Doc looked at the door after Mack had closed it. The grain of the unpainted pine seemed to squirm to his weary eyes.

19. Sweet Thursday (1)

LOOKING backward in time, you can usually find the day it started, the day of Sarajevo, the day of Munich, the moment of Stalingrad or Valley Forge. You fix the day and hour by some incident that happened to yourself. You remember exactly what you were doing when the Japanese bombed Pearl Harbor.

There is no doubt that forces were in motion on that Thursday in Cannery Row. Some of the causes and directions have been in process for generations. There are always some people who claim they felt it coming. Those who remember say it felt like earthquake weather.

It was a Thursday, and it was one of those days in Monterey when the air is washed and polished like a lens, so that you can see the houses in Santa Cruz twenty miles across the bay and you can see the redwood trees on a mountain above Watsonville. The stone point of Frémont's Peak, clear the other side of Salinas, stands up nobly against the east. The sunshine had a goldy look and red geraniums burned the air around them. The delphiniums were like little openings in the sky.

There aren't many days like that anyplace. People treasure them. Little kids are likely to give off tin-whistle screams for no reason, and businessmen find it necessary to take a drive to look at a piece of property. Old people sit looking off into the distance and remember inaccurately that the days of their youth were all like that. Horses roll in the green pastures on such a day and hens make a terrible sunny racket.

Thursday was that magic kind of day. Miss Winch, who took pride in her foul disposition before noon, said good morning to the postman.

Joe Elegant awakened early, intending to work on his novel, on the scene where the young man digs up his grandmother to see if she was as beautiful as he remembered. You will recall his novel, *The Pi Root of Oedipus.* But Joe Elegant saw the golden light on the vacant lot and a dew diamond in the heart of every mallow leaf. He went out in the damp grass in his bare feet and scampered like a kitten until he got to sneezing.

Miss Graves, who sings lead in the butterfly pageant in Pacific Grove, saw her first leprechaun up in back of the reservoir—but you can't tell everything that happened every place on that Sweet Thursday.

For Mack and the boys it was the morning of Truth, and since Mack was to bear the brunt of it, his friends cooked him a hot breakfast and Eddie mixed real bourbon whisky in the coffee. Hazel polished Mack's shoes and brushed his best blue jeans. Whitey No. 1 brought out his father's hat for Mack to wear—a narrow-brimmed black hat, the crown peaked up to a point. Whitey No. 1's father had been a switchman on the Southern Pacific, and this hat proved it. He stuffed toilet paper in back of the sweatband until it fitted Mack perfectly.

Mack didn't talk. He knew how much depended on him, and he was brave and humble at the same time. The boys put the carefully printed tickets in his hand and saw him off, and then they sat down in the weeds to wait. They knew Mack was quaking inside.

Mack went down the chicken walk and across the railroad track. He passed the old boiler and rapped on the rusty pipes in a wild show of bravado.

In front of the grocery he studied a display of screw drivers with loving intensity before he went in.

Cacahuete was behind the counter, studying a copy of *Down Beat*. He wore a purple windbreaker with gold piping. A lean and handsome boy, he had the wild and sullen light of genius in his eyes.

"Hi!" said Mack.

"Jar!" said Cacahuete.

"Joseph and Mary around?"

"Upstairs."

"I want to see him personal," said Mack.

Cacahuete gave him a long, surly stare, then went to the back of the store and called, "*Tio mio!*"

"What do you want?"

"Mack wants to see you."

"What about?"

"Who knows?"

Joseph and Mary came down the stairs in a pale blue silk bathrobe.

"'Morning, Mack. These kids have no manners."

Cacahuete shrugged and took his *Down Beat* to the top of the potato bin.

"You're out early," said the Patrón.

Mack began with ceremonial seriousness, "You ain't been here long, Joseph and Mary, but you've made a lot of friends, good friends."

The Patrón inspected this statement and made note of its slight inaccuracy. Still, he had nothing to lose by going along with it. "I like the people around here," he said. "They treat me good." His eyelids lowered sleepily, which meant he was as alert as a radar screen.

Mack said, "In a little town you get kind of hidebound. But you're a man of the world. You been all over. You know how things is."

The Patrón smiled and acknowledged his wisdom and waited.

"I and the boys want to ask your advice," said Mack. "You ain't likely to get a wild hair."

A vague uneasiness stirred in the Patrón. "What's it about?" he asked tentatively.

Mack drew a deep breath. "A smart businessman like you might think it was silly, but maybe you been here long enough to get it. It's a sentimental thing. It's about Doc. I and the boys owe Doc a debt we ain't never going to be able to repay."

"How much?" asked the Patrón. He up-ended a broom and tore out a straw with which to pick his teeth. "Take a powder," he said softly to Cacahuete, and his nephew slithered upstairs.

"It ain't money," said Mack, "it's gratitude. For years Doc's took care of us—get sick he cures us, get broke he's there with a buck."

"Everybody says the same," the Patrón observed. He could not put his finger on the attack, and yet he felt there was an attack.

The sound of his own voice had a warming, reassuring effect on Mack. He was the professional practicing his profession. "We might of went right on hustling Doc for years," he said, "if only Doc didn't get his ass in a sling."

"He's in trouble?"

"You know he's in trouble," said Mack. "Poor bastard sits there beating his brains out with them sooplapods."

"You told me."

"Well, us boys want to do something about it. We ain't going to see our darling friend crap out if we can help it. I bet he done a couple of nice things for you too."

The Patrón said, "Do you know you can't rig a chess game?"

"We had that out," said Mack impatiently. "Doc's business ain't been good. He can't crack open them sooplapods without he gets a great big goddam microscope—cost about four hundred bucks."

The Patrón said hastily, "If you're passing the hat I'll throw in ten bucks."

"Thanks!" said Mack passionately. "I knew you was a good guy. But that ain't it. I and the boys want to do it ourself. We don't want your ten bucks—we want your advice."

The Patrón went behind the counter, opened the icebox, took out two cans of beer, speared them open, and slid one up the counter to Mack.

"Thanks," said Mack, and he beered down his dry mouth and throat. "Haaah!" he said. "That's fine. Now here's what we want to know. We got something and we want to raffle it. Then we want to take that raffle money and get that microscope for Doc. We want you should give us a hand with the tickets and stuff like that."

"What you going to raffle?" the Patrón asked.

This was the moment, the horrible moment. Mack's hand shook a little as he poured down the second half of the cool sharp beer. His insides quaked. "The Palace Flophouse—our home," he said.

The Patrón took a pocket comb out of stock and ran it through his black shining hair. "It ain't worth four hundred bucks," he said.

Mack nearly cried with relief. He could have kissed the Patrón's hand. He loved Joseph and Mary. A strong and tender tone issued from his throat. "We know that," he said, "but it's our home. Oh, I know it ain't very valuable, but when you got something that ain't worth much—why, you raffle it, don't you? If you got a good cause you can raffle an old pair of socks."

A new respect showed in the Patrón's eyes. "You got something there," he said, and then, "Who's going to win it?"

Mack felt confident now. He knew his man. He was ready to use his knowledge. He said confidentially, "I don't never try to kid a smart hombre. I could tell you we was going to draw honest but you'd know that was double malarky. No, we got a idear."

The Patrón leaned forward. Some of his wariness was lulled. He was still no pushover but he was softened up. "What's the idear?" he asked.

"Well, we got to have someplace to live, don't we? Now this is between I and the boys and you—okay?"

"Okay," said the Patrón.

"We'll sell Doc a ticket or maybe just put a ticket in his name, and we'll rig the raffle so he wins."

"I don't get it," said the Patrón.

"Look!" said Mack. "Doc gets his microscope, don't he? And we go right on habiting in the Palace Flophouse but it's Doc's. It's a sap to his old age—a kind of insurance. I and the boys figure that's the least we can do for him."

"S'pose he sells it?" said the Patrón.

"Oh, not Doc! He wouldn't put us out in the street."

A smile spread over the Patrón's large handsome face. He

could find no fault with it. "I guess I never give you proper credit," he said. "You're smart. Maybe we can do some business —I mean, later. You got the raffle tickets?"

"We made them up last night." Mack laid a little pile of cards on the table.

"How much apiece?"

"Says right on them," Mack said. "Two bucks."

"My first offer still stands," said the Patrón. "I'll take five and you can leave me some to sell."

"Think you could use twenty?"

"I could unload nearly fifty," said the Patrón. "I'll put them out with the Espaldas Mojadas."

Mack's knees were weak as he went up the chicken walk. His glazed eyes stared straight ahead. He walked right past the boys and into the Palace Flophouse and sat down heavily on his bed. The boys trooped in behind him and stood around.

"Got him!" said Mack. "He don't know he owns it. He bought five tickets and he's going to sell fifty to his wetbacks!"

There is a point of relief and triumph in which words have no place. Eddie went outside, and they could hear his shovel strike the ground. Mack and the boys knew Eddie was digging up a keg.

And this was only one of the happenings on that Sweet Thursday.

20. *Sweet Thursday (2)*

FAUNA always drew the shades of her bedroom tight down. Because of the late hours of business, she had to sleep until noon to get her proper rest. On the morning of Sweet Thursday the sun played a trick on her. The windowshade had a hole in it no bigger than the point of a pin. The playful sun picked up the doings of Cannery Row, pushed them through the pinhole, turned them upside down, and projected them in full color on the wall of Fauna's bedroom. Wide Ida waddled across the wall upside down, wearing a print dress strewn with red poppies and on her head a black beret. The Pacific Gas & Electric truck rolled across her wall upside down, its wheels in the air. Mack strode toward the grocery head down. And a little later, Doc, weary, feet over his head, walked along the wallpaper carrying a quart of beer that would have spilled if it had not been an illusion. At first Fauna tried to go back to sleep, but she was afraid she might miss something. It was the little colored ghost of upside-down Doc that drew her from her couch.

It is a common experience that a problem difficult at night is resolved in the morning after the committee of sleep has worked on it. And this had happened to Fauna. She was glad when she raised the shade and saw how beautiful was the day. The roof of the Hediondo Cannery where seagulls had perched glowed like a pearl.

Fauna brushed her hair severely back and put on a close-fitting hat of black sequins. She wore her dark-gray knitted suit and carried gloves. In the kitchen she put six bottles of beer in a paper bag, and then, as an afterthought, she rooted out one of the shrunken monkey heads as a present. When she climbed the stairs of Western Biological and stood at the top, puffing a little, you might have thought she was soliciting for the Red Cross instead of for the Bear Flag.

Doc was frying sausages, sprinkling a little chocolate over them. It gave them an odd and oriental flavor, he thought.

"You're up early," he greeted Fauna.

"I figured one quart of beer wouldn't last long."

"It didn't," said Doc. "Have a couple of sausages?"

"Don't mind if I do," said Fauna. For she knew that he who gives to you is in debt to you. "This here's a monkey head that I picked up in my travels."

"Interesting," said Doc.

"You know, there's some folks think they're people's heads," said Fauna.

"Don't see how they could. See the shape of the eyes and ears? Look at the nose."

"Oh, some folks don't look at people very close," said Fauna. "I'll have a bottle of beer with you."

The taste of the chocolate sausages intrigued her. "I never tasted nothing like it," she observed. "Did you ever eat grasshoppers, Doc?"

"Yes," said Doc. "In Mexico. They're kind of peppery."

Fauna was not one to beat around bushes. "You must get sick of everybody wanting something from you," she said.

Doc smiled. "I'd be sicker if they didn't," he said. "What can I do for you? Say, thanks for the cake and the beer last night!"

Fauna asked, "What did you think of the kid?"

"Strange," said Doc. "Somehow I can't see her working at the Bear Flag."

"Neither can I," said Fauna. "She ain't no good at it but it looks like I'm stuck with her. Trouble with Suzy is, she's got a streak of lady in her and I don't know how to root it out."

Doc munched his sausages and sipped his beer thoughtfully. "I never thought of it, but that could be a drawback," he said.

"She's a nice kid," said Fauna. "I like her fine. But she's a liability in a business way."

"Why don't you kick her out?"

"Oh, I can't," said Fauna. "She's had a tough time. I never had no gift for kicking people out. What I'd like is if she'd pick up and go. She got no future as a floozy."

"She threw the book at me," said Doc.

"You see?" said Fauna. "She's a character. That ain't no good in a house."

"She slapped me in the face with a few basic truths," said Doc. "That's a quick eye she's got."

"And a quicker tongue," said Fauna. "Would you do me a favor?"

"Why, of course," said Doc. "Anything I can."

"I can't go to nobody else," Fauna went on, "they wouldn't understand."

"What is it?"

"Doc," said Fauna, "I knocked around and I seen all kinds. I tell you, if you got a streak of lady in you it spoils you for anything else. Now you never come over to the Bear Flag. You play the field. I personally think that costs more but I ain't one to mess in the way people want to live."

"I don't think I'm following you," said Doc.

"Okay, I'll lay out the deck. When you're making a play for

one of them babes, them amateurs, you got to do quite a lot of talking before you make the sack—ain't that right?"

Doc smiled ruefully. "Right," he said.

"Well, do you always mean every word of it?"

Doc pinched his lower lip. "Why—why—I guess right at the moment I do."

"But afterward?"

"Afterward, if I were to think about it—"

"That's what I mean," said Fauna. "So if you happen to tell a little teensy-beensy bit of baloney you don't blow your brains out."

"You'd do well in the analysis business," said Doc. "What do you want me to do?"

"This kid Suzy's lousy with new roses. She ain't a good hustler because of that streak of lady. I don't know if she'd make a good lady or not. I want her off my neck. Doc, would it do you any harm to make a play for her? I mean, like you do with them dames that come in here."

"What good could that possibly do?" he asked.

"Well, maybe I'm wrong, but the way I figure it, you can use new roses if you want to. If you made a pitch for the kid, like she was a lady, why, she might turn lady on you."

"I still can't see what good it would do," said Doc.

"It would get her the hell out of the Bear Flag," said Fauna. "She wouldn't want to congregate with no more floozies."

"How about me?" said Doc.

"You don't marry them others, do you?"

"No, but—"

"Take a whang at her, will you, Doc?" Fauna begged. "Can't do you no harm. Why, hell, she might scram out of here and take up typewriting or telephone operating. Will you do that for me, Doc?"

He said, "It doesn't seem honest."

Fauna changed her tack. "I was talking to her last night and she said she couldn't remember when a guy had treated her like a girl. What harm would that do?"

"Might make her miserable."

"Might make her fly the coop."

"Maybe she likes it the way it is."

"She don't. I tell you she's a blowed-in-the-glass lady. Look,

Doc, you take her out to dinner and I'll buy the dinner. You don't have to make no pass. Just be nice to her."

"I'll have to think about it."

"Think you might do it?"

"I might."

"That's a good kid if you treat her right. You'd be doing me a big favor."

"Suppose she won't go?"

"She will. I won't give her no choice."

Doc looked out the window and a warmth crept through him, and suddenly he felt better than he could remember feeling.

"I'll think about it," he said.

"I'll throw in three bottles of champagne whenever you say the word," said Fauna.

After lunch Joe Elegant read Fauna his latest chapter. He explained the myth and the symbol. "You see," he said, "the grandmother stands for guilt."

"Ain't she dead and buried?"

"Yes."

"That's a kind of a messy guilt."

"It's the reality below reality," said Joe Elegant.

"Balls!" said Fauna. "Listen, Joe, whyn't you write a story about something real?"

"Maybe *you* can tell *me* about the *art* of writing?" he said.

"I sure as hell can," said Fauna. "There's this guy, and he makes love to this dame."

"Very original," said Joe.

"When a man says words he believes them, even if he thinks he's lying."

"For goodness' sake! What are you talking about?"

"I bet I get rid of a certain person and put up a new gold star. You want to take that bet?"

"How did Doc like the cake?" Joe Elegant asked.

"He loved it," said Fauna.

And this was the second event of that Sweet Thursday.

21. *Sweet Thursday Was One Hell of a Day*

FISSION took place in the Palace Flophouse, and from there a chain reaction flared up in all directions. Cannery Row caught fire. Mack and the boys had the energy and the enthusiasm of plutonium. Only very lazy men could have done so much in so short a time. Oh, the meetings, the messages carried, the plans and counterplans! Mack had to make more and more raffle tickets. What started as a kind of gentle blackmail assumed the nature of an outpouring of popular love for Doc. People bought tickets, sold tickets, traded tickets. Emissaries covered the Southern Pacific Depot, the Greyhound Bus Station. Joe Blaikey, the constable, carried tickets in his pocket and canceled parking summonses if the lawbreaker bought a two-dollar chance on the Palace Flophouse.

Whitey No. 1 invaded the foreign and fancy purlieus of Pebble Beach and Carmel and the Highlands. Whitey No. 2's method was characteristically direct. The first man to refuse him got a rock through his windshield, and the news traveled.

To the boys it had become a crusade. And the winning ticket, of course, with Doc's name on it, was in a tomato can, buried in the vacant lot. By tacit agreement no one mentioned the raffle to Doc. To Doc's friends Mack and the boys mentioned the rigging of the lottery, but to strangers—who cared? It was a perfect example of the collective goodness and generosity of a community.

But if communities have a group Good Fairy they also have an Imp who works parallel with and sometimes in collaboration with the Good Fairy. Cannery Row's Imp saw the Good Fairy stirring to life, and he sprang to action. Into the ears of his clients he whispered a few words, and his constituents grinned with evil pleasure and their thoughts went like this: The Patrón is a wise guy. He's a newcomer, nice clothes, makes his money off poor helpless wetbacks because he's smart. Lee Chong must have sold him the Palace Flophouse and he's forgot it or he never knew it. Once Doc wins it the Patrón won't dare make a move.

It is such fun to outsmart a smart guy. The Imp of the Row had a good professional time and for once his job seemed almost virtuous. People bought more tickets from the Patrón than from anyone else. They wanted to watch his face so they could compare it with his face when he found out.

Now ordinarily Mack and the boys would have strung out the ticket sales over weeks, but time was breathing down their necks. If the Patrón got his tax bill from the county their plan would blow up in their faces. They had to take a chance with Friday—Saturday was the deadline. The boys spread the word that there would be medium-heavy refreshments at the Palace Flophouse on Saturday night and that contributions of any nature would be welcome.

Mack called on Doc the afternoon of Sweet Thursday. "If you ain't doing anything Saturday night," he said, "I and the boys are throwing a little wing-ding. R.S.V.P."

"*Moi, je respond oui.*"

"Come again?"

"I'll be there," said Doc.

Then Mack remembered a mission with which he had been entrusted. "I guess I could squirm it out of you, Doc, like I done once before," he said, "but I'll come right out in the open. When's your birthday?"

A shudder went through Doc. "Please don't give me a party," he begged. "The last one you gave nearly ruined me."

"This hasn't got nothing to do with a party—it's a bet," said Mack. "I stand to win a buck. When is it?" Mack prodded him.

Doc picked the first date that came to him. "July fourth," he said.

"Why, that's like the Fourth of July!"

"A little," said Doc, and he felt greatly relieved.

Later that afternoon Fauna and the girls called formally at the Palace Flophouse in answer to the note Mack had sent asking them to drink a jolt of good stuff. Suzy did not attend. She had been quiet all morning, and then she mooned away on the path that leads along the sea to the lighthouse on Point Pinos. She looked in the tide pools, and she picked a bunch of the tiny flowers that grow as close to the ocean as they can.

Suzy was restless and unhappy. She felt excitement and nausea at the same time. She wanted to smile and she wanted to cry, and she was scared and happy and hopeless. Doc had asked her to have dinner with him, at Sonny Boy's on the pier, and Fauna had urged her to go.

Suzy's first reaction had been violent. "I won't do it!" she said.

"Sure you'll go," said Fauna. "I may have to persuade you with a indoor-ball bat—but you'll go."

"You can't make me."

"Want to test that? Why, I've wore my brain down to the knuckles, trying to do something nice for you."

"I ain't got nothing to wear," said Suzy.

"Neither has Doc. If he can go like he does, what right's a chippy to get grand?"

"But hell, Fauna, he's—he's got it inside. People like me got to put on a puff because they got nothing else. I'm afraid I'll turn mean because I don't know how to be nice."

"Suzy," said Fauna, "I'm going to give you a piece of advice, and if you won't take it, I may just call Joe Blaikey and get you floated right out of town. Don't throw the first punch! Wait'll you're hit before you put up your dukes. Most of the time they ain't nobody laid a glove on you."

"Suppose I could wear my suit? It's got a big spot," said Suzy.

"Ask Joe Elegant to spot-clean it and press it. Tell him I said so."

And thus it was that Suzy went walking out lighthouse way on Sweet Thursday.

The meeting in the Palace wasn't really necessary, for word of the raffle had got around and Fauna had bought ten tickets and made each girl buy one.

Eddie had borrowed glasses from Wide Ida's—for once, with her permission. She was invited to the meeting too, and she brought two quarts of Pine Canyon whisky.

"It don't cost hardly nothing," she explained.

Formality took hold of the meeting. Agnes and Mabel kept their knees together when they sat down, and Fauna's look of thunder made Becky snap hers shut so quickly she spilled her drink.

"She's going to be a wallager," said Mack. "I can't wait to see Doc's face when he wins."

Wide Ida asked, "How you going to explain it to him he wins when he didn't buy no ticket?"

"Why, we'll say a friend did it and don't want his name mentioned. I saw Doc a little while ago. He said he'd sure be here."

Fauna said, "Did you find out when is his birthday?"

"Sure. July fourth."

Fauna exhaled with the sound of escaping gas. "Holy apples! He's a gone goose. He got a born-on Oregon boot. I never seen nothing work out so nice!"

"What're you talking about?" said Mack.

Fauna's eyes were misty. "Mack," she said huskily, "I don't want to horn in on your party, but why couldn't we make it an engagement party too?"

"Who's engaged?"

"Well, they ain't yet—but they will be."

"Who?"

"Doc and Suzy. It's right in their horoscopes."

"S'pose they won't?"

"They will," said Fauna. "You can just depend on that—they will!"

The little group sat in silence, and then Mack said softly, "Did I say it was going to be a wallager? This here's a *tom*-wallager! They ain't been nothing so stupendous since the Second World War! You *sure* Doc'll go for it?"

"You let me take care of that—and don't none of you blab it to him. One time I managed a fighter, Kiss of Death Kelly, welterweight. I'll have Doc in the ring."

Eddie asked, "How about Suzy?"

"Suzy's already in the ring," said Fauna.

They parted quietly, but in their breasts a flame of emotion burned. There never was a day like that Sweet Thursday. And it wasn't over yet.

22. *The Arming*

At four-thirty in the afternoon Fauna ordered Suzy to the office bedroom with full field equipment. Suzy dumped her clothes on Fauna's bed.

"That's a hell of a way to keep wrinkles out," Fauna observed. She picked up the gray woolen skirt and jacket, laid them out, inspected them for spots, smelled them for cleaning fluid. "Nice piece of goods," she said.

"Community chest," said Suzy. "I was in the charity ward."

"Well, somebody wasn't." Her eyes noted the brown shoes. She went to the door and yelled, "Joe! Joe Elegant!"

He looked in. "I'm not supposed to be on duty," he said.

"I'm a thorn in the side of the worker," said Fauna. "You run up the street to Wildock's and get new heel taps on these here. Tell them to fix this scuffed place and give them a nice shine. Wait and bring them back."

Joe complained as he went, but he went.

Fauna said to Suzy, "You got any gloves?"

"No."

"I'll lend you some. Here—these white ones. And here's a handkerchief. I don't want no lipstick marks on it. Now you listen to me, Suzy girl—take care of your shoes, wear clean gloves, carry a white handkerchief, and keep your stocking seams straight. If you do that you can get away with murder. This here's a nice suit—the kind of cloth that the older it gets the better it looks—if your heels ain't run over. Call Becky in!"

When Becky entered Fauna said, "Ain't you got a white piqué dickey and cuffs?"

"I just done them up."

"I want you should lend them to Suzy. Get some thread and sew the cuffs in this here jacket."

"She'll have to wash them."

"She will."

While Becky basted in the cuffs Fauna said, "Turn out your purse, Suzy." She inspected the pile on the bed. "You don't need that aspirin. Here, take my comb—throw that one away. Ain't nothing tackier than a comb missing teeth. Put these here Kleenex in. Here, use my compact and touch up the shine on your nose once in a while. Let's see your nails! Hmmm, pretty good. You washed your hair?"

"Get her a wig," said Becky, and she bit the thread.

"Don't get smart. Come on now—get off your behind and do something with her hair, and not fancy neither." To Suzy she said, "Becky got a light hand with hair. You can't take that coat. Community chest slipped up there." She tapped her teeth with a pencil and then went to her closet and brought out two baum martens that were biting each other's heads off. "Just hang these here bo' martens over your shoulder," Fauna said. "And if you lose them or hurt them I'll cut your tripes out. Now, where are we? No perfume. Douse some of this Florida water on—kind of old-fashioned and young-smelling."

Becky stood behind Suzy's chair, brushing and combing and molding. "She got big ears," Becky said. "Maybe I can kind of hide them a little."

"You got a nice hand with hair," Fauna said.

The final briefing took place at six o'clock, with the bedroom door closed.

"Turn around," said Fauna. "Keep your ankles close together. Now, walk! That's good. You got a real nice walk. Like I said, you're a good-looking kid if you work at it a little."

Suzy looked at herself in the mirror and she smiled, for it seemed to her that she really was pretty, and the idea startled her and pleased her too, and when she looked pleased she was even prettier. Then her mouth turned down and blind panic came over her.

"What's the matter?" Fauna demanded.

"What can I talk about? Fauna, I don't want to go! I don't belong with a guy like Doc. Jesus, Fauna, tell him I'm sick. I ain't going."

Fauna let her talk herself out and then she said quietly, "Maybe you'd like to cry now and get your eyes red after all my trouble? Go on, cry!"

"I'm sorry," said Suzy. "You been nice. I ain't no good, Fauna. You're just wasting your time. I know what I'll do—minute he says something I don't understand I'll get mad. I'm scared."

"'Course you're scared," said Fauna. "But if you didn't care nothing about Doc you wouldn't be scared. You didn't invent it. There ain't never been no dame went out first time with a guy she liked that wasn't scared. Maybe Doc's scared too."

"Oh nuts!" said Suzy.

Fauna said, "If I was your age with your face and shape and what I know, there wouldn't be no man in the world could get away! I got the know-how—but that's all I got. Oh well! I'm going to tell you a few thousand things, Suzy, that if you would listen you'd get anything you want. But hell, you won't listen! Nobody listens, and when they learn the hard way it's too late. Maybe it's a good thing—I don't know."

"I'll listen."

"Sure, but you won't learn. You know, Suzy, they ain't no way in the world to get in trouble by keeping your mouth shut. You look back at every mess you ever got in and you'll find your tongue started it."

"That's true," said Suzy. "But I can't seem to stop."

"You got to learn it like you learn anything else—just practice. Next thing is opinions. You and me is always busting out with opinions. Hell, Suzy, we ain't got no opinions! We just say stuff we heard or seen in the movies. We're scared we'll miss something, like running for a bus. That's the second rule: lay off opinions because you ain't really got any."

"You got them numbered, huh?" said Suzy.

"I should write a book," said Fauna. "'If She Could, I Could.' Now take number three. There don't hardly nobody listen, and it's so easy! You don't have to do nothing when you listen. If you do listen it's pretty interesting. If a guy says something that pricks up your interest, why, don't hide it from him. Kind of try to wonder what he's thinking instead of how you're going to answer him back."

"You're sure putting the finger on me," Suzy said softly.

"I only got a little more, but it's the hardest of all, and the easiest."

"What number?"

"I lost track. Don't pretend to be something you ain't, and don't make like you know something you don't, or sooner or later you'll sure fall on your ass. And there's one more part to this one, whatever number it is: they ain't nobody was ever insulted by a question. S'pose Doc says something and you don't know what it means. Ask him! The nicest thing in the world you can do for anybody is let them help you."

Suzy was silent, looking down at her hands.

Fauna said, "You got nice nails. How do you keep them so nice?"

Suzy said, "That's easy. My grandma taught me. You keep a old lemon rind, and every time you wash your hands you scrounge your fingernails around in it. And then you shake a little face powder on your hand and you polish your nails on the ham of your hand and you push down the quick with a little piece of lemon wood."

"See what I mean?" said Fauna.

"What?"

"I just asked you a question."

Suzy blushed. "I sure fell into that."

"No, you didn't. I wanted to know. It's best if you ask when you want to know."

"Thanks," said Suzy. "You're a hell of a dame. I wonder if I could learn?"

"You can if you just remember a lot of things: first, you got to remember you're Suzy and you ain't nobody else but Suzy. Then you got to remember that Suzy is a good thing—a real valuable thing—and there ain't nothing like it in the world. It don't do no harm just to say that to yourself. Then, when you got that, remember that there's one hell of a lot Suzy don't know. Only way she can find out is if she sees it, or reads it, or asks it. Most people don't look at nothing but themselves, and that's a rat race."

"What's the fourth thing?" Suzy asked.

"I'm proud of you!" Fauna said. "You listened. The next thing you'll have to do some thinking about. Nobody don't give a particular damn about Suzy one way or the other. It's hard to get them thinking about you because they're too busy thinking about themselves. There's two, three, copper-bottom ways to get their attention: Talk about them. If you see something nice or good or pretty, tell them. Don't make it a fake though. Don't fight nobody unless there ain't no other way. Don't never start a fight, and if one starts, let it get going good before you jump in. Best way in the whole world to defend yourself is to keep your dukes down! Now, when you got their attention, first thing they want is to do something for you. Let them. Don't get proud and say you don't need it or want it. That's a slap in the puss. Thing people like most in the world is to give you something and have you like it and need it. That ain't sloppy. That works. You give it a try."

"You think Doc would fall for that stuff?"

"Just give it a try."

Suzy said, "Fauna, didn't you never get married?"

"No."

"Why not?"

Fauna smiled. "Time I learned what I just told you, it was too late."

"I love you," said Suzy.

"Now you see! You got me softened up like butter. I want you should keep them furs."

"But—"

"Watch it!"

"Yeah, I see. I sure do thank you. And would you maybe write down all that stuff so I can get it by heart?"

"Sure I will. Now look, Suzy—tonight, just before you say something, say it first to yourself, and kind of dust it off."

"You mean cussing?"

"I mean cussing and I mean—well, sometimes if you look at it you don't say it. One whole hell of a lot that passes for talk is just running off at the mouth. I guess you're about ready now."

"Is there anything I can do for you, Fauna?"

"Yes. I want you should repeat after me, 'I'm Suzy and nobody else.' "

" 'I'm Suzy and nobody else.' "

" 'I'm a good thing.' "

" 'I'm a good thing.' "

" 'There ain't nothing like me in the whole world.' "

" 'There ain't nothing'—goddam it, Fauna, now my eyes'll be red!"

"They look pretty that way," said Fauna.

At seven o'clock Doc, dressed in an open-collared shirt, leather jacket, and army pants, rang the bell at the Bear Flag. He looked at Suzy and he said, "I've got to make a telephone call, do you mind?" And he ran back to the laboratory.

Ten minutes later he returned. He had on clean slacks, a tweed jacket, and a tie he hadn't used in years.

Fauna saw him standing under the porch light.

"Honey," she said to Suzy, "you win the first round on points."

23. One Night of Love

SONNY BOY is truly the only Greek born in America named Sonny Boy. He operates a restaurant and bar on the wharf in Monterey. Sonny Boy is plump and getting plumper. Although he was born near Sutro Park in San Francisco and went to public schools, Sonny Boy has singlehandedly kept alive the mystery of the Near East. His perfectly round face hints Orient Express and beautiful spies. His bushy voice is congenitally confidential. Sonny Boy can say "good evening" and make it sound like an international plot. His restaurant makes friends for him and supports him. Perhaps Sonny Boy, in one sense, wears a long black cape and dines with Balkan countesses where two seas kiss the Golden Horn—but he also runs a good restaurant. He probably knows more secrets than any man in the community, for his martinis are a combination truth serum and lie detector. *Veritas* is not only *in vino* but regularly batters its way out.

Doc stopped his old car in front of Sonny Boy's, got out, walked around, opened the other door, and helped Suzy out.

She was a little shocked but she remained silent. The sentence, "You think I'm a cripple, for Chrissake!" rose to her throat, but she followed Fauna's advice—whispered it and pushed it back. The fact of his hand on her elbow did a magic thing to her, pushed back her shoulders and raised her chin. The gritty light of resistance went out of her eyes.

Doc opened the door of the bar and stood aside to let Suzy enter. The regulars on the stools turned to look. The eyes crept from pretty face to pretty legs, took in the martens on the way. For one second panic halted her, but she saw no look of recognition in the eyes of the regulars.

Sonny Boy turned sideways to get around the end of the bar. "'Evening, folks," he said. "Your table is ready. Would you like to have a cocktail here, or shall I send one over?"

"Oh, let's sit at the table," said Doc.

Sonny Boy bowed Suzy through the door to the restaurant, and she strolled ahead with her nice walk. Sonny Boy, rolling along beside Doc, said in his conspiratorial whisper, "Your secretary called. It's all fixed. You got a secretary, Doc?"

Doc overcame his surprise. "Part time," he said.

"Who's the lady? She new around here?"

"She's new around here," said Doc. He caught up with Suzy.

"This way," said Sonny Boy. He led them to a round table in front of the stone fireplace. A pine fire crackled and sent out its fragrance. The table had a centerpiece of wild iris. The breadsticks stood like soldiers in their glasses. The napkins were folded to make little crowns. It was the best table in the house, private, but downstage and well lighted.

Suzy's eyes darted around the room. No other table had flowers. Something wonderful happened in Suzy. She didn't walk around the table and sit down. She waited, and when Doc held her chair she seated herself, looked smiling up at him, and said, "Thank you."

Sonny Boy hovered over the table. "Good you telephoned," he said. "I had trouble getting pompano, but I got it. How's about a cocktail? The wine's cooling."

Doc said, "One time I had some kind of—"

"I remember!" said Sonny Boy. "The Webster F. Street Lay-Away Plan—a martini made with chartreuse instead of vermouth. Very good."

"Very effective, as I remember it," said Doc. "Two doubles."

"Coming right up," said Sonny Boy. "I told Tony to be here to play piano like you said, but he's sick."

Doc looked at Suzy to see whether she knew Fauna had made the arrangements. She didn't.

It is probable that if Doc hadn't ordered the Webster F. Street Lay-Away Plans he would have got them anyway. They arrived with a speed that indicated they were already mixed.

The shock of a necktie was leaving Doc. He looked across the table and smiled at Suzy and he wondered, What is beauty in a girl that it can come and go? This Suzy did not faintly resemble the tough hustler who had screamed at him the night before. He raised the cocktail glass. "You're pretty," he said. "I'm glad you came with me. Here's to both of us."

Suzy swallowed a gulp, held back her tears, and waited for the spasm to pass.

"I should have warned you," said Doc, "there's a rumor that this drink is made of rattlesnake venom and raw opium."

Suzy got her breath. "It's good," she said. "But I was watching its right hand and walked into a left hook!"

Her mind cried, I shouldn't of said that! I forgot already. Then she saw Doc's amusement and it was all right.

Suzy noticed a waiter drifting delicately within earshot. She had discovered something for herself. When in doubt, move slowly. Her head turned toward the waiter and he drifted away. She was delighted with her discovery—everything-in-slow-motion. She lifted her glass slowly, looked at it carefully, then sipped and held it a moment before she put it down. S-l-o-w-ness—it gave meaning to everything. It made everything royal. She remembered how all the unsure and worried people she knew jumped and picked and jittered. Just doing everything slowly, forcing herself, she felt a new kind of security. Don't forget, she told herself. Don't ever forget this. Slow! Slow!

Doc gave her a cigarette and held a match, and she leaned forward so slowly that the flame was touching his fingers before she had lighted it. A lovely warmth stole through her body. She felt bold, not defensively bold, but safe.

She asked, "Do they know—what I am?"

The Lay-Away Plan works equally on all. Doc said, "They know you're with me. That's all they need to know. Shall we have one more?"

It came before he got his finger raised for attention. If this was conspiracy, Sonny Boy wanted to be in on it. If felicity, he liked that too.

"I like a fire," Suzy said. "Once we had a fireplace where I lived."

Doc said, "You're pretty. Yes, by George! You're pretty!"

Suzy swallowed the first words that rose and swallowed the second ones and ended up by dropping her eyes and saying "Thank you" softly.

Sonny Boy personally escorted the waiter, who carried the ice bucket with the chilled Chablis. Then he stood back and surveyed the table. "How is everything, Doc?"

"Just fine," said Doc.

"You ready to eat?"

"Any time," said Doc.

And Suzy's discovery continued to hold good: Take it slow and keep your eyes open and your mouth shut.

The cold, cracked crab, the pompano, were new to her, and they required an eating technique she didn't know. She did everything a little behind Doc, and he wasn't conscious that she watched every move he made.

When champagne and fruit and cheese arrived, Suzy knew she had to be alone. A thought so overwhelming had come to her that her knees shook and the blood pounded in her temples. Slow! she warned herself. Take it easy. She looked at the leaping flames and then pivoted her head to Doc. "Will you excuse . . . ?"

"Of course!" He jumped up and drew back her chair. Suzy moved regally toward the Ladies' Room. She could not feel her feet against the floor.

Doc watched her passage. Strange, strange, he thought. What is it? "Maidenly" is the word. A kind of lonely and terrible modesty. What has made the change? Then he thought, It's an act. Fauna coached her. But he knew that wasn't true. Acting couldn't get into the eyes like that. Coaching couldn't draw the blood to her cheeks. He spun the champagne bottle in its bucket, and he found himself wishing she would hurry back. His eyes found a window that reflected the door to the Ladies' Room.

Behind that door Suzy dampened a paper towel and put it against her forehead. She stared at herself in the mirror and she didn't know the face. She thought of the dinner. "I hate fish," she said out loud. "It makes me break out. But I ain't broke out." Finally she was ready to inspect the thought that had sent her out: the symbol, the mystery, the signpost with an inexorable pointing finger. It was so plain no one could miss it.

Fate was not only pointing the way but booting from behind. She thought of the dishes being taken away: the heaped legs and claws of crab and— They had eaten their horoscopes! Cancer and Pisces—fish and crab.

"Great God Almighty!" she said, and she was limp in the hands of Fate.

Sonny Boy came to the table. "Everything all right?"

"Fine," said Doc.

"Just like you ordered."

"Huh?"

"Your secretary told me."

"Fine," said Doc, "just the way I wanted it."

When Suzy came back she was dedicated. You can only fight Fate so far, and when you give in to it you're very strong; because all of your force flows in one direction.

Doc held her chair and then he popped the champagne cork and smelled it.

Suzy said, "Can I have it?"

"Of course."

She turned the cork in her fingers and looked at it. It was very beautiful. She put it in her purse and took an iris from the vase.

"Do you like champagne?"

"I love it," she said and wondered what it would taste like. And she did love it.

Doc said, "You know, out in the sand dunes there are little valleys covered with pines. Sometime, when you can, let's take meat and things out there and cook our supper. It's very nice."

"The fire reminded you," said Suzy.

"That's clever of you—so it did."

She said, "Doc, will you sometime teach me about the stuff you got in your place?"

"Sure I will." A surge of affection filled him. But he was a little afraid too of her terrible modesty. He looked away from her eyes to the wild iris in her hand. "There's an old Welsh story," he said. "It's about a poor knight who made a wife completely out of flowers—"

The wine was strong in Suzy now. She said the sentence

twice to herself before she said it aloud to Doc. "I hope she didn't wilt."

The low voice of Doc's guts burst through at last. "I'm lonely," he said. He said it as a simple matter of fact and he said it in wonder. Then he apologized. "I guess I'm a little drunk." He felt very shy. He filled the glasses. "What the hell! Let's have some brandy too."

Suzy turned half away from him so that her face was outlined in leaping pine flames. "You know that place you said—out in the sand dunes?"

"Yes."

"Could we look at it?"

"Whenever you want."

"On our way home?"

"You'll ruin your shoes."

"I know," said Suzy.

"You could take them off."

"I will," said Suzy.

24. *Waiting Friday*

NOT everyone believes that Friday is unlucky, but nearly everybody agrees it is a waiting day. In business, the week is really over. In school, Friday is the half-open gate to freedom. Friday is neither a holiday nor a workday, but a time of wondering what Saturday will bring. Trade and amusement fall off. Women look through their closets to see what they have to wear. Supper is leftovers from the week.

Joe Elegant ordered sand dabs for supper at the Bear Flag. The Espaldas Mojadas returned from their latest triumph and were ushered with great courtesy to the rooms over the grocery. The Patrón distributed bottles of tequila. Also, he kept a saucer of Seconal at hand. Sometimes a passion of homesickness got into his wetbacks. Sleep, he thought, was better than fighting.

Doc slept late, and when he went to the grocery for his morning beer he found Joseph and Mary alert and gay, and the sound of singing drifted down the stairs.

"Have a good time?" the Patrón asked.

"What do you mean?" Doc demanded.

"Didn't you have a nice party last night?"

"Oh sure," said Doc. He said it with finality.

"Doc, I'd like you to teach me more of that chess."

"You still think you can cheat at it, do you?"

"No, I just like to figure it out. I got a case of Bohemia beer from Mexico, all cold."

"Wonderful!" said Doc. "That's the best beer in the Western Hemisphere."

"It's a present," said the Patrón.

"Why?"

"I don't know. Maybe I just feel good."

"Thanks," said Doc. He began to feel uneasy.

There were eyes on him. Going back to Western Biological, he felt eyes on him. It's the brandy, he thought. I shouldn't drink brandy. Makes me nervous.

He scrambled two eggs and shook curry powder over them. He consulted the tide chart in Thursday's *Monterey Herald.* There was a fair tide at 2:18 p.m., enough for chitons and brittlestars if the wind wasn't blowing inshore by then. The Bohemia beer settled his nerves without solving his restlessness. And for once the curried eggs didn't taste very good.

Fauna knocked and entered. She flicked her hand at the rattlesnakes. "How do you feel, Doc?"

"All right."

"Get drunk?"

"A little."

"How was the dinner?"

"Wonderful. You know what to order."

"I ought to. Say, you want to box or should we lay it on the line? See what I mean about her?"

"Yes. How does she feel?"

"She ain't up yet."

"I'm going collecting."

"Want me to tell her that?"

"Why should you? Wait—I've got her purse. Want to take it to her?"

"Hell, she ain't crippled. Maybe she'll want to get it herself."

"I won't be here."

"You'll be back."

"Say," he said, "what the hell is this?"

She knew he might turn angry now. "I got a lot to do. You ain't mad at me?"

"Why should I be?"

"Well, if you need anything, let me know."

"Fauna," he began. "Oh, let it go."

"What do you want?"

"I was going to ask you something—but I don't want to know."

Suzy was hunched over a cup of coffee when Fauna got back.

"'Morning," said Fauna. And then, "I said good morning."

"Oh yeah," said Suzy. "'Morning."

"Look at me!"

"Why not?" Suzy raised her eyes.

"You can look down now," said Fauna.

"You don't know nothing," said Suzy.

"Okay, I don't know nothing. When did I ever get nosy with you? Joe," she called, "bring me a cup of coffee!" She slid a tin box of aspirins across the oil-cloth tablecover.

"Thanks." Suzy took three and washed them down with coffee.

"He's going out collecting bugs," said Fauna quietly.

"You went over there?"

"I met him in the street. Have a nice time?"

Suzy looked up at her with eyes so wide that she seemed to be turned inside out. "He didn't make no pass," she said breathlessly. "Went out on the sand dunes and he didn't make no pass."

Fauna smiled. "But he talked nice?"

"Didn't talk much, but he talked nice."

"That's good."

"Maybe I'm nuts, Fauna, but I told him."

"Oh, you ain't nuts."

"I told him everything. He didn't even ask."

Fauna asked quietly, "What did he talk about?"

"He said there's a fella in old times made a wife out of flowers."

"What for, for God's sake?"

"Well, I don't know. But it was all right when he said it."

"What else did he say?"

Suzy spoke slowly. "Out in the sand dunes I done most of the talking. But he give me a boost every now and then when I run down."

Fauna said, "He can do that better than anybody."

Suzy's eyes were shining with excitement. "I almost forgot," she said. "I never took no stock in stars and stuff like that, but you know what we had for dinner?"

"Champagne?"

"Fish and crab!" said Suzy. "And I didn't break out."

"Well?"

"Remember what you said, how I'm fish and he's crab?"

Fauna turned her head away. "I got something up my nose," she said. "I wonder if I'm catching cold."

"Do you think that's a sign, Fauna? Do you?"

"Everything's signs," said Fauna. "Everything."

There was a glory in Suzy's eyes. "Right after we ate we was talking, and he said, 'I'm lonely.'"

"Now that ain't like him," Fauna said. "That's a dirty trick!"

"No, ma'am," Suzy contradicted her. "He didn't say it like that. I heard that one before too. He said it like it was pushed out of him. It surprised him, like he didn't know he was going to say it. What do you think, Fauna? Tell me, what do you think?"

"I think there's going to be like a new gold star."

"Well, s'pose—and there ain't no harm in supposing—s'pose I moved over there. It would be—well, it would be right across the street from here. Everybody knows I worked here. Wouldn't that kind of bother him?"

"He knows you work here, don't he? Suzy girl, you got to promise me something. Don't you never try to run away from nothing, because you can't. If you're all right nobody ain't going to tear you down. Guy that runs away, why, he's a fugitive. And a fugitive never gets away."

"How about Doc?" said Suzy.

"Look, if you ain't good enough for him, he ain't good for you."

"I don't want to lay no bear trap for him, Fauna."

Fauna was smiling to herself. She said, "I guess a man is the only kind of varmint sets his own trap, baits it, and then steps in it. You just set still, Suzy girl. Don't do nothing. Nobody can't say you trapped him if you don't do nothing."

"Well, he didn't really say—"

"They never do," said Fauna.

Suzy said weakly, "I can't hardly breathe."

"You know, you ain't cussed once this morning," Fauna said.

"Ain't I?"

"Some of my gold stars was damn good hookers," said Fauna. "But when I put up your gold star, Suzy, the whoring business ain't lost nothing. Like the Patrón says, you're too small in the butt and too big in the bust."

"I don't want nobody to get the idea I'm hustling Doc."

"You're damn right you ain't. I'll see to that." She looked speculatively at Suzy. "You know, I'd like you to get out of town tonight and kind of freshen up."

"Where'll I go?"

"You could go on an errand for me to San Francisco if you wanted to. I got a little package up there in a safe-deposit box. I'll give you some dough. And I want you should buy some clothes and a hat. Get a nice suit. It'll last you for years. Look! Walk up and down Montgomery Street and see what the nice-looking dames is wearing—you know, the kind of material. They're pretty smart women up there. Before you buy, look around a little—make it nice. Come on back tomorrow."

Suzy said, "You getting me out of the way?"

"Yeah," said Fauna. "You got the idea."

"Why?"

"Suzy girl, that ain't none of your business. There's a two o'clock bus and a four o'clock bus."

"I'll take the four o'clock."

"Why?"

"Well, you said Doc's going out collecting bugs. Maybe while he's gone I could kind of swamp out his joint. It ain't had a scrubbing for years."

"That might make him mad."

"I'll start him a nice stew cooking slow," said Suzy. "I make a real nice stew." She came around the table.

"Get your hands off me!" said Fauna. "Go on now! And don't you ever say that thing again that made a sucker out of me. My best fur!"

"You mean, 'I love you'?"

"That's it. Don't you say it."

"Okay," said Suzy.

25. Old Jingleballicks

Doc got back from his collecting about four-thirty. He had over a hundred chitons bound with string to little glass plates to keep them from curling, and submerged in sea water in his collecting buckets were hundreds of brittlestars.

Now, killing is one of the delicate operations of a marine zoologist. You want the animal to resemble its living self, but this is impossible. In death the color changes, just as it does with us. Also, if any violent means of killing is used there is constriction, and in the case of brittlestars the death struggle causes the animal to shed its arms.

In the front room of Western Biological, Doc poured out part of the sea water from his wooden bucket. Then he moved the brittlestars to a large, flat-bottomed glass dish and poured some sea water on top of them. The little animals with the snakelike arms whipped about for a moment and then settled down. When they were quite still and resting Doc added a little fresh water to the dish. The arms stirred nervously. He waited a while and then added a little more fresh water. To a sea animal, fresh water is a poison, and if it is slowly introduced it is as subtle as morphine. It relaxes and soothes until the little creature goes to sleep and dies without violence.

Doc sat down to wait for the poison to act. He sensed that there was something wrong. What could it be? Had he forgotten something? He felt all right, the small hangover of the morning was gone. Of course! It was the case of Bohemia beer over at the Patrón's. His subconscious must have been reminding him of the beer. He looked out the window toward the grocery. And there was something wrong with that too. And finally he saw. His windows were clean. He turned and looked around the laboratory. The records were piled neatly on the shelves, not falling all over themselves. The floor was shining, and that smell—that was soap.

He moved to the kitchen. His dishes were clean, the pans scoured and shining. A delicious odor came from a pot on the gas stove. He lifted the lid. Brown meat juice bubbled up through carrots and onions, and a stick of white celery swam like a fish.

Doc went back to his table and sat down. His cot was made up and smooth and the turned-down sheet was clean. Suddenly a sense of desolation came over him—a great sadness that was like warmth. The toes of his lined-up shoes peeked out at him from under the bed.

The poor kid, he thought. Oh, the poor damn kid! I wonder if she's trying to repay—I hope I haven't done anything bad. My God, I hope she didn't misunderstand anything! What did I say? I know I didn't do anything, but what did I say? I wouldn't hurt Suzy for the world. He glanced around again. She sure does a job of cleaning, he thought. The stew smells wonderful too. He poured a little more fresh water into the glass dish. The arms of the brittlestars were arranging themselves in small spirals. They hardly moved when the fresh poison was introduced.

The clean laboratory made Doc nervous and apprehensive. And there was something missing from himself, something lost. The lowest voice of all was still. In his black depths he was somehow comforted. He went to the record shelf: not Bach . . . no, not Buxtehude . . . not Palestrina either. His hand strayed to an album not used in a long time. He had opened it before he knew what he was doing. And then he smiled and put the first record on the turntable: Mozart's *Don Giovanni.* It started its overture, and Doc, still smiling, went to the kitchen and stirred the stew. "Don Giovanni," he said. "Is that what I think of myself? No! I do not. But why do I feel so good, and so bad?" He looked at his desk. The yellow pads were piled neatly and the pencils were sharpened. "I believe I'll try." And at that point there were fumbling steps on his porch and Old Jingleballicks burst in.

It is madness to write about Old Jingleballicks, but since he came in at this point it is necessary. People coming out of a session with Old Jay felt slightly dizzy, and the wise ones, after a time, just didn't believe it. His name cannot be mentioned, for it occurs on too many bronze plaques that begin, "Donated by——."

Old Jay was born so rich that he didn't know he was rich at all. He thought everybody was that way. He was a scientist, but whether brilliant or a screwball nobody ever knew, and since he had contributed to so many learned foundations and financed so many projects and served on so many boards of trustees, nobody dared openly to wonder. He gave millions away but he was likely to sponge on a friend. His scholastic honors were many, and there were people who thought privately and venomously that they were awarded in hope of a donation, that he was, in fact, like a football player whose grades have little relation to his scholarship.

He was a stubby man with a natural tonsure of yellow hair. His eyes were bright as a bird's eyes, and he was interested in everything. He was so close to reality that he had completely lost touch with realism. Sometimes he amused Doc, and at other times his endless and myopic enthusiasms could drive a man to despair. Old Jingleballicks shouted at everyone under the impression that this made for clarity.

"Did you get my wire?" he cried.

"No."

"Came for your birthday. Always remember it. Same day they burned Giordano Bruno."

"It's not my birthday," said Doc.

"Well, what day is this?"

"Friday."

"Oh! Well, I'll wait over."

"It's in December. I only have one cot."

"All right. I'll sleep on the floor." He wandered to the kitchen, took the lid off the pot, and began eating the stew—blowing on it violently to cool it.

"That's not done," said Doc, and he was irritated to find that he was shouting back.

"Done enough!" cried Old Jay and went on eating.

Doc said, "Hitzler came through. He said you were seen on a lawn in Berkeley, on your knees, pulling a worm out of the ground with your teeth."

Old Jay swallowed a half-cooked carrot. "Not so!" he shouted. "Say, this stew's not done."

"That's what I told you."

"Oh! Well, you see I've watched robins getting worms. Little beggars dig in their heels, so to speak. I got to wondering how much actual pull was involved. Had a scale with a clamp in my teeth. Average night crawler resists to the extent of one pound six ounces. I tried forty-eight individuals. Think of it! A three-ounce bird pulls twenty-two ounces, over seven times his own weight. No wonder they eat so much. Just eating keeps them hungry. Like robins?"

"Not particularly," said Doc. "Are you going to eat all my dinner?"

"I guess so," said Old Jingleballicks. "But it's not done. You got anything to drink?"

"I'll get some beer," said Doc.

"Fine! Get a lot."

"Don't you want to contribute a little?"

"I'm short," said Old Jay.

Doc said, "You are not. You're a free-loader."

"Oh!" said Jingleballicks.

"I said, don't you want to contribute!"

"I'm a little short," said Old Jay.

Doc said angrily, "You are not. You're a free-loader. You never pay. You ran the lab while I was in the Army and damn near bankrupted me. I don't say you stole most of the museum glass, I just say it's missing. Did you take those specimen jars?"

"Well, yes," said Old Jingleballicks. And then he said thoughtfully, "I wish you were a charity or an institution."

"What!"

"Then I could endow you," said Old Jingleballicks.

"Well, I'm not an institution. So what do you do? You go to a lot of trouble to keep from paying a couple of dollars for beer." And suddenly despair and humor crashed head on in Doc and he burst into weary laughter. "Oh Lord," he said, "you're just not possible! You're a ridiculous idea."

"Your stew is burning," said Old Jingleballicks.

Doc leaped to the stove and pulled the pot from the burner. "You ate all the juice," he said bitterly. "Of course it burned!"

"It was very good," said Old Jay.

In the grocery Doc said, "Give me a dozen cans of beer."

"Don't you want the Bohemia?"

"Hell no!" Doc said. "I have a guest who—" And then an evil thought came to him. "A very interesting man," Doc said. "Why don't you come over and have a drink with us? Old—I mean, my friend can explain chess to you better than I can."

"Why not?" said the Patrón. "Maybe I better bring a little liquor."

"Why not?" said Doc.

Crossing the street, the Patrón asked, "You going to the party tomorrow?"

"Sure."

"I like you, Doc, but I don't get you. You ain't real," said the Patrón.

"How do you mean?"

"Well, everything you do is—well, you're like that chess. I don't get you at all."

Doc said, "Do you suppose nobody's real to anybody else? You're going to meet a man who can't possibly exist."

"Don't talk like that," said the Patrón nervously.

Old Jay shouted as they went up the stairs, "I bring you tidings of great joy. The human species is going to disappear!"

"This is Joseph and Mary Rivas," said Doc. "Joseph and Mary, this is Old Jingleballicks."

"Why can't you rig a chess game?" the Patrón asked.

"Oh, you can, you can! Or at least you can rearrange your opponent. Comes to the same thing. Now, where was I? Oh yes—we are about to join the great reptiles in extinction."

"Good!" said Doc.

"You mean there ain't gonna be no more people?" said the Patrón.

"Right, young man. We have played the final joke on ourselves. Open the beer! Man, in saving himself, has destroyed himself."

"Who's destroyed?" the Patrón demanded.

"There must be chuckling on Olympus," said Old Jingleballicks. "We go not to Armageddon but to the gas chamber, and we generate our own gas—"

Doc said, "I intended to work on my paper."

"Good! I'll help," said Old Jingleballicks.

"Oh God! *No!*" said Doc.

"Man has solved his problems," Old Jay went on. "Predators he has removed from the earth; heat and cold he has turned aside; communicable disease he has practically eliminated. The old live on, the young do not die. The best wars can't even balance the birth rate. There was a time when a small army could cut a population in half in a year. Starvation, typhus, plague, tuberculosis, were trusty weapons. A scratch with a spear point meant infection and death. Do you know what the incidence of death from battle wounds is today? One per cent. A hundred years ago it was eighty per cent. The population grows and the productivity of the earth decreases. In a foreseeable future we shall be smothered by our own numbers. Only birth control could save us, and that is one thing mankind is never going to practice."

"Broth-er!" said the Patrón. "What makes you so damn happy about it?"

"It is a cosmic joke. Preoccupation with survival has set the stage for extinction."

"I didn't get one goddam word of that," said Joseph and Mary.

Doc's hands were full. In his left he held a small glass of whisky and in his right a can of beer. He sipped from the one and gulped from the other. "Every instinct tells me to stay out of this," he said, "and every impulse makes me want to get into it."

"Good!" said Old Jay. "Is that whisky?"

"Old Tennis Shoes," said Joseph and Mary. "Want some?"

"Perhaps a little later."

"Okay."

"It's a little later now," said Old Jingleballicks.

"I guess you can hustle with anything," said the Patrón. "I got a feeling I'm being took."

"Well, the impulse wins," said Doc. "You have forgotten one thing, Old Jingleballicks. Indeed, there have been species which became extinct through their own miscalculations, but they were species with a small range of variability. Now consider the lemming—"

"That is a very specialized case," said Old Jingleballicks.

"How do you know we aren't? What do lemmings do when their population exceeds the food supply? Whole masses of them swim out to sea and drown, until a balance of food and population is reached."

"I deny your right to use lemmings," said Old Jingleballicks. "Hand me the bottle, will you?"

"Deny and be damned!" Doc said. "Is the lemming migration a disease? Is it a memory? Or is it a psychic manifestation forced on part of the group for the survival of the whole?"

Old Jay howled back at him, "I will not be robbed of extinction! This is a swindle." He turned to the Patrón. "Don't listen to that man. He's a charlatan."

"He sure in hell is," said Joseph and Mary admiringly.

Doc leveled a finger between the eyes of Old Jay, holding his whisky glass like the butt of a pistol. "Disease, you say? Infection? Down almost to nonexistence? But tell me, are not neurotic disturbances on the increase? And are they curable or does the cure spread them? Now you wait! Don't you try to talk now. Do you suppose that the tendency toward homosexuality might not also have a mathematical progression? And could this not be the human solution?"

"You can't prove it," Old Jingleballicks cried. "It's all talk —overemphasis. Why, you might as well accuse me of neurotic tendencies and be done with it!" His eyes brimmed with tears. "My friend, my thought-friend, my true friend," he whimpered.

Doc said, "I wouldn't even think of such a thing."

"You wouldn't?"

"Certainly not."

"When are you going to start dinner?" said Old Jingleballicks.

"You've eaten my dinner," said Doc.

"I've got a fine idea," said Old Jay. "While you start dinner, William and Mary can get a fresh bottle of whisky and I'll set up the chessmen."

"It's not William and Mary, it's Joseph and Mary."

"Who is? Oh! My friend, I'm going to teach you the greatest of all games, the ethereal creation of human intelligence. Shall we sugar it up with a little side bet?"

"Why, you dishonest old fraud!" Doc shouted.

"Ten dollars, Mary?"

The Patrón shrugged his shoulders in apology to Doc. "You have to pay to learn things," he said.

"Make it twenty-five," Old Jingleballicks said. "You want to live forever?"

Doc opened a can of salmon and a can of spaghetti and stirred the two together in a frying pan. He grated nutmeg over it. Sadly he put the burned stewpot to soak in the sink.

A little after dark the Patrón went back to the grocery and sent Cacahuete to deliver a third bottle of whisky. Upstairs he joined the wetbacks as in advancing and retreating lines they danced the sad and stately measures of the Tehuanos. "Sandunga," they sang, "Sandunga mama mia . . ."

In the darkening laboratory Doc and Old Jay went softly into the third bottle of Old Tennis Shoes.

"You've had the bed long enough," Doc said. "I want it now."

"All right. As I grow older I expect less and less—and get nothing, even from my so-called friends."

"Look here! You've eaten and spoiled my first dinner, stuffed my second, swilled my beer, taken two drinks for one of the whisky, appropriated my bed, broken two phonograph records, and I saw you put my fountain pen in your pocket. And how you razzle-dazzled the Patrón out of twenty-five dollars I don't know. You shouldn't have told him that under certain circumstances a knight can jump three squares in one direction—that's not honest."

"I know," said Old Jingleballicks. He patted the pillow lovingly. "Now you lie down here and get comfortable. I'll bring you a drink. Feel better now?"

"Oh, I'm all right," said Doc.

"Say, is that place across the street still running?"

A jagged rage whipped Doc upright. "You stay out of there!" he said. "You old fool! Lie down and go to sleep."

"Why shouldn't I go? Am I to deny myself the loveliness of women if the price is right? I can hear the tinkle of their sweet voices and see the heaving of their white roundness—"

"Oh, shut up!" Doc said.

"What's the matter, dear friend? I don't remember that you ever starved for love even when it was less near and less reasonable."

"You go to hell," said Doc. "But you go to hell here."

26. The Developing Storm

At the very moment Doc and Old Jingleballicks were quarreling over a matter neither of them understood, Mack was sitting, body comfortable but spirit disturbed, in Fauna's office bedroom. In his hand he held a Venetian glass bud vase of whisky. He was pouring out to Fauna a problem that had not come up in his life for many years.

"Don't think that there ain't been parties before at the Palace, and fights," he said. "Why, when the news come that Gay had went to his reward we give a memorial shindig that they don't hardly do no better at the Salinas Rodeo. Gay would of been proud of it—if he could of got in."

Fauna said, "There's talk around that three mourners went to join Gay before nightfall next day."

"Well, you got to expect a certain amount of accidents," said Mack modestly. "That was all fine. But this here's something special. Not only are loyal hearts framing their dear friend for a hunk of charity, but we got a doubleheader. Right in the Palace Flophouse the holy bounds of matrimony got its spikes dug in on the starting line. This here's a halcyon brawl. I and the boys got real delicate feelings about it."

"But no clothes," said Fauna.

"Right! We think somebody got to set a standard. If the loyal friends look like mugs, what'll the mugs look like?"

Fauna nodded. "I see what you mean. How far you want to go—monkeysuits?"

"God no!" Mack said. "Just pants and coats made out of the same stuff and nobody gets in without he's got a necktie on, and none of them bow ties that light up neither. This is a goddam solemn moment, Fauna."

She scratched her scalp with her pencil.

Mack went on, "I ain't as young as I was. I don't know how many more parties I can take."

"Don't none of us get no younger," said Fauna. She tapped her teeth with the pencil. As it happened, she also had a problem, and she intended to ask Mack's advice. Now, suddenly, the two problems crashed together and a solution for both was born. Into Fauna's eyes came the light of triumph as she murmured, "I got it!"

"Give it to me gentle," said Mack. "I didn't get much sleep today."

Fauna got up and found the stick with which she directed astrological traffic or whacked a protruding piece of bad posture. She talked better with the wand in her hand. "This here calls for a drink," she said, and she poured it.

Mack turned the stem of the bud vase in his fingers and sighted through his drink. The red glass made the brown whisky look green.

Fauna said, "There was a queen a long time ago and she was loaded. Didn't think nothing of paying a couple hundred bucks for a housedress. Got so many bracelets she couldn't bend her arms. You know what she done when she had a birthday or a hanging or something?"

"Overalls," said Mack.

"No, but you're close. Dressed like she's a milkmaid. They'd wash up a cow and the queen'd sit on a gold stool and take a whang at milking. And there's another old dame. Just the top cream of the top cream. Gives them parties can't nobody get in. She wears a headrag. Done it for years. If you look over the crowd and don't see a headrag—she ain't there."

Mack's hand shook as he raised the bud vase to his lips. "Is it what I think?"

"Masquerade!" cried Fauna. "There's only two kinds of people in the world gives a masquerade—people who got too much and people who ain't got nothing."

Mack smiled inwardly to himself. "Can I have a freshener?" he asked.

"Help yourself," said Fauna. "Masquerade has got other things too. People get kind of bored with who they are. Makes them something else for a while."

Mack spoke with reverence. "They used to say, if you got something you can't figure out, give it to Mack. Fauna, it's your dice. You're a bull-bitch idear dame. God te-tum-tum His wonders to perform."

"Like it?"

"Like it! Fauna, this here's one *Life* magazine would give its ass for an invite."

"We got to have a theme."

"How do you mean?"

"Well, we can't let people just run wild. You don't know what kind of stuff they'd wear. I don't want no tramp and gunnysack party."

"I guess you're right. You got any idears?"

"How about 'At the court of the Fairy Queen'?"

"No," said Mack. "First place, we got no right to hurt Joe Elegant's feelings; second place, the cops—"

"Well, how about then 'Snow White and the Seven Dwarfs.'"

"I seen the picture," said Mack. "I think you got something. Some of them dwarfs looked like mugs. I can't see Hazel as no fairy, but he'd do fine as a great big overgrowed dwarf."

"That's what's nice about it," said Fauna. "Gives you some leeway."

"Do you think this might call for a drink?"

"I sure as hell do! You spread the word, Mack, will you? You come either as a dwarf, a prince, or a princess, or you damn well don't get in. Hold that vase steady."

"But not Doc," said Mack.

"You know," said Fauna, "five'll get you seven Doc wears a tie."

27. O Frabjous Day!

THE communications system on Cannery Row is mysterious to the point of magic and rapid to the speed of light. Fauna and Mack came to the decision that the party should be a masquerade on Friday evening at 9:11½. By 9:12 the magic had started, and by 9:30 everyone who was not asleep, drunk, or away, knew about it. One particularly mean woman who hadn't had a man for a long time commented, "How will you know whether they're in costume or not?"—a statement clearly drawn from her own state of misery. But mainly the news was received with wonder and joy. Mack's tom-wallager had achieved the stature of a bull-bitch tom-wallager.

Consider what was in store for the ticket holders: a party at the Palace Flophouse; a raffle that amounted to a potlatch; an engagement of exciting proportions unknown in the annals of the Row; and, on top of this, a costume party! Any one of these would have been enough. Together they threatened to be a celebration close to a catastrophe.

Fauna breathed a sigh of relief for it solved her greatest problem. She wanted to dress Suzy in a certain way, and Suzy, being the tough monkey she was, would have resisted. Now it was easy. There's little difference between the wardrobe of Snow White and that of a lovely young bride.

There will be those who will consider that Fauna took too much upon herself in engineering a marriage without the knowledge or collusion of either party, and such skeptics will be perfectly right. But it was Fauna's conviction, born out of long experience, that most people, one, did not know what they wanted; two, did not know how to go about getting it; and three, didn't know when they had it.

Fauna was one of those rare people who not only have convictions but are quite willing to take responsibility for them. She knew that Doc and Suzy should be together. And since they were too confused, or thoughtless, or shy to bring about that happy state, Fauna was prepared to do it for them. Her critics will cry, "Suppose she is wrong! Maybe this association has no chance of success." And Fauna's answer to this, if she had heard it, would have been, "They ain't doing so good now. It might work. What they got to lose? And when you look at it, what chance has anybody got? Doc put on a tie, didn't he? And if I'm wrong it's my fault. Sure, they'll fight now and then. Who don't? But maybe they'll get something too. What's the odds for anybody?"

And if it was suggested that people should have the right to choose for themselves after thinking it over, she would have replied, "Who thinks? I can think because I ain't part of it."

And if she had been accused of being a busybody she would have said, "Damn right! Done it all my life!" You couldn't win an argument with Fauna because she would agree with you and then go right on as she had planned. She had taken up astrology because she had found that people who won't take advice from a wise and informed friend will blindly follow the orders of planets—which, by all reports, are fairly remote and aloof. Doc would refuse astrology, so he had to be sandbagged. Fauna expected no thanks. She had given that up long ago. Doc could not interpret the black voice of his guts, but it sounded loud in Fauna's ears. She knew his loneliness. When she was with him, that low voice drowned out all the others.

On Saturday morning she made every girl in the house bring out every article of clothing she possessed and lay it on the bed in her office.

Now Mabel was a natural-born, blowed-in-the-glass hustler. In any time, under any system, after a period of orientation, Mabel would have found herself doing exactly what she was doing in Cannery Row. This was not a matter of Fate, but rather a combination of aptitudes and inclinations. Born in a hovel or a castle, Mabel would have gravitated toward hustling.

The heap of finery on Fauna's bed was impressive. Some of those dresses could have got a girl booked for vagrancy just going out to mail a letter.

Mabel took Fauna aside and spoke to her privately. "My grandma come from the old country," she said when the door of her room was closed. Mabel opened the bottom drawer of her bureau and lifted out a brown paper parcel sealed against air with strips of cellophane tape. "Grandma left it to Mama, and Mama left it to me," she said as she tore the paper. "We ain't none of us needed it." She removed layer after layer of tissue paper and at last spread a dress out on her bed—a wedding dress of sheerest white linen embroidered with sprays of white flowers—stitches so tiny they seemed to grow out of the cloth. The bodice was close-fitting and the skirt very full. Mabel opened a box and laid beside the dress a silver wedding crown. "I guess she wouldn't hurt it none," said Mabel. "Tell her not to spill nothing on it. I'll polish up the crown, it's kind of tarnished—real silver!"

Fauna was speechless for once. Her fingers went to the light and lovely fabric. She was a hard woman to break up, but the dress nearly did it. "Snow White!" she said breathlessly. "I better be careful or I'll get to believing my own pitch. Mabel, I'm going to give you my jet earrings."

"I don't want nothing."

"You want my jet earrings!"

"Aw shoot!" said Mabel.

"Looks like it might nearly fit her," Fauna observed.

"Well, we can kind of tack it where it don't."

"You know, you're a good girl. You want I should go to work on you?"

"Hell no!" said Mabel. "I like it here. There's a veil too in this here bag."

"I don't know if we can get away with a veil, but we'll try," said Fauna.

"Oh hell, she don't know a veil from a hole in the ground," said Mabel.

If only people would give the thought, the care, the judgment to international affairs, to politics, even to their jobs, that they lavish on what to wear to a masquerade, the world would run in greased grooves. On the surface Cannery Row was quieter than usual, but below the surface it seethed. In one corner of the Palace Flophouse, Whitey No. 2 gave careful lessons to little Johnny Carriaga in the art of palming cards. Johnny had been borrowed for the occasion—or, more truthfully, rented—since Alberto Carriaga had received sixty-two cents, the price of a gallon of wine, for the use of his firstborn. It was planned that Johnny should be dressed as Cupid, with paper wings, bow and arrow, and quiver. The quiver was added as a hiding place for the winning raffle ticket. For although nearly everyone on the Row knew the raffle was rigged, a certain pride made it necessary to carry the deception off with dignity. Because of a small distrust of Johnny the arrows in the quiver were tipped with rubber suction cups.

Whitey No. 2 had cut a card the exact size of a raffle ticket. "Now try it again, Johnny," he said. "No, I can see the edge of it. Look! Sort of squeeze the edges in your palm, like this. Now try it again. That's right! That's good. Now let's see you get it out of the quiver. You make a pass with the bow—like this—so they look at your other hand, and you say—"

"I know," said Johnny. " 'I'm Cupid, God of Love, and I draw a bead on unsuspecting hearts.' "

"God! That's beautiful," said Eddie. "I wonder where Mack got that?"

"He made it up," said Whitey No. 2. "Now when you shove up the bow with your right hand, you get the ticket out of the quiver with your left. Try it."

" 'I-am-Cupid-God-of-Love,' " said Johnny, and he brandished the bow.

"That's good," said Whitey No. 2. "It will take a little more practice though. Don't look at your left hand, Johnny. Look at the bow. Now here's the bowl. Dig around the cards without dropping the ticket. Go on, practice."

"I want thirty-five cents," said Johnny.

"What!"

"If I don't get thirty-five cents I'll tell."

"Mack," said Whitey No. 2, "this here kid's jumped the price."

"Give it to him," said Mack. "I'll flip him double or nothing later."

"Not with that two-headed nickel, you won't," said Johnny.

"Seems like kids got no respect for their elders nowadays," Eddie observed. "If I ever said that, my old man would of clobbered me."

"Maybe your old man wasn't rigging no raffle," said Johnny.

Whitey No. 1 said, "This kid ain't honest. You know where bad kids go, Johnny?"

"I sure do, and I been there," said Johnny.

"Give him the thirty-five cents," said Mack.

*

What hidden, hoarded longings there are in all of us! Behind the broken nose and baleful eye may be a gentle courtier; behind the postures and symbols and myths of Joe Elegant there may be the hunger to be a man. If one could be, for only an evening, whatever in the world one wished, what would it be? What secret would come out?

To a certain extent the theme of the Palace Flophouse raffle and engagement party was chosen because of Hazel. He was definitely dwarf material. But when he had reviewed the story, asked questions, and got as clear a picture as he ever got of anything, Hazel elected to be Prince Charming. He saw himself in white silk knee breeches and an Eton jacket, his left hand fondling the hilt of a small sword.

They offered him Grumpy, lovable old Grumpy, the prize part of all. They offered him Sweet Pea the Skunk, but Hazel stuck to his dream. It was Prince Charming or he wouldn't attend. Friendships have foundered on less.

"All right," said Mack, "you go ahead. I was going to help you with your costume, but I know when I'm stumped. Hazel, if you're Prince Charming, you're on your own."

"Who cares?" said Hazel. "Who wants your help? I'll bet you're mad because you wanted to be Prince Charming."

"Not me," said Mack. "I'm going as a tree."

"How do you mean?"

"It's a forest, ain't it?" said Mack. "I want a little anenmity. You can't see the tree for the forest."

Hazel went to sit under the cypress tree. He was gloomy and he was frightened because ideas did not come to him, and when he sought them they ran screaming away. But he was determined. He could not let the office down. A man sentenced to be President could not go as a dwarf. It wasn't dignified. Later in the morning he went to the back door of the Bear Flag and called for help from Joe Elegant.

Joe smiled. "I'll help you," he said maliciously.

All over the Row trunks were being opened, and the smell of mothballs penetrated as far as the middle of the street. And all over the Row the story was being rewritten to fit the wardrobe. By unspoken agreement no one planned to be Snow White.

In Western Biological, Doc awakened wracked with pain

from sleeping on the floor. He lay still for a moment, trying to isolate the part of him that hurt worst. Not the least of his agony was his memory of forcing Old Jingleballicks to take his bed. A crazy, alcoholic generosity, probably masochistic in origin, had prompted the sacrifice. He raised up on one shattered elbow and looked at the old bastard sleeping so sweetly—his halo of yellow hair surrounding his polished pink pate, his breath puffing in small comfortable snores.

"Wake up!" Doc shouted in fury.

The pale eyes flickered. "What's for breakfast?" said Old Jay.

"Don't you even have the decency to have a hangover?"

"Certainly I do," said Old Jay with dignity. "How's about some beer?"

"Does your head ache?"

"Yes."

"Do your joints ache?"

"Yes."

"Do you have low-blood-pressure depression?"

"Overwhelming."

"Then I've got you," said Doc. "You get the beer."

The pale eyes rolled despairingly. "I'll pay half if you get it."

"No."

"Tell you what I'll do—I'll loan you the money."

"No."

Old Jingleballicks' eyes were bleak. "Reach me my pants," he said, and he fished out a quarter and a dime and held them out.

"No," said Doc.

"God in heaven! What *do* you want?"

"I want two dollars."

"Why, that would be six bottles!"

"Exactly. You're trapped, Old Jingleballicks, and you know it."

Old Jay dug deep and found two one-dollar bills. "Maybe I can write it off to entertainment," he said.

Doc pulled on pants and shirt and went across the street. He took his time. He drank a bottle of beer quickly and then sipped a second while he heard the news of the day from Joseph and Mary.

Back in the laboratory he put the four cold remaining bottles on the table.

"Where's my change?" asked Old Jay.

"I drank your change," said Doc. He was beginning to feel good. He saw the stricken look. "You cheap old fraud," he said happily, "for once you've been had." And he went on, "I wish I could understand you. You must have millions and yet you pinch and squirm and cheat. Why?"

"Please give me beer. I'm dying," said Old Jingleballicks.

"Then die a little longer," said Doc. "I love to see you die!"

"It's not my fault," Old Jay said. "It's a state of mind. You might call it the American state of mind. The tax laws are creating a whole new kind of man—a psyche rather than a psychosis. Two or three generations and we'll maybe set the species. Can I have beer now?"

"No."

"If a man has any money he doesn't ask, 'Can I afford this?' but, 'Can I deduct it?' Two men fight over a luncheon check when both of them are going to deduct it anyway—a whole nation conditioned to dishonesty by its laws, because honesty is penalized. But it's worse than that. If you'll just hand me a bottle I'll tell you."

"Tell me first."

"I didn't write the tax laws," Old Jay said, trembling. "The only creative thing we have is the individual, but the law doesn't permit me to give money to an individual. I must give it to a group, an organization—and the only thing a group has ever created is bookkeeping. To participate in my gift the individual must become part of the group and thus lose his individuality and his creativeness. I didn't write the law. I hate a law that stifles generosity and makes charity good business. Corporations are losing their financial efficiency because waste pays. I deplore it, but I do it. I know you need a microscope, but I can't give it to you because with taxes a four-hundred-dollar microscope costs me twelve hundred dollars—if I give it to you—and nothing if I give it to an institution. Why, if you, through creative work, should win a prize, most of the money would go in taxes. I don't mind taxes, God knows! But I do mind the kind of law that makes of charity not the full warmness of sharing but a stinking expediency. And now, if you don't hand me a beer, I shall be forced—"

"Here's your beer," said Doc.

"What's for breakfast?"

"God knows. The party at the Palace Flophouse tonight is a masquerade. 'Snow White and the Seven Dwarfs.'"

"Why?"

"I don't know."

"I shall go as a red dwarf," said Old Jingleballicks.

"A dying star," said Doc. "It kind of fits you with that hair."

When the beer was gone they decided that beer made breakfast redundant. Doc went back for six more bottles, and in a burst of generosity he brought back the Bohemia.

"Now there's beer for you," said Old Jingleballicks. "The Mexicans are a great and noble people. The Pyramid of the Sun and this beer—whole civilizations have produced less. You started to tell me about your paper last night but you got deflected by a girl. I'd like to see that girl."

"I'd like to tell you about my paper. I want to draw some parallels between emotional responses in cephalopods and in humans, and I'd like to observe the pathological changes that go with these responses. Now the body walls of octopi are semi-transparent. With proper equipment it might be possible to observe these changes as they happen. Sometimes the simpler organisms can give us a key to the more complex. Dementia praecox, for example, was considered purely a psychotic manifestation until it was observed that there were physical symptoms as well."

"Why don't you write your paper?"

"I seem to be afraid to. A kind of terror comes over me when I start."

"What have you got to lose if you fail?"

"Nothing."

"What have you got to gain if you succeed?"

"I don't know."

Old Jingleballicks regarded Doc benignly. "Have you got enough beer in you so you aren't quarrelsome?"

"I'm never quarrelsome."

"The hell you aren't! Took my head off last night. You hurt my feelings."

"I'm sorry. What did you want to say?"

"Will you let me finish if I start?"

"I'll try."

Old Jay said, "You feel to me like a woman who has never had a baby but knows all the words. There's a lack of fulfillment in you. I think you have violated something or withheld something from yourself—almost as though you were eating plenty but no Vitamin A. You aren't hungry, but you're starving. That's what I think."

"I can't imagine anything I lack. I have freedom, comfort, and the work I like. What have I missed?"

"Well, last night, in every conversation, a girl named Suzy crept in—"

"For God's sake!" said Doc. "Do you know what Suzy is? An illiterate little tramp, a whore! I took her out to dinner because Fauna asked me to. I found her interesting the way I'd find a new species of octopus interesting, that's all. You've always been a goddam fool, Old Jingleballicks, but you've never been a romantic damn fool."

"Who's talking about romance? I was speaking of hunger. Maybe you can't be wholly yourself because you've never given yourself wholly to someone else."

"Of all the esoteric goddam nonsense!" Doc cried. "Why I give floor room to you I don't know."

"Then try to figure out why you get mad," said Old Jay.

"What?"

"Well, aren't you putting a lot of energy into denying something which, if it is not true, deserves no denial?"

"Sometimes I think you're just plain nuts," said Doc.

"Know what I'm going to do?" said Old Jay. "I'm going to buy a bottle of whisky."

"I don't believe it!" said Doc.

28. *Where Alfred the Sacred River Ran*

VERY few people know that Hazel had given the Palace Flophouse its name years ago when the boys had first moved in. Inspired by the glory of having a home, Hazel compounded the name of something he knew about and something he didn't, the known and the unknown, the homely and the exotic; and, ever after, the name had stuck, so that it was known by certain people from one end of the state to the other. And the Palace Flophouse had justified its name over the years. It had been shelter and home base to the boys. Also, some surprising events had occurred there.

The building itself was not impressive—redwood board and bat, tarpaper roof, twenty-eight feet long, fourteen feet wide, two square windows, and two doors, one on each side. Into this simple box Mack and the boys had moved some remarkable articles, the products of their wits, their work, and sometimes their misfortune. The great cast-iron stove was in excellent condition and bid fair to outlast the Colosseum which it resembled. The grandfather clock, once the home of a dog, stood empty now—and Eddie wanted to be buried in it. Each of the beds was canopied as a substitute for mending the roof, and Gay's bed was kept just as it was when he went away—patchwork quilt turned down to reveal a gray tennis-flannel sheet; His copy of *Amazing True Desert Stories*, folded open to page 62, lay on top of the apple box just as Gay had left it; and his prize possession, a collector's item, a ring gear and pinions of a 1914 Willys-Knight, lay on a black velvet cloth in the bottom of the box. On the shelf over his bed the boys kept some kind of nosegay in a swanky swig glass, for Gay had loved flowers. He ate them—particularly red roses, mustard flowers, wild turnip blossoms, and the petals of one variety of dahlia. No one had ever been allowed to sit or sleep in Gay's bed. He might return one day, the boys thought, even though he was reported dead and his Army insurance paid.

Now there had been tom-wallagers in the Palace Flophouse but never such a bull-bitch tom-wallager as was now in the process of exploding. The outside was freshly whitewashed.

Beds were pushed together, and the interior was a bower of pine boughs crossed to make a canopy. The great stove was laid out as a bar and the oven was full of cracked ice. In front of the back door a little stage was built, with a painter's drop-cloth for a curtain and the door for an entrance—for certain theatrical effects, not counting the raffle itself, were planned for that area.

This forest bower was lighted by Japanese lanterns, and a string of lanterns led down to the chicken walk above the railroad track. The boys were pleased with their effort.

Mack surveyed the scene and put a name to it that was remembered. "A veritable fairyland," he said.

The Patrón had contributed his prize group of musicians, the original Espaldas Mojadas—two guitars, gourds, bones, castanets, and Haitian drum, and last, a guitarón as big as a rowboat. Cacahuete Rivas, the nephew of the Patrón, was scheduled to join his trumpet to the band later, but now he was on the beach, practicing his solo softly.

As evening came to Cannery Row the boys were tired but content. Following Mack's lead, they all agreed to be trees. After all, they were the hosts. Their one sorrow was that Hazel had left them. His yearning to be Prince Charming had overcome his love for his friends. In Joe Elegant's tiny bedroom he was being transformed.

"Caught me with my pants down," Mack apologized for the twentieth time. "Hazel's such a mug you forget he's sensitive. Hell, I could of worked out some kind of charming rig if I'd give it some thought. Don't seem right without him here to mess things up."

It is customary at most masquerades for the arriving guests to be shy, ill at ease, and sober, and to stand around uneasily for maybe an hour before the party warms up. In this matter of starting a party Cannery Row is far ahead of some other centers of culture. The party was to start at nine p.m. sharp. The guests would be notified by the trumpet of Cacahuete Rivas, playing "Whistle While You Work."

At least two hours before the signal a series of small earnest parties, at Wide Ida's, the Bear Flag, and in private homes, were practicing for the main event. This party was going to begin in full bloom. Of course Mack and the boys were so weighed down with responsibility that they didn't get the best out of their liquor; still, they made progress, and they watched the big hand of the alarm clock on the back of the stove.

In the Bear Flag the pageantry was spread all over the floor. Snow White was going to have, as ladies of honor, some of the best-known and most respected hookers north of San Luis Obispo. The ladies were dressing in filmy gowns of red, yellow, and green, and each one was to carry a bottle of whisky garlanded with ribbons to match her dress. Fauna was going as a witch. It was her own idea. The only costume she really needed was a broom, but she had made a peaked black hat and a black alpaca wraparound to carry the part off. But Fauna had a payoff. When the big moment came she was prepared to fling off her black gown, switch broom for wand, and emerge as the fairy godmother.

Wide Ida's was dwarf country. Eight Happys, four Sneezys, six Dopeys, and nineteen Grumpys clustered about the bar, earnestly singing "Harvest Moon" in one and a half part harmony.

Joseph and Mary had elected to go as Dracula. He hadn't seen Snow White, but to him a moving picture was a moving picture.

At Western Biological, Doc and Old Jingleballicks were hopelessly enmeshed in a discussion of tobacco mosaic. When the dam had burst a flood followed. A garbage can stood in the middle of the floor, and in it, nestled in crushed ice, the six remaining bottles of a case of champagne bought by Old Jay.

Doc and Old Jay had completely forgotten the party. When Cacahuete's trumpet sounded the call to arms they were shouting so loud they didn't hear it. When the youth and beauty of Cannery Row walked gaily up the lantern-lit chicken walk Old Jay and Doc were still screaming at each other.

Suddenly Doc dropped his voice, and it had the effect of a loud noise. "I think I will go away," he said. "I have tried with every sinew and I have failed."

"Nonsense!" said Old Jay. "Young man, you are at the threshold of a great career."

"But what do I care for honors?"

"How do you know? You never got any," said Old Jay.

"Don't try to hold me back, Old Jingle."

"I won't. There's too many of you already. Do you realize you haven't cooked any dinner?"

"I bought a pound of hamburger and you ate it raw before I got it near a pan."

"You shouldn't starve yourself, young friend," said Old Jingleballicks.

Eddie hurled himself up the steps and flung open the door. "Doc!" he cried. "For God's sakes! She's started! They're going to draw!"

Doc picked a bottle from the ice. "Arm yourself, Old Jingleballicks. Forward!"

They had to help Old Jay up the chicken walk.

The drawing was being held for them. Dwarfs, animals, monsters, were drawn up in a half-circle, facing the curtain.

"I guess we're all here," said Mack. He looked behind the curtain. "You all right, Johnny?"

"Goddam cold," said Johnny.

And at that moment Hazel entered proudly, his chin up, his eyes flashing with dignity. Joe Elegant had worked all day to get his revenge on mankind, and Hazel was the result. The basis of his costume was long gray underwear, to which were sewed hearts, diamonds, spades, and clubs in red and black. Hazel's army shoes had yellow pompoms on the toes. An Elizabethan ruff of stiff paper was around his neck, and on his head a Knight Templar's hat with a white ostrich plume. From the belt around his middle hung a long scabbard. His right hand proudly held a cavalry saber at salute.

Joe Elegant had concentrated his revenge in one area. The drop seat of the costume had been removed and in its place, right on the essential surface of Hazel himself, was painted a bull's eye in concentric circles of red and blue.

Hazel was a breathtaking sight. He did not glance around. He knew he was right—he knew it by the silence. Smartly he turned the saber to parade rest and crossed his hands on the hilt. His breath caught in his throat.

"I," he said huskily, "I am Prince Charming." And the company could see now that his cheeks were rouged and his eyelashes beaded. "I proteck dam—damsels," he announced. And only then did he turn his proud head for the applause and approval he knew he merited.

There were tears in Mack's eyes. "You done fine, Hazel baby," he said. "Couldn't nobody do better. Who helped you?"

"Joe Elegant," said Hazel. "What a nice guy!"

Whitey No. 2 moved up at Mack's imperceptible signal. "You want I should go now?"

"Right now," said Mack softly. "Kick the bejeezus out of him."

Hazel moved proudly in on their soft talk. "Mr. Joe Elegant presents his compliments," he said. "He is sorry he cannot attend as he had to leave town on business. Let's see—is that all?—yep, that's all."

"We'll thank him when he comes back," said Mack grimly.

The guests looked at Hazel with stricken eyes, and no one laughed. One glance at Mack's jutting chin and doubled fists stopped that impulse.

"Get on with it," Wide Ida growled.

Mack pulled himself together, advanced to the curtain, and turned to face the guests.

"Fellow citizens," he said, "right here in Cannery Row lives a guy that there can't nobody want a better friend. For years we have took his bounty without sharing nothing back at him. Now this guy needs a certain article that runs into dough. Therefore it is the pleasure of I and the boys to raffle off the Palace Flophouse to buy a microscope for Doc. We got three hundred and eighty bucks. Curtain!"

Doc shouted, "Mack! You're crazy!"

"Shut up!" said Mack. "Curtain."

The cloth was pulled aside to reveal Johnny Carriaga dressed in an aluminum supporter and a pair of blue paper wings. Johnny brandished his bow. "I-am-Cupid-God-of-Love!" he shouted. Then the winning ticket slipped from his palm and fluttered to the floor. Johnny scrambled after it, yelling, "I draw-a-bead-on-unexpected-hearts." He grabbed the ticket and turned to Mack. "What do I do now?" he asked.

Mack gave up. "Oh, what the hell!" Then he shouted, "Is that the ticket you have drawn, Cupid?"

"I have plucked from the many." Johnny hadn't been near the bowl but he yelled it anyway.

"Give it to me, you little bastard," said Mack quietly. "Friends," he said, "do my eyes deceive me? This *is* a surprise! Well, well! Folks, it gives me great pleasure to announce that the Palace Flophouse has passed into the hands of Doc."

Doc was jarred toward sobriety. He moved close to Mack. "You're crazy!" he said.

"Like a fox," said Mack.

"Who told you you owned it? I didn't tell."

"How do you mean, Doc?"

"I didn't think Chong told anybody but me. He was afraid you'd do something like this."

Mack said, "Let's you and I step outside."

Under the lanterns they faced each other. Doc popped the champagne cork and handed the bottle to Mack, who cupped his mouth over the glistening foam.

"What was you saying, Doc?" he asked quietly.

"Chong wanted you and the boys to have a home. He deeded it to you and put up the money for ten years' taxes."

"Well, whyn't he tell us?"

"He was afraid if you knew you owned it you'd mortgage it or sell it and then you wouldn't have a home."

Mack was shaken. "Doc," he said, "would you do me the favor? Don't tell the boys."

"Why, sure."

"Shake on it?"

"Shake! Have a drink."

Suddenly Mack laughed. "Doc," he said, "I and the boys want to ask will you rent the joint to us?"

"Sure I will, Mack."

"I hope they never find out. They'd skin me," said Mack.

"Wouldn't it be simpler if we just forgot the raffle?"

"No, sir!" said Mack. "Chong was right. I wouldn't trust the boys not to sell her sometime when they need a buck. I wouldn't trust myself."

The visit of Old Jingleballicks had put Doc's system to an outrageous test. Meals had been infrequent, sleep fitful, emotions on stilts, and the intake of alcohol enormous. The raffle had jarred him out of a pleasant swimming state into something resembling sobriety, but not very closely. A fog of unreality like a dream feeling was not in him but all around him. He went inside the Palace and saw the dwarfs and monsters and the preposterous Hazel all lighted by the flickering lanterns. None of it seemed the fabric of sweet reality. The music was deafening. Old Jay danced by, clutching a pale brunette to his stomach as though she were a pain—a disgusting sight, and as unreal as the rest.

Anyone untrained in tom-wallagers might well have been startled at this tom-wallager. Eddie waltzed to the rumba music, his arms embracing an invisible partner. Wide Ida lay on the floor Indian wrestling with Whitey No. 2, at each try displaying acres of pink panties, while a wild conga line of dwarfs and animals milled about. Johnny Carriaga ran wild. Standing on a box, he fired at random but not at unsuspecting hearts. Mrs. Alfred Wong had a rubber-tipped arrow stuck between her shoulderblades. Then Johnny winged a lantern, and it crashed in flames and set fire to three dwarfs, so that they had to be put out with a punch bowl.

Mack and Doc were swept into the conga line. To Doc the room began to revolve slowly and then to rise and fall like the deck of a stately ship in a groundswell. The music roared and tinkled. Hazel beat out rhythm on the stove with his sword until Johnny, aiming carefully, got a bull's eye on Hazel. Hazel leaped in the air and came down on the oven door, scattering crushed ice all over the floor. One of the guests had got wedged in the grandfather clock. From the outside the Palace Flophouse seemed to swell and subside like rising bread.

Doc cupped his hands close to Mack's ear. "Where's Fauna and the girls?" he shouted.

"Later," Mack cried.

"What?"

"Coming later," and he added, "Better get here pretty soon before the joint burns down."

"What?"

"Skip it," Mack shouted.

At this point Whitey No. 1 fought his way to Mack's side and yelled, "Mack, they're coming!"

Mack rushed to the Espaldas Mojadas and raised both hands at them. Johnny aimed his last arrow at the guitarón and took the fret out clean.

"Hold it!" Mack screamed.

The music stopped, and silence fell on the room. Then the unrealest part of all began to happen.

Very softly the sound of a sweet muted trumpet whispered, and the crazy thing was playing the "Wedding March" from *Lohengrin*, and even as Doc listened the sly brass began playing with it, slid into minors, took a short rhythm ride, and moaned away at blues. The dancers were very still, almost stuffed. Doc found the source of the music—Cacahuete Rivas in the corner of the room, muting his trumpet with a damp sponge.

Then in this dream the paint-splashed curtain was pulled aside, and Fauna, the witch, came through the door, straddling a broom.

Doc thought, God! I'd hate to testify about this. I'd get the booby-hatch!

Fauna barked, "This here's a very happy occasion." She looked around. "Doc, come here."

He moved vaguely toward her.

Four girls from the Bear Flag came through the door, dressed in blinding colors. They ranged themselves two on each side of the door, facing inward, holding their beribboned whisky bottles to make an arch.

Fauna dismounted from her broom and ripped off her black wrapper, displaying a sheath of silver lamé. In her hand miraculously appeared a silver wand tipped with a gold star. She struck a pose, riding on her toes as though prepared for flight. "I am your fairy godmother," she shouted. "I bring you Snow White, the bride!"

Then Suzy appeared in the doorway, a transformed Suzy in a wedding gown. The silver crown was on her head, and from its points a veil was suspended. She looked lovely and young and excited. Her lips were parted.

Fauna yelled, "Doc, come get your girl!"

Doc shook his head to try to wake up. It was a dream, a craziness, the crown, the veil, the virginity. "What in hell is going on?"

It happens that two people standing apart can dip into each other's thoughts. Suzy read his mind or his face. An embarrassed red crept up her neck and darkened her cheeks. She closed her eyes.

And Doc's mind read her pain. His world spun like a top. He heard himself say, "Fairy Godmother, I accept—my—girl."

Suzy opened her eyes and looked in Doc's eyes. Then her jaw muscles tightened and her eyes grew fierce; her sweet mouth hardened to a line. She took off the crown and veil, looked at them a moment, and placed them gently on an apple box.

The crazy trumpet put a samba beat to the "Wedding March" and a guitar took up the throbbing.

"Listen, you mugs," said Suzy over the music, "I could live with a stumblebum in a culvert and be a good wife. I could marry a yellow dog and be nice to him. But good Christ! Not Doc!" Suddenly she turned and darted out the door.

Fauna plunged after her. There was no chicken walk out the back way. Suzy slipped and rolled down the embankment and Fauna rolled after her. On the railroad track they gathered themselves together.

"You goddam grandstanding bitch!" said Fauna bitterly. "What do you mean—'not Doc'?"

"I love him," said Suzy.

29. Oh, Woe, Woe, Woe!

ONE of the common reactions to shock is lethargy. If, after an automobile accident, one man is howling and writhing and another sits quietly staring into space, it is usually the quiet man who is badly hurt. A community can go into shock too. Cannery Row did. People drew into themselves, kept their doors closed, and didn't visit. Everyone felt guilty, even those who had not planned the party. Merely to have seen it was enough.

Mack and the boys were doubled up with a sense of unhappy fate. It was their third try at doing something nice for Doc, and it was their third failure. They did not know where to turn to escape their own scorn.

Wide Ida became fiercely taciturn. Her customers drank in silence to escape the guilty rage they knew was just under her muscular surface.

Fauna grieved like a lost setter dog. In a lifetime of preposterous plans she had discovered some failures but never before a catastrophe.

Even the Patrón experienced little flashes of an emotion new to him. Always before he had managed to swap guilt for blame of circumstance or enemy, but now his accusing finger bent like a comedy pistol and aimed at his own heart. It was an interesting pain, but a pain nevertheless. He became kindly and thoughtful of all around him—an attitude that frightened people who knew him. There is nothing reassuring about the smile of a tiger.

As for Doc, he was undergoing reorganization so profound that he didn't know it was happening. He was like a watch taken apart on a jeweler's table—all jewels and springs and balances laid out ready for reassembling. For pain or frustration the human has many anodynes, not the least of which is anger.

Doc quarreled viciously with Old Jingleballicks, ordered him out, and told him never to return. Then Doc fought with the expressman over the quality of the service he had been getting, although it hadn't varied in ten years. Finally he let the word be passed that he was working and did not want to see anyone from Cannery Row or anyplace else. He sat over his yellow pad, the neat pile of Suzy's sharpened pencils beside him, and in his eyes the bleak look of shock.

Suzy was at once the cause and the victim of the disintegration of the Row. It cannot be said that trouble builds character, for just as often it destroys character. But if certain character traits, mixed with certain dreams, are subjected to the fire, sometimes . . . sometimes . . .

Ella, the waitress-manager of the Golden Poppy, was no less tired at ten in the morning than at midnight. She was always tired. She not only accepted this but thought everybody was that way. She could not conceive of feet that did not hurt, of a back that did not ache, or of a cook with a good disposition. At breakfast the row of gobbling mouths ruined her appetite and she never got it back. In the slack time around ten she cleaned and mopped the moist restaurant and swept the crumbs from under the counter stools.

Joe Blaikey came in for his morning coffee.

"Just making a fresh pot. Want to wait?" Ella said.

"Sure," said Joe. "Say, Ella, you heard what happened down in Cannery Row Saturday night?"

"No. What?"

"I don't know. There was a party. I was going to it. Time I got there it was over. Nobody wants to talk about it."

"I didn't hear," said Ella. "Fight, you think?"

"Hell no. They'd talk about a fight. They love a fight. Everybody seems to feel kind of ashamed of something. Let me know if you hear anything, will you?"

"Okay. Coffee's about ready, Joe."

Suzy came in, dressed in her San Francisco suit—gray herringbone tweed, very neat and smart. She sat down on a stool.

"Hi," said the cop.

"Hi," said Suzy. "Cup of coffee."

"Just going through the grounds now. Say, that's a cute outfit," said Ella.

"Frisco," said Suzy.

"You moving out?"

"No," said Suzy, "I'm staying."

Joe said, "What happened down on the Row the other night?"

Suzy shrugged her shoulders.

"You won't talk neither, huh?"

"Nope."

"Damnedest thing I ever saw!" said Joe. "Mostly they'd break their necks to tell. Suzy, if anybody got killed you better spill it. You ever hear of that material-witness stuff?"

"Nobody got killed," said Suzy. And then, "Your name's Ella, ain't it?"

"Till now."

"Remember you said you wasn't never off shift?"

"Well, I ain't," said Ella.

"Would you give me a try? Watch me a couple weeks. Then maybe you could go to a movie."

"Sister, you come to the wrong place. This joint don't make enough profit to hire no waitress."

"I'll do it for my meals, and I don't eat much."

Joe Blaikey looked away. It was his method of paying attention.

Ella said, "What's the gag, sister?"

"No gag. I want a job and I'll sling hash for my keep."

Joe turned his head back slowly. "You'd better tell—" he suggested.

"Sure I'll tell," said Suzy. "I'm going to fix myself up and I ain't going to run away to do it."

"What made up your mind?"

"That ain't none of your business. Is it against the law?"

"Happens so seldom it ought to be," said Joe.

"Come on, Ella," Suzy begged, "give me a break."

Ella asked, "What do you think, Joe?"

Joe's eyes went over Suzy's face. He dwelt for a moment on the dyed hair. He said, "You're letting your hair grow out?"

"Yeah."

"Give her a break, Ella," he said.

Ella smiled a tired smile. "In them clothes?"

"I'll go change. Take me maybe fifteen minutes. I can cook too, Ella. I'm a pretty good fry cook."

"Go change your clothes," said Ella.

Joe Blaikey waited in the street for Suzy to come back. He moved up beside her. "Don't bitch Ella up," he said gently.

"I won't."

"You look excited."

"Joe," said Suzy, "you remember once you said if I wanted to blow town you'd lend me the dough?"

"I thought you was staying."

"I am. I wonder could you stake me not to blow town."

"How much?"

"Twenty-five bucks."

"Where you going to live?"

"I'll let you know."

Joe said, "I staked kids before. What the hell have I got to lose?"

"You'll get it back."

"I know I will," said Joe.

The boiler that for many years had rested among the mallow weeds in the vacant lot between the Bear Flag and the grocery was the first boiler the Hediondo Cannery ever had, and the Hediondo was the first cannery Monterey ever had. When it was understood that pilchards could be placed raw in cans, doused with tomato sauce or oil, sealed and then cooked in live steam, a new industry came to Monterery. Hediondo started with small capital and skimped and pioneered its way first to success and finally to oblivion. Its first boiler for producing the cooking steam was the triumphant improvisation of William Randolph, engineer, fireman, and president. The boiler itself he got for nothing. It was the whole front end of a locomotive of the Pajaro Valley and Coast Railroad. This engine, encountering a split rail one night, leaped a trestle and dived twenty feet into a mudhole. The railroad company stripped its wheels and valves, whistle and bell, and left the great cylinder standing in the mud.

William Randolph found it, hauled it to Monterey, and set it in concrete at the new Hediondo Cannery. For years it produced low-pressure steam for cooking canned fish, while its tubes blew out at intervals and were replaced.

In 1932, when the cannery was rich and expanding, the old boiler was finally abandoned in the vacant lot to save a moving bill. Old Mr. Randolph was still alive and, although retired, he still hated waste. He stripped out the tubes, leaving only the big cylinder, sixteen feet long and seven feet in diameter. The smokestack was still on it, and its firedoor, two feet wide and eighteen inches high, still swung on rusty pins.

Many people had used the boiler for temporary shelter, but Mr. and Mrs. Sam Malloy were the first permanent residents. Mr. Malloy, who was good with his hands, after stripping out the remaining tubes, added a number of little comforts.

A boiler as a home has disadvantages as well as advantages. Some people would balk at getting down on hands and knees to crawl in through the firedoor. The floor, being rounded, makes for difficulty both in walking and in arranging furniture. The third inconvenience lies in a lack of light.

The advantages of a boiler can be listed as follows: it is absolutely rainproof; it is cozy; and it has wonderful ventilation. By adjusting the damper and firedoor you can have as much draft as you like.

Under the smokestack Mr.1 Malloy had built a little brick fireplace for cold winter nights. In addition to all of these advantages, the boiler was fireproof, windproof, earthquake-proof, and almost bombproof. These more than balanced the lack of running water, electricity, and interior plumbing.

There are those, particularly in Carmel-by-the-Sea, who say that Suzy's choice of the boiler as a home was a symbolic retreat to the womb, and, while this may be true, it is also true that this womb had economic factors. At the Golden Poppy, Suzy had her meals free, and in the boiler she had free shelter.

Suzy took the money Joe Blaikey loaned her and went to Holman's Department Store in Pacific Grove. She bought a hammer, saw, assorted nails, two sheets of plywood, a box of pale blue kalsomine and a brush, a tube of Duco cement, a pair of pink cottage curtains with blue flowers, three sheets, two pillow cases, two towels and a washcloth, a teakettle, two cups and saucers, and a box of teabags. At Joe's Surplus she bought a used army cot and mattress pad, bowl and pitcher and chamberpot, two army blankets, a small mirror, and a kerosene lamp. These supplies exhausted her capital, but at the end of her first week of work at the Golden Poppy, Suzy paid Joe back two dollars and a quarter out of tips.

The Row, in its shame, pretended not to see what was going on at the boiler or to hear the sound of hammering late at night. This was good manners rather than a lack of curiosity.

Fauna held out for ten days, and when she did give in to her natural nosiness she went secretly, late on a Tuesday night, when the Bear Flag was closed for lack of customers. From the window of the Ready Room, Fauna could see a little glow of light coming from the firedoor of the boiler. The smokestack put out a lazy curl of smoke that smelled of pine pitch. Fauna went silently out the front door and up through the mallow weeds.

"Suzy," she called softly.

"Who is it?"

"Me, Fauna."

"What do you want?"

"To see if you're all right."

"I'm all right."

Fauna got down on her knees and poked her head through the firedoor. The transformation was complete. The curving walls were pale blue, and the curtains were stuck to the walls with Duco cement. It was a pleasant feminine apartment. Suzy sat on her cot in the light from the little fireplace. She had built a dressing table for her mirror and bowl and pitcher, and beside it stood a fruit jar filled with lupines and poppies.

"You sure fixed it up nice," said Fauna. "Ain't you going to invite me in?"

"Come on in, but don't get stuck in the door."

"Give me a hand, will you?"

Suzy pulled and boosted her through the firedoor. "Here," she said, "sit down on the cot. I'm going to get a chair pretty soon."

"We could make you a hook rug," said Fauna. "That would look nice."

"No," said Suzy. "I want to do it myself. Would you like I should make you a cup of tea?"

"Don't mind if I do," said Fauna absently, and then, "You sure you ain't mad?"

"I ain't mad. You know, I never had no place of my own before."

"Well, you've fixed it up real nice," said Fauna. "I can lend you anything you need. You can use the bathroom over at the Bear Flag."

"They got a shower down at the Golden Poppy," said Suzy.

"Now look," Fauna said. "You got me down and my claws wedged. Don't put the boots to me."

"I ain't."

"This here's a nice cup of tea. I got to tell you one thing, Suzy. I don't care if you want to hear it or not. I been wrong quite a lot, but you're going about this wrong. Don't rub Doc's nose in it. That just makes a man mad."

"What are you talking about?"

"Well, settling here. He can't look out his window without you're in his hair." Fauna braced herself for the explosion, and it did not come.

Suzy looked at her hands. "I got real nice nails," she said. "Down at the Poppy where I got my hands in water all the time I squidge lotion on. Keeps them soft. Fauna, you told me not to run away, and I didn't. I felt like digging a hole in the ground and crawling in and I didn't, because I think what you said was right. I'm going to do it right here in sight."

"That ain't what I said."

"Don't bust in!" said Suzy. "You said about Doc. Now I'm telling you once, and you can tell it all over the Row if you want, then I won't have to tell it to nobody again. You just forget Doc. Doc ain't got nothing to do with me. He come along and I wasn't up to him—wasn't good enough for him. Now maybe it won't never happen again, but if it does—if there's a guy—I'm goddam well going to be good enough for him, inside and outside, public and private; but mostly I'm going to feel good enough. Now, you got that?"

"You better watch that cussing," said Fauna.

"I don't cuss no more."

"You just—"

"Don't try to mix me up," said Suzy. "Did you get what I said?"

"Why, sure, Suzy girl! But I don't see why you won't let your friends give you a hand."

"'Cause then it wouldn't be me done it. Then I wouldn't be no good."

"You borrowed dough from Joe Blaikey."

"Sure, from a cop. The same cop that was going to float me. He ain't a friend, he's a cop. When I get him paid back maybe he can be a friend."

"You sure make it tough on yourself."

"How else? You can't cut off a leg with a banana."

"You wasn't never no hustler, Suzy. At least you wasn't no good at it."

"I know what I was, and I know what I'm going to be."

"Doc?" Fauna asked.

"That's done, I tell you! Get it through your thick head—that's done!"

"Well, I guess I better be going," Fauna said unhappily. She put the teacup on the little dressing table, got down on her hands and knees, and crawled to the firedoor. "Give me a boost through, will you, Suzy?"

Suzy stuffed her through the opening the way you'd stuff a sausage. And then she called, "Fauna!"

Fauna put her head in through the door.

"You been the best friend I ever had. If I'm tough, it ain't at you, it's at me. I was always mad at everybody. Turns out it was me I was mad at. When I get friends with myself, maybe I can get friends with somebody without no chip."

Fauna said, "S'pose Doc come a-begging?"

"I ain't no mantrap," said Suzy. "I wouldn't have him if he come walking on his hands. You can't cure a sock in the puss with a sock in the puss. But if ever I like a guy again, and he lays it on the line, why, I'm going to have something to lay on the other side."

"I miss you, Suzy."

"I'll be back when I'm right. I love you."

"Oh, shut up!" said Fauna. And she clanged the firedoor shut.

30. A President Is Born

Of all our murky inventions, guilt is at once the most devious, the most comic, the most painful. Was it planted by the group pressure of the tribe to keep the potentially dangerous individual off balance? Is it set in the psycho-tissue, watered and cultivated by ductless glands? Is guilt the unconscious device by which a man cries for attention in an unperceiving world, or can it be that the final human pleasure is pain? Whatever its origin, we scream like cats in copulation, wolf-bay the moon, whip ourselves with the exquisite thorns of contempt, and generally have a hell of a good time at it.

In the pleasures and passions of guilt, Hazel should have been voted the human least likely to succeed. Guilt is a selfish pastime and Hazel had never been aware enough of himself to indulge in it. He watched life as a small boy watches a train go by—mouth open, breathing high and light, pleased, astonished, and a little confused.

Hazel had never amounted to a damn. Mack once described Hazel's education: "He done four years in grammar school and four years in reform school—and he didn't learn nothing either place."

Reform school, you see, where vice and crime are not extracurricular, failed to have any more effect on Hazel than the fourth grade had. He came out as innocent as he had gone in. Hazel didn't pay enough attention to be evil. If Mack and the boys and Doc hadn't been his friends, there's no telling what might have happened to him. Hazel thought Mack was the world's greatest human, while Doc he didn't consider human at all. Sometimes he said his prayers to Doc.

But Hazel was changing. Imperceptibly he had begun to pay attention. Perhaps Fauna had planted the germ by reading Hazel's horoscope. After his first protest he never mentioned it again, which should in itself have been suspicious.

Hazel did not want to be President of the United States. If there had been any avenue of escape he would have taken it, but his horoscope closed all doors. When a man is finally boxed and he has no choice, he begins to decorate his box. So Hazel, condemned to the presidency, since he could not escape it, began to ornament it. A man can climb high on the steps of responsibility.

Hazel began to prepare himself for the time when his call should come. He read every word of a copy of *Time* magazine, then went back to the beginning and read it again. He thought about it a great deal and came to the conclusion that it was nuts—which proves that Hazel's problem had been inattention, not unintelligence.

He bought a *World Almanac* and read the lives of the Presidents, and he began to wonder what he would do if the British impressed our sailors or the "Fifty-four-Forty" issue ever came up again.

He had accepted his duty and it made him sick. Sometimes in the morning he would awaken happy in the thought that it was a bad dream. Then he would count his toes and relapse into acceptance of his fate and his duty. What made it worst of all was the loneliness. He couldn't discuss it with anyone. He was set apart and above ordinary experience. When he had offered to fight Mack it was not in anger. He was preparing to defend the weak. When he had flown in the face of his friends, and refused to be a dwarf, and insisted on being Prince Charming, Hazel was not being vain. The dignity of his position was greater than himself. He could not let his future down.

In an ordinary time one of the boys would have noticed

Hazel's suffering face, the weariness, the pained nobility, and they would have given him two tablespoons of Epsom salts. But in these times all men's souls were being tried, and women's too, and a tried soul doesn't look around much.

Hazel's attempts to figure out what had happened at the masquerade were fruitless. He remembered how he had been dignified and beautiful and then all hell had broken loose. And the aftermath was horrible. The spirit of the Palace Flophouse, tested under the torques and stresses of so many years, was broken, shattered like granite, which withstands so long the hammer blows, then suddenly disintegrates.

Mack, who considered life hardly worse than a bad cold, was sickened to death—his eyes were lackluster and his valiant soul was shot. And if Mack was that way, you can imagine what the boys were like—jellyfish washed up on an inhospitable shore.

"What happened?" Hazel asked, and eyes glanced at him and glanced away and no one had the will to explain. For several days Hazel thought it might be the bull-bitch hangover of all time, but it continued into the day of reviving thirst and there was no thirst. Hazel began to be afraid for his friends.

He sat under the cypress tree and he not only kept his mind on the subject, he actually thought about it. It was a time for greatness, and only Hazel had the strength to rise to that bright bait. When he stood up and brushed the cypress dirt from his jeans, he had completed the change. No longer was he Hazel the Innocent, Hazel the Unaware, Hazel the Dope. His shoulders squared to take the weight, and the calm beauty of strength shone from his eyes.

It was dusky in the Palace, moldy and sad. The boys lay on their beds, listless and ruined. Mack stared up at his canopy, and he was the worst of all, for there was no expression in his face. He had not crashed in flames, he was eroding away.

When Hazel sat down quietly on the side of his bed Mack didn't even take a kick at him, although his shoes were on.

Hazel said, "Mack, Mack darling, you should shake the lead out of your pants now."

Mack did not answer, but he closed his eyes and two tears squeezed out and hung there until they dried.

Hazel said gently, "Mack, you want I should kick the hell out of you?"

Mack moved his head quietly back and forth in negation.

Hazel did not hold back. He threw his trump card in, and the hell with it. "I been over to Doc's," he said. "He's setting there with a pencil in his hand. He ain't wrote nothing. He ain't done nothing. He ain't thought nothing. Get off your behind, Mack, he needs us."

Mack spoke sepulchrally. "He needs us like a mud-dauber's nest up his pants leg. Don't blame me, Hazel. I can't fight back no more. I'm down for the count."

"What's happened, Mack?"

Mack's voice was hollow. "When we done it before we wrecked his joint and busted him, but that was mere chaff."

"How do you mean, mere chaff?"

"Oh, it was things busted—glass, records, dishes, books, stuff like that. But this time we've put a knife in his belly. If you keep trying to pat a guy on the head and instead you knock his brains out, you lose confidence." He sighed and turned over and covered his face with his arms.

"You ain't got the right to give up," Hazel said.

"I got the right to do any goddam thing I want."

"Now that sounds better!"

"Or not do nothing," said Mack.

"Look, Doc got to go to La Jolla, you know that. He got to make the spring tides next week. Then, when his new microscope comes, he'll have devilfish and write his paper. We got to help him, Mack."

"Fauna says she used to manage a welterweight name of Kiss of Death Kelly. That's me—Kiss of Death Mack. Everything I touch withers like the sere and yellow leaf."

"Get up!"

"I won't," said Mack.

"Get up, I tell you!"

Mack didn't even respond.

Hazel went outside and looked around. He walked to a broken tar barrel lying in the weeds and pulled out a curved oaken stave. He went back and stood beside Mack's bed.

He judged distance and lift. He hit Mack so hard that his pants split. And only then did Hazel realize how serious it was, for Mack didn't even move. He only groaned.

Hazel fought down panic, and then he remembered his

Fate—a sacrifice to Washington where he would have to eat oysters. "All right, Mack," he said softly. "I'll have to do her myself."

He turned and walked out of the door with quiet dignity.

Mack rolled up on one elbow. "Did you hear what that crazy bastard said? Oh, what the hell! Can't do no worse than I done. Mother, make my bed soon, for I'm sick to the death and I fain would lie down."

"You're already down," said Whitey No. 2.

31. The Thorny Path of Greatness

WHEN people change direction it is a rare one who does not spend the first half of his journey looking back over his shoulder. Hazel had chosen, or had been forced to choose, a new path. He had said, "I'll have to do her myself." It had seemed easy. But, sitting under the sheltering branches of the black cypress tree, he had to admit he didn't know who or what in the hell "she" was. He thought with longing of the old time when he was a dope, when he was cared for and thought for and loved. He had paid off, of course, by accepting ridicule, but it had been a lovely time, a warm time.

Doc had said long ago, "I like to have you sit with me, Hazel. You are the well—the original well. A man can give you his deepest secrets. You don't hear or remember. And if you did, it wouldn't make any difference because you don't pay attention. Why, you're better than a well because you listen—but you don't hear. You are a priest without penalties, an analyst without diagnosis."

Those were the good days before Hazel's responsibility. But responsibility required judgment, the choosing between courses, and what was that but thought? Hazel undertook thought, but he did it secretly. No one knew. He was a little ashamed of it. In the sweet old days he would have sat down under the black cypress and then he would have reclined with his head on his arm and in less than a minute he would have been asleep. The new Hazel clasped his knees with his arms and mourned into the future. His mind climbed and slipped like an ant in the treacherous crater of an ant lion's trap. He must plan, he must judge, he must choose. No sleep came. He didn't even itch. He had to do her. But what was she? He never knew how his solution came to him. He dropped off to sleep, forehead on knees, then suddenly his muscles leaped as though under a blow. He had a sense of falling—and there was his course laid out before him. It wasn't an honorable course, but it was the only one he had. It almost amounted to treachery.

You will remember that it was Hazel's pleasant social custom to ask questions but not to listen to the answers. People expected that, depended on it. Suppose, he thought, I was to ask and then listen but not let on I'm listening. It was sneaky, but the intention was clean and the end infinitely to be desired.

He would not only listen, he would remember, and he would put all the answers together. Maybe then he would be able to think her and do her. One question would be enough, he thought. Maybe two.

Hazel was weary from his effort. He reclined, put his head on his arm, and slept the good sleep of work well done.

32. *Hazel's Quest*

Joe Elegant came cautiously back from his journey ready to take another one at a moment's notice. He expected reprisals for Hazel's costume, and there were no reprisals. In gratitude he made popovers at the Bear Flag three evenings in a row—and the girls didn't even know what they were eating. He wanted to know what had happened but he was afraid to ask. Thus Joe Elegant was glad when Hazel called on him in his little lean-to in the rear of the Bear Flag.

"Sit here," he said. "I'll get you a piece of cake."

While he was gone Hazel regarded the works of Henri the

artist on the wall—one from the chicken-feather period and one from the later nutshell time. And he looked at the card table on which Joe Elegant worked at a portable typewriter. There was a neat pile of manuscript on the table, green paper typed with a green ribbon. A sheet of paper was in the machine. It began: "My dear Anthony West, It was sweet of you—"

Joe came back with a wedge of cake and a glass of milk for Hazel, and while Hazel munched and drank, Joe's large damp eyes bracketed him but never hit him.

"How'd it go?" he asked.

"What?"

"Why, your costume?"

"Fine, fine. Everybody was real surprised."

"I'll bet they were. Did Mack say anything?"

"He said I done fine. He almost cried."

Joe Elegant smiled with quiet malice.

Hazel asked vacuously, "Say, what would you think was the matter with Doc?"

Joe crossed his legs professionally and his fingers rippled through the green-typed green pages. "It's the whole and the part and the part is the whole," he said.

"Come again?"

"It's many things and one thing. Doc's libido is driving him one way and his conscience is pulling him another. His myth is the sea, the wind, and the tide, and he relates to it by collecting animals. He carries his treasures to his laboratory. He wants to hide them and perhaps to place the dragon Fafnir on guard."

Hazel nearly said, "He sells them," but that would have given him away as listening. "I knew a dame named Fafnir," he said. "Bertha Fafnir. Third grade. Used to do pitchers of turkeys on the blackboard Thanksgiving. Had starched underskirts, they rustled kind of."

Joe Elegant scowled faintly at the interruption. "Distill the myth and you get the symbol," he went on. "The symbol is the paper he wants to write, but that in itself has impurities, needs distillation. Why? Because it is a substitute, that's why. His symbol is false. That's why he can't write his paper. Frustration! He has taken the wrong path. And so he brings in false solutions. 'I need a microscope,' he says. 'I need to go to

La Jolla for the spring tides.' He will not go to La Jolla. He will never write his paper."

"Why not?"

"Wrong symbol. We must go back to the myth, the sea. The sea is his mother. His mother is dead but she is living. He is carrying treasures from his mother's womb and trying to save them. Do you understand?"

"Sure," said Hazel listlessly.

"He needs love. He needs understanding," said Joe Elegant.

"Who don't?" Hazel asked.

"I feel that I could help him if he would let me."

"I kind of thought he'd took a shine to Suzy," said Hazel.

Joe Elegant let a shadow of distaste tighten his mouth. "That would only be a new false path, a new frustration."

Hazel observed, "Some people like one thing, some another."

"Very original!" said Joe Elegant.

It was only a few steps from Joe Elegant's lean-to through the kitchen to the Ready Room. In the Ready Room sat Becky with her feet up, reading her mail. Becky subscribed to "Pen Pals" and had a lively correspondence all over the world. The sheet of rice paper in her hands was from Japan. "Dear Pen Pal," it began, "Your interest missive receipt. How gondola the Goldy State. Japan girl do hair-kink likewise, but not using blitch. My friend, Mitzi Mitzuki very West in minded. Would try if you mailing small little container hydrogen peroxide double pressure."

"Hi!" said Hazel.

Becky laid down her letter. "Ever been to Japan?"

"Nope."

"Me neither. How's Mack?"

"Fine. Say, Becky, what would you say was the matter with Doc?"

"Love," said Becky. "Doc's aching away. Or if he ain't, he ought to be. Nice fella like that."

"He sets like he been pole-axed."

"That'll do it. Poor fella! If it was me, why, I'd go to him and I'd put my cool hand on his brow and I'd say, 'Doc—' "

The door of Fauna's room opened. "I thought I heard

voices. Hello, Hazel. Ain't none of the other girls around? Becky's poorly."

"I come to ask you something," said Hazel.

"Well, come on in here. Set down. Want a snort? Is it private? I'll shut the door."

"Yes," said Hazel, and that covered all the questions.

The snort brightened his eye. "What would you say was wrong with Doc?"

"I wouldn't of said it a while ago," said Fauna, "but when he put on that tie—and then, the other night—"

"Hell, he was drunk," said Hazel. "A guy will say anything when he's drunk."

"No, he will not," said Fauna.

"You think it's Suzy?"

"Yes, sir! And if she wasn't nuts, she could go to La Jolla with him and help him work. Why, hell! She'd be in."

"He's trying to write his paper."

"He got himself all bollixed up," said Fauna. "I bet he ain't even thinking about his paper."

"He ain't thinking about nothing."

"That's what I mean. If he could stop not thinking about Suzy, why, he could start thinking about his paper. That's my opinion anyway."

"You think if she went to La Jolla—?"

"I do. But she won't go."

"He wouldn't take her," said Hazel.

"If everybody wasn't such damn fools he wouldn't get asked," said Fauna. "I don't know what we're coming to. Have one more snort?"

"I can't," said Hazel, "I got to see a guy."

It was only a coincidence that Joseph and Mary Rivas was also reading a letter when Hazel entered the grocery. Joseph and Mary was reading and cursing at the same time, cursing in obscure Spanish. The letter was from James Petrillo, and it spoke in no uncertain terms. If the threat in the letter could be carried out, it looked as though what the U.S. government could not do in keeping wetbacks out, the musicians' union could. The Patrón was in a stew. Ordinarily what he could not eliminate he joined. But Petrillo did not give him that choice. Joseph and Mary's mind strayed toward assassination.

Hazel said, "How're you?"

"Lousy!" said the Patrón.

"Ain't nobody feeling too good," Hazel observed. "Doc's setting over there like he's punch-drunk. What you think's the matter with him?"

"Christ knows!" said the Patrón. "I got troubles of my own. Funny thing," he said, "you know, last night I was coming home from Monterey, late, and there was a shadow up in the vacant lot. It moved into that bright spot the street light throws up by the boiler, and I swear to God it was Doc sneaking around up there."

"No!" said Hazel.

"I say yes." The Patrón looked over the vegetables and the piled canned goods and his eyes dwelt on the cardboard Coca-Cola girl in a swing. "Know something?" he said speculatively. "Before the party I would have said she was just one more tramp. Then she belted loose and moved into the boiler. And then, well—it looks like Doc seen something there. Maybe Suzy's got something I missed. I been thinking I might just take a whack at her."

"You can't," said Hazel. "She's Doc's."

"Hell," said the Patrón, "dames don't belong to nobody. I might just whistle under her window."

"She ain't got no windows," said Hazel.

The Patrón smiled. Petrillo's poison was going out of him. "Yes, sir!" he said. "Maybe I missed something."

"You stay away from her," said Hazel.

Joseph and Mary drooped his eyes, and an Indian looked out for a second. Then he smiled again. "Have it your own way," he said lightly. "I hear she's got a job."

This was the Golden Poppy: long, narrow, high-ceilinged; small octagonal tiles on the floor; dark wood counter with small round stools; units at intervals on the counter—juke-box slot, paper-napkin holder, salt, pepper, sugar, mustard, catsup; rear door to the kitchen with window and service shelf; cash register at the front, cigarette machine beside the door; long mirror behind the counter fronted by coffee maker, griddle, toasters, covered cakes and pies, stacked breakfast foods, doughnuts, rack of canned soup and soup heater, fight cards, movie schedule, bus timetable.

There was nothing to be done about the Golden Poppy. It was a dour and gloomy place dedicated to good coffee and sad, soggy food. It could not compete with the gay and phony little restaurants springing up in Monterey, with their checked tablecloths, showcard murals, low ceilings, and candles in cork floats.

The Golden Poppy did not try. There were many people who preferred it to the newcomers—customers who liked cold, damp doughnuts, stringy stews, and canned soup. These diners distrusted fishnets on the walls and jokes on the menu. To them food was a necessary but solemn sacrament about which there should be no nonsense.

The rush hours were seven to eight-thirty, breakfast; eleven-thirty to one-thirty, lunch; six to eight, dinner. In between these hours there were the coffee customers, the sandwich and doughnut people. In the evening came two rush times: at nine-thirty when the early movie let out, and at eleven-thirty when the second show broke. At twelve-thirty the Golden Poppy curled its petals, except on Saturday nights, when it stayed open until two for the early drunks.

The coming of Suzy to the Golden Poppy had a curious but reasonable effect on Ella. She had, over the years, maintained an iron interdict against weariness and pain. If she had allowed herself to realize how miserable she was she would have cut her throat.

Suzy did more than help, she took over: joked with the salesmen, whistled over the sandwich toaster, remembered that Mr. Garrigas liked cream of celery soup and remembered his name too.

For a day or so Ella had watched Suzy and refused acidly when Suzy suggested that she go home and lie down for a couple of hours. Then her interdict cracked, and the crack widened. Abysmal fatigue, aching legs, and abdominal pains crept through. Ella was an exhausted woman when she came at last to admit it. Going home to lie down for an hour was first a sin, and then a luxury, and finally a drug.

Now when Suzy said after the nine-thirty rush, "Go on home and get a good night's sleep," it seemed perfectly natural. Not only could Suzy hold the fort, but her terse, professional gaiety was drawing in new customers.

At eleven-fifteen Suzy had the four Silexes filled with fresh coffee, the hamburgers between waxed paper in the icebox, the tomatoes sliced, and the sandwich bread in the drawer below the griddle. At eleven-thirty the customers came in a rush from the second show.

Suzy grew six extra hands: club sandwiches, melted cheese sandwiches, cheeseburgers, and coffee, coffee, coffee! The cash register jangled and the change appeared standing up between the tits of the rubber mat.

"How's about a date Saturday?"

"Sure! Love to."

"Is it a date?"

"Can my husband come?"

"You married?"

"I won't be if I keep that date."

"You're a swell-looking kid."

"You're kind of pretty yourself. Here's your change."

"Keep it."

"Thanks. Cheeseburger coming up. Sorry, eighty-six on the tuna fish sandwiches."

In the seconds between orders, three of her extra hands crashed dishes into the soapy water, rinsed and dried them.

"Hey! Mr. Gelthain, you forgot your umbrella!"

"So I did. Thank you." That would be another quarter tip, and the quarter went into a slotted can marked "Joe."

Every morning when Joe Blaikey came in for his coffee a little pile of silver was put before him and checked in the account book. It was amazing how it added up.

At five minutes of twelve Hazel came in and waited against the wall until a stool was vacant.

"Hi, Hazel. What'll it be?"

"Cup of coffee."

"It's on the house, Hazel. How you been?"

"Okay."

Gradually the customers thinned out and then were gone. Suzy's flashing hands put the Golden Poppy to bed: scrubbed the grill, washed down the counter, wiped the necks of the catsup bottles. She looked up to see Hazel sweeping out.

"Say, what the hell are you doing?"

"I figured we're both going the same way. I'll walk with you."

"Why not?" said Suzy. "You can carry my books."

"What?"

"Just a joke."

"Ha, ha!" said Hazel seriously.

They walked down Alvarado Street, all closed up except where the bars splashed neon culture on the sidewalk. At the tip of the Presidio they stopped and leaned their elbows on the iron railing and looked at the fishing boats in the black water of the bay. They crossed the tracks, went past the Army warehouse, and entered the upper end of Cannery Row. And at last Hazel said, "You're a swell dame."

"Come again?"

"Say, what you think's the matter with Doc?"

"How would I know?"

"You sore at him?"

"How'd you like to mind your own business?"

"It's all right," said Hazel quickly. "I ain't bright. Everybody knows that."

"What's that got to do with keeping out of my hair?"

"Nobody pays no attention to me," said Hazel. He offered this as a recommendation. "Doc says I don't listen. He likes that."

They walked on in silence for a while. Then Hazel said timidly, "He done everything in the world for me. Once he went character witness for me and I ain't got no character. Once I'd of lost a foot, but he opened her up and shook powder on her and I still got her."

Suzy didn't answer. Their footsteps were loud on the pavement and echoed back from the iron fronts of dead canneries.

"Doc's in trouble," Hazel said.

Their footsteps filled the street.

"Anybody in trouble, why, they go to Doc. Nobody goes to him now he's in trouble."

Step, step, step.

"I got to help him," said Hazel. "But I ain't bright."

"What the hell do you want me to do?" said Suzy.

"Well, couldn't you go over and set with him?"

"No."

"If you was in trouble he'd help you."

"I ain't in trouble. How do you know he's in trouble?"

"I'm telling you. I thought you liked him."

"I like him all right. If he was in real trouble like if he was sick or bust his leg, I'd probably take him some soup."

"Jeeze! If he bust his leg he couldn't go to the spring tides," said Hazel.

"Well, he ain't busted his leg."

They passed Wide Ida's. Hazel asked, "You want a beer?"

"No, thanks." Then she said, "Ain't you going up to the Palace?"

"No," said Hazel, "I got to see a guy."

Suzy said, "Once, when I was a kid, I made an ashtray for my old man and old lady—"

"They like it?"

"They didn't need no ashtray."

"Didn't they smoke?"

"Yes," said Suzy. "Good night."

Hazel was approaching a state of collapse. In his whole life he had never sustained a thought for more than two minutes. Now his resources reeled under the strain of four hours of concentration. And it was not yet over. He had to make two more visits, and then he had to retire under the black cypress tree to sift his findings. So far he could see no light anywhere. His mental pictures were like those children's kaleidoscopes that change color and design as they are turned. It seemed to Hazel that a slight zizzing sound came from his brain.

It was a catty night. Big toms crept about, their heads and shoulders flattened to the ground, seeking other toms. Lady cats preened themselves in sweet innocence, unaware of what they hoped was likely to happen to them. On the rocks off Hopkins Marine Station the sea lions barked with a houndish quaver. The silver canneries were silent under the street lights. And from somewhere on the beach Cacahuete Rivas's trumpet softly mourned the "Memphis Blues."

Hazel had stopped for a moment in appreciation of the

secret night. He looked up at the boiler where Suzy had gone, and into the streak of street light he saw a figure move. From the shape and posture he thought it must be the Patrón. In a way it was none of Hazel's business. He walked up the stairs and knocked on the door of Western Biological.

Doc sat on his bed regarding a heap of collecting paraphernalia: nets, buckets and jars, formaldehyde and Epsom salts and menthol, rubber boots and rubber gloves, glass plates and string. On his table stood a small new traveling aquarium with a tiny pump and motor run by two dry cells. Morosely he watched the mist of white air bubbles sift through the sea water.

"Come in," he said to Hazel. "I'm glad to see you."

"Just come to pass the time of day," said Hazel.

"Good. I'm glad. A man feels silly talking to himself, and at the same time it's private. You're the perfect answer, Hazel."

"Say, Doc, I just remembered. "What's ass—astrophysic?"

"You don't really want me to tell you, do you?"

"Not very much. I just wondered. I signed up for it."

Doc shuddered. "I don't think I want to hear about that," he said.

"I brang you a pint."

"That's friendly of you. Will you join me?"

"Sure," said Hazel. "You're really going to La Jolla, huh?"

"Well, I guess I have to. That's one of the things I've been trying to figure out. I've made such a stink about it."

"Lot of people think you won't go."

"Well, that's one of the reasons I have to."

"Don't you want to?"

"I don't know," said Doc softly.

He got up from the bed and disengaged a wire from the dry cell. "No point in wasting juice," he said. "I've been tearing myself down like a Model T Ford in a backyard. Got the pieces all laid out. Still don't know why it won't run. Don't even know whether I can get it together again."

"I could help," said Hazel. "I know about Model T's."

"It might turn out you know about people too," said Doc.

Hazel looked shyly down at his feet. No one had ever accused him of knowing anything before.

Doc chuckled. "That's my good Hazel!"

"Say, Doc, what you think is the matter with you?" Hazel was appalled at his daring, but he had asked. And Doc seemed to find the question reasonable.

"God knows," he said. "Some kind of obscure self-justification, I guess. I wanted to make a contribution to learning. Maybe that was a substitution for fathering children. Right now, my contribution, even if it came off, seems kind of weak. I think maybe I've talked myself into something, and now maybe I have to do it."

Hazel groped among his bits and pieces. "Mack's sorry about what him and Fauna done. He's just sick."

"He shouldn't be," said Doc. "I'm the one who messed it up."

"You mean you would of took Suzy on?"

"I guess so. I've thought about it ever since. For a couple of days there I felt different and better than I ever have in my life. A kind of built-in pain was gone. I felt wide open."

"About Suzy?"

"I guess so. I'm supposed to have this wild free brain without conventional barriers. And what did I do? I balanced a nasty ledger. I weighed education, experience, background, even probable blood lines. Some of the worst people I ever knew had the best of all those. Well, there it is. Saying it has made it even clearer. I guess I've thrown it away."

"Why don't you give it one more try, Doc?"

"How?"

"Why don't you take a candy bar or a bunch of carnations and knock on her door?"

"Right from the beginning, huh? Sounds kind of silly."

"Well, dames is all dame," said Hazel.

"You may have made a discovery. Have you seen her?"

"Yeah. She got that boiler fixed up real pretty. She got a job down at the Golden Poppy."

"How is she? What did she say?"

Hazel cast about again among his broken pieces. Her vehemence came back to him. "When she was a kid she made an ashtray for her papa and mama—" Hazel let it hang there because it sounded ridiculous.

"Well, what about it?"

"They didn't need no ashtray," said Hazel.

"She told you that?"

"Yep."

"Let's have a drink."

"I can't, Doc. I got one more—I mean, I got to see a guy."

"This late at night?"

"Yeah." And then Hazel confessed. "You been good to me, Doc. I wouldn't do no bad thing to you."

"Of course you wouldn't."

"But I done it."

"What!"

"Remember you always said you liked me 'cause I didn't listen?"

"Sure I remember."

Hazel's eyes were shy and ashamed. "I listened," he said.

"That's all right."

"Doc—"

"Yes?"

"Joseph and Mary's hanging around the boiler."

Hazel couldn't remember ever having been so tired. He had put his mind to unaccustomed tricks, and it was just as he had been afraid it would be. He had got nothing. He had started out hoping to find some kind of light to guide him. What he had got reminded him of Henri's painting in nutshells. He wanted to sleep a long time, perhaps never to awaken to a world in which he now felt himself a stranger. He had made a mess of it. He wondered if he would make as bad a mess in Washington.

He walked wearily through the vacant lot and up the chicken walk to the Palace Flophouse. He wanted to slip into bed in the dark and hide his failure in sleep.

Mack and the boys were waiting up for him.

"Where the hell you been?" said Mack. "We looked all over for you."

"Just walking around," said Hazel listlessly.

Mack moved and groaned. "Jesus! You hit me a crack," he said. "Damn near killed me."

"I shouldn't of did it," said Hazel. "You want I should rub it?"

"Hell no! What you been up to? When you get making plans, the sky is falling on my tail, said Henny Penny."

Whitey No. 2 asked, "Who you been with?"

"Everybody. Just walking around."

"Well, who?"

"Oh, Joe Elegant and Fauna and Suzy and Doc."

"You seen Suzy?" Mack demanded.

"Sure. Went down to the Poppy for a cup of coffee."

"Look who's buying coffee!"

"It was on the house," said Hazel.

"Well, what did she say?"

"She says in the third grade she made an ashtray."

"Oh, Jesus!" said Mack. "Did she say anything about Doc?"

"Yeah, I guess so."

"You guess so!"

"Don't ask me if you're going to be mean to me. That'll just get *me* mean."

Mack shifted painfully to his other buttock.

Hazel felt ringed with hostility. "I guess I'll go outside," he said miserably.

"Wait! What'd she say about Doc?"

"Said she didn't want no part of him, except—I'm going to go on out."

"Except what?"

"Except he got sick or bust a leg."

Mack shook his head. "Sometimes you get me thinking the way you do. God Almighty! I shouldn't of let you out alone."

"I didn't do no harm."

"I bet you didn't do no good neither. I bet right now you're trying to figure out germ warfare—how to get Doc sick."

"I'm tired," said Hazel. "I just want to go to bed."

"Who's stopping you?"

Hazel didn't even take off his clothes before he went to bed, but he didn't sleep either; at least not until the dawn crept out from Salinas. His brain was blistered and his responsibility rode him with surcingle and spurs.

33. *The Distant Drum*

Doc sat for a long time after Hazel left him. His chest rustled with feeling and his throat was dry. His top mind looked at him—a scientist, a thinker trained, conditioned to method, to exactness. No single thing could be permitted in unless it could be measured or tasted or heard or seen. The laws of science were Doc's laws, and he sought to obey them. To break these laws was not only a sin to him but a danger, for violation would let in anarchy. He was frightened and cold.

His middle mind screamed with joy at his discomfiture. "I told you! All through the years I've told you you were fooling yourself. Let's see you get back to analysis, I dare you!"

And the low-humming mind in his entrails was busy too, aching and yet singing that the ache was necessary and good.

Middle mind had its way. Doc thought, Let's look at this. Here is a man with work to do. The girl—what is she? Let's suppose every good thing should come of a relationship with her. It still would be no good. There is no possible way for this girl and me to be successful—no way under the sun. Not only is she illiterate, but she has a violent temper. She has all of the convictions of the uninformed. She is sure of things she has not investigated, not only sure for herself, but sure for everyone. In two months she will become a prude. Then where will freedom go? Your thinking will be like tennis against a bad player. Let's stop this nonsense! Forget it! You can't have it and you don't want it.

Middle mind hooted, "You can't *not* have it too. Whatever happens, you've got her. Take a feel of your pulse, listen to your pounding heart. Why? You just heard the iron door of the boiler clang, that's why. You haven't even thought what that means yet, but you've got a pain in your gut because of that clang and because it's three-thirteen in the morning."

Low mind said, "Nothing's bad. It's all part of one thing—the good and bad. Do you know any man and woman—no matter how close—who don't have good and bad? Let me out! Or, by God, I'll set my claws in you and I'll tear at you for all your life! Let me out, I say! Feel this, this red burning? That's rage. Will you let it out or will it fester here until it makes you sick and crazy? Look at the time. You heard that iron door."

Doc looked at his watch—3:17. "Why that son-of-a-bitch!" he said aloud. He snapped off his light and went to the window and looked out toward the strip of light the street lamp threw on the vacant lot. Then he opened his front door and crept down the stairs. Crossing the street, he followed a broad shadow and hid in it.

The Patrón was sitting on a big rusty pipe trying to work out a puzzle. He had it laid out and the pieces didn't make sense. Here was himself, young, good-looking, snappy dresser, and making dough. And here was a dame, a dime-a-dozen dame, living in a boiler, working for her keep. The Patrón knew methods too, and, if not scientific, they had served him well enough so that he could depend on them. You sweet talk, you promise, you offer, and in reserve you always hold force. Every dame needs a little force. He felt the swelling knuckles of his right hand. This dame was nuts. She didn't listen to his pitch, and when he brought up force she slammed the iron door and damn near took his fingers off. He was going to lose the nails of all four fingers. The dirty bitch! Thus, musing bitterly, he did not hear Doc's approach.

Doc's fingers locked in the collar of the Patrón's striped shirt and yanked him to his feet. By reflex the Patrón lashed out with his foot and kicked Doc's legs from under him. The two fell together and rolled in the mallow weeds. Joseph and Mary tried for the groin with his knee, while Doc's delicate strong fingers laced around the throat. The Patrón felt the thumbs seeking the hollow below his Adam's apple. He tore at the white face with his fingers and Doc's thumbs went home. Flaring lights whirled in the Patrón's eyes and his brain turned red. He knew that in two seconds his thorax would collapse under the thumbs and he would be dead. He had seen it happen. He knew it and, so knowing, he went limp and in sweating terror felt the thumbs relax.

The Patrón lay still, and his sickened mind figured the chances—the groin again or butt of head to chin? But if he missed the terrible thumbs would come again. He was weak and afraid—afraid even to speak for fear the wrong word might draw the seeking thumbs. "Doc," he whispered, "I give up. You got me."

"Go near that girl again and I'll tear your throat out," Doc whispered back.

"I won't. I swear to God I won't."

In the grocery under the seven-watt light, the Patrón tried to get the cork out of a pint with his mashed fingers but had to pass the bottle to Doc.

Doc felt the sickness that follows rage—and he also felt silly. He took a gulp of whisky and passed the bottle over the counter. Joseph and Mary drank and then bent over, coughing and spluttering. Doc had to run around the counter to beat him on the back. When he could speak, Joseph and Mary looked at Doc with wonder.

"I can't understand it," he said. "Where'd you learn that trick? What'd you want to do it for? You might of killed me."

"I guess I wanted to," said Doc. "I must have wanted to." He laughed embarrassedly. "I thought you were making a pass at Suzy."

"I was," said Joseph and Mary. "Jesus, Doc, I didn't know you was that way with her."

"I'm not," said Doc. "Give me a drink."

"You wasn't playing tiddlywinks," said Joseph and Mary. "Now don't get excited. She give me the bum's rush. Hell, she damn near took off my fingers with that door. You ain't got any competition from me, Doc. She's all yours."

"She won't even see me," said Doc.

"Won't? What in hell *is* the matter with her?"

"Who knows?"

They rested their elbows on the counter and faced each other.

"Beats me," said Joseph and Mary. "What you going to do?"

Doc smiled. "Hazel said take her flowers and a candy bar."

"He might have something there. I can't figure her." Gingerly the Patrón let a little whisky dribble down his throat and winced as it passed the bruised place. "I guess she's just nuts," he said. "And if she's nuts, a guy's got to do nuts things. You don't think you could say the hell with her?"

"I have, over and over."

"Don't do no good?"

"Not a bit. I know it's damn foolishness, but there it is."

"I knew guys like that. There ain't nothing to do about it, I guess." His eyes sharpened. "I remember something," he said. "When I was talking to her through that damn firedoor tonight she says, 'When I find a guy that's up to his eyes I'll dive in,' she says. And I says, 'For Doc?' 'Hell no!' she says. 'He's sliced like package bacon.' "

"I guess she's right," said Doc.

"That ain't what I was thinking. Look, Doc, when you had the hooks in me, if I'd went on—well, would you of?"

"I guess so. I can hardly believe it of myself, but I guess I would have. I never did anything like that before. Why?"

"Well, I just thought—a guy that'll do a killing with his hands ain't sliced too thin. Let's finish the pint, Doc, and then I'll help you."

"Help me what?"

"Flowers," said Joseph and Mary. "We got an hour before daylight. Up above Lighthouse Avenue there's front yards just lousy with flowers."

34. *The Deep-Dish Set-Down*

Joe Elegant was only the cook at the Bear Flag, not the bouncer, with the result that his services were never required late at night. He retired early and set his alarm clock for four. This gave him three or four hours every morning over his portable to tap out green letters on green paper.

The book was going well. His hero had been born in a state of shock and nothing subsequent had reassured him. When a symbol wasn't slapping him in the mouth, a myth was kicking his feet out from under him. It was a book of moods, of dank rooms with cryptic wallpaper, of pale odors, of decaying dreams. There wasn't a character in the whole of *The Pi Root of Oedipus* who wouldn't have made the observation ward. The hero had elderly aunts beside whom the Marquis de Sade was an altar boy. The pile of green manuscript was three inches thick, and Joe Elegant was beginning to plan his photograph for the back of the dust cover: open collar, he thought, and a small, wry smile, and one hand relaxed in front of him with an open poison ring on the third finger. He knew which reviewers he could depend on and why. He typed: "A pool scummed with Azolla. In the open water in the middle of the pond a dead fish floated belly up . . ."

Joe Elegant sighed, leaned back, and scratched his stomach. He yawned, went into the Bear Flag's kitchen, and started a pot of coffee. While it was heating he walked out into a glorious morning. The pelicans were drumming in for a run of tom cod, and little pink Kleenex clouds hung over the bay. Joe saw the flowers in front of the boiler door and moved over to inspect them—a huge bouquet of tulips, early roses, jonquils, and iris. They might have been anyone's offering, except that their stems were in a museum jar.

Joe Elegant's life had not been in danger since the engagement and raffle party, but he hadn't felt much friendliness in Cannery Row either. He carried his news into the Bear Flag and served it to Fauna on a tray along with her coffee and crullers. By eight o'clock the news was in the Palace Flophouse, and the early men were ingesting it with their whisky sours at the La Ida.

The best seats were in the Ready Room with its windows overlooking the vacant lot. Mack was there behind a drape, munching Fauna's crullers. The girls were there in their best kimonos. Becky had put on her mules with the ostrich feathers. At eight-thirty the audience heard the boiler door screech and shushed one another.

Suzy, on her hands and knees, poked her head out of the firedoor and rammed her nose into the giant floral tribute. For a long moment she stared at the flowers, and then she reached out and dragged them inside. The iron door closed after her.

At nine o'clock Suzy re-emerged and walked rapidly toward Monterey. At nine-thirty she was back. She went into the boiler and in a moment came out, pushing her suitcase ahead of her. The audience was filled with dismay, but only for a moment. Suzy climbed the steps and rang the bell at the Bear Flag. Fauna chased the girls to their rooms and Mack out the back way before she answered the door.

Suzy said, "You told me I could use your bathroom."

"Help yourself," said Fauna.

In an hour, when the splashing had ceased, Fauna knocked on the bathroom door. "Want a little toilet water, honey?"

"Thanks," said Suzy.

In a few minutes she emerged, scrubbed and shining.

"Like a cup of coffee?" Fauna asked.

"Wish I could," said Suzy. "I got to run. Thanks for the bath. There ain't nothing like a good deep-dish set-down bath."

Fauna, from behind a drape, watched her crawl back into the boiler.

In her office bedroom Fauna scribbled a note and sent it by Joe Elegant to Western Biological. It read: "She ain't going to work today."

35. Il n'y a pas de Mouches sur la Grandmère

Doc laid his best clothes out on his cot. There were pale acid spots on the washed khaki trousers, the white shirt was yellow with age, and he noticed for the first time that his old tweed jacket was frayed through at both elbows. The tie he had worn to the dinner at Sonny Boy's was spotted. He found a black army tie in the bottom of his suitcase. For the first time in his life he was dissatisfied with his clothing. It was silly to feel serious about it, but there was no doubt that he was serious. For a time he sat down and regarded his wardrobe and his life, and he found them both ridiculous. And not less ridiculous was the quaking certainty that he was frightened.

He spoke aloud to the rattlesnakes, and they ran out their forked tongues to listen.

"You are looking at a fool," he said. "I am a reasonable man, a comparatively intelligent man—IQ one hundred and eighty-two, University of Chicago, Master's and Ph.D. An informed man in his own field and not ignorant in some other fields. Regard this man!" he said. "He is about to pay a formal call on a girl in a boiler. He has a half-pound box of chocolates for her. This man is scared stiff. Why? I'll tell you why. He is afraid this girl will not approve of him. He is terrified of her. He knows this is funny, but he cannot laugh at it."

The eyes of the snakes looked dustily at him—or seemed to.

Doc went on, "Let me put it this way: there is nothing I can do. They say of an amputee that he remembers his leg. Well, I remember this girl. I am not whole without her. I am not alive without her. When she was with me I was more alive than I have ever been, and not only when she was pleasant either. Even when we were fighting I was whole. At the time I didn't realize how important it was, but I do now. I am not a dope. I know that if I should win her I'll have many horrible times. Over and over, I'll wish I'd never seen her. But I also know that if I fail I'll never be a whole man. I'll live a gray half-life, and I'll mourn for my lost girl every hour of the rest of my life. As thoughtful reptiles you will wonder, 'Why not wait? Look further! There are better fish in the sea!' But you are not involved. Let me tell you that to me not only are there no better fish, there are no other fish in the sea at all. The sea is lonely without this fish. Put that in your pipe and smoke it!"

He took off his clothes and had a shower and scrubbed himself until his skin was soap-burned and red. He brushed his teeth until his gums bled. His hands were frayed with formaline, but he gouged at his discolored nails just the same, and he brushed at his overgrown hair and he shaved so close that his face was on fire. At last he was ready—and still he looked for things to do, to put off his departure.

His stomach was crowding up against his chest, forcing him to breathe shallowly. I should take a big slug of whisky, he thought. But it would be on my breath and she would know why I'd taken it. I wonder if she's frightened too? You never know. Women can conceal these things better than men. Oh God, what a fool I am! I can't go this way. I'm falling to pieces. My voice would tremble. Why, the little—no, don't do that. You can't build your courage by running her down. You're going to her, not she to you. Why do I say "you" when it is "I"? Am I afraid of "I"?

And then he knew what to do. He went to his records and he found the *Art of the Fugue*. If I can't get courage from his greatness, he thought, I might as well give up. He sat unmoving while Bach built a world and peopled it and organized it and finally fought his world and was destroyed by it. And when the music stopped, as the man had stopped when death came to him, stopped in the middle of a phrase, Doc had his courage back. "Bach fought savagely," he said. "He was not defeated. If he had lived he would have gone on fighting the impossible fight."

Doc cried to no one, "Give me a little time! I want to think. What did Bach have that I am hungry for to the point of starvation? Wasn't it gallantry? And isn't gallantry the great art of the soul? Is there any more noble quality in the human than gallantry?" He stopped and then suddenly he seemed to be wracked with inner tears. "Why didn't I know before?" he asked. "I, who admire it so, didn't even recognize it when I saw it. Old Bach had his talent and his family and his friends. Everyone has something. And what has Suzy got? Absolutely nothing in the world but guts. She's taken on an atomic world with a slingshot, and, by God, she's going to win! If she doesn't win there's no point in living any more.

"What do I mean, win?" Doc asked himself. "I know. If you are not defeated, you win."

Then he stabbed himself in vengeance for having run Suzy down. "I know what I'm doing. In the face of my own defeat I'm warming myself at her gallantry. Let me face this clearly, please! I need her to save myself. I can be whole only with Suzy."

He stood up and he did not feel silly any more and his mission was not ridiculous. "So long," he said to the rattlesnakes. "Wish me luck!" He took his box of candy and went jauntily down the steps of Western Biological. Crossing the street, he knew he was being observed from every window from which he was visible, and he didn't care. He waved a salute to his unseen audience.

Going through the vacant lot among the mallow weeds, he thought, How do you knock on an iron door? He stooped and picked a rusty tenpenny nail from the ground and he arrived almost gaily at the boiler and tapped a little drumbeat on the iron wall. The firedoor was slightly ajar.

Suzy's voice sounded with a metallic ring. "Who is it?"

"It's I," said Doc. "Or me—somebody like that."

The firedoor opened and Suzy looked out. "Thanks for the flowers," she said.

"I brought you another present."

She looked at the candy box in his hand. Being on her hands and knees, she had to twist her neck to look up at him. Doc couldn't tell whether there was suspicion and doubt on her face or only strained muscles from her position.

"Candy?" she asked.

"Yes."

"I don't—" she began, and then Fauna's words crowded in on her with short punches. "What the hell," she said. "Thanks."

Doc was losing his poise. Suzy had straightened her neck and from her position she couldn't see above his knees. Doc tried for lightness again, and he sounded clumsy to himself. "This is a formal call," he said. "Aren't you going to ask me in?"

"Do you think you can get in?"

"I can try."

"There ain't much room inside."

Doc remained silent.

"Oh, for God's sakes come on in!" said Suzy. She backed her head out of the opening.

Doc got down on his hands and knees. He threw the candy box through the firedoor, then crawled through the opening. He thought with amusement, A man who can do this with dignity need never again fear anything, and at that moment his trouser cuff caught on the door and pulled it closed against his ankle. He was all inside except one foot and he could not free himself. "I seem to be hung up," he said.

"Hold it," said Suzy. She straddled him and worked the cuff loose from the door corner. "I think you tore your pants," she said as she backed off over his shoulders. "Maybe I can mend 'em for you."

Doc's eyes were getting used to the dim interior. A little light came in from the smokestack and met a little more that entered from the firedoor.

"It's hard to see at first," said Suzy. "I got a lamp here. Wait, I'll light it up."

"No need," said Doc. He could see now and something in him collapsed with pity at the pretension of the curtains, the painted walls, and the home-built dressing table with its mirror and bottles. My God, what a brave thing is the human! he thought. And then Suzy brought his rising compassion crashing down.

"There's a welder eats at the Poppy. Know what he's going to do first any day he can? Bring his torch and cut windows in the sides."

Her voice echoed with enthusiasm. "I'll put in little window frames and some flower boxes with red geraniums," she said. " 'Course, I'll have to paint the outside then, white, I think, with green trim. Maybe a trellis like in front. I got a nice hand with roses."

Then she was silent. Constraint and formality sifted in and filled the boiler.

Doc thought in wonder, It's not a boiler at all. Somehow she has managed to make a home of this. He said, "You've done a wonderful job here."

"Thanks."

He spoke his thought. "It's a real home."

"It's comfortable," she said. "I never had no room of my own."

"Well, you have now."

"Sometimes I set in here and think how they'd have to blast to get me out if I didn't want to come."

Doc gathered his courage. "Suzy, I'm sorry for what happened."

"I don't want to talk about it. It wasn't none of your fault."

"Yes, it was."

"I don't think so," she said with finality.

"I would do anything to—"

"Look, Doc," she said, "you won't let it alone, so maybe I got to rub your nose in it a little. It wasn't no fault of yours, but it sure as hell give me a lesson. I had myself a bawl and now it's done. There ain't nothing for you to do. I don't need nothing. Anybody's sorry for me, they're wasting their time. I ain't never had it so good in my life. Got that? Well, don't forget it! There ain't nothing for you nor nobody to do 'cause I'm doing it all myself. If you can get that through your knocker, okay. If you can't, you better take a powder."

He said, "What a conceited fool I've been!"

Then silence hung in the boiler. Suzy broke it when she felt that his nose was sufficiently rubbed in it.

"Know what?" she said brightly. "They got a night class, typing, at the high school. I signed up. Next Saturday I get a rent typewriter. I can learn."

"I'll bet you can too. Maybe you'll type my paper for me."

"You're going to write it after all?"

"I've got to, Suzy. It's all I have. I'm a dead duck without it. I'm going to La Jolla Saturday for the spring tides. I'm glad. Are you?"

"Why not?" she asked. "I don't like to see nobody kicked in the face." She drew up formality like a coverlet. "You want I should make you a nice cup of tea? I got a Sterno stove."

"I'd like it."

She had the situation in hand now, and she talked on easily while she lighted the stove and put her little teakettle on to boil.

"I'm making good tips down at the Poppy," she said. "Paid off Joe Blaikey in two weeks. Ella's thinking about taking a week's vacation. She ain't never had a vacation. Hell, I can run the joint easy. 'Scuse that 'hell.' I don't hardly never cuss no more."

"You're doing fine," said Doc. "Could you tell me, without rubbing my nose in it, what you want in a man? Might help me—another time."

"Tea's ready," said Suzy. She passed him the steaming cup. "Leave it steep a little longer," she said. "Sugar's in the cup on the dressing table."

When he was stirring the sugar in she said, "If I thought it wasn't a pitch you was making I'd tell you."

"I don't think it's a pitch."

"Okay then. Maybe what I want ain't anywhere in the world, but I want it, so I think there is such a thing. I want a guy that's wide open. I want him to be a real guy, maybe even a tough guy, but I want a window in him. He can have his dukes up every other place but not with me. And he got to need the hell out of me. He got to be the kind of guy that if he ain't got me he ain't got nothing. And brother, that guy's going to have something!"

"Except for toughness, you're kind of describing me," said Doc.

"You keep out of this! You told me and I was too dumb to listen. You like what you got. You told me straight. I'd spoil it. Took me a long time to wise up, but I sure wised up."

"Maybe what I said wasn't true."

"When you said it with your face it was true all right."

Doc felt beaten. There was no anger in her tone, nothing but acceptance, together with an undertone of excitement. That was it, excitement, almost amounting to gaiety.

He said, "You know, Suzy, you sound happy."

"I am," said Suzy. "And you know who done it for me?"

"Who?"

"Fauna. That's a hunk of dame! She made me proud, and I ain't never been proud before in my life."

"How did she do it?" Doc asked. "I need some of that myself."

"She told me, and made me say it—'There ain't nothing in the world like Suzy'—and she says Suzy is a good thing. And goddam it, it's true! Now let's knock it off, huh?"

"Okay," said Doc. "I guess I ought to be going."

"Yeah," said Suzy, "I got to go to work. Say, remember that guy you told me about that lived out where we went that night?"

"The seer? Sure, what about him?"

"Joe Blaikey had to pick him up."

"What for?"

"Stealing. From the Safeway store. Joe hated to do it."

"I'll see what I can do. So long, Suzy."

"You ain't mad?"

"No, Suzy, but I'm sorry."

"So'm I. But hell, you can't have everything. So long, Doc. Hope you do good at La Jolla."

When Doc crossed the street this time he hoped no one was watching. He went into the laboratory, walked to his cot, and lay down. He was sick with loss. He couldn't think. Only one thing was sure: he had to go to La Jolla. If he didn't he would die, because there would be nothing left in him to believe in, even to defend. He squinched his eyes closed and looked at the bright points of light swimming on his retinas.

There were footsteps on his porch and the snakes whirred their rattles but not violently.

Hazel opened the door and looked in. He saw Doc's expression and the hope died out of him.

"No soap?" he asked.

"No soap," said Doc.

"There got to be some way."

"There isn't," said Doc.

"Anything I can do?"

"No. Yes, there is too. You know Joe Blaikey?"

"The cop? Sure."

"Well, he picked up a man in the sand dunes. Find Joe and tell him I'm interested in the man. Tell him to be nice to him. I'll be down to see him as soon as I can. Tell Joe the man is harmless." Doc rolled on his side and dug in his pocket. "Here's two dollars. Ask Joe to let you see the man and give him—no, stop at the Safeway and buy a dozen candy bars and take them to the seer and then give him the change."

"Seer?"

"That's the man's name," said Doc wearily.

"I'll do her right now," Hazel said proudly. He went out at a dogtrot.

Doc was arranging himself comfortably in his misery again when there was a knock on the door.

"Come in," he cried.

There was no answer but a second knock and a wild buzzing from the snakes.

"Oh Christ!" said Doc. "I hope not schoolchildren on a culture tour."

It was a telegram, a long one, collect. It said:

EUREKA! GREEK WORD MEANING I HAVE FOUND IT. YOU ARE NOW AN INSTITUTION. HAVE SET UP CEPHALOPOD RESEARCH SECTION AT CALIFORNIA INSTITUTE OF TECHNOLOGY. YOU ARE IN CHARGE. SIX THOUSAND A YEAR AND EXPENSES. GET TO WORK ON YOUR DEVILFISH. AM MAKING ARRANGEMENTS FOR YOU TO READ PAPER CALIFORNIA ACADEMY SCI-

ENCES AT END OF YEAR. ALL CLEARLY DEDUCTIBLE. CONGRATULATIONS. WISH I COULD HEAR YOUR WORDS WHEN YOU HAVE TO PAY FOR THIS WIRE.

Doc laid the telegram beside him on the cot. "The son-of-a-bitch," he said.

36. Lama Sabachthani?

HAZEL sat on the end of the steel cot in the Monterey jail and looked with interest at the seer.

"Open up one of them Baby Ruths," he said. "If you're a friend of Doc's, can't nothing bad happen to you."

"I don't know him," said the seer.

"Well, he knows you. That's your good luck."

"I don't know any doctors."

"He ain't that kind. He's a doctor of bugs and stuff like that."

"Oh yes, I do remember. I gave him dinner."

"And he give you candy bars."

"I probably won't eat them."

"Why, for Chrissake, not?"

"Tell my friend Doc that greed poisoned me. I love candy bars. I stole only one at a time and eased my conscience of a little crime. But yesterday an appetite like a whip overcame me. I stole three. The manager of the Safeway says he knew I was stealing one at a time. He let it go. But when I took three he couldn't let it pass. I don't blame him. Who knows what I would have done next? Some other appetite might have driven me. I'll punish myself by smelling these bars and not eating them."

"I think you're nuts!" said Hazel.

"I guess so. I have no basis of comparison so I don't know how other people feel."

"You talk a little like Doc," said Hazel. "I don't get none of it."

"How is he?"

"Not too hot. He got troubles."

"Yes, I could see that. I remember now. He wore loneliness like a shroud. I was afraid for him."

"Jesus, you do talk like him! He got dame trouble."

"That was bound to be. When a man is cold he looks for warmth. When he is lonely there's only one cure. Why doesn't he take the woman?"

"She won't have him unless."

"I see. Sometimes they're that way."

"Who?"

"Women. What do you mean, unless?"

Hazel looked at the seer with level penetrating eyes. This man talked like Doc. Maybe he could help. But with this thought there came also caution.

"I'd like to ask you something," Hazel said.

"What?"

"Well, this ain't none of it true. It's a kind of a—a what-chamacallit—"

"Hypothetical question?"

"I guess so."

"S'pose there's a guy and he's in trouble."

"Yes?"

"Well, he can't get out of it. But he got a friend maybe he don't know about."

"That's you," said the seer.

"No it ain't! It's some other guy. I forget his name." He hurried on, "Well, s'pose the guy's in trouble and there's one way he can get out but he can't do it. You think his friend ought to do it?"

"Certainly."

"Even if it hurt like hell?"

"Certainly."

"Even if it might maybe not work?"

"Certainly. I don't know what the situation is with your Doc, but I know how it should be with you. If you love him you must do anything to help him—anything. Even kill him to save him incurable pain. This is the highest and most terrible duty of friendship. I gather that what you must do is violent. You must first make sure it can be successful, and you must, second, make sure within yourself that you know you will be punished. It is quite possible that even if you are successful your friend will never speak to you again. That takes a lot of love—maybe the greatest love. Make sure you love him that much."

Hazel caught his breath. "Hell, there ain't no such guy. It's hypa—it's malarky, a kind of a riddle."

"I guess you do love him that much," the seer said.

No one knows how greatness comes to a man. It may lie in his blackness, sleeping, or it may lance into him like those driven fiery particles from outer space. These things, however, are known about greatness: need gives it life and puts it in action; it never comes without pain; it leaves a man changed, chastened, and exalted at the same time—he can never return to simplicity.

Under the black cypress tree Hazel writhed on the ground. From between his clenched teeth came little whimpers. As the night drew on and the moon went down leaving blackness, so desolation fell on Hazel, so that he cried out against the agony of his greatness as that Other did, feeling forsaken.

Hour after hour the struggle went on, and only about three o'clock in the morning was Hazel saturated. Then he accepted it as he had accepted the poisoned presidency of the United States. He was calm, for there was no escape. If anyone had seen him it would have been a dull man who did not find him beautiful.

Hazel picked his chosen instrument from the ground—an indoor-ball bat. He crept like a night-colored cat out of the black shadow of the cypress tree.

In less than three minutes he returned. He lay on his stomach under the tree and wept.

37. Little Chapter

Dr. Horace Dormody hated night calls, like everybody else, but Doc was his friend and he responded to the frenzied voice on the telephone. In the lab he looked at Doc's white face and then at his right arm.

"It's broken all right. I don't know how badly. Think you could get to my car? I want to X-ray."

And later he said, "Well, that's that. It's clean and it will take time. Now, tell me your cock-and-bull story again."

"I was asleep," said Doc. "Only thing I can think is that I must have turned over and it was caught between the cot and the wall."

"You mean you weren't in a fight?"

"I tell you I was asleep. What are you grinning about? What's so funny?"

Dr. Horace said, "Have it your own way. It's none of my business—unless the other fellow shows up. The tissue over the break is smashed. It looks as though it's been hit with a club."

"I can't have it!" Doc cried. "I've got to go to La Jolla tomorrow for the spring tides!"

"And turn over rocks?"

"Sure."

"Try and do it," said Dr. Horace. "Is the cast getting hot?"

"Yes," said Doc despondently.

38. Hooptedoodle (2), or The Pacific Grove Butterfly Festival

When things get really bad there are some who seek out others who have it worse, for consolation. It is hard to see how this works but it seems to. You balance your trouble against another's, and if yours is lighter you feel better.

You would say the situation in Cannery Row was just about hopeless. Consider, then, the plight of the town of Pacific Grove, and you will understand why the lights burned all night in the Masonic Hall and why there was talk of getting rid of the city government. It wasn't a small thing. The whole town was involved. The butterflies had not arrived.

Pacific Grove benefits by one of those happy accidents of nature that gladden the heart, excite the imagination, and instruct the young.

On a certain day in the shouting springtime great clouds of orangy Monarch butterflies, like twinkling aery fields of flowers, sail high in the air on a majestic pilgrimage across Monterey Bay and land in the outskirts of Pacific Grove in the pine woods. The butterflies know exactly where they are going. In their millions they land on several pine trees—always the same trees. There they suck the thick, resinous juice which oozes from the twigs, and they get cockeyed. The first comers suck their fill and then fall drunken to the ground, where they lie like a golden carpet, waving their inebriate legs in the air and giving off butterfly shouts of celebration, while their places on the twigs are taken by new, thirsty millions. After about a week of binge the butterflies sober up and fly away, but not in clouds: they face their Monday morning singly or in pairs.

For a long time Pacific Grove didn't know what it had. Then gradually it was remarked that an increasing number of tourists were drawn to see the butterflies. Where there are tourists there is money, and it is a sin to let it drift away. Pacific Grove had a gravy train right in its lap. And the butterflies came free. It is only natural that the Great Butterfly Festival evolved, and where there is a festival there is bound to be a pageant.

There was ointment trouble at first. Pacific Grove is not only a dry town, but ardently dry. The sale of various tonics of good alcoholic content is the highest in the state, but there is no liquor. The fact that the visiting butterflies came to the dry oasis to get drunk seemed a little unfair, but the town solved this, first, by ignoring it, and then, by hotly denying it. The Butterfly Pageant explains the whole thing: There was once a butterfly princess (sung by Miss Graves), and she wandered away and was lost. Somehow a bunch of Indians (citizens in long brown underwear) got in it. I forget how. Anyway, the loyal subjects searched and searched and at last they found their princess and in their millions came to rescue her. (When they lie flat on their backs their legs are waving greetings to their queen.) It all works out very nicely. The pageant is in the ball park and tourists can buy butterflies made out of every conceivable material from pine cones to platinum. The town makes a very nice thing of it. Why, the symbol of Pacific Grove on its advertising is the Monarch butterfly.

In all history there has been only one slip up. In 1924, I think it was, the butterflies did not come, and the frantic town was forced to print hundreds of thousands of paper butterflies in two colors and spread them all over. Today a wise city government keeps a huge supply of paper Monarchs on hand in case tragedy should strike again.

Now the time of the arrival is set, give one or two days in either direction. The pageant has been practicing for months, the Indians are trained, the prince has his tights out of mothballs, and the princess flowers toward coloratura luxury.

Perhaps it was an omen. Two days before the insects were due, Miss Graves lost her voice. She was a nice young woman, rather pretty and rather tired. She taught fourth grade, which is enough to tire anyone. Sprays and injections had no effect. Perhaps it was psychosomatic pressure that closed her throat and bottled up all but a dry squawk. Her eyes were feverish with despondency.

And then the days went by and the butterflies did not arrive. At first there was panic in Pacific Grove, and then a blind anger set in and the citizens looked about for someone to blame. The city government was a pushover. It was time for a change. Storekeepers whose bookkeeping was shaky blamed it on the mayor. Moving-picture attendance had fallen off. The city council took the rap for that. The matter became a growl, and the growl a roar: "Turn the rascals out!"

Then there was a hotel fire in King City, sixty miles away, and guess who came boiling out with an overcoat and a blonde? Mayor Cristy of Pacific Grove didn't even trouble to resign. He left town, and just as well. There was talk of tar and feathers. He must have heard. The town hadn't been so upset since the Great Roque War.

The religious block blamed the whole thing on sin without going into details. The cynics wanted to throw the whole council out, together with the chief of police and the water commissioner. More solid citizens placed the blame where it belonged, on Roosevelt-Truman socialism. And the butterflies did not come.

Then the first grade had its scandal. William Taylor 4th brought his crayons home wrapped in the dust cover of the Kinsey report. On being confronted, he panicked and said he got it from the teacher, Miss Bucke. She was questioned, and it developed that her father had signed a petition for the release of Eugene V. Debs in 1918. It had got so nobody could trust anybody.

And Miss Graves went on croaking.

And the butterflies did not come.

So you see, the trouble on Cannery Row wasn't as horrible as you thought.

39. Sweet Thursday Revisited

Again it was a Sweet Thursday in the spring. The sun took a leap toward summer and loosed the furled petals of the golden poppies. Before noon you could smell the spice of blue lupines from the fields around Fort Ord.

It was a sweet day for all manner of rattlesnakes. On the parade ground a jack rabbit, crazy with spring, strolled in March Hare madness across the rifle range and drew joyous fire from two companies before he skidded to safety behind a sand dune. That jack rabbit's moment of grandeur cost the government eight hundred and ninety dollars and gladdened the hearts of one hell of a lot of soldiers.

Miss Graves awakened breathless with expectancy. She sang a scale in half-tones and found that her voice was back and all was well with the world. And she was right. At eleven o'clock the Monarch butterflies came boiling in from across the bay and landed in their millions on the pine trees, where they sucked the thick sweet juice and got cockeyed. The butterfly committee met in emergency session in the firehouse and got out the crowns of fairies and the long brown underwear of Indians. The mayor pro tem of Pacific Grove wrote a proclamation for the evening paper.

The tide was very low that morning, preparing for the spring tides, and the warm sun dried the seaweed so that billions of flies came on excursion to feed.

People felt good. Judge Albertson discharged the seer on the recommendation of the Safeway manager.

Dr. Horace Dormody whistled through his mask over an appendectomy and told a political joke to the anesthetist, but he didn't mention Doc's broken arm. A patient's problems, no matter how funny, were sacred to Dr. Horace. But he couldn't help chuckling discreetly to himself now and then.

How did the word spread about Doc's arm? Who knows? Fauna heard it with her crullers. Alice, Mabel, and Becky got it with their orange juice. The Patrón heard it from Cacahuete, who thereupon rushed to the beach and played three loud and uninhibited choruses of "Sweet Georgia Brown," using six changes of key.

Wide Ida was siphoning Pine Canyon whisky into Old Crow bottles when she heard it.

Mack and the boys had the news early, and it gave them something pressing to do.

Suzy opened up the Poppy that morning. The counter was crowded with breakfasters who dawdled over coffee. It was well into the morning before Suzy heard that Doc had broken his arm. And then she couldn't do anything about it because Ella was getting a permanent. But after she heard it some midmorning customers got curious service from a Suzy who looked blankly over their heads when they spoke to her. She called Mr. MacMinimin Mr. Gross, and she called Mr. Gross "you" and served his eggs straight up which sickened him.

Mack was first on the scene. He didn't even put on his shoes. He regarded the new cast, which still hadn't cooled off, and listened to the only explanation Doc could think of—that he had got his arm caught between the cot and the wall.

"What you going to do?" Mack asked.

"I don't know. I have to get south, I have to!"

Mack was about to make an offer when a thought came to him that made him say, "Maybe something'll turn up." He bolted for the Palace Flophouse.

Once there, he went to Hazel's bed and found it pristine and unwrinkled.

"He ain't been in," said Whitey No. 1.

"Well, what do you think of that?" Mack said with admiration. "Why, the sweet son-of-a-bitch!"

Mack went out to the cypress tree and crawled under its low hanging limbs, and he dragged Hazel out the way you'd drag a puppy from under a bed and half carried him up to the Palace Flophouse.

Hazel was far gone in emotional fatigue. "I had to," he said hopelessly.

"Anybody seen Suzy?" Mack asked.

"I seen her go to work early," said Eddie.

"Well, you better go break the news to her. Do it offhand," said Mack. "Now, Hazel, how'd you do it?"

"You mad with me?"

"Hell no," said Mack. "'Course we don't know how she'll work out, but it's a step in the right direction." He turned to the two Whiteys. "I want you should notice Hazel didn't bust Doc's leg. That was good judgment. Doc can walk but he can't work. You, Whitey," he said to Whitey No. 2, "I want you should get over to Doc's and bang around. If anybody offers to drive him down to La Jolla you take care of it. Where's the indoor-ball bat?"

"I throwed it in the bay," said Hazel.

"So that's what it was! Whitey, you get yourself a couple of feet of gas pipe."

Hazel went into collapse. Mack sat on the edge of his bed and placed and replaced cold damp rags on Hazel's feverish brow.

Hazel struggled for speech. "Mack," he said, "I can't do her. I don't care if the stars or even the cops say I got to, I can't do her. I ain't got the poop."

"What you talking about? You already done her."

"I don't mean that. You tell Fauna she got to get somebody else for President of the United States."

Mack stared down at him in amazement. "I'll be damned," he said. "I thought you'd forgot."

"I practiced," said Hazel brokenly. "I don't want to let nobody down, Mack, but I just ain't no good at it. Try and get me off, will you, Mack? Please? Pretty goddam please?"

Mack's eyes brimmed with compassion. "Well, you sweet bastard," he said. "You poor little rabbit. Don't you worry. Ain't nobody going to force you. You done noble stuff. Wasn't nobody with guts but you."

"It ain't oysters," Hazel said. "Hell, I could do that. I'd eat old socks if I had to. It's just—the job's too big for me. I'd mess up the whole country."

Mack said, "You just lay there, Hazel baby, Mack's going to take care of it. There ain't nobody brave as you. Whitey," he said to Whitey No. 1, "you set here on Hazel's bed and kind of pet him. Don't let him get up until I get back." And Mack hurried out.

"You got to do something and do it quick," Mack said to Fauna. "S'pose Hazel gets another noble idea—why, hell, he might kill somebody."

"Yeah," said Fauna, "I can see how it is. Just let me get my stuff together. You think he'd like a nice monkey head?"

"He'd love it," said Mack. "He needs it."

Fauna held her chart in front of Hazel's eyes. "Anybody can make a mistake," she said. "They was a fly speck on the chart. Saturn wasn't in the bicuspid at all."

Hazel said suspiciously, "How do I know you ain't malarkying me now just to make me feel good?"

"How many toes you got?"

"I counted them—nine."

"Count them again."

Hazel slipped off his shoes. "Looks like the same as before," he said.

"Look at that little toe kind of bent under. Hell, Hazel, I may of made a mistake with a fly speck, but you miscounted your toes! You got ten. One bent under."

A slow smile began to spread over Hazel's face, a smile of

relieved delight. Then for a moment the shadow of worry came back. "Who you think they'll get instead of me?"

"Nobody knows," said Fauna.

"Well, he better be good," said Hazel ominously. And then he abandoned himself to pure relief. "'I got a little shadow that goes in and out with me,'" he sang.

Fauna rolled up her chart and went home.

Just before noon the expressman picked his unaccustomed way up to the chicken walk to the Palace Flophouse.

"I got a great big crate for you guys," he said. "I ain't got no call to deliver it up a rope ladder. Come on down and get it."

"It's here!" Mack cried. "God works in his tum-te-dum way his tum-tums to perform."

Hazel and Whitey No. 1 and Mack were wrestling the big wooden case up the chicken walk when Eddie joined them.

"Suzy come!" he cried. "I come with her. Seemed like she was about to take off any minute. She's in there with him now."

"Give us a hand," said Mack. "How's she look?"

"Fireball," said Eddie.

They carried the case into the Palace and Mack attacked it with a hand ax.

"There she is," he said when the lid was off.

"She's with Doc. Say, what you got?"

"Look!" said Mack. And he and the boys gazed down on the instrument, the great black tube of an eight-inch reflector, eyepieces socketed beside it, and its tripod cradled.

"Biggest one in the whole damn catalogue," said Mack proudly. "Jesus, Doc'll be happy! Eddie, tell us everything that happened, don't leave nothing out."

What a day it was! A day of purple and gold, the proud colors of the Salinas High School. A squadron of baby angels maneuvered at twelve hundred feet, holding a pink cloud on which the word J-O-Y flashed on and off. A seagull with a broken wing took off and flew straight up into the air, squawking, "Joy! Joy!"

Suzy was ahead of her racing feet when Eddie intercepted

her. She answered yes and no to Eddie's casual comments on the weather, but not only did she not hear the comments, she didn't know Eddie was beside her.

She went up the steps of Western Biological without seeing Whitey No. 2 standing guard with a sashweight. Her coming relieved him of a duty, but he stuck around to hear.

At the top of the steps Suzy became a breathless, shy girl, and, as anybody knows, there is nothing more indestructible and deadly than a shy young girl. She paused to get her breath and then knocked on the door and went in and forgot to close the door—which was good for Whitey No. 2.

Doc was sitting on his cot gloomily regarding the pile of collecting paraphernalia on the floor.

"I heard you was hurt," Suzy said gently. "I come to see if there was anything I could do."

For a moment Doc's face lightened, then gloom descended. "This shoots the spring tides," he said, staring at the white cast. "I don't know what I'll do."

"Does it hurt much?" Suzy asked.

"Some. It will hurt more later, I guess."

"I'll go down to La Jolla with you."

"And turn over rocks that weigh fifty or a hundred pounds?"

"I ain't put together with spit," said Suzy.

"Can you drive a car?"

"Sure," said Suzy.

"You can't do it," he said. And then, from way down in the deep part of him, there came a bubbling shout, "Sure you can! I need you, Suzy. I need you to go with me. It will be terribly hard work and I'm pretty near helpless."

"You can tell me what to do and what to look for."

"Sure I can. And I'm not entirely helpless. I can use my left hand."

"It's a cinch," said Suzy. "When do we start?"

"I've got to go tonight. If we drive all night we can make the tide at seven-eighteen tomorrow morning. Think you can make it?"

"Cinch," said Suzy. "If you need me."

"I need you all right. I'd be lost without you. But you'll be a tired kid."

"Who cares?" said Suzy.

"I want to ask you something," said Doc. "Old Jingleballicks has set up a foundation for me at Cal Tech."

"Why not?"

"I don't have to work there."

"Fine."

"I don't know whether I oughtn't to throw it in his face."

"Why don't you?"

"On the other hand, there's all the wonderful equipment."

"Fine," said Suzy.

"I don't like to work for anybody."

"Give it back."

"But there's an invitation to read my paper before the Academy of Science."

"Do it then."

"I don't know whether I can even write the paper. What shall I do, Suzy?"

"What do you want to do?"

"I don't know."

"What's wrong with that? Say, Doc, I got to do a couple of things. Take me maybe two hours. That too long?"

"Just as long as we start by evening."

"I'll come back soon's I finish."

Doc said, "Suzy, I love you."

She was headed for the door. She whirled and faced him. Her brows were straight and her mouth taut. Then she took a slow breath and her lips became full and turned up at the corners and her eyes shone with incredible excitement.

"Brother," said Suzy, "you got yourself a girl!"

40. I'm Sure We Should All Be as Happy as Kings

In the Palace Flophouse, Suzy sat on a straight chair surrounded by the boys. She wore a look of furious concentration. Her feet were on two bricks and she held a barrel hoop in her hands. Propped in front of her was a board on which were chalked "ignition key," "speedometer," "choke," and "gas gauge." On the floor on her right side stood an apple box with a mop handle sticking upright out of it.

"Try her again," said Mack. "Turn the key and reach up with your right toe for the starter."

Suzy put her foot on a chalk spot on the floor.

"Chug-a-chug-a-chug," said Hazel happily.

"Push out your clutch."

Suzy pushed her left foot down on a brick.

"Now bring the gear to you and back."

She moved the mop handle to low gear.

"Ease up the gas and let in the clutch. Now clutch out, away from you and forward. Give it gas. Now clutch out and straight back. There, you done it good. Now do it again."

At the end of an hour and a half Suzy had driven the straight chair roughly a hundred and fifty miles.

"You'll do all right," said Mack. "Take it slow. If you can get two miles out of town without ramming into something, you can tell him the truth. He ain't going to turn back then. He'll tell you what to do. I'll get her started and kind of lined up with the street."

"You're a bunch of nice guys," said Suzy.

"Hell, if Hazel can go to all the trouble to break—oop, sorry—the least we can do is see he gets some good out of it. Come on now—whang her through the gears again!"

The evening was as lovely as the day had been. The setting sun pinked up the little white caps on the bay and lighted the serious pelicans pounding home to the sea rocks. The metal cannery walls seemed a soft and precious platinum.

Doc's old car stood in front of Western Biological, its back-seat loaded with buckets and pans and nets and crow bars. All Cannery Row was there. The Patrón had set out pints of Old Tennis Shoes along the curb. Fauna's hair blazed in the setting sun. The girls gave Suzy quick little hugs. Becky was in romantic tears.

Joe Elegant looked out his lean-to door. He thought he would go to Rome after his book was published.

Doc held a list in his hand and checked equipment.

Only Mack and the boys were missing. And here they came down the chicken walk, balancing among them the tripod and the long black tube. They crossed the track and the lot and they set the tripod down beside the automobile.

Mack cleared his throat. "Friends," he said, "on behalf of I and the boys it gives me pleasure to present Doc with this here."

Doc looked at the gift—a telescope strong enough to bring the moon to his lap. His mouth fell open. Then he smothered the laughter that rose in him.

"Like it?" said Mack.

"It's beautiful."

"Biggest one in the whole goddam catalogue," said Mack.

Doc's voice was choked. "Thanks," he said. He paused. "After all, I guess it doesn't matter whether you look down or up—as long as you look."

"We'll put her inside for you," said Mack. "Give me one of them pints. To Doc!" he cried, and under his breath he whispered to Suzy, "Turn the key. Now, starter."

The ancient engine roared. Doc was sipping from a pint.

"Clutch out—to you and back," Mack said. "Let in the clutch."

Suzy did.

The old car deliberately climbed the curb, ripped off the stairs of Western Biological, careened into the street, and crawled away, scattering lumber as it went.

Doc turned in the seat and looked back. The disappearing sun shone on his laughing face, his gay and eager face. With his left hand he held the bucking steering wheel.

Cannery Row looked after the ancient car. It made the first turn and was gone from sight behind a warehouse just as the sun was gone.

Fauna said, "I wonder if I'd be safe to put up her gold star tonight. What the hell's the matter with you, Mack?"

Mack said, "Vice is a monster so frightful of mien, I'm sure we should all be as happy as kings." He put his arm around Hazel's shoulders. "I think you'd of made a hell of a president," he said.

THE WINTER OF OUR DISCONTENT

To Beth, my sister,
whose light burns clear

Readers seeking to identify the fictional people and places here described would do better to inspect their own communities and search their own hearts, for this book is about a large part of America today.

PART ONE

Chapter I

WHEN the fair gold morning of April stirred Mary Hawley awake, she turned over to her husband and saw him, little fingers pulling a frog mouth at her.

"You're silly," she said. "Ethan, you've got your comical genius."

"Oh say, Miss Mousie, will you marry me?"

"Did you wake up silly?"

"The year's at the day. The day's at the morn."

"I guess you did. Do you remember it's Good Friday?"

He said hollowly, "The dirty Romans are forming up for Calvary."

"Don't be sacrilegious. Will Marullo let you close the store at eleven?"

"Darling chicken-flower—Marullo is a Catholic and a wop. He probably won't show up at all. I'll close at noon till the execution's over."

"That's Pilgrim talk. It's not nice."

"Nonsense, ladybug. That's from my mother's side. That's pirate talk. It *was* an execution, you know."

"They were not pirates. You said yourself, whalers, and you said they had letters of what-you-call-it from the Continental Congress."

"The ships they fired on thought they were pirates. And those Roman G.I.'s thought it was an execution."

"I've made you mad. I like you better silly."

"I am silly. Everybody knows that."

"You always mix me up. You've got every right to be proud —Pilgrim Fathers and whaling captains right in one family."

"Have they?"

"What do you mean?"

"Would my great ancestors be proud to know they produced a goddam grocery clerk in a goddam wop store in a town they used to own?"

"You are not. You're more like the manager, keep the books and bank the money and order the goods."

"Sure. And I sweep out and carry garbage and kowtow to Marullo, and if I was a goddam cat, I'd be catching Marullo's mice."

She put her arms around him. "Let's be silly," she said. "Please don't say swear words on Good Friday. I do love you."

"Okay," he said after a moment. "That's what they all say. Don't think that lets you lie jaybird naked with a married man."

"I was going to tell you about the children."

"They in jail?"

"Now you're silly again. Maybe it's better if they tell you."

"Now why don't you—"

"Margie Young-Hunt's going to read me again today."

"Like a book? Who's Margie Young-Hunt, what is she, that all our swains—"

"You know if I was jealous—I mean they say when a man pretends he don't notice a pretty girl—"

"Oh, that one. Girl? She's had two husbands."

"The second one died."

"I want my breakfast. Do you believe that stuff?"

"Well Margie saw about Brother in the cards. Someone near and dear, she said."

"Someone near and dear to me is going to get a kick in the pants if she doesn't haul freight—"

"I'm going—eggs?"

"I guess so. Why do they call it Good Friday? What's good about it?"

"Oh! You!" she said. "You always make jokes."

The coffee was made and the eggs in a bowl with toast beside them when Ethan Allen Hawley slid into the dinette near the window.

"I feel good," he said. "Why do they call it Good Friday?"

"Spring," she said from the stove.

"Spring Friday?"

"Spring fever. Is that the children up?"

"Fat chance. Lazy little bastards. Let's get 'em up and whip 'em."

"You talk terrible when you're silly. Will you come home twelve to three?"

"Nope."

"Why not?"

"Women. Sneak 'em in. Maybe that Margie."

"Now Ethan, don't you talk like that. Margie's a good friend. She'd give you the shirt off her back."

"Yah? Where'd she get the shirt?"

"That's Pilgrim talk again."

"I bet you anything we're related. She's got pirate blood."

"Oh! You're just silly again. Here's your list." She tucked it in his breast pocket. "Seems like a lot. But it's Easter weekend, don't forget—and two dozen eggs, don't forget. You're going to be late."

"I know. Might miss a two-bit sale for Marullo. Why two dozen?"

"For dyeing. Allen and Mary Ellen asked specially. You better go."

"Okay, bugflower—but can't I just go up and beat the hell out of Allen and Mary Ellen?"

"You spoil them rotten, Eth. You know you do."

"Farewell, oh ship of state," he said, and slammed the screen door after him and went out into the green-gold morning.

He looked back at the fine old house, his father's house and his great-grandfather's, white-painted shiplap with a fanlight over the front door, and Adam decorations and a widow's walk on the roof. It was deep-set in the greening garden among lilacs a hundred years old, thick as your waist, and swelling with buds. The elms of Elm Street joined their tops and yellowed out in new-coming leaf. The sun had just cleared the bank building and flashed on the silvery gas tower, starting the kelp and salt smell from the old harbor.

Only one person in early Elm Street, Mr. Baker's red setter, the banker's dog, Red Baker, who moved with slow dignity, pausing occasionally to sniff the passenger list on the elm trunks.

"Good morning, sir. My name is Ethan Allen Hawley. I've met you in pissing."

Red Baker stopped and acknowledged the greeting, with a slow sway of his plumed tail.

Ethan said, "I was just looking at my house. They knew how to build in those days."

Red cocked his head and reached with a hind foot to kick casually at his ribs.

"And why not? They had the money. Whale oil from the seven seas, and spermaceti. Do you know what spermaceti is?"

Red gave a whining sigh.

"I see you don't. A light, lovely rose-smelling oil from the head cavity of the sperm whale. Read *Moby Dick*, dog. That's my advice to you."

The setter lifted his leg on the cast-iron hitching post at the gutter.

Turning to walk away, Ethan said over his shoulder, "And make a book report. You might teach my son. He can't even spell spermaceti, or—or anything."

Elm Street runs at an angle into High Street two blocks from the old Ethan Allen Hawley house. Halfway down the first block a delinquent gang of English sparrows were fighting on the new-coming lawn of the Elgar house, not playing but rolling and picking and eye-gouging with such ferocity and so noisily that they didn't see Ethan approach. He stopped to watch the battle.

"Birds in their little nests agree," he said. "So why can't we? Now there's a bunch of horse crap for you. You kids can't get along even on a pretty morning. And you're the bastards Saint Francis was nice to. Screw!" He ran at them, kicking, and the sparrows rose with a whispered roar of wings, complaining bitterly in door-squeak voices. "Let me tell you this," Ethan said after them. "At noon the sun will darken and a blackness will fall on the earth and you will be afraid." He came back to the sidewalk and proceeded on his way.

The old Phillips house in the second block is a boarding house now. Joey Morphy, teller at the First National, came out of the front door. He picked his teeth and straightened his Tattersall waistcoat and said, "Hi," to Ethan. "I was just going to call on you, Mr. Hawley," he said.

"Why do they call it Good Friday?"

"It's from the Latin," said Joey. "Goodus, goodilius, goodum, meaning lousy."

Joey looked like a horse and he smiled like a horse, raising a long upper lip to show big square teeth. Joseph Patrick Morphy, Joey Morphy, Joey-boy—"the Morph"—a real popular guy for one only a few years at New Baytown. A joker who got off his gags veily-eyed like a poker player, but he whinnied at other people's jokes, whether or not he had heard them. A wise guy, the Morph, had the inside dope on everything—and everybody from Mafia to Mountbatten—but he gave it out with a rising inflection, almost like a question. That took the smart-aleck tone out of it, made his listener a party to it so that he could repeat it as his own. Joey was a fascinating monkey—a gambler but no one ever saw him lay down a bet, a good bookkeeper and a wonderful bank teller. Mr. Baker, First National president, trusted Joey so completely that he let the teller do most of the work. The Morph knew everyone intimately and never used a first name. Ethan was Mr. Hawley. Margie Young-Hunt was Mrs. Young-Hunt to Joey, even though it was whispered that he was laying her. He had no family, no connections, lived alone in two rooms and private bath in the old Phillips house, ate most of his meals at the Foremaster Grill and Bar. His banking past was known to Mr. Baker and the bonding company and it was immaculate, but Joey-boy had a way of telling things that had happened to someone else in a way that made you suspect they had happened to Joey, and if that was so, he had really been around. Not taking credit made people like him even more. He kept his fingernails very clean, dressed well and sharply, and always had a clean shirt and a shoeshine.

The two men strolled together down Elm Street toward High.

"I've been meaning to ask you. You related to Admiral Hawley?"

"Don't you mean Admiral Halsey?" Ethan asked. "We've had lots of captains but I never heard of an admiral in the family."

"I heard your granddad was a whaling captain. Kind of connected up in my mind with the admiral, I guess."

"Town like this has got myths," said Ethan. "Like they say people on my dad's side did some pirating way back and my mother's family came over in the *Mayflower*."

"Ethan Allen," Joey said. "My God—you related to him too?"

"Might be. Must be," said Ethan. "What a day—ever see a prettier? What was it you wanted to see me about?"

"Oh, yes. I guess you're closing the store twelve to three. Would you make me a couple of sandwiches about half past eleven? I'll run in and get them. And a bottle of milk."

"Bank's not closing?"

"Bank is. I'm not. Little Joey'll be right in there, chained to the books. Big weekend like this—everybody and his dog cashing checks."

"I never thought of that," said Ethan.

"Oh, sure. Easter, Memorial Day, Fourth of July, Labor Day—any long weekend. If I wanted to stick up a bank, I'd do it just before a long weekend. The stuff's right there all laid out, waiting."

"You ever get stuck up, Joey?"

"No. But I had a friend that did twice."

"What did he say about it?"

"Said he was scared. Just took orders. Laid down on the floor and let 'em have it. Said the money was better insured than he was."

"I'll bring you the sandwiches when I close up. I'll knock on the back door. What kind you want?"

"Don't bother, Mr. Hawley. I'll slip across the alley—one ham and one cheese on rye, lettuce and mayonnaise, and maybe one bottle of milk and a Coke for later."

"Got some nice salami—that's Marullo."

"No, thanks. How's the one-man Mafia holding up?"

"All right, I guess."

"Well, even if you don't like guineas, you got to admire a guy can build a pushcart into all the property he owns. He's pretty cute. People don't know how much he's got salted away. Maybe I shouldn't say that. Banker's not supposed to tell."

"You didn't tell."

They had come to the corner where Elm angles into High Street. Automatically they stopped and turned to look at the pink brick and plaster mess that was the old Bay Hotel, now being wrecked to make room for the new Woolworth's. The yellow-painted bulldozer and the big crane that swung the wrecking ball were silent like waiting predators in the early morning.

"I always wanted to do that," Joey said. "Must be a kick to swing that steel ball and see a wall go down."

"I saw enough go down in France," Ethan said.

"Yeah! Your name's on the monument down by the waterfront."

"Did they ever catch the robbers that stuck up your friend?" Ethan was sure the friend was Joey himself. Anyone would have been.

"Oh, sure. Caught 'em like mice. It's lucky robbers aren't smart. If Joey-boy wrote a book how to rob a bank, the cops would never catch anybody."

Ethan laughed. "How'd you go about it?"

"I got a pipeline, Mr. Hawley. I just read the papers. And I used to know a guy pretty well was a cop. You want the two-dollar lecture?"

"'Bout six bits' worth. I've got to open the store."

"Ladies and gentlemen," said Joey, "I am here this morning —No, look! How do they catch bank robbers? Number one—record, got caught before. Number two—get fighting over the profits and someone blows it. Number three—dames. Can't let dames alone, and that ties into number four—they got to spend that money. Watch new spenders and you got them."

"So what's your method, professor, sir?"

"Simple as socks. Everything opposite. Never rob a bank if you ever got caught or booked for anything. No confederates —do it alone and don't tell a soul, nobody. Forget dames. And don't spend it. Put it away, maybe for years. Then when you've got some excuse for having some money, bring it out a little at a time and invest. Don't spend."

"How about if the robber got recognized?"

"If he covers his face and don't talk, who's going to recognize him? You ever read descriptions by eyewitnesses? They're nuts. My cop friend says sometimes when they'd plant him in the line-up, he got picked out over and over again. People swore their eyes out he did whatever it was. That'll be six bits, please."

Ethan put his hand in his pocket. "I'll have to owe you."

"I'll take it out in sandwiches," said Joey.

The two crossed High Street and entered the alley that right-angled from the other side. Joey went in the back door of the First National Bank on his side of the alley, and Ethan unlocked the alley door of Marullo's Fruit and Fancy Groceries on his side. "Ham and cheese?" he called.

"On rye—lettuce and mayonnaise."

A little light, grayed by the dusty iron-barred window, came into the storeroom from the narrow alley. Ethan paused in the twilight place shelved to the ceiling and stacked with the cartons and wooden cases of canned fruits, vegetables, fish, processed meats, and cheese. He sniffed for mice among the seminal smells of flour and dried beans and peas, the paper-and-ink odor of boxed cereals, thick rich sourness of cheeses, and sausage, reek of hams and bacon, ferment of cabbage trimmings, lettuce, and beet tops from the silvery garbage cans beside the back door. Perceiving no rusty must of mouse, he opened the alley door again and rolled the covered garbage cans into the alley. A gray cat darted to get in, but he drove it away.

"No, you don't," he remarked to the cat. "Mice and rats are fee for cats, but you're a sausage nibbler. Aroint! You hear me—aroint!" The seated cat was licking a curled pink paw but at the second "aroint" he hightailed away and scrambled over the board fence behind the bank. "That must be a magic word," Ethan said aloud. He returned to the storeroom and closed the door after him.

Now through the dusty room to the swinging door of the grocery—but at the cubicle of the toilet he heard the whispering of seeping water. He opened the plywood door, switched on the light, and flushed the toilet. Then he pushed open the wide door with wire-netted glass peekhole and wedged it open, kicking the wood block firmly in with his toe.

The store was greeny from the drawn shades over the big front windows. Again shelves to the ceiling, filled neatly with gleaming canned and glassed foods, a library for the stomach. On one side—counter, cash register, bags, string, and that glory in stainless steel and white enamel, the cold cabinet, in which the compressor whispered to itself. Ethan flipped a switch and flooded the cold cuts, cheeses, sausage, chops, steaks, and fish with a cold bluish neon glare. A reflected cathedral light filled the store, a diffused cathedral light like that of Chartres. Ethan paused to admire it, the organ pipes of canned tomatoes, the chapels of mustard and olives, the hundred oval tombs of sardines.

"Unimum et unimorum," he intoned in a nasal litanic tone. "Uni unimouse quod unibug in omnem unim, domine—ahhhhhmen," he sang. And he could hear his wife commenting, "That's silly and besides it might hurt somebody's feelings. You can't go around hurting feelings."

A clerk in a grocery store—Marullo's grocery store—a man with a wife and two darling children. When is he alone, when can he be alone? Customers in the daytime, wife and kiddies in the evening; wife at night, customers in the daytime, wife and kiddies in the evening. "Bathroom—that's when," Ethan said loudly, and right now, before I open the sluice. Oh! the dusky, musky, smelly-welly, silly-billy time—the slovenly-lovely time. "Now whose feelings can I hurt, sugarfoot?" he said to his wife. "There ain't nobody nor nobody's feelings here. Just me and my unimum unimorum until—until I open that goddam front door."

From a drawer behind the counter by the cash register he took a clean apron and unfolded it and straightened the tapes, put it around his thin middle, brought the tapes around and back again. He reached behind his back with both hands and fumbled a bowknot.

The apron was long, halfway down his shins. He raised his right hand, cupped loosely, palm upward, and he declaimed, "Hear me oh ye canned pears, ye pickles and ye piccalilli—'As soon as it was day, the elders of the people and the chief priests and the scribes came together and led Him into their council—' *as soon as it was day.* The buggers went to work early, didn't they? They didn't waste no time nohow. Let's see now. 'And it was about the sixth hour'—that's maybe twelve o'clock— 'and there was a darkness over all the earth until the ninth hour. And the sun was darkened.' Now how do I remember that? Good God, it took Him a long time to die—a dreadful long time." He dropped his hand and looked wondering at the crowded shelves as though they might answer him. "You don't speak to me now, Mary, my dumpling. Are you one of the Daughters of Jerusalem? 'Weep not for me,' He said. 'Weep for yourselves and for your children. . . . For if they do these things in a green tree, what shall be done in the dry?' Still breaks me up. Aunt Deborah wrought better than she knew. It's not the sixth hour yet—not yet."

He raised the green shades on the big windows, saying, "Come in, day!" And then he unlocked the front doors. "Enter, world." He swung the iron-barred doors open and latched them open. And the morning sun lay softly on the pavement as it should, for in April the sun arose right where the High Street ran into the bay. Ethan went back to the toilet for a broom to sweep the sidewalk.

A day, a livelong day, is not one thing but many. It changes not only in growing light toward zenith and decline again, but in texture and mood, in tone and meaning, warped by a thousand factors of season, of heat or cold, of still or multi winds, torqued by odors, tastes, and the fabrics of ice or grass, of bud or leaf or black-drawn naked limbs. And as a day changes so do its subjects, bugs and birds, cats, dogs, butterflies and people.

Ethan Allen Hawley's quiet, dim, and inward day was done. The man who swept the morning pavement with metronomic strokes was not the man who could sermonize to canned goods, not a unimum unimorum man, not even a silly-billy man. He gathered cigarette ends and gum wrappers, bud cases from the pollenizing trees, and simple plain dust in the sweep of his broom and moved the windrow of derelict toward the gutter, to await the town men with their silver truck.

Mr. Baker took his measured decent way from his house on Maple Street toward the red brick basilica of a First National Bank. And if his steps were not of equal length, who was to know that out of ancient habit he avoided breaking his mother's back?

"Good morning, Mr. Baker," Ethan said and held his stroke to save the banker's neat serge pants from dust.

"Morning, Ethan. Fine morning."

"Fine," said Ethan. "Spring's in, Mr. Baker. Groundhog was right again."

"He was, he was." Mr. Baker paused. "I've been wanting to talk to you, Ethan. That money your wife got by her brother's will—over five thousand, isn't it?"

"Sixty-five hundred after taxes," Ethan said.

"Well, it's just lying in the bank. Ought to be invested. Like to talk to you about that. Your money should be working."

"Sixty-five hundred dollars can't do much work, sir. It can only stand by for emergencies."

"I'm not a believer in idle money, Ethan."

"Well, this also serves—just standing and waiting."

The banker's voice became frosty. "I don't understand." His inflection said he did understand and found it stupid, and his tone twisted a bitterness in Ethan, and the bitterness spawned a lie.

The broom traced a delicate curve against the pavement. "It's this way, sir. That money is Mary's temporary security if anything should happen to me."

"Then you should use part of it to insure your life."

"But it's only temporary, sir. That money was Mary's brother's estate. Her mother is still living. She may live many years."

"I understand. Old people can be a burden."

"They can also sit on their money." Ethan glanced at Mr. Baker's face as he said his lie, and he saw a trace of color rise out of the banker's collar. "You see, sir, if I invested Mary's money I might lose it, the way I lost my own, the way my father lost the pot."

"Water under the bridge, Ethan—water under the bridge. I know you got burned. But times are changing, new opportunities opening up."

"I had my opportunity, Mr. Baker, more opportunity than good sense. Don't forget I owned this store right after the war. Had to sell half a block of real estate to stock it—the last of our business property."

"I know, Ethan. I'm your banker. Know your business the way your doctor knows your pulse."

"Sure you know. Took me less than two years to damn near go bankrupt. Had to sell everything but my house to pay my debts."

"You can't take all the blame for that. Fresh out of the Army—no business experience. And don't forget you ran smack into a depression, only we called it recession. Some pretty seasoned businessmen went under."

"I went under all right. It's the first time in history a Hawley was ever a clerk in a guinea grocery."

"Now that's what I don't understand, Ethan. Anybody can

go broke. What I don't see is why you stay broke, a man of your family and background and education. It doesn't have to be permanent unless your blood has lost its guts. What knocked you out, Ethan? What kept you knocked out?"

Ethan started an angry retort— Course you don't understand; you've never had it—and then he swept a small circle of gum wrappers and cigarette butts into a pyramid and moved the pyramid toward the gutter. "Men don't get knocked out, or I mean they can fight back against big things. What kills them is erosion; they get nudged into failure. They get slowly scared. I'm scared. Long Island Lighting Company might turn off the lights. My wife needs clothes. My children—shoes and fun. And suppose they can't get an education? And the monthly bills and the doctor and teeth and a tonsillectomy, and beyond that suppose I get sick and can't sweep this goddam sidewalk? Course you don't understand. It's slow. It rots out your guts. I can't think beyond next month's payment on the refrigerator. I hate my job and I'm scared I'll lose it. How could you understand that?"

"How about Mary's mother?"

"I told you. She sits on it. She'll die sitting on it."

"I didn't know. I thought Mary came from a poor family. But I know when you're sick you need medicine or maybe an operation or maybe a shock. Our people were daring men. You know it. They didn't let themselves get nibbled to death. And now times are changing. There are opportunities our ancestors never dreamed of. And they're being picked up by foreigners. Foreigners are taking us over. Wake up, Ethan."

"And how about the refrigerator?"

"Let it go if you have to."

"And how about Mary and the children?"

"Forget them for a while. They'll like you better if you climb out of the hole. You're not helping them by worrying about them."

"And Mary's money?"

"Lose it if you have to but risk it. With care and good advice you don't have to lose it. Risk isn't loss. Our people have always been calculated-risk people and they didn't lose. I'm going to shock you, Ethan. You're letting down the memory of old Cap'n Hawley. You owe his memory something. Why, he and my daddy owned the *Belle-Adair* together, one of the last built and finest of all whaling bottoms. Get off your ass, Ethan. You owe the *Belle-Adair* something you haven't paid in guts. The hell with the finance company."

Ethan coaxed a reluctant piece of cellophane over the gutter's edge with his broom tip. He said softly, "The *Belle-Adair* burned to the waterline, sir."

"I know she did, but did that stop us? It did not."

"She was insured."

"Of course she was."

"Well, I wasn't. I saved my house and nothing else."

"You'll have to forget that. You're brooding on something past. You've got to scrape up some courage, some daring. That's why I said you should invest Mary's money. I'm trying to help you, Ethan."

"Thank you, sir."

"We'll get that apron off you. You owe that to old Cap'n Hawley. He wouldn't believe it."

"I guess he wouldn't."

"That's the way to talk. We'll get that apron off."

"If it wasn't for Mary and the children—"

"Forget them, I tell you—for their own good. There's some interesting things going to happen here in New Baytown. You can be part of it."

"Thank you, sir."

"Just let me think about it."

"Mr. Morphy says he's going to work when you close at noon. I'm making him some sandwiches. Want me to make you some?"

"No thanks. I'm letting Joey do the work. He's a good man. There's some property I want to look up. In the County Clerk's office, that is. Nice and private there from twelve till three. Might be something in that for you. We'll talk soon. So long." He took a long first step to miss a crack and crossed the alley entrance to the front door of the First National Bank, and Ethan smiled at his retreating back.

He finished his sweeping quickly, for people were trickling and fresheting to work now. He set the stands of fresh fruit at the entrance of the store. Then, making sure no one was passing, he removed three stacked cans of dog food and, reaching behind, brought out the grim little bag of currency, replaced the dog food, and, ringing "no sale" on the cash register, distributed the twenties, tens, fives, and one-dollar bills in their places under the small retaining wheels. And in the oaken cups at the front of the cash drawer he segregated the halves, quarters, dimes, nickels, and pennies, and slammed the drawer shut. Only a few customers showed up, children sent for a loaf of bread or a carton of milk or a pound of forgotten coffee, little girls with sleep-messy hair.

Margie Young-Hunt came in, pert-breasted in a salmon sweater. Her tweed skirt clung lovingly in against her thighs and tucked up under her proud fanny, but it was in her eyes, her brown myopic eyes, that Ethan saw what his wife could never see because it wasn't there when wives were about. This was a predator, a huntress, Artemis for pants. Old Cap'n Hawley called it a "roving eye." It was in her voice too, a velvet growl that changed to a thin, mellow confidence for wives.

"Morning, Eth," Margie said. "What a day for a picnic!"

"Morning. Want to take a bet you ran out of coffee?"

"If you guess I ran out of Alka-Seltzer, I'm going to avoid you."

"Big night?"

"In a small way. Traveling-salesman story. A divorced woman's safe. Brief case of free samples. Guess you'd call him a drummer. Maybe you know him. Name of Bigger or Bogger, travels for B.B.D. and D. Reason I mention it is he said he was coming in to see you."

"We buy from Waylands mostly."

"Well, maybe Mr. Bugger's just drumming up business, if he feels better than I do this morning. Say, could you give me a glass of water? I'll take a couple of fizzers now."

Ethan went to the storeroom and brought back a Dixie cup of water from the tap. She dropped three of the flat tablets in and let them fizz. Then, "Mud in your eye," she said and tossed it back. "Get to work, you devils," she said.

"I hear you're going to read Mary's fortune today."

"Oh, Lord! I nearly forgot. I should go in the business. I could make my own fortune."

"Mary loves it. Are you good at it?"

"Nothing to be good at. You let people—women, that is—

talk about themselves and then tell it back to them and they think you've got second sight."

"And tall dark strangers?"

"There's that, sure. If I could read men, I wouldn't have pulled the bellywhoppers I have. Brother! did I misread a couple of characters."

"Didn't your first husband die?"

"No, my second, peace be to his ashes, the son of a— No, let it ride. Peace be to his ashes."

Ethan greeted the entering elderly Mrs. Ezyzinski solicitously and lingered over the transference of a quarter of a pound of butter, even passed a complimentary word or two about the weather, but Margie Young-Hunt, relaxed and smiling, inspected the gold-sealed cans of *pâté de foie gras* and the minuscule jewel-cases of caviar in back of the counter by the cash register.

"Now," said Margie when the old lady tottered out, muttering to herself in Polish.

"Now—what?"

"I was just thinking—if I knew as much about men as I do about women, I'd put out my shingle. Why don't you teach me about men, Ethan?"

"You know enough. Maybe too much."

"Oh, come on! Don't you have a silly bone in your body?"

"Want to start now?"

"Maybe some evening."

"Good," he said. "A group. Mary and you and the two kids. Subject: men—their weakness and stupidity and how to use them."

Margie ignored his tone. "Don't you ever work late—accounts first of the month, that stuff?"

"Sure. I take the work home."

She raised her arms over her head and her fingers moused in her hair.

"Why?" she asked.

"Cat's why to make kittens' britches."

"See what you could teach me if you would?"

Ethan said, "'And after that they had mocked Him, they took the robe off from Him and put His own raiment on Him and led Him away to crucify Him. And as they came out they found a man of Cyrene, Simon by name. Him they compelled to bear His cross. And when they were come unto a place called Golgotha—that is to say, a place of a skull—' "

"Oh, for God's sake!"

"Yes—yes—that is correct. . . ."

"Do you know what a son of a bitch you are?"

"Yes, O Daughter of Jerusalem."

Suddenly she smiled. "Know what I'm going to do? I'm going to read one hell of a fortune this morning. You're going to be a big shot, did you know? Everything you touch will turn to gold—a leader of men." She walked quickly to the door and then turned back, grinning. "I dare you to live up to it and I dare you not to. So long, Savior!" How strange the sound of heeltaps on pavement, striking in anger.

At ten o'clock everything changed. The big glass doors of the bank folded open and a river of people dipped in for money and brought the money to Marullo's and took away the fancy foods Easter calls for. Ethan was busy as a water skater until the sixth hour struck.

The angry firebell from its cupola on the town hall clanged the sixth hour. The customers drifted away with their bags of baked meats. Ethan brought in the fruit stands and closed the front doors, and then for no reason except that a darkness fell on the world and on him, he pulled down the thick green shades and the darkness fell on the store. Only the neon in the cold counter glared a ghostly blue.

Behind the counter he cut four fat slices of rye bread and buttered them liberally. He slid open the cold doors and picked out two slices of processed Swiss cheese and three slices of ham. "Lettuce and cheese," he said, "lettuce and cheese. When a man marries he lives in the trees." He mortared the top slices of bread with mayonnaise from a jar, pressed the lids down on the sandwiches, and trimmed the bits of lettuce and ham fat from the edges. Now a carton of milk and a square of waxed paper for wrapping. He was folding the ends of the paper neatly when a key rattled in the front door and Marullo came in, wide as a bear and sack-chested so that his arms seemed short and stood out from his body. His hat was on the back of his head so that his stiff iron-gray bangs showed like a cap. Marullo's eyes were wet and sly and sleepy, but the gold caps on his front teeth shone in the light from the cold counter. Two top buttons of his pants were open, showing his heavy gray underwear. He hooked little fat thumbs in the roll of his pants under his stomach and blinked in the half-darkness.

"Morning, Mr. Marullo. I guess it's afternoon."

"Hi, kid. You shut up good and quick."

"Whole town's shut. I thought you'd be at mass."

"No mass today. Only day in the year with no mass."

"That so? I didn't know that. Anything I can do for you?"

The short fat arms stretched and rocked back and forth on the elbows. "My arms hurt, kid. Arthritis. . . . Gets worse."

"Nothing you can do?"

"I do everything—hot pads, shark oil, pills—still hurts. All nice and shut up. Maybe we can have a talk, eh, kid?" His teeth flashed.

"Anything wrong?"

"Wrong? What's wrong?"

"Well, if you'll wait a minute, I'll just take these sandwiches to the bank. Mr. Morphy asked for them."

"You're a smart kid. You give service. That's good."

Ethan went through the storeroom, crossed the alley, and knocked on the back door of the bank. He passed the milk and sandwiches in to Joey.

"Thanks. You didn't need to."

"It's service. Marullo told me."

"Keep a couple of Cokes cold, will you? I got dry zeros in my mouth."

When Ethan returned, he found Marullo peering into a garbage can.

"Where do you want to talk, Mr. Marullo?"

"Start here, kid." He picked cauliflower leaves from the can. "You cutting off too much."

"Just to make them neat."

"Cauliflower is by weight. You throwing money in the garbage. I know a smart Greek fella owns maybe twenty restaurants. He says the big secret is watch the garbage cans. What you throw out, you don't sell. He's a smart fella."

"Yes, Mr. Marullo." Ethan moved restlessly toward the front of the store with Marullo behind him bending his elbows back and forth.

"You sprinkling good the vegetables like I said?"

"Sure."

The boss lifted a head of lettuce. "Feels dry."

"Well, hell, Marullo, I don't want to waterlog them—they're one-third water now."

"Makes them look crisp, nice and fresh. You think I don't know? I start with one pushcart—just one. I know. You got to learn the tricks, kid, or you go broke. Meat, now—you paying too much."

"Well, we advertise Grade A beef."

"A, B, C—who knows? It's on the card, ain't it? Now, we going to have a nice talk. We got dead wood on our bills. Anybody don't pay by the fifteenth—off the books."

"We can't do that. Some of these people have been trading here for twenty years."

"Listen, kid. Chain stores won't let John D. Rockefeller charge a nickel."

"Yes, but these people are good for it, most of them."

"What's 'good for it'? It ties up money. Chain stores buy carloads. We can't do that. You got to learn, kid. Sure—nice people! Money is nice too. You got too much meat scraps in the box."

"That was fat and crust."

"Okay if you weigh before you trim. You got to look after number one. You don't look after number one, whose'll do it? You got to learn, kid." The gold teeth did not glitter now, for the lips were tight little traps.

Anger splashed up in Ethan before he knew it and he was surprised. "I'm not a chiseler, Marullo."

"Who's a chiseler? That's good business, and good business is the only kind of business that stays in business. You think Mr. Baker is giving away free samples, kid?"

Ethan's top blew off with a bang. "You listen to me," he shouted. "Hawleys have been living here since the middle seventeen hundreds. You're a foreigner. You wouldn't know about that. We've been getting along with our neighbors and being decent all that time. If you think you can barge in from Sicily and change that, you're wrong. If you want my job, you can have it—right here, right now. And don't call me kid or I'll punch you in the nose—"

All Marullo's teeth gleamed now. "Okay, okay. Don't get mad. I just try to do you a good turn."

"Don't call me kid. My family's been here two hundred years." In his own ears it sounded childish, and his rage petered out.

"I don't talk very good English. You think Marullo is guinea name, wop name, dago name. My *genitori*, my name, is maybe two, three thousand years old. Marullus is from Rome, Valerius Maximus tells about it. What's two hundred years?"

"You don't come from here."

"Two hundred years ago you don't neither."

Now Ethan, his rage all leaked away, saw something that makes a man doubtful of the constancy of the realities outside himself. He saw the immigrant, guinea, fruit-peddler change under his eyes, saw the dome of forehead, the strong beak nose, deep-set fierce and fearless eyes, saw the head supported on pillared muscles, saw pride so deep and sure that it could play at humility. It was the shocking discovery that makes a man wonder: If I've missed this, what else have I failed to see?

"You don't have to talk dago talk," he said softly.

"Good business. I teach you business. Sixty-eight years I got. Wife she's died. Arthritis! I hurt. I try to show you business. Maybe you don't learn. Most people they don't learn. Go broke."

"You don't have to rub it in because I went broke."

"No. You got wrong. I'm try to learn you good business so you don't go broke no more."

"Fat chance. I haven't got a business."

"You're still a kid."

Ethan said, "You look here, Marullo. I practically run this store for you. I keep the books, bank the money, order the supplies. Keep customers. They come back. Isn't that good business?"

"Sure—you learned something. You're not no kid no more. You get mad when I call you kid. What I'm going to call you? I call everybody kid."

"Try using my name."

"Don't sound friendly. Kid is friendly."

"It's not dignified."

"Dignified is not friendly."

Ethan laughed. "If you're a clerk in a guinea store, you've got to have dignity—for your wife, for your kids. You understand?"

"Is a fake."

"Course it is. If I had any real dignity, I wouldn't think about it. I nearly forgot something my old father told me not long before he died. He said the threshold of insult is in direct relation to intelligence and security. He said the words 'son of a bitch' are only an insult to a man who isn't quite sure of his mother, but how would you go about insulting Albert Einstein? He was alive then. So you go right on calling me kid if you want to."

"You see, kid? More friendly."

"All right then. What were you going to tell me about business that I'm not doing?"

"Business is money. Money is not friendly. Kid, maybe you too friendly—too nice. Money is not nice. Money got no friends but more money."

"That's nonsense, Marullo. I know plenty of nice, friendly, honorable businessmen."

"When not doing business, kid, yes. You going to find out. When you find out is too late. You keep store nice, kid, but if it's your store you maybe go friendly broke. I'm teaching true lesson like school. Goo-by, kid." Marullo flexed his arms and went quickly out the front door and snapped it after him, and Ethan felt darkness on the world.

A sharp metallic rapping came on the front door. Ethan pushed aside the curtain and called, "We're closed till three."

"Let me in. I want to talk to you."

The stranger came in—a spare man, a perpetually young man who had never been young, a smart dresser, hair gleaming thinly against his scalp, eyes merry and restless.

"Sorry to bother you. Got to blow town. Wanted to see you alone. Thought the old man'd never go."

"Marullo?"

"Yeah. I was across the street."

Ethan glanced at the immaculate hands. On the third finger of the left hand he saw a big cat's eye set in a gold ring.

The stranger saw the glance. "Not a stick-up," he said. "I met a friend of yours last night."

"Yes?"

"Mrs. Young-Hunt. Margie Young-Hunt."

"Oh?"

Ethan could feel the restless sniffing of the stranger's mind, searching for an opening, for a bond on which to build an association.

"Nice kid. She gave you a big build-up. That's why I thought— My name's Biggers. I cover this territory for B.B.D. and D."

"We buy from Waylands."

"I know you do. That's why I'm here. Thought you might like to spread it out a little. We're new in this district. Building up fast. Have to make some concessions to get a foot in the door. It would pay you to take advantage of that."

"You'd have to see Mr. Marullo about that. He's always had a deal with Waylands."

The voice didn't lower but its tone became confidential. "You do the ordering?"

"Well, yes. You see Marullo has arthritis, and besides he has other interests."

"We could shave prices a little."

"I guess Marullo's got them shaved as close as they'll shave. You'd better see him."

"That's what I didn't want to do. I want the man that does the ordering, and that's you."

"I'm just a clerk."

"You do the ordering, Mr. Hawley. I can cut you in for five per cent."

"Marullo might go for a discount like that if the quality was the same."

"You don't get it. I don't want Marullo. This five per cent would be in cash—no checks, no records, no trouble with the tax boys, just nice clean green cabbage from my hand to your hand and from your hand to your pocket."

"Why can't Marullo get the discount?"

"Price agreements."

"All right. Suppose I took the five per cent and turned it over to Marullo?"

"I guess you don't know them like I do. You turn it over to him, he'll wonder how much more you aren't turning over. That's perfectly natural."

Ethan lowered his voice. "You want me to double-cross the man I work for?"

"Who's double-crossed? He don't lose anything and you make a buck. Everybody's got a right to make a buck. Margie said you were a smart cooky."

"It's a dark day," Ethan said.

"No, it's not. You got the shades pulled down." The sniffing mind smelled danger—a mouse confused between the odor of trap wire and the aroma of cheese. "Tell you what," Biggers said, "you think about it. See if you can throw some business our way. I'll drop in to see you when I'm in the district. I make it every two weeks. Here's my card."

Ethan's hand remained at his side. Biggers laid the card on top of the cold counter. "And here's a little memento we got out for new friends." From his side pocket he brought a bill-fold, a rich and beautiful affair of pin seal. He placed it beside the card on the white porcelain. "Nice little item. Place for your driver's license, lodge cards."

Ethan did not reply.

"I'll drop by in a couple of weeks," Biggers said. "You think about it. I'll sure be here. Got a date with Margie. There's quite a kid." With no reply, he said, "I'll let myself out. See you soon." Then suddenly he came close to Ethan. "Don't be a fool. Everybody does it," he said. "Everybody!" And he went rapidly out the door and closed it quietly after him.

In the darkened silence Ethan could hear the low hum of the transformer for the neon light in the cold counter. He turned slowly to the piled and tiered audience on the shelves.

"I thought you were my friends! You didn't raise a hand for me. Fair-weather oysters, fair-weather pickles, fair-weather cake-mix. No more unimus for you. Wonder what Saint Francis would say if a dog bit him, or a bird crapped on him. Would he say, 'Thank you, Mr. Dog, *grazie tanto*, Signora Bird'?" He turned his head toward a rattling and a knocking and a pounding on the alley door, went quickly through the storeroom, muttering, "More customers than if we were open."

Joey Morphy staggered in, clutching his throat. "For God's sake," he groaned. "Succor—or at least Pepsi-Cola, for I dieth of dryth. Why is it so dark in here? Are mine eyes failething too?"

"Shades pulled down. Trying to discourage thirsty bankers."

He led the way to the cold counter and dug out a frosted bottle, uncapped it, and reached for another. "Guess I'll have one too."

Joey-boy leaned against the lighted glass and poured down half the bottle before he lowered it. "Hey!" he said. "Somebody's lost Fort Knox." He picked up the billfold.

"That's a little gift from the B.B.D. and D. drummer. He's trying to hustle some of our business."

"Well, he ain't hustling peanuts. This here's quality, son. Got your initials on it, too, in gold."

"It has?"

"You mean you don't know?"

"He just left a minute ago."

Joey flipped open the folded leather and rustled the clear plastic identification envelopes. "You better start joining something," he said. He opened the back. "Now here's what I call real thoughtful." Between first and second fingers he extracted a new twenty-dollar bill. "I knew they were moving in but didn't know with tanks. That's a remembrance worth remembering."

"Was that in there?"

"You think I planted it?"

"Joey, I want to talk to you. The guy offered me five per cent of any business I threw their way."

"Well, bully-bully! Prosperity at last. And it wasn't no idle promise. You should set up the Cokes. This is your day."

"You don't mean I should take it—"

"Why not, if they don't add it on the cost? Who loses?"

"He said I shouldn't tell Marullo or he'd think I was getting more."

"He would. What's the matter with you, Hawley? You nuts? I guess it's that light. You look green. Do I look green? You weren't thinking of turning it down?"

"I had trouble enough not kicking him in the ass."

"Oh! It's like that—you and the dinosaurs."

"He said everybody does it."

"Not everybody can get it. You're just one of the lucky ones."

"It's not honest."

"How not? Who gets hurt? Is it against the law?"

"You mean you'd take it?"

"Take it—I'd sit up and beg for it. In my business they got all the loopholes closed. Practically everything you can do in a bank is against the law—unless you're president. I don't get you. What are you hoggle-boggling about? If you were taking it away from Alfio lad, I'd say it wasn't quite straight—but you're not. You do them a favor, they do you a favor—a nice crisp green favor. Don't be crazy. You've got a wife and kids to think of. Raising kids ain't going to get any cheaper."

"I wish you'd go away now."

Joey Morphy put his unemptied bottle down hard on the counter. "Mr. Hawley—no, Mr. Ethan Allen Hawley," he said coldly, "if you think I would do anything dishonest or suggest that you do—why you can go and screw yourself."

Joey stalked toward the storeroom.

"I didn't mean that. I didn't mean it. Honest to God I didn't, Joey. I just had a couple of shocks today and besides—this is a dreadful holiday—dreadful."

Morphy paused. "How do you mean? Oh! yes, I know. Yes, I do know. You believe I know?"

"And every year, ever since I was a kid, only it gets worse because—maybe because I know more what it means, I hear those lonely 'lama sabach thani' words."

"I do know, Ethan, I do. It's nearly over—nearly over now, Ethan. Just forget I stomped out, will you?"

And the iron firebell clanged—one single stroke.

"It's over now," said Joey-boy. "It's all over—for a year." He drifted quietly out through the storeroom and eased the alley door shut.

Ethan raised the shades and opened the store again, but there wasn't much trade—a few bottle-of-milk and loaf-of-bread kids, a small lamb chop and can of peas for Miss Borcher for her hot-plate supper. People were just not moving about in the street. During the half-hour before six o'clock, while Ethan was getting things ready to close up, not a soul came in. And he locked up and started away before he remembered the groceries for home—had to go back and assemble them in two big bags and lock up over again. He had wanted to walk down to the bayside and watch the gray waves among the pilings of the dock and smell the sea water and speak to a seagull standing beak into the wind on a mooring float. He remembered a lady-poem written long ago by someone whipped to frenzy by the gliding spiral of a gull's flight. The poem began: "Oh! happy fowl—what thrills thee so?" And the lady poet had never found out, probably didn't want to know.

The heavy bags of groceries for the holidays discouraged the walk. Ethan moved wearily across the High Street and took his way slowly along Elm toward the old Hawley house.

Chapter II

MARY came from the stove and took one of the big grocery bags from him.

"I've got so much to tell you. Can't wait."

He kissed her and she felt the texture of his lips. "What's the matter?" she asked.

"Little tired."

"But you were closed three hours."

"Plenty to do."

"I hope you aren't gloomy."

"It's a gloomy day."

"It's been a wonderful day. Wait till you hear."

"Where are the kids?"

"Upstairs with the radio. They've got something to tell you too."

"Trouble?"

"Now why do you say that?"

"I don't know."

"You don't feel well."

"Damn it, I do too."

"With all the lovely things—I'll wait till after dinner for our part. Are you going to be surprised."

Allen and Mary Ellen boiled down the stairs and into the kitchen. "He's home," they said.

"Pop, you got Peeks in the store?"

"You mean that cereal, sure, Allen."

"I wish you'd bring some. It's the one with a mouse mask on the box that you cut out."

"Aren't you a little old for a mouse mask?"

Ellen said, "You send the box top and ten cents and you get a ventriloquism thing and instructions. We just heard it on the radio."

Mary said, "Tell your father what you want to do."

"Well, we're going to enter the National I Love America Contest. First prize is go to Washington, meet the President—*with* parents—lots of other prizes."

"Fine," said Ethan. "What is it? What do you have to do?"

"Hearst papers," Ellen cried. "All over the country. You just write an essay why you love America. All the winners get to go on television."

"It's the grapes," said Allen. "How about going to Washington, hotel, shows, meet the President, the works. How's that for the grapes?"

"How about your schoolwork?"

"It's this summer. They announce the winners Fourth of July."

"Well, that might be all right. Do you really love America or do you love prizes?"

"Now, Father," said Mary, "don't go spoiling it for them."

"I just wanted to separate the cereal from the mouse mask. They get all mixed up."

"Pop, where would you say we could look it up?"

"Look it up?"

"Sure, like what some other guys said—"

"Your great-grandfather had some pretty fine books. They're in the attic."

"Like what?"

"Oh, like Lincoln's speeches and Daniel Webster and Henry Clay. You might take a look at Thoreau or Walt Whitman or Emerson—Mark Twain too. They're all up there in the attic."

"Did you read them, Pop?"

"He was my grandfather. He used to read them to me sometimes."

"Maybe you could help us with the essays."

"Then they wouldn't be yours."

"Okay," said Allen. "Will you remember to bring home some Peeks? They're full of iron and stuff."

"I'll try."

"Can we go to the movies?"

Mary said, "I thought you were going to dye the Easter eggs. I'm boiling them now. You can take them out on the sun porch after dinner."

"Can we go up in the attic and look at the books?"

"If you turn out the light after. Once it burned for a week. You left it on, Ethan."

When the children had gone, Mary said, "Aren't you glad they're in the contest?"

"Sure, if they do it right."

"I can't wait to tell you—Margie read me in cards today, three times, because she said she never saw anything like it. Three times! I saw the cards come up myself."

"Oh! Lord!"

"You won't be so suspicious when you hear. You always poke fun about tall dark strangers. You can't guess what it was about. Well—you want to guess?"

He said, "Mary, I want to warn you."

"Warn me? Why, you don't even know. My fortune is *you.*"

He spoke a harsh, bitter word under his breath.

"What did you say?"

"I said, 'Slim pickings.' "

"That's what you think, but that's not what the cards think. Three times, she threw them."

"Cards think?"

"They know," said Mary. "Here she read my cards and it was all about you. You're going to be one of the most important men in this town—that's what I said, *most* important. And it's not going to be long either. It's very soon. Every card she turned showed money and more money. You're going to be a rich man."

"Darling," he said, "please let me warn you, please!"

"You're going to make an investment."

"With what?"

"Well, I was thinking about Brother's money."

"No," he cried. "I wouldn't touch it. That's yours. And it's going to stay yours. Did you think that up or did—"

"She never mentioned it. And the cards didn't. You are going to invest in July and from then on, it's one thing after another—one right after another. But don't it sound nice? That's the way she said it— 'Your fortune is Ethan. He is going to be a very rich man, maybe the biggest man in this town.' "

"God damn her! She's got no right."

"Ethan!"

"Do you know what she's doing? Do you know what you're doing?"

"I know I'm a good wife and she's a good friend. And I don't want to quarrel with the children hearing. Margie Young is the best friend I've got. I know you don't like her. What I think is you're jealous of my friends—that's what I think. I had a happy afternoon and you want to spoil it. That's not nice." Mary's face was mottled with angry disappointment, and vengeful toward this obstacle to her daydreaming.

"You just sit there, Mr. Smart, and tear people down. You think Margie made it all up. She didn't, because I cut the cards three times—but even supposing she did, why would she do it except to be kind and friendly and offer a little help. You tell me that, Mr. Smart! You find some nasty reason."

"I wish I knew," he said. "It might be pure mischief. She hasn't a man or a job. It might be mischief."

Mary lowered her voice and spoke with scorn. "You talk about mischief—you wouldn't know mischief if it slapped you in the face. You don't know what Margie goes through. Why, there are men in this town after her all the time. Big men, married men, whispering and urging—nasty. Sometimes she don't know where to turn. That's why she needs me, a woman friend. Oh, she told me things—men you just wouldn't believe. Why some of them even pretend they don't like her in public, and then they sneak to her house or call her up and try to get her to meet them—sanctimonious men, always preaching morals and then doing like that. You talk about mischief."

"Did she say who they were?"

"No, she didn't and that's another proof. Margie don't want to hurt anybody even if they hurt her. But she said there was one I just wouldn't believe. She said it would turn my hair gray if I knew."

Ethan took a deep breath and held it and let it out as a huge sigh.

"Wonder who it could be," Mary said. "The way she said it was like it was somebody we know well and just couldn't believe."

"But she would tell under certain circumstances," Ethan said softly.

"Only if she was forced. She said that herself. Only if she had to if like her—honor, or her good name, you know . . . Who do you s'pose it could be?"

"I think I know."

"You know? Who?"

"Me."

Her mouth fell open. "Oh! You fool," she said. "If I don't watch you, you trap me every time. Well it's better than gloomy."

"A pretty kettle. Man confesses to sins of the flesh with wife's best friend. Is laughed to scorn."

"That's not nice talk."

"Perhaps man should have denied it. Then at least his wife would have honored him with suspicion. My darling, I swear to you by all that's holy, that never by word or deed have I ever made a pass at Margie Young-Hunt. Now will you believe I'm guilty?"

"You!"

"You don't think I'm good enough, desirable enough, in other words you don't think I could make the grade?"

"I like jokes. You know it—but that's not something to joke about. I hope the children haven't got into the trunks up there. They never put anything back."

"I'll try once more, fair wife. A certain woman, initials M. Y.-H., has surrounded me with traps, for reasons known only to herself. I am in grave danger of falling into one or more of them."

"Why don't you think of your fortune? The cards said July and they said it three times—I saw it. You are going to get money and lots of money. Think about that."

"Do you love money so much, cottontail?"

"Love money? What do you mean?"

"Do you want money enough so that even necromancy, thaumaturgy, juju, or any other dark practices are justified?"

"You said it! You started it. I'm not going to let you hide in your words. Do I love money? No, I don't love money. But I don't love worry either. I'd like to be able to hold up my head in this town. I don't like the children to be hang-dog because they can't dress as good—as well—as some others. I'd love to hold up my head."

"And money would prop up your head?"

"It would wipe the sneers off the faces of your holy la-de-das."

"No one sneers at Hawley."

"That's what you think! You just don't see it."

"Maybe because I don't look for it."

"Are you throwing your holy Hawleys up at me?"

"No, my darling. It's not much of a weapon any more."

"Well, I'm glad you found it out. In this town or any other town a Hawley grocery clerk is still a grocery clerk."

"Do you blame me for my failure?"

"No. Of course I don't. But I do blame you for sitting wallowing in it. You could climb out of it if you didn't have your old-fashioned fancy-pants ideas. Everybody's laughing at you. A grand gentleman without money is a bum." The word exploded in her head, and she was silent and ashamed.

"I'm sorry," Ethan said. "You have taught me something—maybe three things, rabbit footling mine. Three things will never be believed—the true, the probable, and the logical. I know now where to get the money to start my fortune."

"Where?"

"I'll rob a bank."

The little bell of the timer on the stove took up a slow-spaced pinging.

Mary said, "Go call the children. The casserole's ready. Tell them to turn out the light." She listened to his tread.

Chapter III

MY wife, my Mary, goes to her sleep the way you would close the door of a closet. So many times I have watched her with envy. Her lovely body squirms a moment as though she fitted herself into a cocoon. She sighs once and at the end of it her eyes close and her lips, untroubled, fall into that wise and remote smile of the ancient Greek gods. She smiles all night in her sleep, her breath purrs in her throat, not a snore, a kitten's purr. For a moment her temperature leaps up so that I can feel the glow of it beside me in the bed, then drops and she has gone away. I don't know where. She says she does not dream. She must, of course. That simply means her dreams do not trouble her, or trouble her so much that she forgets them before awakening. She loves to sleep and sleep welcomes her. I wish it were so with me. I fight off sleep, at the same time craving it.

I have thought the difference might be that my Mary knows she will live forever, that she will step from the living into another life as easily as she slips from sleep to wakefulness. She knows this with her whole body, so completely that she does not think of it any more than she thinks to breathe. Thus she has time to sleep, time to rest, time to cease to exist for a little.

On the other hand, I know in my bones and my tissue that I will one day, soon or late, stop living and so I fight against sleep, and beseech it, even try to trick it into coming. My moment of sleep is a great wrench, an agony. I know this because I have awakened at this second still feeling the crushing blow. And once in sleep, I have a very busy time. My dreams are the problems of the day stepped up to absurdity, a little like men dancing, wearing the horns and masks of animals.

I sleep much less in time than Mary does. She says she needs a great deal of sleep and I agree that I need less but I am far from believing that. There is only so much energy stored in a body, augmented, of course, by foods. One can use it up quickly, the way some children gobble candy, or unwrap it slowly. There's always a little girl who saves part of her candy and so has it when the gobblers have long since finished. I think my Mary will live much longer than I. She will have saved some of her life for later. Come to think of it, most women live longer than men.

Good Friday has always troubled me. Even as a child I was deep taken with sorrow, not at the agony of the crucifixion, but feeling the blighting loneliness of the Crucified. And I have never lost the sorrow, planted by Matthew, and read to me in the clipped, tight speech of my New England Great-Aunt Deborah.

Perhaps it was worse this year. We do take the story to ourselves and identify with it. Today Marullo instructed me, so that for the first time I understood it, in the nature of business. Right afterward I was offered my first bribe. That's an odd thing to say at my age, but I don't remember any other. I must think about Margie Young-Hunt. Is she an evil thing? What is her purpose? I know she has promised me something and threatened me if I don't accept it. Can a man think out his life, or must he just tag along?

So many nights I have lain awake, hearing my Mary's little purring beside me. If you stare into darkness, red spots start swimming on your eyes, and the time is long. Mary so loves her sleep that I have tried to protect her in it, even when the electric itch burned on my skin. She wakens if I leave the bed. It worries her. Because her only experience with sleeplessness has been in illness, she thinks I am not well.

This night I had to get up and out. Her breath purred gently and I could see the archaic smile on her mouth. Maybe she dreamed of good fortune, of the money I was about to make. Mary wants to be proud.

It is odd how a man believes he can think better in a special place. I have such a place, have always had it, but I know it isn't thinking I do there, but feeling and experiencing and remembering. It's a safety place—everyone must have one, although I never heard a man tell of it. Secret, quiet movement often awakens a sleeper when a deliberate normal action does not. Also I am convinced that sleeping minds wander into the thoughts of other people. I caused myself to need the bathroom, and when it was so, got up and went. And afterward I went quietly downstairs, carrying my clothes, and dressed in the kitchen.

Mary says I share other people's troubles that don't exist. Maybe that is so, but I did see a little possible scene play out in the dim-lighted kitchen—Mary awakening and searching the house for me, and her face troubled. I wrote a note on the grocery pad, saying, "Darling—I'm restless. Have gone for a walk. Be back soon." I think I left it squarely in the center of the kitchen table so that if the light was turned on at the wall switch it would be the first thing seen.

Then I eased the back door open and tasted the air. It was chilly, smelled of a crusting of white frost. I muffled up in a heavy coat and pulled a knitted sailor's cap down over my ears. The electric kitchen clock growled. It said quarter of three. I had been lying watching the red spots in the dark since eleven.

Our town of New Baytown is a handsome town, an old town, one of the first clear and defined whole towns in America. Its first settlers and my ancestors, I believe, were sons of those restless, treacherous, quarrelsome, avaricious seafaring men who were a headache to Europe under Elizabeth, took the West Indies for their own under Cromwell, and came finally to roost on the northern coast, holding charters from the returned Charles Stuart. They successfully combined piracy and puritanism, which aren't so unalike when you come right down to it. Both had a strong dislike for opposition and both had a roving eye for other people's property. Where they merged, they produced a hard-bitten, surviving bunch of monkeys. I know about them because my father made me know. He was a kind of high amateur ancestor man and I've always noticed that ancestor people usually lack the qualities of the ones they celebrate. My father was a gentle, well-informed, ill-advised, sometimes brilliant fool. Singlehanded he lost the land, money, prestige, and future; in fact he lost nearly everything Allens and Hawleys had accumulated over several hundred years, lost everything but the names—which was all my father was interested in anyway. Father used to give me what he called "heritage lessons." That's why I know so much about the old boys. Maybe that's also why I'm a clerk in a Sicilian grocery on a block Hawleys used to own. I wish I didn't resent it so much. It wasn't depression or hard times that wiped us out.

All that came from starting to say New Baytown is a pretty town. I turned right on Elm Street instead of left and walked fast up to Porlock, which is a cockeyed parallel with High. Wee Willie, our fat constable, would be dozing in his police car on the High, and I didn't want to pass the time of night with him. "What you doing up so late, Eth? Got yourself a little piece of something?" Wee Willie gets lonesome and loves to talk, and then later he talks about what he talked about. Quite a few small but nasty scandals have grown out of Willie's loneliness. The day constable is Stonewall Jackson Smith. That's not a nickname. He was christened Stonewall Jackson, and it does set him apart from all the other Smiths. I don't know why town cops have to be opposites but they usually are. Stoney Smith is a man who wouldn't give away what day it is unless he were on the stand under oath. Chief Smith runs the police work of the town and he's dedicated, studies the latest methods, and has taken the F.B.I. training in Washington. I guess he's as good a policeman as you are likely to find, tall and quiet and with eyes like little gleams of metal. If you were going in for crime, the chief would be a man to avoid.

All this came from my going over to Porlock Street to avoid talking to Wee Willie. It's on Porlock that the beautiful houses of New Baytown are. You see in the early eighteen hundreds we had over a hundred whaling bottoms. When the ships came back from a year or two out as far as the Antarctic or the China Sea, they would be loaded with oil and very rich. But they would have touched at foreign ports and picked up things as well as ideas. That's why you see so many Chinese things in the houses on Porlock Street. Some of those old captain-owners had good taste too. With all their money, they brought in English architects to build their houses. That's why you see so much Adam influence and Greek revival architecture on Porlock Street. It was that period in England. But with all the fanlights and fluted columns and Greek keys, they never neglected to put a widow's walk on the roof. The idea was that the faithful home-bound wives could go up there to watch for returning ships, and maybe some of them did. My family, the Hawleys, and the Phillipses and the Elgars and the Bakers were older. They stayed put on Elm Street and their houses were what is called Early American, peak roofs and shiplap siding. That's the way my house, the old Hawley house, is. And the giant elms are as old as the houses.

Porlock Street has kept its gas street lamps, only there are electric globes in them now. In the summer tourists come to see the architecture and what they call "the old-world charm" of our town. Why does charm have to be old-world?

I forget how the Vermont Allens got mixed up with the Hawleys. It happened pretty soon after the Revolution. I could find out, of course. Up in the attic somewhere there will be a record. By the time father died, my Mary was pretty tired of Hawley family history, so when she suggested that we store all the things in the attic, I understood how she felt. You can get pretty tired of other people's family history. Mary isn't even New Baytown born. She came from a family of Irish extraction but not Catholic. She always makes a point of that. Ulster family, she calls them. She came from Boston.

No she didn't, either. I got her in Boston. I can see both of us, maybe more clearly now than then, a nervous, frightened Second Lieutenant Hawley with a weekend pass, and the soft, petal-cheeked, sweet-smelling darling of a girl, and triply all of those because of war and textbooks. How serious we were, how deadly serious. I was going to be killed and she was prepared to devote her life to my heroic memory. It was one of a million identical dreams of a million olive uniforms and cotton prints. And it might well have ended with the traditional Dear John letter except that she devoted her life to her warrior. Her letters, sweet with steadfastness, followed me everywhere, round, clear handwriting in dark blue ink on light blue paper, so that my whole company recognized her letters and every man was curiously glad for me. Even if I hadn't wanted to marry Mary, her constancy would have forced me to for the perpetuation of the world dream of fair and faithful women.

She has not wavered, not in the transplanting from Boston Irish tenancy to the old Hawley house on Elm Street. And she never wavered in the slow despondency of my failing business, in the birth of our children, or in the paralysis of my long clerkship. She is a waiter—I can see that now. And I guess she had at lengthy last grown weary of waiting. Never before had the iron of her wishes showed through, for my Mary is no mocker and contempt is not her tool. She has been too busy making the best of too many situations. It only seemed remarkable that the poison came to a head because it had not before. How quickly the pictures formed against the sound of frost-crunching footsteps on the night street.

There's no reason to feel furtive walking in the early morning in New Baytown. Wee Willie makes little jokes about it but most people seeing me walking toward the bay at three in the morning would suppose I was going fishing and not give it another thought. Our people have all sorts of fishing theories, some of them secret like family recipes, and such things are respected and respectable.

The street lights made the hard white frost on the lawns and sidewalks glint like millions of tiny diamonds. Such a frost takes a footprint and there were none ahead. I have always from the time I was a child felt a curious excitement walking in new unmarked snow or frost. It is like being first in a new world, a deep, satisfying sense of discovery of something clean and new, unused, undirtied. The usual night-folk, the cats, don't like to walk on frost. I remember once, on a dare, I stepped out barefoot on a frosty path and it felt like a burn to my feet. But now in galoshes and thick socks I put the first scars on the glittering newness.

Where Porlock crosses Torquay, that's where the bicycle factory is, just off Hicks Street, the clean frost was scarred with long foot-dragged tracks. Danny Taylor, a restless, unsteady ghost, wanting to be somewhere else and dragging there and wanting to be somewhere else. Danny, the town drunk. Every town has one, I guess. Danny Taylor—so many town heads shook slowly from side to side—good family, old family, last of the line, good education. Didn't he have some trouble at the Academy? Why doesn't he straighten up? He's killing himself with booze and that's wrong because Danny's a gentleman. It's a shame, begging money for booze. It's a comfort that his parents aren't alive to see it. It would kill them—but they're dead already. But that's New Baytown talking.

In me Danny is a raw sorrow and out of that a guilt. I should be able to help him. I've tried, but he won't let me. Danny is as near to a brother as I ever had, same age and growing up, same weight and strength. Maybe my guilt comes because

I am my brother's keeper and I have not saved him. With a feeling that deep down, excuses—even valid ones—give no relief. Taylors—as old a family as Hawleys or Bakers or any of the others. In childhood I can remember no picnic, no circus, no competition, no Christmas without Danny beside me as close as my own right arm. Maybe if we had gone to college together this wouldn't have happened. I went to Harvard—luxuriated in languages, bathed in the humanities, lodged in the old, the beautiful, the obscure, indulged myself with knowledge utterly useless in running a grocery store, as it developed. And always I wished Danny could be with me on that bright and excited pilgrimage. But Danny was bred for the sea. His appointment to the Naval Academy was planned and verified and certain even when we were kids. His father sewed up the appointment every time we got a new Congressman.

Three years with honors and then expelled. It killed his parents, they say, and it killed most of Danny. All that remained was this shuffling sorrow—this wandering night sorrow cadging dimes for a pint of skull-buster. I think the English would say, "He's let the side down," and that always wounds the let-downer more than the side. Danny's a night wanderer now, an early-morning man, a lonely, dragging thing. When he asks for a quarter for skull-buster his eyes beg you to forgive him because he can't forgive himself. He sleeps in a shack in back of the boat works where Wilburs used to be shipbuilders. I stooped over his track to see whether he was headed home or away. By the scuff of the frost he was going out and I might meet him any place. Wee Willie wouldn't lock him up. What would be the good?

There was no question where I was going. I had seen and felt and smelled it before I got out of bed. The Old Harbor is pretty far gone now. After the new breakwater went in and the municipal pier, sand and silt crept in and shallowed that once great anchorage sheltered by the jagged teeth of Whitsun Reef. And where once were shipways and rope-walks and warehouses and whole families of coopers to make the whale-oil casks, and docks too over which the bowsprits of whalers could project to their chain stays and figure- or fiddleheads. Three-masters they were usually, square-rigged; the after mast carried square sails as well as boom-and-gaff spanker—deep-hulled ships built to suffer the years at sea in any weather. The flying jib boom was a separate spar and the double dolphin-striker served as spritsail gaffs as well.

I have a steel engraving of the Old Harbor chockablock with ships, and some faded photographs on tin, but I don't really need them. I know the harbor and I know the ships. Grandfather rebuilt it for me with his stick made from a narwhal's horn and he drilled me in the nomenclature, rapping out the terms with his stick against a tide-bared stump of a pile of what was once the Hawley dock, a fierce old man with a white whisker fringe. I loved him so much I ached from it.

"All right," he'd say, in a voice that needed no megaphone from the bridge, "sing out the full rig, and sing it loud. I hate whispering."

And I would sing out, and he'd whack the pile with his narwhal stick at every beat. "Flying jib," I'd sing (whack), "outer jib" (whack), "inner jib, jib" (whack! whack!).

"Sing out! You're whispering."

"Fore skys'l, fore royal, fore topgal'n't s'l, fore upper tops'l, fore lower tops'l, fores'l"—and every one a whack.

"Main! Sing out."

"Main skys'l"—whack.

But sometimes, as he got older, he would tire. "Belay the main," he would shout. "Get to the mizzen. Sing out now."

"Aye, sir. Mizzen skys'l, mizzen royal, mizzen t'gal'n't, mizzen upper tops'l, mizzen lower tops'l, crossjack—"

"And?"

"Spanker."

"How rigged?"

"Boom and gaff, sir."

Whack—whack—whack—narwhal stick against the waterlogged pile.

As his hearing got fuzzier, he accused more and more people of whispering. "If a thing's true, or even if it ain't true and you mean it, sing out," he would cry.

Old Cap'n's ears may have gone wonky toward the end of his life, but not his memory. He could recite you the tonnage and career of every ship, it seemed like, that ever sailed out of the Bay, and what she brought back and how it was divided, and the odd thing was that the great whaling days were nearly over before he was master. Kerosene he called "skunk oil," and kerosene lamps were "stinkpots." By the time electric lights came, he didn't care much or maybe was content just to remember. His death didn't shock me. The old man had drilled me in his death as he had in ships. I knew what to do, inside myself and out.

On the edge of the silted and sanded up Old Harbor, right where the Hawley dock had been, the stone foundation is still there. It comes right down to the low-tide level, and high water laps against its square masonry. Ten feet from the end there is a little passage about four feet wide and four feet high and five feet deep. Its top is vaulted. Maybe it was a drain one time, but the landward entrance is cemented in with sand and broken rock. That is my Place, the place everybody needs. Inside it you are out of sight except from seaward. There's nothing at Old Harbor now but a few clammers' shacks, rattlety things, mostly deserted in the winter, but clammers are a quiet lot anyway. They hardly speak from day's end to end and they walk with their heads down and their shoulders bowed.

That was the place I was headed for. I spent nighttide there before I went in the service, and the nighttide before I married my Mary, and part of the night Ellen was born that hurt her so bad. I was compelled to go and sit inside there and hear the little waves slap the stone and look out at the sawtooth Whitsun rocks. I saw it, lying in bed, watching the dance of the red spots, and I knew I had to sit there. It's big changes take me there—big changes.

South Devon runs along the shore, and there are lights aimed at the beach put there by good people to keep lovers from getting in trouble. They have to go somewhere else. A town ordinance says that Wee Willie has to patrol once an hour. There wasn't a soul on the beach—not a soul, and that was odd because someone is going fishing, or fishing, or coming in nearly all the time. I lowered myself over the edge and found the outcrop stone and doubled into the little cave. And I had hardly settled myself before I heard Wee Willie's car go by. That's twice I had avoided passing the time of night with him.

It sounds uncomfortable and silly, sitting cross-legged in a niche like a blinking Buddha, but some way the stone fits me, or I fit. Maybe I've been going there so long that my behind has conformed to the stones. As for its being silly, I don't mind that. Sometimes it's great fun to be silly, like children playing statues and dying of laughter. And sometimes being silly breaks the even pace and lets you get a new start. When I am troubled, I play a game of silly so that my dear will not catch trouble from me. She hasn't found me out yet, or if she has, I'll never know it. So many things I don't know about my Mary, and among them, how much she knows about me. I don't think she knows about the Place. How would she? I've never told anyone. It has no name in my mind except the Place —no ritual or formula or anything. It's a spot in which to wonder about things. No man really knows about other human beings. The best he can do is to suppose that they are like himself. Now, sitting in the Place, out of the wind, seeing under the guardian lights the tide creep in, black from the dark sky, I wondered whether all men have a Place, or need a Place, or want one and have none. Sometimes I've seen a look in eyes, a frenzied animal look as of need for a quiet, secret place where soul-shivers can abate, where a man is one and can take stock of it. Of course I know of the theories of back to the womb and the death-wish, and these may be true of some men, but I don't think they are true of me, except as easy ways of saying something that isn't easy. I call whatever happens in the Place "taking stock." Some others might call it prayer, and maybe it would be the same thing. I don't believe it's thought. If I wanted to make a picture of it for myself, it would be a wet sheet turning and flapping in a lovely wind and drying and sweetening the white. What happens is right for me, whether or not it is good.

There were plenty of matters to consider and they were jumping and waving their hands for attention like kids in school. Then I heard the slow puttering of a boat engine, a one-lunger, a fishing craft. Her masthead light moved south beyond the Whitsun rocks. I had to put everything aside until she turned her red and green lights safe in the channel, a local boat to have found the entrance so easily. She dropped anchor in the shallows and two men came ashore in her skiff. Little wavelets brushed the beach and the disturbed gulls took time to settle back on the mooring floats.

Item: There was Mary, my dear, to think of, asleep with the smile of mystery on her lips. I hoped she wouldn't awaken and look for me. But if she did, would she ever tell me? I doubt it. I think that Mary, for all that she seems to tell everything, tells very little. There was the fortune to consider. Did Mary want a fortune or did she want it for me? The fact that it was a fake fortune, rigged by Margie Young-Hunt for reasons I didn't know, made no difference at all. A fake fortune was just as good as any and it is possible that all fortunes are a little fake. Any man of reasonable intelligence can make money if that's what he wants. Mostly it's women or clothes or admiration he really wants and they deflect him. The great artists of finance like Morgan and Rockefeller weren't deflected. They wanted and got money, just simple money. What they did with it afterward is another matter. I've always felt they got scared of the ghost they raised and tried to buy it off.

Item: By money, Mary meant new curtains and sure education for the kids and holding her head a little higher and, face it, being proud rather than a little ashamed of me. She had said it in anger and it was true.

Item: Did I want money? Well, no. Something in me hated being a grocery clerk. In the Army I made captain, but I know what got me into O.T.C. It was family and connections. I wasn't picked for my pretty eyes, but I did make a good officer, a good officer. But if I had really liked command, imposing my will on others and seeing them jump, I might have stayed in the Army and I'd have been a colonel by now. But I didn't. I wanted to get it over. They say a good soldier fights a battle, never a war. That's for civilians.

Item: Marullo was telling me the truth about business, business being the process of getting money. And Joey Morphy was telling it straight, and Mr. Baker and the drummer. They all told it straight. Why did it revolt me and leave a taste like a spoiled egg? Am I so good, or so kind, or so just? I don't think so. Am I so proud? Well, there's some of that. Am I lazy, too lazy to be involved? There's an awful lot of inactive kindness which is nothing but laziness, not wanting any trouble, confusion, or effort.

There is a smell and a feel of dawn long before the light. It was in the air now, a tempering of the wind; a new star or a planet cleared the horizon to eastward. I should know what star or planet but I don't. The wind freshens or steadies in the false dawn. It really does. And I would have to be going back soon. This rising star was too late to have much of a go before daylight. What is the saying— "The stars incline, they do not command"? Well, I've heard that a good many serious financiers go to astrologers for instruction in stock purchase. Do the stars incline toward a bull market? Is A.T. and T. influenced by the stars? Nothing as sweet and remote in my fortune as a star. A beat-up tarot deck of fortune-telling cards in the hands of an idle, mischievous woman, and she had rigged the cards. Do the cards incline but not command? Well, the cards inclined me out to the Place in the middle of the night, and they inclined me to give more thought than I wanted to, to a subject I detested. That's quite a bit of inclining right there. Could they incline me to a business cleverness I never had, to acquisitiveness foreign to me? Could I incline to want what I didn't want? There are the eaters and the eaten. That's a good rule to start with. Are the eaters more immoral than the eaten? In the end all are eaten—all—gobbled up by the earth, even the fiercest and the most crafty.

The roosters up on Clam Hill had been crowing for a long time and I had heard and not heard. I wished I could stay to see the sun rise straight out from the Place.

I said there was no ritual involved with the Place but that is not entirely true. Sometime on each visit I reconstruct Old Harbor for my mind's pleasure—the docks, the warehouses, the forests of masts and underbrush of rigging and canvas. And my ancestors, my blood—the young ones on the deck, the fully grown aloft, the mature on the bridge. No nonsense of Madison Avenue then or trimming too many leaves from cauliflowers. Some dignity was then for a man, some stature. A man could breathe.

That was my father talking, the fool. Old Cap'n remembered the fights over shares, the quibbling with stores, suspicion of every plank and keelson, the lawsuits, yes, and the killings—over women, glory, adventure? Not at all. Over money. It was a rare partnership, he said, that lasted more than one voyage, and blistering feuds ever afterward, continuing after the cause was forgotten.

There was one bitterness old Cap'n Hawley did not forget, a crime he could not forgive. He must have told me about it many times, standing or sitting on the rim of Old Harbor. We spent a goodly time there, he and I. I remember him pointing with his narwhal stick.

"Take that third rock on Whitsun Reef," he said. "Got her? Now, line her up with the tip of Porty Point at high water. See it there? Now—half a cable-length out on that line is where she lies, at least her keel."

"The *Belle-Adair*?"

"The *Belle-Adair*."

"Our ship."

"Half ours, a partnership. She burned at anchor—burned to the waterline. I never believed it was an accident."

"You think she was fired, sir?"

"I do."

"But—but you can't do that."

"I couldn't."

"Who did?"

"I don't know."

"Why?"

"Insurance."

"Then it's no different now."

"No different."

"There must be some difference."

"Only in a single man alone—only in one man alone. There's the only power—one man alone. Can't depend on anything else."

He never spoke to Cap'n Baker again, my father told me, but he didn't carry it to his son, Mr. Banker Baker. He wouldn't do that any more than he would burn a ship.

Good God, I've got to get home. And I got. I almost ran and I went up the High Street without thinking. It was still dark enough but a rim of lightness lay on the edge of the sea and made the waves gray iron. I rounded the war memorial and passed the post office. In a doorway Danny Taylor stood as I knew he must, hands in pockets, collar of his ragged coat turned up, and his old peaked shooter's cap with the earflaps turned down. His face was blue-gray with cold and sickness.

"Eth," he said, "I'm sorry to bother you. Sorry. I've got to have some skull-buster. You know I wouldn't ask if I didn't have to."

"I know. I mean I don't know, but I believe you." I gave him a dollar bill. "Will that do it?"

His lips were trembling the way a child's lips do when it's about to cry. "Thank you, Eth," he said. "Yes—that will put me away all day and maybe all night." He began to look better just thinking of it.

"Danny—you've got to stop this. Think I've forgotten? You were my brother, Danny. You still are. I'll do anything in the world to help you."

A little color came into his thin cheeks. He looked at the money in his hand and it was as though he had taken his first gulp of skull-buster. Then he looked at me with hard cold eyes.

"In the first place it's nobody's goddam business. And in the second place you haven't got a bean, Eth. You're as blind as I am, only it's a different kind of blindness."

"Listen to me, Danny."

"What for? Why, I'm better off than you are. I've got my ace in the hole. Remember our country place?"

"Where the house burned down? Where we used to play in the cellar hole?"

"You remember it all right. It's mine."

"Danny, you could sell it and get a new start."

"I won't sell it. The county takes a little bit of it for taxes every year. The big meadow is still mine."

"Why won't you sell it?"

"Because it's me. It's Daniel Taylor. Long as I have it no Christy sons of bitches can tell me what to do and no bastards can lock me up for my own good. Do you get it?"

"Listen, Danny—"

"I won't listen. If you think this dollar gives you the right to preach to me—here! Take it back."

"Keep it."

"I will. You don't know what you're talking about. You've never been a—drunk. I don't tell you how to wrap bacon do I? Now if you'll go your own way, I'll knock on a window and get some skull-buster. And don't forget—I'm better off than you are. I'm not a clerk." He turned around and put his head in the corner of the closed doorway like a child who abolishes the world by looking away from it. And he stayed there until I gave up and walked on.

Wee Willie, parked in front of the hotel, stirred out of his nap and rolled down the window of his Chevrolet. "Morning, Ethan," he said. "You up early or out late?"

"Both."

"Must have found yourself a fancy piece."

"Sure did, Willie, an houri."

"Now, Eth, don't tell me you'd take up with no streetwalker."

"I swear it."

"Can't believe nothing no more. I bet you was fishing. How's Missus?"

"Asleep."

"That's where I'll be, come shift."

I went on without reminding him that's where he'd been.

I walked quietly up my back steps and switched on the kitchen light. My note was on the table a little left of center. I'd swear I left it right in the middle.

I put the coffee on and sat waiting for it to perk, and it had just begun to bounce when Mary came down. My darling looks like a little girl when she awakens. You couldn't think she is the mother of two big brats. And her skin has a lovely smell, like new-cut grass, the most cozy and comforting odor I know.

"What are you doing up so early?"

"Well may you ask. Please to know I have been up most of the night. Regard my galoshes there by the door. Feel them for wetness."

"Where did you go?"

"Down by the sea there is a little cave, my rumpled duck. I crawled inside and I studied the night."

"Now wait."

"And I saw a star come out of the sea, and since it had no owner I took it for our star. I tamed it and turned it back to fatten."

"You're being silly. I think you just got up and that woke me."

"If you don't believe me, ask Wee Willie. I spoke to him. Ask Danny Taylor. I gave him a dollar."

"You shouldn't. He'll just get drunk."

"I know. That was his wish. Where can our star sleep, sweet fern?"

"Doesn't coffee smell good? I'm glad you're silly again. It's awful when you're gloomy. I'm sorry about that fortune thing. I don't want you to think I'm not happy."

"Don't give it a worry, it's in the cards."

"What?"

"No joke. I'm going to make our fortune."

"I never know what you're thinking."

"That's the greatest difficulty with telling the truth. Can I beat the children a little to celebrate the day before Resurrection? I promise to break no bones."

"I haven't washed my face," she said. "I couldn't imagine who was rattling around in the kitchen."

When she had gone up to the bathroom, I put my note to her in my pocket. And I still didn't know. Does anyone ever know even the outer fringe of another? What are you like in there? Mary—do you hear? Who are you in there?

Chapter IV

THAT Saturday morning seemed to have a pattern. I wonder whether all days have. It was a withdrawn day. The little gray whisper of my Aunt Deborah came to me, "Of course, Jesus is dead. This is the only day in the world's days when He is dead. And all men and women are dead too. Jesus is in Hell. But tomorrow. Just wait until tomorrow. Then you'll see something."

I don't remember her very clearly, the way you don't remember someone too close to look at. But she read the Scripture to me like a daily newspaper and I suppose that's the way she thought of it, as something going on happening eternally but always exciting and new. Every Easter, Jesus really rose from the dead, an explosion, expected but nonetheless new. It wasn't two thousand years ago to her; it was now. And she planted something of that in me.

I can't remember wanting to open the store before. I think I hated every sluggish sloven of a morning. But this day I wanted to go. I love my Mary with all my heart, in some ways much better than myself, but it is also true that I do not always listen to her with complete attention. When she tells the chronicle of clothes and health and conversations which please and enlighten her, I do not listen at all, so that sometimes she exclaims, "But you should have known. I told you. I remember very clearly telling you on Thursday morning." And there's no doubt at all about that. She did tell me. She tells me everything in certain areas.

This morning I not only didn't listen, I wanted to get away from it. Maybe I wanted to talk myself and I didn't have anything to say—because, to give her fair due, she doesn't listen to me either, and a good thing sometimes. She listens to tones and intonations and from them gathers her facts about health and how my mood is and am I tired or gay. And that's as good a way as any. Now that I think of it, she doesn't listen to me because I am not talking to her, but to some dark listener within myself. And she doesn't really talk to me either. Of course when the children or some other hell-raising crises are concerned, all that changes.

I've thought so often how telling changes with the nature of the listener. Much of my talk is addressed to people who are dead, like my little Plymouth Rock Aunt Deborah or old Cap'n. I find myself arguing with them. I remember once in weary, dusty combat I called out to old Cap'n, "Do I have to?" And he replied very clearly, "Course you do. And don't whisper." He didn't argue—never did. Just said I must, and so I did. Nothing mysterious or mystic about that. It's asking for advice or an excuse from the inner part of you that is formed and certain.

For pure telling, which is another way of saying asking, my mute and articulate canned and bottled goods in the grocery serve very well. So does any passing animal or bird. They don't argue and they don't repeat.

Mary said, "You're not going already? Why you have half an hour. That's what comes of getting up so early."

"Whole flock of crates to open," I said. "Things to put on the shelves before I open. Great decisions. Should pickles and tomatoes go on the same shelf? Do canned apricots quarrel with peaches? You know how important color relations are on a dress."

"You'd make a joke about anything," Mary said. "But I'm glad. It's better than grumping. So many men grump."

And I was early. Red Baker wasn't out yet. You can set your watch by that dog, or any dog. He'd start his stately tour in exactly half an hour. And Joey Morphy wouldn't, didn't show. The bank wouldn't be open for business but that didn't mean Joey wouldn't be there working on the books. The town was very quiet but of course a lot of people had gone away for the Easter weekend. That and the Fourth of July and Labor Day are the biggest holidays. People go away even when they don't want to. I believe even the sparrows on Elm Street were away.

I did see Stonewall Jackson Smith on duty. He was just coming from a cup of coffee in the Foremaster Coffee Shop. He was so lean and brittle that his pistols and handcuffs seemed outsize. He wears his officer's cap at an angle, jaunty, and picks his teeth with a sharpened goose quill.

"Big business, Stoney. Long hard day making money."

"Huh?" he said. "Nobody's in town." What he meant was that he wished he weren't.

"Any murders, Stoney, or other grisly delights?"

"It's pretty quiet," he said. "Some kids wrecked a car at the bridge. But, hell, it was their own car. Judge'll make 'em pay for repairing the bridge. You heard about the bank job at Floodhampton?"

"No."

"Not even on television?"

"We don't have one, yet. Did they get much?"

"Thirteen thousand, they say. Yesterday just before closing. Three fellas. Four-state alarm. Willie's out on the highway now, bitching his head off."

"He gets plenty of sleep."

"I know, but I don't. I was out all night."

"Think they'll catch them?"

"Oh! I guess so. If it's money they usually do. Insurance companies keep nagging. Never let up."

"It would be nice work if they didn't catch you."

"Sure would," he said.

"Stoney, I wish you'd look in on Danny Taylor. He looks awful sick."

"Just a question of time," Stoney said. "But I'll go by. It's a shame. Nice fella. Nice family."

"It kills me. I like him."

"Well you can't do nothing with him. It's going to rain, Eth. Willie hates to get wet."

For the first time in my memory, I went into the alley with pleasure and opened the back door with excitement. The cat was by the door, waiting. I can't remember a morning when that lean and efficient cat hasn't been waiting to try to get in the back door and I have never failed to throw a stick at him or run him off. To the best of my knowledge, he has never got in. I call the cat "he" because his ears are torn up from fighting. Are cats strange animals or do they so resemble us that we find them curious as we do monkeys? Perhaps six or eight hundred times that cat has tried to get in and he has never made it.

"You're due for a cruel surprise," I told the cat. He was sitting in a circle of his tail, and the tip flicked up between his front feet. I went into the dark store, took a can of milk from the shelf, punched it open, and squirted it into a cup. Then I carried the cup to the storeroom and set it just inside and left the door open. He watched me gravely, looked at the milk, and then walked away and slid over the fence in back of the bank.

I was watching him go when Joey Morphy came into the alley with the key to the bank's back door ready in his hand. He looked seedy—grainy—as though he hadn't been to bed.

"Hi, Mr. Hawley."

"I thought you were closed today."

"Looks like I never close. Thirty-six-dollar mistake in the books. I worked till midnight last night."

"Short?"

"No—over."

"That should be good."

"Well, it ain't. I got to find it."

"Are banks that honest?"

"Banks are. It's only some men that aren't. If I'm going to get any holiday, I've got to find it."

"Wish I knew something about business."

"I can tell you all I know in one sentence. Money gets money."

"That doesn't do me much good."

"Me either. But I can sure give advice."

"Like what?"

"Like never take the first offer, and like, if somebody wants to sell, he's got a reason, and like, a thing is only as valuable as who wants it."

"That the quick course?"

"That's it, but it don't mean nothing without the first."

"Money gets money?"

"That cuts a lot of us out."

"Don't some people borrow?"

"Yeah, but you have to have credit and that's a kind of money."

"Guess I better stick to groceries."

"Looks like. Hear about the Floodhampton bank?"

"Stoney told me. Funny, we were just talking about it yesterday, remember?"

"I've got a friend there. Three guys—one talked with an

accent, one with a limp. Three guys. Sure they'll get them. Maybe a week. Maybe two."

"Tough!"

"Oh, I don't know. They aren't smart. There's a law against not being smart."

"I'm sorry about yesterday."

"Forget it. I talk too much. That's another rule—don't talk. I'll never learn that. Say, you look good."

"I shouldn't. Didn't get much sleep."

"Somebody sick?"

"No. Just one of those nights."

"Don't I know. . . ."

I swept out the store and raised the shades and didn't know I was doing it or hating it. Joey's rules popped around and around in my head. And I discussed matters with my friends on the shelves, perhaps aloud, perhaps not. I don't know.

"Dear associates," I said, "if it's that simple, why don't more people do it? Why does nearly everyone make the same mistakes and over and over? Is there always something forgotten? Maybe the real basic weakness might be some form of kindness. Marullo said money has no heart. Wouldn't it be true then that any kindness in a money man would be a weakness? How do you get nice ordinary Joes to slaughter people in a war? Well, it helps if the enemy looks different or talks different. But then how about civil war? Well the Yankees ate babies and the Rebs starved prisoners. That helps. I'll get around to you, sliced beets and tinned button mushrooms, in a moment. I know you want me to talk about you. Everyone does. But I'm on the verge of it—point of reference, that's it. If the laws of thinking are the laws of things, then morals are relative too, and manner and sin—that's relative too in a relative universe. Has to be. No getting away from it. Point of reference.

"You dry cereal with the Mickey Mouse mask on the box and a ventriloquism gadget for the label and ten cents. I'll have to take you home, but right now you sit up and listen. What I told dear Mary as a joke is true. My ancestors, those highly revered ship-owners and captains, surely had commissions to raid commerce in the Revolution and again in 1812. Very patriotic and virtuous. But to the British they were pirates, and what they took they kept. That's how the family fortune started that was lost by my father. That's where the money that makes money came from. We can be proud of it."

I brought in a carton of tomato paste, slashed it open, and stacked the charming slender little cans on their depleted shelf. "Maybe you don't know, because you're kind of foreigners. Money not only has no heart but no honor nor any memory. Money is respectable automatically if you keep it a while. You must not think I am denouncing money. I admire it very much. Gentlemen, may I introduce some newcomers to our community. Let's see, I'll put them here beside you catsups. Make these bread-and-butter pickles welcome in their new home. New Yorkers, born and sliced and bottled. I was discussing money with my friends here. One of your finest families—oh, you'd know the name! Everybody in the world does, I guess. Well, they got their big start selling beef to the British when our country was at war with the British, and their money is as admired as any and so is the family. And another dynasty, probably the greatest bankers of them all. The founder bought three hundred rifles from the Army. The Army had rejected them as dangerously defective and so he got them very cheap, maybe fifty cents apiece. Pretty soon General Frémont was ready to start his heroic trek to the West, and he bought the rifles, sight unseen, for twenty dollars apiece. No one ever heard whether they blew up in the troopers' hands. And that was the money that makes money. It doesn't matter how you get it just as long as you get it and use it to make more. I'm not being cynical. Our lord and master, Marullo of the ancient Roman name, is quite right. Where money is concerned, the ordinary rules of conduct take a holiday. Why do I talk to groceries? Perhaps because you are discreet. You do not repeat my words, or gossip. Money is a crass and ungracious subject only when you have it. The poor find it fascinating. But don't you agree that if one becomes actively interested in money, he should know something of its nature and character and tendencies? I'm afraid that very few men, and they great artists or misers, are interested in money for itself. And you can kick out those misers who are conditioned by fear."

By now there was a large pile of empty cartons on the floor.

I carried them to the storeroom to be trimmed and kept. Lots of people carry supplies home in them and, as Marullo would say, "It saves bags, kid."

There's that "kid" again. I don't mind it any more. I want him to call me "kid," even to think of me as "kid." While I was stacking the cartons, there came a battering on the front door. I looked at my big old silver railroad watch, and do you know for the first time in my life I had not opened on the moment of nine. Here it was plainly quarter after nine. All that discussion with the groceries had thrown me. Through the glass-and-iron screen of the door I could see it was Margie Young-Hunt. I had never really looked at her, had never inspected her. Maybe that's why she did the fortune—just to make sure I knew she existed. I shouldn't change too quickly.

I threw open the doors.

"Didn't mean to rout you out."

"But I'm late."

"Are you?"

"Sure. It's after nine."

She sauntered in. Her behind stuck out nice and round and bounced slowly, one up and one down with each step. She was well enough stacked in front so she didn't have to emphasize them. They were there. Margie is what Joey-boy would call a "dish," and my own son Allen too, maybe. Perhaps I was seeing her for the first time. Her features regular, nose a little long, lips outlined fuller than they were, the lower particularly. Her hair dyed a rich chestnut brown that doesn't occur in nature, but pretty. Her chin was fragile and deep-cut but there was plenty of muscle in the cheeks and very wide cheekbones. Margie's eyes had had care. They were that hazel to blue to steel color that changes with the light. It was a durable face that had taken it and could take it, even violence, even punching. Her eyes flicked about, to me, to the groceries, and back to me. I imagined she was a very close observer and a good rememberer too.

"I hope you don't have the same problem as yesterday."

She laughed. "No—no. I don't get a drummer every day. This time I really ran out of coffee."

"Most people do."

"What do you mean?"

"Well, the first ten people every morning ran out of coffee."

"Is that true?"

"Sure. Say, I want to thank you for sending your drummer in."

"It was his idea."

"But you did it. What kind of coffee?"

"Doesn't matter. I make lousy coffee no matter what kind I get."

"Do you measure?"

"Sure, and it's still lousy. Coffee just isn't—I nearly said 'my cup of tea.'"

"You did say it. Try this blend." I picked a can from the shelf and as she reached to take it from me—just that little gesture—every part of her body moved, shifted, announced itself quietly. I'm here, the leg. Me, the thigh. Not better than me, the soft belly. Everything was new, newly seen. I caught my breath. Mary says a woman can put out signals or not, just as she wishes. And if that's so, Margie had a communications system that ran from her pointed patent-leather toe to her curving soft chestnut hair.

"You seem to have got over your mullygrabs."

"I had 'em bad yesterday. Don't know where they come from."

"Don't I know! Sometimes with me not for the usual reason."

"You did quite a job with that fortune."

"Sore about it?"

"No. I'd just like to know how you did it."

"You don't believe in that stuff."

"It's not belief. You hit some things right on the nose. Things I'd been thinking and things I've been doing."

"Like what?"

"Like it's time for a change."

"You think I rigged the cards, don't you?"

"Doesn't matter. If you did—what made you? Have you thought of that?"

She looked me full in the eyes, suspicious, probing, questioning. "Yeah!" she said softly. "I mean no, I never thought of that. If I rigged them, what made me? That would be like unrigging the rig."

Mr. Baker looked in the door. "Morning, Margie," he said. "Ethan, have you given any thought to my suggestion?"

"I sure have. And I'd like to talk to you."

"Anytime at all, Ethan."

"Well, I can't get out during the week. You know, Marullo's hardly ever here. Going to be home tomorrow?"

"After church, sure. That's an idea. You bring Mary about four. While the ladies jaw about Easter hats, we'll slip off and—"

"I've got a hundred things I want to ask. Guess I better write them down."

"Anything I know, you're welcome to. See you then. Morning, Margie."

When he went out, Margie said, "You're beginning fast."

"Maybe just limbering up. Say—know what would be interesting? How about if you turned the cards blindfolded or something and see how close they come to yesterday."

"No!" she said. "That wouldn't work. You kidding me, or do you really go for it?"

"Way I look at it, it doesn't matter about believing. I don't believe in extrasensory perception, or lightning or the hydrogen bomb, or even violets or schools of fish—but I know they exist. I don't believe in ghosts but I've seen them."

"Now you're kidding."

"I'm not."

"You don't seem like the same man."

"I'm not. Maybe nobody is, for long."

"What caused it, Eth?"

"I don't know. Maybe I'm sick of being a grocery clerk."

"It's about time."

"Do you really like Mary?"

"Sure I do. Why would you ask that?"

"You just don't seem to be the same kind of—well, you're so different from her."

"I see what you mean. But I do like her. I love her."

"So do I."

"Lucky."

"I know I am."

"I meant her. Well, I'll go make my lousy coffee. I'll think about that card deal."

"Sooner the better, before it cools."

She tapped out, her neat buttocks jumping like live rubber. I had never seen her before. I wonder how many people I've looked at all my life and never seen. It's scary to think about. Point of reference again. When two people meet, each one is changed by the other so you've got two new people. Maybe that means—hell, it's complicated. I agreed with myself to think about such things at night when I couldn't sleep. Forgetting to open on time scared me. That's like dropping your handkerchief at the scene of the murder, or your glasses like those what-you-callems in Chicago. What does that mean? What crime? What murder?

At noon I made four sandwiches, cheese and ham, with lettuce and mayonnaise. Ham and cheese, ham and cheese—when a man marries, he lives in the trees. I took two of the sandwiches and a bottle of Coke to the back door of the bank and handed them in to Joey-boy. "Find the mistake?"

"Not yet. You know, I'm so close to it, I'm blind."

"Why not lay off till Monday?"

"Can't. Banks are a screwy lot."

"Sometimes if you don't think about something, it comes to you."

"I know. Thanks for the sandwiches." He looked inside to make sure there was lettuce and mayonnaise.

Saturday afternoon before Easter in the grocery business is what my august and illiterate son would call "for the birds." But two things did happen that proved to me at least that some deep-down underwater change was going on in me. I mean that yesterday, or any yesterday before that, I wouldn't have done what I did. It's like looking at wallpaper samples. I guess I had unrolled a new pattern.

The first thing was Marullo coming in. His arthritis was hurting him pretty bad. He kept flexing his arms like a weight-lifter.

"How it goes?"

"Slow, Alfio." I had never called him by his first name before.

"Nobody in town—"

"I like it better when you call me 'kid.'"

"I thought you don't like it."

"I find I do, Alfio."

"Everybody gone away." His shoulders must have been burning as though there were hot sand in the joints.

"How long ago did you come from Sicily?"

"Forty-seven years. Long time."

"Ever been back?"

"No."

"Why don't you go on a visit?"

"What for? Everything changed."

"Don't you get curious about it?"

"Not much."

"Any relatives alive?"

"Sure, my brother and his kids and they got kids."

"I'd think you'd want to see them."

He looked at me, I guess, as I'd looked at Margie, saw me for the first time.

"What you got on your mind, kid?"

"Hurts me to see your arthritis. I thought how its warm in Sicily. Might knock the pain out."

He looked at me suspiciously. "What's with you?"

"How do you mean?"

"You look different."

"Oh! I got a little bit of good news."

"Not going to quit?"

"Not right away. If you wanted to make a trip to Italy, I could promise I'd be here."

"What's good news?"

"Can't tell you yet. It's like this. . . ." I balanced my palm back and forth.

"Money?"

"Could be. Look, you're rich enough. Why don't you go back to Sicily and show 'em what a rich American looks like? Soak up some sun. I can take care of the store. You know that."

"You ain't quitting?"

"Hell, no. You know me well enough to know I wouldn't run out on you."

"You changed, kid. Why?"

"I told you. Go bounce the bambinos."

"I don't belong there," he said, but I knew I'd planted something—really something. And I knew he'd come in late that night and go over the books. He's a suspicious bastard.

He'd hardly left when—well, it was like yesterday—the B.B.D. and D. drummer came in.

"Not on business," he said. "I'm staying the weekend out at Montauk. Thought I'd drop in."

"I'm glad you did," I said. "I want to give you this." I held out the billfold with the twenty sticking out.

"Hell, that's good will. I told you I'm not on business."

"Take it!"

"What you getting at?"

"It constitutes a contract where I come from."

"What's the matter, you sore?"

"Certainly not."

"Then why?"

"Take it! The bids aren't all in."

"Jesus—did Waylands make a better offer?"

"No."

"Who, then—them damn discount houses?"

I pushed the twenty-dollar bill into his breast pocket behind his peaked handkerchief. "I'll keep the billfold," I said. "It's nice."

"Look I can't make an offer without I talk to the head office. Don't close till maybe Tuesday. I'll telephone you. If I say it's Hugh, you'll know who it is."

"It's your money in the pay phone."

"Well, hold it open, will you?"

"It's open," I said. "Doing any fishing?"

"Only for dames. I tried to take that dish Margie out there. She wouldn't go. Damn near snapped my head off. I don't get dames."

"They're curiouser and curiouser."

"You can say that again," he said, and I haven't heard that expression in fifteen years. He looked worried. "Don't do anything till you hear from me," he said. "Jesus, I thought I was conning a country boy."

"I will not sell my master short."

"Nuts. You just raised the ante."

"I just refused a bribe if you feel the urge to talk about it."

I guess that proves I was different. The guy began to look at me with respect and I liked it. I loved it. The bugger thought I was like him, only better at it.

Just before I was ready to close up Mary telephoned. "Ethan," she said, "now don't get mad—"

"At what, flower feet?"

"Well, she's so lonely and I thought—well, I asked Margie to dinner."

"Why not?"

"You're not mad?"

"Hell, no."

"Don't swear. Tomorrow's Easter."

"That reminds me, press your prettiest. We're going to Baker's at four o'clock."

"At their house?"

"Yes, for tea."

"I'll have to wear my Easter church outfit."

"Good stuff, fern tip."

"You're not mad about Margie?"

"I love you," I said. And I do. I really do. And I remember thinking what a hell of a man a man could become.

Chapter V

When I walked up Elm Street and turned in at the walk of buried ballast stones, I stopped and looked at the old place. It felt different. It felt mine. Not Mary's, not Father's, not old Cap'n's, but mine. I could sell it or burn it or keep it.

I'd taken only two of the back steps when the screen door whapped open and Allen boiled out yelling, "Where's the Peeks? Didn't you bring me the Peeks?"

"No," I said. And, wonder layered with wonders, he didn't scream his pain and loss. He didn't appeal to his mother to agree that I had promised.

He said, "Oh!" and went quietly away.

"Good evening," I said to his retreating back and he stopped and said, "Good evening," as though it were a foreign word he'd just learned.

Mary came into the kitchen. "You've had a haircut," she said. She identifies any strangeness in me as a fever or a haircut.

"No, pin curl, I have not."

"Well, I've been going like spit to get the house ready."

"Ready?"

"I told you, Margie's coming for dinner."

"I know, but why all the festive hurly-burly?"

"We haven't had a dinner guest in ages."

"That's true. That's really true."

"Are you going to put on your dark suit?"

"No, Old Dobbin, my decent gray."

"Why not the dark?"

"Don't want to spoil the press for church tomorrow."

"I can press it tomorrow morning."

"I'll wear Old Dobbin, as sweet a suit as you'll find in the county."

"Children," she called, "don't you touch anything! I've put out the nut dishes. You don't want to wear the dark?"

"No."

"Margie will be dressed to the nines."

"Margie likes Old Dobbin."

"How do you know?"

"She told me."

"She did not."

"Wrote a letter to the paper about it."

"Be serious. You *are* going to be nice to her?"

"I'm going to make love to her."

"I'd think you'd like to wear the dark—with her coming."

"Look, flower girl, when I came in, I didn't give a damn what I wore or nothing. In two short moments you have made it impossible for me to wear anything but Old Dobbin."

"Just to be mean?"

"Sure."

"Oh!" she said in the same tone Allen had used.

"What's for dinner? I want to wear a tie to match the meat."

"Roast chicken. Can't you smell it?"

"Guess I can. Mary—I—" But I didn't go on. Why do it? You can't buck a national instinct. She'd been to the Chicken Bargain Day at the Safe Rite Store. Cheaper than Marullo's. Of course I got them wholesale and I have explained to Mary the come-on bargains at the chain stores. The bargain draws you in and you pick up a dozen other things that aren't bargains just because they're under your hand. Everyone knows it and everyone does it.

My lecture to Mary Manyflowers died afoaling. The New Ethan Allen Hawley goes along with the national follies and uses them when he can.

Mary said, "I hope you don't think I was disloyal."

"My darling, what can be virtuous or sinful about a chicken?"

"It was awful cheap."

"I think you did the wise—the wifely thing."

"You're making fun."

Allen was in my bedroom waiting for me. "Can I look at your Knight Templar sword?"

"Sure. It's in the corner of the closet."

He knew perfectly well where it was. While I skinned off my clothes, he got it out of the leather case and unsheathed it and held the shiny plated blade up in the light and looked at his noble posture in the mirror.

"How's the essay going?"

"Huh?"

"Don't you mean, 'I beg your pardon, sir'?"

"Yes, sir."

"I said, how's the essay?"

"Oh! Fine."

"You going to do it?"

"Sure."

"Sure?"

"Sure, sir."

"You can look at the hat, too. In that big leather case on the shelf. Feather's kind of yellowy."

I got in the big old wide-bottomed tub with the lion's feet. They made them big enough to luxuriate in in those days. I scrubbed Marullo and the whole day off my skin with a brush and I shaved in the tub without looking, feeling for the whiskers with my fingertips. Everyone would agree that's pretty Roman and decadent. While I combed my hair, I looked in the mirror. I hadn't seen my face in a long time. It's quite possible to shave every day and never really to see your face, particularly if you don't care much for it. Beauty is only skin deep, and also beauty must come from inside. It better be the second if I was to get anywhere. It isn't that I have an ugly face. To me, it just isn't interesting. I made a few expressions and gave it up. They weren't noble or menacing or proud or funny. It was just the same damn face making faces.

When I came back to the bedroom, Allen had the plumed Knight Templar hat on, and if it makes me look that silly I must resign. The leather hatbox was open on the floor. It has a support made of velvet-covered cardboard like an upside-down porridge bowl.

"I wonder if they can bleach that ostrich plume or do I have to get a new one?"

"If you get a new one, can I have this?"

"Why not? Where's Ellen? I haven't heard her young screechy voice."

"She's writing on her I Love America essay."

"And you?"

"I'm thinking about it. Will you bring some Peeks home?"

"I'll probably forget it. Why don't you drop in at the store and pick it up someday?"

"Okay. Mind if I ask something—sir?"

"I'd be flattered."

"Did we use to own all High Street for two blocks?"

"We did."

"And did we have whaling ships?"

"Yep."

"Well, why don't we now?"

"We lost them."

"How come?"

"Just up and lost them."

"That's a joke."

"It's a pretty darned serious joke, if you dissect it."

"We're dissecting a frog at school."

"Good for you. Not so good for the frog. Which of these beauty-ties shall I wear?"

"The blue one," he said without interest. "Say, when you get dressed can you—have you got time to come up in the attic?"

"I'll make time if it's important."

"Will you come?"

"I will."

"All right. I'll go up now and turn on the light."

"Be with you in a couple of tie-tying moments."

His footsteps sounded hollowly on the uncarpeted attic stairs.

If I think about it while I tie a bow, the tie has a rotating tendency, but if I let my fingers take their own way, they do it perfectly. I commissioned my fingers and thought about the attic of the old Hawley house, my house, my attic. It is not a dark and spidery prison for the broken and the abandoned. It has windows with small panes so old that the light comes through lavender and the outside is wavery—like a world seen through water. The books stored there are not waiting to be thrown out or given to the Seamen's Institute. They sit comfortably on their shelves waiting to be rediscovered. And the chairs, some unfashionable for a time, some rump-sprung, are large and soft. It is not a dusty place either. Housecleaning is attic-cleaning also, and since it is mostly closed away, dust does not enter. I remember as a child scrambling among the brilliants of books or, battered with agonies, or in the spectral half-life that requires loneliness, retiring to the attic, to lie curled in a great body-molded chair in the violet-lavender light from the window. There I could study the big adze-squared beams that support the roof—see how they are mortised one into another and pinned in place with oaken dowels. When it rains from rustling drip to roar on the roof, it is a fine secure place. Then the books, tinted with light, the picture books of children grown, seeded, and gone; *Chatterboxes* and the Rollo series; a thousand acts of God—*Fire*, *Flood*, *Tidal Waves*, *Earthquakes*—all fully illustrated; the Gustave Doré Hell, with Dante's squared cantos like bricks between; and the heartbreaking stories of Hans Christian Andersen, the blood-chilling violence and cruelty of the Grimm Brothers, the Morte d'Arthur of majesty with drawings by Aubrey Beardsley, a sickly, warped creature, a strange choice to illustrate great, manly Malory.

I remember thinking how wise a man was H. C. Andersen. The king told his secrets down a well, and his secrets were safe. A man who tells secrets or stories must think of who is hearing or reading, for a story has as many versions as it has readers. Everyone takes what he wants or can from it and thus changes it to his measure. Some pick out parts and reject the rest, some strain the story through their mesh of prejudice, some paint it with their own delight. A story must have some points of contact with the reader to make him feel at home in it. Only then can he accept wonders. The tale I may tell to Allen must be differently built from the same tale told to my Mary, and that in turn shaped to fit Marullo if Marullo is to join it. But perhaps the Well of Hosay Andersen is best. It only receives, and the echo it gives back is quiet and soon over.

I guess we're all, or most of us, the wards of that nineteenth-century science which denied existence to anything it could not measure or explain. The things we couldn't explain went right on but surely not with our blessing. We did not see what we couldn't explain, and meanwhile a great part of the world was abandoned to children, insane people, fools, and mystics, who were more interested in what is than in why it is. So many old and lovely things are stored in the world's attic, because we don't want them around us and we don't dare throw them out.

A single unshaded light hung from a roof beam. The attic is floored with hand-hewn pine planks twenty inches wide and two inches thick, ample support for the neat stacks of trunks and boxes, of paper-wrapped lamps and vases and all manner of exiled finery. And the light glowed softly on the generations of books in open bookcases—all clean and dustless. My Mary is a stern and uncompromising dust harrier and she is neat as a top sergeant. The books are arranged by size and color.

Allen rested his forehead on the top of a bookcase and glared down at the books. His right hand was on the pommel of the Knight Templar sword, point downward like a cane.

"You make a symbolic picture, my son. Call it 'Youth, War, and Learning.' "

"I want to ask you—you said there was books to look up stuff."

"What kind of stuff?"

"Patriotic jazz, for the essay."

"I see. Patriotic jazz. How's this for beat? 'Is life so dear or peace so sweet as to be purchased at the price of chains and slavery? Forbid it, Almighty God! I know not what course others may take, but as for me, give me liberty or give me death!' "

"Great! That's the berries."

"Sure is. There were giants on the earth in those days."

"I wisht I lived then. Pirate ships. Oh boy! Bang-bang! Strike your colors! Pots of gold and ladies in silk dresses and jewels. I sure wisht I lived then. Some of our folks done—did it. You said so yourself."

"Kind of genteel piracy—they called them privateers. I guess it wasn't as sweet as it sounds from a distance. Salt beef and biscuit. There was scurvy on the earth in those days too."

"I wouldn't mind that. I'd get the gold and bring it home. I guess they won't let you do it any more."

"No—it's bigger and better organized now. They call it diplomacy."

"There's a boy in our school that won two television prizes—fifty dollars and two hundred dollars. How's that?"

"He must be smart."

"Him? Course not. It's a trick, he says. You got to learn the trick and then you get a gimmick."

"Gimmick?"

"Sure—like you're a cripple or you support your old mother raising frogs. That gives you audience interest so they choose you. He's got a magazine with every contest in the whole country in it. Can I get one of those magazines, Pop?"

"Well, piracy is out, but I guess the impulse lingers."

"How do you mean?"

"Something for nothing. Wealth without effort."

"Can I get that magazine?"

"I thought such things were in disrepute since the payola scandals."

"Hell, no. I mean no, sir. They just changed it around a little. I'd sure like to cut in on some of that loot."

"It is loot, isn't it?"

"It's all dough, no matter how you get it."

"I don't believe that. It doesn't hurt the money to get it that way but it hurts the one who gets it."

"I don't see how. It's not against the law. Why, some of the biggest people in this country—"

"Charles, my son, my son."

"How do you mean, Charles?"

"Do you have to be rich, Allen? Do you have to?"

"Do you think I like to live without no motorbike? Must be twenty kids with motorbikes. And how you think it is if your family hasn't even got a car, leave alone no television?"

"I'm deeply shocked."

"You don't know how it is, Dad. One day in class I did a theme how my great-granddad was a whaling captain."

"He was."

"Whole class bust out laughing. Know what they call me? Whaley. How'd you like that?"

"Pretty bad."

"It wouldn't be so bad if you were a lawyer or in a bank or like that. Know what I'm going to do with the first chunk of loot I win?"

"No, what?"

"I'm going to buy you an automobile so you won't feel so lousy when other people all got one."

I said, "Thank you, Allen." My throat was dry.

"Oh, that's all right. I can't get a license yet anyway."

"You'll find all the great speeches of our nation in that case, Allen. I hope you'll read some of them."

"I will. I need to."

"You surely do. Good hunting." I went quietly down the stairs and moistened my lips as I went. And Allen was right. I felt lousy.

When I sat down in my big chair under the reading light, Mary brought the paper to me.

"What a comfort you are, wiggles."

"That suit looks real nice."

"You're a good loser and a good cook."

"The tie matches your eyes."

"You're up to something. I can tell. I'll trade you a secret for a secret."

"But I don't have one," she said.

"Make one up!"

"I can't. Come on, Ethan, tell me."

"Any eary children listening in?"

"No."

"Well, Margie Young-Hunt came in today. Out of coffee, so she said. I think she's carrying a torch for me."

"Come on, tell."

"Well, we were talking about the fortune and I said it would be interesting to do it again and see if it was the same."

"You didn't!"

"I did so. And she said it would be interesting."

"But you don't like things like that."

"I do when they're good."

"Think she'll do it tonight?"

"If you care to offer me a penny for my thoughts, I think that's why she's coming."

"Oh, no! I asked her."

"After she set you up for it."

"You don't like her."

"On the contrary—I'm beginning to like her very much, and to respect her."

"I wish I could tell when you're joking."

Ellen came in then quietly so that you couldn't tell whether she had been listening but I suspect she had. Ellen is a girl-girl-girl and thirteen to boot, sweet and sad, gay and delicate, sickly when she needs it. She is in that stage like dough beginning to set. She may be pretty, or not. She is a leaner, leans on me, breathes on me too, but her breath is sweet like a cow's breath. She's a toucher, too.

Ellen leaned on the arm of my chair and her thin little shoulder touched mine. She ran one pink finger down my coat sleeve and onto the hairs on my wrist and it tickled. The blond hairs on her arm shone like gold dust under the lamp. A devious one, she is, but then I guess all girl-girl-girls are.

"Nail polish," I said.

"Mama lets me if it's only pink. Your nails are rough."

"Aren't they?"

"But they're clean."

"I scrubbed them."

"I hate dirty nails like Allen's."

"Maybe you just hate Allen lock, stock, and bobtail."

"I do."

"Good for you. Why don't you kill him?"

"You're silly." She crawled her fingers behind my ear. She's probably making some boy kids very nervous already.

"I hear you are working on your essay."

"Stinker told you."

"Is it good?"

"Oh, yes! Very good. I'll let you read it when it's done."

"Honored. I see you're dressed for the occasion."

"This old thing? I'm saving my new dress for tomorrow."

"Good idea. There'll be boys."

"I hate boys. I do hate boys."

"I know you do. Hostility is your motto. I don't like 'em much myself. Now lean off me a minute. I want to read the paper."

She flounced like a 1920 movie star and instantly took her revenge. "When are you going to be rich?"

Yes, she'll give some man a bad time. My instinct was to grab her and paddle her but that's exactly what she wanted. I do believe she had eye shadow on. There was as little pity in her eyes as you'll find in a panther's eyes.

"Next Friday," I said.

"Well, I wish you'd hurry up. I'm sick of being poor." And she slipped quickly out. A listener at doors too. I do love her, and that's odd because she is everything I destest in anyone else—and I adore her.

No newspaper for me. I hadn't even unfolded it when Margie Young-Hunt arrived. She was done up—hairdresser done up. I guess Mary would know how it's done, but I don't.

In the morning the out-of-coffee Margie was set for me like

a bear trap. The same evening she drew a bead on Mary. If her behind bounced, I couldn't see it. If anything was under her neat suit, it was hiding. She was a perfect guest—for another woman—helpful, charming, complimentary, thoughtful, modest. She treated me as though I had taken on forty years since the morning. What a wonderful thing a woman is. I can admire what they do even if I don't understand why.

While Margie and Mary went through their pleasant litany, "What have you done with your hair?" . . . "I like it" . . . "That's your color. You should always wear it"—the harmless recognition signals of women—I thought of the most feminine story I ever heard. Two women meet. One cries, "What have you done with your hair? It looks like a wig." "It is a wig." "Well, you'd never know it."

Maybe these are deeper responses than we know or have any right to know.

Dinner was a series of exclamations about the excellence of the roast chicken and denials that it was edible. Ellen studied our guest with a recording eye, every detail of hair-dress and make-up. And I knew then how young they start the minute examination on which they base what is called their intuition. Ellen avoided my eyes. She knew she had shot to kill and she expected revenge. Very well, my savage daughter. I shall revenge myself in the cruelest way you can imagine. I shall forget it.

And it was a good dinner, over-rich and too much of it, as company dinners must be, and a mountain of dishes not ordinarily used. And coffee afterward, which we do not ordinarily have.

"Doesn't it keep you awake?"

"Nothing keeps me awake."

"Not even me?"

"Ethan!"

And then the silent, deadly war of the dishes. "Let me help."

"Not at all. You're the guest."

"Well, let me carry them."

Mary's eyes sought out the children and her spirit moved on them with fixed bayonet. They knew what was coming, but they were helpless.

Mary said, "The children always do it. They love to. And they do it so well. I'm proud of them."

"Well, isn't that nice? You don't see it much any more."

"I know. We feel very fortunate that they want to help."

I could read their ferrety little minds, looking for an escape, thinking of making a fuss, getting sick, dropping the beautiful old dishes. Mary must have read their evil little minds also. She said, "The remarkable thing is that they never break anything, don't even chip a glass."

"Well, you are blessed!" Margie said. "How did you teach them?"

"I didn't. It's just natural with them. You know, some people are just naturally clumsy; well, Allen and Ellen are just naturally clever with their hands."

I glanced at the kids to see how they were handling it. They knew they were being taken. I think they wondered whether Margie Young-Hunt knew it. They were still looking for an escape. I dropped the beam full on them.

"Of course they like to hear compliments," I said, "but we're holding them up. They'll miss the movie if we don't let them get to it."

Margie had the grace not to laugh and Mary gave me a quick and startled look of admiration. They hadn't even asked to go to the movie.

Even if teen-age children aren't making a sound, it's quieter when they're gone. They put a boiling in the air around them. As they left, the whole house seemed to sigh and settle. No wonder poltergeists infest only houses with adolescent children.

The three of us circled warily around the subject each one knew was coming. I went to the glass-fronted cabinet and took out three long-stemmed, lily-shaped glasses, cotton twist, brought home from England, heaven knows how long ago. And I poured from a basket-covered gallon jug, dark and discolored with age.

"Jamaica rum," I said. "Hawleys were seamen."

"Must be very old," said Margie Young-Hunt.

"Older than you or me or my father."

"It'll take the top of your head off," Mary said. "Well, this must be a party. Ethan only gets it out for weddings and funerals. Do you think it's all right, dear? Just before Easter, I mean?"

"The Sacrament isn't Coca-Cola, my darling."

"Mary, I've never seen your husband so gay."

"It's the fortune you read," said Mary. "It's changed him overnight."

What a frightening thing is the human, a mass of gauges and dials and registers, and we can read only a few and those perhaps not accurately. A flare of searing red pain formed in my bowels and moved upward until it speared and tore at the place just under my ribs. A great wind roared in my ears and drove me like a helpless ship, dismasted before it could shorten sail. I tasted bitter salt and I saw a pulsing, heaving room. Every warning signal screamed danger, screamed havoc, screamed shock. It caught me as I passed behind my ladies' chairs and doubled me over in quaking agony, and just as suddenly it was gone. I straightened up and moved on and they didn't even know it had happened. I understand how people once believed the devil could take possession. I'm not sure I don't believe it. Possession! The seething birth of something foreign with every nerve resisting and losing the fight and settling back beaten to make peace with the invader. Violation—that's the word, if you can think of the sound of a word edged with blue flame like a blowtorch.

My dear's voice came through. "It doesn't really harm to hear nice things," she said.

I tried my voice and it was strong and good. "A little hope, even hopeless hope, never hurt anybody," I said, and I put the jug away in its cabinet, and went back to my chair and drank half the glass of ancient, fragrant rum and sat down and crossed my knees and locked my fingers in my lap.

"I don't understand him," Mary said. "He's always hated fortune-telling, made jokes about it. I just don't understand."

My nerve ends were rustling like dry, windblown winter grass and my laced fingers had whitened from pressure.

"I'll try to explain it to Mrs. Young—to Margie," I said. "Mary comes from a noble but poor Irish family."

"We weren't all that poor."

"Can't you hear it in her speech?"

"Well, now that you mention it—"

"Well, Mary's sainted, or should be, grandmother was a good Christian, wasn't she, Mary?"

It seemed to me a little hostility was growing in my dear. I went on. "But she had no trouble believing in fairy people, although in strict, unbending Christian theology the two don't mix."

"But that's different."

"Of course it is, darling. Nearly everything's different. Can you disbelieve in something you don't know about?"

"Look out for him," Mary said. "He'll catch you in a word trap."

"I will not. I don't know about fortunes or fortune-telling. How can I not believe in it? I believe it exists because it happens."

"But you don't believe it's true."

"What's true is that people get it done, millions of them, and pay for it. That's enough to know to be interested, isn't it?"

"But you don't—"

"Wait! It isn't that I don't believe but that I don't know. They're not the same thing. I don't know which comes first—the fortune or the fortune-telling."

"I think I know what he means."

"You do?" Mary was not pleased.

"Suppose the fortune-teller was sensitive to things that are going to happen anyway. Is that what you mean?"

"That's different. But how can cards know?"

I said, "The cards can't even move without someone turning them."

Margie did not look at me but I knew she sensed Mary's growing unease and she wanted instructions.

"Couldn't we work out a test?" I asked.

"Well, that's a funny thing. These things seem to resent a test and go away, but there's no harm trying. Can you think of a test?"

"You haven't touched your rum." They lifted their glasses together and sipped and put them down. I finished mine and got out the bottle.

"Ethan, do you think you should?"

"Yes, dearling." I filled my glass. "Why can't you turn the cards blindfolded?"

"They have to be read."

"How would it be if Mary turned them or I did, and you read them?"

"There's supposed to be a closeness between the reader and the cards, but I don't know—we could try."

Mary said, "I think if we do it at all, we ought to do it the right way." She's always that way. She doesn't like change—little change, I mean. The big ones she can handle better than anyone, blows up at a cut finger but would be calm and efficient with a cut throat. I had a throb of unease because I had told Mary we discussed this, and here we were seeming to think of it for the first time.

"We talked about it this morning."

"Yes, when I came in for coffee. I've been thinking about it all day. I brought the cards."

It is Mary's tendency to confuse intentness with anger and anger with violence and she is terrified of violence. Some drinking uncles put that fear on her, and it's a shame. I could feel her fear rising.

"Let's not fool with it," I said. "Let's play some cassino instead."

Margie saw the tactic, knew it, had probably used it. "All right with me."

"My fortune's set. I'm going to be rich. Let it go at that."

"You see, I told you he didn't believe in it. He leads you all around the bush and then he won't play. He makes me so mad sometimes."

"I do? You never show it. You are always my darling wife."

Isn't it strange how sometimes you can feel currents and cross-currents—not always, but sometimes. Mary doesn't use her mind for organized thought and maybe this makes her more receptive of impressions. A tension was growing in the room. It crossed my mind that she might not be best friends with Margie any more—might never feel easy with her.

"I'd really like to know about the cards," I said. "I'm ignorant. I always heard that gypsies do it. Are you a gypsy? I don't think I ever knew one."

Mary said, "Her maiden name was Russian but she's from Alaska."

Then that accounted for the wide cheekbones.

Margie said, "I have a guilty secret I've never told you, Mary, how we came to be in Alaska."

"The Russians owned it," I said. "We bought it from them."

"Yes, but did you know it was a prison, like Siberia, only for worse crimes?"

"What kind of crimes?"

"The worst. My great-grandmother was sentenced to Alaska for witchcraft."

"What did she do?"

"She raised storms."

I laughed. "I see you come by it naturally."

"Raising storms?"

"Reading cards—same thing, maybe."

Mary said, "You're joking. That isn't true."

"It may be joking, Mary, but it's true. That was the worst crime, worse than murder. I've still got her papers—only of course they're in Russian."

"Can you speak Russian?"

"Only a little now."

I said, "Maybe witchcraft still is the worst crime."

"See what I mean?" said Mary. "He jumps this side and that side. You never know what he's thinking. Last night he—he got up before daylight this morning. Went for a walk."

"I'm a scoundrel," I said. "An unmitigated, unredeemable rascal."

"Well, I would like to see Margie turn the cards—but her own way without you mixing in. If we keep talking, the children will be home and then we can't."

"Excuse me a moment," I said. I climbed the stairs to our bedroom. The sword was on the bed and the hatbox open on the floor. I went to the bathroom and flushed the toilet. You can hear the water rushing all over the house. I wet a cloth in cold water and pressed it against my forehead and particularly against my eyes. They seemed to bulge from inside pressure. The cold water felt good. I sat on the toilet seat and put my face down against the damp washcloth and when it warmed up I wet it again. Going through the bedroom, I picked the plumed Knight Templar's hat from its box and marched down the stairs wearing it.

"Oh, you fool," said Mary. And she looked glad and relieved. The ache went out of the air.

"Can they bleach ostrich feathers?" I asked. "It's turned yellow."

"I think so. Ask Mr. Schultz."

"I'll take it down Monday."

"I wish Margie would turn the cards," said Mary. "I would dearly love that."

I put the hat on the newel post of the banister, and it looked like a drunken admiral if there is such a thing.

"Get the card table, Eth. It takes lots of room."

I brought it from the hall closet and snapped the legs open.

"Margie likes a straight chair."

I set a dining chair. "Do we have to do anything?"

"Concentrate," said Margie.

"On what?"

"As near as possible on nothing. The cards are in my purse over on the couch."

I'd always thought of fortune-telling cards as greasy and thick and bent, but these were clean and shining, as though they were coated with plastic. They were longer and narrower than playing cards and many more than fifty-two. Margie sat straight at the table and fanned them—bright-colored pictures and intricate suits. The names were in French: *l'empereur*, *l'ermite*, *le chariot*, *la justice*, *le mat*, *le diable*—earth, sun, moon, and stars, and suits of swords, cups, batons, and money, I guess, if *deniero* means money, but the symbol was shaped like a heraldic rose, and each suit with its *roi*, *reine*, and *chevalier*. Then I saw strange cards—disturbing cards—a tower riven by lightning, a wheel of fortune, a man hanging by his feet from a gallows, called *le pendu*, and Death—*la mort*, a skeleton with a scythe.

"Kind of gloomy," I said. "Do the pictures mean what they seem to?"

"It's how they fall in relation. If they fall upside down they reverse their meaning."

"Is there a variation in meaning?"

"Yes. That's the interpretation."

The moment she had the cards Margie became formal. Under the lights her hands showed what I had seen before, that she was older than she looked.

"Where did you learn it?" I asked.

"I used to watch my grandmother and later I took it up as a trick for parties—I suppose a way of getting attention."

"Do you believe in it?"

"I don't know. Sometimes remarkable things come out. I don't know."

"Could the cards be a concentration ritual—psychic exercise?"

"Sometimes I think that's true. When I find I give a value to a card it didn't have before, that's when it is usually accurate." Her hands were like living things as they shuffled and cut and shuffled and cut again and passed them to me to cut.

"Who am I doing?"

"Read Ethan," Mary cried. "See if it matches yesterday's."

Margie looked at me. "Light hair," she said, "blue eyes. Are you under forty?"

"Just."

"The king of batons." She found it in the deck. "This is you" —a picture of a crowned and robed king holding a huge red and blue scepter and *Roi de Bâton* printed under him. She laid it out face up and reshuffled the deck. Then she turned the cards rapidly, speaking in a singsong voice as she did. A card on top of my card—"This covers you." Crosswise on top—"This crosses you." One above—"This crowns you." One below—"This is your foundation. This before, this behind you." She had formed a cross of cards on the table. Then rapidly she turned up four in a line to the left of the cross, saying, "Yourself, your house, your hopes, your future." The last card was the man hanged upside down, le pendu, but from where I sat across the table he was right side up.

"So much for my future."

"It can mean salvation," she said. Her forefinger traced the line of her lower lip.

Mary demanded, "Is the money there?"

"Yes—it's there," she said absently. And suddenly she gathered the cards, shuffled them over and over, and laid them out again, muttering her ritual under her breath. She didn't seem to study individual cards but to see the whole group at once, and her eyes were misty and remote.

A good trick, I thought, a killer at ladies' clubs—or anywhere else. So must the Pythoness have looked, cool and composed and confusing. If you can hold people tense, hardly breathing, expectant for a long time, they'll believe anything—not acting, so much as technique, timing. This woman was wasting her talent on traveling salesmen. But what did she want of us or of me? Suddenly she gathered the cards, patted them square, and put them in the red box, which said: *I. Muller & Cie, Fabrique de Cartes.*

"Can't do it," she said. "Happens sometimes."

Mary said breathlessly, "Did you see something you don't want to tell?"

"Oh, I'll tell all right! Once when I was a little girl I saw a snake change its skin, a Rocky Mountain rattler. I watched the whole thing. Well, looking at the cards, they disappeared and I saw that snake changing its skin, part dusty and ragged and part fresh and new. You figure it out."

I said, "Sounds like a trance state. Ever have it happen before?"

"Three times before."

"Make any sense the other times?"

"Not that I know of."

"Always the snake?"

"Oh, no! Other things, but just as crazy."

Mary said enthusiastically, "Maybe it's a symbol of the change in fortune that's coming to Ethan."

"Is he a rattlesnake?"

"Oh! I see what you mean."

"Makes me feel crawly," Margie said. "Once I kind of liked snakes and then when I grew up I hated them. They give me the willies. I'd better be going."

"Ethan can see you home."

"Wouldn't think of it."

"I'd be glad to."

Margie smiled at Mary. "You keep him right here with you," she said. "You don't know what it's like to be without one."

"Nonsense," said Mary. "You could get a husband by crooking your finger."

"That's what I did before. It's no good. If they come that easy, they're not worth having. Keep him home. Someone might grab him." She got into her coat as she talked—a fast scrammer. "Lovely dinner. I hope you'll ask me back. Sorry about the fortune, Ethan."

"Will we see you in church tomorrow?"

"No. I'm going up to Montauk tonight."

"But it's too cold and wet."

"I love the mornings on the sea up there. Good night." She was out before I could even hold the door for her, out as though something was after her.

Mary said, "I didn't know she was going up there tonight."

And I couldn't tell her: Neither did she.

"Ethan—what do you make of that fortune tonight?"

"She didn't tell one."

"You forget, she said there would be money. But what do you make of it? I think she saw something she didn't want to tell. Something that scared her."

"Maybe she once saw the snake and it stayed in her mind."

"You don't think it had a—meaning?"

"Honey roll, you're the fortune expert. How would I know?"

"Well, anyway, I'm glad you don't hate her. I thought you did."

"I'm tricky," I said. "I conceal my thoughts."

"Not from me you don't. They'll stay right through the second show."

"Come again?"

"The children. They always do. I thought you were wonderful about the dishes."

"I'm devious," I said. "And, in due course, I have designs on your honor."

Chapter VI

It has been my experience to put aside a decision for future pondering. Then one day, fencing a piece of time to face the problem, I have found it already completed, solved, and the verdict taken. This must happen to everyone, but I have no way of knowing that. It's as though, in the dark and desolate caves of the mind, a faceless jury had met and decided. This secret and sleepless area in me I have always thought of as black, deep, waveless water, a spawning place from which only a few forms ever rise to the surface. Or maybe it's a great library where is recorded everything that has ever happened to living matter back to the first moment when it began to live.

I think some people have closer access to this place than others—poets, for example. Once, when I had a paper route and no alarm clock, I worked out a way to send a signal and to get a reply. Lying in bed at night, I would see myself standing on the edge of the black water. I pictured a white stone held in my hand, a circular stone. I would write on its surface in very black letters "4 o'clock," then drop the stone and watch it sink, turning over and over, until it disappeared. It worked for me. On the second of four I awakened. Later I could use it to arouse me at ten minutes of four or quarter after. And it never failed me.

And then sometimes a strange, sometimes hideous thing thrusts up to the surface as though a sea serpent or a kraken emerged from the great depths.

Only a year ago Mary's brother Dennis died in our house, died dreadfully, of an infection of the thyroid that forced the juices of fear through him so that he was violent and terrified and fierce. His kindly Irish horse-face grew bestial. I helped to hold him down, to pacify and reassure him in his death-dreaming, and it went on for a week before his lungs began to fill. I didn't want Mary to see him die. She had never seen death, and this one, I knew, might wipe out her sweet memory of a kindly man who was her brother. Then, as I sat waiting by his bed, a monster swam up out of my dark water. I hated him. I wanted to kill him, to bite out his throat. My jaw muscles tightened and I think my lips fleered back like a wolf's at the kill.

When it was over, in panic guilt I confessed what I had felt to old Doc Peele, who signed the death certificate.

"I don't think it's unusual," he said. "I've seen it on people's faces, but few admit it."

"But what causes it? I liked him."

"Maybe an old memory," he said. "Maybe a return to the time of the pack when a sick or hurt member was a danger. Some animals and most fish tear down and eat a weakened brother."

"But I'm not an animal—or a fish."

"No, you're not. And perhaps that's why you find it foreign. But it's there. It's all there."

He's a good old man, Doc Peele, a tired old man. He's birthed and buried us for fifty years.

Back to that Congress in the Dark—it must have been working overtime. Sometimes a man seems to reverse himself so that you would say, "He can't do that. It's out of character." Maybe it's not. It could be just another angle, or it might be that the pressures above or below have changed his shape. You see it in war a lot—a coward turning hero and a brave man crashing in flames. Or you read in the morning paper about a nice, kind family man who cuts down wife and children with an ax. I think I believe that a man is changing all the time. But there are certain moments when the change becomes noticeable. If I wanted to dig deep enough, I could probably trace the seeds of my change right back to my birth or before. Recently many little things had begun to form a pattern of larger things. It's as though events and experiences nudged and jostled me in a direction contrary to my normal one or the one I had come to think was normal—the direction of the grocery clerk, the failure, the man without real hope or drive, barred in by responsibilities for filling the bellies and clothing the bodies of his family, caged by habits and attitudes I thought of as being moral, even virtuous. And it may be that I had a smugness about being what I called a "Good Man."

And surely I knew what was going on around me. Marullo didn't have to tell me. You can't live in a town the size of New Baytown and not know. I didn't think about it much. Judge

Dorcas fixed traffic tickets for favors. It wasn't even secret. And favors call for favors. The Town Manager, who was also Budd Building Supplies, sold equipment to the township at a high price, and some of it not needed. If a new paved street went in, it usually turned out that Mr. Baker and Marullo and half a dozen other business leaders had bought up the lots before the plan was announced. These were just facts of nature, but I had always believed they weren't facts of my nature. Marullo and Mr. Baker and the drummer and Margie Young-Hunt and Joey Morphy in a concentration had been nudging me and altogether it amounted to a push, so that "I've got to put aside a little time to think it out."

My darling was purring in her sleep, with the archaic smile on her lips, and she had the extra glow of comfort and solace she gets after love, a calm fulfilledness.

I should have been sleepy after wandering around the night before, but I wasn't. I've noticed that I am rarely sleepy if I know I can sleep long in the morning. The red dots were swimming on my eyes, and the street light threw the shadows of naked elm branches on the ceiling, where they made slow and stately cats' cradles because the spring wind was blowing. The window was open halfway and the white curtains swelled and filled like sails on an anchored boat. Mary must have white curtains and often washed. They give her a sense of decency and security. She pretends a little anger when I tell her it's her lace-curtain Irish soul.

I felt good and fulfilled too, but whereas Mary dives for sleep, I didn't want to go to sleep. I wanted to go on fully tasting how good I felt. I wanted to think about the I Love America Essay Contest my offspring were entering. But behind these and others, I wanted to consider what was happening to me and what to do about it, so naturally I got out the last thing first and I found that the dark jury of the deep had already decided for me. There it was, laid out and certain. It was like training for a race and preparing and finally being down at start with your spikes set in their holes. No choice then. You go when the pistol cracks. I found I was ready with my spikes set, waiting only for the shot. And apparently I was the last to know. All day people had remarked that I looked well, by that meaning I looked different, more confident, changed. That drummer had a look of shock in the afternoon. Marullo had inspected me uneasily. And Joey-boy felt the need to apologize for something I had done. Then Margie Young-Hunt—maybe she was the sharpest with her rattlesnake dream. Some way she had penetrated and discovered a certainty about me before I was certain of it. And the symbol was a rattlesnake. I found I was grinning in the dark. And afterward, confused, she used the oldest trick—the threat of infidelity, a bait cast in a flowing tide to find what fish are feeding there. I didn't remember the secret whisper of her hidden body—no, the picture was of her clawed hands that showed age and nervousness and the cruelty that comes to one when control of a situation is lost.

Sometimes I wish I knew the nature of night thoughts. They're close kin to dreams. Sometimes I can direct them, and other times they take their head and come rushing over me like strong, unmanaged horses.

Danny Taylor came in. I didn't want to think about him and be sad but he came anyway. I had to use a trick a tough old sergeant taught me once, and it works. There was a day and a night and a day in the war that was all one piece, one unit of which the parts were just about all the dirty dreadfulness that can happen in that sick business. While it was going on I'm not sure I knew its agony because I was busy and unutterably tired, but afterward that unit of a day and a night and a day came back to me over and over again in my night thoughts until it was like that insanity they call battle fatigue and once named shell-shock. I used every trick I could not to think of it, but it crept back in spite of me. It waited through the day to get at me in the dark. Once mawkish with whisky I told it to my top sergeant, an old pro who had been in wars we have forgotten ever happened. If he had worn his ribbons, there'd have been no room for buttons—Mike Pulaski, a polack from Chicago, no relation to the hero. By good fortune, he was decently drunk or he might have clammed up out of a conditioned conviction about fraternizing with an officer.

Mike heard me out, staring at a spot between my eyes. "Yeah!" he said. "I know about that. Trouble is, a guy tries to shove it out of his head. That don't work. What you got to do is kind of welcome it."

"How do you mean, Mike?"

"Take it's something kind of long—you start at the beginning and remember everything you can, right to the end. Every time it comes back you do that, from the first right through the finish. Pretty soon it'll get tired and pieces of it will go, and before long the whole thing will go."

I tried it and it worked. I don't know whether the headshrinkers know this but they should.

When Danny Taylor came into my night I gave him Sergeant Mike's treatment.

When we were kids together, same age, same size, same weight, we used to go to the grain and feed store on High Street and get on the scales. One week I'd be half a pound heavier and the next Danny would catch up with me. We used to fish and hunt and swim together and go out with the same girls. Danny's family was well fixed like most of the old families of New Baytown. The Taylor house is that white one with the tall fluted columns on Porlock Street. Once the Taylors had a country house too—about three miles from town.

The country all around us is rolling hills covered with trees, some scrub pine and some with second-growth oak, and hickory and some cedars. Once, long before I was born, the oaks were monsters, so big that the local-built ships had cut their keels and ribs and planking within a short distance of the shipyards until it was all gone. In this roly-poly country the Taylors once had a house set in the middle of a big meadow, the only level place for miles around. It must once have been a lake bottom because it was flat as a table and surrounded by low hills. Maybe sixty years ago, the Taylor house burned down and was never rebuilt. As kids Danny and I used to ride out there on bicycles. We played in the stone cellar and built a hunting lodge of bricks from the old foundation. The gardens must have been wonderful. We could see avenues of trees and a suggestion of formal hedges and borders among the scrabble of the returned forest. Here and there would be a stretch of stone balustrade, and once we found a bust of Pan on a tapering stand. It had fallen on its face and buried its horns and beard in the sandy loam. We stood it up and cleaned it and celebrated it for a time, but greed and girls got the better of us. We finally carted it into Floodhampton and sold it to a junk man for five dollars. It must have been a good piece, maybe an old one.

Danny and I were friends as all boys must have friends. Then his appointment to the Naval Academy came through. I saw him once in uniform and not again for years. New Baytown was and is a tight, close-made town. Everyone knew Danny was expelled and no one discussed it. Taylors died out, well, just as Hawleys died out. I'm the only one left, and, of course, Allen, my son. Danny didn't come back until they were all dead, and he came back a drunk. At first I tried to help but he didn't want me. He didn't want anybody. But, in spite of it, we were close—very close.

I went over everything I could remember right up to that very morning when I gave him the dollar to let him find his local oblivion.

The structure of my change was feeling, pressures from without, Mary's wish, Allen's desires, Ellen's anger, Mr. Baker's help. Only at the last when the move is mounted and prepared does thought place a roof on the building and bring in words to explain and to justify. Suppose my humble and interminable clerkship was not virtue at all but a moral laziness? For any success, boldness is required. Perhaps I was simply timid, fearful of consequences—in a word, lazy. Successful business in our town is not complicated or obscure and it is not widely successful either, because its practicers have set artificial limits for their activities. Their crimes are little crimes and so their success is small success. If the town government and the business complex of New Baytown were ever deeply investigated it would be found that a hundred legal and a thousand moral rules were broken, but they were small violations—petty larceny. They abolished part of the Decalogue and kept the rest. And when one of our successful men had what he needed or wanted, he reassumed his virtue as easily as changing his shirt, and for all one could see, he took no hurt from his derelictions, always assuming that he didn't get caught. Did any of them think about this? I don't know. And if small crimes could be condoned by self, why not a quick, harsh, brave one? Is murder by slow, steady pressure any less murder than a quick and merciful knife-thrust? I don't feel guilt for the German lives I took. Suppose for a limited time I abolished all the rules, not just some of them. Once the objective was reached, could they not all be reassumed? There is no doubt that business is a kind of war. Why not, then, make it all-out war in pursuit of peace? Mr. Baker and his friends did not shoot my father, but they advised him and when his structure collapsed they inherited. And isn't that a kind of murder? Have any of the great fortunes we admire been put together without ruthlessness? I can't think of any.

And if I should put the rules aside for a time, I knew I would wear scars but would they be worse than the scars of failure I was wearing? To be alive at all is to have scars.

All this wondering was the weather vane on top of the building of unrest and of discontent. It could be done because it had been done. But if I opened up that door, could I ever get it closed again? I did not know. I could not know until I had opened it. . . . Did Mr. Baker know? Had Mr. Baker even thought of it? . . . Old Cap'n thought the Bakers burned the *Belle-Adair* for the insurance. Could that and my father's misfortune be the reason Mr. Baker wanted to help me? Were these his scars?

What was happening could be described as a great ship being turned and bunted and shoved about and pulled around by many small tugs. Once turned by tide and tugs, it must set a new course and start its engines turning. On the bridge which is the planning center, the question must be asked: All right, I know now where I want to go. How do I get there, and where are lurking rocks and what will the weather be?

One fatal reef I knew was talk. So many betray themselves before they are betrayed, with a kind of wistful hunger for glory, even the glory of punishment. Andersen's Well is the only confidant to trust—Andersen's Well.

I called out to old Cap'n. "Shall I set the course, sir? Is it a good course? Will it get me there?"

And for the first time he denied me his command. "You'll have to work it out yourself. What's good for one is bad for another, and you won't know till after."

The old bastard might have helped me then, but perhaps it wouldn't have made any difference. No one wants advice—only corroboration.

Chapter VII

WHEN I awakened, old sleepy Mary was up and gone and coffee and bacon were afoot. I could smell them. And you'd have to search for a better day for a resurrection, a green and blue and yellow day. From the bedroom window I could see that everything was resurrecting, grass, trees. They chose a proper season for it. I put on my Christmas dressing gown and my birthday slippers. In the bathroom I found some of Allen's hair goo and slicked it on, so that my combed and brushed scalp felt tight like a cap.

Easter Sunday breakfast is an orgy of eggs and pancakes, and bacon curling about everything. I crept up on Mary and patted her silk-covered fanny and said, "*Kyrie eleison!*"

"Oh!" she said. "I didn't hear you coming." She regarded my dressing gown, paisley pattern. "Nice," she said. "You don't wear it enough."

"I haven't time. I haven't had time."

"Well, it's nice," she said.

"Ought to be. You picked it. Are the kids sleeping through these wonderful smells?"

"Oh, no. They're out back, hiding eggs. I wonder what Mr. Baker wants."

The quick jump never fails to startle me. "Mr. Baker, Mr. Baker. Oh! He probably wants to help me start my fortune."

"Did you tell him? About the cards?"

"Course not, darling. But maybe he guessed." Then I said seriously, "Look, cheesecake, you do think I have a great business brain, don't you?"

"What do you mean?" She had a pancake up for turning, and it stayed up.

"Mr. Baker thinks I should invest your brother's legacy."

"Well, if Mr. Baker—"

"Now wait. I don't want to do it. That's your money and your safety."

"Doesn't Mr. Baker know more about that than you do, dear?"

"I'm not sure. All I know is my father thought he knew. That's why I'm working for Marullo."

"Still, I think Mr. Baker—"

"Will you be guided by me, sweetheart?"

"Well, of course—"

"In everything?"

"Are you being silly?"

"I'm dead serious—dead!"

"I believe you are. But you can't go around doubting Mr. Baker. Why, he's—he's—"

"He's Mr. Baker. We'll listen to what he has to say and then—I still will want that money right in the bank where it is."

Allen shot through the back door as though fired by a sling-shot. "Marullo," he said. "Mr. Marullo's outside. He wants to see you."

"Now what?" Mary demanded.

"Well, ask him in."

"I did. He wants to see you outside."

"Ethan, what is it? You can't go out in your robe. It's Easter Sunday."

"Allen," I said, "you tell Mr. Marullo I'm not dressed. Tell him he can come back later. But if he's in a hurry, he can come in the front door if he wants to see me alone." He dashed.

"I don't know what he wants. Maybe the store's been robbed."

Allen shot back. "He's going around front."

"Now, dear, don't you let him spoil your breakfast, you hear me?"

I went through the house and opened the front door. Marullo was on the porch, dressed in his best for Easter mass, and his best was black broadcloth and big gold watch chain. He held his black hat in his hand and he smiled at me nervously like a dog out of bounds.

"Come in."

"No," he said. "I just got one word to say. I heard how that fella offered you a kickback."

"Yes?"

"I heard how you threw him out."

"Who told you?"

"I can't tell." He smiled again.

"Well, what about it? You trying to say I should have taken it?"

He stepped forward and shook my hand, pumped it up and down twice very formally. "You're a good fella," he said.

"Maybe he didn't offer enough."

"You kidding? You're a good fella. That's all. You're a good fella." He reached in his bulging side pocket and brought out a bag. "You take this." He patted my shoulder and then in a welter of embarrassment turned and fled; his short legs pumped him away and his fat neck flamed where it bulged over his stiff white collar.

"What was it?"

I looked in the bag—colored candy Easter eggs. We had a big square glass jar of them at the store. "He brought a present for the kids," I said.

"Marullo? Brought a present. I can't believe it."

"Well, he did."

"Why? He never did anything like that."

"I guess he just plain loves me."

"Is there something I don't know?"

"Duck blossom, there are eight million things none of us know." The children were staring in from the open back door. I held out the bag to them. "A present from an admirer. Don't get into them until after breakfast."

As we were getting dressed for church, Mary said, "I wish I knew what that was all about."

"Marullo? I'll have to admit, darling, I wish I knew what it was all about too."

"But a bag of cheap candy—"

"Do you suppose it might be a grave simplicity?"

"I don't understand."

"His wife is dead. He has neither chick nor child. He's getting old. Maybe—well, maybe he's lonely."

"He never has been here before. While he's lonesome, you should ask him for a raise. He doesn't drop in on Mr. Baker. It makes me nervous."

I gauded myself like the flowers of the field, decent dark

suit, my burying black, shirt and collar so starchly white they threw the sun's light back in the sun's face, cerulean tie with cautious polka dots.

Was Mrs. Margie Young-Hunt whomping up ancestral storms? Where did Marullo get his information? It could only be Mr. Bugger to Mrs. Young-Hunt to Mr. Marullo. I do not trust thee Margie Young, the reason why I cannot tongue. But this I know and know right spung, I do not trust thee Mrs. Young. And with that singing in my head I delved in the garden for a white flower for my Easter buttonhole. In the angle made by the foundation and the sloping cellar door there is a protected place, the earth warmed by the furnace and exposed to every scrap of winter sunlight. There white violets grow, brought from the cemetery where they grow wild over the graves of my ancestors. I picked three tiny lion-faced blossoms for my buttonhole and gathered a round dozen for my darling, set their own pale leaves about them for a nosegay, and bound them tight with a bit of aluminum foil from the kitchen.

"Why, they're lovely," Mary said. "Wait till I get a pin, I'll wear them."

"They're the first—the very first, my creamy fowl. I am your slave. Christ is risen. All's right with the world."

"Please don't be silly about sacred things, dear."

"What in the world have you done with your hair?"

"Do you like it?"

"I love it. Always wear it that way."

"I wasn't sure you'd like it. Margie said you'd never notice. Wait till I tell her you did." She set a bowl of flowers on her head, the yearly vernal offering to Eostre. "Like it?"

"I love it."

Now the young got their inspection, ears, nostrils, shoeshines, every detail, and they resisted every moment of it. Allen's hair was so plastered that he could hardly blink. The heels of his shoes were unpolished but with infinite care he had trained a line of hair to roll on his crested brow like a summer wave.

Ellen was girl of a girlness. All in sight was in order. I tried my luck again. "Ellen," I said, "you're doing something different with your hair. It becomes you. Mary, darling, don't you like it?"

"Oh! She's beginning to take pride," Mary said.

We formed a procession down our path to Elm Street, then left to Porlock, where our church is, our old white-steepled church, stolen intact from Christopher Wren. And we were part of a growing stream, and every woman in passing had delight of other women's hats.

"I have designed an Easter hat," I said. "A simple, off-the-face crown of thorns in gold with real ruby droplets on the forehead."

"Ethan!" said Mary sternly. "Suppose someone should hear you."

"No, I guess it couldn't be popular."

"I think you're horrid," Mary said, and so did I, worse than horrid. But I did wonder how Mr. Baker would respond to comment on his hair.

Our family rivulet joined other streams and passed stately greetings and the stream was a river pouring into St. Thomas's Episcopal Church, a medium-high church, maybe a little higher than center.

When the time comes that I must impart the mysteries of life to my son, which I have no doubt he knows, I must remember to inform him about hair. Armed with a kindly word for hair, he will go as far as his concupiscent little heart desires. I must warn him, however. He may kick, beat, drop, tousle, or bump them, but he must never—never—mess their hair. With this knowledge he can be king.

The Bakers were just ahead of us going up the steps, and we passed decorous greetings. "I believe we're seeing you at tea."

"Yes, indeed. A very happy Easter to you."

"Can that be Allen? How he's grown. And Mary Ellen. Well, I can't keep track—they shoot up so."

There's something very dear about a church you grew in. I know every secret corner, secret odor of St. Thomas's. In that font I was christened, at that rail confirmed, in that pew Hawleys have sat for God knows how long, and that is no figure of speech. I must have been deeply printed with the sacredness because I remember every desecration, and there were plenty of them. I think I can go to every place where my initials are scratched with a nail. When Danny Taylor and I punched the letters of a singularly dirty word with a pin in the

Book of Common Prayer, Mr. Wheeler caught us and we were punished, but they had to go through all the prayerbooks and the hymnals to make sure there weren't more.

Once, in that chair stall under the lectern, a dreadful thing happened. I wore the lace and carried the cross and sang a beefy soprano. Once the bishop was officiating, a nice old man, hairless as a boiled onion, but to me glowing with rays of holiness. So it was that, stunned with inspiration, I set the cross in its socket at the end of processional and forgot to throw the brass latch that held it in. At the reading of the second lesson I saw with horror the heavy brass cross sway and crash on that holy hairless head. The bishop went down like a pole-axed cow and I lost the lace to a boy who couldn't sing as well, a boy named Skunkfoot Hill. He's an anthropologist now, somewhere in the West. The incident seemed to prove to me that intentions, good or bad, are not enough. There's luck or fate or something else that takes over accidents.

We sat the service through and heard the news announced that Christ was risen indeed. It ran shivers up my spine as always. I took communion with a good heart. Allen and Mary Ellen weren't yet confirmed and they got pretty restless and had to be given the iron eye to stop their jittering. When Mary's eyes are hostile, they can pierce even the armor plate of adolescence.

Then in the drenching sunshine we shook hands and greeted and shook hands and wished the season's best to the community of our neighbors. All those we had spoken to coming in, we regreeted going out—a continuation of the litany, of a continuous litany in the form of decorous good manners, a quiet supplication to be noticed and to be respected.

"Good morning. And how are you this fine day?"

"Very well, thank you. How is your mother?"

"She's getting old—getting old—the aches and daggers of getting old. I'll tell her you asked for her."

The words are meaningless except in terms of feeling. Does anyone act as the result of thought or does feeling stimulate action and sometimes thought implement it? Ahead of our small parade in the sun went Mr. Baker, avoiding stepping on cracks; his mother, dead these twenty years, was safe from a broken back. And Mrs. Baker, Amelia, tripping along beside him, trying to match his uneven stride with her fluttering feet, a small, bright-eyed bird of a woman, but a seed-eating bird.

Allen, my son, walked beside his sister, but each of them tried to give the impression that they were total strangers. I think she despises him and he detests her. This may last all their lives while they learn to conceal it in a rose cloud of loving words. Give them their lunches, my sister, my wife—their hard-boiled eggs and pickles, their jelly-and-peanut-butter sandwiches, their red barrel-smelling apples, and turn them free in the world to spawn.

And that's just what she did. They walked away, carrying their paper bags, each one to a separate private world.

"Did you enjoy the service, my darling?"

"Oh, yes! I always do. But you—sometimes I wonder if you believe—no, I mean it. Well, your jokes—sometimes—"

"Pull up your chair, my dimpsy darling."

"I have to get lunch on."

"Bugger lunch."

"That's what I mean. Your jokes."

"Lunch is not sacred. If it were warmer, I could carry you to a rowboat and we would go out past the breakwater and fish for porgies."

"We're going to the Bakers'. Do you know whether you believe in the church or not, Ethan? Why do you call me silly names? You hardly ever use my name."

"To avoid being repetitious and tiresome, but in my heart your name rings like a bell. Do I believe? What a question! Do I lift out each shining phrase from the Nicene creed, loaded like a shotgun shell, and inspect it? No. It isn't necessary. It's a singular thing, Mary. If my mind and soul and body were as dry of faith as a navy bean, the words, 'The Lord is my Shepherd, I shall not want. He maketh me to lie down in green pastures,' would still make my stomach turn over and put a flutter in my chest and light a fire in my brain."

"I don't understand."

"Good girl. Neither do I. Let's say that when I was a little baby, and all my bones soft and malleable, I was put in a small Episcopal cruciform box and so took my shape. Then, when I broke out of the box, the way a baby chick escapes an egg, is it strange that I had the shape of a cross? Have you ever noticed that chickens are roughly egg-shaped?"

"You say such dreadful things, even to the children."

"And they to me. Ellen, only last night, asked, 'Daddy, when will we be rich?' But I did not say to her what I know: 'We will be rich soon, and you who handle poverty badly will handle riches equally badly.' And that is true. In poverty she is envious. In riches she may be a snob. Money does not change the sickness, only the symptoms."

"You talk this way about your own children. What must you say of me?"

"I say you are a blessing, a dearling, the brightness in a foggy life."

"You sound drunk—anyway intoxicated."

"I am."

"You aren't. I could smell it."

"You are smelling it sweetheart."

"What's come over you?"

"Ah! you do know, don't you? A change—a bloody big storm of a change. You are only feeling the outmost waves."

"You worry me, Ethan. You really do. You're wild."

"Do you remember my decorations?"

"Your medals—from the war?"

"They were awarded for wildness—for wilderness. No man on earth ever had less murder in his heart than I. But they made another box and crammed me in it. The times, the moment, demanded that I slaughter human beings and I did."

"That was wartime and for your country."

"It's always some kind of time. So far I have avoided my own time. I was a goddam good soldier, potkin—clever and quick and merciless, an effective unit for wartime. Maybe I could be an equally efficient unit in this time."

"You're trying to tell me something."

"Sadly enough, I am. And it sounds in my ears like an apology. I hope it is not."

"I'm going to set out lunch."

"Not hungry after that nor'easter of a breakfast."

"Well, you can nibble something. Did you see Mrs. Baker's hat? She must have got it in New York."

"What has she done with her hair?"

"You noticed that? It's almost strawberry."

" 'To be a light to lighten the gentiles, and to be the glory of thy peo-ple Israel.' "

"Why would Margie want to go to Montauk this time of year?"

"She loves the early morning."

"She's not an early riser. I joke with her about that. And don't you think it was queer, Marullo bringing candy eggs?"

"Do you connect the two events? Margie gets up early and Marullo brings eggs."

"Don't be silly."

"I'm not. For once I'm not. If I tell you a secret, will you promise not to tell?"

"It's a joke!"

"No."

"Well, I promise."

"I think Marullo is going to make a trip to Italy."

"How do you know? Did he tell you?"

"Not exactly. I put things together. I *put* things together."

"But that'll leave you alone in the store. You'll have to get someone to help you."

"I can handle it."

"You do practically everything now. You'll have to get someone in to help."

"Remember—it isn't sure and it's a secret."

"Oh, I never forget a promise."

"But you'll hint."

"Ethan, I will not."

"Do you know what you are? A dear little baby rabbit with flowers on your head."

"You help yourself in the kitchen. I'm going to freshen up."

When she was gone, I sprawled out in my chair and I heard in my secret ears, "Lord, now lettest Thou Thy servant de-part in pee-ace, according to Thy word." And darned if I didn't go to sleep. Dropped off a cliff into the dark, right there in the living room. I don't do that often. And because I had been thinking of Danny Taylor, I dreamed of Danny Taylor. We were not small or great but grown, and we were at the flat dry lake-bottom with the old house foundations and cellar hole.

And it was early summer, for I remarked the fatness of the leaves and the grass so heavy that it bent of its weight, the kind of day that makes you feel fat and crazy too. Danny went behind a young juniper straight and slender as a column. I heard his voice, distorted and thick like words spoken under water. Then I was with him and he was melting and running down over his frame. With my palms I tried to smooth him upward, back in place, the way you try to smooth wet cement when it runs out of the form, but I couldn't. His essence ran between my fingers. They say a dream is a moment. This one went on and on and the more I tried, the more he melted.

When Mary awakened me I was panting with effort.

"Spring fever," she said. "That's the first sign. When I was a growing girl, I slept so much my mother sent for Doctor Grady. She thought I had sleeping sickness, but I was only growing in the spring."

"I had a daymare. I wouldn't wish a dream like that on anyone."

"It's all the confusion. Go up and comb your hair and wash your face. You look tired, dear. Are you all right? It's nearly time to go. You slept two hours. You must have needed it. I wish I knew what's on Mr. Baker's mind."

"You will, darling. And promise me you will listen to every word."

"But he might want a word alone with you. Businessmen don't like ladies listening."

"Well, he can't have it that way. I want you there."

"You know I have no experience in business."

"I know—but it's your money he'll be talking about."

You can't know people like the Bakers unless you are born knowing them. Acquaintance, even friendship, is a different matter. I know them because Hawleys and Bakers were alike in blood, place of origin, experience, and past fortune. This makes for a kind of nucleus walled and moated against outsiders. When my father lost our money, I was not edged completely out. I am still acceptable as a Hawley to Bakers for perhaps my lifetime because they feel related to me. But I am a poor relation. Gentry without money gradually cease to be gentry. Without money, Allen, my son, will not know Bakers and his son will be an outsider, no matter what his name and antecedents. We have become ranchers without land, commanders without troops, horsemen on foot. We can't survive. Perhaps that is one reason why the change was taking place in me. I do not want, never have wanted, money for itself. But money is necessary to keep my place in a category I am used to and comfortable in. All this must have worked itself out in the dark place below my thinking level. It emerged not as a thought but as a conviction.

"Good afternoon," Mrs. Baker said. "So glad you could come. You've neglected us, Mary. Hasn't it been a glorious day? Did you enjoy the service? For a clergyman I think he's such an interesting man."

"We don't see you nearly often enough," Mr. Baker said. "I remember your grandfather sitting in that very chair and reporting that the dirty Spaniards had sunk the *Maine*. He spilled his tea, only it wasn't tea. Old Cap'n Hawley used to lace his rum with a little tea. He was a truculent man, some thought a quarrelsome man."

I could see that Mary was first shaken and then pleased at this warmth. Of course she didn't know I had promoted her to be an heiress. A reputation for money is almost as negotiable as money itself.

Mrs. Baker, her head jerking with some nervous disorder, poured tea into cups as thin and fragile as magnolia petals, and her pouring hand was the only steady part of her.

Mr. Baker stirred with a thoughtful spoon. "I don't know whether I love tea or the ceremony of it," he said. "I like all ceremonies—even the silly ones."

"I think I understand," I said. "This morning I felt comfortable in the service because it had no surprises. I knew the words before they were said."

"During the war, Ethan—listen to this, ladies, and see if you can remember anything like it—during the war I served as a consultant to the Secretary of War. I spent some time in Washington."

"I hated it," said Mrs. Baker.

"Well, there was a big military tea, a real doozer, maybe five hundred guests. The ranking lady was the wife of a five-star general and next in importance was the lady of a lieutenant general. Mrs. Secretary, the hostess, asked the five-star lady to pour the tea and Mrs. Three-Stars to pour coffee. Well, the top lady refused because, and I quote her, 'Everyone knows coffee outranks tea.' Now, did you ever hear that?" He chuckled. "As it turned out, whisky outranked everybody."

"It was such a restless place," Mrs. Baker said. "People moved before they had time to gather a set of habits, or manners."

Mary told her story of an Irish tea in Boston with the water boiling in round tubs over an open fire and served with tin ladles. "And they don't steep. They boil," she said. "That tea will unsettle varnish on a table."

There must be ritual preliminaries to a serious discussion or action, and the sharper the matter is, the longer and lighter must the singing be. Each person must add a bit of feather or a colored patch. If Mary and Mrs. Baker were not to be a part of the serious matter, they would long since have set up their own pattern of exchange. Mr. Baker had poured wine on the earth of conversation and so had my Mary, and she was pleased and excited by their attentiveness. It remained for Mrs. Baker and for me to contribute and I felt it only decent to be last.

She took her turn and drew her source from the teapot as the others had. "I remember when there were dozens of kinds of tea," she offered brightly. "Why, everyone had recipes for nearly everything. I guess there wasn't a weed or a leaf or a flower that wasn't made into some kind of tea. Now there are only two, India and China, and not much China. Remember tansy and camomile and orange-leaf and flower—and—and cambric?"

"What's cambric?" Mary asked.

"Equal parts hot water and hot milk. Children love it. It doesn't taste like milk and water." That accounted for Mrs. Baker.

It was my turn, and I intended to make a few carefully meaningless remarks about the Boston Tea Party, but you can't always do what you intended. Surprises slip out, not waiting for permission.

"I went to sleep after service," I heard me say. "I dreamed of Danny Taylor, a dreadful dream. You remember Danny."

"Poor chap," said Mr. Baker.

"Once we were closer than brothers. I had no brother. I

guess we were brothers in a way. I don't carry it out, of course, but I feel I should be my brother Danny's keeper."

Mary was annoyed with me for breaking the pattern of the conversation. She took a small revenge. "Ethan gives him money. I don't think it's right. He just uses it to get drunk."

"Wellll!" said Mr. Baker.

"I wonder—anyway the dream was a noonmare. I give him so little—a dollar now and then. What else can he do with a dollar but get drunk? Maybe with a decent amount he could get well."

"No one would dare do that," Mary cried. "That would be after killing him. Isn't that so, Mr. Baker?"

"Poor chap," Mr. Baker said. "A fine family the Taylors were. It makes me sick to see him this way. But Mary's right. He'd probably drink himself to death."

"He is anyway. But he's safe from me. I don't have a decent amount to give him."

"It's the principle," Mr. Baker said.

Mrs. Baker contributed a feminine savagery: "He should be in an institution where they could look after him."

All three were annoyed with me. I should have stayed with the Boston Tea Party.

Strange how the mind goes romping, playing blindman's buff or pin-the-tail-on-the-donkey when it should be using every observation to find a path through the minefield of secret plans and submerged obstacles. I understood the house of Baker and the house of Hawley, the dark walls and curtains, the funereal rubber plants unacquainted with sun; the portraits and prints and remembrances of other times in pottery and scrimshaw, in fabrics and wood which bolt it to reality and to permanence. Chairs change with style and comfort but chests and tables, bookcases and desks, relate to a solid past. Hawley was more than a family. It was a house. And that was why poor Danny held onto Taylor Meadow. Without it, no family—and soon not even a name. By tone and inflection and desire, the three sitting there had canceled him. It may be that some men require a house and a history to reassure themselves that they exist—it's a slim enough connection, at most. In the store I was a failure and a clerk, in my house I was Hawley, so I too must be unsure. Baker could offer a hand to Hawley. Without my house, I too would have been canceled. It was not man to man but house to house. I resented the removal from real of Danny Taylor, but I couldn't stop it. And this thought sharpened and tempered me. Baker was going to try to refurbish Hawley for Baker's participation in Mary's fancied inheritance. Now I was on the edge of the minefield. My heart hardened against my selfless benefactor. I felt it harden and grow wary and dangerous. And with its direction came the feeling of combat, and the laws of controlled savagery, and the first law is: Let even your defense have the appearance of attack.

I said, "Mr. Baker, we don't need to go over the background. You know better than I do the slow, precise way in which my father lost the Hawley substance. I was away at war. How did it happen?"

"It wasn't his intention, but his judgment—"

"I know he was unworldly—but how did it happen?"

"Well, it was a time of wild investment. He invested wildly."

"Did he have any advice?"

"He put money in munitions that were already obsolete. Then when the contracts were canceled, he lost."

"You were in Washington. Did you know about the contracts?"

"Only in a general way."

"But enough so you didn't invest."

"No, I didn't."

"Did you advise my father about investments?"

"I was in Washington."

"But you knew he had borrowed the money on the Hawley property, the money to invest?"

"Yes, I knew that."

"Did you advise against it?"

"I was in Washington."

"But your bank foreclosed."

"A bank doesn't have any choice, Ethan. You know that."

"Yes, I know. Only it's a shame you couldn't have advised him."

"You shouldn't blame him, Ethan."

"Now that I understand it, I don't. I didn't mean to blame him, but I never quite knew what happened."

I think Mr. Baker had prepared an opening. Having lost his chance, he had to grope about for his next move. He coughed, blew his nose and wiped it with a paper handkerchief from a flat pocket package, wiped his eyes with a second sheet, polished his glasses with a third. Everyone has his own method for gaining time. I've known a man to take five minutes to fill and light a pipe.

When he was ready again, I said, "I know I have no right in myself to ask you for help. But you yourself brought up the long partnership of our families."

"Good people," he said. "And usually men of excellent judgment, conservative—"

"But not blindly so, sir. I believe that once they decided on a course they drove through."

"That they did."

"Even if it came to sinking an enemy—or burning a ship?"

"They were commissioned, of course."

"In 1801, I believe, sir, they were questioned about what constituted an enemy."

"There's always some readjustment after a war."

"Surely. But I'm not taking up old scores for talk. Frankly, Mr. Baker, I want to—to rehabilitate my fortunes."

"That's the spirit, Ethan. For a time I thought you'd lost the old Hawley touch."

"I had; or maybe I'd not developed it. You've offered help. Where do I start?"

"The trouble is, you need capital to start."

"I know that. But if I had some capital, where would I start?"

"This must be tiresome for the ladies," he said. "Maybe we should go into the library. Business is dull to ladies."

Mrs. Baker stood up. "I was just about to ask Mary to help me select some wallpaper for the big bedroom. The samples are upstairs, Mary."

"I'd like Mary to hear—"

But she went along with them, as I knew she would. "I don't know a thing about business," she said. "But I do know about wallpaper."

"But you're concerned, darling."

"I just get mixed up, Ethan. You know I do."

"Maybe I'll get more mixed up without you, darling."

Mr. Baker had probably suggested the wallpaper bit. I think his wife does not choose the paper. Surely no woman picked the dark and geometric paper in the room where we sat.

"Now," he said when they were gone, "your problem is capital, Ethan. Your house is clear. You can mortgage it."

"I won't do that."

"Well, I can respect that, but it's the only collateral you have. There is also Mary's money. It's not much, but with some money you can get more money."

"I don't want to touch her money. That's her safety."

"It's in a joint account and it's not earning anything."

"Let's say I overcame my scruples. What have you in mind?"

"Have you any idea what her mother's worth?"

"No—but it seems substantial."

He cleaned his glasses with great care. "What I say is bound to be in confidence."

"Of course."

"Fortunately I know you are not a talker. No Hawley ever was, except perhaps your father. Now, I know as a businessman that New Baytown is going to grow. It has everything to make it grow—a harbor, beaches, inland waters. Once it starts, nothing can stop it. A good businessman owes it to his town to help it develop."

"And take a profit."

"Naturally."

"Why hasn't it developed?"

"I think you know that—the mossbacks on the council. They're living in the past. They hold back progress."

It always interested me to hear how philanthropic the taking of a profit can be. Stripped of its forward-looking, good-of-the-community clothing, Mr. Baker's place was just what it had to be. He and a few others, a very few, would support the town's present administrations until they had bought or controlled all the future facilities. Then they would turn the council and the Town Manager out and let progress reign, and only then would it be discovered that they owned every avenue through which it could come. From pure sentiment, he was willing to cut me in for a small share. I don't know whether or not he had intended to let me know the timetable, or whether his enthusiasm got the better of him, but it did come through the generalities. The town election is July seventh. By that time, the forward-looking group must have the wheels of progress under control.

I don't suppose there is a man in the world who doesn't love to give advice. As I maintained a small reluctance, my teacher grew more vehement and more specific.

"I'll have to think about it, sir," I said. "What's easy for you is a mystery to me. And of course I'll have to discuss it with Mary."

"Now that's where I think you're wrong," he said. "There's too much petticoat in business today."

"But it's her inheritance."

"Best thing you can do for her is make her some money for a surprise. They like it better that way."

"I hope I don't sound ungrateful, Mr. Baker. I think slowly. I'll just have to mull it over. Did you hear Marullo is going to Italy?"

His eyes sharpened. "For good?"

"No, just a visit."

"Well, I hope he makes some arrangement to protect you in case something happened to him. He's not a young man. Has he made a will?"

"I don't know."

"If a bunch of his wop relations moved in, you might find yourself out of a job."

I retired into a protective vagueness. "You've given me a lot to chew on," I said. "But I wonder if you can give me some little idea of when you will start."

"I can tell you this: Development is pretty much dependent on transportation."

"Well, the big thruways are moving out."

"Still a long way to come. The kind of men with the kind of money we want to attract will want to come by air."

"And we have no airport?"

"That's right."

"Furthermore, we have no place for an airport without pushing hills around."

"An expensive operation. The cost of labor would be prohibitive."

"Then what is your plan?"

"Ethan, you'll have to trust me and forgive me. I can't tell you that at this time. But I do promise that if you can raise some capital, I'll see that you get in on the ground floor. And I can tell you that there is a very definite situation, but it has to be solved."

"Well, I guess that's better than I deserve."

"The old families must stick together."

"Is Marullo part of the group?"

"Certainly not. He goes his own way with his own crowd."

"They do pretty well, don't they?"

"Better than I think is healthy. I don't like to see these foreigners creeping in."

"And July seventh is the sound-off."

"Did I say that?"

"No, I guess I just imagined it."

"You must have."

And with that Mary came back from the wallpaper. We did our courteous duties and walked slowly toward home.

"They just couldn't have been nicer. What did he say?"

"Same old thing. I should use your money to get a start, and I won't do it."

"I know you're thinking of me, dear. But I say if you don't take his advice you're a fool."

"I don't like it, Mary. Suppose he's wrong. You'd be without protection."

"I tell you this, Ethan, if you don't do it, I'll take the money and hand it over to him. I promise you I will."

"Let me think about it. I don't want to involve you in business."

"You don't have to. That money's in a joint account. You know what the fortune said."

"Oh, Lord—the fortune again."

"Well, I believe it."

"If I lost your money, you'd hate me."

"I wouldn't. You are my fortune! That's what Margie said."

"What Margie said, is in my head, in letters red, until I'm dead."

"Don't make a joke."

"Maybe I'm not. Don't let fortune spoil the sweetness of our failure."

"I don't see how a little money could spoil anything. Not a lot of money—just enough." I didn't answer. "Well—do you?"

I said, "O prince's daughter, there is no such thing as just enough money. Only two measures: No Money and Not Enough Money."

"Why, that's not true."

"That *is* true. Remember the Texas billionaire who died recently? He lived in a hotel room and out of a suitcase. He left no will, no heirs, but he didn't have enough money. The more you have, the less enough it is."

She said sarcastically, "I suppose you find it sinful for me to want new living-room curtains and a water heater big enough so four people can bathe the same day and I can wash dishes too."

"I was not reporting on sin, you juggins. I was stating a fact, a law of nature."

"You seem to have no respect for human nature."

"Not human nature, my Mary—nature. Squirrels bank ten times as many hickory nuts as they can ever use. The pocket gopher, with a stomach full to bursting, still loads his cheeks like sacks. And how much of the honey the clever bees collect do the clever bees eat?"

When Mary is confused or perplexed, she spurts anger the way an octopus spurts ink, and hides in the dark cloud of it.

"You make me sick," she said. "You can't let anyone have a little happiness."

"My darling, it isn't that. It's a despairing unhappiness I'm afraid of, the panic money brings, the protectiveness and the envy."

She must have been unconsciously fearful of the same thing. She struck at me, probed for a hurting place, and found it and twisted the jagged words. "Here's a grocery clerk without a bean worried about how bad it will be when he's rich. You act as though you could pick up a fortune any time you want to."

"I think I can."

"How?"

"That's the worry."

"You don't know how or you'd have done it before. You're just bluffing. You always bluff."

The intent to wound raises rage. I could feel the fever rise in me. Ugly, desperate words moved up like venom. I felt a sour hatefulness.

Mary said, "Look! There it goes! Did you see it?"

"Where? What?"

"Went right past the tree there and into our yard."

"What was it, Mary? Tell me! What did you see?"

In the dusk I saw her smile, that incredible female smile. It is called wisdom but it isn't that but rather an understanding that makes wisdom unnecessary.

"You didn't see anything, Mary."

"I saw a quarrel—but it got away."

I put my arm about her and turned her. "Let's go around the block before we go in."

We strolled in the tunnel of the night and we didn't speak again, or need to.

Chapter VIII

As a child I hunted and killed small creatures with energy and joy. Rabbits and squirrels, small birds, and later ducks and wild geese came crashing down, rumpled distortions of bone and blood and fur and feathers. There was a savage creativeness about it without hatred or rancor or guilt. The war retired my appetite for destruction; perhaps I was like a child overindulged in sweets. A shotgun's blast was no longer a shout of fierce happiness.

In this first spring a bouncing pair of rabbits paid daily visits to our garden. They loved best my Mary's carnations, ate them down to raw crowns.

"You'll have to get rid of them," Mary said.

I brought out my 12-bore, sticky with grease, and found some old thickened shells with number five shot. In the evening I sat on the back steps and when the rabbits were in line I blasted both of them with one shot. Then I buried the furry ruins under the big lilac and I was miserable in the stomach.

It was simply that I had grown unused to killing things. A man can get used to anything. Slaughtering or undertaking or even execution; rack and pincers must be just a job when one gets used to it.

When the children had gone to bed I said, "I'm going out for a while."

Mary didn't ask where or why, as she would have a few days ago. "Shall you be late?"

"No, not late."

"I won't wait up, I'm sleepy," she said. And it seemed that, having accepted a direction, she was farther along than I. I still had the rabbit misery. Perhaps it is natural for a man who has destroyed something to try to restore a balance by creating something. But was that my impulse?

I fumbled my way into the stinking kennel where Danny Taylor lived. A lighted candle burned in a saucer beside his Army cot.

Danny was in bad shape, blue and gaunt and sick. His skin had a pewter sheen. It was hard not to be sick at the smell of the dirty place and the dirty man, under a filthy comforter. His eyes were open and glazed. I expected him to babble in delirium. It was a shock when he spoke clearly and in the tone and manner of Danny Taylor.

"What do you want here, Eth?"

"I want to help you."

"You know better than that."

"You're sick."

"Think I don't know it? I know it better than anyone." He groped behind his cot and brought out a bottle of Old Forester one-third full. "Have a shot?"

"No, Danny. That's expensive whisky."

"I have friends."

"Who gave it to you?"

"That's none of your business, Eth." He took a drink and kept it down, but for a moment it was not easy. And then his color came back. He laughed. "My friend wanted to talk business but I fooled him. I passed out before he could get it said. He didn't know how little it takes. Do you want to talk business Eth? 'Cause I can pass out again quick."

"Do you have any feeling about me, Danny? Any trust? Any—well, feeling?"

"Sure I do, but when it comes right down to it I am a drunk, and a drunk feels strongest about liquor."

"If I could raise the money, would you go for a cure?"

The frightening thing was how quickly he had become normal and easy and—like himself. "I might say I would, Eth. But you don't know drunks. I'd take the money and drink it up."

"Well, suppose I paid it right to the hospital, or wherever."

"I'm trying to tell you. I'd go with the best intentions, and in a few days I'd get out. You can't trust a drunk, Eth. That's what you can't understand. No matter what I did or said—I'd still get out."

"Don't you want to come out of it, Danny?"

"I guess I don't. I guess you know what I want." He hoisted the bottle again, and again I was astonished at the speed of the reaction. Not only did he become the old Danny I knew but his senses and perceptions were sharpened, so clear in fact that he read my thought. "Don't trust it," he said. "It's only for a little time. Alcohol stimulates and then depresses. I hope you won't stay around to see that. Right now, I don't believe it will happen. I never do when I'm up." Then his eyes, wet and shining in the candlelight, looked into me. "Ethan," he said. "You offered to pay for a cure for me. You haven't the money, Ethan."

"I could get it. Mary inherited some from her brother."

"And you would give me that?"

"Yes."

"Even though I tell you never to trust a drunk? Even if I assure you I would take your money and break your heart?"

"You're breaking my heart now, Danny. I had a dream about you. We were out at the old place—remember?"

He raised the bottle and then put it down, saying, "No, not yet—not yet. Eth—never—never trust a drunk. When he—when I'm—horrible—a dead thing—there's still a clever, secret mind at work, and it's not a friendly mind. Right now, right at this moment, I'm a man who was your friend. I lied to you about passing out. Oh, I passed out all right, but I know about the bottle."

"Wait," I said, "before you go any further, else it will look—well, you might suspect me. It was Baker brought the bottle, wasn't it?"

"Yes."

"He wanted you to sign something."

"Yes, but I passed out." He chuckled to himself and again lifted the bottle to his lips, but in the candlelight I saw the smallest bubble. He had taken only a drop.

"That's one of the things I wanted to tell you, Danny. Was it the old place he wanted?"

"Yes."

"How does it happen you haven't sold it?"

"I thought I told you. It makes me a gentleman, lacking only the conduct of a gentleman."

"Don't sell it, Danny. Hold onto it."

"What's it to you? Why not?"

"For your pride."

"I don't have any pride left, only position."

"Yes, you have. When you asked me for money, you were ashamed. That means pride."

"No, I told you. That was a trick. Drunks are clever, I tell you. It embarrassed you, and you gave me a buck because you thought I was ashamed. I wasn't ashamed. I just wanted a drink."

"Don't sell it, Danny. It's valuable. Baker knows it. He doesn't buy anything without value."

"What's valuable about it?"

"It's the only place nearby level enough for an airfield."

"I see."

"If you'll hold out, it can be a whole new start for you, Danny. Hold onto it. You could take the cure and when you came out you'd have a nest egg."

"But no nest. Maybe I'd rather sell it and drink it up and—'When the bough breaks the cradle will fall, and down will come baby, cradle and all.'" He sang shrilly and laughed. "Do you want the place, Eth? Is that why you came here?"

"I want you to be well."

"I am well."

"I want to explain, Danny. If you were a bum, you could be free to do whatever you want. But you have something a group of forward-looking citizens want and need."

"Taylor Meadow. And I'm going to hold onto it. I'm forward-looking too." He glanced affectionately at the bottle.

"Danny, I told you, it's the only place for an airport. It's a key place. They have to have it—either that or level the hills, and they can't afford that."

"Then I have them by the ying-yang and I'm going to twist."

"You've forgotten, Danny. A man of property is a precious vessel. Already I've heard that the kindest thing would be to put you in an institution where you would get the care you need."

"They wouldn't dare."

"Oh, yes they would—and feel virtuous about it. You know the process. The judge, you know him, would rule you incompetent to handle property. He would appoint a guardian, and I can guess which one. And all this would be expensive, so of course your property would have to be sold to pay the costs, and guess who would be there to buy it."

His eyes were shiny and he listened with his mouth parted. Now he looked away.

"You're trying to scare me, Eth. You picked the wrong time.

Catch me in the morning when I'm cold and the world is green vomit. Right now—my strength it is the strength of ten because the bottle's here." He waved it like a sword and his eyes went to slits gleaming in the candlelight. "Did I tell you, Eth? I think I did—a drunk has a special evil kind of intelligence."

"But I've told you what will happen."

"I agree with you. I know it's true. You've made your point. But instead of scaring me, you're roused my imp. Whoever thinks a drunk is helpless is crazy. A drunk is a very special vehicle with special abilities. I can fight back, and right now I seem to want to."

"Good boy! That's what I want to hear."

He sighted at me over the neck of the whisky bottle as though it were the bead on the end of a rifle. "You'd loan me Mary's money?"

"Yes."

"Without security?"

"Yes."

"Knowing the chance of getting it back is a thousand to one against?"

"Yes."

"There's an ugly thing in a drunk, Eth. I don't believe you." He licked his dry lips. "Would you put the money in my hands?"

"Whenever you say."

"I've told you not to."

"But I will."

This time he tipped the bottle back and the big bubble rose inside the glass. When he stopped drinking, his eyes were even shinier but they were cold and impersonal as a snake's eyes. "Can you get the money this week, Eth?"

"Yes."

"Wednesday?"

"Yes."

"Have you got a couple of bucks now?"

I had just that—a dollar bill, a half, a quarter, two dimes and a nickel, and three pennies. I poured them into his outstretched hand.

He finished the bottle and dropped it on the floor. "Somehow I never put you down for clever, Eth. Do you know even a basic cure would cost about a thousand dollars?"

"All right."

"This is fun, Eth. This isn't chess, it's poker. I used to be pretty good at poker—too good. You're betting I'll put up my meadow as collateral. And you're betting that a thousand dollars' worth of booze will kill me, and there you'll be with an airport in your lap."

"That's a nasty thing, Danny."

"I warned you I was nasty."

"Couldn't you think I meant it the way I said it?"

"No. But I've got a way to—keep it the way you said it. You remember me in the old days, Eth. Do you think I don't remember you? You're the kid with the built-in judge. Okay. I'm getting dry. The bottle's empty. I'm going out. My price is one thousand bucks."

"All right."

"In cash on Wednesday."

"I'll bring it."

"No note, no signature, no nothing. And don't think you remember me, Ethan, from the old days. My friend here has changed all that. I have no loyalty, no fairness. What you'll get is nothing but hearty laughter."

"I would only ask you to try."

"Sure, I'll promise, Eth. But I hope I've convinced you what a drunk's promise is worth. Just bring the cash. Stay as long as you like. My house is your house. I'm going out. See you Wednesday, Eth." He eased himself up out of the old Army cot, flung the comforter behind it, and walked out with a rolling gait. His pants were not zipped up.

I sat for a while, watching the candle gutter down into the grease of the saucer. Everything he had said was true, except one thing on which I placed my bet. He hadn't changed that much. Somewhere in the wreckage was Danny Taylor. I didn't believe he could amputate Danny. I loved Danny and I was prepared to—do just what he said. I was. From a distance I heard him singing in a clear, high falsetto:

> "Speed, bonnie boat, like a bird on the wing.
> 'Onward!' the sailors cry!
> Carry the lad that's born to be king
> Over the sea to Skye."

After a lonely while I blew out the candle and walked home by way of High Street. Willie wasn't asleep yet in the police car.

"Seems to me you're out a lot, Eth," he said.

"You know how it is."

"Sure. Spring. Young man's fancy."

Mary was asleep, smiling, but when I slipped in beside her, she half awakened. The misery was in my stomach—the cold, hurting misery. Mary turned on her side and gathered me into her warm grass-smelling body and I needed her. I knew the misery would get less, but right now I needed her. I don't know whether she really awakened but even sleeping she knew my need.

And afterward she was awake and she said, "I suppose you're hungry."

"Yes, Helen."

"What do you want?"

"Onion sandwich—no, two onion sandwiches on rye bread."

"I'll have to have one to stand you."

"Don't you want one?"

"Of course."

She padded down the stairs and came back in a little while with sandwiches and a carton of milk and two glasses.

It was a pretty hot onion. "Mary, muldoon," I began.

"Wait till you swallow."

"Did you mean that about not wanting to know about business?"

"Why—yes."

"Well, I have a lead. I want a thousand dollars."

"Was it something Mr. Baker told you?"

"In a way. But private too."

"Well, you just write a check."

"No, darling, I want you to get it in cash. And you might pass the word at the bank that you're getting new furniture or rugs or something."

"But I'm not."

"You will."

"Is it a secret?"

"You said you wanted it that way."

"Yes—well—I do. Yes. It's better that way. This is a burny onion. Would Mr. Baker approve?"

"He would if he did it."

"When do you want it?"

"Tomorrow."

"I can't eat this onion. I guess I smell bad enough now, though."

"You're my darling."

"I can't get over Marullo."

"How do you mean?"

"Coming to the house. Bringing candy."

"God works in a mysterious way."

"Now don't be sacrilegious. Easter isn't over."

"Yes 'tis. It's one-fifteen."

"Good Lord! We better get to sleep."

"Ah! There's the rub—Shakespeare."

"You'd make a joke about anything."

But it was no joke. The misery stayed, not thought about but aching away, and sometimes I would have to ask myself, Why do I ache? Men can get used to anything, but it takes time. Once long ago I took a job wheeling nitroglycerin in a dynamite plant. The pay was high because the stuff is tricky. At first I worried with every step I took, but in a week or so it was only a job. Why, I'd even got used to being a grocery clerk. There's something desirable about anything you're used to as opposed to something you're not.

In the dark with the red spots swimming in my eyes, I inquired of myself concerning what they used to call matters of conscience, and I could find no wound. I asked whether, having set my course, I could change direction or even reverse the compass ninety degrees and I thought I could but I didn't want to.

I had a new dimension, and I was fascinated with it. It was like discovering an unused set of muscles or having come true the child's dream that I could fly. Often I can replay events, scenes, conversations, and pick up from the repeat details which escaped me at first showing.

Mary found strangeness in Marullo's coming to the house with candy eggs, and I trust Mary's sense of strangeness. I had thought of it as a thank offering because I had not cheated him. But Mary's question made me reinspect for something I knew but had passed by. Marullo did not reward for things past; he bribed for things to come. He was not interested in me except in so far as I could be of use to him. I went back over his business instruction and the talk about Sicily. Somewhere he had lost his certainty. In some way he wanted something of me or needed something. There was a way to find out. If I should ask for something he would ordinarily refuse and get it from him, then I would know that he was off balance and deeply troubled. I put Marullo aside and went to Margie. Margie—that gives you an idea of her age. "Margie, I'm always dreaming of you, Margie. I'd give the world to . . ."

I replayed the Margie scenes against the swimming spots on the ceiling, trying to add no more than was really there. For a long time, maybe two years, there had been a Mrs. Young-Hunt who was a friend of my wife, part of the conversations I did not listen to. Then suddenly Margie Young-Hunt had emerged, and then Margie. She must have come to the store before Good Friday, but I could not remember it. On that day it was as though she announced herself. Before that it is possible that she didn't see me any more than I saw her. But from that time on she was present—a mover and a shaker. What did she want? Could it be pure mischief of a woman with too little to do? Or did she move to a plan? It did seem to me that she had announced herself to me—made me conscious of her and kept me aware of her. It seemed to me that she started the second fortune-telling in good faith, intending it to be the usual performance, polished and professional. Then something happened, something that tore it up. Mary had said nothing to cause her tension, nor had I. Had she really seen the vision of the snake? That would be the simplest explanation and probably the true one. Maybe she was truly intuitive, an intruder into the minds of others. The fact that she had caught me midway in a metamorphosis made me likely to believe this, but it could have been an accident. But what made her run to Montauk when she had not intended to go, join up with the drummer, spill the beans to Marullo? Somehow I didn't believe she spilled things she didn't intend to spill. Somewhere in the attic bookcases there was an account of the life of—was it Bering? No, Baranov, Alexander Baranov, the Russian governor somewhere near 1800. Maybe there would be some reference to Alaska as a prison for witches. It was too unlikely a story to be made up. I must look. I thought maybe I could creep up there now without waking Mary.

Then I heard a creak of the old oak stair treads, then a second and a third, so I knew it was not a settling of the house from a change of temperature. It had to be Ellen walking in her sleep.

Of course I love my daughter, but sometimes she frightens me for she seems to have been born clever, at once jealous and loving. She was always jealous of her brother and often I feel she is jealous of me. It seemed to me that her preoccupation with sex began very early. Maybe fathers always feel this. When she was a very little girl, her uninhibited interest in male genitalia was embarrassing. Then she went into the secrecy of change. Here was no angelic innocent girlhood of the magazines. The house boiled with nervousness, the walls vibrated with unease. I've read that in the Middle Ages pubescent girls were thought to be susceptible to witchcraft and I'm not sure it is not so. For a time we had what we called as a joke a poltergeist. Pictures fell from their hangings, dishes crashed to the floor. There were poundings in the attic and thumpings in the cellar. I don't know what caused it, but I was interested enough to keep my eye on Ellen, on her secret comings and goings. She was like a night cat. I satisfied myself that she was not responsible for the fallings and crashings and thumpings, but also I found they never happened when she was out of the house. She might be sitting staring into space when the poltergeist came, but she was always there.

As a child I remember hearing that the old Hawley house was haunted long ago by the ghost of one of the puritan-pirate ancestors but, according to accounts, he was a decent ghost who walked and wandered and groaned as he should. The stairs creaked under his invisible weight and he rapped on the wall when a death was imminent, all proper and in good taste. The poltergeist was something quite different—malicious, malignant, and mischievous and vengeful. He never broke a valueless thing. Then he went away. I never really believed in him. He was a family joke, except that there he was and there were the broken pictures and shattered china.

When he left, Ellen began walking in her sleep as she was now. I could hear her slow but certain footsteps going downstairs. And at the same time my Mary sighed deeply and murmured beside me. And a breeze sprang up and moved the shadows of leafing limbs on the ceiling.

I slipped quietly from bed and slid into my bathrobe, for I, like everyone else, believed that a sleepwalker should not be startled awake.

This sounds as though I didn't like my daughter, but I do. I love her, but I am somewhat in fear of her because I don't understand her.

If you use our stairs near the edge on the side of the wall, they do not creak. I discovered that as a tomcatting boy coming home from the back fences of the town. I still use the knowledge if I do not want to disturb Mary. I used it now—moved silently down the staircase, trailing my fingers against the wall for guidance. A dim and lacy sublight penetrated from the street-lamp side and dissipated to semidarkness away from the window. But I could see Ellen. She seemed to have a glow, perhaps her white nightgown. Her face was shadowed but her arms and hands picked up light. She was standing at the glass-fronted cabinet where the worthless family treasures are kept, the carved scrimshaw, the sperm whales and boats complete with oars and irons and crews, harpooner in the bow—all carved from whales' bone—like teeth and the curved tusks of walrus; a small model of the *Belle-Adair*, shiny with varnish, her furled sails and cordage brown and dusty. There were bits of the *chinoiserie* the old captains brought from the Orient after they had stripped the China area of sperm whales, bits and pieces, ebony and ivory, laughing and serious gods, Buddhas, serene and dirty, carved flowers in rose quartz and soapstone and some jade—yes, some good jade—and thin cups, translucent and lovely. Some of the things might be valuable—like the small shapeless horses which yet had life—but if they were valuable it was an accident, must have been. How would those sailing, whale-killing men know good from bad—or would they? Or did they?

The cabinet had always been the holy place of the *parenti* to me—Roman masks of the ancestors, or the lares and penates back to a stone fallen from the moon. We even had a mandrake root—a perfect little man, sprouted from the death-ejected sperm of a hanged man, and also we had a veritable mermaid, pretty ratty by now, but cleverly made by sewing the front end of a monkey and the after end of a fish together. It had shrunk with the years and the stitches showed, but its little teeth still showed in a ferocious smile.

I presume that every family has a magic thing, a continuity thing that inflames and comforts and inspires from generation to generation. Ours was a—how shall I say?—a kind of mound of translucent stone, perhaps quartz or jadeite or even soapstone. It was circular, four inches in diameter and an inch and a half at its rounded peak. And carved on its surface was an endless interweaving shape that seemed to move and yet went no place. It was living but had no head or tail, nor beginning or end. The polished stone was not slick to the touch but slightly tacky like flesh, and it was always warm to the touch. You could see into it and yet not through it. I guess some old seaman of my blood had brought it back from China. It was magic—good to see, to touch, to rub against your cheek or to caress with your fingers. This strange and magic mound lived in the glass cabinet. As child and boy and man I was allowed to touch it, to handle it, but never to carry it away. And its color and convolutions and texture changed as my needs changed. Once I supposed it was a breast, to me as a boy it became yoni, inflamed and aching. Perhaps later it evolved to brain or even enigma, the headless, endless, moving thing—the question which is whole within itself, needing no answer to destroy it, no beginning or end to limit it.

The glass case had a brass lock from colonial times and a square brass key, always in the lock.

My sleeping daughter had the magic mound in her hands, caressing it with her fingers, petting it as though it were alive. She pressed it against her unformed breast, placed it on her cheek below her ear, nuzzled it like a suckling puppy, and she hummed a low song like a moan of pleasure and of longing. There was destruction in her. I had been afraid at first that she might want to crash it to bits or hide it away, but now I saw that it was mother, lover, child, in her hands.

I wondered how I might awaken her without fright. But why are sleepwalkers awakened? Is it for fear that they may hurt themselves? I've never heard of injury in this state, except through awakening. Why should I interfere? This was no nightmare full of pain or fear but rather pleasure and association beyond waking understanding. What call had I to spoil it? I moved quietly back and sat down in my big chair to wait.

The dim room seemed swarming with particles of brilliant light moving and whirling like clouds of gnats. I guess they were not really there but only prickles of weariness swimming in the fluid of my eyes, but they were very convincing. And it did seem true that a glow came from my daughter Ellen, not only from the white of her gown but from her skin as well. I could see her face and I should not have been able to in the darkened room. It seemed to me that it was not a little girl's face at all—nor was it old, but it was mature and complete and formed. Her lips closed firmly, which they did not normally do.

After a time Ellen put the talisman firmly and precisely back in its place and she closed the glass-fronted case and twisted the brass key that kept it closed. Then she turned and walked past my chair and up the stairs. Two things I may have imagined—one, that she did not walk like a child but like a fulfilled woman, and second, that as she went the luminescence drained away from her. These may be impressions, children of my mind, but a third thing is not. As she ascended the stairs, there was no creak of wood. She must have been walking near to the wall, where the treads do not complain.

In a few moments I followed her and found her in her bed, asleep and properly covered. She breathed through her mouth and her face was a sleeping child's face.

On compulsion I went down the stairs again and opened the glass case. I took the mound in my hands. It was warm from Ellen's body. As I had done in childhood, I traced the endless flowing form with my forefingertip and I took comfort in it. I felt close to Ellen because of it.

I wonder, did the stone bring her somehow close to me—to the Hawleys?

Chapter IX

ON Monday perfidious spring dodged back toward winter with cold rain and raw gusty wind that shredded the tender leaves of too trusting trees. The bold and concupiscent bull sparrows on the lawns, intent on lechery, got blown about like rags, off course and off target, and they chattered wrathfully against the inconstant weather.

I greeted Mr. Red Baker on his tour, his tail blown sideways like a battle flag. He was an old acquaintance, squinting his eyes against the rain. I said, "From now on you and I can be friends on the surface, but I feel it only right to tell you that our smiles conceal a savage contest, a conflict of interests." I could have said more but he was anxious to finish his chores and get under cover.

The Morph was on time. He may have been waiting for me —probably was. "Hell of a day," he said, and his oiled-silk raincoat flapped and billowed around his legs. "I hear you did a social turn with my boss."

"I needed some advice. He gave me tea too."

"He'll do that."

"You know how advice is. You only want it if it agrees with what you wanted to do anyway."

"Sounds like investment."

"My Mary wants some new furniture. When a woman wants something she first dresses it up as a good investment."

"Not only women, either," said Morph. "I do it myself."

"Well, it's her money. She wants to shop around for bargains."

At the corner of High Street we watched a tin sign tear loose from Rapp's Toy Store and go skidding and screeching along, sounding like a traffic accident.

"Say, I heard your boss is going to make a trip home to Italy."

"I don't know. Seems odd to me he never went before. Those families are awful close."

"Got time for a cup of coffee?"

"I ought to get swept out. Should be a busy morning after the holiday."

"Oh, come on! Live big. The personal friend of Mr. Baker can afford time for a cup of coffee." He didn't say it meanly the way it looks in print. He could make anything sound innocent and well-intentioned.

In all the years I had never gone into the Foremaster Grill for a cup of coffee in the morning and I was probably the only man in town who didn't. It was a custom, a habit, and a club. We climbed on stools at the counter and Miss Lynch, I went to school with her, slid coffee to us without spilling any in the saucer. A tiny bottle of cream leaned against the cup but she rolled two paper-wrapped cubes of sugar like dice so that Morph cried out, "Snake eyes."

Miss Lynch—Miss Lynch. The "miss" was part of her name by now, and part of herself. I guess she will never be able to excise it. Her nose gets redder every year, but it's sinus, not booze.

"Morning, Ethan," she said. "You celebrating something?"

"He dragged me in," I said, and then as an experiment in kindness, "Annie."

Her head snapped around as though at a pistol shot and then, as the idea got through, she smiled and, do you know, she looked exactly as she had in the fifth grade, red nose and all.

"It's good to see you, Ethan," she said and wiped her nose on a paper napkin.

"When I heard it, I was surprised," Morph said. He picked at the paper on the sugar cube. His nails were polished. "You get an idea and then it's fixed and you think it's true. Gives you a turn when it's not."

"I don't know what you're talking about."

"I guess I don't either. Goddam these wrappers. Why can't they just put it loose in a bowl?"

"Maybe because people might use more."

"I guess so. I knew a guy once lived on sugar for a while. He'd go in the Automat. Ten cents for a cup of coffee, drink half, fill it up with sugar. At least he didn't starve to death."

As usual, I wondered if that guy wasn't Morph—a strange one, tough, ageless man with a manicure. I think he was a fairly well-educated man, but only because of his processes, his technique of thinking. His erudition hid in a demi-world dialect, a language of the bright, hard, brassy illiterate. "Is that why you use one lump of sugar?" I asked.

He grinned. "Everybody's got a theory," he said. "I don't care how beat a guy is, he'll have a theory why he's beat. A theory can lead you down the garden path 'cause you'll follow it in spite of road signs. I guess that's what fooled me about your boss."

I hadn't had coffee away from home in a long time. It wasn't very good. It didn't taste like coffee at all but it was hot, and I spilled some on my shirt, so I know it was also brown.

"I guess I don't know what you mean."

"I been trying to track where I got the idea. I guess it's because he says he's been here forty years. Thirty-five years or thirty-seven years, okay, but not forty years."

"I guess I'm not too bright."

"That would make it 1920. You still don't dig it? Well, in a bank you've got to case people quick, check hustlers, you know. Pretty soon you get a built-in set of rules. You don't even think about it. It just clicks into place—and you can be wrong. Maybe he did come in 1920. I could be wrong."

I finished my coffee. "Time to sweep out," I said.

"You fool me too," Morph said. "If you asked questions I'd be hard to get. But you don't, so I got to tell you. Nineteen twenty-one was the first emergency immigration law."

"And?"

"In 1920 he could come in. In 1921 he probably couldn't."

"And?"

"So—anyway my weasel brain says—he came in after 1921 by the back door. So he can't go home because he can't get a passport to get back."

"God, I'm glad I'm not a banker."

"You'd probably be better than I am. I talk too much. If he's going back, I'm real wrong. Wait up—I'm coming. Coffee's on me."

" 'By, Annie," I said.

"Come in again, Eth. You never come in."

"I will."

As we crossed the street Morph said, "Don't let on to his guinea eminence that I pulled a blooper about him being deportation bait, will you?"

"Why should I?"

"Why did I? What's in that jewel case?"

"Knight Templar's hat. Feather's yellow. Going to see if it can be whited up."

"You belong to that?"

"It's in the family. We been Masons since before George Washington was Grand Master."

"He was? Does Mr. Baker belong?"

"It's in his family too."

We were in the alley now. Morph fished for the key to the bank's back door. "Maybe that's why we open the safe like a lodge meeting. Might as well be holding candles. It's kind of holy."

"Morph," I said. "you're full of bull this morning. Easter didn't clean you up at all."

"I'll know in eight days," he said. "No, I mean it. Comes nine o'clock on the nose we stand uncovered in front of the holy of holies. Then the time lock springs and Father Baker genuflects and opens the safe and we all bow down to the Great God Currency."

"You're nuts, Morph."

"Maybe so. Goddam this old lock. You could open it with an ice pick but not with the key." He jiggled the key and kicked at the door until it finally burst open. He took a piece of Kleenex from his pocket and jammed it into the spring lock's seat.

I caught myself about to ask, Isn't that dangerous?

He answered without the question. "Damn thing won't lock itself open. Course Baker checks to see it's locked after the safe's open. Don't blow my dirty suspicions to Marullo, will you? He's too solvent."

"Okay, Morph," I said and turned to my own door on my own side of the alley, and looked around for the cat that always tried to get in, but he wasn't there.

Inside, the store looked changed and new to me. I saw things I had never seen before and didn't see things that had worried and irritated me. And why not? Bring new eyes to a world or even new lenses, and presto—new world.

The leaky valve of the old box toilet hissed softly. Marullo wouldn't get a new valve because the water wasn't metered and who cared. I went to the front of the store and lifted a slotted two-pound weight from the old-fashioned balance scale. In the toilet I hung the weight on the chain above the oaken tassel. The toilet flushed and kept on flushing. I went back to the front of the store to listen and could hear it bubbling and scolding in the bowl. It's a sound you can't mistake for anything else. Then I returned the weight to its bar on the scale and took my place in my pulpit behind the counter. My congregation in the shelves stood waiting. Poor devils, they couldn't get away. I particularly noticed the Mickey Mouse mask smiling down from its box in the pew of breakfast foods. That reminded me of my promise to Allen. I found the extension hand for grabbing things from top shelves and took a box down and stood it under my coat in the storeroom. When I was back in the pulpit, the next Mickey Mouse in line smiled down at me.

I reached behind the canned goods and brought out the gray linen sack of small change for the cash register, then, remembering something, reached farther until my hand found the old greasy .38-caliber revolver that had been there ever since I can remember. It was a silvered Iver Johnson with most of the silver peeled off. I broke it and saw the cartridges green with verdigris. The cylinder was so sluggish with ancient grease that it turned with difficulty. I put the disreputable and probably dangerous piece in the drawer below the cash register, pulled out a clean apron, and wrapped it around my middle, folding the top over neatly to conceal the strings.

Is there anyone who has not wondered about the decisions and acts and campaigns of the mighty of the earth? Are they born in reasoning and dictated by virtue or can some of them be the products of accidents, of daydreaming, of imagining, of the stories we tell ourselves? I know exactly how long I had been playing a game of imagining because I know it started with the Morph's rules for successful bank robbery. I had gone over his words with a childish pleasure adults ordinarily will not admit. It was a play game that ran parallel with the store's life and everything that happened seemed to fall into place in the game. The leaking toilet, the Mickey Mouse mask Allen wanted, the account of the opening of the safe. New curves and angles dropped into place, the Kleenex nudged in the door lock in the alley. Little by little the game grew, but entirely in the mind until this morning. Putting the scale weight on the toilet chain was the first physical contribution I had made to the mental ballet. Getting the old pistol out was the second. And now I began to wonder about the timing. The game was growing in precision.

I still carry my father's big silver Hamilton railroad watch with thick hands and big black numbers, a wonderful watch for time-telling, if not for beauty. This morning I put it in my shirt pocket before I swept out the store. And I checked the time so that at five minutes to nine I had the front doors open and had just taken the first deliberate broom strokes at the sidewalk. It's amazing how much dirt accumulates over a weekend, and what with the rain, the dirt was slush.

What a wonderful precision instrument is our bank—like my father's railroad watch. At five minutes of nine Mr. Baker came into the wind from Elm Street. Harry Robbit and Edith Alden must have been watching. They backed out of the Foremaster Grill and joined him midstreet.

"Morning, Mr. Baker," I called. "Morning, Edith. Morning, Harry."

"Good morning, Ethan. You're going to need a hose for that!" They entered the bank.

I leaned my broom in the store entrance, took the weight from the scale, went behind the cash register, opened the drawer, and went through fast but deliberate pantomime. I walked to the storeroom, hung the weight on the toilet chain. Hooked the skirt of my apron over the belly band, put on my raincoat, and stepped to the back door and opened it a crack. As the black minute hand of my watch crossed twelve the clock bell of the firehouse began bonging. I counted eight steps across the alley and then in my mind twenty steps. I moved my hand but not my lips—allowed ten seconds, moved my hand again. All this I saw in my mind—I counted while my hands made certain movements—twenty steps, quick but deliberate, then eight more steps. I closed the alley door, took off my raincoat, unhooked my apron, went into the toilet, took the weight off the chain and stopped the flushing, moved back of the counter, opened the drawer, opened my hatbox and closed and strapped it, went back to the entrance, took up my broom, and looked at the watch. It was two minutes and twenty seconds past nine o'clock; pretty good, but with a little practice it could be cut under two minutes.

I was only half finished with the sidewalk when Stoney, the chief constable, came across from the Foremaster Grill.

"Morning, Eth. Gimme a quick half-pound of butter, pound of bacon, bottle of milk, and a dozen eggs. My wife run out of everything."

"Sure thing, Chief. How's everything?" I got the things together and snapped open a bag.

"Okay," he said. "I come by a minute ago but I heard you was in the can."

"It'll take me a week to get over all those hard-boiled eggs."

"That's the truth," said Stoney. "Man's got to go, he's got to go."

So that was all right.

As he was about to leave, he said, "What's with your friend, Danny Taylor?"

"I don't know—is he on one?"

"No, he looked pretty good, fairly clean. I was sitting in the car. He had me witness his signature."

"For what?"

"I don't know. Had two papers but turned back so I couldn't see."

"Two papers?"

"Yeah, two. He signed twice and I witnessed twice."

"Was he sober?"

"Seemed like. Had his hair cut and a necktie on."

"I wish I could believe it, Chief."

"So do I. Poor fella. I guess they never stop trying. I got to get home." And he galloped away. Stoney's wife is twenty years younger than he is. I went back and brushed the larger pieces of filth off the sidewalk.

I felt lousy. Maybe the first time is always hard.

I was right about the heavy custom. It seemed to me that everybody in town had run out of everything. And since our deliveries of fruits and vegetables didn't come in until about noon, the pickings were pretty slim. But even with what we had, the customers kept me jumping.

Marullo came in about ten o'clock and for a wonder he gave

me a hand, weighing and wrapping and ringing up money on the cash register. He hadn't helped around the store for a long time. Mostly he just wandered in and looked around and went out—like an absentee landlord. But this morning he helped to open the crates and boxes of fresh stuff when it came in. It seemed to me that he was uneasy and that he studied me when I wasn't looking. We didn't have time to talk but I could feel his eyes on me. I thought it must be hearing that I had refused the bribe. Maybe Morph was right. A certain kind of man, if he hears you have been honest, probes for the dishonesty that prompted it. The what's-he-getting-out-of-it? attitude must be particularly strong in men who play their own lives like a poker hand. The thought gave me a little chuckle but a deep one that didn't even raise a bubble to the surface.

About eleven o'clock, my Mary came in, shining in a new cotton print. She looked pretty and happy and a little breathless, as though she had done a pleasant but dangerous thing—and she had. She gave me a brown manila envelope.

"I thought you might be wanting this," she said. She smiled at Marullo the bright birdlike way she does when she doesn't really like someone. And she didn't like or trust Marullo—never had. I always put it down to the fact that a wife never likes her husband's boss or his secretary.

I said, "Thank you, dear. You're very thoughtful. Sorry I can't take you for a boat ride on the Nile right now."

"You *are* busy," she said.

"Well, didn't you run out of everything?"

"Sure I did. Here, I've got a list. Will you bring things home tonight? I know you're too rushed to put them up now."

"But no hard-boiled eggs—"

"No, darling. Not for a whole year."

"Those Easter bunnies were sure busy."

"Margie wants to take us to dinner at the Foremaster tonight. She says she never gets to entertain us."

"Fine," I said.

"She says her place is too small."

"Is it?"

"I'm keeping you from your work," she said.

Marullo's eyes were on the brown envelope in my hand. I put it up under my apron and stuffed it in my pocket. He knew it was a bank envelope. And I could feel his mind hunting like a terrier after rats in a city dump.

Mary said, "I didn't get a chance to thank you for the candy, Mr. Marullo. The children loved it."

"Just good wishes of the Easter," he said. "You dress like springtime."

"Why, thank you. I got wet too. I thought the rain was over, but it came back."

"Take my raincoat, Mary."

"I wouldn't think of it. It's just a shower now. You get back to your customers."

The pace got worse. Mr. Baker looked in and saw the line of people waiting and went out. "I'll come back later," he called.

And still they came, right up until noon, and then, as usually happens, all custom stopped. People were eating lunch. The traffic died out in the street. For the first time all morning no one was wanting something. I drank more milk from the carton I had opened. Anything I took from the store I marked down and just deducted it from my pay. Marullo let me have things wholesale. It makes a big difference. I don't think we could have lived on my pay if he hadn't.

He leaned back against the counter and folded his arms and that hurt, so he shoved his hands in his pockets until that hurt.

I said, "I'm sure glad you helped out. Never saw such a rush. But I guess they can't go on living on left-over potato salad."

"You do a nice job, kid."

"I do a job."

"No, they come back. They like you."

"They're just used to me. I've been here forever." And then I tried a little tiny probe. "I'll bet you're looking forward to that hot Sicilian sun. It is hot in Sicily. I was there in the war."

Marullo looked away. "I don't make my mind yet."

"Why not?"

"Well, I been away so long time—forty years. I don't know nobody there."

"But you have relatives."

"They don't know me neither."

"I sure wish I could take a vacation in Italy—without a rifle and a field pack. Forty years is a long time, though. What year did you come over?"

"Nineteen twenty—long time ago."

Morph seemed to have hit it on the nose. Maybe bankers and cops and customs men get an instinct. Then another, maybe a little deeper probe came to my mind. I opened the drawer and took out the old revolver and tossed it on the counter. Marullo put his hands behind him. "What you got there, kid?"

"I just thought you ought to get a permit for it if you haven't got one. The Sullivan Act is a tough one."

"Where'd it come from?"

"It's been here all along."

"I never saw it. It don't belong to me. It's yours."

"Not mine. I never saw it before either. It's got to belong to somebody. Long as it's here don't you think you better apply for a permit? You sure it's not yours?"

"I tell you I never saw it. I don't like guns."

"That's funny. I thought all big Mafia men loved 'em."

"How you mean, Mafia? You trying to say I'm Mafia?"

I made a big innocent joke about it. "The way I heard it, all Sicilians belong to Mafia."

"That's crazy. I don't even know no Mafia."

I tossed the gun into the drawer. "Live and learn!" I said. "Well, I sure don't want it. Maybe I better turn it over to Stoney. Tell him I just came on it behind something, because that's what I did."

"You do that," said Marullo. "I never saw it in my life. I don't want it. It's not mine."

"Okay," I said. "Out it goes."

It takes quite a few documents to get a Sullivan Act permit —almost as many as to get a passport.

My boss had ants. Maybe too many small things had happened too close together.

The elderly Miss Elgar, the princess royal of New Baytown, came in close-hauled, with a set jib. Between Miss Elgar and the world were two plates of safety glass, a space between. She negotiated for a dozen eggs. Having known me as a little boy, she never thought of me as anything else. I could see that she was amazed and pleased that I could make change.

"I thank you, Ethan," she said. Her eyes slid over the coffee-grinder and over Marullo and gave equal attention to each. "How's your father, Ethan?"

"Fine, Miss Elgar," I said.

"Give him my greetings, that's a good boy."

"Yes, ma'am. I surely will, ma'am." I wasn't about to reregulate her time sense. They say she still winds the grandfather clock every Sunday night and it has been electrified for years. It wouldn't be bad to be that way, suspended in time—not bad at all, an endless afternoon of now. She nodded gravely to the coffee-grinder before she left.

"Crazy in the head," Marullo said and screwed his forefinger into his temple.

"Nobody changes. Nobody gets hurt."

"Your father is dead. Why don't you tell her he's dead?"

"If she'd believed me, she'd forget it. She always asks after him. It's not so long ago she stopped inquiring after my grandfather. She was his friend, they say, the old goat."

"Crazy in the head," Marullo observed. But for some reason having to do with Miss Elgar's unusual feeling about time, he had got hold of himself. It's hard to know how simple or complicated a man is. When you become too sure, you're usually wrong. I think, from habit and practice, Marullo had reduced his approaches to men to three: command, flattery, and purchase. And the three must have worked often enough to allow him to depend on them. Somewhere in his dealing with me he had lost the first.

"You're a good kid," he said. "You're a good friend too."

"Old Cap'n, he was my grandfather, used to say, 'If you want to keep a friend never test him.'"

"That's smart."

"He was smart."

"All over Sunday I been thinking, kid—even in church I was thinking."

I knew he had been worried about the kickback, at least I thought he had, so I jumped it out to save him time.

"About that fine present, huh?"

"Yeah." He looked at me with admiration. "You're smart too."

"Not smart enough to be working for myself."

"You been here how long—twelve years?"

"That's it—too long. 'Bout time for a change, don't you think?"

"And you never took none of the petty cash and you never took nothing home without you wrote it down."

"Honesty is a racket with me."

"Don't make no joke. What I say is true. I check. I know."

"You may pin the medal on my left lapel."

"Everybody steals—some more, some less—but not you. I know!"

"Maybe I'm waiting to steal the whole thing."

"Don't make jokes. What I say is true."

"Alfio, you've got a jewel. Don't polish me too much. The paste may show through."

"Why don't you be partners with me?"

"On what? My salary?"

"We work it out some way."

"Then I couldn't steal from you without robbing myself."

He laughed appreciatively. "You're smart, kid. But you don't steal."

"You didn't listen. Maybe I plan to take it all."

"You're honest, kid."

"That's what I'm telling you. When I'm most honest, nobody believes me. I tell you, Alfio, to conceal your motives, tell the truth."

"What kind of talk you do?"

"*Ars est celare artem.*"

He moved his lips over that and then broke into a laugh.

"Ho," he cried. "Ho! Ho! *Hic erat demonstrandum.*"

"Want a cold Coke?"

"No good for here!" He flung his arms across his abdomen.

"You aren't old enough for a bad stomach, not over fifty."

"Fifty-two, and I got a bad stomach."

"Okay," I said. "Then you came over at twelve if it was 1920. I guess they start Latin early in Sicily."

"I was choirboy," he said.

"I used to carry the cross in the choir myself. I'm going to have a Coke. Alfio," I said, "you work out a way for me to buy in here and I'll look at it. But I warn you, I don't have money."

"We work it out."

"But I'm going to have money."

His eyes were on my face and couldn't seem to remove themselves. And Marullo said softly, "*Io lo credo.*"

Power but not of glory surged through me. I opened a Coke and, tipping it back, looked down its brown barrel at Marullo's eyes.

"You're a good kid," he said and he shook my hand and wandered away, out of the store.

On an impulse I called after him, "How does your arm feel?"

He turned with a look of astonishment. "It don't hurt no more," he said. And he went on and repeated the words to himself, "It don't hurt no more."

He came back excitedly. "You got to take that dough."

"What dough?"

"That five per cent."

"Why?"

"You got to take it. You can buy in with me a little and a little, only hold out for six per cent."

"No."

"What you mean no, if I say yes?"

"I won't need it, Alfio. I'd taken it if I needed to, but I don't need it."

He sighed deeply.

The afternoon wasn't as busy as the morning, but it wasn't light either. There's always a slack time between three and four —usually twenty minutes to half an hour, I don't know why. Then it picks up again, but that's people going home from work and wives whomping up a last-ditch dinner.

In the slack period Mr. Baker came in. He waited, regarding the cheese and sausage in the cold chamber, until the store was clear of two customers, both sloppy shoppers, the kind who don't know what they want, the kind who pick up and put down, hoping that something will jump into their arms and demand to be bought.

At last the shoppers were finished and gone.

"Ethan," he said, "did you know Mary drew out a thousand dollars?"

"Yes, sir. She told me she was going to."

"Do you know what she wants it for?"

"Sure, sir. She's been talking about it for months. You know how women are. The furniture gets a little worn, but just the minute they decide to get new, the old stuff is just impossible."

"Don't you think it's foolish to spend it now on that kind of stuff? I told you yesterday there was going to be an opening."

"It's her money, sir."

"I wasn't talking about gambling, Ethan. I was talking about sure-fire investment. I believe with that thousand she could get her furniture in a year and still have a thousand."

"Mr. Baker, I can't very well forbid her to spend her own money."

"Couldn't you persuade her, couldn't you reason with her?"

"It never occurred to me."

"That sounds like your father, Ethan. That sounds wishy-washy. If I'm going to help you get on your feet I can't have you wishy-washy."

"Well, sir."

"And it isn't like she was going to spend it locally. No, she's going to wander around the discount houses and pay cash. There's no telling what she'll pick up. Local man might charge more but he'd be here if she got a lemon. You should put your foot down, Ethan. Try to get her to redeposit it! Or you tell her to put the money in my hands. She'll never regret it."

"It's money her brother left her, sir."

"I know that. I tried to reason with her when she drew it. She just turned blue-eyed vague—said she wanted to look around. Can't she look around without a thousand dollars in her pocket? You ought to know better, if she doesn't."

"I guess I'm out of practice, Mr. Baker. We haven't had any money since we were married."

"Well, you'd better learn and learn quick or you won't have any very long. The spending habit is like a dope with some women."

"Mary hasn't had a chance to develop the habit, sir."

"Well, she will. Just let her taste blood and she'll turn killer."

"Mr. Baker, I don't think you mean that."

"I do too."

"There's never been a more careful wife with money. She's had to be."

For some reason he had worked up a storm. "It's you I'm disappointed in, Ethan. If you're going to get any place you've got to be the boss in your own house. You could hold off new furniture another little while."

"I could, but she can't." The thought came to me that maybe bankers develop X-ray eyes for money, that maybe he could see the envelope through my clothes. "I'll try to reason with her, Mr. Baker."

"If she hasn't spent it already. Is she home now?"

"She said she was going to get a bus to Ridgehampton."

"Good God! There goes a thousand bucks."

"Well, she still has some capital."

"That's not the point. Your only entrance is money."

"Money gets money," I said softly.

"That's right. Lose sight of that and you're a gone goose, a clerk for the rest of your life."

"I'm sorry it happened."

"Well, you better lay down the law."

"Women are funny, sir. Maybe your talking about making money yesterday gave her the idea it was easy to get."

"Well, you disabuse her, because without it you can't get any."

"Would you like a cold Coke, sir?"

"Yes, I would."

He couldn't drink it out of the bottle. I had to open a package of paper picnic cups, but it cooled him a little. He muttered like retreating thunder.

Two Negro ladies from the crossing came in and he had to swallow his Coke and his rage. "You talk to her," he said savagely and he strode out and crossed the street to go home. I wondered if he was mad because he was suspicious, but I didn't think so. No, I think he was mad because he felt he'd lost his habit of command. You can get furious at someone who doesn't take your advice.

The Negro ladies were pleasant. There's a community of colored at the crossing, very nice people. They don't trade with us much because they have their own store, only now and then they do some comparative shopping to see if their racial loyalty isn't costing them too much. They did more pricing than buying and I understand why—pretty women, too, such long, straight, slender legs. It's a wonder what a lack of malnutrition in childhood can do for the human body, or the human spirit, for that matter.

Just before closing time I telephoned Mary. "Pigeon-flake, I'm going to be a little late."

"Don't forget we're having dinner with Margie at the Foremaster."

"I remember."

"How late are you going to be?"

"Ten or fifteen minutes. I want to walk down and look at the dredger in the harbor."

"Why?"

"I'm thinking of buying it."

"Oh!"

"Want me to pick up some fish?"

"Well, if you see some nice flounder. That's about all that's running."

"All right—I'm running."

"Now don't dawdle. You'll have to bathe and change. The Foremaster, you know."

"I won't, my fair, my lovely. Mr. Baker gave me hell for letting you spend a thousand dollars."

"Why, that old goat!"

"Mary—Mary! The walls have ears."

"You tell him what he can do."

"But he can't. Besides, he thinks you're a nitwit."

"What?"

"And I'm a wishy-washy, a washy-wishy—a you know how I am."

She was laughing her lovely trill, something that raises goose lumps of pleasure on my soul.

"Hurry home, darling," she said. "Hurry home." And how's that for a man to have! When I hung up, I stood by the phone all weak and leaky and happy if there is such a condition. I tried to think how it had been before Mary, and I couldn't remember, or how it would be without her, and I could not imagine it except that it would be a condition bordered in black. I guess everyone at some time or other writes his epitaph. Mine would be "Good-by Charley."

The sun was below the western hills but a great powdery cloud scooped its light and threw it on the harbor and the breakwater and the sea beyond so that the whitecaps were pink as roses. The piles in the water by the city pier are triple logs iron-banded at the top and sloping like pylons to shear the winter ice. On top of each one a gull stood motionless, usually a male with white immaculate vest and clean gray wings. I wonder if each one owns his place and can sell or rent it at will.

A few fishing boats were in. I know all the fishermen, have known them all my life. And Mary was right. They only had flounder. I bought four nice ones from Joe Logan and stood by while he filleted them for me, his knife slipping along the spine as easily as it would through water. In the spring there is one sure subject—when will the weakfish come? We used to say, "When lilacs bloom the weakfish coome," but you can't depend on it. Seems to me that all my life the weaks have not arrived or have just left. And what beautiful fish they are when you get one, slender as trout, clean, silver as—silver. They smell good. Well, they weren't running. Joe Logan hadn't taken a single one.

"Me, I like blowfish," Joe said. "Funny thing, when you call them blowfish nobody will touch them, but call them sea chicken and customers fight for them."

"How's your daughter, Joe?"

"Oh, she seems to get better and then she fades off. It's killing me."

"Too bad. I'm sorry."

"If there was anything to do—"

"I know—poor kid. Here's a bag. Just drop the flounders in it. Give her my love, Joe."

He looked me long in the eyes as though he hoped to draw something out of me, some medicine. "I'll do that, Eth," he said. "I'll tell her."

Back of the breakwater the county dredger was working, its giant screw augering up mud and shells and the pumps pushing the junk through pipe on pontoons and flinging it behind the black-tarred bulkheads on the shore. Its running lights were on and its riding lights too and two red balls were hoisted to show that it was working. A pale cook in white cap and apron leaned his bare arms on the rail and looked down into the troubled water and occasionally he spat into the roil. The wind was inshore. It brought from the dredger the stink of mud and long-dead shells and tarnished weed together with the sweet smell of baking cinnamon in apple pie. The great auger turned with majesty, boring out the channel.

Then with a flash of pink the sails of a lithe yacht caught the afterglow and came about and lost the light. I wandered back and turned left past the new marina and the old yacht club and the American Legion Hall with brown-painted machine guns mounted beside its steps.

At the boat yard they were working late trying to get the stored craft painted and ready against the coming summer. The unusual cold of the early spring had set them back with the painting and varnishing.

I walked well past the boat works and then down through the weed-grown lot to the harbor's edge and then slowly back toward Danny's lean-to shack. And I whistled an old tune against his wishing me to.

And it seemed he did. His shack was empty but I knew as surely as if I saw him that Danny was lying hidden in the weeds, perhaps between the huge square timbers that were scattered about. And since I knew he would come back as soon as I was gone, I took the brown envelope from my pocket and propped it on his dirty bed and I went away, still whistling, except for one moment when I called softly, "Good-by, Danny. Good luck." And I went on whistling back to the street and over to Porlock and past the great houses to Elm and so to my own—the Hawley house.

I found my Mary in the eye of a storm, quiet and slowly rotating herself with debris and great winds surging around her. She directed the devastation in her white nylon slip and slippers; her new-washed hair clustered on curlers on her head like a large litter of suckling sausages. I can't remember when we had been out to dinner at a restaurant. We couldn't afford it and had lost the habit. Mary's wild excitement fluttered the children on the edges of her personal hurricane. She fed them, washed them, issued orders, rescinded orders. The ironing board was standing in the kitchen with my dear and valued clothing pressed and hanging on the backs of chairs. Mary would pause in her gallop to swipe the iron at a dress she was pressing. The children were almost too excited to eat, but they had their orders.

I have five suits called best—a good number for a grocery

clerk to have. I fingered them on the chair backs. They were called Old Blue, Sweet George Brown, Dorian Grey, Burying Black, and Dobbin.

"Which one shall I wear, cuddles?"

"Cuddles? Oh! Well, it's not formal and it's Monday night. I'd say it would be Sweet George or Dorian, yes, Dorian, that's formal enough without being formal."

"And my polka-dot bow tie?"

"Of course."

Ellen broke in. "Papa! You're not going to wear a bow tie! You're too old."

"I am not. I'm young and gay and giddy."

"You'll be a laughing stork. I'm glad I'm not going."

"I am too. Where do you get the idea that I'm an old stork?"

"Well you aren't old, but you're too old for a bow tie."

"You're a nasty little conformist."

"Well, if you want to be a laughing stork."

"That's what I want to be. Mary, don't you want me to be a laughing stork?"

"Let your father alone, he has to bathe. I laid a shirt out on the bed."

Allen said, "I'm halfway through my I Love America essay."

"That's good, because come summer I'm going to put you to work."

"Work?"

"In the store."

"Oh!" He didn't seem too enthusiastic.

Ellen gave an opening gasp but when she had our attention she didn't say anything. Mary repeated the eighty-five things the children were to do and not to do while we were gone and I went upstairs for my tub.

I was tying my dear blue polka-dot, my only blue polka-dot tie when Ellen leaned in against the door. "It wouldn't be so bad if you were younger," she said with dreadful femininity.

"You're going to give some happy husband a rough time, my dear."

"Even the seniors in high school wouldn't wear it."

"Prime Minister Macmillan does."

"That's different. Daddy, is it cheating to copy something out of a book?"

"Explain!"

"Well, if a person, if I was writing my essay and I took stuff out of a book—how about that?"

"It would depend on how you did it."

"Like you said—explain."

"Don't you mean 'as I said'?"

"Yes."

"Well, if you put quotation marks around it and a footnote telling who wrote it, it could add dignity and authority. I guess half the writing in America is quotations if it isn't anthologies. Now do you like my tie?"

"S'pose you didn't put those marks . . ."

"Then it would be stealing like any other kind of stealing. You didn't do that, did you?"

"No."

"Then what is your problem?"

"Could they put you in jail?"

"Might—if you got money for it. Don't do it, my girl. Now what do you think about my tie?"

"I guess you're just impossible," she said.

"If you plan to join the others, you might tell your blinking brother that I brought him his bleeding Mickey Mouse mask and shame on him."

"You never listen, really listen."

"I do too."

"No, you don't. You'll be sorry."

"Good-by, Leda. Say hello to the swan."

She lounged away, a baby-fatted volupt. Girls kill me. They turn out to be girls.

My Mary was just beautiful, just beautiful and shining. A light from inside her oozed out of her pores. She took my arm as we walked down Elm Street under the arching trees with the street lights playing on us and I swear our legs moved with the proud and tender steps of thoroughbreds coming to the barrier.

"You must come to Rome! Egypt isn't big enough for you. The great world calls."

She giggled. I swear she giggled as would have done honor to our daughter.

"We're going to go out more often, my darling."

"When?"

"When we are rich."

"When is that?"

"Soon. I'm going to teach you to wear shoes."

"Will you light your cigars with ten-dollar bills?"

"Twenties."

"I like you."

"Shucks, ma'am. You oughten to say that. You plumb embarrass me."

Not long ago the owners of the Foremaster installed bow windows on the street, with small square panes of bottle glass, designed to make the place look old and authentic—and it did so look—but people sitting inside at the tables had their faces altered by the warping glass. One face would be all jaw, another one big vacant eye, but it all added to the age and the authenticity of the old Foremaster and so did the geraniums and lobelias in the window boxes.

Margie was waiting for us, hostess to her fingertips. She introduced her companion, a Mr. Hartog of New York, sunlamp tanned and set with teeth like an ear of Country Gentleman. Mr. Hartog looked wrapped and shellacked, but he answered all sentences with an appreciative laugh. That was his contribution and it wasn't a bad one.

"How d'you do?" said Mary.

Mr. Hartog laughed.

I said, "I hope you know your companion is a witch."

Mr. Hartog laughed. We all felt good.

Margie said, "I've asked for a table by the window. That one there."

"You also had them put special flowers, Margie."

"Mary, I have to do something to repay all your kindness."

They went on like this during and after Margie had seated us, and Mr. Hartog laughed at every period, clearly a brilliant man. I made a plan to get a word from him, but later.

The set table seemed fine and very white and the silver which wasn't silver looked extra silvery.

Margie said, "I'm the hostess and that means I'm the boss and I say martinis whether you want them or not." Mr. Hartog laughed.

The martinis came, not in little glasses but big as bird baths with twists of lemon peel. The first taste bit like a vampire bat, made its little anesthesia, and after that the drink mellowed and toward the bottom turned downright good.

"We're going to have two," said Margie. "The food's pretty good here but not that good."

Then I told how I had always planned to open a bar where you could only get your second martini. I would make a fortune.

Mr. Hartog laughed and four more bird baths appeared at our table while I was still chewing the first lemon peel.

With the first taste of his second drink, Mr. Hartog developed the power of speech. He had a low, vibrant voice, like that of an actor or a singer or a salesman of some product people don't want. You might even call it a bedside voice.

"Mrs. Young-Hunt tells me you're in business here," he said. "It's a fascinating town—unspoiled."

I was about to tell him exactly what my business consisted in when Margie took the ball. "Mr. Hawley is the coming power of this county," she said.

"So? What line are you in, Mr. Hawley?"

"Everything," said Margie. "Absolutely everything, but not openly, you understand." Her eyes had a liquor shine. I looked at Mary's eyes and they were just beginning to surface, so I judged the others had had a couple before we came, or at least Margie had.

"Well, that saves me from denying it," I said.

Mr. Hartog came back to his laugh. "You have a lovely wife. That's half the battle."

"That's the whole battle."

"Ethan, you'll make him think we fight."

"Oh, we do!" I gulped half the glass and felt the warmth spring up behind my eyes. And I was looking at the bottle end of one of the tiny window panes. It caught the candlelight and seemed to revolve slowly. Maybe it was self-hypnosis, for I heard my own voice go on, listened to myself from outside myself. "Mrs. Margie is the Witch of the East. A martini is not a drink. It's a potion." The gleaming glass still held me.

"Oh, dear! I always thought of myself as Ozma. Wasn't the Witch of the East a wicked witch?"

"She was indeed."

"And didn't she melt?"

Through the crooked glass I saw a man's figure walking past on the sidewalk. He was all misshaped by the distortion, but he carried his head a little to the left and walked curiously on the outsides of his feet. Danny did that. I saw myself leap up and run after him. I saw myself run to the corner of Elm Street but he had disappeared, perhaps in the back garden of the second house. I called, "Danny! Danny! Give me back the money. Please, Danny, give it to me. Don't take it. It's poisoned. I poisoned it!"

I heard a laugh. It was Mr. Hartog's laugh. Margie said, "Well, I would rather be Ozma."

I wiped the tears from my eyes with my napkin and explained, "I should drink it, not bathe my eyes in it. It burns."

"Your eyes are all red," Mary said.

I couldn't get back to the party but I heard myself talk and tell stories and I heard my Mary laugh like golden glory so I guess I was funny, and even charming, but I couldn't ever get back to the table. And I think Margie knew it. She kept looking at me with a concealed question, damn her. She was a witch.

I don't know what we had to eat. I remember white wine so perhaps it was fish. The brittle glass revolved like a propeller. And there was brandy, so I must have had coffee—and then it was over.

Going out, when Mary and Mr. Hartog had gone ahead, Margie asked, "Where did you go?"

"I don't know what you mean."

"You went away. You were only part here."

"Aroint ye, witch!"

"Okay, bud," she said.

On our way home I searched the shadows of the gardens. Mary clung to my arm and her footsteps were a little jerky. "What a nice time," she said. "I never had a better time."

"It was nice."

"Margie's a perfect hostess. I don't know how I'll match that dinner."

"She surely is."

"And you, Ethan. I knew you could be funny but you had

us laughing all the time. Mr. Hartog said he was weak from laughing about Mr. Red Baker."

Had I told that? Which one? I must have. Oh, Danny—give back the money! Please!

"You're better than a show," my Mary said. And in our own doorway I grabbed her so tight that she whimpered. "You're tipped, darling. You're hurting. Please don't let's wake the children."

It was my intention to wait until she slept and then to creep out, to go to his shack, to look for him, even to put the police on him. But I knew better. Danny was gone. I knew Danny was gone. And I lay in the darkness and watched the little red and yellow spots swimming in the water of my eyes. I knew what I had done, and Danny knew it too. I thought of my small rabbit slaughter. Maybe it's only the first time that's miserable. It has to be faced. In business and in politics a man must carve and maul his way through men to get to be King of the Mountain. Once there, he can be great and kind—but he must get there first.

Chapter X

THE Templeton Airfield is only about forty miles from New Baytown, and that's about five minutes' flying time for the jets. They come over with increasing regularity, swarms of deadly gnats. I wish I could admire them, even love them the way my son Allen does. If they had more than one purpose, maybe I could, but their only function is killing and I've had a bellyful of that. I haven't learned, as Allen has, to locate them by looking ahead of the sound they make. They go through the sound barrier with a boom that makes me think the furnace has exploded. When they go over at night they get into my dreams and I awaken with a sad sick feeling as though my soul had an ulcer.

Early in the morning a flight of them boomed through and I jumped awake, a little trembly. They must have made me dream of those German 88-millimeter all-purpose rifles we used to admire and fear so much.

My body was prickly with fear sweat as I lay in the gathering morning light and listened to the slender spindles of malice whining away in the distance. I thought how that shudder was under the skin of everybody in the world, not in the mind, deep under the skin. It's not the jets so much as what their purpose is.

When a condition or a problem becomes too great, humans have the protection of not thinking about it. But it goes inward and minces up with a lot of other things already there and what comes out is discontent and uneasiness, guilt and a compulsion to get something—anything—before it is all gone. Maybe the assembly-line psychoanalysts aren't dealing with complexes at all but with those warheads that may one day be mushroom clouds. It does seem to me that nearly everyone I see is nervous and restless and a little loud and gaily crazy like people getting drunk on New Year's Eve. Should auld acquaintance be forgot and kiss your neighbor's wife.

I turned my head toward mine. She was not smiling in her sleep. Her mouth was drawn down and there were lines of weariness around her squinched-shut eyes and so she was sick, because that's the way she looks when she is sick. She is the wellest wife in the world until she is sick, which isn't often, and then she is the sickest wife in the world.

Another flight of jets exploded through sound. We had maybe a half-million years to get used to fire and less than fifteen to build thinking about this force so extravagantly more fierce than fire. Would we ever have the chance to make a tool of this? If the laws of thinking are the laws of things, can fission be happening in the soul? Is that what is happening to me, to us?

I remember a story Aunt Deborah told me long ago. Early in the last century some of my people were Cambellites. Aunt Deborah was a child then, but she remembered how the end of the world was coming at a certain time. Her parents gave everything away, everything they owned but the bed sheets. Those they put on and at the predicted time they went to the hills to meet the End of the World. Dressed in sheets, hundreds of people prayed and sang. The night came and they sang louder and danced and as it got near time there was a shooting star, she said, and everybody screamed. She could still remember the screaming. Like wolves, she said, like hyenas, although she had never heard a hyena. Then the moment came. White-dressed men and women and children held their breaths. The moment went on and on. The children got blue in the face—and then it passed. It was done and they were cheated out of their destruction. In the dawn they crept down the hill and tried to get back the clothes they had given away, and the pots and pans and their ox and their ass. And I remember knowing how bad they must have felt.

I think what brought that back was the jets—all that enormous effort and time and money to stockpile all that death. Would we feel cheated if we never used it? We can shoot rockets into space but we can't cure anger or discontent.

My Mary opened her eyes. "Ethan," she said, "you're talking in your mind. I don't know what it's about but it's loud. Stop thinking, Ethan."

I was going to suggest that she give up drink but she looked too miserable. I don't always know when not to joke, but this time I said, "Head?"

"Yes."

"Stomach?"

"Yes."

"All over?"

"All over."

"I'll get you something."

"Get me a grave."

"Stay down."

"I can't. I've got to get the children off to school."

"I'll do it."

"You've got to go to work."

"I'll do it, I tell you."

After a moment she said, "Ethan, I don't think I can get up. I feel too bad."

"Doctor?"

"No."

"I can't leave you alone. Can Ellen stay with you?"

"No, she has examinations."

"Could I call up Margie Young-Hunt to come over?"

"Her phone is out. She's getting a new thingamabob."

"I can go by and ask her."

"She'd kill anybody that waked her this early."

"I could slip a note under her door."

"No, I don't want you to."

"Nothing to it."

"No, no. I don't want you to. I don't want you to."

"I can't leave you alone."

"That's funny. I feel better. I guess it was shouting at you that did it. Well, it's true," she said, and to prove it she got up and put on her dressing gown. She did look better.

"You're wonderful, my darling."

I cut myself shaving and went down to breakfast with a red tatter of toilet paper sticking to my face.

No Morph standing on the porch picking his teeth when I went by. I was glad. I didn't want to see him. I hurried just in case he might try to catch up with me.

When I opened the alley door I saw the brown bank envelope that had been pushed under it. It was sealed and bank envelopes are tough. I had to get out my pocket knife to slit it open.

Three sheets of paper from a five-cent lined school pad, written on with a soft lead pencil. A will: "I, being in my right mind . . ." and "In consideration I . . ." A note of hand: "I agree to repay and pledge my . . ." Both papers signed, the writing neat and precise. "Dear Eth: This is what you want."

The skin on my face felt as hard as a crab's back. I closed the alley door slowly as you'd close a vault. The first two sheets of paper I folded carefully and placed in my wallet, and the other —I crumpled it and put it in the toilet and pulled the chain. It's a high box toilet with a kind of step in the bowl. The balled paper resisted going over the edge, but finally it did.

The alley door was a little open when I emerged from the cubicle. I thought I had closed it. Going toward it, I heard a small sound and, looking up, I saw that damn cat on one of the top storage shelves hooking out with its claws for a hanging side of bacon. It took a long-handled broom and quite a chase to drive it out into the alley. As it streaked past me, I swiped at it and missed and broke the broom handle against the doorjamb.

There was no sermon for the canned goods that morning. I couldn't raise a text. But I did get out a hose to wash down the front sidewalk and the gutter too. Afterward I cleaned the whole store, even corners long neglected and choked with flug. And I sang too:

"Now is the winter of our discontent
Made glorious summer by this sun of York."

I know it's not a song, but I sang it.

PART TWO

Chapter XI

NEW BAYTOWN is a lovely place. Its harbor, once a great one, is sheltered from the northeast screamers by an offshore island. The village is strewn about a complex of inland waters fed by the tides, which at ebb and flow drive wild races through narrow channels from the harbor and the sea. It is not a crowded or an urban town. Except for the great houses of the long-gone whalers, the dwellings are small and neat, distributed among fine old trees, oaks of several kinds, maples and elms, hickory and some cypresses, but except for the old planted elms on the original streets, the native timber is largely oak. Once the virgin oaks were so many and so large that several shipyards drew planks and knees, keels and keelsons, from nearby.

Communities, like people, have periods of health and times of sickness—even youth and age, hope and despondency. There was a time when a few towns like New Baytown furnished the whale oil that lighted the Western World. Student lamps of Oxford and Cambridge drew fuel from this American outpost. And then petroleum, rock oil gushed out in Pennsylvania and cheap kerosene, called coal oil, took the place of whale oil and retired most of the sea hunters. Sickness or the despair fell on New Baytown—perhaps an attitude from which it did not recover. Other towns not too far away grew and prospered on other products and energies, but New Baytown, whose whole living force had been in square-rigged ships and whales, sank into torpor. The snake of population crawling out from New York passed New Baytown by, leaving it to its memories. And, as usually happens, New Baytown people persuaded themselves that they liked it that way. They were spared the noise and litter of summer people, the garish glow of neon signs, the spending of tourist money and tourist razzle-dazzle. Only a few new houses were built around the fine inland waters. But the snake of population continued to writhe out and everyone knew that sooner or later it would engulf the village of New Baytown. The local people longed for that and hated the idea of it at the same time. The neighboring towns were rich, spilled over with loot from tourists, puffed with spoils, gleamed with the great houses of the new rich. Old Baytown spawned art and ceramics and pansies, and the damn broadfooted brood of Lesbos wove handmade fabrics and small domestic intrigues. New Baytown talked of the old days and of flounder and when the weakfish would start running.

In the reedy edges of the inner waters, the mallards nested and brought out their young flotillas, muskrats dug communities and swam lithely in the early morning. The ospreys hung, aimed, and plummeted on fish, and sea gulls carried clams and scallops high in the air and dropped them to break them open for eating. Some otters still clove the water like secret furry whispers; rabbits poached in the gardens and gray squirrels moved like little waves in the streets of the village. Cock pheasants flapped and coughed their crowing. Blue herons poised in the shallow water like leggy rapiers and at night the bitterns cried out like lonesome ghosts.

Spring is late and summer late at New Baytown, but when it comes it has a soft, wild, and special sound and smell and feeling. In early June the world of leaf and blade and flowers explodes, and every sunset is different. Then in the evening the bobwhites state their crisp names and after dark there is a wall of sound of whippoorwill. The oaks grow fat with leaf and fling their long-tasseled blossoms in the grass. Then dogs from various houses meet and go on picnics, wandering bemused and happy in the woods, and sometimes they do not come home for days.

In June man, hustled by instinct, mows grass, riffles the earth with seeds, and locks in combat with mole and rabbit, ant, beetle, bird, and all others who gather to take his garden from him. Woman looks at the curling-edge petals of a rose and melts a little and sighs, and her skin becomes a petal and her eyes are stamens.

June is gay—cool and warm, wet and shouting with growth and reproduction of the sweet and the noxious, the builder and the spoiler. The girls in body-form slacks wander the High Street with locked hands while small transistor radios sit on their shoulders and whine love songs in their ears. The young boys, bleeding with sap, sit on the stools of Tanger's Drugstore ingesting future pimples through straws. They watch the girls with level goat-eyes and make disparaging remarks to one another while their insides whimper with longing.

In June businessmen drop by Al 'n' Sue's or the Foremaster for a beer and stay for whisky and get sweatily drunk in the afternoon. Even in the afternoon the dusty cars creep to the desolate dooryard of the remote and paintless house with every blind drawn, at the end of Mill Street, where Alice, the village whore, receives the afternoon problems of June-bitten men. And all day long the rowboats anchor off the breakwater and happy men and women coax up their dinners from the sea.

June is painting and clipping, plans and projects. It's a rare man who doesn't bring home cement blocks and two-by-fours and on the backs of envelopes rough out drawings of Taj Mahals. A hundred little boats lie belly down and keel up on the shore, their bottoms gleaming with copper paint, and their owners straighten up and smile at the slow, unmoving windrows. Still school grips the intransigent children until near to the end of the month and, when examination time comes, rebellion foams up and the common cold becomes epidemic, a plague which disappears on closing day.

In June the happy seed of summer germinates. "Where shall we go over the glorious Fourth of July? . . . It's getting on time we should be planning our vacation." June is the mother of potentials, ducklings swim bravely perhaps to the submarine jaws of snapping turtles, lettuces lunge toward drought, tomatoes rear defiant stems toward cutworms, and families match the merits of sand and sunburn over fretful mountain nights loud with mosquito symphonies. "This year I'm going to rest. I won't get so tired. This year I won't allow the kids to make my free two weeks a hell on wheels. I work all year. This is my time. I work all year." Vacation planning triumphs over memory and all's right with the world.

New Baytown had slept for a long time. The men who governed it, politically, morally, economically, had so long continued that their ways were set. The Town Manager, the council, the judges, the police were eternal. The Town Manager sold equipment to the township, and the judges fixed traffic tickets as they had for so long that they did not remember it as illegal practice—at least the books said it was. Being normal men, they surely did not consider it immoral. All men are moral. Only their neighbors are not.

The yellow afternoon had the warm breath of summer. A few early season people, those without children to hold them glued until school was out, were moving in the streets, strangers. Some cars came through, towing small boats and big outboard motors on trailers. Ethan would have known with his eyes closed that they were summer people by what they bought—cold cuts and process cheese, crackers and tinned sardines.

Joey Morphy came in for his afternoon refreshment as he did every day now that the weather was warming. He waved the bottle toward the cold counter. "You should put in a soda fountain," he said.

"And grow four new arms, or split into two clerks like a *puendo* pod? You forget, neighbor Joey, I don't own the store."

"You should."

"Must I tell you my sad story of the death of kings?"

"I know your story. You didn't know your asparagus from a hole in the double-entry bookkeeping. You had to learn the hard way. Now wait—but you learned."

"Small good it does me."

"If it was your store now, you'd make money."

"But it isn't."

"If you opened up next door, you'd take all the customers with you."

"What makes you think so?"

"Because people buy from people they know. It's called good will and it works."

"Didn't work before. Everybody in town knew me. I went broke."

"That was technical. You didn't know how to buy."

"Maybe I still don't."

"You do. You don't even know you've learned. But you've still got a broke state of mind. Junk it, Mr. Hawley. Junk it, Ethan."

"Thanks."

"I like you. When is Marullo going to Italy?"

"He hasn't said. Tell me, Joey—how rich is he? No, don't. I know you're not supposed to talk about clients."

"I can rupture a rule for a friend, Ethan. I don't know all his affairs, but if our account means anything, I'd say he is. He's got his fingers in all kinds of things—piece of property here, vacant lot there, some beach-front houses, and a bundle of first mortgages big around as your waist."

"How do you know?"

"Safe-deposit box. He rents one of our big ones. When he opens it, he has one key and I have the other. I'll admit I've peeked. Guess I'm a peeping Tom at heart."

"But it's all on the level, isn't it? I mean—well you read all the time about—well, drugs and rackets and things like that."

"I wouldn't know about that. He don't tell his business around. Draws some out, puts some back. And I don't know where else he banks. You notice I don't tell his balance."

"I didn't ask."

"Could you let me have a beer?"

"Only to take out. I can put it in a paper cup."

"I wouldn't ask you to break the law."

"Nuts!" Ethan punched holes in a can. "Just hold it down beside you if anybody comes in."

"Thanks. I've put a lot of thought on you, Ethan."

"Why?"

"Maybe because I'm a Nosy Parker. Failure is a state of mind. It's like one of those sand traps an ant lion digs. You keep sliding back. Takes one hell of a jump to get out of it. You've got to make that jump, Eth. Once you get out, you'll find success is a state of mind too."

"Is it a trap too?"

"If it is—it's a better kind."

"Suppose a man makes the jump, and someone else gets tromped."

"Only God sees the sparrow fall, but even God doesn't do anything about it."

"I wish I knew what you're trying to tell me to do."

"I wish I did too. If I did, I might do it myself. Bank tellers don't get to be president. A man with a fistful of stock does. I guess I'm trying to say, Grab anything that goes by. It may not come around again."

"You're a philosopher, Joey, a financial philosopher."

"Don't rub it in. If you don't have it, you think about it. Man being alone thinks about things. You know most people live ninety per cent in the past, seven per cent in the present, and that only leaves them three per cent for the future. Old Satchel Paige said the wisest thing about that I ever heard. He said, 'Don't look behind. Something may be gaining on you.' I got to get back. Mr. Baker's going to New York tomorrow for a few days. He's busy as a bug."

"What about?"

"How do I know? But I separate the mail. He's been getting a lot from Albany."

"Politics?"

"I only separate it. I don't read it. Is business always this slow?"

"Around four o'clock, yes. It'll pick up in ten minutes or so."

"You see? You've learned. I bet you didn't know that before you went broke. Be seeing you. Grab the gold ring for a free ride."

The little buying spurt between five and six came on schedule. The sun, held back by daylight-saving, was still high and the streets light as midafternoon when he brought in the fruit bins and closed the front doors and drew the green shades. Then, reading from a list, he gathered the supplies to carry home and put them all in one big bag. With his apron off and his coat and hat on, he boosted up and sat on the counter and stared at the shelves of the congregation. "No message!" he said. "Only remember the words of Satchel Paige. I guess I have to learn about not looking back."

He took the folded lined pages from his wallet, made a little envelope for them of waxed paper. Then, opening the enamel door to the works of the cold counter, he slipped the waxy envelope in a corner behind the compressor and closed the metal door on it.

Under the cash register on a shelf he found the dusty and dog-eared Manhattan telephone book, kept there for emergency orders to the supply house. Under U, under United States, under Justice, Dept of . . . His finger moved down the column past "Antitrust Div US Court House, Customs Div, Detention Hdqtrs, Fed Bur of Investgatn," and under it,

"Immigration & Naturalization Svce, 20 W Bway, BA 7-0300, Nights Sat Sun & Holidays OL 6-5888."

He said aloud, "OL 6-5888–OL 6-5888 because it's late." And then he spoke to his canned goods without looking at them. "If everything's proper and aboveboard, nobody gets hurt."

Ethan went out the alley door and locked it. He carried his bag of groceries across the street to the Foremaster Hotel and Grill. The grill was noisy with cocktailers but the tiny lobby where the public phone booth stood was deserted even by the room clerk. He closed the glass door, put his groceries on the floor, spread his change on the shelf, inserted a dime, and dialed O.

"Operator."

"Oh! Operator—I want to call New York."

"Will you dial the number, please?"

And he did.

Ethan came from work, carrying his bag of groceries. How good the long afternoons are! The lawn was so tall and lush that it took his footprints. He kissed Mary damply.

"Pollywog," he said, "the lawn is running wild. Do you think I could get Allen to cut it?"

"Well, it's examination time. You know how that is, and school closing and all."

"What's that unearthly squalling sound in the other room?"

"He's practicing with his voice-throwing gadget. He's going to perform at the school closing show."

"Well, I guess I'll have to cut the lawn myself."

"I'm sorry, dear. But you know how they are."

"Yes, I'm beginning to learn how they are."

"Are you in a bad temper? Did you have a hard day?"

"Let's see. No, I guess not. I've been on my feet all day. The thought of pushing the lawnmower doesn't make me jump with joy."

"We should have a power mower. The Johnsons have one you can ride on."

"We should have a gardener and a gardener's boy. My grandfather did. Ride on? Allen might cut the lawn if he could ride."

"Don't be mean to him. He's only fourteen. They're all like that."

"Who do you suppose established the fallacy that children are cute?"

"You *are* in a bad temper."

"Let's see. Yes, I guess I am. And that squalling is driving me crazy."

"He's practicing."

"So you said."

"Now don't take your bad temper out on him."

"All right, but it would help if I could." Ethan pushed through the living room, where Allen was squawking vaguely recognizable words from a vibrating reed held on his tongue. "What in the world is that?"

Allen spat it into his palm. "From that box of Peeks. It's ventriloquism."

"Did you eat the Peeks?"

"No. I don't like it. I've got to practice, Dad."

"Hold up a moment." Ethan sat down. "What do you plan to do with your life?"

"Huh?"

"The future. Haven't they told you in school? The future is in your hands."

Ellen slithered into the room and draped herself on the couch like a knob-kneed cat. She rippled out a steel-cutting giggle.

"He wants to go on television," she said.

"There was a kid only thirteen won a hundred and thirty thousand dollars on a quiz program."

"Turned out it was rigged," said Ellen.

"Well, he still had a hundred and thirty grand."

Ethan said softly, "The moral aspects don't bother you?"

"Well, it's still a lot of dough."

"You don't find it dishonest?"

"Shucks, everybody does it."

"How about the ones who offer themselves on a silver platter and there are no takers? They have neither honesty nor money."

"That's the chance you take—the way the cooky crumbles."

"Yes, it's crumbling, isn't it?" Ethan said. "And so are your manners. Sit up! Have you dropped the word 'sir' from the language?"

The boy looked startled, checked to see if it was meant, then lounged upright, full of resentment. "No, sir," he said.

"How are you doing in school?"

"All right, I guess."

"You were writing an essay about how you love America. Has your determination to destroy her stopped that project?"

"How do you mean, destroy—sir?"

"Can you honestly love a dishonest thing?"

"Heck, Dad, everybody does it."

"Does that make it good?"

"Well, nobody's knocking it except a few eggheads. I finished the essay."

"Good, I'd like to see it."

"I sent it off."

"You must have a copy."

"No, sir."

"Suppose it gets lost?"

"I didn't think of that. Dad, I wish I could go to camp the way all the other kids do."

"We can't afford it. Not all the other kids go—only a few of them."

"I wish we had some money." He stared down at his hands and licked his lips.

Ellen's eyes were narrowed and concentrated.

Ethan studied his son. "I'm going to make that possible," he said.

"Sir?"

"I can get you a job to work in the store this summer."

"How do you mean, work?"

"Isn't your question, 'What do you mean, work?' You will carry and trim shelves and sweep and perhaps, if you do well, you can wait on customers."

"I want to go to camp."

"You also want to win a hundred thousand dollars."

"Maybe I'll win the essay contest. At least that's a trip to Washington anyway. Some kind of vacation after all year in school."

"Allen! There are unchanging rules of conduct, of courtesy, of honesty, yes, even of energy. It's time I taught you to give them lip service at least. You're going to work."

The boy looked up. "You can't."

"I beg your pardon?"

"Child labor laws. I can't even get a work permit before I'm sixteen. You want me to break the law?"

"Do you think all the boys and girls who help their parents are half slave and half criminal?" Ethan's anger was as naked and ruthless as love. Allen looked away.

"I didn't mean that, sir."

"I'm sure you didn't. And you won't again. You stubbed your nose on twenty generations of Hawleys and Allens. They were honorable men. You may be worthy to be one someday."

"Yes, sir. May I go to my room, sir?"

"You may."

Allen walked up the stairs slowly.

When he had disappeared, Ellen whirled her legs like propellers. She sat up and pulled down her skirt like a young lady.

"I've been reading the speeches of Henry Clay. He sure was good."

"Yes, he was."

"Do you remember them?"

"Not really, I guess. It's been a long time since I read them."

"He's great."

"Somehow it doesn't seem schoolgirl reading."

"He's just great."

Ethan got up from his chair with a whole long and weary day pushing him back.

In the kitchen he found Mary red-eyed and angry.

"I heard you," she said. "I don't know what you think you're doing. He's just a little boy."

"That's the time to start, my darling."

"Don't darling me. I won't stand a tyrant."

"Tyrant? Oh, Lord!"

"He's just a little boy. You went for him."

"I think he feels better now."

"I don't know what you mean. You crushed him like an insect."

"No, darling. I gave him a quick glimpse of the world. He was building a false one."

"Who are you to know what the world is?"

Ethan walked past her and out the back door.

"Where are you going?"

"To cut the lawn."

"I thought you were tired."

"I am—I was." He looked over his shoulder and up at her standing inside the screened door. "A man is a lonely thing," he said, and he smiled at her a moment before he got out the lawnmower.

Mary heard the whirring blades tearing through the soft and supple grass.

The sound stopped by the doorstep. Ethan called, "Mary, Mary, my darling. I love you." And the whirling blades raged on through the overgrown grass.

Chapter XII

Margie Young-Hunt was an attractive woman, informed, clever; so clever that she knew when and how to mask her cleverness. Her marriages had failed, the men had failed; one by being weak, and the second weaker—he died. Dates did not come to her. She created them, mended her fences by frequent telephone calls, by letters, get-well cards, and arranged accidental meetings. She carried homemade soup to the sick and remembered birthdays. By these means she kept people aware of her existence.

More than any woman in town she kept her stomach flat, her skin clean and glowing, her teeth bright, and her chin-line taut. A goodly part of her income went to hair, nails, massage, creams, and unguents. Other women said, "She must be older than she looks."

When supporting muscles of her breasts no longer responded to creams, massage, and exercise, she placed them in shapely forms that rode high and jauntily. Her make-up took increasing time. Her hair had all the sheen, luster, wave the television products promise. On a date, dining, dancing, laughing, amusing, drawing her escort with a net of small magnets, who could know her cold sense of repetition? After a decent interval and an outlay of money, she usually went to bed with him if she discreetly could. Then back to her fence-mending. Sooner or later the shared bed must be the trap to catch her future security and ease. But the prospective game leaped clear of the quilted jaws. More and more of her dates were the married, the infirm, or the cautious. And Margie knew better than anyone that her time was running out. The tarot cards did not respond when she sought help for herself.

Margie had known many men, most of them guilty, wounded in their vanity, or despairing, so that she had developed a contempt for her quarry as a professional hunter of vermin does. It was easy to move such men through their fears and their vanities. They ached so to be fooled that she no longer felt triumph—only a kind of disgusted pity. These were her friends and associates. She protected them even from the discovery that they were her friends. She gave them the best of herself because they demanded nothing of her. She kept them secret because at the bottom she did not admire herself. Danny Taylor was one of these, and Alfio Marullo another, and Chief Stonewall Jackson Smith a third, and there were others. They trusted her and she them, and their secret existence was the one warm honesty to which she could retire to restore herself. These friends talked freely and without fear to her, for to them she was a kind of Andersen's Well—receptive, unjudging, and silent. As most people have secret vices, Margie Young-Hunt concealed a secret virtue. And because of this quiet thing it is probable that she knew more about New Baytown, and even Wessex County, than anyone, and her knowledge was unwarped because she would not—could not—use it for her own profit. But in other fields, everything that came to her hand was usable.

Her project Ethan Allen Hawley began casually and out of idleness. In a way he was correct in thinking it was mischievous, a testing of her power. Many of the sad men who came to her for comfort and reassurance were hogtied with impotence, bound and helpless in sexual traumas that infected all other areas of their lives. And she found it easy by small flatteries and reassurances to set them free to fight again against their whip-armed wives. She was genuinely fond of Mary Hawley, and through her she gradually became aware of Ethan, bound in another kind of trauma, a social-economic bind that had robbed him of strength and certainty. Having no work, no love, no children, she wondered whether she could release and direct this crippled man toward some new end. It was a game, a kind of puzzle, a test, a product not of kindness but simply of curiosity and idleness. This was a superior man. To direct him would prove her superiority, and this she needed increasingly.

Probably she was the only one who knew the depth of the change in Ethan and it frightened her because she thought it was her doing. The mouse was growing a lion's mane. She saw the muscles under his clothes, felt ruthlessness growing behind his eyes. So must the gentle Einstein have felt when his dreamed concept of the nature of matter flashed over Hiroshima.

Margie liked Mary Hawley very much and she had little

sympathy and no pity for her. Misfortune is a fact of nature acceptable to women, especially when it falls on other women.

In her tiny immaculate house set in a large, overgrown garden very near to Old Harbor, she leaned toward the make-up mirror to inspect her tools, and her eyes saw through cream, powder, eye-shadowing, and lashes sheathed in black, saw the hidden wrinkles, the inelasticity of skin. She felt the years creep up like the rising tide about a rock in a calm sea. There is an arsenal of maturity, of middle age, but these require training and technique she did not yet have. She must learn them before her structure of youth and excitement crumbled and left her naked, rotten, ridiculous. Her success had been that she never let down, even alone. Now, as an experiment, she allowed her mouth to droop as it wanted to, her eyelids to fall half-staff. She lowered her high-held chin and a plaited rope came into being. Before her in the mirror she saw twenty years clamber over her and she shuddered as the icy whispering told her what lay waiting. She had delayed too long. A woman must have a showcase in which to grow old, lights, props, black velvet, children, graying and fattening, snickering and pilfering, love, protection, and small change, a serene and undemanding husband or his even more serene and less demanding will and trust fund. A woman growing old alone is useless cast-off trash, a wrinkled obscenity with no hobbled retainers to cluck and mutter over her aches and to rub her pains.

A hot spot of fear formed in her stomach. She had been lucky in her first husband. He was weak and she soon found the valve of his weakness. He was hopelessly in love with her, so much so that when she needed a divorce he did not ask for a remarriage clause in his alimony settlement.

Her second husband thought she had a private fortune and so she had. He didn't leave her much when he died, but, with the alimony from her first husband, she could live decently, dress well, and cast about at leisure. Suppose her first husband should die! There was the fear spot. There was the night- or daymare—the monthly-check-mare.

In January she had seen him at that great wide cross of Madison Avenue and Fifty-seventh Street. He looked old and gaunt. She was haunted with his mortality. If the bastard died, the money would stop. She thought she might be the only person in the world who wholeheartedly prayed for his health.

His lean, silent face and dead eyes came on her memory screen now and touched off the hot spot in her stomach. If the son of a bitch should die . . . !

Margie, leaning toward the mirror, paused and hurled her will like a javelin. Her chin rose; the ropes dropped back; her eyes shone; the skin snuggled close to her skull; her shoulders squared. She stood up and waltzed in a deft circle on the deep-piled red carpet. Her feet were bare, with gleaming pinkened toenails. She must rush, she must hurry, before it was too late.

She flung open her closet and laid hands on the sweet, provocative dress she had been saving for the Fourth of July weekend, the shoes with pencil heels, the stockings more sheer than no stockings at all. There was no languor in her now. She dressed as quickly and efficiently as a butcher whets his knife and she checked against a full-length mirror the way that same butcher tests his blade against his thumb. Speed but no rush, speed for the man who will not wait, and then—the casual slowness of the informed, the smart, the chic, the confident, the lady with pretty legs and immaculate white gloves. No man she passed failed to look after her. Miller Brothers' truckdriver whistled as he lumbered by with lumber and two high-school boys leveled slitted Valentino eyes at her and painfully swallowed the saliva that flooded their half-open mouths.

"How about that?" said one.

And, "Yeah!" the other replied.

"How'd you like—"

"Yeah!"

A lady does not wander—not in New Baytown. She must be going someplace, have some business, however small and meaningless. As she walked in dotted steps along the High Street, she bowed and spoke to passers-by and reviewed them automatically.

Mr. Hall—he was living on credit, had been for some time.

Stoney—a tough, male man, but what woman could live on a cop's salary or pension? Besides, he was her friend.

Harold Beck with real estate and plenty of it, but Harold was queer as a duck. He himself was probably the only person in the world who didn't know it.

MacDowell— "So nice to see you, sir. How's Milly?" Impossible—Scottish, tight, tied to his wife—an invalid, the kind who lives forever. He was a secret. No one knew what he was worth.

Dew-eyed Donald Randolph—wonderful on the next bar stool, a barroom gentleman whose manners penetrated deep into his drunkenness, but useless unless you wanted to keep house on a bar stool.

Harold Luce—it was said that he was related to the publisher of *Time* magazine but who said it, himself? A flinty man who had a reputation for wisdom based on his lack of the power of speech.

Ed Wantoner—a liar, a cheat, and a thief. Supposed to be loaded and his wife was dying, but Ed trusted no one. He didn't even trust his dog not to run away. Kept it tied up and howling.

Paul Strait—a power in the Republican party. His wife was named Butterfly—not a nickname. Butterfly Strait, christened Butterfly, and that's the truth. Paul did well if New York State had a Republican governor. He owned the city dump, where it cost a quarter to dump a load of garbage. It was told that when the rats got so bad and big as to be dangerous, Paul sold tickets for the privilege of shooting them, rented flashlights and rifles—stocked .22-caliber cartridges to shoot them with. He looked so like a president that many people called him Ike. But Danny Taylor while quietly drunk had referred to him as the Noblest Paul of them Aul, and that stuck. Noble Paul became his name when he wasn't present.

Marullo—he's sicker than he was. He's gray sick. Marullo's eyes were those of a man shot in the stomach with a .45. He had walked past the doorway of his own store without going in. Margie entered the store, bouncing her neat buttocks.

Ethan was talking to a stranger, a youngish dark-haired man, Ivy League pants and hat with a narrow brim. Fortyish, hard, tough, and devoted to whatever he was doing. He leaned over the counter and seemed about to inspect Ethan's tonsils.

Margie said, "Hi! You're busy. I'll come back later."

There are endless idle but legitimate things a strolling woman can do in a bank. Margie crossed the alley mouth and went into the marble and brushed-steel temple.

Joey Morphy lighted up the whole barred square of his

teller's window when he saw her. What a smile, what a character, what a good playmate, and what a lousy prospect as a husband. Margie properly appraised him as a born bachelor who would die fighting to remain one. No double grave for Joey.

She said, "Please, sir, do you have any fresh unsalted money?"

"Excuse me, ma'am, I'll see. I'm almost positive I saw some somewhere. How much of it would you like to have?"

"About six ounces, m'sieur." She took a folding book from her white kid bag and wrote a check for twenty dollars.

Joey laughed. He liked Margie. Once in a while, not too often, he took her out to dinner and laid her. But he also liked her company and her sense of play.

Joey said, "Mrs. Young-Hunt, that reminds me of a friend I had who was in Mexico with Pancho Villa. Remember him?"

"Never knew him."

"No jazz. It's a story the guy told me. He said when Pancho was in the north, he worked the mint printing twenty-peso notes. Made so many his men stopped counting them. They weren't so hot at counting anyway. Got to weighing them on a balance scale."

Margie said, "Joey, you can't resist autobiography."

"Hell, no, Mrs. Young-Hunt. I'd have been about five years old. It's a story. Seems a fine stacked dame, Injun but stacked, came in and said, 'My general, you have executed my husband and left me a poor widow with five children, and is that any way to run a popular revolution?'

"Pancho went over her assets the way I'm doing now."

"You got no mortgage, Joey."

"I know. It's a story. Pancho said to an aide-de-camp, 'Weigh out five kilos of money for her.'

"Well, that's quite a bundle. They tied it together with a piece of wire and the woman went out, dangling the bale of kale. Then a lieutenant stepped out and saluted and he said, 'My general (they say it *mi gral*—like *hral*), we did not shoot her husband. He was drunk. We put him in the jail around the corner.'

"Pancho had never taken his eyes off the dame walking away with the bundle. He said, 'Go out and shoot him. We cannot disappoint that poor widow.'"

"Joey, you're impossible."

"It's a true story. I believe it." He turned her check around. "Do you want this in twenties, fifties, or hundreds?"

"Give it to me in two-bitses."

They enjoyed each other.

Mr. Baker looked out of his frosted-glass office.

Now there was a bet. Baker had made a grammatically correct but obscure pass at her once. Mr. Baker was Mr. Money. Sure he had a wife, but Margie knew the Bakers of this world. They could always raise a moral reason for doing what they wanted to do anyway. She was glad she had turned him down. It left him still in the book.

She gathered the four five-dollar bills Joey had given her and moved toward the gray banker, but at that moment the man she had seen talking to Ethan came in quietly, passed in front of her, presented a card, and was taken into Mr. Baker's office and the door closed.

"Well, kiss my foot," she said to Joey.

"Prettiest foot in Wessex County," Joey said. "Want to go out tonight? Dance, eat, all that?"

"Can't," she said. "Who is that?"

"Never saw him before. Looks like a bank-examiner type. It's times like this I'm glad I'm honest and even gladder I can add and subtract."

"You know, Joey, you're going to make some faithful woman a hell of a fine fugitive."

"That is my prayerful hope, ma'am."

"See you."

She went out, crossed the alley, and entered Marullo's grocery again.

"Hi, Eth."

"Hello, Margie."

"Who was the handsome stranger?"

"Don't you carry your crystal ball?"

"Secret agent?"

"Worse than that. Margie, is everybody afraid of cops? Even if I haven't done anything I'm scared of cops."

"Was that curly-haired piece of the true cross a dick?"

"Not exactly. Said he was a federal man."

"What you been up to, Ethan?"

"Up to? Me? Why 'up to'?"

"What did he want?"

"I only know what he asked but I don't know what he wanted."

"What did he ask?"

"How long do I know my boss? Who else knows him? When did he come to New Baytown?"

"What did you tell him?"

"When I joined up to fight the foe, I didn't know him. When I came back he was here. When I went broke, he took over the store and gave me a job."

"What do you suppose it's about?"

"God knows."

Margie had been trying to look past his eyes. She thought, He's pretending to be a simpleton. I wonder what the guy really wanted!

He said it so quietly it frightened her. "You don't believe me. You know, Margie, no one ever believes the truth."

"The whole truth? When you carve a chicken, Eth, it's all chicken, but some is dark meat and some white."

"I guess so. Frankly, I'm worried, Margie. I need this job. If anything happened to Alfio I'd be pounding the street."

"Aren't you forgetting you're going to be rich?"

"Kind of hard to remember when I'm not."

"Ethan, I wonder if you remember back. It was in the spring right near Easter. I came in and you called me Daughter of Jerusalem."

"That was Good Friday."

"You do remember. Well, I found it. It's Matthew, and it's pretty wonderful and—scary."

"Yes."

"What got into you?"

"My Great-Aunt Deborah. She got me crucified once a year. It still goes on."

"You're kidding. You weren't kidding then."

"No, I wasn't. And I'm not now."

She said playfully, "You know, the fortune I read you is coming true."

"I know it is."

"Don't you think you owe me something?"

"Sure."

"When are you going to pay?"

"Would you care to step into the back room?"

"I don't think you could do it."

"You don't?"

"No, Ethan, and you don't either. You've never had a quick jump in the hay in your life."

"I could learn, maybe."

"You couldn't fornicate if you wanted to."

"I could try."

"It would take love or hatred to arouse you, and either one would require a slow and stately procedure."

"Maybe you're right. How did you know?"

"I never know how I know."

He slid the door of the cold cabinet open, took out a Coke, which instantly grew a jacket of frost, opened it, and handed the bottle to her while he opened a second.

"What is it you want of me?"

"I've never known a man like that. Perhaps I want to see what it's like to be loved or hated that much."

"You're a witch! Why don't you whistle up a wind?"

"I can't whistle. I can raise a puny little storm in most men with my eyebrows. How do I go about lighting your fire?"

"Maybe you have."

He studied her closely and did not try to conceal his inspection. "Built like a brick outhouse," he said, "soft and smooth and strong and good."

"How do you know? You've never felt me."

"If I ever do, you'd better run like hell."

"My love."

"Come off it. There's something wrong here. I'm conceited enough to know the caliber of my attractiveness. What do you want? You're a fine broth of a dame but you're also smart. What do you want?"

"I told your fortune and it's coming true."

"And you want to suck along?"

"Yes."

"Now I can believe you." He raised his eyes. "Mary of my heart," he said, "look on your husband, your lover, your dear friend. Guard me against evil from within me and from harm without. I pray for your help, my Mary, for a man has a strange and wind-troubled need and the ache of the ages is on him to spread his seeds everywhere. *Ora pro me.*"

"You're a fake, Ethan."

"I know it. But can't I be a humble fake?"

"I'm afraid of you now. I wasn't before."

"I can't think why."

She had that tarot look and he saw it.

"Marullo."

"What about him?"

"I'm asking."

"Be with you in a moment. Half a dozen eggs, square of butter, right. How are you for coffee?"

"Yes, a can of coffee. I like to have it on the shelf. How is that Whumpdum corned-beef hash?"

"I haven't tried it. They say it's very good. Be with you in a moment, Mr. Baker. Didn't Mrs. Baker get some of that Whumpdum corned-beef hash?"

"I don't know, Ethan. I eat what's put before me. Mrs. Young-Hunt, you get prettier every day."

"Kind sir."

"It's true. And—you dress so well."

"I was thinking the same about you. Now you're not pretty but you have a wonderful tailor."

"I guess I have. He charges enough."

"Remember the old boy who said, 'Manners maketh man'? Well that's changed now. Tailors make men in any image they want."

"The trouble with a well-made suit, it lasts too long. This is ten years old."

"I can't believe it, Mr. Baker. How is Mrs. Baker?"

"Well enough to complain. Why don't you call on her, Mrs. Young-Hunt? She gets lonely. There aren't many people in this generation who can carry on a literate conversation. It was Wickham who said it. It's the motto of Winchester College."

She turned to Ethan. "You show me another American banker who knows that."

Mr. Baker grew ruddy. "My wife subscribed to Great Books. She's a great reader. Please call on her."

"I'd love to. Put my things in a bag, Mr. Hawley. I'll pick them up on my way home."

"Right, ma'am."

"That's quite a remarkable young woman," Mr. Baker said.

"She and Mary hit it off."

"Ethan, did that government man come here?"

"Yes."

"What does he want?"

"I don't know. He asked some questions about Mr. Marullo. I didn't know the answers."

Mr. Baker released the image of Margie as slowly as an anemone opens and casts out the shell of a sucked-clean crab. "Ethan, have you seen Danny Taylor?"

"No, I haven't."

"Do you know where he is?"

"No, I don't."

"I have to get in touch with him. Can't you think where he might be?"

"I haven't seen him for—well, since May. He was going to try the cure again."

"Do you know where?"

"He didn't say. But he wanted to try."

"Was it a public institution?"

"I don't think so, sir. He borrowed some money from me."

"What!"

"I loaned him a little money."

"How much?"

"*I beg your pardon?*"

"Sorry, Ethan. You are old friends. Sorry. Did he have other money?"

"I think so."

"You don't know how much?"

"No sir. I just had a feeling he had more."

"If you know where he is, please tell me."

"I would if I knew, Mr. Baker. Maybe you could make a list of the places and phone."

"Did he borrow cash?"

"Yes."

"Then that's no good. He'd change his name."

"Why?"

"They always do from good families. Ethan, did you get the money from Mary?"

"Yes."

"She didn't mind?"

"She didn't know."

"Now you're being smart."

"I learned from you, sir."

"Well, don't forget it."

"Maybe I'm learning little by little. Mostly I'm learning how much I don't know."

"Well, that's healthy. Is Mary well?"

"Oh, she's strong and tough. Wish I could take her on a little vacation. We haven't been out of town in years."

"That will come, Ethan. I think I'll go to Maine over the Fourth of July. I can't take the noise any more."

"I guess you bankers are the lucky ones. Weren't you in Albany lately?"

"What gave you that idea?"

"I don't know—heard it someplace. Maybe Mrs. Baker told Mary."

"She couldn't. She didn't know it. Try to think where you heard it."

"Maybe I only imagined it."

"This troubles me, Ethan. Think hard where you heard it."

"I can't, sir. What does it matter if it isn't true?"

"I'll tell you in confidence why I'm worried. It's because it is true. The Governor called me in. It's a serious matter. I wonder where the leak could be."

"Anyone see you there?"

"Not that I know of. I flew in and out. This is serious. I'm going to tell you something. If it gets out I'll know where it came from."

"Then I don't want to hear it."

"You haven't any choice now that you know about Albany. The state is looking into county and town affairs."

"Why?"

"I guess because the smell has got as far as Albany."

"No politics?"

"I guess anything the Governor does can be called politics."

"Mr. Baker, why can't it be in the open?"

"I'll tell you why. Upstate the word got out and by the

time the examiners got to work most of the records had disappeared."

"I see. I wish you hadn't told me. I'm not a talker but I wish I didn't know."

"For that matter, I wish the same thing, Ethan."

"The election is July seventh. Will it break before that?"

"I don't know. That's up to the state."

"Do you suppose Marullo is mixed in it? I can't afford to lose my job."

"I don't think so. That was a federal man. Department of Justice. Didn't you ask for his credentials?"

"Didn't think of it. He flashed them but I didn't look."

"Well, you should. You always should."

"I wouldn't think you'd want to go away."

"Oh, that doesn't matter. Nothing happens over Fourth of July weekend. Why, the Japs attacked Pearl Harbor on a weekend. They knew everyone would be away."

"I wish I could take Mary someplace."

"Maybe you can later. I want you to whip your brains and try to find where Taylor is."

"Why? Is it so important?"

"It is. I can't tell you why right now."

"I sure wish I could find him, then."

"Well, if you could turn him up maybe you wouldn't need this job."

"If it's that way, I'll sure try, sir."

"That's the boy, Ethan. I'm sure you will. And if you do locate him, you call me—any time, day or night."

Chapter XIII

I WONDER about people who say they haven't time to think. For myself, I can double think. I find that weighing vegetables, passing the time of day with customers, fighting or loving Mary, coping with the children—none of these prevents a second and continuing layer of thinking, wondering, conjecturing. Surely this must be true of everyone. Maybe not having time to think is not having the wish to think.

In the strange, uncharted country I had entered, perhaps I had no choice. Questions boiled up, demanding to be noticed. And it was a world so new to me that I puzzled over matters old residents probably solved and put away when they were children.

I had thought I could put a process in motion and control it at every turn—even stop it when I wanted to. And now the frightening conviction grew in me that such a process may become a thing in itself, a person almost, having its own ends and means and quite independent of its creator. And another troublesome thought came in. Did I really start it, or did I simply not resist it? I may have been the mover, but was I not also the moved? Once on the long street, there seemed to be no crossroads, no forked paths, no choice.

The choice was in the first evaluation. What are morals? Are they simply words? Was it honorable to assess my father's weakness, which was a generous mind and the ill-founded dream that other men were equally generous? No, it was simply good business to dig the pit for him. He fell into it himself. No one pushed him. Was it immoral to strip him when he was down? Apparently not.

Now a slow, deliberate encirclement was moving on New Baytown, and it was set in motion by honorable men. If it succeeded, they would be thought not crooked but clever. And if a factor they had overlooked moved in, would that be immoral or dishonorable? I think that would depend on whether or not it was successful. To most of the world success is never bad. I remember how, when Hitler moved unchecked and triumphant, many honorable men sought and found virtues in him.

And Mussolini made the trains run on time, and Vichy collaborated for the good of France, and whatever else Stalin was, he was strong. Strength and success—they are above morality, above criticism. It seems, then, that it is not what you do, but how you do it and what you call it. Is there a check in men, deep in them, that stops or punishes? There doesn't seem to be. The only punishment is for failure. In effect no crime is committed unless a criminal is caught. In the move designed for New Baytown some men had to get hurt, some even destroyed, but this in no way deterred the movement.

I could not call this a struggle with my conscience. Once I perceived the pattern and accepted it, the path was clearly marked and the dangers apparent. What amazed me most was that it seemed to plan itself; one thing grew out of another and everything fitted together. I watched it grow and only guided it with the lightest touch.

What I had done and planned to do was undertaken with full knowledge that it was foreign to me, but necessary as a stirrup is to mount a tall horse. But once I had mounted, the stirrup would not be needed. Maybe I could not stop this process, but I need never start another. I did not need or want to be a citizen of this gray and dangerous country. I had nothing to do with the coming tragedy of July 7. It was not my process, but I could anticipate and I could use it.

One of our oldest and most often disproved myths is that a man's thoughts show in his face, that the eyes are the windows of the soul. It isn't so. Only sickness shows, or defeat or despair, which are different kinds of sickness. Some rare people can feel beneath, can sense a change or hear a secret signal. I think my Mary felt a change, but she misinterpreted it, and I think Margie Young-Hunt knew—but she was a witch and that is a worrisome thing. It seemed to me that she was intelligent as well as magic—and that's even more worrisome.

I felt sure that Mr. Baker would go on a holiday, probably on Friday afternoon of the Fourth of July weekend. The storm would have to break Friday or Saturday to give it time to take effect before election and it was logical to suppose that Mr. Baker would want to be away when the shock came. Of course that didn't matter much to me. It was more an exercise in anticipation, but it did make several moves necessary on

Thursday, just in case he left that night. My Saturday matter was so finely practical that I could move through it in my sleep. If I had any fear of that, it was more like a small stage fright.

On Monday, June 27, Marullo came in soon after I had opened up. He walked about, looking strangely at the shelves, the cash register, the cold counter, and he walked back to the storeroom and looked about. You would have thought from his expression that he was seeing it for the first time.

I said, "Going to take a trip over the Fourth?"

"Why do you say that?"

"Well, everybody does who can afford it."

"Oh! Where would I go?"

"Where's anybody go? Catskills, even out to Montauk and fish. School tuna running."

The very thought of fighting a thirty-pound plunging fish drove arthritic pains up his arms so that he flexed them and winced.

I very nearly asked him when he planned to go to Italy, but that seemed too much. Instead, I moved over to him and took him gently by his right elbow. "Alfio," I said, "I think you're nuts. Why don't you go into New York to the best specialist? There must be something to stop that pain."

"I don't believe it."

"What have you got to lose? Go ahead. Try it."

"What do you care?"

"I don't. But I've worked here a long time for a stupid son of a bitch dago. If a yellow dog hurt that much, I'd get to feeling it myself. You come in here and move your arms and it's half an hour before I can straighten up."

"You like me?"

"Hell, no. I'm buttering you up for a raise."

He looked at me with hound's eyes, rimmed with red, and dark brown iris and pupil all one piece. He seemed about to say something but changed his mind about it. "You're a good kid," he said.

"Don't depend on it."

"A good kid!" he said explosively and as though shocked by his show of emotion he went out of the store and walked away.

I was weighing out two pounds of string beans for Mrs.

Davidson when Marullo came charging back. He stood in the doorway and shouted at me.

"You take my Pontiac."

"What?"

"Go someplace Sunday and Monday."

"I can't afford it."

"You take the kids. I told the garage for you to get my Pontiac. Tank full of gas."

"Wait a minute."

"You go to hell. Take the kids." He tossed something like a spitball at me and it fell among the string beans. Mrs. Davidson watched him plunge away again down the street. I picked the green wad from the string beans—three twenty-dollar bills folded in a tight square.

"What's the matter with him?"

"He's an excitable Italian."

"He must be, throwing money!"

He didn't show up the rest of the week, so that was all right. He'd never gone away before without telling me. It was like watching a parade go by, just standing and watching it go by and knowing what the next float would be but watching for it just the same.

I hadn't expected the Pontiac. He never loaned his car to anybody. It was a strange time. Some outside force or design seemed to have taken control of events so that they were crowded close the way cattle are in a loading chute. I know the opposite can be true. Sometimes the force or design deflects and destroys, no matter how careful and deep the planning. I guess that's why we believe in luck and unluck.

On Thursday, the thirtieth of June, I awakened as usual in the black pearl light of the dawn, and that was early now in the lap of midsummer. Chair and bureau were dark blobs and pictures only lighter suggestions. The white window curtains seemed to sigh in and out as though they breathed, because it's a rare dawn that does not wave a small wind over the land.

Coming out of sleep, I had the advantage of two worlds, the layered firmament of dream and the temporal fixtures of the mind awake. I stretched luxuriously—a good and tingling sensation. It's as though the skin has shrunk in the night and one must push it out to daytime size by bulging the muscles, and there's an itching pleasure in it.

First I referred to my remembered dreams as I would glance through a newspaper to see if there was anything of interest or import. Then I explored the coming day for events that had not happened. Next I followed a practice learned from the best officer I ever had. He was Charley Edwards, a major of middling age, perhaps a little too far along to be a combat officer but he was a good one. He had a large family, a pretty wife and four children in steps, and his heart could ache with love and longing for them if he allowed it to. He told me about it. In his deadly business he could not afford to have his attention warped and split by love, and so he had arrived at a method. In the morning, that is if he were not jerked from sleep by an alert, he opened his mind and heart to his family. He went over each one in turn, how they looked, what they were like; he caressed them and reassured them of his love. It was as though he picked precious things one by one from a cabinet, looked at each, felt it, kissed it, and put it back; and last he gave them a small good-by and shut the door of the cabinet. The whole thing took half an hour if he could get it and then he didn't have to think of them again all day. He could devote his full capacity, untwisted by conflicting thought and feeling, to the job he had to do—the killing of men. He was the best officer I ever knew. I asked his permission to use his method and he gave it to me. When he was killed, all I could think was that his had been a good and effective life. He had taken his pleasure, savored his love, and paid his debts, and how many people even approached that?

I didn't always use Major Charley's method, but on a day like this Thursday, when I knew my attention should be as uninterrupted as possible, I awakened when the day opened its door a crack and I visited my family as Major Charley had.

I visited them in chronological order, bowed to Aunt Deborah. She was named for Deborah the Judge of Israel and I have read that a judge was a military leader. Perhaps she responded to her name. My great-aunt could have led armies. She did marshal the cohorts of thought. My joy in learning for no visible profit came from her. Stern though she was, she was charged with curiosity and had little use for anyone who was not. I gave her my obeisance. I offered a spectral toast to old Cap'n and ducked my head to my father. I even made my duty to the untenanted hole in the past I knew as my mother. I never knew her. She died before I could, and left only a hole in the past where she should be.

One thing troubled me. Aunt Deborah and old Cap'n and my father would not come clear. Their outlines were vague and wavery where they should have been sharp as photographs. Well, perhaps the mind fades in its memories as old tintypes do—the background reaching out to engulf the subjects. I couldn't hold them forever.

Mary should have been next but I laid her aside for later.

I raised Allen. I could not find his early face, the face of joy and excitement that made me sure of the perfectability of man. He appeared what he had become—sullen, conceited, resentful, remote and secret in the pain and perplexity of his pubescence, a dreadful, harrowing time when he must bite everyone near, even himself, like a dog in a trap. Even in my mind's picture he could not come out of his miserable discontent, and I put him aside, only saying to him, I know. I remember how bad it is and I can't help. No one can. I can only tell you it will be over. But you can't believe that. Go in peace—go with my love even though during this time we can't stand each other.

Ellen brought a surge of pleasure. She will be pretty, prettier even than her mother, because when her little face jells into its final shape she will have the strange authority of Aunt Deborah. Her moods, her cruelties, her nervousness are the ingredients of a being quite beautiful and dear. I know, because I saw her standing in her sleep holding the pink talisman to her little breast and looking a woman fulfilled. And as the talisman was important and still is to me, so it is to Ellen. Maybe it is Ellen who will carry and pass on whatever is immortal in me. And in my greeting I put my arms around her and she, true to form, tickled my ear and giggled. My Ellen. My daughter.

I turned my head to Mary, sleeping and smiling on my right. That is her place so that, when it is good and right and ready, she can shelter her head on my right arm, leaving my left hand free for caressing.

A few days before, I snicked my forefinger with the curved banana knife at the store, and a callusy scab toughened the ball of my fingertip. And so I stroked the lovely line from ear to shoulder with my second finger but gently enough not to startle and firmly enough not to tickle. She sighed as she always does, a deep, gathered breath and a low release of luxury. Some people resent awakening, but not Mary. She comes to a day with expectancy that it will be good. And, knowing this, I try to offer some small gift to justify her conviction. And I try to hold back gifts for occasions, such as the one I now produced from my mind's purse.

Her eyes opened, hazed with sleep. "Already?" she asked, and she glanced at the window to see how near the day had come. Over the bureau the picture hangs—trees and a lake and a small cow standing in the water of the lake. I made out the cow's tail from my bed, and knew the day had come.

"I bring you tidings of great joy, my flying squirrel."

"Crazy."

"Have I ever lied to you?"

"Maybe."

"Are you awake enough to hear the tidings of great joy?"

"No."

"Then I will withhold them."

She turned on her left shoulder and made a deep crease in her soft flesh. "You joke so much. If it's like you're going to cement over the lawn—"

"I am not."

"Or you're starting a cricket farm—"

"No. But you do remember old discarded plans."

"Is it a joke?"

"Well, it's a thing so strange and magic that you are going to have to buttress your belief."

Her eyes were clear and wakeful now and I could see the little trembles around her lips preparing for laughter. "Tell me."

"Do you know a man of Eyetalian extraction named Marullo?"

"Crazy—you're being silly."

"You will find it so. Said Marullo has gone from here for a time."

"Where?"

"He didn't say."

"When will he be back?"

"Stop confusing me. He didn't say that either. What he did say and, when I protested, what he ordered was that we should take his car and go on a happy trip over the holiday."

"You're joking me."

"Would I tell a lie that would make you sad?"

"But why?"

"That I can't tell you. What I can swear to from Boy Scout oath to papal oath is that the mink-lined Pontiac with a tank full of virgin gasoline awaits your highness's pleasure."

"But where shall we go?"

"That, my lovely insect-wife is what you are going to decide, and take all day today, tomorrow, and Saturday to plan it."

"But Monday's a holiday. That's two full days."

"That's correct."

"Can we afford it? It might mean a motel or something."

"Can or not, we will. I have a secret purse."

"Silly, I know your purse. I can't imagine him lending his car."

"Neither can I, but he did."

"Don't forget he brought candy Easter."

"Perhaps it is senility."

"I wonder what he wants."

"That's not worthy of my wife. Perhaps he wants us to love him."

"I'll have to do a thousand things."

"I know you will." I could see her mind plowing into the possibilities like a bulldozer. I knew I had lost her attention and probably couldn't get it back, and that was good.

At breakfast before my second cup of coffee she had picked up and discarded half the pleasure areas of eastern America. Poor darling hadn't had much fun these last few years.

I said, "Chloe, I know I'm going to have trouble getting your attention. A very important investment is offered. I want some more of your money. The first is doing well."

"Does Mr. Baker know about it?"

"It's his idea."

"Then take it. You sign a check."

"Don't you want to know how much?"

"I guess so."

"Don't you want to know what the investment is? The

figures, the flotage, the graphs, the probable return, the fiscal dinkum, and all that?"

"I wouldn't understand it."

"Oh, yes you would."

"Well, I wouldn't want to understand it."

"No wonder they call you the Vixen of Wall Street. That ice-cold, diamond-sharp business mind—it's frightening."

"We're going a trip," she said. "We're going a trip for two days."

And how the hell could a man not love her, not adore her? "Who is Mary—what is she?" I sang and collected the empty milk bottles and went to work.

I felt the need to catch up with Joey, just to get the feel of him, but I must have been a moment late or he a moment early. He was entering the coffee shop when I turned into the High Street. I followed him in and took the stool beside him. "You got me into this habit, Joey."

"Hi, Mr. Hawley. It's pretty good coffee."

I greeted my old school girl friend. "Morning, Annie."

"You going to be a regular, Eth?"

"Looks like. One cuppa and black."

"Black it is."

"Black as the eye of despair."

"What?"

"Black."

"You see any white in that, Eth, I'll give you another."

"How are things, Morph?"

"Just the same, only worse."

"Want to trade jobs?"

"I would, just before a long weekend."

"You're not the only one with problems. People stock up on food too."

"I guess they do. I hadn't thought of that."

"Picnic stuff, pickles, sausages, and, God help us, marshmallows. This a big one for you?"

"With the Fourth on Monday and nice weather, you kidding? And what makes it worse, God Almighty feels the need of rest and recreation in the mountains."

"Mr. Baker?"

"Not James G. Blaine."

"I want to see him. I need to see him."

"Well, try to catch him if you can. He's jumping like a quarter in a tambourine."

"I can bring sandwiches to your battle station, Joey."

"I might just ask you to."

"I pay this time," I said.

"Okay."

We crossed the street together and went into the alley. "You sound lowy, Joey."

"I am. I get pretty tired of other people's money. I got a hot date for the weekend and I'll probably be too pooped to warm up to it." He nudged a gum wrapper into the lock, went in, saying, "See you," and closed the door. I pushed the back door open. "Joey! You want a sandwich today?"

"No thanks," he called out of the dim, floor-oil-smelling interior. "Maybe Friday, Saturday sure."

"Don't you close at noon?"

"I told you. The bank closes but Morphy don't."

"Just call on me."

"Thanks—thanks, Mr. Hawley."

I had nothing to say to my forces on the shelves that morning except "Good morning gentlemen—at ease!" At a few moments before nine, aproned and broomed, I was out front, sweeping the sidewalk.

Mr. Baker is so regular you can hear him tick and I'm sure there's a hairspring in his chest. Eight fifty-six, fifty-seven, there he came down Elm Street; eight fifty-eight, he crossed; eight fifty-nine—he was at the glass doors, where I, with broom at carry arms, intercepted him. "Mr. Baker, I want to talk to you."

"Morning, Ethan. Can you wait a minute? Come on in."

I followed him, and it was just as Joey said—like a religious ceremony. They practically stood at attention as the clock hand crossed nine. There came a click and buzzing from the great steel safe door. Then Joey dialed the mystic numbers and turned the wheel that drew the bolts. The holy of holies swung stately open and Mr. Baker took the salute of the assembled money. I stood outside the rail like a humble communicant waiting for the sacrament.

Mr. Baker turned. "Now, Ethan. What can I do for you?"

I said softly, "I want to talk to you privately, and I can't leave the store."

"Won't it wait?"

" 'Fraid not."

"You ought to have some help."

"I know it."

"If I get a moment I'll drop over. Any word about Taylor?"

"Not yet. But I've put out some lines."

"I'll try to get over."

"Thank you, sir." But I knew he would come.

And he did, in less than an hour, and stood about until the present customers were gone.

"Now—what is it, Ethan?"

"Mr. Baker, with a doctor or a lawyer or a priest there's a rule of secrecy. Is there such a thing with a banker?"

He smiled. "Have you ever heard a banker discuss a client's interests, Ethan?"

"No."

"Well, ask sometime and see how far you get. And besides that custom, I'm your friend, Ethan."

"I know. I guess I'm a little jumpy. It's been a long time since I've had a break."

"A break?"

"I'll lay them out face up, Mr. Baker. Marullo's in trouble."

He moved close to me. "What kind of trouble?"

"I don't know exactly, sir. I think it might be illegal entry."

"How do you know?"

"He told me—not in so many words. You know how he is."

I could almost see his mind leaping about, picking up pieces and fitting them together. "Go on," he said. "That's deportation."

"I'm afraid so. He's been good to me, Mr. Baker. I wouldn't do anything to hurt him."

"You owe yourself something, Ethan. What was his proposition?"

"It's not merely a proposition. I had to put it together out of a lot of excited gobbledegook. But I gathered that if I had a quick five thousand in cash, I could own the store."

"That sounds as if he's going to run for it—but you don't know that."

"I don't know anything really."

"So there's no chance of a collusion charge. He didn't tell you anything specific."

"No, sir."

"Then how did you arrive at that figure?"

"Easy, sir. That's all we've got."

"But you might get it for less?"

"Maybe."

His quick eye went over the store and valued it. "If you are right in your assumption you're in a good bargaining position."

"I'm not much good at that."

"You know I don't favor under-the-table deals. Maybe I could talk to him."

"He's out of town."

"When will he be back?"

"I don't know, sir. Remember, it's only my impression he might drop in, and if I had cash, he might deal. He likes me, you know."

"I know he does."

"I'd hate to think I was taking advantage."

"He can always get it from someone else. He could get ten thousand easy from—anybody."

"Then maybe I'm overhopeful."

"Now, don't think small. You have to look after number one."

"Number two. It's Mary's money."

"So it is. Well, what did you have in mind?"

"Well, I thought you could maybe draw some papers up and leave the date and the amount blank. Then I thought I'd draw the money Friday."

"Why Friday?"

"Well, again it's only a guess, but he did say something about how everybody's away over the holiday. I kind of figured he might show up then. Don't you have his account?"

"No, by God. He drew it out just recently. Buying stocks, he said. I didn't think anything of it because he's done that before and always brought back more than he took out." He looked full in the eyes of a high-colored Miss Rheingold on the cold counter, but he didn't respond to her laughing invitation. "You know you could take a terrible beating on this?"

"How do you mean?"

"For one thing, he could sell it to half a dozen different people and, for another, it might be neck-deep in mortgage. And no title search."

"I could maybe find out in the county clerk's office. I know how busy you are, Mr. Baker. I'm taking advantage of your friendship for my family. Besides, you're the only friend I have who knows about such things."

"I'll call Tom Watson about the title deed. Damn it, Ethan, it's a bad time. I want to take a little trip tomorrow night. If it's true and he's a crook, you could be taken. Taken to the cleaners."

"Maybe I better give it up, then. But good God, Mr. Baker, I'm tired of being a grocery clerk."

"I didn't say give it up. I said you're taking a chance."

"Mary would be so happy if I owned the store. But I guess you're right. I shouldn't gamble with her money. I suppose what I should do is call up the federal men."

"That would lose you any advantage you have."

"How?"

"If he is deported he can sell his holdings through an agent and this store will bring a lot more than you can pay. You don't *know* he's going to jump. How could you tell them he is if you don't know? You don't even know he's picked up."

"That's true."

"As a matter of fact, you don't know anything about him—really know. All you've told me is vague suspicions, isn't that so?"

"Yes."

"And you'd better forget those."

"Wouldn't it look bad—paying in cash with no record?"

"You could write on the check—oh, something like 'For investment in grocery business with A. Marullo.' That would be a record of your intention."

"Suppose none of this works."

"Then redeposit the money."

"You think it's worth the risk?"

"Well—everything's a risk, Ethan. It's a risk to carry that much money around."

"I'll take care of that."

"I wish I didn't have to be out of town."

What I said about timing still held. In all that time nobody came into the store, but half a dozen came in now—three women, an old man, and two kids. Mr. Baker moved close and spoke softly. "I'll make it in hundred-dollar bills and note the numbers. Then if they catch him you can get it back." He nodded gravely to the three women, said, "Good morning, George," to the old man, and roughed his fingers through the kids' coarse hair. Mr. Baker is a very clever man.

Chapter XIV

JULY first. It parts the year like the part in a head of hair. I had foreseen it as a boundary marker for me—yesterday one kind of me, tomorrow a different kind. I had made my moves that could not be recalled. Time and incidents had played along, had seemed to collaborate with me. I did not ever draw virtue down to hide what I was doing from myself. No one made me take the course I had chosen. Temporarily I traded a habit of conduct and attitude for comfort and dignity and a cushion of security. It would be too easy to agree that I did it for my family because I knew that in their comfort and security I would find my dignity. But my objective was limited and, once achieved, I could take back my habit of conduct. I knew I could. War did not make a killer of me, although for a time I killed men. Sending out patrols, knowing some of the men would die, aroused no joy in sacrifice in me as it did in some, and I could never joy in what I had done, nor excuse or condone it. The main thing was to know the limited objective for what it was, and, once it was achieved, to stop the process in its tracks. But that could only be if I knew what I was doing and did not fool myself—security and dignity, and then stop the process in its tracks. I knew from combat that casualties are the victims of a process, not of anger nor of hate or cruelty. And I believe that in the moment of acceptance, between winner and loser, between killer and killed, there is love.

But Danny's scribbled papers hurt like a sorrow, and Marullo's grateful eyes.

I had not lain awake as men are said to do on the eve of battle. Sleep came quickly, heavily, completely, and released me just as freely in the predawn, refreshed. I did not lie in the darkness as usual. My urge was to visit my life as it had been. I slipped quietly from bed, dressed in the bathroom, and went down the stairs, walking near to the wall. It did surprise me when I went to the cabinet, unlocked it, and recognized the rosy mound by touch. I put it in my pocket and closed and locked the cabinet. In my whole life I had never carried it away and I had not known I would do it this morning. Memory directed me through the dark kitchen and out the back door into the graying yard. The arching elms were fat with leaves, a true black cave. If I had then had Marullo's Pontiac I would have driven out of New Baytown to the awakening world of my first memory. My finger traced the endless sinuous design on the flesh-warm talisman in my pocket—talisman?

That Deborah who sent me as a child to Golgotha was a precise machine with words. She took no nonsense from them nor permitted me a laxity. What power she had, that old woman! If she wanted immortality, she had it in my brain. Seeing me trace the puzzle with my finger, she said, "Ethan, that outlandish thing could well become your talisman."

"What's a talisman?"

"If I tell you, your half-attention will only half learn. Look it up."

So many words are mine because Aunt Deborah first aroused my curiosity and then forced me to satisfy it by my own effort. Of course I replied, "Who cares?" But she knew I would creep to it alone and she spelled it so I could track it down. T-a-l-i-s-m-a-n. She cared deeply about words and she hated their misuse as she would hate the clumsy handling of any fine thing. Now, so many cycles later, I can see the page—can see myself misspelling "talisman." The Arabic was only a squiggly line with a bulb on the end of it. The Greek I could pronounce because of the blade of that old woman. "A stone or other object engraved with figures or characters to which are attributed the occult powers of the planetary influences and celestial configurations under which it was made, usually worn as an amulet to avert evil from or bring fortune to the bearer." I had then to look for "occult," "planetary," "celestial," and "amulet." It was always that way. One word set off others like a string of firecrackers.

When later I asked her, "Do you believe in talismans?" she replied, "What has my belief to do with it?"

I put it in her hands. "What does this figure or character mean?"

"It's your talisman, not mine. It means what you want it to mean. Put it back in the cabinet. It will wait for you."

Now, as I walked in the cavern of the elms, she was as alive as ever she had been and that's true immortality. Over and under itself the carving went, and around and over and under, a serpent with neither head nor tail nor beginning nor ending. And I had taken it away with me for the first time—to avert evil? To bring fortune? I don't believe in fortune-telling either, and immortality has always felt to me like a sickly promise for the disappointed.

The light-rimmed boundary of the east was July, for June had gone away in the night. July is brass where June is gold, and lead where June is silver. July leaves are heavy and fat and crowding. Birdsong of July is a flatulent refrain without passion, for the nests are empty now and dumpy fledglings teeter clumsily. No, July is not a month of promise or of fulfillment. Fruit is growing but unsweet and uncolored, corn is a limp green bundle with a young and yellow tassel. The squashes still wear umbilical crowns of dry blossom.

I walked to Porlock Street, Porlock the plump and satisfied. The gathering brass of dawn showed rosebushes heavy with middle-aged blooms, like women whose corseting no longer conceals a thickening stomach, no matter how pretty their legs may remain.

Walking slowly, I found myself not saying but feeling good-by—not farewell. Farewell has a sweet sound of reluctance. Good-by is short and final, a word with teeth sharp to bite through the string that ties past to the future.

I came to the Old Harbor. Good-by to what? I don't know. I couldn't remember. I think I wanted to go to the Place, but man commensal with the sea would know that the tide was at flood and the Place under dark water. Last night I saw the moon only four days grown like a thickened, curved surgeon's needle, but strong enough to pull the tide into the cave mouth of the Place.

No need to visit Danny's shack in hope. The light had come enough to see the grasses standing upright in the path where Danny's feet had stumbled them flat.

Old Harbor was flecked with summer craft, slim hulls with sails covered in grommeted coats of canvas, and here and there a morning man made ready, clearing boom and coiling jib- and mainsheets, unbagging his Genoa like a great white rumpled nest.

The new harbor was busier. Charter boats tied close for

boarding passengers, the frantic summer fishermen who pay a price and glut the decks with fish and in the afternoon wonder vaguely what to do with them, sacks and baskets and mountains of porgies and blows and blackfish, sea robins, and even slender dogfish, all to be torn up greedily, to die, and to be thrown back for the waiting gulls. The gulls swarm and wait, knowing the summer fishermen will sicken of their plenty. Who wants to clean and scale a sack of fish? It's harder to give away fish than it is to catch them.

The bay was oil-smooth now and the brass light poured over it. The cans and nuns stood unswaying on the channel edge, each one with its mirror twin upside down below it in the water.

I turned at the flagpole and war memorial and found my name among the surviving heroes, the letters picked out in silver—CAPT. E. A. HAWLEY—and below in gold the names of the eighteen New Baytown men who didn't make it home. I knew the names of most of them and once I knew the men—no different then from the rest, but different now in gold. For a brief moment I wished I could be with them in the lower files, Capt. E. A. Hawley in gold, the slobs and malingerers, the cowards and the heroes all lumped together in gold. Not only the brave get killed, but the brave have a better chance at it.

Fat Willie drove up and parked beside the monument and took the flag from the seat beside him.

"Hi, Eth," he said. He shackled the brass grommets and raised the flag slowly to the top of the staff, where it slumped limp as a hanged man. "She barely made it," Willie said, panting a little. "Look at her. Two more days for her, and then the new one goes up."

"The fifty-star?"

"You bet. We got a nylon, big devil, twice as big as this and don't weigh no more than half."

"How's tricks, Willie?"

"I can't complain—but I do. This glorious Fourth is always a mess. Coming on a Monday, there'll be just that much more accidents and fights and drunks—out-of-town drunks. Want a lift up to the store?"

"Thanks. I've got to stop at the post office and I thought I'd get a cup of coffee."

"Okay. I'll ride you. I'd even coffee you but Stoney's mean as a bull bitch."

"What's his problem?"

"God knows. Went away a couple of days and he come back mean and tough."

"Where'd he go?"

"He didn't say, but he come back mean. I'll wait while you get your mail."

"Don't bother, Willie. I've got to address some things."

"Suit yourself." He backed out and slid away up the High Street.

The post office was still dusky and the floor newly oiled, and a sign up: DANGER. SLICK FLOOR.

We'd had Number 7 drawer since the old post office was built. I dialed G ½ R and took out a pile of plans and promises addressed to "Box-Holder." And that's all there was—waste-basket fodder. I strolled up the High, intending to have a cup of coffee, but at the last moment I didn't want it, or didn't want to talk, or—I don't know why. I just didn't want to go to the Foremaster coffee shop. Good God, what a mess of draggle-tail impulses a man is—and a woman too, I guess.

I was sweeping the sidewalk when Mr. Baker ticked out of Elm Street and went in for the ceremony of the time lock. And I was halfheartedly arranging muskmelons in the doorway stands when the old-fashioned green armored car pulled up in front of the bank. Two guards armed like commandos got out of the back and carried gray sacks of money into the bank. In about ten minutes they came out and got into the riveted fortress and it drove away. I guess they had to stand by while Morph counted it and Mr. Baker checked and gave a receipt. It's an awful lot of trouble taking care of money. As Morph says, you could get a downright distaste for other people's money. And by the size and weight, the bank must have anticipated a large holiday withdrawal. If I was a run-of-the-mill bank robber, now would be the time to stick it up. But I wasn't a run-of-the-mill bank robber. I owed everything I knew to Pal Joey. He could have been a great one if he had wished. I did wonder why he didn't want to, just to try out his theory.

Business piled up that morning. It was worse than I had thought it might be. The sun turned hot and fierce and very little wind moved, the kind of weather that drives people on their vacations whether they want to go or not. I had a line of customers waiting to be served. One thing I knew, come hell or high water, I had to get some help. If Allen didn't work out, I'd fire him and get someone else.

When Mr. Baker came in about eleven, he was in a hurry. I had to stand off some customers and go into the storeroom with him.

He put a big envelope and a small one in my hands, and he was so rushed that he barked a kind of shorthand. "Tom Watson says the deed's okay. He doesn't know whether it's papered. He doesn't think so. Here are conveyances. Get signatures where I've checked. The money's marked and the numbers noted. Here's a check all made out. Just sign it. Sorry I have to rush, Ethan. I hate doing business like this."

"You really think I should go ahead?"

"Goddammit, Ethan, after all the trouble I've gone to—"

"Sorry, sir. Sorry. I know you're right." I put the check on a canned-milk carton and signed it with my indelible pencil.

Mr. Baker wasn't too rushed to inspect the check. "Offer two thousand at first. And raise your offer two hundred at a time. You realize, of course, you've only got a five-hundred balance in the bank. God help you if you run short."

"If it's clear, can't I borrow on the store?"

"Sure you can if you want interest to eat you up."

"I don't know how to thank you."

"Don't go soft, Ethan. Don't let him poor-mouth you. He can be a spellbinder. All dagos can. Just remember number one."

"I am sure grateful."

"Got to go," he said. "Want to hit the highway before the noon traffic." And out he went and nearly knocked Mrs. Willow down in the doorway where she had been over every cantaloupe twice.

The day didn't get any less frantic. I guess the heat that splashed the streets made people edgy and downright quarrelsome. Instead of a holiday, you'd have thought they were stocking up for a catastrophe. I couldn't have got a sandwich over to the Morph if I'd wanted to.

I not only had to wait on people, I had to keep my eyes open. A lot of the customers were summer people, strangers in town, and they steal if you don't watch them. They can't seem to help it. And it's not always stuff they need either. The little jars of luxuries take the worst beating, foie gras and caviar and button mushrooms. That's why Marullo had me keep such stuff back of the counter, where the customers aren't supposed to go. He taught me it's not good business to catch a shoplifter. Makes everyone restless, maybe because—well, in his thoughts anyway—everyone is guilty. About the only way is to charge the loss off to somebody else. But if I saw someone drifting too close to certain shelves, I could forestall the impulse by saying, "Those cocktail onions are a bargain." I've seen the customer jump as though I'd read his mind. What I hate worst about it is the suspicion. It's unpleasant to be suspicious. Makes me angry, as though one person were injuring many.

The day wore on to a kind of sadness, and time slowed down. After five Chief Stoney came in, lean and grim and ulcerish. He bought a TV dinner—country steak, carrots, mashed potatoes, cooked and frozen in a kind of aluminum tray.

I said, "You look like you had a touch of sun, Chief."

"Well, I ain't. I feel fine." He looked miserable.

"Want two of those?"

"Just one. My wife's gone visiting. A cop don't get holidays."

"Too bad."

"Maybe it's just as well. With this mob hanging around, I don't get home much."

"I heard you were away."

"Who told you?"

"Willie."

"He better learn to keep his big mouth shut."

"He didn't mean harm."

"Hasn't got brains enough to mean harm. Maybe not brains enough to stay out of jail."

"Who has?" I said it on purpose and I got even more response than I had anticipated.

"Just what do you mean by that, Ethan?"

"I mean we've got so many laws you can't breathe without breaking something."

"That's the truth. Gets so you don't really know."

"I was going to ask you, Chief—cleaning up, I found an old

revolver, all dirty and rusty. Marullo says it's not his, and it sure isn't mine. What do I do with it?"

"Turn it over to me, if you don't want to apply for a license."

"I'll bring it down from home tomorrow. I stuck it in a can of oil. What do you do with things like that, Stoney?"

"Oh, check to see if they're hot and then throw them in the ocean." He seemed to be feeling better, but it had been a long, hot day. I couldn't let him be.

"Remember a couple of years ago there was a case somewhere upstate? Police were selling confiscated guns."

Stoney smiled the sweet smile of an alligator and with the same gay innocence. "I had one hell of a week, Eth. One hell of a week. If you're going about needling me, why, don't do it, because I've had one hell of a week."

"Sorry, Chief. Anything a sober citizen can do to help, like getting drunk with you?"

"I wish to Christ I could. I'd rather get drunk than anything I can think of."

"Why don't you?"

"Do you know? No, how could you? If I only knew what it's for and where it's from."

"What you talking about?"

"Forget it, Eth. No—don't forget it. You're a friend of Mr. Baker. Has he got any deals on?"

"I'm not that good a friend, Chief."

"How about Marullo? Where is Marullo?"

"Went in to New York. He wants to get his arthritis checked over."

"God almighty. I don't know. I just don't know. If there was just a line, why, I'd know where to jump."

"You're not talking sense, Stoney."

"No, I'm not. I talked too much already."

"I'm not too bright but if you want to unload—"

"I don't. No, I don't. They're not going to pin a leak on me even if I knew who they were. Forget it, Eth. I'm just a worried man."

"You couldn't leak to me, Stoney. What was it—grand jury?"

"Then you do know?"

"A little."

"What's behind it?"

"Progress."

Stoney came close to me and his iron hand grasped my upper arm so tightly that it hurt. "Ethan," he said fiercely, "do you think I'm a good cop?"

"The best."

"I aim to be. I want to be. Eth—do you think it's right to make a man tell on his friends to save himself?"

"No, I don't."

"Neither do I. I can't admire such a government. What scares me, Eth, is—I won't be such a good cop any more because I won't admire what I'm doing."

"Did they catch you out, Chief?"

"It's like you said. So many laws you can't take a deep breath without you break one. But Jesus Christ! The guys were my friends. You won't leak, Ethan?"

"No I won't. You forgot your TV dinner, Chief."

"Yeah!" he said. "I'll go home and take off my shoes and watch how those television cops do it. You know, sometimes an empty house is a nice rest. See you, Eth."

I liked Stoney. I guess he is a good officer. I wonder where the line falls.

I was closing up shop, drawing in the fruit bins from the doorway, when Joey Morphy sauntered in.

"Quick!" I said, and I closed the double front doors and drew the dark green shades. "Speak in a whisper."

"What's got into you?"

"Someone might want to buy something."

"Yeah! I know what you mean. God! I hate long holidays. Brings out the worst in everybody. They start out mad and come home pooped and broke."

"Want a cold drink while I draw the coverlets over my darling?"

"I don't mind. Got some cold beer?"

"To take out only."

"I'll take it out. Just open the can."

I punched two triangular holes in the tin and he upended it, opened his throat, and drained it into him. "Ah!" he said and set the can on the counter.

"We're going on a trip."

"You poor devil. Where?"

"I don't know. We haven't fought over that yet"

"Something's going on. Do you know what it is?"

"Give me a clue."

"I can't. I just feel it. Hair on the back of my neck kind of itches. That's a sure sign. Everybody's a little out of synch."

"Maybe you just imagine it."

"Maybe. But Mr. Baker doesn't take holidays. He was in one hell of a hurry to get out of town."

I laughed. "Have you checked the books?"

"Know something? I did."

"You're kidding."

"Once I knew a postmaster, little town. Had a punk kid working there, name of Ralph—pale hair, glasses, little tiny chin, adenoids big as goiters. Ralph got tagged for stealing stamps—lots of stamps, like maybe eighteen hundred dollars' worth. Couldn't do a thing. He was a punk."

"You mean he didn't take them?"

"If he didn't it was just the same as if he did. I'm jumpy. I'm never going to get tagged if I can help it."

"Is that why you never married?"

"Come to think of it, by God, that's one of the reasons."

I folded my apron and put it in the drawer under the cash register. "Takes too much time and effort to be suspicious, Joey. I couldn't take the time."

"Have to in a bank. You only lose once. All it needs is a whisper."

"Don't tell me you're suspicious."

"It's an instinct. If anything's just a little bit out of norm, my alarm goes off."

"What a way to live! You don't really mean that."

"I guess I don't. I just thought if you'd heard something, you'd tell me—that is, if it was any of my business."

"I think I'd tell anybody anything I know. Maybe that's why nobody ever tells me anything. Going home?"

"No, I think I'll go eat across the street."

I switched the front lights off. "Mind coming out through the alley? Look, I'll make sandwiches in the morning before the rush. One ham, one cheese on rye bread, lettuce *and* mayonnaise, right? And a quart of milk."

"You ought to work in a bank," he said.

I guess he wasn't any lonelier than anybody else just because he lived alone. He left me at the door of the Foremaster and for a moment I wished I could go with him. I thought home might be a mess.

And it was. Mary had planned the trip. Out near Montauk Point there's a dude ranch with all the fancy fixings you see in what they call adult Westerns. The joke is that it's the oldest working cattle ranch in America. It was a cattle ranch before Texas was discovered. First charter came from Charles II. Originally the herds that supplied New York grazed there and the herdsmen were drawn by lot, like jurors, for limited service. Of course now it's all silver spurs and cowboy stuff, but the red cattle still graze on the moors. Mary thought it would be nice to spend Sunday night in one of the guest houses.

Ellen wanted to go into New York, stay at a hotel, and spend two days in Times Square. Allen didn't want to go at all, any place. That's one of his ways of getting attention and proving that he exists.

The house boiled with emotion—Ellen in slow, dripping, juicy tears, Mary tired and flushed with frustration, Allen sitting sullen and withdrawn with his little radio blasting in his ear, a thumping whining song of love and loss in a voice of sub-hysteria. "You promised to be true, and then you took and threw, my lovin' lonely heart right on the floor."

"I'm about ready to give up," Mary said.

"They're just trying to help."

"They seem to go out of their way to be difficult."

"I never get to do anything." Ellen sniffled.

In the living room Allen turned up the volume. ". . . my lovin' lonely heart right on the floor."

"Couldn't we lock them in the cellar and go off by ourselves, carotene, dear."

"You know, at this point I wish we could." She had to raise her voice to be heard over the pounding roar of the lovin' lonely heart.

Without warning a rage came up in me. I turned and strode toward the living room to tear my son to shreds and throw his lonely lovin' corpse on the floor and trample it. As I went loping through the door the music stopped. "We interrupt this program to bring you a special bulletin. Officials of New Baytown and Wessex County were this afternoon subpoenaed to appear before a grand jury to answer charges ranging from fixing traffic tickets to taking bribes and kickbacks on town and county contracts. . . ."

There it came—the Town Manager, the council, the magistrates, the works. I listened without hearing—sad and heavy. Maybe they had been doing what they were charged with, but they'd been doing it so long they didn't think it was wrong. And even if they were innocent they couldn't be cleared before the local election, and even if a man is cleared the charge is remembered. They were surrounded. They must have known it. I listened for a mention of Stoney and it didn't come so I guess he had traded them for immunity. No wonder he felt so raw and alone.

Mary was listening at the door. "Well!" she said. "We haven't had so much excitement in a long time. Do you think it's true, Ethan?"

"Doesn't matter," I said. "That's not what it's for."

"I wonder what Mr. Baker thinks."

"He went on a holiday. Yes, I wonder what he feels."

Allen grew restive because his music was interrupted.

The news and dinner and dishes put off our trip problems until it was too late for a decision or for further tears and quarreling.

In bed I got to shivering all over. The cold, passionless savagery of the attack chilled right through the warm summer night.

Mary said, "You're all goose lumps, dear. Do you think you have a virus?"

"No, my fancy, I guess I was just feeling what those men must feel. They must feel awful."

"Stop it, Ethan. You can't take other people's troubles on your shoulders."

"I can because I do."

"I wonder if you'll ever be a businessman. You're too sensitive, Ethan. It's not your crime."

"I was thinking maybe it is—everybody's crime."

"I don't understand."

"I don't much either, sweetheart."

"If there was only someone who could stay with them."

"Repeat, please, Columbine!"

"How I would love to take a holiday just with you. It's been forever."

"We're short on unattached elderly female relatives. Put your mind to it. If only we could can them or salt or pickle them for a little while. Mary, madonna, put your mind to it. I ache to be alone with you in a strange place. We could walk the dunes and swim naked at night and I would tousle you in a fern bed."

"Darling, I know, darling. I know it's been hard on you. Don't think I don't know."

"Well, hold me close. Let's think of some way."

"You're still shivering. Do you feel cold?"

"Cold and hot, full and empty—and tired."

"I'll try to think of something. I really will. Of course I love them but—"

"I know, and I could wear my bow tie—"

"Will they put them in jail?"

"I wish we could—"

"Those men?"

"No. It won't be necessary. They can't even appear before next Tuesday, and Thursday is election. That's what it's for."

"Ethan, that's cynical. You aren't like that. We'll have to go away if you're getting cynical because—that wasn't a joke, the way you said it. I know your jokes. You meant that."

A fear struck me. I was showing through. I couldn't let myself show through. "Oh say, Miss Mousie will you marry me?"

And Mary said, "Oho! Oho!"

My sudden fear that I might be showing through was very great. I had made myself believe that the eyes are not the mirror of the soul. Some of the deadliest little female contraptions I ever saw had the faces and the eyes of angels. There is a breed that can read through skin and through bone right into the center, but they are rare. For the most part people are not curious except about themselves. Once a Canadian girl of Scottish blood told me a story that had bitten her and the telling bit me. She said that in the age of growing up when she felt that all eyes were on her and not favorably, so that she went from blushes to tears and back again, her Highland grandfather, observing her pain, said sharply. "Ye wouldna be sae worrit wi' what folk think about ye if ye kenned how seldom they do." It cured her and the telling reassured me of privacy, because it's true. But Mary, who ordinarily lives in a house of flowers of her own growing, had heard a tone, or felt a cutting wind. This was a danger, until tomorrow should be over.

If my plan had leaped up full-grown and deadly I would have rejected it as nonsense. People don't do such things, but people play secret games. Mine began with Joey's rules for robbing a bank. Against the boredom of my job I played with it and everything along the way fell into it—Allen and his mouse mask, leaking toilet, rusty pistol, holiday coming up, Joey wadding paper in the lock of the alley door. As a game I timed the process, enacted it, tested it. But gunmen shooting it out with cops—aren't they the little boys who practiced quick draws with cap pistols until they got so good they had to use the skill?

I don't know when my game stopped being a game. Perhaps when I knew I might buy the store and would need money to run it. For one thing, it is hard to throw away a perfect structure without testing it. And as for the dishonesty, the crime—it was not a crime against men, only against money. No one would get hurt. Money is insured. The real crimes were against men, against Danny and against Marullo. If I could do what I had done, theft was nothing. And all of it was temporary. None of it would ever have to be repeated. Actually, before I knew it was not a game, my procedure and equipment and timing were as near perfection as possible. The cap-pistol boy found a .45 in his hand.

Of course an accident was possible but that is so in crossing the street or walking under a tree. I don't think I had any fear. I had rehearsed that out of me, but I did have a breathlessness, like the stage fright of an actor standing in the wings on his opening night. And it was like a play in that every conceivable mischance had been inspected and eliminated.

In my worry that I would not sleep, I slept, deeply and as far as I know without dreams, and overslept. I had planned to use the dark pre-day for the calming medicine of contemplation. Instead, when my eyes jerked open, the tail of the cow in the lake had been visible at least half an hour. I awakened with a jar like the blow of driven air from high explosive. Sometimes such an awakening sprains muscles. Mine shook the bed so that Mary awakened, saying, "What's the matter?"

"I've overslept."

"Nonsense. It's early."

"No, my ablative absolute. This is a monster day for me. The world will be grocery-happy today. Don't you get up."

"You'll need a good breakfast."

"Know what I'll do? I'll get a carton of coffee at the Foremaster and I'll raven Marullo's shelves like a wolf."

"You will?"

"Rest, little mouse of a mouseness, and try to find a way for us to escape from our darling children. We need that. I mean it."

"I know we do. I'll try to think."

"I was dressed and gone before she could suggest any of the seasonal things for my protection and comfort.

Joey was in the coffee shop and he patted the stool beside him.

"Can't, Morph. I'm late. Annie, could you give me a quart of coffee in a carton?"

"It'll have to be two pints, Eth."

"Good. Even gooder."

She filled and covered the little paper buckets and put them in a bag.

Joey finished and walked across with me.

"You'll have to say mass without the bishop this morning."

"Guess so. Say, how about that news?"

"I can't take it in."

"You remember I said I smelled something."

"I thought about that when I heard it. You've got quite a nose."

"It's part of the trade. Baker can come back now. Wonder if he will."

"Come back?"

"You get no smell there?"

I looked at him helplessly. "I'm missing something and I don't even know what it is."

"Jesus God."

"You mean I should see something?"

"That's what I mean. The law of the fang is not repealed."

"Oh, Lord! There must be a whole world I miss. I was trying to remember whether it's both lettuce and mayonnaise you like."

"Both." He stripped the cellophane cover from his pack of Camels and wadded it to push in the lock.

"Got to go," I said. "We've got a special sale on tea. Send in a box top, you get a baby! Know any ladies?"

"I sure do, and that's about the last prize they want. Don't bother to bring them, I'll come for the sandwiches." He went in his door and there was no click of the spring lock. I did hope that Joey never discovered that he was the best teacher I had ever had. He not only informed, he demonstrated and, without knowing it, prepared a way for me.

Everyone who knew about such things, the experts, agreed that only money gets money. The best way is always the simplest. The shocking simplicity of the thing was its greatest strength. But I really believe it was only a detailed daydream until Marullo through none of his fault walked in his own darkness over a cliff. Once it seemed almost certain that I could get the store for my own, only then did the high-flown dreaming come down to earth. A good but ill-informed question might be: If I could get the store, why did I need money? Mr. Baker would understand, so would Joey—so, for that matter, would Marullo. The store without running capital was worse than no store at all. The Appian Way of bankruptcy is lined with the graves of unprotected ventures. I have one grave there already. The silliest soldier would not throw his whole strength at a break-through without mortars or reserves or replacements, but many a borning business does just that. Mary's money in marked bills bulged against my bottom in my hip pocket, but Marullo would take as much of that as he could get. Then the first of the month. The wholesale houses are not openhanded with credit for unproved organizations. Therefore I would still need money, and that money was waiting for me behind ticking steel doors. The process of getting it, designed as daydreams, stood up remarkably when inspected. That robbery was unlawful troubled me very little. Marullo was no problem. If he were not the victim he might have planned it himself. Danny was troubling, even though I could with perfect truth assume that he was finished anyway. Mr.

Baker's ineffectual attempt to do the same thing to Danny gave me more justification than most men need. But Danny remained a burning in my guts and I had to accept that as one accepts a wound in successful combat. I had to live with that, but maybe it would heal in time or be walled off with forgetfulness the way a shell fragment gets walled off with cartilage.

The immediate was the money, and that move was as carefully prepared and timed as an electric circuit.

The Morphy laws stood up well and I remembered them and had even added one. First law: Have no past record. Well, I had none. Number two: No accomplices or confidants. I certainly had none. Number three: No dames. Well, Margie Young-Hunt was the only person I knew who could be called a dame, and I was not about to drink champagne out of her slipper. Number four: Don't splurge. Well, I wouldn't. Gradually I would use it to pay bills to wholesalers. I had a place for it. In my Knight Templar's hatbox there was a support of velvet-covered cardboard, the size and shape of my head. This was already lifted free and the edges coated with contact cement so it could be restored in an instant.

Recognition—a Mickey Mouse mask. No one would see anything else. An old cotton raincoat of Marullo's—all tan cotton raincoats look alike—and a pair of those tear-off cellophane gloves that come on a roll. The mask had been cut several days ago and the box and cereal flushed down the toilet, as the mask and gloves would be. The old silvered Iver Johnson pistol was smoked with lampblack and in the toilet was a can of crankcase oil to throw it in for delivery to Chief Stoney at the first opportunity.

I had added my own final law: Don't be a pig. Don't take too much and avoid large bills. If somewhere about six to ten thousand in tens and twenties were available, that would be enough and easy to handle and to hide. A cardboard cakebox on the cold counter would be the swap bag and when next seen it would have a cake in it. I had tried that terrible reedy ventriloquism thing to change my voice and had given it up for silence and gestures. Everything in place and ready.

I was almost sorry Mr. Baker wasn't here. There would be only Morph and Harry Robbit and Edith Alden. It was planned to the split second. At five minutes to nine I would place the broom in the entrance. I'd practiced over and over. Apron tucked up, scale weight on the toilet chain to keep it flushing. Anyone who came in would hear the water and draw his own conclusion. Coat, mask, cakebox, gun, gloves. Cross the alley on the stroke of nine, shove open the back door, put on mask, enter just after timeclock buzzes and Joey swings open the door. Motion the three to lie down, with the gun. They'd give no trouble. As Joey said, the money was insured, he wasn't. Pick up the money, put it in cakebox, cross alley, flush gloves and mask down toilet, put gun in can of oil, coat off. Apron down, money in hatbox, cake in cakebox, pick up broom, and go on sweeping sidewalk, available and visible when the alarm came. The whole thing one minute and forty seconds, timed, checked, and rechecked. But carefully as I had planned and timed, I still felt a little breathless and I swept out the store prior to opening the two front doors. I wore yesterday's apron so that new wrinkles would not be noticeable.

And would you believe it, time stood still as though a Joshua in a wing collar had shot the sun in its course. The minute hand of my father's big watch had set its heels and resisted morning.

It was long since I had addressed my flock aloud, but this morning I did, perhaps out of nervousness.

"My friends," I said, "what you are about to witness is a mystery. I know I can depend on you to keep silent. If any of you have any feeling about the moral issue involved, I challenge you and will ask you to leave." I paused. "No objections? Very well. If I ever hear of an oyster or a cabbage discussing this with strangers, the sentence is death by dinner fork.

"And I want to thank you all. We have been together, humble workers in the vineyard, and I a servant as you are. But now a change is coming. I will be master here henceforth, but I promise I will be a good and kind and understanding master. The time approaches, my friends, the curtain rises—farewell." And as I moved to the front doors with the broom, I heard my own voice cry, "Danny—Danny! Get out of my guts." A great shudder shook me so that I had to lean on the broom a moment before I opened up the doors.

My father's watch said nine with its black, stumpy hour hand and minus six with its long, thin minute hand. I could feel its heart beat against my palm as I looked at it.

Chapter XV

It was a day as different from other days as dogs are from cats and both of them from chrysanthemums or tidal waves or scarlet fever. It is the law in many states, certainly in ours, that it must rain on long holiday weekends, else how could the multitudes get drenched and miserable? The July sun fought off a multitude of little feathered clouds and drove them scuttling, but thunderheads looked over the western rim, the strong-arm rain-bearers from the Hudson River Valley, armed with lightning and already mumbling to themselves. If the law was properly obeyed, they would hold back until a maximum number of ant-happy humans were on the highways and the beaches, summer-dressed and summer-green.

Most of the other stores did not open until nine-thirty. It had been Marullo's thought to catch a pinch of trade by having me jump the gun half an hour. I thought I would change that. It caused more ill feeling among the other stores than the profit justified. Marullo didn't care about that, if he ever knew about it. He was a foreigner, a wop, a criminal, a tyrant, a squeezer of the poor, a bastard, and eight kinds of son of a bitch. I having destroyed him, it was only natural that his faults and crimes should become blindingly apparent to me.

I felt old long hand edging around on my father's watch and I found I was sweeping viciously with tensed muscles, waiting for the moment of swift, smooth movement of my mission. I breathed through my mouth, and my stomach pushed against my lungs as I remember it did waiting for an attack.

For Saturday-morning-Fourth-of-July-weekend, there were few people about. A stranger—old man—went by, carrying a fishing rod and a green plastic tackle box. He was on his way to the town pier to sit all day dangling a limp strip of squid in the water. He didn't even look up, but I forced his attention.

"Hope you catch some big ones."

"Never catch anything," he said.

"Stripers come in sometimes."

"I don't believe it."

A red-hot optimist, but at least I had set the hook in his attention.

And Jennie Single rolled along the sidewalk. She moved as though she had casters instead of feet, probably New Baytown's least reliable witness. Once she turned on her gas oven and forgot to light it. She'd have blown herself through the roof if she could have remembered where she had put the matches.

"Morning, Miss Jenny."

"Good morning, Danny."

"I'm Ethan."

"Course you are. I'm going to bake a cake."

I tried to gouge a scar in her memory. "What kind?"

"Well, it's Fannie Farmer but the label fell off the package so I really don't know."

What a witness she would make, if I needed a witness. And why did she say "Danny"?

A piece of tinfoil on the pavement resisted the broom. I had to stoop down and lift it with a fingernail. Those assistant bank mice were really mousing the hour with Cat Baker away. They were the ones I wanted. It was less than one minute to nine when they burst from the coffee shop and sprinted across the street.

"Run—run—run!" I called and they grinned self-consciously as they charged the bank doors.

Now it was time. I must not think of the whole thing—just one step at a time and each in its place, as I had practiced. I folded my anxious stomach down where it belonged. First lean the broom against the doorjamb where it could be seen. I moved with slow, deliberate speed.

From the corner of my eye I saw a car come along the street and I paused to let it go by.

"Mr. Hawley!"

I whirled the way cornered gangsters do in the movies. A dusty dark green Chevrolet had slid to the curb and, great God! that Ivy League government man was getting out. My stone-built earth shuddered like a reflection in water. Paralyzed, I saw him cross the pavement. It seemed to take ages, but it was simple as that. My long-planned perfect structure turned to dust before my eyes the way a long-buried artifact does when the air strikes it. I thought of rushing for the toilet and going through with it. It wouldn't work. I couldn't repeal the Morphy law. Thought and light must travel at about the same speed. It's a shock to throw out a plan so long considered, so many times enacted that its consummation is just one more repetition, but I tossed it out, threw it away, closed it off. I had no choice. And light-speed thought said, Thank God he didn't come one minute later. That would have been the fatal accident they write about in crime stories.

And all this while the young man moved stiffly four steps across the pavement.

Something must have showed through to him.

"What's the matter, Mr. Hawley? You look sick."

"Skitters," I said.

"That'll wait for no man. Run for it. I'll wait."

I dashed for the toilet, closed the door, and pulled the chain to make a rush of water. I hadn't switched on the light. I sat there in the dark. My quaking stomach played along. In a moment I really had to go, and I did, and slowly the beating pressure in me subsided. I added a bylaw to the Morphy code. In case of accident, change your plan—instantly.

It has happened to me before that in crisis or great danger I have stepped out and apart and as an interested stranger watched myself, my movements and my mind, but immune to the emotions of the thing observed. Sitting in the blackness, I saw the other person fold his perfect plan and put it in a box and close the lid and shove the thing not only out of sight but out of thought. I mean that by the time I stood up in the darkness and zipped and smoothed and laid my hand on the flimsy plywood door, I was a grocery clerk prepared for a busy day. It was no secretiveness. It was really so. I wondered what the young man wanted, but only with the pale apprehension that comes from a low-grade fear of cops.

"Sorry to keep you waiting," I said. "Can't remember what I ate to cause that."

"There's a virus going around," he said. "My wife had it last week."

"Well, this virus carried a gun. I nearly got caught short. What can I do for you?"

He seemed embarrassed, apologetic, almost shy. "A guy does funny things," he said.

I overcame an impulse to say, It takes all kinds—and I'm glad I did because his next words were, "In my business you meet all kinds."

I walked behind the counter and kicked the leather Knight Templar hatbox closed. And I leaned my elbows on the counter.

Very odd. Five minutes earlier I saw myself through the eyes of other people. I had to. What they saw was important. And as he came across the pavement, this man had been a huge, dark, hopeless fate, an enemy, an ogre. But with my project tucked away and gone as a part of me, I saw him now as an object apart—no longer linked with me for good or bad. He was, I think, about my age, but shaped in a school, a manner, perhaps a cult—a lean face and hair carefully trimmed short and standing straight up, white shirt of a coarse woven linen with the collar buttoned down and a tie chosen by his wife, and without doubt patted and straightened by her as he left the house. His suit a gray darkness and his nails home cared for but well cared for, a wide gold wedding ring on his left hand, a tiny bar in his buttonhole, a suggestion of the decoration he would not wear. His mouth and dark blue eyes were schooled to firmness, which made it all the more strange that they were not firm now. In some way a hole had been opened in him. He was not the same man whose questions had been short, squared bars of steel spaced perfectly, one below its fellow.

"You were here before," I said. "What is your business?"

"Department of Justice."

"Your business is justice?"

He smiled. "Yes, at least that's what I hope. But I'm not on official business—not even sure the department would approve. But it's my day off."

"What can I do for you?"

"It's kind of complicated. Don't know quite where to begin. It's not in the book. Hawley, I've been in the service twelve years and I've never had anything like this before."

"Maybe if you tell me what it is I can help you do it."

He smiled at me. "Hard to set it up. I've been driving three hours from New York and I've got to drive three hours back in holiday traffic."

"Sounds serious."

"It is."

"I think you said your name was Walder."

"Richard Walder."

"I'm going to be swamped with customers, Mr. Walder. Don't know why they haven't started. Hot-dog-and-relish trade. You'd better start. Am I in trouble?"

"In my job you meet all kinds. Tough ones, liars, cheats, hustlers, stupid, bright. Mostly you can get mad at them, get an attitude to carry you through. Do you see?"

"No, I guess not. Look, Walder, what in hell's bothering you? I'm not completely stupid. I've talked to Mr. Baker at the bank. You're after Mr. Marullo, my boss."

"And I got him," he said softly.

"What for?"

"Illegal entry. It's not my doing. They throw me a dossier and I follow it up. I don't judge him or try him."

"He'll be deported?"

"Yes."

"Can he make a fight? Can I help him?"

"No. He doesn't want to. He's pleading guilty. He wants to go."

"Well, I'll be damned!"

Six or eight customers came in. "I warned you," I called to him, and I helped them select what they needed or thought they did. Thank heaven I had ordered a mountain of hot-dog and hamburger rolls.

Walder called, "What do you get for piccalilli?"

"It's marked on the label."

"Thirty-nine cents, ma'am," he said. And he went to work, measuring, bagging, adding. He reached in front of me to ring up cash on the register. When he moved away I took a bag from the pile, opened the drawer, and, using the bag like a pot-holder I picked up the old revolver, took it back to the toilet, and dropped it in the can of crankcase oil that waited for it.

"You're good at this," I said when I came back.

"I used to have a job at Grand Union after school."

"It shows."

"Don't you have anybody to help?"

"I'm going to bring my boy in."

Customers always come in coveys, never in evenly spaced singles. A clerk gets set in the interval to meet the next flight. Another thing, when two men do something together they become alike, differences of mind become less ragged. The Army discovered that black and white no longer fight each other when they have something else to fight in company. My subcutaneous fear of a cop dissipated when Walder weighed out a pound of tomatoes and totted up a list of figures on a bag.

Our first flight took off.

"Better tell me quick what you want," I said.

"I promised Marullo I'd come out here. He wants to give you the store."

"You're nuts. I beg your pardon, ma'am. I was speaking to my friend."

"Oh, yes. Of course. Well, there are five of us—three children. How many frankfurters will I need?"

"Five apiece for the children, three for your husband, two for you. That's twenty."

"You think they'll eat five?"

"They think they will. Is it a picnic?"

"Uh-huh."

"Then get five extra for dropping in the fire."

"Where do you keep the Plug-O for sinks?"

"Back there with the cleansers and ammonia."

It was broken up like that and was bound to be. Edited of customers, it was like this:

"I guess I'm in a state of shock. I just do my job and it's with mugs for the most part. If you get conditioned by crooks and liars and cheats, why, an honest man can shock the hell out of you."

"What do you mean, honest? My boss never gave away anything. He's a tough monkey."

"I know he is. We made him that way. He told me and I believe him. Before he came over he knew the words on the bottom of the Statue of Liberty. He'd memorized the Declaration of Independence in dialect. The Bill of Rights was words of fire. And then he couldn't get in. So he came anyway. A nice man helped him—took everything he had and dropped him in the surf to wade ashore. It was quite a while before he understood the American way, but he learned—he learned. 'A guy got to make a buck! Look out for number one!' But he learned. He's not dumb. He took care of number one."

This was interspersed with customers so it didn't build to a dramatic climax—just a series of short statements.

"That's why he wasn't hurt when somebody turned him in.

"Turned him in?"

"Sure. All it takes is a telephone call."

"Who did that?"

"Who knows? The department's a machine. You set the dials and it follows through all the steps like an automatic washer."

"Why didn't he run for it?"

"He's tired, right to his bones he's tired. And he's disgusted. He's got some money. He wants to go back to Sicily."

"I still don't get it about the store."

"He's like me. I can take care of chiselers. That's my job. An honest man gums up my works, throws me sky high. That's what happened to him. One guy didn't try to cheat him, didn't steal, didn't whine, didn't chisel. He tried to teach the sucker to take care of himself in the land of the free but the boob couldn't learn. For a long time you scared him. He tried to figure out your racket, and he discovered your racket was honesty."

"Suppose he was wrong?"

"He doesn't think he was. He wants to make you a kind of monument to something he believed in once. I've got the conveyance out in the car. All you have to do is file it."

"I don't understand it."

"I don't know whether I do or not. You know how he talks—like corn popping. I'm trying to translate what he tried to explain. It's like a man is made a certain way with a certain direction. If he changes that, something blows, he strips a gear, he gets sick. It's like a—well, like a do-it-yourself police court. You have to pay for a violation. You're his down payment, kind of, so the light won't go out."

"Why did you drive out here?"

"Don't know exactly. Had to—maybe—so the light won't go out."

"Oh, God!"

The store clouded up with clamoring kids and damp women. There wouldn't be any more uncluttered moments until noon at least.

Walder went out to his car, and came back and parted a wave of frantic summer wives to get to the counter. He laid down one of those cardboard bellows envelopes tied with a tape.

"Got to go. Four hours' drive with this traffic. My wife's mad. She said it could wait. But it couldn't wait."

"Mister, I been waiting ten minutes to get waited on."

"Be right with you, ma'am."

"I asked him if he had any message and he said, 'Tell him good-by.' You got any message?"

"Tell him good-by."

The wave of ill-disguised stomachs closed in again and it was just as well for me. I dropped the envelope in the drawer below the cash register and with it—desolation.

Chapter XVI

THE day went quickly and yet was endless. Closing time had no relation to opening time, so long ago it was that I could hardly remember it. Joey came in as I was about to close the front doors and without asking him I punched a beer can and handed it to him, and then I opened one for myself and I have never done that before. I tried to tell him about Marullo and the store, and found I could not, not even the story I had accepted in exchange for the truth.

"You look tired," he said.

"I guess I am. Look at those shelves—stripped. They bought things they didn't want and didn't need." I unloaded the cash register into the gray canvas bag, added the money Mr. Baker had brought, and on top I put the bellows envelope and tied up the bag with a piece of string.

"You oughtn't to leave that around."

"Maybe not. I hide it. Want another beer?"

"Sure."

"Me too."

"You're too good an audience," he said. "I get to believing my own stories."

"Like what?"

"Like my triple-deck instincts. I had one this morning. Woke up with it. Guess I dreamed it, but it was real strong, hair on the back of my neck and everything. I didn't think the bank was going to get stuck up today. I knew it. I knew it, lying in bed. We keep little wedges under the foot alarms so we won't tramp them by mistake. First thing this morning I took them out. I was that sure of it, braced for it. Now how do you explain that?"

"Maybe somebody planned it and you read his mind and he gave it up."

"You make it easy for a guy to guess wrong with honor."

"How do you figure it?"

"God knows. I think I've been Mr. Know-It-All to you so much I got to believe it. But it sure shook me up."

"You know, Morph, I'm too tired even to sweep out."

"Don't leave that dough here tonight. Take it home."

"Okay, if you say so."

"I still got the feeling something's screwy."

I opened the leather box and put the money sack in with my plumed hat and strapped it closed. Joey, watching me, said, "I'm going in to New York and get a room at a hotel and I'm going to watch the waterfall across Times Square for two solid days with my shoes off."

"With your date?"

"I called that off. I'll order up a bottle of whisky and a dame. Don't have to talk to either of them."

"I told you—maybe we're going on a little trip."

"Hope so. You need it. Ready to go?"

"Couple of things to do. You go on, Joey. Get your shoes off."

First thing to do was to call Mary and tell her I had to be a little late.

"Yes, but hurry, hurry, hurry. News, news, news."

"Can't you tell me now, sweetheart?"

"No. I want to see your face."

I hung the Mickey Mouse mask on the cash register by its rubber band so that it covered the little window where the numbers show. Then I put on my coat and hat and turned out the lights and sat on the counter with my legs dangling. A naked black banana stalk nudged me on one side and the cash register fitted against my left shoulder like a bookend. The shades were up so that the summer late light strained through the crossed-wire grating, and it was very quiet, a quiet like a rushing sound, and that's what I needed. I felt in my left side pocket for the lump the cash register pushed against me. The talisman—I held it in my two hands and stared down at it. I had thought I needed it yesterday. Had I forgot to put it back or was my keeping it with me no accident? I don't know.

As always it put its power on me as I traced its design with my finger. At midday it was the pink of a rose, but in the evening it picked up a darker tone, a purplish blush as though a little blood had got in it.

It wasn't thought I needed but rearrangement, change of

design, as though I were in a garden from which the house had been moved in the night. Some kind of makeshift had to be set up to shelter me until I could rebuild. I had retired into busyness until I could let new things enter slowly and count and identify them as they came. The shelves, all day assaulted, showed many gaps where their defenses had been breeched by the hungry horde, a snaggle-toothed effect, a walled town after artillery fire.

"Let us pray for our departed friends," I said. "The thin red line of catsup, the gallant pickles and condiments down to the small bald capers of vinegar. We cannot dedicate, we cannot consecrate—no not that. It is rather to us the living—no not that. Alfio—I wish you luck and surcease from pain. You are wrong, of course, but wrongness can be a poultice to you. You made a sacrifice for having been a sacrifice."

People passing in the street flickered the light inside the store. I dug back in the debris of the day for Walder's words and for his face when he said them: "A do-it-yourself police court. You have to pay for a violation. You're his down payment, kind of, so the light won't go out." That's what the man said. Walder in his safe world of crooks shaken by one gleaming shaft of honesty.

So the light won't go out. Did Alfio say it that way? Walder didn't know, but he did know that's what Marullo meant.

I traced the serpent on the talisman and came back to the beginning, which was the end. That was an old light—Marulli three thousand years ago found their way through the lupariae to the Lupercal on the Palatine to offer a votive to Lycean Pan, protector of the flocks from wolves. And that light had not gone out. Marullo, the dago, the wop, the guinea, sacrificed to the same god for the same reason. I saw him again raise his head out of the welter of fat neck and aching shoulders, I saw the noble head, the hot eyes—and the light. I wondered what my payment would be and when demanded. If I took my talisman down to the Old Harbor and threw it in the sea—would that be acceptable?

I did not draw the shades. On long holidays we left them up so the cops could look in. The storeroom was dark. I locked the alley door and was halfway across the street when I remembered the hatbox behind the counter. I did not go back for it. It would be a kind of question asked. The wind was rising that Saturday evening, blowing shrill and eagerly from the southeast as it must to bring the rain to soak the vacationers. I thought to put out the milk for that gray cat on Tuesday and invite it in to be a guest in my store.

Chapter XVII

I DON'T know for sure how other people are inside—all different and all alike at the same time. I can only guess. But I do know how I will squirm and wriggle to avoid a hurtful truth and, when finally there is no choice, will put it off, hoping it will go away. Do other people say primly, "I'll think about that tomorrow when I am rested," and then draw on a hoped-for future or an edited past like a child playing with violence against the inevitability of bedtime?

My dawdled steps toward home led through a minefield of the truth. The future was sowed with fertile dragon's teeth. It was not unnatural to run for a safe anchorage in the past. But on that course, set square across it was Aunt Deborah, a great wing shot on a covey of lies, her eyes gleaming question marks.

I had looked in the window of the jewelry store at expanding watch bands and glasses frames as long as was decent. The humid, windy evening was breeding a thunderstorm.

There were many like Great-Aunt Deborah early in the last century, islands of curiosity and knowledge. Maybe it was being cut off from a world of peers that drove the few into books or perhaps it was the endless waiting, sometimes three years, sometimes forever, for the ships to come home, that pushed them into the kind of books that filled our attic. She was the greatest of great-aunts, a sibyl and a pythoness in one, said magic nonsense words to me, which kept their magic but not their nonsense when I tracked them down.

"Me beswac fah wyrm thurh faegir word," she said and the tone was doom. And, "Seo leo gif heo blades onbirigth abit aerest hire ladteow." Wonder-words they must be, since I still remember them.

The Town Manager of New Baytown went crab-scuttling by me, head down, and only gave me good evening in return for mine first offered.

I could feel my house, the old Hawley house, from half a block away. Last night it huddled in a web of gloom but this thunder-bordered eve it radiated excitement. A house, like an opal, takes on the colors of the day. Antic Mary heard my footsteps on the walk and she flickered out the screen door like a flame.

"You'll never guess!" she said, and her hands were out, palms in, as though she carried a package.

It was in my mind so I replied "Seo leo gif heo blades onbirigth abit aerest hire ladteow."

"Well, that's a pretty good guess but it's not right."

"Some secret admirer has given us a dinosaur."

"Wrong, but it's just as wonderful. And I won't tell till you wash up, because you'll have to be clean to hear it."

"What I hear is the love music of a blue-bottom baboon." And I did—it blatted from the living room, where Allen importuned his soul in a phlegm of revolt. "Just when I was ready, to ask you to go steady, they said I didn't know my mind. Your glance gives me ants whenever we romance, and they say I couldn't know my mind."

"I think I'll burn him up, heaven wife."

"No, you won't. Not when you hear."

"Can't you tell me dirty?"

"No."

I went through the living room. My son responded to my greeting with the sharp expression of a piece of chewed gum.

"I hope you got your lonely lovin' heart swept up."

"Huh?"

"Huh, *sir!* Last I heard, somebody had took and threw it on the floor."

"Number one," he said, "number one in the whole country. Sold a million copies in two weeks."

"Great! I'm glad the future is in your hands." I joined the next chorus as I went up the stairs. " 'Your glance gives me ants whenever we romance, and they say I couldn't know my mind.' "

Ellen was stalking me with a book in her hand, one finger between the pages. I know her method. She would ask me what she thought I might think an interesting question and then let slip whatever it was Mary wanted to tell me. It's a kind of triumph for Ellen to tell first. I wouldn't say she is a tattletale, but she is. I waved crossed fingers at her.

"King's X."

"But, Daddy—"

"I said King's X, Miss Hothouse Rhubarb, and I meant

King's X." I slammed the door and shouted, "A man's bathroom is his castle." And I heard her laugh. I don't trust children when they laugh at my jokes. I scrubbed my face raw and brushed my teeth until my gums bled. I shaved, put on a clean shirt and the bow tie my daughter hated, as a declaration of revolt.

My Mary was flittered with impatience when I faced her.

"You won't believe it."

"Seo leo gif heo blades onbirigth. Speak."

"Margie is the nicest friend I ever had."

"I quote—'The man who invented the cuckoo clock is dead. This is old news but good!' "

"You'll never guess—she's going to keep the children so we can have our trip."

"Is this a trick?"

"I didn't ask. She offered."

"They'll eat her alive."

"They're crazy about her. She's going to take them to New York on the train Sunday, stay all night in a friend's apartment, and Monday see the new fifty-star flag-raising in Rockefeller Center and the parade and—everything."

"I can't believe it."

"Isn't that the nicest thing?"

"The very nicest. And we will flee to the Montauk moors, Miss Mousie?"

"I've already called and reserved a room."

"It's delirium. I shall burst. I feel myself swelling up."

I had thought to tell her about the store, but too much news is constipating. Better to wait and tell her on the moor.

Ellen came slithering into the kitchen. "Daddy, that pink thing's gone from the cabinet."

"I have it. I have it here in my pocket. Here, you may put it back."

"You told us never to take it away."

"I still tell you that, on pain of death."

She snatched it almost greedily and carried it in both hands to the living room.

Mary's eyes were on me strangely, somberly. "Why did you take it, Ethan?"

"For luck, my love. And it worked."

Chapter XVIII

It rained on Sunday, July third, as it must, fat drops more wet than usual. We nudged our way in the damp segmented worms of traffic, feeling a little grand and helpless and lost, like cage-bred birds set free, and frightened as freedom shows its teeth. Mary sat straight, smelling of fresh-ironed cotton.

"Are you happy—are you gay?"

"I keep listening for the children."

"I know. Aunt Deborah called it happy-lonesome. Take flight, my bird! Those long flaps on your shoulders are wings, you juggins."

She smiled and nuzzled close. "It's good, but I still listen for the children. I wonder what they are doing now?"

"Almost anything you can guess except wondering what we are doing."

"I guess that's right. They aren't really interested."

"Let us emulate them, then. When I saw your barge slide near, O Nile serpent, I knew it was our day. Octavian will beg his bread tonight from some Greek goatherd."

"You're crazy. Allen never looks where he's going. He might step right out in traffic against a light."

"I know. And poor little Ellen with her club foot. Well, she has a good heart and a pretty face. Perhaps someone will love her and amputate her feet."

"Oh! let me worry a little. I'll feel better if I do."

"I never heard it better put. Shall we together go over all the horrid possibilities?"

"You know what I mean."

"I do. But you, highness, brought it to the family. It only travels in the female line. The little bleeders."

"No one loves his children more than you."

"My guilt is as the guilt of ten because I am a skunk."

"I like you."

"Now that's the kind of worrying I approve of. See that stretch? Look how the gorse and heather hold and the sand cuts out from under like solid little waves. The rain hits the earth and jumps right up in a thin mist. I've always thought it is like Dartmoor or Exmoor, and I've never seen them except through the eyes of print. You know the first Devon men must have felt at home here. Do you think it's haunted?"

"If it isn't, you'll haunt it."

"You must not make compliments unless you mean them."

"It's not for now. Watch for the side road. It will say 'Moorcroft.'"

It did, too, and the nice thing about that lean spindle end of Long Island is that the rain sinks in and there is no mud.

We had a doll's house to ourselves, fresh and ginghamy, and nationally advertised twin beds, fat as muffins.

"I don't approve of those."

"Silly—you can reach across."

"I can do one whole hell of a lot better than that, you harlot."

We dined in greasy dignity on broiled Maine lobsters sloshed down with white wine—lots of white wine to make my Mary's eyes to shine, and I plied her with cognac seductively until my own head was buzzing. *She* remembered the number of our doll house and *she* could find the keyhole. I wasn't too buzzed to have my way with her, but I think she could have escaped if she had wanted to.

Then, aching with comfort, she drowsed her head on my right arm and smiled and made small yawny sounds.

"Are you worried about something?"

"What a thought. You're dreaming before you're asleep."

"You're working so hard to make me happy. I can't get past into you. Are you worried?"

A strange and seeing time, the front steps of sleep.

"Yes, I'm worried. Does that reassure you? I wouldn't want you to repeat it, but the sky is falling and a piece of it fell on my tail."

She had drifted sweetly off with her Panic smile. I slipped my arm free and stood between the beds. The rain was over except for roof drip, and the quarter-moon glistened its image in a billion droplets. "*Beaux rêves*, my dearling dear. Don't let the sky fall on us!"

My bed was cool and oversoft but I could see the sharp moon driving through the sea-fleeing clouds. And I heard the ghost-cry of a bittern. I crossed the fingers of both hands—

King's X for a little while. Double King's X. It was only a pea that fell on my tail.

If the dawn came up with any thunder, I didn't hear it. All golden green it was when I came to it, dark of heather and pale with fern and yellowy red with wet dune sand, and not far away the Atlantic glittering like hammered silver. A twisted gaffer oak beside our house had put out near its root a lichen big as a pillow, a ridge-waved thing of gray pearly white. A curving graveled path led among the small township of doll houses to the shingled bungalow that had spawned them all. Here were office, postcards, gifts, stamps, and also dining room with blue-checkered tablecloths where we dolls could dine.

The manager was in his counting house, checking some kind of list. I had noticed him when we registered, a man of wisped hair and little need to shave. He was a furtive and a furthy man at once, and he had so hoped from our gaiety our outing was clandestine that I nearly signed his book "John Smith and wife" to give him pleasure. He sniffed for sin. Indeed he seemed to see with his long tender nose as a mole does.

"Good morning," I said.

He leveled his nose at me. "Slept well?"

"Perfectly. I wonder if I can carry a tray of breakfast to my wife."

"We only serve in the dining room, seven-thirty to nine-thirty."

"But if I carry it myself—"

"It's against the rules."

"Couldn't we break them this once? You know how it is." I threw that in because that's how he hoped it was.

His pleasure was reward enough. His eyes grew moist and his nose trembled. "Feeling a little shy, is she?"

"Well, you know how it is."

"I don't know what the cook will say."

"Ask him and tell him a dollar stands tiptoe on the misty mountaintop."

The cook was a Greek who found a dollar attractive. In time I toted a giant napkin-covered tray along the graveled path and set it on a rustic bench while I picked a bouquet of microscopic field flowers to grace the royal breakfast of my dear.

Perhaps she was awake, but she opened her eyes anyway and said, "I smell coffee. Oh! Oh! What a nice husband—and—and flowers"—all the little sounds that never lose their fragrance.

We breakfasted and coffeed and coffeed again, my Mary propped up in bed, looking younger and more innocent than her daughter. And each of us spoke respectfully of how well we had slept.

My time had come. "Get comfortable. I have news both sad and glad."

"Good! Did you buy the ocean?"

"Marullo is in trouble."

"What?"

"A long time ago he came to America without asking leave."

"Well—what?"

"Now they are asking him to leave."

"Deported?"

"Yes."

"But that's awful."

"It's not nice."

"What will we do? What will you do?"

"Playtime is over. He sold me the store—or rather he sold you the store. It's your money. He has to convert his property and he likes me; he practically gave it to me—three thousand dollars."

"But that's awful. You mean—you mean you own the store?"

"Yes."

"You're not a clerk! Not a clerk!"

She rolled face down in the pillows and wept, big, full-bosomed sobs, the way a slave might when the collar is struck off.

I went out on the doll's front stoop and sat in the sun until she was ready, and when she had finished and washed her face and combed her hair and put on her dressing gown, she opened the door and called to me. And she was different, would always be different. She didn't have to say it. The set of her neck said it. She could hold up her head. We were gentlefolks again.

"Can't we do anything to help Mr. Marullo?"

"I'm afraid not."

"How did it happen? Who found out?"

"I don't know."

"He's a good man. They shouldn't do it to him. How is he taking it?"

"With dignity. With honor."

We walked on the beach as we had thought we might, sat in the sand, picked up small bright shells and showed them to each other, as we must do, spoke with conventional wonder about natural things, the sea, the air, the light, the wind-cooled sun, as though the Creator were listening in for compliments.

Mary's attention was split. I think she wanted to be back home in her new status, to see the different look in the eyes of women, the changed tone of greetings in the High Street. I think she was no more "poor Mary Hawley, she works so hard." She had become Mrs. Ethan Allen Hawley and would ever be. And I had to keep her that. She went through the day because it was planned and paid for, but the real shells she turned over and inspected were the shining days to come.

We had our lunch in the blue-checked dining room, where Mary's manner, her certainty of position and place, disappointed Mr. Mole. His tender nose was out of joint that had so joyously quivered at the scent of sin. His disillusion was complete when he had to come to our table and report a telephone call for Mrs. Hawley.

"Who knows we're here?"

"Why, Margie, of course. I had to tell her because of the children. Oh! I do hope— He doesn't look where he's going, you know."

She came back trembling like a star. "You'll never guess. You couldn't."

"I can guess it's good."

"She said, 'Have you heard the news? Have you heard the radio?' I could tell by her voice it wasn't bad news."

"Could you tell it and then flash back to how she said it?"

"I can't believe it."

"Could you let me try to believe it?"

"Allen has won honorable mention."

"What? Allen? Tell me!"

"In the essay contest—in the whole country—honorable mention."

"No!"

"He has. Only five honorable mentions—and a watch, and he's going on television. Can you believe it? A celebrity in the family."

"I can't believe it. You mean all that slob stuff was a sham? What an actor! His lonely lovin' heart wasn't throwed on the floor at all."

"Don't make fun. Just think, our son is one of five boys in the whole United States to get honorable mention—and television."

"And a watch! Wonder if he can tell time."

"Ethan, if you make fun, people will think you're jealous of your own son."

"I'm just astonished. I thought his prose style was about the level of General Eisenhower's. Allen doesn't have a ghost-writer."

"I know you, Eth. You make a game of running them down. But it's you who spoil them. It's just your secret way. I want to know—did you help him with his essay?"

"Help him! He didn't even let me see it."

"Well—that's all right then. I didn't want you looking smug because you wrote it for him."

"I can't get over it. It goes to show we don't know much about our own children. How's Ellen taking it?"

"Why, proud as a peacock. Margie was so excited she could hardly talk. The newspapers want to interview him—and television, he's going to be on television. Do you realize we don't even have a set to see him on? Margie says we can watch on hers. A celebrity in the family! Ethan, we ought to have a television."

"We'll get one. I'll get one first thing tomorrow morning, or why don't you order one?"

"Can we—Ethan, I forgot you own the store, I clean forgot. Can you take it in? A celebrity."

"I hope we can live with him."

"You let him have his day. We should start home. They're coming in on the seven-eighteen. We should be there, you know, to kind of receive him."

"And bake a cake."

"I will."

"And string crepe paper."

"You aren't being jealous mean, are you?"

"No. I'm overcome. I think crepe paper is a fine thing, all over the house."

"But not outside. That would look—ostentatious. Margie said why don't we pretend we don't know and let him tell us?"

"I disagree. He might turn shy. It would be as though we didn't care. No, he should come home to cheers and cries of triumph and a cake. If there was anything open, I'd get sparklers."

"The roadside stands—"

"Of course. On the way home—if they have any left."

Mary put down her head a moment as though she were saying grace. "You own the store and Allen's a celebrity. Who would have thought all that could happen all at once? Ethan, we should get started home. We ought to be there when they come. Why are you looking that way?"

"It just swept over me like a wave—how little we know about anyone. It gives me a shiver of mullygrubs. I remember at Christmas when I should be gay I used to get the Welsh rats."

"What's that?"

"It's the way I heard it when Great-Aunt Deborah pronounced *Weltschmerz*."

"What's that?"

"A goose walking over your grave."

"Oh! That! Well, don't get it. I guess this is the best day of our whole lives. It would be—ungrateful if we didn't know it. Now you smile and chase off those Welsh rats. That's funny, Ethan, 'Welsh rats.' You pay the bill. I'll put our things together."

I paid our bill with money that had been folded in a tight little square. And I asked Mr. Mole, "Do you have any sparklers left at the gift counter?"

"I think so. I'll see. . . . Here they are. How many do you want?"

"All you have," I said. "Our son has become a celebrity."

"Really? What kind?"

"There's only one kind."

"You mean like Dick Clark or like that?"

"Or Chessman or Dillinger."

"You're joking."

"He'll be on television."

"What station? What time?"

"I don't know—yet."

"I'll watch for it. What's his name?"

"The same as mine. Ethan Allen Hawley—called Allen."

"Well it's been an honor to have you and Mrs. Allen with us."

"Mrs. Hawley."

"Of course. I hope you'll come again. Lots of celebrities have stayed here. They come for—the quiet."

Mary sat straight and proud on the golden road toward home in the slow and glittering snake of the traffic.

"I got a whole box of sparklers. Over a hundred."

"Now that's more like you, dear. I wonder if the Bakers are back yet."

Chapter XIX

MY son conducted himself well. He was relaxed and kind to us. He took no revenge, ordered no executions. His honors and our compliments he accepted as his due, without vanity and also without overdone humility. He advanced to his chair in the living room and switched on his radio before the hundred sparklers had fizzed out to black sticks. It was obvious that he forgave us our trespasses. I never saw a boy accept greatness with more grace.

It was truly a night of wonders. If Allen's easy ascent into heaven was surprising, how much more so was Ellen's reaction. Some years of close and enforced observation told me Miss Ellen would be tattered and storm-blown with envy, would in fact look out for some means of minimizing his greatness. She fooled me. She became her brother's celebrator. It was Ellen who told how they were sitting in an elegant apartment on Sixty-seventh Street, after an evening of magic, casually watching the C.B.S. late news on television, when the word of Allen's triumph was announced. It was Ellen who recounted what they said and how they looked and how you could have knocked them over with a feather. Allen sat remote and calm during Ellen's telling of how he would appear with the four other honorables, how he would read his essay while millions looked and listened, and Mary clucked happily in the pauses. I glanced at Margie Young-Hunt. She was indrawn as she was during card-reading. And a dark quiet crept into the room.

"No escaping it," I said. "This calls for ice-cold root beer all around."

"Ellen will get it. Where is Ellen? She drifts in and out like smoke."

Margie Young-Hunt stood up nervously. "This is a family party. I've got to go."

"But Margie, you're part of it. Where did Ellen go?"

"Mary, don't make me admit I'm a trifle on the pooped side."

"You have had it, dear. I keep forgetting. We had such a rest, you'll never know—and thanks to you."

"I loved it. I wouldn't have missed it."

She wanted to be away, and quickly. She took our thanks and Allen's thanks and fled.

Mary said quietly, "We didn't tell about the store."

"Let it ride. It would be robbing His Pink Eminence. It's his right. Where did Ellen go?"

"She went to bed," said Mary. "That's thoughtful, darling, and you're right. Allen, it's been a big day. Time you went to bed."

"I think I'll sit here a while," Allen said kindly.

"But you need rest."

"I'm resting."

Mary looked to me for help.

"These are the times that try men's souls. I can dust him, or we can let him have his victory even over us."

"He's just a little boy, really. He needs his rest."

"He needs several things, but rest isn't one of them."

"Everyone knows children need their rest."

"The things everyone knows are most likely to be wrong. Did you ever know a child to die of overwork? No—only adults. Children are too smart for that. They rest when they need rest."

"But it's after midnight."

"So it is, darling, and he will sleep until noon tomorrow. You and I will be up at six."

"You mean you'll go to bed and leave him sitting there?"

"He needs his revenge on us for having borne him."

"I don't know what you're talking about. What revenge?"

"I want to make a treaty with you because you're growing angry."

"So I am. You're being stupid."

"If within half an hour after we go to bed he does not creep to his nest, I will pay you forty-seven million, eight hundred and twenty-six dollars and eighty cents."

Well, I lost, and I must pay her. It was thirty-five minutes after we said good night that the stair creaked under our celebrity.

"I hate you when you're right," my Mary said. She had prepared herself to spend the night listening.

"I wasn't right, dear. I lost by five minutes. It's just that I remember."

She went to sleep then. She didn't hear Ellen creep down the stairs, but I did. I was watching my red dots moving in the dark. And I did not follow, for I heard the faint click of the brass key in the lock of the cabinet and I knew my daughter was charging her battery.

My red spots were active. They dashed about and ran away when I centered on them. Old Cap'n was avoiding me. He hadn't come clear since—well, since Easter. It's not like Aunt Harriet—"up in heben she be"—but I do know that when I am not friends with myself old Cap'n doesn't come clear. That's a kind of test of my personal relations with myself.

This night I forced him. I lay straight and rigid, far over on my side of the bed. I tightened every muscle of my body, particularly my neck and jaw, and doubled my fists on my belly and I forced him, bleak little eyes, white spiky mustache, and the forward-curving shoulders that proved he had once been a powerful man of his body and had used it. I even made him put on the blue cap with the short shiny visor and the gold H contrived of two anchors, the cap he hardly ever wore. The old boy was reluctant, but I made him come and I set him on the crumbling sea wall of Old Harbor near the Place. I sat him firmly on a heap of ballast stone and fixed his cupped hands on the head of the narwhal cane. That cane could have knocked over an elephant.

"I need something to hate. Being sorry and understanding—that's pap. I'm looking for a real hate to take the heat off."

Memory's a spawner. Start with one clear detailed print, and it springs into action and it can go forward or back like a film, once it starts.

Old Cap'n moved. He pointed with his cane. "Line the third rock beyond the breakwater with the tip of Porty Point at high water, then out that line half a cable-length she lies, what's left of her."

"How far is half a cable-length, sir?"

"How far? Why, half a hundred fathom, of course. She was anchored to swing and the tide flowing. Two bad-luck years. Half the oil casks empty. I was ashore when she caught fire, about midnight. When the oil fired she lit the town like midday and flames running on the oil slick as far as Osprey Point.

Couldn't beach her for fear of burning the docks. She burned to the water in an hour. Her keel and false keel are down there now—and sound. Shelter Island virgin oak they were, and her knees too."

"How'd it start?"

"I never thought it started. I was ashore."

"Who'd want to burn her?"

"Why, her owners."

"You owned her."

"I was half-owner. I couldn't burn a ship. I'd like to see those timbers—like to see what shape they're in."

"You can go now, Cap'n, sir."

"That's slim fare to hate on."

"It's better than nothing. I'll get that keel up—soon as I'm rich. I'll do that for you—line the third rock with Porty Point at high water, fifty fathoms out." I was not sleeping. My fists and forearms were rigid and pressed against my stomach to prevent old Cap'n from fading, but when I let him go, sleep lapped over me.

When Pharaoh had a dream he called in the experts and they told him how it was and would be in the kingdom, and that was right because he was the kingdom. When some of us have a dream, we take it to an expert and he tells us how it is in the country of ourselves. I had a dream that didn't need an expert. Like most modern people, I don't believe in prophecy or magic and then spend half my time practicing it.

In the springtime Allen, feeling low and lonely, announced that he was an atheist to punish God and his parents. I told him not to go out on a limb or he wouldn't have leeway to not walk under ladders and cancel black cats with spit and thumb and wish on the new moon.

People who are most afraid of their dreams convince themselves they don't dream at all. I can explain my dream easily enough, but that doesn't make it any less frightening.

An order came through from Danny, I don't know how. He was going away by aircraft and he wanted certain things of me, things I had to make myself. He wanted a cap for Mary. It had to be of dark brown sueded lambskin with the wool on the inside. It had to be of skin like an old pair of sheep-lined slippers I have, had to be like a baseball cap with a long beak. Also he wanted a wind gauge—not the little whirling metal cups but handmade from the thin, stiff cardboard of government postcards, mounted on strips of bamboo. And he called me to meet him before he took off. I carried old Cap'n's narwhal stick with me. It stands in the elephant's-foot umbrella stand in our hall.

When we got the elephant's foot as a present I looked at the big ivory-colored toenails, I told my children, "The first kid who puts nail polish on those toenails gets clobbered—understand?" They obeyed me, so I had to paint them myself—bright red fingernail enamel from Mary's harem table.

I went to meet Danny in Marullo's Pontiac and the airport was the New Baytown post office. When I parked I laid the twisted stick on the back seat and two mean-looking cops in a squad car drove up and said, "Not on the seat."

"Is it against the law?"

"So you want to be a wise guy!"

"No. I was just asking."

"Well, don't put it on the seat."

Danny was in the back of the post office, sorting packages. He was wearing the lambskin cap and whirling the cardboard wind gauge. His face was thin and his lips very chapped but his hands were swollen like hot-water bottles, as though they had been wasp-stung.

He stood up to shake hands and my right hand was folded in the warm, rubbery mass. He put something in my hand, something small and heavy and cool, about the size of a key but not a key—a shape, a metal thing that felt sharp-edged and polished. I don't know what it was because I didn't look at it, I only felt it. I leaned near and kissed him on the mouth and with my lips felt his dry lips all chapped and rough. I awakened then, shaken and cold. The dawn had come. I could see the lake but not the cow standing in it, and I could still feel the chapped dry lips. I got up instantly because I didn't want to lie there thinking about it. I didn't make coffee but I went to the elephant's foot and saw that the wicked club called a cane was still there.

It was the throbbing time of dawn, and hot and humid, for the morning wind had not started to blow. The street was gray and silver and the sidewalk greasy with the deposit of humanity.

The Foremaster coffee shop wasn't open, but I didn't want coffee anyway. I went through the alley and opened my back door—looked in the front and saw the leather hatbox behind the counter. I opened a coffee can, poured the coffee in the garbage pail. Then I punched two holes in a can of condensed milk and squirted it into the coffee can, propped the back door open, and put the can in the entrance. The cat was in the alley all right, but he wouldn't come to the milk until I went into the front of the store. From there I could see him, gray cat in gray alley, lapping the milk. When he raised his head he was mustached with milk. He sat down and wiped his mouth and licked his pads.

I opened the hatbox and took out the Saturday receipts, all listed and held together with paper clips. From the brown bank envelope I removed thirty one-hundred-dollar bills and replaced the other twenty of them. This three thousand dollars would be my margin of safety until the store's economy could balance. Mary's other two thousand would go back to her account and, as soon as I could do it safely, I would replace the three thousand. The thirty bills I put in my new wallet, which made it very fat in my hip pocket. Then I brought cases and cartons from the storeroom, ripped and tore them open, and began to replenish my exhausted shelves, while on a strip of wrapping paper I listed the goods that had to be reordered. Cartons and boxes I piled in the alley for the collection truck, and I refilled the coffee can with milk but the cat did not return. Either he had had enough or he took pleasure only in what he could steal.

It must be that there are years unlike other years, as different in climate and direction and mood as one day can be from another day. This year of 1960 was a year of change, a year when secret fears come into the open, when discontent stops being dormant and changes gradually to anger. It wasn't only in me or in New Baytown. Presidential nominations would be coming up soon and in the air the discontent was changing to anger and with the excitement anger brings. And it wasn't only the nation; the whole world stirred with restlessness and uneasiness as discontent moved to anger and anger tried to find an outlet in action, any action so long as it was violent—Africa,

Cuba, South America, Europe, Asia, the Near East, all restless as horses at the barrier.

I knew that Tuesday, July fifth, was going to be a day larger than other days. I even think I knew what things would happen before they happened, but since they did I will never be sure whether I really knew.

I think I knew that the seventeen-jewel, shockproof Mr. Baker, who ticked the hours, would come rattling at my front door an hour before the bank opening time. He did before I had opened for business. I let him in and closed the doors after him.

"What an awful thing," he said. "I was out of touch. I came back as soon as I heard."

"Which awful thing, sir?"

"Why, the scandal! Those men are my friends, my old friends. I've got to do something."

"They won't even be questioned before election—just charged."

"I know. Couldn't we issue a statement of our belief in their innocence? Even a paid advertisement if necessary."

"In what, sir? The *Bay Harbor Messenger* doesn't come out until Thursday."

"Well, something should be done."

"I know."

It was so formal. He must have known I knew. And yet he met my eyes and he seemed genuinely worried.

"The crazy fringe will ruin town elections unless we do something. We've got to offer new candidates. We don't have any choice. It's a terrible thing to do to old friends, but they'd be the first to know we can't let the egghead fringe get in."

"Why don't you talk to them?"

"They're bruised and mad. They haven't had time to think it out. Did Marullo come?"

"He sent a friend. I bought the store for three thousand."

"That's good. You got a bargain. Get the papers?"

"Yes."

"Well, if he jumps, the bills are listed."

"He won't jump. He wants to go. He's tired."

"I never trusted him. Never knew what he had his fingers in."

"Was he a crook, sir?"

"He was tricky, played both sides of the street. He's worth a lot if he can dispose of his property, but three thousand—that's a giveaway."

"He liked me."

"He must have. Who did he send, the Mafia?"

"A government man. You see, Marullo trusted me."

Mr. Baker clasped his brow, and that was out of character. "Why didn't I think of it? You're the man. Good family, reliable, property-owner, businessman, respected. You don't have an enemy in town. Of course you're the man."

"The man?"

"For town manager."

"I've only been a businessman since Saturday."

"You know what I mean. Around you we could get respectable new faces. Why, it's the perfect way."

"From grocery clerk to town manager?"

"Nobody ever thought of a Hawley as a grocery clerk."

"I did. Mary did."

"But you aren't. We can announce it today before that crazy fringe gets set."

"I'll have to consider it from keelson to skys'l."

"There's no time."

"Who had you thought of before?"

"Before what?"

"Before the council burned. I'll talk to you later. Saturday was a big day. I could have sold the scales."

"You can make a nice thing of this store, Ethan. I advise you to build it up and sell it. You're going to be too big to wait on customers. Is there any word at all about Danny?"

"Not yet. Not so far."

"You shouldn't have given him money."

"Perhaps not. I thought I was doing a good deed."

"Of course you did. Of course you did."

"Mr. Baker, sir—what happened to the *Belle-Adair*?"

"What happened? Why, she burned."

"In the harbor—how did it start, sir?"

"Funny time to ask. I only know what I heard. I was too little even to remember. Those old ships got oil-soaked. I suppose some sailor dropped a match. Your grandfather was master. I think he was ashore. Just came in."

"Bad voyage."

"That's what I heard."

"Any trouble collecting the insurance?"

"Well, they always send investigators. No, as I remember, it took some time but we collected, Hawleys and Bakers."

"My grandfather thought she was set afire."

"Why, for heaven's sake?"

"To get the money. The whaling industry was gone."

"I never heard that he said that."

"You never heard it?"

"Ethan—what are you getting at? Why are you bringing up something that happened so long ago?"

"It's a horrible thing to burn a ship. It's a murder. I'm going to bring up her keel someday."

"Her keel?"

"I know just where she lies. Half a cable offshore."

"Why would you do that?"

"I'd like to see if the oak is sound. It was Shelter Island virgin oak. She's not all dead if her keel's alive. You'd better go, if you're going to bless the opening of the safe. And I've got to open up."

Then his balance wheel started and he ticked off to the bank.

I think now I had expected Biggers too. Poor fellow must spend most of his time watching doorways. And he must have been waiting somewhere in peeking range for Mr. Baker to leave.

"I hope you're not going to jump down my throat."

"Why should I?"

"I can understand why you were huffy. I guess I wasn't very—diplomatic."

"Maybe that was it."

"Have you chewed on my proposition?"

"Yes."

"What do you think?"

"I think six per cent would be better."

"I don't know whether B. B. will go for it."

"It's up to them."

"They might go five and a half."

"And you might go the other half."

"Jesus, man. I thought you were being a country boy. You cut deep."

"Take it or leave it."

"Well, what kind of volume would it be?"

"There's a partial list over by the cash register."

He studied the strip of wrapping paper. "Looks like I'm hooked. And, brother, I'm bleeding. Can I get the full order today?"

"Tomorrow would be better and bigger."

"You mean you'll switch the whole account?"

"If you play nice."

"Brother, you must have your boss by the throat. Can you get away with it?"

"Just have to see."

"Well, maybe I could get a crack at the drummer's friend. Brother, you must be cold as a herring. I tell you that dame's a dish."

"Friend of my wife."

"Oh! Yeah! I see how it could be. Too close to home is bad news. You're smart. If I didn't know it before, I know it now. Six per cent. Jesus! Tomorrow in the morning."

"Maybe late this afternoon if I get time."

"Make it tomorrow morning."

On Saturday business came in bursts. This Tuesday the whole tempo had changed. People took time. They wanted to talk about the scandal, saying it was bad, awful, sad, disgraceful, but enjoying it too. We haven't had a scandal for a long time. Nobody mentioned the Democratic National Convention coming up in Los Angeles—not even once. Of course New Baytown is a Republican town, but I think mostly they were interested in what was close to home. We knew the men whose graves we danced on.

Chief Stonewall Jackson came in during the noon hour and he looked tired and sad.

I put the can of oil on the counter and fished out the old pistol with a piece of wire.

"Here's the evidence, Chief. Take it away, will you? It makes me nervous."

"Well, wipe it off, will you? Look at that! That's what they used to call a two-dollar pistol—top-latch Iver Johnson. You got anybody that can mind the store?"

"No, I haven't."

"Where's Marullo?"

"He's out of town."

"Guess maybe you might have to close up for a while."

"What is this, Chief?"

"Well, Charley Pryor's boy ran away from home this morning. Got a cold drink there somewhere?"

"Sure. Orange, cream, lemon, Coke?"

"Give me a Seven-Up. Charley's a funny kind of guy. His boy Tom is eight. He figures the world's against him and he's going to run away to be a pirate. Anybody else would of give him a crack acrost the behind, but not Charley. Aren't you going to open this?"

"Sorry. There you are. What's Charley got to do with me? I like him, of course."

"Well, Charley don't do things like other people. He figures the best way to cure Tom is to help him. So after breakfast they get a bedroll together and a big lunch. Tom wants to take a Jap sword for self-protection, but it drags so he settles for a bayonet. Charley loads him in the car and drives him out of town to give him a good start. He let him out over near Taylor Meadow—you know, the old Taylor place. That's about nine o'clock this morning. Charley watched the kid a while. First thing he did was sit down and eat six sandwiches and two hard-boiled eggs. And then he went on acrost the meadow with his brave little bindle and his bayonet and Charley drove home."

Here it came. I knew it, I knew it. It was almost a relief to get it over.

"'Bout eleven he come slobbering out on the road and hooked a ride home."

"I think I can guess, Stoney—is it Danny?"

"'Fraid so. Down in the cellar hole of the old house. Case of whisky, only two empties, and a bottle of sleeping pills. Sorry I got to ask you this, Eth. Been there a long time and something got at him, at his face. Cats, maybe. You remember any scars or marks on him?"

"I don't want to look at him, Chief."

"Well, who does? How about scars?"

"I remember a barb-wire cut above the knee on his left leg, and—and"—I rolled up my sleeve—"a heart just like this tattooed. We did it together when we were kids. Cut in with a razor blade and rubbed ink in. It's still pretty clear, see?"

"Well—that may do it. Anything else?"

"Yes—big scar under his left arm, piece of the rib cut out. He had pleural pneumonia before the new drugs and they put in a drain."

"Well, of course if there was a rib cut, that'll do it. I won't even have to go back myself. Let the coroner get off his ass. You'll have to swear to those marks if it's him."

"Okay. But don't make me look at him, Stoney. He was—you know—he was my friend."

"Sure, Eth. Say is there anything in what I hear about you running for town manager?"

"It's news to me. Chief—could you stay here two minutes—"

"I got to go."

"Just two minutes while I run across the street and get a drink?"

"Oh! Sure! I get it. Sure—go ahead. I got to get along with the new town manager."

I got the drink and a pint too to bring back with me. When Stoney had gone, I printed BACK AT TWO on a card, closed the doors, and drew the shades.

I sat on the leather hatbox behind the counter in my store, sat in the dim green darkness of my store.

Chapter XX

At ten minutes to three I went out the back door and around the corner to the front of the bank. Morph in his bronze cage drew in the sheaf of money and checks, the brown envelope, and the deposit slips. He spread the little bank books with a Y of fingers and wrote small angled numbers with a steel pen that whispered on the paper. As he pushed the books out to me he looked up with veiled and cautious eyes.

"I'm not going to talk about it, Ethan. I know he was your friend."

"Thanks."

"If you slip out quick you might avoid the Brain."

But I didn't. For all I know Morph may have buzzed him. The frosted-glass door of the office swung open and Mr. Baker, neat and spare and gray, said quietly, "Can you spare a moment, Ethan?"

No use to put it off. I walked into his frosty den and he closed the door so softly that I did not hear the latch click. His desk was topped with plate glass, under which were lists of typed numbers. Two customers' chairs in echelon stood by his tall chair like twin suckling calves. They were comfortable but lower than the desk chair. When I sat down I had to look up at Mr. Baker and that put me in the position of supplication.

"Sad thing."

"Yes."

"I don't think you ought to take all the blame. Probably would have happened anyway."

"Probably."

"I'm sure you thought you were doing the right thing."

"I thought he had a chance."

"Of course you did."

My hatred was rising in my throat like a yellow taste, more sickening than furious.

"Apart from the human tragedy and waste, it raises a difficulty. Do you know whether he had relatives?"

"I don't think so."

"Anybody with money has relatives."

"He had no money."

"He had Taylor Meadow, free and clear."

"Did he? Well, a meadow and a cellar hole—"

"Ethan, I told you we planned an airfield to service the whole district. The meadow is level. If we can't use it, it will cost millions to bulldoze runways in the hills. And now, even if he has no heirs, it will have to go through the courts. Take months."

"I see."

His ire fissured. "I wonder if you do see! With your good intentions you've thrown the thing sky high. Sometimes I think a do-gooder is the most dangerous thing in the world."

"Perhaps you're right. I ought to get back to the store."

"It's your store."

"It is, isn't it? I can't get used to it. I forget."

"Yes, you forget. The money you gave him was Mary's money. She'll never see it now. You threw it away."

"Danny was fond of my Mary. He knew it was her money."

"Fat lot of good that will do her."

"I thought he was making a joke. He gave me these." I pulled the two pieces of ruled paper from my inside pocket, where I had put them, knowing I would have to draw them out like this.

Mr. Baker straightened them on his glass-topped desk. As he read them a muscle beside his right ear twitched so that his ear bobbed. His eyes went back over them, this time looking for a hole.

When the son of a bitch looked at me there was fear in him. He saw someone he hadn't known existed. It took him a moment to adjust to the stranger, but he was good. He adjusted.

"What is your asking price?"

"Fifty-one per cent."

"Of what?"

"Of the corporation or partnership or whatever."

"That's ridiculous."

"You want an airfield. I have the only one available."

He wiped his glasses carefully on a piece of pocket Kleenex, then put them on. But he didn't look at me. He looked a circle all around me and left me out. Finally he asked, "Did you know what you were doing, Ethan?"

"Yes."

"Do you feel good about it?"

"I guess I feel as the man felt who took him a bottle of whisky and tried to get him to sign a paper."

"Did he tell you that?"

"Yes."

"He was a liar."

"He told me he was. He warned me he was. Maybe there's some trick in these papers." I swept them gently from in front of him and folded the two soiled pencil-written sheets.

"There's a trick all right, Ethan. Those documents are without a flaw, dated, witnessed, clear. Maybe he hated you. Maybe his trick was the disintegration of a man."

"Mr. Baker, no one in my family ever burned a ship."

"We'll talk, Ethan, we'll do business. We'll make money. A little town will spring up on the hills around the meadow. I guess you'll have to be town manager now."

"I can't, sir. That would constitute a conflict of interest. Some pretty sad men are finding that out right now."

He sighed—a cautious sigh as though he feared to awaken something in his throat.

I stood up and rested my hand on the curved and padded leather back of the supplicant's chair. "You'll feel better, sir, when you have got used to the fact that I am not a pleasant fool."

"Why couldn't you have taken me into your confidence?"

"An accomplice is dangerous."

"Then you do feel you have committed a crime."

"No. A crime is something someone else commits. I've got to open the store, even if it is my own store."

My hand was on the doorknob when he asked quietly, "Who turned Marullo in?"

"I think you did, sir." He leaped to his feet, but I closed the door after me and went back to my store.

Chapter XXI

NO ONE in the world can rise to a party or a plateau of celebration like my Mary. It isn't what she contributes but what she receives that makes her glow like a jewel. Her eyes shine, her smiling mouth underlines, her quick laughter builds strength into a sickly joke. With Mary in the doorway of a party everyone feels more attractive and clever than he was, and so he actually becomes. Beyond this Mary does not and need not contribute.

The whole Hawley house glowed with celebration when I came home. Bright-colored plastic flags were strung in canopies from center light to picture molding, and lines of colored plastic bannerets hung from the banisters.

"You wouldn't believe it," Mary cried. "Ellen got them from the Esso Service Station. George Sandow loaned them."

"What's it about?"

"About everything. It's a glory thing."

I don't know whether she had heard of Danny Taylor or had heard and retired him. Certainly I didn't invite him to the feast, but he paced about outside. I knew I would have to go out to meet him later but I did not ask him in.

"You'd think it was Ellen had won honorable mention," Mary said. "She's even prouder than if *she* was the celebrity. Look at the cake she baked." It was a tall white cake with HERO written on its top in red, green, yellow, and blue letters. "We're having roast chicken *and* dressing *and* giblet gravy *and* mashed potatoes, even if it is summer."

"Good, darling, good. And where's the young celebrity?"

"Well, it's changed him too. He's taking a bath and changing for dinner."

"It's a day of portent, sibyl. Somewhere you will find a mule has foaled and a new comet come into the sky. A bath before dinner. Imagine!"

"I thought you might like to change too. I have a bottle of wine and I thought maybe a speech or a toast or something like that, even if it's just the family." She fairly flooded the house with party. I found myself rushing up the stairs to bathe and be a part of it.

Passing Allen's door, I knocked, heard a grunt, and went in.

He was standing in front of his mirror, holding a hand-glass so he could see his profile. With some dark stuff, maybe Mary's mascara, he had painted on a narrow black mustache, had darkened his brows and raised the outer ends to satanic tips. He was smiling a world-wise, cynical charm into the mirror when I entered. And he was wearing my blue polka-dot bow tie. He did not seem embarrassed at being caught.

"Rehearsing for a turn," he said and put the hand-mirror down.

"Son, in all the excitement I don't think I've told you how proud I am."

"It's—well, it's only a start."

"Frankly, I didn't think you were even as good a writer as the President. I'm as much surprised as I am pleased. When are you going to read your essay to the world?"

"Sunday, four-thirty *and* a national hookup. I have to go into New York. Special plane flying me."

"Are you well rehearsed?"

"Oh, I'll do all right. It's just a start."

"Well, it's more like a jump to be one of five in the whole country."

"National hookup," he said. He began to remove the mustache with a cotton pad and I saw with amazement that he had a make-up kit, eye-shadow, grease paint, cold cream.

"Everything's happened at once to all of us. Do you know I've bought the store?"

"Yeah! I heard."

"Well, when the bunting and the tinsel come down, I'm going to need your help."

"How do you mean?"

"I told you before, to help me in the store."

"I couldn't do that," he said, and he inspected his teeth in the hand-mirror.

"You couldn't do what?"

"I've got a couple of guest shots and then 'What's My Line?' and 'Mystery Guest.' Then there's a new quiz coming up called Teen Twisters. I might even get to M.C. that. So you see I won't have time." He sprayed something sticky on his hair from a pressure can.

"So your career is all set, is it?"

"Like I told you, it's just a start."

"I'll not let loose the dogs of war tonight. We'll discuss it later."

"There's a guy from N.B.C. been trying to get you on the phone. Maybe it's a contract because like I'm not of age."

"Have you thought of school, my son?"

"Who needs it if you got a contract?"

I got out fast and closed the door and in my bathroom I ran the water cold and iced my skin and let the cold penetrate deep to control my shaking rage. And when I emerged clean and shining and smelling of Mary's perfume, my control was back. In the few moments before dinner, Ellen sat on the arm of my chair and then rolled over in my lap and put her arms around me.

"I do love you," she said. "Isn't it exciting? And isn't Allen wonderful? It's like he's born to it." And this was the girl I had thought very selfish and a little mean.

Just before the cake I toasted the young hero and wished him luck and I finished, " 'Now is the winter of our discontent made glorious summer by this son of York.' "

"That's Shakespeare," Ellen said.

"Yes, muggins, but what play, who says it, and where?"

"I wouldn't know," said Allen. "That's for squares."

I helped carry the dishes to the kitchen. Mary still carried her glow. "Don't fret," she said. "He'll find his line. He'll be all right. Please be patient with him."

"I will, my holy quail."

"There was a man calling from New York. I guess about Allen. Isn't it exciting, their sending a plane for him? I can't get used to you owning the store. I know—it's all over town you're going to be town manager."

"I'm not."

"Well, I heard it a dozen times."

"I have a business deal that makes it impossible. I have to go out for a while, my darling. I have a meeting."

"Maybe I'll get to wish you were back a clerk. You were home nights then. What if the man calls back?"

"He can wait."

"He didn't want to. Will you be late?"

"Can't tell. Depends on how it goes."

"Wasn't it sad about Danny Taylor? Take a raincoat."

"Sure was."

In the hall I put on my hat and on an impulse picked old Cap'n's narwhal cane from the elephant foot. Ellen materialized beside me.

"Can I go with you?"

"Not tonight."

"I do love you."

I stared deep into my daughter for a moment. "I love you too," I said. "I'll bring you jewels—any favorites?"

She giggled. "You going to carry a cane?"

"For self-protection." I held the spiraled ivory at parry, like a broadsword.

"You going to be gone long?"

"Not long."

"Why do you take the cane?"

"Pure decoration, a boast, a threat, a fear, a vestigial need to bear arms."

"I'll wait up for you. Can I hold the pink thing?"

"Oh, no you won't, my little dung-flower. Pink thing? You mean the talisman? Sure you may."

"What's a talisman?"

"Look it up in the dictionary. Know how to spell it?"

"T-a-l-e-s-m-a-n."

"No, t-a-l-*i*-s-m-a-n."

"Why don't you tell me?"

"You'll know it better if you look it up."

She locked her arms around me and squeezed and as quickly let me go.

The night closed thick and damp about me, humid air about the consistency of chicken broth. The street lights hiding among the fat leaves of Elm Street sprouted damp, hairy halos of moisture.

A man with a job sees so little of the normal daylight world.

No wonder he must get his news and his attitudes from his wife. She knows what happened and who said what about it, but it is strained through her womanness, wherefore most working men see the daylight world through women's eyes. But in the night, when his store or his job is closed, then is a man's world risen—for a time.

The twisted staff of narwhal ivory felt good in my hand, its heavy silver knob polished by old Cap'n's palm.

Once long ago when I lived in a daylight world, the world being too much with me, I would have gone to grass. Face downward and very close to the green stems, I became one with ants and aphids and sow bugs, no longer a colossus. And in a ferocious jungle of the grass I found the distraction that meant peace.

Now in the night I wanted Old Harbor and the Place, where an inevitable world of cycles of life and time and of tide could smooth my raggedness.

I walked quickly to the High Street, and only glanced across at my green-curtained store as I passed the Foremaster. In front of the fire station fat Willie sat in the police car, red of face and sweating like a pig.

"You on the prowl again, Eth?"

"Yep."

"Terrible sad about Danny Taylor. Nice fella."

"Terrible," I said and hurried on.

A few cars cruised about, building a breeze, but there were no strollers. No one risked the sweat of walking.

I turned at the monument and walked toward Old Harbor and saw the anchor lights of a few yachts and offshore fishing craft. Then I saw a figure turn out of Porlock Street and come toward me and I knew by walk and posture it was Margie Young-Hunt.

She stopped in front of me, gave me no chance of passing. Some women can look cool on a hot night. Perhaps it was the breezy movement of her cotton skirt.

She said, "I guess you're looking for me." She replaced a strand of hair that wasn't out of place.

"Why do you say that?"

She turned and took my arm and with her fingers urged me to walk on. "That's the kind I get. I was in the Foremaster. I saw you go by and I thought you might be looking for me, so I whipped around the block and intercepted you."

"How'd you know which way I would turn?"

"I don't know. I knew. Listen to the cicadas—that's more hot weather and no wind. Don't worry, Ethan, we'll be out of the light in a moment. You can come to my place if you want. I'll give you a drink—a tall cold drink, from a tall hot woman."

I let her fingers guide me into the shadows of a grove of outgrown privet. Some kind of yellow blossoms near the ground burned the darkness.

"This is my house—a garage with a pleasure dome over it."

"What makes you think I was looking for you?"

"Me or someone like me. Ever see a bullfight, Ethan?"

"Once at Arles just after the war."

"My second husband used to take me. He loved them. I think bullfights are for men who aren't very brave and wish they were. If you saw one you'll know what I mean. Remember after all the cape work when the bull tries to kill something that isn't there?"

"Yes."

"Remember how he gets confused and uneasy, sometimes just stands and looks for an answer? Well, then they have to give him a horse or his heart will break. He has to get his horns into something solid or his spirit dies. Well, I'm that horse. And that's the kind of men I get, confused and puzzled. If they can get a horn into me, that's a little triumph. Then they can go back to *muleta* and *espada*."

"Margie!"

"Just a moment. I'm trying to find my key. Smell the honeysuckle!"

"But I've just had a triumph."

"You have? Hooked a cape—trampled it?"

"How do you know?"

"I just know when a man is looking for me, or some other Margie. Watch the stairs, they're narrow. Don't hit your head at the top. Now, here's the switch—you see? A pleasure dome, soft lights, smell of musk—down to a sunless sea!"

"I guess you're a witch all right."

"You know goddam well I am. A poor, pitiful small-town witch. Sit there, near the window. I'll turn on the fake breeze.

I'm going to what they call 'slip into something comfortable,' then I'll get you a tall cool skull-buster."

"Where'd you hear that word?"

"You know where I heard it."

"Did you know him well?"

"Part of him. The part of a man a woman can know. Sometimes that's the best part, but not often. It was with Danny. He trusted me."

The room was a memory album of other rooms, bits and pieces of other lives like footnotes. The fan at the window made a small whispering roar.

She came back soon in long, loose, billowing blue and brought a cloud of scent. When I breathed it in she said, "Don't worry. It's a cologne Mary has never smelled on me. Here's a drink—gin and tonic. I rubbed the glass with tonic. It's gin, just gin. If you rattle the ice, you'll think it's cool."

I drank it down like beer and felt its dry heat reach out over my shoulders and down my arms so that my skin shimmered.

"I guess you needed that," she said.

"I guess so."

"I'll make a brave bull of you—enough resistance so you'll think you have a triumph. That's what a bull needs."

I stared at my hands, crisscrossed with scratches and tiny cuts from opening boxes, and my nails, not too clean.

She took the ivory stick from the couch where I had dropped it. "I hope you don't need this for your drooping passion."

"Are you my enemy, now?"

"Me, New Baytown's playmate, your enemy?"

I was silent so long that I could feel her growing restless. "Take your time," she said. "You've got all your life to answer. I'll get you a drink."

I took the full glass from her and my lips and mouth were so dry I had to sip from it before I could speak, and when I did my throat wore a husk.

"What do you want?"

"I might have settled for love."

"From a man who loves his wife?"

"Mary? You don't even know her."

"I know she's tender and sweet and kind of helpless."

"Helpless? She's tough as a boot. She'll go right on long after you've rattled your engine to pieces. She's like a gull that uses the wind to stay aloft and never beats a wing."

"That's not true."

"Comes a big trouble, she'll breeze through while you burn up."

"What do you want?"

"Aren't you going to make a pass? Aren't you going to beat out your hatred with your hips on good old Margie?"

I set my half-emptied glass down on a side table, and quick as a snake she lifted it and put an ash tray under it, and dried the ring of moisture with her hand.

"Margie—I want to know about you."

"No kidding. You want to know what I thought of your performance."

"I can't figure what you want until I know who you are."

"I believe the man means it—the dollar tour. Through Margie Young-Hunt with gun and camera. I was a good little kid, a smart little kid and a medium lousy dancer. Met what they call an older man and married him. He didn't love me—he was in love with me. That's on a silver platter for a good smart little kid. I didn't like to dance much and I sure as hell didn't like to work. When I dumped him he was so mixed up he didn't even put a remarriage clause in the settlement. Married another guy and led a big world whirl that killed him. For twenty years that check has zeroed in on the first of every month. For twenty years I haven't done a lick of work, except pick up a few presents from admirers. Doesn't seem like twenty years, but it is. I'm not a good little kid any more."

She went to her little kitchen and brought three ice cubes in her hand, dumped them into her glass, and sloshed gin over them. The muttering fan brought in the smell of sea flats exposed by the dropping tide. She said softly, "You're going to make a lot of money, Ethan."

"You know about the deal?"

"Some of the noblest Romans of them all are creepers."

"Go on."

She made a sweeping gesture with her hand and her glass went flying; the ice cubes bounced back from the wall like dice.

"Lover boy had a stroke last week. When he cools, the

checks stop. I'm old and lazy and I'm scared. I set you up as a backlog, but I don't trust you. You might break the rules. You might turn honest. I tell you I'm scared."

I stood up and found my legs were heavy, not wavery—just heavy and remote.

"What have you got to work with?"

"Marullo was my friend too."

"I see."

"Don't you want to go to bed with me? I'm good. That's what they tell me."

"I don't hate you."

"That's why I don't trust you."

"We'll try to work something out. I hate Baker. Maybe you can clip him."

"What language. You're not working on your drink."

"Drink's for happy times with me."

"Does Baker know what you did to Danny?"

"Yes."

"How'd he take it?"

"All right. But I wouldn't like to turn my back."

"Alfio should have turned his back to you."

"What do you mean by that?"

"Only what I guess. But I'd make book on my guess. Don't worry, I won't tell him. Marullo is my friend."

"I think I understand; you're building up a hate so you can use the sword. Margie, you've got a rubber sword."

"Think I don't know it Eth? But I've got my money on a hunch."

"Do you want to tell me?"

"Might as well. I'm betting ten generations of Hawleys are going to kick your ass around the block, and when they leave off you'll have your own wet rope and salt to rub in the wounds."

"If that were so—where does it leave you?"

"You're going to need a friend to talk to and I'm the only person in the world who fills the bill. A secret's a terribly lonesome thing, Ethan. And it won't cost you much, maybe only a small percentage."

"I think I'll go now."

"Drink your drink."

"I don't want it."

"Don't bump your head going downstairs, Ethan."

I was halfway down when she followed me. "Did you mean to leave your stick?"

"Lord, no."

"Here it is. I thought it might be a kind of—sacrifice."

It was raining and that makes honeysuckle smell sweet in the night. My legs were so wobbly that I really needed the narwhal stick.

Fat Willie had a roll of paper towels on the seat beside him to mop the sweat from his head.

"I'll give you odds I know who she is."

"You'd win."

"Say, Eth, there's been a guy looking for you—guy in a big Chrysler, with a chauffeur."

"What'd he want?"

"I don't know. Wanted to know if I seen you. I didn't give a peep."

"You'll get a Christmas present, Willie."

"Say, Eth, what's the matter with your feet?"

"Been playing poker. They went to sleep."

"Yeah! they'll do that. If I see the guy, shall I tell him you've went home?"

"Tell him to come to the store tomorrow."

"Chrysler Imperial. Big son of a bitch, long as a freight car."

Joey-boy was standing on the sidewalk in front of the Foremaster, looking limp and humid.

"Thought you were going into New York for a cold bottle."

"Too hot. Couldn't put my heart in it. Come in and have a drink, Ethan. I'm feeling low."

"Too hot for a drink, Morph."

"Even a beer?"

"Beer heats me up."

"Story of my life. When the cards are down—no place to go. Nobody to talk to."

"You should get married."

"That's nobody to talk to in spades."

"Maybe you're right."

"Damn right I am. There's nobody as lonely as an all-married man."

"How do you know?"

"I see 'em. I'm looking at one. Guess I'll get a bag of cold beer and see if Margie Young-Hunt will play. She don't keep hours."

"I don't think she's in town, Morph. She told my wife—at least I think she did—that she was going up to Maine till the heat is over."

"Goddam her. Well—her loss is the barkeep's gain. I'll tell him the sad episodes of a misspent life. He don't listen either. So long, Eth. Walk with God! That's what they say in Mexico."

The narwhal stick tapped on the pavement and punctuated my wondering about why I told Joey that. She wouldn't talk. That would spoil her game. She had to keep the pin in her hand grenade. I don't know why.

I could see the Chrysler standing at the curb by the old Hawley house when I turned into Elm Street from the High, but it was more like a hearse than a freight car, black but not gleaming by reason of the droplets of rain and the greasy splash that rises from the highways. It carried frosted parking lights.

It must have been very late. No lights shone from the sleeping houses on Elm Street. I was wet and I must somewhere have stepped in a puddle. My shoes made a juicy squidging sound as I walked.

I saw a man in a chauffeur's cap through the musty windshield. I stopped beside the monster car and rapped with my knuckles on the glass and the window slid down with an electric whine. I felt the unnatural climate of air-conditioning on my face.

"I'm Ethan Hawley. Are you looking for me?" I saw teeth in the dimness—gleaming teeth picked out by our street light.

The door sprang open of itself and a lean, well-tailored man stepped out. "I'm Dunscombe, Brock and Schwin, television branch. I have to talk to you." He looked toward the driver. "Not here. Can we go inside?"

"I guess so. I think everyone's asleep. If you talk quietly . . ."

He followed me up our walk of flagstones set in the spongy lawn. The night light was burning in the hall. As we went in I put the narwhal stick in the elephant's foot.

I turned on the reading light over my big sprung-bottomed chair.

The house was quiet, but it seemed to me the wrong kind of

quiet—a nervous quiet. I glanced up the stairwell at the bedroom doors above.

"Must be important to come this late."

"It is."

I could see him now. His teeth were his ambassadors, unhelped by his weary but wary eyes.

"We want to keep this private. It's been a bad year, as you well know. The bottom fell out with the quiz scandals and then the payola fuss and the Congressional committees. We have to watch everything. It's a dangerous time."

"I wish you'd tell me what you want."

"You've read your boy's I Love America essay?"

"No, I haven't. He wanted to surprise me."

"He has. I don't know why we didn't catch it, but we didn't." He held out a folded blue cover to me. "Read the underlining."

I sank into my chair and opened it. It was either printed or typed by one of those new machines that looks like type, but it was marred with harsh black pencil lines down both margins.

I LOVE AMERICA

by

ETHAN ALLEN HAWLEY II

"What is an individual man? An atom, almost invisible without a magnifying glass—a mere speck upon the surface of the universe; not a second in time compared to immeasurable, never-beginning and never-ending eternity, a drop of water in the great deep which evaporates and is borne off by the winds, a grain of sand, which is soon gathered to the dust from which it sprung. Shall a being so small, so petty, so fleeting, so evanescent oppose itself to the onward march of a great nation which is to subsist for ages and ages to come, oppose itself to that long line of posterity which springing from our loins will endure during the existence of the world? Let us look to our country, elevate ourselves to the dignity of pure and disinterested patriots, and save our country from all impending dangers. What are we—what is any man—worth who is not ready and willing to sacrifice himself for his country?"

I riffled through the pages and saw the black marks everywhere.

"Do you recognize it?"

"No. It sounds familiar—sounds like maybe somewhere in the last century."

"It is. It's Henry Clay, delivered in 1850."

"And the rest? All Clay?"

"No—bits and pieces, some Daniel Webster, some Jefferson, and, God help me, a swatch from Lincoln's Second Inaugural. I don't know how that got past. I guess because there were thousands of them. Thank Christ we caught it in time—after all the quiz troubles and Van Doren and all."

"It doesn't sound like the prose style of a boy."

"I don't know how it happened. And it might have gone through if we hadn't got the postcard."

"Postcard?"

"Picture postcard, picture of the Empire State Building."

"Who sent it?"

"Anonymous."

"Where was it mailed from?"

"New York."

"Let me see it."

"It's under lock and key in case there's any trouble. You don't want to make trouble, do you?"

"What is it you want?"

"I want you to forget the whole thing. We'll just drop the whole thing and forget it—if you will."

"It's not a thing easy to forget."

"Hell, I mean just keep your lip buttoned—don't give us any trouble. It's been a bad year. Election year anybody will dig up anything."

I closed the rich blue covers and handed it back to him. "I won't give you any trouble."

His teeth showed like matched pearls. "I knew it. I told them. I looked you up. You have a good record—good family."

"Will you go away now?"

"You've got to know I understand how you feel."

"Thank you. And I know how you feel. What you can cover up doesn't exist."

"I don't want to go away leaving you angry. Public relations is my line. We could work something out. Scholarship or like that—something dignified."

"Has sin gone on strike for a wage raise? No, just go away now—please!"

"We'll work something out."

"I'm sure you will."

I let him out and sat down again and turned out the light and sat listening to my house. It thudded like a heart, and maybe it was my heart and a rustling old house. I thought to go to the cabinet and take the talisman in my hand—had stood up to get it.

I heard a crunching sound and a whinny like a frightened colt, and quick steps in the hall and silence. My shoes squidged on the stairs. I went in to Ellen's room and switched on the light. She was balled up under a sheet, her head under her pillow. When I tried to lift the pillow she clung to it and I had to yank it away. A line of blood ran from the corner of her mouth.

"I slipped in the bathroom."

"I see. Are you badly hurt?"

"I don't think so."

"In other words, it's none of my business."

"I didn't want him to go to jail."

Allen was sitting on the edge of his bed, naked except for jockey shorts. His eyes—they made me think of a mouse in a corner, ready at last to fight a broom.

"The stinking sneak!"

"Did you hear it all?"

"I heard what that stinking sneak did."

"Did you hear what you did?"

The driven mouse attacked. "Who cares? Everybody does it. It's the way the cooky crumbles."

"You believe that?"

"Don't you read the papers? Everybody right up to the top—just read the papers. You get to feeling holy, just read the papers. I bet you took some in your time, because they all do. I'm not going to take the rap for everybody. I don't care about anything. Except that stinking sneak."

Mary awakens slowly, but she was awake. Perhaps she hadn't been asleep. She was in Ellen's room, sitting on the edge of the bed. The street light made her plain enough with shadows of leaves moving on her face. She was a rock, a great granite rock set in a tide race. It was true. She was tough as a boot, unmoving, unyielding, and safe.

"Will you be coming to bed, Ethan?"

So she had been listening too.

"Not now, my darling dear."

"Are you going out again?"

"Yes—to walk."

"You need your sleep. It's still raining. Do you have to go?"

"Yes. There's a place. I have to go there."

"Take your raincoat. You forgot it before."

"Yes, my darling."

I didn't kiss her then. I couldn't with the balled and covered figure beside her. But I touched her shoulder and I touched her face and she was tough as a boot.

I went to the bathroom for a moment for a package of razor blades.

I was in the hall, reaching in the closet for a raincoat as Mary wished, when I heard a scuffle and a scramble and a rush and Ellen flung herself at me, grunting and snuffling. She buried her bleeding nose against my breast and pinned my elbows down with encircling arms. And her whole little body shook.

I took her by the forelock and pulled her head up under the hall night light.

"Take me with you."

"Silly, I can't. But if you'll come in the kitchen, I'll wash your face."

"Take me with you. You're not coming back."

"What do you mean, skookum? Of course I'm coming back. I'm always coming back. You go up to bed and rest. Then you'll feel better."

"You won't take me?"

"Where I'm going they wouldn't let you in. Do you want to stand outside in your nightgown?"

"You can't."

She grappled me again and her hands caressed and stroked my arms, my sides, dug her balled fists into my side pockets so that I was afraid she might find the razor blades. She was always a caressing girl, a stroking girl, and a surprising girl. Suddenly she released me and stood back with her head raised and her eyes level and without tears. I kissed her dirty little cheek and felt the dried blood against my mouth. And then I turned to the door.

"Don't you want your stick?"

"No, Ellen. Not tonight. Go to bed, darling. Go to bed."

I ran away fast. I guess I ran away from her and from Mary. I could hear Mary coming down the stairs with measured steps.

Chapter XXII

THE tide was on the rise. I waded into the warm bay water and clambered into the Place. A slow ground swell moved in and out of the entrance, flowed through my trousers. The fat billfold in my hip pocket swelled against my hip and then grew thinner under my weight as it water-soaked. The summer sea was crowded with little jellyfish the size of gooseberries, dangling their tendrils and their nettle cells. As they washed in against my legs and belly I felt them sting like small bitter fires, and the slow wave breathed in and out of the Place. The rain was only a thin mist now and it accumulated all the stars and town lamps and spread them evenly—a dark, pewter-colored sheen. I could see the third rock, but from the Place it did not line up with the point over the sunken keel of the *Belle-Adair*. A stronger wave lifted my legs and made them feel free and separate from me, and an eager wind sprang from nowhere and drove the mist like sheep. Then I could see a star—late rising, too late rising over the edge. Some kind of craft came chugging in, a craft with sail, by the slow, solemn sound of her engine. I saw her mast light over the toothy tumble of the breakwater but her red and green were below my range of sight.

My skin blazed under the lances of the jellyfish. I heard an anchor plunge, and the mast light went out.

Marullo's light still burned, and old Cap'n's light and Aunt Deborah's light.

It isn't true that there's a community of light, a bonfire of the world. Everyone carries his own, his lonely own.

A rustling school of tiny feeding fish flicked along the shore.

My light is out. There's nothing blacker than a wick.

Inward I said, I want to go home—no not home, to the other side of home where the lights are given.

It's so much darker when a light goes out than it would have been if it had never shone. The world is full of dark derelicts. The better way—the Marulli of that old Rome would have known it—there comes a time for decent, honorable retirement, not dramatic, not punishment of self or family—just good-by, a warm bath and an opened vein, a warm sea and a razor blade.

The ground swell on the rising tide whished into the Place and raised my legs and hips and swung them to the side and carried my wet folded raincoat out with it.

I rolled on one hip and reached in my side pocket for my razor blades and I felt the lump. Then in wonder I remembered the caressing, stroking hands of the light-bearer. For a moment it resisted coming out of my wet pocket. Then in my hand it gathered every bit of light there was and seemed red—dark red.

A surge of wave pushed me against the very back of the Place. And the tempo of the sea speeded up. I had to fight the water to get out, and I had to get out. I rolled and scrambled and splashed chest deep in the surf and the brisking waves pushed me against the old sea wall.

I had to get back—had to return the talisman to its new owner.

Else another light might go out.

TRAVELS WITH CHARLEY

IN SEARCH OF AMERICA

This book is dedicated to Harold Guinzburg with respect born of an association and affection that just growed.

—JOHN STEINBECK

Part One

WHEN I very young and the urge to be someplace else was on me, I was assured by mature people that maturity would cure this itch. When years described me as mature, the remedy prescribed was middle age. In middle age I was assured that greater age would calm my fever and now that I am fifty-eight perhaps senility will do the job. Nothing has worked. Four hoarse blasts of a ship's whistle still raise the hair on my neck and set my feet to tapping. The sound of a jet, an engine warming up, even the clopping of shod hooves on pavement brings on the ancient shudder, the dry mouth and vacant eye, the hot palms and the churn of stomach high up under the rib cage. In other words, I don't improve; in further words, once a bum always a bum. I fear the disease is incurable. I set this matter down not to instruct others but to inform myself.

When the virus of restlessness begins to take possession of a wayward man, and the road away from Here seems broad and straight and sweet, the victim must first find in himself a good and sufficient reason for going. This to the practical bum is not difficult. He has a built-in garden of reasons to choose from. Next he must plan his trip in time and space, choose a direction and a destination. And last he must implement the journey. How to go, what to take, how long to stay. This part of the process is invariable and immortal. I set it down only so that newcomers to bumdom, like teen-agers in new-hatched sin, will not think they invented it.

Once a journey is designed, equipped, and put in process, a new factor enters and takes over. A trip, a safari, an exploration, is an entity, different from all other journeys. It has personality, temperament, individuality, uniqueness. A journey is a person in itself; no two are alike. And all plans, safeguards, policing, and coercion are fruitless. We find after years of struggle that we do not take a trip; a trip takes us. Tour masters, schedules, reservations, brassbound and inevitable, dash themselves to wreckage on the personality of the trip. Only when this is recognized can the blown-in-the-glass bum relax and go along with it. Only then do the frustrations fall away. In this a journey is like marriage. The certain way to be wrong is to think you control it. I feel better now, having said this, although only those who have experienced it will understand it.

*

My plan was clear, concise, and reasonable, I think. For many years I have traveled in many parts of the world. In America I live in New York, or dip into Chicago or San Francisco. But New York is no more America than Paris is France or London is England. Thus I discovered that I did not know my own country. I, an American writer, writing about America, was working from memory, and the memory is at best a faulty, warpy reservoir. I had not heard the speech of America, smelled the grass and trees and sewage, seen its hills and water, its color and quality of light. I knew the changes only from books and newspapers. But more than this, I had not felt the country for twenty-five years. In short, I was writing of something I did not know about, and it seems to me that in a so-called writer this is criminal. My memories were distorted by twenty-five intervening years.

Once I traveled about in an old bakery wagon, double-doored rattler with a mattress on its floor. I stopped where people stopped or gathered, I listened and looked and felt, and in the process had a picture of my country the accuracy of which was impaired only by my own shortcomings.

So it was that I determined to look again, to try to rediscover this monster land. Otherwise, in writing, I could not tell the small diagnostic truths which are the foundations of the larger truth. One sharp difficulty presented itself. In the intervening twenty-five years my name had become reasonably well known. And it has been my experience that when people have heard of you, favorably or not, they change; they become, through shyness or the other qualities that publicity inspires, something they are not under ordinary circumstances. This being so, my trip demanded that I leave my name and my identity at home. I had to be peripatetic eyes and ears, a kind of moving gelatin plate. I could not sign hotel registers, meet people I knew, interview others, or even ask searching questions. Furthermore, two or more people disturb the ecologic complex of an area. I had to go alone and I had to be self-contained, a kind of casual turtle carrying his house on his back.

With all this in mind I wrote to the head office of a great corporation which manufactures trucks. I specified my purpose and my needs. I wanted a three-quarter-ton pick-up truck, capable of going anywhere under possibly rigorous conditions, and on this truck I wanted a little house built like the cabin of a small boat. A trailer is difficult to maneuver on mountain roads, is impossible and often illegal to park, and is subject to many restrictions. In due time, specifications came through, for a tough, fast, comfortable vehicle, mounting a camper top —a little house with double bed, a four-burner stove, a heater, refrigerator and lights operating on butane, a chemical toilet, closet space, storage space, windows screened against insects—exactly what I wanted. It was delivered in the summer to my little fishing place at Sag Harbor near the end of Long Island. Although I didn't want to start before Labor Day, when the nation settles back to normal living, I did want to get used to my turtle shell, to equip it and learn it. It arrived in August, a beautiful thing, powerful and yet lithe. It was almost as easy to handle as a passenger car. And because my planned trip had aroused some satiric remarks among my friends, I named it Rocinante, which you will remember was the name of Don Quixote's horse.

Since I made no secret of my project, a number of controversies arose among my friends and advisers. (A projected journey spawns advisers in schools.) I was told that since my photograph was as widely distributed as my publisher could make it, I would find it impossible to move about without being recognized. Let me say in advance that in over ten thousand miles, in thirty-four states, I was not recognized even once. I believe that people identify things only in context. Even those people who might have known me against a background I am supposed to have, in no case identified me in Rocinante.

I was advised that the name Rocinante painted on the side of my truck in sixteenth-century Spanish script would cause curiosity and inquiry in some places. I do not know how many people recognized the name, but surely no one ever asked about it.

Next, I was told that a stranger's purpose in moving about the country might cause inquiry or even suspicion. For this reason I racked a shotgun, two rifles, and a couple of fishing rods in my truck, for it is my experience that if a man is going hunting or fishing his purpose is understood and even applauded. Actually, my hunting days are over. I no longer kill or catch anything I cannot get into a frying pan; I am too old for sport killing. This stage setting turned out to be unnecessary.

It was said that my New York license plates would arouse interest and perhaps questions, since they were the only outward identifying marks I had. And so they did—perhaps twenty or thirty times in the whole trip. But such contacts followed an invariable pattern, somewhat as follows:

Local man: "New York, huh?"

Me: "Yep."

Local man: "I was there in nineteen thirty-eight—or was it thirty-nine? Alice, was it thirty-eight or thirty-nine we went to New York?"

Alice: "It was thirty-six. I remember because it was the year Alfred died."

Local man: "Anyway, I hated it. Wouldn't live there if you paid me."

There was some genuine worry about my traveling alone, open to attack, robbery, assault. It is well known that our roads are dangerous. And here I admit I had senseless qualms. It is some years since I have been alone, nameless, friendless, without any of the safety one gets from family, friends, and accomplices. There is no reality in the danger. It's just a very lonely, helpless feeling at first—a kind of desolate feeling. For this reason I took one companion on my journey—an old French gentleman poodle known as Charley. Actually his name is Charles le Chien. He was born in Bercy on the outskirts of Paris and trained in France, and while he knows a little poodle-English, he responds quickly only to commands in French. Otherwise he has to translate, and that slows him down. He is a very big poodle, of a color called *bleu*, and he is blue when he is clean. Charley is a born diplomat. He prefers negotiation to fighting, and properly so, since he is very bad at fighting. Only once in his ten years has he been in trouble—when he met a dog who refused to negotiate. Charley lost a piece of his right ear that time. But he is a good watch dog—has a roar like a lion, designed to conceal from night-wandering strangers the fact that he couldn't bite his way out of a *cornet du papier*. He is a good friend and traveling companion, and would rather travel about than anything he can imagine. If he occurs at length in this account, it is because he contributed much to the trip. A dog, particularly an exotic like Charley, is a bond between strangers. Many conversations en route began with "What degree of a dog is that?"

The techniques of opening conversation are universal. I knew long ago and rediscovered that the best way to attract attention, help, and conversation is to be lost. A man who seeing his mother starving to death on a path kicks her in the stomach to clear the way, will cheerfully devote several hours of his time giving wrong directions to a total stranger who claims to be lost.

*

UNDER the big oak trees of my place at Sag Harbor sat Rocinante, handsome and self-contained, and neighbors came to visit, some neighbors we didn't even know we had. I saw in their eyes something I was to see over and over in every part of the nation—a burning desire to go, to move, to get under way, anyplace, away from any Here. They spoke quietly of how they wanted to go someday, to move about, free and unanchored, not toward something but away from something. I saw this look and heard this yearning everywhere in every state I visited. Nearly every American hungers to move. One small boy about thirteen years old came back every day. He stood apart shyly and looked at Rocinante; he peered in the door, even lay on the ground and studied the heavy-duty springs. He was a silent, ubiquitous small boy. He even came at night to stare at Rocinante. After a week he could stand it no longer. His words wrestled their way hell-bent through his shyness. He said, "If you'll take me with you, why, I'll do anything. I'll cook, I'll wash all the dishes, and do all the work and I'll take care of you."

Unfortunately for me I knew his longing. "I wish I could," I said. "But the school board and your parents and lots of others say I can't."

"I'll do anything," he said. And I believe he would. I don't think he ever gave up until I drove away without him. He had the dream I've had all my life, and there is no cure.

Equipping Rocinante was a long and pleasant process. I took far too many things, but I didn't know what I would find. Tools for emergency, tow lines, a small block and tackle, a trenching tool and crowbar, tools for making and fixing and improvising. Then there were emergency foods. I would be late in the northwest and caught by snow. I prepared for at least a week of emergency. Water was easy; Rocinante carried a thirty-gallon tank.

I thought I might do some writing along the way, perhaps essays, surely notes, certainly letters. I took paper, carbon, typewriter, pencils, notebooks, and not only those but dictionaries, a compact encyclopedia, and a dozen other reference books, heavy ones. I suppose our capacity for self-delusion is boundless. I knew very well that I rarely make notes, and if I do I either lose them or can't read them. I also knew from thirty years of my profession that I cannot write hot on an event. It has to ferment. I must do what a friend calls "mule it over" for a time before it goes down. And in spite of this self-knowledge I equipped Rocinante with enough writing material to take care of ten volumes. Also I laid in a hundred and fifty pounds of those books one hasn't got around to reading—and of course those are the books one isn't ever going to get around to reading. Canned goods, shotgun shells, rifle cartridges, tool boxes, and far too many clothes, blankets and pillows, and many too many shoes and boots, padded nylon sub-zero underwear, plastic dishes and cups and a plastic dishpan, a spare tank of bottled gas. The overloaded springs sighed and settled lower and lower. I judge now that I carried about four times too much of everything.

Now, Charley is a mind-reading dog. There have been many trips in his lifetime, and often he has to be left at home. He knows we are going long before the suitcases come out, and he paces and worries and whines and goes into a state of mild hysteria, old as he is. During the weeks of preparation he was underfoot the whole time and made a damned nuisance of himself. He took to hiding in the truck, creeping in and trying to make himself look small.

Labor Day approached, the day of truth when millions of kids would be back in school and tens of millions of parents would be off the highways. I was prepared to set out as soon after that as possible. And about that time hurricane Donna was reported tromping her way out of the Caribbean in our direction. On Long Island's tip, we have had enough of that to be highly respectful. With a hurricane approaching we prepare to stand a siege. Our little bay is fairly well protected, but not that well. As Donna crept toward us I filled the kerosene lamps, activated the hand pump to the well, and tied down everything movable. I have a twenty-two-foot cabin boat, the *Fayre Eleyne.* I battened her down and took her to the middle of the bay, put down a huge old-fashioned hook anchor and half-inch chain, and moored her with a long swing. With that rig she could ride a hundred-and-fifty-mile wind unless her bow pulled out.

Donna sneaked on. We brought out a battery radio for reports, since the power would go off if Donna struck. But there was one added worry—Rocinante, sitting among the trees. In a waking nightmare I saw a tree crash down on the truck and crush her like a bug. I placed her away from a possible direct fall, but that didn't mean that the whole top of a tree might not fly fifty feet through the air and smash her.

By early morning we knew by radio that we were going to get it, and by ten o'clock we heard that the eye would pass over us and that it would reach us at 1:07—some exact time like that. Our bay was quiet, without a ripple, but the water was still dark and the *Fayre Eleyne* rode daintily slack against her mooring.

Our bay is better protected than most, so that many small craft came cruising in for mooring. And I saw with fear that many of their owners didn't know how to moor. Finally two boats, pretty things, came in, one towing the other. A light anchor went down and they were left, the bow of one tethered to the stern of the other and both within the swing of the *Fayre*

Eleyne. I took a megaphone to the end of my pier and tried to protest against this foolishness, but the owners either did not hear or did not know or did not care.

The wind struck on the moment we were told it would, and ripped the water like a black sheet. It hammered like a fist. The whole top of an oak tree crashed down, grazing the cottage where we watched. The next gust stove one of the big windows in. I forced it back and drove wedges in top and bottom with a hand ax. Electric power and telephones went out with the first blast, as we knew they must. And eight-foot tides were predicted. We watched the wind rip at earth and sea like a surging pack of terriers. The trees plunged and bent like grasses, and the whipped water raised a cream of foam. A boat broke loose and tobogganed up on the shore, and then another. Houses built in the benign spring and early summer took waves in their second-story windows. Our cottage is on a little hill thirty feet above sea level. But the rising tide washed over my high pier. As the wind changed direction I moved Rocinante to keep her always to leeward of our big oaks. The *Fayre Eleyne* rode gallantly, swinging like a weather vane away from the changing wind.

The boats which had been tethered one to the other had fouled up by now, the tow line under propeller and rudder and the two hulls bashing and scraping together. Another craft had dragged its anchor and gone ashore on a mud bank.

Charley dog has no nerves. Gunfire or thunder, explosions or high winds leave him utterly unconcerned. In the midst of the howling storm, he found a warm place under a table and went to sleep.

The wind stopped as suddenly as it had begun, and although the waves continued out of rhythm they were not wind-tattered, and the tide rose higher and higher. All the piers around our little bay had disappeared under water, and only their piles or hand rails showed. The silence was like a rushing sound. The radio told us we were in the eye of Donna, the still and frightening calm in the middle of the revolving storm. I don't know how long the calm lasted. It seemed a long time of waiting. And then the other side struck us, the wind from the opposite direction. The *Fayre Eleyne* swung sweetly around and put her bow into the wind. But the two lashed boats dragged anchor, swarmed down on *Fayre Eleyne*, and bracketed her. She was dragged fighting and protesting downwind and forced against a neighboring pier, and we could hear her hull crying against the oaken piles. The wind registered over ninety-five miles now.

I found myself running, fighting the wind around the head of the bay toward the pier where the boats were breaking up. I think my wife, for whom the *Fayre Eleyne* is named, ran after me, shouting orders for me to stop. The floor of the pier was four feet under water, but piles stuck up and offered handholds. I worked my way out little by little up to my breast pockets, the shore-driven wind slapping water in my mouth. My boat cried and whined against the piles, and plunged like a frightened calf. Then I jumped and fumbled my way aboard her. For the first time in my life I had a knife when I needed it. The bracketing wayward boats were pushing *Eleyne* against the pier. I cut anchor line and tow line and kicked them free, and they blew ashore on the mudbank. But *Eleyne*'s anchor chain was intact, and that great old mud hook was still down, a hundred pounds of iron with spear-shaped flukes wide as a shovel.

Eleyne's engine is not always obedient, but this day it started at a touch. I hung on, standing on the deck, reaching inboard for wheel and throttle and clutch with my left hand. And that boat tried to help—I suppose she was that scared. I edged her out and worked up the anchor chain with my right hand. Under ordinary conditions I can barely pull that anchor with both hands in a calm. But everything went right this time. I edged over the hook and it tipped up and freed its spades. Then I lifted it clear of the bottom and nosed into the wind and gave it throttle and we headed into that goddamn wind and gained on it. It was as though we pushed our way through thick porridge. A hundred yards offshore I let the hook go and it plunged down and grabbed bottom, and the *Fayre Eleyne* straightened and raised her bow and seemed to sigh with relief.

Well, there I was, a hundred yards offshore with Donna baying over me like a pack of white-whiskered hounds. No skiff could possibly weather it for a minute. I saw a piece of branch go skidding by and simply jumped in after it. There was no danger. If I could keep my head up I had to blow ashore, but I admit the half-Wellington rubber boots I wore got pretty heavy. It couldn't have been more than three minutes before I grounded and that other Fayre Eleyne and a neighbor pulled me out. It was only then that I began to shake all over, but looking out and seeing our little boat riding well and safely was nice. I must have strained something pulling that anchor with one hand, because I needed a little help home; a tumbler of whisky on the kitchen table was some help too. I've tried since to raise that anchor with one hand and I can't do it.

The wind died quickly and left us to wreckage—power lines down, and no telephone for a week. But Rocinante was not damaged at all.

Part Two

In long-range planning for a trip, I think there is a private conviction that it won't happen. As the day approached, my warm bed and comfortable house grew increasingly desirable and my dear wife incalculably precious. To give these up for three months for the terrors of the uncomfortable and unknown seemed crazy. I didn't want to go. Something had to happen to forbid my going, but it didn't. I could get sick, of course, but that was one of my main but secret reasons for going at all. During the previous winter I had become rather seriously ill with one of those carefully named difficulties which are the whispers of approaching age. When I came out of it I received the usual lecture about slowing up, losing weight, limiting the cholesterol intake. It happens to many men, and I think doctors have memorized the litany. It had happened to so many of my friends. The lecture ends, "Slow down. You're not as young as you once were." And I had seen so many begin to pack their lives in cotton wool, smother their impulses, hood their passions, and gradually retire from their manhood into a kind of spiritual and physical semi-invalidism. In this they are encouraged by wives and relatives, and it's such a sweet trap.

Who doesn't like to be a center for concern? A kind of second childhood falls on so many men. They trade their violence for the promise of a small increase of life span. In effect, the head of the house becomes the youngest child. And I have searched myself for this possibility with a kind of horror. For I have always lived violently, drunk hugely, eaten too much or not at all, slept around the clock or missed two nights of sleeping, worked too hard and too long in glory, or slobbed for a time in utter laziness. I've lifted, pulled, chopped, climbed, made love with joy and taken my hangovers as a consequence, not as a punishment. I did not want to surrender fierceness for a small gain in yardage. My wife married a man; I saw no reason why she should inherit a baby. I knew that ten or twelve thousand miles driving a truck, alone and unattended, over every kind of road, would be hard work, but to me it represented the antidote for the poison of the professional sick man. And in my own life I am not willing to trade quality for quantity. If this projected journey should prove too much then it was time to go anyway. I see too many men delay their exits with a sickly, slow reluctance to leave the stage. It's bad theater as well as bad living. I am very fortunate in having a wife who likes being a woman, which means that she likes men, not elderly babies. Although this last foundation for the journey was never discussed, I am sure she understood it.

The morning came, a bright one with the tawny look of autumn in the sunlight. My wife and I parted very quickly, since both of us hate good-bys, and neither one of us wanted to be left when the other had gone. She gunned her motor and exploded away for New York and I, with Charley beside me, drove Rocinante to the Shelter Island Ferry, and then to a second ferry to Greenport and a third from Orient Point to the coast of Connecticut, across Long Island Sound, for I wanted to avoid New York traffic and get well on my way. And I confess to a feeling of gray desolation.

On the ferry deck the sun was sharp and the coast of the mainland only an hour away. A lovely sloop stood away from us, her genoa set like a curving scarf, and all the coastal craft trudged up the Sound or wallowed heavily toward New York. Then a submarine slipped to the surface half a mile away, and the day lost part of its brightness. Farther away another dark creature slashed through the water, and another; of course they are based in New London, and this is their home. And perhaps they are keeping the world's peace with this venom. I wish I could like submarines, for then I might find them beautiful, but they are designed for destruction, and while they may explore and chart the sea bottom, and draw new trade lines under the Arctic ice, their main purpose is threat. And I remember too well crossing the Atlantic on a troop ship and knowing that somewhere on the way the dark things lurked searching for us with their single-stalk eyes. Somehow the light goes bleak for me when I see them and remember burned men pulled from the oil-slicked sea. And now submarines are armed with mass murder, our silly, only way of deterring mass murder.

Only a few people stood in the wind on the top deck of the clanking iron ferry boat. A young man in a trench coat, with cornsilk hair and delphinium eyes red-edged by the dull wind, turned to me and then pointed. "That's the new one," he said. "She can stay down three months."

"How can you tell them?"

"I know them. I'm on them."

"Atomic?"

"Not yet, but I've got an uncle on one, and maybe pretty soon."

"You're not in uniform."

"Just had a leave."

"Do you like to serve on them?"

"Sure I do. The pay's good and there's all kinds of—future."

"Would you like to be down three months?"

"You'd get used to it. The food's good and there's movies and—I'd like to go under the Pole, wouldn't you?"

"I guess I would."

"And there's movies and all kinds of—future."

"Where are you from?"

"From over there—New London—born there. My uncle's in the service and two cousins. I guess we're a kind of submarine family."

"They worry me."

"Oh, you'd get over that, sir. Pretty soon you wouldn't even think you were submerged—that is, if you haven't got something wrong with you. Ever had claustrophobia?"

"No."

"Well, then. You soon get used to it. Care to go below for a cup of coffee? There's plenty of time."

"Sure I would."

And could be he's right and I'm wrong. It's his world, not mine any more. There's no anger in his delphinium eyes and no fear and no hatred either, so maybe it's all right. It's just a job with good pay and a future. I must not put my memories and my fear on him. Maybe it won't be true again, but that's his lookout. It's his world now. Perhaps he understands things I will never learn.

We drank our coffee out of paper cups, and through the square ferry windows he pointed out the dry docks and the skeletons of new submarines.

"Nice thing about it is if there's a storm you can submerge, and it's quiet. Sleep like a baby and all hell busting loose up above." He gave me directions for getting out of town, some of the few accurate ones I got on the whole trip.

"So long," I said. "I hope you have a good—future."

"It's not bad, you know. Good-by, sir."

And driving along a back Connecticut road, tree-bordered and gardened, I knew he had made me feel better and surer.

For weeks I had studied maps, large-scale and small, but maps are not reality at all—they can be tyrants. I know people who are so immersed in road maps that they never see the countryside they pass through, and others who, having traced a route, are held to it as though held by flanged wheels to rails. I pulled Rocinante into a small picnic area maintained by the state of Connecticut and got out my book of maps. And suddenly the United States became huge beyond belief and impossible ever to cross. I wondered how in hell I'd got myself mixed up in a project that couldn't be carried out. It was like starting to write a novel. When I face the desolate impossibility of writing five hundred pages a sick sense of failure falls on me and I know I can never do it. This happens every time. Then gradually I write one page and then another. One day's work is all I can permit myself to contemplate and I eliminate the possibility of ever finishing. So it was now, as I looked at the bright-colored projection of monster America. The leaves of the trees about the camp ground were thick and heavy, no longer growing but hanging limp and waiting for the first frost to whip them with color and the second to drive them to the earth and terminate their year.

Charley is a tall dog. As he sat in the seat beside me, his head was almost as high as mine. He put his nose close to my ear and said, "Ftt." He is the only dog I ever knew who could pronounce the consonant *F.* This is because his front teeth are crooked, a tragedy which keeps him out of dog shows; because his upper front teeth slightly engage his lower lip Charley can pronounce *F.* The word "Ftt" usually means he would like to salute a bush or a tree. I opened the cab door and let him out, and he went about his ceremony. He doesn't have to think about it to do it well. It is my experience that in some areas Charley is more intelligent than I am, but in others he is abysmally ignorant. He can't read, can't drive a car, and has no grasp of mathematics. But in his own field of endeavor, which he was now practicing, the slow, imperial smelling over and anointing of an area, he has no peer. Of course his horizons are limited, but how wide are mine?

We drove on in the autumn afternoon, heading north. Because I was self-contained, I thought it might be nice if I could invite people I met along the way to my home for a drink, but I had neglected to lay in liquor. But there are pretty little bottle stores on the back roads of this state. I knew there were some dry states but had forgotten which they were, and it was just as well to stock up. A small store was set well back from the road in a grove of sugar maples. It had a well-kept garden and flower boxes. The owner was a young-old man with a gray face, I suspect a teetotaller. He opened his order book and straightened the carbons with patient care. You never know what people will want to drink. I ordered bourbon, scotch, gin, vermouth, vodka, a medium good brandy, aged applejack, and a case of beer. It seemed to me that those might take care of most situations. It was a big order for a little store. The owner was impressed.

"Must be quite a party."

"No—it's just traveling supplies."

He helped me to carry the cartons out and I opened Rocinante's door.

"You going in that?"

"Sure."

"Where?"

"All over."

And then I saw what I was to see so many times on the journey—a look of longing. "Lord! I wish I could go."

"Don't you like it here?"

"Sure. It's all right, but I wish I could go."

"You don't even know where I'm going."

"I don't care. I'd like to go anywhere."

Eventually I had to come out of the tree-hidden roads and do my best to bypass the cities. Hartford and Providence and such are big cities, bustling with manufacturing, lousy with traffic. It takes far longer to go through cities than to drive several hundred miles. And in the intricate traffic pattern, as you try to find your way through, there's no possibility of seeing anything. But now I have been through hundreds of towns and cities in every climate and against every kind of scenery, and of course they are all different, and the people have points of difference, but in some ways they are alike. American cities are like badger holes, ringed with trash—all of them—surrounded by piles of wrecked and rusting automobiles, and almost smothered with rubbish. Everything we use comes in boxes, cartons, bins, the so-called packaging we love so much. The mountains of things we throw away are much greater than the things we use. In this, if in no other way, we can see the wild and reckless exuberance of our production, and waste seems to be the index. Driving along I thought how in France or Italy every item of these thrown-out things would have been saved and used for something. This is not said in criticism of one system or the other but I do wonder whether there will come a time when we can no longer afford our wastefulness—chemical wastes in the rivers, metal wastes everywhere, and atomic wastes buried deep in the earth or sunk in the sea. When an Indian village became too deep in its own filth, the inhabitants moved. And we have no place to which to move.

I had promised my youngest son to say good-by in passing his school at Deerfield, Massachusetts, but I got there too late to arouse him, so I drove up the mountain and found a dairy, bought some milk, and asked permission to camp under an apple tree. The dairy man had a Ph.D. in mathematics, and he must have had some training in philosophy. He liked what he was doing and he didn't want to be somewhere else—one of the very few contented people I met in my whole journey.

I prefer to draw a curtain over my visit to Eaglebrook school. It can be imagined what effect Rocinante had on two hundred teen-age prisoners of education just settling down to serve their winter sentence. They visited my truck in droves, as many as fifteen at a time in the little cabin. And they looked courteous curses at me because I could go and they could not. My own son will probably never forgive me. Soon after I drove off, I stopped to make sure there were no stowaways.

My route went north in Vermont and then east in New Hampshire in the White Mountains. The roadside stands were piled with golden pumpkins and russet squashes and baskets of red apples so crisp and sweet that they seemed to explode with juice when I bit into them. I bought apples and a gallon jug of fresh-pressed cider. I believe that everyone along the highways sells moccasins and deerskin gloves. And those who don't sell goat-milk candy. Until then, I had not seen the factory-outlet stores in the open country selling shoes and clothes. The villages are the prettiest, I guess, in the whole nation, neat and white-painted, and—not counting the motels and tourist courts—unchanged for a hundred years except for traffic and paved streets.

The climate changed quickly to cold and the trees burst into color, the reds and yellows you can't believe. It isn't only color but a glowing, as though the leaves gobbled the light of the autumn sun and then released it slowly. There's a quality of fire in these colors. I got high in the mountains before dusk. A sign beside a stream offered fresh eggs for sale, and I drove up a farm road and bought some eggs and asked permission to camp beside the stream and offered to pay.

The farmer was a spare man, with what we think of as a Yankee face and the flat vowels we consider Yankee pronunciation.

"No need to pay," he said. "The land's not working. But I would like to look at that rig you've got there."

I said, "Let me find a level place and put it in order, then come down for a cup of coffee—or something."

I backed and filled until I found a level place where I could hear the eager stream rattling; it was almost dark. Charley had said "Ftt" several times, meaning this time that he was hungry. I opened Rocinante's door, turned on the light, and found utter chaos inside. I have stowed a boat very often against roll and pitch, but the quick stops and starts of a truck are a different hazard. The floor was littered with books and papers. My typewriter roosted uncomfortably on a pile of plastic dishes, a rifle had fallen down and nudged itself against the stove, and one entire ream of paper, five hundred sheets, had drifted like snow to cover the whole place. I lighted the gas mantle lamp, stuffed the debris in a little closet, and put on water for coffee. In the morning I would have to reorganize my cargo. No one can tell how to do it. The technique must be learned the way I learned it, by failures. The moment it was dark it became bitterly cold, but the lamp and the gas burners of the stove warmed my little house cozily. Charley ate his supper, did his tour of duty, and retired into a carpeted corner under the table which was to be his for the next three months.

There are so many modern designs for easy living. On my boat I had discovered the aluminum, disposable cooking utensils, frying pans and deep dishes. You fry a fish and throw the pan overboard. I was well equipped with these things. I opened a can of corned-beef hash and patted it into a disposable dish and set it on an asbestos pad over a low flame, to heat very slowly. The coffee was barely ready when Charley let out his lion roar. I can't say how comforting it is to be told that someone is approaching in the dark. And if the approacher happened to have evil in his heart, that great voice would give him pause if he did not know Charley's basically pacific and diplomatic nature.

The farm owner knocked on my door and I invited him in.

"You've got it nice in here," he said. "Yes, sir, you've got it nice."

He slipped in the seat beside the table. This table can be lowered at night and the cushions can be converted to make a double bed. "Nice," he said again.

I poured him a cup of coffee. It seems to me that coffee smells even better when the frost is in. "A little something on the side?" I asked. "Something to give it authority?"

"No—this is fine. This is nice."

"Not a touch of applejack? I'm tired from driving, I'd like a spot myself."

He looked at me with the contained amusement that is considered taciturnity by non-Yankees. "Would you have one if I didn't?"

"No, I guess not."

"I wouldn't rob you then—just a spoonful."

So I poured each of us a good dollop of twenty-one-year-old applejack and slipped in on my side of the table. Charley moved over to make room and put his chin down on my feet.

There's a gentility on the road. A direct or personal question is out of bounds. But this is simple good manners anywhere in the world. He did not ask my name nor I his, but I had seen his quick eyes go to the firearms in their rubber slings, to the fishing rods pinioned against the wall.

Khrushchev was at the United Nations, one of the few reasons I would have liked to be in New York. I asked, "Have you listened to the radio today?"

"Five-o'clock report."

"What happened at the U.N.? I forgot to listen."

"You wouldn't believe it," he said. "Mr. K. took off his shoe and pounded the table."

"What for?"

"Didn't like what was being said."

"Seems a strange way to protest."

"Well, it got attention. That's about all the news talked about."

"They should give him a gavel so he could keep his shoes on."

"That's a good idea. Maybe it could be in the shape of a shoe so he wouldn't be embarrassed." He sipped the applejack with a deep appreciation. "That's pretty nice," he said.

"How do folks around here feel about all this talking back to the Russians?"

"I don't know about other people. But I think if you're talking back it's kind of like a rear-guard action. I'd like to see us do something so they had to talk back to us."

"You've got something there."

"Seems to me we're always defending ourselves."

I refilled the coffee cups and poured a little more applejack for both of us. "You think we should attack?"

"I think we should at least take the ball sometimes."

"I'm not taking a poll, but how does the election seem to be going around here?"

"I wish I knew," he said. "People aren't talking. I think this might be the secretest election we ever had. People just won't put out an opinion."

"Could it be they haven't got one?"

"Maybe, or maybe they just don't want to tell. I remember other elections when there would be pretty peppery arguments. I haven't heard even one."

And that's what I found all over the country—no arguments, no discussion.

"Is it the same—other places?" He must have seen my license plates, but he would not mention that.

"That seems right to me. Do you think people are scared to have an opinion?"

"Maybe some. But I know some that don't scare, and they don't say, either."

"That's been my experience," I said. "But I don't know, really."

"I don't either. Maybe it's all part of the same thing. No thanks, no more. I can smell your supper's nearly ready. I'll step along."

"Part of what same thing?"

"Well, you take my grandfather and his father—he was still alive until I was twelve. They knew some things they were sure about. They were pretty sure give a little line and then what *might* happen. But now—what might happen?"

"I don't know."

"Nobody knows. What good's an opinion if you don't know? My grandfather knew the number of whiskers in the Almighty's beard. I don't even know what happened yesterday, let alone tomorrow. He knew what it was that makes a rock or a table. I don't even understand the formula that says nobody knows. We've got nothing to go on—got no way to think about things. I'll step along. Will I see you in the morning?"

"I don't know. I'm going to start early. I want to get clear across Maine to Deer Isle."

"Say, that's a pretty place isn't it?"

"I don't know yet. I haven't been there."

"Well, it's nice. You'll like it. Thanks for the—coffee. Good night."

Charley looked after him and sighed and went back to sleep. I ate my corned-beef hash, then made down my bed and dug out Shirer's *Rise and Fall of the Third Reich*. But I found I couldn't read, and when the light was off I couldn't sleep. The clattering stream on the rocks was a good reposeful sound, but the conversation of the farmer stayed with me—a thoughtful, articulate man he was. I couldn't hope to find many like him. And maybe he had put his finger on it. Humans had perhaps a million years to get used to fire as a thing and as an idea. Between the time a man got his fingers burned on a lightning-struck tree until another man carried some inside a cave and found it kept him warm, maybe a hundred thousand years, and from there to the blast furnaces of Detroit—how long?

And now a force was in hand how much more strong, and

we hadn't had time to develop the means to think, for man has to have feelings and then words before he can come close to thought and, in the past at least, that has taken a long time.

Roosters were crowing before I went to sleep. And I felt at last that my journey was started. I think I hadn't really believed in it before.

Charley likes to get up early, and he likes me to get up early too. And why shouldn't he? Right after his breakfast he goes back to sleep. Over the years he has developed a number of innocent-appearing ways to get me up. He can shake himself and his collar loud enough to wake the dead. If that doesn't work he gets a sneezing fit. But perhaps his most irritating method is to sit quietly beside the bed and stare into my face with a sweet and forgiving look on his face; I come out of deep sleep with the feeling of being looked at. But I have learned to keep my eyes tight shut. If I even blink he sneezes and stretches, and that night's sleep is over for me. Often the war of wills goes on for quite a time, I squinching my eyes shut and he forgiving me, but he nearly always wins. He liked traveling so much he wanted to get started early, and early for Charley is the first tempering of darkness with the dawn.

I soon discovered that if a wayfaring stranger wishes to eavesdrop on a local population the places for him to slip in and hold his peace are bars and churches. But some New England towns don't have bars, and church is only on Sunday. A good alternative is the roadside restaurant where men gather for breakfast before going to work or going hunting. To find these places inhabited, one must get up very early. And there is a drawback even to this. Early-rising men not only do not talk much to strangers, they barely talk to one another. Breakfast conversation is limited to a series of laconic grunts. The natural New England taciturnity reaches its glorious perfection at breakfast.

I fed Charley, gave him a limited promenade, and hit the road. An icy mist covered the hills and froze on my windshield. I am not normally a breakfast eater, but here I had to be or I wouldn't see anybody unless I stopped for gas. At the first lighted roadside restaurant I pulled in and took my seat at a counter. The customers were folded over their coffee cups like ferns. A normal conversation is as follows:

WAITRESS: "Same?"
CUSTOMER: "Yep."
WAITRESS: "Cold enough for you?"
CUSTOMER: "Yep."
(Ten minutes.)
WAITRESS: "Refill?"
CUSTOMER: "Yep."

This is a really talkative customer. Some reduce it to "Burp" and others do not answer at all. An early morning waitress in New England leads a lonely life, but I soon learned that if I tried to inject life and gaiety into her job with a blithe remark she dropped her eyes and answered "Yep" or "Umph." Still, I did feel that there was some kind of communication, but I can't say what it was.

The best of learning came on the morning radio, which I learned to love. Every town of a few thousand people has its station, and it takes the place of the old local newspaper. Bargains and trades are announced, social doings, prices of commodities, messages. The records played are the same all over the country. If "Teen-Age Angel" is top of the list in Maine, it is top of the list in Montana. In the course of a day you may hear "Teen-Age Angel" thirty or forty times. But in addition to local news and chronicles, some foreign advertising creeps in. As I went farther and farther north and it got colder I was aware of more and more advertising for Florida real estate and, with the approach of the long and bitter winter, I could see why Florida is a golden word. As I went along I found that more and more people lusted toward Florida and that thousands had moved there and more thousands wanted to and would. The advertising, with a side look at Federal Communications, made few claims except for the fact that the land they were selling was in Florida. Some of them went out on a limb and promised that it was above tide level. But that didn't matter; the very name Florida carried the message of warmth and ease and comfort. It was irresistible.

I've lived in good climate, and it bores the hell out of me. I like weather rather than climate. In Cuernavaca, Mexico, where I once lived, and where the climate is as near to perfect as is conceivable, I have found that when people leave there they usually go to Alaska. I'd like to see how long an Aroostook

County man can stand Florida. The trouble is that with his savings moved and invested there, he can't very well go back. His dice are rolled and can't be picked up again. But I do wonder if a down-Easter, sitting on a nylon-and-aluminum chair out on a changelessly green lawn slapping mosquitoes in the evening of a Florida October—I do wonder if the stab of memory doesn't strike him high in the stomach just below the ribs where it hurts. And in the humid ever-summer I dare his picturing mind not to go back to the shout of color, to the clean rasp of frosty air, to the smell of pine wood burning and the caressing warmth of kitchens. For how can one know color in perpetual green, and what good is warmth without cold to give it sweetness?

I drove as slowly as custom and the impatient law permitted. That's the only way to see anything. Every few miles the states provided places of rest off the roads, sheltered places sometimes near dark streams. There were painted oil drums for garbage, and picnic tables, and sometimes fireplaces or barbecue pits. At intervals I drove Rocinante off the road and let Charley out to smell over the register of previous guests. Then I would heat my coffee and sit comfortably on my back step and contemplate wood and water and the quick-rising mountains with crowns of conifers and the fir trees high up, dusted with snow. Long ago at Easter I had a looking-egg. Peering in a little porthole at the end, I saw a lovely little farm, a kind of dream farm, and on the farmhouse chimney a stork sitting on a nest. I regarded this as a fairy-tale farm as surely imagined as gnomes sitting under toadstools. And then in Denmark I saw that farm or its brother, and it was true, just as it had been in the looking-egg. And in Salinas, California, where I grew up, although we had some frost the climate was cool and foggy. When we saw colored pictures of a Vermont autumn forest it was another fairy thing and we frankly didn't believe it. In school we memorized "Snowbound" and little poems about Old Jack Frost and his paintbrush, but the only thing Jack Frost did for us was put a thin skin of ice on the watering trough, and that rarely. To find not only that this bedlam of color was true but that the pictures were pale and inaccurate translations, was to me startling. I can't even imagine the forest colors when I am not seeing them. I wondered whether constant association could cause inattention, and asked a native New Hampshire woman about it. She said the autumn never failed to amaze her; to elate. "It is a glory," she said, "and can't be remembered, so that it always comes as a surprise."

In the stream beside the resting place I saw a trout rise from the dark water of a pool and make outflowing silver rings, and Charley saw it too and waded in and got wet, the fool. He never thinks of the future. I stepped into Rocinante to bring out my poor mite of garbage for the oil drum, two empty cans; I had eaten from one and Charley from the other. And among the books I had brought along, I saw a well-remembered cover and brought it out to the sunlight—a golden hand holding at once a serpent and a mirror with wings, and below in scriptlike letters "*The Spectator*, Edited by Henry Morley."

I seem to have had a fortunate childhood for a writer. My grandfather, Sam'l Hamilton, loved good writing, and he knew it too, and he had some bluestocking daughters, among them my mother. Thus it was that in Salinas, in the great dark walnut bookcase with the glass doors, there were strange and wonderful things to be found. My parents never offered them, and the glass doors obviously guarded them, and so I pilfered from that case. It was neither forbidden nor discouraged. I think today if we forbade our illiterate children to touch the wonderful things of our literature, perhaps they might steal them and find secret joy. Very early I conceived a love for Joseph Addison which I have never lost. He plays the instrument of language as Casals plays a cello. I do not know whether he influenced my prose style, but I could hope he did. In the White Mountains in 1960, sitting in the sun, I opened the well-remembered first volume, printed in 1883. I turned to Number 1 of *The Spectator*—Thursday, March 1, 1711. It was headed:

> *"Non fumum ex fulgore, sed ex fumo dare lucem*
> *Cogitat, et speciosa dehinc miracula promat."*—Horace.

I remember so well loving Addison's use of capital letters for nouns. He writes under this date:

"I have observed that a Reader seldom peruses a Book with Pleasure 'till he knows whether the Writer of it be a black or fair Man, of a mild or cholerick Disposition, Married or a Batchelor, with other Particulars of the like Nature, that conduce very much to the right Understanding of an Author. To gratify this Curiosity, which is so natural to a Reader, I design this Paper and my next, as Prefatory Discourses to my following Writings and shall give some Account in them of the several persons that are engaged in this Work. As the chief trouble of Compiling, Digesting and Correcting will fall to my Share, I must do myself the justice to open the Work with my own History."

Sunday, January 29, 1961. Yes, Joseph Addison, I hear and I will obey within Reason, for it appears that the Curiosity you speak of has in no Way abated. I have found many Readers more interested in what I wear than in what I think, more avid to know how I do it than in what I do. In regarding my Work, some Readers profess greater Feeling for what it makes than for what it says. Since a Suggestion from the Master is a Command not unlike Holy Writ, I shall digress and comply at the same Time.

Among the generality of men I am tall—six feet even—although among the males of my family I am considered a dwarf. They range from six feet two inches to six feet five, and I know that both my sons, when they stretch their full height, will overtop me. I am very wide of shoulder and, in the condition I now find myself, narrow of hip. My legs are long in proportion to my trunk and are said to be shapely. My hair is a grizzled gray, my eyes blue and my cheeks ruddy, a complexion inherited from my Irish mother. My face has not ignored the passage of time, but recorded it with scars, lines, furrows, and erosions. I wear a beard and mustache but shave my cheeks; said beard, having a dark skunk stripe up the middle and white edges, commemorates certain relatives. I cultivate this beard not for the usual given reasons of skin trouble or pain of shaving, nor for the secret purpose of covering a weak chin, but as pure unblushing decoration, much as a peacock finds pleasure in his tail. And finally, in our time a beard is the one thing a woman cannot do better than a man, or if she can her success is assured only in a circus.

My costume for traveling was utilitarian if a trifle bizarre. Half-Wellington rubber boots with cork inner soles kept my feet warm and dry. Khaki cotton trousers, bought in an army-surplus store, covered my shanks, while my upper regions rejoiced in a hunting coat with corduroy cuffs and collar and a game pocket in the rear big enough to smuggle an Indian princess into a Y.M.C.A. My cap was one I have worn for many years, a blue serge British naval cap with a short visor and on its peak the royal lion and unicorn, as always fighting for the crown of England. This cap is pretty ratty and salt-crusted, but it was given me by the skipper of a motor torpedo boat on which I sailed out of Dover during the war—a gentle gentleman and a murderer. After I left his command he attacked a German E-boat and held his fire trying to take it whole since none had ever been captured, and in the process he got himself sunk. I have worn his cap ever since in his honor and in his memory. Besides, I like it. It agrees with me. Down East this cap did not draw a second glance, but when later, in Wisconsin, North Dakota, Montana, I had left the sea far behind, I thought it drew attention, and I bought what we used to call a stockman's hat, a Stetson, not too wide of brim, a rich but conservative western hat of the kind my cow-harrying uncles used to wear. Only when I came down to another sea in Seattle did I reassume the naval cap.

Thus far with Addison's injunction, but my Reader has me back in that New Hampshire picnic place. As I sat there fingering the first volume of *The Spectator* and considering how the mind usually does two things at once that it knows about and probably several it doesn't, a luxurious car drove in and a rather stout and bedizened woman released a rather stout and bedizened Pomeranian of the female persuasion. I would not have known this latter fact, but Charley knew. Emerging from behind the garbage can, he found her beautiful, his French blood flared up, and he proceeded to gallantries unmistakable even to the slack eyes of mademoiselle's mistress. This creature let out a shriek like a wounded rabbit, emerged from the car with an explosive ooze, and would have snatched her darling to her bosom if she could have bent down that far. The best she could do was to fetch a slap at tall Charley's head. He quite naturally and casually took a nip at her hand before proceeding toward romance. Until that moment I never quite knew the meaning of the phrase "to make the welkin ring." In the first place I didn't know what a welkin was. I looked it up later. And that bull bitch of a woman sure as hell made it ring. I grabbed her hand and saw that the skin wasn't even broken, so I grabbed her dog, which promptly bit me good and drew blood before I could get the little monster by the throat and gently throttle it.

Charley regarded the whole scene as nonsense. He wet on the garbage can for the twentieth time and called it a day.

It took time to calm the lady. I brought out the bottle of brandy, which might have killed her, and she took a slug that should have killed her.

After all I've done for him you'd think Charley would have come to my aid, but he dislikes neurotics and he detests drunks. He climbed in Rocinante, crawled under the table, and went to sleep. Sic semper cum Frogs.

At last milady flailed away with her hand brake on, and the kind of a day I had built lay in ruins. Addison had crashed in flames, the trout no longer ringed the pool, and a cloud covered the sun and put a chill in the air. I found myself driving faster than I wanted to and it began to rain, a cold steel rain. I didn't give the lovely villages the attention they deserved, and before long I had crossed into Maine and continued eastward.

I wish any two states could get together on a speed limit. Just about the time you get used to fifty miles an hour you cross a state line and it's sixty-five. I wonder why they can't settle down and agree. However, in one matter all states agree —each one admits it is the finest of all and announces that fact in huge letters as you cross the state line. Among nearly forty I didn't see a single state that hadn't a good word to say for itself. It seemed a little indelicate. It might be better to let visitors find out for themselves. But maybe we wouldn't if it weren't drawn to our attention.

*

PREPARATION for the winter in New England is drastic. The summer population must be large and the roads and highways gorged with refugees from the sticky heat of Boston and New York. Now the hot-dog stands, the ice-cream parlors, the curiosity shops, deerskin-moccasin-and-glove places, were all shuttered and closed, many of them with cards saying "Open Next Summer." I can never get used to the thousands of antique shops along the roads, all bulging with authentic and attested trash from an earlier time. I believe the population of the thirteen colonies was less than four million souls, and every one of them must have been frantically turning out tables, chairs, china, glass, candle molds, and oddly shaped bits of iron, copper, and brass for future sale to twentieth-century tourists. There are enough antiques for sale along the roads of New England alone to furnish the houses of a population of fifty million. If I were a good businessman, and cared a tittle for my unborn great grandchildren, which I do not, I would gather all the junk and the wrecked automobiles, comb the city dumps, and pile these gleanings in mountains and spray the whole thing with that stuff the Navy uses to mothball ships. At the end of a hundred years my descendants would be permitted to open this treasure trove and would be the antique kings of the world. If the battered, cracked, and broken stuff our ancestors tried to get rid of now brings so much money, think what a 1954 Oldsmobile, or a 1960 toastmaster will bring—and a vintage Waring Mixor—Lord, the possibilities are endless! Things we have to pay to have hauled away could bring fortunes.

If I seem to be over-interested in junk, it is because I am, and I have a lot of it, too—half a garage full of bits and broken pieces. I use these things for repairing other things. Recently I stopped my car in front of the display yard of a junk dealer near Sag Harbor. As I was looking courteously at the stock, it suddenly occurred to me that I had more than he had. But it can be seen that I do have a genuine and almost miserly interest in worthless objects. My excuse is that in this era of planned obsolescence, when a thing breaks down I can usually find something in my collection to repair it—a toilet, or a motor, or a lawn mower. But I guess the truth is that I simply like junk.

Before I started my tour, I had known that at intervals of every few days I would have to stop at auto courts or motels, not so much to sleep but for the sake of hot, luxurious bathing. In Rocinante I heated water in a tea kettle and took sponge baths, but bathing in a bucket delivers little cleanliness and no pleasure whatever. A deep-dish sit-down in a tub with scalding water is a pure joy. Quite early on my trip, however, I invented a method for washing clothes which you will go a long way to better. It came about this way. I had a large plastic garbage bucket with cover and bail. Since the normal movement of the truck tipped it over, I tethered it by a length of strong elastic rope of cotton-covered rubber to the clothes pole in my little closet, where it could jiggle to its heart's content without spilling. After a day of this, I opened it to dispose of the stuff at a roadside garbage can and found the most thoroughly mixed and kneaded garbage I have ever seen. I suppose all great inventions spring from some such experience. The next morning, I washed the plastic bucket, put in two shirts, underwear, and socks, added hot water and detergent, and hung it by its rubber rope to the clothes pole, where it jigged and danced crazily all day. That night I rinsed the clothes in a stream, and you've never seen clothes so clean. Inside Rocinante I strung a nylon line close to the window and hung the clothes to dry. From that time on, my clothing was washed on one day of driving and dried on the next. I even went overboard and washed sheets and pillow cases that way. So much for daintiness, but it didn't take care of hot baths.

Not far outside of Bangor I stopped at an auto court and rented a room. It wasn't expensive. The sign said "Greatly Reduced Winter Rates." It was immaculate; everything was done in plastics—the floors, the curtain, table tops of stainless burnless plastic, lamp shades of plastic. Only the bedding and the towels were of a natural material. I went to the small restaurant run in conjunction. It was all plastic too—the table linen, the butter dish. The sugar and crackers were wrapped in cellophane, the jelly in a small plastic coffin sealed with cellophane. It was early evening and I was the only customer. Even the waitress wore a sponge-off apron. She wasn't happy, but then she wasn't unhappy. She wasn't anything. But I don't believe anyone is a nothing. There has to be something inside, if only to keep the skin from collapsing. This vacant eye, listless hand, this damask cheek dusted like a doughnut with plastic powder, had to have a memory or a dream.

On a chance I asked, "How soon you going to Florida?"

"Nex' week," she said listlessly. Then something stirred in that aching void. "Say, how do you know I'm going?"

"Read your mind, I guess."

She looked at my beard. "You with a show?"

"No."

"Then how do you mean read my mind?"

"Maybe I guessed. Like it down there?"

"Oh, sure! I go every year. Lots of waitress jobs in the winter."

"What do you do down there, I mean for fun?"

"Oh, nothing. Just fool around."

"Do you fish or swim?"

"Not much. I just fool around. I don't like that sand, makes me itch."

"Make good money?"

"It's a cheap crowd."

"Cheap?"

"They rather spen' it on booze."

"Than what?"

"Than tips. Just the same here with the summer people. Cheap."

Strange how one person can saturate a room with vitality, with excitement. Then there are others, and this dame was one of them, who can drain off energy and joy, can suck pleasure dry and get no sustenance from it. Such people spread a grayness in the air about them. I'd been driving a long time, and perhaps my energy was low and my resistance down. She got me. I felt so blue and miserable I wanted to crawl into a plastic cover and die. What a date she must be, what a lover! I tried to imagine that last and couldn't. For a moment I considered giving her a five-dollar tip, but I knew what would happen. She wouldn't be glad. She'd just think I was crazy.

I went back to my clean little room. I don't ever drink alone. It's not much fun. And I don't think I will until I am an alcoholic. But this night I got a bottle of vodka from my stores and took it to my cell. In the bathroom two water tumblers were sealed in cellophane sacks with the words: "These glasses are sterilized for your protection." Across the toilet seat a strip of paper bore the message: "This seat has been sterilized with ultraviolet light for your protection." Everyone was protecting me and it was horrible. I tore the glasses from their covers. I violated the toilet-seat seal with my foot. I poured half a tumbler of vodka and drank it and then another. Then I lay deep in hot water in the tub and I was utterly miserable, and nothing was good anywhere.

Charley caught it from me, but he is a gallant dog. He came into the bathroom and that old fool played with the plastic bath mat like a puppy. What strength of character, what a friend! Then he rushed to the door and barked as though I were being invaded. And if it hadn't been for all that plastic he might have succeeded.

I remember an old Arab in North Africa, a man whose hands had never felt water. He gave me mint tea in a glass so coated with use that it was opaque, but he handed me companionship, and the tea was wonderful because of it. And without any protection my teeth didn't fall out, nor did running sores develop. I began to formulate a new law describing the relationship of protection to despondency. A sad soul can kill you quicker, far quicker, than a germ.

If Charley hadn't shaken and bounced and said "Ftt," I might have forgotten that every night he gets two dog biscuits and a walk to clear his head. I put on clean clothes and went out with him into the star-raddled night. And the Aurora Borealis was out. I've seen it only a few times in my life. It hung and moved with majesty in folds like an infinite traveler upstage in an infinite theater. In colors of rose and lavender and purple it moved and pulsed against the night, and the frost-sharpened stars shone through it. What a thing to see at a time when I needed it so badly! I wondered for a moment whether I should grab that waitress and kick her behind out to look at it, but I didn't dare. She could make eternity and infinity melt and run out through your fingers. The air had a sweet burn of frost, and Charley, moving ahead, saluted in detail a whole row of clipped privet, and he steamed as he went. When he came back, he was pleased and glad for me. I gave him three dog biscuits, rumpled up the sterile bed, and went out to sleep in Rocinante.

It is not unlike me that in heading toward the West I should travel east. That has always been my tendency. I was going to Deer Isle for a very good reason. My longtime friend and associate, Elizabeth Otis, has been going to Deer Isle every year. When she speaks of it, she gets an other-world look in her eyes and becomes completely inarticulate. When I planned my trip she said, "Of course you'll stop at Deer Isle."

"It's out of my way."

"Nonsense," she said in a tone I know very well. I gathered from her voice and manner that if I didn't go to Deer Isle I had better never show my face in New York again. She then telephoned Miss Eleanor Brace, with whom she always stays, and that was that. I was committed. All I knew about Deer Isle was that there was nothing you could say about it, but if I didn't go I was crazy. Also, Miss Brace was waiting for me.

I got thoroughly lost in Bangor, what with traffic and trucks, horns blaring and lights changing. I vaguely remembered that I should be on U.S. Highway 1, and I found it and drove ten miles in the wrong direction, back toward New York. I had been given written directions on how to go, detailed directions, but have you ever noticed that instructions from one who knows the country get you more lost than you are, even when they are accurate? I also got lost in Ellsworth, which I am told is impossible. Then the roads narrowed and the lumber trucks roared past me. I was lost almost all day, even though I found Blue Hill and Sedgwick. Late in the despairing afternoon I stopped my truck and approached a majestic Maine state trooper. What a man he was, granite as any quarried about Portland, a perfect model for some future equestrian statue. I wonder if future heroes will be carved in marble jeeps or patrol cars?

"I seem to be lost, officer. I wonder if you could direct me?"

"Where is it you want to go?"

"I'm trying to get to Deer Isle."

He looked at me closely, and when he was satisfied that I wasn't joking he swung on his hips and pointed across a small stretch of open water, and he didn't bother to speak.

"Is that it?"

He nodded from up to down and left his head down.

"Well, how do I get there?"

I have always heard that Maine people are rather taciturn, but for this candidate for Mount Rushmore to point twice in an afternoon was to be unbearably talkative. He swung his chin in a small arc in the direction I had been traveling. If the afternoon had not been advancing I would have tried for another word from him even if doomed to failure. "Thank you," I said, and sounded to myself as though I rattled on forever.

First there was a very high iron bridge, as high-arched as a rainbow, and after a bit a low stone bridge built in the shape of an S-curve, and I was on Deer Isle. My written directions said that I must take every road branch that turned right, and the word "every" was underlined. I climbed a hill and turned right into pine woods on a smaller road, and turned right on a very narrow road and turned right again on wheel tracks on pine needles. It is so easy once you have been over it. I couldn't believe I would find the place, but in a hundred yards there was the great old house of Miss Eleanor Brace, and there she was to welcome me. I let Charley out, and suddenly an angry streak of gray burned across the clearing in the pines and bucketed into the house. That was George. He didn't welcome me and he particularly didn't welcome Charley. I never did rightly see George, but his sulking presence was everywhere. For George is an old gray cat who has accumulated a hatred of people and things so intense that even hidden upstairs he communicates his prayer that you will go away. If the bomb should fall and wipe out every living thing except Miss Brace, George would be happy. That's the way he would design a world if it were up to him. And he could never know that Charley's interest in him was purely courteous; if he did, he would be hurt in his misanthropy, for Charley has no interest in cats whatever, even for chasing purposes.

We didn't give George any trouble because for two nights we stayed in Rocinante, but I am told that when guests sleep in the house George goes into the pine woods and watches from afar, grumbling his dissatisfaction and pouring out his dislike. Miss Brace admits that for the purposes of a cat, whatever they are, George is worthless. He isn't good company, he is not sympathetic, and he has little aesthetic value.

"Perhaps he catches mice and rats," I suggested helpfully.

"Never," said Miss Brace. "Wouldn't think of it. And do you want to know something? George is a girl."

I had to restrain Charley because the unseen presence of George was everywhere. In a more enlightened day when witches and familiars were better understood, George would have found his, or rather her, end in a bonfire, because if ever there was a familiar, an envoy of the devil, a consorter with evil spirits, George is it.

One doesn't have to be sensitive to feel the strangeness of Deer Isle. And if people who have been going there for many years cannot describe it, what can I do after two days? It is an island that nestles like a suckling against the breast of Maine, but there are many of those. The sheltered darkling water seems to suck up light, but I've seen that before. The pine woods rustle and the wind cries over open country that is like Dartmoor. Stonington, Deer Isle's chief town, does not look like an American town at all in place or in architecture. Its houses are layered down to the calm water of the bay. This town very closely resembles Lyme Regis on the coast of Dorset, and I would willingly bet that its founding settlers came from Dorset or Somerset or Cornwall. Maine speech is very like that in West Country England, the double vowels pronounced as they are in Anglo-Saxon, but the resemblance is doubly strong on Deer Isle. And the coastal people below the Bristol Channel are secret people, and perhaps magic people. There's aught behind their eyes, hidden away so deep that perhaps even they do not know they have it. And that same thing is so in Deer Islers. To put it plainly, this Isle is like Avalon; it must disappear when you are not there. Or take for example the mystery of the coon cats, huge tailless cats with gray coats barred with black, which is why they are called coon cats. They are wild; they live in the woods and are very fierce. Once in a while a native brings in a kitten and raises it, and it is a pleasure to him, almost an honor, but coon cats are rarely even approximately tame. You take a chance of being raked or bitten all the time. These cats are obviously of Manx origin, and even interbreeding with tame cats they contribute taillessness. The story is that the great ancestors of the coon cats were brought by some ship's captain and that they soon went wild. But I wonder where they get their size. They are twice as big as any Manx cat I ever saw. Could it be that they bred with bobcat or lynx? I don't know. Nobody knows.

Down by the Stonington Harbor the summer boats were being pulled up for storage. And not only here but in other inlets nearby are very large lobster pounds crawling with those dark-shelled Maine lobsters from the dark water which are the best lobsters in the world. Miss Brace ordered up three, not more than a pound and a half, she said, and that night their excellence was demonstrated beyond a doubt. There are no lobsters like these—simply boiled, with no fancy sauces, only melted butter and lemon, they have no equals anywhere. Even shipped or flown alive away from their dark homes, they lose something.

At a wonderful store in Stonington, half hardware store and half ship's chandler, I bought a kerosene lamp with a tin reflector for Rocinante. I had the fear that I might somewhere run out of butane gas, and how would I read in bed then? I screwed the lamp bracket to the wall over my bed and trimmed the wick to make a golden butterfly of flame. And often on my trip I used it for warmth and color as well as light. It was exactly the same lamp that was in all the rooms at the ranch when I was a child. And no pleasanter light was ever designed, although old timers say that whale oil makes a nicer flame.

I have demonstrated that I can't describe Deer Isle. There is something about it that opens no door to words. But it stays with you afterward, and, more than that, things you didn't know you saw come back to you after you have left. One thing I remember very clearly. It might have been caused by the season with a quality of light, or the autumn clarity. Everything stood out separate from everything else, a rock, a rounded lump of sea-polished driftwood on a beach, a roof line. Each pine tree was itself and separate even if it was a part of a forest. Drawing a very long bow of relationships, could I say that the people have that same quality? Surely I never met such ardent individuals. I would hate to try to force them to do anything they didn't want to do. I heard many stories about the Isle—I remember it is Isle and not Island—and was given much taciturn advice. I will repeat only one admonishment from a native of Maine, and I will not put a name to that person for fear of reprisal.

"Don't ever ask directions of a Maine native," I was told.

"Why ever not?"

"Somehow we think it is funny to misdirect people and we don't smile when we do it, but we laugh inwardly. It is our nature."

I wonder if that is true. I could never test it, because through my own efforts I am lost most of the time without any help from anyone.

I have spoken with approval, even affection, of Rocinante but not of the pick-up truck on which the camper top rode. It was a new model, with a powerful V-6 engine. It had automatic transmission and an oversized generator to give me lights inside the cabin if I should need them. The cooling system was so loaded with antifreeze that it could have withstood polar weather. I believe that American-made automobiles for passengers are made to wear out so that they must be replaced. This is not so with the trucks. A trucker requires many more thousands of miles of good service than a passenger-car owner. He is not to be dazzled with trimming or fins or doodads and he is not required by his status to buy a new model every year or so to maintain social face. Everything about my truck was made to last. Its frame was heavy, the metal rigid, the engine big and sturdy. Of course I treated it well in matters of oil changes and greasing, and I did not drive it to its limit or force it to do acrobatics required of sports cars. The cab was double-walled, and a good heater had been installed. When I returned after more than ten thousand miles the engine was only well broken in. And it never failed or stuttered even once during the journey.

I moved up the coast of Maine, through Millbridge and Addison and Machias and Perry and South Robbinston, until there was no more coast. I never knew or had forgotten how much of Maine sticks up like a thumb into Canada with New Brunswick on the east. We know so little of our own geography. Why, Maine extends northward almost to the mouth of the St. Lawrence, and its upper border is perhaps a hundred miles north of Quebec. And another thing I had conveniently forgotten was how incredibly huge America is. As I drove north through the little towns and the increasing forest rolling away to the horizon, the season changed quickly and out of all proportion. Perhaps it was my getting away from the steadying hand of the sea, and also perhaps I was getting very far north. The houses had a snow-beaten look, and many were crushed and deserted, driven to earth by the winters. Except in the towns there was evidence of a population which had once lived here and farmed and had its being and had then been driven out. The forests were marching back, and where farm wagons once had been only the big logging trucks rumbled along.

And the game had come back, too; deer strayed on the roads and there were marks of bear.

There are customs, attitudes, myths and directions and changes that seem to be part of the structure of America. And I propose to discuss them as they were first thrust on my attention. While these discussions go on you are to imagine me bowling along on some little road or pulled up behind a bridge, or cooking a big pot of lima beans and salt pork. And the first of these has to do with hunting. I could not have escaped hunting if I had wanted to, for open seasons spangle the autumn. We have inherited many attitudes from our recent ancestors who wrestled this continent as Jacob wrestled the angel, and the pioneers won. From them we take a belief that every American is a natural-born hunter. And every fall a great number of men set out to prove that without talent, training, knowledge, or practice they are dead shots with rifle or shotgun. The results are horrid. From the moment I left Sag Harbor the guns were booming at the migrating ducks, and as I drove in Maine the rifle shots in the forests would have frightened off any number of redcoats so long as they didn't know what was happening. This is bound to get me a bad name as a sportsman, but let me say at once that I have nothing against the killing of animals. Something has to kill them, I suppose. In my youth I often crawled miles on my belly through freezing wind for the pure glory of blasting a mudhen which even soaked in salt water made poor eating. I don't greatly care for venison or bear or moose or elk except for the livers. The recipes, the herbs, the wine, the preparation that goes into a good venison dish would make an old shoe a gourmet's delight. If I were hungry, I would happily hunt anything that runs or crawls or flies, even relatives, and tear them down with my teeth. But it isn't hunger that drives millions of armed American males to forests and hills every autumn, as the high incidence of heart failure among the hunters will prove. Somehow the hunting process has to do with masculinity, but I don't quite know how. I know there are any number of good and efficient hunters who know what they are doing; but many more are overweight gentlemen, primed with whisky and armed with high-powered rifles. They shoot at anything that moves or looks as though it might, and their success in killing one another may well prevent a population explosion. If the casualties were limited to their own kind there would be no problem, but the slaughter of cows, pigs, farmers, dogs, and highway signs makes autumn a dangerous season in which to travel. A farmer in upper New York State painted the word cow in big black letters on both sides of his white bossy, but the hunters shot it anyway. In Wisconsin, as I was driving through, a hunter shot his own guide between the shoulder blades. The coroner questioning this nimrod asked, "Did you think he was a deer?"

"Yes, sir, I did."

"But you weren't sure he was a deer."

"Well, no sir. I guess not."

With the rolling barrage going on in Maine, of course I was afraid for myself. Four automobiles were hit on opening day, but mainly I was afraid for Charley. I know that a poodle looks very like a buck deer to one of these hunters, and I had to find some way of protecting him. In Rocinante there was a box of red Kleenex that someone had given me as a present. I wrapped Charley's tail in red Kleenex and fastened it with rubber bands. Every morning I renewed his flag, and he wore it all the way west while bullets whined and whistled around us. This is not intended to be funny. The radios warned against carrying a white handkerchief. Too many hunters seeing a flash of white have taken it for the tail of a running deer and cured a head cold with a single shot.

But this legacy of the frontiersman is not a new thing. When I was a child on the ranch near Salinas, California, we had a Chinese cook who regularly made a modest good thing of it. On a ridge not far away, a sycamore log lay on its side supported by two of its broken branches. Lee's attention was drawn to this speckled fawn-colored chunk of wood by the bullet holes in it. He nailed a pair of horns to one end and then retired to his cabin until deer season was over. Then he harvested the lead from the old tree trunk. Some seasons he got fifty or sixty pounds of it. It wasn't a fortune but it was wages. After a couple of years, when the tree was completely shot away, Lee replaced it with four gunny sacks of sand and the same antlers. Then it was even easier to harvest his crop. If he had put out fifty of them it would have been a fortune, but Lee was a humble man who didn't care for mass production.

*

Maine seemed to stretch on endlessly. I felt as Peary must have when he approached what he thought was the North Pole. But I wanted to see Aroostook County, the big northern county of Maine. There are three great potato-raising sections —Idaho, Suffolk County on Long Island, and Aroostook, Maine. Lots of people had talked of Aroostook County, but I had never met anyone who had actually been there. I had been told that the crop is harvested by Canucks from Canada who flood over the border at harvest time. My way went endlessly through forest country and past many lakes, not yet frozen. As often as I could I chose the small wood roads, and they are not conducive to speed. The temperature lifted and it rained endlessly and the forests wept. Charley never got dry, and smelled as though he were mildewed. The sky was the color of wet gray aluminum and there was no indication on the translucent shield where the sun might be, so I couldn't tell direction. On a curving road I might have been traveling east or south or west instead of the north I wanted. That old fake about the moss growing on the north sides of trees lied to me when I was a Boy Scout. Moss grows on the shady side, and that may be any side. I determined to buy a compass in the next town, but there wasn't any next town on the road I was traveling. The darkness crept down and the rain drummed on the steel roof of the cab and the windshield wipers sobbed their arcs. Tall dark trees lined the road, crowding the gravel. It seemed hours since I had passed a car or a house or a store, for this was the country gone back to forest. A desolate loneliness settled on me—almost a frightening loneliness. Charley, wet and shivering, curled up in his corner of the seat and offered no companionship. I pulled in behind the approach to a concrete bridge, but couldn't find a level place on the sloping roadside.

Even the cabin was dismal and damp. I turned the gas mantle high, lit the kerosene lamp, and lighted two burners of my stove to drive the loneliness away. The rain drummed on the metal roof. Nothing in my stock of foods looked edible. The darkness fell and the trees moved closer. Over the rain drums I seemed to hear voices, as though a crowd of people muttered and mumbled offstage. Charley was restless. He didn't bark an alarm, but he growled and whined uneasily, which is very unlike him, and he didn't eat his supper and he left his water dish untouched—and that by a dog who drinks his weight in water every day and needs to because of the outgo. I succumbed utterly to my desolation, made two peanut-butter sandwiches, and went to bed and wrote letters home, passing my loneliness around. Then the rain stopped falling and the trees dripped and I helped to spawn a school of secret dangers. Oh, we can populate the dark with horrors, even we who think ourselves informed and sure, believing nothing we cannot measure or weigh. I knew beyond all doubt that the dark things crowding in on me either did not exist or were not dangerous to me, and still I was afraid. I thought how terrible the nights must have been in a time when men knew the things were there and were deadly. But no, that's wrong. If I knew they were there, I would have weapons against them, charms, prayers, some kind of alliance with forces equally strong but on my side. Knowing they were not there made me defenseless against them and perhaps more afraid.

Long ago I owned a little ranch in the Santa Cruz mountains in California. In one place a forest of giant madrone trees joined their tops over a true tarn, a black, spring-fed lake. If there is such a thing as a haunted place, that one was haunted, made so by dim light strained through the leaves and various tricks of perspective. I had working for me a Filipino man, a hill man, short and dark and silent, of the Maori people perhaps. Once, thinking he must have come from a tribal system which recognizes the unseen as a part of reality, I asked this man if he was not afraid of the haunted place, particularly at night. He said he was not afraid because years before a witch doctor gave him a charm against evil spirits.

"Let me see that charm," I asked.

"It's words," he said. "It's a word charm."

"Can you say them to me?"

"Sure," he said and he droned, "*In nomine Patris et Fillii et Spiritus Sancti.*"

"What does it mean?" I asked.

He raised his shoulders. "I don't know," he said. "It's a charm against evil spirits so I am not afraid of them."

I've dredged this conversation out of a strange-sounding

Spanish but there is no doubt of his charm, and it worked for him.

Lying in my bed under the weeping night I did my best to read to take my mind out of misery, but while my eyes moved on the lines I listened to the night. On the edge of sleep a new sound jerked me awake, the sound of footsteps, I thought, moving stealthily on gravel. On the bed beside me I had a flash-light two feet long, made for coon hunters. It throws a powerful beam at least a mile. I got up from bed and lifted my 30/30 carbine from the wall and listened again near the door of Rocinante—and I heard the steps come closer. Then Charley roared his warning and I opened the door and sprayed the road with light. It was a man in boots and a yellow oilskin. The light pinned him still.

"What do you want?" I called.

He must have been startled. It took him a moment to answer. "I want to go home. I live up the road."

And now I felt the whole silly thing, the ridiculous pattern that had piled up layer on layer. "Would you like a cup of coffee, or a drink?"

"No, it's late. If you'll take that light out of my face I'll get along."

I snapped off the light and he disappeared but his voice in passing said, "Come to think of it, what are you doing here?"

"Camping," I said, "just camped for the night." And I went to sleep the moment I hit the bed.

The sun was up when I awakened and the world was remade and shining. There are as many worlds as there are kinds of days, and as an opal changes its colors and its fire to match the nature of a day, so do I. The night fears and loneliness were so far gone that I could hardly remember them.

Even Rocinante, dirty and pine-needle-covered as she was, seemed to leap over the road with joy. Now there were open fields among the lakes and forests, fields with the crumbly friable soil potatoes love. Trucks with flat beds loaded with empty potato barrels moved on the roads, and the mechanical potato digger turned up long windrows of pale-skinned tubers.

In Spanish there is a word for which I can't find a counterword in English. It is the verb *vacilar*, present participle *vacilando.* It does not mean vacillating at all. If one is vacilando, he is going somewhere but doesn't greatly care whether or not he gets there, although he has direction. My friend Jack Wagner has often, in Mexico, assumed this state of being. Let us say we wanted to walk in the streets of Mexico City but not at random. We would choose some article almost certain not to exist there and then diligently try to find it.

I wanted to go to the rooftree of Maine to start my trip before turning west. It seemed to give the journey a design, and everything in the world must have design or the human mind rejects it. But in addition it must have purpose or the human conscience shies away from it. Maine was my design, potatoes my purpose. If I had not seen a single potato my status as *vacilador* would not have been affected. As it turned out I saw almost more potatoes than I needed to see. I saw mountains of potatoes—oceans—more potatoes than you would think the world's population could consume in a hundred years.

I've seen many migrant crop-picking people about the country: Hindus, Filipinos, Mexicans, Okies away from their states. Here in Maine a great many were French Canadians who came over the border for the harvest season. It occurs to me that, just as the Carthaginians hired mercenaries to do their fighting for them, we Americans bring in mercenaries to do our hard and humble work. I hope we may not be overwhelmed one day by peoples not too proud or too lazy or too soft to bend to the earth and pick up the things we eat.

These Canucks were a hardy people. They traveled and camped by families and groups of families, perhaps even clans: men, women, boys, girls, and small children too. Only the nurslings did not work at picking up the potatoes and placing them in the barrels. Americans drove the trucks and used a windlass and a kind of davit to pull the filled barrels aboard. Then they drove away to deposit the crop in the potato barns with earth heaped high about their sides to prevent freezing.

My knowledge of Canuck French derives from motion pictures usually with Nelson Eddy and Jeanette MacDonald, and it consists largely of "By gar." It's odd, but I didn't hear a single one of the potato pickers say "By gar," and they must have seen the pictures and known what is right. The women and girls wore pants usually of corduroy and thick sweaters, and they covered their heads with bright-colored scarves to protect their hair from the dust that rises from the fields with the smallest wind. Most of these people traveled in big trucks covered with dark canvas tarpaulins, but there were some trailers and a few camper tops like Rocinante. At night some slept in the trucks and trailers, but also there were tents pitched in pleasant places, and the smells that came from their cooking fires indicated that they had not lost their French genius for making soup.

Fortunately the tents and trucks and two trailers were settled on the edge of a clear and lovely lake. I parked Rocinante about ninety-five yards away but also on the lake's edge. Then I put on coffee to boil and brought out my garbage-bucket laundry, which had been jouncing for two days, and rinsed the detergent out at the edge of the lake. Attitudes toward strangers crop up mysteriously. I was downwind from the camp and the odor of their soup drifted to me. Those people might have been murderers, sadists, brutes, ugly apish sub-humans for all I knew, but I found myself thinking, "What charming people, what flair, how beautiful they are. How I wish I knew them." And all based on the delicious smell of soup.

In establishing contact with strange people, Charley is my ambassador. I release him, and he drifts toward the objective, or rather to whatever the objective may be preparing for dinner. I retrieve him so that he will not be a nuisance to my neighbors—*et voilà!* A child can do the same thing, but a dog is better.

The incident came off as smoothly as one might expect of a tested and well-rehearsed script. I sent out my ambassador and drank a cup of coffee while I gave him time to operate. Then I strolled to the camp to relieve my neighbors of the inconvenience of my miserable cur. They were nice-looking people, a dozen of them, not counting children, three of the girls pretty and given to giggling, two of the wives buxom and a third even buxomer with child, a patriarch, two brothers-in-law, and a couple of young men who were working toward being brothers-in-law. But the operating chieftain, with deference of course to the patriarch, was a fine-looking man of about thirty-five, broad-shouldered and lithe, with the cream-and-berries complexion of a girl and crisp black curling hair.

The dog had caused no trouble, he said. The truth was that

they had remarked that he was a handsome dog. I of course found myself prejudiced in spite of his deficiencies, being his owner, but the dog had one advantage over most dogs. He was born and raised in France.

The group closed ranks. The three pretty girls giggled and were instantly smothered by the navy-blue eye of the chieftain, backed by a hiss from the patriarch.

Was that the truth? Where in France?

In Bercy, on the outskirts of Paris, did they know it?

No, unfortunately they had never been to the fatherland.

I hoped they might remedy that.

They should have known Charley for a French national by his manners. They had observed my *roulotte* with admiration.

It was simple but comfortable. If they found it convenient, I should be pleased to show it to them.

I was very kind. It would give them pleasure.

If the elevated tone indicates to you that it was carried on in French, you are wrong. The chieftain spoke a very pure and careful English. The one French word used was *roulotte*. The asides among themselves were in Canuck. My French is ridiculous, anyway. No, the elevated tone was a part and parcel of the pageantry of establishing a rapport. I gathered Charley to me. Might I expect them after their supper, which I smelled on the fire?

They would be honored.

I set my cabin in order, heated and ate a can of chili con carne, made sure the beer was cold, and even picked a bouquet of autumn leaves and put them in a milk bottle on the table. The roll of paper cups laid in for just such an occasion had got squashed flat by a flying dictionary my first day out, but I made coasters from folded paper towels. It's amazing what trouble you will go to for a party. Then Charley barked them in and I was host in my own house. Six people can squeeze in behind my table, and they did. Two others beside me stood up, and the back door was wreathed with children's faces. They were very nice people but quite formal. I opened beer for the big ones and pop for the outsiders.

In due course these people told me quite a bit about themselves. They came over the border every year for the potato harvest. With everyone working, it made a nice little pool against the winter. Did they have any trouble with immigration people at the border? Well, no. The rules seemed to relax during the harvest season, and besides, the way was smoothed by a contractor to whom they paid a small percentage of their pay. But they didn't really pay him. He collected directly from the farmers. I've known quite a few migrant people over the years—Okies and Mexican wetbacks, and the Negroes who move into New Jersey and Long Island. And wherever I've seen them there has always been a contractor in the background to smooth the way for them for a consideration. Years ago the farmers tried to draw more labor than they needed so that they could lower wages. This seems to be no longer true, for government agencies channel only as many laborers as are needed, and some kind of minimum wage is maintained. In other cases the migrants have been driven to movement and seasonal work by poverty and terrible need.

Surely my guests for the evening were neither mistreated nor driven. This clan, having put their own small farm to bed for the winter in the Province of Quebec, came over the line to make a small nest egg. They even carried a little feeling of holiday with them almost like the hops- and strawberry-pickers from London and the Midland cities of England. These were a hardy and self-sufficient people, quite capable of taking care of themselves.

I opened more beer. After the night of desolate loneliness I felt very good to be surrounded by warm and friendly but cautious people. I tapped an artesian well of good feeling and made a small speech in my pidgin type of French. It began: "Messy dam. *Je vous porte un cher souvenir de la belle France—en particulier du Departement de Charente.*"

They looked startled but interested. Then John the chieftain slowly translated my speech into high-school English and put it back into Canadian French. "Charente?" he asked. "Why Charente?" I leaned down and opened a compartment under my sink and lifted out a bottle of very old and reverend brandy brought along for weddings, frost bite, and heart attacks. John studied the label with the devout attention a good Christian might give to the holy sacrament. And his words were reverent:

"Jesus Christ," he said. "I forgot. Charente—that's where Cognac is." Then he read the purported year of the bottle's nativity and softly repeated his first words.

He passed the bottle to the patriarch in his corner, and the old man smiled so sweetly that for the first time I could see he lacked front teeth. The brother-in-law growled in his throat like a happy tomcat and the pregnant ladies twittered like *alouettes* singing to the sun. I handed John a corkscrew while I laid out the crystal—three plastic coffee cups, a jelly glass, a shaving mug, and several wide-mouthed pill bottles. I emptied their capsules into a saucepan and rinsed out the odor of wheat germ with water from the tap. The cognac was very, very good, and from the first muttered "*Sante*" and the first clicking sip you could feel the Brotherhood of Man growing until it filled Rocinante full—and the sisterhood also.

They refused seconds and I insisted. And the division of thirds was put on the basis that there wasn't enough to save. And with the few divided drops of that third there came into Rocinante a triumphant human magic that can bless a house, or a truck for that matter—nine people gathered in complete silence and the nine parts making a whole as surely as my arms and legs are part of me, separate and inseparable. Rocinante took on a glow it never quite lost.

Such a fabric cannot be prolonged and should not be. The patriarch gave some kind of signal. My guests squirmed out of their squeezed-up seats behind the table and the adieux, as they should be, were short and formal. Then they went into the night, their way home lighted by the chieftain John carrying a tin kerosene lantern. They walked in silence among sleepy stumbling children and I never saw them again. But I like them.

I didn't make down my bed because I wanted to start very early. I curled up behind the table and slept a little while until in the dim false dawn Charley looked into my face and said "Ftt." While I heated my coffee, I made a little sign on cardboard and stuck it in the neck of the empty brandy bottle, then passing the sleeping camp I stopped and stood the bottle where they would see it. The sign read: "*Enfant de France, Mort pour la Patrie.*" And I drove as quietly as I could, for on this day I intended to drive a little west and then take the long road south down the long reach of Maine. There are times that one treasures for all one's life, and such times are burned clearly and sharply on the material of total recall. I felt very fortunate that morning.

On such a trip as mine, so much there is to see and to think about that event and thought set down as they occurred would roil and stir like a slow-cooking *minestrone.* There are map people whose joy is to lavish more attention on the sheets of colored paper than on the colored land rolling by. I have listened to accounts by such travelers in which every road number was remembered, every mileage recalled, and every little countryside discovered. Another kind of traveler requires to know in terms of maps exactly where he is pin-pointed every moment, as though there were some kind of safety in black and red lines, in dotted indications and squirming blue of lakes and the shadings that indicate mountains. It is not so with me. I was born lost and take no pleasure in being found, nor much identification from shapes which symbolize continents and states. Besides, roads change, increase, are widened or abandoned so often in our country that one must buy road maps like daily newspapers. But since I know the passions of the mapifiers I can report that I moved north in Maine roughly or parallel to U.S. Highway 1 through Houlton, Mars Hill, Presque Isle, Caribou, Van Buren, turned westward, still on U.S. 1, past Madawaska, Upper Frenchville, and Fort Kent, then went due south on State Highway 11 past Eagle Lake, Winterville, Portage, Squa Pan, Masardis, Knowles Corner, Patten, Sherman, Grindstone, and so to Millinocket.

I can report this because I have a map before me, but what I remember has no reference to the numbers and colored lines and squiggles. I have thrown this routing in as a sop and shall not make a habit of it. What I remember are the long avenues in the frost, the farms and houses braced against the winter, the flat, laconic Maine speech in crossroads stores where I stopped to buy supplies. The many deer that crossed the road on nimbling hooves and leaped like bounding rubber away from the passing Rocinante. The roaring lumber trucks. And always I remember that this huge area had once been much more settled and was now abandoned to the creeping forest, the animals, the lumber camps and the cold. The big towns are getting bigger and the villages smaller. The hamlet store, whether grocery, general, hardware, clothing, cannot compete with the supermarket and the chain organization. Our treasured and nostalgic picture of the village general store, the cracker-barrel store where an informed yeomanry gather to express opinions and formulate the national character, is very rapidly disappearing. People who once held family fortresses against wind and weather, against scourges of frost and drought and insect enemies, now cluster against the busy breast of the big town.

The new American finds his challenge and his love in traffic-choked streets, skies nested in smog, choking with the acids of industry, the screech of rubber and houses leashed in against one another while the townlets wither a time and die. And this, as I found, is as true in Texas as in Maine. Clarendon yields to Amarillo just as surely as Stacyville, Maine, bleeds its substance into Millinocket, where the logs are ground up, the air smells of chemicals, the rivers are choked and poisoned, and the streets swarm with this happy, hurrying breed. This is not offered in criticism but only as observation. And I am sure that, as all pendulums reverse their swing, so eventually will the swollen cities rupture like dehiscent wombs and disperse their children back to the countryside. This prophecy is underwritten by the tendency of the rich to do this already. Where the rich lead, the poor will follow, or try to.

Some years ago at Abercrombie and Fitch I bought a cattle caller, an automobile horn manipulated by a lever with which nearly all cow emotions can be imitated, from the sweet lowing of a romantic heifer to the growling roar of a bull in the prime and lust of his bullhood. I had this contraption on Rocinante, and it was most effective. When its call goes out, every bovine within hearing distance raises its head from grazing and moves toward the sound.

In the silver chill of the Maine afternoon, as I bucketed and lumbered over the pitted surface of a wood road, I saw four lady mooses moving with stately heaviness across my bow. As I came near they broke into a heavy-cushioned trot. On an impulse I pressed down the lever of the cattle caller and a bellow came out like that of a Miura bull as he poises before firing himself at the butterfly sweep of his first veronica. The ladies, who were on the point of disappearing into the forest, heard the sound, stopped, turned, and then came for me with gathering speed and with what looked to me like romance in their eyes—but four romances, each weighing well over a thousand pounds! And much as I favor love in all its aspects, I trod my accelerator and got the hell out of there fast. And I remembered a story of the great Fred Allen. His character was a Maine man telling of a moose hunt. "I sat on a log and blew my moose call and waited. Then suddenly I felt something like a warm bath mat on my neck and head. Well sir, it was a moosess licking me and there was a light of passion in her eyes."

"Did you shoot her?" he was asked.

"No, sir. I went away from there fast, but I have often thought that somewhere in Maine there's a moose with a broken heart."

Maine is just as long coming down as it is going up, maybe longer. I could and should have gone to Baxter State Park, but I didn't. I had dawdled too long and it was getting cold and I had visions of Napoleon at Moscow and the Germans at Stalingrad. So I retreated smartly—Brownville Junction, Milo, Dover-Foxcroft, Guilford, Bingham, Skowhegan, Mexico, Rumford, where I joined a road I had already traveled through the White Mountains. Perhaps this was weak of me, but I wanted to get on with it. The rivers were full of logs, bank to bank for miles, waiting their turn at the abbatoir to give their woody hearts so that the bulwarks of our civilization such as *Time* magazine and the *Daily News* can survive, to defend us against ignorance. The mill towns, with all respect, are knots of worms. You come out of serene country and suddenly you are tossed and battered by a howling hurricane of traffic. For a time you fight your way blindly in the mad crush of hurtling metal and then suddenly it dies away and you are in serene and quiet countryside again. And there is no margin or overlap. It is a mystery but a happy one.

In the short time since I had passed, the foliage of the White Mountains had changed and tattered. The leaves were falling, rolling in dusky clouds, and the conifers on the slopes were crusted with snow. I drove long and furiously, to Charley's great disgust. Any number of times he said "Ftt" to me and I ignored him, and barreled on across the upraised thumb of New Hampshire. I wanted a bath and a new bed and a drink and a little human commerce, and I thought to find it on the Connecticut River. It is very strange that when you set a goal for yourself, it is hard not to hold toward it even if it is inconvenient and not even desirable. The way was longer than I had thought and I was very tired. My years spoke for my attention with aching shoulders but I was aimed at the Connecticut River and I ignored the weariness, and this was utter nonsense. It was nearly dark when I found the place I wanted, not far from Lancaster, New Hampshire. The river was wide and pleasant, bordered with trees and edged with a pleasant meadow. And near the bank there stood what I was lusting for—a row of neat little white houses on the green meadow by the river, and a small, compactly housed office and lunch room with a sign on the roadside that bore the welcome words "Open" and "Vacancy." I swung Rocinante off the road and opened the cab door to let Charley out.

The afternoon light made mirrors of the windows of the office and lunch room. My whole body ached from the road as I opened the door and went in. Not a soul was there. The register was on the desk, stools at the lunch counter, pies and cakes under plastic covers; the refrigerator hummed; a few dirty dishes soaked in soapy water in the stainless-steel sink, and a faucet dripped slowly into it.

I banged the little bell on the desk, then called out, "Anybody here?" No answer, nothing. I sat down on a stool to await the return of the management. The numbered keys to the little white houses hung on a board. The daylight slipped away and the place darkened. I went outside to collect Charley and to verify my impression that the sign said "Open" and "Vacancy." By now it was getting dark. I brought out a flashlight and looked through the office for a note saying "Back in ten minutes," but there was none. I felt strangely like a Peeping Tom; I didn't belong there. Then I went outside and moved Rocinante out of the driveway, fed Charley, made some coffee, and waited.

It would have been simple to take a key, leave a note on the desk saying that I had done so, and open one of the little houses. It wasn't right. I couldn't do it. On the highway a few cars went by and crossed the bridge over the river, but none turned in. The windows of the office and grill flashed under approaching headlights and then blacked out again. I had planned to eat a light supper and then to fall dog-weary into bed. I made my bed, found I wasn't hungry after all, and lay down. But sleep would not come to me. I listened for the return of the management. At last I lighted my gas mantle and tried to read, but with listening I could not follow the words. At last I dozed, awakened in the dark, looked out—nothing, nobody. My little sleep was troubled and uneasy.

At dawn I arose and created a long, slow, time-wasting breakfast. The sun came up, searching out the windows. I walked down to the river to keep Charley company, returned, even shaved and took a sponge bath in a bucket. The sun was well up by now. I went to the office and entered. The refrigerator hummed, the faucet dripped into the cold soapy water of the sink. A new-born, heavy-winged fat fly crawled fretfully over a plastic pie cover. At nine-thirty I drove away and no one had come, nothing had moved. The sign still read "Open" and "Vacancy." I drove across the iron bridge, rattling the steel-tread plates. The empty place disturbed me deeply, and, come to think of it, it still does.

On the long journey doubts were often my companions. I've always admired those reporters who can descend on an area, talk to key people, ask key questions, take samplings of opinions, and then set down an orderly report very like a road map. I envy this technique and at the same time do not trust it as a mirror of reality. I feel that there are too many realities. What I set down here is true until someone else passes that way and rearranges the world in his own style. In literary criticism the critic has no choice but to make over the victim of his attention into something the size and shape of himself.

And in this report I do not fool myself into thinking I am dealing with constants. A long time ago I was in the ancient city of Prague and at the same time Joseph Alsop, the justly famous critic of places and events, was there. He talked to informed people, officials, ambassadors; he read reports, even the fine print and figures, while I in my slipshod manner roved about with actors, gypsies, vagabonds. Joe and I flew home to America in the same plane, and on the way he told me about Prague, and his Prague had no relation to the city I had seen and heard. It just wasn't the same place, and yet each of us was honest, neither one a liar, both pretty good observers by any standard, and we brought home two cities, two truths. For this reason I cannot commend this account as an America that you will find. So much there is to see, but our morning eyes describe a different world than do our afternoon eyes, and surely our wearied evening eyes can report only a weary evening world.

Sunday morning, in a Vermont town, my last day in New England, I shaved, dressed in a suit, polished my shoes, whited my sepulcher, and looked for a church to attend. Several I eliminated for reasons I do not now remember, but on seeing a John Knox church I drove into a side street and parked Rocinante out of sight, gave Charley his instructions about watching the truck, and took my way with dignity to a church of blindingly white ship lap. I took my seat in the rear of the spotless, polished place of worship. The prayers were to the point, directing the attention of the Almighty to certain weaknesses and undivine tendencies I know to be mine and could only suppose were shared by others gathered there.

The service did my heart and I hope my soul some good. It had been long since I had heard such an approach. It is our practice now, at least in the large cities, to find from our psychiatric priesthood that our sins aren't really sins at all but accidents that are set in motion by forces beyond our control. There was no such nonsense in this church. The minister, a man of iron with tool-steel eyes and a delivery like a pneumatic drill, opened up with prayer and reassured us that we were a pretty sorry lot. And he was right. We didn't amount to much to start with, and due to our own tawdry efforts we had been slipping ever since. Then, having softened us up, he went into a glorious sermon, a fire-and-brimstone sermon. Having proved that we, or perhaps only I, were no damn good, he painted with cool certainty what was likely to happen to us if we didn't make some basic reorganizations for which he didn't hold out much hope. He spoke of hell as an expert, not the mush-mush hell of these soft days, but a well-stoked, white-hot hell served by technicians of the first order. This reverend brought it to a point where we could understand it, a good hard coal fire, plenty of draft, and a squad of open-hearth devils who put their hearts into their work, and their work was me.

I began to feel good all over. For some years now God has been a pal to us, practicing togetherness, and that causes the same emptiness a father does playing softball with his son. But this Vermont God cared enough about me to go to a lot of trouble kicking the hell out of me. He put my sins in a new perspective. Whereas they had been small and mean and nasty and best forgotten, this minister gave them some size and bloom and dignity. I hadn't been thinking very well of myself for some years, but if my sins had this dimension there was some pride left. I wasn't a naughty child but a first rate sinner, and I was going to catch it.

I felt so revived in spirit that I put five dollars in the plate, and afterward, in front of the church, shook hands warmly with the minister and as many of the congregation as I could. It gave me a lovely sense of evil-doing that lasted clear through till Tuesday. I even considered beating Charley to give him some satisfaction too, because Charley is only a little less sinful than I am. All across the country I went to church on Sundays, a different denomination every week, but nowhere did I find the quality of that Vermont preacher. He forged a religion designed to last, not predigested obsolescence.

I crossed into New York State at Rouses Point and stayed as near to Lake Ontario as I could because it was my intention to look at Niagara Falls, which I had never seen, and then to slip into Canada, from Hamilton to Windsor, keeping Lake Erie on the south, and to emerge at Detroit—a kind of end run, a small triumph over geography. We know, of course, that each of our states is an individual and proud of it. Not content with their names, they take descriptive titles also—the Empire State, the Garden State, the Granite State—titles proudly borne and little given to understatement. But now for the first time I became aware that each state had also its individual prose style, made sharply evident in its highway signs. Crossing state lines one is aware of this change of language. The New England states use a terse form of instruction, a tight-lipped, laconic style sheet, wasting no words and few letters. New York State shouts at you the whole time. Do this. Do that. Squeeze left. Squeeze right. Every few feet an imperious command. In Ohio the signs are more benign. They offer friendly advice, and are more like suggestions. Some states use a turgid style which can get you lost with the greatest ease. There are states which tell you what you may expect to find in the way of road conditions ahead, while others let you find out for yourself. Nearly all have abandoned the adverb for the adjective. Drive Slow. Drive Safe.

I am an avid reader of all signs, and I find that in the historical markers the prose of statehood reaches its glorious best, and most lyric. I have further established, at least to my own satisfaction, that those states with the shortest histories and the least world-shaking events have the most historical markers. Some Western states even find glory in half-forgotten murders and bank robberies. The towns not to be left behind proudly announce their celebrated sons, so the traveler is informed by signs and banners—Birthplace of Elvis Presley, of Cole Porter, of Alan P. Huggins. This is no new thing, of course. I seem to remember that small cities in ancient Greece quarreled bitterly over which was the birthplace of Homer. Within my memory an outraged home-town citizenry wanted Red Lewis back for tarring and feathering after he wrote *Main Street*. And today Sauk Centre celebrates itself for having produced him. We, as a nation, are as hungry for history as was England when Geoffrey of Monmouth concocted his History of British Kings, many of whom he manufactured to meet a growing demand. And as in states and communities, so in individual Americans this hunger for decent association with the past. Genealogists are worked to death winnowing the debris of ancestry for grains of greatness. Not long ago it was proved that Dwight D. Eisenhower was descended from the royal line of Britain, a proof if one were needed that everyone is descended from everyone. The then little town where I was born, which within my grandfather's memory was a blacksmith shop in a swamp, recalls with yearly pageantry a glowing past of Spanish dons and rose-eating senoritas who have in public memory wiped out the small, desolate tribe of grub- and grasshopper-eating Indians who were our true first settlers.

I find this interesting, but it does make for suspicion of history as a record of reality. I thought of these things as I read the historical markers across the country, thought how the myth wipes out the fact. On a very low level the following is the process of a myth. Visiting in the town where I was born, I talked with a very old man who had known me as a child. He remembered vividly seeing me, a peaked, shivering child walking past his house one freezing morning, my inadequate overcoat fastened across my little chest with horse-blanket pins. This in its small way is the very stuff of myths—the poor and suffering child who rises to glory, on a limited scale of course. Even though I didn't remember the episode, I knew it could not be true. My mother was a passionate sewer-on of buttons. A button off was more than sloppiness; it was a sin. If I had pinned my coat, my mother would have whaled me. The story could not be true, but this old gentleman so loved it that I could never convince him of its falsity, so I didn't try. If my home town wants me in horse-blanket pins, nothing I can do is likely to change it, particularly the truth.

It rained in New York State, the Empire State, rained cold and pitiless, as the highway-sign writers would put it. Indeed the dismal downpour made my intended visit to Niagara Falls seem redundant. I was then hopelessly lost in the streets of a small but endless town in the neighborhood of Medina, I think. I pulled to the side of the street and got out my book of road maps. But to find where you are going, you must know where you are, and I didn't. The windows of the cab were tightly closed and opaque with streaming rain. My car radio played softly. Suddenly there was a knock on the window, the door was wrenched open, and a man slipped into the seat beside me. The man was quite red of face, quite whisky of breath. His trousers were held up by red braces over the long gray underwear that covered his chest.

"Turn that damn thing off," he said, and then turned off my radio himself. "My daughter saw you out the window," he continued. "Thought you was in trouble." He looked at my maps. "Throw those things away. Now, where is it you want to go?"

I don't know why it is a man can't answer such a question with the truth. The truth was that I had turned off the big highway 104 and into the smaller roads because the traffic was heavy and passing vehicles threw sheets of water on my windshield. I wanted to go to Niagara Falls. Why couldn't I have admitted it? I looked down at my map and said, "I'm trying to get to Erie, Pennsylvania."

"Good," he said. "Now, throw those maps away. Now you

turn around, go two traffic lights, that'll bring you to Egg Street. Turn left there and about two hundred yards on Egg turn right at an angle. That's a twisty kind of street and you'll come to an overpass, but don't take it. You turn left there and it will curve around like this—see? Like this." His hand made a curving motion. "Now, when the curve straightens out you'll come to three branching roads. There's a big red house on the left-hand branch so you don't take that, you take the right-hand branch. Now, have you got that so far?"

"Sure," I said. "That's easy."

"Well repeat it back so I'll know you're going right."

I had stopped listening at the curving road. I said, "Maybe you better tell me again."

"I thought so. Turn around and go two traffic lights to Egg Street, turn left for two hundred yards and turn right at an angle on a twisty street till you come to an overpass but don't take it."

"That clears it up for me," I said quickly. "I sure do thank you for helping me out."

"Hell," he said, "I ain't even got you out of town yet."

Well, he got me out of town by a route which, if I could have remembered it, let alone followed it, would have made the path into the Labyrinth at Knossos seem like a throughway. When he was finally satisfied and thanked, he got out and slammed the door, but such is my social cowardice that I actually did turn around, knowing he would be watching out the window. I drove around two blocks and blundered my way back to 104, traffic or not.

*

NIAGARA FALLS is very nice. It's like a large version of the old Bond sign on Times Square. I'm very glad I saw it, because from now on if I am asked whether I have seen Niagara Falls I can say yes, and be telling the truth for once.

When I told my adviser that I was going to Erie, Pennsylvania, I had no idea of going there, but as it turned out, I was. My intention was to creep across the neck of Ontario, bypassing not only Erie but Cleveland and Toledo.

I find out of long experience that I admire all nations and

hate all governments, and nowhere is my natural anarchism more aroused than at national borders where patient and efficient public servants carry out their duties in matters of immigration and customs. I have never smuggled anything in my life. Why, then, do I feel an uneasy sense of guilt on approaching a customs barrier? I crossed a high toll bridge and negotiated a no man's land and came to the place where the Stars and Stripes stood shoulder to shoulder with the Union Jack. The Canadians were very kind. They asked where I was going and for how long, gave Rocinante a cursory inspection, and came at last to Charley.

"Do you have a certificate of rabies vaccination on the dog?"

"No, I haven't. You see he's an old dog. He was vaccinated long ago."

Another official came out. "We advise you not to cross the border with him, then."

"But I'm just crossing a small part of Canada and reentering the U.S."

"We understand," they said kindly. "You can take him into Canada but the U.S. won't let him back."

"But technically I am still in the U.S. and there's no complaint."

"There will be if he crosses the line and tries to get back."

"Well, where can I get him vaccinated?"

They didn't know. I would have to retrace my way at least twenty miles, find a vet, have Charley vaccinated, and then return. I was crossing only to save a little time, and this would wipe out the time saved and much more.

"Please understand, it is your own government, not ours. We are simply advising you. It's the rule."

I guess this is why I hate governments, all governments. It is always the rule, the fine print, carried out by fine-print men. There's nothing to fight, no wall to hammer with frustrated fists. I highly approve of vaccination, feel it should be compulsory; rabies is a dreadful thing. And yet I found myself hating the rule and all governments that made rules. It was not the shots but the certificate that was important. And it is usually so with governments—not a fact but a small slip of paper. These were such nice men, friendly and helpful. It was a slow time at the border. They gave me a cup of tea and Charley half a dozen cookies. And they seemed genuinely sorry that I had to go to Erie, Pennsylvania, for the lack of a paper. And so I turned about and proceeded toward the Stars and Stripes and another government. Exiting I had not been required to stop, but now the barrier was down.

"Are you an American citizen?"

"Yes, sir, here's my passport."

"Do you have anything to declare?"

"I haven't been away."

"Have you a rabies vaccination certificate for your dog?"

"He hasn't been away either."

"But you are coming from Canada."

"I have not been in Canada."

I saw the steel come into eyes, the brows lower to a level of suspicion. Far from saving time, it looked as though I might lose much more than even Erie, Pennsylvania.

"Will you step into the office?"

This request had the effect on me a Gestapo knock on the door might have. It raises panic, anger, and guilty feelings whether or not I have done wrong. My voice took on the strident tone of virtuous outrage which automatically arouses suspicion.

"Please step into the office."

"I tell you I have not been in Canada. If you were watching, you would have seen that I turned back."

"Step this way, please, sir."

Then into the telephone: "New York license so-and-so. Yes. Pick-up truck with camper top. Yes—a dog." And to me: "What kind of dog is it?"

"Poodle."

"Poodle—I said poodle. Light brown."

"Blue," I said.

"Light brown. Okay. Thanks."

I do hope I did not sense a certain sadness at my innocence.

"They say you didn't cross the line."

"That's what I told you."

"May I see your passport?"

"Why? I haven't left the country. I'm not about to leave the country." But I handed over my passport just the same. He leafed through it, pausing at the entry-and-exit stamps of other journeys. He inspected my photograph, opened the yellow smallpox vaccination certificate stapled to the back cover. At the bottom of the last page he saw pencilled in a faint set of letters and figures. "What is this?"

"I don't know. Let me see. Oh, that! Why, it's a telephone number."

"What's it doing in your passport?"

"I guess I didn't have a slip of paper. I don't even remember whose number it is."

By now he had me on the run and he knew it. "Don't you know it is against the law to deface a passport?"

"I'll erase it."

"You should not write anything in your passport. That's the regulation."

"I won't ever do it again. I promise." And I wanted to promise him I wouldn't lie or steal or associate with persons of loose morals, or covet my neighbor's wife, or anything. He closed my passport firmly and handed it back to me. I'm sure he felt better having found that telephone number. Suppose after all his trouble he hadn't found me guilty of anything, and on a slow day.

"Thank you, sir," I said. "May I proceed now?"

He waved his hand kindly. "Go ahead," he said.

And that's why I went toward Erie, Pennsylvania, and it was Charley's fault. I crossed the high iron bridge and stopped to pay toll. The man leaned out the window. "Go on," he said, "it's on the house."

"How do you mean?"

"I seen you go through the other way a little while ago. I seen the dog. I knew you'd be back."

"Why didn't you tell me?"

"Nobody believes it. Go ahead. You get a free ride one way."

He wasn't government, you see. But government can make you feel so small and mean that it takes some doing to build back a sense of self-importance. Charley and I stayed at the grandest auto court we could find that night, a place only the rich could afford, a pleasure dome of ivory and apes and peacocks and moreover with a restaurant, and room service. I ordered ice and soda and made a scotch and soda and then another. Then I had a waiter in and bespoke soup and a steak and a pound of raw hamburger for Charley, and I overtipped mercilessly. Before I went to sleep I went over all the things I wished I had said to that immigration man, and some of them were incredibly clever and cutting.

*

FROM the beginning of my journey, I had avoided the great high-speed slashes of concrete and tar called "thruways," or "super-highways." Various states have different names for them, but I had dawdled in New England, the winter grew apace, and I had visions of being snowbound in North Dakota. I sought out U.S. 90, a wide gash of a super-highway, multiple-lane carrier of the nation's goods. Rocinante bucketed along. The minimum speed on this road was greater than any I had previously driven. I drove into a wind quartering in from my starboard bow and felt the buffeting, sometimes staggering blows of the gale I helped to make. I could hear the sough of it on the square surfaces of my camper top. Instructions screamed at me from the road once: "Do not stop! No stopping. Maintain speed." Trucks as long as freighters went roaring by, delivering a wind like the blow of a fist. These great roads are wonderful for moving goods but not for inspection of a countryside. You are bound to the wheel and your eyes to the car ahead and to the rear-view mirror for the car behind and the side mirror for the car or truck about to pass, and at the same time you must read all the signs for fear you may miss some instructions or orders. No roadside stands selling squash juice, no antique stores, no farm products or factory outlets. When we get these thruways across the whole country, as we will and must, it will be possible to drive from New York to California without seeing a single thing.

At intervals there are places of rest and recreation, food, fuel and oil, postcards, steam-table food, picnic tables, garbage cans all fresh and newly painted, rest rooms and lavatories so spotless, so incensed with deodorants and with detergents that it takes a time to get your sense of smell back. For deodorants are not quite correctly named; they substitute one smell for another, and the substitute must be much stronger and more penetrating than the odor it conquers. I had neglected my own country too long. Civilization had made great strides in my absence. I remember when a coin in a slot would get you a stick of gum or a candy bar, but in these dining palaces were vending machines where various coins could deliver handkerchiefs, comb-and-nail-file sets, hair conditioners and cosmetics, first-aid kits, minor drugs such as aspirin, mild physics, pills to keep you awake. I found myself entranced with these gadgets. Suppose you want a soft drink; you pick your kind—Sungrape or Cooly Cola—press a button, insert the coin, and stand back. A paper cup drops into place, the drink pours out and stops a quarter of an inch from the brim—a cold, refreshing drink guaranteed synthetic. Coffee is even more interesting, for when the hot black fluid has ceased, a squirt of milk comes down and an envelope of sugar drops beside the cup. But of all, the hot-soup machine is the triumph. Choose among ten—pea, chicken noodle, beef and veg., insert the coin. A rumbling hum comes from the giant and a sign lights up that reads "Heating." After a minute a red light flashes on and off until you open a little door and remove the paper cup of boiling-hot soup.

It is life at a peak of some kind of civilization. The restaurant accommodations, great scallops of counters with simulated leather stools, are as spotless as and not unlike the lavatories. Everything that can be captured and held down is sealed in clear plastic. The food is oven-fresh, spotless and tasteless; untouched by human hands. I remembered with an ache certain dishes in France and Italy touched by innumerable human hands.

These centers for rest, food, and replenishment are kept beautiful with lawns and flowers. At the front, nearest the highway, are parking places for passenger automobiles together with regiments of gasoline pumps. At the rear the trucks draw up, and there they have their services—the huge overland caravans. Being technically a truck, Rocinante took her place in the rear, and I soon made acquaintance with the truckers. They are a breed set apart from the life around them, the long-distance truckers. In some town or city somewhere their wives and children live while the husbands traverse the nation carrying every kind of food and product and machine. They are clannish and they stick together, speaking a specialized language. And although I was a small craft among monsters of transportation they were kind to me and helpful.

I learned that in the truck parks there are showers and soap and towels—that I could park and sleep the night if I wished. The men had little commerce with local people, but being avid radio listeners they could report news and politics from all parts of the nation. The food and fuel centers on the parkways or thruways are leased by the various states, but on other highways private enterprise has truckers' stations that offer discounts on fuel, beds, baths, and places to sit and shoot the breeze. But being a specialized group, leading special lives, associating only with their own kind, they would have made it possible for me to cross the country without talking to a local town-bound man. For the truckers cruise over the surface of the nation without being a part of it. Of course in the towns where their families live they have whatever roots are possible—clubs, dances, love affairs, and murders.

I liked the truckers very much, as I always like specialists. By listening to them talk I accumulated a vocabulary of the road, of tires and springs, of overweight. The truckers over long distances have stations along their routes where they know the service men and the waitresses behind the counters, and where occasionally they meet their opposite numbers in other trucks. The great get-together symbol is the cup of coffee. I found I often stopped for coffee, not because I wanted it but for a rest and a change from the unrolling highway. It takes strength and control and attention to drive a truck long distances, no matter how much the effort is made easier by air brakes and power-assisted steering. It would be interesting to know and easy to establish with modern testing methods how much energy in foot pounds is expended in driving a truck for six hours. Once Ed Ricketts and I, collecting marine animals, turning over rocks in an area, tried to estimate how much weight we lifted in an average collecting day. The stones we turned over were not large—weighing from three to fifty pounds. We estimated that on a rich day, when we had little sense of energy expended, each of us had lifted four to ten tons of rock. Consider then the small, unnoticed turning of the steering wheel, perhaps the exertion of only one pound for each motion, the varying pressure of foot on accelerator, not more than half a pound perhaps but an enormous total over a period of six hours. Then there are the muscles of shoulders and neck, constantly if unconsciously flexed for emergency, the eyes darting from road to rear-view mirror, the thousand decisions so deep that the conscious mind is not aware of them. The output of energy, nervous and muscular, is enormous. Thus the coffee break is a rest in many senses.

Quite often I sat with these men and listened to their talk and now and then asked questions. I soon learned not to expect knowledge of the country they passed through. Except for the truck stops, they had no contact with it. It was driven home to me how like sailors they were. I remember when I first went to sea being astonished that the men who sailed over the world and touched the ports to the strange and exotic had little contact with that world. Some of the truckers on long hauls traveled in pairs and took their turns. The one off duty slept or read paperbacks. But on the roads their interests were engines, and weather, and maintaining the speed that makes a predictable schedule possible. Some of them were on regular runs back and forth while others moved over single operations. It is a whole pattern of life, little known to the settled people along the routes of the great trucks. I learned only enough about these men to be sure I would like to know much more.

If one has driven a car over many years, as I have, nearly all reactions have become automatic. One does not think about what to do. Nearly all the driving technique is deeply buried in a machine-like unconscious. This being so, a large area of the conscious mind is left free for thinking. And what do people think of when they drive? On short trips perhaps of arrival at a destination or memory of events at the place of departure. But there is left, particularly on very long trips, a large area for day-dreaming or even, God help us, for thought. No one can know what another does in that area. I myself have planned houses I will never build, have made gardens I will never plant, have designed a method for pumping the soft silt and decayed shells from the bottom of my bay up to my point of land at Sag Harbor, of leeching out the salt, thus making a rich and productive soil. I don't know whether or not I will do this, but driving along I have planned it in detail even to the kind of pump, the leeching bins, the tests to determine disappearance of salinity. Driving, I have created turtle traps in my mind, have written long, detailed letters never to be put to paper, much less sent. When the radio was on, music has stimulated memory of times and places, complete with characters and stage sets, memories so exact that every word of dialogue is recreated. And I have projected future scenes, just as complete and convincing—scenes that will never take place. I've written short stories in my mind, chuckling at my own humor, saddened or stimulated by structure or content.

I can only suspect that the lonely man peoples his driving dreams with friends, that the loveless man surrounds himself with lovely loving women, and that children climb through the dreaming of the childless driver. And how about the areas of regrets? If only I had done so-and-so, or had not said such-and-such—my God, the damn thing might not have happened. Finding this potential in my own mind, I can suspect it in others, but I will never know, for no one ever tells. And this is why, on my journey which was designed for observation, I stayed as much as possible on secondary roads where there was much to see and hear and smell, and avoided the great wide traffic slashes which promote the self by fostering daydreams. I drove this wide, eventless way called U.S. 90 which bypassed Buffalo and Erie to Madison, Ohio, and then found the equally wide and fast U.S. 20 past Cleveland and Toledo, and so into Michigan.

On these roads out of the manufacturing centers there moved many mobile homes, pulled by specially designed trucks, and since these mobile homes comprise one of my generalities, I may as well get to them now. Early in my travels I had become aware of these new things under the sun, of their great numbers, and since they occur in increasing numbers all over the nation, observation of them and perhaps some speculation is in order. They are not trailers to be pulled by one's own car but shining cars long as pullmans. From the beginning of my travels I had noticed the sale lots where they were sold and traded, but then I began to be aware of the parks where they sit down in uneasy permanence. In Maine I took to stopping the night in these parks, talking to the managers and to the dwellers in this new kind of housing, for they gather in groups of like to like.

They are wonderfully built homes, aluminum skins, double-walled, with insulation, and often paneled with veneer of hardwood. Sometimes as much as forty feet long, they have two to five rooms, and are complete with air-conditioners, toilets, baths, and invariably television. The parks where they sit are sometimes landscaped and equipped with every facility. I talked with the park men, who were enthusiastic. A mobile home is drawn to the trailer park and installed on a ramp, a heavy rubber sewer pipe is bolted underneath, water and electric power connected, the television antenna raised, and the family is in residence. Several park managers agreed that last year one in four new housing units in the whole country was a mobile home. The park men charge a small ground rent plus fees for water and electricity. Telephones are connected in nearly all of them simply by plugging in a jack. Sometimes the park has a general store for supplies, but if not the supermarkets which dot the countryside are available. Parking difficulties in the towns have caused these markets to move to the open country where they are immune from town taxes. This is also true of the trailer parks. The fact that these homes can be moved does not mean that they do move. Sometimes their owners stay for years in one place, plant gardens, build little walls of cinder blocks, put out awnings and garden furniture. It is a whole way of life that was new to me. These homes are never cheap and often are quite expensive and lavish. I have seen some that cost $20,000 and contained all the thousand appliances we live by—dishwashers, automatic clothes washers and driers, refrigerators and deep freezes.

The owners were not only willing but glad and proud to show their homes to me. The rooms, while small, were well proportioned. Every conceivable unit was built in. Wide windows, some even called picture windows, destroyed any sense of being closed in; the bedrooms and beds were spacious and the storage space unbelievable. It seemed to me a revolution in living and on a rapid increase. Why did a family choose to live in such a home? Well, it was comfortable, compact, easy to keep clean, easy to heat.

In Maine: "I'm tired of living in a cold barn with the wind whistling through, tired of the torment of little taxes and payments for this and that. It's warm and cozy and in the summer the air-conditioner keeps us cool."

"What is the usual income bracket of the mobiles?"

"That is variable but a goodly number are in the ten-thousand- to twenty-thousand-dollar class."

"Has job uncertainty anything to do with the rapid increase of these units?"

"Well perhaps there may be some of that. Who knows what is in store tomorrow? Mechanics, plant engineers, architects, accountants, and even here and there a doctor or a dentist live in the mobile. If a plant or a factory closes down, you're not trapped with property you can't sell. Suppose the husband has a job and is buying a house and there's a layoff. The value goes out of his house. But if he has a mobile home he rents a trucking service and moves on and he hasn't lost anything. He may never have to do it, but the fact that he can is a comfort to him."

"How are they purchased?"

"On time, just like an automobile. It's like paying rent."

And then I discovered the greatest selling appeal of all—one that crawls through nearly all American life. Improvements are made on these mobile homes every year. If you are doing well you turn yours in on a new model just as you do with an automobile if you can possibly afford to. There's status to that. And the turn-in value is higher than that of automobiles because there's a ready market for used homes. And after a few years the once expensive home may have a poorer family. They are easy to maintain, need no paint since they are usually of aluminum, and are not tied to fluctuating land values.

"How about schools?"

The school buses pick the children up right at the park and bring them back. The family car takes the head of the house to work and the family to a drive-in movie at night. It's a healthy life out in the country air. The payments, even if high and festooned with interest, are no worse than renting an apartment and fighting the owner for heat. And where could you rent such a comfortable ground-floor apartment with a place for your car outside the door? Where else could the kids have a dog? Nearly every mobile home has a dog, as Charley discovered to his delight. Twice I was invited to dinner in a mobile home and several times watched a football game on television. A manager told me that one of the first considerations in his business was to find and buy a place where television reception is good. Since I did not require any facilities, sewer, water, or electricity, the price to me for stopping the night was one dollar.

The first impression forced on me was that permanence is neither achieved nor desired by mobile people. They do not buy for the generations, but only until a new model they can afford comes out. The mobile units are by no means limited to the park communities. Hundreds of them will be found sitting beside a farm house, and this was explained to me. There was a time when, on the occasion of a son's marriage and the addition of a wife and later of children to the farm, it was customary to add a wing or at least a lean-to on the home place. Now in many cases a mobile unit takes the place of additional building. A farmer from whom I bought eggs and home-smoked bacon told me of the advantages. Each family has a privacy it never had before. The old folks are not irritated by crying babies. The mother-in-law problem is abated because the new daughter has a privacy she never had and a place of her own in which to build the structure of a family. When they move away, and nearly all Americans move away, or want to, they do not leave unused and therefore useless rooms. Relations between the generations are greatly improved. The son is a guest when he visits the parents' house, and the parents are guests in the son's house.

Then there are the loners, and I have talked with them also. Driving along, you see high on a hill a single mobile home placed to command a great view. Others nestle under trees fringing a river or a lake. These loners have rented a tiny piece of land from the owner. They need only enough for the unit and the right of passage to get to it. Sometimes the loner digs a well and a cesspool, and plants a small garden, but others transport their water in fifty-gallon oil drums. Enormous ingenuity is apparent with some of the loners in placing the water supply higher than the unit and connecting it with plastic pipe so that a gravity flow is insured.

One of the dinners that I shared in a mobile home was

cooked in an immaculate kitchen, walled in plastic tile, with stainless-steel sinks and ovens and stoves flush with the wall. The fuel is butane or some other bottled gas which can be picked up anywhere. We ate in a dining alcove paneled in mahogany veneer. I've never had a better or a more comfortable dinner. I had brought a bottle of whisky as my contribution, and afterward we sat in deep comfortable chairs cushioned in foam rubber. This family liked the way they lived and wouldn't think of going back to the old way. The husband worked as a garage mechanic about four miles away and made good pay. Two children walked to the highway every morning and were picked up by a yellow school bus.

Sipping a highball after dinner, hearing the rushing of water in the electric dishwasher in the kitchen, I brought up a question that had puzzled me. These were good, thoughtful, intelligent people. I said, "One of our most treasured feelings concerns roots, growing up rooted in some soil or some community." How did they feel about raising their children without roots? Was it good or bad? Would they miss it or not?

The father, a good-looking, fair-skinned man with dark eyes, answered me. "How many people today have what you are talking about? What roots are there in an apartment twelve floors up? What roots are in a housing development of hundreds and thousands of small dwellings almost exactly alike? My father came from Italy," he said. "He grew up in Tuscany in a house where his family had lived maybe a thousand years. That's roots for you, no running water, no toilet, and they cooked with charcoal or vine clippings. They had just two rooms, a kitchen and a bedroom where everybody slept, grandpa, father and all the kids, no place to read, no place to be alone, and never had had. Was that better? I bet if you gave my old man the choice he'd cut his roots and live like this." He waved his hands at the comfortable room. "Fact is, he cut his roots away and came to America. Then he lived in a tenement in New York—just one room, walk-up, cold water and no heat. That's where I was born and I lived in the streets as a kid until my old man got a job upstate in New York in the grape country. You see, he knew about vines, that's about all he knew. Now you take my wife. She's Irish descent. Her people had roots too."

"In a peat bog," the wife said. "And lived on potatoes." She gazed fondly through the door at her fine kitchen.

"Don't you miss some kind of permanence?"

"Who's got permanence? Factory closes down, you move on. Good times and things opening up, you move on where it's better. You got roots you sit and starve. You take the pioneers in the history books. They were movers. Take up land, sell it, move on. I read in a book how Lincoln's family came to Illinois on a raft. They had some barrels of whisky for a bank account. How many kids in America stay in the place where they were born, if they can get out?"

"You've thought about it a lot."

"Don't have to think about it. There it is. I've got a good trade. Long as there's automobiles I can get work, but suppose the place I work goes broke. I got to move where there's a job. I get to my job in three minutes. You want I should drive twenty miles because I got roots?"

Later they showed me magazines designed exclusively for mobile dwellers, stories and poems and hints for successful mobile living. How to stop a leak. How to choose a place for sun or coolness. And there were advertisements for gadgets, fascinating things, for cooking, cleaning, washing clothes, furniture and beds and cribs. Also there were full-page pictures of new models, each one grander and more shiny than the next.

"There's thousands of them," said the father, "and there's going to be millions."

"Joe's quite a dreamer," the wife said. "He's always figuring something out. Tell him your ideas, Joe."

"Maybe he wouldn't be interested."

"Sure I would."

"Well, it's not a dream like she said, it's for real, and I'm going to do it pretty soon now. Take a little capital, but it would pay off. I been looking around the used lots for the unit I want at the price I want to pay. Going to rip out the guts and set it up for a repair shop. I got enough tools nearly already, and I'll stock little things like windshield wipers and fan belts and cylinder rings and inner tubes, stuff like that. You take these courts are getting bigger and bigger. Some of the mobile people got two cars. I'll rent me a hundred feet of ground right near and I'll be in business. There's one thing you can say about cars, there's nearly always something wrong with them that's got to be fixed. And I'll have my house, this here one right beside my shop. That way I would have a bell and give twenty-four-hour service."

"Sounds like a good deal," I said. And it does.

"Best thing about it," Joe went on, "if business fell off, why, I'd just move on where it was good."

His wife said, "Joe's got it all worked out on paper where everything's going to go, every wrench and drill, even an electric welder. Joe's a wonderful welder."

I said, "I take back what I said, Joe. I guess you've got your roots in a grease pit."

"You could do worse. I even worked that out. And you know, when the kids grow up, we could even work our way south in the winter and north in the summer."

"Joe does good work," said his wife. "He's got his own steady customers where he works. Some men come fifty miles to get Joe to work on their cars because he does good work."

"I'm a real good mechanic," said Joe.

Driving the big highway near Toledo I had a conversation with Charley on the subject of roots. He listened but he didn't reply. In the pattern-thinking about roots I and most other people have left two things out of consideration. Could it be that Americans are a restless people, a mobile people, never satisfied with where they are as a matter of selection? The pioneers, the immigrants who peopled the continent, were the restless ones in Europe. The steady rooted ones stayed home and are still there. But every one of us, except the Negroes forced here as slaves, are descended from the restless ones, the wayward ones who were not content to stay at home. Wouldn't it be unusual if we had not inherited this tendency? And the fact is that we have. But that's the short view. What are roots and how long have we had them? If our species has existed for a couple of million years, what is its history? Our remote ancestors followed the game, moved with the food supply, and fled from evil weather, from ice and the changing seasons. Then after millennia beyond thinking they domesticated some animals so that they lived with their food supply. Then of necessity they followed the grass that fed their flocks in endless wanderings. Only when agriculture came into practice—and that's not very long ago in terms of the whole history—did a place achieve meaning and value and permanence. But land is a tangible, and tangibles have a way of getting into few hands. Thus it was that one man wanted ownership of land and at the same time wanted servitude because someone had to work it. Roots were in ownership of land, in tangible and immovable possessions. In this view we are a restless species with a very short history of roots, and those not widely distributed. Perhaps we have overrated roots as a psychic need. Maybe the greater the urge, the deeper and more ancient is the need, the will, the hunger to be somewhere else.

Charley had no answer to my premise. Also, he was a mess. I had promised myself to keep him combed and clipped and beautiful, and I hadn't done it. His fur was balled and dirty. Poodles do not shed any more than sheep do. At night, when I had planned this virtuous grooming, I was always too busy with something else. Also I discovered a dangerous allergy I didn't know he had. One night I had pulled up at a trucker's park where huge cattle trucks put up and cleaned their beds; around the park there was a mountain of manure and a fog of flies. Although Rocinante was screened the flies got in in their millions and hid in corners and would not be dislodged. For the first time I got out the bug bomb and sprayed heavily, and Charley broke into a sneezing attack so violent and prolonged that I had finally to carry him out in my arms. In the morning the cab was full of sleepy flies and I sprayed it and Charley had another attack. After that, whenever flying visitors invaded I had to close Charley out and air out the house or cab after the pests were dead. I never saw such a severe allergy.

Since I hadn't seen the Middle West for a long time many impressions crowded in on me as I drove through Ohio and Michigan and Illinois. The first was the enormous increase in population. Villages had become towns and towns had grown to cities. The roads squirmed with traffic; the cities were so dense with people that all attention had to be devoted to not hitting anyone or not being hit. The next impression was of an electric energy, a force, almost a fluid of energy so powerful as to be stunning in its impact. No matter what the direction, whether for good or for bad, the vitality was everywhere. I don't think for a second that the people I had seen and talked to in New England were either unfriendly or discourteous, but they spoke tersely and usually waited for the newcomer to open communication. Almost on crossing the Ohio line it seemed to me that people were more open and more outgoing. The waitress in a roadside stand said good morning before I had a chance to, discussed breakfast as though she liked the idea, spoke with enthusiasm about the weather, sometimes even offered some information about herself without my delving. Strangers talked freely to one another without caution. I had forgotten how rich and beautiful is the countryside—the deep topsoil, the wealth of great trees, the lake country of Michigan handsome as a well-made woman, and dressed and jeweled. It seemed to me that the earth was generous and outgoing here in the heartland, and perhaps the people took a cue from it.

One of my purposes was to listen, to hear speech, accent, speech rhythms, overtones and emphasis. For speech is so much more than words and sentences. I did listen everywhere. It seemed to me that regional speech is in the process of disappearing, not gone but going. Forty years of radio and twenty years of television must have this impact. Communications must destroy localness, by a slow, inevitable process. I can remember a time when I could almost pinpoint a man's place of origin by his speech. That is growing more difficult now and will in some foreseeable future become impossible. It is a rare house or building that is not rigged with spiky combers of the air. Radio and television speech becomes standardized, perhaps better English than we have ever used. Just as our bread, mixed and baked, packaged and sold without benefit of accident or human frailty, is uniformly good and uniformly tasteless, so will our speech become one speech.

I who love words and the endless possibility of words am saddened by this inevitability. For with local accent will disappear local tempo. The idioms, the figures of speech that make language rich and full of the poetry of place and time must go. And in their place will be a national speech, wrapped and packaged, standard and tasteless. Localness is not gone but it is going. In the many years since I have listened to the land the change is very great. Traveling west along the northern routes I did not hear a truly local speech until I reached Montana. That is one of the reasons I fell in love again with Montana.

The West Coast went back to packaged English. The Southwest kept a grasp but a slipping grasp on localness. Of course the deep south holds on by main strength to its regional expressions, just as it holds and treasures some other anachronisms, but no region can hold out for long against the highway, the high-tension line, and the national television. What I am mourning is perhaps not worth saving, but I regret its loss nevertheless.

Even while I protest the assembly-line production of our food, our songs, our language, and eventually our souls, I know that it was a rare home that baked good bread in the old days. Mother's cooking was with rare exceptions poor, that good unpasteurized milk touched only by flies and bits of manure crawled with bacteria, the healthy old-time life was riddled with aches, sudden death from unknown causes, and that sweet local speech I mourn was the child of illiteracy and ignorance. It is the nature of a man as he grows older, a small bridge in time, to protest against change, particularly change for the better. But it is true that we have exchanged corpulence for starvation, and either one will kill us. The lines of change are down. We, or at least I, can have no conception of human life and human thought in a hundred years or fifty years. Perhaps my greatest wisdom is the knowledge that I do not know. The sad ones are those who waste their energy in trying to hold it back, for they can only feel bitterness in loss and no joy in gain.

As I passed through or near the great hives of production—Youngstown, Cleveland, Akron, Toledo, Pontiac, Flint, and later South Bend and Gary—my eyes and mind were battered by the fantastic hugeness and energy of production, a complication that resembles chaos and cannot be. So might one look down on an ant hill and see no method or direction or purpose in the darting hurrying inhabitants. What was so wonderful was that I could come again to a quiet country road, tree-bordered, with fenced fields and cows, could pull up Rocinante beside a lake of clear, clean water and see high overhead the arrows of southing ducks and geese. There Charley could with his delicate exploring nose read his own particular literature on bushes and tree trunks and leave his message there, perhaps as important in endless time as these pen scratches I put down on perishable paper. There in the quiet, with the wind flicking tree branches and distorting the water's mirror, I cooked improbable dinners in my disposable aluminum pans, made coffee so rich and sturdy it would float a nail, and, sitting on my own back doorsteps, could finally come to think about what I had seen and try to arrange some pattern of thought to accommodate the teeming crowds of my seeing and hearing.

I'll tell you what it was like. Go to the Ufizzi in Florence, the Louvre in Paris, and you are so crushed with the numbers, once the might of greatness, that you go away distressed, with a feeling like constipation. And then when you are alone and remembering, the canvases sort themselves out; some are eliminated by your taste or your limitations, but others stand up clear and clean. Then you can go back to look at one thing untroubled by the shouts of the multitude. After confusion I can go into the Prado in Madrid and pass unseeing the thousand pictures shouting for my attention and I can visit a friend—a not large Greco, *San Pablo con un Libro*. St. Paul has just closed the book. His finger marks the last page read and on his face are the wonder and will to understand after the book is closed. Maybe understanding is possible only after. Years ago when I used to work in the woods it was said of lumber men that they did their logging in the whorehouse and their sex in the woods. So I have to find my way through the exploding production lines of the Middle West while sitting alone beside a lake in northern Michigan.

As I sat secure in the silence, a jeep scuffed to a stop on the road and good Charley left his work and roared. A young man in boots, corduroys, and a red and black checked mackinaw climbed out and strode near. He spoke in the harsh unfriendly tone a man uses when he doesn't much like what he has to do.

"Don't you know this land is posted? This is private property."

Normally his tone would have sparked a tinder in me. I would have flared an ugliness of anger and he would then have been able to evict me with pleasure and good conscience. We might even have edged into a quarrel with passion and violence. That would be only normal, except that the beauty and the quiet made me slow to respond with resentment, and in my hesitation I lost it. I said, "I knew it must be private. I was about to look for someone to ask permission or maybe pay to rest here."

"The owner don't want campers. They leave papers around and build fires."

"I don't blame him. I know the mess they make."

"See that sign on that tree? No trespassing, hunting, fishing, camping."

"Well," I said, "that sounds as if it means business. If it's your job to throw me off, you've got to throw me off. I'll go peacefully. But I've just made a pot of coffee. Do you think your boss would mind if I finished it? Would he mind if I offered you a cup? Then you could kick me off quicker."

The young man grinned. "What the hell," he said. "You don't build no fires and you don't throw out no trash."

"I'm doing worse than that. I'm trying to bribe you with a cup of coffee. It's worse than that, too. I'm suggesting a dollop of Old Granddad in the coffee."

He laughed then. "What the hell!" he said. "Let me get my jeep off the road."

Well, the whole pattern was broken. He squatted cross-legged in the pine needles on the ground and sipped his coffee. Charley sniffed close and let himself be touched, and that's a rare thing for Charley. He does not permit strangers to touch him, just happens to be somewhere else. But this young man's fingers found the place behind the ears Charley delights to have rubbed, and he sighed contentedly and sat down.

"What you doing—going hunting? I see your guns in the truck."

"Just driving through. You know how you see a place and it's just right, and you're just tired enough, I guess you can't help stopping."

"Yeah," he said. "I know what you mean. You got a nice outfit."

"I like it and Charley likes it."

"Charley? Never heard of a dog named Charley. Hello, Charley."

"I wouldn't want to get you in trouble with your boss. Think I ought to drag ass now?"

"What the hell?" he said. "He ain't here. I'm in charge. You ain't doing no harm."

"I'm trespassing."

"Know something? Fella camped here, kind of a nut. So I came to kick him off. He said something funny. He says, 'Trespassing ain't a crime and ain't a misdemeanor.' He says it's a tort. Now what the hell does that mean? He was a kind of a nut."

"Search me," I said, "I'm not a nut. Let me warm up your coffee." I warmed it two ways.

"You make swell coffee," said my host.

"Before it gets too dark I've got to find a place to park. Know any place up the road where they'll let me stay the night?"

"If you pull over that way behind those pine trees nobody could see you from the road."

"But I'd be committing a tort."

"Yeah. I wish to Christ I knew what that meant."

He drove ahead of me in the jeep and helped me find a level place in the pine grove. And after dark he came into Rocinante and admired her facilities and we drank some whisky together and had a nice visit and told each other a few lies. I showed him some fancy jigs and poppers I'd bought at Abercrombie and Fitch, and gave him one, and I gave him some paperback thrillers I'd finished with, all loaded with sex and sadism, and also a copy of *Field and Stream*. In return he invited me to stay as long as I wished and said that he'd come by tomorrow and we'd do a little fishing, and I accepted for one day at least. It's nice to have friends, and besides I wanted a little time to think about the things I'd seen, the huge factories and plants and the scurry and production.

The guardian of the lake was a lonely man, the more so because he had a wife. He showed me her picture in a plastic shield in his wallet, a prettyish blonde girl trying her best to live up to the pictures in the magazines, a girl of products, home permanents, shampoos, rinses, skin conditioners. She hated being out in what she called the Sticks, longed for the great and gracious life in Toledo or South Bend. Her only company was found in the shiny pages of *Charm* and *Glamour*. Eventually she would sulk her way to success. Her husband would get a job in some great clanging organism of progress, and they would live happily ever after. All this came through in small, oblique spurts in his conversation. She knew exactly what she wanted and he didn't, but his want would ache in him all his life. After he drove away in his jeep I lived his life for him and it put a mist of despair on me. He wanted his pretty little wife and he wanted something else and he couldn't have both.

Charley had a dream so violent that he awakened me. His legs jerked in the motions of running and he made little yipping cries. Perhaps he dreamed he chased some gigantic rabbit and couldn't quite catch it. Or maybe in his dream something chased him. On the second supposition I put out my hand and awakened him, but the dream must have been strong. He muttered to himself and complained and drank half a bowl of water before he went back to sleep.

The guardian came back soon after sun-up. He brought a rod and I got out my own and rigged a spinning reel, and had to find my glasses to tie on the bright painted popper. The monofilament line is transparent, said to be invisible to fish, and is completely invisible to me without my glasses.

I said, "You know, I don't have a fishing license."

"What the hell," he said, "we probably won't catch anything anyway."

And he was right, we didn't.

We walked and cast and walked and did everything we knew to interest bass or pike. My friend kept saying, "They're right down there if we can just get the message through." But we never did. If they were down there, they still are. A remarkable amount of my fishing is like that, but I like it just the same. My wants are simple. I have no desire to latch onto a monster symbol of fate and prove my manhood in titanic piscine war. But sometimes I do like a couple of cooperative fish of frying size. At noon I refused an invitation to come to dinner and meet the wife. I was growing increasingly anxious to meet my own wife, so I hurried on.

There was a time not too long ago when a man put out to sea and ceased to exist for two or three years or forever. And when the covered wagons set out to cross the continent, friends and relations remaining at home might never hear from the wanderers again. Life went on, problems were settled, decisions were taken. Even I can remember when a telegram meant just one thing—a death in the family. In one short lifetime the telephone has changed all that. If in this wandering narrative I seem to have cut the cords of family joys and sorrows, of Junior's current delinquency and junior Junior's new tooth, of business triumph and agony, it is not so. Three times a week from some bar, supermarket, or tire-and-tool cluttered service station, I put calls through to New York and reestablished my identity in time and space. For three or four minutes I had a name, and the duties and joys and frustrations a man carries with him like a comet's tail. It was like dodging back and forth from one dimension to another, a silent explosion of breaking through a sound barrier, a curious experience, like a quick dip into a known but alien water.

It was established that my wife was to fly out to meet me in Chicago for a short break in my journey. In two hours, in theory at least, she would slice through a segment of the earth it had taken me weeks to clamber over. I became impatient, stuck to the huge toll road that strings the northern border of Indiana, bypassed Elkhart and South Bend and Gary. The nature of the road describes the nature of the travel. The straightness of the way, the swish of traffic, the unbroken speed are hypnotic, and while the miles peel off an imperceptible exhaustion sets in. Day and night are one. The setting sun is neither an invitation nor a command to stop, for the traffic rolls constantly.

Late in the night I pulled into a rest area, had a hamburger at the great lunch counter that never closes, and walked Charley on the close-clipped grass. I slept an hour but awakened long before daylight. I had brought city suits and shirts and shoes, but had forgotten to bring a suitcase to transport them from truck to hotel room. Indeed, I don't know where I could have stored a suitcase. In a garbage can under an arc light I found a clean corrugated paper carton and packed my city clothes. I wrapped my clean white shirts in road maps and tied the carton with fishing line.

Knowing my tendency to panic in the roar and crush of traffic, I started into Chicago long before daylight. I wanted to end up at the Ambassador East, where I had reservations, and, true to form, ended up lost. Finally, in a burst of invention, I hired an all-night taxi to lead me, and sure enough I had passed very near my hotel. If the doorman and bellhops found my means of traveling unusual, they gave no sign. I handed out my suits on hangers, my shoes in the game pocket of a hunting coat, and my shirts in their neat wrapping of New England road maps. Rocinante was whisked away to a garage for storage. Charley had to go to a kennel to be stored, bathed, and Hollanderized. Even at his age he is a vain dog and loves to be beautified, but when he found he was to be left and in Chicago, his ordinary aplomb broke down and he cried out in rage and despair. I closed my ears and went away quickly to my hotel.

I think I am well and favorably known at the Ambassador East, but this need not apply when I arrive in wrinkled hunting clothes, unshaven and lightly crusted with the dirt of travel and bleary-eyed from driving most of the night. Certainly I had a reservation, but my room might not be vacated until noon. The hotel's position was explained to me carefully. I understood it and forgave the management. My own position was that I would like a bath and a bed, but since that was impossible I would simply pile up in a chair in the lobby and go to sleep until my room was ready.

I saw in the desk man's eyes his sense of uneasiness. Even I knew I would be no ornament to this elegant and expensive pleasure dome. He signaled an assistant manager, perhaps by telepathy, and all together we worked out a solution. A gentleman had just checked out to catch an early airplane. His room was not cleaned and prepared, but I was welcome to use it until mine was ready. Thus the problem was solved by intelligence and patience, and each got what he wanted—I had my chance at a hot bath and a sleep, and the hotel was spared the mischance of having me in the lobby.

The room had not been touched since its former occupant had left. I sank into a comfortable chair to pull off my boots and even got one of them off before I began to notice things and then more things and more. In a surprisingly short time I forgot the bath and the sleep and found myself deeply involved with Lonesome Harry.

An animal resting or passing by leaves crushed grass, footprints, and perhaps droppings, but a human occupying a room for one night prints his character, his biography, his recent history, and sometimes his future plans and hopes. I further believe that personality seeps into walls and is slowly released. This might well be an explanation of ghosts and such manifestations. Although my conclusions may be wrong, I seem to be sensitive to the spoor of the human. Also, I am not shy about admitting that I am an incorrigible Peeping Tom. I have never passed an unshaded window without looking in, have never closed my ears to a conversation that was none of my business. I can justify or even dignify this by protesting that in my trade I must know about people, but I suspect that I am simply curious.

As I sat in this unmade room, Lonesome Harry began to take shape and dimension. I could feel that recently departed guest in the bits and pieces of himself he had left behind. Of course Charley, even with his imperfect nose, would have known more. But Charley was in a kennel preparing to be clipped. Even so, Harry is as real to me as anyone I ever met, and more real than many. He is not unique, in fact is a member of a fairly large group. Therefore he becomes of interest in any investigation of America. Before I begin to patch him together, lest a number of men grow nervous, let me declare that his name is not Harry. He lives in Westport, Connecticut. This information comes from the laundry strips from several shirts. A man usually lives where he has his shirts laundered. I only suspect that he commutes to work in New York. His trip to Chicago was primarily a business trip with some traditional pleasures thrown in. I know his name because he signed it a number of times on hotel stationery, each signature with a slightly different slant. This seems to indicate that he is not entirely sure of himself in the business world, but there were other signs of that.

He had started a letter to his wife which also ended in the wastebasket. "Darling: Everything is going OK. Tried to call your aunt but no answer. I wish you were here with me. This is a lonesome town. You forgot to put in my cuff links. I bought a cheap pair at Marshall Field. I'm writing this while I wait for C.E. to call. Hope he brings the cont . . ."

It's just as well that Darling didn't drop in to make Chicago less lonesome for Harry. His guest was not C.E. with a contract. She was a brunette and wore very pale lipstick—cigarette butts in the ash tray and the edge of a highball glass. They drank Jack Daniel's, a whole bottle—the empty bottle, six soda bottles, and a tub that had held ice cubes. She used a heavy perfume and did not stay the night—the second pillow used but not slept on, also no lipstick on discarded tissues. I like to think her name was Lucille—I don't know why. Maybe because it was and is. She was a nervous friend—smoked Harry's recessed, filtered cigarettes but stubbed each one out only one-third smoked and lighted another, and she didn't put them out, she crushed them, frayed the ends. Lucille wore one of those little smidgins of hats held on by inturned combs. One of the combs broke loose. That and a bobby pin beside the bed told me Lucille is a brunette. I don't know whether or not Lucille is professional, but at least she is practiced. There is a fine businesslike quality about her. She didn't leave too many things around, as an amateur might. Also she didn't get drunk. Her glass was empty but the vase of red roses—courtesy of the management—smelled of Jack Daniel's, and it didn't do them any good.

I wonder what Harry and Lucille talked about. I wonder whether she made him less lonesome. Somehow I doubt it. I think both of them were doing what was expected of them. Harry shouldn't have slugged his drinks. His stomach isn't up to it—Tums wrappers in the wastebasket. I guess his business is a sensitive one and hard on the stomach. Lonesome Harry must have finished the bottle after Lucille left. He had a hang-over—two foil tubes of Bromo Seltzer in the bathroom.

Three things haunted me about Lonesome Harry. First, I don't think he had any fun; second, I think he was really lonesome, maybe in a chronic state; and third, he didn't do a single thing that couldn't be predicted—didn't break a glass or a mirror, committed no outrages, left no physical evidence of joy. I had been hobbling around with one boot off finding out about Harry. I even looked under the bed and in the closet. He hadn't even forgotten a tie. I felt sad about Harry.

Part Three

CHICAGO was a break in my journey, a resumption of my name, identity, and happy marital status. My wife flew in from the East for her brief visit. I was delighted at the change, back to my known and trusted life—but here I run into a literary difficulty.

Chicago broke my continuity. This is permissible in life but not in writing. So I leave Chicago out, because it is off the line, out of drawing. In my travels, it was pleasant and good; in writing, it would contribute only a disunity.

When that time was over and the good-bys said, I had to go through the same lost loneliness all over again, and it was no less painful than at first. There seemed to be no cure for loneliness save only being alone.

Charley was torn three ways—with anger at me for leaving him, with gladness at the sight of Rocinante, and with pure pride in his appearance. For when Charley is groomed and clipped and washed he is as pleased with himself as is a man with a good tailor or a woman newly patinaed by a beauty parlor, all of whom can believe they are like that clear through. Charley's combed columns of legs were noble things, his cap of silver blue fur was rakish, and he carried the pompon of his tail like the baton of a bandmaster. A wealth of combed and clipped mustache gave him the appearance and attitude of a French rake of the nineteenth century, and incidentally concealed his crooked front teeth. I happen to know what he looks like without the tailoring. One summer when his fur grew matted and mildewed I clipped him to the skin. Under those sturdy towers of legs are spindly shanks, thin and not too straight; with his chest ruff removed one can see the sagging stomach of the middle-aged. But if Charley was aware of his deep-down inadequacy, he gave no sign. If manners maketh man, then manner and grooming maketh poodle. He sat straight and nobly in the seat of Rocinante and he gave me to understand that while forgiveness was not impossible, I would have to work for it.

He is a fraud and I know it. Once when our boys were little

and in summer camp we paid them the deadly parents' visit. When we were about to depart, a lady parent told us she had to leave quickly to keep her child from going into hysterics. And with brave but trembling lips she fled blindly, masking her feeling to save her child. The boy watched her go and then with infinite relief went back to his gang and his business, knowing that he too had played the game. And I know for a fact that five minutes after I had left Charley he had found new friends and had made his arrangements for his comfort. But one thing Charley did not fake. He was delighted to be traveling again, and for a few days he was an ornament to the trip.

*

ILLINOIS did a fair autumn day for us, crisp and clean. We moved quickly northward, heading for Wisconsin through a noble land of good fields and magnificent trees, a gentleman's countryside, neat and white-fenced and I would guess subsidized by outside income. It did not seem to me to have the thrust of land that supports itself and its owner. Rather it was like a beautiful woman who requires the support and help of many faceless ones just to keep going. But this fact does not make her less lovely—if you can afford her.

It is possible, even probable, to be told a truth about a place, to accept it, to know it and at the same time not to know anything about it. I had never been to Wisconsin, but all my life I had heard about it, had eaten its cheeses, some of them as good as any in the world. And I must have seen pictures. Everyone must have. Why then was I unprepared for the beauty of this region, for its variety of field and hill, forest, lake? I think now I must have considered it one big level cow pasture because of the state's enormous yield of milk products. I never saw a country that changed so rapidly, and because I had not expected it everything I saw brought a delight. I don't know how it is in other seasons, the summers may reek and rock with heat, the winters may groan with dismal cold, but when I saw it for the first and only time in early October, the air was rich with butter-colored sunlight, not fuzzy but crisp and clear so that every frost-gay tree was set off, the rising hills were not compounded, but alone and separate. There was a penetration of the light into solid substance so that I seemed to see into things, deep in, and I've seen that kind of light elsewhere only in Greece. I remembered now that I had been told Wisconsin is a lovely state, but the telling had not prepared me. It was a magic day. The land dripped with richness, the fat cows and pigs gleaming against green, and, in the smaller holdings, corn standing in little tents as corn should, and pumpkins all about.

I don't know whether or not Wisconsin has a cheese-tasting festival, but I who am a lover of cheese believe it should. Cheese was everywhere, cheese centers, cheese co-operatives, cheese stores and stands, perhaps even cheese ice cream. I can believe anything, since I saw a score of signs advertising Swiss Cheese Candy. It is sad that I didn't stop to sample Swiss Cheese Candy. Now I can't persuade anyone that it exists, that I did not make it up.

Beside the road I saw a very large establishment, the greatest distributor of sea shells in the world—and this in Wisconsin, which hasn't known a sea since pre-Cambrian times. But Wisconsin is loaded with surprises. I had heard of the Wisconsin Dells but was not prepared for the weird country sculptured by the Ice Age, a strange, gleaming country of water and carved rock, black and green. To awaken here might make one believe it a dream of some other planet, for it has a non-earthly quality, or else the engraved record of a time when the world was much younger and much different. Clinging to the sides of the dreamlike waterways was the litter of our times, the motels, the hot-dog stands, the merchants of the cheap and mediocre and tawdry so loved by summer tourists, but these incrustations were closed and boarded against the winter and, even open, I doubt that they could dispel the enchantment of the Wisconsin Dells.

I stopped that night on a hilltop that was a truckers' place but of a special kind. Here the gigantic cattle trucks rested and scraped out the residue left by their recent cargoes. There were mountains of manure and over them mushroom clouds of flies. Charley moved about smiling and sniffing ecstatically like an American woman in a French perfume shop. I can't bring myself to criticize his taste. Some people like one thing and some another. The odors were rich and earthy, but not disgusting.

As the evening deepened, I walked with Charley among his mountains of delight to the brow of the hill and looked down on the little valley below. It was a disturbing sight. I thought too much driving had distorted my vision or addled my judgment, for the dark earth below seemed to move and pulse and breathe. It was not water but it rippled like a black liquid. I walked quickly down the hill to iron out the distortion. The valley floor was carpeted with turkeys, it seemed like millions of them, so densely packed that they covered the earth. It was a great relief. Of course, this was a reservoir for Thanksgiving.

To mill so close together is in the nature of turkeys in the evening. I remembered how on the ranch in my youth the turkeys gathered and roosted in clots in the cypress trees, out of reach of wildcats and coyotes, the only indication I know of that turkeys have any intelligence at all. To know them is not to admire them, for they are vain and hysterical. They gather in vulnerable groups and then panic at rumors. They are subject to all the sicknesses of other fowl, together with some they have invented. Turkeys seem to be manic-depressive types, gobbling with blushing wattles, spread tails, and scraping wings in amorous bravado at one moment and huddled in craven cowardice the next. It is hard to see how they can be related to their wild, clever, suspicious cousins. But here in their thousands they carpeted the earth waiting to lie on their backs on the platters of America.

I know it is a shame that I had never seen the noble twin cities of St. Paul and Minneapolis, but how much greater a disgrace that I still haven't, although I went through them. As I approached, a great surf of traffic engulfed me, waves of station wagons, rip tides of roaring trucks. I wonder why it is that when I plan a route too carefully it goes to pieces, whereas if I blunder along in blissful ignorance aimed in a fancied direction I get through with no trouble. In the early morning I had studied maps, drawn a careful line along the way I wished to go. I still have that arrogant plan—into St. Paul on Highway 10, then gently across the Mississippi. The S-curve in the Mississippi here would give me three crossings of the river. After this pleasant jaunt I meant to go through Golden Valley, drawn by its name. That seems simple enough, and perhaps it can be done, but not by me.

First the traffic struck me like a tidal wave and carried me along, a bit of shiny flotsam bounded in front by a gasoline truck half a block long. Behind me was an enormous cement mixer on wheels, its big howitzer revolving as it proceeded. On my right was what I judged to be an atomic cannon. As usual I panicked and got lost. Like a weakening swimmer I edged to the right into a pleasant street only to be stopped by a policeman, who informed me that trucks and such vermin were not permitted there. He thrust me back into the ravening stream.

I drove for hours, never able to take my eyes from the surrounding mammoths. I must have crossed the river but I couldn't see it. I never did see it. I never saw St. Paul or Minneapolis. All I saw was a river of trucks; all I heard was a roar of motors. The air saturated with Diesel fumes burned in my lungs. Charley got a coughing fit and I couldn't take time to pat him on the back. At a red light I saw that I was on an Evacuation Route. It took some time for that to penetrate. My head was spinning. I had lost all sense of direction. But the signs—"Evacuation Route"—continued. Of course, it is the planned escape route from the bomb that hasn't been dropped. Here in the middle of the Middle West an escape route, a road designed by fear. In my mind I could see it because I have seen people running away—the roads clogged to a standstill and the stampede over the cliff of our own designing. And suddenly I thought of that valley of the turkeys and wondered how I could have the gall to think turkeys stupid. Indeed, they have an advantage over us. They're good to eat.

It took me nearly four hours to get through the Twin Cities. I've heard that some parts of them are beautiful. And I never found Golden Valley. Charley was no help. He wasn't involved with a race that could build a thing it had to escape from. He didn't want to go to the moon just to get the hell away from it all. Confronted with our stupidities, Charley accepts them for what they are—stupidities.

Sometime in these bedlam hours I must have crossed the river again because I had got back on U.S. 10 and was moving north on the east side of the Mississippi. The country opened out and I stopped at a roadside restaurant, exhausted. It was a German restaurant complete with sausages, sauerkraut, and beer steins hanging in rows over the bar, shining but unused. I was the only customer at that time of day. The waitress was no Brunhild but a lean, dark-faced little thing, either a young and troubled girl or a very spry old woman, I couldn't tell which. I ordered bratwurst and sauerkraut and distinctly saw the cook unwrap a sausage from a cellophane slip cover and drop it in boiling water. The beer came in a can. The bratwurst was terrible and the kraut an insulting watery mess.

"I wonder if you can help me?" I asked the young-ancient waitress.

"What's your trouble?"

"I guess I'm a little lost."

"How do you mean lost?" she said.

The cook leaned through his window and rested bare elbows on the serving counter.

"I want to go to Sauk Centre and I don't seem to be getting there."

"Where'd you come from?"

"Minneapolis."

"Then what you doing this side of the river?"

"Well, I seem to have got lost in Minneapolis, too."

She looked at the cook. "He got lost in Minneapolis," she said.

"Nobody can get lost in Minneapolis," the cook said. "I was born there and I know."

The waitress said, "I come from St. Cloud and I can't get lost in Minneapolis."

"I guess I brought some new talent to it. But I want to go to Sauk Centre."

The cook said, "If he can stay on a road he can't get lost. You're on Fifty-two. Cross over at St. Cloud and stay on Fifty-two."

"Is Sauk Centre on Fifty-two?"

"Ain't no place else. You must be a stranger around here, getting lost in Minneapolis. I couldn't get lost blindfolded."

I said a little snappishly, "Could you get lost in Albany or San Francisco?"

"I never been there but I bet I wouldn't get lost."

"I been to Duluth," the waitress said. "And Christmas I'm going to Sioux Falls. I got a aunt there."

"Ain't you got relatives in Sauk Centre?" the cook asked.

"Sure, but that's not so far away—like he says San Francisco. My brother's in the Navy. He's in San Diego. You got relations in Sauk Centre?"

"No, I just want to see it. Sinclair Lewis came from there."

"Oh! Yeah. They got a sign up. I guess quite a few folks come to see it. It does the town some good."

"He's the first man who told me about this part of the country."

"Who is?"

"Sinclair Lewis."

"Oh! Yeah. You know him?"

"No, I just read him."

I'm sure she was going to say "Who?" but I stopped her. "You say I cross at St. Cloud and stay on Fifty-two?"

The cook said, "I don't think what's-his-name is there any more."

"I know. He's dead."

"You don't say."

*

THERE was a sign in Sauk Centre all right: "Birthplace of Sinclair Lewis."

For some reason I went through there fast and turned north on 71 to Wadena and it got dark and I pounded on to Detroit Lakes. There was a face before me, a lean and shriveled face like an apple too long in the barrel, a lonely face and sick with loneliness.

I didn't know him well, never knew him in the boisterous days when he was called Red. Toward the end of his life he called me several times in New York and we would have lunch at the Algonquin. I called him Mr. Lewis—still do in my mind. He didn't drink any more and took no pleasure in his food, but now and then his eyes would glitter with steel.

I had read *Main Street* when I was in high school, and I

remember the violent hatred it aroused in the countryside of his nativity.

Did he go back?

Just went through now and again. The only good writer was a dead writer. Then he couldn't surprise anyone any more, couldn't hurt anyone any more. And the last time I saw him he seemed to have shriveled even more. He said, "I'm cold. I seem to be always cold. I'm going to Italy."

And he did, and he died there, and I don't know whether or not it's true but I've heard he died alone. And now he's good for the town. Brings in some tourists. He's a good writer now.

If there had been room in Rocinante I would have packed the W.P.A. Guides to the States, all forty-eight volumes of them. I have all of them, and some are very rare. If I remember correctly, North Dakota printed only eight hundred copies and South Dakota about five hundred. The complete set comprises the most comprehensive account of the United States ever got together, and nothing since has even approached it. It was compiled during the depression by the best writers in America, who were, if that is possible, more depressed than any other group while maintaining their inalienable instinct for eating. But these books were detested by Mr. Roosevelt's opposition. If W.P.A. workers leaned on their shovels, the writers leaned on their pens. The result was that in some states the plates were broken up after a few copies were printed, and that is a shame because they were reservoirs of organized, documented, and well-written information, geological, historical, and economic. If I had carried my guides along, for example, I would have looked up Detroit Lakes, Minnesota, where I stopped, and would have known why it is called Detroit Lakes, who named it, when, and why. I stopped near there late at night and so did Charley, and I don't know any more about it than he does.

The next day a long-cultivated ambition was to blossom and fruit.

Curious how a place unvisited can take such hold on the mind so that the very name sets up a ringing. To me such a place was Fargo, North Dakota. Perhaps its first impact is in the name Wells-Fargo, but my interest certainly goes beyond that. If you will take a map of the United States and fold it in the middle, eastern edge against western, and crease it sharply, right in the crease will be Fargo. On double-page maps sometimes Fargo gets lost in the binding. That may not be a very scientific method for finding the east-west middle of the country, but it will do. But beyond this, Fargo to me is brother to the fabulous places of the earth, kin to those magically remote spots mentioned by Herodotus and Marco Polo and Mandeville. From my earliest memory, if it was a cold day, Fargo was the coldest place on the continent. If heat was the subject, then at that time the papers listed Fargo as hotter than any place else, or wetter or drier, or deeper in snow. That's my impression, anyway. But I know that a dozen or half a hundred towns will rise up in injured wrath to denounce me with claims and figures for having much more dreadful weather than Fargo. I apologize to them in advance. As a sop to hurt feelings, I must admit that when I passed through Moorhead, Minnesota, and rattled across the Red River into Fargo on the other side, it was a golden autumn day, the town as traffic-troubled, as neon-plastered, as cluttered and milling with activity as any other up-and-coming town of forty-six thousand souls. The countryside was no different from Minnesota over the river. I drove through the town as usual, seeing little but the truck ahead of me and the Thunderbird in my rear-view mirror. It's bad to have one's myth shaken up like that. Would Samarkand or Cathay or Cipango have suffered the same fate if visited? As soon as I had cleared the outskirts, the broken-metal-and-glass outer ring, and moved through Mapleton I found a pleasant place to stop on the Maple River not far from Alice—what a wonderful name for a town, Alice. It had 162 inhabitants in 1950 and 124 at the last census—and so much for the population explosion at Alice. Anyway, on the Maple River I drew into a little copse, of sycamores I think, that overhung the stream, and paused to lick my mythological wounds. And I found with joy that the fact of Fargo had in no way disturbed my mind's picture of it. I could still think of Fargo as I always had—blizzard-riven, heat-blasted, dust-raddled. I am happy to report that in the war between reality and romance, reality is not the stronger.

Although it was only mid-morning, I cooked a sumptuous

dinner for myself, but I don't remember what it was. And Charley, who still had vestiges of his Chicago grooming, waded in the water and became his old dirty self again.

After the comfort and the company of Chicago I had had to learn to be alone again. It takes a little time. But there on the Maple River, not far from Alice, the gift of it was coming back. Charley had forgiven me in a nauseatingly superior way, but now he had settled down to business also. The pull-out place beside the water was pleasant. I brought out my garbage-can washing machine and rinsed clothes that had been jiggling in detergent for two days. And then, because a pleasant breeze was blowing, I spread my sheets to dry on some low bushes. I don't know what kind of bushes they were, but the leaves had a rich smell like sandalwood, and there's nothing I like better than scented sheets. And I made some notes on a sheet of yellow paper on the nature and quality of being alone. These notes would in the normal course of events have been lost as notes are always lost, but these particular notes turned up long afterward wrapped around a bottle of ketchup and secured with a rubber band. The first note says: "Relationship Time to Aloneness." And I remember about that. Having a companion fixes you in time and that the present, but when the quality of aloneness settles down, past, present, and future all flow together. A memory, a present event, and a forecast all equally present.

The second note lies obscurely under a streak of ketchup, or catsup, but the third is electric. It says: "Reversion to pleasure-pain basis," and this is from some observation of another time.

A number of years ago I had some experience with being alone. For two succeeding years I was alone each winter for eight months at a stretch in the Sierra Nevada mountains on Lake Tahoe. I was a caretaker on a summer estate during the winter months when it was snowed in. And I made some observations then. As the time went on I found that my reactions thickened. Ordinarily I am a whistler. I stopped whistling. I stopped conversing with my dogs, and I believe that subtleties of feeling began to disappear until finally I was on a pleasure-pain basis. Then it occurred to me that the delicate shades of feeling, of reaction, are the result of communication, and without such communication they tend to disappear. A man with nothing to say has no words. Can its reverse be true—a man who has no one to say anything to has no words as he has no need for words? Now and then there appear accounts of babies raised by animals—wolves and such. It is usually reported that the youngster crawls on all fours, makes those sounds learned from his foster parents, and perhaps even thinks like a wolf. Only through imitation do we develop toward originality. Take Charley, for example. He has always associated with the learned, the gentle, the literate, and the reasonable both in France and in America. And Charley is no more like a dog than he is like a cat. His perceptions are sharp and delicate and he is a mind-reader. I don't know that he can read the thoughts of other dogs, but he can read mine. Before a plan is half formed in my mind, Charley knows about it, and he also knows whether he is to be included in it. There's no question about this. I know too well his look of despair and disapproval when I have just thought that he must be left at home. And so much for the three notes below the red stain on the ketchup bottle.

Soon Charley moved downstream and found some discarded bags of garbage, which he went through with discrimination. He nosed over an empty bean can, sniffed in its opening, and rejected it. Then he took up the paper bag in his teeth and gently shook it so that more treasures rolled out, among them a balled-up piece of heavy white paper.

I opened it and smoothed the angry creases from its surface. It was a court order addressed to Jack So-and-so, informing him that if he didn't pay his back alimony he would be in contempt and punishable. The court sat in an eastern state, and this was North Dakota. Some poor guy on the lam. He shouldn't have left this spoor around, in case anyone was looking for him. I snapped my Zippo lighter and burned the evidence with full knowledge that I compounded the contempt. Good Lord, the trails we leave! Suppose someone, finding the ketchup bottle, tried to reconstruct me from my notes. I helped Charley sort over the garbage, but there was no other written material, only the containers of prepared foods. The man was no cook. He lived out of cans, but then perhaps his former wife did also.

It was only shortly after noon but I was so relaxed and comfortable that I hated to move. "Should we stay the night, Charley?" He inspected me and wagged his tail as a professor wags a pencil—once to the left, once to the right, and return to center. I sat on the bank, took off socks and boots, and dipped my feet in water so cold it burned until the freezing went deep and deadened feeling. My mother believed that cold water on the feet forced the blood to your head so that you thought better. "Time for examination, *mon vieux Chamal*," I said aloud, "which is another way of saying I feel comfortingly lazy. I came out on this trip to try to learn something of America. Am I learning anything? If I am, I don't know what it is. So far can I go back with a bag full of conclusions, a cluster of answers to riddles? I doubt it, but maybe. When I go to Europe, when I am asked what America is like, what will I say? I don't know. Well, using your olfactory method of investigation, what have you learned, my friend?"

Two complete wags. At least he didn't leave the question open.

"Does all America so far smell alike? Or are there sectional smells?" Charley began to turn around and around to the left, and then he reversed and turned eight times to the right before he finally settled and put his nose on his paws and his head within reach of my hand. He has a hard time getting down. When he was young a car hit him and broke his hip. He wore a cast for a long time. Now in his golden age his hip troubles him when he is tired. After too long a run he limps on his right hind leg. But because of his long turning before lying down, we sometimes call him a whirl poodle—much to our shame. If my mother's rule was right I was thinking pretty well. But she also said, "Cold feet—warm heart." And that's a different matter.

I had parked well away from the road and from any traffic for my time of rest and recount. I am serious about this. I did not put aside my sloth for the sake of a few amusing anecdotes. I came with the wish to learn what America is like. And I wasn't sure I was learning anything. I found I was talking aloud to Charley. He likes the idea but the practice makes him sleepy.

"Just for ducks, let's try a little of what my boys would call this generality jazz. Under heads and subheads. Let's take food as we have found it. It is more than possible that in the cities we have passed through, traffic-harried, there are good and distinguished restaurants with menus of delight. But in the eating places along the roads the food has been clean, tasteless, colorless, and of a complete sameness. It is almost as though the customers had no interest in what they ate as long as it had no character to embarrass them. This is true of all but the breakfasts, which are uniformly wonderful if you stick to bacon and eggs and pan-fried potatoes. At the roadsides I never had a really good dinner or a really bad breakfast. The bacon or sausage was good and packaged at the factory, the eggs fresh or kept fresh by refrigeration, and refrigeration was universal." I might even say roadside America is the paradise of breakfast except for one thing. Now and then I would see a sign that said "home-made sausage" or "home-smoked bacons and hams" or "new-laid eggs" and I would stop and lay in supplies. Then, cooking my own breakfast and making my own coffee, I found that the difference was instantly apparent. A freshly laid egg does not taste remotely like the pale, battery-produced refrigerated egg. The sausage would be sweet and sharp and pungent with spices, and my coffee a wine-dark happiness. Can I then say that the America I saw has put cleanliness first, at the expense of taste? And—since all our perceptive nerve trunks including that of taste are not only perfectible but also capable of trauma—that the sense of taste tends to disappear and that strong, pungent, or exotic flavors arouse suspicion and dislike and so are eliminated?

"Let's go a little farther into other fields, Charley. Let's take the books, magazines, and papers we have seen displayed where we have stopped. The dominant publication has been the comic book. There have been local papers and I've bought and read them. There have been racks of paperbacks with some great and good titles but overwhelmingly outnumbered by the volumes of sex, sadism, and homicide. The big-city papers cast their shadows over large areas around them, the *New York Times* as far as the Great Lakes, the *Chicago Tribune* all the way here to North Dakota. Here, Charley, I give you a warning, should you be drawn to generalities. If this people has so atrophied its taste buds as to find tasteless food not only acceptable but desirable, what of the emotional life of the nation? Do they find their emotional fare so bland that it must be spiced with sex and sadism through the medium of the paperback? And if this is so, why are there no condiments save ketchup and mustard to enhance their foods?

"We've listened to local radio all across the country. And apart from a few reportings of football games, the mental fare has been as generalized, as packaged, and as undistinguished as the food." I stirred Charley with my foot to keep him awake.

I had been keen to hear what people thought politically. Those whom I had met did not talk about the subject, didn't seem to want to talk about it. It seemed to me partly caution and partly a lack of interest, but strong opinions were just not stated. One storekeeper did admit to me that he had to do business with both sides and could not permit himself the luxury of an opinion. He was a graying man in a little gray store, a crossroads place where I stopped for a box of dog biscuits and a can of pipe tobacco. This man, this store might have been anywhere in the nation, but actually it was back in Minnesota. The man had a kind of gray wistful twinkle in his eyes as though he remembered humor when it was not against the law, so that I dared go out on a limb. I said, "It looks then as though the natural contentiousness of people had died. But I don't believe that. It'll just take another channel. Can you think, sir, of what that channel might be?"

"You mean where will they bust out?"

"Where do they bust out?"

I was not wrong, the twinkle was there, the precious, humorous twinkle. "Well, sir," he said, "we've got a murder now and then, or we can read about them. Then we've got the World Series. You can raise a wind any time over the Pirates or the Yankees, but I guess the best of all is we've got the Russians."

"Feelings pretty strong there?"

"Oh, sure! Hardly a day goes by somebody doesn't take a belt at the Russians." For some reason he was getting a little easier, even permitted himself a chuckle that could have turned to throat-clearing if he saw a bad reaction from me.

I asked, "Anybody know any Russians around here?"

And now he went all out and laughed. "Course not. That's why they're valuable. Nobody can find fault with you if you take out after the Russians."

"Because we're not doing business with them?"

He picked up a cheese knife from the counter and carefully ran his thumb along the edge and laid the knife down. "Maybe that's it. By George, maybe that's it. We're not doing business."

"You think then we might be using the Russians as an outlet for something else, for other things."

"I didn't think that at all, sir, but I bet I'm going to. Why, I remember when people took everything out on Mr. Roosevelt. Andy Larsen got red in the face about Roosevelt one time when his hens got the croup. Yes, sir," he said with growing enthusiasm, "those Russians got quite a load to carry. Man has a fight with his wife, he belts the Russians."

"Maybe everybody needs Russians. I'll bet even in Russia they need Russians. Maybe they call it Americans."

He cut a sliver of cheese from a wheel and held it out to me on the knife blade. "You've give me something to think about in a sneaking kind of way."

"I thought you gave it to me."

"How?"

"About business and opinions."

"Well, maybe so. Know what I'm going to do? Next time Andy Larsen comes in red in the face, I'm going to see if the Russians are bothering his hens. It was a great loss to Andy when Mr. Roosevelt died."

Now I don't say that an awful lot of people have this man's sense of things. Maybe they don't, but maybe they do—also in their privacy or in non-business areas.

Charley raised his head and roared a warning without bothering to get to his feet. Then I heard a motor approaching, and trying to get up found my feet were long gone in sleep in the cold water. I couldn't feel them at all. While I rubbed and massaged them and they awakened to painful pins and needles, a vintage sedan pulling a short coupled trailer like a box turtle lumbered down from the road and took a position on the water about fifty yards away. I felt annoyance at this invasion of my privacy, but Charley was delighted. He moved on stiff legs with little delicate mincing steps to investigate the newcomer and in the manner of dogs and people did not look directly at the object of his interest. If I seem to be ridiculing Charley, look you at what I was doing in the next half hour and also what my neighbor was doing. Each of us went about our business, with slow deliberateness, each being very careful not to stare at the other and at the same time sneaking glances, appraising, evaluating. I saw a man, not young, not old, but with a jaunty springy step. He was dressed in olive-drab trousers and a leather jacket, and he wore a cowboy hat but with a flat crown and the brim curled and held to a peak by the chin strap. He had a classic profile, and even in the distance I could see that he wore a beard that tied into his sideburns and so found his hair. My own beard is restricted to my chin. The air had grown quickly chill. And I don't know whether my head was cold or that I didn't want to remain uncovered in the presence of a stranger. At any rate, I put on my old naval cap, made a pot of coffee, and sat on my back steps glancing with great interest at everything except my neighbor, who swept out his trailer and threw out a dishpan of soapy water while he pointedly unwatched me. Charley's interest was captured and held by various growlings and barkings that came from inside the trailer.

There must be in everyone a sense of proper and civil timing, for I had just resolved to speak to my neighbor, in fact had just stood up to move toward him, when he strolled toward me. He too had felt that the period of waiting was over. He moved with a strange gait reminiscent to me of something I couldn't place. There was a seedy grandeur about the man. In the time of chivalric myth this would be the beggar who turns out to be a king's son. As he came near I stood up from my iron back stoop to greet him.

He did not give me a sweeping bow, but I had the impression that he might have—either that or a full regimental salute.

"Good afternoon," he said. "I see you are of the profession."

I guess my mouth fell open. It's years since I have heard the term. "Well, no. No, I'm not."

Now it was his turn to look puzzled. "Not? But—my dear chap, if you're not, how do you know the expression?"

"I guess I've been on the fringes."

"Ah! Fringes. Of course. Backstage no doubt—direction, stage manager?"

"Flops," I said. "Would you like a cup of coffee?"

"Delighted." He never let down. That's one nice thing about

those of the profession—they rarely do. He folded himself on the divan seat behind my table with a grace I never achieved in all my traveling. And I set out two plastic mugs and two glasses, poured coffee, and set a bottle of whisky within easy reach. It seemed to me a mist of tears came into his eyes, but it might be that they were in mine.

"Flops," he said. "Who hasn't known them hasn't played."

"Shall I pour for you?"

"Please do—no, no water." He cleared his palate with black coffee and then munched delicately on the whisky while his eye swept my abode. "Nice place you have here, very nice."

"Tell me, please, what made you think I was in the theater?"

He chuckled dryly. "Very simple, Watson. You know I've played that. Both parts. Well, first I saw your poodle, and then I observed your beard. Then on approaching I saw that you wore a naval cap with the British Royal Arms."

"Was that what broadened your *a*'s?"

"That might be, old chap. That certainly might be. I fall into such things, hardly knowing I'm doing it." Now, close up, I saw that he was not young. His movements were pure youth but there was that about his skin texture and the edges of his lips that was middle-aged or past it. And his eyes, large warm brown irises set on whites that were turning yellow, corroborated this.

"Your health," I said. We emptied our plastic glasses, chased with coffee, and I refilled.

"If it isn't too personal or too painful—what did you do in the theater?"

"I wrote a couple of plays."

"Produced?"

"Yes. They flopped."

"Would I know your name?"

"I doubt it. Nobody else did."

He sighed. "It's a hard business. But if you're hooked, you're hooked. I was hooked by my granddaddy and my daddy set the hook."

"Both actors?"

"And my mother and grandmother."

"Lord. That *is* show business. Are you"—I searched for the old word—"resting now?"

"Not at all. I'm playing."

"What, for God's sake, and where?"

"Wherever I can trap an audience. Schools, churches, service clubs. I bring culture, give readings. I guess you can hear my partner over there complaining. He's very good too. Part Airedale and part coyote. Steals the show when he feels like it."

I began to feel delighted with this man. "I didn't know such things went on."

"They don't, some of the time."

"Been at it long?"

"Three years less two months."

"All over the country?"

"Wherever two or three are gathered together. I hadn't worked for over a year—just tramped the agencies and casting calls and lived up my benefits. With me there's no question of doing something else. It's all I know—all I ever have known. Once long ago there was a community of theater people on Nantucket island. My daddy bought a nice lot there and put up a frame house. Well, I sold that and bought my outfit there and I've been moving ever since, and I like it. I don't think I'll ever go back to the grind. Of course, if there should be a part—but hell, who'd remember me for a part—any part?"

"You're striking close to home there."

"Yes, it's a hard business."

"I hope you won't think I'm inquisitive even if I am. I'd like to know how you go about it. What happens? How do people treat you?"

"They treat me very well. And I don't know how I go about it. Sometimes I even have to rent a hall and advertise, sometimes I speak to the principal of the high school."

"But aren't people scared of gypsies, vagabonds, and actors?"

"I guess they are at first. At the beginning they take me for a kind of harmless freak. But I'm honest and I don't charge much, and after a little the material takes over and gets into them. You see, I respect the material. That makes the difference. I'm not a charlatan, I'm an actor—good or bad, an actor." His color had deepened with whisky and vehemence, and perhaps at being able to talk to someone with a little likeness of experience. I poured more into his glass this time and watched with pleasure his enjoyment of it. He drank and sighed.

"Don't get something like this very often," he said. "I hope I haven't given you the impression that I'm rolling in receipts. Sometimes it's a little rough."

"Go on about it. Tell more."

"Where was I?"

"You were saying you respected your material and that you were an actor."

"Oh, yes. Well, there's one more thing. You know when show people come into what they call the sticks, they have a contempt for the yokels. It took me a little time, but when I learned that there aren't any yokels I began to get on fine. I learned respect for my audience. They feel that and they work with me, and not against me. Once you respect them, they can understand anything you can tell them."

"Tell about your material. What do you use?"

He looked down at his hands and I saw that they were well-kept and very white, as though he wore gloves most of the time. "I hope you won't think I'm stealing material," he said. "I admire the delivery of Sir John Gielgud. I heard him do his monologue of Shakespeare—*The Ages of Man.* And then I bought a record of it to study. What he can do with words, with tones, and inflections!"

"You use that?"

"Yes, but I don't steal it. I tell about hearing Sir John, and what it did to me, and then I say I'm going to try to give an impression of how he did it."

"Clever."

"Well, it does help, because it gives authority to the performance, and Shakespeare doesn't need billing, and that way I'm not stealing his material. It's like I'm celebrating him, which I do."

"How do they respond?"

"Well, I guess I'm pretty much at home with it now, because I can watch the words sink in, and they forget about me and their eyes kind of turn inward and I'm not a freak to them any more. Well—what do you think?"

"I think Gielgud would be pleased."

"Oh! I wrote to him and told him what I was doing and how I was doing it, a long letter." He brought a lumpy wallet from his hip pocket and extracted a carefully folded piece of aluminum foil, opened it, and with careful fingers unfolded a small sheet of notepaper with the name engraved at the top. The message was typed. It said, "Dear . . . : Thank you for your kind and interesting letter. I would not be an actor if I were not aware of the sincere flattery implied in your work. Good luck and God bless you. John Gielgud."

I sighed, and I watched his reverent fingers fold the note and close it in its armor of foil and put it away. "I never show that to anyone to get a show," he said. "I wouldn't think of doing that."

And I'm sure he wouldn't.

He whirled his plastic glass in his hand and regarded the rinse of whisky left in it, a gesture often designed to draw emptiness to the attention of a host. I uncorked the bottle.

"No," he said. "No more for me. I learned long ago that the most important and valuable of acting techniques is the exit."

"But I'd like to ask more questions."

"All the more reason for the exit." He drained the last drop. "Keep them asking," he said, "and exit clean and sharp. Thank you and good afternoon."

I watched him swing lightly toward his trailer and I knew I would be haunted by one question. I called out,—"Wait a moment."

He paused and turned back to me.

"What does the dog do?"

"Oh, a couple of silly tricks," he said. "He keeps the performance simple. He picks it up when it goes stale." And he continued on to his home.

So it went on—a profession older than writing and one that will probably survive when the written word has disappeared. And all the sterile wonders of movies and television and radio will fail to wipe it out—a living man in communication with a living audience. But how did he live? Who were his companions? What was his hidden life? He was right. His exit whetted the questions.

*

THE night was loaded with omens. The grieving sky turned the little water to a dangerous metal and then the wind got up—not the gusty, rabbity wind of the sea coasts I know but a great bursting sweep of wind with nothing to inhibit it for a thousand miles in any direction. Because it was a wind strange to me, and therefore mysterious, it set up mysterious responses in me. In terms of reason, it was strange only because I found it so. But a goodly part of our experience which we find inexplicable must be like that. To my certain knowledge, many people conceal experiences for fear of ridicule. How many people have seen or heard or felt something which so outraged their sense of what should be that the whole thing was brushed quickly away like dirt under a rug?

For myself, I try to keep the line open even for things I can't understand or explain, but it is difficult in this frightened time. At this moment in North Dakota I had a reluctance to drive on that amounted to fear. At the same time, Charley wanted to go—in fact, made such a commotion about going that I tried to reason with him.

"Listen to me, dog. I have a strong impulse to stay amounting to celestial command. If I should overcome it and go and a great snow should close in on us, I would recognize it as a warning disregarded. If we stay and a big snow should come I would be certain I had a pipeline to prophecy."

Charley sneezed and paced restlessly. "All right, *mon cur*, let's take your side of it. You want to go on. Suppose we do, and in the night a tree should crash down right where we are presently standing. It would be you who have the attention of the gods. And there is always that chance. I could tell you many stories about faithful animals who saved their masters, but I think you are just bored and I'm not going to flatter you." Charley leveled at me his most cynical eye. I think he is neither a romantic nor a mystic. "I know what you mean. If we go, and no tree crashes down, or stay and no snow falls—what then? I'll tell you what then. We forget the whole episode and the field of prophecy is in no way injured. I vote to stay. You vote to go. But being nearer the pinnacle of creation than you, and also president, I cast the deciding vote."

We stayed and it didn't snow and no tree fell, so naturally we forgot the whole thing and are wide open for more mystic feelings when they come. And in the early morning swept clean of clouds and telescopically clear, we crunched around on the thick white ground cover of frost and got under way. The caravan of the arts was dark but the dog barked as we ground up to the highway.

Someone must have told me about the Missouri River at Bismarck, North Dakota, or I must have read about it. In either case, I hadn't paid attention. I came on it in amazement. Here is where the map should fold. Here is the boundary between east and west. On the Bismarck side it is eastern landscape, eastern grass, with the look and smell of eastern America. Across the Missouri on the Mandan side, it is pure west, with brown grass and water scorings and small outcrops. The two sides of the river might well be a thousand miles apart. As I was not prepared for the Missouri boundary, so I was not prepared for the Bad Lands. They deserve this name. They are like the work of an evil child. Such a place the Fallen Angels might have built as a spite to Heaven, dry and sharp, desolate and dangerous, and for me filled with foreboding. A sense comes from it that it does not like or welcome humans. But humans being what they are, and I being human, I turned off the highway on a shaley road and headed in among the buttes, but with a shyness as though I crashed a party. The road surface tore viciously at my tires and made Rocinante's overloaded springs cry with anguish. What a place for a colony of troglodytes, or better, of trolls. And here's an odd thing. Just as I felt unwanted in this land, so do I feel a reluctance in writing about it.

Presently I saw a man leaning on a two-strand barbed-wire fence, the wires fixed not to posts but to crooked tree limbs stuck in the ground. The man wore a dark hat, and jeans and long jacket washed palest blue with lighter places at knees and elbows. His pale eyes were frosted with sun glare and his lips scaly as snakeskin. A .22 rifle leaned against the fence beside him and on the ground lay a little heap of fur and feathers—rabbits and small birds. I pulled up to speak to him, saw his eyes wash over Rocinante, sweep up the details, and then retire into their sockets. And I found I had nothing to say to him. The "Looks like an early winter," or "Any good fishing hereabouts?" didn't seem to apply. And so we simply brooded at each other.

"Afternoon!"

"Yes, sir," he said.

"Any place nearby where I can buy some eggs?"

"Not real close by 'less you want to go as far as Galva or up to Beach."

"I was set for some scratch-hen eggs."

"Powdered," he said. "My Mrs. gets powdered."

"Lived here long?"

"Yep."

I waited for him to ask something or to say something so we could go on, but he didn't. And as the silence continued, it became more and more impossible to think of something to say. I made one more try. "Does it get very cold here winters?"

"Fairly."

"You talk too much."

He grinned. "That's what my Mrs. says."

"So long," I said, and put the car in gear and moved along. And in my rear-view mirror I couldn't see that he looked after me. He may not be a typical Badlander, but he's one of the few I caught.

A little farther along I stopped at a small house, a section of war-surplus barracks, it looked, but painted white with yellow trim, and with the dying vestiges of a garden, frosted-down geraniums and a few clusters of chrysanthemums, little button things yellow and red-brown. I walked up the path with the certainty that I was being regarded from behind the white window curtains. An old woman answered my knock and gave me the drink of water I asked for and nearly talked my arm off. She was hungry to talk, frantic to talk, about her relatives, her friends, and how she wasn't used to this. For she was not a native and she didn't rightly belong here. Her native clime was a land of milk and honey and had its share of apes and ivory and peacocks. Her voice rattled on as though she was terrified of the silence that would settle when I was gone. As she talked it came to me that she was afraid of this place and, further, that so was I. I felt I wouldn't like to have the night catch me here.

I went into a state of flight, running to get away from the unearthly landscape. And then the late afternoon changed everything. As the sun angled, the buttes and coulees, the cliffs and sculptured hills and ravines lost their burned and dreadful look and glowed with yellow and rich browns and a hundred variations of red and silver gray, all picked out by streaks of coal black. It was so beautiful that I stopped near a thicket of dwarfed and wind-warped cedars and junipers, and once stopped I was caught, trapped in color and dazzled by the clarity of the light. Against the descending sun the battlements were dark and clean-lined, while to the east, where the uninhibited light poured slantwise, the strange landscape shouted with color. And the night, far from being frightful, was lovely beyond thought, for the stars were close, and although there was no moon the starlight made a silver glow in the sky. The air cut the nostrils with dry frost. And for pure pleasure I collected a pile of dry dead cedar branches and built a small fire just to smell the perfume of the burning wood and to hear the excited crackle of the branches. My fire made a dome of yellow light over me, and nearby I heard a screech owl hunting and a barking of coyotes, not howling but the short chuckling bark of the dark of the moon. This is one of the few places I have ever seen where the night was friendlier than the day. And I can easily see how people are driven back to the Bad Lands.

Before I slept I spread a map on my bed, a Charley-tromped map. Beach was not far away, and that would be the end of North Dakota. And coming up would be Montana, where I had never been. That night was so cold that I put on my insulated underwear for pajamas, and when Charley had done his duties and had his biscuits and consumed his usual gallon of water and finally curled up in his place under the bed, I dug out an extra blanket and covered him—all except the tip of his nose—and he sighed and wriggled and gave a great groan of pure ecstatic comfort. And I thought how every safe generality I gathered in my travels was canceled by another. In the night the Bad Lands had become Good Lands. I can't explain it. That's how it was.

*

THE next passage in my journey is a love affair. I am in love with Montana. For other states I have admiration, respect, recognition, even some affection, but with Montana it is love, and it's difficult to analyze love when you're in it. Once, when I raptured in a violet glow given off by the Queen of the

World, my father asked me why, and I thought he was crazy not to see. Of course I know now she was a mouse-haired, freckle-nosed, scabby-kneed little girl with a voice like a bat and the loving kindness of a gila monster, but then she lighted up the landscape and me. It seems to me that Montana is a great splash of grandeur. The scale is huge but not overpowering. The land is rich with grass and color, and the mountains are the kind I would create if mountains were ever put on my agenda. Montana seems to me to be what a small boy would think Texas is like from hearing Texans. Here for the first time I heard a definite regional accent unaffected by TV-ese, a slow-paced warm speech. It seemed to me that the frantic bustle of America was not in Montana. Its people did not seem afraid of shadows in a John Birch Society sense. The calm of the mountains and the rolling grasslands had got into the inhabitants. It was hunting season when I drove through the state. The men I talked to seemed to me not moved to a riot of seasonal slaughter but simply to be going out to kill edible meat. Again my attitude may be informed by love, but it seemed to me that the towns were places to live in rather than nervous hives. People had time to pause in their occupations to undertake the passing art of neighborliness.

I found I did not rush through the towns to get them over with. I even found things I had to buy to make myself linger. In Billings I bought a hat, in Livingston a jacket, in Butte a rifle I didn't particularly need, a Remington bolt-action 222, second-hand but in beautiful condition. Then I found a telescope sight I had to have, and waited while it was mounted on the rifle, and in the process got to know everyone in the shop and any customers who entered. With the gun in a vise and the bolt out, we zeroed the new sight on a chimney three blocks away, and later when I got to shooting the little gun I found no reason to change it. I spent a good part of a morning at this, mostly because I wanted to stay. But I see that, as usual, love is inarticulate. Montana has a spell on me. It is grandeur and warmth. If Montana had a seacoast, or if I could live away from the sea, I would instantly move there and petition for admission. Of all the states it is my favorite and my love.

At Custer we made a side trip south to pay our respects to General Custer and Sitting Bull on the battlefield of Little Big

Horn. I don't suppose there is an American who doesn't carry Remington's painting of the last defense of the center column of the 7th Cavalry in his head. I removed my hat in memory of brave men, and Charley saluted in his own manner but I thought with great respect.

The whole of eastern Montana and the western Dakotas is memory-marked as Injun country, and the memories are not very old either. Some years ago my neighbor was Charles Erskine Scott Wood, who wrote *Heavenly Discourse*. He was a very old man when I knew him, but as a young lieutenant just out of military academy he had been assigned to General Miles and he served in the Chief Joseph campaign. His memory of it was very clear and very sad. He said it was one of the most gallant retreats in all history. Chief Joseph and the Nez Percés with squaws and children, dogs, and all their possessions, retreated under heavy fire for over a thousand miles, trying to escape to Canada. Wood said they fought every step of the way against odds until finally they were surrounded by the cavalry under General Miles and the large part of them wiped out. It was the saddest duty he had ever performed, Wood said, and he had never lost his respect for the fighting qualities of the Nez Percés. "If they hadn't had their families with them we could never have caught them," he said. "And if we had been evenly matched in men and weapons, we couldn't have beaten them. They were men," he said. "Real men."

*

I MUST confess to a laxness in the matter of National Parks. I haven't visited many of them. Perhaps this is because they enclose the unique, the spectacular, the astounding—the greatest waterfall, the deepest canyon, the highest cliff, the most stupendous works of man or nature. And I would rather see a good Brady photograph than Mount Rushmore. For it is my opinion that we enclose and celebrate the freaks of our nation and of our civilization. Yellowstone National Park is no more representative of America than is Disneyland.

This being my natural attitude, I don't know what made me turn sharply south and cross a state line to take a look at Yellowstone. Perhaps it was a fear of my neighbors. I could hear them say, "You mean you were that near to Yellowstone and didn't go? You must be crazy." Again it might have been the American tendency in travel. One goes, not so much to see but to tell afterward. Whatever my purpose in going to Yellowstone, I'm glad I went because I discovered something about Charley I might never have known.

A pleasant-looking National Park man checked me in and then he said, "How about that dog? They aren't permitted in except on leash."

"Why?" I asked.

"Because of the bears."

"Sir," I said, "this is an unique dog. He does not live by tooth or fang. He respects the right of cats to be cats although he doesn't admire them. He turns his steps rather than disturb an earnest caterpillar. His greatest fear is that someone will point out a rabbit and suggest that he chase it. This is a dog of peace and tranquility. I suggest that the greatest danger to your bears will be pique at being ignored by Charley."

The young man laughed. "I wasn't so much worried about the bears," he said. "But our bears have developed an intolerance for dogs. One of them might demonstrate his prejudice with a clip on the chin, and then—no dog."

"I'll lock him in the back, sir. I promise you Charley will cause no ripple in the bear world, and as an old bear-looker, neither will I."

"I just have to warn you," he said. "I have no doubt your dog has the best of intentions. On the other hand, our bears have the worst. Don't leave food about. Not only do they steal but they are critical of anyone who tries to reform them. In a word, don't believe their sweet faces or you might get clobbered. And don't let the dog wander. Bears don't argue."

We went on our way into the wonderland of nature gone nuts, and you will have to believe what happened. The only way I can prove it would be to get a bear.

Less than a mile from the entrance I saw a bear beside the road, and it ambled out as though to flag me down. Instantly a change came over Charley. He shrieked with rage. His lips flared, showing wicked teeth that have some trouble with a dog biscuit. He screeched insults at the bear, which hearing, the bear reared up and seemed to me to overtop Rocinante.

Frantically I rolled the windows shut and, swinging quickly to the left, grazed the animal, then scuttled on while Charley raved and ranted beside me, describing in detail what he would do to that bear if he could get at him. I was never so astonished in my life. To the best of my knowledge Charley had never seen a bear, and in his whole history had showed great tolerance for every living thing. Besides all this, Charley is a coward, so deep-seated a coward that he has developed a technique for concealing it. And yet he showed every evidence of wanting to get out and murder a bear that outweighed him a thousand to one. I don't understand it.

A little farther along two bears showed up, and the effect was doubled. Charley became a maniac. He leaped all over me, he cursed and growled, snarled and screamed. I didn't know he had the ability to snarl. Where did he learn it? Bears were in good supply, and the road became a nightmare. For the first time in his life Charley resisted reason, even resisted a cuff on the ear. He became a primitive killer lusting for the blood of his enemy, and up to this moment he had had no enemies. In a bearless stretch, I opened the cab, took Charley by the collar, and locked him in the house. But that did no good. When we passed other bears he leaped on the table and scratched at the windows trying to get out at them. I could hear canned goods crashing as he struggled in his mania. Bears simply brought out the Hyde in my Jekyll-headed dog. What could have caused it? Was it a pre-breed memory of a time when the wolf was in him? I know him well. Once in a while he tries a bluff, but it is a palpable lie. I swear that this was no lie. I am certain that if he were released he would have charged every bear we passed and found victory or death.

It was too nerve-wracking, a shocking spectacle, like seeing an old, calm friend go insane. No amount of natural wonders, of rigid cliffs and belching waters, of smoking springs could even engage my attention while that pandemonium went on. After about the fifth encounter I gave up, turned Rocinante about, and retraced my way. If I had stopped the night and bears had gathered to my cooking, I dare not think what would have happened.

At the gate the park guard checked me out. "You didn't stay long. Where's the dog?"

"Locked up back there. And I owe you an apology. That dog has the heart and soul of a bear-killer and I didn't know it. Heretofore he has been a little tender-hearted toward an underdone steak."

"Yeah!" he said. "That happens sometimes. That's why I warned you. A bear dog would know his chances, but I've seen a Pomeranian go up like a puff of smoke. You know, a well-favored bear can bat a dog like a tennis ball."

I moved fast, back the way I had come, and I was reluctant to camp for fear there might be some unofficial non-government bears about. That night I spent in a pretty auto court near Livingston. I had my dinner in a restaurant, and when I had settled in with a drink and a comfortable chair and my bathed bare feet on a carpet with red roses, I inspected Charley. He was dazed. His eyes held a faraway look and he was totally exhausted, emotionally no doubt. Mostly he reminded me of a man coming out of a long, hard drunk—worn out, depleted, collapsed. He couldn't eat his dinner, he refused the evening walk, and once we were in he collapsed on the floor and went to sleep. In the night I heard him whining and yapping, and when I turned on the light his feet were making running gestures and his body jerked and his eyes were wide open, but it was only a night bear. I awakened him and gave him some water. This time he went to sleep and didn't stir all night. In the morning he was still tired. I wonder why we think the thoughts and emotions of animals are simple.

*

I REMEMBER as a child reading or hearing the words "The Great Divide" and being stunned by the glorious sound, a proper sound for the granite backbone of a continent. I saw in my mind escarpments rising into the clouds, a kind of natural Great Wall of China. The Rocky Mountains are too big, too long, too important to have to be imposing. In Montana to which I had returned, the rise is gradual, and were it not for a painted sign I never would have known when I crossed it. It wasn't very high as elevations go. I passed it as I saw the sign, but I stopped and backed up and got out and straddled it. As I stood over it facing south it had a strange impact on me that rain falling on my right foot must fall into the Pacific Ocean, while that on my left foot would eventually find its way after uncountable miles to the Atlantic. The place wasn't impressive enough to carry a stupendous fact like that.

It is impossible to be in this high spinal country without giving thought to the first men who crossed it, the French explorers, the Lewis and Clark men. We fly it in five hours, drive it in a week, dawdle it as I was doing in a month or six weeks. But Lewis and Clark and their party started in St. Louis in 1804 and returned in 1806. And if we get to thinking we are men, we might remember that in the two and a half years of pushing through wild and unknown country to the Pacific Ocean and then back, only one man died and only one deserted. And we get sick if the milk delivery is late and nearly die of heart failure if there is an elevator strike. What must these men have thought as a really new world unrolled—or was the progress so slow that the impact was lost? I can't believe they were unimpressed. Certainly their report to the government is an excited and an exciting document. They were not confused. They knew what they had found.

I drove across the upraised thumb of Idaho and through real mountains that climbed straight up, tufted with pines and deep-dusted with snow. My radio went dead and I thought it was broken, but it was only that the high ridges cut off the radio waves. The snow started to fall, but my luck held, for it was only a light gay snow. The air was softer than it had been on the other side of the Great Divide and I seemed to remember reading that the warm airs from over the Japanese current penetrate deep inland. The underbrush was thick and very green, and everywhere was a rush of waters. The roads were deserted except for an occasional hunting party in red hats and yellow jackets, and sometimes with a deer or an elk draped over the hood of the car. A few mountain cabins were incised into the steep slopes, but not many.

I was having to make many stops for Charley's sake. Charley was having increasing difficulty in evacuating his bladder, which is Nellie talk for the sad symptoms of not being able to pee. This sometimes caused him pain and always caused him embarrassment. Consider this dog of great *élan*, of impeccable manner, of *ton*, *enfin* of a certain majesty. Not only did he hurt, but his feelings were hurt. I would stop beside the road and let him wander, and turn my back on him in kindness. It took him a very long time. If it had happened to a human male I would have thought it was prostatitis. Charley is an elderly gentleman of the French persuasion. The only two ailments the French will admit to are that and a bad liver.

And so, while waiting for him and pretending to inspect plants and small water courses, I tried to reconstruct my trip as a single piece and not as a series of incidents. What was I doing wrong? Was it going as I wished? Before I left, I was briefed, instructed, directed, and brain-washed by many of my friends. One among them is a well-known and highly respected political reporter. He had been grass-rooting with the presidential candidates, and when I saw him he was not happy, because he loves his country, and he felt a sickness in it. I might say further that he is a completely honest man.

He said bitterly, "If anywhere in your travels you come on a man with guts, mark the place. I want to go to see him. I haven't seen anything but cowardice and expediency. This used to be a nation of giants. Where have they gone? You can't defend a nation with a board of directors. That takes men. Where are they?"

"Must be somewhere," I said.

"Well, you try to root a few out. We need them. I swear to God the only people in this country with any guts seem to be Negroes. Mind you," he said, "I don't want to keep Negroes out of the hero business, but I'm damned if I want them to corner the market. You dig me up ten white, able-bodied Americans who aren't afraid to have a conviction, an idea, or an opinion in an unpopular field, and I'll have the major part of a standing army."

His obvious worry in this matter impressed me, so I did listen and look along the way. And it is true I didn't hear many convictions. I saw only two real-man fights, with bare fists and enthusiastic inaccuracy, and both of those were over women.

Charley came back apologizing for needing more time. I wished I could help him but he wanted to be alone. And I remembered another thing my friend said.

"There used to be a thing or a commodity we put great store by. It was called the People. Find out where the People have gone. I don't mean the square-eyed toothpaste-and-hair-dye people or the new-car-or-bust people, or the success-and-coronary people. Maybe they never existed, but if there ever were the People, that's the commodity the Declaration was talking about, and Mr. Lincoln. Come to think of it, I've known a few, but not many. Wouldn't it be silly if the Constitution had been talking about a young man whose life centers around a whistle, a wink, and Wildroot?"

I remember retorting, "Maybe the People are always those who used to live the generation before last."

Charley was pretty stiff. I had to help him into the cab of Rocinante. And we proceeded up the mountain. A very light dry snow blew like white dust on the highway, and the evening was coming earlier now, I thought. Just under the ridge of a pass I stopped for gasoline in a little put-together, do-it-yourself group of cabins, square boxes, each with a stoop, a door, and one window, and no vestige of a garden or gravel paths. The small combined store, repair shop, and lunch room behind the gas pumps was as unprepossessing as any I have ever seen. The blue restaurant signs were old and autographed by the flies of many past summers. "Pies like mother would of made if mother could of cooked." "We don't look in your mouth. Don't look in our kitchen." "No checks cashed unless accompanied by fingerprints." The standard old ones. There would be no cellophane on the food here.

No one came to the gas pump, so I went into the lunch room. A sound of a quarrel came from the back room, which was probably the kitchen—a deep voice and a lighter male voice yammering back and forth. I called, "Anybody home?" and the voices stopped. Then a burly man came through the door, still scowling from the fracas.

"Want something?"

"Fill-up of gas. But if you have a cabin, I might stay the night."

"Take your pick. Ain't a soul here."

"Can I have a bath?"

"I'll bring you a bucket of hot water. Winter rates two dollars."

"Good. Can I get something to eat?"

"Baked ham and beans, ice cream."

"Okay. I've got a dog."

"It's a free country. The cabins are all open. Take your pick. Sing out if you need something."

No effort had been spared to make the cabins uncomfortable and ugly. The bed was lumpy, the walls dirty yellow, the curtains like the underskirts of a slattern. And the close room had a mixed aroma of mice and moisture, mold and the smell of old, old dust, but the sheets were clean and a little airing got rid of the memories of old inhabitants. A naked globe hung from the ceiling and the room was heated by kerosene stove.

There was a knock on the door, and I admitted a young man of about twenty, dressed in gray flannel slacks, two-tone shoes, a polka-dotted ascot, and a blazer with the badge of a Spokane high school. His dark, shining hair was a masterpiece of overcombing, the top hair laid back and criss-crossed with long side strands that just cleared the ears. He was a shock to me after the ogre of the lunch counter.

"Here's your hot water," he said, and his was the voice of the other quarreler. The door was open, and I saw his eyes go over Rocinante and linger on the license plate.

"You really from New York?"

"Yep."

"I want to go there sometime."

"Everybody there wants to come out here."

"What for? There's nothing here. You can just rot here."

"If it's rotting you want, you can do it any place."

"I mean there's no chance for advancing yourself."

"What do you want to advance toward?"

"Well, you know, there's no theater and no music, no one to—talk to. Why it's even hard to get late magazines unless you subscribe."

"So you read *The New Yorker*?"

"How did you know? I subscribe."

"And *Time* magazine?

"Of course."

"You don't have to go anywhere."

"Beg pardon?"

"You've got the world at your fingertips, the world of fashion, of art, and the world of thought right in your own back yard. Going would only confuse you further."

"One likes to see for one's self," he said. I swear he said it.

"That your father?"

"Yes, but I'm more like an orphan. All he likes is fishing and hunting and drinking."

"And what do you like?"

"I want to get ahead in the world. I'm twenty years old. I've got to think of my future. There he is yelling for me. He can't say anything without yelling. You going to eat with us?"

"Sure."

I bathed slowly in the crusted galvanized bucket. For a moment I thought of digging out New York clothes and putting on a puff for the boy, but I dropped that one and settled for clean chino slacks and a knitted shirt.

The burly proprietor's face was red as a ripe raspberry when I went into the lunch counter. He thrust his jaw at me. "As if I ain't carrying enough trouble, you got to be from New York."

"Is that bad?"

"For me it is. I just got that kid quieted down and you put burrs under his blanket."

"I didn't give New York a good name."

"No, but you come from there and now he's all riled up again. Oh, hell, what's the use? He's no damn good around here. Come on, you might as well eat with us out back."

Out back was kitchen, larder, pantry, dining room—and the cot covered with army blankets made it bedroom too. A great gothic wood stove clicked and purred. We were to eat at a square table covered with white, knife-scarred oilcloth. The keyed-up boy dished up bowls of bubbling navy beans and fat-back.

"I wonder if you could rig me a reading light?"

"Hell, I turn off the generator when we go to bed. I can give you a coal-oil lamp. Pull up. Got a canned baked ham in the oven."

The moody boy served the beans listlessly.

The red-faced man spoke up. "I thought he'd just finish high school and that would be the end of it, but not him, not Robbie. He took a night course—now get this—not in high school. He paid for it. Don't know where he got the money."

"Sounds pretty ambitious."

"Ambitious my big fat foot. You don't know what the course

was—hairdressing. Not barbering—hairdressing—for women. Now maybe you see why I got worries."

Robbie turned from carving the ham. The slender knife was held rigidly in his right hand. He searched my face for the look of contempt he expected.

I strove to look stern, thoughtful, and noncommittal all at once. I pulled at my beard, which is said to indicate concentration. "Whatever I say, one or the other of you is going to sic the dog on me. You've got me in the middle."

Papa took a deep breath and let it out slowly. "By God, you're right," he said, and then he chuckled and the tension went out of the room.

Robbie brought the plates of ham to the table and he smiled at me, I think in gratitude.

"Now that we got our hackles down, what do you think of this hair-dressing beautician stuff?" Papa said.

"You're not going to like what I think."

"How do I know if you don't say it?"

"Well, okay, but I'm going to eat fast in case I have to run for it."

I went through my beans and half my ham before I answered him.

"All right," I said. "You've hit on a subject I've given a lot of thought to. I know quite a few women and girls—all ages, all kinds, all shapes—no two alike except in one thing—the hairdresser. It is my considered opinion that the hairdresser is the most influential man in any community."

"You're making a joke."

"I am not. I've made a deep study of this. When women go to the hairdresser, and they all do if they can afford it, something happens to them. They feel safe, they relax. They don't have to keep up any kind of pretense. The hairdresser knows what their skin is like under the make-up, he knows their age, their face-liftings. This being so, women tell a hairdresser things they wouldn't dare confess to a priest, and they are open about matters they'd try to conceal from a doctor."

"You don't say."

"I do say. I tell you I'm a student of this. When women place their secret lives in the hairdresser's hands, he gains an authority few other men ever attain. I have heard hairdressers quoted with complete conviction in art, literature, politics, economics, child care, and morals."

"I think you're kidding but on the level."

"I'm not smiling when I say it. I tell you that a clever, thoughtful, ambitious hairdresser wields a power beyond the comprehension of most men."

"Jesus Christ! You hear that, Robbie? Did you know all that?"

"Some of it. Why, in the course I took there was a whole section on psychology."

"I never would of thought of it," Papa said. "Say, how about a little drink?"

"Thanks, not tonight. My dog's not well. I'm going to push on early and try to find a vet."

"Tell you what—Robbie will rig up a reading light for you. I'll leave the generator on. Will you want some breakfast?"

"I don't think so. I'm going to get an early start."

When I came to my cabin after trying to help Charley in his travail, Robbie was tying a trouble light to the iron frame of my sad bed.

He said quietly, "Mister, I don't know if you believe all that you said, but you sure gave me a hand up."

"You know, I think most of it might be true. If it is, that's a lot of responsibility, isn't it, Robbie?"

"It sure is," he said solemnly.

It was a restless night for me. I had rented a cabin not nearly as comfortable as the one I carried with me, and once installed I had interfered in a matter that was none of my business. And while it is true that people rarely take action on advice of others unless they were going to do it anyway, there was the small chance that in my enthusiasm for my hairdressing thesis I might have raised up a monster.

In the middle of the night Charley awakened me with a soft apologetic whining, and since he is not a whining dog I got up immediately. He was in trouble, his abdomen distended and his nose and ears hot. I took him out and stayed with him, but he could not relieve the pressure.

I wish I knew something of veterinary medicine. There's a feeling of helplessness with a sick animal. It can't explain how it feels, though on the other hand it can't lie, build up its symptoms, or indulge in the pleasures of hypochondria. I don't mean they are incapable of faking. Even Charley, who is as honest as they come, is prone to limp when his feelings are hurt. I wish someone would write a good, comprehensive book of home dog medicine. I would do it myself if I were qualified.

Charley was a really sick dog, and due to get sicker unless I could find some way to relieve the growing pressure. A catheter would do it, but who has one in the mountains in the middle of the night? I had a plastic tube for siphoning gasoline, but the diameter was too great. Then I remembered something about pressure causing muscular tension which increases the pressure, etc., so that the first step is to relax the muscles. My medicine chest was not designed for general practice, but I did have a bottle of sleeping pills—seconal, one and a half grains. But how about dosage? That is where the home medicine book would be helpful. I took a capsule apart and unloaded half of it and fitted it together again. I slipped the capsule back beyond the bow in Charley's tongue where he could not push it out, then held up his head and massaged it down his throat. Then I lifted him on the bed and covered him. At the end of an hour there was no change in him, so I opened a second capsule and gave him another half. I think that, for his weight, one and a half grains is a pretty heavy dose, but Charley must have a high tolerance. He resisted it for three quarters of an hour before his breathing slowed and he went to sleep. I must have dozed off, too. The next thing I knew, he hit the floor. In his drugged condition his legs buckled under him. He got up, stumbled, and got up again. I opened the door and let him out. Well, the method worked all right, but I don't see how one medium-sized dog's body could have held that much fluid. Finally he staggered in and collapsed on a piece of carpet and was asleep immediately. He was so completely out that I worried over the dosage. But his temperature had dropped and his breathing was normal and his heart beat was strong and steady. My sleep was restless, and when dawn came I saw that Charley had not moved. I awakened him and he was quite agreeable when I got his attention. He smiled, yawned, and went back to sleep.

I lifted him into the cab and drove hell for leather for Spokane. I don't remember a thing about the country on the way. On the outskirts I looked up a veterinary in the phone book, asked directions, and rushed Charley into the examination room as an emergency. I shall not mention the doctor's name, but he is one more reason for a good home book on dog medicine. The doctor was, if not elderly, pushing his luck, but who am I to say he had a hangover? He raised Charley's lip with a shaking hand, then turned up an eyelid and let it fall back.

"What's the matter with him?" he asked, with no interest whatever.

"That's why I'm here—to find out."

"Kind of dopey. Old dog. Maybe he had a stroke."

"He had a distended bladder. If he's dopey, it's because I gave him one and a half grains of seconal."

"What for?"

"To relax him."

"Well, he's relaxed."

"Was the dosage too big?"

"I don't know."

"Well, how much would you give?"

"I wouldn't give it at all."

"Let's start fresh—what's wrong with him?"

"Probably a cold."

"Would that cause bladder symptoms?"

"If the cold was there—yes, sir."

"Well, look—I'm on the move. I'd like a little closer diagnosis."

He snorted. "Look here. He's an old dog. Old dogs get aches and pains. That's just the way it is."

I must have been snappish from the night. "So do old men," I said. "That doesn't keep them from doing something about it." And I think for the first time I got through to him.

"Give you something to flush out his kidneys," he said. "Just a cold."

I took the little pills and paid my bill and got out of there. It wasn't that this veterinary didn't like animals. I think he didn't like himself, and when that is so the subject usually must find an area for dislike outside himself. Else he would have to admit his self-contempt.

On the other hand, I yield to no one in my distaste for the

self-styled dog-lover, the kind who heaps up his frustrations and makes a dog carry them around. Such a dog-lover talks baby talk to mature and thoughtful animals, and attributes his own sloppy characteristics to them until the dog becomes in his mind an alter ego. Such people, it seems to me, in what they imagine to be kindness, are capable of inflicting long and lasting tortures on an animal, denying it any of its natural desires and fulfillments until a dog of weak character breaks down and becomes the fat, asthmatic, befurred bundle of neuroses. When a stranger addresses Charley in baby talk, Charley avoids him. For Charley is not a human; he's a dog, and he likes it that way. He feels that he is a first-rate dog and has no wish to be a second-rate human. When the alcoholic vet touched him with his unsteady, inept hand, I saw the look of veiled contempt in Charley's eyes. He knew about the man, I thought, and perhaps the doctor knew he knew. And maybe that was the man's trouble. It would be very painful to know that your patients had no faith in you.

After Spokane, the danger of early snows had passed, for the air was changed and mulsed by the strong breath of the Pacific. The actual time on the way from Chicago was short, but the overwhelming size and variety of the land, the many incidents and people along the way, had stretched time out of all bearing. For it is not true that an uneventful time in the past is remembered as fast. On the contrary, it takes the time-stones of events to give a memory past dimension. Eventlessness collapses time.

The Pacific is my home ocean; I knew it first, grew up on its shore, collected marine animals along the coast. I know its moods, its color, its nature. It was very far inland that I caught the first smell of the Pacific. When one has been long at sea, the smell of land reaches far out to greet one. And the same is true when one has been long inland. I believe I smelled the sea rocks and the kelp and the excitement of churning sea water, the sharpness of iodine and the under odor of washed and ground calcareous shells. Such a far-off and remembered odor comes subtly so that one does not consciously smell it, but rather an electric excitement is released—a kind of boisterous joy. I found myself plunging over the roads of Washington, as dedicated to the sea as any migrating lemming.

I remembered lush and lovely eastern Washington very well and the noble Columbia River, which left its mark on Lewis and Clark. And, while there were dams and power lines I hadn't seen, it was not greatly changed from what I remembered. It was only as I approached Seattle that the unbelievable change became apparent.

Of course, I had been reading about the population explosion on the West Coast, but for West Coast most people substitute California. People swarming in, cities doubling and trebling in numbers of inhabitants, while the fiscal guardians groan over the increasing weight of improvements and the need to care for a large new spate of indigents. It was here in Washington that I saw it first. I remembered Seattle as a town sitting on hills beside a matchless harborage—a little city of space and trees and gardens, its houses matched to such a background. It is no longer so. The tops of hills are shaved off to make level warrens for the rabbits of the present. The highways eight lanes wide cut like glaciers through the uneasy land. This Seattle had no relation to the one I remembered. The traffic rushed with murderous intensity. On the outskirts of this place I once knew well I could not find my way. Along what had been country lanes rich with berries, high wire fences and mile-long factories stretched, and the yellow smoke of progress hung over all, fighting the sea winds' efforts to drive them off.

This sounds as though I bemoan an older time, which is the preoccupation of the old, or cultivate an opposition to change, which is the currency of the rich and stupid. It is not so. This Seattle was not something changed that I once knew. It was a new thing. Set down there not knowing it was Seattle, I could not have told where I was. Everywhere frantic growth, a carcinomatous growth. Bulldozers rolled up the green forests and heaped the resulting trash for burning. The torn white lumber from concrete forms was piled beside gray walls. I wonder why progress looks so much like destruction.

Next day I walked in the old port of Seattle, where the fish and crabs and shrimps lay beautifully on white beds of shaved ice and where the washed and shining vegetables were arranged in pictures. I drank clam juice and ate the sharp crab cocktails at stands along the waterfront. It was not much changed—a little more run-down and dingy than it was twenty years ago. And here a generality concerning the growth of American cities, seemingly true of all of them I know. When a city begins to grow and spread outward, from the edges, the center which was once its glory is in a sense abandoned to time. Then the buildings grow dark and a kind of decay sets in; poorer people move in as the rents fall, and small fringe businesses take the place of once flowering establishments. The district is still too good to tear down and too outmoded to be desirable. Besides, all the energy has flowed out to the new developments, to the semi-rural supermarkets, the outdoor movies, new houses with wide lawns and stucco schools where children are confirmed in their illiteracy. The old port with narrow streets and cobbled surfaces, smoke-grimed, goes into a period of desolation inhabited at night by the vague ruins of men, the lotus eaters who struggle daily toward unconsciousness by way of raw alcohol. Nearly every city I know has such a dying mother of violence and despair where at night the brightness of the street lamps is sucked away and policemen walk in pairs. And then one day perhaps the city returns and rips out the sore and builds a monument to its past.

The rest during my stay in Seattle had improved Charley's condition. I wondered whether in his advancing age the constant vibration of the truck might not have been the cause of his trouble.

Quite naturally, as we moved down the beautiful coast my method of travel was changed. Each evening I found a pleasant auto court to rest in, beautiful new places that have sprung up in recent years. Now I began to experience a tendency in the West that perhaps I am too old to accept. It is the principle of do it yourself. At breakfast a toaster is on your table. You make your own toast. When I drew into one of these gems of comfort and convenience, registered, and was shown to my comfortable room after paying in advance, of course, that was the end of any contact with the management. There were no waiters, no bell boys. The chambermaids crept in and out invisibly. If I wanted ice, there was a machine near the office. I got my own ice, my own papers. Everything was convenient, centrally located, and lonesome. I lived in the utmost luxury. Other guests came and went silently. If one confronted them with "Good evening," they looked a little confused and then responded, "Good evening." It seemed to me that they looked at me for a place to insert a coin.

Somewhere in Oregon, on a rainy Sunday, the gallant Rocinante bespoke my attention. I have not spoken of my faithful vehicle except in formal terms of passing praise. Is it not always so? We value virtue but do not discuss it. The honest bookkeeper, the faithful wife, the earnest scholar get little of our attention compared to the embezzler, the tramp, the cheat. If Rocinante has been neglected in this account, it is because she performed perfectly. Neglect did not extend to the mechanical, however. Meticulously I had changed the oil and attended to the greasing. I hate to see a motor neglected or mistreated or worked beyond its capacity.

Rocinante responded to my kindness as she must, with purring motor and perfect performance. In only one thing was I thoughtless, or perhaps overzealous. I carried too much of everything—too much food, too many books, tools enough to assemble a submarine. If I found sweet-tasting water I filled her tank, and thirty gallons of water weigh three hundred pounds. A spare container of butane gas for safety's sake weighs seventy-five pounds. Her springs were deeply depressed but seemingly safe, and on hard-pitching roads I slowed and eased her through, and because of her ready goodness I treated her like the honest bookkeeper, the faithful wife: I ignored her. And in Oregon on a rainy Sunday, moving through an endless muddy puddle, a right rear tire blew out with a damp explosion. I have known and owned mean, ugly-natured cars which would have done this thing out of pure evil and malice, but not Rocinante.

All in the day's work, I thought; that's the way the ball bounces. Well, this ball had bounced in eight inches of muddy water, and the spare tire, under the cab, had been let down into the mud. The changing tools had been put away under the floor under the table, so that my total load had to be unpacked. The new jack, never used and bright with factory paint, was stiff and unruly, and it was not designed for the overhang of Rocinante. I lay on my stomach and edged my way, swam my way under the truck, holding my nostrils clear of the surface of the water. The jack handle was slippery with greasy mud. Mud balls formed in my beard. I lay panting like a wounded duck, quietly cursing as I inched the jack forward under an axle that I had to find by feel, since it was under water. Then, with super-human gruntings and bubblings, my eyes starting from their sockets, I levered the great weight. I could feel my muscles tearing apart and separating from their anchoring bones. In actual time, not over an hour elapsed before I had the spare tire on. I was unrecognizable under many layers of yellow mud. My hands were cut and bleeding. I rolled the bad tire to a high place and inspected it. The whole side wall had blown out. Then I looked at the left rear tire, and to my horror saw a great rubber bubble on its side and, farther along, another. It was obvious that the other tire might go at any moment, and it was Sunday and it was raining and it was Oregon. If the other tire blew, there we were, on a wet and lonesome road, having no recourse except to burst into tears and wait for death. And perhaps some kind birds might cover us with leaves. I peeled off mud and clothes together and changed to new finery, which got muddy in the process.

No car has ever had such obsequious treatment as did Rocinante as we moved slowly on. Every irregularity in the road hurt me clear through. We crawled along at not more than five miles an hour. And that ancient law went into effect which says that when you need towns they are very far apart. I needed more than a town. I needed two new heavy-duty rear tires. The men who had designed my truck had not anticipated the load I would carry.

After forty years in the painful wet desert with no cloud by day nor pillar of fire by night to guide us, we came to a damp little shut-up town whose name escapes me because I never learned it. Everything was closed—everything but one small service station. The owner was a giant with a scarred face and an evil white eye. If he were a horse I wouldn't buy him. He was a mostly silent man. "You got trouble," he said.

"You're telling me. Don't you sell tires?"

"Not your size. Have to send to Portland for those. Could phone tomorrow and get them maybe the next day."

"Isn't there any place in town that might have them?"

"There's two. Both closed. I don't think they got that size. You going to need bigger tires." He scratched his beard, peered long at the bubbles on the left rear, and poked them with a forefinger like a file. Finally he went into his little office, pushed a litter of brake linings and fan belts and catalogues aside, and from underneath dug out a telephone. And if ever my faith in the essential saintliness of humans becomes tattered, I shall think of that evil looking man.

After three calls he found a dealer who had one of the kind and size required, but this man was tied up with a wedding and couldn't tear himself away. Three calls later, he turned up a rumor of another tire, but it was eight miles away. The rain continued to fall. The process was endless because between each call there was a line of cars waiting to be filled with gas and oil, and all this had to be done with a stately slowness.

A brother-in-law was finally aroused. He had a farm up the road a piece. He didn't want to get out in the rain, but my evil saint exerted some kind of pressure on him. That brother-in-law drove to the two places far apart where the tires might be, found them, and brought them to me. In a little less than four hours I was equipped, riding on big heavy-duty tires of a kind that should have been there in the first place. I could have knelt in the mud and kissed the man's hands, but I didn't. I tipped him rather royally and he said, "You didn't ought to do that. Jus' remember one thing," he said. "Them new tires is bigger. They're gonna change your speedometer reading. You'll be goin' faster'n the needle says and you get some itchy cop, why, he might pick you up."

I was so full of humble gratefulness, I could hardly speak. That happened on Sunday in Oregon in the rain, and I hope that evil-looking service-station man may live a thousand years and people the earth with his offspring.

*

Now, there is not any question that Charley was rapidly becoming a tree expert of enormous background. He could probably get a job as a consultant with the Davies people. But from the first I had withheld from him any information about the giant redwoods. It seemed to me that a Long Island poodle who had made his devoirs to *Sequoia sempervirens* or *Sequoia gigantia* might be set apart from other dogs—might even be like that Galahad who saw the Grail. The concept is staggering. After this experience he might be translated mystically to another plane of existence, to another dimension, just as the redwoods seem to be out of time and out of our ordinary thinking. The experience might even drive him mad. I had thought of that. On the other hand, it might make of him a consummate bore. A dog with an experience like that could become a pariah in the truest sense of the word.

The redwoods, once seen, leave a mark or create a vision that stays with you always. No one has ever successfully painted or photographed a redwood tree. The feeling they produce is not transferable. From them comes silence and awe. It's not only their unbelievable stature, nor the color which seems to shift and vary under your eyes, no, they are not like any trees we know, they are ambassadors from another time. They have the mystery of ferns that disappeared a million years ago into the coal of the carboniferous era. They carry their own light and shade. The vainest, most slap-happy and irreverent of men, in the presence of redwoods, goes under a spell of wonder and respect. Respect—that's the word. One feels the need to bow to unquestioned sovereigns. I have known these great ones since my earliest childhood, have lived among them, camped and slept against their warm monster bodies, and no amount of association has bred contempt in me. And the feeling is not limited to me.

A number of years ago, a newcomer, a stranger, moved to my country near Monterey. His senses must have been blunted and atrophied with money and the getting of it. He bought a grove of sempervirens in a deep valley near the coast, and then, as was his right by ownership, he cut them down and sold the lumber, and left on the ground the wreckage of his slaughter. Shock and numb outrage filled the town. This was not only murder but sacrilege. We looked on that man with loathing, and he was marked to the day of his death.

Of course, many of the ancient groves have been lumbered off, but many of the stately monuments remain and will remain, for a good and interesting reason. States and governments could not buy and protect these holy trees. This being so, clubs, organizations, even individuals, bought them and dedicated them to the future. I don't know any other similar case. Such is the impact of the sequoias on the human mind. But what would it be on Charley?

Approaching the redwood country, in southern Oregon, I kept him in the back of Rocinante, hooded as it were. I passed several groves and let them go as not quite adequate—and then on a level meadow by a stream we saw the grandfather, standing alone, three hundred feet high and with the girth of a small apartment house. The branches with their flat, bright green leaves did not start below a hundred and fifty feet up. Under that was the straight, slightly tapering column with its red to purple to blue. Its top was noble and lightning-riven by some ancient storm. I coasted off the road and pulled to within fifty feet of the godlike thing, so close that I had to throw back my head and raise my eyes to vertical to see its branches. This was the time I had waited for. I opened the back door and let Charley out and stood silently watching, for this could be dog's dream of heaven in the highest.

Charley sniffed and shook his collar. He sauntered to a weed, collaborated with a sapling, went to the stream and drank, then looked about for new things to do.

"Charley," I called. "Look!" I pointed at the grandfather. He wagged his tail and took another drink. I said, "Of course. He doesn't raise his head high enough to see the branches to prove it's a tree." I strolled to him and raised his muzzle straight up. "Look, Charley. It's the tree of all trees. It's the end of the Quest."

Charley got a sneezing fit, as all dogs do when the nose is elevated too high. I felt the rage and hatred one has toward non-appreciators, toward those who through ignorance destroy a treasured plan. I dragged him to the trunk and rubbed his nose against it. He looked coldly at me and forgave me and sauntered away to a hazelnut bush.

"If I thought he did it out of spite or to make a joke," I said to myself, "I'd kill him out of hand. I can't live without knowing." I opened my pocket knife and moved to the creekside, where I cut a branch from a small willow tree, a Y-branch well tufted with leaves. I trimmed the branch ends neatly and finally sharpened the butt end, then went to the serene grandfather of Titans and stuck the little willow in the earth so that its greenery rested against the shaggy redwood bark. Then I whistled to Charley and he responded amiably enough. I pointedly did not look at him. He cruised casually about until he saw the willow with a start of surprise. He sniffed its new-cut leaves delicately and then, after turning this way and that to get range and trajectory, he fired.

*

I STAYED two days close to the bodies of the giants, and there were no trippers, no chattering troupes with cameras. There's a cathedral hush here. Perhaps the thick soft bark absorbs sound and creates a silence. The trees rise straight up to zenith; there is no horizon. The dawn comes early and remains dawn until the sun is high. Then the green fernlike foliage so far up strains the sunlight to a green gold and distributes it in shafts or rather in stripes of light and shade. After the sun passes zenith it is afternoon and quickly evening with a whispering dusk as long as was the morning.

Thus time and the ordinary divisions of the day are changed. To me dawn and dusk are quiet times, and here in the redwoods nearly the whole of daylight is a quiet time. Birds move in the dim light or flash like sparks through the stripes of sun, but they make little sound. Underfoot is a mattress of needles deposited for over two thousand years. No sound of footsteps can be heard on this thick blanket. To me there's a remote and cloistered feeling here. One holds back speech for fear of disturbing something—what? From my earliest childhood I've felt that something was going on in the groves, something of which I was not a part. And if I had forgotten the feeling, I soon got it back.

At night, the darkness is black—only straight up a patch of gray and an occasional star. And there's a breathing in the black, for these huge things that control the day and inhabit the night are living things and have presence, and perhaps feeling, and, somewhere in deep-down perception, perhaps communication. I have had lifelong association with these things. (Odd that the word "trees" does not apply.) I can accept them and their power and their age because I was early exposed to them. On the other hand, people lacking such experience begin to have a feeling of uneasiness here, of danger, of being shut in, enclosed and overwhelmed. It is not only the size of these redwoods but their strangeness that frightens them. And why not? For these are the last remaining members of a race that flourished over four continents as far back in geologic time as the upper Jurassic period. Fossils of these ancients have been found dating from the Cretaceous era while in the Eocene and Miocene they were spread over England and Europe and America. And then the glaciers moved down and wiped the Titans out beyond recovery. And only these few are left—a stunning memory of what the world was like once long ago. Can it be that we do not love to be reminded that we are very young and callow in a world that was old when we came into it? And could there be a strong resistance to the certainty that a living world will continue its stately way when we no longer inhabit it?

*

I FIND it difficult to write about my native place, northern California. It should be the easiest, because I knew that strip angled against the Pacific better than any place in the world. But I find it not one thing but many—one printed over another until the whole thing blurs. What it is is warped with memory of what it was and that with what happened there to me, the whole bundle wracked until objectiveness is nigh impossible. This four-lane concrete highway slashed with speeding cars I remember as a narrow, twisting mountain road where the wood teams moved, drawn by steady mules. They signaled their coming with the high, sweet jangle of hame bells. This was a little little town, a general store under a tree and a blacksmith shop and a bench in front on which to sit and listen to the clang of hammer on anvil. Now little houses, each one like the next, particularly since they try to be different, spread for a mile in all directions. That was a woody hill with live oaks dark green against the parched grass where the coyotes sang on moonlit nights. The top is shaved off and a television relay station lunges at the sky and feeds a nervous picture to thousands of tiny houses clustered like aphids beside the roads.

And isn't this the typical complaint? I have never resisted

change, even when it has been called progress, and yet I felt resentment toward the strangers swamping what I thought of as my country with noise and clutter and the inevitable rings of junk. And of course these new people will resent the newer people. I remember how when I was a child we responded to the natural dislike of the stranger. We who were born here and our parents also felt a strange superiority over newcomers, barbarians, *forestieri*, and they, the foreigners, resented us and even made a rude poem about us:

> The miner came in forty-nine,
> The whores in fifty-one.
> And when they got together,
> They made a Native Son.

And we were an outrage to the Spanish-Mexicans and they in their turn on the Indians. Could that be why the sequoias make folks nervous? Those natives were grown trees when a political execution took place on Golgotha. They were well toward middle age when Caesar destroyed the Roman republic in the process of saving it. To the sequoias everyone is a stranger, a barbarian.

Sometimes the view of change is distorted by a change in oneself. The room which seemed so large is shrunk, the mountain has become a hill. But this is no illusion in this case. I remember Salinas, the town of my birth, when it proudly announced four thousand citizens. Now it is eighty thousand and leaping pell mell on in a mathematical progression—a hundred thousand in three years and perhaps two hundred thousand in ten, with no end in sight. Even those people who joy in numbers and are impressed with bigness are beginning to worry, gradually becoming aware that there must be a saturation point and the progress may be a progression toward strangulation. And no solution has been found. You can't forbid people to be born—at least not yet.

I spoke earlier of the emergence of the trailer home, the mobile unit, and of certain advantages to their owners. I had thought there were many of them in the East and the Middle West, but California spawns them like herrings. The trailer courts are everywhere, lapping up the sides of hills, spilling into river beds. And they bring with them a new problem.

These people partake of all the local facilities, the hospitals, the schools, police protection, welfare programs, and so far they do not pay taxes. Local facilities are supported by real-estate taxes, from which the mobile home is immune. It is true that the state imposes a license fee, but that fee does not come to the counties or the towns except for road maintenance and extension. Thus the owners of immovable property find themselves supporting swarms of guests, and they are getting pretty angry about it. But our tax laws and the way we think about them were long developing. The mind shies away from a head tax, a facility tax. The concept of real property is deeply implanted in us as the source and symbol of wealth. And now a vast number of people have found a way to bypass it. This might be applauded, since we generally admire those who can escape taxes, were it not that the burden of this freedom falls with increasing weight on others. It is obvious that within a very short time a whole new method of taxation will have to be devised, else the burden on real estate will be so great that no one will be able to afford it; far from being a source of profit, ownership will be a penalty, and this will be the apex of a pyramid of paradoxes. We have in the past been forced into reluctant change by weather, calamity, and plague. Now the pressure comes from our biologic success as a species. We have overcome all enemies but ourselves.

When I was a child growing up in Salinas we called San Francisco "the City." Of course it was the only city we knew, but I still think of it as the City, and so does everyone else who has ever associated with it. A strange and exclusive word is "city." Besides San Francisco, only small sections of London and Rome stay in the mind as the City. New Yorkers say they are going to town, Paris has no title but Paris. Mexico City is the Capital.

Once I knew the City very well, spent my attic days there, while others were being a lost generation in Paris. I fledged in San Francisco, climbed its hills, slept in its parks, worked on its docks, marched and shouted in its revolts. In a way I felt I owned the City as much as it owned me.

San Francisco put on a show for me. I saw her across the bay, from the great road that bypasses Sausalito and enters the Golden Gate Bridge. The afternoon sun painted her white and gold—rising on her hills like a noble city in a happy dream. A city on hills has it over flat-land places. New York makes its own hills with craning buildings, but this gold and white acropolis rising wave on wave against the blue of the Pacific sky was a stunning thing, a painted thing like a picture of a medieval Italian city which can never have existed. I stopped in a parking place to look at her and the necklace bridge over the entrance from the sea that led to her. Over the green higher hills to the south, the evening fog rolled like herds of sheep coming to cote in the golden city. I've never seen her more lovely. When I was a child and we were going to the City, I couldn't sleep for several nights before, out of bursting excitement. She leaves a mark.

Then I crossed the great arch hung from filaments and I was in the city I knew so well.

It remained the City I remembered, so confident of its greatness that it can afford to be kind. It had been kind to me in the days of my poverty and it did not resent my temporary solvency. I might have stayed indefinitely, but I had to go to Monterey to send off my absentee ballot.

In my young days in Monterey County, a hundred miles south of San Francisco, everyone was a Republican. My family was Republican. I might still be one if I had stayed there. President Harding stirred me toward the Democratic party and President Hoover cemented me there. If I indulge in personal political history, it is because I think my experience may not be unique.

I arrived in Monterey and the fight began. My sisters are still Republicans. Civil war is supposed to be the bitterest of wars, and surely family politics are the most vehement and venomous. I can discuss politics coldly and analytically with strangers. That was not possible with my sisters. We ended each session panting and spent with rage. On no point was there any compromise. No quarter was asked or given.

Each evening we promised, "Let's just be friendly and loving. No politics tonight." And ten minutes later we would be screaming at each other. "John Kennedy was a so-and-so—"

"Well, if that's your attitude, how can you reconcile Dick Nixon?"

"Now let's be calm. We're reasonable people. Let's explore this."

"I have explored it. How about the scotch whisky?"

"Oh, if you take that line, how about the grocery in Santa Ana? How about Checkers, my beauty?"

"Father would turn in his grave if he heard you."

"No, don't bring him in, because he would be a Democrat today."

"Listen to you. Bobby Kennedy is out buying sacks full of votes."

"You mean no Republican ever bought a vote? Don't make me laugh."

It was bitter and it was endless. We dug up obsolete convention weapons and insults to hurl back and forth.

"You talk like a Communist."

"Well, you sound suspiciously like Genghis Khan."

It was awful. A stranger hearing us would have called the police to prevent bloodshed. And I don't think we were the only ones. I believe this was going on all over the country in private. It must have been only publicly that the nation was tongue-tied.

The main purpose of this homecoming seemed to be fighting over politics, but in between I visited old places. There was a touching reunion in Johnny Garcia's bar in Monterey, with tears and embraces, speeches and endearments in the *poco* Spanish of my youth. There were Jolón Indians I remembered as shirttail *chamacos.* The years rolled away. We danced formally, hands locked behind us. And we sang the southern county anthem, "There wass a jung guy from Jolón—got seek from leeving halone. He wan to Keeng Ceety to gat sometheeng pretty—*Puta chingada cabrón.*" I hadn't heard it in years. It was old home week. The years crawled back in their holes. It was the Monterey where they used to put a wild bull and a grizzly bear in the ring together, a place of sweet and sentimental violence, and a wise innocence as yet unknown and therefore undirtied by undiapered minds.

We sat at the bar, and Johnny Garcia regarded us with his tear-blown Gallego eyes. His shirt was open and a gold medal on a chain hung at his throat. He leaned close over the bar and said to the nearest man, "Look at it! Juanito here gave it to me years ago, brought it from Mexico—la Morena, La Virgincita de Guadeloupe, and look!" He turned the gold oval. "My name and his."

I said, "Scratched with a pin."

"I have never taken it off," said Johnny.

A big dark *paisano* I didn't know stood on the rail and leaned over the bar. "*Favor?*" he asked, and without looking Johnny extended the medal. The man kissed it, said "*Gracias,*" and went quickly out through the swinging doors.

Johnny's chest swelled with emotion and his eyes were wet. "Juanito," he said. "Come home! Come back to your friends. We love you. We need you. This is your seat, *compadre*, do not leave it vacant."

I must admit I felt the old surge of love and oratory and I haven't a drop of Galician blood. "*Cuñado mio,*" I said sadly, "I live in New York now."

"I don't like New York," Johnny said.

"You've never been there."

"I know. That's why I don't like it. You have to come back. You belong here."

I drank deeply, and darned if I didn't find myself making a speech. The old words unused for so long came rattling back to me. "Let your heart have ears, my uncle, my friend. We are not baby skunks, you and I. Time has settled some of our problems."

"Silence," he said. "I will not hear it. It is not true. You still love wine, you still love girls. What has changed? I know you. *No me cagas, niño.*"

"*Te cago nunca*. There was a great man named Thomas Wolfe and he wrote a book called *You Can't Go Home Again*. And that is true."

"Liar," said Johnny. "This is your cradle, your home." Suddenly he hit the bar with the oaken indoor ball bat he used in arguments to keep the peace. "In the fullness of time—maybe a hundred years—this should be your grave." The bat fell from his hand and he wept at the prospect of my future demise. I puddled up at the prospect myself.

I gazed at my empty glass. "These Gallegos have no manners."

"Oh, for God's sake," Johnny said. "Oh, forgive me!" and he filled us up.

The line-up at the bar was silent now, dark faces with a courteous lack of expression.

"To your home-coming, *compadre*," Johnny said. "John the Baptist, get the hell out of those potato chips."

"*Conejo de mi Alma*," I said. "Rabbit of my soul, hear me out."

The big dark one came in from the street, leaned over the bar and kissed Johnny's medal, and went out again.

I said irritably, "There was a time when a man could be listened to. Must I buy a ticket? Must I make a reservation to tell a story?"

Johnny turned to the silent bar. "Silence!" he said fiercely, and took up his indoor ball bat.

"I will now tell you true things, brother-in-law. Step into the street—strangers, foreigners, thousands of them. Look to the hills, a pigeon loft. Today I walked the length of Alvarado Street and back by the Calle Principál and I saw nothing but strangers. This afternoon I got lost in Peter's Gate. I went to the Field of Love back of Joe Duckworth's house by the Ball Park. It's a used-car lot. My nerves are jangled by traffic lights. Even the police are strangers, foreigners. I went to the Carmel Valley where once we could shoot a thirty-thirty in any direction. Now you couldn't shoot a marble knuckles down without wounding a foreigner. And Johnny, I don't mind people, you know that. But these are rich people. They plant geraniums in big pots. Swimming pools where frogs and crayfish used to wait for us. No, my goatly friend. If this were my home, would I get lost in it? If this were my home could I walk the streets and hear no blessing?"

Johnny was slumped casually over the bar. "But here, Juanito, it's the same. We don't let them in."

I looked down the line of faces. "Yes, here it is better. But can I live on a bar stool? Let us not fool ourselves. What we knew is dead, and maybe the greatest part of what we were is dead. What's out there is new and perhaps good, but it's nothing we know."

Johnny held his temples between his cupped hands and his eyes were bloodshot.

"Where are the great ones? Tell me, where's Willie Trip?"

"Dead," Johnny said hollowly.

"Where is Pilon, Johnny, Pom Pom, Miz Gragg, Stevie Field?"

"Dead, dead, dead," he echoed.

"Ed Ricketts, Whitey's Number One and Two, where's Sonny Boy, Ankle Varney, Jesús María Corcoran, Joe Portagee, Shorty Lee, Flora Wood, and that girl who kept spiders in her hat?"

"Dead—all dead," Johnny moaned.

"It's like we was in a bucket of ghosts," said Johnny.

"No. They're not true ghosts. We're the ghosts."

The big dark one came in and Johnny held out his medal for kissing without being asked.

Johnny turned and walked with widespread legs back to the bar mirror. He studied his face for a moment, picked up a bottle, took out the cork, smelled it, tasted it. Then he looked at his fingernails. There was a stir of restlessness along the bar, shoulders hunched, legs were uncrossed.

There's going to be trouble, I said to myself.

Johnny came back and delicately set the bottle on the bar between us. His eyes were wide and dreamy.

Johnny shook his head. "I guess you don't like us any more. I guess maybe you're too good for us." His fingertips played slow chords on an invisible keyboard on the bar.

For just a moment I was tempted. I heard the wail of trumpets and the clash of arms. But hell, I'm too old for it. I made the door in two steps. I turned. "Why does he kiss your medal?"

"He's placing bets."

"Okay. See you tomorrow, Johnny."

The double door swung to behind me. I was on Alvarado Street, slashed with neon light—and around me it was nothing but strangers.

*

In my flurry of nostalgic spite, I have done the Monterey Peninsula a disservice. It is a beautiful place, clean, well run, and progressive. The beaches are clean where once they festered with fish guts and flies. The canneries which once put up a sickening stench are gone, their places filled with restaurants, antique shops, and the like. They fish for tourists now, not pilchards, and that species they are not likely to wipe out. And Carmel, begun by starveling writers and unwanted painters, is now a community of the well-to-do and the retired. If Carmel's founders should return, they could not afford to live there, but it wouldn't go that far. They would be instantly picked up as suspicious characters and deported over the city line.

The place of my origin had changed, and having gone away I had not changed with it. In my memory it stood as it once did and its outward appearance confused and angered me.

What I am about to tell must be the experience of very many in this nation where so many wander and come back. I called on old and valued friends. I thought their hair had receded a little more than mine. The greetings were enthusiastic. The memories flooded up. Old crimes and old triumphs were brought out and dusted. And suddenly my attention wandered, and looking at my ancient friend, I saw that his wandered also. And it was true what I had said to Johnny Garcia—I was the ghost. My town had grown and changed and my friend along with it. Now returning, as changed to my friend as my town was to me, I distorted his picture, muddied his memory. When I went away I had died, and so became fixed and unchangeable. My return caused only confusion and uneasiness. Although they could not say it, my old friends wanted me gone so that I could take my proper place in the pattern of remembrance—and I wanted to go for the same reason. Tom Wolfe was right. You can't go home again because home has ceased to exist except in the mothballs of memory.

My departure was flight. But I did do one formal and sentimental thing before I turned my back. I drove up to Fremont's Peak, the highest point for many miles around. I climbed the last spiky rocks to the top. Here among these blackened granite outcrops General Frémont made his stand against a Mexican army, and defeated it. When I was a boy we occasionally found cannon balls and rusted bayonets in the area. This solitary stone peak overlooks the whole of my childhood and youth, the great Salinas Valley stretching south for nearly a hundred miles, the town of Salinas where I was born now spreading like crab grass toward the foothills. Mount Toro, on the brother range to the west, was a rounded benign mountain, and to the north Monterey Bay shone like a blue platter. I felt and smelled and heard the wind blow up from the long valley. It smelled of the brown hills of wild oats.

I remembered how once, in that part of youth that is deeply concerned with death, I wanted to be buried on this peak where without eyes I could see everything I knew and loved, for in those days there was no world beyond the mountains. And I remembered how intensely I felt about my interment. It is strange and perhaps fortunate that when one's time grows nearer one's interest in it flags as death becomes a fact rather than a pageantry. Here on these high rocks my memory myth repaired itself. Charley, having explored the area, sat at my feet, his fringed ears blowing like laundry on a line. His nose, moist with curiosity, sniffed the wind-borne pattern of a hundred miles.

"You wouldn't know, my Charley, that right down there, in that little valley, I fished for trout with your namesake, my Uncle Charley. And over there—see where I'm pointing—my mother shot a wildcat. Straight down there, forty miles away, our family ranch was—old starvation ranch. Can you see that darker place there? Well, that's a tiny canyon with a clear and lovely stream bordered with wild azaleas and fringed with big oaks. And on one of those oaks my father burned his name with a hot iron together with the name of the girl he loved. In the long years the bark grew over the burn and covered it. And just a little while ago, a man cut that oak for firewood and his splitting wedge uncovered my father's name and the man sent it to me. In the spring, Charley, when the valley is carpeted with blue lupines like a flowery sea, there's the smell of heaven up here, the smell of heaven."

I printed it once more on my eyes, south, west, and north, and then we hurried away from the permanent and changeless past where my mother is always shooting a wildcat and my father is always burning his name with his love.

*

It would be pleasant to be able to say of my travels with Charley, "I went out to find the truth about my country and I found it." And then it would be such a simple matter to set down my findings and lean back comfortably with a fine sense of having discovered truths and taught them to my readers. I wish it were that easy. But what I carried in my head and deeper in my perceptions was a barrel of worms. I discovered long ago in collecting and classifying marine animals that what I found was closely intermeshed with how I felt at the moment. External reality has a way of being not so external after all.

This monster of a land, this mightiest of nations, this spawn of the future, turns out to be the macrocosm of microcosm me. If an Englishman or a Frenchman or an Italian should travel my route, see what I saw, hear what I heard, their stored pictures would be not only different from mine but equally different from one another. If other Americans reading this account should feel it true, that agreement would only mean that we are alike in our Americanness.

From start to finish I found no strangers. If I had, I might be able to report them more objectively. But these are my people and this my country. If I found matters to criticize and to deplore, they were tendencies equally present in myself. If I were to prepare one immaculately inspected generality it would be this: For all of our enormous geographic range, for all of our sectionalism, for all of our interwoven breeds drawn from every part of the ethnic world, we are a nation, a new breed. Americans are much more American than they are Northerners, Southerners, Westerners, or Easterners. And descendants of English, Irish, Italian, Jewish, German, Polish are essentially American. This is not patriotic whoop-de-do; it is carefully observed fact. California Chinese, Boston Irish, Wisconsin German, yes, and Alabama Negroes, have more in common than they have apart. And this is the more remarkable because it has happened so quickly. It is a fact that Americans from all sections and of all racial extractions are more alike than the Welsh are like the English, the Lancashireman like the Cockney, or for that matter the Lowland Scot like the Highlander. It is astonishing that this has happened in less than two hundred years and most of it in the last fifty. The American identity is an exact and provable thing.

Starting on my return journey, I realized by now that I could not see everything. My impressionable gelatin plate was getting muddled. I determined to inspect two more sections and then call it a day—Texas and a sampling of the Deep South. From my reading, it seemed to me that Texas is emerging as a separate force and that the South is in the pain of labor with the nature of its future child still unknown. And I have thought that such is the bitterness of the labor that the child has been forgotten.

This journey had been like a full dinner of many courses, set before a starving man. At first he tries to eat all of everything, but as the meal progresses he finds he must forgo some things to keep his appetite and his taste buds functioning.

I bucketed Rocinante out of California by the shortest possible route—one I knew well from the old days of the 1930s. From Salinas to Los Banos, through Fresno and Bakersfield, then over the pass and into the Mojave Desert, a burned and burning desert even this late in the year, its hills like piles of black cinders in the distance, and the rutted floor sucked dry by the hungry sun. It's easy enough now, on the high-speed road in a dependable and comfortable car, with stopping places for shade and every service station vaunting its refrigeration. But I can remember when we came to it with prayer, listening for trouble in our laboring old motors, drawing a plume of steam from our boiling radiators. Then the broken-down wreck by the side of the road was in real trouble unless someone stopped to offer help. And I have never crossed it without sharing something with those early families foot-dragging through this terrestrial hell, leaving the white skeletons of horses and cattle which still mark the way.

The Mojave is a big desert and a frightening one. It's as though nature tested a man for endurance and constancy to prove whether he was good enough to get to California. The shimmering dry heat made visions of water on the flat plain. And even when you drive at high speed, the hills that mark the boundaries recede before you. Charley, always a dog for water, panted asthmatically, jarring his whole body with the effort, and a good eight inches of his tongue hung out flat as a leaf and dripping. I pulled off the road into a small gulley to give him water from my thirty-gallon tank. But before I let him drink I poured water all over him and on my hair and shoulders and shirt. The air is so dry that evaporation makes you feel suddenly cold.

I opened a can of beer from my refrigerator and sat well inside the shade of Rocinante, looking out at the sun-pounded plain, dotted here and there with clumps of sagebrush.

About fifty yards away two coyotes stood watching me, their tawny coats blending with sand and sun. I knew that with any quick or suspicious movement of mine they could drift into invisibility. With the most casual slowness I reached down my new rifle from its sling over my bed—the .222 with its bitter little high-speed, long-range stings. Very slowly I brought the rifle up. Perhaps in the shade of my house I was half hidden by the blinding light outside. The little rifle has a beautiful telescope sight with a wide field. The coyotes had not moved.

I got both of them in the field of my telescope, and the glass brought them very close. Their tongues lolled out so that they seemed to smile mockingly. They were favored animals, not starved, but well furred, the golden hair tempered with black guard hairs. Their little lemon-yellow eyes were plainly visible in the glass. I moved the cross hairs to the breast of the right-hand animal, and pushed the safety. My elbows on the table steadied the gun. The cross hairs lay unmoving on the brisket. And then the coyote sat down like a dog and its right rear paw came up to scratch the right shoulder.

My finger was reluctant to touch the trigger. I must be getting very old and my ancient conditioning worn thin. Coyotes are vermin. They steal chickens. They thin the ranks of quail and all other game birds. They must be killed. They are the enemy. My first shot would drop the sitting beast, and the other would whirl to fade away. I might very well pull him down with a running shot because I am a good rifleman.

And I did not fire. My training said, "Shoot!" and my age replied, "There isn't a chicken within thirty miles, and if there are any they aren't my chickens. And this waterless place is not quail country. No, these boys are keeping their figures with kangaroo rats and jackrabbits, and that's vermin eat vermin. Why should I interfere?"

"Kill them," my training said. "Everyone kills them. It's a public service." My finger moved to the trigger. The cross was steady on the breast just below the panting tongue. I could imagine the splash and jar of angry steel, the leap and struggle until the torn heart failed, and then, not too long later, the shadow of a buzzard, and another. By that time I would be long gone—out of the desert and across the Colorado River. And beside the sagebush there would be a naked, eyeless skull, a few picked bones, a spot of black dried blood and a few rags of golden fur.

I guess I'm too old and too lazy to be a good citizen. The second coyote stood sidewise to my rifle. I moved the cross hairs to his shoulder and held steady. There was no question of missing with that rifle at that range. I owned both animals. Their lives were mine. I put the safety on and laid the rifle on the table. Without the telescope they were not so intimately close. The hot blast of light tousled the air to shimmering.

Then I remembered something I heard long ago that I hope is true. It was unwritten law in China, so my informant told me, that when one man saved another's life he became responsible for that life to the end of its existence. For, having interfered with a course of events, the savior could not escape his responsibility. And that has always made good sense to me.

Now I had a token responsibility for two live and healthy coyotes. In the delicate world of relationships, we are tied together for all time. I opened two cans of dog food and left them as a votive.

I have driven through the Southwest many times, and even more often have flown over it—a great and mysterious wasteland, a sun-punished place. It is a mystery, something concealed and waiting. It seems deserted, free of parasitic man, but this is not entirely so. Follow the double line of wheel tracks through sand and rock and you will find a habitation somewhere huddled in a protected place, with a few trees pointing their roots at under-earth water, a patch of starveling corn and squash, and strips of jerky hanging on a string. There is a breed of desert men, not hiding exactly but gone to sanctuary from the sins of confusion.

At night in this waterless air the stars come down just out of reach of your fingers. In such a place lived the hermits of the early church piercing to infinity with unlittered minds. The great concepts of oneness and of majestic order seem always to be born in the desert. The quiet counting of the stars, and observation of their movements, came first from desert places. I have known desert men who chose their places with quiet and slow passion, rejecting the nervousness of a watered world. These men have not changed with the exploding times except to die and be replaced by others like them.

And always there are mysteries in the desert, stories told and retold of secret places in the desert mountains where surviving clans from an older era wait to re-emerge. Usually these groups guard treasures hidden from the waves of conquest, the golden artifacts of an archaic Montezuma, or a mine so rich that its discovery would change the world. If a stranger discovers their existence, he is killed or so absorbed that he is never seen again. These stories have an inevitable pattern untroubled by the question, If none return, how is it known what is there? Oh, it's there all right, but if you find it you will never be found.

And there is another monolithic tale which never changes. Two prospectors in partnership discover a mine of preternatural richness—of gold or diamonds or rubies. They load themselves with samples, as much as they can carry, and they mark the place in their minds by landmarks all around. Then, on the way out to the other world, one dies of thirst and exhaustion, but the other crawls on, discarding most of the treasure he has grown too weak to carry. He comes at last to a settlement, or perhaps is found by other prospecting men. They examine his samples with great excitement. Sometimes in the story the survivor dies after leaving directions with his rescuers, or again he is nursed back to strength. Then a well-equipped party sets out to find the treasure, and it can never be found again. That is the invariable end of the story—it is never found again. I have heard this story many times, and it never changes. There is nourishment in the desert for myth, but myth must somewhere have its roots in reality.

And there are true secrets in the desert. In the war of sun and dryness against living things, life has its secrets of survival. Life, no matter on what level, must be moist or it will disappear. I find most interesting the conspiracy of life in the desert to circumvent the death rays of the all-conquering sun. The beaten earth appears defeated and dead, but it only appears so. A vast and inventive organization of living matter survives by seeming to have lost. The gray and dusty sage wears oily armor to protect its inward small moistness. Some plants engorge themselves with water in the rare rainfall and store it for future use. Animal life wears a hard, dry skin or an outer skeleton to defy the desiccation. And every living thing has developed techniques for finding or creating shade. Small reptiles and rodents burrow or slide below the surface or cling to the shaded side of an outcropping. Movement is slow to preserve energy, and it is a rare animal which can or will defy the sun for long. A rattlesnake will die in an hour of full sun. Some insects of bolder inventiveness have devised personal refrigeration systems. Those animals which must drink moisture get it at second hand—a rabbit from a leaf, a coyote from the blood of a rabbit.

One may look in vain for living creatures in the daytime, but when the sun goes and the night gives consent, a world of creatures awakens and takes up its intricate pattern. Then the hunted come out and the hunters, and hunters of the hunters. The night awakes to buzzing and to cries and barks.

When, very late in the history of our planet, the incredible accident of life occurred, a balance of chemical factors, combined with temperature, in quantities and in kinds so delicate as to be unlikely, all came together in the retort of time and a new thing emerged, soft and helpless and unprotected in the savage world of unlife. Then processes of change and variation took place in the organisms, so that one kind became different from all others. But one ingredient, perhaps the most important of all, is planted in every life form—the factor of survival. No living thing is without it, nor could life exist without this magic formula. Of course, each form developed its own machinery for survival, and some failed and disappeared while others peopled the earth. The first life might easily have been snuffed out and the accident may never have happened again —but, once it existed, its first quality, its duty, preoccupation, direction, and end, shared by every living thing, is to go on living. And so it does and so it will until some other accident cancels it. And the desert, the dry and sun-lashed desert, is a good school in which to observe the cleverness and the infinite variety of techniques of survival under pitiless opposition. Life could not change the sun or water the desert, so it changed itself.

The desert, being an unwanted place, might well be the last stand of life against unlife. For in the rich and moist and wanted areas of the world, life pyramids against itself and in its confusion has finally allied itself with the enemy non-life. And what the scorching, searing, freezing, poisoning weapons of non-life have failed to do may be accomplished to the end of its destruction and extinction by the tactics of survival gone sour. If the most versatile of living forms, the human, now fights for survival as it always has, it can eliminate not only itself but all other life. And if that should transpire, unwanted places like the desert might be the harsh mother of repopulation. For the inhabitants of the desert are well trained and well armed against desolation. Even our own misguided species might re-emerge from the desert. The lone man and his sun-toughened wife who cling to the shade in an unfruitful and uncoveted place might, with their brothers in arms—the coyote, the jackrabbit, the horned toad, the rattlesnake, together with a host of armored insects—these trained and tested fragments of life might well be the last hope of life against non-life. The desert has mothered magic things before this.

*

MUCH earlier I spoke of the changes at state lines, changes in Highway English, in prose forms on the signs, changes in permitted speeds. The states' rights guaranteed under the Constitution seem to be passionately and gleefully exercised. California searches vehicles for vegetables and fruits which might carry pernicious insects and diseases, and regulations of these are enforced with almost religious intensity.

Some years ago I knew a gay and inventive family from Idaho. Planning to visit relatives in California, they took a truckload of potatoes to sell along the way to help pay expenses. They had disposed of over half their cargo when they were stopped at the California line and their potatoes refused entrance. They were not financially able to abandon their potatoes, so they cheerfully set up camp right on the state line, where they ate potatoes, sold potatoes, bartered potatoes. At the end of two weeks the truck was empty. Then they went through the inspector's station in good standing and continued on their way.

The separateness of the states, which has been bitterly called Balkanization, creates many problems. Rarely do two states have the same gasoline tax, and these taxes largely support the building and maintenance of highways. The enormous interstate trucks make use of the roads and by their very weight and speed increase the maintenance costs. Thus the states have weighing stations for trucks where the loads are assessed and taxed. And if there is a differential in gasoline tax, the tanks are measured and the tax applied. The signs say, "All trucks stop." Being a truck, I stopped, only to be waved on over the scales. They were not looking for such as I. But sometimes I stopped and talked to the inspectors when they were not too busy. And this brings me to the subject of state police. Like most Americans I am no lover of cops, and the consistent investigation of city forces for bribery, brutality, and a long and picturesque list of malfeasances is not designed to reassure me. However, my hostility does not extend to the state troopers now maintained in most parts of the country. By the simple expedient of recruiting intelligent and educated men, paying them adequately, and setting them beyond political coercion, many states have succeeded in creating elite corps of men, secure in their dignity and proud of their service. Eventually our cities may find it necessary to reorganize their police on the pattern of the state police. But this will never happen while political organizations retain the slightest power to reward or to punish.

Across the Colorado River from Needles, the dark and jagged ramparts of Arizona stood up against the sky, and behind them the huge tilted plain rising toward the backbone of the continent again. I know this way so well from many crossings—Kingman, Ash Fork, Flagstaff with its mountain peak behind it, then Winslow, Holbrook, Sanders, down hill and up again, and then Arizona passed. The towns were a little larger and more brightly lighted than I remembered them, the motels bigger and more luxurious.

I crossed into New Mexico, rushed past Gallup in the night,

and camped on the Continental Divide—and much more spectacular it is here than in the north. The night was very cold and dry, and the stars were cut glass. I drove into a little canyon out of the wind and parked by a mound of broken bottles—whisky and gin bottles, thousands of them. I don't know why they were there.

And I sat in the seat and faced what I had concealed from myself. I was driving myself, pounding out the miles because I was no longer hearing or seeing. I had passed my limit of taking in or, like a man who goes on stuffing in food after he is filled, I felt helpless to assimilate what was fed in through my eyes. Each hill looked like the one just passed. I have felt this way in the Prado in Madrid after looking at a hundred paintings—the stuffed and helpless inability to see more.

This would be a time to find a sheltered place beside a stream to rest and refurbish. Charley, in the dark seat beside me, mentioned a difficulty with a little moaning sigh. I had even forgotten him. I let him out and he staggered to the hill of broken bottles, sniffed at them, and took another way.

The night air was very cold, shivery cold, so that I lighted the cabin and turned up the gas to warm the air. The cabin was not neat. My bed was unmade and breakfast dishes lay desolate in the sink. I sat on the bed and stared into gray dreariness. Why had I thought I could learn anything about the land? For the last hundreds of miles I had avoided people. Even at necessary stops for gasoline I had answered in monosyllables and retained no picture. My eye and brain had welshed on me. I was fooling myself that this was important or even instructive. There was a ready remedy, of course. I reached out the whisky bottle without getting up, poured half a tumbler, smelled it, and poured it back in the bottle. No remedy was there.

Charley had not returned. I opened the door and whistled him and got no response. That shook me out of it. I grabbed my searchlight and turned its spearing beam up the canyon. The light flashed on two eyes about fifty yards away. I ran up the trail and found him standing staring into space, just as I had been.

"What's the matter, Charley, aren't you well?"

His tail slowly waved his replies. "Oh, yes. Quite well, I guess."

"Why didn't you come when I whistled?"

"I didn't hear you whistle."

"What are you staring at?"

"I don't know. Nothing I guess."

"Well, don't you want your dinner?"

"I'm really not hungry. But I'll go through the motions."

Back in the cabin he flopped down on the floor and put his chin down on his paws.

"Come on up on the bed, Charley. Let's be miserable together." He complied but without enthusiasm and I riffled my fingers in his topknot and behind his ears the way he likes it. "How's that?"

He shifted his head. "A little more to the left. There. That's the place."

"We'd be lousy explorers. A few days out and we get the mullygrubs The first white man through here—I think he was named Narváez and I'm under the impression his little jaunt took six years. Move over. I'll look it up. Nope, it was eight years—1528 to 1536. And Narváez himself didn't make it this far. Four of his men did, though. I wonder if they ever got the mullygrubs. We're soft, Charley. Maybe it's time for a little gallantry. When's your birthday?"

"I don't know. Maybe it's like horses, the first of January."

"Think it might be today?"

"Who knows?"

"I could make you a cake. Have to be hotcake mix because that's what I have. Plenty of syrup and a candle on top."

Charley watched the operation with some interest. His silly tail made delicate conversation. "Anybody saw you make a birthday cake for a dog that he don't even know when's his birthday would think you were nuts."

"If you can't manage any better grammar than that with your tail, maybe it's a good thing you can't talk."

It turned out pretty well—four layers of hotcakes with maple syrup between and a stub of a miner's candle on top. I drank Charley's health in straight whisky as he ate and licked up the syrup. And then we both felt better. But there was Narváez' party—eight years. There were men in those days.

Charley licked the syrup from his whiskers. "What makes you so moony?"

"It's because I've stopped seeing. When that happens you think you'll never see again."

He stood up and stretched himself, first fore and then aft. "Let's take a stroll up the hill," he suggested. "Maybe you've started again."

We inspected the pile of broken whisky bottles and then continued up the trail. The dry, frozen air came out of us in plumes of steam. Some fairly large animal went leaping up the broken stone hill, or maybe a small animal and a big little avalanche.

"What does your nose say that was?"

"Nothing I recognize. Kind of a musky smell. Nothing I'm going to chase, either."

So dark was the night that it was prickled with fiery clots. My light brought an answering flash up the steep rocky bank. I climbed up, slipping and floundering, lost the echoed light and found it again, a good little new-split stone with a piece of mica in it—not a fortune but a good thing to have. I put it in my pocket and we went to bed.

Part Four

When I started this narrative, I knew that sooner or later I would have to have a go at Texas, and I dreaded it. I could have bypassed Texas about as easily as a space traveler can avoid the Milky Way. It sticks its big old Panhandle up north and it slops and slouches along the Rio Grande. Once you are in Texas it seems to take forever to get out, and some people never make it.

Let me say in the beginning that even if I wanted to avoid Texas I could not, for I am wived in Texas and mother-in-lawed and uncled and aunted and cousined within an inch of my life. Staying away from Texas geographically is no help whatever, for Texas moves through our house in New York, our fishing cottage at Sag Harbor, and when we had a flat in Paris, Texas was there too. It permeates the world to a ridiculous degree. Once, in Florence, on seeing a lovely little Italian princess, I said to her father, "But she doesn't look Italian. It may seem strange, but she looks like an American Indian." To which her father replied, "Why shouldn't she? Her grandfather married a Cherokee in Texas."

Writers facing the problem of Texas find themselves floundering in generalities, and I am no exception. Texas is a state of mind. Texas is an obsession. Above all, Texas is a nation in every sense of the word. And there's an opening covey of generalities. A Texan outside of Texas is a foreigner. My wife refers to herself as the Texan that got away, but that is only partly true. She has virtually no accent until she talks to a Texan, when she instantly reverts. You would not have to scratch deep to find her origin. She says such words as yes, air, hair, guess, with two syllables—yayus, ayer, hayer, gayus. And sometimes in a weary moment the word ink becomes ank. Our daughter, after a stretch in Austin, was visiting New York friends. She said, "Do you have a pin?"

"Certainly, dear," said her host. "Do you want a straight pin or a safety pin?"

"Aont a fountain pin," she said.

I've studied the Texas problem from many angles and for

many years. And of course one of my truths is inevitably canceled by another. Outside their state I think Texans are a little frightened and very tender in their feelings, and these qualities cause boasting, arrogance, and noisy complacency—the outlets of shy children. At home Texans are none of these things. The ones I know are gracious, friendly, generous, and quiet. In New York we hear them so often bring up their treasured uniqueness. Texas is the only state that came into the Union by treaty. It retains the right to secede at will. We have heard them threaten to secede so often that I formed an enthusiastic organization—The American Friends for Texas Secession. This stops the subject cold. They want to be able to secede but they don't want anyone to want them to.

Like most passionate nations Texas has its own private history based on, but not limited by, facts. The tradition of the tough and versatile frontiersman is true but not exclusive. It is for the few to know that in the great old days of Virginia there were three punishments for high crimes—death, exile to Texas, and imprisonment, in that order. And some of the deportees must have descendants.

Again—the glorious defense to the death of the Alamo against the hordes of Santa Anna is a fact. The brave bands of Texans did indeed wrest their liberty from Mexico, and freedom, liberty, are holy words. One must go to contemporary observers in Europe for a non-Texan opinion as to the nature of the tyranny that raised need for revolt. Outside observers say the pressure was twofold. The Texans, they say, didn't want to pay taxes and, second, Mexico had abolished slavery in 1829, and Texas, being part of Mexico, was required to free its slaves. Of course there were other causes of revolt, but these two are spectacular to a European, and rarely mentioned here.

I have said that Texas is a state of mind, but I think it is more than that. It is a mystique closely approximating a religion. And this is true to the extent that people either passionately love Texas or passionately hate it and, as in other religions, few people dare to inspect it for fear of losing their bearings in mystery and paradox. Any observations of mine can be quickly cancelled by opinion or counter-observation. But I think there will be little quarrel with my feeling that Texas is one thing. For all its enormous range of space, climate, and physical appearance, and for all the internal squabbles, contentions, and strivings, Texas has a tight cohesiveness perhaps stronger than any other section of America. Rich, poor, Panhandle, Gulf, city, country, Texas is the obsession, the proper study and the passionate possession of all Texans. Some years ago, Edna Ferber wrote a book about a very tiny group of very rich Texans. Her description was accurate, so far as my knowledge extends, but the emphasis was one of disparagement. And instantly the book was attacked by Texans of all groups, classes, and possessions. To attack one Texan is to draw fire from all Texans. The Texas joke, on the other hand, is a revered institution, beloved and in many cases originating in Texas.

The tradition of the frontier cattleman is as tenderly nurtured in Texas as is the hint of Norman blood in England. And while it is true that many families are descended from contract colonists not unlike the present-day braceros, all hold to the dream of the longhorn steer and the unfenced horizon. When a man makes his fortune in oil or government contracts, in chemicals or wholesale groceries, his first act is to buy a ranch, the largest he can afford, and to run some cattle. A candidate for public office who does not own a ranch is said to have little chance of election. The tradition of the land is deep fixed in the Texas psyche. Businessmen wear heeled boots that never feel a stirrup, and men of great wealth who have houses in Paris and regularly shoot grouse in Scotland refer to themselves as little old country boys. It would be easy to make sport of their attitude if one did not know that in this way they try to keep their association with the strength and simplicity of the land. Instinctively they feel that this is the source not only of wealth but of energy. And the energy of Texans is boundless and explosive. The successful man with his traditional ranch, at least in my experience, is no absentee owner. He works at it, oversees his herd and adds to it. The energy, in a climate so hot as to be staggering, is also staggering. And the tradition of hard work is maintained whatever the fortune or lack of it.

The power of an attitude is amazing. Among other tendencies to be noted, Texas is a military nation. The armed forces of the United States are loaded with Texans and often dominated by Texans. Even the dearly loved spectacular sports are run almost like military operations. Nowhere are there larger bands or more marching organizations, with corps of costumed girls whirling glittering batons. Sectional football games have the glory and the despair of war, and when a Texas team takes the field against a foreign state, it is an army with banners.

If I keep coming back to the energy of Texas, it is because I am so aware of it. It seems to me like that thrust of dynamism which caused and permitted whole peoples to migrate and to conquer in earlier ages. The land mass of Texas is rich in recoverable spoil. If this had not been so, I think I believe the relentless energy of Texans would have moved out and conquered new lands. This conviction is somewhat borne out in the restless movement of Texas capital. But now, so far, the conquest has been by purchase rather than by warfare. The oil deserts of the Near East, the opening lands of South America have felt the thrust. Then there are new islands of capital conquest: factories in the Middle West, food-processing plants, tool and die works, lumber and pulp. Even publishing houses have been added to the legitimate twentieth-century Texas spoil. There is no moral in these observations, nor any warning. Energy must have an outlet and will seek one.

In all ages, rich, energetic, and successful nations, when they have carved their place in the world, have felt hunger for art, for culture, even for learning and beauty. The Texas cities shoot upward and outward. The colleges are heavy with gifts and endowments. Theaters and symphony orchestras sprout overnight. In any huge and boisterous surge of energy and enthusiasm there must be errors and miscalculations, even breach of judgment and taste. And there is always the non-productive brotherhood of critics to disparage and to satirize, to view with horror and contempt. My own interest is attracted to the fact that these things are done at all. There will doubtless be thousands of ribald failures, but in the world's history artists have always been drawn where they are welcome and well treated.

By its nature and its size Texas invites generalities, and the generalities usually end up as paradox—the "little ol' country boy" at a symphony, the booted and blue-jeaned ranchman in Neiman-Marcus, buying Chinese jades.

Politically Texas continues its paradox. Traditionally and nostalgically it is Old South Democrat, but this does not prevent its voting conservative Republican in national elections while electing liberals to city and county posts. My opening statement still holds—everything in Texas is likely to be canceled by something else.

Most areas in the world may be placed in latitude and longitude, described chemically in their earth, sky and water, rooted and fuzzed over with identified flora and peopled with known fauna, and there's an end to it. Then there are others where fable, myth, preconception, love, longing, or prejudice step in and so distort a cool, clear appraisal that a kind of high-colored magical confusion takes permanent hold. Greece is such an area, and those parts of England where King Arthur walked. One quality of such places as I am trying to define is that a very large part of them is personal and subjective. And surely Texas is such a place.

I have moved over a great part of Texas and I know that within its borders I have seen just about as many kinds of country, contour, climate, and conformation as there are in the world saving only the Arctic, and a good north wind can even bring the icy breath down. The stern horizon-fenced plains of the Panhandle are foreign to the little wooded hills and sweet streams in the Davis Mountains. The rich citrus orchards of the Rio Grande valley do not relate to the sagebrush grazing of South Texas. The hot and humid air of the Gulf Coast has no likeness in the cool crystal in the northwest of the Panhandle. And Austin on its hills among the bordered lakes might be across the world from Dallas.

What I am trying to say is that there is no physical or geographical unity in Texas. Its unity lies in the mind. And this is not only in Texans. The word Texas becomes a symbol to everyone in the world. There's no question that this Texas-of-the-mind fable is often synthetic, sometimes untruthful, and frequently romantic, but that in no way diminishes its strength as a symbol.

The foregoing investigation into the nature of the idea of Texas is put down as a prelude to my journeying across Texas with Charley in Rocinante. It soon became apparent that this stretch had to be different from the rest of the trip. In the first place I knew the countryside, and in the second I had friends and relatives by marriage, and such a situation makes objectivity practically impossible, for I know no place where hospitality is practiced so fervently as in Texas.

But before that most pleasant and sometimes exhausting human trait took hold, I had three days of namelessness in a beautiful motor hotel in the middle of Amarillo. A passing car on a gravel road had thrown up pebbles and broken out the large front window of Rocinante and it had to be replaced. But, more important, Charley had been taken with his old ailment again, and this time he was in bad trouble and great pain. I remembered the poor incompetent veterinary in the Northwest, who did not know and did not care. And I remembered how Charley had looked at him with pained wonder and contempt.

In Amarillo the doctor I summoned turned out to be a young man. He drove up in a medium-priced convertible. He leaned over Charley. "What's his problem?" he asked. I explained Charley's difficulty. Then the young vet's hands went down and moved over hips and distended abdomen—trained and knowing hands. Charley sighed a great sigh and his tail wagged slowly up from the floor and down again. Charley put himself in this man's care, completely confident. I've seen this instant rapport before, and it is good to see.

The strong fingers probed and investigated and then the vet straightened up. "It can happen to any little old boy," he said.

"Is it what I think it is?"

"Yep. Prostatitis."

"Can you treat it?"

"Sure. I'll have to relax him first, and then I can give him medication for it. Can you leave him for maybe four days?"

"Whether I can or not, I will."

He lifted Charley in his arms and carried him out and laid him in the front seat of the convertible, and the tufted tail twittered against the leather. He was content and confident, and so was I. And that is how I happened to stay around Amarillo for a while. To complete the episode, I picked up Charley four days later, completely well. The doctor gave me pills to give at intervals while traveling so that the ailment never came back. There's absolutely nothing to take the place of a good man.

I do not intend to dwell long on Texas. Since the death of Hollywood the Lone Star State has taken its place at the top for being interviewed, inspected, and discussed. But no account of Texas would be complete without a Texas orgy, showing men of great wealth squandering their millions on tasteless and impassioned exhibitionism. My wife had come from New York to join me, and we were invited to a Texas ranch for Thanksgiving. It is owned by a friend who sometimes comes to New York, where we give him an orgy. I shall not name him, following the tradition of letting the reader guess. I presume that he is rich, although I have never asked him about it. As invited, we arrived at the ranch on the afternoon before the Thanksgiving orgy. It is a beautiful ranch, rich in water and trees and grazing land. Everywhere bulldozers had pushed up earth dams to hold back the water, making a series of life-giving lakes down the center of the ranch. On well-grassed flats the blooded Herefords grazed, only looking up as we drove by in a cloud of dust. I don't know how big the ranch is. I didn't ask my host.

The house, a one-story brick structure, stood in a grove of cottonwoods on a little eminence over a pool made by a dammed-up spring. The dark surface of the water was disturbed by trout that had been planted there. The house was comfortable, had three bedrooms, each room with a bath—both tub and shower. The living room, paneled in stained pine, served also as a dining room, with a fireplace at one end and a glass-fronted gun case against the side. Through the open kitchen door the staff could be seen—a large dark lady and a giggleful girl. Our host met us and helped carry our bags in.

The orgy began at once. We had a bath and on emerging were given scotch and soda, which we drank thirstily. After that we inspected the barn across the way, the kennels in which there were three pointers, one of them not feeling so well. Then to the corral, where the daughter of the house was working on the training of a quarter horse, an animal of parts named Specklebottom. After that we inspected two new dams with water building slowly behind them, and at several drinking stations communed with a small herd of recently purchased cattle. This violence exhausted us and we went back to the house for a short nap.

We awakened from this to find neighboring friends arriving, they brought a large pot of chili con carne, made from a family recipe, the best I have ever tasted. Now other rich people began to arrive, concealing their status in blue jeans and riding boots. Drinks were passed and a gay conversation ensued having to do with hunting, riding, and cattle-breeding, with many bursts of laughter. I reclined on a window seat and in the gathering dusk watched the wild turkeys come in to roost in the cottonwood trees. They fly up clumsily and distribute themselves and then suddenly they blend with the tree and disappear. At least thirty of them came in to roost.

As the darkness came the window become a mirror in which I could watch my host and his guests without their knowledge. They sat about the little paneled room, some in rocking chairs and three of the ladies on a couch. And the subtlety of their ostentation drew my attention. One of the ladies was making a sweater while another worked a puzzle, tapping her teeth with the eraser of a yellow pencil. The men talked casually of grass and water, of So-and-So who had bought a new champion bull in England and flown it home. They were dressed in jeans of that light blue, lighter and a little frayed at the seams, that can be achieved only by a hundred washings.

But the studied detail did not stop there. Boots were scuffed on the inside and salted with horse sweat, and the heels run over. The open collars of the men's shirts showed dark red lines of sunburn on their throats, and one guest had gone to the trouble and expense of breaking his forefinger, which was splinted and covered with laced leather cut from a glove. My host went to the extreme of serving his guests from a bar which consisted of a tub of ice, quart bottles of soda, two bottles of whisky and a case of pop.

The smell of money was everywhere. The daughter of the house, for example, sat on the floor cleaning a .22 rifle, telling a sophisticated and ribald story of how Specklebottom, her stallion, had leaped a five-bar corral gate and visited a mare in the next county. She thought she had property rights in the foal, Specklebottom's blood line being what it was. The scene verified what we have all heard about fabulous Texas millionaires.

I was reminded of a time in Pacific Grove when I was painting the inside of a cottage my father had built there before I was born. My hired helper worked beside me, and neither of us being expert we were well splattered. Suddenly we found ourselves out of paint. I said, "Neal, run up to Holman's and get a half-gallon of paint and a quart of thinner."

"I'll have to clean up and change my clothes," he said.

"Nuts! Go as you are."

"I can't do it."

"Why not? I would."

Then he said a wise and memorable thing. "You got to be awful rich to dress as bad as you do," he said.

And this isn't funny. It's true. And it was true at the orgy. How unthinkably rich these Texans must be to live as simply as they were.

I took a walk with my wife, around the trout pool and over against the hill. The air was chill and the wind blowing from the north had winter in it. We listened for frogs, but they had shacked up for the winter. But we heard a coyote howl upwind and we heard a cow bawling for her late weaned bairn. The pointers came to the wire mesh of the kennel, wriggling like happy snakes and sneezing with enthusiasm, and even the sickly one came out of his house and fleered at us. Then we stood in the high entrance of the great barn and smelled at the sweetness of alfalfa and the bready odor of rolled barley. At the corral the stock horses snorted at us and rubbed their heads against the bars, and Specklebottom took a kick at a gelded friend just to keep in practice. Owls were flying this night, shrieking to start their prey, and a nighthawk made soft rhythmic whoops in the distance. I wished that Able Baker Charley Dog could have been with us. He would have admired this night. But he was resting under sedatives in Amarillo curing his prostatitis. The sharp north wind clashed the naked branches of the cottonwoods. It seemed to me that winter, which had been on my tail during the whole trip, had finally caught up with me. Somewhere in our, or at least my, recent zoologic past, hibernation must have been a fact of being. Else why does cold night air make me so sleepy? It does and it did, and we went in to the house where the ghosts had already retired and we went to bed.

I awakened early. I had seen two trout rods leaning against the screen outside our room. I went down the grassed hill, slipping in the frost to the edge of the dark pool. A fly was ready fastened on the line, a black gnat, a little frayed but still hairy enough. And as it touched the surface of the pool the water boiled and churned. I brought in a ten-inch rainbow trout and skidded him up on the grass and knocked him on the head. I cast four times and had four trout. I cleaned them and threw the innards to their friends.

In the kitchen the cook gave me coffee and I sat in an alcove while she dipped my fish in corn meal and fried them crisp in bacon fat and served them to me under a coverlet of bacon that crumbled in my mouth. It was a long time since I had eaten trout like that, five minutes from water to pan. You take him in your fingers delicately by head and tail and nibble him from off his backbone, and finally you eat the tail, crisp as a potato chip. Coffee has a special taste of a frosty morning, and the third cup is as good as the first. I would have lingered in the kitchen discussing nothing with the staff, but she cleared me out because she had to stuff two turkeys for the Thanksgiving orgy.

In the mid-morning sunshine we went quail-hunting, I with my old and shiny 12-bore with the dented barrel, which I carried in Rocinante. That gun was no great shakes when I bought it second-hand fifteen years ago, and it has never got any better. But I suppose it is as good as I am. If I can hit them the gun will pull them down. But before we started I looked with a certain longing through the glass door at a Luigi Franchi 12-gauge double with a Purdy lock so beautiful that I was filled with covetousness. The carving on the steel had the pearly gleam of a Damascus blade, while the stock flowed into lock and lock into barrels as though they had grown that way from a magic planted seed. I'm sure that if my host had seen my envy he would have loaned me the beauty, but I didn't ask. Suppose I tripped and fell, or dropped it, or knocked its lovely tubes against a rock? No, it would be like carrying the crown jewels through a mine field. My old beat-up gun is no bargain, but at least anything that can happen to it has, and there's no worrying.

For a week our host had noted where the coveys were gathering. We spread out and moved through brush and thicket, down into water, out, and up, while the spring-steel pointers worked ahead of us and a fat old bitch pointer named Duchess with flame in her eyes outworked them all, and us too. We found quail tracks in the dust, quail tracks in the sand and mud of stream beds, bits of quail-feather fluff in the dry tips of the sage. We walked for miles, slowly, guns up and ready to throw shot at a drumming flight. And we never saw a quail. The dogs never saw or smelled a quail. We told stories and some lies about previous quail hunts, but it did no good. The quail had gone, really gone. I am only a reasonable quail shot but the men with me were excellent, the dogs were professional, keen, hard, and hard-working. No quail. But there's one nice thing about hunting. Even with no birds, you'd rather go than not.

My host thought my heart was breaking. He said, "Look. You take that little 222 of yours this afternoon and shoot yourself a wild turkey."

"How many are there?" I asked.

"Well, two years ago I planted thirty. I think there are about eighty now."

"I counted thirty in the band that flew up near the house last night."

"There's two other bands," he said.

I really didn't want a turkey. What would I do with it in Rocinante? I said, "Wait a year. When they top a hundred birds, I'll come down and hunt with you."

We came back to the house and showered and shaved, and because it was Thanksgiving we put on white shirts and jackets and ties. The orgy came off on schedule at two o'clock. I'll skip through the details quickly in order not to shock the readers, and also I see no reason to hold these people up to scorn. After two good drinks of whisky, the two brown and glazed turkeys were brought in, carved by our host and served by us. We said grace and afterward drank a toast all around and ate ourselves into a proper insensibility. Then, like decadent Romans at Petronius's board, we took a walk and retired for the necessary and inevitable nap. And that was my Thanksgiving orgy in Texas.

Of course I don't think they do it every day. They couldn't. And somewhat the same thing happens when they visit us in New York. Of course they want to see shows and go to night clubs. And at the end of a few days of this they say, "We just don't see how you can live like this." To which we reply, "We don't. And when you go home, we won't."

And now I feel better for having exposed to the light of scrutiny the decadent practices of the rich Texans I know. But I don't for one moment think they eat chili con carne or roast turkey every day.

*

WHEN I laid the ground plan of my journey, there were definite questions to which I wanted matching answers. It didn't seem to me that they were impossible questions. I suppose they could all be lumped into the single question: "What are Americans like today?"

In Europe it is a popular sport to describe what the Americans are like. Everyone seems to know. And we are equally happy in this game. How many times have I not heard one of my fellow countrymen, after a three-week tour of Europe, describe with certainty the nature of the French, the British, the Italians, the Germans, and above all the Russians? Traveling about, I early learned the difference between an American and the Americans. They are so far apart that they might be opposites. Often when a European has described the Americans with hostility and scorn he has turned to me and said, "Of course, I don't mean you. I am speaking of those others." It boils down to this: the Americans, the British are that faceless clot you don't know, but a Frenchman or an Italian is your acquaintance and your friend. He has none of the qualities your ignorance causes you to hate.

I had always considered this a kind of semantic deadfall, but moving about in my own country I am not at all sure that is so. Americans as I saw them and talked to them were indeed individuals, each one different from the others, but gradually I began to feel that the Americans exist, that they really do have generalized characteristics regardless of their states, their social and financial status, their education, their religious, and their political convictions. But if there is indeed an American image built of truth rather than reflecting either hostility or wishful thinking, what is this image? What does it look like? What does it do? If the same song, the same joke, the same style sweeps through all parts of the country at once, it must be that all Americans are alike in something. The fact that the same joke, the same style, has no effect in France or England or Italy makes this contention valid. But the more I inspected this American image, the less sure I became of what it is. It appeared to me increasingly paradoxical, and it has been my experience that when paradox crops up too often for comfort, it means that certain factors are missing in the equation.

Now I had moved through a galaxy of states, each with its own character, and through clouds and myriads of people, and ahead of me lay an area, the South, that I dreaded to see and yet knew I must see and hear. I am not drawn to pain and violence. I never gaze at accidents unless I can help, or attend street fights for kicks. I faced the South with dread. Here, I knew, were pain and confusion and all the manic results of bewilderment and fear. And the South being a limb of the nation, its pain spreads out to all America.

I knew, as everyone knows, the true but incomplete statement of the problem—that an original sin of the fathers was being visited on the children of succeeding generations. I have many Southern friends, both Negro and white, many of them of superb minds and characters, and often, when not the problem but the mere suggestion of the Negro-white subject has come up, I have seen and felt them go into a room of experience into which I cannot enter.

Perhaps I, more than most people from the so-called North, am kept out of real and emotional understanding of the agony not because I, a white, have no experience with Negroes but because of the nature of my experience.

In Salinas in California, where I was born and grew and went to school gathering the impressions that formed me, there was only one Negro family. The name was Cooper and the father and mother were there when I was born, but they had three sons, one a little older than I, one my age, and one a year younger, so that in grade school and high school there was always a Cooper in the grade ahead, one in my class, and one in the class below. In a word, I was bracketed with Coopers. The father, universally called Mr. Cooper, ran a little trucking business—ran it well and made a good living. His wife was a warm and friendly woman who was good for a piece of gingerbread any time we wanted to put the hustle on her.

If there was any color prejudice in Salinas I never heard or felt a breath of it. The Coopers were respected, and their self-respect was in no way forced. Ulysses, the oldest, was one of the best pole-vaulters our town ever developed, a tall, quiet boy. I remember the lean grace of his movements in a track suit and I remember envying his smooth and perfect timing. He died in his third year in high school and I was one of his pallbearers, and I think I was guilty of the sin of pride at being chosen. The second son, Ignatius, my classmate, was not my favorite, I discover now, because he was far and away the best student. In arithmetic and later in mathematics he topped our grades, and in Latin he not only was a better student but he didn't cheat. And who can like a classmate like that? The youngest Cooper—the baby—was all smiles. It's odd that I do not remember his first name. He was a musician from the start, and when I last saw him he was deep in composition which seemed, to my partially instructed ear, bold and original and good. But beyond this giftedness, the Cooper boys were my friends.

Now, these were the only Negroes I knew or had contact with in the days of my flypaper childhood, and you can see how little I was prepared for the great world. When I heard, for example, that Negroes were an inferior race, I thought the authority was misinformed. When I heard that Negroes were dirty I remembered Mrs. Cooper's shining kitchen. Lazy? The drone and clop of Mr. Cooper's horse-drawn dray in the street outside used to awaken us in the dawn. Dishonest? Mr. Cooper was one of the very few Salinians who never let a debt cross the fifteenth of the month.

I realize now that there was something else about the Coopers that set them apart from other Negroes I have seen and met since. Because they were not hurt or insulted, they were not defensive or combative. Because their dignity was intact, they had no need to be overbearing, and because the Cooper boys had never heard that they were inferior, their minds could grow to their true limits.

That was my Negro experience until I was well grown, perhaps too far grown to reform the inflexible habits of childhood. Oh, I have seen plenty since and have felt the shattering waves of violence and despair and confusion. I have seen Negro children who really cannot learn, particularly those who in their gelatin plate of babyness have been told they were inferior. And, remembering the Coopers and how we felt about them, I think my main feeling is sorrow at the curtain of fear and anger drawn down between us. And I've just thought of an amusing possibility. If in Salinas anyone from a wiser and more sophisticated world had asked, "How would you like your sister to marry a Cooper?" I think we would have laughed. For it might have occurred to us that a Cooper might not have wanted to marry our sister, good friends though we all were.

Thus it remains that I am basically unfitted to take sides in the racial conflict. I must admit that cruelty and force exerted against weakness turn me sick with rage, but this would be equally true in the treatment of any weak by any strong.

Beyond my failings as a racist, I knew I was not wanted in the South. When people are engaged in something they are not proud of, they do not welcome witnesses. In fact, they come to believe the witness causes the trouble.

In all this discussion of the South I have been speaking only about the violence set loose by the desegregation movements—the children going to school, the young Negroes demanding the questionable privilege of lunch counters, buses, and toilets. But I am particularly interested in the school business, because it seems to me that the blight can disappear only when there are millions of Coopers.

Recently a dear Southern friend instructed me passionately in the theory of "equal but separate." "It just happens," he said, "that in my town there are three new Negro schools not equal but superior to the white schools. Now wouldn't you think they would be satisfied with that? And in the bus station the washrooms are exactly the same. What's your answer to that?"

I said, "Maybe it's a matter of ignorance. You could solve it and really put them in their places if you switched schools and toilets. The moment they realized that your schools weren't as good as theirs, they would realize their error."

And do you know what he said? He said, "You troublemaking son of a bitch." But he said it smiling.

*

WHILE I was still in Texas, late in 1960, the incident most reported and pictured in the newspapers was the matriculation of a couple of tiny Negro children in a New Orleans school. Behind these small dark mites were the law's majesty and the law's power to enforce—both the scales and the sword were allied with the infants—while against them were three hundred years of fear and anger and terror of change in a changing world. I had seen photographs in the papers every day and motion pictures on the television screen. What made the newsmen love the story was a group of stout middle-aged women who, by some curious definition of the word "mother," gathered every day to scream invectives at children. Further, a small group of them had become so expert that they were known as the Cheerleaders, and a crowd gathered every day to enjoy and to applaud their performance.

This strange drama seemed so improbable that I felt I had to see it. It had the same draw as a five-legged calf or a two-headed foetus at a sideshow, a distortion of normal life we have always found so interesting that we will pay to see it, perhaps to prove to ourselves that we have the proper number of legs or heads. In the New Orleans show, I felt all the amusement of the improbable abnormal, but also a kind of horror that it could be so.

At this time the winter which had been following my track ever since I left home suddenly struck with a black norther. It brought ice and freezing sleet and sheeted the highways with dark ice. I gathered Charley from the good doctor. He looked half his age and felt wonderful, and to prove it he ran and jumped and rolled and laughed and gave little yips of pure joy. It felt very good to have him with me again, sitting up right in the seat beside me, peering ahead at the unrolling road, or curling up to sleep with his head in my lap and his silly ears available for fondling. That dog can sleep through any amount of judicious caresses.

Now we stopped dawdling and laid our wheels to the road and went. We could not go fast because of the ice, but we drove relentlessly, hardly glancing at the passing of Texas beside us. And Texas was achingly endless—Sweetwater and Balinger and Austin. We bypassed Houston. We stopped for gasoline and coffee and slabs of pie. Charley had his meals and his walks in gas stations. Night did not stop us, and when my eyes ached and burned from peering too long and my shoulders were side hills of pain, I pulled into a turnout and crawled like a mole into my bed, only to see the highway writhe along behind my closed lids. No more than two hours could I sleep, and then out into the bitter cold night and on and on. Water beside the road was frozen solid, and people moved about with shawls and sweaters wrapped around their ears.

Other times I have come to Beaumont dripping with sweat and lusting for ice and air-conditioning. Now Beaumont with all its glare of neon signs was what they called froze up. I went through Beaumont at night, or rather in the dark well after midnight. The blue-fingered man who filled my gas tank looked in at Charley and said, "Hey, it's a dog! I thought you had a nigger in there." And he laughed delightedly. It was the first of many repetitions. At least twenty times I heard it—"Thought you had a nigger in there." It was an unusual joke—always fresh—and never Negro or even Nigra, always Nigger or rather Niggah. That word seemed terribly important, a kind of safety word to cling to lest some structure collapse.

And then I was in Louisiana, with Lake Charles away to the side in the dark, but my lights glittered on ice and glinted on diamond frost, and those people who forever trudge the roads at night were mounded over with cloth against the cold. I dogged it on through La Fayette and Morgan City and came in the early dawn to Houma, which is pronounced Homer and is in my memory one of the pleasantest places in the world. There lives my old friend Doctor St. Martin, a gentle, learned man, a Cajun who has lifted babies and cured colic among the shell-heap Cajuns for miles around. I guess he knows more about Cajuns than anyone living, but I remembered with longing other gifts of Doctor St. Martin. He makes the best and most subtle martini in the world by a process approximating magic. The only part of his formula I know is that he uses distilled water for his ice and distills it himself to be sure. I have eaten black duck at his table—two St. Martin martinis and a brace of black duck with a burgundy delivered from the bottle as a baby might be delivered, and this in a darkened house where the shades have been closed at dawn and the cool night air preserved. At that table with its silver soft and dull, shining as pewter, I remember the raised glass of the grape's holy blood, the stem caressed by the doctor's strong artist fingers, and even now I can hear the sweet little health and welcome in the singing language of Acadia which once was French and now is itself. This picture filled my frosty windshield, and if there had been traffic would have made me a dangerous driver. But it was pale yellow frozen dawn in Houma and I knew that if I stopped to pay my respects, my will and my determination would drift away on the particular lotus St. Martin purveys and we would be speaking of timeless matters when the evening came, and another evening. And so I only bowed in the direction of my friend and scudded on toward New Orleans, for I wanted to catch a show of the Cheerleaders.

Even I know better than to drive a car near trouble, particularly Rocinante, with New York license plates. Only yesterday a reporter had been beaten and his camera smashed, for even convinced voters are reluctant to have their moment of history recorded and preserved.

So, well on the edge of town I drove into a parking lot. The attendant came to my window. "Man, oh man, I thought you had a nigger in there. Man, oh man, it's a dog. I see that big old black face and I think it's a big old nigger."

"His face is blue-gray when he's clean," I said coldly.

"Well I see some blue-gray niggers and they wasn't clean. New York, eh?"

It seemed to me a chill like the morning air came into his voice. "Just driving through," I said. "I want to park for a couple of hours. Think you can get me a taxi?"

"Tell you what I bet. I bet you're going to see the Cheerleaders."

"That's right."

"Well, I hope you're not one of those trouble-makers or reporters."

"I just want to see it."

"Man, oh man, you going to see something. Ain't those Cheerleaders something? Man, oh man, you never heard nothing like it when they get going."

I locked Charley in Rocinante's house after giving the attendant a tour of the premises, a drink of whisky, and a dollar. "Be kind of careful about opening the door when I'm away," I said. "Charley takes his job pretty seriously. You might lose a hand." This was an outrageous lie, of course, but the man said, "Yes, sir. You don't catch me fooling around with no strange dog."

The taxi driver, a sallow, yellowish man, shriveled like a chickpea with the cold, said, "I wouldn't take you more than a couple of blocks near. I don't go to have my cab wrecked."

"Is it that bad?"

"It ain't is it. It's can it get. And it can get that bad."

"When do they get going?"

He looked at his watch. "Except it's cold, they been coming in since dawn. It's quarter to. You get along and you won't miss nothing except it's cold."

I had camouflaged myself in an old blue jacket and my British navy cap on the supposition that in a seaport no one ever looks at a sailor any more than a waiter is inspected in a restaurant. In his natural haunts a sailor has no face and certainly no plans beyond getting drunk and maybe in jail for fighting. At least that's the general feeling about sailors. I've tested it. The most that happens is a kindly voice of authority saying, "Why don't you go back to your ship, sailor? You wouldn't want to sit in the tank and miss your tide, now would you, sailor?" And the speaker wouldn't recognize you five minutes later. And the Lion and Unicorn on my cap made me even more anonymous. But I must warn anyone testing my theory, never try it away from a shipping port.

"Where you from?" the driver asked with a complete lack of interest.

"Liverpool."

"Limey, huh? Well, you'll be all right. It's the goddamn New York Jews cause all the trouble."

I found myself with a British inflection and by no means one of Liverpool. "Jews—what? How do they cause trouble?"

"Why, hell, mister. We know how to take care of this. Everybody's happy and getting along fine. Why, I *like* niggers. And them goddamn New York Jews come in and stir the niggers up. They just stay in New York there wouldn't be no trouble. Ought to take them out."

"You mean lynch them?"

"I don't mean nothing else, mister."

He let me out and I started to walk away. "Don't try to get too close, mister," he called after me. "Just you enjoy it but don't mix in."

"Thanks," I said, and killed the "awfully" that came to my tongue.

As I walked toward the school I was in a stream of people all white and all going in my direction. They walked intently like people going to a fire after it has been burning for some time. They beat their hands against their hips or hugged them under coats, and many men had scarves under their hats and covering their ears.

Across the street from the school the police had set up wooden barriers to keep the crowd back, and they paraded back and forth, ignoring the jokes called to them. The front of the school was deserted but along the curb United States marshals were spaced, not in uniform but wearing armbands to identify them. Their guns bulged decently under their coats but their eyes darted about nervously, inspecting faces. It seemed to me that they inspected me to see if I was a regular, and then abandoned me as unimportant.

It was apparent where the Cheerleaders were, because people shoved forward to try to get near them. They had a favored place at the barricade directly across from the school entrance, and in that area a concentration of police stamped their feet and slapped their hands together in unaccustomed gloves.

Suddenly I was pushed violently and a cry went up: "Here she comes. Let her through. . . . Come on, move back. Let her through. Where you been? You're late for school. Where you been, Nellie?"

The name was not Nellie. I forget what it was. But she shoved through the dense crowd quite near enough to me so that I could see her coat of imitation fleece and her gold earrings. She was not tall, but her body was ample and full-busted. I judge she was about fifty. She was heavily powdered, which made the line of her double chin look very dark.

She wore a ferocious smile and pushed her way through the milling people, holding a fistful of clippings high in her hand to keep them from being crushed. Since it was her left hand I looked particularly for a wedding ring, and saw that there was none. I slipped in behind her to get carried along by her wave, but the crush was dense and I was given a warning too. "Watch it, sailor. Everybody wants to hear."

Nellie was received with shouts of greeting. I don't know how many Cheerleaders there were. There was no fixed line between the Cheerleaders and the crowd behind them. What I could see was that a group was passing newspaper clippings back and forth and reading them aloud with little squeals of delight.

Now the crowd grew restless, as an audience does when the clock goes past curtain time. Men all around me looked at their watches. I looked at mine. It was three minutes to nine.

The show opened on time. Sound of sirens. Motorcycle cops. Then two big black cars filled with big men in blond felt hats pulled up in front of the school. The crowd seemed to hold its breath. Four big marshals got out of each car and from somewhere in the automobiles they extracted the littlest Negro girl you ever saw, dressed in shining starchy white, with new white shoes on feet so little they were almost round. Her face and little legs were very black against the white.

The big marshals stood her on the curb and a jangle of jeering shrieks went up from behind the barricades. The little girl did not look at the howling crowd but from the side the whites of her eyes showed like those of a frightened fawn. The men turned her around like a doll, and then the strange procession moved up the broad walk toward the school, and the child was even more a mite because the men were so big. Then the girl made a curious hop, and I think I know what it was. I think in her whole life she had not gone ten steps without skipping, but now in the middle of her first skip the weight bore her down and her little round feet took measured, reluctant steps between the tall guards. Slowly they climbed the steps and entered the school.

The papers had printed that the jibes and jeers were cruel and sometimes obscene, and so they were, but this was not the big show. The crowd was waiting for the white man who dared to bring his white child to school. And here he came along the guarded walk, a tall man dressed in light gray, leading his frightened child by the hand. His body was tensed as a strong leaf spring drawn to the breaking strain; his face was grave and gray, and his eyes were on the ground immediately ahead of him. The muscles of his cheeks stood out from clenched jaws, a man afraid who by his will held his fears in check as a great rider directs a panicked horse.

A shrill, grating voice rang out. The yelling was not in chorus. Each took a turn and at the end of each the crowd broke into howls and roars and whistles of applause. This is what they had come to see and hear.

No newspaper had printed the words these women shouted. It was indicated that they were indelicate, some even said obscene. On television the sound track was made to blur or had crowd noises cut in to cover. But now I heard the words, bestial and filthy and degenerate. In a long and unprotected life I have seen and heard the vomitings of demoniac humans before. Why then did these screams fill me with a shocked and sickened sorrow?

The words written down are dirty, carefully and selectedly filthy. But there was something far worse here than dirt, a kind of frightening witches' Sabbath. Here was no spontaneous cry of anger, of insane rage.

Perhaps that is what made me sick with weary nausea. Here was no principle good or bad, no direction. These blowzy women with their little hats and their clippings hungered for attention. They wanted to be admired. They simpered in happy, almost innocent triumph when they were applauded. Theirs was the demented cruelty of egocentric children, and somehow this made their insensate beastliness much more heartbreaking. These were not mothers, not even women. They were crazy actors playing to a crazy audience.

The crowd behind the barrier roared and cheered and pounded one another with joy. The nervous strolling police watched for any break over the barrier. Their lips were tight but a few of them smiled and quickly unsmiled. Across the street the U.S. marshals stood unmoving. The gray-clothed man's legs had speeded for a second, but he reined them down with his will and walked up the school pavement.

The crowd quieted and the next cheer lady had her turn. Her voice was the bellow of a bull, a deep and powerful shout with flat edges like a circus barker's voice. There is no need to set down her words. The pattern was the same; only the rhythm and tonal quality were different. Anyone who has been near the theater would know that these speeches were not spontaneous. They were tried and memorized and carefully rehearsed. This was theater. I watched the intent faces of the listening crowd and they were the faces of an audience. When there was applause, it was for a performer.

My body churned with weary nausea, but I could not let an illness blind me after I had come so far to look and to hear. And suddenly I knew something was wrong and distorted and out of drawing. I knew New Orleans, I have over the years had many friends there, thoughtful, gentle people, with a tradition of kindness and courtesy. I remembered Lyle Saxon, a huge man of soft laughter. How many days I have spent with Roark Bradford, who took Louisiana sounds and sights and created God and the Green Pastures to which He leadeth us. I looked in the crowd for such faces of such people and they were not there. I've seen this kind bellow for blood at a prize fight, have orgasms when a man is gored in the bull ring, stare with vicarious lust at a highway accident, stand patiently in line for the privilege of watching any pain or any agony. But where were the others—the ones who would be proud they were of a species with the gray man—the ones whose arms would ache to gather up the small, scared black mite?

I don't know where they were. Perhaps they felt as helpless as I did, but they left New Orleans misrepresented to the world. The crowd, no doubt, rushed home to see themselves on television, and what they saw went out all over the world, unchallenged by the other things I know are there.

*

THE show was over and the river of us began to move away. Second show would be when school-closing bell rang and the little black face had to look out at her accusers again. I was in New Orleans of the great restaurants. I know them all and most of them know me. And I could no more have gone to Gallatoir's for an omelet and champagne than I could have danced on a grave. Even setting this down on paper has raised the weary, hopeless nausea in me again. It is not written to amuse. It does not amuse me.

I bought a poor-boy sandwich and got out of town. Not too far along I found a pleasant resting place where I could sit and munch and contemplate and stare out over the stately brown, slow-moving Father of Waters as my spirit required. Charley did not wander about but sat close and pressed his shoulder against my knee, and he does that only when I am ill, so I suppose I was ill with a kind of sorrow.

I lost track of time, but a while after the sun had passed top a man came walking and we exchanged good afternoons. He was a neatly dressed man well along in years, with a Greco face and fine wind-lifted white hair and a clipped white mustache. I asked him to join me, and when he accepted I went into my house and set coffee to cooking and, remembering how Roark Bradford liked it, I doubled the dosage, two heaping tablespoons of coffee to each cup and two heaping for the pot. I cracked an egg and cupped out the yolk and dropped white and shells into the pot, for I know nothing that polishes coffee and makes it shine like that. The air was still very cold and a cold night was coming, so that the brew, rising from cold water to a rolling boil, gave the good smell that competes successfully with other good smells.

My guest was satisfied, and he warmed his hands against the plastic cup. "By your license, you're a stranger here," he said. "How do you come to know about coffee?"

"I learned on Bourbon Street from giants in the earth," I said. "But they would have asked the bean of a darker roast and they would have liked a little chicory for bite."

"You do know," he said. "You're not a stranger after all. And can you make diablo?"

"For parties, yes. You come from here?"

"More generations than I can prove beyond doubt, except classified under *ci gît* in St. Louis."

"I see. You're of that breed. I'm glad you stopped by. I used to know St. Louis, even collected epitaphs."

"Did you, sir? You'll remember the queer one, then."

"If it's the same one, I tried to memorize it. You mean that one that starts, 'Alas that one whose darnthly joy . . . ?'"

"That's it. Robert John Cresswell, died 1845 aged twenty-six."

"I wish I could remember it."

"Have you a paper? You can write it down."

And when I had a pad on my knee he said, "Alas that one whose darnthly joy had often to trust in heaven should canty thus sudden to from all its hopes benivens and though thy love for off remore that dealt the dog pest thou left to prove thy sufferings while below."

"It's wonderful," I said. "Lewis Carroll could have written it. I almost know what it means."

"Everyone does. Are you traveling for pleasure?"

"I was until today. I saw the Cheerleaders."

"Oh, yes, I see," he said, and a weight and a darkness fell on him.

"What's going to happen?"

"I don't know. I just don't know. I don't dare think about it. Why do I have to think about it? I'm too old. Let the others take care of it."

"Can you see an end?"

"Oh, certainly an end. It's the means—it's the means. But you're from the North. This isn't your problem."

"I guess it's everybody's problem. It isn't local. Would you have another cup of coffee and talk to me about it? I don't have a position. I mean I want to hear."

"There's nothing to learn," he said. "It seems to change its face with who you are and where you've been and how you feel—not think, but feel. You didn't like what you saw?"

"Would you?"

"Maybe less than you because I know all of its aching past and some of its stinking future. That's an ugly word, sir, but there's no other."

"The Negroes want to be people. Are you against that?"

"Bless you, no, sir. But to get to be people they must fight those who aren't satisfied to be people."

"You mean the Negroes won't be satisfied with any gain?"

"Are you? Is anyone you know?"

"Would you be content to let them be people?"

"Content enough, but I wouldn't understand it. I've got too many *ci gîts* here. How can I tell you? Well, suppose your dog here, he looks a very intelligent dog—"

"He is."

"Well, suppose he could talk and stand on his hind legs.

Maybe he could do very well in every way. Perhaps you could invite him to dinner, but could you think of him as people?"

"Do you mean, how would I like my sister to marry him?"

He laughed. "I'm only telling you how hard it is to change a feeling about things. And will you believe that it will be just as hard for Negroes to change their feeling about us as it is for us to change about them? This isn't new. It's been going on a long time."

"Anyway, the subject skims the joy off a pan of conversation."

"That it does, sir. I think I'm what you might call an enlightened Southerner mistaking an insult for a compliment. As such a new-born hybrid, I know what will happen over the ages. It's starting now in Africa and in Asia."

"You mean absorption—the Negroes will disappear?"

"If they outnumber us, we will disappear, or more likely both will disappear into something new."

"And meanwhile?"

"It's the meanwhile frightens me, sir. The ancients placed love and war in the hands of closely related gods. That was no accident. That, sir, was a profound knowledge of man."

"You reason well."

"The ones you saw today do not reason at all. They're the ones who may alert the god."

"Then you do think it can't happen in peace?"

"I don't know," he cried. "I guess that's the worst. I just don't know. Sometimes I long to assume my rightful title Ci Gît."

"I wish you would ride along with me. Are you on the move?"

"No. I have a little place just off there below that grove. I spend a lot of time there, mostly reading—old things—mostly looking at—old things. It's my intentional method of avoiding the issue because I'm afraid of it."

"I guess we all do some of that."

He smiled. "I have an old Negro couple as old as I am to take care of me. And sometimes in the evening we forget. They forget to envy me and I forget they might, and we are just three pleasant . . . things living together and smelling the flowers."

"Things," I repeated. "That's interesting—not man and

beast, not black and white, but pleasant things. My wife told me of an old old man who said, 'I remember a time when Negroes had no souls. It was much better and easier then. Now it's confusing.' "

"I don't remember, but it must be so. It is my guess that we can cut and divide our inherited guilt like a birthday cake," he said, and save for the mustache he looked like the Greco San Pablo who holds the closed book in his hands. "Surely my ancestors had slaves, but it is possible that yours caught them and sold them to us."

"I have a puritan strain that might well have done so."

"If by force you make a creature live and work like a beast, you must think of him as a beast, else empathy would drive you mad. Once you have classified him in your mind, your feelings are safe." He stared at the river, and the breeze stirred his hair like white smoke. "And if your heart has human vestiges of courage and anger, which in a man are virtues, then you have fear of a dangerous beast, and since your heart has intelligence and inventiveness and the ability to conceal them, you live with terror. Then you must crush his manlike tendencies and make of him the docile beast you want. And if you can teach your child from the beginning about the beast, he will not share your bewilderment."

"I've been told the good old-time Negro sang and danced and was content."

"He also ran away. The fugitive laws suggest how often."

"You're not what the North thinks of as a Southerner."

"Perhaps not. But I'm not alone." He stood up and dusted his trousers with his fingers. "No—not alone. I'll go along to my pleasant things now."

"I have not asked your name, sir, nor offered mine."

"Ci Gît," he said. "Monsieur Ci Gît—a big family, a common name."

When he went away I felt a sweetness like music, if music could pleasure the skin with a little chill.

To me, it had been a day larger than a day, not to be measured against other days with any chance of matching. With little sleep the night before I knew I should stop. I was very tired, but sometimes fatigue can be a stimulant and a compulsion. It forced me to fill my gas tank and compelled me to stop and offer a ride to an old Negro who trudged with heavy heels in the grass-grown verge beside the concrete road. He was reluctant to accept and did so only as though helpless to resist. He wore the battered clothes of a field hand and an ancient broadcloth coat highly polished by age and wear. His face was coffee-colored and cross-hatched with a million tiny wrinkles, and his lower lids showed red rims like a bloodhound's eyes. He clasped his hands in his lap, knotted and lumpy as cherry twigs, and all of him seemed to shrink in the seat as though he sucked in his outline to make it smaller.

He never looked at me. I could not see that he looked at anything. But first he asked, "Dog bite, captain, sir?"

"No. He's friendly."

After a long silent while I asked, "How are things going with you?"

"Fine, just fine, captain, sir."

"How do you feel about what's going on?"

He didn't answer.

"I mean about the schools and the sit-ins."

"I don't know nothing about that, captain, sir."

"Work on a farm?"

"Crop a cotton lot, sir."

"Make a living at it?"

"I get along fine, captain, sir."

We went in silence for a stretch upriver. The trees and the tropic grass were burned and sad from the ferocious northern freeze. After a time I said, more to myself than to him, "After all, why should you trust me? A question is a trap and an answer is your foot in it." I remembered a scene—something that happened in New York—and was moved to tell him about it, but I quickly abandoned the impulse because out of the corner of my eye I could see that he had drawn away and squeezed himself against the far side of the cab. But the memory was strong.

I lived then in a small brick house in Manhattan, and, being for the moment solvent, employed a Negro. Across the street and on the corner there was a bar and restaurant. One winter dusk when the sidewalks were iced I stood in my window looking out and saw a tipsy woman come out of the bar, slip on the ice, and fall flat. She tried to struggle up but slipped and fell again and lay there screaming maudlinly. At that moment the Negro who worked for me came around the corner, saw the woman, and instantly crossed the street, keeping as far from her as possible.

When he came in I said, "I saw you duck. Why didn't you give that woman a hand?"

"Well, sir, she's drunk and I'm Negro. If I touched her she could easy scream rape, and then it's a crowd, and who believes me?"

"It took quick thinking to duck that fast."

"Oh, no sir!" he said. "I've been practicing to be a Negro a long time."

And now in Rocinante I was foolishly trying to destroy a lifetime of practice.

"I won't ask you any more questions," I said.

But he squirmed with restlessness. "Would you let me down here, please, captain? I live nearby."

I let him down and saw in the mirror how he took up his trudging beside the road. He didn't live nearby at all, but walking was safer than riding with me.

Weariness flagged me down and I stopped in a pleasant motel. The beds were good but I could not sleep. The gray man walked across my eyes, and the faces of the Cheerladies, but mostly I saw the old man squeezed as far away from me as he could get, as though I carried the infection, and perhaps I did. I came out to learn. What was I learning? I had not felt one moment free from the tension, a weight of savage fear. No doubt I felt it more being newcome, but it was there; I hadn't brought it. Everyone, white and black, lived in it and breathed it—all ages, all trades, all classes. To them it was a fact of existence. And it was building pressure like a boil. Could there be no relief until it burst?

I had seen so little of the whole. I didn't see a great deal of World War II—one landing out of a hundred, a few separated times of combat, a few thousand dead out of millions—but I saw enough and felt enough to believe war was no stranger. So here—a little episode, a few people, but the breath of fear was everywhere. I wanted to get away—a cowardly attitude, perhaps, but more cowardly to deny. But the people around me lived here. They accepted it as a permanent way of life, had never known it otherwise nor expected it to stop. The Cockney children in London were restless when the bombing stopped and disturbed a pattern to which they had grown accustomed.

I tossed about until Charley grew angry with me and told me "Ftt" several times. But Charley doesn't have our problems. He doesn't belong to a species clever enough to split the atom but not clever enough to live in peace with itself. He doesn't even know about race, nor is he concerned with his sisters' marriage. It's quite the opposite. Once Charley fell in love with a dachshund, a romance racially unsuitable, physically ridiculous, and mechanically impossible. But all these problems Charley ignored. He loved deeply and tried dogfully. It would be difficult to explain to a dog the good and moral purpose of a thousand humans gathered to curse one tiny human. I've seen a look in dogs' eyes, a quickly vanishing look of amazed contempt, and I am convinced that basically dogs think humans are nuts.

I didn't choose my first customer the next day. He picked me. He sat on a stool next to me eating a hamburger whose twin I held in my hand. He was somewhere between thirty and thirty-five, long and stringy, and nice-looking. His long lank hair was nearly ash-blond, worn long and treasured since he whopped it with a pocket comb unconsciously and often. He wore a light gray suit that was travel-wrinkled and stained; he carried the jacket over his shoulder. His white shirt was open at the collar, permitted so by pulling down the knot of his pale paisley tie. His speech was the deepest south I had heard so far. He asked where I was going and, when I told him I aimed toward Jackson and Montgomery, begged a ride with me. When he saw Charley he thought at first I had a nigger in there. It had got to be a pattern.

We settled ourselves comfortably. He combed back his hair and complimented me on Rocinante. "Of course," he said, "I could tell right off you're from the North."

"You've got a good ear," I said, I thought facetiously.

"Oh, I get around," he admitted.

I think I was responsible for what happened. If I could have kept my mouth shut I might have learned something of value. There's the restless night to blame and the length of the journey and the nervousness. Then, too, Christmas was coming and I found myself thinking of getting home more often than was helpful.

We established that I was traveling for pleasure and that he was on the lookout for a job.

"You come up the river," he said. "Did you see the doings in New Orleans?"

"Yes, I did."

"Wasn't they something, especially that Nellie? She really ripped the roof off."

"Yes, she did."

"Does your heart good to see somebody do their duty."

I think it was there that I went haywire. I should have grunted and let him read what he wanted in it. But a nasty little worm of anger began to stir in me. "They doing it out of duty?"

"Sure, God bless them. Somebody got to keep the goddamn niggers out of our schools." The sublimity of self-sacrifice activating the Cheerleaders overwhelmed him. "Comes a time when a man's got to sit down and think, and that's the time you got to make up your mind to sell your life for something you believe in."

"Did you decide to do it?"

"I sure did, and a lot more like me."

"What do you believe in?"

"I'm not just about to allow my kids to go to school with no niggers. Yes, sir. I'll sell my life first but I aim to kill me a whole goddamn flock of niggers before I go."

"How many children do you have?"

He swung around toward me. "I don't have any but I aim to have some and I promise you they won't go to school with no niggers."

"Do you propose to sell your life before or after you have children?"

I had to watch the road so I only got a glimpse of his expression, and it wasn't pleasant. "You sound to me like a nigger-lover. I might of known it. Trouble-makers—come down here and tell us how to live. Well, you won't get away with it, mister. We got an eye on you Commie nigger-lovers."

"I just had a brave picture of you selling your life."

"By God, I was right. You are a nigger-lover."

"No, I'm not. And I'm not a white-lover either, if it includes those noble Cheerladies."

His face was very near to me. "You want to hear what I think of you?"

"No. I heard Nellie use the words yesterday." I put on the brake and pulled Rocinante off the road.

He looked puzzled. "What you stopping for?"

"Get out," I said.

"Oh, you want to go round."

"No. I want to get rid of you. Get out."

"You going to make me?"

I reached into the space between the seat and the door where there is nothing.

"Okay, okay," he said, and got out and slammed the door so hard that Charley wailed with annoyance.

I started instantly, but I heard him scream, and in the mirror saw his hating face and his open spit-ringed mouth. He shrilled "Nigger-lover, nigger-lover, nigger-lover," as long as I could see him and I don't know how long after. It's true I goaded him, but I couldn't help it. I guess when they're drafting peacemakers they'd better pass me by.

I picked up one more passenger between Jackson and Montgomery, a young Negro student with a sharp face and the look and feel of impatient fierceness. He carried three fountain pens in his breast pocket, and his inner pocket bulged with papers. I knew he was a student because I asked him. He was alert. License plate and speech relaxed him as much as he is ever likely to relax.

We discussed the sit-ins. He had taken part in them, and in the bus boycott. I told him what I had seen in New Orleans. He had been there. He had expected what I was shocked at.

Finally we spoke of Martin Luther King and his teaching of passive but unrelenting resistance.

"It's too slow," he said. "It will take too long."

"There's improvement, there's constant improvement. Ghandi proved it's the only weapon that can win against violence."

"I know all that. I've studied it. The gains are drops of water and time is passing. I want it faster, I want action—action now."

"That might defeat the whole thing."

"I might be an old man before I'm a man at all. I might be dead before."

"That's true. And Ghandi's dead. Are there many like you who want action?"

"Yes. I mean, some—I mean, I don't know how many."

We talked of many things then. He was a passionate and articulate young man with anxiety and fierceness just below the surface. But when I dropped him in Montgomery he leaned through the window of the cab and he laughed. "I'm ashamed," he said. "It's just selfishness. But I want to see it—me—not dead. Here! Me! I want to see it—soon." And then he swung around and wiped his eyes with his hand and he walked quickly away.

With all the polls and opinion posts, with newspapers more opinion than news so that we no longer know one from the other, I want to be very clear about one thing. I have not intended to present, nor do I think I have presented, any kind of cross-section so that a reader can say, "He thinks he has presented a true picture of the South." I don't. I've only told what a few people said to me and what I saw. I don't know whether they were typical or whether any conclusion can be drawn. But I do know it is a troubled place and a people caught in a jam. And I know that the solution when it arrives will not be easy or simple. I feel with Monsieur Ci Gît that the end is not in question. It's the means—the dreadful uncertainty of the means.

*

In the beginning of this record I tried to explore the nature of journeys, how they are things in themselves, each one an individual and no two alike. I speculated with a kind of wonder on the strength of the individuality of journeys and stopped on the postulate that people don't take trips—trips take people. That discussion, however, did not go into the life span of journeys. This seems to be variable and unpredictable. Who has not known a journey to be over and dead before the traveler returns? The reverse is also true: many a trip continues long after movement in time and space have ceased. I remember a man in Salinas who in his middle years traveled to Honolulu and back, and that journey continued for the rest of his life. We could watch him in his rocking chair on his front porch, his eyes squinted, half-closed, endlessly traveling to Honolulu.

My own journey started long before I left, and was over before I returned. I know exactly where and when it was over. Near Abingdon, in the dog-leg of Virginia, at four o'clock of a windy afternoon, without warning or good-by or kiss my foot, my journey went away and left me stranded far from home. I tried to call it back, to catch it up—a foolish and hopeless matter, because it was definitely and permanently over and finished. The road became an endless stone ribbon, the hills obstructions, the trees green blurs, the people simply moving figures with heads but no faces. All the food along the way tasted like soup, even the soup. My bed was unmade. I slipped into it for naps at long uneven intervals. My stove was unlighted and a loaf of bread gathered mold in my cupboard. The miles rolled under me unacknowledged. I know it was cold, but I didn't feel it; I know the countryside must have been beautiful, but I didn't see it. I bulldozed blindly through West Virginia, plunged into Pennsylvania and grooved Rocinante to the great wide turnpike. There was no night, no day, no distance. I must have stopped to fill my gas tank, to walk and feed Charley, to eat, to telephone, but I don't remember any of it.

It is very strange. Up to Abingdon, Virginia, I can reel back the trip like film. I have almost total recall, every face is there, every hill and tree and color, and sound of speech and small scenes ready to replay themselves in my memory. After Abingdon—nothing. The way was a gray, timeless, eventless tunnel, but at the end of it was the one shining reality—my own wife, my own house in my own street, my own bed. It was all there, and I lumbered my way toward it. Rocinante could be fleet, but I had not driven her fast. Now she leaped under my heavy relentless foot, and the wind shrieked around the corners of the house. If you think I am indulging in fantasy about the trip, how can you explain that Charley knew it was over too? He at least is no dreamer, no coiner of moods. He went to sleep with his head in my lap, never looked out the window, never said "Ftt," never urged me to a turn-out. He carried out his functions like a sleepwalker, ignored whole rows of garbage cans. If that doesn't prove the truth of my statement, nothing can.

New Jersey was another turnpike. My body was in a nerveless, tireless vacuum. The increasing river of traffic for New York carried me along, and suddenly there was the welcoming maw of Holland Tunnel and at the other end home.

A policeman waved me out of the snake of traffic and flagged me to a stop. "You can't go through the tunnel with that butane," he said.

"But officer, it's turned off."

"Doesn't matter. It's the law. Can't take gas into the tunnel."

And suddenly I fell apart, collapsed into a jelly of weariness. "But I want to get home," I wailed. "How am I going to get home?"

He was very kind to me, and patient too. Maybe he had a home somewhere. "You can go up and take George Washington Bridge, or you can take a ferry."

It was rush hour, but the gentle-hearted policeman must have seen a potential maniac in me. He held back the savage traffic and got me through and directed me with great care. I think he was strongly tempted to drive me home.

Magically I was on the Hoboken ferry and then ashore, far downtown with the daily panic rush of commuters leaping and running and dodging in front, obeying no signals. Every evening is Pamplona in lower New York. I made a turn and then another, entered a one-way street the wrong way and had to back out, got boxed in the middle of a crossing by a swirling rapids of turning people.

Suddenly I pulled to the curb in a no-parking area, cut my motor, and leaned back in the seat and laughed, and I couldn't stop. My hands and arms and shoulders were shaking with road jitters.

An old-fshioned cop with a fine red face and a frosty blue eye leaned in toward me. "What's the matter with you, Mac, drunk?" he asked.

I said, "Officer, I've driven this thing all over the country—

mountains, plains, deserts. And now I'm back in my own town, where I live—and I'm lost."

He grinned happily. "Think nothing of it, Mac," he said. "I got lost in Brooklyn only Saturday. Now where is it you were wanting to go?"

And that's how the traveler came home again.

CHRONOLOGY

NOTE ON THE TEXTS

NOTES

Chronology

1902 Born John Ernst Steinbeck on February 27 in Salinas, California; the third child and only son (sisters are Esther, b. 1892, and Beth, b. 1894) of Olive Hamilton Steinbeck, a former schoolteacher, and John Ernst Steinbeck, manager of a flour mill. (Paternal grandfather, John Adolph Grossteinbeck, a German cabinetmaker from Düsseldorf, moved to Jerusalem with his brother Frederic in 1854 and married Almira Dickson, daughter of Sarah Eldridge Dickson and evangelist Walter Dickson, Americans who had gone to the Holy Land to convert the Jews. After Arab raiders killed Frederic and raped Sarah Dickson and her daughter, Mary, in 1858, John and Almira came to the United States, where they used the name Steinbeck. They settled in Massachusetts and then in Florida, where John Ernst Steinbeck was born, before moving to California after the Civil War. Maternal grandfather, Samuel Hamilton, born in Ballykelly in northern Ireland, immigrated to the United States at age 17 and settled in New York City, where in 1849 he married Elizabeth Fagen, an American of northern Irish ancestry; they moved to California in the early 1850s, where eventually Hamilton homesteaded a 1760-acre ranch near King City and was a skilled blacksmith.)

1903–9 Spends summers by the sea in family's Pacific Grove cottage near Monterey and on uncle Tom Hamilton's ranch near King City. Sister Mary is born in 1905. Steinbeck enjoys roaming in fields and along seashore; from father learns to love gardening. Receives a red Shetland pony named Jill from family in 1906, and cares for her himself. Home is full of books; parents and older sisters read out loud to him, and he becomes acquainted at an early age with novels of Robert Louis Stevenson and Walter Scott, the Bible, Greek myths, *The Pilgrim's Progress,* and *Paradise Lost.* Begins reading books himself and especially enjoys Sir Thomas Malory's *Le Morte d'Arthur.* Attends public schools in Salinas; does well in school and skips fifth grade. Enjoys reading Mark Twain and Jack London. Often cared for by older sisters while mother takes active part in town affairs.

1910 When the mill is closed in Salinas, father decides against taking job offer with a company farther north because it would mean uprooting the family. Father opens a feed and grain store which fails in 1918, and works briefly as accountant for sugar refinery before being appointed treasurer of Monterey County (holds position, through continual reelection, until shortly before his death).

1918 In junior year of high school Steinbeck develops pleural pneumonia and nearly dies; nursed by mother on ranch farther south in Salinas Valley. Writes stories and reads them out loud to close friends.

1919–24 Graduates from Salinas High School. Begins sporadic attendance at Stanford University in October as an English major. Meets Carlton "Dook" Sheffield and Carl Wilhelmson, who become lifelong friends. In spring 1920 undergoes operation for acute appendicitis. After working as surveyor in mountains above Big Sur, works in the summer as carpenter's helper at Spreckels Sugar Mill (continues to work over the next several years at the mill and on its many sugar beet ranches, where his duties include running chemical tests on sugar beets and supervising day laborers). Returns to Stanford full time in January 1923; studies English versification with William Herbert Carruth in spring 1923, and enrolls for summer study at Stanford-affiliated Hopkins Marine Station in Pacific Grove, where he takes courses in English and zoology. Studies creative writing with Edith Mirrielees at Stanford for two terms in 1924. Influenced by philosophy lectures of Harold Chapman Brown. Publishes stories "Fingers of Cloud: A Satire on College Protervity" and "Adventures in Arcademy: A Journey into the Ridiculous" in the February and June issues of *The Stanford Spectator*, student literary magazine.

1925–26 Leaves Stanford without a degree in June 1925, having completed less than three years of coursework. After working during the summer as caretaker of a lodge near Lake Tahoe, sails on a freighter by way of the Panama Canal to New York City. Settles in Brooklyn (moves to Gramercy Park area of Manhattan in 1926). Works as laborer on the construction of Madison Square Garden and as reporter for the *New York American*. Submits short stories to Robert M. McBride & Company, New York publishing firm, which rejects them. Returns to California by freighter in summer 1926, working as assistant steward in return for passage. Hired in the fall to work as caretaker of Lake Tahoe estate of Mrs. Alice Brigham.

1927 Lives alone on Brigham estate during winter. Story "The Gifts of Iban" appears in *The Smoker's Companion* in March under pseudonym "John Stern." Works with close friend Webster (Toby) Street on Street's play "The Green Lady" (material becomes the basis for *To a God Unknown*).

1928 Finishes first novel, *Cup of Gold*, in January. Leaves caretaker job in May and begins work at fish hatchery in Tahoe City in June. Meets Carol Henning, a tourist visiting the hatchery, during summer. Fired from hatchery job for wrecking superintendent's truck. In September moves to San Francisco, where he lives in "a dark little attic" on Powell Street and gets job as warehouse worker for company owned by sister Mary's husband, Bill Dekker.

1929 With help of college acquaintance Amasa (Ted) Miller, *Cup of Gold* is accepted for publication by Robert M. McBride. Gives up warehouse job and with father's financial help spends most of year writing in Pacific Grove and Palo Alto (father frequently sends money during the next several years). *Cup of Gold* published in August. Moves back to San Francisco in the fall and shares an apartment with Carl Wilhelmson.

1930 Marries Carol Henning in January. They stay briefly with Dook Sheffield and his wife in Eagle Rock, near Los Angeles, and then, successively, in a shack and two rented houses in the vicinity, before moving in September to family's three-room cottage in Pacific Grove where they live rent-free and feed themselves in part through fishing and raising vegetables. Manuscript of *To a God Unknown* rejected by Robert M. McBride. Meets marine biologist Edward F. Ricketts, owner of Pacific Biological Laboratory, who becomes close friend and major intellectual influence. Writes experimental novella "Dissonant Symphony" and, under pseudonym Peter Pym, crime novel "Murder at Full Moon"; neither is accepted for publication, and he later destroys manuscript of "Dissonant Symphony."

1931 Works on series of related stories, *The Pastures of Heaven*. Begins lifelong association with New York literary agency McIntosh & Otis (agent Elizabeth Otis becomes close friend).

1932 *The Pastures of Heaven* accepted for publication by Cape and Smith in February. Through Ricketts, becomes acquainted with myth scholar Joseph Campbell. Carol works part time as bookkeeper-secretary at Ricketts' laboratory in spring and summer; after she loses job because Ricketts cannot afford to pay her, Steinbeck and Carol move to Montrose area, north of Eagle Rock, staying with the Sheffields until they find a house to rent. Following bankruptcy of Cape and Smith, *The Pastures of Heaven* published by Brewer, Warren, and Putnam (where Cape and Smith editor Robert O. Ballou had moved).

1933 Despite father's financial help, Steinbeck and Carol are unable to make ends meet and are forced in February to give up the Montrose house. Mother becomes seriously ill in March, and after being hospitalized, suffers massive stroke; Steinbeck and Carol move to family home in Salinas. Steinbeck spends most of his time taking care of his mother at hospital and, after her release in June, at home. Writes the first of the four stories later joined together as *The Red Pony.* Father collapses in August and remains incapacitated for nearly a year; cared for by Carol at Pacific Grove cottage while Steinbeck spends much time in Salinas caring for mother. *To a God Unknown* published in September by Robert O. Ballou under his own imprint. During summer and fall completes first draft of *Tortilla Flat,* partly based on anecdotes told to him by Susan Gregory, a high school Spanish teacher in Monterey. Meets journalist Lincoln Steffens and his wife, Ella Winter, who are living in Carmel (continues to visit them until Steffens' death in 1936). "The Red Pony" (later titled "The Gift") and "The Great Mountains" appear in *North American Review,* November–December (both later become part of *The Red Pony*).

1934 Mother dies in February. Steinbeck and Carol live with father in Pacific Grove cottage, until arrangements are made for father to move back into Salinas home with caretakers in March. Steinbeck meets fugitive labor organizers Cicil McKiddy and Carl Williams in Seaside, California; interviews them about their involvement with 1933 cotton workers' strike in the San Joaquin Valley, organized by Communist-led Cannery and Agricultural Workers' Industrial Union, and about strike leader Pat Chambers. Manuscript of *Tortilla Flat* rejected by Robert O. Ballou and by Louis Kronenberger at Knopf. During summer completes nine short stories, eight of which are later collected in *The Long Valley.* Begins writing *In Dubious Battle,* based in part on interviews with McKiddy and Williams, in August. *Tortilla Flat* is accepted for publication by Pascal Covici of Covici-Friede. Enunciates "aggregation" theory of groups in unpublished essay "Argument of Phalanx": "Men are not final individuals but units in the greater beast, the phalanx . . . The nature of the phalanx is not the sum of the natures of unit-men, but a new individual having emotions and ends of its own, and these are foreign and incomprehensible to unit-men."

1935 *In Dubious Battle* accepted by Covici-Friede. Father dies in May. *Tortilla Flat,* published in May, becomes Steinbeck's first commercially successful book. Forms friendship with Joseph Henry Jackson, book reviewer for *San Francisco Chronicle.* Meets Pascal Covici for the first time in August. With royalties from *Tortilla Flat,* travels with Carol to Mexico in September; they rent an apartment in Mexico City (writes to friend: "This well of just pure life is charging us up again"). Meets painter Diego Rivera. Learns that film rights for *Tortilla Fiat* have been sold to Paramount for $4,000. Returns to United States at year's end, traveling to New York to sign Paramount contract and then to Pacific Grove before Christmas.

1936 *In Dubious Battle* published by Covici-Friede in January. Begins work on children's book (project eventually leads him to write *Of Mice and Men*); much of manuscript is destroyed by his dog in May. Visited by John O'Hara, who had contracted to write a dramatic adaptation (eventually abandoned) of *In Dubious Battle*; O'Hara becomes lifelong friend. In May begins to build house in Los Gatos, north of Monterey. Goes on six-day trip with Ricketts collecting octopuses along Baja California coast. Moves into Los Gatos house on Greenwood Lane, completed in July. Completes *Of Mice and Men* in August. Commissioned by *San Francisco News* to write articles on migrant farm workers; after meeting with federal officials at Resettlement Administration in San Francisco, tours San Joaquin Valley in bakery truck, accompanied by former preacher Eric H. Thomsen, regional director of federal migrant camp program. At Arvin Sanitary Camp ("Weedpatch") in Kern County, meets camp director Tom Collins, and from his conversation and written reports on migrant workers gathers material later incorporated into *The Grapes of Wrath.* Articles published as "The Harvest Gypsies" in seven installments in October. Begins researching and writing novel about migrants (later referred to as "The Oklahomans"). Limited editions of *Nothing So Monstrous* (excerpt from *The Pastures of Heaven*, with a new epilogue) and *Saint Katy the Virgin* published by Covici-Friede.

1937 *Of Mice and Men* published in March; becomes a best seller and Book-of-the-Month Club selection. Sails in March with Carol through Panama Canal to Philadelphia; after two-and-a-half-week stay in New York, they travel to Denmark, Sweden, Finland, and the Soviet Union, returning to New York in July. Works with director George S. Kaufman on dramatic adaptation of *Of Mice and Men*. Visits Farm Security Administration office in Washington, D.C., and talks with deputy administrator Dr. Will Alexander. Stories "The Promise," "The Gift," and "The Great Mountains" published as *The Red Pony* in a limited edition by Covici-Friede. Travels in California in October doing research on migrants; joined at migrant camp in Gridley by Tom Collins, who accompanies him on rest of trip. *Of Mice and Men* opens on Broadway November 23, starring Wallace Ford and Broderick Crawford; it runs for 207 performances (Steinbeck never sees the production).

1938 Dramatic adaptation of *Tortilla Flat* by Jack Kirkland opens on Broadway in January (closes after four performances). Meets documentary filmmaker Pare Lorentz. Makes two trips to San Joaquin Valley in February and March, where he joins Tom Collins in investigating condition of migrant workers in the wake of devastating floods in Visalia. Article based on trips is rejected by *Life*. Invited by Lorentz, travels to Hollywood where he meets film directors King Vidor, Lewis Milestone, and Mervyn Le Roy and actor James Cagney. Article published in April as "Starvation Under the Orange Trees" in the *Monterey Trader*. *Their Blood Is Strong*, expanded version of "The Harvest Gypsies," published as pamphlet by Simon J. Lubin Society of California to raise money for migrant workers. In May abandons unfinished satirical novel ("L'Affaire Lettuceberg") about vigilantes, suggested by brutal Salinas lettuce strike of September 1936. Learns that *Of Mice and Men* has won the New York Drama Critics Circle Award as best play of 1937. In late May begins 100-day period of work on novel that becomes *The Grapes of Wrath*. Keeps journal of novel's composition (published posthumously in 1989 as *Working Days*); of the title, suggested by Carol, Steinbeck writes: "I like it because it is a march and this book is a kind of march—because it is in our own revolutionary tradition and because in reference to this book it has a large meaning." Visited unexpectedly by Charlie Chaplin, who is living in Pebble Beach, near Carmel, and they establish friendship. Purchases 47-acre ranch (the "Old Biddle Ranch") outside Los Gatos; begins construction of new house on property in September. In August, Covici-Friede goes bankrupt and Pascal Covici joins Viking Press as senior editor; short story collection *The Long Valley* is published by Viking in September and sells well. (Viking becomes the publisher of all of Steinbeck's subsequent books.) Physically exhausted, completes manuscript of *The Grapes of Wrath* in November.

1939 Suffers for most of the year from sometimes crippling leg pain. Elizabeth Otis, his agent, urges him to make changes in the language of *The Grapes of Wrath*; during two days of intensive work agrees to some revisions. Later writes to Covici, "This book wasn't written for delicate ladies. If they read it at all they're messing in something not their business. I've never changed a word to fit the prejudices of a group and I never will." Argues further with Covici over proposal to change the novel's ending: "You know that I have never been touchy about changes, but I have too many thousands of hours on this book, every incident has been too carefully chosen and its weight judged and fitted. The balance is there. One other thing—I am not writing a satisfying story. I've done my damndest to rip a reader's nerves to rags, I don't want him satisfied." In March hears rumor that he is being investigated by the F.B.I.; worries about possible violence against him by Associated Farmers organization. *The Grapes of Wrath*, published in April by Viking with large advance sale, becomes the number-one national best seller; screen rights are sold for $75,000. Novel is banned or burned in Buffalo, New York, East St. Louis, Illinois, and Kern County, California, is denounced in Congress by Oklahoma representative Lyle Boren, and is the subject of a protest meeting at the Palace Hotel in San Francisco. Steinbeck is overwhelmed by flood of public attention and correspondence. Travels to Chicago in April to work with Pare Lorentz on *The Fight for Life*, documentary about Chicago Maternity Center. Rents apartment in Hollywood in June. Through old friend Max Wagner, now working in Hollywood, meets singer Gwendolyn ("Gwyn") Conger, and begins affair with her. Forms friendships with songwriter Frank Loesser and his wife, Lynn Loesser, actor Burgess Meredith, Nunnally Johnson (screenwriter for *The Grapes of Wrath*), and writer Robert Benchley. Difficulties with Carol lead to temporary separation; they reconcile and go on car trip in Pacific Northwest, visiting Vancouver in company with composer John Cage and his wife, Xenia. Travels with Carol in September to Chicago, visiting Lorentz and science writer Paul de Kruif in connection with *The Fight for Life*. Plans to devote himself to study of science and to write science textbooks in collaboration with Ricketts; becomes full partner in Ricketts' laboratory, and makes marine collecting trips with him in San Francisco Bay area. In December sees previews of John Ford's film version of *The Grapes of Wrath* ("No punches were pulled—in fact . . . it is a harsher thing than the book") and Lewis Milestone's film of *Of Mice and Men* ("Milestone has done a curious lyrical thing. It hangs together and is underplayed").

1940 In March, embarks with Ricketts, Carol, and small crew on marine collecting expedition in Gulf of California on boat *Western Flyer*, returning to Monterey April 20. Writes Eleanor Roosevelt, thanking her for remarking after her visit to a migrant workers camp in April that she had "never believed that *The Grapes of Wrath* was exaggerated." Wins Pulitzer Prize for *The Grapes of Wrath* (gives prize money to friend Ritchie Lovejoy to enable him to complete a novel). Impressed by singer Woody Guthrie, who records "The Ballad of Tom Joad," based on *The Grapes of Wrath*. Travels with Carol to Mexico in May to work on script for *The Forgotten Village*, an independent feature film produced and directed by Herbert Kline, about the struggle to bring modern medicine to a remote village. Meets with Lewis Milestone in Hollywood about film version of *The Red Pony*. Disturbed by influence of German propaganda in Latin America, writes to President Franklin D. Roosevelt, who receives him for brief visit in which Steinbeck proposes the formation of a propaganda office focusing on the Western Hemisphere. Visits Roosevelt again in September and proposes scheme to undermine Axis powers by distributing counterfeit German money in occupied countries of Europe. Takes flying lessons. Returns to Mexico in October to work on *The Forgotten Village*.

1941 Buys small house on Eardley Street in Monterey. Tells Carol in April about affair with Gwyn Conger. Separates from Carol at end of April; lives in Eardley Street house. *The Forgotten Village,* book version of film script, illustrated with stills, published in May. Works on book about Gulf of California trip, describing it to Pascal Covici as "a new kind of writing," and completes manuscript in July. Sells Los Gatos ranch at end of August. Works on screenplay for *The Red Pony.* In autumn moves to East Coast with Gwyn; they stay in a house on Burgess Meredith's farm in Suffern, New York, before moving in November into Bedford Hotel in Manhattan. Writes radio speeches for Foreign Information Service under direction of Robert E. Sherwood; travels frequently between New York and Washington. *Sea of Cortez: A Leisurely Journey of Travel and Research,* narrative by Steinbeck with a detailed scientific appendix by Ricketts, published in December. Film of *The Forgotten Village* banned for indecency by New York State Board of Censors because of scenes of childbirth and breast-feeding (ban lifted after public hearing).

1942 *The Moon Is Down*, set in unnamed occupied Nordic country, published in March; opens as play on Broadway in April. Moves into rented house at Sneden's Landing in Rockland County, New York, in April. Becomes friendly with playwright Maxwell Anderson, singer Burl Ives, and radio comedian Fred Allen. Sells film rights to *The Moon Is Down.* Appointed special consultant to the Secretary of War and accepts assignment from the Army Air Forces to write book about the training of bomber crews. Visits 20 air bases across the United States with photographer John Swope; their work is published as *Bombs Away: The Story of a Bomber Team.* Rents house in Sherman Oaks, California, in September to work on film based on *Bombs Away,* but production is plagued by difficulties and film is never made. With old friend Jack Wagner (brother of Max Wagner), writes script for film *A Medal for Benny.* Film of *Tortilla Flat*, directed by Victor Fleming and starring Spencer Tracy, released.

1943 Writes novella (unpublished) as basis for film *Lifeboat,* directed by Alfred Hitchcock. Moves into apartment on East 51st Street in New York City with Gwyn. Divorce from Carol becomes final on March 18. Marries Gwyn on March 29 in New Orleans. Accredited as war correspondent for New York *Herald Tribune,* following intensive security investigation by army counterintelligence. Travels to England on troop ship in June; meets photographer Robert

Capa, renews acquaintance with foreign correspondent William L. Shirer, and spends time with Burgess Meredith. Receives clearance in early August to go to North Africa; travels in Algeria and Tunisia, writing reports and working on an army film project. Sails on PT boat from Tunisia to Sicily as part of special operations unit commanded by actor Douglas Fairbanks Jr. that carries out coastal raids designed to harass and mislead the Germans. Reports from Salerno beachhead in Italy in mid-September. Rejoins Fairbanks' unit and participates in operations, including capture of Italian island of Ventotene. After a few weeks in London returns to New York City in early October, suffering from effects of combat, including burst eardrums and partial amnesia. Begins "The Good Little Neighbor," a novella set in Mexico that was never finished. *The Portable Steinbeck*, edited by Pascal Covici, published by Viking Press. Film of *The Moon Is Down*, directed by Irving Pichel, released.

1944 Sees screening of Hitchcock's *Lifeboat*; angered by changes in his original story and tries unsuccessfully to have his name removed from the credits. Travels with Gwyn to Mexico by way of Chicago and New Orleans in mid-January. Begins to develop film project *The Pearl* (based on Mexican folktale briefly recounted in *Sea of Cortez*), to be directed by Emilio Fernandez. Returns to New York in March. Has busy social life with friends, including Robert Capa and John O'Hara; meets Ernest Hemingway but is dismayed by his boorish behavior. Discusses plans for a musical comedy, "The Wizard of Maine," with Frank Loesser. Receives Academy Award nomination for best original story for *Lifeboat*. Completes *Cannery Row* in six weeks, with central character modeled on Ricketts. Writes to Sheffield about the book: "One thing—it never mentions the war—not once. . . . The crap I wrote over seas had a profoundly nauseating effect on me. Among other unpleasant things modern war is the most dishonest thing imaginable." Son Thom born August 2. In October moves back to California, settling in Soto House, large 19th-century adobe house near waterfront in Monterey.

1945 *Cannery Row* published in January; it sells well despite mixed reviews. Completes draft of novella *The Pearl* and goes to Mexico with Gwyn in February to work with Fernandez on the film; they return in mid-March. Troubled by resentment he has experienced in Monterey, writes to

Covici: "You remember how happy I was to come back here. It really was a home coming. Well there is no home coming nor any welcome. What there is is jealousy and hatred and the knife in the back. . . . Our old friends won't have us back. . . . And the town and the region—that is the people of it—just pure poison." Returns to Mexico in April with Jack Wagner, followed by Gwyn and Thom; works on shooting script for *The Pearl* in luxurious rented house in Cuernavaca. Does research in Mexican archives for proposed film about Emiliano Zapata. With Jack Wagner, receives Academy Award nomination for best original story for *A Medal for Benny* (directed by Irving Pichel). Begins to work on *The Wayward Bus.* Gwyn leaves Mexico for New York because of ill health; Steinbeck visits her there for over a month, then returns to Cuernavaca in October for filming of *The Pearl.* Having sold Monterey house, Steinbeck and Gwyn buy pair of adjacent brownstones on East 78th Street in New York City; he drives back to New York in early December.

1946 Settles into new home. (Rents out second brownstone to Nathaniel Benchley and wife, Marjorie, who become close friends of Steinbeck and Gwyn.) Son John born June 12. After difficult pregnancy, Gwyn continues to be in poor health. Steinbeck returns to Mexico it August for further work on film of *The Pearl.* After finishing *The Wayward Bus,* sails to Europe with Gwyn in October, visiting Sweden, Denmark, Norway, and France. Awarded King Haakon Liberty Cross in Norway for *The Moon Is Down.*

1947 Works on play "The Last Joan" (abandoned by April). *The Wayward Bus* published in February. Amid marital difficulties Gwyn goes to California for a month. With Robert Capa, Steinbeck plans trip to Russia for the New York *Herald Tribune.* Hospitalized after seriously injuring knee and foot when second-story railing in apartment breaks. Still walking with a cane, travels to France in June with Gwyn and Capa; after Gwyn returns home in July, goes on with Capa for brief stay in Sweden before proceeding to Soviet Union; visits Moscow, Stalingrad, Ukraine, and Georgia; returns by way of Prague and Budapest. Begins research for novel *The Salinas Valley* (later *East of Eden*). *The Pearl* published in November.

1948 Invests in World Video, television venture which collapses after a few months. Film of *The Pearl* released in the United States. Goes to Monterey for several weeks in

February to research *East of Eden*. *A Russian Journal*, with text by Steinbeck and photographs by Capa, published in April. Hospitalized in April for removal of varicose veins. Ed Ricketts is severely injured in automobile accident on May 7 and dies on May 11; Steinbeck writes to friend Bo Beskow, "there died the greatest man I have known and the best teacher. It is going to take a long time to reorganize my thinking and my planning without him." After returning from funeral in Monterey, is told by Gwyn that she wants a divorce; moves into Bedford Hotel. Spends much of summer in Mexico, researching screenplay for *Viva Zapata!*, to be directed by Elia Kazan. Returns to California in September, settling again in Pacific Grove house. Divorce becomes final in October. Devotes himself to gardening and home repairs; drinks heavily, and suffers from deep depression. Travels to Mexico in November with Kazan. Learns in December that he has been elected to the American Academy of Arts and Letters.

1949 Film of *The Red Pony*, directed by Lewis Milestone and with screenplay by Steinbeck, released. Returns briefly to Mexico in February. Over Memorial Day weekend meets Elaine Scott, wife of actor Zachary Scott; sees her frequently thereafter while working in Hollywood on *Zapata* screenplay. Sons come to stay for two months in summer, first in series of annual visits mandated by custody agreement. Begins work on *Everyman* (later *Burning Bright*), play in novella form. Finishes draft of *Viva Zapata!* screenplay. Elaine Scott files for divorce; Steinbeck moves to New York City and Elaine joins him there with her daughter Waverly; they settle in large apartment on East 52nd Street.

1950 Finishes *Burning Bright* in January. Leads active social life, meeting Elaine's many friends in the theater (she had previously worked as stage manager and in casting for the Theatre Guild and as stage manager for the original production of *Oklahoma!*). In February works with Kazan in Los Angeles on *Zapata*. Travels with Elaine to Texas in the spring to meet her family in Fort Worth (her father, Waverly Anderson, is a prominent oilman). Rents house for summer in Rockland County, near Burgess Meredith, Maxwell Anderson, and cartoonist Bill Mauldin. *Burning Bright*, produced by Richard Rodgers and Oscar Hammerstein II and starring Kent Smith and Barbara Bel Geddes, opens on Broadway in October to generally poor reviews; novel version published in November. Marries Elaine on December 28, and they honeymoon in Bermuda.

1951 Steinbeck and Elaine move in February into brownstone on East 72nd Street (their home for the next 13 years). On February 12 begins *East of Eden*. In his journal, says he intends to tell "the story of my country and the story of me" to his two young sons in order to demonstrate "the greatest story of all—the story of good and evil, of strength and weakness, of love and hate, of beauty and ugliness . . . how these doubles are inseparable. . . ." Summers in Nantucket with Elaine and sons. *The Log from the Sea of Cortez*, with new introductory memoir "About Ed Ricketts," published in September. Completes draft of *East of Eden* in November.

1952 Renews acquaintance with playwright Arthur Miller, with whom he forms close friendship. *Viva Zapata!* released. Travels from March to September in Morocco, Algeria, Spain, France, Switzerland, Italy, England, Scotland, and Ireland, writing articles for *Collier's*, with Elaine collaborating as photographer. Attacked by Italian Communist newspaper *L'Unita* while in Rome for failure to denounce U.S. policy in Korea, and writes lengthy retort (incident recounted in *Collier's* article "Duel Without Pistols"). *East of Eden* is published in September; receives mixed reviews but sells well. Writes and delivers on-camera introduction to omnibus film *O. Henry's Full House*. Writes speeches for supporters of Adlai Stevenson's presidential campaign and foreword to *Speeches of Adlai Stevenson*.

1953 Travels with Elaine and writer Barnaby Conrad to the Virgin Islands, for first of nine annual Caribbean vacations. Receives Academy Award nominations for best story and best screenplay for *Viva Zapata!* Collaborates with Cy Feuer and Ernest Martin, who are to produce musical *Bear Flag*, a continuation of *Cannery Row*; works on novel derived from idea for the musical, later titled *Sweet Thursday*. In September rents cottage in Sag Harbor, Long Island, where he consults with neighbor Ernest Martin on progress of musical. Suffers from depression and consults psychologist Gertrudis Brenner.

1954 During Virgin Islands vacation enjoys company of economist John Kenneth Galbraith and his wife, Catherine. Richard Rodgers and Oscar Hammerstein take over both writing and production of *Bear Flag* (now titled *Pipe Dream*). Sails with Elaine to Europe in March; they travel in Portugal and Spain, and in May begin four-month stay in Paris; suffers minor stroke on his way to Paris. Shocked by news that Robert Capa has been killed by a land mine in Vietnam. *Sweet Thursday* published in June. Travels to Munich to visit facilities of Radio Free Europe; writes statement on freedom of expression for broadcast behind the Iron Curtain. Writes weekly articles for literary supplement of *Le Figaro*; honored at dinner given by the Académie Française. Leaves Paris in September to travel in England (where he meets editor Malcolm Muggeridge and agrees to contribute occasional pieces to *Punch*), southern France, Italy, and Greece; returns with Elaine to America in December on the *Andrea Doria*.

1955 Invites William Faulkner to dinner in New York, but Faulkner drinks heavily and is uncommunicative (later they become friendly). Buys house in Sag Harbor, Long Island. Film of *East of Eden*, directed by Elia Kazan, with screenplay by Paul Osborn based on the novel's final segment, opens in March. Joins staff of *Saturday Review* as "Editor-at-Large" (contributes 17 articles and editorials by 1960). *Pipe Dream* opens on Broadway in September.

1956 Flies with Elaine to Trinidad in January. Covers Democratic and Republican political conventions in Chicago and San Francisco for Louisville *Courier-Journal* and its syndicated papers. Meets Adlai Stevenson, who becomes close friend; again contributes speech material to Stevenson campaign. Beginning in November serves on writers' committee (chaired by William Faulkner) of government-sponsored People to People program. Finishes comic novel *The Short Reign of Pippin IV* in November. Begins version of Sir Thomas Malory's *Morte d'Arthur* in modern English (never completed; it is published posthumously in 1976 as *The Acts of King Arthur and His Noble Knights*). Collection of essays in French written for *Le Figaro Littéraire* and other magazines published in Paris as *Un Américain à New York et à Paris*.

1957 Reads Malory intensively; does medieval research in Morgan Library in New York, assisted and advised by bookstore manager Chase Horton. Writes defense of Arthur Miller, then standing trial for contempt of Congress as a result of House Un-American Activities Committee investigation: "The Congress is truly on trial along with

Arthur Miller . . . . I feel profoundly that our country is better served by individual courage and morals than by the safe and public patriotism which Dr. Johnson called 'the last refuge of scoundrels.'" Sails in March to Italy with Elaine and sister Mary Dekker, partly under auspices of United States Information Agency, staying mostly in Florence and Rome. Continues Arthurian research, including investigation of Thomas Malory's life. Writes about the trip for Louisville *Courier-Journal. The Short Reign of Pippin IV* published in April. After leaving Italy, travels in France, England, Denmark, and Sweden. Meets leading Malory scholar Eugène Vinaver in Manchester, England, and sees Dag Hammarskjöld and Soviet novelist Mikhail Sholokhov in Stockholm. Flies to Tokyo in September with John Hersey and John Dos Passos to attend P.E.N. conference; becomes ill with severe influenza shortly after arrival.

1958 Travels to the Bahamas with Burgess Meredith and others as part of unsuccessful treasure salvage project. Spends June in England with Elaine. Sees Vinaver again and meets playwright Robert Bolt; continues Malory research. Works on novella "Don Keehan," based on *Don Quixote* (eventually abandoned). *Once There Was a War,* collection of war dispatches from 1943, published in September.

1959 Sails with Elaine to England in February; meets novelist Erskine Caldwell on board ship. Spends next eight months in rented cottage near Bruton, Somerset. Works on Malory project. Discouraged by unsympathetic response of Elizabeth Otis and Chase Horton to Malory book. In August goes on motor trip through Wales. Returns to United States in October. Suffers an undiagnosed attack (possibly from a small stroke) and is briefly hospitalized. Letter to Adlai Stevenson on destructive aspects of American affluence creates controversy when it is published in the press ("If I wanted to destroy a nation, I would give it too much, and I would have it on its knees, miserable, greedy, and sick").

1960 Puts aside Malory book, intending to return to it later. Begins novel eventually titled *The Winter of Our Discontent* in March; completes first draft in mid-July. Becomes involved in unsuccessful effort to draft Adlai Stevenson for Democratic presidential nomination. In September sets out on eleven-week journey ("Operation Windmills") with dog Charley across America, in pick-up truck he names Rocinante. Travels through New England, the Great Lakes region, and the Dakotas to the West Coast, where he is joined temporarily by Elaine in Seattle, then returns to New York by way of California, Texas, and Louisiana.

1961 Attends inauguration of President John F. Kennedy. Continues working on *Travels with Charley,* account of his cross-country journey, in February during vacation on Barbados. Sons Thom and John move in permanently with Steinbeck and Elaine because of difficulties with Gwyn. Accompanies Mohole expedition off the Mexican coast and writes account that appears in *Life* in April (project attempted to drill hole through the oceanic crust into the earth's mantle). *The Winter of Our Discontent* published in spring; Steinbeck is depressed by reviews, "even the favorable ones." In September begins ten-month stay in Europe with wife, sons, and their tutor, future playwright Terrence McNally. On arrival in London shocked by news of death of Dag Hammarskjöld in plane crash. Tours England, Wales, and Scotland in rented car, and after brief stay in Paris continues on through southern France to Italy; in Milan, at end of November, suffers attack (either a small stroke or heart attack). Family spends Christmas in Rome.

1962 Stays on Capri with Elaine, recuperating for several months, while sons travel with McNally. Pays tribute to his Stanford creative writing teacher Edith Mirrielees in preface to Viking reissue of her book *Story Writing.* Resumes travels in Italy and Greece in April; gives speech to Greek students at American College in Athens. *Travels with Charley in Search of America* published in midsummer. Through McNally meets playwright Edward Albee, with whom he forms friendship. Learns on October 25 that he has won Nobel Prize for Literature. Writes to Swedish friend Bo Beskow: "I suppose you know of the attack on the award to me not only by Time Magazine with which I have had a long-time feud but also from the cutglass critics, that grey priesthood which defines literature and has little to do with reading. They have never liked me and now are really beside themselves with rage." Travels to Stockholm for award ceremonies; makes short visit to London.

1963 Attends honorary dinner in New York for longtime friend Carl Sandburg in January. Moves with Elaine out of brownstone into high-rise apartment on same block in March. Dog Charley dies in April. Undergoes surgery for detached retina in June; while recuperating in hospital, visited regularly and read to by John O'Hara. At the suggestion of President Kennedy, makes two-month cultural exchange visit to Eastern Europe; in October travels with Elaine to Finland, the Soviet Union (including visits to Ukraine, Armenia, and Georgia), Poland, Austria, Hungary, Czechoslovakia, and West Germany. Tour joined (as Steinbeck had requested) by Edward Albee in Moscow. Steinbeck publicly protests pirating of Western books in the Soviet Union; sees Soviet writers including Ilya Ehrenburg, Victor Nekrasov, and Yevgeny Yevtushenko, and visits grave of Boris Pasternak despite official interference. Spends time with Erskine Caldwell, also staying in Moscow. Learns in Warsaw of assassination of President Kennedy. In West Berlin meets German writers Günter Grass and Uwe Johnson. Travels with Elaine to Washington in December for State Department debriefing; they attend private dinner with President Lyndon Johnson and Lady Bird Johnson (Elaine had known Lady Bird at University of Texas), establishing friendship.

1964 Asked by Jacqueline Kennedy to write book about John F. Kennedy; has long correspondence with her, but declines project. Estranged from sons, who return to live with Gwyn and bring suit with her for additional child support (large increase denied by New York Family Court in April). Spends Easter in Rome with Elaine. Begins work on text originally designed to accompany collection of photographs of America (eventually published as essay collection *America and Americans*). Helps write Lyndon Johnson's speech accepting the Democratic presidential nomination. Receives Presidential Medal of Freedom in September. Resumes work on Malory book. Pascal Covici dies October 14; Steinbeck speaks at memorial service along with Arthur Miller and Saul Bellow. Attends reunion with relatives in Watsonville, California. Works on President Johnson's inaugural address. Spends Christmas in County Galway, Ireland, with film director John Huston.

1965 Spends several weeks in London and Paris in early January; in Paris learns of sister Mary Dekker's death. Asked by President Johnson to make trip to Vietnam as special emissary, but declines. Writes to Elizabeth Otis proposing publication of journal written during composition of *East of Eden* (published posthumously in 1969 as *Journal of a*

Novel). Begins regular column for *Newsday* (it runs, with some interruptions, from November 1965 to May 1967). Travels with Elaine to England in December; accompanied by Eugène Vinaver and his wife on tour of libraries in northern England. Spends Christmas with John Huston in Ireland.

1966 Travels with Elaine to Israel in February for *Newsday*; visits graves of relatives there. Appointed by President Johnson to council of the National Endowment for the Arts in April. *America and Americans* published. Son John finishes basic training and asks father's help in getting assigned to serve with American forces in Vietnam; Steinbeck writes, "I was horrified when you asked me to get you orders to go out, but I couldn't have failed you there . . . But if I had had to request that you *not* be sent, I think I would have been far more unhappy." Writes to Lyndon Johnson in May in support of his Vietnam policy. After *The New York Times* publishes poem by Yevtushenko attacking Steinbeck's failure to oppose the Vietnam War, Steinbeck writes public letter describing war as "Chinese-inspired" and criticizing the Soviet Union for arming North Vietnam. Makes unsuccessful attempt to start new novel, "A Piece of It Fell on My Tail." Sees Yevtushenko, who is on reading tour of America, in November; they are partially reconciled. In December goes to Southeast Asia as reporter for *Newsday* with Elaine; met in Saigon by son John. Over six-week period tours wide area of South Vietnam, frequently going on combat missions and reporting sympathetically on American war effort.

1967 Visits Thailand, Laos, Indonesia, Hong Kong, where he suffers slipped disk, and Japan; returns home in April. Spends weekend at White House in May, and at President Johnson's request discusses his journey with Vice-President Hubert Humphrey, Secretary of State Dean Rusk, and Secretary of Defense Robert McNamara. Suffers debilitating pain as a result of back injury, and in October enters hospital for surgery. While awaiting operation, learns of son John's arrest in Washington, D.C., in connection with marijuana found in his apartment; John visits his father in hospital, but rejects offer of legal assistance. (While still in the army, John had written a magazine article about widespread marijuana use among soldiers in Vietnam; following his arrest, his comments on the subject are given wide press exposure; he is acquitted of the drug charge in mid-December.) Steinbeck undergoes successful back operation and spinal fusion on October 23; released from hospital in early December. Flies to Grenada with Elaine for Christmas.

1968 After a month in Grenada, recuperates in New York apartment. Goes to Sag Harbor in spring. Suffers minor stroke on Memorial Day weekend in Sag Harbor, followed by heart attack later in July. Enters New York Hospital July 17, and suffers another heart attack while there. Leaves hospital and returns to Sag Harbor in August. Writes to Elizabeth Otis: "I am pretty sure by now that the people running the war have neither conception nor control of it . . . I know we cannot win this war, nor any war for that matter." Returns to city apartment in November. Dies at home of cardiorespiratory failure at 5:30 P.M. on December 20. Funeral service is held at St. James Episcopal Church on Madison Avenue. Elaine takes ashes to Pacific Grove; after family service at Point Lobos on December 26, they are later buried in the family plot in Garden of Memories Cemetery, Salinas.

Note on the Texts

This volume contains four novels by John Steinbeck, *The Wayward Bus* (1947), *Burning Bright* (1950), *Sweet Thursday* (1954), and *The Winter of Our Discontent* (1961), along with the travel book *Travels with Charley in Search of America* (1962).

While in Mexico in the summer of 1945, Steinbeck sketched out some notes for a story and wrote a brief scenario in Spanish entitled "El Camion Vacilador." His initially modest intentions for the story quickly grew into something larger and more ambitious; in July 1945 he wrote to Pascal Covici, his editor at Viking, that he was hoping to write "something like the *Don Quixote* of Mexico." The following year he completed the novel, which was published by Viking in 1947. The text in this volume is taken from the 1947 Viking edition of *The Wayward Bus.*

Burning Bright is Steinbeck's adaptation of his play of the same title, which opened on Broadway on October 18, 1950, and closed after 13 performances. The bulk of the play, originally entitled "Everyman" and then "In the Forests of the Night," was written in about a month in early 1950. The short novel based on the play was published by Viking in 1950; this edition contains the text printed here.

Using the working title "Bear Flag," Steinbeck began writing *Sweet Thursday* late in 1952, and it took him slightly less than a year to complete his first draft. Like *Burning Bright*, it was conceived and written with the intention of also being performed on stage; by early 1954, Oscar Hammerstein had agreed to adapt the novel for a Broadway production, with Richard Rogers writing the music. *Sweet Thursday* was published by Viking in June 1954. Entitled *Pipe Dream*, the theatrical adaptation of the book opened on Broadway in November 1955 to generally negative reviews and ran through the middle of the following year. The 1954 Viking edition of *Sweet Thursday* contains the text printed here.

Although he had drafted notes for a novel that would become *The Winter of Our Discontent* in 1957, Steinbeck did not begin working in earnest on the book until early in 1960. Once he was hard at work on it, the narrative progressed quickly, with Steinbeck completing his first full draft in June 1960. His final novel published during his lifetime, *The Winter of Our Discontent* was brought out by Viking in 1961; the text in this volume is taken from this edition.

Travels with Charley in Search of America, based on Steinbeck's eleven-week cross-country journey in the fall of 1960, was shaped from his journal of the trip and from letters written while traveling to his wife, Elaine. Steinbeck worked on *Travels with Charley* throughout 1961; at times disheartened by the progress he was making, the favorable response to prepublication excerpts in *Holiday* magazine buoyed his spirit as he worked to complete the book. The text printed here is taken from the first edition of *Travels with Charley in Search of America*, published by Viking in 1962.

The texts of the original printings chosen for inclusion here are presented without change, except for the correction of typographical errors. Spelling, punctuation, and capitalization are often expressive features and are not altered, even when inconsistent or irregular. The following errors have been corrected: 8.7, Tufts'; 53.17, said,; 247.11, droped; 345.39, siad; 367.28, quater; 369.31, Not; 385.27, going explode; 404.13, "Now; 419.18, peaked; 428.22, Queen?'; 428.31, Give's; 446.16, Doc?'"; 450.14, Monterery; 476.14, pelicians; 517.19, wouldn't"; 518.38, made; 625.13, "miss'; 641.5, mariana; 669.35, that that; 702.10, its; 715.3, hard board; 734.1, docks; 767.28, prcess;; 770.23, man: Anyway; 858.10, dog dog; 873.25, said,; 893.32, hazlenut; 909.14, world If; 926.10, then; 929.3, every; 937.26, Their.

Notes

In the notes below, the reference numbers denote page and line of this volume (the line count includes headings). No note is made for material included in standard desk-reference books such as Webster's *Collegiate*, *Biographical*, and *Geographical* dictionaries. Quotations from Shakespeare are keyed to *The Riverside Shakespeare* (Boston: Houghton Mifflin, 1974), edited by G. Blakemore Evans. References to the Bible have been keyed to the King James version. For reference to other studies and further biographical background than is contained in the Chronology, see Jackson J. Benson, *The True Adventures of John Steinbeck, Writer* (New York: Viking Press, 1984); Jay Parini, *John Steinbeck: A Biography* (New York: Henry Holt, 1995); *Steinbeck: A Life in Letters* (New York: Viking Press, 1975), edited by Elaine Steinbeck and Robert Wallsten; *Letters to Elizabeth: A Selection of Letters from John Steinbeck to Elizabeth Otis* (San Francisco: Book Club of California, 1978), edited by Florian J. Shasky and Susan F. Riggs; *Conversations with John Steinbeck* (Jackson: University Press of Mississippi, 1988), edited by Thomas Fensch; Thomas Fensch, *Steinbeck and Covici: The Story of a Friendship* (Middlebury, Vermont: Paul S. Eriksson, 1979); Tetsumaro Hayashi, *A New Steinbeck Bibliography, 1929–1971*, and *A New Steinbeck Bibliography: 1971–1981* (Metuchen, New Jersey: Scarecrow Press, 1983); Michael J. Meyer, *The Hayashi Steinbeck Bibliography, 1982–1996* (Lanham, Maryland: Scarecrow Press, 1998); Robert Harmon, *John Steinbeck: An Annotated Guide to Bibliographical Sources* (Lanham, Maryland: Scarecrow Press, 1996); Robert DeMott, *Steinbeck's Reading* (New York: Garland Publishing, 1984); Robert DeMott, *Steinbeck's Typewriter: Essays on His Art* (Troy, New York: Whitston Publishing, 1996); Roy Simmonds, *A Biographical and Critical Introduction of John Steinbeck* (Lewiston, New York: Edwin Mellen Press, 2000); Richard Astro, *John Steinbeck and Edward F. Ricketts: The Shaping of a Novelist* (Minneapolis: University of Minnesota Press, 1974); Michael Hemp, *Cannery Row: The History of Old Ocean View Avenue* (Monterey, California: The History Company, 1986); Bruce Arris, *Inside Cannery Row: Sketches from the Steinbeck Era* (San Francisco: Lexikos, 1988); Katharine A. Rodger, *Renaissance Man of Cannery Row: The Life and Letters of Edward F. Ricketts* (Tuscaloosa: University of Alabama Press, 2002); *Breaking Through: Essays, Journals, and Travelogues of Edward F. Ricketts* (Berkeley: University of California Press,

2006), edited by Katharine A. Rodger; William McPheron, *John Steinbeck: From Salinas to Stockholm* (Stanford: Stanford University Libraries, 2000); Susan Shillinglaw, *A Journey into Steinbeck's California*, Photographs by Nancy Burnett (Berkeley, California: Roaring Forties Press, 2006); *Dictionary of Literary Biography, Volume 309: John Steinbeck: A Documentary Volume* (Detroit: Thomson Gale, 2005), edited by Luchen Li; *Critical Companion to John Steinbeck: A Literary Reference to His Life and Work* (New York: Facts on File, 2005), edited by Jeffrey Schultz and Luchen Li; *A John Steinbeck Encyclopedia* (Westport, Connecticut: Greenwood Press, 2006), edited by Brian Railsback and Michael J. Meyer; *John Steinbeck: The Contemporary Reviews* (New York: Cambridge University Press, 1996), edited by Joseph R. McElrath, Jesse S. Crisler, and Susan Shillinglaw; John Ditsky, *John Steinbeck and the Critics* (Rochester: Camden House, 2000); continuing issues of *Steinbeck Review* (formerly *Steinbeck Studies*).

THE WAYWARD BUS

1.2–8 *I pray you all gyve audience . . .* EVERYMAN] The opening lines of the 15th-century morality play *Everyman*, in which a dying man is abandoned by all companions save one (Good Deeds) on his journey to death.

2.2 GWYN] Gwyndolyn Conger Steinbeck (c. 1916–1975), John Steinbeck's wife from 1943 to 1948.

3.2 San Ysidro] Like other geographic locations in the novel, this is fictitious, not to be confused with the San Ysidro now part of greater San Diego.

7.16 Clark Gable] Hollywood star (1901–1960) who rose to preeminence in the 1930s with such films as *Mutiny on the Bounty* and *Gone with the Wind*.

8.7 the Van Johnsons . . . Sonny Tufts] Van Johnson (b. 1916), actor whose films included *Weekend at the Waldorf* (1945) and *No Leave No Love* (1946); Sonny Tufts (1911–1970), actor who enjoyed brief stardom in films such as *Bring On the Girls* (1945) and *Easy Come Easy Go* (1947). Like Frank Sinatra, Johnson and Tufts became successful at a time when Clark Gable and other earlier stars were serving in the military.

8.32 Aztec calendar stone] Or "Aztec Sun Stone"; a large basaltic 16th-century carving (13 feet in diameter and weighing 24 tons) unearthed in the 17th century at the Central Plaza of Mexico City, depicting the 18-month Aztec calendar.

15.27 Virgin of Guadalupe] Or "Our Lady of Guadalupe"; a representation of a dark-skinned Virgin Mary who appeared to one of the first Christian converts in North America, Juan Diego, on December 9, 1531, on

Tepeyac, a hill in present-day Mexico. Steinbeck retold the tale in his short story, "The Miracle of Tepayac" (*Collier's*, 1948).

19.22–23 Kit Carson] Christopher "Kit" Carson (1809–1868), frontiersman, Indian fighter, and soldier, who fought the Spanish in California with John C. Frémont, fought with the Union in New Mexico during the Civil War, and conducted a campaign against the Navajo. Fictionalized versions of Carson's career appeared in dime novels, comic books, and movies.

30.1 Eugene Debs] Eugene Victor Debs (1855–1926), labor activist and five-time Socialist candidate for President between 1900 and 1920.

30.19 picketed a scrap-iron ship bound for Japan] Between 1937 and 1940 American labor unions and political activists sought to prevent the shipment of scrap iron to Japan to protest the Japanese invasion of China. On October 16, 1940, President Franklin D. Roosevelt imposed an embargo that ended scrap metal shipments to Japan from U.S. ports.

30.35–37 Mexico . . . expropriated the oil] A dispute between the Mexican government (under President Lázaro Cárdenas) and the Standard Oil Company of New Jersey culminated in the Mexican seizure of foreign-owned oil properties in March 1938.

69.15–16 Lions Club] Lions Clubs International, a service club for businessmen founded by Melvin Jones in 1917.

71.4–5 Bob Hope . . . Bing Crosby] Bob Hope (1903–2003), comedian, and Bing Crosby (1903–1977), singer and movie actor, costarred in a series of very popular comedies including *Road to Singapore* (1940), *Road to Zanzibar* (1941), and *Road to Morocco* (1942).

84.8 *Captain Hornblower*] C. S. Forester (1899–1966) wrote a series of novels set in the period of the Napoleonic Wars and describing the rise of Horatio Hornblower through the ranks of the Royal Navy from midshipman to admiral; the first three novels, *Beat to Quarters* (1937), *A Ship of the Line* (1938), and *Flying Colours* (1939), were published together in 1939 as *Captain Horatio Hornblower*.

84.9–10 stories of Saroyan] William Saroyan (1908–1981), Armenian-American short story writer born in Fresno, California, whose story settings sometimes overlapped with those of Steinbeck.

93.17 Bellodgia] A moderately priced perfume, launched in 1927 by the Design House of Caron.

94.21 Oakes murder trial] The reference is to a sensational 1943 murder case involving Sir Harry Oakes (1874–1943), a multimillionaire who had been bludgeoned to death at his Nassau, Bahamas, estate; Alfred Fouquereaux de Marigny was acquitted after a trial that revealed shortcomings in the investigation.

109.25–26 Wee Kirk i' the Heather] Chapel on the grounds of Forest Lawn Memorial Park in Glendale, California, where many Hollywood stars are interred.

117.12–13 Spencer Tracy just came along . . . and they loved him] The film described is imaginary.

160.7 *zaguán*] Front hall or entryway.

175.23 *rebozos*] Shawls.

176.37–38 "Foxy Grandpa" . . . "Little Nemo" . . . "Happy Hooligan" . . . "Buster Brown."] Early comic strip characters: *Foxy Grandpa* (1900–1918), created by Charles Edward "Bunny" Schultze; *Little Nemo in Slumberland* (1905–1927), created by Winsor McCay; *Happy Hooligan* (1900–1932), created by Frederick Burr Opper; and *Buster Brown* (1902–1921), created by Richard Felton Outcault.

201.33 Bob Taft] Robert A. Taft (1889–1953) was a Republican senator from Ohio, 1939–53. A leading conservative, Taft was an unsuccessful candidate for the Republican presidential nomination in 1940, 1948, and 1952.

203.13 like Cary Grant done in that movie] The reference is probably to Leo McCarey's *The Awful Truth* (1937), starring Cary Grant and Irene Dunne.

212.24–28 Blue Lodge . . . Scottish Rite] Degrees of the Order of the Freemasons, listed in ascending order of rank.

BURNING BRIGHT

229.3–7 *Tyger*! . . . BLAKE] From *Songs of Innocence and Experience: Shewing the Two Contrary States of the Human Soul* (1794).

230. 1–4 To, for, and because of Elaine] Elaine Anderson Scott (1914–2003), to whom Steinbeck was married from 1950 until his death in 1968.

SWEET THURSDAY

303.7–8 As with the oysters . . . every one."] Cf. Lewis Carroll's *Through the Looking-Glass, and What Alice Found There* (1871), chapter 4: "'O Oysters,' said the Carpenter, / 'You've had a pleasant run! / Shall we be trotting home again?' / But answer came there none— / And this was scarcely odd, because / They'd eaten every one."

305.12–13 "Rock of Ages . . . St. James Infirmary."] "Rock of Ages" (1776), written by Augustus M. Toplady; "Asleep in the Deep" (1897), written by Arthur J. Lamb, with melody by Henry W. Petrie; "St James Infirmary," a song of indeterminate authorship, was recorded by many artists including Louis Armstrong in 1928.

305.22–23 Bear Flag] The Bear Flag, so named because it featured a grizzly bear, was raised at Sonoma, California, on June 14, 1846, by a group of American settlers led by Capt. John C. Frémont in a revolt against Mexican rule. In 1911 California's state legislature adopted it as the state flag.

314.16 Espaldas Mojadas] Wetbacks.

314.17–18 "Ven á Mi . . . que Llora."] Spanish song titles: "Come to Me, My Sorrowful Girl," "Woman from San Luis," and "The Little White Cloud that Cries."

314.19 *charro*] Gaudy.

316.19 William Byrd] English composer (1543–1623) whose works included three Latin Masses, written 1593–95.

316.23–24 Diamond Jim Brady] James Buchanan Brady (1856–1917), American businessman, financier, and philanthropist whose excessive eating was legendary.

318.1 Bhagavad-gita] "Song of the Lord"; a passage of 700 verses constituting the sixth book of the Sanskrit epic *Mahabharata* (c. 500–200 B.C.E.). It consists of a dialogue between the god Krishna and the hero Arjuna, occurring in a timeless moment before the climactic struggle between good and evil.

338.14 Jack Dempsey] Dempsey (1895–1983) was the world heavyweight boxing champion, 1919–26. Known as "The Manassa Mauler," 50 of his 60 wins were by knockouts.

343.27 *Sorrows of Werther*] *The Sorrows of Young Werther* (1774), novel of love and suicide by Johann Wolfgang von Goethe (1749–1832).

350.24 Harun al-Rashid] Fifth Abbasid caliph (ca. 763–809, ruled 786–809), renowned as a patron of arts and letters, who makes frequent appearances as a character in *The Thousand and One Nights.*

357.26–27 "lets concealment . . . his damask cheek"] Cf. *Twelfth Night*, II.iv.111–12: "But let concealment, like a worm i' the bud, / Feed on her damask cheek."

360.8 *Flower in a Crannied Wall*] Poem (1869) by Alfred, Lord Tennyson (1809–1892).

365.23 Romie Jacks] One of seven surviving children of the wealthy Scottish-born Monterey County land baron David Jacks and his wife, Marie Christina Soledad Romie, Romie Jacks served as manager of the family-owned Abbot (later Cominos) Hotel in Salinas, California.

370.32 Sterling North] Thomas Sterling North (1906–1974), author of numerous books for adults and children, including the best seller *So Dear To My Heart* (1947).

384.32 Jiggs and Maggie] *Bringing Up Father*, comic strip created by

George McManus (1884?–1954) that ran from 1913 to 2000; it was often called *Jiggs and Maggie*, after its two main characters.

391.1–2 *Down Beat*] American jazz magazine established in 1935 in Chicago, Illinois.

391.11 *Tio mio*] My uncle.

419.34 Buxtehude . . . Palestrina] Dieterich Buxtehude (c. 1637–1707), German-Danish organist and eminent composer of the Baroque period; Giovanni Pierluigi da Palestrina (c. 1525–1594), influential Italian Renaissance composer.

420.32 Giordano Bruno] Italian philosopher, priest, astronomer, astrologer, and occultist (1548–1600) who was burned at the stake in Rome as a heretic.

425.21 Tehuanos] Inhabitants, predominantly Zapotec Indians, of Tehuantepec in Oaxaca, in southeastern Mexico.

425.21–22 Sandunga] "La Sandunga," unofficial regional anthem of the Isthmus of Tehuantepec, was written by governor and military commander Máximo Ramó Ortiz (d. 1855). The song expresses the grief of a Tehuana (Zapotecan woman) over the death of her mother.

429.1 *O Frabjous Day!*] Cf. "Jabberwocky" (1871), in Lewis Carroll's *Through the Looking Glass*, chapter 1.

438.1 *Where Alfred the Sacred River Ran*] Cf. Samuel Taylor Coleridge, "Kubla Khan" (1816): "Where Alph, the sacred river, ran / Through caverns measureless to man."

439.36 "Whistle While You Work"] Song featured in Walt Disney's *Snow White and the Seven Dwarfs* (1937), with music by Frank Churchill and lyrics by Larry Morey.

445.4–5 "Wedding March" from *Lohengrin*] The "Bridal Chorus" from Richard Wagner's opera (1850), traditionally played at weddings and commonly known as "Here Comes the Bride."

455.26–27 if the British impressed our sailors] During the administrations of Washington, Adams, Jefferson, and Madison, the Royal Navy impressed thousands of seamen from American ships, claiming they were British subjects. (The British refused to recognize American naturalization, and often disregarded protection documents issued to native-born American sailors). American anger over impressment became one of the causes of the War of 1812.

455.27 "Fifty-four-Forty"] In 1844 James K. Polk was elected President on a platform calling for setting the northern boundary of Oregon at 54°40′N. The Anglo-American dispute over the boundary was settled in 1846 by a treaty setting the border at 49°N.

477.18–19 *Il n'y a pas de Mouches sur la Grandmère*] There are no flies on grandmother.

485.6 *Lama Sabacthani?*] Cf. Matthew 27:46: "And about the ninth hour Jesus cried with a loud voice, saying, Eli, Eli, lama sabachthani? that is to say, My God, my God, why hast thou forsaken me?"

491.9 Kinsey report] Alfred C. Kinsey (1894–1956), zoologist at Indiana University and founder of its Institute for Sex Research, published *Sexual Behavior in the Human Male* (1948) and *Sexual Behavior in the Human Female* (1953).

491.11–12 petition for release of Eugene Debs in 1918] Eugene V. Debs (1855–1926), four-time Socialist Party presidential candidate, was convicted in 1918 under the Espionage Act for inciting disloyalty in the armed forces by making an anti-war speech in Canton, Ohio. He was sentenced to ten years in prison, but was freed on December 25, 1919, after President Warren G. Harding commuted his sentence.

497.29–30 *I'm Sure We Should All Be as Happy as Kings*] Cf. Poem 25 ("Happy Thought") in Robert Louis Stevenson, *A Child's Garden of Verses* (1885): "The world is so full of a number of things, / I'm sure we should all be as happy as kings."

THE WINTER OF OUR DISCONTENT

508.6–9 spermaceti . . . *Moby Dick*] Cf. Herman Melville, *Moby-Dick* (1851), chapter 77, "The Great Heidelburgh Tun": ". . . the tun of the whale contains by far the most precious of all his oily vintages; namely, the highly prized spermaceti, in its absolutely pure, limpid, and odoriferous state."

509.32 Admiral Halsey] William F. Halsey (1882–1959), a famous naval commander in the war against Japan.

510.37 Woolworth's] The F. W. Woolworth Company was a nationwide retail company whose five-and-dime stores became a nearly universal presence in America. The first Woolworth's store was founded in 1878 by Frank Winfield Woolworth; the chain closed in 1997.

512.39 Chartres] Cathedral in France completed in 1220, considered a masterpiece of Gothic architecture.

513.27–514.1 'As soon as it was day . . . done in the dry?] Cf. Luke 22: 66–23:31.

518.15 Artemis] Virginal goddess of the hunt in Greek mythology.

519.38–519.3 And after that . . . place of a skull] Cf. Matthew 27: 31–33.

523.8–9 Valerius Maximus] Roman historian and moralist (c. 20 B.C.E.–c. 50 A.D.); his *Memorabilia*, in nine books, is a miscellany of anecdotes about various subjects.

528.24 'lama sabach thani'] See note 485.6.

539.32 Adam influence] Robert Adam (1728–1792), Scottish architect whose neo-classic style had an international influence on architecture and interior design.

546.13 Morgan and Rockefeller] John Pierpont Morgan (1837–1913) and John D. Rockefeller, Sr. (1839–1937), two of the wealthiest capitalists in American history.

546.23 O.T.C.] Harvard's Reserve Officers' Training Corps was founded in 1916, the first college unit in the nation.

556.30 laws of thinking . . . laws of things] Cf. John Elof Boodin (1869–1950), *A Realistic Universe: An Introduction to Metaphysics* (1916): "Somehow, the laws of thought must be the laws of things if we are going to attempt a science of reality."

557.22–23 General Frémont . . . trek to the West] In the 1830s and 1840s, John C. Frémont (1813–1890) took part in numerous expeditions west of the Mississippi River, at different times exploring Oregon, the Sierra Nevada Mountains, and California, where in 1846 he helped American settlers revolt against Mexican authorities and establish the Bear Flag Republic.

563.30 curiouser and curiouser] Cf. Lewis Carroll's *Alice's Adventures in Wonderland* (1865), chapter 2, "The Pool of Tears": "'Curiouser and curiouser!' cried Alice (she was so much surprised, that for the moment she quite forgot how to speak good English)."

569.5 *Chatterboxes* . . . the Rollo series] *Chatterbox*, a 19th-century children's magazine; the Rollo series, a 29-volume series of didactic novels about a young boy named Rollo, written by clergyman and educator Jacob Abbot (1803–1879) and aimed at a juvenile audience.

569.7 the Gustave Doré Hell] The illustrator Gustave Doré (1832–1883) issued his edition of Dante's *Inferno* in Paris in 1861. An American edition appeared in 1865.

569.10–11 Morte d'Arthur . . . Aubrey Beardsley] The illustrations by Aubrey Beardsley (1872–1898) for Sir Thomas Malory's *Le Morte D' Arthur* appeared originally in an edition published by J. M. Dent in London, 1893–94.

570.13–16 'Is life so dear . . . give me death!'] Final sentences of a speech by Patrick Henry (1736–1799), delivered March 23, 1775, in the Virginia Convention.

580.20–21 l'empereur, l'ermite, le chariot, la justice, le mat, le diable] The emperor, the hermit, the chariot, justice, the fool, the devil.

581.38 Pythoness] The priestess of Apollo at Delphi.

591.13 *Kyrie eleison*] Lord have mercy.

599.34–35 "Lord, now lettest Thou . . . to Thy word."] Cf. Luke 2:29.

601.16 sunk the *Maine*] On February 15, 1898, the battleship USS *Maine* was destroyed by an explosion in Havana harbor that killed 262 of its crew. The U.S. Navy board of inquiry into the loss of the *Maine* concluded in March 1898 that the explosion of the ship's magazine was caused by the detonation of an underwater mine, but stated that it could not determine responsibility. The United States declared war on Spain on April 25, 1898.

616.36–39 "Speed, bonnie boat . . . to Skye."] The chorus of the song "Skye Boat" (lyrics by Sir Harold Boulton, published in 1884), which commemorates the crossing of Charles Edward Stuart (1720–1788), known as Bonnie Prince Charlie, the unsuccessful Jacobite pretender to the British throne, to the Isle of Skye in the Hebrides after his defeat at the battle of Culloden on April 16, 1746.

618.14 There's the rub] Cf. *Hamlet*, III.1.64.

619.38 Bering . . . Baranov] Vitus Jonassen Bering (1681–1741), Danish-born navigator and explorer in the service of the Russian Navy, charted much of the Siberian and Alaskan coasts. Alexander Baranov (1747–1819) served as Russian governor in Alaska, 1799–1818.

626.22 first emergency immigration law] The Emergency Quota Act (1921) restricted immigration by setting limits based on the number of foreign-born people already in the United States in 1910, with immigration not to exceed three percent of each nationality.

633.8 Sullivan Act] A New York State law dating from 1911 that requires a permit for a private citizen to own a handgun.

635.24 *Ars est celare artem.*] "It is art to conceal art."—Ovid, *Ars Amatoria* (*The Art of Love,* A.D. 8).

635.40 *Io lo credo*] I believe it.

642.38 Prime Minister Macmillan] Harold Macmillan (1894–1986) served as Prime Minister of Great Britain from 1957 to 1963.

643.27 Leda . . . swan] In Greek mythology, the mortal Leda, wife of King Tyndareus of Sparta, is seduced by Zeus in the form of a swan.

645.36–38 Witch of the East . . . Ozma] The Wicked Witch of the East is a character in *The Wonderful Wizard of Oz* (1900) by L. Frank Baum (1856–1919); Princess Ozma, who eventually becomes ruler of the Land of Oz, appeared in *The Marvelous Land of Oz* (1904) and several other sequels, including *Ozma of Oz* (1917).

649.11 Cambellites] Campbellites, a restorationist Churches of Christ congregation, named for two of its founders in 1830, father and son Thomas and Alexander Campbell; the church refused to hold any creeds other than the Bible, rejected original sin, and practiced adult and youth baptism.

651.23–24 "Now is the winter . . . of York."] Cf. *Richard III*, I.i.1–2.

652.21 petroleum] The first commercially successful oil well was drilled in August 1859 near Titusville, Pennsylvania.

655.20 sad story of the death of kings] Cf. *Richard II*, III.ii.156.

656.25 Nosy Parker] Prying person; busybody.

657.28 words of Satchel Paige] Leroy Robert (Satchel) Paige (1906–1982), pitcher in both the Negro Baseball League and the American League, once said: "Don't look back. Something might be gaining on you."

666.24 Valentino eyes] Rudolph Valentino (1895–1926) Italian-born film star known for his roles in such films as *The Four Horsemen of the Apocalypse* (1921), *The Sheik* (1921), and *Blood and Sand* (1922).

667.9–10 publisher of *Time* magazine] Henry R. Luce (1898–1967), co-founder, publisher, and editor of *Time* from 1923 to 1964.

668.14 Pancho Villa] Steinbeck uses the same anecdote in *The Wayward Bus*; see pgs. 133–34 in this volume.

670.28 It's Matthew] See note 513.38.

672.2 *Ora pro me.*] Pray for me.

672.34 Wickham] William of Wykeham (1324–1404), Bishop of Winchester, Chancellor of England, and founder of New College, Oxford (1379), and Winchester College (1394).

672.37 Great Books] The Great Books of the Western World, a uniform collection of classic works available by subscription from The Great Books Foundation, a nonprofit educational organization established in 1947.

680.35 Deborah the Judge of Israel] Cf. Judges 4–5. Deborah was a prophetess and the only female judge mentioned in the Bible; under her guidance Barak conquered Sisera and delivered Israel from Canaanite rule.

684.40 James G. Blaine] Blaine (1830–1893), prominent American politician who served as congressman, senator, and secretary of state.

691.7 Golgotha] Hill on which Jesus was crucified, from the Aramaic for "skull."

693.31 The fifty-star] The 50-star flag became the nation's official flag on July 4, 1959.

700.5–6 Montauk Point . . . dude ranch] Deep Hollow Ranch in Montauk, eastern Long Island, which bills itself as America's oldest cattle ranch, became a dude ranch in 1937 while continuing its working tradition.

705.25 Appian Way] Roman road which linked Rome with southern Italy.

713.34–35 words . . . Statue of Liberty] Cf. Emma Lazarus, "The New

Colossus" (1883). The poem was engraved on a plaque in 1903 and placed on the statue's pedestal.

720.27–29 "Me beswac . . . hire ladteow."] The first quotation, spoken by Eve in the original text, means "The serpent betrayed me with fair words," and is from the Old English poem *Genesis*, a verse paraphrase of part of the Book of Genesis written around 1000; the second quotation, which means "The tamed lion, if she tastes blood, will bite first her master," is from an Old English translation by King Alfred (849–899) of Boethius's *De Consolatione Philosophiae* (*Of the Consolation of Philosophy*), c. A.D. 524.

723.18 O Nile serpent] Cf. *Antony and Cleopatra*, I.v.25.

724.35 *Beaux rêves*] French: pleasant dreams.

729.22 *Weltschmertz*] German: world-weariness.

729.38–39 Dick Clark . . . Chessman . . . Dillinger] Dick Clark (b. 1929) was host of the syndicated television variety show *American Bandstand* (1957 to 1988); Caryl Chessman (1921–1960) was convicted in 1948 on 17 counts of robbery, kidnapping, and rape, and after a series of appeals and stays was executed at San Quentin Prison on May 2, 1960; John Dillinger (1903–1934), was an American bank robber declared Public Enemy No. 1 by the FBI, whose agents shot him dead outside a Chicago movie theater in 1934.

733.8-9 Aunt Harriet—"up in heben she be"] Cf. Hoagy Carmichael, "Old Rockin' Chair's Got Me" (1929), also known as "Rocking Chair": "My dear old aunt Harriet, in Heaven she be."

736.34 Presidential nominations] The Democratic National Convention met at the Los Angeles Memorial Sports Arena, July 11–15, 1960, and nominated John F. Kennedy for president and Lyndon B. Johnson for vice-president. The Republican National Convention met at Chicago's International Amphitheater, July 25–28, 1960, and nominated Richard M. Nixon for president and Henry Cabot Lodge for vice-president.

747.38–39 'What's My Line?' . . . 'Mystery Guest.'] *What's My Line* (1950–1967) was a nationally broadcast weekly CBS television game show in which four panelists tried to figure out the unusual occupations of various contestants. Each show featured a celebrity mystery guest whom the panelists attempted to identify while blindfolded.

748.1 Teen Twisters] No quiz show of this name existed; the recording artist Chubby Checker (b. 1941) released an album called *For Teen Twisters Only* in 1961.

751.27 *muleta and espada*] *Muleta*, a short red cape used by matadors; *espada*, a matador's sword.

757.8 quiz scandals] In November 1959 Charles Van Doren (b. 1926), an instructor at Columbia University and son of the distinguished writer and professor Mark Van Doren, testified to the House Subcommittee on Legislative Oversight that *Twenty-One*, a popular NBC television quiz show on which he had earned $138,000 in prize money, was rigged. Similar revelations surfaced about other TV quiz shows, including *Dotto* and *The $64,000 Challenge*.

757.9 payola fuss . . . Congressional committees] In 1959 Congressional hearings were convened to investigate the practice of record companies paying radio station disc jockeys to give airtime to their records. Congress amended the Federal Communications Act in 1960 to outlaw under-the-table payments and require broadcasters to disclose if airplay for a song had been purchased.

757.23–36 "What is an individual . . . his country?"] The passage is from Henry Clay's speech on the Compromise of 1850 delivered in the Senate on July 22, 1850.

TRAVELS WITH CHARLEY

766.1 *Harold Guinzburg*] Harold K. Guinzburg (1899–1961), cofounder, with George S. Oppenheim, of Viking Press, Steinbeck's publisher for most of his career.

784.40 Khrushchev was at the United Nations,] Nikita Khrushchev (1894–1971), first secretary of the Soviet Communist Party, 1953–64, and premier of the Soviet Union, 1958–64, attended several sessions of the United Nations General Assembly in the fall of 1960. On October 11, 1960, he pounded his shoe on his desk to protest remarks made a Filipino delegate.

786.29 Shirer's *Rise and Fall of the Third Reich*] William L. Shirer's (1904–1993) best-selling account of Nazi Germany, which won the National Book Award in 1961; in a 1962 letter, Steinbeck declared it "wonderful . . . a fine history."

788.20 "Teen-Age Angel"] "Teen Angel," written by Jean Dinning and performed by Mark Dinning, was at the top of the U.S. Billboard Hot 100 chart in February 1960.

789.34 "Snowbound"] *Snow-Bound: A Winter Idyll* (1866), long poem by John Greenleaf Whittier (1807–1892).

790.14 The Spectator . . . Henry Morley] Morley (1822–1894) edited a collection of *The Spectator*, the English periodical founded by Joseph Addison (1672–1719) and Sir Richard Steele (1672–1729), produced 1711–12 and briefly resumed in 1714.

790.32–33 *"Non fumum ex fulgore, . . . miracula promat."*—Horace.] "He intends to produce not smoke from a flash of lightning, but he intends to produce light out of smoke, so as thereafter to yield splendid sights."—*Ars Poetica*, lines 143–44.

793.13 Sic semper cum Frogs.] "Thus ever with Frogs," a parody of John Wilkes Booth's exclamation after assassinating Abraham Lincoln ("Sic semper tyrannis").

797.37 Elizabeth Otis] Elizabeth R. Otis (1900–1981), co-founder in 1928, with Mavis McIntosh, of McIntosh and Otis, the literary agency that represented John Steinbeck from 1931 on.

805.1–3 Peary . . . North Pole] Rear Admiral Robert E. Peary (1856–1920) led the first expedition to reach the North Pole on April 6, 1909, after making several earlier attempts.

806.35–36 "*In nomine Patris . . . et Spiritus Sancti.*"] "In the name of the Father, and of the Son, and of the Holy Spirit."

808.13 *vacilador*] In a letter to the film producer Charles Brackett in 1956, Steinbeck wrote: "The word *vacilador*, or the verb *vacilar*, is not translatable unfortunately, and it's a word we really need in English because to be 'vacilando' means you're aiming at some place, but you don't care much whether you get there." (The original Spanish working title for *The Wayward Bus* had been *El Camion Vacilador.*)

808.35 Nelson Eddy and Jeanette MacDonald] Nelson Eddy (1901–1967) and Jeanette MacDonald (1903–1965) starred in a series of Hollywood musicals in the 1930s and 1940s; Steinbeck's reference is to *Rose-Marie,* their 1936 film set in the Canadian Rockies.

811.30–31 *Je vous porte . . . Departement de Charente.*] "I bring you a dear souvenir of beautiful France, particularly, the Department of Charente." Charente, in the western region of France, is noted for its brandy.

812.8 *alouettes*] Larks.

812.37–38 "*Enfant de France, Mort pour la Patrie.*"] "A Son of France, Dead for His Country."

815.6 Fred Allen] Comedian and radio personality (1894–1956), a friend of Steinbeck's.

817.33 Joseph Alsop] Political correspondent and syndicated columnist (1910–1989). Steinbeck visited Prague in September 1947.

818.12 John Knox church] A Presbyterian church, named after the Scottish Protestant reformer John Knox (1513?–1572).

820.18–19 Red Lewis . . . *Main Street*] Sinclair Lewis (1885–1951), American novelist born in Sauk Centre, Minnesota. His fictionalized portrayal of his hometown in *Main Street* (1920) initially created much local bitterness.

820.21–22 Geoffrey of Monmouth . . . History of British Kings] Geoffrey (c. 1100–c. 1155) completed *Histories of the Kings of Britain* (*Historia Regum Britanniae*) around 1138.

828.32 Ed Ricketts] Marine biologist (1897–1948) who was Steinbeck's close friend from 1930 on and had a major influence on his work. The two often collected specimens together, as described in the 1941 book they co-wrote, *Sea of Cortez: A Leisurely Journal of Travel and Research.*

840.18 *San Pablo con un Libro*] "Saint Paul with a Book" by El Greco (1541–1614).

855.13 W.P.A. Guides to the States] Part of President Franklin D. Roosevelt's Works Projects Administration (WPA), the Federal Writers' Project created the American Guide Series, with a volume for each of the 48 states as well as the Alaska Territory, Puerto Rico, and Washington, D.C.; the state guides were printed individually by each state.

856.8 Mandeville] Sir John Mandeville, attributive author of the 14th century *Travels of Sir John Mandeville.*

866.19–20 Sir John Gielgud . . . *The Ages of Man*] The Shakespearean actor Gielgud (1904–2000) won a Tony Award for *The Ages of Man*, his one-man performance of excerpts from Shakespeare's works, in 1959; the recording was nominated for a Grammy in the same year.

872.14 John Birch Society] An extreme right-wing political organization founded in Indiana in 1958 by candy manufacturer Robert Welch (1899–1985) and named after John Birch (1918–1945), an American intelligence officer killed by the Chinese Communists at the end of World War II.

873.8–9 Charles Erskine Scott Wood . . . *Heavenly Discourse*] Wood (1852–1944) served as a soldier in campaigns against the Nez Percé, Bannock, and Piute Indians; he later became a successful lawyer and author, and was active in radical politics. *Heavenly Discourse* (1927), a collection of satirical dialogues originally published in *The Masses*, was a best seller. Steinbeck lived near Wood's Los Gatos home, "The Cats," from 1938 to 1941.

873.11–12 General Miles . . . Chief Joseph campaign] General Nelson Miles (1839–1925), Union Civil War commander and Indian fighter; he forced the surrender of Nez Percé Chief Joseph in 1877. Chief Joseph (Hin-mah-too-yah-lat-kekt, 1840–1904), along with several other chiefs, led his people on a 1,400-mile trek through the Northwest that eluded the army repeatedly until his surrender in northern Montana on October 5, 1877.

879.8 Wildroot] Wildroot Cream Oil, hair product for men.

899.3 scotch whisky] John F. Kennedy's father, Joseph Kennedy, had been in the whisky importing business, and was alleged to have had ties to organized crime.

899.4–5 grocery in Santa Ana] Nixon's parents owned a grocery store in Whittier, which is north of Santa Ana, and he was born in Yorba Linda.

899.5 Checkers] In a televised speech on September 23, 1952, Richard

Nixon, then the Republican candidate for vice-president, defended himself against charges of unethically receiving $18,000 in funds from political supporters. During the speech he acknowledged receiving the gift of a dog that his daughter Tricia had named Checkers, and said: "And you know the kids love this dog and I just want to say this right now, that regardless of what they say about it, we're gonna keep it."

899.278 *chamacos*] Lads.

903.36 General Frémont made his stand] The American military exploration party led by Captain John C. Frémont (1813–1890) fortified a position on Gavilán (or Hawk's) Peak in March 1846 after being ordered to leave California by Mexican General José Castro. After three days, Frémont abandoned the position and began marching toward Oregon. Gavilán was later renamed Frémont Peak.

914.17 Narváez] The Spanish explorer Panfilo de Narváez (c. 1470–1528) set out from near present-day Tampa Bay, Florida, in 1528 and began a trek across the South and Southwest. In 1536 four survivors from the expedition reached the Spanish settlement of Culiacan in present-day Mexico.

918.6 Edna Ferber wrote a book] Ferber's novel *Giant* (1952) focused on the Texas oil industry and drew attention to racial problems. It was filmed in 1956.

933.13–14 the Cheerleaders] Name given to a group of white parents led by B. J. "Una" Gaillot, a New Orleans housewife, that publicly harassed black and white students entering schools desegregated under federal court order in November 1960.

938.12 Lyle Saxon] Saxon (1891–1946) was a feature writer for the New Orleans *Times-Picayune* from 1918 to 1926, and author of books about Louisiana and the South, including *Father Mississippi* (1927), *Fabulous New Orleans* (1928), and *Old Louisiana* (1929).

938.13–15 Roark Bradford . . . Green Pastures] Bradford (1896–1948) was a journalist and author of black dialect and Southern plantation fiction. His collection *Ol' Man Adam An' His Chillun* (1928), in which a black preacher retells stories from the Bible, was adapted for the stage in 1930 by Marc Connelly as *The Green Pastures.*

Library of Congress Cataloging-in-Publication Data

Steinbeck, John, 1902–1968.
Travels with Charley & later novels / John Steinbeck
p. cm.
Contents: The wayward bus — Burning bright — Sweet Thursday — The winter of our discontent — Travels with Charley
ISBN: 978-1-59853-004-9 (alk. paper)
I. Title: II. Title: Travels with Charley and later novels.

PS3537.T3234A6 2007
813′.52—dc22 2006048757

THE LIBRARY OF AMERICA SERIES

The Library of America fosters appreciation and pride in America's literary heritage by publishing, and keeping permanently in print, authoritative editions of America's best and most significant writing. An independent nonprofit organization, it was founded in 1979 with seed money from the National Endowment for the Humanities and the Ford Foundation.

1. Herman Melville, *Typee, Omoo, Mardi* (1982)
2. Nathaniel Hawthorne, *Tales and Sketches* (1982)
3. Walt Whitman, *Poetry and Prose* (1982)
4. Harriet Beecher Stowe, *Three Novels* (1982)
5. Mark Twain, *Mississippi Writings* (1982)
6. Jack London, *Novels and Stories* (1982)
7. Jack London, *Novels and Social Writings* (1982)
8. William Dean Howells, *Novels 1875–1886* (1982)
9. Herman Melville, *Redburn, White-Jacket, Moby-Dick* (1983)
10. Nathaniel Hawthorne, *Collected Novels* (1983)
11. Francis Parkman, *France and England in North America*, vol. I (1983)
12. Francis Parkman, *France and England in North America*, vol. II (1983)
13. Henry James, *Novels 1871–1880* (1983)
14. Henry Adams, *Novels, Mont Saint Michel, The Education* (1983)
15. Ralph Waldo Emerson, *Essays and Lectures* (1983)
16. Washington Irving, *History, Tales and Sketches* (1983)
17. Thomas Jefferson, *Writings* (1984)
18. Stephen Crane, *Prose and Poetry* (1984)
19. Edgar Allan Poe, *Poetry and Tales* (1984)
20. Edgar Allan Poe, *Essays and Reviews* (1984)
21. Mark Twain, *The Innocents Abroad, Roughing It* (1984)
22. Henry James, *Literary Criticism: Essays, American & English Writers* (1984)
23. Henry James, *Literary Criticism: European Writers & The Prefaces* (1984)
24. Herman Melville, *Pierre, Israel Potter, The Confidence-Man, Tales & Billy Budd* (1985)
25. William Faulkner, *Novels 1930–1935* (1985)
26. James Fenimore Cooper, *The Leatherstocking Tales*, vol. I (1985)
27. James Fenimore Cooper, *The Leatherstocking Tales*, vol. II (1985)
28. Henry David Thoreau, *A Week, Walden, The Maine Woods, Cape Cod* (1985)
29. Henry James, *Novels 1881–1886* (1985)
30. Edith Wharton, *Novels* (1986)
31. Henry Adams, *History of the U.S. during the Administrations of Jefferson* (1986)
32. Henry Adams, *History of the U.S. during the Administrations of Madison* (1986)
33. Frank Norris, *Novels and Essays* (1986)
34. W.E.B. Du Bois, *Writings* (1986)
35. Willa Cather, *Early Novels and Stories* (1987)
36. Theodore Dreiser, *Sister Carrie, Jennie Gerhardt, Twelve Men* (1987)

37A. Benjamin Franklin, *Silence Dogood, The Busy-Body, & Early Writings* (1987)

37B. Benjamin Franklin, *Autobiography, Poor Richard, & Later Writings* (1987)

38. William James, *Writings 1902–1910* (1987)
39. Flannery O'Connor, *Collected Works* (1988)
40. Eugene O'Neill, *Complete Plays 1913–1920* (1988)
41. Eugene O'Neill, *Complete Plays 1920–1931* (1988)
42. Eugene O'Neill, *Complete Plays 1932–1943* (1988)
43. Henry James, *Novels 1886–1890* (1989)
44. William Dean Howells, *Novels 1886–1888* (1989)
45. Abraham Lincoln, *Speeches and Writings 1832–1858* (1989)
46. Abraham Lincoln, *Speeches and Writings 1859–1865* (1989)
47. Edith Wharton, *Novellas and Other Writings* (1990)
48. William Faulkner, *Novels 1936–1940* (1990)
49. Willa Cather, *Later Novels* (1990)

50. Ulysses S. Grant, *Memoirs and Selected Letters* (1990)
51. William Tecumseh Sherman, *Memoirs* (1990)
52. Washington Irving, *Bracebridge Hall, Tales of a Traveller, The Alhambra* (1991)
53. Francis Parkman, *The Oregon Trail, The Conspiracy of Pontiac* (1991)
54. James Fenimore Cooper, *Sea Tales: The Pilot, The Red Rover* (1991)
55. Richard Wright, *Early Works* (1991)
56. Richard Wright, *Later Works* (1991)
57. Willa Cather, *Stories, Poems, and Other Writings* (1992)
58. William James, *Writings 1878–1899* (1992)
59. Sinclair Lewis, *Main Street & Babbitt* (1992)
60. Mark Twain, *Collected Tales, Sketches, Speeches, & Essays 1852–1890* (1992)
61. Mark Twain, *Collected Tales, Sketches, Speeches, & Essays 1891–1910* (1992)
62. *The Debate on the Constitution: Part One* (1993)
63. *The Debate on the Constitution: Part Two* (1993)
64. Henry James, *Collected Travel Writings: Great Britain & America* (1993)
65. Henry James, *Collected Travel Writings: The Continent* (1993)
66. *American Poetry: The Nineteenth Century*, Vol. 1 (1993)
67. *American Poetry: The Nineteenth Century*, Vol. 2 (1993)
68. Frederick Douglass, *Autobiographies* (1994)
69. Sarah Orne Jewett, *Novels and Stories* (1994)
70. Ralph Waldo Emerson, *Collected Poems and Translations* (1994)
71. Mark Twain, *Historical Romances* (1994)
72. John Steinbeck, *Novels and Stories 1932–1937* (1994)
73. William Faulkner, *Novels 1942–1954* (1994)
74. Zora Neale Hurston, *Novels and Stories* (1995)
75. Zora Neale Hurston, *Folklore, Memoirs, and Other Writings* (1995)
76. Thomas Paine, *Collected Writings* (1995)
77. *Reporting World War II: American Journalism 1938–1944* (1995)
78. *Reporting World War II: American Journalism 1944–1946* (1995)
79. Raymond Chandler, *Stories and Early Novels* (1995)
80. Raymond Chandler, *Later Novels and Other Writings* (1995)
81. Robert Frost, *Collected Poems, Prose, & Plays* (1995)
82. Henry James, *Complete Stories 1892–1898* (1996)
83. Henry James, *Complete Stories 1898–1910* (1996)
84. William Bartram, *Travels and Other Writings* (1996)
85. John Dos Passos, *U.S.A.* (1996)
86. John Steinbeck, *The Grapes of Wrath and Other Writings 1936–1941* (1996)
87. Vladimir Nabokov, *Novels and Memoirs 1941–1951* (1996)
88. Vladimir Nabokov, *Novels 1955–1962* (1996)
89. Vladimir Nabokov, *Novels 1969–1974* (1996)
90. James Thurber, *Writings and Drawings* (1996)
91. George Washington, *Writings* (1997)
92. John Muir, *Nature Writings* (1997)
93. Nathanael West, *Novels and Other Writings* (1997)
94. *Crime Novels: American Noir of the 1930s and 40s* (1997)
95. *Crime Novels: American Noir of the 1950s* (1997)
96. Wallace Stevens, *Collected Poetry and Prose* (1997)
97. James Baldwin, *Early Novels and Stories* (1998)
98. James Baldwin, *Collected Essays* (1998)
99. Gertrude Stein, *Writings 1903–1932* (1998)
100. Gertrude Stein, *Writings 1932–1946* (1998)
101. Eudora Welty, *Complete Novels* (1998)
102. Eudora Welty, *Stories, Essays, & Memoir* (1998)
103. Charles Brockden Brown, *Three Gothic Novels* (1998)
104. *Reporting Vietnam: American Journalism 1959–1969* (1998)
105. *Reporting Vietnam: American Journalism 1969–1975* (1998)
106. Henry James, *Complete Stories 1874–1884* (1999)

107. Henry James, *Complete Stories 1884–1891* (1999)
108. *American Sermons: The Pilgrims to Martin Luther King Jr.* (1999)
109. James Madison, *Writings* (1999)
110. Dashiell Hammett, *Complete Novels* (1999)
111. Henry James, *Complete Stories 1864–1874* (1999)
112. William Faulkner, *Novels 1957–1962* (1999)
113. John James Audubon, *Writings & Drawings* (1999)
114. *Slave Narratives* (2000)
115. *American Poetry: The Twentieth Century,* Vol. 1 (2000)
116. *American Poetry: The Twentieth Century,* Vol. 2 (2000)
117. F. Scott Fitzgerald, *Novels and Stories 1920–1922* (2000)
118. Henry Wadsworth Longfellow, *Poems and Other Writings* (2000)
119. Tennessee Williams, *Plays 1937–1955* (2000)
120. Tennessee Williams, *Plays 1957–1980* (2000)
121. Edith Wharton, *Collected Stories 1891–1910* (2001)
122. Edith Wharton, *Collected Stories 1911–1937* (2001)
123. *The American Revolution: Writings from the War of Independence* (2001)
124. Henry David Thoreau, *Collected Essays and Poems* (2001)
125. Dashiell Hammett, *Crime Stories and Other Writings* (2001)
126. Dawn Powell, *Novels 1930–1942* (2001)
127. Dawn Powell, *Novels 1944–1962* (2001)
128. Carson McCullers, *Complete Novels* (2001)
129. Alexander Hamilton, *Writings* (2001)
130. Mark Twain, *The Gilded Age and Later Novels* (2002)
131. Charles W. Chesnutt, *Stories, Novels, and Essays* (2002)
132. John Steinbeck, *Novels 1942–1952* (2002)
133. Sinclair Lewis, *Arrowsmith, Elmer Gantry, Dodsworth* (2002)
134. Paul Bowles, *The Sheltering Sky, Let It Come Down, The Spider's House* (2002)
135. Paul Bowles, *Collected Stories & Later Writings* (2002)
136. Kate Chopin, *Complete Novels & Stories* (2002)
137. *Reporting Civil Rights: American Journalism 1941–1963* (2003)
138. *Reporting Civil Rights: American Journalism 1963–1973* (2003)
139. Henry James, *Novels 1896–1899* (2003)
140. Theodore Dreiser, *An American Tragedy* (2003)
141. Saul Bellow, *Novels 1944–1953* (2003)
142. John Dos Passos, *Novels 1920–1925* (2003)
143. John Dos Passos, *Travel Books and Other Writings* (2003)
144. Ezra Pound, *Poems and Translations* (2003)
145. James Weldon Johnson, *Writings* (2004)
146. Washington Irving, *Three Western Narratives* (2004)
147. Alexis de Tocqueville, *Democracy in America* (2004)
148. James T. Farrell, *Studs Lonigan: A Trilogy* (2004)
149. Isaac Bashevis Singer, *Collected Stories I* (2004)
150. Isaac Bashevis Singer, *Collected Stories II* (2004)
151. Isaac Bashevis Singer, *Collected Stories III* (2004)
152. Kaufman & Co., *Broadway Comedies* (2004)
153. Theodore Roosevelt, *The Rough Riders, An Autobiography* (2004)
154. Theodore Roosevelt, *Letters and Speeches* (2004)
155. H. P. Lovecraft, *Tales* (2005)
156. Louisa May Alcott, *Little Women, Little Men, Jo's Boys* (2005)
157. Philip Roth, *Novels & Stories 1959–1962* (2005)
158. Philip Roth, *Novels 1967–1972* (2005)
159. James Agee, *Let Us Now Praise Famous Men, A Death in the Family* (2005)
160. James Agee, *Film Writing & Selected Journalism* (2005)
161. Richard Henry Dana, Jr., *Two Years Before the Mast & Other Voyages* (2005)
162. Henry James, *Novels 1901–1902* (2006)
163. Arthur Miller, *Collected Plays 1944–1961* (2006)

164. William Faulkner, *Novels 1926–1929* (2006)
165. Philip Roth, *Novels 1973–1977* (2006)
166. *American Speeches: Part One* (2006)
167. *American Speeches: Part Two* (2006)
168. Hart Crane, *Complete Poems & Selected Letters* (2006)
169. Saul Bellow, *Novels 1956–1964* (2007)
170. John Steinbeck, *Travels with Charley and Later Novels* (2007)
171. Capt. John Smith, *Writings with Other Narratives* (2007)
172. Thornton Wilder, *Collected Plays & Writns on Theater* (2007)

This book is set in 10 point Linotron Galliard, a face designed for photocomposition by Matthew Carter and based on the sixteenth-century face Granjon. The paper is acid-free lightweight opaque and meets the requirements for permanence of the American National Standards Institute. The binding material is Brillianta, a woven rayon cloth made by Van Heek-Scholco Textielfabrieken, Holland. Composition by Dedicated Business Services. Printing by Malloy Incorporated. Binding by Dekker Bookbinding. Designed by Bruce Campbell.